FRANS G. BENGTSSON 1894–1954 was one of Sweden's greatest writers. A poet, novelist, essayist and historian, Bengtsson gained a unique reputation in Scandinavia for his incisive biographies and his translations of English, French and Icelandic poetry. *The Long Ships* was his first novel, and heralded by critics as a masterpiece of historical fiction.

From the reviews of *The Long Ships*:

'A novel with the potential to please every literate human being in the entire world – something for everyone. Bengtsson recreates the world of 1000 AD with telling detail and persuasive historiography, with a keen grasp of the eternal bits that pebble the record of human vanity, and with the unflagging verve of a born storyteller – but above all, and this is the most remarkable of the book's many virtues, with an intimate detachment, a neighbourly distance, a sincere irony, that feels at once ancient and postmodern. It is this astringent tone, undeceived, versed in human folly, at once charitable and cruel, that is the source of the novel's unique flavor, the poker-faced humor that is most beloved by those who love this book'   MICHAEL CHABON

'[A] wonderful adventure novel'   *Observer*

'This extraordinary saga of epic adventure on land and sea . . . is a masterpiece of historical fiction . . . Not least of the rewards of reading Mr Bengtsson's gorgeous romance is the sly humor that is sprinkled through it'
                                                New York Times

'A boldly illuminated picture of the Northmen . . . confidently recommended'   *The Times*

'A remarkable panorama of a vanished way of life'   *TLS*

'Offers lusty Vikings lusting and looting, bedding and battling across Europe from the Ebro to the Dneiper'   *Time*

'The author and his excellent translator bring that old, warrior world alive with such vigorous enjoyment and simplicity that the deeds of those men roving about the world in their dragon ships seem as marvellous as those of our atomic age'   *Daily Telegraph*

'[Bengtsson] keeps his readers eager for the next chapter. He has a sharp eye for the picturesque and the comic in daily living, and though his style is sophisticated he often writes with a kind of festive abandon'   *New York Herald Tribune*

'The literary equivalent of an action- and intrigue-filled adventure movie that won't insult your intelligence . . . Orm is a charismatic character, and Bengtsson is an infectiously enthusiastic and surprisingly funny writer – even readers with zero interest in the Europe of a millennium ago will want to keep turning the pages. All novels should be so lucky as to age this well'   *NPR*

'A banquet of adventure by sea and land, with man-size help-ings of battle and murder, robbery and rape'   *New Statesman*

'Still the king of books about Vikings . . . the Vikings liked to row and sail and fight. That's what they do in this action-packed epic'   *Bookmarks Magazine*

FRANS G. BENGTSSON

The Long Ships

A Saga of the Viking Age

Translated by Michael Meyer

HARPER

Harper
An Imprint of HarperCollins*Publishers*
77–85 Fulham Palace Road,
Hammersmith, London W6 8JB

www.harpercollins.co.uk

This paperback edition 2014
1

First published in Great Britain by Collins 1954

Maps © John Gilkes

A catalogue record for this book
is available from the British Library

ISBN: 978-0-00-756070-7

Set in Meridien by Palimpsest Book Production Limited,
Falkirk, Stirlingshire

Printed and bound in Great Britain by
Clays Ltd, St Ives plc

MIX
Paper from
responsible sources
FSC **FSC™ C007454**
www.fsc.org

FSC™ is a non-profit international organisation established to promote
the responsible management of the world's forests. Products carrying the
FSC label are independently certified to assure consumers that they come
from forests that are managed to meet the social, economic and
ecological needs of present and future generations,
and other controlled sources.

Find out more about HarperCollins and the environment at
www.harpercollins.co.uk/green

HARP SONG OF THE DANE WOMEN

What is a woman that you forsake her,
And the hearth-fire and the home-acre,
To go with the old grey Widow-maker?

She has no house to lay a guest in—
But one chill bed for all to rest in,
That the pale suns and the stray bergs nest in.

She has no strong white arms to fold you,
But the ten-times-fingering weed to hold you—
Out on the rocks where the tide has rolled you.

Yet, when the signs of summer thicken,
And the ice breaks, and the birch-buds quicken,
Yearly you turn from our side, and sicken—

Sicken again for the shouts and the slaughters.
You steal away to the lapping waters,
And look at your ship in her winter-quarters.

You forget our mirth, and talk at the tables,
The kine in the shed and the horse in the stables—
To pitch her sides and go over her cables.

Then you drive out where the storm-clouds swallow,
And the sound of your oar-blades, falling hollow,
Is all we have left through the months to follow.

Ah, what is Woman that you forsake her,
And the hearth-fire and the home-acre,
To go with the old grey Widow-maker?

RUDYARD KIPLING

CONTENTS

PART TWO

IN KING ETHELRED'S KINGDOM

PART THREE

IN THE BORDER COUNTRY

PART FOUR

THE BULGAR GOLD

TRANSLATOR'S NOTE

The action of *The Long Ships* covers, approximately, the years A.D. 980–1010. At that time, the southern provinces of Sweden belonged to Denmark, so that Orm, although born and bred in Skania, regarded himself as a Dane.*

The Vikings harried the countries of northern and western Europe more or less continuously for a period of over 200 years, from the end of the eighth century until the beginning of the eleventh. Most of the raids on western Europe were carried out by Danes and Norwegians; for the Swedes regarded the Baltic as their domain, and founded a kingdom in Russia at the end of the ninth century which endured for 350 years, until the coming of the Mongols. Ireland was, at first, the favourite western hunting-ground of the Vikings; it was not until 838, forty years after the first attack on Ireland, that they began to raid England in large numbers. For the next sixty years, however, they – especially the great Ragnar Hairy-Breeks and his terrible sons – troubled England cruelly, until Alfred withstood them and forced them to come to terms. Then, from 896 until 979, England enjoyed eighty years of almost unbroken respite from their fury. In France, the Northmen were so feared that, in 911, Charles the Simple ceded part of his kingdom to them; this came to be known as Normandy, the Northmen's land. Vikings peopled Iceland in 860, and Greenland in 986. In the latter year a

---

* Denmark also claimed suzerainty over Norway, though the Norwegians regarded themselves as independent.

Viking ship heading for Greenland went off its course and reached America, which, because of the good grapes they found there, the men named 'Wineland the Good.' Several other Viking ships sailed to America during the next twenty years.

The Battle of Jörundfjord, or Hjörungavag, so frequently referred to in the following pages, was one of the most famous battles fought in the north during the Viking Age. It was fought between the Norwegians and the Jomsvikings. The Jomsvikings (to quote Professor C. Turville-Petre) were 'a closed society of Vikings, living according to their own laws and customs. None of them might be younger than eighteen years, and none older than fifty; they must not quarrel among themselves, and each must avenge the other as his brother.' No woman was allowed within their citadel, Jomsborg, which was sited on the southern shore of the Baltic, probably in the region of where Swinemunde now stands. According to Icelandic sources, Canute's father, King Sven Forkbeard, invited the Jomsvikings to a feast. As the ale flowed, King Sven swore an oath to invade England and kill Ethelred the Unready, or else drive him into exile. The Jomsviking chieftain, Sigvalde, swore in his turn to sail to Norway and kill the rebel Jarl Haakon, or else drive him into exile. All the other Jomsvikings, including the two Skanian chieftains, Bue Digre and Vagn Akesson, swore to follow him. They sailed to Norway with sixty ships, but Haakon got wind of their approach and, when at last they turned into Jörundfjord, they found him waiting for them with a fleet of no less than 180 ships. At first, despite being thus outnumbered, the Jomsvikings looked likely to prevail; but the weather turned against them and, after a bitter struggle, they were routed and slaughtered almost to a man.

This was in 989. In the following spring, another vital battle was fought in Sweden, on Fyris Plain before Uppsala, when the dreaded Styrbjörn, the exiled nephew of King Erik of Sweden, sought to win his uncle's kingdom, but was killed by a chance spear in the first moments of the fight. It is to the echoes of these two battles that *The Long Ships* opens.

M.M.

How the shaven men fared in Skania in King Harald Bluetooth's time

Many restless men rowed north from Skania with Blue and Vagn, and found ill fortune at Jörundfjord; others marched with Styrbjörn to Uppsala and died there with him. When the news reached their homeland that few of them could be expected to return, elegies were declaimed and memorial stones set up; whereupon, all sensible men agreed that what had happened was for the best, since they could now hope to have a more peaceful time than before, and less parcelling out of land by the axe and sword. There followed a time of plenty, with fine rye harvests and great herring catches, so that most people were well contented; but there were some who thought that the crops were tardy, and they went a-viking in Ireland and England, where fortune smiled on their wars; and many of them stayed there.

About this time the shaven men had begun to arrive in Skania both from the Saxons' land and from England, to preach the Christian faith. They had many strange tales to relate, and at first people were curious and listened to them eagerly, and women found it pleasant to be baptized by these foreigners, and to be presented with a white shift. Before long, however, the foreigners began to run short of shifts, and people wearied of their sermons, finding them tedious and their matter doubtful; besides which, they spoke a rough-sounding dialect that they had learned in Hedeby or in the western islands, which gave their speech a foolish air.

So then there was something of a decline in conversions, and the shaven men, who talked incessantly of peace and were above all very violent in their denunciation of the gods, were one by one seized by devout persons and were hung up on sacred ash-trees and shot at with arrows, and offered to the birds of Odin. Others went northwards to the forests of the Göings, where men were less religiously inclined; there, they were welcomed warmly, and were tied up and led to the markets in Smaland, where they were bartered for oxen and for beaver skins. Some of them, upon finding themselves slaves of the Smalanders, let their hair grow and waxed discontented with their God Jehovah, and gave good service to their masters; but the majority continued to denounce the gods and to spend their time baptizing women and children instead of breaking stones and grinding corn, and made such annoyance of themselves that soon it became impossible for the Göings to obtain, as hitherto, a yoke of three-year-old oxen for a sturdy priest without giving a measure of salt or cloth into the bargain. So feeling increased against the shaven men in the border country.

One summer, the word went round the whole of the Danish kingdom that King Harald Bluetooth had embraced the new religion. In his youth, he had done so tentatively, but had soon regretted his decision and recanted; this time, however, he had adopted it seriously. For King Harald was by now an old man, and had for some years been tormented by terrible pains in his back, so that he had almost lost his pleasure in ale and women; but wise bishops, sent by the Emperor himself, had rubbed him with bear's-grease, blessed and made potent with the names of apostles, and had wrapped him in sheepskins and given him holy herbal water to drink instead of ale, and had made the sign of the cross between his shoulders and exorcised many devils out of him, until at last his aches and pains had departed; and so the King became a Christian.

Thereupon, the holy men had assured him that still worse torments would come to plague him if he should ever again offer sacrifice, or show himself in any way unzealous in the new religion. So King Harald (as soon as he had become active again, and found himself capable of fulfilling his obligations towards a young Moroccan slave-girl, whom Olof of the Precious Stones, the King of Cork, had sent him as a goodwill present), issued a proclamation that all his subjects should get themselves christened without delay; and, although such an order sounded strangely from the lips of one who was himself descended from Odin, still many obeyed his command, for he had ruled long and prosperously, so that his word counted for much in the land. He meted out especially severe punishments to anyone who had been guilty of violence against any priest; so that the number of priests in Skania now began to multiply greatly, and churches rose upon the plain, and the old gods fell into disuse, except in times of peril at sea or of cattle-plague.

In Göinge, however, the King's proclamation was the occasion of much merriment. The people of the border forests were blessed with a readier sense of fun than the sober dwellers of the plain, and nothing made them laugh so much as a royal proclamation. For in the border country, few men's authority extended beyond the limit of their right arm, and from Jellinge to Göinge was a long march even for the mightiest of kings to undertake. In the old days, in the time of Harald Hildetand and Ivar of the Broad Embrace, and even before that, kings had been wont to come to Göinge to hunt the wild ox in the great forests there, but seldom on any other errand. But since those times, the wild ox had died out, and the king's visits had ceased; so that nowadays, if any king was bold enough to murmur a complaint that the people of those parts were turbulent or that they paid insufficient taxes, and threatened to journey thither himself to remedy matters, the answer would be sent to him that there were, unfortunately, no wild oxen to be seen in the district nowadays, but that as soon as any should appear he would at once be informed, and a royal welcome would be prepared for him. Accordingly, it had for long been a saying among the border people that no king would be seen in their country until the wild oxen returned.

So in Göinge, things remained as they had always been, and Christianity made no headway there. Such priests as did venture into those parts were sold over the border as in the old days; though some of the Göings were of the opinion that it would be better to kill them on the spot, and start a good war against the skinflints of Sunnerbo and Allbo, for the Smalanders gave such poor prices for priests nowadays that it was hardly worth a man's trouble to lead them to market.

PART ONE

The Long Voyage

CHAPTER ONE

Concerning Thane Toste and his household

Along the coast the people lived together in villages, partly to be sure of food, that they might not depend entirely on the luck of their own catch, and partly for greater security; for ships rounding the Skanian peninsula often sent marauding parties ashore, both in the spring, to replenish cheaply their stock of fresh meat for the westward voyage, and in the winter, if they were returning empty-handed from unsuccessful wars. Horns would be blown during the night when raiders were thought to have landed, so that the neighbours might come to the assistance of those attacked; and the stay-at-homes of a good village would occasionally even capture a ship or two for themselves, from strangers who had not been sufficiently prudent, and so have fine prizes to show the wanderers of the village when the long ships came home for their winter rest.

But men who were wealthy and proud, and who owned their own ships, often found it irksome to have neighbours on their doorstep, and preferred to live apart; for, even when they were at sea, they could keep their homes defended by good warriors whom they paid to stay in their houses and guard them. In the region of the Mound, there were many such great lords, and the rich thanes of that district had the reputation of being the proudest in all the Danish kingdom. When they were at home, they readily picked quarrels with one another, although their homesteads lay well spaced apart; but often they were abroad, for they had been used from their childhood to look out over the sea and to regard it as their own private pasture, where any whom they found trespassing would have to answer for it.

In these parts there lived a thane called Toste, a worthy man and a great sailor who, although he was advanced in years, still commanded his ship and set out each summer for foreign shores. He had kinsmen in Limerick in Ireland, among the Vikings who had settled there, and he sailed west each year to trade with them and to help their chieftain, a descendant of Ragnar of the Hairy Breeks, to collect tribute from the Irish and from their monasteries and churches. Of late, however, things had begun to go less well for the Vikings in Ireland, ever since Muirkjartach of the Leathern Coats, the King of Connaught, had marched round the island with his shield-arm towards the sea as a sign of defiance. For the natives now defended themselves better than before and followed their kings more willingly, so that it had become a difficult business to extort tribute from them; and even the monasteries and churches, that had previously been easy to plunder, had now built high stone towers to which the priests betook themselves, and from which they could not be driven by fire or by force of arms. In view of all this, many of Toste's followers were now of the opinion that it might be more profitable to go a-viking in England or France, where times were good and more might be won with less effort; but Toste preferred to do as he had been used to do, thinking himself too old to start journeying to countries where he might not feel so well at home.

His wife was called Asa. She came from the border forest and had a ready tongue, besides being somewhat smart of temper, so that Toste was sometimes heard to remark that he could not see much evidence of time having smoothed out the wrinkles in her nature, as it was said to do. But she was a skilful housewife, and took good care of the farm when Toste was away. She had borne him five sons and three daughters; but their sons had not met with the best of luck. The eldest of them had come to grief at a wedding, when, merry with ale, he had attempted to prove that he could ride bareback on a bull; and the next one had been washed overboard on his first voyage. But the unluckiest of all had been their fourth son, who was called Are; for, one summer, when he was nineteen years old, he had got two of their neighbours' wives with child while their husbands were abroad, which had been the instance of much trouble and sly jibing, and had put Toste to considerable expense when the husbands returned home. This dejected Are's spirits and made him shy; then he killed a man who had chaffed him overlong for his dexterity, and had to flee the country. It was rumoured that he had sold himself to Swedish merchants and had sailed with them to the east, so that he might meet no more people who knew of his misfortune, but nothing had been heard of him since. Asa, however, had dreamed of a black horse with blood on its shoulders, and knew by this that he was dead.

So after that, Asa and Toste had only two sons left. The elder of these was called Odd. He was a short youth, coarsely built and bow-legged, but strong and horny-handed, and of a reflective temper; he was soon accompanying Toste on his voyages, and showed himself to be a skilful shipman, as well as a hard fighter. At home, though, he was often contrary in his behaviour, for he found the long winters tedious, and Asa and he bickered continually. He was sometimes heard to say that he would rather be eating rancid salt-meat on board ship than Yuletide joints at home; but Asa remarked that he never seemed to take less than anyone else of the food she set before them. He dozed so much every day that he would often complain that he had slept poorly during the night; it did not even seem to help, he would say, when he took one of the servant-girls into the bed-straw with him. Asa did not like his sleeping with her servants; she said it might give them too high an opinion of themselves and make them impudent towards their mistress; she observed that it would be more satisfactory if Odd acquired a wife. But Odd replied that there was no hurry about that; in any case, the women that suited his taste best were the ones in Ireland, and he could not very well bring any of them home with him for, if he did, Asa and they would soon be going for one another tooth and nail. At this, Asa became angry and asked whether this could be her own son who addressed her thus, and expressed the wish that she might shortly die; to which Odd retorted that she might live or die as she chose, and he would not presume to advise her which state to choose, but would endure with resignation whatever might befall.

Although he was slow of speech, Asa did not always succeed in having the last word, and she used to say that it was in truth a hard thing for her to have lost three good sons and to have been left with the one whom she could most easily have spared.

Odd got on better with his father, however, and, as soon as the spring came, and the smell of tar began to drift across from the boathouse to the jetty, his humour would improve, and sometimes he would even try, though he had little talent for the craft, to compose a verse or two – of how the auk's meadow was now ripe for ploughing; or how the horses of the sea would shortly waft him to the summer land.

But he never won himself any great name as a bard, least of all among those daughters of neighbouring thanes who were of marriageable age; and he was seldom observed to turn his head as he sailed away.

His brother was the youngest of all Toste's children, and the jewel of his mother's eye. His name was Orm. He grew quickly, becoming long and scatter-limbed, and distressing Asa by his lack of flesh; so that whenever he failed to eat a good deal more than any of the grown men, she would become convinced that she would soon lose him, and often said that his poor appetite would assuredly be his downfall. Orm was, in fact, fond of food, and did not grudge his mother her anxiety regarding his appetite; but Toste and Odd were sometimes driven to protest that she reserved all the tit-bits for him. In his childhood, Orm had once or twice fallen sick, ever since when Asa had been convinced that his health was fragile, so that she was continually fussing over him with solicitous admonitions, making him believe that he was racked with dangerous cramps and in urgent need of sacred onions, witches' incantations and hot clay platters, when the only real trouble was that he had overeaten himself on corn porridge and pork.

As he grew up, Asa's worries increased. It was her hope that he would, in time, become a famous man and a chieftain; and she expressed to Toste her delight that Orm was shaping into a big, strong lad, wise in his discourse, in every respect a worthy scion of his mother's line. She was, though, very fearful of all the perils that he might encounter on the highway of manhood, and reminded him often of the disasters that had overtaken his brothers, making him promise always to beware of bulls, to be careful on board ship, and never to lie with other men's wives; but, apart from these dangers, there was so much else that might befall him that she hardly knew where to begin to counsel him. When he reached the age of sixteen, and was ready to sail with the others,

Asa forbade him to go, on the ground that he was still too young and too fragile of health; and, when Toste asked her whether she had it in her mind to bring him up to be a chieftain of the kitchen and a hero of old women, she exploded into such a rage that Toste himself became frightened, and let her have her way, and was glad to be allowed to take his own leave, and, indeed, lost little time in doing so. That autumn, Toste and Odd returned late from their voyage, and had lost so many of their crew that they scarcely had enough left to man the oars; nevertheless, they were well contented with the results of their expedition, and had much to relate. In Limerick, they had met with small success, for the Irish kings in Munster had by now become so powerful that the Vikings who lived there had their work cut out to hold on to what they had. Then, however, some friends of Toste (who had anchored his ship off the coast) had asked whether he might feel inclined to accompany them on a secret visit to a great midsummer fair which was held each year at Merioneth, in Wales, a district to which the Vikings had not previously penetrated, but which could be reached with the assistance of two experienced guides whom Toste's friends had discovered. Their followers being enthusiastic, Odd had persuaded Toste to fall in with this suggestion; so seven shiploads of them had landed near Merioneth and, after following a difficult route inland, had managed to arrive at the fair without giving wind of their approach. There had been fierce fighting, and a good many men had been killed, but in the end the Vikings had prevailed and had captured a great quantity of booty, as well as many prisoners. These they had sold in Cork, making a special voyage thither for the purpose, for it had long been the custom for slave-traders to gather in Cork from all the corners of the world to bid for the captives whom the Vikings brought there; and the king of those parts, Olof of the Precious Stones, who was a Christian and very old and wise, would himself purchase any that caught his fancy, so that he might give their kinsmen the opportunity to ransom them, on which transaction he could be sure of making a pretty profit. From Cork, they had set out for home, in company with a number of other Viking ships in case of pirates, for they had little appetite for further fighting, weakly manned as they now were, besides having much treasure aboard. So they had succeeded in coming unscathed round the Skaw, where the men of the Vik and of Westfold lurked in ambush to surprise richly laden ships returning homewards from the south and west.

After the survivors of the crew had been allotted their share of the booty, a great quantity remained for Toste; who, when he had weighed it and locked it into his treasure-chest, announced that an expedition such as this would serve as a fitting conclusion to his wanderings, and that henceforth he would remain at home, the more willingly since he was beginning to grow somewhat stiff of limb; Odd was by now capable of managing the affairs of the expeditions fully as well as he, and would, besides, have Orm to help him. Odd thought that this was a good idea; but Asa was of a very different opinion, observing that, whilst a fair amount of silver had been won, it could hardly be expected to last for long, considering how many mouths she had to feed each winter; besides which, how could they be sure that Odd would not spend all the prize-money he won in future expeditions on his Irish women, or indeed whether, left to himself, he would ever bother to come home to them at all? As regards the stiffness which Toste complained of in his back, he ought by now to know that this was not the result of his voyages but of the months that he spent idling in front of the fire throughout each winter; and to be falling over his sprawling legs for six months in every year was quite sufficient for her. She could not understand (she continued) what men were coming to nowadays; her own great-uncle, Sven Rat-Nose, a mighty man among the Göings, had fallen like a hero fighting the Smalanders three years after drinking the whole company under the table at his eldest grandson's wedding; whereas, now, you heard talk of cramps from men in the prime of life who were apparently quite willing to die, unashamedly, on their backs in straw, like cows. However, she concluded, all this could be settled in good time, and meanwhile Toste and Odd and the others who had come home with them were to drown their worries in good ale, of a brew that would please their palates; and Toste was to put these nonsensical ideas out of his head and drink to an equally profitable expedition next year; and then they would all enjoy a comfortable winter together, so long as nobody invented any more of such stupid notions to provoke her, which she trusted they would not.

When she had left them to prepare the ale, Odd remarked that, if all her female ancestors had had tongues like her, Sven Rat-Nose

12

had probably fixed on the Smalanders as the lesser evil. Toste demurred, saying that he agreed up to a point, but that she was in many respects a good wife, and ought, perhaps, not to be provoked unnecessarily, and that Odd should do his best to humour her.

That winter, they all noticed that Asa went about her household duties with less than her usual ardour and bustle, and that her tongue ran less freely than it was wont to do. She was more than ever solicitous towards Orm, and would sometimes stand and gaze at him, as though contemplating a vision. Orm had by now grown big, and could compete in matters of strength with all those of his age, as well as with many older youths. He was red-haired and fair-skinned, broad between the eyes, snub-nosed and wide-mouthed, with long arms and rather rounded shoulders: he was quick and agile, and surer than most with a spear or with a bow. He was fiery of tongue, and would rush blindly on any man that roused him, so that even Odd, who had previously enjoyed teasing him to a white fury, had now begun to treat him with caution; for Orm's strength made him a dangerous opponent. But in general, except when he was angry, he was quiet and tractable, and always ready to do whatever Asa asked of him, though he occasionally had words with her when her fussing irked him.

Toste now gave him a man's weapons – a sword and a broad axe and a good helmet – and Orm made himself a shield; but he found difficulty in obtaining a chain-shirt, for nobody in the household was of his size, and there was, at that time, a shortage of good mail-smiths in the land, most of them having migrated to England or to the Jarl at Rouen, where their work was better paid. Toste said that, for the time being, Orm would have to be content with a leather tunic, until such time as he could get himself a good shirt in Ireland; for there, dead men's armour was always to be had cheaply in any harbour.

They were talking on this subject at table one day, when of a sudden Asa buried her face in her arms and began to weep. They all fell silent and stared at her, for it was not often that tears were seen on her cheeks; and Odd asked her if she had the toothache. Asa dried her face, and turned towards Toste. She said that all this talk of dead men's armour seemed to her to be a bad omen, and that she was already certain that disaster would overtake Orm as soon as he accompanied them to sea, for thrice in her dreams she

13

had seen him lying bleeding on a ship's bench, and they all knew that her dreams could be relied upon to come true. She begged Toste, therefore, to listen to her earnest prayer and not to expose their son's life to unnecessary peril, but to allow him to remain at home with her for this one summer; for she believed that danger threatened him in the very near future and that, if he could only survive this immediate hazard, the risk would subsequently decrease.

Orm asked her whether she could see in her dream in which part of his body he was wounded. Asa replied that, each time she dreamed this dream, the sight of him lying thus had awakened her in a cold terror; but she had seen his hair bloody and his face pale, and the vision had weighed heavily upon her, the more so each time that it returned, although she had not previously wished to speak of it.

Toste sat silent for a while, pondering over what she had said; then he remarked that he knew little about dreams, and had never himself paid much attention to them.

'For the Ancients used to observe,' he said, 'that, as the Spinstress spinneth, so shall it be. If, though, you, Asa, have dreamed the same dream thrice, then it may be that this is intended to serve as a warning to us; and, in truth, we have already lost our share of sons. Therefore, I shall not oppose your will in this matter, and Orm shall remain at home this summer, if it is also his wish. For my own part, I begin to feel that I should not mind sailing once more to the west; so, perhaps, after all, your suggestion may turn out to be the best solution for us all.'

Odd concurred with Toste, for he had several times noticed that Asa's dreams foretold the future correctly. Orm was not overjoyed at their decision, but he was accustomed to obey Asa's will in important matters; so nothing more was said.

When spring came, and sufficient men had been hired from the hinterland to fill the gaps in their crew, Toste and Odd sailed away as usual, while Orm remained at home. He behaved somewhat sulkily towards his mother, and sometimes pretended to be sick in order to frighten her, but, as soon as she began to fuss over him and dose him with medicines, he would find himself believing that he was in fact ill, so that he gained but little pleasure from his game. Asa could not bring herself to forget her dream and, despite all the

14

worry he caused her, it comforted her to have him safe with her at home.

Nevertheless, and in spite of his mother, he sailed forth that summer on his first voyage.

CHAPTER TWO

Concerning Krok's expedition: and how Orm set forth on his first voyage

In the fortieth year of King Harald Bluetooth's reign, six summers before the Jomsvikings' expedition to Norway, three ships, fitted with new sails and boldly manned, set sail from the Listerland and headed southwards to plunder the country of the Wends. They were commanded by a chieftain called Krok. He was a dark-complexioned man, tall and loose-limbed and very strong; and he had a great name in his part of the country, for he possessed a talent for evolving audacious plans, and enjoyed deriding men whose enterprises had gone astray and telling them what he would have done if he had been in their shoes. He had never in fact achieved anything of note, for he preferred to talk of the feats he intended to perform in the near future; but at length, he had so fired the young men of the district with his talk of the booty that brave warriors might win in the course of a properly conducted expedition against the Wends, that they had got together and fitted out ships and had chosen him to be their chieftain. There was, he had told them, much treasure to be found in Wendland; above all, one could be certain of a fine haul of silver, amber and slaves.

Krok and his men reached the Wendish coast and discovered the mouth of a river, up which they rowed against a strong current until they came to a wooden fortress, with piles forming a boom across the river. Here they went ashore in a grey dawn twilight, and attacked the Wends, having first slipped through their outlying defences. But the fortress was strongly manned, and its defenders shot arrows at them cunningly, and Krok's men were tired with their heavy rowing, so there was a bitter struggle before the Wends were finally put to flight. In the course of it, Krok lost many good men; and, when the booty was examined, it was found to consist of a few iron kettles and some sheepskin coats. They rowed back down the river, and made an attempt on another village farther to the west, but it, too, was well defended and, after another sharp struggle, in which they sustained further losses, they won a few sides of smoked pork, a torn chain-shirt and a necklace of small, worn silver coins.

They buried their dead on the shore, and held counsel, and Krok had some difficulty in explaining to them why the expedition had not turned out as he had foretold. But he succeeded in calming their temper with well-chosen words, reminding them that no man could insure against bad luck or the whims of circumstance, and that no true Viking allowed himself to become dispirited by a little adversity. The Wends, he explained, were becoming redoubtable adversaries; and he had a good plan to put to them which would certainly redound to the advantage of them all. This was that they should make an attempt against Bornholm, for the richness of that island's inhabitants was well known to them all, and it would be weakly defended, many of its warriors having recently gone to England. A shore-thrust here would meet with little opposition, and would be sure to yield a rich harvest of gold, brocades and fine weapons.

They found this well spoken, and their spirits rose again; so they set sail and headed for Bornholm, which they reached early one morning. They rowed along the eastern coast of the island in a calm sea and a rising haze, searching for a good landing-place, pulling briskly and keeping well together, for they were in high good humour; but they kept silence, for they hoped to land unobserved. Suddenly, they heard ahead of them the clank of rowlocks and the plash of oar-blades dipping evenly, and out of the haze appeared a single long ship approaching round a headland. It made towards them, without slackening its stroke, and they all stared at it, for it was large and splendid to behold, with a red dragon-head at its prow, and twenty-four pairs of oars; and they were glad that it was unaccompanied. Krok ordered all his men who were not engaged at the oars to take up their weapons and stand ready for boarding; for here there was plainly much to be won. But the lone ship headed straight towards them, as though its helmsman had not observed their presence; and a stoutly built man, standing in the prow, with a broad beard visible beneath his bossed helmet, cupped his hand to his mouth as they approached and roared in a harsh voice: 'Get out of our way, unless you want to fight!'

Krok laughed, and his men laughed with him; and he shouted back: 'Have you ever seen three ships give way to one?'

'Ay, and more than three!' roared the fat man impatiently. 'For most men give way to Styrbjörn. But be quick about it and make your choice. Get out of our way or fight!'

When Krok heard the fat man's words, he made no reply, but silently turned his ship aside; and his men rested their oars while the lone ship rowed past them, nor did any of them unsheath his sword. They saw a tall young man in a blue cloak, with fair down lining his jaw, rise from his resting-place beside the helmsman and stand surveying them with sleepy eyes, grasping a spear in his hand. He yawned broadly, dropped his spear and laid himself again to rest; and Krok's men realized that this was Björn Olofsson, commonly called Styrbjörn, the banished nephew of King Erik of Uppsala, who seldom sought refuge from storm and never from battle, and whom few men willingly encountered at sea. His ship proceeded on its course, its long oars sweeping evenly, and disappeared southwards into the haze. But Krok and his men found their previous high spirits difficult to recover.

They rowed to the eastern skerries, which were uninhabited, and there they landed and cooked a meal, and held long counsel. Many of them thought that they would do best to turn for home, seeing that bad luck had followed them even to Bornholm. For, if Styrbjörn was in these waters, the island was sure to be swarming with Jomsvikings, in which case there would be nothing left for any other raiders. Some of them said that there was little use in going to sea with the sort of chieftain who gave way to a single ship.

Krok was at first less eloquent than usual; but he had ale brought ashore for them all and, after they had drunk, he delivered a speech of encouragement. In one sense, he was ready to admit, it might be considered unfortunate that they had encountered Styrbjörn in this manner; but, if you looked at it another way, it was extremely fortunate that they had encountered him when they did, for if they had come ashore and met them or other Jomsvikings there, they would have had to pay dearly for it. All Jomsvikings, and none more so than Styrbjörn's men, were half berserk, sometimes being even proof against iron, and able to lay about them with both hands full as well as the best warriors from Lister. That he had been reluctant to order an assault on Styrbjörn's ship might, at first sight, appear odd to idle-thinking men, nevertheless, he regarded his reluctance as fully justified, and considered it fortunate that he had made his decision so promptly. For a homeless and exiled pirate would hardly be likely to have sufficient treasure stored away in any one place to be worth a bloody battle; and he would remind them that they had not come to sea to win empty honour, but to secure hard booty. In view of all this, he had thought it more proper to consider the general good than his own reputation as a warrior, and, if they would reflect, he felt sure that they would agree that he had acted in this affair in a manner befitting a chieftain.

As he thus cunningly dispersed the fog of dejection which had settled on his men's spirits, Krok began to feel his own courage rising anew; and he proceeded to exhort them strongly against making for home. For the people of Lister, he said, were inclined to be uncharitable, and the women in particular would ply them with painful queries regarding their exploits and the prizes they had won, and why they had returned so soon. No man proud of his good name would thus willingly lay himself open to the shafts of their mockery; therefore, he suggested, it would be better if they could postpone their return until they had won something worth bringing home. The important thing now, he concluded, was that they should remain together, face their adversities with courage and resolution, and determine on some worthy goal to which to proceed; on which matter, before he spoke any further, he would like to hear the views of his wise comrades.

One of the men then proposed that they should go to the land of the Livonians and the Kures* where there was a rich harvest to be reaped; but this suggestion won little support, for men of greater experience knew that large shiploads of Swedes descended annually on those regions, and it was not to be reckoned that they would

---

* Modern Lithuania and Latvia.

proffer a warm welcome to any strangers who arrived on the same errand. Another man had heard that the greatest single hoard of silver in the world was to be found in Gotland, and he thought that they should try their hand there; but others of his companions, who knew better, said that nowadays, since the Gotlanders had become rich, they lived in large villages, which could only be successfully attacked by a powerful army.

A third man then rose to address them, a warrior called Berse, who was a wise speaker and prized by all for his sound judgment. He said that the Eastern Sea was becoming a crowded and un-rewarding pasture, for far too many men were plundering its coasts and islands, so that even such peoples as the Wends were learning how to defend themselves. It would be a poor thing to turn meekly for home – on that point, he was of the same opinion as Krok – but it was, he thought, worth considering whether they might not sail out to the lands in the west. He had never himself travelled to those parts, but certain men from Skania, whom he had met at a fair during the previous summer, had been in England and Brittany with Toke Gormsson and Sigvalde Jarl, and had had much to say in praise of those countries. They wore gold rings and costly garments, and according to their report certain companies of Vikings had anchored their ships in Frankish estuaries for months on end while they plundered the hinterland, and these men had frequently had burgomasters and abbots to wait on them at table and the daughters of counts to make them merry in bed. How strictly his informants had kept to the truth he could not, of course, say, but, as a general rule, you could believe about half of what Skanians told you; and these men had made an impression on him of considerable prosperity, for they had invited him, a stranger from Blekinge, to join them in a grand drinking-bout and had not at-tempted to steal his belongings while he slept, so that their story could not be altogether false; besides which, it was more or less confirmed by reports he had heard from other quarters. Now, where Skanians had prospered, men of Blekinge ought to fare at least as well; therefore, he concluded, he, for his part, would suggest that they should sail to the lands of the west, if a majority among his comrades were of the same mind.

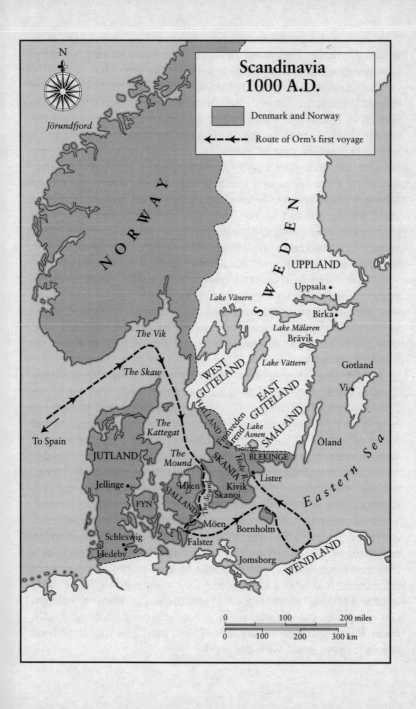

Scandinavia
1000 A.D.

Denmark and Norway

Route of Orm's first voyage

N

NORWAY

SWEDEN

UPPLAND

Jörundfjord

The Vik

The Skaw

Lake Vänern

Uppsala

Birka

Lake Mälaren

Brävik

WEST
GUTELAND

Lake Vättern

Gotland

Vi

EAST
GUTELAND

The Kattegat

HALLAND

SMÅLAND

Finnveden

Värend

Lake
Asnen

Öland

The Mound

SKANIA

Holtr R.

Goinge

BLEKINGE

JUTLAND

Jellinge

HVEN

Kivik

Skanör

Lister

Eastern Sea

FYN

SJÄLLAND

The Sound

Schleswig

Möen

Falster

Bornholm

Hedeby

Jomsborg

WENDLAND

To Spain

0   100   200 miles

0   100   200   300 km

Many of them applauded his proposal and cried assent; but others doubted whether they were sufficiently provisioned to carry them through until they came to their goal.

Then Krok spoke again. He said that Berse had made exactly the suggestion that he himself thought of putting forward. Berse had spoken of the daughters of counts and of wealthy abbots, for the return of whose persons they would receive large ransoms; and he would like to add that in Ireland, there were, as was well known, no less than a hundred and sixty kings, some great, some small, but all of whom possessed much gold and many fine women, and whose soldiers fought wearing only linen garments, so that they could not be difficult to overcome. The most difficult part of their voyage would be passing through the Sound, where they might find themselves attacked by the natives of those parts; but three strongly manned ships, which Styrbjörn himself had not dared to challenge, would be likely to command respect even in the Sound; besides which, most of the Vikings of that region would, at this time of the year, already have sailed westwards; and in any case, there would be no moon during the next few nights. As regards food, any that they needed they could easily obtain as soon as they had successfully negotiated the Sound.

By this time they had all recovered their former high spirits. They said the plan was a good one, and that Krok was the wisest and cleverest of all chieftains; and they were all proud to discover how little trepidation they felt at the prospect of a voyage to the lands of the west, for no ship from their district had attempted such a journey within living memory. They set sail and came to Möen, and rested there for a day and a night, keeping a good lookout and waiting for a favourable wind. Then they headed up through the Sound in stormy weather, and came that evening to its neck without meeting any enemies. Later, during the night, they anchored in the lee of the Mound and decided to go ashore in search of provisions. Three companies landed secretly, each in a different place. Krok's company was lucky, for they came at once on a sheep-fold near a large house, and managed to kill the shepherd and his dog before they could give the alarm. Then they caught the sheep and cut the throats of as many as they could take with them, but this caused the animals to bleat loudly, so that Krok bade his men make haste with the work.

They returned to the ship by the way they had come, making as much speed as they could, each man bearing a sheep over his shoulder. They heard behind them the clamour of people who had awoken in the house, and soon there arose the harsh yowling of dogs that had been unleashed on their scent. Then they heard from farther off a woman's voice, which piercing through the noise of the dogs and men cried: 'Wait! Stay with me!' and screamed: 'Orm!' several times, and then again cried: 'Wait!' very shrilly and despairingly. Krok's men had difficulty in moving quickly with their loads, for the path was stony and steep, and the night was cloudy and still almost pitch-dark. Krok himself went last in the line, carrying his sheep over his shoulder and holding an axe in his other hand. He was anxious, if possible, to avoid becoming involved in a fight for the sake of a sheep, for it was not worth while to risk life and limbs for so little; so he drove his men forward with harsh words of rebuke when they stumbled or slackened speed.

The ship lay hard by some flat rocks, being held away from them by the oars. They were ready to pull out as soon as Krok returned, for the other landing-parties had already returned empty-handed; some of them were waiting on the beach in case Krok should need any assistance. They were only a few paces from the ship when two great dogs came bounding down the path. One of them leaped at Krok, but he jumped aside and struck it with his axe; the other flashed past him with a huge leap at the man just in front of him, knocked him over by its impetus and buried its teeth in his throat. Two of the others hastened forward and killed the dog, and when they and Krok bent over the man who had been bitten they saw that his throat was badly torn and that he was rapidly bleeding to death.

In the same instant a spear hissed past Krok's head, and two men came running down the slope and out on to the flat rocks; they had run so fast that they had outstripped all their companions. The foremost of them, who was bareheaded and bore no shield, but carried a short sword in his hand, tripped and fell headlong on the rocks; two spears flew over him and hit his companion, who crumpled to the ground. But the bareheaded man was at once on his feet again; baying like a wolf, he hewed at one man who had leaped forward with his sword raised when he had fallen, and felled him with a blow on the temples. Then he sprang at Krok, who

23

stood just behind him; all this happened very quickly. He aimed savagely at Krok, but Krok was still carrying his sheep, and he slipped it round to meet the blow, in the same instant striking his adversary with the reverse edge of his axe on the forehead, so that he fell to the ground senseless. Krok bent over him, and saw that he was no more than a youth, red-haired and snub-nosed and pale-complexioned. He felt with his fingers the place where the axe-head had landed and found that the skull was unfractured.

'I shall take the calf with me as well as the sheep,' he said. 'He can row in the place of the man he killed.'

So they picked him up and carried him on to the ship, and threw him beneath an oar-bench; then, when they had all come aboard, except the two men whom they had left dead behind them, they pulled out to sea just as a large crowd of pursuers appeared on the beach. The sky had now begun to lighten, and some spears were thrown at the ship; but they did no damage. The men pulled strongly at their oars, happy in the knowledge that they had fresh meat on board; and they had already gone a good way from land when the figures on the beach were joined by a woman in a long blue shift with her hair streaming behind her, who ran to the edge of the rocks and stretched out her arms towards the ship, crying something. Her cry reached them as a thin sound across the water, but she stood there long after they had ceased to hear her.

In this wise, Orm, the son of Toste, who later came to be known as Red Orm or Orm the Far-Travelled, set forth on his first voyage.

CHAPTER THREE

How they sailed southwards, and how they found themselves a good guide

Krok's men were very hungry when they reached Weather Island, for they had had to row the whole way there. They lay to and went ashore to gather fuel and cook themselves a good dinner; they found there only a few old fishermen, who on account of their poverty were not afraid of plunderers. When they came to cut up the sheep, they praised their fatness, and the evident excellence of the spring pasturing on the Mound. They stuck the joints on their spears and held them in the fire, and their mouths watered as the fat began to crackle, for it was a long time since their nostrils had known such a cheering smell. Many of them exchanged stories of the last occasions on which they had been present at so tasty a meal, and they all agreed that their voyage to the lands of the west had begun promisingly. Then they began to eat so that the juice of the meat ran over their beards.

By this time, Orm had regained his senses, but he was still sick and dizzy, and when he came ashore with the others, it was all he could do to keep on his legs. He sat down and held his head between his hands, and made no reply to the words that were addressed to him. But after a while, when he had vomited and drunk water, he felt better, and when he smelt the odour of the frying meat, he raised his head like a man who has just woken up, and looked at the men around him. The man who was sitting nearest to him grinned in a friendly way, and cut off a bit of his meat and offered it to him.

'Take this and eat it,' he said. 'You never tasted better in your life.'

'I know its quality,' replied Orm. 'I provided it.'

He took the meat and held it between his fingers without eating it. He looked thoughtfully round the circle, at each man in turn, and then said: 'Where is the man I hit? Is he dead?'

'He is dead,' replied his neighbour, 'but no one here stands to avenge him, and you are to row in his stead. His oar lies in front of mine, so it will be well that you and I should be friends. My name is Toke; what is yours?'

Orm told him his name, and asked him: 'The man I killed. Was he a good fighter?'

'He was, as you observed, somewhat slow of movement,' replied Toke, 'and he was not so handy with a sword as I am myself. But that would be asking a lot of a man, for I am one of the finest swordsmen in our company. Still, he was a strong man, and steadfast and of a good name; he was called Ale, and his father sows twelve bushels of rye, and he had been called to sea twice already. If you can row as well as he did, you are no mean oarsman.'

When Orm heard this, it seemed to cheer his spirits, and he began to eat. But after a few minutes, he asked: 'Who was it who struck me down?'

Krok was sitting a short way from him and heard his question. He laughed and raised his axe, finished his mouthful and said: 'This is the maid who kissed you. Had she bitten you, you would not have asked her name.'

Orm gazed at Krok with rounded eyes, that looked as though they had never blinked, and then said with a sigh: 'I had no helmet and was breathless from running; otherwise, it might have gone differently.'

'You are a conceited puppy, Skanian,' said Krok, 'and fancy yourself a soldier. But you are yet young and lack a soldier's prudence. For prudent men do not forget their helmets when they run out after sheep; nay, not even when their own wives are stolen from them. But you seem to be a man whom Fortune smiles on, and it may be that you will bring us all into her good favour. We have already seen three manifestations of her love for you. Firstly, you slipped on the rocks as two spears were flying towards you; then Ale, whom you slew, has no kinsman or close comrade among us who is bound to avenge him; and thirdly, I did not kill you, because I wished to have an oarsman to replace him. Therefore I believe you to be a man of great good luck, who can thereby be of use to us; wherefore I now give you the freedom of our company, provided only that you agree to take Ale's oar.'

They all thought that Krok had spoken well. Orm munched his meat reflectively; then he said: 'I accept the freedom you offer me; nor do I think I need feel ashamed to do so, although you stole my sheep. But I will not row as a slave, for I am of noble blood; and, though I am young, yet I hold myself to be a good soldier, for I slew Ale, and he was one. I therefore claim back my sword.'

This provoked a long and complicated discussion. Some of them regarded Orm's demand as altogether unreasonable, and said that he ought to think himself lucky to have been granted his life; but others remarked that self-esteem was no great fault in a young man, and that the claims of those whom Fortune smiled on should not be lightly ignored. Toke laughed and said he was amazed that so many men, three full ships' companies, could be anxious about whether or not one boy was to be allowed to carry a sword. A man called Calf, who had spoken against granting Orm's request, wanted to fight Toke for saying this, and Toke said that he would be glad to oblige him as soon as he had finished the good kidney that he was just then occupied with; but Krok forbade them to fight over such a matter. The end of it all was that Orm got his sword back, but that his future behaviour would determine whether he was to be treated as a slave or as a comrade. But Orm was to pay Krok for his sword, which was a fine weapon, as soon as he won anything on the voyage.

By this time a light breeze had sprung up, and Krok said that it was time for them to avail themselves of it and set sail. So they all went aboard and the ship made its way up through the Kattegat with its sails filled with the wind. Orm stared back across the sea and said that it was lucky for Krok that they had few ships left at home in these parts at this time of year; for, if he knew his mother, she would else by now have been on their tails with half the people of the Mound assisting her.

Then he washed the wound in his head and rinsed the clotted blood from his hair; and Krok said that the scar on his forehead would be a fine thing to show womenfolk. Then Toke produced an old leather helmet with iron bands. He said it was not much of a

27

helmet for these times, but that he had found it among the Wends and that he had nothing better that he could spare. It would, he said, not be of much use against an axe, but still, it would be better than nothing. Orm tried it on and found that it would fit him when the swelling had gone down. Orm thanked Toke; and they both knew now that they would be friends.

They rounded the Skaw with a good following wind, and there, after ancient custom, they sacrificed to Agir and all his kin, offering sheep's flesh and pork and ale, and were followed for a long while afterwards by shrieking gulls, which they took to be a good omen. They rowed down the Jutland coast, where the country was deserted and the ribs of wrecked ships were often to be seen in the sand; further south, they went ashore on two small islands, where they found water and food but little else. They proceeded down the coast, for the most part with favourable winds helping them, so that the men became good-humoured through being relieved of the tiresome labour of constant rowing. Toke said that Orm was, perhaps, weather-lucky, as well as being ordinarily fortunate; and weather-luck was one of the best kinds of luck that a man could have, so that if this were in fact so, Orm could indeed hope for a prosperous future. Orm thought that Toke might be right; but Krok was unwilling to agree with them on this point.

'It is I who bring us this good weather,' he said. 'For we have had good weather and winds from the very beginning, long before Orm joined us; indeed, if I had not known my weather-luck to be reliable, I should not have ventured on this expedition. But Orm's luck is good, if not of the same quality as my own; and the more lucky men we have aboard, the better it will be for us all.'

Berse the Wise agreed, and said that men without luck had the hardest burden of all to bear.

'For man can triumph over man, and weapon over weapon; against the Gods, we can pit sacrifice, and against witchcraft, contrary magic; but against bad luck, no man has anything to oppose.'

Toke said that, for his part, he did not know whether he had great good luck, except that his luck in fishing had always been good. He had always done well enough against men whom he had quarrelled with; but that might be the result of his strength and skill rather than of his luck.

'But what worries me,' he said, 'is whether on this expedition we shall have gold-luck and woman-luck: for I have heard great tales of all the fine things that are to be found here in the west, and it is beginning to seem a long time since I felt a gold ring or a woman. Even if we only find silver instead of gold, and no princesses, such as Berse has spoken of, but simple Frankish housewives, I shall not complain; for I am not a fussy man.'

Krok said that Toke would have to be patient for a little longer, however strong his desire for either commodity; and Toke agreed that it certainly seemed likely that he would have to wait for a while; for it did not look as though either gold or women grew on trees in these parts.

They sailed along flat coasts, where nothing was to be seen except sand and marshlands, and an occasional fishing-hut. Then they passed promontories on which tall crosses stood, and knew they had come to the Christians' land and to the Frankish coasts. For the wise men among them knew that these crosses had first been set up by the great Emperor Charles, the father of all emperors, to keep Nordic seafarers away from his land; but the gods of the north had proved stronger than his. They put into creeks to take refuge from threatening squalls, and to rest overnight, and saw waters more salt and green than any they had seen before, rising and falling with the ebb and the flood tides. There were no ships to be seen, and no people; only here and there the traces of some old building. Many villages had flourished in these parts, before the first Northmen came, but everything had long since been plundered and laid waste, so that nowadays men had to travel far to the south before they could find any prizes worth the taking.

They came down to where the sea narrowed between England and the mainland; and there was talk among them of turning towards the English coast. For they knew that King Edgar had recently died and that he had been succeeded by sons who were not yet of age, which had made the land much sought after by the Vikings. But Krok and Berse and others among the wisest of them held that the country of the Franks was still the best, if one went far enough south; for the King of Frankland and the Emperor of Germany were at war with each other on a point of dispute concerning their frontiers, and the coastal regions of countries at war always provided good hunting-grounds for Northmen.

29

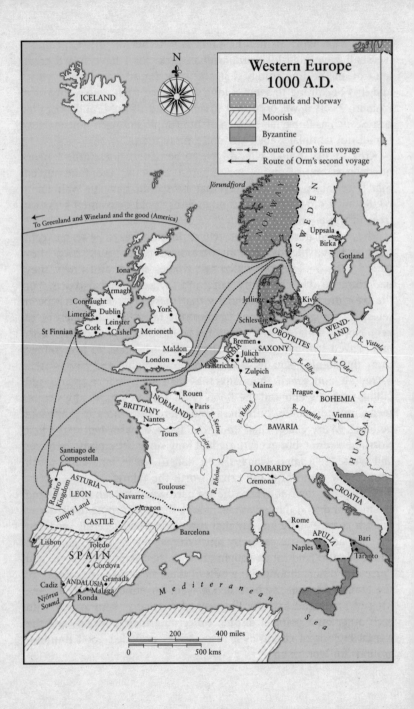

Western Europe
1000 A.D.

Denmark and Norway

Moorish

Byzantine

←--- Route of Orm's first voyage
←——— Route of Orm's second voyage

ICELAND

Jörundfjord

NORWAY

SWEDEN

Uppsala

Birka

Gotland

← To Greenland and Wineland and the good (America)

Iona

Armagh

Connaught

Limerick   Dublin

St Finnian   Cork   Leinster   York

Cashel   Merioneth

Jellinge   Kivik

Schleswig   OBOTRITES

WEND-
LAND

Bremen   SAXONY   R. Vistula

Maldon   Jülich   R. Elbe   R. Oder

London   Maastricht   Aachen

Zulpich

Mainz   Prague   BOHEMIA

Rouen   R. Rhine

BRITTANY   Paris   Vienna

Nantes   R. Seine   R. Danube

Tours   R. Loire   BAVARIA   HUNGARY

LOMBARDY   CROATIA

Santiago de
Compostella   Toulouse   Cremona

ASTURIA   R. Rhône

Ramiro   Navarre   Rome

Kingdom   LEON

Empty Land   Aragon   APULIA   Bari

CASTILE   Barcelona   Naples   Taranto

Lisbon   Toledo

SPAIN   Cordova

Cadiz   Granada

ANDALUSIA   Malaga   M e d i t e r r a n e a n

Njörva   Ronda   S e a
Sound

0   200   400 miles

0   500 kms

So they continued down the Frankish coast; but here they lay further out to sea and kept a sharp look-out on every quarter, for they had now come to that region which certain Northmen had won from the King of the Franks. Here ancient crosses were constantly to be seen on promontories and at river mouths, but even more frequent were pikes with bearded heads set on them, to signify that the rulers of that land had no desire to welcome seamen from their own northern climes upon their coasts. Krok and his men thought that this showed scant hospitality on the part of the men who were now enjoying the fruits of the land; but, they said, it was only what was to be expected of men from Skania and Själland; and they asked Orm whether he had any kinsmen in these parts. Orm replied that he had none, as far as he knew, since his kinsmen always sailed to Ireland; but that he would bear in mind, when he got home, this idea of putting heads on poles, for they would make fine scarecrows to protect his sheep. They all laughed at this, and thought that he was well able to speak up for himself.

They hid in ambush at the mouth of a river, and took some fishing boats, but they found little worth in them and could elicit no reply from the men in the boats when they asked where the rich villages were around there. When they had killed a couple of them and still could get no intelligible answer from the others, they let them go alive, since they were of miserable appearance and would be of no use as rowers, and would fetch no price as slaves. More than once they slipped ashore under the cover of night, but they won little, for the people lived in large and well-guarded villages, and several times they had to make haste back to their ships to avoid being surrounded and outnumbered. They hoped that they would soon come to the end of the region where the Northmen held sway.

One evening, they met four long ships rowing from the south; they looked to be heavily laden, and Krok let his ships move near to them so that he might see how strongly they were manned. It was a calm evening, and they rowed slowly towards each other; the strangers set a long shield upon their mast-top, with its point turned upwards, as a sign that they came as friends, and Krok's men conversed with them at the distance of a spear's throw, while each chieftain tried to calculate the other's strength. The strangers said that they were from Jutland, and that they were on their way home after a long voyage. They had plundered in Brittany with seven ships during the previous summer, and had then ventured far to the south; afterwards, they had wintered on an island off the mouth of the Loire, and had ventured up the river, but then a cruel plague had broken out among them, and now they were making their way home with such ships as they had strength to man. When asked what they had won, they replied that a wise seaman never counts his wealth until he has brought it safely home; but this they could tell him (since at this meeting they reckoned themselves strong enough to hold what they had won), that they had no complaint to make about the amount of their catch. There was always the possibility of a bad season, compared with the way things had been in the old days, and that held true however far southwards one might travel; but anyone who happened on a part of Brittany that had hitherto escaped plunder would be able to find good reward for his pains.

Krok asked whether they had any wine or good ale that they would be willing to exchange for pork or dried fish; meanwhile, he tried to come nearer their ships, for he was sorely tempted to hazard an attack on them and by this means get a fine return for his whole voyage at one swoop. But the Jutish captain at once brought his ship round to bar their path, with his prow facing them, and replied that he preferred to keep his swine and ale for his own use.

'But by all means come nearer,' he said to Krok, 'if there is anything else you care to sample.'

Krok weighed a spear in his hand and seemed uncertain which course to take; but at that moment a commotion broke out on one of the Jutish ships. Two men could be seen struggling with each other by the gunwale; then they fell into the water, still locked in each other's arms. Both of them sank, and one was seen no more; but the other rose to the surface at a distance from the ship, only to dive again when a spear was thrown at him by one of the men he had left. There was much shouting on the Jutish ship, but when Krok's men asked them what was the matter, they received no reply. Dusk was now beginning to descend and, after a brief exchange of words, the strangers began to row forward again before Krok could decide whether or not to join battle. Then Toke, who sat at his larboard oar just behind Orm on Krok's own ship, cried to Krok:

'Come and look at this! My fishing-luck gets better all the time!'

One hand was gripping Toke's oar, and one Orm's, and a face lay in the water between the hands, staring up at the ship. It was big-eyed and very pale, black-haired and black-bearded.

'This is a bold fellow and a good swimmer,' said one of the men. 'He has dived under our ship to get away from the Jutes.'

'And a wise man, too,' said another, 'for he sees that we are better men than they.'

A third said: 'He is black like a troll, and yellow like a corpse and does not look the sort of man who brings good luck with him. It is dangerous to take such a man aboard.'

They discussed the advantages and disadvantages of doing so, and some of them shouted questions at the man in the water; but he lay there without moving, clinging tightly to the oars and blinking his eyes and swaying with the sea. At last Krok ordered him to be brought aboard; he could always be killed later, he explained to those who opposed the idea, if the course of things showed that it would be best to do so.

So Toke and Orm drew in their oars and hauled the man aboard; he was yellow-skinned and strongly built, and naked to his waist, with only a few rags to cover him. He tottered on his feet and could hardly stand, but he clenched his fist and shook it at the Jutish ships as they merged into the distance, spitting after them and grinding his teeth. Then he cried something and fell headlong as the ship rolled, but was quickly on his feet again, and beat his breast and stretched his arms towards the sky and cried in a different voice, but in words which none of them could understand. When Orm was old, and told of all the things that had befallen him, he used to say that he never heard so terrible a grinding of teeth, or so pitiful and ringing a voice, as when this stranger cried out to the sky.

They all wondered at him, and questioned him profusely as to who he was and what had happened to him. He understood some of what they said, and was able to reply brokenly in the Nordic tongue, and they thought he said he was a Jute and that he disliked rowing on Saturdays and that it was for this reason that he hated the men he had now escaped from; but this made no sense to them, and some of them were of the opinion that he was crazy. They gave him food and drink, and he ate greedily of beans and fish; but when they offered him salt pork, he rejected it with disgust. Krok said that he would do to man an oar, and that when the voyage was over they could sell him for a good sum; meanwhile, Berse could, out of his wisdom, try to make something of what the stranger said and discover whether he had any useful information to give them about the lands from which he had come.

So during the next few days Berse sat and talked a good deal with the stranger, and they conversed as well as they could. Berse was a calm and patient man, a great eater and a skilful bard, who had gone to sea to get away from a shrewish wife; he was wise and full of cunning, and bit by bit he succeeded in piecing together most of what the stranger had to say. This he told to Krok and the others.

'He is not crazy,' said Berse, 'though he seems so; nor is he a Jute, though we thought him to be one. He says that he is a Jew. They are a people from the East who killed the man whom the Christians regard as their god. This killing took place long ago, but the Christians still cherish a great hatred against the Jews because of it, and like to kill them, and will not accept any ransom for them or show them any clemency. For this reason, most of the Jews live in the lands ruled by the Caliph of Cordova, since in his kingdom the man they killed is not regarded as a god.'

Berse added that he had heard some talk of this before, and many others said that they, too, had heard rumours relating to it. Orm said that he had heard that the dead man had been nailed to a tree, as the sons of Ragnar Hairy-Breeks had done in the old days with the chief priest of England. But how they could continue to regard him as a god after the Jews had killed him, none of them could understand; for obviously no true god could be killed by men. Then Berse went on to tell them more of what he had managed to grasp of the Jew's story:

'He has been a slave of the Jutes for a year, and there he underwent much suffering, because he would not row on Saturdays; for the God of the Jews gets very angry with a Jew who does anything on that day. But the Jutes could not understand this, though he often tried to explain it to them, and they beat him and starved him when he refused to row. It was while he was in their hands that he learned the little he knows of our tongue; but when he speaks of them, he curses them in his own language, because he does not know sufficient words to do so in ours. He says that he wept much when he was among them and cried to his god for help; then, when he saw our ship approaching, he knew that his cry had been heard.

When he jumped overboard, he dragged with him a man who had often beaten him. He asked his God to be a shield to him, and not to let the other man escape; that, he says, is why no spear hit him, and how he found the strength to dive under our ship; and so powerful is the name of his god that he will not name him to me, however much I try to persuade him to do so. That is what he says of the Jutes and his escape from them; and he has more to tell us about something else, which he thinks we shall find useful. But much of what he says about this I cannot clearly understand.'

They were all curious to know what else the Jew had to say, which might be useful to them; and at last Berse managed to discover the gist of it.

'He says,' Berse told them, 'that he is a wealthy man in his own country, which lies within the Caliph of Cordova's kingdom. His name is Solomon, and he is a silversmith, besides apparently being a great poet. He was captured by a Christian chieftain who came from the north and plundered the region where he lives. This chieftain made him send for a large sum of money to ransom himself, and then sold him to a slave-trader, for the Christians do not like to keep their word to Jews, because they killed their god. The slave-trader sold him at sea to merchants, from whom he was captured by the Jutes; and it was his bad fortune to be set at once to pull an oar on a Saturday. Now he hates these Jutes with a bitter hatred; but even that is mild compared with the hatred he feels towards the Christian chieftain who betrayed him. This chieftain is very rich and lives only a day's march from the sea; and he says that he will gladly show us how to get there, so that we may plunder the chieftain of all he possesses and burn down his house and take out his eyes and loose him naked among the stones and trees. He says that there is wealth for us all there.'

They all agreed that this was the best news they had heard for many a day; and Solomon, who had been sitting beside Berse while he was recounting all this and had been following him as well as he could, leaped to his feet with a great cry and a joyful countenance, and cast himself full length on the deck before Krok and put a tuft of his beard into his mouth and chewed it; then he seized one of Krok's feet and placed it upon his neck, all the while babbling like a drunken man in words that no one could understand. When he had calmed himself a little, he began to search among the words of their language that he knew; he said that he wished to serve Krok and his men faithfully until they had won these riches and he had gained his revenge; but he asked for a definite promise that he himself should be allowed to pluck out the eyes of the Christian chieftain. Both Krok and Berse agreed that this was a reasonable request.

On each of the three ships, the men now began hotly to discuss all this, and it put them in the best of spirits. They said that the stranger might not bring much luck to himself, to judge by what happened to him, but that he might bring all the more to them; and Toke thought that he had never hooked a better fish. They treated the Jew as a friend, and collected a few clothes for him to wear, and gave him ale to drink, though they had not much left. The country to which he wished to guide them was called Leon, and they knew roughly where it lay; on their right hand between the land of the Franks and that of the Cordovan Caliph; perhaps five days good sailing southwards from the Breton cape, which they could now see. They sacrificed again to the sea-people, were rewarded with a good wind, and sailed on into the open sea.

CHAPTER FOUR

How Krok's men came to Ramiro's kingdom, and how they paid a rewarding visit

When Orm was old, and spoke of the adventures that had befallen him, he used to say that he had had little to complain of during the time that he was in Krok's service, although he had joined his company so unwillingly. The blow he had received on his skull troubled him only for a few days; and he got on well with the men, so that, before long, they ceased to regard him as their prisoner. They remembered gratefully the good sheep that they had obtained from him, and he had other qualities that made him a good ship-mate. He knew as many ballads as Berse, and had learned from his mother to speak them with the intonation of the bards; besides which, he could tell lie-stories so cunningly that you had to believe in them, though he admitted that, in this particular craft, he was Toke's inferior. So they prized him as a good comrade, and a clever one, well able to while away the dreary hours agreeably for them during the long days when they had a good wind in their sail and were resting from their oars.

Some of the sailors were disgruntled because Krok had left Brittany without having first tried to get new supplies of fresh meat; for the food they had aboard was now beginning to smell old. The pork was rancid, the stockfish mildewed, the meal stale, the bread maggoty and the water sour; but Krok and those of his followers who had sailed on expeditions of this sort before asserted that this was as good fare as any sailor could wish for. Orm ate his rations with a good appetite, though, while he did so, he used often to tell the others of the delicacies to which he was accustomed at home. Berse remarked that it seemed to him to be a wise dispensation of the gods that a man could, when at sea, eat and enjoy food that, at home, he would not offer to his slaves or his dogs, but only to pigs; for, were it not so arranged, long sea-voyages would be exceedingly nauseating.

Toke said that the thing that troubled him most was the fact that the ale was now finished. He was, he assured them, not a fussy man, and he reckoned that he could stomach most things when necessity demanded it, not excluding his sealskin shoes, but only if he had good ale to wash them down. It would, he said, be a fearful prospect to envisage a life without ale, either on sea or ashore; and he questioned the Jew much concerning the quality of the ale in the country to which they were journeying without, however, being able to extract any very clear information from him on the subject. He told the others stories of great feasts and drinking-bouts that he had been present at, and mourned that he had not, on those occasions, drunk even more than he had.

Their second night at sea, a strong wind arose, driving high breakers, and they were glad that the sky remained clear, for they were steering by the stars. Krok began to wonder whether it would be wise to come out into the limitless sea; but the wisest sailors among them said that, however far you might sail to the south, you would always have land on your left, save only in the Njörva Sound,* where the waters led in to Rome, which stood at the centre of the world. Men who sailed from Norway to Iceland, said Berse, had a more difficult task, for they had no land in whose lee to shelter, but only the open sea, stretching away for ever on either bow.

The Jew knew all about the stars, and declared himself skilful at navigation; but in the event, he proved to be of little use to them, for his stars had different names to the ones they were used to, besides which, he was sea-sick. Orm suffered likewise, and he and Solomon hung over the gunwale together in great misery, thinking that they would die. The Jew wailed most piteously in his own language in the intervals of his vomiting; Orm told him to shut up, but he answered that he was crying to his god, who was in the storm wind. Then Orm grabbed him by the scruff of his neck and told him that, though he himself was in poor shape, he yet had

* The Straits of Gibraltar.

enough strength to throw him over the side if he uttered one cry more, for there was sufficient wind about already without his bringing his god any nearer to them.

This quietened Solomon; and, towards morning, the wind lessened and the sea grew calm, and they both began to feel better. Solomon was very green in the face, but he grinned at Orm in a friendly way and seemed not to bear him any ill-will for his conduct of the night before, and pointed his finger across the sea at the sunrise. He sought among the words he knew and said that those were the red wings of the morning far out in the sea, and that his god was there. Orm replied that his god appeared to him to be the sort of divinity who was best kept at a respectable distance.

Later that morning, they discerned mountains far ahead of them. They pulled in to the shore, but had difficulty in finding a sheltered bay in which to anchor; and the Jew said that this part of the coast was strange to him. They went ashore, and came at once into conflict with the inhabitants of the place, who were numerous; but these soon fled, and Krok's men ransacked their huts, returning with some goats and other food, as well as one or two prisoners. Fires were lit, and they all rejoiced at having reached land without mishap, and were glad to have the taste of roast meat once more on their tongues. Toke searched high and low for ale, but succeeded in discovering only a few skins of wine, which was so harsh and sour that, he said, he could feel his belly shrivelling as he swallowed it; so much so that he could not drink it all himself, but gave away what was left and sat alone for the rest of the evening singing sadly to himself, with tears in his beard. Berse warned them not to disturb him, for he was a dangerous man when he had drunk himself to weeping-point.

Solomon questioned the prisoners, and told the Vikings that they were now in the country of the Count of Castile, and that the place to which he wished to lead them lay far to the west. Krok said that they would have to wait for another wind to carry them in that direction, and that in the meantime they could do no more than rest and eat; though, he added, the situation might become awkward if strong hostile forces should attack them here, while the wind was blowing landwards, or if enemy ships should block their exit from the bay. But Solomon explained, as best he could, that there was little danger of this, for the Count of Castile had hardly any ships at sea, and it would take him some time to gather a sufficient force to cause them trouble. In former years, he told them, this Count of Castile had been a powerful ruler, but nowadays he was forced to bow the knee to the Moorish Caliph in Cordova, and even had to pay him tribute; for, saving only the Emperor Otto of Germany and the Emperor Basil of Constantinople, there was now no monarch in the world as powerful as the Caliph of Cordova. At this, the men laughed loudly, saying that the Jew was doubtless saying what he supposed to be the truth, but that he obviously knew little about the subject. Had he, they asked, never heard of King Harald of Denmark, and did he not know that there was no king in the world as mighty as he?

Orm was still groggy after his sea-sickness and had little appetite for food, which made him afraid that he might be sickening for something serious, for he worried continually about his health. He soon curled up in front of one of the fires, and fell into a deep sleep; but during the night, when the whole camp was still, Toke came and woke him. With tears streaming down his cheeks, he protested that Orm was the only friend he had, and said that he would like, if he might, to sing him a song that he had just remembered; it was about two bear cubs, he explained, and he had learned it as a child at his mother's knee, and it was the most beautiful song he had ever heard. So saying, he sat down on the ground beside Orm, dried his tears and began to sing. Now it was a peculiarity with Orm that he found it difficult to be sociable when he had just been woken out of a sound sleep; however, he voiced no protest, but merely turned over on to his other side and tried to go back to sleep.

Toke could not remember much of his song, and this made him miserable again. He complained that he had been sitting alone all the evening, and that nobody had come to keep him company. What had hurt him most, he said, was the fact that Orm had not once given him so much as a friendly glance, to cheer him up; for he had always hitherto regarded Orm as his best friend, from the first moment that he had set eyes upon him; now, though, he realized that he was, after all, only a good-for-nothing blackguard like all Skanians; and when a puppy like him forgot his manners, a good sound hiding was the only remedy.

So saying, he got to his feet to look round for a stick; but Orm, who was by this time fully awake, sat up. When Toke saw him do this, he tried to aim a kick at him; but, as he raised his foot, Orm snatched a brand out of the fire and threw it in Toke's face. Toke ducked in the middle of aiming his kick, and fell on his back, but he was on his feet again in an instant, white in the face and blind with rage. Orm, too, had leaped to his feet, so that they now stood facing each other. It was bright moonlight, but Orm's eyes were flickering a dangerous red as he threw himself furiously upon Toke, who tried to draw his sword; Orm had lain his aside, and had not had time to lay his hand on it. Now, Toke was a huge and powerful man, broad in the loins, and with tremendous hands, while Orm had not yet grown to his full strength, although he was already strong enough to deal with most men. He secured a lock on Toke's neck with one arm, and pinned Toke's right wrist with his other hand, to stop him drawing his sword; but Toke took a good grip on Orm's clothing, lifted him from his feet with a sudden jerk, and threw him over his head like a starfish. Orm, however, managed to hold his lock, though it felt as though his spine would snap at any moment, and, twisting round, got one of his knees into the small of Toke's back. Then he threw himself backwards, dragging Toke down on top of him, and, exerting all his strength, succeeded in turning him over, so that he had Toke under him with his face in the dust. By this time, several of the others had been roused, and Berse ran towards them with a rope, muttering that what else could you expect if you allowed Toke to sozzle himself like that. They bound him fast, hand and foot, though he struggled wildly to stop them. However he quietened down after a short while, and before long he was shouting to Orm that he had now remembered the rest of the song. He began to sing it, but Berse threw water over him, whereupon he fell asleep.

On awaking the next morning, Toke swore fearfully at finding himself tied up, being unable to remember anything of what had happened. When they told him, he was full of remorse for the way he had behaved, and explained that it was his great misfortune that drink sometimes made him difficult. Ale, he said, translated him completely, and now, regrettably, it seemed that wine was going to have the same effect. He inquired anxiously whether Orm now regarded him as his enemy, in view of his conduct of the previous night. Orm replied that he did not, adding that he would be delighted to continue the fight amiably any time that Toke felt so disposed;

but he begged that Toke would promise him one thing, namely, that he would abstain from song, for the rasp of a nightjar, or the croaking of an old crow on an outhouse roof, was far more melodious than his nocturnal serenading. Toke laughed, and promised that he would try to improve his talents in that respect; for he was a kindly man except when ale or wine distorted his nature.

All the men thought that Orm had come out of the affair remarkably well, especially considering his youth; for few of those who came within the range of Toke's arm once he had reached the weeping stage escaped unscathed. So Orm rose in the estimation of his fellows, as well as in his own. After this incident, they began to call him Red Orm, not only because of his red hair but also because he had proved himself a man of mettle, and one not to be provoked without sound cause.

After some days, a good wind sprang up, and they put out to sea. They kept well away from the land, to avoid dangerous currents, and headed westwards along the coast of Ramiro's kingdom until they had rounded the cape. Then they rowed southwards along a steep and broken coast, proceeding through a small archipelago, which reminded the men of their own group of islands off Blekinge. At length, they reached the mouth of a certain river, for which the Jew had been keeping a look-out. They entered the river on the flood tide, and rowed up it until they were halted by weirs; there they went ashore and held counsel. Solomon described the journey that lay ahead of them, saying that bold men might march in less than a day to the fortress of the man upon whom he wished to be revenged, one of King Ramiro's margraves, a man called Ordono, the most villainous and scoundrelly bandit (he said) in all the shores of Christendom.

Krok and Berse questioned him closely concerning the fortress, asking him details of its strength and situation, and how large an army the margrave kept to defend it. Solomon replied that it lay in such a craggy and deserted tract of country that the Caliph's army, which consisted largely of cavalry, never came near it. This made it an excellent hideout for a bandit, and there was great wealth contained within its walls. It was built of oak-trunks and was protected by an earthen dyke, surmounted by a stockage; and its defenders might be reckoned to number, at the outside, 200 men. Solomon thought that they probably did not keep careful watch because its situation was so remote; and, indeed, the majority of the margrave's men were often absent marauding in the south.

Krok said the number of the defenders worried him less than the dyke and the stockade, which would make a surprise assault difficult. Some of the men thought it would be a simple matter to set fire to the stockade, but Berse reminded them that the whole fortress might then catch, in which case they would gain little profit from whatever wealth it might contain. In the end, they decided that they would trust to their luck and determine what plan to follow when they reached the place. It was agreed that forty men should remain on board the ships, while the rest were to set out when evening fell, for it would then be cooler. Then they drew lots to determine which of them should stay with the ships, for they were all keen to be on the spot when the looting began.

They saw to their weapons, and slept during the heat of the day in a grove of oak-trees. Then they fortified themselves with food and drink and, as evening fell, the company set out, numbering in all 136 men. Krok marched at their head, with the Jew and Berse, and the rest followed, some wearing chain-shirts and others leathern jackets. Most of them were armed with sword and spear, though a few carried axes; and each man had a shield and helmet. Orm marched beside Toke, who said it was a good thing to have this opportunity to loosen one's joints before the fighting began, after so many sedentary weeks upon the oar-bench.

They marched through a barren wilderness, in which no signs of human life could be seen; for these border regions between the Christian and the Andalusian kingdoms had for long been deserted. They kept to the northern bank of the river, fording a number of small streams; meanwhile the darkness thickened and, after some hours, they rested and waited for the moon to rise. Then they turned northwards along a valley, making swift progress over flat terrain, and Solomon proved himself a good guide for, before the skies grew grey, they reached the approaches to the fortress. There they hid in the scrub and rested again for a while, peering forward into the gloom to discern what they could by the pale light of the moon. The sight of the stockade somewhat daunted them, for it consisted of rough tree-trunks more than twice the height of a man; and the huge gate, which was fortified on top, looked exceedingly formidable.

Krok observed that it would be no easy task to set fire to this, adding that he would, in any event, prefer to storm the place without using fire, if it were at all possible; but that there might be no other way, in which case they would have to pile brushwood against the stockade and set light to it, and hope that the whole building would not catch. He asked Berse if he had any better suggestion to put forward, but Berse shook his head, and sighed, and said that he could not think of any alternative, though he, too, disliked resorting to the use of fire. Nor had Solomon anything better to propose; he muttered that he would have to rest content with seeing the infidel burn, although he had hoped to obtain a more satisfying mode of revenge.

At this point in the discussion Toke crawled forward to Krok and Berse and asked what the delay was for, as he was beginning to grow thirsty and, the sooner they stormed the fortress, the sooner he would be able to get something to drink. Krok told him that the problem they were debating was how to force an entry. To this, Toke replied that, if they would give him five spears, he could, he thought, show them that he was capable of more things than merely rowing and drinking ale. The others asked what plan he had in mind, but he would only answer that, if all went well, he would procure their entry into the fortress, though the owners of the spears would have to be prepared to re-shaft them when they got them back. Berse, who knew Toke of old, advised that he should be given his head; so the spears were brought, and Toke cut off their shafts just where the iron joined the wood, so that he had a short stump left below each blade. He then announced that he was ready to begin; and he and Krok began to steal quietly towards the rampart, taking cover behind rocks and bushes, with a handful of picked men following them. They heard a few cocks crow from within the fortress but, apart from this, the night was completely quiet.

They crept up to the rampart a short way along from the gate; then Toke climbed up to the foot of the stockade and drove one of his spears between two of the piles, a good ell's length from the ground, twisting it with all his strength to make it fast. Higher up in the next chink along, he drove a second blade; then, when he had noiselessly made sure that both of them would take the strain, he stepped carefully up on to the shortened shafts and fixed a third spear-head higher up in the next chink. But, placed as he was, he found himself unable to make this blade fast without creating a

44

noise. Krok, who had by now realized what Toke had in mind, signed to him to come down, whispering that they would have to do a bit of hammering now, even at the risk of disturbing certain sleepers from their slumber. Then, carrying the two remaining spear-heads in his hand, he took Toke's place on the steps that he had already made fast, and drove the third blade home with a couple of blows from the flat of his axe, immediately afterwards doing likewise with the fourth and fifth spear-heads, fastening them higher up and further along. As soon as he had driven the last blade home, he climbed up them and so reached the top of the stockade.

As he did so, they heard cries and alarms from within the fortress and a great baying of horns; but others of the Vikings followed Krok swiftly up Toke's ladder, as fast as they could clamber, and joined him at the top. Along the inside of the stockade there ran a wooden bridge, for bowmen to stand on. Krok and his followers jumped down on to this, encountering some men, armed with bows and spears and still drowsy with sleep, who ran out to intercept them, and cut them down. By this time, they were being assailed with arrows from the ground, and two of them were hit, but Krok and the others ran along the bridge to the gate, and there dropped to the ground, in the hope of being able to open it from within and thus admit the rest of their comrades. Hard fighting ensued, however, for many of the defenders of the fortress had already run to defend the gate, and reinforcements were coming to their aid with every minute that passed. One of the twenty men who had followed Krok up the ladder was hanging from the stockade with an arrow in his eye, and three others had been hit in their passage along the bridge; but all those who had managed to reach the ground safely packed themselves together in a tight phalanx and, raising their battle-cry, fought their way with spear and sword to the gate. Here it was very dark, and they found themselves hard pressed indeed, with enemies behind as well as in front of them.

Then they heard their battle-cry answered from without, for the men waiting on the hillside had run forward to the rampart as soon as they had seen that the attempt to scale the stockade had succeeded, and many of them were hacking at the gate with their axes, while others clambered up Toke's ladder and dropped down inside the fortress to assist their companions who were fighting within the gate. There the strife was fierce and chaotic, friends and foes hardly knowing which was which. Krok felled several men with his axe, but was himself then struck on the side of the neck with a club wielded by a huge man with a black, plaited beard, who appeared to be the defenders' chieftain. Krok's helmet partially parried the force of the blow, but he staggered and fell on his knees. At length Toke and Orm succeeded in fighting their way through a tangle of men and shields, so tightly packed that it was impossible to use a spear, with the ground so greasy with blood that their feet several times all but went from under them, and managed to draw the bolts of the gate. Their comrades poured in to join them, and such of the defenders in the gateway as did not flee were overwhelmed and slaughtered.

Then a terrible panic descended on the Christians, and they fled with death snarling at their heels. Solomon, who had been among the first to break in through the gate, charged ahead of the Vikings like a fanatic, stumbling over the bodies of the slain. Seizing a sword that lay upon the ground and whirling it above his head, he shrieked to his companions through the uproar, bidding them all make haste to the citadel. Krok, who was still dazed from the blow that had felled him, and was unable to regain his feet, cried to them from where he lay in the gateway to follow the Jew. Many of the Vikings ran into the houses that lined the inside of the rampart to slake their thirst or to look for women; but the majority of them pursued the fleeing defenders to the great citadel which stood in the centre of the fortress. The gate of the citadel was crowded with Christians trying to get in but, before it could be closed, their pursuers swarmed in among them, so that fighting broke out again within the citadel; for the Christians saw that they had no option but to defend themselves. The big man with the plaited beard fought bravely, felling two men who attacked him, but at length he was forced into a corner and sustained blows which brought him to his knees, sorely wounded. On seeing him fall, Solomon rushed forward and threw himself upon him, seizing him by the beard and spitting on him, and slobbering like a drunken man; but the bearded man stared at him as though uncomprehendingly, rolled on to his side, closed his eyes and died.

Seeing this, Solomon broke into loud lamentations at having been cheated of his full revenge, in that he had not been allowed to kill the man himself. Such Christians as remained alive defended themselves no longer when they saw that their leader had fallen, but surrendered to the mercy of their conquerors. Some of them were spared, so that they might be sold as slaves. Having helped themselves handsomely to meat and drink, which included ale as well as wine, the Vikings ransacked the fortress for booty, and disputes broke out concerning the women whom they discovered crouching in various corners, for they had been without women for many weeks. All the booty they found was heaped into an enormous pile – money, jewels, weapons, garments, brocades, coats of mail, household goods, bridles, silver plate and much besides – and, when it had all been counted, the value of it was found to exceed their wildest expectations. Solomon explained to them that it represented the fruits of years of plundering at the expense of the Andalusians. Krok, who was now able to stand on his feet again, and had a rag soaked with wine bandaged round his head, rejoiced at the sight of it, and was only afraid lest it might prove difficult to find space for so much on board their ships. However, Berse assured him that they would be able to find room for it all.

'For no man,' he said, 'complains of the weight of the cargo, when it is his own booty that is putting strain upon his oar.'

They spent the rest of the day indulging their appetites, in high good humour; then, they slept and, when night came, started on their return march towards the ships. All the prisoners were heavily laden with booty, and the men themselves had much to carry. Some Andalusian prisoners had been found in the dungeons of the citadel; they wept with joy at being freed, but looked wretchedly feeble and were incapable of carrying anything. So they were granted their liberty, and accompanied the Vikings on their way back to the ships, whence they were to proceed southwards with Solomon to their own country. Some donkeys had been captured, and Krok mounted one of them and rode at the head of the column, with his feet reaching to the ground. The other donkeys were led behind him, laden with food and ale; but their loads were speedily lightened, for the men stopped frequently to rest and refresh themselves.

Berse tried to hurry them on, that they might reach the ships as soon as possible. He was afraid lest they might be pursued, for some of the defenders of the fortress had managed to escape, and could have ridden far enough to have procured help; but the men paid little attention to his exhortations, for they were in high spirits, and most

47

of them were befuddled with drink. Orm had taken a bale of silk, a bronze mirror and a large glass bowl, which was proving awkward to carry. Toke had a big wooden box balanced on his shoulder, finely embossed and full of various objects; with his other hand, he was leading a girl who had taken his fancy, and whom he wanted to hold on to for as long as possible. He was in excellent spirits, and expressed to Orm the hope that the girl might turn out to be the margrave's daughter; but then he grew melancholy, beginning to doubt whether there would be room for her on board the ship. He was unsteady on his feet, on account of the quantity he had drunk, but the girl seemed already to be solicitously disposed towards him, and supported him when he stumbled. She was well proportioned and very young, and Orm said that he had seldom seen a finer girl, and that it would be a good thing to have woman-luck as good as Toke's. But Toke replied that, despite their friendship, he could not share her with Orm, for she appealed to him very particularly and he wished to keep her for himself, if the gods should permit this to be.

At last, they reached the ships, and the men who had remained on board were greatly jubilant at the sight of such rich booty, for it had been agreed that this was to be divided amongst them all. Solomon received many expressions of thanks from them all, and various costly presents; then he departed, together with the prisoners whom they had freed, since he was anxious to get clear of the Christians' country as soon as he could. Toke, who had not yet stopped drinking, began to weep when he heard that Solomon had left them, saying that now he had nobody to help him to converse with his girl. He drew his sword and wanted to run after him; but Orm and the others succeeded in quietening him without having to resort to violence, and in the end he nestled contentedly down beside his girl, having first bound her fast to him so that she should not steal away or be stolen while he slept.

The next morning, they began to share out the booty, which proved to be no simple task. Everybody wanted to have as big a share as the next man; but it was decided that Krok and Berse and the helmsman and one or two others should have three times as much as the rest. Even then, although the business of sharing everything out fairly was allotted to the wisest among them, it was difficult to satisfy everyone. Berse said that, since it was largely due to Toke that the fortress had been taken, he too, ought to have a triple share; and they all agreed that this should be so. But Toke replied that he would be content with his single share, if he might be allowed to bring his girl on board and keep her there without anyone objecting.

'For I should dearly like to bring her home with me,' he said, 'even though I cannot be completely sure that she is the margrave's daughter. I am already getting on excellently with her and, when she is able to speak our language, and we can understand each other's conversation, it will be better still.'

Berse remarked that this might not turn out to be such an advantage as Toke supposed, and Krok added that the ships were going to be so heavily laden with all the booty they had won that, even allowing for the fact that they lost eleven men in the fight, he doubted whether there would be room for the girl on board; as things were they would probably have to leave some of the less valuable booty behind.

At this, Toke rose to his feet, lifted the girl on to his shoulder and commanded them all to have a good look at her and to note how beautiful she was, and what a fine figure she had.

'I do not doubt,' he said, 'that she is well able to excite the lust of any man. Now, if there be any man here who covets her, I shall be happy to fight him for her, here and now, either with sword or with axe, whichever weapon he cares to choose. Let the winner keep the girl; and the man who dies will, by his absence, lighten the ship more than she will burden it; and in this way, I can fairly take her with me.'

The girl held tightly with one hand to the beard on Toke's cheek, and went red and wriggled her legs and put her other hand over her eyes; but then she took it away again, seeming to enjoy being looked at. They all thought that Toke's proposition had been cunningly devised. But none of them elected to fight with him, despite the beauty of the girl, for they all liked him and, besides, feared him for his strength and his skill at arms.

When all the booty had been shared out and stored aboard, it was decided that Toke should be permitted to bring his girl aboard Krok's ship, although it was heavily laden; for they agreed that he had deserved such a reward for his part in the storming of the fortress. Then they held counsel regarding the question of the homeward voyage, and agreed that they should return along the Asturian and Frankish coasts if the weather was bad, but that, if it were good, they should try to make for Ireland, thence to proceed homewards round the Scottish islands; for, with such booty as they had, it would be taking an unnecessary risk to sail through unfrequented waters, where they might encounter other ships.

They ate and drank as much as they could hold, having now an abundance of food and drink, more indeed than they could take with them; and all the men were merry and excited, telling each other what they would buy with their new-found wealth when they reached home. Krok was, by this time, himself again; but the captain of one of the others ships had fallen in the fortress, and Berse took command of his vessel. Toke and Orm sat down to their old oars in Krok's ship, finding it easy work with the current to help them; and Toke kept a close eye on his girl, who spent most of the time sitting by him, and was careful to see that nobody came near her without good cause.

CHAPTER FIVE

How Krok's luck changed twice, and how Orm became left-handed

They rowed down to the mouth of the river on the ebb tide, and offered up a skin of wine and a pot of flesh for the homeward voyage. Then they set sail, shipped their oars and moved out under a gentle wind into the long sweep of the bay. The heavily laden ships lay deep in the water, and made slow progress; and Krok remarked that they would have to row until their arms ached before they saw their home shores again. Orm, afterwards, in his old age, used to say that these were the unluckiest words he had ever heard spoken, for, from that moment, Krok's luck, which had hitherto been so good, suddenly broke, just as though a god had heard him speak and had decided there and then to make him a true prophet.

Seven ships appeared round the southern point of the bay, heading northwards. On sighting Krok's ships, however, they turned into the bay and approached them at a great pace, their oars moving nimbly through the water. They were ships such as Krok's men had never before set eyes on, being long and low and very light in the water, and were filled with armed men, wearing black beards and strange coverings on their helmets. The men who were rowing them, two at each oar, were naked, and their skins a polished black-brown. They headed towards the Vikings amid hoarse cries and the sharp tumult of small drums.

Krok's three ships at once came abreast of each other, keeping close to the land on their side of the bay, in order to avoid being encircled. Krok was unwilling to give the order to lower sail; for, he said, should the wind rise, it would be to their advantage. Toke made haste to hide his girl among the bales of booty, piling them around and even on top of her, so as to protect her from spears and arrows. Orm helped him; then they took their places at the gunwale with the others. By this time, Orm was well armed, for he had provided himself with a mail-shirt and a shield and a good helmet from the fortress. A man standing near them wondered whether these strangers might perhaps be Christians, bent on revenge; but Orm thought it more likely that they were the Caliph's men, since no cross was visible on their shields or standards. Toke said that he was glad that he had quenched his thirst before the fighting began, for it looked as though it might be hot.

'And such of us as survive the day,' he said, 'will have a story worth telling our children; for these men have a savage air about them, and they far outnumber us.'

By this time the foreigners had approached to within a short distance, and they now assailed the Vikings with showers of arrows. They rowed cunningly, slipping round the Viking ships and attacking them from all sides. The ship which Berse was commanding lay next to the shore, so that they could not surround her; but Krok's own ship lay at the extreme right of the three, furthest from the land, and was at once engaged in hard fighting. Two of the strangers' ships drew alongside her on the seaward side, the one lying beyond the other. They grappled the three vessels together with chains and iron hooks; then the men from the outer ship, yelling wildly, jumped across to the inner one, whence they all swarmed on to the Viking ship. They poured abroad her in overwhelming numbers, fighting very fiercely and skilfully, so that Krok's ship, by now very low in the water, lagged sadly behind her two companions. Then a third enemy ship managed to slip round her bows and grapple her on the shoreward side. So the situation now was that Berse's ship and the third Viking vessel had managed to get clear of the bay, though they had four enemy ships harrying them and were hard pressed to hold them off, while Krok's ship was engaging three opponents single-handed. At this stage of the battle, the wind rose, so that both Berse's ships were driven still further from the shore, with fierce fighting raging aboard them and broad ribbons of blood trailing behind them in the water.

But the men in Krok's ship had no time to worry about how their companion vessels were faring, for they had their hands more than full with their own adversaries. So many foemen had climbed aboard over one of the gunwales that the ship had keeled over and was in danger of sinking; and, although many of the raiders were hewn down and fell into the water or back into their own ship, a high proportion of them remained aboard, while others were swarming to their assistance from both sides. Krok fought bravely, and such of the foreigners as challenged him soon ceased their whooping; but, before long, he recognized that the enemy's superiority in numbers was too great. Then he threw aside his shield, sprang on to the gunwale and, swinging his axe with both hands, severed two of the chains that bound his ship to the enemy; but a man whom he had felled clutched hold of one of his legs and, in the same instant, he received a spear through the shoulders and toppled headlong into the enemy ship, where many of his foes fell upon him, so that he was taken prisoner and bound fast.

After this, many of Krok's men were slain, though they defended themselves to the limit of their strength, and at last the whole ship was overrun, apart from a few men who were hemmed forward, including Toke and Orm. Toke had an arrow in his thigh, but was still on his feet, while Orm had received a blow on his forehead and could scarcely see for the blood that was running down into his eyes. Both of them were very weary. Toke's sword broke on the boss of a shield, but as he stepped backwards his foot struck against a firkin of wine which had been captured in the fortress and had been stored in the bows. Throwing aside the stump of his sword, he seized the firkin with both hands and raised it above his head.

'This shall not be wasted,' he muttered, and hurled it against the nearest of his foes, crushing two of them and tripping up several others who fell over their bodies.

Then he cried to Orm and the others that there was nothing more to be done in the ship and, with those words, jumped head first into the sea, in the hope of swimming ashore. Orm and as many of the others as could disengage the enemy followed suit. Arrows and spears pursued them, and two of them were hit. Orm dived, came up, and swam as hard as he could; but, as he was often to observe in his old age, few things are more difficult than swimming in a mail-shirt when a man is tired and his shirt is tight. Before long, neither Toke nor Orm had the strength left to swim further, and they were on the point of sinking when one of the enemy's ships overtook them, and they were dragged on board and bound fast, without being able to offer any resistance.

So the Vikings were defeated, and their victors rowed ashore to examine what they had won and to bury their dead. They cleared the decks of the ship they had captured, throwing the corpses overboard, and began to rummage through its cargo, while the prisoners were led ashore and sat down on the beach, well guarded, with their arms bound. There were nine of them, all wounded. They waited for death, staring silently out to sea; but there was not sign of Berse's ship or of their pursuers.

Toke sighed and began to mumble to himself. Then he said:

> 'Once, thirsty, I
> Wasted good ale.
> Soon shall I taste
> Valhalla's mead.'

Orm lay on his back, gazing up at the sky. He said:

> 'At home in the house
> That saw me grow
> Would I were seated now
> Eating sour milk and bread.'

But none of them was sicker at heart than Krok; for, ever since the beginning of their expedition, he had regarded himself as a lucky man, and as a hero, and now he had seen his luck crumble within the hour. He watched them throwing his dead followers overboard from what had been his ship, and said:

> 'The ploughers of the sea
> Earned for their toil
> Misfortune and a foul
> And early death.'

Toke observed that this was a remarkable coincidence, that three poets should be found in so small a company.

'Even if you cannot fully match my skill at composing verses,'

54

he said, 'yet be of good cheer. Remember that it is granted to the poets to drink from the largest horn at the banquet of the gods.'

At this moment, they heard a piercing shriek from the ship, followed by a great hubbub, signifying that the foreigners had discovered Toke's girl in her hiding-place. They brought her ashore, and an argument seemed to be developing as to who should have her, for several men began quarrelling in high-pitched voices, their black beards going up and down. Toke said: 'Now the crows are disputing for possession of the hen, while the hawk sits nursing his broken wing.'

The girl was led forward to the chieftain of the foreigners, a fat man with a grizzled beard and gold rings in his ears, clad in a red cloak and holding in his hand a silver hammer with a long white shaft. He studied her, stroking his beard; then he addressed her, and they could see that the two of them understood each other's language. The girl had plenty to say, pointing several times in the direction of the prisoners; but to two of his questions, when he also pointed towards them, she made a negative gesture with her hands and shook her head. The chieftain nodded, and then gave her an order which she seemed reluctant to obey, for she raised her arms towards the sky and cried out; but when he spoke to her again, in a severe voice, she became submissive and took her clothes off and stood naked before him. All the men standing around them sighed and tugged their beards, and murmured with enraptured voices, for, from the crown of her head to the soles of her feet, she was exceedingly beautiful. The chieftain ordered her to turn round, and examined her closely, fingering her hair, which was long and brown, and feeling her skin. Then he stood up, and laid a signet ring, which he wore on one of his forefingers, against her belly and breasts and lips; after which, addressing some remark to his men, he took off his red cloak and wrapped it about her. On hearing his words, all his followers placed their hands against their foreheads and bowed, murmuring obsequiously. Then the girl dressed again, retaining, however, the red cloak, and food and drink were given to her, and everybody treated her with reverence.

The prisoners watched all this in silence; and, when it reached the stage where the girl was given the cloak and was offered food and drink, Orm remarked that she seemed to have the best luck of all Krok's company. Toke agreed, and said that it was a hard thing for him so see her in all her beauty only now for the first time, when she was already another man's; for he had had little time with her, and they had always had to hurry; and now, he said, he could weep to think that he would never have the opportunity to split the skull of the pot-bellied greybeard who had soiled her body with his greasy fingers.

'But I cling to the hope,' he added, 'that the old gentleman will get little joy out of her; for, from the first moment that I saw her, I found her intelligent and of excellent taste, even though we could not understand each other's conversation; so that I think it cannot be long before she will stick a knife into the guts of that old billy-goat.'

All this while, Krok had been sitting in deep silence, weighed down by his fate, with his face turned towards the sea, unable to take any interest in what was happening on shore. But now, all of a sudden, he uttered a cry, and as he did so the foreigners began to gabble excitedly among themselves, for four ships had appeared far out in the bay, rowing towards the land. They were the ships that had fought Berse, and were rowing slowly; and soon they could see that one of them was lying very deep in the water, badly damaged, with the centre of one of its gunwales smashed in, and many of its oars broken.

At this spectacle, the prisoners, though dispirited at their own plight, faint from their wounds and much troubled by thirst, broke into shouts of delighted laughter. For they realized at once that Berse had succeeded in ramming this ship, once the wind had risen out in the open sea, and that the enemy had had to break off the fight when they found themselves with only three sound ships left, and had rowed back with the damaged one. Some of them now began to hope that Berse might return and rescue them. But Krok said: 'He has lost many men, for he had enemies aboard and his hands full when I last saw him. And he must have guessed that few of us can be left alive since he has not seen our ship come out of the bay; so he is more likely to try and reach home safely with what he has, either in both his ships or, if he has too few men left to man both, in one of them. Should he reach Blekinge safely, even if only with one ship, the story of Krok's expedition will be told in the Listerland, and will be well remembered in the years to come. Now, however, these men will surely kill us, for their anger will be greater now that two of our ships have escaped their clutches.'

In this, though, Krok was proved a false prophet. They were given food and drink, and a man came to look at their wounds; and then they realized that they were to become slaves. Some of them regarded this as preferable to death, while others were doubtful whether it might not prove a worse fate. The foreign chieftain had his galley-slaves brought ashore, and let them speak with the Vikings. They seemed to hail from many different lands, and addressed them in various strange mumblings, but none of them spoke any language that the prisoners could understand. The foreigners remained in this place for a few days, putting their damaged ship in order.

Many of the oarsmen in this ship had been killed when Berse had rammed it, and the captured Vikings were set to replace them. They were well used to rowing, and at first they did not find the work too arduous for them, especially as, in this ship, there were two men to each oar. But they had to row almost naked, of which they were much ashamed, and each man had one leg chained. Their skin was almost white, compared with that of the other slaves, and their backs were sorely flayed by the sun, so that they came to regard each sunrise as another turn of the rack. After a time, however, they became tanned like their fellows, and ceased to count the days, and were conscious of nothing but rowing and sleeping, feeling hunger and thirst, drinking and eating and rowing again, until at last they reached the stage where, when harder rowing than usual had made them weary, they would fall asleep at their oars and continue rowing, without falling out of time or needing to be aroused by the overseer's whip. This showed them to have become true galley-slaves.

They rowed in heat and in fierce rain, and sometimes in a pleasant cool, though it was never cold. They were the Caliph's slaves, but they had little knowledge of whither they were rowing or what purpose their labour might be serving. They rowed beside steep coasts and rich lowlands, and toiled painfully up broad and swiftly-flowing rivers, on the banks of which they saw brown and black men and occasionally, but always at a distance, veiled women. They passed through the Njörva Sound, and journeyed to the limits of the Caliph's dominions, seeing many rich islands and fine cities, the names of which they did not know. They anchored in great harbours, where they were shut up in slave-houses until the time came for them to put out to sea again; and they rowed hard in pursuit of foreign ships till their hearts seemed to be about to burst, and lay

57

panting on the deck while battles that they had no strength to watch raged on the grapplings above them.

They felt neither grief nor hope, and cried to no gods, for they had work enough to do minding their oars and keeping a watchful eye open for the man with the whip who supervised their rowing. They hated him with a fierce intensity when he flicked them with his whip, and even more when they were rowing their hearts out and he strode among them with big lumps of bread soaked in wine, which he stuffed into their mouths, for then they knew that they would have to row without rest for as long as their strength sustained them. They could not understand what he said, but they soon learned to know from the tone of his voice how many lashes he was preparing to administer as a reward for negligence; and their only comfort was to hope that he would have a hard end, with his windpipe slit or his back flayed until his bones could be seen through the blood.

In his old age, Orm used to say that this period in his life was lengthy to endure, but brief to tell of, for one day resembled another, so that, in a sense, it was as though time was standing still for them. But there were signs to remind him that time was, in fact, passing; and one of these was his beard. When he first became a slave, he was the only one among them so young as to be beardless; but before long, his beard began to grow, becoming redder even than his hair, and in time it grew so long that it swept the handle of his oar as he bowed himself over his stroke. Longer than that it could not grow, for the sweep of his oar curtailed its length; and, of all the methods of trimming one's beard, he would say, that was the last that he would choose.

The second sign was the increase in his strength. He was already strong when they first chained him to his place, and used to rowing in Krok's ship, but a slave has to work harder than a free man, and the long bouts of rowing tried him sorely and sometimes, in the first few weeks, made him sick and dizzy. He saw men burst their hearts, spewing bloody froth over their beards, and topple backwards over the benches with their bodies shaking violently, and die and be thrown overboard; but he knew that he had only two choices to make, either to row while his fellows rowed, even if it meant rowing himself to death, or to receive the kiss of the overseer's whip upon his back. He said that he always chose the former, though it was little to go for, because once, during the first few days of his slavery, he had felt the whip, and he knew that, if he felt it again, a white madness would descend upon him, and then his death would be certain.

So he rowed to the limit of his strength, even when his eyes blurred and his arms and his back ached like fire. After some weeks, however, he found that he was ceasing to be aware of his tiredness. His strength waxed, and soon he had to be careful not to pull too hard for fear of snapping his oar, which now felt like a stick in his hands; for a broken oar meant a sharp lesson from the whip. Throughout his long term as one of the Caliph's galley-slaves, he rowed a larboard oar, which involved sitting with the oar on his right and taking the strain of the stroke on his left hand. Always afterwards, as long as he lived, he wielded his sword and such-like weapons with his left hand, though he still used his right arm for casting spears. The strength which he gained through this labour, which was greater than that of other men, remained with him, and he still had much of it left when he was old.

But there was a third sign, apart from the growth of his beard and of his strength, to remind him that time was passing as he laboured at his oar; for he found himself gradually beginning to understand something of the foreign tongues that were being spoken around him, at first only a word here and there, but, in time, much more. Some of the slaves were from distant lands in the south and east, and spoke tongues like the yapping of dogs which none but themselves could understand; others were prisoners from the Christian lands in the north, and spoke the languages of those regions. Many, however, were Andalusians, who had been put to the oar because they had been pirates or rebels, or because they had angered the Caliph with seditious teaching concerning their god and prophet; and these, like their masters, spoke Arabic. The overseer with the whip expressed himself in this tongue and, since it was always a wise thing for every slave to try to understand what this man wanted from them, he proved a good language-master to Orm, without causing himself any exertion in the process.

It was a cumbrous language to understand, and even more so to speak, for it consisted of guttural sounds that came from the depths of the throat, and resembled nothing so much as the grunting of oxen, or the croaking of frogs. Orm and his comrades never ceased to wonder that these foreigners should have chosen to give

59

themselves the trouble of having to produce such complicated noises, instead of talking in the simple and natural manner of the north. However, he showed himself to be quicker than any of the others in picking it up, partly, perhaps, because he was younger than they, but partly also because he had always shown an aptitude for pronouncing difficult and unfamiliar words that he had found in the old ballads, even when he had not been able to understand their meaning.

So it came to pass that Orm was the first of them who was able to understand what was being said to them, and the only one who could speak a word or two in reply. The consequence was that he became his companions' spokesman and interpreter, and that all orders were addressed to him. He was, besides, able to discover many things for the others by asking questions, as well as he could, of such of the other slaves as spoke Arabic and were able to tell him what he wanted to know. Thus, although he was the youngest of the Northmen, and a slave as they were, he came to regard himself as their chieftain, for neither Krok nor Toke were able to learn a word of the strange language; and Orm always afterwards used to say that, after good luck, strength and skill at arms, nothing was so useful to a man who found himself among foreigners as the ability to learn a language.

The ship was manned by fifty soldiers, and the galley-slaves numbered seventy-two; for there were eighteen pairs of oars. From bench to bench they would often murmur of the possibility of working themselves free from their chains, over-powering the soldiers, and so winning their freedom; but the chains were strong, and were carefully watched, and guards were always posted when the ship was lying at anchor. Even when they engaged an enemy ship, some of the soldiers were always detailed to keep an eye on the slaves, with orders to kill any that showed signs of restlessness. When they were led ashore in any of the Caliph's great military harbours, they were shut up in a slave-house until the ship was ready to depart again, being kept all the time under strict surveillance, and were never allowed to be together in large numbers; so that there seemed to be no future for them but to row for as long as life remained in their bodies, or until some enemy ship might chance to conquer their own and set them at liberty. But the Caliph's ships were many, and always outnumbered their enemies, so that this eventuality was scarcely to be reckoned with. Such of them as showed themselves refractory, or relieved their hatred with curses, were flogged to death or thrown overboard alive; though, occasionally, when the culprit was a strong oarsman, he was merely castrated and set again to his oar, which, although the slaves were never permitted a woman, they held to be the worst punishment of all.

When, in his old age, Orm used to tell of his years as a galley-slave, he still remembered all the positions that his fellow Vikings occupied in the ship, as well as those of most of the other slaves; and, as he told his story, he would take his listeners from oar to oar, describing what sort of man sat at each, and which among them died, and how others came to take their places, and which of them received the most whippings. He said that it was not difficult for him to remember these things, for in his dreams he often returned to the slave-ship, and saw the wealed backs straining before his eyes, and heard the men groaning with the terrible labour of their rowing, and, always, the feet of the overseer approaching behind him. His bed needed all the good craftsmanship that had gone into its making to keep it from splitting asunder as he would grip one of its beams to heave at the oar of his sleep; and he often said that there was no happiness in the world to compare with that of awakening from such a dream and finding it to be only a dream.

Three oars in front of Orm, also on the larboard side, sat Krok; and he was now a much changed man. Orm and the others knew that being a galley-slave fell harder on him than on the rest of them, because he was a man accustomed to command, and one who had always believed himself to be lucky. He was very silent, seldom replying when his neighbours addressed him; and although, with his great strength, he found no difficulty in doing the work required of him, he rowed always as though half asleep and deep in reflection on other matters. His stroke would gradually become slower, and his oar would fall out of time, and he would be savagely lashed by the overseer; but none of them ever heard him utter any cry as he received his punishment, or even mumble a curse. He would pull hard on his oar, and take up the stroke again; but his gaze would follow the overseer's back thoughtfully as the latter moved forward, as a man watches a troublesome wasp that he cannot lay his hands on.

Krok shared his oar with a man called Gunne, who complained

loudly of the many whippings he received on Krok's account; but Krok paid little heed to his lamentations. At length, on one occasion, when the overseer had flogged them both cruelly and Gunne's complaints were louder and his resentment greater than usual, Krok turned his eyes towards him, as though noticing his presence for the first time, and said; 'Be patient, Gunne. You will not have to endure my company for much longer. I am a chieftain, and was not born to serve other men; but I have one task yet to accomplish, if only my luck will stretch sufficiently to allow me to do what I have to do.'

He said no more, and what task it was that he had to perform, Gunne could not wring from him.

Just in front of Orm there sat two men named Halle and Ogmund. They spoke often of the good days that they spent in the past, of the food and the ale and the fine girls at home in the north, and conjured up various fitting deaths for the overseer; but they could never think of a way to bring any of them about. Orm himself was seated with a dark-brown foreigner who, for some misdemeanour, had had his tongue cut out. He was a good oarsman, and seldom needed the whip, but Orm would have preferred to be next to one of his own countrymen, or at any rate somebody able to talk. The worst of it, as far as Orm was concerned, was that the tongueless man, though unable to talk, was able all the more to cough, and his cough was more frightful than any that Orm had ever heard; when he coughed, he became grey in the face and gulped like a landed fish, and altogether wore such a wretched and woebegone appearance that it seemed impossible that he could live much longer. This made Orm anxious concerning his own health. He did not prize the life of a galley-slave very highly, but he was unwilling to be carried off by a cough; the tongueless man's performance made him certain in his mind of that. The more he reflected on the possibility of his dying like this, the more it dejected his spirits, and he wished that Toke had been seated nearer to him.

Toke was placed several oars behind Orm, so that they seldom had a chance to speak to one another, only, indeed, while they were being led ashore or back to the ship; for, in the slave-house, they were tethered together in groups of four in tiny cells, according to their places in the ship. Toke had, by now, regained something of his former humour, and could still manage to find something to laugh at, though he was usually at loggerheads with the man who shared his oar, whose name was Tume and who, in Toke's view, did less than his share of the rowing and ate more than his share of the rations. Toke composed abusive lampoons, some about Tume and some about the overseer, and sang them as shanties while he rowed, so that Orm and the others could hear them.

Most of the time, however, he occupied his thoughts with trying to plan some method of escape. The first time that Orm and he had a chance to speak to each other, he whispered that he had a good plan almost worked out. All he needed was a small bit of iron. With this, he could prise open one of the links in his ankle-chain, one dark night, when the ship was in port and everybody except the watchmen would be asleep. Having done this, he would pass the iron on to the other Vikings, each of whom would quietly break his chain. When they had all freed themselves, they would throttle the watchmen in the dark, without making a noise, and steal their weapons; then, once ashore, they would be able to fend for themselves.

Orm said that this would be a fine idea, if only it were practicable; and he would be glad to lend a hand in throttling the guards, if they got that far, which he rather doubted. Where, though, could they find a suitable piece of iron, and how could naked men, who were always under close observation, manage to smuggle it aboard without being detected? Toke sighed, and admitted that these were difficulties that would require careful consideration; but he could not think of any better plan, and said they would merely have to bide their time until an opportunity should present itself.

He succeeded in having a surreptitious word with Krok, too, and told him of his plan; but Krok listened to him abstractedly, and showed little interest or enthusiasm.

Not long afterwards, the ship was put into dry dock in one of the Caliph's shipyards to be scraped and pitched. Many of the slaves were detailed to assist with the work, chained in pairs; and the Northmen, who knew the ways of ships, were among these. Armed guards kept watch over them; and the overseer walked his rounds with his whip, to speed the work, two guards, armed with swords and bows, following him everywhere he went to protect him. Close to the ship, there stood a large cauldron full of simmering pitch, next to which was a barrel containing drinking water for the slaves.

Krok and Gunne were drinking from this barrel when one of

the slaves approached supporting his oar-companion, who had lost his foothold while engaged in the work and had so injured his foot that he was unable to stand on it. He was lowered to the ground, and had begun to drink, when the overseer came up to see what was afoot. The injured man was lying on his side, groaning; whereupon, the overseer, thinking that the man was shamming, gave him a cut with his whip to bring him to his feet. The man, however, remained where he was, with everybody's eyes fixed upon him.

Krok was standing a few paces behind them, on the far side of the barrel. He shifted towards them, dragging Gunne with him; and suddenly it seemed as though all his previous apathy had dropped away from him. When he was close enough, and saw that there was sufficient slack in the chain, he sprang forward, seized the overseer by the belt and the neck and lifted him above his head. The overseer cried out in terror, and the nearest of the guards turned and ran his sword through Krok's body. Krok seemed not to feel the blow. Taking two sideward paces, he flung the overseer head downwards into the boiling pitch, as the other guard's sword bit into his head. Krok tottered, but he kept his eyes fixed on what could be seen of the overseer. Then, he gave a laugh, and said: 'Now my luck has turned again,' and fell to the ground and died.

All the slaves raised a great shout of joy, to see the overseer meet such an end; but the gladness of the Vikings was mingled with grief, and in the months that followed they often recalled Krok's deed and the last words that he had uttered. They all agreed that he had died in a manner befitting a chieftain; and they expressed the hope that the overseer had lived long enough in the cauldron to get a good feel of the pitch. Toke wrought a strophe in Krok's honour, which ran thus:

> 'Worse than the whip-lash burned
> The whipper, when his head
> Was drowned deep in the hot wash—
> Tub of the sea-mare's bows.
> Krok, who, by cruel fate
> Had slaved at a foreign oar.
> Won his revenge and freedom,
> His luck had turned again.'

When they rowed out to sea again, they had a new overseer to supervise their labours; but he seemed to have taken note of the fate of his predecessor, for he was somewhat sparing in the use of his whip.

CHAPTER SIX

Concerning the Jew Solomon and the Lady Subaida, and how Orm got his sword Blue-Tongue

The tongueless man who rowed beside Orm grew worse and worse until at last he could row no more; so, when the ship anchored in one of the Caliph's military harbours in the south, called Malaga, he was led ashore, and they waited for another man to be brought to replace him. Orm had had to do nearly all the work on his oar during the last few weeks, and was curious to know whether he would now have a more congenial workmate. The next morning, the new man appeared. He was dragged to the ship by four soldiers, who had their work cut out to get him up the gangway, and nobody needed to peer closely at him to know that he still had his tongue. He was a young man, handsome, beardless and finely limbed, and he shrieked curses more frightful than anything that had been heard in the ship before.

He was carried to his place and held fast there while the chain was fixed round his ankle. At this, tears streamed down his cheeks, though they seemed to be the effect of anger rather than of sorrow. The ship's captain and the overseer came to have a look at him, whereupon he immediately began to abuse them with curses and imprecations, calling them many names that Orm had never heard before, so that all the slaves expected to see him receive a fearful flogging. The captain and the overseer, however, merely stroked their beards and looked thoughtful, while they studied a letter that the soldiers had brought with them. They nodded their heads at this and shook them at that sentence, and whispered discreetly among themselves, while all the time the newcomer howled abuse at them, calling them sons of whores, pork-eaters and copulators of female asses. At last, the overseer threatened him with the whip and told him to keep his mouth shut. Then when the captain and the overseer had moved away, the newcomer began to weep in earnest, so that his whole body shook with it.

Orm did not know what to make of all this, but thought he would get little help from this fellow, unless they used the whip on him. Still, he felt it would be something to have a companion who could at any rate talk, after his experience with the tongueless man. At first, however, the newcomer disdained to hold any converse with him, and rejected Orm's friendly approaches. As Orm had feared, he turned out to be no oarsman, and could not adapt himself to his new mode of life at all, finding especial cause for complaint in the food that was supplied to them, which seemed to Orm to be very good, though insufficient. But Orm was forbearing with him, and did the rowing for both of them, and muttered words of encouragement to him, in so far as he was able to in Arabic. Several times he asked the man who he was and why he had been sentenced to this ship, but received in response merely haughty glances and shoulder-shrugs. At length the man condescended to address him, and announced that he was a man of breeding and not accustomed to being cross-examined by slaves who could not even talk properly. At this, Orm said: 'For those words you have just uttered, I could take you by the neck so that you felt it; but it is better that there should be peace between us, and that you and I should be friends. In this ship we are all slaves, you no less than the rest of us; nor are you the only man aboard who is of good lineage. I am so myself; my name is Orm, and I am a chieftain's son. It is true that I speak your language poorly, but you speak mine worse, for you do not know a word of it. It therefore appears to me that there is nothing to choose between us; indeed, if either of us has the advantage, I do not think it is you.'

'Your intonation is deplorable,' replied the newcomer. 'However, you seem to be a man of some intelligence. It is possible that, among your own people, you are reckoned to be well-born; but in this respect, you can hardly compare with me, for on my mother's side I am directly descended from the Prophet, peace be to His immortal soul! Know, too, that the tongue which I speak is Allah's own, all other tongues having been invented by evil spirits to hinder the spread of the true learning. So you see that there can be no comparison between us. Khalid is my name, the son of Yezid; my father was a high officer of the Caliph, and I own great possessions and do no work, apart from supervising my gardens, entertaining my friends and composing music and poetry. It is true, I admit, that I now temporarily find myself otherwise occupied, but this shall not be for long, may worms eat out the eyes of he who set me here! I have written songs which are sung throughout Malaga, and there are few poets living as skilful as I.'

Orm commented that there must be many poets in the Caliph's kingdom, as he had met one already. Khalid replied that there were a lot in the sense that many men attempted to write verses, but that very few of them could be considered true poets.

After this conversation, they got on better together, although Khalid continued to be a poor oarsmen, and was sometimes hardly able to pull at all, because his hands were skinned by the oar. A little later, he told Orm how he had come to be sent to the ship. He had to repeat himself several times, and use paraphrases to explain what he meant, for he was difficult to follow; but in the end Orm grasped the gist of what he had to say.

Khalid told him that his present plight arose from the fact of the most beautiful maiden in all Malaga being the daughter of the governor of the city, a man of low birth and evil disposition. The beauty of his daughter, however, was such that not even a poet could conceive of anything lovelier, and on one occasion Khalid had been lucky enough to see her unveiled at a harvest feast. From that moment, he had loved her above all other women, and had written songs in her honour that had melted in his mouth as he sang them. At length, by dint of taking up residence on the roof of a house near where she lived, he had succeeded in catching another glimpse of her when she was sitting alone on her roof. He had shouted ecstatic greetings to her and, by stretching out his arms appealingly towards her, had prevailed on her to lift her veil once more. This was a sign that she reciprocated his love; and the surpassing magnificence of her beauty had almost caused him to faint.

Thus assured that the lady was favourably disposed towards him, he had given rich gifts to her maid-in-waiting, and so had managed to convey messages to her. Then the governor had gone to Cordova to present his annual accounts to the Caliph, and the lady had sent Khalid a red flower; whereupon he had disguised himself as an old crone and, with the connivance of the maid-in-waiting, had gained admission to the lady's presence, where he had enjoyed lively sport with her. One day, however, not long afterwards, her brother had drawn upon him in the city and, in the ensuing fight, had, by reason of Khalid's skill at arms, been wounded. On the governor's return, Khalid had been arrested and brought before him.

At this point in his story, Khalid went black with fury, spat viciously and shrieked horrible curses upon the governor. Then he proceeded: 'Legally, he had no case against me. Granted I had lain with his daughter, but in return for that I immortalized her in exquisite songs, and even he seemed to realize that a man of my birth could hardly be expected to propose marriage to the daughter of a common Berber. I had wounded his son, but only after he had attacked me; indeed, but for the temperateness of my nature, he would not have escaped with his life. For all this, the governor, if he had been a true lover of justice, should have been grateful to me. Instead, he took counsel in his wickedness, which is surpassing even in Malaga, and this is the result. Hearken well, O unbeliever, and be amazed.'

Orm listened to all this with interest, although many of the words were unfamiliar to him, and the men on the nearest benches listened too, for Khalid told his story in a loud voice.

'He had one of my poems read aloud, and asked whether I had written it. I replied that everyone in Malaga knew the poem and knew that I was the author of it, for it is a pæan in praise of the city, the best that was ever written. In the poem occur these lines:

> "This I know well; that had the Prophet e'er
> Tasted the harvest that the grape-vines bear,
> He would not blindly have forbidden us
> (In his strict book) to taste the sweet grape's juice.
> His whiskers berry-drenched, his beaker flowing,
> With praise of wine he had enhanced his teaching."'

Having recited these lines, Khalid burst into tears, and explained that it was for their sake that he had been condemned to serve in the galleys. For the Caliph, who was the protector of the true faith and the earthly representative of the Prophet, had ordained that any who blasphemed against the Prophet or criticized his teaching should be severely punished, and the governor had hit upon this method of securing his revenge, under the pretext of demanding justice.

'But I solace myself by reflecting that this state of affairs cannot last for long,' said Khalid. 'For my family is more powerful than his, and has, besides, the Caliph's ear, so that I shall shortly be liberated. That is why nobody in this ship dares to bring the whip to me, for they know that no man can, with impunity, lay his hand on one who is descended from the Prophet.'

Orm asked when this Prophet had lived, and Khalid replied that he had died more than 350 years ago. Orm remarked that he must indeed have been a mighty man if he could still, after so long an interval, protect his kinsmen and decide what his people might or might not drink. No man had ever wielded such power in Skania, not even King Ivar of the Broad Embrace, who was the mightiest man that had lived in the north.

'No man in my country,' he said, 'lays down the law about what another man may drink, be he king or commoner.'

Orm's knowledge of Arabic increased by leaps and bounds now that he had Khalid as his companion, for the latter talked incessantly and had many interesting things to tell of. After some days, he enquired where Orm's country was and how he had come to be in the ship. Then Orm told him the story of Krok's expedition, and how he had joined it, and of all that had ensued. When he had recounted his adventures, as well as he could, he concluded: 'As you see, much of what happened was the result of our meeting with the Jew Solomon. I think it possible that he was a man of luck, for he was freed from his slavery, and, as long as he remained with us, our fortunes prospered. He said that he was an important man in a town called Toledo, where he was a silversmith, as well as being the leading poet.'

Khalid said that he had certainly heard of him, for his skill as a silversmith was renowned; nor was he a bad poet, as poets went in Toledo.

'Not so long ago,' he said, 'I heard one of his poems sung by a wandering minstrel from the north, in which he described how he had fallen into the hands of an Asturian margrave, who used him ill, and how he had escaped and had led the fierce pirates against the fortress, storming it and killing the margrave and sticking his head on a pole for the crows to peck at, after which he had returned home to his own country with the margrave's gold. It was a competent work, in a simple style, though lacking the delicacy of expression that we of Malaga aim at.'

'He does not belittle his achievments,' said Orm. 'If he is prepared to go to so much trouble to revenge himself on an enemy, he ought to be willing to do something to help the friends who rendered him such service. It was we who liberated him from his slavery, stormed the fortress and executed his revenge; and, if he is in reality an important man in his country, he is, perhaps, in a position to render us who sit here a service comparable to that which we performed for him. Nor do I see how else we shall ever regain our freedom, if he does not help us.'

Khalid said that Solomon was famous for his wealth, and that the Caliph regarded him highly, although he did not follow the true religion. Orm now began to hope, but he said nothing to his countrymen of what Khalid had told him. The outcome of their conversation was that Khalid undertook to send a message, together with Orm's greetings, to Solomon in Toledo, as soon as he was released himself.

But the days passed, and still no order arrived for Khalid's liberation. The delay made him more unruly than ever, and he inveighed furiously against the indifference shown by his kinsmen. He began to compose a long poem on the pernicious influence of wine, hoping that he might be able to get this copied out when they were in port and forwarded to the Caliph, so that his real feelings on the subject might become known. But when it came to the point where he had to sing the praises of water and lemon-juice, and to acclaim their superiority to wine, his verses began to halt somewhat. However, although he continued to shriek imprecations at the ship's crew whenever his dark fits settled on him, he was still never touched with the whip, and Orm took this to be a hopeful sign that he would not remain with them for much longer.

One morning, when they were in one of the eastern harbours, the ship having returned with many others from a hard chase after African pirates, four men walked aboard and, when Khalid saw them, he became faint with joy and paid no heed to Orm's questions regarding their identity. One of the men was an official with a big turban and a cloak reaching to his feet. He handed a letter to the captain of the ship, who touched it with his forehead and read it reverently. Another member of the four seemed to be some kinsman of Khalid's, for, as soon as the latter had been released from his ankle-chain, they threw themselves into each other's arms, weeping and exchanging kisses and chattering like madmen. The other two men were servants, bearing clothes and baskets. They dressed Khalid in a fine robe and offered him food. Orm shouted to him to remember his promise, but Khalid was already rebuking his kinsman for having forgotten to bring a barber with him, and did not hear. Then Khalid went ashore with his suite, the captain and crew bidding him obsequious farewells, which he acknowledged with condescension as though barely aware of their presence, and disappeared arm in arm with his kinsman.

Orm was sorry to see him depart, for Khalid had been an entertaining companion, and he feared that, in his new-found freedom, he would be above remembering to fulfil his promise. Another man was chained beside Orm in Khalid's place, a shop-keeper who had been found guilty of using false weights. He tired quickly, and was little use at the oar, and had to be whipped frequently, at which he moaned and mumbled little pieties to himself. Orm gained small pleasure from his company, and this was the period of his life in the galley that he found most tedious. He set all his hopes on Khalid and Solomon but, as more and more time passed, these began to fade.

At last, however, in Cadiz, their lucky day arrived. An officer came on board with a troop of men, and all the Northmen were released from their ankle-chains and were given clothes and shoes, and were removed to another ship, which proceeded up the great river to Cordova. They were made to lend a hand rowing against the stream, but were not fettered or whipped, and were frequently relieved; moreover, they were allowed to sit together, and so could talk without hindrance for the first time for many a day. They had been galley-slaves for two years and the greater part of a third; and Toke, who sang and laughed almost the whole time, said that he did not know what would become of them now, but that one thing he did know, that it was high time that he drank the thirst out of himself. Orm said that it would be better if he could wait until he

72

had someone's permission to do so, for it would be a bad thing if they had any violence now, which they would be liable to have, if Orm's memory served him rightly, once Toke began quenching his thirst. Toke agreed that he would do better to wait, though he added that the waiting would be difficult. They all wondered what was going to happen to them, and Orm now repeated to them the details of his conversation wth Khalid concerning the Jew. Then they were loud in the Jew's praise, and in Orm's also; and, although Orm was the youngest of them, they all now acknowledged him to be their chieftain.

Orm asked the officer what was going to be done with them, and whether he knew of a Jew called Solomon, but all the officer could tell him was that he had been commanded to conduct them to Cordova; and he had never heard of Solomon.

They arrived at the Caliph's city, and saw it spreading out on both banks of the river, with many houses huddled together and white palaces and palm courts and towers. They marvelled greatly at its size and splendour, which surpassed anything that they could have imagined, and its wealth seemed to them sufficient to provide rich booty for all the seamen from the whole of the Danish kingdom.

They were led through the city, gazing in wonder on the throngs of people; though they complained that there were too few women among them, and that not much could be seen of those that were abroad, because they were all cloaked and veiled.

'A woman would have her work cut out not to appear beautiful in my eyes,' said Toke, 'if only I had a chance to talk to one of them; for it is now three years since we fell among these foreigners, and in all that time we have not been allowed to smell a single woman.'

'If they set us free,' said Ogmund, 'we ought to be able to do well for women in this country; for their men are of miserable appearance compared with us.'

'Every man in this land is allowed to have four wives,' said Orm, 'if he has embraced the Prophet and his teaching. But, once having done so, he can never drink wine again.'

'It is a difficult choice to make,' said Toke, 'for their ale is too thin for my palate. But it may be that we have not yet sampled their best brew. And four women is just about what I need.'

They came to a large house, where there were many soldiers, and there they slept the night. The next morning, a stranger appeared and led them to another house not far distant, where they were well bathed and barbered, and where cool drinks were offered to them in beautiful tiny cups. Then they were given softer garments, which chafed them less; for their clothes felt rough against their skin, since they had for so long been naked. They looked at each other, laughing at the change that had been wrought in their appearance; then, marvelling greatly at all this, they were conducted into a dining-room, where a man came forward, greeting them and bidding them welcome. They recognized him at once as Solomon, although he now wore a very different appearance to when they had last seen him, for he had all the bearing and accoutrements of a rich and mighty prince.

He greeted them hospitably, bidding them eat and drink and regard his house as their own; but he had forgotten most of what he had formerly known of the Nordic tongue, so that only Orm was able to converse with him. Solomon said that he had done all that he could on their behalf, as soon as he had heard of their plight, because they had once performed a very great service for him, which he was glad to be able to repay. Orm thanked him as eloquently as he could; but, he told Solomon, what they were most eager to know was whether they were now free men, or whether they were still slaves.

Solomon replied that they were still the Caliph's slaves, and must remain so; in that matter, he could not help them; but they were now to serve in the Caliph's private bodyguard, which was recruited from the pick of prisoners that the Caliph captured in battle, and of the slaves that he purchased from abroad. The Caliphs of Cordova, he went on, had always possessed such a bodyguard, regarding it as safer than being surrounded by armed subjects of their own, since the latter might more easily be bribed by their kinsmen or their friends to lay violent hands on the Caliph's person when discontent pricked the land.

But before they joined the bodyguard, Solomon told them, they would first be his guests for a while, in order that they might in some measure recover themselves after their labours; so they stayed at his house for five days, and were treated as heroes are treated at the table of Odin. They partook of many delicate dishes, and drink was brought to them whenever they cared to call for it; musicians played for them, and they made themselves tipsy with wine every evening, no Prophet having forbidden Solomon to taste of that drink. Orm and his fellows, however, kept a watchful eye on Toke the whole time, lest he should drink too much and so weep and become dangerous. Their host offered each of them a young slave-girl to keep them company in bed, and this delighted them most of all. They agreed unanimously that the Jew was a fine man, and a chieftain, every bit as good as if he had been of Nordic blood; and Toke said that he had seldom made a more fortunate catch than when he had drawn this noble Semite out of the sea. They slept late in the mornings, in feather-beds softer than anything they had previously known; and, at table, they quarrelled merrily as to which among them had the prettiest slave-girl, and none of them would allow that his was not the choicest of them all.

On the third evening of their stay there, Solomon bade Orm and Toke accompany him into the city, saying that there was someone else whom they had to thank for their liberation, and who had perhaps done more for them than he had. They went with him along many streets, and Orm asked whether Khalid, the great poet of Malaga, had perhaps come to Cordova, and whether it was he whom they were on their way to visit; but Solomon replied that they were going to meet a nobler personage than Khalid.

'And only a foreigner,' he added feelingly, 'could look upon this Khalid as a great poet, though he noises it abroad that he is one. Sometimes I try to calculate how many truly great poets there can be said to be nowadays in the Caliph's dominions; and I do not think that that honour can rightly be allowed to more than five of us, among which number Khalid could not possibly find inclusion, although he has a certain facility for playing with rhymes. None the less, you do right, Orm, to regard him as your friend, for without his help I should never have discovered what became of you and your men; so, if you should meet him and he should refer to himself as a poet, you need not correct him.'

Orm remarked that he knew enough about men not to argue with poets concerning their respective merits; but Toke broke into their conversation with the complaint that he wanted to know why he had been pressed into this evening ramble when it was impossible for him to understand a word of what was being said, and when he had been enjoying himself so much in Solomon's house. Solomon merely replied that it was necessary that he should accompany them, it having so been ordered.

They arrived at a walled garden with a narrow gate, which was opened to admit them. They entered, walking among beautiful trees and many strange plants and flowers, and came to a place where a great fountain was playing and clear water ran through rich grasses in small coiling streams. From the opposite direction to that from which they had come, a litter was being carried towards them by four slaves, followed by two slave-girls and two black men carrying drawn swords.

Solomon halted, and Orm and Toke did likewise. The litter was lowered to the ground, and the slave-girls ran forward and stood reverently one on either side of it. Then a veiled lady stepped forth. Solomon bowed low to her thrice, with his hands pressed against his forehead, so that Orm and Toke realized that she must be of royal blood; they remained upright, however, for it seemed to them a wrong thing that any man should abase himself before a woman.

The lady inclined her head graciously in Solomon's direction. Then she turned towards Orm and Toke, and murmured something beneath her veil; and her eyes were friendly. Solomon bowed to her again, and said: 'Warriors from the north, thank Her Highness Subaida, for it is by her power that you stand liberated.'

Orm said to the lady: 'If you have helped to free us, we owe you a great debt of thanks. But who you are, and why you have showed us such favour, we do not know.'

'Yet we have met,' she answered, 'and perchance you will remember my face.'

So saying, she lifted her veil, at which the Jew abased himself again. Toke tugged at his beard and muttered to Orm: 'It is my girl from the fortress, and she is more beautiful now than ever. Her luck must indeed have been good, for, since we last saw her, she has become a queen. I should like to know whether she is pleased to see me again.'

The lady glanced towards Toke, and said: 'Why do you address your friend, and not me?'

Orm replied to her that Toke could not understand Arabic, but that he said that he remembered her and thought her even more beautiful now than when he had last seen her.

'And we both rejoice,' he added, 'to see that luck and power have come your way, for you appear to us to be deserving of the one and worthy of the other.'

She looked at Orm, and smiled, and said: 'But you, O red man, have learned the language of this country, as I have done. Which is the better man, you or your friend who was once my master?'

'We both reckon ourselves to be good men,' replied Orm. 'But I am young, and am less experienced than he; and he performed mighty feats when we took the fortress which was your home. Therefore, I hold him to be the better man of us, as yet; though he cannot tell you so himself in the language of this land. But better than either of us was Krok, our chieftain; but he is dead.'

She said that she remembered Krok, and that good chieftains seldom lived to be old. Orm told her how he had died, and she nodded, and said: 'Fate has woven our destinies together in a curious way. You took my father's house, and slew him and most of his people, for which I should rightly make you atone with your lives. But my father was a cruel man, especially towards my mother, and I hated and feared him like a hairy devil. I was glad when he was killed, and was not sorry to find myself among foreigners, nor to be made love to by your friend, although it was a pity that we were never able to talk to each other. I did not much care for the smell of his beard, but he had merry eyes and a kind laugh, and these I liked; and he used me gently, even when he was drunk and impatient with lust. He left no bruises on my body, and gave me only a light burden to bear on the march to the ship. I would have been willing to accompany him to your country. Tell him this.'

Orm repeated all that she had said to Toke, who listened with a contented expression. When Orm had finished, Toke said: 'You see how lucky I am with women! But she is the best I ever saw, and you may tell her that I said so. Do you suppose that she intends to make me an important man in this country of hers?'

Orm replied that she had said nothing about that; then, after repeating Toke's compliment to her, he begged her to tell them what had happened to her since they had parted on the seashore.

'The ship's captain brought me hither to Cordova,' she said. 'Nor did he lay his hand on me, although he had forced me to stand naked before him, for he knew that I would make a fine gift for him to present to his master, the Grand Vizier. Now, therefore, I belong to the Grand Vizier of the Caliph, who is called Almansur and is the most powerful man in the whole of the Caliph's dominions. He, after first instructing me in the teaching of the Prophet, raised me from a slave-girl to be his chief wife, since he found that my beauty exceeded that of all his other women. Praised be Allah for it! So, you have brought me luck, for, if you had not come to destroy my father's fortress, I would still be living in daily dread of my father, and would have had some bad man forced on me as a husband, for all my beauty. When, therefore, Solomon, who makes my finest jewellery, informed me that you were still alive, I resolved to give you such assistance as lay within my power.'

'We have three persons to thank for freeing us from the galley-benches,' said Orm. 'Yourself, Solomon, and a man from Malaga called Khalid. Now, though, we know that it was your word that counted for most; therefore, we give our chief thanks to you. It was lucky for us that we met such people as you and these two poets, for otherwise we should still be straining upon our benches, with naught but death to hope for. We shall be proud to enter your lord's service, and to aid him against his enemies. But we are surprised that you succeeded in persuading him to release us, for all the power you wield; for we seamen from the north are regarded here as great enemies, and have been so ever since the days of the sons of Ragnar Hairy-Breeks.'

Subaida replied: 'You did my lord Almansur a great service when you took my father's fortress, for he would not else have known that I existed. Besides this, it is well known among the people of this country that the men of the north keep their word and are brave warriors. Both the Caliph Abderrachman the Great, and his father, the Emir Abdullah, had many Northmen in their bodyguards, for in those days your countrymen harried our Spanish coasts sorely; but of late, few Northmen have been seen in these parts, so there are now none of them in the royal bodyguard. If you serve my lord Almansur faithfully and well, you will be richly rewarded, and the captain of the guard will give you and your men full armour and fine weapons. But first, I have a gift for each of you.'

She beckoned to one of the slaves who stood beside the litter, and he brought forward two swords, with splendidly ornamented scabbards and belts embossed with heavy silver buckles. One of these she gave to Toke, and the other to Orm. They accepted them joyfully, for they had felt naked with no swords at their waists during the years that had passed. They drew them forth from their scabbards, examining the blades closely, and weighing them in their hands. Solomon looked at the swords, and said: 'These were forged in Toledo, where the best smiths in the world, both in silver and in steel, work. They still make swords straight there, as was the fashion in the time of the Gothic kings, before the servants of the Prophet came to this land. No smith alive forges a finer sword than these.'

Toke laughed aloud for joy, and began to mutter to himself. At length, he said:

> 'Long have the warrior's hands
> Known the oar's timber.
> See how they laugh to hold
> Once more the war-man's blade.'

Orm was anxious not to be outdone as a poet, so he reflected for a few minutes and then, holding his sword before his face, said:

> 'The sword the fair one gave me
> I raise with my left hand,
> Like Tyr among the immortals.
> The serpent has won back his sting.'

Subaida laughed, and said: 'Giving a man a sword is like giving a woman a looking-glass; they have eyes left for nothing else. But it is good to see gifts so gratefully received. May they bring you luck.'

Then, their meeting ended, for Subaida said that the time had come for her to bid them farewell, though it might chance that sometime they would meet again. So she stepped into her litter, and was borne away.

As they returned with Solomon to his house, the three of them were loud in their praise of Subaida and of the costly presents she had given them. Solomon explained that he had known her for more than a year, and had often sold her jewellery. He had realized from the first that she was the same girl that Toke had won in the cruel margrave's fortress, although her beauty had greatly increased since then. Toke said: 'She is fair and kind, and does not forget those who take her fancy. It is a hard thing for me to see her again, knowing that she is the wife of a great lord. Still, I am glad she does not belong to that pot-bellied old goat with the silver hammer who captured us. I should not have liked that. But all in all, I cannot complain, for the girl Solomon has found for me suits me very well.'

Orm questioned the Jew concerning Subaida's lord, Almansur, asking how he could be the mightiest man in the land. Surely the Caliph must be more powerful than he? Solomon, however, explained how the matter lay. The previous Caliph, Hacham the Learned, the son of Abderracham the Great, had been a great ruler, despite the fact that he had spent most of his time reading books and conversing with learned men. On his death, he had left no heir save an infant son, named Hischam, who was the present Caliph. Now Hacham had ordained that his most trusted counsellor, together with his favourite wife, who was the child's mother, should rule until Hischam came of age. Unfortunately, these two had so enjoyed the exercise of their power that they had imprisoned the young Caliph in a castle, on the pretext that he was of too holy a nature to be bothered with earthly matters. This counsellor had, in his capacity as regent of the realm, won many victories against the Christians in the north, as a result of which he had received the title of Almansur, meaning 'the conqueror.' The Queen, the young Caliph's mother, had for a long time past loved Almansur above all other earthly things, but he had become weary of her, for she was older than he and inclined, besides, to be captious about the division of power; so now she had been imprisoned, like her son, and Almansur ruled alone in the land as the Caliph's regent. Many of his subjects hated him for what he had done to the Caliph and the Queen Mother, but many loved him for the victories he had gained against the Christians; and he was a good master to his bodyguard, for he relied on them as a shield against all who treasured envy and hatred towards him. Orm and his men might, therefore, expect to prosper in Almansur's palace while there was peace, in addition to all the fighting that they could wish for, since, each spring, Almansur set forth with a mighty army, either against the King of Asturia and the Count of Castile, or against the King of Navarre and the Counts of Aragon, far away in the north near the border country of the Franks. All these monarchs lived in perpetual dread of him, and were glad to pay him tribute in order to make him postpone his visits.

'But they do not find it easy to buy him off,' continued Solomon, 'the reason for this being that he is a very unhappy man. He is powerful and victorious, and has succeeded in every enterprise to which he has laid his hand; but, in spite of all this, everyone knows that he is plagued by an incessant fear. For he has turned his hand against the Caliph, who is the shadow of the Prophet, and has stolen his power from him; on account of which, he lives in daily dread of the wrath of Allah, and has no peace in his soul. Each year he seeks to propitiate Allah by waging new wars against the Christians, and that is why he never accepts tributes from all the Christian princes at once, but only allows each of them to buy him off for a few months at a time, so that he can always have some of them available for him to put zealously to the sword. Of all the warriors that have ever been born in this land, he is the mightiest; and he has sworn a great oath that he will die in the field, with his face turned towards the false worshippers who believe that the son of Joseph was God. He takes little interest in verses of music, so that these are lean times for poets compared with the favours we enjoyed under Hacham the Wise; but, in his leisure hours, he finds some pleasure in gold and silver work, and in precious stones, so I cannot complain. I bought this house in Cordova that I might the better serve his pleasure; and long may he flourish and long may fortune smile upon him for, to a silversmith, he is indeed a good master.'

All this and more Solomon recounted to Orm, and Orm repeated it to Toke and the others; and they agreed that this Almansur must be a notable prince. But his fear of Allah they could not understand, for it was unknown among the Northmen for anyone to be afraid of the gods.

Before the time came for them to leave the Jew's house, he gave them sage counsel on many matters; above all, he warned Toke never to let it become known that he had formerly been Subaida's master.

'For princes enjoy the sight of their women's former lovers no more than we do,' he said, 'and it was bold of her to allow you to see her again, even though there were witnesses present to swear, if necessary, that nothing untoward occurred. In this, as in all other respects, Almansur is a sharp-eyed master, so that Toke will do well to keep a tight rein on his tongue.'

Toke replied that there was no fear of his doing otherwise; and that his most immediate concern was to think of a good name for his sword. For such a sword as his had surely come from the hand of as great a smith as he who had forged Sigurd's sword Gram, or Mimming, which had belonged to Didrik, or Skofnung, which Rolf the Jade had wielded. Therefore, it must have a name, as theirs had had. But he could not hit upon any name that pleased him, although he tried assiduously to think of one. Orm, however, called his sword Blue-Tongue.

They left Solomon with many expressions of thanks, and were conducted to Almansur's palace, where they were received by an officer of the royal household, and were given armour and a full complement of weapons, and commenced their service in Almansur's bodyguard. And the seven men from the north elected Orm to be their chieftain.

CHAPTER SEVEN

How Orm served Almansur, and how he sailed with St James's bell

Orm entered the imperial bodyguard at Cordova in the year commonly reckoned as the eighth of the reign of the Caliph Hischam, that is, three years before Blue Digre and Vagn Akesson sailed with the Jomsvikings against the Norwegians. He remained in Almansur's service for four years.

The men of the imperial bodyguard were greatly respected in Cordova, and were more finely attired than the ordinary citizens. Their mail-shirts were light and thin, but more resilient and of finer workmanship than any that Orm and his men had ever previously seen. Their helmets shone like silver, and on occasion they wore scarlet cloaks over their armour; and their shields were engraved round the edge with an arc of lettering, cunningly worked. This same legend was sewn upon Almansur's great banners, which were always borne at the head of his army when he marched to war, and the meaning of it was: 'Allah alone is victorious.'

The first occasion on which Orm and his men entered Almansur's presence, to be shown to him by the commander of the guard, they were surprised at his appearance, for they had imagined him to be of the proportions of a hero. He was, in fact, an unprepossessing man, pinched and half-bald, with a yellow-green face and heavy eyebrows. He was seated on a broad bed among a heap of cushions, and tugged meditatively at his beard as he addressed rapid commands to two secretaries seated on the floor before him, who took down everything he said. On a table beside his bed there stood a copper box and, next to the box, a bowl of fruit and a large wicker cage, in which several tiny monkeys were playing and leaping round on a wheel. While the secretaries were writing down what he had just said, he took fruit from the bowl and put it between the bars of the cage and watched the monkeys fighting for the gift and stretching out their dwarfish hands for more; but, instead of smiling at their antics, he stared at them with sad eyes, and pushed more fruit between the bars and began again to dictate to his secretaries.

After a while, he gave the secretaries permission to rest, and bade the commander of the guard approach with his men. He turned his face from the cage and gazed at Orm and the other Vikings. His eyes were black and as though grief-stricken, but it seemed as if something burned and glittered deep down in their depths, so that the men found it difficult to meet his gaze for more than a few seconds. He studied them critically, one by one, and nodded his head.

'These men have the bearing of warriors,' he said to the commander. 'Do they understand our language?'

The commander indicated Orm, and said that he understood Arabic, but that the rest knew little or none, and that they regarded him as their chieftain.

Almansur said to Orm: 'What is your name?'

Orm told him his name, and added that, in his language, it meant Serpent. Almansur then asked him: 'Who is your King?'

'Harald, the son of Gorm,' replied Orm, 'and he is the lord of all the Danish kingdom.'

'I do not know of him,' said Almansur.

'Be glad of it, lord,' replied Orm, 'for, whithersoever his ships sail, kings pale at the sound of his name.'

Almansur gazed at Orm for a few moments; then he said: 'You are quick-tongued, and deserve the name you bear. Is your King a friend of the Franks?'

Orm smiled, and answered: 'He was their friend when his own country was disturbed by insurrection. But, when fortune smiles upon him, he burns their cities, both in Frankland and in Saxony. And he is a King whom fortune dotes on.'

'Perchance he is a good King,' said Almansur. 'Who is your god?'

'That is a more difficult question to answer, lord,' replied Orm. 'My gods are the gods of my people, and we think them strong, as

84

we ourselves are. There are many of them, but some of them are old, and few men trouble to worship these, apart from poets. The strongest of them is called Thor. He is red, as I am, and is held to be the friend of all mortal men. But the wisest of them is Odin, who is the god of soldiers, and they say that it is thanks to him that we Northmen are the best warriors in the world. Whether, though, any of our gods have done anything for me, I do not know; certain it is that I have not done much for them. And they seem to me to have little sway in this land.'

'Now, listen carefully, infidel,' said Almansur, 'to what I am about to say. There is no god save Allah. Say not that there are many, nor that there are three; it shall be well for you on the Judgment Day if you do not say these things. There is but one Allah, the Eternal, the Sublime; and Mohammed is His Prophet. This is the truth, and this you shall believe. When I wage war against the Christians, I wage it for Allah and the Prophet, and ill betide any man of my army who does not honour them. From henceforth, therefore, you and your men shall worship none but the true god.'

Orm replied: 'We men of the North do not worship our gods except in time of necessity, for we think it foolish to weary them with babbling. In this land, we have worshipped no god since the time when we sacrificed to the sea-god to bless our homeward voyage with luck; and that proved to be of little use to us for, not long afterwards, your ships appeared, and we whom you see here became your captives. Perchance it may be that our gods wield but little power in this land; therefore, lord, I for my part shall willingly obey your command and worship your god while I am your servant. If it be your pleasure, I shall ask my comrades what is their feeling in this matter.'

Almansur nodded his assent, and Orm said to his men: 'He says that we must worship his god. He has only one god, who is called Allah, and who dislikes all other gods. My own belief is that his god is powerful in this country, and that our gods are weak so far away from our homeland and theirs. We shall receive better treatment if we follow the custom of the people in this matter, and I think it would be foolish of us to go against Almansur's wishes.'

The men agreed that they had little choice, and that it would be madness to anger so mighty a lord as Almansur; at length, therefore, Orm turned to Almansur and informed him that they were all willing to worship Allah and promise to invoke no other god.

Almansur then summoned two priests into his presence, together with a magistrate, before whom Orm and his men were made to repeat the holy creed of the servants of Mohammed, as pronounced to Orm by Almansur: namely, that there is no God save Allah, and that Mohammed is his Prophet. All the men save Orm found difficulty in enunciating the words, although they were carefully spelt out to them.

When this ceremony was completed, Almansur appeared to be well pleased, and told the priests that he felt that he had thereby done a good service to Allah, with which they agreed. Then, putting his hand into the copper box that stood on the table, he took from it a handful of gold coins, and gave fifteen pieces to each of the men, but thirty to Orm. They thanked him, and were conducted by the commander back to their own quarters.

Toke said: 'Now we have bidden farewell to our gods. This may be a right thing to do in a foreign land, where other gods reign; but, if I ever reach home again, I shall bother more about them than about this Allah. Still, I dare say he is the best god in these parts, and he has already provided us with gold. If he can manage to provide a few women too, he will rise even higher in my estimation.'

A short while afterwards, Almansur declared war against the Christians and set out northwards with his imperial bodyguard and a mighty army. He plundered for three months in Navarre and Aragon, during which time Orm and his men won both gold and women, so that they declared themselves well satisfied to serve such a master. Each subsequent spring and autumn, they found themselves in the field under Almansur's banners, resting in Cordova during the worst of the summer heat, and during those months of the year which the people of the south call winter. They did their best to accustom themselves to the habits of the country, and found little cause for complaint in their employment, for Almansur often rewarded them with rich gifts, to secure their loyalty, and everything that they won by storm or plunder they were permitted to keep for themselves, apart from one-fifth, which they had to yield to him.

Sometimes, however, they found it somewhat irksome to be followers of Allah and servants of the Prophet. Whenever, on their expeditions, they found wine or pork in the Christians' houses, they were forbidden to enjoy either commodity, though they longed for both. This decree, which appeared to them more extraordinary than any they had previously heard of, they seldom dared to disobey, for Almansur punished any disobedience very strictly. In addition to this, they found themselves having to pray to Allah and abase themselves before the Prophet far too often for their taste; for, every morning and evening, when Almansur was in the field, the whole of his army would fall to its knees, facing the direction in which the City of the Prophet was said to lie, and every man had to bow several times, pressing his forehead against the earth. This seemed to them a debasing ridiculous thing for a man to have to do, but they agreed that there was nothing for it but to conform to this custom as best as they could, and do as the rest of the army did.

They excelled in battle, and won a great name for themselves in the bodyguard. They held themselves to be the best men in it and, when the time came for the dividing up of booty, no man challenged their right to whatever they chose. There were eight of them, all told: Orm and Toke, Halle and Ogmund, Tume, who had rowed with Toke, Gunne, who had rowed with Krok, Rapp, who was one-eyed, and Ulf, who was the oldest of them. Once, long before, he had had one of the corners of his mouth split at a Christmas feast, ever since when he had been known as Grinulf, because his mouth sat awry and was broader than other men's. Their luck was so good that only one of them lost his life during all the four years that they were in Almansur's service.

They travelled far and wide; for, the more Almansur's beard became flecked with grey, the more vehemently he harried the Christians, spending less and less time peacefully at home in his palace at Cordova. They were with him when he marched far northwards to Pamplona, in the kingdom of Navarre, where twice they attempted vainly to storm the city; but the third time, they took it and gave it to the sword. Here Tume, who had shared Toke's oar in the galley, was killed by a stone from a catapult. They sailed in Almansur's own ship to Majorca, when the governor of that island had shown himself refractory, and stood guard while his head was struck off, together with those of thirty of his kinsmen. They fought in dust and heat a grim conflict at Henares, where the Count of Castile's men pressed them hard but were at length encircled and annihilated. There, on the evening following the battle, the dead Christians were piled together and built into a great mound of corpses, from the summit of which one of Almansur's priests called the servants of the Prophet to prayer. Then they marched on a huge expedition to the Kingdom of Leon, where they harried King Sancho the Fat so sorely that, in the end, his own men found him dispensable (for he was so fat that he could no longer sit on a horse, and deposed him, and came with tribute to Almansur.

Throughout all these campaigns, Orm and his men never ceased to marvel at Almansur's sacrifice and power, and at the great luck which always attended his enterprises; but most of all they marvelled at the extent of his fear of Allah, and the variety of measures that he was for ever devising to placate his God. All the dirt that gathered on his shoes and clothing when he was in the field was carefully scraped off each evening by his servants and placed in a silken bag; and, at the conclusion of every campaign, this bagful of dirt was brought back to Cordova. He had ordained that all this dirt that he had collected in his wars against the Christians was to be buried with him when he died, because the Prophet had said: 'Blessed are those who have trodden dusty ways to fight against the unbelievers.'

Despite all this, however, Almansur's dread of Allah no whit decreased, and finally he decided to undertake a mightier enterprise than any that he had yet attempted, namely, to destroy the holy city of the Christians in Asturia in which the apostle James, the great miracle-worker, lay buried. In the autumn of the twelfth year of the reign of the Caliph Hischam, which was the fourth year that Orm and his men spent in Almansur's service, he assembled an army larger than any that had ever before been seen in Spain, and marched northwards, proceeding through the Empty Land, which was the old dividing barrier between the Andalusians and the Asturian Christians.

They reached the Christian settlements on the far side of the Empty Land, which no Andalusian had penetrated in mortal memory, and each day saw them engaged in hard fighting, for the Christians defended themselves cunningly among the mountains and ravines. Then, one evening, when the army had pitched camp and Almansur was resting in his great tent after evening prayer, the Christians launched a surprise attack. At first they threatened to overwhelm the Mohammedans, for a troop of them broke into the camp and created a panic, the air becoming wild with war-cries and shrieks for help. Hearing these, Almansur hastened forth from his tent, wearing his helmet and carrying his sword, but without his armour, to see what was afoot. Now, that evening, Orm and two of his men, Halle and Rapp the One-Eyed, were standing guard at the entrance to the tent. As Almansur emerged, several of the enemy's horsemen appeared, galloping towards the tent at full speed. When they saw Almansur, they recognized him by his green helmet-veil (for he was the only man in the army who wore that colour), and, yelling triumphantly, cast their spears at him. It was a dark night, and Almansur was old and could not have evaded them; but Orm, who was standing nearest to him, flung himself suddenly at his back, bowling him over on to his face and taking two of the spears on his shield and a third in his shoulder. A fourth grazed Almansur's side as he lay on the ground, and drew blood. Halle and Rapp rushed forward to meet the enemy, casting their spears at them and bringing one man from his horse; then, others swarmed to their assistance, from all directions, and the Christians were killed or put to flight.

Orm pulled the spear out of his shoulder, and assisted Almansur to his feet, wondering dubiously how his master would feel about being knocked face downwards on to the ground. Almansur, however, was hugely pleased with his wound. It was the first that he had ever received, and he reckoned it as a piece of great good luck that he had been allowed to spill his blood for Allah's sake, without sustaining any serious injury in the process. He ordered three of his cavalry commanders to be summoned before him, and rebuked them publicly before his assembled officers for not having kept better watch over the camp. They prostrated themselves at his feet, and confessed their negligence; whereupon Almansur, as was his wont when he was in a good humour, allowed them time to say their prayers and bind up their beards before being led to execution.

To Halle and Rapp, he gave a fistful of gold each. Then, while all the officers of the army were still drawn up before him, he bade Orm step forward. Almansur stared at him, and said: 'Red-bearded man, you have laid your hand upon your master, which it is forbidden for any soldier to do. What answer have you to make to this charge?'

Orm replied: 'The air was alive with spears, and there was naught else to be done. But it is my belief, lord, that your honour is so great that what has happened cannot harm it. Besides which, you fell with your face towards your enemies, so that no man can say that you shrank from them.'

Almansur sat fingering his beard silently. Then he nodded and said: 'It is a good answer. And you saved my life; and I have work yet to accomplish.'

He ordered a neck-chain to be brought from his coffers; it was of gold, and heavy. He said: 'I see that a spear found your shoulder. Perchance it may prove painful. Here is balm for the pain.'

So saying, he hung the chain around Orm's neck, which was an exceedingly rare honour for him to grant. After this incident, Orm and his men stood even higher in Almansur's favour than before. Toke examined the chain, and expressed his delight that Orm had won so rich a gift.

'Without doubt,' he said, 'this Almansur is the best master that a man could wish to serve. All the same, I think it was lucky for you, and for the rest of us, that you did not push him on to his back.'

Next day, the army continued its march; and at length they came to the holy city of the Christians, where the apostle James lay buried, with a great church built over his grave. Here there was heavy fighting, for the Christians, believing that the apostle would come to their aid, fought to the limit of their endurance; but in the end, Almansur overcame them, and the city was taken and burnt. Hither, Christians from all parts of their country had brought their most valuable treasures for safe keeping, for the city had never before been threatened by any enemy; consequently, an enormous quantity of booty was captured, together with many prisoners. It was Almansur's especial wish to raze the great church that stood over the apostle's grave, but this was of stone and would not burn. Instead, therefore, he set his prisoners, aided by men from his own army, to pull it down. Now, in the tower of this church, there hung twelve bells, each one bearing the name of an apostle. They had a most melodious note, and were greatly prized by the Christians, in particular the largest of them all, which was called James.

Almansur commanded that these bells should be taken back to Cordova by the Christian captives, there to be placed in the great mosque with their mouths facing upwards, so that they might be filled with sweet-scented oil and burn perpetually as great lamps to the glory of Allah and the Prophet. They were enormously heavy, and great litters were built to hold them; sixty prisoners were set to carry each bell in one of these litters, working in shifts. But the James bell was so heavy that no litter could be built to take it, and they knew it would not be possible to convey it by ox-cart across the mountain passes. Almansur, however, was very unwilling to leave it behind, for he regarded it as the finest item of spoil that he had ever won.

Accordingly, he had a platform built for the bell to be placed upon, in order that this platform might be dragged on rollers to a nearby river, whence it and the bell could be removed to Cordova by ship. When the platform was ready, and the rollers had been placed beneath it, iron bars were passed through the hasps of the bell, and a number of men tried to lift it on to the platform; but the southerners lacked either the strength or the enthusiasm for the work; and, when longer bars were tried, so that more men might help with the lifting, the bars broke and the bell remained on the ground. Orm and his men, who had come to watch the work, began to laugh; then Toke said: 'Six grown men ought to be able to lift that without much trouble,' and Orm said: 'Four should be able to manage it.'

Then he and Toke and Ogmund and Rapp the One-Eyed walked up to the bell, ran a short bar through the hasps, and lifted the bell up and on to the platform.

Almansur, who had been riding past on his horse, stopped to watch them do this. He called Orm to him, and said: 'Allah has blessed you and your men with great strength, praised be His name! It would seem that you are the men to see that this bell is safely conveyed to the ship, and to guard it on its passage to Cordova; for I know no other men capable of handling it.'

Orm bowed, and replied that this task did not appear to him to be difficult.

Then Almansur had a body of good slaves chosen from among the prisoners, and ordered them to draw the bell down to the river at a point where it began to be navigable, after which they were to serve as oarsmen on a ship awaiting them there, which had been captured from the Asturians. Two officials from Almansur's staff were sent with them, to be in charge during the voyage.

Ropes were tied to the platform, and Orm and his men set off with the bell and its slaves, some of the prisoners drawing it, and others placing rollers before it. It was a tedious journey, for the path they had to follow led, for the most part, downhill, so that sometimes the bell slid forwards under its own momentum, and in the early stages some of the slaves who were changing the rollers were crushed. Orm, however, made them fasten a drag-rope to the rear of the platform, so that they might be able to control it where the going was steep. Thereafter, they made better progress, and so eventually came down to the river where the ship lay at anchor.

It was a merchant ship, smallish, but strongly built, with a good deck, ten pairs of oars, a mast and a sail. Orm and his men lifted the bell aboard, and made it fast with ropes and chocks; then they put the slaves in their places at the oars, and moved off down the river. This river ran westwards, north of that river up which Krok's ships had rowed on their way to the margrave's fortress; and the Northmen were happy to find themselves once again in charge of a ship.

The Vikings took it in turns to keep an eye on the rowers, whom they found mulish and very clumsy at their work. They were disappointed to find that there were no ankle-chains in the ship, for this meant that someone had to keep watch throughout the night; and in spite of this, a couple of the prisoners, who had felt the whip, managed to escape. Orm's men agreed that they had never seen such miserable rowing before, and that, if it went on like this, they would never reach Cordova.

When they came to the mouth of the river, they found there many of Almansur's great warships, which had been unable, on account of their size, to sail up the river, although most of the soldiers from them had marched inland to join in the general plundering. Orm's men were glad to see these ships, and he immediately sent both the officials to borrow as many ankle-chains as possible from the various captains, until he had obtained all that he needed. Then the slaves were fettered to their places. Orm also took this opportunity of laying in stores for the voyage, for it was a long way to Cordova. Having done this, they lay at anchor by the warships in a sheltered bay, to wait for good sailing weather.

In the evening Orm went ashore, together with Toke and Gunne, leaving the rest of his men to guard the ship. They walked down the shore in the direction of some small warehouses, in which traders had established themselves for the purpose of bargaining for the loot that had been won, and to sell necessaries to the ships. They had all but reached the first warehouse when six men from one of the ships entered it, and Gunne suddenly halted in his tracks.

'We have business to transact with those men,' he said. 'Did you notice the first two?'

Neither Orm nor Toke had observed their faces.

Gunne said: 'They were the men who killed Krok.'

Orm paled, and a tremor ran through his body.

'If that is so,' he said, 'they have lived long enough.'

They drew their swords. Orm and Toke still carried those which the lady Subaida had given to them, and Toke had not yet succeeded in finding any name for his sword as good as Blue-Tongue.

'Our duty to Krok comes before our duty to Almansur,' said Orm. 'All of us have vengeance to reap here. But mine comes first, because I am his successor as chieftain. You two run behind the warehouse, to stop them escaping that way.'

The warehouse had a door in each of its shorter walls. Orm entered through the nearest, and found the six men inside, talking to the trader. The latter, when he saw Orm enter with his sword drawn, slunk away behind some sacks, but the six men from the ship drew their weapons and shrieked questions at him. It was dark and confined in the warehouse, but Orm at once picked out one of the men who had killed Krok.

'Have you said your evening prayer?' he cried, and hewed at the man's neck so that his head flew from his shoulders.

Two of the others immediately attacked Orm, so that he had his work cut out to defend himself. Meanwhile, the other three ran to the back door; but Toke and Gunne were there before them. Toke felled one of them on the spot, crying out Krok's name, and aimed a savage blow at the next man; but there was little room to manœuvre, because the warehouse was small and crowded with goods, to say nothing of the men who were fighting in it. One man jumped up on to a bench and tried to aim a blow at Orm, but his sword caught in a rafter, and Orm flung his shield into the man's face. The spike on his shield entered the other's eye, and he fell on his face and lay still. After that, the fight did not last much longer. The second of the two men who had killed Krok was felled by Gunne; of the others, Orm had killed two and Toke three; but the trader, who had burrowed himself almost out of sight in his corner, they allowed to escape unharmed, because he had nothing to do with this affair.

When they came out of the warehouse with their swords all bloody, they saw men approaching to discover what the noise had been about; but, on seeing the Viking's aspect, they turned and ran. Toke held his sword erect before his face; thick blood ran down its blade and fell from the hilt in large drops.

'Now I name thee, O sister of Blue-Tongue!' he said. 'Hereafter shalt thou be known as Red-Jowl.'

Orm stared after the men from the ships as they ran away into the distance.

'We, too, must make haste,' he said, 'for now we are outlaws in this land. But it is a small price to pay for vengeance.'

They hastened to the ship, and told the others what had happened. Then, at once, although it had by now grown dark, they weighed anchor and put out to sea. They rejoiced in the knowledge that Krok had been avenged, though at the same time they realized that they had no time to lose in getting clear of this country and its waters. They did their best to whip up a good pace from the slaves, and Orm himself took over the steering-oar, while Almansur's two secretaries, who were unaware of what had happened, hurled questions at him but received scant reply. At last, the ship came safely out of the bay into the open sea; and a wind sprang up from the south, so that they were able to raise a sail. They steered northwards and away from the land, until the day broke; and there was no sign of any ship pursuing them.

They saw a group of islands off their larboard bow, and Orm put in to one of them. Here, he sent both the secretaries ashore, bidding them convey his greetings to Almansur.

'It would be churlish of us to quit the service of such a master,' he said, 'without wishing him farewell. Tell him, therefore, on behalf of us all, that it has been our fate to have killed six of his men in revenge for Krok, who was our chieftain; although six men's lives are a small return for his death. We are taking this ship with us, and the slaves that man it, for we think that he will scarcely notice its loss. Also, we are taking the bell, because it makes the ship ride stable, and we have dangerous seas ahead of us. We all think that he has been a good master to us and, if we had not had to kill these men, we should gladly have remained longer in his service; but, as things have turned out, this is the only course left open to us, if we are to escape with our lives.'

The secretaries undertook to deliver this message, word for word as Orm had spoken it. Then, he added: 'It would be well, too, if, when you return to Cordova, you could bear our greetings to a wealthy Jew called Solomon, who is a poet and a silversmith. And thank him from us for having befriended us so generously; for we shall never see him again.'

'And tell the lady Subaida,' said Toke, 'that two men from the north, whom she knows, send her their thanks and greetings. Tell her, too, that the swords she gave us have served us well, and that their edges are yet undented, despite all the work that they have done. But, for your own sakes, do not deliver this message when Almansur is within hearing.'

The secretaries had their writing materials with them, and noted all this down; then, they were left on the island with enough food to sustain them until such time as some ship should find them, or they should manage to make their way to the mainland.

When the slaves working the oars saw that the ship was putting out towards the open sea, they made a noisy clamour and complaint, and it was evident that they wished to be left on the island with the secretaries. Orm's men had to go round with switches and rope-ends to silence them and make them row; for the wind had dropped, and they were anxious to lose no time in getting clear of these dangerous waters.

'It is lucky we have them fast in foot-irons,' said Gunne, 'or we should have had the lot of them overboard by now, for all our swords. It is a pity we did not borrow a proper scourge when we took the fetters. The teeth of these switches and rope-ends are too blunt for mules like these.'

'You are right,' said Toke, 'strangely enough; for we little thought, in the days when we sat on the galley benches, that we should ever come to mourn the absence of an overseer's whip.'

'Well, they say that no back is so tender as one's own,' replied Gunne. 'But I fear these backs will have to itch somewhat more sharply, if we are ever to escape from here.'

Toke agreed, and they went round the benches again, flogging the slaves smartly to make the ship move faster. But they still made laboured progress, for the slaves could not keep the stroke. Orm noticed this, and said: 'Rope-ends alone will never teach men to row, if they are not used to oars. Let us see if we cannot persuade the bell to lend us her aid.'

As he spoke, he took an axe, and struck the bell with its blunt edge as the slaves dipped their oars. The bell gave out a great peal, and the slaves pulled in response. In this way, they soon began to keep better time. Orm made his men take turns in sounding the stroke. They found that if they struck with a wooden club padded with leather, the bell pealed more melodiously; and this discovery pleased them mightily.

After a while, however, a wind sprang up and they had no further need to row. The wind gradually increased, blowing more and more gustily, until it approached the gale strength; and things now began to look dangerous. Grinulf remarked that this was only what was to be expected if men put out to sea without first propitiating the people of the water. But others spoke against him, recalling the sacrifice they had offered on a previous occasion and how shortly afterwards they had encountered the ships of Almansur. Gunne ventured the opinion that they might perhaps sacrifice to Allah, for safety's sake, and a few of the men supported this suggestion; but Toke said that, in his view, Allah had little pull in what went on at sea. Then Orm said:

'I do not believe that any man can be certain just how powerful this or that god is, or how much he can do to help us. And I think we should be foolish to neglect one god for the sake of not offending some other. But one thing we know, that there is one god who has served us well on this enterprise; I mean, St James; for it is his bell that keeps our ship from turning turtle and, apart from this, it has helped the rowers to keep time. So let us not forget him.'

They agreed that this was well spoken, and sacrificed meat

and drink to Agir, Allah and St James, which put them in better heart.

By this time they had little idea where they were, save only that they were a good way from Asturia. However, they knew that, if they held their course northwards, in the direction in which the storm was driving them, and avoided diverging too far to the west, they would be sure to strike land eventually, either in Ireland or in England, or perhaps in Brittany. So they screwed up their courage and rowed out the storm. Once or twice they managed to discern familiar stars; and they trusted that they would find their way.

Their chief worry concerned the slaves, who, although they now had no work to do at the oars, became poorly with fear and sea-sickness and the wet and cold, so that all of them were green and their teeth chattered; and a couple of them died. They had little warm clothing on the ship, and each day it blew colder, for the autumn was by now far advanced. Orm and his men pitied the wretchedness of the slaves, and tended them as well as they could; and, to such of them as had stomach to eat, they gave the best food; for they knew that these slaves would be valuable booty, if they could bring them safely to land.

At last, the storm died down, and for a whole day they enjoyed fine weather and a good wind, and held their course to the north-east; and the slaves perked up, encouraged by the sun. But, that evening, the wind dropped completely, and a fog descended on them and began to thicken. It was cold and damp, so that they all trembled with the cold, the slaves most of all; no breath of wind came, and the ship lay tossing in a heavy swell. Orm said:

'This is a pretty pass we have come to. If we stay here and wait for the wind, the slaves will die of cold; but if we make them row, they will die just as surely, in the wretched state they are in now. Though we have precious little to row on while we can see neither sun nor stars.'

'I think we should make them row,' said Rapp, 'to warm them up a little. We can steer with the swell, for that gale was blowing from the south; and we have nothing else to guide us while this fog holds.'

They thought Rapp's advice good, and the slaves were made to take up their oars, which they did amid much grousing; and indeed, they had little strength for the task. The men took turns again at beating time on the bell, and it seemed to their ears to sound more sweetly than before, with a long peal following each stroke, so that she was of good comfort to them in the fog. At intervals, they allowed the slaves to rest awhile and sleep; but, apart from this, they rowed the whole night through, steering with the swell, while the fog hugged them closely and incessantly.

When morning came, Ogmund was at the helm, with Rapp sounding the bell, while the others slept. Suddenly the two men listened, and stared at one another, and then listened anew. A faint peal had sounded from far away. Much astonished, they roused the others, and all strained their ears. The note was repeated several times, and it seemed to them to come from forward.

'It sounds as though we are not the only sailors who are rowing to a bell,' said Toke.

'Let us proceed softly,' said Grinulf. 'For this may be Ran and her daughters, who seduce men at sea with music and enchantments.'

'It sounds to me more like dwarfs at an anvil,' said Halle: 'and it would be no fun to make their acquaintance. Perhaps we are near some island where trolls hold sway.'

The peal still rang out faintly from the distance. All of them were now in a cold sweat, and they waited to hear what Orm should say. The slaves, too, listened, and began to chatter eagerly amongst themselves; but the tongues they spoke were unknown to Orm and his men.

'What this may be, no man can tell,' said Orm. 'But let us not be frightened at so small a thing. Let us row on, as we have done up to now, and keep our eyes skinned. For my part, I have never heard of witchery practised by morning light.'

They agreed with this, and the rowing continued; meanwhile, the distant note began to grow clearer. Light puffs of wind stirred their hair, and the fog thinned; then, suddenly, they all cried out that they spied land. It was a rocky coast, and appeared to be either an island or a promontory. They could not doubt that the sound had come from this spot, although it had now ceased. They saw green grass, and some goats grazing; also two or three huts, beside which men stood staring out to sea.

'These do not look to me like trolls,' said Orm, 'or the

daughters of Ran either. Let us go ashore and find out where we have come to.'

They did so; and the men of the island showed no fear at seeing armed men ashore, but came cheerfully towards them and greeted them. They were six in number, all old men, with white beards and long brown cloaks: and no one could understand what they said.

'To what land have we come?' asked Orm. 'And whose men are you?'

One of the old men understood his words, and cried to the others: 'Lochlannach! Lochlannach!'* Then he answered Orm in the latter's tongue: 'You have come to Ireland, and we are the servants of St Finnian.'

When Orm and his men heard this, they were overcome with joy, for they thought they must be nearly home. They could now see that they had landed on a small island and, beyond it, they could discern the Irish coast. On this small island there lived only the old men and their goats.

The old men conversed among themselves eagerly and in amazement; then the one who understood Norse said to Orm: 'You speak the tongue of the Northmen, and I understand that tongue, for in my young days I associated much with the Northmen before I came to this island. But certain it is that I have never seen men from Lochlann dressed as you and your men are dressed. Where do you come from? Are you white or black Lochlannachs?† And how is it that you come sailing to the sound of a bell? Today is St Brandan's day, and we rang our bell to pay homage to his memory; then we heard your bell reply from the sea, and we supposed that it might be St Brandan himself answering us, for he was a great sailor. But in Jesus Christ's name, are you all baptized men, that you come sailing with this holy sound?'

'The old man can gab,' said Toke. 'There is a mouthful for you to answer there, Orm.'

Orm replied to the old man: 'We are black Lochlannachs, men of King Harald's land: though, whether King Harald still lives, I

* i.e., 'men of the lakes.'
† i.e., Norwegians or Danes.

do not know, for we have been a long while from home. But our cloaks and garments are Spanish, for we have come from Andalusia, where we served a great lord named Almansur. And our bell is called James, and comes from the church in Asturia where the apostle James lies buried, and it is the biggest of all the bells there; but how and why it has accompanied us on our journey is too long a story to be told now. We have heard of this Christ you speak of, but where we come from he is held in no great honour, and we are not baptized. But since you are Christians, you may be glad to hear that we have Christian men at our oars. They are our slaves, and come from the same place as the bell; but they have been badly knocked about on our journey, and are worth but little now. It would be a good thing if they could come ashore here and rest for a while before we continue on our journey homewards. You need fear nothing from us; for you seem to be good men, and we use no violence towards those that do not try to oppose us. We could make use of a few of your goats, but you will suffer no other loss, for we do not intend to stay long here.'

When it was explained to the old men what he had said, they wagged their heads and whispered among themselves; and their spokesman said that they often welcomed seafaring men on their island, and that no man did them harm.

'For we ourselves do harm to no man,' he said, 'and we have no possessions apart from these goats and our boats and huts; the whole isle else is St Finnian's Isle, and he is powerful in the sight of God and holds his hand over us. This year he has blessed our goats generously, so that you shall not lack for sustenance. Welcome therefore to the little we can offer you; and for us old men, who sit here year after year in loneliness, it will be a joy to listen to the story of your travels.'

So the slaves were brought ashore and the ship was beached; and Orm and his men rested on St Finnian's Isle, living in peaceful harmony with the monks. They fished with them, making fine catches, and fed the slaves so that they looked less wretched; and Orm and the others had to recount all their adventures for the monks to hear for, although they had difficulty in following his words, the old men were eager for news of distant lands. But most of all, they marvelled at the bell, which was larger than any they had heard of in Ireland. They acclaimed it as a mighty miracle that St James and St Finnian had spoken to each other with their bells from afar; and sometimes at their holy services they smote the bell of St James instead of their own, and rejoiced aloud as its great clang echoed out across the sea.

CHAPTER EIGHT

Concerning Orm's sojourn among the monks of St Finnian, and how a great miracle occurred at Jellinge

While they were resting with the monks of St Finnian, Orm and his men deliberated deeply as to what course they should take once the slaves had recovered sufficiently for them to be able to proceed on their voyage. They were all eager to get back home, Orm no less than the others; nor was there much danger of encountering pirates at this time of year, when few ships were at sea. But the going was likely to be hard in the winter weather, which in turn might well result in the slaves dying on their hands; it would, therefore, they thought, perhaps be wisest to sell them as soon as possible. For that, they could either sail down to Limerick, where Orm's father was well known, or up to Cork, where Olof of the Precious Stones had for long been the biggest dealer in slaves in these parts. They asked the monks which they thought would be the best plan for them to follow.

When the monks understood what their guests wanted to know, they chattered eagerly to each other, and were apparently much amused; then their spokesman said: 'It is plain that you come from distant parts and know little about the way things are in Ireland now. It will not be easy for you to trade in Limerick, or in Cork either; for Brian Boru is powerful in Ireland now and, although you hail from a far country, you have probably heard of him.'

Orm said that he often heard his father speak of a King Brian, who waged war against the Vikings in Limerick.

'He does not wage war against them any longer,' said the monk. 'At first he was the chieftain of the Dalcassians; then the Vikings in

Limerick waged war against him. After that, he became King of Thomond, and then he waged war against them. In time, he became King of the whole of Munster, and then he stormed Limerick and killed most of the Vikings there; those that were not killed, fled. So now he is the greatest warrior and hero in Ireland, King of Munster, and Lord of Leinster; and such foreigners as remain in our coastal cities pay tribute to him. At present, he is waging war against Malachy, who is King of all our kings in Ireland, to win his wife and his power from him. Olof of the Precious Stones pays him tribute and has to send him soldiers to help him with his war against King Malachy; and even Sigtrygg Silk-Beard of Dublin, who is the most powerful of all the foreign chieftains in Ireland, has paid him tribute on two occasions.'

'These are grave tidings,' said Orm; 'and this King Brian appears indeed to be a mighty chieftain, though it may be that we have seen a mightier. But even if all you say is true, I do not see why this should prevent us from selling our slaves to him.'

'King Brian does not buy slaves,' said the monk, 'for he takes all that he requires from his neighbours and from the men of Lochlann. Besides which, it is known that there are three things which he covets more than anything else in the world, and three things that he abominates – and these last will be to your disadvantage. The things that he covets are these: supreme power, which he has already; the greatest quantity of gold, which he also has; and the most beautiful woman, whom all the world knows to be Gormlaith, the sister of Maelmore, King of Leinster. Her he has yet to win. She was formerly married to King Olof Kvaran of Dublin, who got rid of her because of the sharpness of her tongue; now she is wed to Malachy, the King of our kings, who so disports himself in her boudoirs that he is hardly fit to take the field any more. When Brian has defeated Malachy he will win Gormlaith, for he never fails to get what he wants. But the three things that he most abominates are heathens, men from Lochlann, and poets who praise other kings. His hatred is as violent as his greed, and nothing can assuage either of them; so, since you are heathens and Lochlannachs to boot, we would not advise you to approach him too nearly, for we do not want to see you killed.'

The men listened attentively to all this, and agreed that it would be unrewarding to trade with King Brian. Orm said: 'It seems to me that the James bell was a good guide to us, when it led us to your isle and not to King Brian's kingdom.'

'St Finnian's bell helped you, too,' said the monk; 'and now that you have seen what the saints can do, even for the heathens, would it not be a wise thing for you to start believing in God and become Christians?'

Orm said that he had not given the matter much consideration, and that he did not think there was any urgency about deciding.

'It may be more urgent than you know,' said the monk, 'for there are now only eleven years left till the end of the world, when Christ will appear in the sky and judge all mortal men. Before this happens, all heathens will do well to be baptized; and it would be foolish of you to be among the last to do so. Unbelievers are now going over to God in greater numbers than ever before, so that in a short while there will be few of them left in their darkness; and certain it is that the coming of Christ is presently imminent, for the wickedest heathen of all, King Harald of Denmark, has just been baptized. Now, therefore, is the time for you to do as he has done and abandon your false gods and embrace the true faith.'

All the men stared at him in amazement, and one or two of them burst out laughing and slapped their knees.

'You will soon be telling us,' said Toke, 'that he has become a monk like yourself, and shaved off his hair.'

Orm said: 'We have travelled far and wide in the world, while you rest here with your brothers on this lonely island; nevertheless, you have greater tidings for us than we have to tell you. But this is no small thing that you ask us to believe, when you tell us that King Harald has turned Christian; and I think the most likely explanation is that some seafarer has put this idea into your heads, knowing that you are simple and incredulous and thinking to make sport of you.'

But the monk insisted that he had spoken the truth, and had not merely repeated some sailor's yarn. For they had heard this great news from the mouth of their own Bishop, when he had visited them two years before; and on each of the next seven Sundays they had offered thanks to God, on behalf of all Christians whose homes had been visited by the Vikings, for the great victory He had gained.

This persuaded the men that the monk had told them the truth, though they found it none the less difficult to believe such remarkable tidings.

'He is himself descended from Odin,' they said, staring at one another in amazement; 'how, then, can he bind himself to any other god?'

'All his life he has had great good luck,' they said; 'and this was granted to him by the Aesir; his fleets have sailed against the Christians and have returned home laden with their wealth. What can he want with the Christians' god?'

They shook their heads and sat dumbfounded.

'He is old now,' said Grinulf, 'and it may be that he has become a child again, as King Ane of Uppsala did in former times. For kings drink stronger ale than other men, and have many women; and that can tire a man over the years, so that his understanding darkens and he no longer knows what he is doing. But men who are kings do as they please, even when wisdom has passed from them. Perhaps that is how King Harald has become ensnared into these Christian beliefs.'

The men nodded assent, and recounted stories of people in their homeland who had grown peculiar in their old age and had caused their families great trouble by their crooked fancies; and they all agreed that it was no good thing for a man to live until his teeth fell out and his understanding began to languish. The monks pointed out that worse things than that would befall them, for when the Day of Judgment arrived, in eleven years' time, they would be dragged suddenly out of the earth. But the men replied that they would worry about that when the time came, and that they were not going to bother to go over to Christ for the fear of that.

Orm had much to occupy his mind, for he had to decide what course they would do best to take, seeing that they did not dare to go inland to the markets. At length he said to his men: 'It is a fine thing to be a chieftain when there is booty to be divided up and ale to be handed around, but less desirable when there are plans to be made; and I have not been able to think out anything very good. Certain it is that we must sail now, for the slaves are as fit as they ever will be as the result of their rest here and the good food they have had, and the longer we delay the more difficult our journey will be, because of the weather. The best plan seems to me to be to sail to King Harald, for in his court there are many rich men who will be likely to give us a good price for our slaves; and, if he has in fact turned Christian, we have a fine gift to offer him, which should bring us at once into his favour. For my part, I would rather enter his service than sit at home as the youngest son in my father's house, if indeed the old man and Odd, my brother, are still alive, which I do not know; and those of you who yearn to return to your homes will have an easy journey from his court to Bleckinge, once we have completed the sale and shared out the money. But the main problem will be to see that the slaves do not die, when we come up into the cold of the northern waters.'

Then he told the monks that he was prepared to drive a bargain with them. If they gave him all the goatskins they had, together with such clothes as they could spare, he would let them keep the two feeblest of his slaves; for, if he took them with him on the voyage, they would die, while if they stayed ashore and regained their health, they would be useful to the monks. In addition to this, he was willing to give them some Andalusian silver coins. The monks laughed, and said that this was a better bargain than most Irishmen managed to drive with Lochlannach; but that they would most of all like to have the James bell. Orm, however, replied that he could not spare this, and the bargain was concluded on the basis of his original proposal, so that the slaves were provided with something in the way of winter clothing.

They smoked fish and goat's-meat to provision themselves for the voyage, taking besides a quantity of the turnips that the monks grew. The monks helped them with everything, behaving in the most friendly way towards them, and did not complain about their herd of goats being reduced to such small proportions by their guests; the only things that worried them were that the holy bell was going to remain in heathen hands, and that Orm and his men would not realize what was best for them and become Christians. When the time came to say farewell, they made one last effort to convince their departing friends of the truth about Christ and St Finnian and the Day of Judgment, and all the things that would befall them if they neglected to be converted to the true faith. Orm replied that he had little time just then to attend to such matters, but added that he would be a poor chieftain if he went away without giving them some token of gratitude for all the hospitality they had shown towards him and his men. Then, putting his hand into his belt, he drew out three gold pieces and gave them to the monks.

When Toke saw this, he laughed to see such open-handedness; but then he said that he was as rich a man as Orm, and that he intended in due course to marry into one of the best houses in Lister and become a great man in his district. So he, too, gave the monks three gold pieces, while they stood amazed to see such munificence. The other men did not greatly enthuse over the example of their leaders, but for the sake of their good names they, too, gave something; all except Grinulf. The others chaffed him for his thrift, but he grinned with his crooked mouth, and scratched his beard on his cheek and was content with the way he had acted.

'I am no chieftain,' he said, 'besides which, I am beginning to grow old; no girl is going to marry me and bring me a fine house to live in, and no gammer neither. So I am only being prudent, in being thrifty.'

When the slaves had been led aboard again and chained to their places, Orm sailed away from St Finnian's Isle and headed eastwards along the Irish coast. They had a strong wind to help them, and made good progress. All of them were troubled by the autumn cold, despite the fact that they had swathed themselves in goatskins; for Orm and his men had by now been such a long time in the south that they felt the cold in their bones more than they had been wont to. Nevertheless, they were all in good heart at being so near to their homeland, and their only anxiety was lest they should be intercepted by other of their countrymen who might be in these waters; so they kept a sharp look-out. For the monks had said that Vikings from Denmark were to be seen in greater numbers than ever around the English coasts now that most of Ireland had been closed to them by the might of King Brian, so that England was now regarded as being the best hunting-ground. In order, therefore, to avoid encountering other Viking ships, Orm kept the ship well out from the land as they steered up through the English Channel. They had good luck, for they met no ships; so they emerged into the open sea, and felt the spray of the waves growing colder, and sailed on until they sighted the coast of Jutland. Then they all laughed for joy, for it gladdened their hearts to see Danish soil once more; and they pointed out to one another the various landmarks that they had sighted when they had sailed southwards with Krok long before.

They rounded the Skaw and steered southwards, coming into the lee of the land; and now the slaves had to row again, as well as they could, while the bell of James sang the stroke. Here, Orm spoke with some men in fishing-boats who crossed their course, and discovered from them how far they were from Jellinge, where King Harald Bluetooth held his court. Then they polished their weapons and saw to their clothing, so that they might appear before the king in a manner befitting men of worth.

Early one morning, they rowed up to Jellinge and made their ship fast to a pier. From where they lay, they could see the royal castle, surrounded by a stockade. There were some huts down by the pier, and people came out of them and stared curiously at Orm and his men, for they had the mien and appearance of foreigners. Then the men lifted the bell ashore, using the same platform and rollers that they had employed in Asturia; and while they did so, a crowd of astonished spectators gathered from the huts to gaze upon so great a wonder and to learn where these foreigners had come from. Orm and his men found it very strange to hear their own language being spoken by others again, after having lived among foreigners for so many years. They released the slaves from their chains and harnessed them to the bell, to pull it up to the King.

Suddenly, they heard cries and sounds of confusion from the direction of the castle, and saw a fat man in a long cowl come running towards them down the hill. He was shaven, and wore a silver cross at his breast and terror in his face. He arrived breathlessly at the huts and, flinging his arms wide apart, cried, 'Leeches! Leeches! Is there no merciful soul here who can give us leeches? I must have blood-leeches immediately, fresh and strong.'

They could tell he was a foreigner, but he spoke the Danish tongue deftly, although he was gasping for breath.

'Our leeches up in the castle have fallen sick and lost their appetite,' he continued, panting, 'and leeches are the only thing to relieve him when he has the toothache. In the name of the Father, the Son and the Holy Ghost, is there nobody here who has any leeches?'

No one in the huts had leeches, however, and the fat priest

groaned and began to look desperate. He had by this time arrived down at the pier where Orm's ship was lying at anchor, and there, suddenly, he caught sight of the bell and the men surrounding it. His eyes emerged slowly from their sockets, and he ran forward to examine it more closely.

'What is this?' he cried. 'A bell, a holy bell? Am I dreaming? Is this a real bell, or is it a fabrication of the devil? How has it come here, to this land of darkness and evil spirits? Never in my life have I seen such a magnificent bell, not even in the Emperor's own cathedral at Worms.'

'It is called James, after an apostle,' said Orm; 'and we have brought it here from the apostle's church in Asturia. We heard that King Harald had turned Christian, and thought such a gift would please him.'

'A miracle, a miracle!' cried the priest, bursting into tears of relief and stretching his arms heavenwards. 'God's angels have turned to us in our hour of need, when our leeches sickened. This is better medicine than leeches. But hurry, hurry! Delay is dangerous, for he has the ache badly.'

The slaves dragged the bell slowly up towards the castle, while the priest exhorted the men incessantly to use all the strength they had to pull it faster. He kept up a continual chatter, as though he had taken leave of his senses, mopping his eyes and turning his face skywards and crying out fragments of sacred jargon. Orm and the others gathered that the King had toothache, but could not make out what good their bell was expected to do. But the priest babbled about how lucky something was and called them messengers of God and said that everything would now be all right.

'He has not many teeth left in his mouth, praised be Almightly God!' he said, 'but those that he has cause us as much trouble as all the other machinations contrived by the devil in the whole of this barbarous land. For, despite his age, they often cause him pain, all except the two blue ones; and when they begin to ache he is dangerous to approach, and blasphemes immoderately. There was a time this summer, when one of his molars was hurting him, that he almost sent Brother Willibald to join the martyrs; for he hit him on the head with the big crucifix, which should properly only be used for the soothing of pain. Brother Willibald is himself again now, praise the Lord, but he was sick and dizzy for many weeks.

109

We resigned our lives to the mercy of God, Brother Willibald and I, when we came with Bishop Poppo to this land of darkness with our gospel and our skill in healing; still, it seems a waste to be threatened with martyrdom for the sake of a couple of old teeth. Nor are we permitted to draw any of them out. This he has forbidden us to do, on pain of death, for he says that he is not prepared to become like some old King of the Swedes who ended up drinking milk from a horn. You see the difficulties and dangers we endure from this king in our zeal to spread the faith; Brother Willibald, who is the wisest doctor in the whole diocese of Bremen, and I myself, who am both doctor and precentor, and am called Brother Matthias.'

He paused for breath, mopping the sweat from his face and panted at the slaves to move faster. Then he continued: 'The chief difficulty which we doctors have to put up with in this country is that we have no relics to help us, not even so much as a single one of St Lazarus' teeth, which are irresistible healers of the toothache and are to be found everywhere else in Christendom. For we missionaries to the heathen are not permitted to carry relics with us, lest they should fall into heathen hands and so become sullied. We have to rely on our prayers and the Cross and earthly means of healing, and sometimes these are not enough. So none of us can heal by spiritual medicine here among the Danes, until we have relics to assist us; and the time for that has not yet arrived. For although three bishops and innumerable minor priests have been killed by the people here, and some of the bodies of these martyrs have been recovered and given Christian burial, so that we know where to find them, yet the Holy Church had ordained that no bones of bishops or martyrs may be dug up and used for medicine until they have been dead thirty-six years. Until that time comes, this will be a difficult country for doctors to work in.'

He shook his head and mumbled sadly to himself, but then appeared to perk up again.

'However,' he went on, 'now that God has seen fit to allow this great miracle to take place, things will become easier for Brother Willibald and me. True it is that I have never seen any reference in the Holy Scriptures to any special efficacy of St James as a healer of the toothache; but in his own bell, fresh from his blessed tomb, there must surely reside much power against evil of all kinds, even including bad teeth. Therefore, chieftain, it cannot but be that you are God's messenger to myself and Brother Willibald, and to all of the Christian faith in this land.'

Orm said: 'O wise sir, how can you cure toothache with a bell? My men and I have been in distant lands and have seen many marvellous things; but this would be the most miraculous of all.'

'There are two cures for the toothache that we who are skilled in the craft of healing know of,' replied Brother Matthias, 'and both of them are good. Personally – and I am sure Brother Willibald will feel as I do in the matter – I am of the opinion that the ancient prescription laid down by St Gregory is the most effective. You will soon have an opportunity to witness it in operation.'

By this time they had reached the rampart with its surmounting stockade, and the great outer door was opened for them by an old porter, while another man blew on a horn to signify that visitors had arrived. Brother Matthias placed himself at the head of the procession, and began exultantly to chant a holy song: *Vexilla regis prodeunt*. Behind him marched Orm and Toke, followed by the slaves drawing the bell, with the other men urging them along.

Within the stockade lay many houses, all belonging to members of the King's household. For King Harald lived in greater pomp, and with a more extravagant show of power, than his father had done. He had had King Gorm's huge dining-hall enlarged and had added to its splendour, and had had longhouses built for his servants and followers. The completion of his cookhouse and brewery had been celebrated by poets; and men who knew said that they were even bigger than those of the king in Uppsala. Brother Matthias led the way to the King's own sleep-house; for, now that he was old, King Harald spent most of his time there with his women and his treasure-chests.

The sleep-house was a lofty and very spacious building, though nowadays it was less crowded than it had been of old. For, since Bishop Poppo had repeatedly warned King Harald that he must take good care in every respect to lead a Christian life, the King had dispensed with the services of most of his women, retaining only a few of the younger ones. Such of the older women as had borne him children now lived elsewhere within the walls. On this particular morning, however, there was a great bustle of activity in and about the house, with many people of both sexes running around in anxious confusion. Some of them stopped to stare at the approaching procession, asking themselves what all this could mean; but Brother Matthias, breaking off his song, cantered like a drunken man through the crowd and into the King's chambers, with Orm and Toke following him.

'Brother Willibald, Brother Willibald!' he cried. 'There is yet balm to be found in Gilead! Royal King, rejoice and praise God, for a miracle has been performed for you, and your pain shall soon be driven away. I am as Saul, the son of Kish; for I went out to seek blood-leeches, and found instead a holy thing.'

While Orm's men were, with great difficulty, contriving to bring the bell into the King's bedchamber, Brother Matthias began to recount all that had taken place.

Orm and his men saluted King Harald with great respect, gazing curiously upon him; for his name had been in their ears for as long as they could remember, and they thought it strange to see him, after all these years, in such a sick and sorry state.

His bed stood against the short wall of the room, facing the door. It was stoutly timbered and lofty, and was full of bolsters and skin rugs; and it was of such a size that three or four people might lie in it without crowding each other. King Harald sat on its edge, surrounded by cushions, wrapped in a long robe of otter's fur and wearing on his head a yellow knitted woollen cap. On the floor at his feet squatted two young women, with a pan of hot coals between them, and each of them held one of his feet on her knees and chafed it to keep it warm.

The most ignorant of men, seeing him there, would instinctively have guessed that King Harald was a great king, although the circumstances of royalty were absent and an expression of unkingly misery was upon his face. His big round eyes goggled with melancholy anticipation of imminent agony as his gaze wandered around the faces in his chamber and finally alighted on the bell as it entered the door. He seemed unable to register much interest in the sight that greeted his eyes, and panted in little gasps, as though out of breath; for the pain had temporarily gone, and he was waiting for it to come back and torment him anew. He was heavily built and of powerful appearance, broad-chested and huge-paunched, and his face was large and red, with shiny and unwrinkled skin. His hair was white, but his beard, which was thick and matted and lay down over his chest in tapering tongues, was a greyish yellow; though, in the middle there was a narrow ribbon, coming down from his nether lip, which had retained its full yellowness and contained no grey at all. His face was wet all round his mouth, from the medicines he had taken for the pain, so that both his blue eye-teeth, which were famous for their length as well as for their colour, glistened even more brightly than was their wont, like the tusks on an old boar. His eyes stood goggling from their sockets and were bloodshot; but an awful majesty lurked within them, and in his broad forehead and great grizzled eyebrows.

Bishop Poppo was not present, for he had been keeping vigil by the King's bedside throughout the night, offering up prayers for him, and had had to listen to frightful threats and blasphemies when the pain had grown especially violent, so that in the end he had been compelled to retire and get some rest. But Brother Willibald, who had also been up all night experimenting with various medicines in company with Brother Matthias, had managed to remain awake and was still in cheerful spirits. He was a little, shrivelled man, with a big nose and pursed lips and a red scar across his temples. He nodded eagerly as he listened to Brother Matthias' account of what had taken place, and flung his arms above his head when he saw the bell appear in the doorway.

'This is in sooth a miracle!' he cried, in piercing and exultant tones. 'As the ravens of the sky succoured the prophet Elijah with food when he was alone in the wilderness, so have these wanderers come to our aid with help sent from heaven. All our worldly medicines have only succeeded in banishing the pain for a few minutes; for as soon as our lord the King's impatience causes him to open his mouth, the pain returns at once. So it has been throughout the night. Now, however, his cure is certain. First, then, Brother Matthias, wash the bell well with holy water; then turn it on its side, and wash its interior, for I do not see on its outer surface any of the dust that we shall need. Then, in good time, I will mix this dust with the other ingredients.'

So they turned the bell on to its side, and Brother Matthias swabbed its interior with a cloth dipped in holy water, which he then wrung out into a bowl. There was a lot of old dust in the bell, so that the water he wrung out of the cloth was quite black, which greatly delighted Brother Willibald. Then Brother Willibald set to work mixing his medicines, which he kept in a big leather chest, all the while delivering an instructive discourse to such of the company as were curious to know what he was attempting to do.

'The ancient prescription of St Gregory is the most efficacious in cases such as this,' he said. 'It is a simple formula, and there are no secrets about its preparation. Juice of sloe, boar's gall, saltpetre and bull's-blood, a pinch of horse-radish and a few drops of juniper-water, all mixed with an equal quantity of holy water in which some sacred relic has been washed. The mixture to be kept in the mouth while three verses from the psalms are sung; this procedure to be repeated thrice. This is the surest medicine against the tooth-ache that we who practise the craft of healing know: and it never fails, provided that the sacred relic is sufficiently strong. The Apulian doctors of the old Emperor Otto fancied frog's blood to be more efficacious than bull's-blood, but few physicians are of that opinion nowadays; which is a fortunate thing, for frog's-blood is not easy to procure in winter.'

He took from his chest two small metal bottles, uncorked them, smelt them, shook his head, and sent a servant to the kitchen to fetch fresh galls and fresh bull's blood.

'Only the best will suffice in a case such as this,' he said; 'and, when the relic is as powerful as the one we have here, great care must be taken over the other ingredients.'

All this had occupied several minutes, and King Harald now seemed to be less troubled by his pain. He turned his gaze towards Orm and Toke, evidently puzzled at seeing strangers clad in foreign armour; for they still wore the red cloaks and engraved shields of Almansur, and their helmets had nose-pieces and descended low down over their cheeks and necks. He beckoned to them to come nearer.

'Whose men are you?' he said.

'We are your men, King Harald,' replied Orm. 'But we have come hither from Andalusia, where we served Almansur, the great Lord of Cordova, until blood came between us and him. Krok of Lister was our chieftain when we first set forth, sailing in three ships. But he was killed, and many others with him. I am Orm, the son of Toste, of the Mound in Skania, chieftain of such as remain; and we

114

have come to you with this bell. We thought it would be a good gift for you, O King, when we heard that you had become a Christian. Of its potency in countering the toothache I know nothing, but at sea it has been a powerful ally to us. It was the largest of all the bells over St James's grave in Asturia, where many marvellous things were found; we went there with our master, Almansur, who treasured this bell most dearly.'

King Harald nodded without speaking; but one of the two young women squatting at his feet turned her head and, staring up at Orm and Toke, said very rapidly in Arabic: 'In the name of Allah, the Merciful, the Compassionate! Are you Almansur's men?'

They both gazed at her, amazed at hearing this tongue spoken at King Harald's court. She was fair to look upon, with large brown eyes that stood wide apart in her pale face. Her hair was black and hung from her temples in two long plaits. Toke had never been fluent in Arabic, but it was by now a long time since he had talked with a woman, so that he managed to come out readily with his reply. 'You surely come from Andalusia,' he said. 'I have seen women there like you, though none so fair.'

She gave him a quick smile, showing her white teeth, but then turned her eyes sadly downwards.

'O stranger, who speaks my language,' she said in a soft voice, 'you see what reward my beauty has brought me. Here sit I, an Andalusian of Celbitian blood, now a slave-girl among the darkest heathens and shamefully unveiled, rubbing this old Bluetooth's decaying feet. There is nothing in this country but cold and darkness and skin-rugs and lice, and food such as the dogs of Seville would vomit up. Only in Allah can I seek refuge from the miserable fate to which my beauty has brought me.'

'You look to me to be too good for the work you are doing here,' said Toke warmly. 'You ought to be able to find yourself a man with something better than his toes to offer you.'

Again she smiled like the sun at him, although tears had come into her eyes; but at that moment King Harald roused himself and said angrily: 'Who are you that mumble crow-talk with my woman?'

'I am Toke, the son of Grey Gull of Lister,' replied Toke, 'and my sword and the dexterity of my tongue are all that I possess. But I intended no disrespect to you, O King, in addressing your woman.

She asked me about the bell, and I answered her; and she replied that she thought it was a gift that would give you as much pleasure as she has given you, and be no less useful.'

King Harald opened his mouth to reply, but, as he did so, his face went black and he let out a roar and flung himself backwards among the cushions, so that the two young women working on his feet were thrown head over heels on to their backs; for the pain had returned savagely into his bad tooth.

At this there was great confusion in the bedchamber, and those that stood nearest the King's bed took a step backwards lest he should become violent. But Brother Willibald had by now prepared his potion, and came boldly forward with cheerful mien and encouraging words.

'Now, now, royal King!' he said admonishingly, and made the sign of the cross twice, first over the King and then over the bowl containing the potion, which he held in one of his hands. With his other hand he took a little horn spoon, and chanted in a solemn voice:

> 'The cruel pain
> Within thee burning
> Now shall be quenched
> In the well of healing.
> Soon shalt thou feel
> The ache departing.'

The King stared at him and his bowl, snorted angrily, shook his head and groaned, and then, in his agony, aimed a blow at him and roared violently: 'Away from me, priest! Away with your incantations and broth. Ho, there, Hallbjörn, Arnkel, Grim! Up with your axes and split me this louse of a priest!'

But his men had often heard him talk like this, and paid no heed to his fulminations: and Brother Willibald, no whit daunted, addressed him boldly: 'Be patient, O King, and sit upright and put this in your mouth; for it is rich with the strength of saints. Only three spoonfuls, O King, and you need not swallow them. Sing, Brother Matthias!'

Brother Matthias, who was standing behind Brother Willibald with the great crucifix in his hand, began to intone a sacred hymn:

'Solve vincla reis
profer lumen caecis,
mala nostra pelle,
bona cuncta posce!'

This seemed to subdue the King, for he patiently allowed himself to be lifted into a sitting position. Brother Willibald promply inserted a spoonful of the mixture into his mouth, proceeding as he did so to accompany Brother Matthias in his hymn, while everyone in the bedchamber watched them with great expectancy. The King went purple in the face with the strength of the potion, but kept his mouth closed; then, when three verses had been sung, he obediently spat it out, whereupon Brother Willibald, without desisting from his singing, gave him another spoonful.

All the spectators afterwards agreed that it was only a few seconds after receiving the second spoonful, and before the priests had had time to complete a verse of the hymn, that the King suddenly closed his eyes and went rigid. Then he opened them again and spat out the potion, gave vent to a deep sigh, and roared for ale. Brother Willibald stopped singing and leaned anxiously towards him.

'Is it better, your Majesty? Has the pain ceased?'

'It has,' said the King, spitting again. 'Your medicine was sour, but it appears to have been effective.'

Brother Willibald threw up his arms for joy.

'Hosanna!' he cried. 'A miracle has occurred! St James of Spain has answered our prayer! Praise the Lord, O King, for better times are now beginning! The toothache shall no more cloud your spirit, nor shall anxiety dwell in the hearts of your servants!'

King Harald nodded his head and stroked the corners of his beard. He seized with both hands a large vessel, which a page brought to him, and raised it to his mouth. At first he swallowed carefully, evidently afraid lest the pain might return, but then drank confidently until the vessel was empty. He ordered it to be refilled and offered it to Orm.

'Drink!' he commanded. 'And accept our thanks for the succour you have brought us.'

Orm took the vessel and drank. It was the finest ale he had ever tasted, strong and full-bodied, such as only kings could afford to brew, and he drank it with a will. Toke watched him, and sighed; then, he said:

> 'In my throat there is a feeling
> Of dry-rot most unblest.
> Do physicians know the healing
> For me, that ale is best?'

'If you are a poet, you shall drink,' said King Harald. 'But afterwards you will have to compose a poem about your drink.'

So they filled the vessel again for Toke, and he put it to his mouth and drank, leaning his head further and further backwards; and all those present in the King's bedchamber agreed that they had seen few vessels emptied more smartly. Then he reflected for a while, wiping the froth from his beard, and at length declaimed, in a voice stronger than that in which he had made his request:

> 'Thirsting I rowed for many a year,
> And thirsting I did good slaughter.
> All praise to thee, Gorm's gracious heir!
> Thou knowest my favourite water!'

The men in the bedchamber praised Toke's poem, and King Harald said: 'There are few poets to be found nowadays, and few of those are able to turn out verses without sitting for hours in cogitation. Many men have come to me with odes and lyrics, and it has vexed me sorely to see them while the winter away in my halls with their noses snuffling up my ale, producing nothing whatever once they had declaimed the poem they had brought with them. I like men to whom verses come easily, and who can give me some new delight each day when I dine, in which respect, you, Toke of Lister, are more fluent than any poet I have heard since Einar Skalaglam and Vigfus Viga-Glumsson were my guests. You shall both spend Yule with me, and your men too; and my best ale shall be provided for you, for you have earned it by the gift you brought me.'

Then King Harald gave a great yawn, for he was weary after his troublesome night. He wrapped his fur more closely around him, snuggled himself into a more comfortable position in his bed, and lay ready for rest, with the two young women on either side of him. The skin rugs were spread over him, and Brother Matthias and Brother Willibald made the sign of the cross above his head and mumbled a prayer. Then they all left the room, and the groom of the bedchamber strode into the middle of the palace yard with his sword in his hand and cried three times in a loud voice: 'The King of Denmark sleeps!' so that no noise should be made which might disturb King Harald's slumber.

CHAPTER NINE

How King Harald Bluetooth celebrated Yule

Great men from all over the North came to Jellinge to celebrate Yule with King Harald, so that there was less than room enough for them at the tables and in the bedchambers. But Orm and his men did not complain of this overcrowding, for they had received a good price for their slaves, and had sold them all before the festival commenced. When Orm had divided up the proceeds of the sale, his men felt rich and free indeed, and they began to yearn for Lister and to know whether Berse's two ships had come home, or whether they themselves were the only survivors of Krok's expedition. However, they offered no objection to staying in Jellinge until the festival was over, for it was regarded as a great honour, and one which added lustre to a man's name for the rest of his days, to have celebrated Yule with the King of the Danes.

The principal guest was King Harald's son, King Sven Forkbeard,* who had arrived from Hedeby with a large following. Like all King Harald's sons, he was the child of one of his father's concubines; and there was little love lost between him and his father, so that in general they avoided each other as much as possible. Every Yule, though, King Sven made the journey to Jellinge, and everybody knew why. For it often happened at Yule, when the food was richer and the drink stronger than at any other time in the year, that old men suddenly died, either in bed or on the drinking-bench. This had been the case with old King Gorm, who had lain unconscious

* The father of King Canute the Great.

120

for two days after a surfeit of Yuletide pork, and had then died! and King Sven wanted to be near the royal coffers when his father passed over. For many Yules now he had made the journey in vain, and each year his impatience increased. His followers were a rough crew, overbearing and quarrelsome, and it was difficult to keep the peace between them and the men of King Harald's household, all the more so now that King Harald had turned Christian and many of his men had followed suit. For King Sven still clung to the old religion, and made spiteful mock of his father's conversion, saying that the Danes would have been spared all this folly if the old man had had the sense to know when he had lived long enough.

However, he did not trumpet his opinions too openly when he was at Jellinge, for King Harald was easily roused to anger, and when this happened he was liable to do anything to anybody. They wasted no words on one another once they had made formal salutation, nor, from their seats of honour in the great hall, did they toast each other more than the conventions of politeness absolutely required.

There was a snowstorm on Christmas Eve, but it passed, and the weather grew calm and cold; and on Christmas morning, while the priests were singing mass and the courtyard of the palace lay shrouded in good steam from the preparations afoot in the kitchens, a great long-ship rowed up from the south and made fast to the pier, its sail tattered and its oars glazed with ice. King Harald was at mass, but they sent a messenger to inform him. Wondering who these new guests could be, he went up the stairs to look at the ship. It was steeply built, with a red dragon's head poised arrogantly upon a curved neck at the prow, its jaws caked with ice from the cruel seas it had passed through. They saw men climb ashore wearing garments barked with ice, among them a tall chieftain in a blue cloak and another, of equal stature, clothed in red. King Harald scanned them as closely as he could from where he stood, and said: 'It looks like a Jomsviking, or perhaps a Swedish ship, and it is boldly manned, for its crew approach the King of Danes with no shield of peace upon their masthead. I know of but three men who would dare to come thus: Skoglar-Toste, Vagn Akesson, and Styrbjörn. Moreover, they have brought their ship alongside without removing their dragon-head, though they know well that the trolls of the mainland do not love dragon-heads; and I know of but two men who do not care what the trolls think, and they are Vagn and Styrbjörn. But I see from the ship's condition that its captain disdained to seek shelter from last night's storm, and there is but one man who would have refused to bow to such a tempest. It is my guess, therefore, that this must be my son-in-law Styrbjörn, whom I have not seen these four years; one of them wears a blue cloak, moreover, and Styrbjörn has sworn to wear blue until he has won back his inheritance from King Erik. Who this other with him may be, the man who is as tall as he, I cannot surely say; but Strut-Harald's sons are taller than most men, all three of them, and they are all friends to Styrbjörn. It cannot be Jarl Sigvalde, the eldest of them, for he takes little pleasure in Yule celebrations now, because of the ignominy with which he stained his name when he rowed his ships away from the battle at Jörundfjord; and his brother Hemming is in England. But the third of Strut-Harald's sons is Thorkel the Tall, and it may be that this is he.'

Thus King Harald surmised in his wisdom; and when the strangers reached the palace and it became apparent that he was right, his spirits rose higher than they had been at any time since King Sven arrived. He bade Styrbjörn and Thorkel welcome, ordered the bath-house to be heated for them at once, and offered mulled ale to them and all their men.

'Even the greatest of warriors,' he said, 'need something to warm themselves after such a voyage as you have endured: and there is truth in the old saying:

> "Mulled ale for the frozen man,
> And mulled ale for the weary:
> For mulled ale is the body's friend,
> And makes the sick heart merry."'

Several of Styrbjörn's men were so exhausted by their voyage that they were hardly able to stand: but when tankards of mulled ale were offered them, their hands proved to be steady enough, for not a drop was spilled.

'As soon as you have bathed and rested,' said King Harald, 'the Yule feast shall begin: and I shall go to it with a better appetite than if I had only my son's face to look at across the table.'

'Is Forkbeard here?' said Styrbjörn, glancing around him. 'I should be glad to have a word with him.'

'He still cherishes the hope that some day he will see me die the ale-death,' said King Harald. 'That is why he has come. But if I ever should die at a Yule feast, I think it will be because I am sick of looking at his misshapen face. You will have your chance to speak with him in good time. But tell me one thing. Is there blood between him and you?'

'No blood as yet,' replied Styrbjörn, 'but as to the future, I cannot say. He has promised me men and ships to help me against my kinsmen in Uppsala, but none have yet arrived.'

'There must be no fighting in my house during the holy festival,' said King Harald. 'You must understand that at once, although I know that you will find it tedious to keep the peace. For I am now a follower of Christ, who has been a good ally to me: and Christ will tolerate no strife on Christmas Day, which is his birthday, nor on the holy days which follow.'

Styrbjörn replied: 'I am a man without a country, and as such cannot afford the luxury of being peaceful: for I would rather be the crow than his carrion. But while I am your guest, I think I shall be able to keep the peace as well as any man, whichsoever gods are presiding over the feast; for you have been a good father-in-law to me, and I have never had cause to quarrel with you. But I have news to bring you, namely, that your daughter Tyra is dead. I wish I could have come with more joyful tidings.'

'That is sad news indeed,' said King Harald. 'How did she die?'

'She took it amiss,' said Styrbjörn, 'because I found myself a Wendish concubine. She became so wrathful that she began to spit blood; then she languished and, after a time, died. In all other respects she was an excellent wife.'

'I have noticed of late,' said King Harald, 'that young people cling less keenly to life than old people. But we must not allow this grief to weigh down our spirits during the Yule feast; and in any case, I have more daughters left than I know what to do with. They are a fine-spirited bunch, and will not marry any man who is not of noble birth and high renown; so that you need not remain a widower for long, if you should find any girl among them that takes your fancy. You shall see them all; though I fear that, when they hear that you are single again, they may have some difficulty in keeping the Yule peace.'

'Something other than marriage is uppermost in my mind just now,' said Styrbjörn, 'but we can speak of that later.'

Many glances were cast at Styrbjörn from doorways and loop-holes, as he went with his men to the bath-house; for he rarely accepted hospitality, and was held to be the greatest warrior that had been seen in the North since the days of the sons of Ragnar Hairy-Breeks. He had a short, fair beard and pale blue eyes, and men who had not seen him before murmured with surprise at finding him so slim-built and narrow-waisted. For they all knew that his strength was such that he cleft shields like loaves of bread and split armed men from the neck to the crutch with his sword, which was called Cradle-Song. Wise men said that the ancient luck of the Uppsala kings was his, and that it was this that gave him strength and success in every enterprise he undertook. But it was also known that the curse of his family, and their ancient ill-luck, had in part descended on him, and that it was because of this that he was a chieftain without a country; and that it was for this reason, too, that he was often afflicted with a great heaviness and melancholy. When the fit attacked him, he would shut himself away from all company and sit sighing and mumbling darkly to himself for days on end, unable to endure the presence of any of his fellow beings, save for a woman to comb his hair and an old harpist to give him ale and play him sad music. But so soon as the fit passed from him, he would be eager to go to sea again, and to battle, and then he would bring the strongest of his men to weariness and despair by his recklessness and his bad weather-luck.

So he was feared as no other chieftain in the north was feared, almost as though something of the power and majesty of the gods dwelt in him; and there were those who believed that some time, in the future, when he reached the zenith of his might, he would sail to Miklagard and crown himself emperor there, and voyage in triumph along the round edge of the earth with his terrible navies.

But there were others who claimed that they could see it written in his eyes that he would die young and unlucky.

At length, everything was ready in King Harald's great dining-hall for the Yule feast, and all the men were assembled there in their numbers, seated on benches. No women were allowed to be present at so tremendous a drinking-bout, for it was difficult enough, King Harald thought, to keep the peace when men were by themselves, and it would be many times harder if they had women to brag to in their cups. When everyone was in his place, the groom of the bedchamber announced in a gigantic voice that the peace of Christ and of King Harald reigned in the hall, and that no edged implements might be used except for the purpose of cutting up food; any cut, thrust, or open wound caused by weapon, ale-tankard, meat-bone, wooden platter, ladle, or clenched fist, would be reckoned as plain murder, and would be regarded as sacrilege against Christ and as an unpardonable crime, and the miscreant would have a stone tied round his neck and be drowned in deep water. All weapons apart from eating knives had been left by order in the vestibules, and only the exalted personages who sat at King Harald's own table were allowed to retain their swords; for it was felt that they would be able to control themselves even when drunk.

The hall was built to hold a good 600 men without crowding, and in the middle stood King Harald's own table, with the thirty most eminent of the company seated at it. The tables for the other guests stretched down the length of the hall from one end to the other. Styrbjörn sat on King Harald's right hand, and Bishop Poppo on his left; opposite them, King Sven had Thorkel the Tall on his right, and a red-faced, bald old jarl from the Small Islands called Sibbe on his left. The others sat according to their rank, King Harald himself having settled each man's place personally. Orm, though he could not be reckoned as one of the great chieftains, had yet been allotted a better place than he could have expected, and Toke likewise, for King Harald was grateful to them for their gift of the great bell, and was an admirer of Toke's poetry. So Orm sat three places from the Bishop, and Toke four; for Orm had told King Harald that he would like, if possible, to sit next to Toke, in case the latter became troublesome through drink. Facing them across the table were men of King Sven's company.

The Bishop read grace, King Harald having commanded him to be brief about it, and then they drank three toasts: to the honour of Christ, to the luck of King Harald, and to the return of the sun. Even those of the company who were not Christians joined in the toast to Christ, for it was the first of the toasts and they were thirsty for their ale; some of them, however, made the sign of the hammer over their tankards and murmured the name of Thor before they drank. When the toast to King Harald's luck was drunk, King Sven got ale in his windpipe and had a coughing fit, causing Styrbjörn to ask whether the brew was too strong for his taste.

Then the Yule pork was brought in, and warriors and chieftains alike fell silent when they saw it appear, and took a deep breath and sighed with joyous anticipation: many loosened their belts, to save doing so later. For although there were those who whispered that King Harald was in his old age less open-handed with gold and silver than he had been of yore, this accusation had never been levelled at him in the matter of meat and drink, and certainly never by anyone who had celebrated Yule in his palace.

Forty-eight acorn hogs, well fattened, were slaughtered for his pleasure every Yule; and it was his custom to say that, if this did not see them through the whole feast-tide, it would at any rate be sufficient to provide a tasty entrée for every guest, and that they could then fill up with beef and mutton. The kitchen servants entered in a long line, two by two, each pair bearing a great smoking pot, except for some who carried troughs of blood-sausage. They were accompanied by boys armed with long forked spits which, once the pots had been set beside the tables, they plunged into the stew, fishing out large hunks of meat which they gave to the guests in order of precedence, so that each had his fair share; in addition to which, every man received a good ell's-length of blood-sausage, or more if he wanted it. There were bread cakes and fried turnips set out on clay plates, and at the foot of each table there stood a butt of ale, so that no man's horn or tankard need ever be empty.

As the pork approached Orm and Toke, they sat quite still, with their faces turned towards the pot, watching the boy closely as he fished for the meat. They sighed blissfully as he lifted out fine pieces of shoulder pork to put on their plates, reminding each other how long it was since they had last eaten such a dinner, and marvelling that they had managed to survive so many years in a country where no pork was allowed to be eaten. But when the blood-sausage arrived, tears came into their eyes, and they declared that they had never eaten a meal worthy of the name since the day they had sailed away with Krok.

'This is the best smell of all,' said Orm in a small voice.

'There is thyme in it,' said Toke huskily.

He plunged his sausage into his mouth, as far as it would go, bit off a length and slowly closed his jaws; then he swung hastily round, grabbing at the boy's coat as he attempted to move on with the trough, and said: 'If it be not contrary to King Harald's orders, give me at once another length of that sausage. I have for some years past now fared indifferently among the Andalusians, where they have no food worthy of the name, and these seven Yules I have longed for blood-sausage and had none.'

'My case,' said Orm, 'is the same.'

The boy laughed at their anxiety, and assured them that King Harald had enough sausage for everybody. He ladled out a good length of the thickest that he had on to each of their plates; then they were contented, and began to eat in earnest.

For some time now, nobody spoke, either at the King's table or anywhere else in the hall, except when somebody asked for more ale or mumbled a word between bites in praise of King Harald's Yuletide meat.

On Orm's right sat a young man who cut his meat with a knife that bore an engraved silver hilt. He was fair-skinned, and had very long and exquisite hair, carefully combed. He belonged to Thorkel the Tall's company, and evidently came of good family, for he was honourably placed at the King's table although he had as yet no beard; besides which, his nobility was apparent from his fine clothing and silver sword-belt. After that first flush of eating was over, he turned to Orm and said: 'It is good at a feast to sit next to men who have travelled widely; and I think I heard that you and your neighbour have voyaged further afield than most of us here.'

Orm replied that this was correct, and that Toke and he had spent six years in Spain.

'For various reasons,' he added, 'our journey took longer than we had anticipated; and many of those who set out with us never returned.'

'You must have had many adventures worth the telling,' said the other. 'I, myself, though I have not travelled as far as either of you, have also recently been on a voyage from which few came back.'

Orm asked him who he was, and what voyage he referred to.

The other replied: 'I come from Bornholm, and my name is Sigurd; and my father was Blue Digre, of whom you may have heard, despite your long sojourn abroad. I was with him at Jörundfjord when he was killed, and I was captured there, together with Vagn Akesson and many others beside. Nor should I be sitting here to-night to tell the tale if it had not been for my long hair; for it was my hair that saved my life when orders had been given for all the prisoners to be killed.'

By this time, a number of their table companions had eaten their fill and were beginning to regain the freedom of their tongues for the purpose of speech. Toke now joined in the conversation, remarking that what the Bornholmer had just said had an unusual ring about it, and promised a good story; for his part, he had always regarded long hair as being more of a handicap to a soldier than an advantage. Thorkel the Tall sat picking his teeth in the aristocratic manner that was now beginning to be fashionable among great men who had travelled widely, with his face turned to one side and the palm of his hand raised before his mouth. He overheard their conversation and observed that long hair had proved unlucky to many a soldier in the past, and that sensible men always took good care to bind their hair up carefully beneath their helmets; however, he added, Sigurd Buesson would show by his story how a shrewd man might take advantage of the length of his hair, and he hoped that everyone in the hall would listen to what he had to say.

King Sven was, by this time, in a better humour, the appearance of Styrbjörn having shadowed his spirits for a while. He sat lolling backwards in his chair, gnawing a pig's trotter, the bones from which he spat out on to the straw that covered the floor. He noted with satisfaction that King Harald, who was engaged in a discussion with Styrbjörn about women, was eating and drinking more than anyone else. He, too, overheard what was being said further down the table and joined in the discussion, pointing out that a wise soldier also always remembers his beard, for when a battle was being fought in windy weather a man's beard could easily get into his eyes just when he was preparing to parry a sword-thrust or to avoid a winging spear; wherefore, he told them, he always made a point of having his hair plaited before marching into battle. But now he would be interested to hear how Sigurd Buesson had taken advantage of his long hair, for men who had fought at Jörundfjord usually had adventures worth relating.

Bishop Poppo had not succeeded in finishing all that had been placed before him, and the ale that he had drunk had given him hiccups; nevertheless, he was capable of utterance and he, too, joined in the discussion, saying that he would be happy to tell them the story of Prince Absalom, whose long hair had proved to be his downfall. This, he said, was a good and instructive story, which stood written in God's own holy book. But King Sven cut him off promptly with the comment that he could keep such stories for women and children, if he could persuade them to listen to him. Words were then exchanged between him and the Bishop on this score; but King Harald said: 'A feast such as this, which lasts for six days, will allow us all time in which to tell our stories: and few things are better than to listen to good stories, when a man has eaten his fill and has ale left in his cup. For it helps the time to pass easily between one meal and the next, and makes for less quarrelling across the tables. But let me say this in the Bishop's favour, that he had good tales to tell, for I myself have listened to many of them with pleasure, concerning saints and apostles and the old kings that used to reign in the eastern lands. He has told me many stories about one of them whose name was Solomon, who was greatly beloved by God and who seems to have been very much like myself, though it is true that he had more women. I think that the Bishop should tell his story first, before the food and drink made him sleepy, for our Yule drinking does not have the same good effect on him that it has on us, since he has not had sufficient time to accustom himself to it. After him, let other men tell of their adventures at Jörundfjord, or with Styrbjörn among the Wends, or elsewhere. We have, besides, here among us, men who have been as far abroad as Spain, whence they have sailed to my court bearing with them a holy bell, which has been of great service to me; and I wish to hear them tell their story before this feast is done.'

They all agreed that King Harald had spoken wisely, and it was done as he suggested; so that evening, after the torches had been brought in, the Bishop told the story of King David and his son Absalom. He spoke loudly, so that everyone could hear him, and he told his tale cunningly, so that all the company except King Sven enjoyed it. When the Bishop had finished talking, King Harald observed that his story was well worth storing away in one's memory, for one reason and another; and Styrbjörn laughed, and raised his glass to King Sven, and said: 'Be wise, O Prince, and pay heed to this tale, and cut thy hair short as bishops do.'

This remark appealed to King Harald, who smote his thigh and fell into such a fit of laughing that the whole bench on his side of the table shook; and when his men and Styrbjörn's followers saw their masters laughing, they all joined in, even those of them who were unaware of the cause, so that the whole hall rang with merriment. King Sven's men, however, were displeased; and he himself glowered sourly and mumbled something into his cup and gnawed his lip-beard and had a dangerous look about him, as though he might at any moment leap to his feet and break into violence. Styrbjörn leaned forward in his seat and stared at him out of his pale eyes, which never blinked, and smiled. There was considerable unrest in the hall, and it looked as though the Christmas peace might shortly be ended. The Bishop stretched out his hands and cried something which nobody heard, and men fixed their eyes upon each other across the table, and groped for the nearest thing that might serve as a weapon. But then King Harald's jesters, two small Irishmen who were famed for their skill in trade, jumped up on to the King's table in motley-coloured tunics, wearing feathers in their hair, and began to flap their broad sleeves and puff their chests and stamp their feet and stretch their necks; then they crew at each other exactly like cocks, so that no man present could remember ever having heard a cock crow as finely as they did; and within a few seconds they had all forgotten their anger and were lolling in their seats helpless with laughter at their antics. So the first day of the feasting ended.

On the next day, when the eating was over and the torches had been carried in, Sigurd Buesson told them of his adventures at Jörundfjord, and how he had been saved by his long hair. They all knew about his expedition; how the Jomsvikings, with men from Bornholm, had sailed out in a mighty fleet under the command of Strut-Harald's sons, with Blue Digre and Vagn Akesson, to win Norway from Jarl Haakon, and how few had returned from that enterprise; so Sigurd did not waste many words on this part of his story, and made no mention of how Sigvalde had fled with his ships from the battle. For it would have been churlish to have spoken of Sigvalde when Thorkel the Tall was among his audience, although they all knew Thorkel to be a bold fighter, and were aware that he had been struck on the head by a large stone during the battle soon after the opposing navies had come to grips, so that he had not been conscious when his brother had rowed away.

Sigurd had been aboard his father's ship, and confined himself to such parts of the battle as he himself had been directly concerned in. He told them of his father's death; how Bue had fought fiercely, but at last, when the Norwegians had boarded his ship in over-whelming numbers, had received a slash on his face from a sword which had taken away his nose and the greater part of his jaw; and how he had then seized up his great treasure-chest and leaped overboard with it in his arms. He told, too, how Bue's kinsman, Aslak Holmskalle, had gone berserk, casting aside his shield and helmet, which was something one seldom saw nowadays, and hewing about him with both hands, impervious to the touch of iron, until an Icelandic bard, a follower of Jarl Haakon's son Erik, had picked up an anvil from the deck and with it had split his skull.

'After that,' continued Sigurd, 'for such of us as remained alive on my father's ship, there was little left to do; for we were few in numbers, and very fatigued, and all our ships had now been over-powered, save only Vagn's own ship, which still fought on. We were hemmed in the forecastle, so weary that before long we could lift neither hand nor foot; and at last there were but nine of us left, all wounded, and there they pinned us with their shields and so took us. We were disarmed and brought ashore; and soon the survivors of Vagn's ship were dragged to join us, Vagn himself being among them. Two men carried him, and he bore both sword-and-spear-wounds, and was pale and weary and said nothing. They made us sit on a log on the beach, with our legs tied together with a long rope, though they left our hands free; and there we sat and waited, while men were sent to Jarl Haakon to discover what should be our fate. He commanded that we were instantly to be put to death, and Jarl Erik, his son, and many of his followers, came to watch our end; for the Norwegians were curious to see how Jomsvikings would conduct themselves in the face of death. There were thirty of us on the log, nine from Bue's ship, eight from Vagn's, and the rest from other ships. Vagn himself sat on our extreme right; and I shall tell you the names of such of the others as were known to me.'

Then he gave them a list of all those whose names he knew, in the order which they sat on the log; and all the company in the great hall listened in silence, for many of those he named were men whom they had known, and some of his listeners had kinsmen among the dead.

He continued: 'Then a man came with a beard-axe and stood in front of Vagn, and said: "Do you know who I am?" Vagn glanced at him, but did not seem to notice him, and said nothing, for he was very weary. Then the other man said: "I am Thorkel Leira. Perhaps you remember the vow you made to kill me and bring my daughter Ingeborg to bed?" Now this was true, for Vagn had vowed thus before setting out, since he had heard that Thorkel's daughter was the most beautiful girl in Norway, besides being one of the richest. "But now," continued Thorkel Leira, with a broad grin, "it looks rather as though I am going to kill you." Vagn curled his lip and said: "There are yet Jomsvikings living." "They shall not live long," replied Thorkel, "and I shall see to it myself, so that there shall be no mistake. You will see all your men die beneath my hand, after which you will shortly follow them." Then he went to the other end of the log and proceeded to behead the prisoners, one after the other as they sat there. He had a good axe and went to work with a will; and he never needed to strike twice. But I think that those who were watching the scene had to admit that Vagn's and Bue's men knew how to conduct themselves in the face of death. Two who were seated not far from me began a discussion as to what it would feel like once one's head was off, and they agreed that it was one of those things that are difficult to foretell. One of them said: "I have a brooch here in my hand. If my brain is still working after I have lost my head, I shall stick it into the ground." Thorkel arrived at him; but as soon as the blow fell on his neck, the brooch dropped from his hand. That left only two men between Thorkel and myself.'

Sigurd Buesson smiled quietly at his listeners, who sat in silent excitement. He raised his cup and drank a deep draught. King Harald said: 'I see that you still have your head on your shoulders; and anyone can hear by the sound of your swallowing that there is nothing wrong with your neck. But that was a sorry situation you were in on that Norwegian log, and it is no easy thing to guess how you managed to escape to tell the tale, however long your hair. This is a fine story, and do not keep us waiting to know how it ended.'

They all raised a shout of agreement, and Sigurd Buesson continued: 'As I sat there on the log, I do not think I was more frightened than the others were; but I felt it would be a pity to die without having done something worthy for men to speak of after I had gone. So when Thorkel came to my place, I said to him: "I am afraid for my hair; I do not want it to be stained with blood." So saying, I drew it forward over my head; and a man who was walking behind Thorkel – I heard later that he was his brother-in-law – ran forward and wound my hair round his fingers and said to Thorkel: "Now, strike!" He did so; but in the same instant, I pulled my head back as quickly as I could, so that the axe fell between me and his brother-in-law and cut off both the latter's hands. One of them remained hanging in my hair.'

Everyone in the hall burst into a great roar of laughter. Sigurd himself laughed with them; then he proceeded: 'You may well laugh; but your laughter, loud as it is, is as silence compared with the merriment of the Norwegians when they saw Thorkel's brother-in-law writhing on the ground, with Thorkel standing scowling above him. Some of them laughed so much that they fell over. Jarl Erik came forward and looked at me and said: "Who are you?" I replied: "My name is Sigurd, and Bue was my father; there are yet Jomsvikings living." The Jarl said: "You are truly of Bue's blood. Will you accept your life from me?" "From such a man as you, Jarl," I replied, "I will accept it." Then they untied me. But Thorkel, ill-pleased at this, roared: "Shall it be thus? Then it were best I lose no time in despatching Vagn." Raising his axe, he rushed towards him, as he sat quietly on the end of the log. But one of Vagn's men, named Skarde, a good man from Kivik, was seated four places from Vagn; and it seemed to him wrong that Vagn should lose his head before his proper turn arrived. So he threw himself forward over the foot-rope, as Thorkel rushed by him, so that Thorkel fell full length over his body, and lay at Vagn's feet. Vagn leaned forward and took up the axe, and there was little weariness to be seen in his face and he buried it in Thorkel's head. "I have fulfilled half my vow," he said; "and still there are Jomsvikings living." The Norwegians laughed louder than ever; and Jarl Erik said: "Will you have your life, Vagn?" "If you grant it to us all," replied Vagn. "It shall be so," said the Jarl. So they freed us all. Twelve of us escaped from the log with our lives.'

Sigurd Buesson was loudly acclaimed for his story, and everyone praised the good use he had made of his hair. They all discussed his story across the tables, admiring his good luck and that of Vagn; and Orm said to Sigurd: 'There is much that is common knowledge in these parts which Toke and I are ignorant of, because we have been out of the country for so long a time. Where is Vagn now, and what happened to him after he escaped from the log with his life? From all that you say, his luck sounds to me greater than that of any other man I ever heard tell of.'

'That is so,' replied Sigurd, 'nor does it stop half-way. We rose high in Jarl Erik's favour, and after a while he sought out Thorkel Leira's daughter, whom he found to be even more beautiful than he had imagined her; nor did she offer any objection to helping him to fulfil the remainder of his promise; so that now they are married, and are well contented. He is thinking of coming back to Bornholm with her, as soon as he can find the time to do so; but the last heard of him was that he was still in Norway and was complaining that it would be many months before he could return home. For he became master of so many fine houses when he married the girl, and of so many great estates attached to them, that it will be no swift matter to sell them for the prices they deserve to command; and it is not Vagn's custom to sell things cheaply when he does not have to do so.'

Toke said: 'There is one thing in your story that I cannot help wondering about. I mean, your father, Bue's, treasure-chest, which he took with him when he jumped overboard. Did you fish it up before you left Norway? Or did someone else get there before you? If it is still lying on the sea-bed, I know what I should do were I to go to Norway. I should drag the sea for that treasure-chest; for Bue's silver must have been worth a great fortune.'

'They fished long for it,' said Sigurd; 'not only the Norwegians, but also such of Bue's men as survived. Many men dragged for it with grappling hooks, but they caught nothing; and one man from the Vik who dived down with a rope was never seen again. Then all of us concluded that Bue was such a Viking as would wish to keep his treasure with him on the sea-bed, and that he would have no mercy on any man who tried to take it from him; for he was a strong man, and he loved his wealth. Wise men know that those who dwell in the Great Halls are stronger than when they were alive; and this may also be true of Bue, although he does not dwell in the Great Halls but on the deep sea-bed beside his treasure-chest.'

'It is a pity that so much silver should be lost,' said Toke. 'But, as you say, even the boldest of men would not willingly choose to be at the bottom of the sea with Broad Bue's arms locked about his waist.'

So that evening drew to its close.

The next evening, King Harald wanted to hear about Styrbjörn's adventures among the Wends and Kures. Styrbjörn said that he was no story-teller; but an Icelander who was of his following took up the tale. His name was Björn Asbrandsson, and he was a famous warrior, besides being a great poet to boot, like all wanderers from Iceland. Although he was somewhat drunk, he managed to improvise some highly skilful verses in King Harald's honour in a metre known as *töglag*. This was the latest and most difficult verse-form that the Icelandic poets had invented, and indeed his poem was so artfully contrived that little could be understood of its content. Everybody, however, listened with an appearance of understanding, for any man who could not understand poetry would be regarded as a poor specimen of a warrior; and King Harald praised the poem, and gave the poet a gold ring. Toke plunged his head between his hands on the table, and sighed disconsolately; this, he muttered, was real poetry, and he could see that he would never be able to succeed in writing the sort of verses that won gold rings.

The man from Iceland, whom some called Björn Champion-of-the-men-of-Breidifjord,[*] and who had been a follower of Styrbjörn for two summers, then went on to tell them of Styrbjörn's various campaigns, and the notable things that had occurred during them. He was a fine talker, and continued for several hours without anyone wearying of his story; and everybody knew that what he was telling them was the truth, since Styrbjörn himself was among his listeners. He gave them many examples of Styrbjörn's boldness, and of his great luck, and also spoke of the rich booty that his followers had won. Finally, he concluded by reciting an ancient poem about Styrbjörn's ancestors, beginning with the gods and ending with his uncle Erik, who was now reigning in Uppsala. To this poem, he had himself added a final strophe, which ran as follows:

'Northwards soon
To crave his birthright
Styrbjörn shall row

---

[*] A good poet and a strong fighter, who is supposed to have ended his days in America.

With a hundred keels.
His gallant men
With victory flaming
Shall make full merry
In Erik's halls.'

This was greeted with tremendous applause, and many of the diners jumped up on to their benches to drink to Styrbjörn's luck. Styrbjörn ordered a costly drinking-cup to be brought to him, and presented it to the poet, saying: 'This is not your bardic crown, O Icelander; that it shall be set upon your brow when I sit on my throne in Uppsala. There shall be wealth worth winning there for every man of my followers; for my uncle Erik is a thrifty man, and has hoarded much that we can put to better use than by allowing it to tarnish in his coffers. When the spring buds open, I shall sail northwards to open those coffers, and any man who wishes to accompany me shall be welcome.'

Both among King Harald's followers and among King Sven's there were many whose blood was fired by this challenge, and who roared at once that they would keep him company; for the extent of King Erik's wealth was famous throughout the north, besides which, Uppsala had not been plundered since the time of Ivar of the Broad Embrace. Jarl Sibbe of the Small Islands was drunk and was having difficulty in controlling both his head and his wine-cup; but he joined in the thunder of acclamation, roaring that he would bring five ships to row north with Styrbjörn, for, he said, he was now beginning to grow stiff and sleepy, and it was better for a man to die among warriors than upon straw like a cow. King Harald said that he was, alas, too old to take the field, and that he had to keep his soldiers at home to maintain peace in his kingdom; however, he would not stand in the way of his son, Sven, if the latter wished to ally his men and ships to Styrbjörn's enterprise.

King Sven spat meditatively, took a swig from his cup, fingered his beard, and said that it would be difficult for him to spare either men or ships, since he could not neglect his obligations towards his own people, whom he could not leave a defenceless prey to the Saxons and Obotrites.

'I think it fairer,' he added, 'that if any assistance be lent, it should be provided by my father; for now that he is old, his men must have little to do but wait for the next meal-time and listen to the twittering of priests.'

King Harald exploded with fury at this remark, and there was uproar in the hall: he said that it was easy to see that Sven would be glad to see him left defenceless in Jellinge.

'But it shall be as I command!' he screamed, and his face was scarlet; 'For I am the King of the Danes, and I alone! So, Sven, you shall lend ships and men to Styrbjörn!'

Hearing these words, King Sven sat silent, for he was afraid of his father's wrath; besides which, it was clear that many of his men were eager to follow Styrbjörn to Uppsala. Then Styrbjörn spoke.

'I am delighted,' he said, 'to see how anxious you both are to help me. I think the best solution would be that you, Harald, should decide how many ships Sven shall lend; and that you, my good friend Sven, shall determine the extent to which your father shall aid me.'

This suggestion caused great merriment among all the feasters, so that the tension in the hall decreased; and finally it was agreed that Harald and Sven should each send twelve well-manned ships to fight with Styrbjörn, in addition to whatever help he might succeed in persuading the Skanians to lend him; in return for which, Harald and Sven were to have a share of the treasure that lay in King Erik's coffers. So that evening too, drew to its close.

The next day, since they had finished the Yule pork, cabbage soup and mutton appeared on the tables, which they all agreed to be an excellent change. In the evening, a man from Halland told them about a great wedding that he had been present at in Finnveden, among the wild people of Smaland. During the celebrations, a dispute had broken out concerning a horse-deal, and knives had quickly appeared; whereupon the bride and her attendant maidens had laughed delightedly and applauded, and had encouraged the disputants to settle the matter there and then. However, when the bride, who belonged to a well-known local family, saw her uncle's eye gouged out by one of the bridegroom's kinsmen, she seized a torch from the wall and hit her bridegroom over the head with it, so that his hair caught fire. One of the bridesmaids had, with great presence of mind, forced her petticoat over his head and twisted it tight, thereby saving his life, though he screamed fearfully and his head, when it appeared again, was burned black and raw. Meanwhile, the fire had caught the straw on the floor, and eleven drunken or wounded men lying in it had been burned to death; so that this wedding was generally agreed to have been one of the best they had had for years in Finnveden, and one that would be long remembered. The bride and bridegroom were now living together in blissful happiness, although he had not been able to grow new hair to replace that which he had lost in the fire.

When this story was finished, King Harald said that it was good to hear of such merry goings-on among the Smalanders, for they were in general a sour and treacherous people; and, he went on, Bishop Poppo ought to thank God every time he said his prayers that he had been sent to Denmark, where men knew how to behave themselves, when he might have fallen instead among the robber folk of Finnveden or Värend.

'But to-morrow,' he concluded, 'let us hear about the country of the Andalusians, and the strange adventures that befell Orm the son of Toste and Toke the son of Grey-Gull on their voyage; for this, I think, will amuse us all.'

So that evening ended.

The next morning Orm and Toke debated as to which of them should tell the story of their travels.

'You are our chieftain,' said Toke, 'so you must also be our historian.'

'You were on the expedition before I joined it,' said Orm. 'Besides which, you have a readier gift for words than I. Anyway, it is time you had a chance to talk your fill, for I seem to have noticed during these last evenings that once or twice you have found difficulty in listening in silence to all these stories that we have had to hear.'

'It is not the speaking that worries me,' said Toke, 'for I think I have as ready a tongue as most men. The thing that troubles me is that I cannot tell a story unless I am well supplied with ale, for my throat becomes dry easily, and our story is not one that can be told in a few sentences. I have managed to control myself for four evenings, on each of which I have quitted the King's table soberly and peacefully. None the less, it has not been easy for me, although I have had little occasion for talking. It would be a pity if I were to lapse into one of my melancholy moods and gain the reputation of being an ill-conducted man, and one unworthy to eat at the tables of kings.'

'Well,' said Orm, 'we must hope for the best. Even if you should become tipsy during your narration, I do not think that such fine ale as King Harald provides will be likely to make you violent or quarrelsome.'

'It shall be as it shall be,' said Toke, and shook his head doubtfully.

So that evening, Toke told the story of Krok's expedition, and of all that had befallen them on their travels; how Orm had come to join them, how they had discovered the Jew in the sea, and how they had plundered the fortress in Ramiro's kingdom; of the sea-battle they had fought against the Andalusians, and how they had become galley-slaves; and he told them how Krok had died. Then he described how they had been freed from their slavery, and the services that the Jew had performed for them, and how they had received their swords from Subaida.

When he reached this point in his story, both King Harald and Styrbjörn expressed their wish to see these swords; so Orm and Toke passed Blue-Tongue and Red-Jowl up the table. King Harald and Styrbjörn drew them from their scabbards and weighed them in their hands, studying them carefully; and both agreed that they had never in their lives seen finer swords than these. Then the swords were passed round the whole table, for many of the guests were curious to examine such fine weapons, and Orm fidgeted nervously until he had Blue-Tongue back at his waist again, for he felt half naked without her cheek against his thigh.

Almost opposite Orm and Toke there sat two of Sven's followers named Sigtrygg and Dyre, who were brothers. Sigtrygg belonged to King Sven's own ship. He was a huge, coarse-framed man, with a broad and extraordinarily bushy beard which reached right up to his eyebrows. Dyre was younger, but he, too, was rated as being one of King Sven's boldest warriors. Orm had noticed that Sigtrygg had, for some time during Toke's account of their adventures, been throwing dark glances in their direction, and had once or twice appeared to be about to interrupt with some remark. When the swords reached him in the course of their passage round the table, he examined them closely and nodded to himself, and seemed reluctant to pass them back.

King Sven, who liked to hear about distant lands, now exhorted Toke to proceed with his story. Toke, who had been utilizing the interval well, replied that he would be glad to continue as soon as the men opposite him had finished looking at his sword and that of Orm. At this, Sigtrygg and Dyre returned the swords, without saying anything, and Toke took up his tale again.

He told them of Almansur and of his might and wealth, and how they had entered his service as members of his imperial bodyguard and had had to worship the Prophet, bowing towards the east each evening and renouncing many of the good things of life; and he told of the wars in which they had partaken, and of the booty they had won. When he came to the story of their march through the Empty Land towards St James's burial place, and described to them how Orm had saved Almansur's life and how Almansur had given him the great gold chain as a token of gratitude, King Harald said: 'If you still have that chain, Orm, I should be interested to see it; for, if it is as surpassing an example of the goldsmith's art as your sword is of the smith's, it must indeed be a marvel to look upon.'

'I have it still, King Harald,' replied Orm, 'I intend to keep it always; and I have always thought it wise to show it to other men as little as possible, for it is of such beauty as to awaken the covetousness of any man who is not a king or the wealthiest of lords. It would be churlish of me to refuse to show it to you, O King, and to King Styrbjörn and King Sven and the Jarls; but I beg that it shall not be passed round for the other guests to see.'

Then he opened his tunic and drew out the chain, which he wore around his neck, and handed it to Sigurd Buesson. Sigurd passed it to Hallbjörn, the groom of the bedchamber, who sat on his right, and Hallbjörn passed it across Bishop Poppo's place to King Harald: for the Bishop's place now stood empty, he having had his fill of the Yuletide drinking and being now confined to his bed, where Brother Willibald was tending him.

King Harald measured the chain, and held it against the light, that he might the better examine its beauty. Then he announced that he had spent his whole life collecting jewels and precious ornaments, but that he could not remember ever having seen a finer work of art than this. The chain consisted of thick lozenges of pure gold, each lozenge being long and narrow, a good thumb in length and the breadth of a thumb-nail at its middle point, where it was widest, and from which it tapered inwards towards its end; and each lozenge was joined to its fellow by a small gold ring. The chain comprised thirty-six such lozenges; every first lozenge had a precious red stone set in its centre, and every second, a green.

When Styrbjörn held it in his hand, he said that this was worthy to have come from Weland's smithy; he added, however, that there might be articles of equal beauty in his uncle's coffers. When it reached King Sven, he observed that it was the sort of prize for which warriors gladly gave their blood and the daughters of kings their maidenheads.

Then Thorkel the Tall examined the chain, and, after he had praised it as the others had done, he leaned down the table to hand it back to Orm. As he did so, Sigtrygg thrust out his hand to take it; but Orm was quicker, and his hand reached it first.

'Who are you to snatch at it?' he said to Sigtrygg. 'I have not heard you are a king or a jarl, and I do not want it to be handled by any but them.'

'I wish to fight with you for this ornament,' said Sigtrygg.

'I can believe that,' replied Orm, 'for you are plainly a covetous and unmannerly churl. My advice to you is to keep your fingers to yourself and not to meddle with people who know how to behave themselves.'

'You are afraid to fight with me,' thundered Sigtrygg. 'But fight you shall, or else surrender your chain to me; for you have long stood in debt to me, and I demand this chain in payment.'

'You have a weak head for ale, and it makes you talk foolishly' said Orm, 'for I never saw you in my life before this feast began, so that I cannot possibly be in your debt. The best thing you can do,' he added sharply, 'is to sit still and hold your tongue, before I beg King Harald's leave to tweak your nose where you sit. I am a man of peace, and loth to dirty my fingers on such a snout as yours; but even the most patient of men would feel an urge to teach you manners.'

Now Sigtrygg was a renowned warrior, feared by all for his strength and ferocity, and by no means accustomed to being addressed in such a manner as this. He leaped up from his bench bellowing like a bull and pouring out a flood of abuse; but louder still rang King Harald's voice through the hall, as he called furiously for silence and demanded to know the cause of this disturbance.

'Your good ale, O King,' said Orm, 'together with this man's greed for gold, have combined to drive his wits out of him; for he screams

141

that he will have my chain and claims that I stand in his debt, though I have never before set eyes on him.'

King Harald said angrily that Sven's men were always making trouble, and he demanded sternly of Sigtrygg what had driven him to take leave of his senses and lose control of himself, when he had heard it plainly proclaimed that both the peace of Christ and the peace of King Harald were to be respected in this hall.

'Royal King,' said Sigtrygg 'let me explain how this whole matter stands, and you will see that my claim is just. Seven years ago I suffered a cruel wrong, and now, here at your feast, I have heard that these two men were among the perpetrators of it. That summer, we were sailing home from the southern lands in four ships, Bork of Hven, Silverpalle, Fare-Wide Svensson and myself, when we met three ships sailing southwards. We held converse with them, and from this man Toke's story I now know whose ships they were. Now on my ship there served a Spanish slave, a dark-haired, yellow-skinned man. While we were speaking with the strangers, this man jumped overboard, dragging with him my brother-in-law Oskel, a good man; and nothing more was seen of either of them. But now we have all heard that this slave was taken up on board their ship, and that he was this man whom they call Solomon; and that he served them well indeed. These two men who sit there, Orm and Toke, were the men who pulled him out of the water; we have heard as much from their own lips. For such a slave I could have got a fine price. This man Orm is now the chieftain of such as survive from Krok's company, and it is no more than justice that he should repay me for the loss I thereby incurred. I therefore demand of you, Orm, that you surrender me this chain in payment for the loss of my slave and my brother-in-law, peacefully and of your own free will; failing which, that you meet me in single combat outside this hall, on trodden earth, with shield and sword, now and without delay. Whether or not you give me the chain, I shall in any case kill you; for you have said that you wish to tweak my nose – and to me, Sigtrygg, the son of Stigand, and kinsman of King Sven, no man has even addressed impertinences and lived to see the end of the day on which he uttered them.'

'Two things only have kept my temper cool as I listened to your words,' replied Orm. 'The first is that the chain is mine and shall remain so, whoever may or may not have jumped from your ship into the sea seven years ago. And the second is that Blue-Tongue and I shall have a say in the matter of which of us shall live to see to-morrow's sunrise. But first, let us hear King Harald's pleasure regarding this affair.'

Everyone in the hall was happy to see that there was a good prospect of an armed combat; for a fight between two such men as Orm and Sigtrygg was sure to be worth the watching. Both King Sven and Styrbjörn expressed their opinion that this would add pleasant variety to the Yuletide drinking; but King Harald sat pondering the matter deeply, stroking his beard and wearing an expression of perplexed uncertainty. At length, he said: 'This is a difficult case on which to pronounce judgment. I think it doubtful whether Sigtrygg can fairly claim compensation from Orm for a loss which he sustained through no fault of Orm's. On the other hand, it cannot be denied that no man may reasonably be expected to lose a good slave, to say nothing of a brother-in-law, without expecting to receive some compensation for his loss. In any case, now that insults have been exchanged they are bound to fight it out as soon as they are out of my sight; and such a chain as Orm wears must surely have been the cause of many combats in the past, and will certainly be the cause of many more in the years to come. In the circumstances, therefore, I see no reason why they should not be permitted to settle it here, in armed combat, where we can all enjoy watching them. Therefore, Hallbjörn, see to it that a combat ring be trodden out and roped off here, outside our hall, where the ground is most even, and see to it also that it be well lit with flares and torches; and tell us as soon as it is ready.'

'King Harald,' said Orm, and his voice sounded strangely unhappy. 'I am not willing to be a party to such a contest.'

They all stared at him in amazement, and Sigtrygg and a number of King Sven's followers burst out laughing. King Harald shook his head sadly and said: 'If you are afraid to fight, then there is no alternative but that you surrender your chain to him, and hope that it may divert his wrath. To my ears, your voice had a bolder tone in it than this a few minutes ago.'

'It is not the fighting that worries me,' said Orm, 'but the cold. I have always been a man of delicate health, and cold is the thing that I can least endure. Nothing is more dangerous for my health than to go out from a hot room, after heavy drinking, into the cold night air, especially now that I have spent so many years in southern climes and am unaccustomed to the northern winter. I do not see why, to please this Sigtrygg, I should have to endure being racked with coughs for the rest of the winter; for coughs and colds tend to hang about me, and my mother always used to say that they would be the death of me, if I did not take good care of myself. Therefore, O King, I humbly propose that the fight take place here, in the hall, before your table, where there is plenty of space, and where you yourself will be able to enjoy the spectacle in comfort.'

Many of those present laughed at Orm's anxiety; but Sigtrygg did not join in their mirth, bellowing furiously that he would soon settle any fears Orm might cherish concerning his health. Orm, however, paid no attention to him, but remained quietly seated with his face turned towards King Harald, awaiting his decision. At last King Harald said: 'I am sorry to see that young men are growing soft nowadays. They are not what they used to be. The sons of Ragnar Hairy-Breeks never bothered about such trivial considerations as their health or the weather; nor, indeed, did I myself, in my younger days. Really, I do not know of any young man to-day who is of the old mettle, apart from Styrbjörn. However, I confess that, now that I am old, it would be a convenience for me to be able to watch the fight without having to move from my present chair. It is lucky that the Bishop is ill in bed, for he would never permit this to take place; still, I do not see that the peace which we have come here to celebrate can be said to be broken by anything to which I give my assent; nor do I think that Christ could have any objection to a contest of skill, provided that it be conducted with due propriety and the correct formalities. Therefore, let Orm and Sigtrygg fight here in the cleared hall before my table, with sword and shield, helmet and chainshirt; and let no man assist them, except with the putting on of their armour. If one of them be killed, the matter is decided; but if either of them be no longer able to stand upright, or throw down his sword, or seek shelter beneath the tables, his adversary shall not continue to strike at him, for he shall then be deemed to have lost the fight and the chain with it. And I and Styrbjörn and Hallbjörn my groom shall see that the contest is fairly fought.'

Then men hastened to fetch armour for Orm and Sigtrygg, and the noise in the hall was very great as the rival merits of the champions were extolled and challenged. King Harald's men deemed Orm the better fighter of the two, but King Sven's men were loud in Sigtrygg's praise and said that he had slain nine men in single combat without sustaining a single wound serious enough to require bandaging. Among those who talked loudest was Dyre. He asked Orm whether he was not afraid that the cold of the grave might make him cough; then he turned to his brother and bade him be content to have Orm's chain for his share of the compensation, and allow him, Dyre, to have Orm's sword.

All this while, since they had first interrupted his story, Toke had been sitting in heavy silence mumbling to himself and drinking; but, when he heard Dyre's words, life seemed to return into his brain. He plunged his eating-knife into the table in front of Dyre's place, so that it stood quivering in the wood, tossed his sword, still in its sheath, beside the knife; then he leaned forward across the table, so quickly that Dyre had no time to draw away, seized him by the ears and the beard on his cheeks, and forced his face downwards towards the weapons, saying: 'Here you see weapons as good as Orm's; but if you wish to have them, you must win them yourself, and not beg them from another.'

Dyre was a strong man, and he took hold on Toke's wrists and tried to dislodge his grip, but only succeeded in intensifying the pressure on his ears and beard, so that he groaned and grunted but could not free himself.

'I am holding you here in amicable converse,' said Toke, 'because I have no wish to disturb the King's peace in this hall. But you shall not go free till you have promised to fight with me, for Red-Jowl likes not to hide her beauty from men's eyes when her sister dances naked.'

'Let me go,' snarled Dyre, his mouth pressing against the table, 'that I may waste no time in closing your mouth.'

'That is a promise,' said Toke, and as he spoke he released his grip and blew from between his fingers the wisps of beard that he had dragged from their roots.

The whole of Dyre's face, apart from his ears which were scarlet, was white with fury, and at first he seemed to have lost the power of speech. He rose slowly to his feet and said: 'This matter shall be settled without delay; and your suggestion is a good one, for by this means my brother and I shall have a Spanish sword apiece. Let us go out and piss together, nor forget to bring our swords with us.'

'That was well spoken,' said Toke. 'You and I can dispense with the formalities of kings. For your acceptance of my suggestion, I shall remain in your debt as long as you live; how long that may be, we shall shortly know.'

Then they descended the length of the King's table, each on his opposite side, and strode shoulder to shoulder down the aisle between the long tables that faced each other across the hall, and out through one of the doors in the short wall at the bottom. King Sven saw them go and smiled, for it pleased him to see his men behave arrogantly, because this increased his fame and the fear in which his name was held.

Meanwhile, Orm and Sigtrygg had begun to arm themselves for combat, and the part of the floor where they were to fight had been swept, so that they should not slip on the straw or stumble over the bones which had been thrown there for King Harald's dogs to gnaw. The men who had been eating at the top and bottom of the hall now crowded forward to get a better view, squeezing into spaces on the benches and the long tables on both sides of the cleared square, as well as behind King Harald's table and along the wall on the remaining side. King Harald was in high good-humour, and could scarcely wait for the fight to begin; and when, on turning his head, he noticed two of his women peeping eagerly in at one of the doors, he issued a command that all his women and daughters should come and watch the sport; for it would be a hard thing, he said, if they should be denied the pleasure of witnessing such a spectacle. He made room for some of them on his own royal bench, by his side and on his knees, and for others in the Bishop's empty seat; the two most beautiful of his daughters, however, managed to find a space on either side of Styrbjörn, and found nothing to complain of in the tightness of the crush that pressed them against him; they giggled coyly when he offered them ale, and drank it with a bold air. For those women who could not find room on a royal bench, another bench was placed behind the table in such a position that the King and his companions did not impede their view.

Hallbjörn the groom then commanded a fanfare to be blown, and called for silence. He proclaimed that everyone should keep absolutely still while the fight was in progress, and that no man might shout advice to the contestants, or throw anything into the arena. Both the contestants were now ready, and they entered the arena and stood facing one another. When it was seen that Orm held his sword in his left hand, an excited hubbub of discussion broke out, for a fight between one right-handed and one left-handed man provided difficulties for both of them, since it meant that the blows fell on their sword-arm sides, to which their shields offered less protection.

It was plain that neither of them was the sort of adversary that a man would choose to find himself pitted against; nor did either man appear to cherish any anxiety regarding the outcome of the contest. Orm was half a head taller than Sigtrygg, and had the longer reach, but Sigtrygg was more squarely built and looked rather the more powerful man of the two. They held their shields well forward across their breasts and high enough to be able to cover their necks promptly, should the necessity arise; and each kept his eyes fixed on his opponent's sword, so as to be able to anticipate the other's blows. As soon as they came within striking distance of one another, Orm aimed a slash at Sigtrygg's legs, but Sigtrygg evaded the blow nimbly and replied with a vicious swing which landed with a ringing crash on Orm's helmet. After this opening, both men proceeded more cautiously, parrying each other's blows skilfully with their shields, and King Harald was heard to observe to his women that it was good to see experienced swordsmen such as these at work, instead of the sort who rushed crazily into the fight leaving themselves open; for this meant that the spectacle would last longer.

'It is no easy thing to forecast which of these two is likely to prove the master,' he said. 'But the red man looks to be as safe a swordsman as I have seen for many a month, for all his fear of the cold; and I shall not be surprised if Sven is one kinsman the poorer to-night.'

King Sven, who, like both the Jarls, was sitting on the edge of the table to get a better view of the fight, smiled contemptuously and retorted that nobody who knew Sigtrygg need have any fears regarding the outcome.

'Although my men are not averse to the sport of armed combat,' he said, 'it is seldom that I lose one of them, except when they fight against each other.'

As he spoke, Toke re-entered the hall. He was limping badly, and could be heard muttering a verse to himself; and as he climbed over the bench to his place, it could be seen that one of his legs was black with blood from his thigh to his knee.

'How went it with Dyre?' asked Siguard Buesson.

'It took time,' replied Toke. 'But he finished pissing at last.'

Everybody's eyes were now on the fight, which Sigtrygg seemed eager to bring to a quick conclusion. He was attacking Orm savagely, trying to pierce his defence and concentrating on his legs and face and the fingers of his sword-hand. Orm was defending himself ably, but did not appear to be able to achieve anything very positive himself; and it could be seen that he was having trouble with Sigtrygg's shield. This was larger than his own, and was of tough wood, strengthened with leather; only the centre boss was of iron, and Orm had to take care that his sword should not become embedded in the edge of the shield, for if that were to happen it would give Sigtrygg the chance to snap it or wrench it from his grasp by a twist of his arm. Orm's shield was made entirely of iron, with a sharp spike in its centre.

Sigtrygg sneeringly asked Orm whether it was warm enough for him. Blood was pouring down Orm's cheek from the first blow on his helmet, and he had besides received a thrust in the leg and a slash across the hand, while Sigtrygg was still unmarked. Orm made no reply, but retreated step by step alongside one of the long tables. Crouching behind his shield, Sigtrygg moved swiftly in to the attack, padding forwards and occasionally leaping to one or the other side, while his blows rained ever the more fiercely, so that it seemed to most of the spectators that the end could not now be far distant.

Then Orm suddenly sprang at his opponent and, taking Sigtrygg's blow on his sword, drove his shield against Sigtrygg's with all his strength, so that the spike on his own shield pierced through the leather and into the wood and remained embedded there. He forced the shield downwards so hard that the handles of both of them snapped, whereupon the two men both took a step backwards, freed their swords and, leaping high into the air, slashed at each other in the same instant. Sigtrygg's blow struck Orm in the side, piercing his chain-shirt and causing a deep wound; but Orm's sword buried itself in Sigtrygg's throat, and a great shout filled the hall as the bearded head flew from its shoulders, bounced on the edge of the table and fell with a splash into the butt of ale that stood at its foot.

Orm staggered, and supported himself against the table. He wiped his sword across his knee, replaced it in its sheath and gazed down at the headless body lying at his feet.

'Now you know,' he said, 'whose chain it is.'

CHAPTER TEN

How Orm lost his necklace

The fight for the necklace was busily discussed throughout the palace, in the hall, the kitchens and the women's chambers. All those who had witnessed it were careful to store away in their memories everything that had been said and done, so as to have a good story to tell other men in the years to come. Orm's feat in pinning his opponent's shield was particularly praised, and on the next evening Styrbjörn's Icelander recited some verses in *ljodahattr* on the danger of losing one's head in ale. It was generally agreed that such sport as this was not to be enjoyed every Yule, even at King Harald's court.

Orm and Toke, however, were confined to bed on account of their wounds, and could take little pleasure in anything during the next few days, although Brother Willibald used his most soothing salves upon their injured places. Toke's wound began to fester, making him delirious and violent, so that four men were needed to hold him down while Brother Willibald dressed it; and Orm, who had had two of his ribs broken and had lost a quantity of blood, was feeling very sore and enfeebled, and lacked his usual appetite. This last he took to be an evil symptom, and one that boded ill for his recovery; and he became very downhearted.

King Harald had ordered one of his best bedchambers to be prepared for them, with a walled fireplace to warm it, and hay instead of straw in the mattresses. Many of the King's men, and Styrbjörn's also, came to see them on the day after the combat, to discuss the previous evening's happenings and chuckle over King Sven's discomfiture. They made the room very crowded and noisy, and Brother Willibald had to rebuke them and finally drive them out; so that Orm and Toke were not sure whether it was more dispiriting to have company or to be left to their solitude. Shortly after this they lost the comradeship of their own men, who were all anxious to return home now that the Christmas feasting was over; all, that is, save One-Eyed Rapp, who was an outlaw in the Lister Country, and so preferred to remain at Jellinge. After a few days, a storm having blown up and dispersed the ice, King Sven put sullenly out to sea with few words of farewell. Styrbjörn, too, took his leave of King Harald, being anxious to lose no time in recruiting men for his spring expedition; and Orm's men obtained permission to sail part of the way with them, paying for their passage by taking their turn at the oars. Styrbjörn would have liked Orm and Toke to join his company. He came in person to visit them in their chamber, and said that they had made a good contribution to the Yule festivities and that it would be a pity if they were now to spend a week in bed for the sake of a few scratches.

'Visit me on Bornholm when the cranes begin to stretch their wings,' he said. 'I have room for men of your mettle on the prow of my own ship.'

He left them without waiting for their reply, his head being full of urgent matters; so that this was all the converse they had with Styrbjörn. They lay for a time in silence; then Toke said:

> 'Welcome the day when
> From the ship's deck I shall see
> Crane and stork and goose
> Steer their course to the north.'

But Orm, after reflecting for a while, replied sadly:

> 'Speak not of cranes; ere then
> They will have buried me
> Where mole and curious mouse
> Coldly shall brush my mouth.'

When most of the guests had departed, and there was less confusion in the kitchens, Brother Willibald ordered meat broth to be prepared for both the wounded Vikings twice a day, to fortify them.

Several of the King's women thereupon volunteered to carry it from the kitchens to the bedchamber, being curious to see the men at close quarters. This they were able to do without hindrance, for, now that the feasting was concluded, King Harald had taken to his bed, and both Brother Willibald and Brother Matthias, to say nothing of the Bishop, were fully occupied in praying over him and giving him purges to cleanse his blood and his bowels.

The first woman to put her head into their room was the young Moorish girl with whom they had spoken on the first occasion on which they had entered King Harald's presence with the bell. Toke gave a shout of delight on recognizing her, and straightway bade her approach nearer. She sidled shyly in, carrying a can and spoon, seated herself on the edge of his bed, and began to feed him. Another girl entered behind her, seated herself beside Orm, and started to feed him likewise. She was young and tall, well made and pale-skinned, with grey eyes and a large and beautiful mouth; she had, besides, dark hair, with an amber hoop around it. Orm had not seen her before, but she did not appear to be one of the servants.

Orm, however, found difficulty in swallowing the broth, for his wound prevented him from sitting up. After a few mouthfuls, he got some of the meat into his windpipe and began to cough violently. This made his wound ache, and clouded his humour, causing him to groan with the pain. The corners of the girl's mouth rose in a smile as he glowered sourly at her. When the fit had passed, he said sullenly: 'I have not been put here to be laughed at. Who are you, anyway?'

'My name is Ylva,' she replied, 'and I did not know until this minute that you were the sort of man who could make anyone laugh. How can you, who slew my brother Sven's best warrior, whimper at a spoonful of hot broth?'

'It's not the broth that troubles me,' said Orm. 'A wound like mine is liable to be painful sometimes. I should have thought even a woman might have guessed that. But if you are King Sven's sister, it may be that the broth you have brought me is bad; indeed, now I think of it, it has an unpleasant flavour. Have you come to avenge the injury I did to your brother?'

The girl sprang to her feet and flung the can and spoon into the fireplace, so that the broth spattered all over the room. Her eyes

152

blazed fiercely at Orm; then, suddenly, she calmed herself, and laughed, and sat down again on the edge of the bed.

'You are not afraid to show when you are afraid,' she said. 'That much, at least, must be said in your favour; though, which of us is behaving the more sensibly is a question to which two answers might be given. But I saw you fight Sigtrygg, and it was a good combat; and be sure of this, that I regard no man as my enemy merely because he has injured my brother Sven. It was high time somebody taught this Sigtrygg a lesson. His breath stank loathsomely, and there was talk between him and Sven of his having me to wife. Had this happened, he would not have enjoyed many nights of wedlock, for I am not to be pleasured by any chance berserk whose fancy I may happen to tickle. So at least I owe you some thanks for saving me from that extremity.'

'You are an impudent and brazen wench,' said Orm, 'and, I doubt not, a wildcat to boot; but it is always thus with the daughters of kings. However, I cannot deny that you seem to be too good for such a man as this Sigtrygg was. But I myself have come out of this contest sorely scathed, and I do not know what the end of it will be for me.'

Ylva squeezed the tip of her tongue between her teeth, and nodded and looked thoughtful.

'There may be others besides you and Sigtrygg and Sven who have sustained loss and injury through this contest,' she said. 'I have heard about this necklace of yours which Sigtrygg coveted. They say you got it from a southern king, and that it is the finest jewel that was ever seen. I desire to see it, and you need not fear that I shall try to steal it from you, although, if Sigtrygg had killed you it might have become my own.'

'It is an unlucky thing to possess an object which all men desire to finger,' said Orm sadly.

'If that is the way you feel,' said Ylva, 'why did you not let Sigtrygg have it? You would then have been freed from the cares it brings you.'

'Of one thing I am certain, though I have known you for but a short while,' said Orm. 'That, whatsoever man weds you, there will be long intervals between those occasions on which he will enjoy the last word.'

'I hardly think you are ever likely to be in a position to prove the truth of that remark,' said Ylva. 'The way you look now, I would not lie in the same bed with you if you were to offer me five necklaces. Why have you not got someone to wash your hair and beard? You look worse than a Smalander. But tell me straightway whether you will show me the necklace or no.'

'That is a fine way to speak to a sick man,' said Orm, 'to liken him to a Smalander. I would have you know that I am of noble blood on both my father's and my mother's side. My mother's grandmother's half-brother was Sven Rat-Nose of Göinge, and he, as you may know, was directly descended through his mother from Ivar of the Broad Embrace. It is only because I am sick that I tolerate your impertinences; othewise, I would already have shooed you out of the room. However, I will confess that I should like to be washed, though I am not really well enough to be touched; and, if you are willing to do me that service, I shall have the chance to see whether you can be more skilful at some things than you are at serving soup. Though, it may be that the daughters of kings are not competent to perform such useful duties.'

'You are proposing that I act as your slave-girl,' said Ylva, 'which no man has dared to suggest to me before. It is lucky for you that the blood of Broad-Hug runs in your veins. But I confess it would amuse me to see how you look after you have been washed, so I shall come early to-morrow morning, and you will then see that I can perform such tasks as well as anybody.'

'I must be combed, too,' said Orm. 'Then, when you have done all this to my satisfaction, I may, perhaps, show you the necklace.'

Meanwhile, things were becoming somewhat noisy in Toke's half of the room. The broth and the sight of a woman had considerably raised his spirits. He had managed to pull himself up into a sitting position, and they were endeavouring to converse in her language. This he was able to do but lamely; but he was all the more nimble in the use of his hands, with which he was trying to draw her closer to him. She defended herself against his advances, striking him on the knuckles with her spoon, but made no great effort to move out of distance, and seemed not altogether displeased, while Toke praised her beauty as well as he was able, and cursed his game leg that kept him sedentary.

Orm and Ylva turned to watch them, as their sport became noisier. Ylva smiled at their antics, but Orm shouted crossly to Toke to behave himself and leave the girl alone.

'What do you suppose King Harald will have to say?' he said, 'if he hears that you have been fondling one of his women above her knees?'

'Perhaps he will remark, as you did,' said Ylva, 'that it is an unlucky thing to own something that all men wish to finger. But he will hear nothing about it from my lips, for he has more than enough women for a man of his years; and she, unhappy girl, finds little joy among us here, and weeps often and is hard to comfort, since she understands little of what we say to her. So do not let it worry you that she sports with a man whose compliments she can understand, and who seems, besides, to be a bold fellow.'

Orm, however, insisted that Toke must control his inclinations while they were enjoying King Harald's hospitality.

Toke had, in the meantime, become somewhat calmer, and was now only holding the girl by one of her plaits. He assured Orm that there was no cause for alarm.

'For nobody can accuse me of anything,' he said, 'while my leg is in its present state; besides which, you heard with your own ears the little priest say that King Harald expressly ordered everything possible to be done to make us comfortable, because of the snub we served King Sven. Now I, as everybody knows, am a man to whose comfort women are an essential factor; and this woman seems to me to be an admirable specimen of her kind. I cannot think of anything that could be more likely to hasten my recovery; indeed, I am beginning to feel better already. I have told her to come here as often as she can, for my health's sake; and I do not think she is afraid of me, although I have been flirting somewhat boldly with her.'

Orm grunted doubtfully; but the end of it was that both the women agreed to come the next morning and wash their heads and beards. Then Brother Willibald arrived in a flurry to dress their wounds, and when he saw the spilt broth he shrieked with fury and drove the women from the room. Not even Ylva dared to gainsay him, for everyone was afraid of the man who wielded power over their life and health.

When Orm and Toke were left alone, they lay on their beds in silence, having much to occupy their thoughts. At length, Toke said: 'Our luck has turned good again, now that women have managed to find their way to us. Things are beginning to look more cheerful.'

155

But Orm said: 'We shall have bad luck on our hands if you cannot curb your itches; and I should be easier in my mind if I were sure that you could.'

Toke replied that he had good hopes of his ability to do this, if he really tried in earnest.

'Though, I doubt whether she would be anxious to spurn my advances,' he said, 'if I were fit and able to press them; for an old king cannot be much company for a girl of her spirit, and she has been kept under strict surveillance ever since she first came here. She is called Mirah, and comes from a place called Ronda, and is of good family. She was captured by Vikings who came in the night and bore her away with many others of her village, and sold her to the King of Cork. He, in turn, gave her to King Harald as a friendship-gift, because of her great beauty; but she says that she would have appreciated the honour more if he had given her to someone younger and with whom she could talk. I have seldom seen such a fine girl, so beautifully formed and smooth-skinned; though the girl who sat on your bed is also fine, if perhaps a trifle skinny and less full of figure than she might be. And she seems to be well disposed towards you. Even in such a place as this, our quality is apparent, for we win the favour of women even from our sick-beds.'

But Orm replied that he had no room in his thoughts for woman-love, for he felt more sick and enfeebled than ever, and doubted whether he had much time left.

The next morning, as soon as it was light, the women came to them as they had promised, bringing warm lye, water and hand-cloths, and washed Orm's and Toke's heads and beards meticulously. Ylva had some difficulty in attending to Orm, because he was unable to sit up, but she supported his body with her arm and used him carefully, and emerged from her task with credit, for he got no lye in his eyes or mouth and yet became clean and fine. Then she seated herself on the head of his bed, put his head between her knees, and began to comb him. She asked him is he was uncomfortable, but Orm had to admit that this was not the case. She found difficulty in passing the comb through his hair, for it was thick and coarse, and very tangled as a result of the washing; but she persevered patiently with the task, so that he thought he had never in his life been better combed. She spoke familiarly to him, as though they

156

had been friends for a long time; and Orm felt well content to have her near him.

'You will have your heads washed again before you get up,' she said, 'for the Bishop and his men like to baptize people when they are lying sick on their backs, and I am surprised they have not already spoken to you about it. They baptized my father when he was sorely ill and had small hope of recovery. Most people regard a sick-bed as the best place to be baptized in during the winter, for if a man is ill the priests merely sprinkle his head, whereas if he is well he has to be completely immersed in the sea, which few men fancy when the water is still sharp with ice. It is unpleasant for the priests, too, for they have to stand in the water up to their knees, and become blue in the face, and their teeth chatter so that they can scarcely speak the blessings. For this reason, they prefer in winter to baptize men who cannot move from their beds. Myself the Bishop baptized on Midsummer Day, which they call the Day of the Baptist, and that was not unpleasant. We squatted round him in our white shifts, I and my sisters, while he read over us, and then he lifted his hand and we held our noses and ducked under the water. I remained below the surface longer than any of the others, so that my baptism was held to be the best. Then we were all given garments that had been blessed, and little crosses to wear about our necks. And no harm came to any of us as a result of this.'

Orm replied that he knew all about such strange customs, having dwelt in the Southland, where nobody was permitted to eat pork, and with the monks of Ireland, who had tried to persuade him to allow himself to be baptized.

'But it will take a long time,' he said, 'before anyone convinces me that the observances of such customs can do a man good or can seriously gratify any god. I should like to see the Bishop or priest who could get me to sit in cold water up to my ears, in summer or winter. Nor have I any desire to have water sprinkled over my head, or to be read over; for it is my belief that a man ought to beware of all such forms of sorcery and trollcraft.'

Ylva said that several of King Harald's men had complained of the backache after being baptized, and had requested the Bishop to give them money for the pain, but that, apart from this, they were apparently none the worse for their experience; indeed, there were many who had now come to regard baptism as being advantageous to a man's health. The priests had no objection to a man eating pork, as Orm had doubtless observed during the Yuletide feasting, nor did they lay down any regulations regarding diet, save only that when anyone offered them horse-meat they spat and crossed themselves, and had at first occasionally been heard to mutter that men ought not to eat meat on Fridays; her father, however, had expressed his unwillingness to hear any more talk on that subject. She herself could not say that she had found the new religion in any way inconvenient. There were some, though, who held that the harvest was smaller and the cows' milk thinner nowadays, and that this was because people had begun to neglect the old gods.

She drew her comb slowly through a tuft of his hair which she had just untangled, and held it up against the daylight to examine it closely.

'I do not understand how this can be,' she said, 'but there does not appear to be a single louse in your hair.'

'That is not possible,' said Orm. 'It must be a bad comb.'

She said that it was a good louse-comb, and scraped his head so that his scalp burned, but still she could find no louse.

'If what you say is true, then I am sick indeed,' said Orm, 'and things are even worse than I had feared. This can only mean that my blood is poisoned.'

Ylva ventured the opinion that things might perhaps not be quite as bad as he feared, but Orm was much depressed by her discovery. He lay in silence while she finished her combing, acknowledging her further remarks with dispirited grunts. Meanwhile, however, Toke and Mirah had all the more to say to each other, and appeared to be finding each other more and more congenial.

At last, Orm's hair and beard were combed ready, and Ylva regarded the results of her work with satisfaction.

'Now you look less like a scarecrow,' she said, 'and more like a chieftain. Few women would run from the sight of you now, and you can thank me for that.'

She picked up his shield, rubbed it with her sleeve in the part where it was least scarred, and held it in front of his face. Orm regarded himself in it, and nodded.

'You have combed me well,' he admitted, 'better than I thought a king's daughter could. It may be that you are somewhat above the run of them. You have earned a glimpse of my necklace.'

So saying, he loosened the neck of his shirt, drew forth the chain and handed it to her. Ylva uttered a little cry as her hands closed on it. She weighed it in her fingers and admired its beauty; and Mirah left Toke and ran to look at it, and she, too, murmured aloud with wonder. Orm said to Ylva: 'Hang it round your neck,' and she did as he bade her. The necklace was long, and hung down over the breast-rings of her undergarment. She hastily set the shield upon the wall-seat to see how the necklace looked against her throat.

'It is long enough to go twice round my neck,' she said, and was unable to take her eyes or her fingers from it. 'How should it be worn?'

'Almansur kept it in a chest,' said Orm, 'where no one ever set eyes on it. Since it became mine, I have worn it beneath my shirt until it chafed my skin, and never showed it to any man until this Yuletide, when it straightway brought me pain. No one, I think, can say that it has not now found a more suitable resting-place; therefore, Ylva, regard it as your own, and wear it as you think most fitting.'

She clutched the necklace with both hands, and stared at him with enormous eyes.

'Have you taken leave of your senses?' she cried. 'What have I done that you should give me such a princely gift? The noblest queen in the world would lie with a berserk for the sake of a poorer jewel than this.'

'You have combed me well,' replied Orm; and he smiled at her. 'We who are of Broad-Hug's line give good friendship-gifts or none at all.'

Mirah, too, wished to try on the necklace, but Toke commanded her to return to him, and not to tease her mind with trinkets; and he had already won such power over her that she obeyed him meekly. Ylva said: 'Perhaps I would do best to blood it beneath my clothing, for my sisters and all the women in the palace would claw out my eyes to get it for themselves. But why you have given it to me is beyond my understanding, however much of Broad-Hug's blood may run in your veins.'

Orm sighed, and answered: 'What shall it profit me when the grass grows over my limbs? I know now that I shall surely die, for you

159

have found that not even a louse will live on my body; though, indeed, I had guessed as much already. Perhaps it might have become yours even if I had not been marked for death; though, then I should have required something of you in return for it. You seem to me to be well worthy of such a jewel, and it is my guess that you will prove fully able to defend it if anyone should challenge you to a contest of nails. But, for my part, I would rather live and see it glitter between your breasts.'

CHAPTER ELEVEN

Concerning the wrath of Brother Willibald, and how Orm tried his hand at wooing

Things soon turned out as Ylva had foretold, for a few days later the Bishop began to hint that the two wounded men should allow themselves to be baptized; but he had no success with either of them in this matter. Orm lost his patience almost at once, and told him sharply that he wished to hear no more about it, since he had in any case but a short time left to live; while Toke said that he, for his part, would very soon be fit and well, and so had no need of any spiritual assistance. The Bishop then set Brother Matthias to strive to win them over by patient methods and gradual education, and he made several endeavours to teach them the Creed, ignoring their entreaties to be left in peace. Then Toke had a good spear, slim-bladed and keen-edged, brought to him, and the next time Brother Matthias came to instruct them he found Toke sitting up in bed, supported on one elbow, weighing the spear thoughtfully in his free hand.

'It would be an ill thing to break the peace in King Harald's palace,' said Toke, 'but I do not think anyone can condemn an invalid for doing so in self-defence. It would also be a pity to soil the floor of so fine a chamber as this with the blood of a fat man, and your veins look full; however, I have persuaded myself that, if I can nail you cleanly to a wall with this spear, the blood-gush will be contained within reasonable limits. To do this will not be a simple task for a bed-ridden man to perform, but I shall try my best to execute it competently; and this I swear I shall do the moment you open your mouth to plague us with your prattle. For, as we have told you, we do not wish to hear any more of it.'

161

Brother Matthias turned white, and raised his hands before him in fearful supplication. At first, he seemed to be about to speak; then, however, his limbs began to quake, and he beat a smart retreat from the chamber, slamming the door behind him. After this, they were not disturbed by him any more. But Brother Willibald, who never showed any sign of fear, came at his usual time to dress their wounds, and rebuked them severely for the fright they had given Brother Matthias.

'You are a man of mettle,' said Toke, 'though there is but little of you; and I confess that I prefer you to other men of your kidney, although you are rude and peevish. Perhaps it is because you do not try to badger us into this Christianity, but content yourself with ministering to our wounds.'

Brother Willibald replied that he had been longer than his fellow-priests in this land of darkness, and had managed to free himself from such vain fancies and ambitions.

'When I first came here,' he said, 'I was as fanatical as any other member of the Blessed Benedict's Order in my zeal to baptize every heathen soul. But now I am wiser, and know what is feasible and what is merely vanity. It is right that the children of this land should be baptized, together with such women as have not wallowed too deeply in sin, if indeed any such are to be found; but the grown men of this country are veritable apostles of Satan and must, in the name of Divine Justice, burn in hell fire, however assiduously one may baptize them; for no redemption can suffice to wipe away such vileness as their souls are stained with. Of this I am sure, for I know them well; therefore I do not waste my time trying to convert such men as you.'

His voice became frenzied, and he glared wrathfully from one to the other, brandishing his arms and crying: 'Bloodwolves, murderers and malefactors, adulterate vermin, Gadarene swine, weeds of Satan and minions of Beelzebub, generation of vipers and basilisks, shall you be cleansed by holy baptism and stand as white as snow in the regiments of the blessed angels? Nay, I tell you, it shall not be so. I have lived long in this house and have witnessed too much; I know your ways. No bishop nor holy father shall ever persuade me that such as you can be saved. How should men of the north be allowed to enter the gates of heaven? You would scrabble at the blessed virgins with your lewd fingers, you would raise your war-whoops against the seraphim and archangels, you would bawl for ale before the throne of God himself! No, no, I know what I speak of. Hell alone will serve for such as you, whether you be baptized or no. Praised be Almighty God, the One, the Eternal, Amen!'

He fumbled angrily among his medicines and bandages, and bustled across the room to apply salves to Toke's wound.

'Why do you exert yourself to make us well again,' said Orm, 'if your hatred for us is so great?'

'I do it because I am a Christian, and have learned to repay evil with good,' he replied, 'which is more than you will ever learn to do. Do I not still bear the scar upon my brow where King Harald struck me with the holy crucifix? Yet do I not still daily minister to his contaminated flesh with all the skill that lies at my command? Besides which, it may ultimately be for the best that such fierce fighting-men as you should be kept alive in this land, for you are like to send many of your fellows to hell before you go there yourselves, as you have already done at this Christmas feast. Let wolf rend wolf, that the Lamb of God may dwell in peace.'

When he at length left them, Toke said that it looked as though the blow on the head which the little fellow had received when the King had cracked him with the cross had knocked the wits out of him, for most of what he had shouted at them had no sense in it; with which observation Orm agreed. But both of them admitted that he was marvellously cunning in medicine, and very diligent in the care he showed towards them.

Toke was now beginning to be himself again, and before long he was able to limp round the room and even outside it, while Orm lay alone in his bed, finding time heavy on his hands except when Ylva was there to talk to him. When she was at his side, the thought of his impending death troubled him less, for she was always full of merriment and bright talk, so that he found pleasure in listening to her; but he became sullen again so soon as she said that he was looking better and would soon be up and about. In regard to that matter, he said, he thought he knew best what was most likely to happen. Soon, however, he found himself able to sit up in bed without too much pain; and the next time Ylva combed him, she found a louse in his hair that was large and fresh and full of blood. This made him think deeply, and he said that he did not know what conclusion to come to.

'You must not let the matter of the necklace weigh on your mind,' said Ylva. 'You gave it to me when you thought you were going to die, and the memory of it troubles you now that you see that you are going to live. But I shall gladly give it back to you, though it far surpasses in beauty anything that has ever before been seen in this land. For I do not wish it to be said that I lured your gold from you when you were sick with wounds; which I have already heard muttered more than once.'

'Truly, it would be good to keep such a jewel in one's family,' said Orm. 'But the best solution for me would be to have both you and the jewel; nor will I accept it back on any other condition. But before I ask your father what his feelings are in regard to this, I should like to know whether you yourself are so inclined. For the first time we spoke together you told me that, if you had been forced to marry Sigtrygg, you would have driven a knife into him in his bridal bed; and I should like to be sure that you feel differently towards me.'

Ylva laughed merrily and said that he should not be too confident about this.

'For I am of a stranger temper than you know,' she said, 'and difficult to satisfy. And the daughters of kings are more troublesome than other women when they marry and leave home. Have you heard what befell Agne, the King of the Swedes, long ago, when he took to wife a king's daughter from a land east of the sea, who was not willing to be his bedfellow? The first night after the marriage, he lay with her in a tent beneath a tree, and when he was sound asleep she fastened a rope to his neck-ring, which was a good, strong ring, and hanged him from the tree, though he was a great king and she had but one slave-girl to help her. So ponder the matter carefully, before you seek my hand.'

She leaned forward and stroked his forehead, and pinched his ears and looked into his eyes, smiling, so that Orm felt better than he had done for many days.

But then she suddenly became solemn and thoughtful, and said it was vain to talk of such things before her father had expressed his opinion on the matter; and she thought it would be no easy thing to win his consent unless Orm was better favoured than most men as regards property and cattle and gold.

'He complains incessantly that so many of his daughters are

unwed,' she said, 'but he will never admit than any man is sufficiently rich and noble to be worthy of us. It is not such a fine thing as people imagine to be a king's daughter, for many bold youths wink furtively at us and finger the hem of our skirts when no one is watching, but few of them have the courage to carry their suit to our father, and such as do come crestfallen from the interview. It is a sore pity that he is so intent on getting us worthy husbands, though it is true that a poor man would be no fit mate for me. But you, Orm, who can bestow such a necklace upon me and have the blood of the Broad Embrace in your veins, must doubtless be one of the richest princes in Skania?'

Orm replied that he hoped to be able to prevail upon King Harald into consenting to his suit, for he knew that the King regarded him highly, both because of the bell he had brought him and for the way in which he had vanquished Sigtrygg.

'But I do not know,' he continued, 'how much wealth awaits me in Skania, for it is now seven years since I left my home, and I cannot tell how it stands with my family. It may be that fewer of them are alive than when I saw them last, and that my inheritance is therefore greater. But in any case, I have much gold from the south besides the necklace I have already given you, so that even if I own no more than what I have with me, nobody can call me a poor man. And I can obtain more in the way in which I won this.'

Ylva nodded doubtfully, and said that this did not sound too promising, her father being a very exacting man. Toke, who had come in while the discussion was afoot, agreed with her, and said that this was an occasion when it was necessary to think carefully before deciding what to do.

'It so happens,' he added, 'that I am able to tell the best way to win a weathly woman of noble blood when her father is unwilling but she herself is agreeable. My mother's father was called Nose-Tönne. He used to trade with the Smalanders, and possessed a small house, twelve cows and a great store of wisdom. One day he was on a business trip to Värend, and there saw a girl called Gyda, who was the daughter of a wealthy lord. He determined to win her, partly for the honour it would bring him and partly because he coveted her fine body and thick red hair. But her father, who was named Glum, was a proud man, and he said that Tönne was not good enough to be his son-in-law, though the girl herself thought otherwise. Gyda and Tönne, therefore, wasted no time in inveighing against the old man's folly, but hastily formed a plan, and arranged to meet in the forest while she was nutting there with her maids. The result of this encounter was that she came to be with child, and Tönne had to fight two duels with her brother, the marks of which they both bore till the day they died. In due course, she gave birth to twins; whereupon the old man decided that it was no use kicking against the pricks any longer. So they married, and lived together in great bliss and contentment, and had seven more children, so that all the people of the district praised my grandfather's wisdom and good luck, and his reputation waxed enormously and became very great, especially when old Glum died and left them a big inheritance. And if my grandfather had not hit upon such a wise method of obtaining the woman of his choice, I should not be sitting here to give you this good advice; for my mother was one of the twins who were begotten under the nut-bushes.'

'If a marriage can only be brought about by producing twins,' said Ylva, 'your advice is easier given than followed. And there is a difference between having a farmer from Värend as your father and being daughter to the King of the Danes. I doubt whether such an experiment would turn out as well for us as it did for your grandparents.'

Orm thought there was a good deal to be said both for and against Toke's plan, though it was but cold comfort for a man who was sick and unlusty; however, he said, he would make no decision until he was well enough to walk and could sound King Harald's feelings on the matter.

This took some time; but at length he grew better and his wound healed, and his strength began to return to him. The winter was by now almost past. King Harald also had recovered from the effects of Christmas and was in capital spirits, busily supervising the preparation of his warships; for he was making ready to sail to Skanör to collect his herring-tax, as well as to despatch the ships which he had promised Styrbjörn at the feast. Orm went to him and explained what was in his mind. King Harald listened to his request amiably, showing no displeasure, but straightway inquired how wealthy Orm was, that he could regard himself as eligible for such a match. Orm furnished him with details of his parentage and ancestry, and enumerated his father's possessions, not omitting to mention all that he himself was bringing home from his travels abroad.

'In addition to all this,' he concluded, 'there is much land in Göinge which my mother was due to inherit, though I do not know whether it has yet come into her possession. Nor can I say which of my kinsmen are still alive, or how it is with them. For much may have occurred in Skania during these seven years that I have been away.'

'The jewel you gave my daughter was a princely gift,' said King Harald, 'and you have done me several good services, which I have not forgotten. But to marry a daughter of the King of the Danes is the most ambitious match that a man could hope for, and no man has sought the hand of any of my daughters without offering more than all that you possess. Besides which, you have a brother who stands between you and your father's wealth. Now, if he be alive, and have sons, how then shall you support my daughter? I am beginning to grow somewhat advanced in years, though a man might not mark it, and I am anxious to see my daughters well married while I am yet alive to make a good match for them. For I do not think that Sven will bother his head about them when I am gone.'

Orm was compelled to admit that he had little to offer in return for the hand of such a woman.

'But I may well find, when I reach home,' he said, 'that the whole inheritance is mine. My father was already beginning to show his years when I sailed away, and my brother Odd spent all his summers in Ireland, and showed little inclination to stop at home. And I have heard that the Vikings in Ireland have fared poorly during the past few years, since King Brian became powerful there.'

King Harald nodded, and said that King Brian had caused the death of many Danes in Ireland, and of many seafarers who had ventured into his coastal waters; though, in one sense, this had been something of a blessing, since these men included a good many who had been mischief-makers in their own land.

'But this Brian, this King of Munster,' he said, 'has had his head turned by the surfeit of his successes, so that he is now demanding tribute not only from my good friend King Olof of Cork, but also from my own kinsman, Sigtrygg Silk-Beard of Dublin. Such self-importance sits ill upon the head of an Irish king, and in good time

I shall send a fleet to his island to trip his arrogance. It might be a good thing to bring him here and keep him tethered to the door of my hall, not merely to provide sport for my men when they are drinking, but also to teach him a lesson in Christian humility, and to provide a warning for other kings. For I have always been of the opinion that the King of the Danes ought to be regarded with veneration by all other monarchs.'

'It is my belief, lord,' said Orm, 'that you are the mightiest of kings. Even among the Andalusians and the blue men* there are warriors who know your name and speak of the great deeds that you have done.'

'You have chosen your words well,' said King Harald, 'though previously you showed insufficient humility in begging for the hand of one of my fairest daughters when you were not even certain how you were placed as regards your inheritance and possessions. However, I shall not condemn you too severely for this, since you are young and unreflective. But I shall not immediately accede to your request, nor shall I refuse it. This is my decision. Come to me again in the autumn, when I have returned from my expedition and you are better informed concerning your wealth and expectations; and if I then find them sufficient, you shall have the girl, because of the friendship I bear you. And if not, there will always be a place for you in my bodyguard. Until then, you must contain yourself in patience.'

When Orm told Ylva how his interview with King Harald had resulted, she flew into a great fury. Tears swelled into her eyes, and she shrieked that she would pluck the old man's beard from his chin to punish him for his close-fistedness and obstinacy, and then lose no time in doing as Toke had advised her. But when she had recovered her composure, she thought it wiser, after all, to abandon this plan.

'I am not afraid of his wrath,' she said, 'not even when he bellows like a bull and flings his ale-cup at me; for I am too quick for him, so that he has never yet managed to hit me, and his fits soon pass. But it is so with him that if anyone gainsays him once his mind is set on a thing, he remembers his grievance darkly and will never

* Negroes.

168

cease to seek revenge for it. Therefore, I think it best that we should not oppose him in this matter, lest he turn his wrath against us both and give me away to the first rich man that catches his eye merely to spite me and show which of us is the stronger. But know this, Orm, that I desire no husband but you, and am ready to wait till the autumn for you, though the interval will be long and tedious. If, then, he still opposes our match, I will wait no longer but will follow you whithersoever you lead me.'

'When I hear you speak like that,' said Orm, 'I almost begin to feel myself a man again.'

CHAPTER TWELVE

How Orm came home from his long voyage

King Harald fitted out twenty ships for his expedition. Twelve of these were for Styrbjörn, while with the remainder he intended to assert his authority at Skanör, where a strong force of men was always needed to collect the herring-tax. He chose his crews with great care; and every Dane was eager to serve on the ships that were to sail with Styrbjörn, for they knew that much booty might be gained there.

Many men came down to Jellinge to join the fleet; and, when King Harald had made his choice, Orm and Toke sought among the ones that were left to find folk whom they might hire to row them home in the ship they had stolen from Almansur; but oarsmen were asking a high price, and this they were unwilling to pay, for, now that they had come so near home, they were reluctant to part with any more of what they had won. Eventually, to save themselves the expense, they made an agreement with a man from Fyn called Ake to the effect that he should buy the ship from them and, in return, crew it and convey them both to their respective homes, Orm to the Mound and Toke to Lister, as well as being responsible for providing food for the voyage. There was a tremendous amount of haggling about this, and at one stage it appeared likely to end in a fight between Toke and Ake, for Toke wanted to have a sum of money as well as his passage, since, he asserted, the ship was practically new and thoroughly stable and seaworthy, if somewhat on the small side. Ake, however, refused to accept this valuation; the ship was, he protested, foreign and of inferior workmanship, and, indeed, virtually worthless, so that he was already on the bad end of the bargain. In the end they asked Hallbjörn, the groom, to arbitrate their case, and the matter was concluded without a fight, though Orm and Toke made little profit on the transaction.

Neither of them felt inclined to join Styrbjörn, for they both had other things uppermost in their minds; and Orm's strength returned but slowly to him, so that he thought he would be an invalid for the rest of his days. He was sad, too, to think that he would shortly have to part from Ylva, who was now permanently chaperoned by a couple of old women, to make sure that she and Orm should not see too much of each other. But although the old women performed their duties conscientiously, they were frequently driven to complain that the King had allotted them a task too arduous for their aged bones.

When the fleet was at last ready to sail, King Harald bade the Bishop bless all the ships; but he refused to take him with him, because of the bad weather-luck which all priests were known to bring. The Bishop wanted to go to Skania to visit his priests and his churches there, and to count the number of conversions that had been made; but King Harald told him he would have to wait until another ship sailed to those parts. For he himself, he roundly swore, would never take any bishop to sea with him, nor even a common priest.

'For I am too old to tempt fortune,' he said, 'and all sailors know that sea-robbers and water-trolls and all sea-powers hate nothing so much as a shaven man, and set traps to drown him as soon as he leaves the land. My nephew, Gold-Harald, once sailed homewards from Brittany with a large number of newly captured slaves at his oars, and straightway encountered storms and blizzards and fearful seas, although it was yet but early in the autumn. When his ship was on the point of sinking, he bethought himself and discovered two shaven men among his rowers. He threw them overboard, and enjoyed excellent weather for the rest of the voyage. He could do this, because he was a heathen, but it would ill become me to throw a bishop overboard to calm the weather. So he will have to remain here.'

On the morning that the fleet was due to sail, which was also the morning which Orm and Toke had fixed for their departure, King Harald came down to the jetties to board his ship. He wore a white cloak and a silver helmet, and had a great company of men with him; and his standards were borne before him. When he reached the place where Orm's ship lay, he halted, bade his followers wait awhile, and climbed aboard unaccompanied to have a few words with Orm in private.

'I honour you thus publicly,' he said, 'to show evidence of the friendship I bear you, that no man may suppose any enmity to exist between us because I have not yet granted you my daughter's hand. She is now confined in the women's house, where she is the cause of much disturbance; for she is a high-spirited wench, and would otherwise be quite capable of running down to your ship the moment I turned my back, to try and tempt you to take her with you, which would be a bad thing for both of you. I and you must now part for a while, and unfortunately I have, at the moment, no adequate gift with which to repay you for the bell you brought me; but I am sure that things will be different when you return in the autumn.'

It was a fine spring morning, with a clear sky and a gentle breeze blowing, and King Harald was in a merry humour. He examined the ship closely, noting its foreign workmanship, for he was well versed in the ways of ships and knew as much about decks and rowlocks as any shipwright, so that he found a number of points worth commenting upon. While he was thus engaged, Toke climbed aboard, staggering beneath the weight of an enormous chest. He seemed taken aback to see King Harald there, but lowered his chest carefully to the deck and came forward to greet him.

'That is a fair-sized package you have with you there,' said the King. 'What does it contain?'

'Only a few oddments for the old woman, my mother, in case she is still living,' replied Toke. 'It is a good thing to bring home a gift of some sort when a man has been away for as long as I have.'

King Harald nodded approvingly, and observed that it was good to find young people who still retained respect and affection for their parents. He himself, he added, had noticed little evidence of either quality in his own family.

'And now,' he said, seating himself on the chest that Toke had brought aboard with him, 'I am thirsty, and should like to quaff a cup of ale before we say farewell.'

The chest creaked beneath his weight, and Toke, with an anxious look on his face, took a step towards him; but the chest remained in one piece. Orm drew some ale from a barrel, and offered it to the King, who drank to their luck for the voyage. He wiped the froth from his beard, and remarked that ale always tasted best at sea; he would, therefore, be obliged if Orm would refill his cup once more. Orm did so, and King Harald emptied it slowly; then he nodded farewell to them, climbed ashore, and departed towards his own great flagship, to the mast of which his standard had already been fixed, displaying two ravens with outstretched wings sewn in black upon a background of scarlet silk.

Orm glanced curiously at Toke.

'Why are you so pale?' he asked.

'I have my worries, like other men,' replied Toke. 'You yourself have not the most cheerful of countenances.'

'I know what I am leaving behind,' said Orm, 'but the wisest of men could not tell me to what I am returning, or whether things will turn out as I fear they may.'

At last, all the ships put out to sea, and steered their separate courses. King Harald and his fleet headed eastwards through the archipelago, and Orm's ship rowed northwards along the coast to the tip of Själland. The wind favoured the King's ships, and before long they had begun to disappear into the distance. Toke stood staring after them, until their sails had grown tiny; then he said:

> 'Dread the hour
> When Denmark's despot
> Bulbous sat
> On brittle box-lid.
> Faintly yet I
> Fear my freight be
> Broken-boned
> By Bluetooth's burden.'

He strode to the chest, opened it, and lifted forth his freight, which consisted of the Moorish girl. She looked pale and wretched, for it had been cramped and suffocating in the chest, and she had been in it for a good while. When Toke released hold of her, her knees gave under her and she lay on the deck panting and shaking and looking half-dead, until he helped her to her feet again. She began to sob, glancing fearfully around her.

'Have no fear,' said Toke. 'He is far away by now.'

She sat pale and wild-eyed on the deck, gazing at the ship and the men, without speaking; and the men at the oars gazed back at her with eyes as wide as her own, asking each other what this could mean. But none of them was as pale as Orm, or stared more fearfully, for he looked as though some huge stroke of ill-luck had just smitten him.

Ake, the ship's master, hummed and hawed and tugged his beard.

'You made no mention of this when we struck our bargain,' he said, 'that a woman should be aboard. The least I ask is that you should tell me who she is and why she came aboard in a chest.'

'That does not concern you,' replied Orm blackly. 'Take care of your ship, and we will take care of what concerns us.'

'He who refuses to reply may have dangerous things to hide,' said Ake. 'I am a stranger in Jellinge, and know little of what goes on there, but a man does not have to be wise to see that this is a crooked business and one that may easily bring evil in its wake. Whom have you stolen her from?'

Orm seated himself on a coil of rope, with his hands clasped round his knees and his back towards Ake. Without turning his head, he replied evenly: 'I give you two choices. Either hold your tongue, or be thrown into the sea, head foremost. Make your choice, and be speedy about it, for you yap like a mongrel puppy and disturb my head.'

Ake turned away mumbling, and spat over the side, and they could see as he moved again to his steering-oar that he was brooding darkly and in an evil humour. But Orm sat still and silent, staring as he pondered.

After a while, Toke's girl recovered her spirits, and they gave her something to strengthen her; but this at once made her wretchedly sea-sick, and she hung groaning over the gunwale, refusing to be comforted by the soothing words which Toke proffered her. In the end, he let her be, fastening her to the gunwale with a rope, and came and sat beside Orm.

'Now the worst is past,' he said, 'though this is certainly a troublesome and nerve-racking way of obtaining a woman. I do not think there are many men who would have dared to do as I have done; however, I suppose my luck is greater than that of most people.'

'It is better than mine,' said Orm. 'I grant you that.'

174

'That is not so certain,' said Toke. 'For your luck has always been good; and a king's daughter is a greater prize than the woman I have won. You must not grieve that you have not been able to do as I have done, for even I could hardly have succeeded in kidnapping a girl as closely guarded as yours was.'

Orm laughed between his teeth. He sat silent for a while, and then ordered Rapp to replace Ake at the steering-oar, for the latter's ears looked likely to stretch themselves to tearing-point. Then he said to Toke: 'I had supposed that a firm friendship existed between us two, since we have been together for so long; but, as the old ones truthfully used to say, it takes a long time to prove a man. In this mad enterprise in which you have now involved us both, you have behaved as though I did not exist or was not worth bothering about.'

Toke replied: 'You have one characteristic which ill becomes a chieftain, Orm, and that is the ease with which you take offence. Most men would have praised me for stealing the woman single-handed, without endangering anyone else; but you regard yourself as having been insulted because you were not told about everything beforehand. What kind of friendship is it which breaks on so small a rock as this?'

Orm stared at him, white with fury.

'It is difficult to forbear with such addle-headedness as yours,' he said. 'What do I care about what methods you use to get your women, or whether or not you keep your plans to yourself? What does concern me is that you have earned us King Harald's enmity and wrath, so that, whithersoever we go in the Danish kingdom, we shall find ourselves outlaws. You have got your woman, and have barred me for ever from mine. A man does not have to be quick to take offence to find fault with such evidence of friendship.'

Toke could not find much to say in reply to this charge, and was forced to admit that he had not thought of it in this light before. He tried to mollify Orm by saying that King Harald was old and feeble and could not live much longer; but Orm drew scant comfort from this, and the more he thought about it, the more irrevocably he felt himself to be separated from Ylva, and his anger waxed accordingly.

They put in for the night in a sheltered creek, and lit two fires. Orm, Toke, Rapp and Mirah sat by one of them, and Ake and his crew round the other. None of the Vikings was in a mood for talking,

175

but the other men kept up a greedy murmur of discussion. They spoke, however, in low tones, so that the matter of their talk could not be heard.

After they had eaten, the woman curled up to sleep by the fire, with a cloak covering her body. Orm and Toke sat in silence some way apart from one another. Dusk began to fall, and a cold wind sprang up, turning the sea grey; and a storm-cloud appeared in the west. Orm sighed deeply several times, and tugged hard at his beard. Both he and Toke were black with anger.

'It would be best to settle this matter,' said Toke.

'You have only to say the word,' replied Orm.

Rapp had gone to gather fuel for the fire. Now he returned, and overheard their last words. He was a silent man, who seldom minded anyone's business but his own. Now, however, he said: 'It would be a good thing if you two could leave your fighting till later, for we have other work to do. There are fourteen men in the crew, and we are but three; and that is already difference enough.'

They asked him what he meant by this.

'They are planning to kill us, because of the woman,' said Rapp. 'I heard them discussing it as I was gathering wood.'

Orm laughed.

'This is a fine hare you have started,' he said bitterly to Toke.

Toke shook his head sadly, and stared with troubled eyes at his woman as she slept beside the fire.

'Things are as they are,' he said, 'and the main thing now is to decide the best way out of this affair. I think the wisest course for us to follow would be to kill the lot of them where they sit, while they are still planning how to dispose of us. They are many, but they are far from being such men as we.'

'It looks as though we shall have rough weather to-morrow,' said Rapp. 'And in that case we cannot afford to kill many of them, for we shall need them in the ship, unless we want to spend the rest of our lives in this place. But whatever we do, let us do it at once, or we shall have a rough night of it.'

'They are foolish folk from Fyn,' said Toke, 'and once we have killed Ake and one or two of the others, the rest will tumble over themselves to do our bidding. But it is you, Orm, who must decide what we are to do. Perhaps it might be wisest to wait till they are asleep and attack them then.'

Orm's melancholy had left him, now that there was work to be done. He got to his feet and stood as though making water, so as to be able to survey the group round the other fire without exciting their attention.

'There are twelve of them there,' he said, when he had sat down again, 'which may mean that they have sent two of their number inland to get help, without our noticing their departure. If that is so, we shall soon have a swarm of foes descending on us; so I think we would do best to settle this business without delay. It is plain that they have little fore-sight or lust for combat, or they would have tried to overpower Rapp when he was in the woods alone. But now we shall teach them that they must manage things more skilfully when they have men of our mettle to deal with. I will go alone and speak with them; then, while their eyes are upon me, come silently up behind them, and hew well and quickly, or it will go hard for us. I must go without my shield; there is no help for it.'

He picked up a tanker which they had used at supper, and walked across to Ake's fire to fill it from the barrel which they had brought ashore and set down there. Two or three of the crew had already laid themselves down to sleep by the fire, but most of them were still seated and awake, and their eyes turned towards Orm as he walked towards them. He filled the tankard, blew off the froth and took a deep draught.

'There is bad wood in your barrel,' he said to Ake, 'your ale smacks of it already.'

'It was good enough for King Harald,' retorted Ake sullenly, 'and it should be good enough for you. But I promise you that you will not have to drink much more of it.'

The men laughed at his words, but Orm handed him the tankard as though he had noticed nothing untoward.

'Taste for yourself,' he said, 'and see if I have not spoken the truth.'

Ake took the tankard without moving from where he sat. Then, as he set it to his lips, Orm gave the bottom of the tankard a great kick so that Ake's jaw was broken and his chin fell upon his breast.

'Does it not taste of wood?' said Orm, and in the same instant he whipped his sword from its sheath and felled the man beside him, as the latter jumped to his feet.

The other men, dumbfounded by the suddenness of all this, barely had time to grab for their weapons before Toke and Rapp fell on them from behind; and after that, they had little time to show what mettle they were made of. Four of them were killed, in addition to Ake, two fled into the woods, and the remaining five ran to the ship and prepared to defend themselves there. Orm cried to them to throw down their weapons, vowing that if they did so he would spare their lives. But they stood wavering, uncertain whether to believe him.

'We cannot be sure that you will keep your word,' they shouted back.

'That I can believe,' replied Orm. 'You can only hope that I am less treacherous than you have proved to be.'

They held a whispered conference, and then shouted down that his proposal gave them insufficient assurance, and that they would prefer to keep their weapons and be allowed to depart, leaving the ship and everything else to the Vikings.

'Then I give you this assurance instead,' cried Orm, 'that if you do not instantly do as I say you will all be killed where you stand. Perhaps this knowledge will comfort you.'

So saying, he swung himself up on to the ship and walked slowly towards them, without waiting for Toke and Rapp to follow him. His helmet had been knocked off by a stone that one of the men had thrown, his eyes were narrow with fury, and Blue-Tongue glittered wetly in his hand as he strode towards them, measuring them as though they were hounds that required the whip. Then they obeyed his bidding and threw down their weapons, muttering baleful curses upon Ake, for they were incensed that everything had turned out otherwise than as he had foretold.

It was by now quite dark, and a blustering wind had sprung up, but Orm thought it unwise for them to remain any longer in the bay. If they lingered, he said, they would have half an army of loyal Själlanders descending upon them to recover King Harald's woman and restore her to her rightful master. Therefore, despite the darkness and hard weather, and the fact that they were so few, he felt there was nothing for it but to try their luck against the sea; for the consequences of Toke's folly would, he feared, dog their heels for many a day.

Having no time to lose, they made haste to bring aboard the

178

food-chest and ale-butt. The woman wept and grated her teeth at the prospect of such a voyage as the weather promised, but obeyed without complaint. Orm stood guard over the prisoners with drawn sword as they sat at their oars, while Toke and Rapp lifted the ale aboard. Toke was handling the barrel very clumsily and awkwardly, and Orm shouted angrily at them to be quicker about it.

'The wood is slippery, and my fingers cannot get a proper hold,' replied Toke mournfully, 'for my hand is not as it should be.'

Orm had never heard him speak so heavily before. His sword-hand had been split at the joint of the third and fourth fingers, so that two of his fingers pointed one way and two the other.

'The loss of blood does not trouble me,' he said, 'but this hand will be of little use for rowing to-night, and that is a bad thing, for we shall need to row hard if we are to get out of this bay before daybreak.'

He rinsed his hand in the water, and turned towards the woman.

'You have helped me much already, my poor Mirah,' he said, 'though it may be that I have done the greater share. Let me now see whether you can help me in this matter, also.'

The woman dried her tears and came to look at his hand. She wailed softly when she saw how grave the wound was, but none the less contrived to dress it skilfully. She said she would have been happier with wine to wash it in and cobwebs to lay upon it, but since these were not available she made do with water and grass and chewed bread. Then she bound it up tightly with bandages which she tore from her clothing.

'The most useless things can be turned to useful purposes,' said Orm. 'And now we are both left-handed.'

It was evident from the way he spoke that his anger against Toke had been allayed.

Then they pulled away from the land with seven men at the oars and Toke minding the steering-oar, and the work of getting the ship out of the bay and round the point into the lee of the coast was the hardest that Orm had known since the days when he had toiled as a galley-slave. He kept a spear in readiness at his side to kill the first prisoner who flagged; and, when one of them caught a crab in the trough of a wave and was thrown on to his back, he was up on his bench and pulling again at his oar within the instant. The woman sat huddled at Toke's feet, rolling her eyes in fear and wretchedness. Toke steadied her with his foot and bade her take up the baling-bucket and perform some useful service; but, although she tried to obey him, her work was of no avail, and the ship was half submerged when they at last rounded the point and were able to set sail and bale.

For the rest of the night they were at the mercy of the storm. Orm himself took over the steering-oar, but all he could do was to keep the ship headed towards the north-east and hope that she would not be driven aground before day broke. None of them thought there was much hope of surviving such a tempest, which was worse than that which they had endured on their voyage to Ireland. Then Rapp said: 'We have five prisoners aboard, unarmed and in our power. It is doubtful whether they will be of any further use to us as rowers, but they may help us to calm the storm if we offer them to the sea-people.'

Toke said that this seemed to him an excellent and proper suggestion, though he felt that they might begin by throwing one or two overboard, to see if that had any effect. But Orm said that they could not do this with any of the prisoners, because he had promised them their lives.

'If you want to give someone to the sea-people,' he said to Toke, 'I can only suggest that you offer them your woman. Indeed, I think it might turn out to the advantage of us all if we could rid ourselves of someone who has brought us so much ill-luck.'

But Toke said that he would allow nothing of that sort to happen so long as he had breath in his body and one hand capable of wielding a sword.

So no more was said on that subject. As day dawned, a heavy rain began to fall and stood around them like smoke, and the storm began to lessen. When it became light, they could discern the coast of Halland ahead of them, and at last they succeeded in getting the ship into an inlet with her sail slit and her belly half-full of water.

'These boards have carried me here from St James's tomb,' said Orm, 'and now I have not far to go. But I shall come home without my necklace, and without the James bell, and little profit have I gained from giving them away.'

'You are bringing home a sword and a ship,' said Toke, 'and I have a sword and a woman. And few of those who rowed forth with Krok have as much as that to show for their voyage.'

'We carry with us also a great king's anger,' said Orm, 'and worse than that can hang around no man's neck.'

The hardships of their journey were now past. They set the five prisoners ashore, and allowed them to depart in peace; then, after they had rested for a while, and had put their ship and sail in order, they got good weather and sailed down the coast before a gentle breeze. Even the woman was now in good spirits, and was able to help them with one thing and another, so that Orm found himself able to endure her presence better than before.

As evening fell, they drew in to the flat rocks that lay below Toste's house, against which, when they had last seen the place, Krok's ships had been gently rocking. They walked up the path towards the house, with Orm at their head. A short way from the water's edge, the path crossed a frothing stream, by means of a wooden bridge consisting of three planks. Orm said: 'Be careful of the one on the left. It is rotten.'

Then he gazed at the plank, and said: 'It was rotten long before I left this place, and every time my father crossed this bridge he said that he would have it mended at once. Yet I see that it is still unmended, and still holds together, though it seems to me that I have long been parted from this place. If this bridge still stands, it may be that the old man, my father, has also survived the years that have passed.'

A little further on, they saw a stork's nest in a high tree, with a stork standing upon it. Orm stopped and whistled and the stork beat its wings and clattered its beak in reply.

'He remembers me,' said Orm. 'It is the same stork; and it seems to me that it was but yesterday that he and I last spoke together.'

Then they passed through a barred gate. Orm said: 'Shut the gate securely; for my mother gets angry if the sheep escape, and when she is out of temper our evening fare suffers.'

Dogs began to bark, and men appeared at the door and gaped at the three Vikings as they approached the house. Then a woman pushed her way through the knot of men and came towards them. It was Asa. She was pale, but apart from this looked as brisk and spry as when Orm had last seen her.

'Orm,' she said, and her voice trembled. Then she added: 'God has heard my prayers at last.'

'His ears seem to be deafened with prayers nowadays,' said Orm. 'But I never thought that of you, of all people, would turn Christian.'

'I have been alone,' said Asa. 'But now, all is well.'

'Have your men sailed forth already?' asked Orm.

'I have no men left,' she said. 'Odd stayed away the year after you left, and Toste died three years ago, in the year of the great cattle sickness. But I have managed to survive because I turned to the true religion; for then I knew that my prayers would be answered and that you would come back to me.'

'We have much to speak of,' said Orm, 'but it would be good if we could eat first. These are my men; but the woman is foreign and is not mine.'

Asa said that Orm was now the master of the house and that all his friends were hers; so they entered, and were entertained like heroes. There were tears in her eyes as she carried to the table those dishes which she knew that Orm loved most dearly. They had many things to tell each other, and the telling of them covered many evenings; but no word was said of how Toke had won his woman, for Orm did not wish to temper his mother's joy so soon after his return home. Asa took to Toke immediately and tended his wounded hand with great care and skill, so that it quickly began to mend; and she was fond and motherly towards Mirah, though they could talk but little together, and praised her beauty and black hair. She was disappointed that Orm and his men were not willing to thank God with her for their lucky return; but she was too overjoyed to take offence at their refusal, and said that Orm and the others would understand these things better when they were older and wiser.

At first, Orm found such blitheness and gentleness somewhat strange in Asa, and it was six days before he heard her make one of her sharp-tongued sallies against the servant-maids and could feel that she was beginning to be herself again.

Orm and Toke were now friends again, though neither of them ever mentioned Ylva. As they described to Asa the adventures that had befallen them since Krok's expedition had first rowed forth, Orm felt his old affection for Toke rekindle, and was eloquent in the latter's praise; but whenever his thoughts turned to Ylva, his humour darkened, and then the sight of Toke and his woman gave him little joy. Mirah grew prettier every day, and laughed and sang the whole time, and she and Toke were so happy together that they had little time to notice other people's troubles. Asa prophesied that they would have fine children, and Mirah, when this was explained to her, smiled and said they were doing all they could to ensure that this would be the case. Asa observed that she must now begin to look for a wife for Orm, but Orm replied with a dark countenance that she could take her time about that.

As things now were, it was impracticable for Toke to proceed home by sea, at least as long as King Harald's ships were at Skanör; so he decided to journey to Lister by land, with no company save that of his woman (for Rapp was remaining with Orm), and bought horses to carry them. Early one morning they took their leave, with many expressions of gratitude to Asa for her hospitality; and Orm accompanied them for a short distance to show them the right path for the Lister country.

'Here we must part,' said Orm, 'and with all my heart I wish you a good journey. But it is not easy to be hopeful about the future, for King Harald will not rest until he has hunted you down, whithersoever you may flee.'

'I fear it is our fate to be unlucky with kings,' replied Toke, 'though we are as meek-minded as other men. Almansur, King Sven, and now King Harald; we have made enemies of them all, and the man who brought our heads to any one of them would be well rewarded. None the less, I intend to hold on to mine.'

So they parted. Toke and Mirah rode eastwards and disappeared in the woods; and Orm rode back to the house to tell Asa of the danger that hung over them from King Harald's wrath.

PART TWO

In King Ethelred's Kingdom

CHAPTER ONE

Concerning the battle that was fought at Maldon, and what came after it

That spring, many ships were timbered along the coasts of the northern countries, and keels were pitched which had long lain dry. Bays and sounds vomited forth navies, with kings and their wrath aboard; and when summer came, there was great unrest upon the seas.

Styrbjörn rowed early up through the Eastern Sea, with many ships and men from Jomsborg, Bornholm and Skania. He put into Lake Mälaren, and came at length to the plain before Uppsala, where he and King Erik joined battle. There he fell, in the first moments of the fight, and men say that he died laughing. For, when he saw the battle array of the Swedes move forward, drawn up in the ancient manner behind horses' heads borne high upon pikes, with King Erik seated in the midst of his army in an old sacred ox-chariot, he threw his head back in a wild frenzy of laughter. In the same instant, a spear came between his beard and the rim of his shield and took him in the throat. When his followers saw this happen, their courage broke, and many of them fled there and then, so that King Erik won a great victory.

Then King Sven Forkbeard rowed down through the Danish islands with ships from Fyn and Jutland to take King Harald as the latter sat counting his herring-tax at Skanör; for King Sven had at last lost patience at his father's unwillingness to die. But King Harald fled to Bornholm and gathered his ships there, and sharp encounters were fought between these two until, at length, King Harald took refuge in his fortress at Jomsborg, sorely wounded. Then much of the Danish kingdom was split with strife, for some men held

King Harald's cause to be just and some King Sven's, while others preferred to fend for themselves and better their own fortunes while the land lay lawless under its warring kings.

But when the summer stood in its flower, King Erik of Uppsala came sailing southwards, with the greatest army that the Swedes had embarked in any man's memory, driving before him the remnants of Styrbjörn's fleet, which had been harrying his coasts and plundering his villages in revenge for their chieftain's death. King Erik had a mind to punish both King Harald and King Sven for the aid which they had lent to Styrbjörn, and many men thought it an unrewarding prospect to oppose the man who had conquered Styrbjörn and who was already being called 'The Victorious.' He pursued King Sven to his islands and beyond to Jutland, leaving his own Jarls to rule the places through which he passed. Soon the rumour spread that King Harald had died of his wounds at Jomsborg, a landless refugee, deserted by the luck that had hitherto favoured all his enterprises; but the other two kings continued to war against each other. King Erik held the upper hand, but King Sven resisted him stubbornly. Men reported that the royal castle at Jellinge changed hands every few weeks, King Sven and King Erik taking it in turns to occupy King Harald's old bedchamber; but it was generally agreed that King Sven was the more likely to have arrived first at his father's treasure-chests.

But in Skania there were many chieftains who felt little inclined to involve themselves in this war of kings, thinking it better to let them settle their own differences, so that honest men might be left to occupy themselves with more profitable undertakings. One such was Thorkel the Tall, who had no desire to serve King Sven and was still less anxious to find himself a minor thane of King Erik. So he sent word to other thanes and chieftains that he had a mind to fare north that summer to Frisia and England, if he could find sufficient good men willing to accompany him. Many thought this a good scheme, for Thorkel was an admired chieftain, and his luck was held to be excellent, ever since he had succeeded in escaping with his life from the battle at Jörundfjord. Masterless men of Styrbjörn's army, who had managed to evade King Erik's clutches, also came to join him, and before long he was lying at anchor in the Sound off the island of Hven with twenty-two ships; but he did not as yet reckon himself sufficiently strong to fare forth.

Among those who had joined his banner was Orm Tostesson, known as Red Orm, from the Mound in Skania. He had brought with him a large and well-manned ship. Thorkel remembered him from the Christmas feast at King Harald's castle, and welcomed him joyfully.

It had so turned out with Orm that he had quickly wearied of sitting at home and arranging the affairs of cattle and farmhands; and he had found it difficult to live peaceably with Asa, although she did her best to make him happy. For she still regarded him as a half-grown boy, and fussed continually over him with motherly counsel, as though he lacked the sagacity to manage things for himself. He did his best to explain to her that he had, for some years, been accustomed to deciding the affairs of other men as well as his own, but this information did not appear to impress her; nor did her zealous endeavours to convert him to her new religion and find him a wife improve his humour.

The news of King Harald's death had come as a great relief to them both; for, when Asa had first learned the truth about how Toke had got his woman, she had been overcome with terror, and had been convinced that there was nothing for it but to sell the house and flee to the estate which she had inherited from her father in the forests on the Smaland border, where even King Harald's arm would scarcely be able to reach them. Her fear had been ended by the news of King Harald's death; but Orm could not keep his thoughts from Ylva, and he worried more about her safety than about his own. Often he wondered what had become of her when her father had died; whether King Sven had taken her under his wing, as a prospective wife for one of his berserks, or whether, perhaps, she had fallen into the hands of the Swedes, the thought of which troubled him no less. Since he was on evil terms with King Sven, he could not think of any way in which he might regain her for himself, least of all while war was raging through and around the islands.

He said nothing about Ylva to Asa, for he had no wish to listen to the fruitless advice which he knew she would immediately shower upon him. But he profited little thereby, for Asa knew several maidens in the district who would admirably suit his needs, and their mothers, being of the same mind as she, brought them to the house and displayed them newly washed, with their plaits fastened with red silk ribbons. The maidens came willingly and sat high-bosomed, a-clink with ornaments, shooting large-eyed glances at him; but he showed no enthusiasm for any of them, for none of them resembled Ylva or was as witty and ready-tongued as she was, so that in the end Asa grew impatient with him, and thought that even Odd had hardly been more difficult to please.

When, therefore, the news came that Thorkel intended to fare forth a-viking, Orm lost no time in procuring himself a good ship and hiring men from the district to come with him, paying little heed to Asa's tears and entreaties. Everybody knew him to be a widely travelled man who had returned with much gold from his voyage, so that he found little difficulty in assembling a good crew. He told Asa that he did not expect to be away for as long this time as when he had previously set forth, and promised her that, when he returned, he would settle down to a peaceful life and take up farming in earnest. Asa wept, and protested that she could not endure such sorrow and loneliness, but Orm assured her that she would live much longer than he, and would help to birch his children, and his grandchildren to boot. But this only caused her to weep the more bitterly. So they parted, and Orm sailed to join Thorkel.

While Thorkel was still lying off Hven, waiting for a favourable wind, a fleet of twenty-eight ships came rowing up from the south; and from their banners and the cut of their stems it was apparent that they were Swedish. The weather was calm and good for fighting, and both sides made ready for battle; but Thorkel shouted across the water to the strangers, proclaiming his identity, and stating that he wished to speak with their chieftain. The Swedes were under the command of two chieftains, of equal sway. One was called Jostein, a man from Uppland, and the other Gudmund, an East Gute. They said they had come up to help King Erik plunder in Denmark, and asked what more he wished to know.

'If our fleets join battle,' shouted Thorkel, 'there will be little booty for the winners, and many men will be killed on both sides. I tell you this, though I am the more likely to prevail.'

'We have five ships more than you,' roared the strangers.

'That may be,' replied Thorkel. 'But mine are all picked men, and we have just eaten our morning meal, while your men are weary from rowing, which makes a man less skilful with his spear and sword. But I have a better suggestion to make, which would redound to the advantage of us all; for I can name a more rewarding place than Denmark to go a-viking in.'

'We have come to aid King Erik,' shouted the Upplander.

'I do not doubt it,' replied Thorkel. 'And if I join battle with you, I shall have given good aid to King Sven. But if, instead of fighting one another, we join forces and sail together to lands ripe for plunder, we shall have served our kings just as usefully as if we stay and battle it out here. For in either case, none of us will take any further part in this war; and the difference will be that, if we do as I suggest, we shall all still be alive, with much fine booty waiting for us to come and collect it.'

'You use words skilfully,' said Gudmund. 'There is wisdom in what you say, and I think we might profitably continue this discussion at closer quarters.'

'I know from report that you are both noble chieftains and honourable men,' said Thorkel. 'Therefore, I am not afraid that you will act treacherously if we meet to debate the matter.'

'I know your brother, Sigvalde,' said Jostein. 'But I have often heard it said that you, Thorkel, are of stouter mettle than he.'

So they agreed to meet on the island to debate the matter, on the beach at the foot of a cliff, in sight of the ships. Jostein and Gudmund were each to bring three men with them, and Thorkel five, bearing swords but no casting weapons. This was done, and, from the ships, the men of the opposing fleets marked how, at first, the chieftains kept their distance from each other, with their men standing close behind them. Then Thorkel ordered ale to be offered to the Swedes, together with pork and bread; and soon they were seen to sit down in a circle and talk as friends.

The more Jostein and Gudmund considered Thorkel's proposition, the more excellent it appeared to them to be, and before long Gudmund was anxiously supporting it. Jostein at first held out against it, saying that King Erik had a savage memory for men who betrayed his trust in them; but Thorkel regaled them with details of the splendid plunder that awaited sea-rovers in the islands of the west, and Gudmund reckoned that they could worry about King Erik's memory when the time came. Then they came to an agreement regarding the division of command during the voyage, and how the booty was to be shared out, so that no disputes should arise later; and Gudmund observed that so much meat and talk gave a man a fine thirst, and praised the excellence of Thorkel's ale. Thorkel shook his head, and said that it was, in truth, the best that he could offer them for the moment, but that it was nothing compared with the ale in England, where the best hops in the world grew. Then even Jostein had to agree that this sounded like a land worth voyaging to. So they took each other by the hand, and swore to be faithful and to keep their word; then, when they had returned to their ships, three sheep were slaughtered over the bows of each chieftain's vessel, as a sacrifice to sea-people for weather-luck and a good voyage. All the crews were well satisfied with the agreement that their chieftains had made; and Thorkel's reputation, which was already great in the eyes of his men, waxed because of the wisdom he had displayed in this matter.

Several more ships came to join Thorkel, from Skania and Halland; and when, at last, a favourable wind arose, the fleet put forth, fifty-five sails strong, and spent the autumn plundering in Frisia, and wintered there.

Orm enquired of Thorkel and other of his comrades whether they knew what had become of King Harald's household. Some said they had heard that Jellinge had been burnt, others that Bishop Poppo had calmed the sea with psalms and escaped by ship, although King Sven had done his best to catch him. But none of them knew what had happened to the King's women.

In England, things were beginning to be as they had been in the old days, in the time of the sons of Ragnar Hairy-Breeks; for King Ethelred had come to the throne. He had not long come of age, and taken the reins of government into his own hands, before men began to call him the Irresolute, or the Redeless; and honest-seafarers from the north flocked joyfully to his coasts to give him the chance to justify his reputation.

At first, they came in small bodies, and were easily repelled. Beacons were lit along the coasts to signify their arrival, and stout warriors armed with broad shields rushed to meet them and drive them back into the sea. But King Ethelred yawned at his table and offered up prayers against the Northmen, and lay cheerfully with his chieftains' women. He screamed with rage when they brought word to him in his boudoir that in spite of his prayers the long ships had returned; he listened, fatigued, to much counsel and complained loudly at being thus inconvenienced, and otherwise did nothing. Then the invaders began to arrive more frequently and in stronger companies, till the King's levies became inadequate to deal with them, and the larger bands of them would sometimes drive deep inland and return to their ships bent double under the weight of their booty; and the word spread abroad, and many believed it, that no kingdom could now compare with King Ethelred's in wealth and fatness for valiant seafarers who came in good strength. For it was, by now, many years since England had been properly plundered, save in her coastal areas.

But as yet no large fleet had sailed there, and no chieftains had learned the art of demanding danegeld in minted silver from King Ethelred's coffers. But in the Year of Grace 991 both these deficiencies were remedied; and thereafter there was no lack of men willing to be instructed in this art as long as King Ethelred was there to pay good silver to such as came and asked for it.

Soon after the Easter of that year, which was the fifth year after King Ethelred's coming-of-age, the beacons were lit along the Kentish coasts. Men gazed pale-faced into the morning mists, and turned and ran to hide what they could and drive their cattle into the forests and take themselves into hiding with them, and word was sent to King Ethelred and his Jarls as fast as horse could ride that the biggest fleet that had been sighted for many years was rowing along his coasts, and that the heathens had already begun to wade ashore.

The levies were assembled, but could achieve nothing against the invaders, who split up into powerful bands and plundered the district, gathering into one place everything that they laid hands on. Then the English fell into a panic lest they should drive inland, and the Archbishop of Canterbury betook himself in person to the King to crave help for his city. However, after the invaders had enjoyed themselves for a short while in the coastal area and had carried off to their ships everything that they found worth taking, they embarked again and sailed away up the coast. Then they landed in the country of the East Saxons and did likewise there.

King Ethelred and his Archbishop, whose name was Sigerik, promptly offered up longer prayers than ever; and then they heard that the heathens, after sacking a few villages, had put out to sea again, they had rich gifts distributed among those priests who had prayed most assiduously, believing themselves to be rid at last of these unwelcome visitors. No sooner had this been done than the Vikings rowed in to a town called Maldon, at the mouth of the river Panta, pitched camp on an island in the middle of the estuary, and prepared to assault the town.

The Jarl of the East Saxons was called Byrhtnoth. He had a great name in his country, and was bigger than other men and very proud and fearless. He assembled a powerful army and marched against them, to see whether blows might prove more effectual than prayers against the invaders. On reaching Maldon, he marched past the town towards the Vikings' camp until only the arm of the river separated the two forces. But now it was difficult for him to attack the Vikings, and equally difficult for them to attack him. The tide came in, filling the river arm to the level of its banks. It was no broader than a spear's-throw, so that the armies were able to hail one another, but it did not appear as though they would be able to come to close grips. So they stood facing each other in merry spring weather.

A herald of Thorkel the Tall's army, a man skilled in speech, stepped forward to the river's edge, raised his shield, and cried across the water: 'The seamen of the north, who fear no man, bid me address you thus. Give us silver and gold, and we will give you peace. You are richer than we, and it will be better for you to buy peace with tribute than to meet men of our mettle with spear and sword. If you have wealth enough, it will not be necessary for us to kill each other. Then, when you have bought your freedom, and freedom for your families and your houses and all that you possess, we shall be your friends and will return to our ships with your freeing money, and will sail away from this place, and will remain faithful to our word.'

But Byrhtnoth himself stepped forward and, brandishing his spear, roared back: 'Hearken well, sea-rover, to our reply! Here is all the tribute you will get from us: pointed spears and keen-edged swords! It would ill become such a Jarl as I, Byrhtnoth, Byrhthelm's son, whose name is without spot, not to defend my country and the land of my King. This matter shall be settled by point and blade, and hard indeed must you hew before you find aught else in this land.'

They stood facing each other until the tide turned and began again to run towards the sea. Then the herald of the Vikings cried across the river: 'Now we have stood idle long enough. Come over to us, and we will let you have our soil as battle-ground; or, if you prefer it, choose a place on your bank, and we will come over to you.'

Jarl Byrhtnoth was unwilling to wade across the river, for the water was cold and he feared lest it might make his men's limbs stiff and their clothing heavy. At the same time, he was eager to join battle before his men should begin to feel tired and hungry. So he cried back: 'I will give you ground here, and do not delay but come now to fight us. And God alone knows which of us will hold the field.'

And these are the words of Byrhtnoth's bard, who was present at this battle and escaped with his life:

> The sea-men's army feared not the flood.
> Blood-wolves waded west through Panta.
> Clear through the current's crystal water
> Bore they their linden-shields to the strand.

Byrhtnoth's men stood awaiting them like a hedge of shields. He had ordered them first to cast their spears, and then to advance with their swords and drive the heathens back into the river. But the Vikings formed into battle-order along the bank as they emerged from the water, each ship's crew keeping together, and, straightway, raised their battle-cries and charged, with the captain of each ship running at the head of his crew. A swarm of spears flew towards them, bringing many of them to the ground, whence they did not rise; but they continued to advance relentlessly until they found themselves shield to shield with the Englishmen. Then there was fierce hewing, and loud alarums; and the Vikings' right and left wings were halted and hard pressed. But Thorkel the Tall and the two captains nearest to him – Orm was one, and the other was Fare-Wide Svensson, a famous chieftain from Själland, whom King Harald had proclaimed outlaw throughout the Danish kingdom, and who had fought with Styrbjörn at the battle on Fyris Plain before Uppsala – assaulted Byrhtnoth's own phalanx and broke it. Thorkel cried to his men to fell the tall man in the silver helmet, for then the day would be theirs. Straightway the fighting became fiercest in this part of the field, and there was little elbowroom for men of small stature. Fare-Wide hewed his way forward, slew Byrhtnoth's standard-bearer, and aimed a blow at Byrhtnoth, wounding him; but he fell himself in the same instant, with a spear through his beard. Many of the chieftains on both sides were killed; and Orm slipped on a fallen shield which was greasy with blood, and tumbled headlong over the body of a man he had just slain. As he fell, he received a blow on the back of his neck from a club, but at once those of his men who were closest to him threw their shields over his body to cover him and protect his back.

When he regained his senses, and was able, with Rapp's assistance, to get to his feet again, the battle had moved away from that part of the field, and the Vikings had gained the upper hand. Byrhtnoth had fallen, and many of his men had fled, but others had formed themselves into a tight ring and, although surrounded, were still resisting valiantly. Thorkel shouted to them over the noise of the battle that he would spare their lives if they cast down their arms; but the cry came back from their midst: 'The fewer we be, the fiercer we shall hew, and the shrewder shall be our aim and our courage crueller.'

They fought on until they all lay dead upon the ground, together with many of their foemen, about their chieftain's corpse. The Vikings marvelled at the valour of these Englishmen, praising the dead; nevertheless, this battle at Maldon, fought three weeks before Whitsun in the year 991, was a grievous setback for King Ethelred, and a disaster for his realm. For now, far and wide about them, the land lay helpless before the fury of the invaders from the north.

The Vikings buried their dead, and pledged them and the victory that they had won. They handed Byrhtnoth's corpse over to the sorrowful envoys who came to beg for it, that they might give it Christian burial; then they sent proclamations to Maldon and other towns in the district, commanding that the inhabitants should pay fire-tribute and ransom without delay, lest a heavier penalty be demanded of them. They rejoiced at the thought of so much wealth lying in store for them, counting it already as their own; and their anger mounted as the days passed and no Englishman came with surrender and gold. So they rowed up to Maldon and set fire to the stockade on the river bank, and stormed the town and sacked it fearfully. Then they wept because so much had been burnt that there was little left for booty. They swore that they would, in the future, be more sparing in their use of fire, for it was silver that they yearned for and not destruction, which swallowed up silver with all else; and they set to work to whip in horses from the whole district, that they might the more speedily descend on those parts of the land which reckoned themselves safe from the invaders' wrath. Soon bands of them rode forth in all directions, and returned to the camp laden with booty; and there was now such dire panic throughout the land that no chieftain dared to emulate Byrhtnoth and challenge them to battle. Prisoners whom they took reported that King Ethelred was sitting pasty-faced behind his walls, mumbling prayers with his priests, wholly redeless.

In the church at Maldon, which was of stone, some of the English were still holding out. They had fled up into the tower when the Vikings had stormed the city, priests and women being among them; and they had drawn the steps up with them as they ascended, that they might not be pursued into their retreat. The Vikings suspected that they had taken much treasure with them, and strove their utmost to persuade them to descend from their tower and bring their treasure with them. But neither by fire nor by force of arms could they achieve anything; and the people had plenty of food and drink with them in the tower and sang psalms and appeared to be in good heart. When the Vikings approached the tower to try to induce them by words to act sensibly and come down and part with their treasure, they cast down stones, curses and filth upon their heads, yelling with triumph when any of their missiles met their mark. All the Vikings agreed that stone churches and their towers were among the most vexatious obstacles than a man could find himself confronted with.

Jostein, who was an old, hard man, very greedy for gold, said that he could only think of one way to break down these people's obstinacy; namely, that they should bring their prisoners to within sight of the tower, and there kill them, one by one, until the people in the tower could endure it no more and so would be forced to surrender. A number of the men agreed with him in this, for he had a great name for wisdom; but Gudmund and Thorkel thought such a plan unwarriorlike, and were unwilling to be parties to it.

It would be better, said Thorkel, to bring them down by guile; he added that he was well acquainted with the foibles of priests, and knew how best to approach them and get them to do what one wanted.

He ordered his men to remove a great cross from above the altar in the church. Then he approached the tower, with two men carrying the cross before him, and, halting at its foot, cried up to the people there that he needed priests to tend the wounded and also, which was more urgent, to instruct him personally in the Christian faith. Of late, he explained, he had begun to feel strongly attracted towards the new religion; and he would act towards them as though he was already a Christian, for he would allow everyone in the tower to leave it unscathed in life and limb.

He had proceeded thus far in his discourse when a stone shot out of the tower and struck his shield-arm near the shoulder, knocking him to the ground and breaking his arm. At this, the two men dropped the cross and assisted him to safety, while the people in the tower cheered in triumph. Jostein, who had been watching, curled his lip and observed that guile in war was not such a simple matter as inexperienced young that sometimes appeared to imagine.

All Thorkel's followers were inflamed with fury at seeing their chieftain wounded thus, and flights of arrows were loosed at the loopholes in the tower; but this achieved nothing, and the situation appeared to be insoluble. Orm said that in the Southland he had sometimes seen Almansur's men drive Christians from their church towers by smoking them out; and they at once set to work to try and do this. Wood and wet straw were piled together inside the church and around the foot of the tower, and were lit; but the tower was high and a breeze dispersed most of the smoke before it could ascend. In the end the Vikings lost patience, and decided to leave things until the inhabitants of the tower should begin to feel the pangs of hunger.

Thorkel was dejected by the failure of his stratagem, and feared lest his men should taunt him on the subject. Apart from this, he was irked at the prospect of having to sit idly in Maldon guarding the camp, for it was clear that it would be some time before he would be able to ride out and plunder; and he was anxious that men knowledgeable in medicine should come and examine his injury. Orm came to commiserate with him, as he sat before a fire drinking mulled ale with his broken arm hanging at his side. Many men thumbed his arm, but none of them knew how to put it in splints.

Thorkel groaned uncomfortably as they thumbed the fracture, and said it would be medicine enough for the moment if they could bind up his arm as well as it would allow, with or without splints.

'Now the words I spoke at the foot of the tower have come true,' he said. 'I need a priest badly; for priests understand such matters as this.'

Orm nodded in agreement, and said that priests were cunning doctors; after the Yule feast at King Harald's, he had had a much worse wound than Thorkel's healed by a priest. Indeed, he added, he would welcome a priest no less than Thorkel, for the blow he had received on his skull from a shoed club was causing him incessant headaches, so that he was beginning to wonder whether something might not have come loose inside his head.

When they were alone, Thorkel said to him: 'I hold you to be the wisest of my ship's captains, and the best warrior, too, now that Fare-Wise is dead. None the less, it is clear that you easily lose your courage when your body is afflicted, even when the injury is but a slight one.'

Orm replied: 'It is so with me that I am a man who has lost his luck. Formerly, my luck was good, for I survived unscathed more dangers than most men face in the whole of their lives, and emerged from all of them with profit. But since I returned from the Southland, everything has gone wrong for me. I have lost my gold chain, my sweetheart, and the man whose company pleased me best; and as for battle, it has come to such a pass that nowadays I can scarcely draw my sword without coming to some harm. Even when I advised you to smoke these English out of their church tower, nothing came of it.'

Thorkel said that he had seen unluckier men than Orm, but Orm shook his head sadly. He sent his men off plundering with Rapp in command, and remained himself in the town with Thorkel, spending most of the time sitting by himself and contemplating his woes.

One morning, not long afterwards, the bells in the church tower rang long and loud, and the people there sang psalms very zealously, causing the Vikings to shout up and ask them what all the fuss might be about. The people had no stones left to throw down at them, but they shouted back that it was now Whitsun, and that this day was for them, a day of rejoicing.

The Vikings found this reply astonishing, and several of them asked the English what on earth they could have to rejoice about, and how they were placed as regards meat and ale. They replied that, in that matter, things were as they were; nevertheless, they would continue to rejoice, because Christ was in Heaven and would surely help them.

Thorkel's men roasted fat sheep over their fires, and the odour of roasting was wafted up to the tower, where all the people were hungry. The men cried up to them to be sensible and come down and taste their roast; but they paid no attention to this invitation, and began shortly to sing afresh.

Thorkel and Orm sat munching together, listening to the singing from the tower.

'Their singing is hoarser than usual,' said Thorkel. 'They are beginning to get dry in the throat. If their drink is finished, it cannot be long before they will have to come down.'

'Their plight is worse than mine, and yet they sing,' said Orm; and he contemplated a fine piece of mutton mournfully before putting it in his mouth.

'I think you would make a poor songster in any church tower,' said Thorkel.

The same day, around dinner-time, Gudmund returned from a-viking inland. He was a large, merry man, with a face which still bore traces of old wounds he had received when a bear had clawed him; and he now rode into the camp, drunken and voluble, with a costly scarlet cloak flung across his shoulders, two heavy silver belts around his waist and a broad grin in the centre of his yellow beard.

This, he cried, as soon as he spied Thorkel, was a land after his own heart, wealthy beyond imagination; as long as he lived, he would never cease to be grateful to Thorkel for having tempted him to come here. He had plundered nine villages and a market, losing only four men; his horses were tottering beneath the weight of their booty, although only the choicest articles had been selected, and following them were ox-carts loaded with strong ale and other delicacies. It would, he added, be necessary in due course to get hold of several more ships, with plenty of cargo-room, to take home all the booty that they would, in a short time and with little expense of effort, have gathered in this excellent land.

'Besides all this,' he concluded, 'I found a procession of people on the road – two bishops and their suites. They said they were envoys from King Ethelred, so I offered them ale and bade them follow me here. The Bishops are old, and ride slowly, but they should be here soon; though what they can want with us is not easy to guess. They say they are coming with an offer of peace from their King, but it is we, and not he, who shall decide when there is to be peace. I suspect that they also want to teach us Christianity; but we shall have little time to listen to their teaching with such fine plunder to be had everywhere.'

Thorkel roused himself at these tidings, and said that priests were what he had most need of just now, for he was anxious to get his arm set properly; and Orm, too, was pleased at the prospect of being able to talk to a priest about his sore head.

'But I shall not be surprised,' Thorkel said, 'if the errand on which they have come is to ransom our prisoners and those people up in the tower.'

A short while afterwards, the Bishops rode into the town. They were of venerable aspect with staffs in their hands and hoods covering their heads. They had with them a great company of outriders and priests, grooms, stewards and musicians; and they pronounced the peace of God upon all who met their eye. All of Thorkel's men who were in the camp came to gaze at them, but some shrank away when the Bishops raised their hands. The people in the tower broke into loud acclamations at the sight of them, and began again to ring their bells.

Thorkel and Gudmund showed them every hospitality; and, when they had rested and had given thanks to God for their lucky journey, they explained their mission.

The Bishop who appeared to be the senior of the two, and who was called the Bishop of St Edmund's Bury, addressed Thorkel and Gudmund and such others of the Vikings as had gathered to hear what he had to say. These, he said, were evil times, and it was a great grief to Christ and His Church that men did not know how to live peacefully with one another in love and tolerance. Fortunately, however, he continued, they now had in England a King who loved peace above all other things, and this despite the magnitude of his power and the legions of warriors that lay awaiting his command. He preferred to win the love of his enemies rather than to destroy them by the sword. King Ethelred regarded the Northmen as zealous young men who lacked counsel and did not know what was best for them; and, after having consulted his own wise counsellors, he had decided on this occasion not to march against them and put them to the sword, but rather to point out peacefully to them the error of their ways. He had, accordingly, sent his envoys to find out how the gallant chieftains of the north, and their followers, could be persuaded to turn their thoughts towards peace and abandon the dangerous paths which they were now treading. It was King Ethelred's desire that they should return to their ships and depart from his coasts to dwell in their own land in peace and content-ment; and, to facilitate this, and win their friendship for all time, he was ready to give them such presents as would fill them all with joy and gratitude. Such royal munificence would, he trusted, so soften the hardness of their young hearts that they would learn to love God's holy law and Christ's gospel. If this should come to pass, good King Ethelred's joy would know no bounds and his love for them would become even greater.

The Bishop was bent with age and toothless, and few of the Vikings could understand what he said; but his words were translated for them by a wise priest of his suite, and all those who stood there listening turned and stared at one another in bewilderment. Gudmund was seated on an ale-butt, drunken and contented, rubbing a little gold cross to polish it, and when they explained to him what the Bishop had said, he began to rock backwards and forwards with delight. He shouted to Thorkel that the latter lose no time in replying to this excellent discourse.

So Thorkel replied, in a manner befitting a chieftain. He said that what they had just heard was, without doubt, something worth pondering on. King Ethelred had already a great name in the Danish kingdom, but it now appeared that he was an even finer king than they had been led to believe; and this proposal of his, to give them all presents, accorded well with the opinion of his worth that they had hitherto held.

'For,' he continued, 'as we told Jarl Byrhtnoth, when we spoke with him across the river, you who dwell in this land are rich, and we poor seafarers are only too anxious to be your friends if you will but share your wealth with us. It is good to hear that King Ethelred himself shares our feelings in this matter; and, seeing that he is so rich and powerful and full of wisdom, I do not doubt that he will show himself most liberal towards us. How much he intends to offer us, we have not yet been told; but we need a lot to make us merry, for we are a melancholy race. I think it best that his gifts should take the form of gold and minted silver, for this will be easiest to count, and easiest, too, for us to carry home. While everything is being settled, we shall be glad if he will permit us to remain here undisturbed, taking from the district what we need for our upkeep and pleasure. There is, though, someone who has as much say in this matter as Gudmund and myself, and that is Jostein. He is at present away plundering with many of his followers, and until he returns we cannot decide how large King Ethelred's gift is to be. But there is one thing which I should like to know at once, and that is whether you have any priest skilled in medicine among your followers; for, as you see, I have this damaged arm which needs plastering.'

The younger Bishop replied that they had with them two men who were learned in the craft of healing, and said he would be glad to bid them attend to Thorkel's arm. He requested, however, that, in return for this service, Thorkel should allow the people who were shut up in the tower to descend and go their ways without hindrance; for it was a heavy thing, he said, to think of them up there tormented by hunger and thirst.

'As far as I am concerned,' said Thorkel, 'they can come down as soon as they like. We have been trying to persuade them to do so ever since we took this town, but they have resisted our offers most obstinately; in fact, it was they who broke my arm. Half of what they have in the tower they must give to us. This is small repayment for the injury to my arm and all the bother they have caused us. But when they have done that, they may go whithersoever they please.'

Soon, therefore, all the people in the tower descended, looking pale and wasted. Some of them wept and threw themselves at the Bishop's feet, while others cried piteously for water and food. Thorkel's men were disappointed to find that there was little of value in the tower; nevertheless, they gave them food and did them no harm.

Orm happened to pass a water-trough, where a number of those who had been in the tower were drinking. Among them was a little bald man in a priest's cowl, with a long nose and a red scar across his forehead. Orm stared at him in astonishment. Then he went up and seized him by the shoulder.

'I am glad to see you again,' he said, 'and I have something to thank you for since the last time we met. But I little thought to meet King Harald's physician in England. How did you come here?'

'I came here from the tower,' retorted Brother Willibald wrathfully, 'where you heathen berserks have compelled me to spend the last fortnight.'

'I have several things to discuss with you,' said Orm. 'Come with me, and I will give you food and drink.'

'I have nothing to discuss with you,' replied Brother Willibald. 'The less I see of the Danes, the better it will be for me. That much, at least, I have learned by now. I will get my meat and drink elsewhere.'

Orm was afraid lest the little priest might, in his anger, dart away and give him the slip, so he picked him up and carried him away under one arm, promising him as he did so that no harm should come to him. Brother Willibald struggled vigorously, demanding sternly to be put down, and informing Orm that leprosy and fearful battle-wounds were the least retribution that would descend on any man who laid his hand on a priest; but Orm ignored his protests and carried him into a house which he had chosen as his quarters after they had stormed the town, and which now contained only a few members of his crew who had been wounded and two old women.

The little priest was obviously famished, but, when meat and drink were placed before him, he sat for some time staring bitterly at the platter and tankard, making no effort to touch them. Then he sighed, muttered something to himself, made the sign of the cross over the food, and began to eat greedily. Orm refilled his tankard with ale, and waited patiently until Brother Willibald had appeased his hunger. The good ale appeared to have no soothing effect upon his temper, for the harshness of the retorts did not diminish; however, he found it in himself to answer Orm's questions, and, before long, he was talking as ebulliently as ever.

He had, he explained, escaped from Denmark with Bishop Poppo when the evil and unchristian King Sven had descended upon Jellinge to destroy God's servants there. The Bishop, sick and fragile, was now living on the charity of the Abbot of Westminster, grieving over the destruction of all his work in the north. Brother Willibald, though, felt that there was, in fact, little to grieve about, when you considered the matter aright; for there could be no doubt that what had happened was a sign from God that holy men should cease their efforts to convert the heathens of the north, and should, instead, leave them to destroy each other by their evil practices, which were, in truth, past all understanding. For his own part, Brother Willibald added, he had no intention of ever again attempting to convert anyone from those parts; and he was prepared to proclaim the fact upon the Cross and Passion of Christ in the presence of anyone who wished to hear it, including, if necessary, the Archbishop of Bremen himself.

His eyes smouldering, he drained his tankard, smacked his lips and observed that ale was more nourishing than meat for a starving man. Orm refilled his tankard, and he continued with his story.

When Bishop Poppo had heard that Danish vikings had landed on the east coast of England, he had been anxious to try and learn from them how things now were in the Danish kingdom; whether any Christians were still alive; whether the rumour that King Harald had died was true, and many other things besides. But the Bishop had felt too weak to undertake the journey from Westminster himself, and so had sent Brother Willibald to get the information for him.

'For the Bishop told me I would run little risk of injury among the heathens, however inflamed their passions might be. He said they would welcome me on account of my knowledge of medicine; in addition to which there would be men among them who had known me at King Harald's court. I had my own feelings on the matter, for he is too good for this world, and knows you less well than I do. However, it is not seemly to contradict one's Bishop; so I did as he bade me. I reached this town one evening, very exhausted, and, after celebrating evensong, laid myself down to sleep in the church house. There I was woken by screaming and thick smoke, and men and women came running in half-naked, crying that the foul fiends had descended on us. Fiends there were none, but worse adversaries, and it seemed to me that little was likely to be gained by greeting them with words of salutation from Bishop Poppo. So I fled with the rest up into the church tower, and there I should have perished, and the others with me, had God not elected to liberate us from our plight upon this blessed Whitsun day.'

He wagged his head mournfully, and regarded Orm with weary eyes.

'All this was fourteen days ago,' he said, 'and since then I have had little sleep. And my body is weak – nay, not weak, for it is as strong as the spirit that inhabits it; still, there are limits to its strength.'

'You can sleep later,' said Orm impatiently. 'Do you know aught of what has happened to Ylva, King Harald's daughter?'

'This much I know,' replied Brother Willibald promptly, 'that unless she shortly mends her ways, she will burn in hell fire for her brazenness of spirit and scandalous conduct. And what hope can one cherish that any daughter of King Harald will ever mend her ways?'

'Do you hate our women, too?' asked Orm. 'What harm has she ever done to you?'

'It matters little what she has done to me,' said the little priest bitterly, 'though she did, in fact, call me a bald old owl merely because I threatened her with the vengeance of the Lord.'

'You threatened her, priest?' said Orm, getting to his feet. 'Why did you threaten her?'

'Because she swore that she would do as she pleased and marry a heathen, even though all the Bishops in the world should strive to stop her.'

Orm clutched his beard and stared open-eyed at the little priest. Then he seated himself again.

'I am the heathen she wishes to marry,' he said quietly. 'Where is she now?'

But he received no answer to his question that evening, for, as he spoke, Brother Willibald drooped slowly down on to the table and fell fast asleep with his head upon his arms. Orm did his best to wake him, but in vain; at length, he picked him up, carried him to the settle, lay him there, and threw a skin over him. He noted with surprise that he was beginning to grow fond of this little priest. For a while he sat alone brooding over his ale. Then, as he found that he had no desire for sleep, his impatience began again to swell within him, and he got up, crossed to the settle, and gave Brother Willibald a vigorous shaking.

But Brother Willibald merely turned over in his sleep and muttered in a drowsy and peevish whisper: 'Worse than fiends!'

When, next morning, the little priest at length awoke, he proved to be somewhat milder of temper, and seemed fairly contented with his situation; so Orm lost no time in extracting from him the details of everything that had happened to Ylva since he had last seen her. She had fled from Jellinge with the Bishop, preferring exile to remaining at home in her brother Sven's care, and had spent the winter with him at Westminster, in great impatience to return home to Denmark as soon as good news should arrive of the situation there. Of late, however, the rumour had reached them that King Harald had died in exile. This had caused Ylva to consider journeying north to the home of her sister Gunhild, who was wedded to the Danish Jarl Palling of Northumberland. The Bishop was unwilling to allow her to undertake such a dangerous journey, preferring that she should remain in the south and marry some chieftain from those parts, whom he would help to find for her. But whenever he had brought this subject up, she had turned white with rage, and had broken into fearful invective against anyone who happened to be near her, not excluding the Bishop himself.

This was what the little priest had to tell Orm concerning Ylva. Orm was happy to know that she had escaped King Sven's clutches, but it vexed him not to be able to think of any means of seeing her. He worried, too, about the blow which he had received on his neck, and the pain which he still suffered as a result of it; but Brother Willibald smiled disparagingly and said that skulls as thick as his would survive worse cracks than that. However, he put blood-leeches behind Orm's ears, with the result that he soon began to feel better. Nevertheless, he could not keep his thoughts from Ylva. It occurred to him to try and talk Thorkel and the other chieftains into undertaking a great plundering expedition against London and Westminster, in the hope that this might enable him to make contact with her; but the chieftains were occupied in tedious conferences with the envoys, settling details regarding the gifts which they were to receive from King Ethelred, and the whole army sat idle-fingered, doing nothing but eat and drink and speculate as to how much so great a King could fittingly be asked to pay.

Both the old Bishops spoke out manfully on their master's behalf, advancing many arguments to show why the sums suggested by the chieftains should be regarded as excessive. They regretted that the Vikings did not appear to realize that there were more valuable things in the world than gold and silver, and that for a rich man to enter the Kingdom of Heaven was more difficult than for an ox to pass through the smoke-hole of a roof. The chieftains heard them out patiently, and then replied that, should any disadvantages accrue to them from the bargain, they would accept them stoically, but they could not accept a sum less than that which they had originally named. If, they added, what the Bishops had said about the Kingdom of Heaven and the smoke-hole was true, they would surely be doing King Ethelred a good service by relieving him of some of the burden of his wealth.

Sighing, the Bishops increased their offer, and at last agreement was reached as to the sum that King Ethelred was to pay. Every man in the fleet was to receive six marks of silver, in addition to what they had already taken by plunder. Every helmsman was to have twelve marks, and every ship's captain sixty; and Thorkel, Gudmund and Jostein were each to receive three hundred marks. The Bishops said that this was a sad day for them, and that they hardly knew what their King would say when he heard the sum they had agreed on. It would, they explained, fall all the more heavily on him because, at this very moment, other envoys of his were negotiating with a Norwegian chieftain named Olaf Tryggvasson, who was, with his fleet, plundering their south coast. They could not be sure, they said, that even King Ethelred's wealth would suffice to meet both demands.

When they heard this, the chieftains began to worry lest they might have asked for too small a sum, and, also, lest the Norwegians should get in before them. They held a brief conference amongst themselves, and then announced that they had decided not to increase their demand, but that the Bishops had better lose no time in fetching the silver, for, they said, they would take it ill if the Norwegians were paid before them.

The Bishop of London, who was a friendly and smiling man, assented to this, and promised that they would do their best.

'I am, however, surprised,' he said, 'to see such valiant chieftains as yourselves bothering your heads about this Norwegian captain, whose fleet is much smaller than yours. Would it not be a good thing for you to row down to the south coast, where this captain is lying, and destroy him and his men, and so win all his treasure? He has lately come from Brittany, in fine ships, and men say that he took much booty there. If you were to do this, it would still further increase the love which our lord the King bears you; and he would, in that case, have no difficulty in finding the sum you demand, since he would not then have to appease this Norwegian captain's greed.'

Thorkel nodded, and looked uncertain, and Gudmund laughed and said that the Bishop's suggestion was certainly worth considering.

'I have never myself met any of these Norwegians,' he said, 'but everyone knows that an encounter with them always provides fine fighting and good tales for the survivors to tell their children. At home, in Bravik, I have heard it said that few men outside East Guteland are their superiors, and it might be worth finding out whether this reputation of theirs is justified. I have, in my ships, berserks from Aland who are beginning to complain that this expedition is providing them with splendid booty and excellent ale, but little in the way of good fighting; and they say they are not used to a peaceful life.'

Thorkel commented that he had, on one occasion, encountered Norwegians, but that he had no objection to doing so again, once his arm was healed; for in a battle with them, much honour and wealth might be won.

Then Jostein burst into a great roar of laughter, and took off his hat and flung it on the ground at his feet. He always wore an old red hat with a broad brim when he was not actually fighting, because his helmet chafed his skull.

'Look at me!' he cried. 'I am old and bald; and, where age is, there is also wisdom, as I am about to show you. This god-man can deceive you, Thorkel, and you, too, Gudmund, with his craft and cunning, but he cannot deceive me, for I am as old and as wise as he is. It will be a fine thing for him and his King if he can persuade us to fight against the Norwegian; for then we shall destroy each other, and King Ethelred will be quit of us all and will not need to squander any of his silver on such as survive the battle. But if you take my advice, you will not let any such thing happen.'

Gudmund and Thorkel had to admit that they had not thought of it in this light, and that Jostein was the wisest of them all; and the envoys found that they could not prevail upon them any further. So they made ready to return to King Ethelred, to tell him how everything had turned out, and to make arrangements to have the silver collected as soon as possible.

But before they departed, they robed themselves in their finest garments, gathered their followers about them and walked out in solemn procession to the field where the battle had taken place. There they read prayers over the bodies of the dead, who lay half-covered by the richly growing grass, while crows and ravens circled above them in their multitudes, complaining harshly at being thus rudely disturbed from their lawful feeding.

CHAPTER TWO

Concerning spiritual things

There was great rejoicing in the camp when the men learned of the agreement that their chieftains had reached with King Ethelred's envoys. They all praised the chieftains for striking such a fine bargain, and acclaimed King Ethelred as the most considerate king towards poor seafarers from the north that there had ever been. Much drinking and merrymaking followed, fat sheep and young women being in great demand; and the scholars among them sat round the fires where the sheep were being roasted and tried to calculate how much silver there would be to each ship, and how much for the whole fleet. This they found a difficult task, and there were frequent disputes as to who had calculated most correctly; but on one point they were all agreed, namely, that none of them had ever before believed that such a quantity of silver could exist anywhere in the world, unless perhaps in the Emperor's palace at Miklagard. Some of them thought it surprising that the helmsmen should receive so large a share, seeing that their work was light and they were never required to sit at an oar; but the helmsmen themselves thought that every right-thinking man would appreciate that they were worth more than any other members of the fleet.

Although the ale was good and strong and the excitement great, still, the arguments seldom took a serious turn; for they all now regarded themselves as rich men, and found life good, and so were less ready than usual to grope for their weapons.

But Orm sat brooding darkly with the little priest, thinking that few men in the world could find themselves more unhappily placed than he.

Brother Willibald had found plenty to occupy him, for there were many wounded men who required his attention, and he applied himself to their needs with zeal and cunning. He also examined Thorkel's arm, and had a good deal to say about the Bishops' doctor and the way that he had treated it; for he was unwilling to allow that anyone but himself possessed any skill or knowledge in the craft of medicine. He said that he would have to leave with the Bishops, but Orm was reluctant to let him go.

'For it is always a good thing to have a doctor around,' he said, 'and it may be, as you say, that you are the best there is. It is true that I should like to send greetings through you to Ylva, this daughter of King Harald; but if I did this, I should never see you again, because of the hatred you bear us Northmen. So I should never know her reply, in any case. I cannot decide what is the best thing for me to do, and this uncertainty is having a serious effect on my appetite and sleep.'

'Do you intend to keep me here by force?' asked Brother Willibald indignantly. 'I have frequently heard you Northmen boast that your fidelity to your word matches your valour in battle; and all of us who were in the tower were promised that we should be free to go as we pleased. But doubtless that has slipped your memory.'

Orm stared blackly ahead of him, and replied that he seldom forgot things.

'But it is hard for me to let you go,' he added, 'for you are a good counsellor to me, even if you can do nothing for me in this matter. You are a wise man, little priest, so answer me this question. If you were in my place, and were faced with the problem that faces me, what would you do?'

Brother Willibald smiled to himself, and nodded sympathetically at Orm. Then he shook his head.

'You seem to be very fixed on wooing this young woman,' he said, 'despite the sharpness of her temper. I am surprised at this, for you godless berserks are usually content with any woman who crosses your path, and seldom mope for a particular one. Is it because she is a princess?'

'She can expect no dowry from her father,' said Orm, 'the way things have turned out for him. And be sure of this, that it is herself, and not her wealth, that I yearn for. Nor is the fact that she is of noble blood any obstacle to our marriage, for I am myself of aristocratic ancestry.'

212

'Perhaps she has given you a love potion,' said Brother Willibald, 'and that is why your passion for her is so unrelenting.'

'Once she gave me a drink,' said Orm, 'but never since. It was the first occasion on which I saw her, and the drink was meat broth. And I drank but little of that, for she lost her temper and threw the cup and the broth into the fireplace. In any case, it was you yourself who ordered the broth to be prepared for me.'

'I was not present while it was being prepared,' said Brother Willibald thoughtfully, 'nor while she was bringing it from the kitchen to your room; and a young man needs but a few drops of one of these potions, when the woman in question is young and well-shaped. But even if it be true that she put witchcraft in the drink, there is nothing I can do about it; for there is no cure for love save love itself. That is the verdict of all the wise doctors that have ever practised since the earliest times.'

'The cure you speak of is the cure I wish to have,' said Orm, 'and what I am asking is whether you can help me to procure it.'

Brother Willibald pointed his finger at him magisterially, and, in his most fatherly manner, said: 'There is only one thing to be done when a man is troubled and cannot work out his own salvation; but you, unfortunate heathen, are in no position to follow my advice. For the only remedy is to pray to God for help, and that you cannot do.'

'Does he often help you?' asked Orm.

'He helps me when I ask him sensible things,' replied Brother Willibald with feeling, 'and that is more than your gods do for you. He does not listen when I complain to him about trivial afflictions, which he thinks I am well able to endure on my own; indeed, I have, with my own eyes, seen the holy and blessed Bishop Poppo, when we were fleeing across the sea, cry most desperately to God and St Peter to relieve him from sea-sickness, and remain unheard. But when I was in the tower with these other good people, and hunger and thirst and the swords of Anti-Christ were threatening us, we cried to God in our need, and he heard us and granted our prayers, although there was none amongst us as blessed in the sight of God as Bishop Poppo. For in God's good time, the envoys arrived and rescued us; and, although they were, in one sense, envoys from King Ethelred to the heathen chieftains, still, they were also envoys from God sent from Heaven

213

to succour us, in answer to the many and earnest prayers that we had offered up to him.'

Orm nodded, and admitted that there might be something in what Brother Willibald said, since he had himself been a witness to all this.

'Now I begin to understand,' he said, 'why my plan to smoke you out of the tower went astray. Doubtless this God, or whoever you cried to, ordered the wind to arise and blow away the smoke.'

Brother Willibald replied that this was exactly what had happened; the finger of God had countered their evil machinations and set them at naught.

Orm sat pondering in silence, tugging his beard uncertainly.

'My mother has become a Christian, in her old age,' he said at length. 'She has learned two prayers, which she repeats often, holding them to be the most potent. She says it is these prayers that saved me from death and brought me home to her again, after undergoing so many perils; though it may be that Blue-Tongue and I did our share in overcoming them, and you, too, little priest. Now I am beginning to feel that I, too, might ask God to help me, since he seems to be such a helpful god. But I do not know what he will ask of me in return, nor how I should address him.'

'You cannot ask God to help you,' said Brother Willibald decisively, 'until you have become a Christian. And you cannot become a Christian until you have been baptized. And you cannot be baptized until you have renounced your false gods and professed yourself a convinced believer in the Father, the Son and the Holy Ghost.'

'Those are a great many conditions,' said Orm. 'More than Allah and his Prophet require of a man.'

'Allah and his Prophet?' exclaimed the little priest in surprise. 'What do you know of them?'

'I have travelled more widely in the world than you,' replied Orm. 'And when I served Almansur in Andalusia, we had to pray to Allah and his Prophet twice a day, and sometimes even thrice. I still remember the prayers, if you would care to hear them.'

Brother Willibald threw up his hands in horror.

'In the Name of the Father, the Son and the Holy Ghost!' he cried. 'Save us from the machinations of Satan and the devices of Allah the abominable! Your state is as parlous as a man's could be,

214

for to worship Allah is the worst heresy of all. Are you still a follower of his?'

'I worshipped him while I was Almansur's servant,' said Orm, 'because my master commanded me to do so, and he was a man whom it was folly to disobey. Since I left him, I have not worshipped any god. Perhaps that is why things have gone less well for me recently.'

'I am surprised that Bishop Poppo did not come to hear of this while you were at King Harald's court,' said Brother Willibald. 'If he had known that you had embraced the black impostor he would have baptized you straightway, so full of zeal and piety is he, even if it had needed twelve of King Harald's berserks to hold you in the water. It is a good and blessed thing to rescue a plain soul from darkness and blindness; and it may be that even the souls of Northmen should be regarded as deserving of charity, though I confess I can hardly bring myself to believe it after all I have suffered at their hands. But all good men are agreed that it is seven times more glorious to have the soul of one who has been seduced by Mahomet. For Satan himself has not caused more mischief than that man.'

Orm asked who Satan might be, and Brother Willibald told him all about him.

'It would appear, then,' said Orm, 'that I have involuntarily angered this Satan by ceasing to worship Allah and his Prophet; and that all my misfortuntes have resulted from this.'

'Exactly,' said the little priest, 'and it is lucky for you that you have come at last to realize the error of your ways. Your present state is as disastrous as could be imagined, for you have incurred the wrath of Satan without having the protection of God. As long as you worship Mahomet, accursed be his name, Satan was your ally, and so, to a certain extent, you prospered.'

'It is as I feared,' said Orm. 'Few men are in such a desperate plight as I. It is too much for any man to be on evil terms with both God and Satan.'

He sat for a while buried in reflection.

At length he said: 'Take me to the envoys. I wish to speak with men who have influence with God.'

The Bishops had returned from the battlefield, where they had been blessing the dead, and were intending to start on their homeward journey on the following day. The elder of them was exhausted with walking round from corpse to corpse, and had gone to rest, but the Bishop of London had invited Gudmund to join him in his lodgings, and was sitting drinking with him in a last effort to persuade him to allow himself to become converted to Christianity.

Ever since they had first arrived at Maldon, the Bishops had striven their utmost to win the Viking chieftains over to their religion. King Ethelred and his Archbishop had commanded them to do so, for, if they should succeed in this, the King's honour would be greatly enhanced in the sight of God and his countrymen. They had not succeeded in making much headway with Thorkel, for he had replied that his weapon-luck was good enough already and was, in any case, considerably superior to that of the Christians. Accordingly, he said, there seemed no point in his looking round for new gods. Nor had they prevailed upon Jostein. He had listened mutely to their arguments, sitting with his hands crossed upon the handle of the great battleaxe which he always carried with him, and which he called Widow's-Grief, regarding them from beneath wrinkled brows as they explained to him the mysteries of Christ and of the Kingdom of God. Then he gave a great roar of laughter, flung his hat upon the floor, and asked the Bishops if they thought that he was a simpleton.

'These twenty-seven winters,' he said, 'I have served as priest at the great Uppsala sacrifice; and you do me little honour in filling my ears with such prattle as this, fit only for children and gammers. With this axe, which you see here, I have hewn off the heads of the harvest sacrifices, and hung their bodies on the sacred trees that front the temple; and there were Christians among them, ay, and priests too, naked on their knees in the snow, wailing. Tell me what profit they gained from worshipping this God you speak of.'

The Bishops shuddered and crossed themselves, and understood that there was no sense in trying to reason with such a man.

But they cherished greater hopes of Gudmund, for he was amiable and good-humoured towards them, and seemed interested in what they had to say; and sometimes, when he had drunk well, he had even thanked them warmly for their beautiful talk and solicitous regard for his spiritual well-being. However, he had not, as yet, committed himself definitely; so the Bishop of London had now invited him to a grand dinner, with food and drink of a very special nature, in the hope of being able to push him to a positive decision.

Gudmund helped himself greedily to everything that was put before him; and, when he had eaten and drunk his fill, the Bishop's musicians played for him, so beautifully that tears began to appear in his beard. Then the Bishop set to work on him, speaking in his most persuasive tones, and choosing his words with care. Gudmund listened, and nodded, and at length admitted that there was much that appealed to him in this Christianity.

'You are a good fellow,' he said to the Bishop. 'You are open-handed and wise, and you drink like a warrior, and your talk is agreeable to listen to. I would like to accede to your request; but you must know that this is no small favour that you are asking of me. For it will be an ill thing if I return home to find myself the laughing-stock of my house-folk and neighbours, for having allowed myself to be deceived by the prattle of priests. Still, it is my belief that a man like you must doubtless wield considerable power and be the possessor of many secrets; and I have here an object which I have recently found, and which I should like you to read one of your prayers over.'

He drew from his shirt the little gold cross, and held it in front of the Bishop's nose.

'I found this in a rich man's house,' he said. 'It cost me two men's lives, and a prettier plaything I never set eyes on. I intend to give this to my small son when I return home. His name is Folke, and women call Filbyter. He is a sturdy little ruffian, with a particular fondness for silver and gold, and once he has got his hands on a thing it is no easy matter to get it away from him. He will hardly be able to contain himself when he sees this cross. It would be a fine thing if you could bless it and make it lucky, for I want him to become rich and powerful, so that he will be able to sit at home in his house and be honoured by men, and see his crops flourish and his cattle wax fat, and have no need to rove the sea for his livelihood, faring ill among foreigners and their arms.'

The Bishop smiled, and took the cross and mumbled over it. Gudmund, greatly delighted, stuffed it back into his shirt.

'You shall return to your home a wealthy man,' said the Bishop, 'thanks to good King Ethelred's open-handedness and meek love of

217

peace. But you must believe me when I tell you that your luck would be even greater if you were to come over to Christ.'

'A man can never have too much luck,' said Gudmund, pulling thoughtfully at his beard. 'I have already decided which neighbour's land I shall purchase when I return home, and what manner of house I shall build on it. It shall be large, with many rooms, built of the finest oak. To have it the way I want it to be is going to cost a lot of silver. But if I have a good hoard of silver left in my coffers after I have built it, I do not think anyone will feel much inclined to laugh at me, howsoever I may have conducted myself while abroad. So, it shall be as you wish. You may baptize me, and I will follow Christ faithfully for the rest of my days, if you increase my share of King Ethelred's silver by a hundred marks.'

'That,' replied the Bishop mildly, 'is not the right attitude of mind for one wishing to be admitted into the brotherhood of Christ. However, I shall not blame you too heavily, since you are doubtless unfamiliar with the text which says: 'Blessed are the poor'; and I fear it would take some time to explain the truth of that to you. But you should bethink yourself that you are already about to receive much silver from King Ethelred, more than any other living man could offer you; and, although he is a great and powerful King, still, even his coffers are not bottomless. It is not within his power to grant this demand of yours, even if he were agreeable to doing so. I think I can promise you a baptismal gift of twenty marks, seeing that you are a chieftain, but that is the maximum that I can offer, and he may regard even that as excessive. But now I beg that you will sample a drink which I have specially ordered to be prepared for us and which is, I think, not known in your country. It consists of hot wine blended with honey and with rare spices from the Eastland called cinnamon and cardamom. Men well versed in the subject of drink assert that no beverage is so pleasing to the palate or so effective at dispersing heavy humours and morbid cogitations.'

Gudmund found the drink good and wholesome; nevertheless, the Bishop's offer still appeared to him to be inadequate. He would not, he explained, be prepared to risk his good name at home in East Guteland for as little as that.

'However, for the sake of the friendship I bear towards you,' he said, 'I shall do it for sixty marks. I cannot offer myself more cheaply than that.'

'The friendship I bear towards you could not be greater,' replied the Bishop, 'and such is my desire to lead you into the brotherhood of Christ, so that you may partake of the wealth which Heaven has to offer, that I will even plunge into my own poor coffers to satisfy your demand. But I own, alas, little in the way of worldly goods, and ten marks is the most that I can add to my original offer.'

Gudmund shook his head at this, and closed his eyes sleepily. At this stage in the bargaining, a commotion was suddenly heard outside the door, and Orm burst in with Brother Willibald struggling under one arm and two porters hanging on to his clothing and clamouring that the Bishop was not to be disturbed.

'Holy Bishop!' he said. 'I am Orm, Toste's son, from the Mound in Skania, a captain of Thorkel the Tall. I wish to be baptized and to accompany you to London.'

The Bishop stared at him in amazement and some alarm. But when he saw that Orm was neither drunk nor out of his wits, he asked him the meaning of his request; for he was not accustomed to Northmen forcing themselves into his presence on errands of this nature.

'I wish to place myself under the protection of God,' said Orm, 'for my plight is worse than that of other men. This priest can explain it all to you better than I can.'

Brother Willibald then begged the Bishop to forgive him for taking part in this intrusion. He had, he explained, not come voluntarily, but had been compelled to do so by the brute force of this heathen berserk, who had dragged him past vigilant porters, despite his desperate struggles and protests; for he himself had realized that the Bishop was engaged upon important business.

The Bishop replied amiably that he need give no more thought to the matter. He pointed a finger at Gudmund, who, with the assistance of a last cupful of spiced wine, had fallen asleep in his chair.

'I have laboured long to persuade him to become a Christian,' he said, 'and yet I have failed, for his soul is wholly occupied with earthly considerations. But now, God has sent me another heathen in his place, and one, moreover, who is not called but comes of his own free will. Welcome, unbeliever! Are you fully prepared to join our brotherhood?'

'I am,' replied Orm, 'for I have already served the Prophet

Mahomet and his god, and I gather that nothing can be more dangerous than that.'

The Bishop's eyes grew round, and he struck the cross on his breast three times and called for holy water.

'Mahomet and his god?' he enquired of Brother Willibald. 'What is the meaning of this?'

Between them, Orm and Brother Willibald explained to the Bishop how the matter stood. The Bishop then announced that he had, in his time, seen much of sin and darkness, but that never before had he set eyes upon a man who had actually served Mahomet. When the holy water arrived, he took a small branch, dipped it in the water, and shook it over Orm, intoning prayers the while to drive the evil spirits out of the latter's body. Orm turned pale as the Bishop did this, and he afterwards said that this sprinkling was a hard thing to endure, for it made his whole body shiver as though the hairs on his neck were trying to stand on end. The Bishop continued to sprinkle him vigorously for some time, but at length desisted and said that that would suffice.

'You are not rolling about in fits,' he informed Orm, 'and I can see no froth on your lips, nor can I detect any unpleasant smell emanating from your body. All this signifies that the evil spirit has departed from you. Praise God for it!'

Then he sprinkled a little on Gudmund, who immediately leaped to his feet, roaring at them to reef sail, but then fell back on his bench and began to snore resonantly.

Orm dried the water from his face, and asked whether this would have the same effect upon him as baptism.

The Bishop replied that there was a considerable difference between baptism and this rite, and that it was by no means so easy for a man to be permitted to undergo baptism, least of all one who had served Mahomet.

'First you must forswear your false gods,' he said, 'and avow your belief in the Father, the Son and the Holy Ghost. In addition to this, you must also be schooled in Christian doctrine.'

'I have no gods to forswear,' said Orm, 'and am ready to bind myself to God and his son and this ghost of theirs. As for schooling in Christian doctrine, I have already had plenty of that, first from the monks in Ireland, and afterwards at King Harald's court, and from my old mother at home, as well as she was able. And now I have heard more about it from this little priest, who is my friend and has taught me a great deal about Satan. So that I think I am as learned on the subject as most men.'

The Bishop nodded approvingly and said that this was good to hear, and that it was not often that one met heathens who were willing to listen to so much instruction about holy matters. Then he rubbed his nose and stole a thoughtful glance at Gudmund, who was sound asleep. He turned again to Orm.

'There is one other point,' he said slowly and with great solemnity. 'You have been dyed more deeply in sin than any man I have ever come across, in that you have served the false prophet, who is the blackest of all the chieftains of Satan. Now, if, after partaking in such abominable practices, you wish to place yourself under the wing of the living God, it is meet that you should bring with you a gift for Him and for His Church, to show that your repentance is genuine and that you have truly abandoned your evil ways.'

Orm replied that was no more than was reasonable, that he should give something to improve his luck and buy the protection of God. He asked the Bishop what would be regarded as a suitable gift.

'That depends,' said the Bishop, 'upon a man's blood and wealth, and upon the magnitude of his sins. Once I baptized a Danish chieftain who had come to this land to claim his inheritance. He gave five oxen, an anker of ale and twenty pounds of beeswax to the Church of God. In the ancient scriptures we read of men of noble birth who gave as much as ten marks of silver, or even twelve, and built a church besides. But they had brought all their household with them to be baptized.'

'I do not wish to give less than other men,' said Orm, 'for you must know that the blood of the Broad Embrace runs in my veins. When I reach home, I will build a church; you shall baptize all my crew, and I will give you fifteen marks of silver. But in return for this, I expect you to speak well of me to God.'

'You are a true chieftain!' cried the Bishop joyfully, 'and I will do all that lies in my power to help you.'

Both of them were delighted with the bargain they had struck; but the Bishop wondered if Orm could have been serious when he had said that all the members of his crew were to be baptized with him.

'If I am to be a Christian,' said Orm, 'I cannot have heathens

221

aboard my ship. For what would God think of me if I were to allow that? They shall do as I do, and when I tell my crew that such and such a thing is to be, they do not contradict me. I have some men aboard who have already been baptized once, or even twice, but once more cannot hurt them.'

He begged that the Bishops and all their followers should honour him by coming aboard his ship the next morning, so that he might convey them up the river to London and Westminster, and they might all be baptized there.

'My ship is large and fine,' he said. 'It will be somewhat crowded, with so many guests aboard, but the voyage will not take long, and the weather is fair and calm.'

He was very pressing about this; but the Bishop said that he could not take a decision in so important a matter before discussing it with his brother in office and with others of their company, so Orm had to contain himself patiently until the following day. He parted from the Bishop with many expressions of thanks, and walked back to his lodgings with Brother Willibald. The latter had not said much in the Bishop's presence, but, as soon as they had left the house, he began to cackle mirthfully.

'What are you so amused at?' asked Orm.

'I was only thinking,' replied the little priest, 'how much trouble you were putting yourself to for the sake of King Harald's daughter. But I think you are acquitting yourself very well.'

'If everything goes as it should,' said Orm, 'you shall not be left unrewarded. For it seems to me that my luck began to improve from the moment I met you again.'

The Bishop, left to himself, sat for a while smiling to himself, and then bade his servants wake Gudmund. This they at length succeeded in doing, though he grumbled at being thus disturbed.

'I have been thinking about that matter we were speaking of,' said the Bishop, 'and, with God's help, I think I can promise you forty marks if you will allow yourself to be baptized.'

On hearing this, Gudmund became wide awake, and, after a brief argument, they shook hands on forty-five marks, together with a pound of the spices which the Bishop used to flavour his wine.

The next day, at Thorkel's lodgings, the chieftains discussed Orm's proposal to convey the Bishops by ship to Westminster. On hearing of the plan, Gudmund announced that he would like to join the party. Seeing that the envoys had promised them a safe conduct, and that peace had been concluded between themselves and King Ethelred, he would, he said, like to be present when the King weighed out his silver, to ensure that the ceremony was carried out in a right and proper manner.

Thorkel thought this a reasonable request, and said he would have liked to accompany them himself, if his arm had been better. But Jostein said that it was quite sufficient that one of the three chieftains should go; otherwise, the English might be tempted to attack them, and it would be rash to weaken the strength of the main body in the camp before the silver was safely in their hands.

The weather was so fine that the Bishops could not find it in themselves to refuse to return by ship. Their only concern was lest they should fall foul of pirates; so at last it was decided that Gudmund should take his ship as well as Orm's, and that they should sail up to Westminster together. There, they were to see the silver weighed out with the least possible delay; and, in the event of their meeting the King himself, they were to thank him for his gift and inform him that they intended to start plundering again, on a more extensive scale than before, if he took too long about handing it over.

Orm summoned his crew together and told them that they were now about to sail up to Westminster with the shield of peace upon their masthead and with King Ethelred's holy envoys aboard.

Several of his men expressed uneasiness at this. They said that it was always dangerous to have a priest on board, as every sailor knew, and that a Bishop might prove even worse.

Orm calmed their fears, however, and assured them that everything would be all right; for, he explained, these godmen were so holy that no harm could possibly come to them, however cunningly the sea-people might contrive against them. He continued: 'When we reach Westminster, I am going to get myself baptized. I have discussed the subject thoroughly with these holy men, and they have convinced me that it is an excellent thing to worship Christ; so I intend to begin doing so as soon as possible. Now, in a ship, it is always best that everyone should be of the same mind and should follow the same customs. It is, therefore, my wish that you shall all be baptized with me. This will be to the advantage of you all. You can be certain of this, for I, who know, tell you that it will be so.

223

If any of you is unwilling to do this, let him speak up at once; but he shall leave my ship and take his belongings with him, and shall not be a follower of mine any more.'

Many of the men glanced doubtfully at each other, and scratched behind their ears; but Rapp the One-Eyed, who was the ship's helmsman, and who was feared by most of the men, was standing in front of the crew as they listened, and he nodded calmly when he heard Orm say this, having heard him speak thus on a similar occasion once before. When the others saw Rapp do this, they offered no objection.

Orm continued: 'I know that there are among you men who have already been baptized at home in Skania, perhaps receiving a shirt or a tunic for your pains, or a little cross to wear on a band round your neck. Sometimes it happens that one hears one of these men say that he cannot see that he has profited much from being baptized. But these were cheap baptisms, fit only for women and children. This time, we are going to be baptized differently, by holier men, and are going to get protection from God and better luck for the rest of our lives. It would not be a right thing that we should gain such advantages without paying for them. I myself am giving a large sum for the protection and luck that I expect to receive; and each of you shall pay a penny.'

There was murmuring at this, and some of the men were heard to say that this was a new idea, that a man should pay to be baptized, and that a penny was no small sum.

'I am not forcing anyone to do this,' said Orm. 'Anyone who thinks this suggestion unreasonable can save his money by meeting me in combat as soon as the baptizing is finished. If he wins, nobody is going to make him pay; and if he loses, he will also save his money.'

Most of the men thought that this was well spoken, and several of them challenged any member of the crew who had a mind to be close-fisted to declare himself. But the ones to whom these words were addressed grinned weakly, thinking that they would have to make the best of whatever advantages their money might bring them.

Gudmund and Orm each took one of the god-men aboard his ship, the elder Bishop and his suite going with Gudmund and the Bishop of London with Orm, who also took with him Brother

224

Willibald. The Bishops blessed their ships, prayed for a lucky voyage, and set up their standards; then the ships put out, and at once got a good breeze and fine weather, which made the men regard the Bishops with increased respect. They entered the River Thames on the flood tide, spent the night in the estuary, and next morning, in a clear dawn light, began to row up the river.

People stood at their hut doors among the trees that lined the river bank, staring at the ships fearfully, and men fishing in the river prepared to flee as the ships hove into sight; however, they were calmed by the sight of the Bishops' standards. Here and there they saw burnt villages, lying deserted after one of the Vikings' visits; then, further up, they came to a place where the river was blocked by four rows of piles, with only a channel left free in the middle. Three large watchships lay there, filled with armed men. The Vikings were forced to stop rowing, for the watch-ships stood in the midst of the channel with all their men prepared for battle, and blocked further progress.

'Are you blind?' roared Gudmund across the water, 'or have you lost your wits? Do you not see that we come with a shield of peace upon our masthead, and the holy Bishops aboard?'

'Do not try to fool us,' replied a voice from the watchships. 'We want no pirates here.'

'We have your own King's envoys aboard,' roared Gudmund.

'We know you,' came the reply. 'You are full of cunning and devilry.'

'We are coming to be baptized,' shouted Orm impatiently.

At this, there was loud laughter on the watch-ships, and a voice shouted back: 'Have you grown tired of your lord and master, the Devil?'

'Yes!' roared Orm furiously, and at this the laughter on the other ships was redoubled.

Then it looked as though there was going to be fighting, for Orm was enraged by their laughter and bade Rapp heave to and grapple the nearest ship, which was doing most of the laughing. But by this time, the Bishops had hastily donned their robes, and now, raising their staffs aloft, they cried to both sides to be still. Orm was unwilling to obey, and Gudmund, too, thought that this was asking too much. Then the Bishops cried across the water to their countrymen, addressing them sternly, so that at last they realized that the holy men were what they appeared to be, and not prisoners or pirates in disguise. So the ships were allowed to pass, and nothing came of the encounter, apart from smart exchanges of insults between the rival crews as the Vikings rowed past.

Orm stood with a spear in his hand, staring at the watch-ships, still white with wrath.

'I should have liked to teach them some manners,' he said to Brother Willibald, who was standing beside him, and who had not shown any evidence of fear when the fighting had seemed about to begin.

'He who lives by the sword shall perish by the sword,' replied the little priest. 'Thus it is written in the holy book, where all wisdom is. How could you have come to King Harald's daughter, if you had fought with King Ethelred's ships? But you are a man of violence, and will always remain one. And you will suffer sorely for it.'

Orm sighed, and threw down his spear.

'When I have won her,' he said, 'I shall be a man of peace.'

But the little priest shook his head sadly.

'Can the leopard change its spots?' he said. 'Or the blue man his skin? Thus, too, is it written in the holy book. But thank God and the blessed Bishops that they have helped you now.'

Soon they rounded a curve in the river and saw London lying before them on the right bank. It was a sight that struck the Vikings speechless with wonder, for the town was so great that, from the river, they could not see its end, and the priests told them it had been calculated that more than thirty thousand men dwelt there. Many of the Vikings found it difficult to imagine what so many men could find to live on in such a crowded place, with no fields or cattle. But the wise ones among them knew, and said, that such town-dwellers were an evil and cunning race, who understood well how to earn a livelihood from honest country-folk without themselves ever setting their hands to a plough or a flail. It was, therefore, these wise men argued, a good thing for bold sailors to pay occasional visits to these people and relieve them of what they had stolen from other folk. So they all gazed spellbound at the town as they rowed slowly up against the tide, thinking that here indeed there must be riches worth the taking.

But Orm and Rapp the One-Eyed said that they had seen bigger cities, and that this was only a village compared with Cordova.

So they rowed on towards the great bridge, which was built of huge tree-trunks, and which was so high that the biggest ships could row under it once they had lowered their masts. Many people rushed out to see them, including armed men, yelling at the tops of their voices about heathens and devils; but they broke into shouts of jubilation when they heard their Bishops cry resonantly to them that all was well, and that peace had been concluded with the men from the sea. As the ships approached, people crowded on to the bridge to catch a glimpse of them at close quarters. When the crews caught sight of several fine young women among them, they shouted enthusiastically to them to make haste and come down, promising that they would find good prizes aboard, silver and merriment and bold men, as well as plenty of priests to pardon their sins in the best Christian manner. One or two of the young women giggled coyly and answered that they had a mind to do as the men bade them, but that it was a long way to jump; whereupon they were immediately grabbed by the hair by their furious kinsfolk, who promised them the birch on their bare bodies for indulging in such lewd chatter with heathen men.

Brother Willibald shook his head sadly, and said that young people were very difficult nowadays, even in Christian communities. And Rapp, too, standing at his steering-oar, shook his head as they passed beneath the bridge, and muttered sullenly that women were always full of useless chatter, wherever you found them.

'They ought to have kept their mouths shut,' he said, 'and to have jumped at once, as they were told to do.'

They were now approaching Westminster, and could see tall spires rising up behind the trees. The Bishops clothed themselves once more in all their finery; and the priests attending them began to chant an ancient hymn, which St Columbanus had been wont to sing when baptizing heathens.

> 'Lo! Here's a host from darkness won—
> —Do not reject them, Lord!—
> Who late in need and peril spun
> Upon the sinful flood.
> To the cross which the wide world o'er hath blazed
> They lift their eyes, and Thy name is praised
> By souls which late with the Devil grazed.
> —Do not reject them, Lord!'

Their voices rang sweetly over the water in the clear evening; and as soon as the men at the oars had grasped the rhythm of the hymn, they began to pull in time to it, and voted it a fine shanty to row by.

As the singing ceased, they brought the ship to starboard, and made her fast to one of the piers beneath the red walls of Westminster.

CHAPTER THREE

Concerning marriage and baptism, and King Ethelred's silver

King Ethelred the Redeless sat miserably in Westminster, surrounded by rede-givers, waiting to hear the outcome of his negotiations with the Northmen. He had gathered all his warriors together about him, partly to protect his own person in these dangerous times, and partly to keep an eye on the people of London, who had begun to murmur somewhat after the defeat of Maldon. He had his Archbishop with him to help and comfort him, but the latter could achieve little in that direction; and the King's uneasiness had so increased, since the envoys had departed, that he had given up hunting entirely, and had lost his desire for masses and women. He spent most of his time swatting flies, at which occupation he was exceedingly skilful.

When, however, he heard that the envoys had returned, having concluded peace with the invaders, he emerged from his melancholy; and, when they told him that the chieftains and their crews had come with the Bishops to be baptized, his excitement knew no bounds. He immediately ordered all the bells in the town to be rung, and commanded that the foreigners should be entertained sumptuously; but when he heard that there were two strong ships' companies of them, he became uneasy again, and could not make up his mind whether such tidings should be regarded as excellent or calamitous. He scratched his beard earnestly, and consulted his priests, courtiers and chamberlains as to their opinions on the matter. Eventually, it was decided that the Vikings should be permitted to encamp in some fields outside the town, but should not be allowed to enter it, and that the guards on the walls should be strengthened; also, that it should be proclaimed in all the churches that the heathens were flocking to London in their multitudes in search of baptism and spiritual education, so that all the people, when they heard this, might sing praise and thanksgiving to their God and King for causing such a miracle to occur. The very next morning, he added, so soon as he had had a few hours to rest and relax after the anxiety of the past fortnight, the envoys would be granted audience; and they might bring with them the chieftains who were to be baptized.

The Northmen proceeded to their camping-ground, and the King's officers made haste to furnish them with everything that they might require, treating them like royal guests. Before long, the air was filled with the crackling of huge fires and the lowing of cattle beneath the slaughter-knife, and there was much demand for white bread, fat cheese, honey, egg-cakes, fresh pork, and ale as such kings and bishops were wont to drink. Orm's men were rowdier than Gudmund's, and more exacting in their demands, for they reckoned that, since they were about to be baptized, they had a right to the best of everything.

Orm, however, had something other than the stomachs of his men uppermost in his thoughts, being anxious to visit another part of the town with Brother Willibald, whom he refused to let out of his sight. He was wretched with anxiety lest Ylva should have come to harm, and could still hardly believe that he would find her safe and sound, despite all Brother Willibald's assurances that this would be the case. He felt certain that she had already promised herself to another, or that she had run away, or been carried off, or that the King, who was said to be much addicted to women, had noted her beauty and had taken her to be his concubine.

They passed through the city gate without hindrance, for the guards dared not oppose the entry of a foreigner accompanied by a priest, and Brother Willibald led the way to the great abbey, where Bishop Poppo was residing as the Abbot's guest. He had just returned from evensong, and looked older and thinner than when Orm had last seen him at King Harald's court, but his face lit up with pleasure when he saw Brother Willibald.

'God be praised that you have returned safely!' he said. 'You have been away for a long time, and I had begun to fear lest misfortune might have overtaken you on your journey. There is much that I wish to learn from you. But who is this man whom you have brought with you?'

'We sat at the same table in King Harald's hall,' said Orm, 'the time you told the story about the king's son who got hanged by his hair. But there were many others there besides me, and much has happened since that evening. I am called Orm Tostesson, and I have come to this land commanding my own ship under Trokel the Tall. And I have come to this place this evening to be baptized and to fetch my woman.'

'He used to be a follower of Mahomet,' put in Brother Willibald eagerly, 'but now he wishes to abandon his allegiance to the Devil. He is the man I made well after the last Christmas feast at King Harlad's, the time they fought with swords in the dining-hall before the drunken kings. It was he and his comrade who threatened Brother Matthias with spears because he tried to instruct them in Christian doctrine. But now he wishes to be baptized.'

'In the Name of the Father, the Son and the Holy Ghost!' exclaimed the Bishop in alarm. 'Has this man served Mahomet?'

'He has been purged and sprinkled by the Bishop of London,' said the little priest soothingly, 'who found no evil spirit left in him.'

'I have come to fetch Ylva, King Harald's daughter,' said Orm impatiently. 'She has been promised to me, both by herself and by King Harald.'

'Who is now dead,' said the little priest, 'leaving the heathens to war among themselves in Denmark.'

'Holy Bishop,' said Orm. 'I should dearly like to see her at once.'

'This matter cannot be settled so simply,' said the Bishop, and bade them seat themselves.

'He has come to London to be baptized, and all his crew with him, for her sake,' said Brother Willibald.

'And he has served Mahomet?' cried the Bishop. 'This is indeed a mighty miracle. God still grants me moments of felicity, even though He has seen fit to condemn me to end my days in exile with all my life's work ruined and set at naught.'

He bade his servant bring them ale, and asked for tidings of recent events in Denmark and of all that had happened at Maldon.

Brother Willibald answered him at considerable length; and Orm, despite his impatience, assisted him with such details as he was able to provide; for the Bishop was a gentle and reverend man, and Orm could not find it in himself to refuse him the information he was so eager to obtain.

When they had told the Bishop everything they knew, he turned to Orm and said: 'So now you have come to take from me my baptismal child, Ylva? It is no small ambition to seek the hand of a king's daughter. But I have heard the girl express her feelings in the matter; and she is, God witness, a person who knows her own mind!'

He shook his head, and smiled silently to himself.

'She is a charge to make an old man hasten towards his grave,' he continued, 'and if you can rule her judgment, you are a wiser man than I am, or than good King Harald was. But the Lord our God moves along mysterious paths; and, once you have been baptized, I shall not stand in your way. Indeed, her marriage would lift a heavy burden from my old shoulders.'

'We have been parted for long enough, she and I,' said Orm. 'Do not keep me from her any longer.'

The Bishop rubbed his nose uncertainly, and remarked that such zeal was understandable in a young man, but that the hour was late, and that it might perhaps be more advisable to postpone the meeting until after the baptism. However, in the end he allowed himself to be persuaded, summoned one of his deacons, and bade him rouse four men, go with them to the Lady Ermentrude, greet her from the Bishop and beg her, despite the lateness of the hour, to permit them to bring King Harald's daughter to him.

'I have done my best to keep her safe from the eyes of men,' he continued, when the deacon had left them, 'which was very necessary with a girl of her comeliness in such a place as this is, now that the King and his court and all his soldiers have taken up residence here. She is lodged with the blessed Queen Bertha's nuns, hard by this abbey; and a troublesome guest she has proved to be, despite the fact that all the nuns treat her most affectionately. Twice she has tried to escape, because, so she said, the life wearied her; and on one occasion, not so long ago, she inflamed the lust of two young men of good family, who had caught a glimpse of her in the nuns' garden and had managed to exchange words with her over the wall. Such was the passion that she aroused in them that they climbed into the convent grounds early one morning, accompanied by their servants and henchmen, and fought a duel with swords among the nuns' flower-beds to decide which of them should have the right of wooing her. They fought so desperately that, in the end, they both had to be carried away, bleeding fearfully from their wounds, while she sat at her window laughing to see such sport. Conduct of this nature is unseemly in a convent, for it may infect the pious sisters' souls and do them great harm. But I confess that her behaviour seems to me to be the result of thoughtlessness rather than of evil intentions.'

'Did they both die?' asked Orm.

'No,' replied the Bishop. 'They recovered, although their wounds were grave. I myself joined in the prayers for them. I was sick and weary at the time, and felt it a heavy burden to have such a charge upon my hands. I admonished her severely and begged her to accept the hand of one or other of the men, seeing that they had fought so desperately for her sake and were both of noble birth. I told her that I should die easier in my mind if I could see her wedded first. But, on hearing this, she fell into a frenzy, and declared that, since both the young men were still living, their duel could not have been very seriously fought, and that she would hear no more of their suits. She said she preferred the sort of man whose enemies needed no prayers or bandages after fighting. It was then that I heard her mention your name.'

The Bishop smiled benevolently at Orm, and bade him not to neglect his ale.

'I had other troubles to contend with in this affair,' he continued, 'for the Abbess, the pious Lady Ermentrude, had it in her mind to birch the girl on her bare skin for having incited these men to combat. But seeing that my poor godchild was only a guest in the convent, and a king's daughter to boot, I succeeded in dissuading her from pursuing this extreme course. It was not an easy task, for abbesses are, in general, unwilling to listen to counsel, and have little confidence in the wisdom of men, even when they happen to be bishops. However, in the end she mitigated her sentence to three days' prayer and fasting, and I think it was probably fortunate that she did so. True it is that the pious Lady Ermentrude is a woman of adamant will and no mean strength of body, being broader in the loins than most of her sex; none the less, God alone can say with certainty which of their two skins would have smarted the more had she attempted to bring the birch to King Harald's daughter. My poor godchild might have prevailed, and so have fallen even further from grace.'

'The first time she and I spoke together,' said Orm, 'it was plain to me that she had never tasted the rod, though I doubted not that she had sometimes deserved it. As I saw more of her, though, the question ceased to trouble me; and I think I shall be able to manage her, even though she may occasionally prove obstinate.'

'The wise King Solomon,' said the Bishop, 'observed that a beautiful woman who lacks discipline is like a sow with a gold ring in her snout. This may well be true, for King Solomon was knowledgeable on the subject of women; and sometimes, when her behaviour has troubled me, I have been sadly reminded of his words. On the other hand, and it has often surprised me that this is so, I have never found it easy to feel angry towards her. I like to think that her conduct reflects no more than the frenzy and intemperance of youth; and it may be that, as you say, you will be able to curb her without resorting to chastisement, even when she is your wife.'

'There is a further point worth considering,' said Brother Willibald. 'I have often observed that women tend to become more tractable after they have borne their first three or four children. Indeed, I have heard married men say that, if God had not ordered it so, the state of wedlock would not be easy to endure.'

Orm and the Bishop expressed their agreement with this observation. Then they heard footsteps approaching the door, and Ylva entered. It was dark in the Bishop's chamber, for no lamps had yet been lighted; but she straightway recognized Orm, and ran towards him crying excitedly. The Bishop, however, despite his years, sprang nimbly to his feet and placed himself between them, with his arms stretched wide.

'Not so, not so!' he cried importunately. 'In God's name, calm yourself, dear child! Enter not into lewd embraces in the sight of priests and in the sacred precincts of an abbey! Besides which, he is not yet baptized. Have you forgotten that?'

Ylva tried to push the Bishop aside, but he stood his ground manfully, and Brother Willibald ran to his assistance and seized her by the arm. She ceased struggling, and smiled happily at Orm over the Bishop's shoulder.

'Orm!' she said. 'I saw the ships row up the river, and knew that men from Denmark were aboard. Then I saw a red beard next to the helmsman of one of them, and began to weep, for it looked like you and yet I knew that it could not be you. And the old woman would not let me come to see.'

234

She rested her head upon the Bishop's shoulder, and began to shake with weeping.

Orm moved towards her, and stroked her hair, but he did not well know what to say, for he knew little about women's tears.

'I shall thrash the old woman, if you so wish it,' he said. 'Only promise me that you will not be sad.'

The Bishop tried to edge him away and to persuade Ylva to sit down, speaking soothing words to her.

'My poor child,' he said, 'do not weep. You have been alone in a foreign land among strange people, but God has been good to you. Seat yourself upon this bench, and you shall have hot wine with honey in it. Brother Willibald shall go at once to prepare it, and there shall be plenty of honey in it; and bright lights also shall be lit. And you shall taste strange nuts from the Southland, called almonds, which my good brother the Abbot has given me. You may eat as many of them as you wish to.'

Ylva seated herself, drew her arm across her face, and burst into a loud and merry peal of laughter.

'The old man is as much a fool as you are, Orm,' she said, 'though he is the best god-man I have yet come across. He thinks I am unhappy, and that he can comfort me with nuts. But even in his Kingdom of Heaven, I do not think there can be many people who are as full of joy as I am at this moment.'

Wax candles were brought in, fair and gleaming, and Brother Willibald followed with the mulled wine. He poured it out into a beaker of green glass, announcing as he did so that it must be drunk at once for its strength and flavour to be fully appreciated; and none of them dared to say that it should be otherwise.

Orm said:

> 'Fair the glow
> Of gleaming candles,
> Roman glass
> And god-men's goodness.
> Fairer yet
> The glow that gleams
> Though the tears
> Of virgin eyes.'

'And that,' he added, 'is the first verse that has come to my lips for many a long day.'

'Were I a poet,' said Ylva, 'I, too, should dearly love to make a verse to enshrine this moment. But alas, I cannot. This I know well, for, when the old Abbess condemned me to spend three days in prayer and fasting, I spent the whole time trying to compose lampoons about her. But I could not, although my father had on occasion tried to teach me the craft, when he was in one of his forthcoming moods. He could not compose verses himself, but he knew how it should be done. And that was the worst part of my punishment, that I was unable to compose a single verse to indict the crone who set me there. But it is all one now, for I shall not be ruled by old women any more.'

'That you shall not,' replied Orm.

There was much besides that he wished to learn from her; so she and the Bishop told him all that had happened during their last days in Denmark, and about their flight from King Sven.

'But one thing I have to confess to you,' said Ylva. 'When Sven was almost upon us, and I did not know whether I should manage to escape his clutches, I hid the necklace. For, above all things, I wanted to prevent that from falling into his hands. And I had no time to get it back before we boarded the ship. I know this news will grieve you, Orm, but I could not think of anything else to do.'

'I would rather have you without the necklace than the necklace without you,' he replied. 'But it is a jewel of royal worth, and I fear you will feel its loss more deeply than I shall. Where did you hide it?'

'That, at least, I can tell you,' she said, 'for I think there is nobody here who will betray the secret. A short way from the great gate of the palace, there is a small rise, covered with heather and juniper, just to the right of the path below the bridge. On that rise, there are three large stones lying together in the undergrowth. Two of them are large, and are buried deep in the ground, so that they are scarcely visible. The third lies balanced on top of them, and is not so heavy but that I managed to shift it. I wrapped the necklace in a cloth, and the cloth in a skin, and put them beneath this stone. It was a hard thing for me to have to leave it there, for it was the only keepsake I had by which to remember you. But I think it must still be lying there safely, more so than if it had accompanied me to this foreign land, for no man ever goes near that place, nor even cattle.'

'I know those stones,' said Brother Willibald. 'I used to go there to gather wild thyme and cat's-foot against the heartburn.'

'It may prove to be a lucky chance that you hid it outside the rampart,' said Orm, 'though I fear it will be a difficult enough task to fetch it from its present hiding-place, so near as it is to the wolf's lair.'

Now that Ylva had eased her mind of this burden, her heart was lightened. She flung her arms round the Bishop's neck, squeezed almonds into his mouth, and begged him to bless them and marry them there and then. But this suggestion so horrified the Bishop that he got an almond lodged in his windpipe, and waved his hands in dismay.

'I am of the same mind as the woman,' said Orm. 'God himself saw to it that we should meet again, and we do not intend to part any more.'

'You do not know what you are saying,' protested the Bishop. 'Such ideas are the devil's prompting.'

'I will not return to the crone,' said Ylva, 'and I cannot stay here. I shall go with Orm in any case, and it will be better if you wed us first.'

'He is not yet baptized!' cried the Bishop in despair. 'Dear child, how can I marry you to a heathen? It is a scandalous thing to see a young girl so hot with lust. Have you never been taught the meaning of modesty.'

'No,' replied Ylva without hesitation. 'My father taught me many things, but modesty was something of which he knew little. But how can there be any harm in my wishing to get married?'

Orm took from his belt six gold pieces, which remained from the small hoard which he had brought home from Andalusia, and laid them on the table before the Bishop.

'I am already paying one Bishop to baptize me,' he said, 'and I am not so poor but that I can afford another to marry me. If you speak well of me to God, and buy candles for His church out of this money, I do not think he will mind if I get married first and baptized later.'

'He has the blood of Broad-Hug in his veins,' said Ylva proudly, 'and if you have any scruples about marrying an unbaptized man, why do you not baptize him yourself here and now? Bid your servants bring water, and sprinkle him as you used to sprinkle the sick in Denmark. What matter if he gets baptized again later, with the others before the King? Twice cannot be worse than once.'

'The sacrament must not be abused,' said the Bishop, chidingly, 'and I do not know if he is yet ready to receive it.'

'He is ready,' said Brother Willibald. 'And he might perhaps receive provisional baptism, though that is a ceremony which is seldom performed nowadays. It is lawful for a Christian woman to marry a man who has been provisionally baptized.'

Orm and Ylva looked admiringly at Brother Willibald, and the Bishop clasped his hands together and his face grew less troubled.

'Old age has clouded my powers of memory,' he said, 'unless it is this good wine that has done it, though its effect is, in general, salutary. In ancient times, it was a common practice for men who were not prepared to allow themselves to be baptized, but who yet held Christ in honour, to be provisionally baptized. It is lucky for all of us that we have Brother Willibald here to remind us of these things.'

'I have felt friendly towards him for some time,' said Orm, 'and now he stands even higher in my affection. From the very first moment that I met him after the battle, my luck turned for the better.'

The Bishop straightway sent a messenger to summon the abbot and two of his canons, who came readily to help him perform the rite, and to see this foreign chieftain. When the Bishop had robed himself, he dipped his hand in holy water and made the sign of the cross over Orm, touching him on the forehead, the breast and the hands, the while pronouncing blessings upon him.

'I must be growing used to this,' said Orm, when the Bishop had finished, 'for this frightened me much less than when the other fellow sprinkled me with the branch.'

All the churchmen agreed that an unbaptized man could not be married in the abbey chapel, but that the ceremony might take place in the Bishop's chamber. So Orm and Ylva were told to kneel before the Bishop, on two hassocks which were provided for them.

'This is a posture I do not think you are used to,' said Ylva.

'I have spent more time than most men on my knees,' replied Orm, 'in the days when I used to serve Mahomet. But it is a good thing not to have beat my brow against the floor!'

When the Bishop came to the part of the service in which he had to exhort them to multiply and to dwell together in peace for the remainder of their days, they nodded their affirmation. But when he commanded Ylva to obey her husband in everything, they looked doubtfully at one another.

'I shall do my best,' said Ylva.

'It will be hard for her at first,' said Orm, 'for she is not accustomed to obedience. But I will remind her of these words of yours if ever they should slip her memory.'

When the ceremony had been completed, and all the churchmen had wished them good luck and many children, it occurred to the Bishop to worry about where they were to spend their bridal night. For there was no room available in the abbey, nor in the houses adjoining it, and he knew of no place in the city where they might find lodgings.

'I will go with Orm,' said Ylva contentedly. 'What is good enough for him will be good enough for me.'

'You cannot lie with him by the camp-fires, among all the other men,' exclaimed the Bishop in alarm.

But Orm said:

> 'The voyager,
> Heir to the sea,
> The good plougher
> Of the auk-bird's meadow,
> Hath a bridal bed
> For his royal spouse
> Better than straw
> Or cushioned couches.'

Brother Willibald accompanied them as far as the city gate, to make sure that the guards allowed them to pass through the postern. There they parted from him, with many expressions of gratitude, and made their way down to the pier where the ships lay. Rapp had left two men on board, to guard against thieves. These men, left to their own devices, had drunk deeply, so that the sound of their sleeping was audible from a good distance. Orm shook them awake, and bade them help him pull the ship into midstream; which, although they were still befuddled, they succeeded at last in doing.

239

Then they dropped anchor, and the ship stood swaying upon the tide.

'I have no further need of you now,' he said to the two men.

'How shall we get ashore?' they asked.

'It is not far for a bold man to swim,' he replied.

They both complained that they were drunk, and that the water was cold.

'I am not in a waiting mood,' said Orm; and with those words, he picked one of them up by the neck and belt and tossed him head first into the river, whereupon the other promptly followed suit, without further ado. From the darkness echoed back the sounds of their coughing and sneezing as they splashed their way towards the bank.

'I do not think anyone will disturb us now,' said Orm.

'This is a bridal bed that I shall not complain of,' said Ylva.

It was late that night before they closed their eyes; but when at last they did so, they slept well.

When, next day, the envoys appeared before King Ethelred with Gudmund and Orm, they found the King in an excellent humour. After bidding them a warm welcome, he praised the chieftains for their zeal to be baptized, and asked whether they were enjoying their sojourn at Westminster. Gudmund had occupied the night with a tremendous drinking bout, the effects of which were still noticeable in his speech, so that he and Orm both felt honestly able to reply that they were.

The Bishops began by relating the outcome of their mission and giving details of the agreement they had reached with the Vikings, while everyone in the hall hung upon their words. The King was seated on a throne beneath a canopy, with his crown upon his head and his sceptre in his hand. Orm thought that this was a new sort of monarch to see after Almansur and King Harald. He was a tall man, of dignified appearance, swathed in a velvet cloak, and pale-complexioned, with a sparse brown beard and large eyes.

When the Bishops named the amount of silver that they had promised the Vikings, King Ethelred smote the arm of his throne violently with his sceptre, whereupon all the gathering in the hall rose to their feet.

'Look!' he exclaimed to the Archbishop, who was seated by his side on a lower chair. 'Four flies at a single blow! And yet this is but poorly shaped for the work.'

The Archbishop said he thought there were not many kings in the world who could have performed such a feat, and that it testified both to his dexterity and to the excellence of his luck. The King nodded delightedly; then, the envoys proceeded with their narration, and everybody began again to listen to them.

When at last they had concluded, the King thanked them, and praised the wisdom and zeal that they had displayed. He asked the Archbishop what he thought the general reaction to the settlement would be. The Archbishop replied that the sum that the Bishops had named would, indeed, be a heavy burden for the land to bear, but that it was, beyond doubt, the best solution of a difficult situation; to which the King nodded his agreement.

'It is, moreover, a good thing,' continued the Archbishop, 'a joy to all Christian folk and highly pleasing to the Lord our God that our pious envoys have succeeded in winning these great war-chieftains and many of their followers over to the army of Christ. Let us not forget to rejoice at this.'

'By no means,' said King Ethelred.

The Bishop of London murmured to Gudmund that it was now his turn to speak, and Gudmund willingly stepped forward. He thanked the King for the hospitality and generosity which he had shown them, and informed him that his fame would, hereafter, stretch as far as the most distant villages of East Guteland, if not further still. But, he went on, there was one thing that he was anxious to know, namely, how long it would be before the silver was actually placed in their hands.

The King regarded him closely while he was speaking and, when he had concluded, asked him what the scar on his face might signify.

Gudmund replied that it was a wound he had received from a bear which he had once attacked rather thoughtlessly, allowing the bear to break the shaft of the spear which he had driven into its chest and then maul him with its claws before he at last managed to fell it with his axe.

King Ethelred's face clouded with sympathy as he listened to the story of this unfortunate incident.

'We have no bears in this land,' he said, 'much to our loss. But my brother, King Hugo of Frankland, has lately sent me two bears

241

which know how to dance, and thereby give us great pleasure. I should have liked to show them to you, but unfortunately my best trainer marched away with Byrhtnoth and was slain by you in the battle. I miss him greatly, for when other men try to make them dance, they move but sluggishly or not at all.'

Gudmund agreed that this was a great misfortune.

'But all men have their worries,' he said, 'and ours is: "When are we going to get the silver?"'

King Ethelred scratched his beard and glanced at the Archbishop.

'You have asked for a considerable sum,' said the Archbishop, 'and not even great King Ethelred has that amount in his coffers. We shall have to despatch messengers throughout the land to collect the balance. This may take two months, or even three.'

Gudmund shook his head at this.

'You must help me now, Skanian,' he said to Orm, 'for we cannot wait as long as that; but I have talked myself dry in the mouth.'

Orm stepper forward, and said that he was young, and poorly qualified to speak before so great a monarch and so wise an assembly, but that he would explain the case as well as he was able.

'It is no small matter,' he said, 'to make chieftains and soldiers wait so long for what has been promised to them. For they are men who quickly change their moods and are little inclined towards meekness, and it sometimes happens that they grow weary of the tedium of waiting when they are still hot with the flush of victory and know that good plunder lies ready for them to gather whithersoever they choose to turn. This Gudmund, whom you see here, is a mild and merry man as long as he is content with the way things are going, but when he is angry the boldest chieftains of the Eastern Sea quake at his approach, and neither man nor bear can withstand his fury. And he has berserks among his followers who are scarcely less fearful than he.'

All the assembly looked at Gudmund, who went red in the face and cleared his throat. Orm continued: 'Thorkel and Jostein are men of similar mettle, and their followers are fully as ferocious as Gudmund's. Therefore, I would suggest that half the sum due to us should be paid immediately. This will enable us to wait more patiently until the balance has been collected.'

The King nodded his head, glanced at the Archbishop, and nodded again.

'And since,' continued Orm, 'both God and yourself, King Ethelred, find it a cause for rejoicing that so many of us have come up to Westminster to be baptized, it might perhaps be a wise thing to allow all such converts to receive their share here and now. If this should happen, many of our comrades might be driven to wonder whether it would not be beneficial to their souls, also, that they should become Christians.'

Gudmund declared in a loud voice that these words exactly expressed his own feelings on the matter.

'If you do as he suggests,' he added, 'I can promise you that every follower of mine who is encamped outside this town will become a Christian at the same time as I do.'

The Archbishop said that this was capital news, and promised that skilled instructors would be sent immediately to prepare the men for conversion. It was then agreed that all the Vikings who had come to London should receive their share of the silver as soon as they had been baptized, and that the army at Maldon should have a third of its silver despatched without delay, the balance to follow in six weeks.

When the meeting had concluded and they had left the hall, Gudmund thanked Orm warmly for the help the latter had given him.

'I have never heard wiser words issue from the mouth of so young a man,' he said. 'There is no doubt that you were born to be a chieftain. It will be very advantageous to me to get my silver now, for I have the feeling that some of those who are going to wait till later may experience some difficulty in obtaining their full amount. I do not intend that you shall go unrewarded for this service; so, when I receive my share, five marks of it shall be yours.'

'I have observed,' replied Orm, 'that, despite the measure of your wisdom, you are in some ways an excessively modest man. If you were a common or petty chieftain, with five or six ships and no name to speak of, five marks might be regarded as a proper sum to offer me for the service I have rendered you. But, seeing that your fame stretches far beyond the frontiers of Sweden, it ill befits you to offer me so niggardly a sum, and it would ill befit me to accept it. For if this were to become known, your good name might suffer.'

'It is possible that you are right in what you say,' said Gudmund doubtfully. 'How much would you give if you were in my place?'

243

'I have known men who would have given fifteen marks in return for such a service,' said Orm. 'Styrbjörn would have given no less; and Thorkel would give twelve. On the other hand, I know some men who would not give anything. But I have no wish to sway your own judgment in this matter; and, whatever the outcome, we shall remain good friends.'

'It is not easy for a man to be sure just how famous he is,' said Gudmund, troubled, and he went his way, buried in calculation.

The following Sunday, they were all baptized in the great church. Most of the priests were anxious that the ceremony should be performed in the river, as had been customary in former times when heathens were baptized in London; but both Gudmund and Orm asserted vigorously that there was to be no immersion as far as they were concerned. The two chieftains walked at the head of the procession, with their heads bared, wearing long white cloaks with a red cross sewn on the front of each; and their men followed, also wearing white cloaks, as many as there were enough for in so large a company. All of them carried their weapons, for Orm and Gudmund had explained that they seldom liked to be parted from their swords, and least of all when they were in a foreign land. The king himself sat in the choir, and the church was thronged with people. Ylva was among the congregation. Orm was unwilling to let her show herself in public, for she now appeared to him more beautiful than ever, and he feared lest someone might steal her away. But she had insisted on coming to the church, because, she said, she was curious to see how reverently Orm would conduct himself when the cold water started running down his neck. She sat next to Brother Willibald, who kept a close eye on her and restrained her when she would have laughed at the white cloaks; and Bishop Poppo was also present, and assisted with the rites, though he felt exceedingly feeble. He himself baptized Orm, and the Bishop of London Gudmund; then six priests took over from them and baptized the rest of the Vikings as expeditiously as possible.

When the ceremony was over, Gudmund and Orm were received privately by the King. He gave each of them a gold ring, and expressed the hope that God would bless all their future enterprises; also, he said, he trusted that they would, in the near future, come and see his bears, which had now begun to show a marked improvement in their dancing.

The next day, the silver was paid out by the King's scribes and treasurers to all the baptized men, which caused great jubilation among them. Orm's men were somewhat less jubilant than the others, because each of them had to pay his chieftain a penny; none of them, however, chose the less expensive alternative of challenging him to combat.

'With the help of these contributions, I shall build a church in Skania,' said Orm, as he stowed the money safely away in his chest.

Then he put fifteen marks in a purse, and went with it to the Bishop of London, who, in return, bestowed a special blessing upon him. Later that afternoon, Gudmund came aboard carrying the same purse in his hand, very drunk and in capital spirits. He said that all his share of the money had now been counted and stored away, and that, all in all, it had been an excellent day's work.

'I have been thinking over what you said the other day,' he continued, 'and I have come to the conclusion that you were right in saying that five marks would be too paltry a sum for a man of my reputation to give you as a reward for the service you rendered me. Take, instead, these fifteen marks. Now that Styrbjörn is dead, I do not think I can be valued at less.'

Orm said that such generosity was more than he could have anticipated; however, he said, he would not refuse such a gift, seeing that it came from the hand of so great a man. In return, he gave Gudmund his Andalusian shield, the same with which he had fought Sigtrygg in King Harald's hall.

Ylva said she was glad to see that Orm had a good head for collecting silver, for it was not a task at which she would shine, and she thought it likely that they would have a good number of mouths to care for in the years to come.

That evening, Orm and Ylva visited Bishop Poppo, and bade him farewell; for they were eager to sail for home as soon as possible. Ylva wept, for she found it hard to part from the Bishop, whom she called her second father: and his eyes, too, filled with tears.

'Were I less feeble,' he said, 'I would come with you, for I think I could, even now, perform some useful work in Skania, old as I am. But these poor bones can endure no further hardships.'

'You have a good servant in Willibald,' said Orm, 'and both Ylva and I delight in his company. Perhaps he could come with us, if you yourself cannot, to fortify us in our beliefs, and to persuade others to do as we have done. Though I fear he is not greatly enamoured of us Northmen.'

The Bishop said that Willibald was the wisest of his priests, and a most zealous worker.

'I know of nobody more skilful at converting heathens,' he said, 'though, in his own zealous enthusiasm, he is occasionally prone to be somewhat uncharitable towards the sins and weaknesses of others. I think it best that we should ask him his own feelings in the matter; for I do not wish to send an unwilling priest with you.'

Brother Willibald was summoned, and the Bishop informed him what they had in mind. Brother Willibald asked, in vexed tones, when they were intending to sail. Orm replied that he wished to depart on the morrow, if the wind remained favourable.

Brother Willibald shook his head gloomily.

'It is ungracious of you to give me so little time to prepare myself,' he said. 'I must take many salves and medicines with me when I depart for the shores of night and violence. But with God's good help, and if I make haste, everything shall be ready; for I am loth to be parted from you young people.'

CHAPTER FOUR

How Brother Willibald taught King Sven a maxim from the scriptures

Orm went to Gudmund and bade him greet Thorkel from him and tell him that he would not be rejoining the army, as he was sailing for home. Gudmund was grieved at this news, and tried to persuade him to change his mind; but Orm said that his recent luck had been too good to last much longer.

'I have nothing more to perform in this land,' he said, 'and, if you had such a woman as Ylva with you, would you house her among an army of idle soldiers whose tongues slobber out of their mouths at every woman they see? My sword would never be in its sheath, and it is my wish to live with her in peace. And that is her wish also.'

Gudmund admitted that Ylva was a woman fit to tempt any man who caught the briefest glimpse of her to wander from the path of discretion. He himself, he added, would like, if he could, to sail home to Bravik without further delay, for it made him uneasy to have so much silver about him. But this he could not do, for he must return to the rest of his men whom he had left at Maldon and must, besides, tell Thorkel and Jostein what agreement they had come to regarding the distribution of the silver.

'My men here are being plundered by quick-witted women,' he said, 'who swarm like flies round their silver, and steal it from their very belts and breeches, once they have made them sufficiently drunk. Therefore, I think it best that I should row down the river with you to-day, if I can get my crew assembled in time.'

They went to King Ethelred and his Archbishop to bid them farewell, and saw the bears dance miraculously on their hind-legs. Then they ordered the horns to be blown, and the men took their places at the oars, where many of them performed very clumsily at first as the result of fatigue and drunkenness. They made swift progress down the river, however, and this time the watch-ships did not bar their path, though there was a lively exchange of repartee between the crews. They spent the night at anchor in the estuary. Then Gudmund and Orm parted, and went their separate ways.

Ylva was a good sailor; nevertheless, she hoped that the sea voyage would not take too long for she found it very cramped in the ship. Orm comforted her by assuring her that the weather was usually good at this time of the year, and would not be likely to delay them.

'The only detour we shall need to make,' he said, 'will be to a certain hill near Jellinge; and that should not take us long.'

Ylva was not sure whether it would be a wise thing to regain the necklace now since nobody knew what the situation was in Jutland nor even who sat upon the throne at Jellinge. But Orm said that he wanted to get this business settled by the time he reached home.

'And, whoever sits at Jellinge,' he added, 'whether it be King Sven, or King Erik, I do not think it likely that we shall find him there at this time of the year when all kings like to fight. We will steal ashore at night and, if all goes well, nobody need know that we have come.'

Brother Willibald enjoyed being at sea, though it disappointed him that nobody fell ill during the voyage. He liked especially to squat beside Rapp when the latter was at the steering-oar, and to ply him with questions concerning the Southland and the adventures he had had there; and, although Rapp was somewhat scant in his replies, these two seemed to be becoming good friends.

They rounded the Jutland cape and headed southwards, encountering no other ships; but then the wind turned against them, so that they had much hard rowing to do, and on one occasion they had to seek the shelter of the coast and wait for the gale to lessen. It was night as they rowed up towards the mouth of the river below Jellinge, but the sky had already begun to grow green with dawn when Orm finally beached the ship, some distance below the castle. He told Brother Willibald, Rapp, and two good men from the crew to follow him; but he bade Ylva remain on board. She was unwilling to obey, but he said that it was to be so.

'In such matters as this, it is I who shall decide,' he said, 'whatever may be the case later. Brother Willibald knows the place as well as you do; and, if we should encounter anyone, and there should be fighting, which is possible now that it is growing light, it will be better that you should be here. We shall not be gone for long.'

They walked up from the beach in the direction of the castle, proceeding across the fields that lay on its southern side. Brother Willibald was just remarking that they had almost reached the place when suddenly, they heard the tramp of feet and men's voices coming from the bridge away to their left, and saw a herd of cattle approaching them, driven by several men.

'It will be safest to kill these fellows,' said Rapp weighing a spear in his hand.

But Brother Willibald grabbed him by the arm and forbade him vehemently to use any violence towards men who had done him no harm. Orm agreed, and said that, if they made haste there should be no need for bloodshed.

So they began to run towards the rise. The cowherds stopped and stared at them in amazement.

'Whose men are you?' they shouted.

'King Harald's,' replied Orm.

'The little priest!' shrieked one of the herdsmen. 'It is the little priest who used to attend King Harald! These men are enemies! Run and rouse the castle!'

Rapp and the two men with him sprang immediately in pursuit of the herdsmen, but the catttle blocked their path, so that the others got a good lead. Meanwhile, Orm ran to the rise with Brother Willibald, who at once showed him the place where the three stones lay. Orm heaved the topmost one aside; and there, beneath it, lay the necklace, just as Ylva had hidden it.

'Now we shall have to show our paces,' he said, as he thrust it into his shirt.

Shouts and alarms could now be heard from the castle; and, when they reached Rapp and his men, they found him cursing himself for having failed to stop the herdsmen from giving the alarm. In his anger, he had flung his spear at one of them, who, as a result, was now lying outside the great gate.

'But it served little purpose,' he said, 'and now I have lost a good spear.'

They raced as fast as they could across the fields towards the ship. Very soon, however, they heard loud whoops behind them, and the pounding of hoofs. Rapp was a sharp-sighted man with his one eye, and he and Orm glanced back over their shoulders as they ran.

'Here comes King Sven himself,' muttered Orm. 'That is no mean honour.'

'And in a hurry,' said Rapp, 'for he has forgotten to plait his beard.'

Brother Willibald was not so young as the others: nevertheless, he sprinted along nimbly with his cassock lifted high above his knees.

'Now is your chance!' cried Orm. 'Mark them with your spears!'

As he spoke, he stopped in his tracks, turned and flung his spear at the foremost of the pursuers, a man on a big horse who was galloping just in front of King Sven. When the man saw the spear winging towards him, he pulled his horse back on to its hind legs. The spear buried itself deeply in the animal's chest, causing it to topple forwards and roll over, crushing its rider beneath it. Rapp's men cast their spears at King Sven, but failed to hit him; and now he was almost upon them, and they had no spears left with which to defend themselves.

Brother Willibald bent down, picked up a large stone, and flung it with all his might.

'Love thy neighbours,' he grunted as it left his hand.

The stone struck King Sven full on the mouth with a loud smack. With a howl of agony, he crumpled up on to the horse's mane, and slithered to the ground.

'That is what I call a good priest,' said Rapp.

The rest of the pursuers crowded round King Sven where he lay on the ground, so that Orm and his men managed to reach the ship unscathed, though somewhat short of breath. Orm cried to the rowers to begin pulling at once, while he and the others were still wading out from the shore. They were dragged aboard, and had come a good way from the shore before the first horseman appeared at the water's edge. The wind had sprung up again in the grey dawn twilight, and was favourable to them, so that, using both sail and oars, they managed to come swiftly out into the sea.

Orm gave the necklace to Ylva, and told her of all that had

happened to them; and even Rapp was less scant of speech than usual, as he praised the excellence of the little priest's throw.

'I hope he felt it,' said Ylva.

'There was blood on his mouth as he fell,' said Rapp. 'I saw it clearly.'

'Little priest,' said Ylva, 'I have a mind to kiss you for striking that blow.'

Orm laughed.

'That is what I have always been most afraid of,' he said, 'that you would become enamoured of priests in your piety.'

Brother Willibald protested vehemently that he had had no wish to be kissed: nevertheless, he appeared to be not altogether displeased at the praises which were being showered upon him.

'That kiss that King Sven received, he will not soon forget,' said Orm, 'and it is not his habit to leave such things unavenged. When we reach home, if we do so safely, my mother will have to pack with speed, for I think it will be safest for us to depart into the forests, where no king ventures. And there I shall build my church.'

And of Orm's subsequent adventures, in the forest country far north towards the border, the story also shall be told; of his zeal for Christianity, and Brother Willibald's triumphs of conversion; of the opposition they encountered from the Smalanders, and their feuds with them; and of how the wild oxen returned to the land.

PART THREE

In the Border Country

CHAPTER ONE

How Orm built his house and church, and how they named his red-haired daughters

Three years had passed since Orm, after selling in haste his father's house on the Mound in order to flee from the wrath of King Sven, had toiled up to the border country with all his household, his wife and mother, his servants and his little priest, his horses and cattle and as much silver and valuables as his beasts could carry. The estate which Asa had inherited from her father in the border country was called Gröning; but it had, for some years now, been a neglected wilderness of sagging roofs and overgrown fields, inhabited only by an ancient and infirm bailiff, his wife, and a gaggle of scrawny geese. Orm found little to be enthusiastic about when he saw the place, and thought it a poor homestead for a man of his quality and for a woman who was King Harald's daughter; and Asa ran to and fro weeping and calling to God in her misery, and inveighing violently against the old couple; for she had not visited the place since the days when she had been a girl and her father had lived there in wealth and prosperity, before he and his two sons had been killed in a feud.

But Ylva was contented; for here, she said, they would be safe from King Sven and his ruffianly following.

'This is a place that will suit me well enough,' she said to Orm, 'if you can prove yourself as skilful at house-building as you have shown yourself to be at fighting and handling a ship.'

Their first winter there they fared meagrely, for there was little food for man or beast, and they found their neighbours hostile. Orm sent men to a thane of the district, Gudmund of Uvaberg, whom men called Gudmund the Thunderer, and who was famed for his wealth and pugnacity, to buy hay and hops; but the men returned to Orm empty-handed, having received short shrift, for a newcomer to the border who was a follower of Christ to boot did not appear to Gudmund to be worthy of his notice. Then Orm saddled his horse and set forth with One-Eyed Rapp and three other good men. They arrived at Uvaberg a little before dawn. He succeeded without much difficulty in gaining entry to Gudmund's house, picked him out of his bed, carried him out through his own front door, and dangled him by one leg over his own well, while Rapp and the others set their backs against the door that the people in the house might not disturb their parley. After Orm and Gudmund had argued the matter for a while over the mouth of the well, a bargain was concluded between them by which Orm was to receive all the hay and hops he required at a fair price; whereupon Orm turned him right ways up again and set him upon his feet, pleased at having been able to settle the transaction without being forced to resort to violence.

The Thunderer's wrath, though considerable, was equalled by the respect in which he now held Orm, and was a good deal less than his astonishment at finding himself alive.

'For, you must know,' he said, 'that I am a dangerous man, even though you are somewhat larger of frame and may, therefore, have to wait a while before you sample the flavour of my wrath. Few men would have dared to let me escape alive after serving me as you have done; indeed, I hardly know if I myself would have been bold enough to do so, had I been in your trousers. But perhaps your wisdom is not commensurate with your strength.'

'I am wiser than you,' said Orm, 'for I am a follower of Christ, and therefore possess His wisdom in addition to my own. It is His wish that a man shall be gentle unto his neighbour, even though that neighbour should do him mischief. So, if you are sensible, you will go on your knees and thank Him; for your well looked to me to be somewhat deep. But if it is your wish that we two should be enemies, you will find that I can be wise in more ways than one; for I have encountered more dangerous adversaries than you, and no man has yet worsted me.'

Gudmund said that he would have to endure much mockery for the indignity that he had been forced to undergo, and that his good name would suffer in consequence; besides which, his leg had been painfully stretched by having to support his weight over the well.

As he was speaking, the news was brought to him that one of his men, who had rushed at Orm with a sword as the latter was carrying Gudmund out of the house, was now being tended by the women for a broken shoulder which Rapp had given him with the blunt edge of his axe. Gudmund then asked what the attitude of Orm and Christ might be to this piece of information, and whether they thought that such an aggregate of injury and insult was not worth some compensation.

Orm pondered this problem for a while. Then he replied that the man whose shoulder had been broken had only himself to blame for his injury, and that he would give him nothing.

'It was lucky for the foolish fellow,' he said, 'that Rapp is as devout a believer in Christian principles as I am; otherwise the man would not now require any attention from your women. He should count himself fortunate to have escaped so lightly. But as regards the injury and insult that you claim to have suffered, I think there is some justice in what you say, and I shall give you compensation. If you will accompany me, I shall introduce you to a holy doctor who is a member of my household at Gröning. He is the cleverest physician in the world, and will speedily cure the pain in your leg; indeed, so holy is he that, after he has treated it, you will find it sounder than its fellow. And it will greatly add to your honour, and to the respect in which your name is held, when it becomes known that you have been attended by a man who was, for a long period, King Harald's personal physician, and treated him for the many ailments from which he suffered, and cured them all marvellously.'

They argued about this at some length, but in the end Gudmund agreed to ride back with Orm to Gröning. There, Father Willibald applied soothing salves to the leg, and swathed it in bandages, while Gudmund plied him eagerly with questions about King Harald; but when the priest tried to tell him about Christ and the advantages of baptism, he became very violent, and told him that he could keep his mouth shut upon that subject. For, he roared, if it became known that he had fallen a victim to such nonsense, it would damage his reputation worse than the news of his suspension over the well, and men would never cease to laugh at him. It was a poor thing, he concluded deafeningly, that anyone should hold so low an opinion of his intelligence as to suppose him capable of being gulled by such foolish prattle.

As he took his leave of Orm, having received payment for his hay and hops, he said: 'It is not my wish that there should be a blood-feud between our houses; but, if the opportunity should arise for me to repay the insult that you have inflicted upon me, be sure that I shall not neglect it. It may be some time before such an opportunity will present itself; but I am a man whose memory is long.'

Orm looked at him, and smiled.

'I know you to be a dangerous man,' he said, 'for you yourself have told me so. Nevertheless, I do not think this vow of yours will cause me to lie awake at night. But know this, that if you attempt to do me a mischief, I shall baptize you, whether I have to hold you by the legs or by the ears to do so.'

Father Willibald was dejected by his failure to convert Gudmund, and declared himself convinced that his work in the north was doomed to failure. Ylva, however, comforted him with the assurance that things would be easier once Orm had built his church. Orm said that he would, in good time, fulfil his promise to do this, but that his more immediate concern was to build himself a house; and this, he vowed, he would start work on immediately. He straightway applied himself earnestly to the task, sending his men into the forest to fell trees, lop them, and drag them back, whereupon he himself chopped them into lengths with his axe. He chose his wood most meticulously, using only thick trunks that had no flaw in them: for he intended, he said, that his house should be of fine appearance and built to endure, and no mere forest shack. Asa's estate comprised the land that lay in a bend of the river, protected by water on three sides; the soil was firm, and not liable to flooding. There was room here for all that he wished to build, and he enjoyed the work so much that, the further it became advanced, the more ambitiously he began to plan. He built his house with a walled fireplace and a slide-board in the roof for the smoke to leave by, the same as he had seen in King Harald's castle; and the roof itself he constructed of peeled ash saplings, surmounted by a layer of birch bark and thick turves. Then he built a brewhouse, a cattle-shed and a store-house, all amply proportioned, and finer than any that had previously been seen in these parts; and at last, when all these were completed, he announced that the most important buildings were now ready, and that he would shortly be able to begin thinking about his church.

That spring, the time arrived for Ylva's confinement. Both Asa and Father Willibald took busy charge of her; they had a deal to do, and fell over one another in their eagerness to ensure that nothing might be left undone. The confinement was a difficult one. Ylva screamed fearfully, vowing that it would be preferable to enter a convent and become a nun than to endure such pain; but Father Willibald laid his crucifix upon her belly and muttered priest-talk over her, and in the end everything went as it should, and she was delivered of twins. They were both girls, which was, at first, a disappointment to Asa and Ylva; but when they were brought to Orm and laid upon his knees, he found little cause for complaint. Everyone agreed that they had bawled and struggled as vigorously as any man-children; and, once Ylva had accepted that they were girls, and could never become boys, she regained her cheerfulness, and promised Orm that, next time, she would give him a son. It soon became evident that both the girls were going to be red-haired, which Orm feared might bode ill for them; for, he said, if they had inherited the colour of his hair, they might also develop a facial resemblance to him, and he was reluctant that his daughters should be condemned to such a fate as that. But Asa and Ylva bade him desist from such unlucky prophesying; there was no reason, they said, to suppose that they would look like him, and it was by no means disadvantageous for a girl to be born with red hair.

When the question arose of what names to give them, Orm declared that one of them must be called Oddny, after his maternal grandmother, which greatly delighted Asa.

'But we must name her sister after some member of your family,' he told Ylva, 'and that you must choose yourself.'

'It is difficult to be sure which name will bring her the most luck,' said Ylva. 'My mother was a war captive, and died when I was seven years old. She was called Ludmilla, and was daughter to a chieftain of the Obotrites; and she was stolen away by force from her own wedding. For all warriors who have visited that country agree that the best time to attack Obotrites or any other Wendish people is when they are celebrating some great wedding, because then they are drunk, and lack their usual skill at arms, and their watchmen lie sleeping because of the great strength of the mead they brew for such occasions, so that rich booty can then be secured without much exertion, both in the form of treasure and of young women. I have never seen a woman as beautiful as she was; and my father always used to say that her luck was good, although she died young, for, three whole years, she remained his favourite wife; and it was no small thing for an Obotrite woman, he used to say, to be permitted into the bed of the King of the Danes and bear him a daughter. Though, it may be that she herself had other feelings concerning this, for, after she was dead, I heard her slave-girls whispering among themselves that, shortly after her arrival in Denmark, she had tried to hang herself; which they thought arose from the fact of her having seen her bridegroom killed before her eyes when they had taken her and were carrying her away to the ships. She loved me very tenderly, but I cannot be sure whether it would be a lucky thing to name the child after her.'

Asa said that such a thing must not be thought of, for there could be no worse luck than being carried away by foreign warriors, and if they gave the child her grandmother's name the same fate might befall her.

But Orm said that the problem could not be settled as easily as that.

'For I myself was stolen away by warriors,' he said, 'but I do not reckon that to have been an unlucky thing for me; for, if that had not happened, I should not have become the man I am, and would never have won my sword nor my gold chain, nor Ylva neither. And if Ludmilla had not been stolen away, King Harald would not have begotten the daughter who now shares my bed.'

They found it difficult to make up their minds about this, for, although Ylva was anxious that her fair and virtuous mother's name should be perpetuated, she was unwilling to expose her daughter to the risk of being stolen by the Smalanders or some such savage people. But when Father Willibald heard what they were arguing about, he declared immediately that Ludmilla was an excellent and lucky name, having been borne by a pious princess who had lived in the country of Moravia in the time of the old Emperor Otto. So they decided to call the child Ludmilla; and all the housefolk prophesied a marvellous future for one so curiously named, for it was a name that none of them had heard before.

As soon as the two infants were strong enough, they were baptized by Father Willibald to the accompaniment of much bawling. They waxed fast, enjoying the best of health, and were soon tumbling around the floor with the huge Irish dogs which Orm had brought with him from Skania, or fighting over the dolls and animals which Rapp and Father Willibald carved out of wood for them. Asa doted upon them both, and exhibited far more patience towards them than towards any other member of the household; but Orm and Ylva sometimes had difficulty in deciding which of the two was the more obstinate and troublesome. It was continually impressed upon Ludmilla that she had been named after a saint, but this had no noticeable effect on the manner in which she conducted herself. The two infants got on well together, however, although they occasionally went for one another's hair; and, when one of them had her bottom smacked, the other would stand by and howl no whit less resonantly than the punished miscreant.

The next year, early in the summer, Orm completed his church. He had sited it on the water's edge, where the bank curved, so that it would shield the other buildings from the river, and he had made it so spacious that there was room for sixty people to sit in it, though nobody could suggest where so large a congregation was likely to come from. Then he built a good rampart across the base of his peninsula, surmounted by a double stockade with a strong gate in the centre of it; for, the more he built, the more he worried for the safety of his house, and he was anxious to be prepared against the danger of attack by robbers, as well as by any ruffians whom King Sven might send their way.

When all this work had been completed, Ylva, to her great joy and that of all the household, gave birth to a son. Asa said that this must be God's reward to them for having built the church, and Orm agreed that this might well be the reason for so excellent a stroke of luck.

The new child was without flaw in limb or body and, from the moment of its arrival, leather-lunged. Everyone agreed that he must, without doubt, be destined to become a chieftain, since he had the blood both of King Harald and of Ivar of the Broad-Embrace in his veins. When they brought him to his father for the first time, Orm took Blue-Tongue down from her hook on the wall, drew her from her sheath, and placed flour and a few grains of salt upon the tip of her blade. Then Asa brought the child's head carefully towards the sword until his tongue and lips touched the offering. Father Willibald watched this procedure frowningly. He made the sign of the cross over the child and said that so unchristian a custom, which involved bringing the child into contact with a weapon of death, was evil, and not to be encouraged. But nobody agreed with him, and even Ylva, weak and exhausted as she was, cried cheerfully from her bed that there was no sense in his argument.

'It is the custom for children of noble birth to be initiated thus,' she said. 'For it brings them the courage of chieftains and a contempt for danger, and weapon-luck, and, besides, skill in the choosing of words. I cannot believe that Christ, from all that you tell us about Him, is the sort of god who would be likely to object to any child receiving such gifts as these.'

'It is a rite honoured by time,' said Orm, 'and the ancients had a great store of wisdom, even though they did not know about Christ. I myself was made to lick a sword-tip for my first meal, and I do not intend that my son, who is King Harald's grandson, shall have a worse start in life than I had.'

So there the matter remained, although Father Willibald shook his head sadly and muttered something to himself about the way the Devil still ruled these northern lands.

CHAPTER TWO

How they planned a christening feast for King Harald's grandson

Orm was now in better spirits than ever before, for every enterprise to which he laid his hand flourished. His fields bore a rich harvest, his cattle waxed fat, his barns and store-houses were full, a son had been born to him (and he had good hopes that it might not be his last), and Ylva and his children enjoyed the best of health. He took good care to see that there was no idleness among his men once dawn had broken; Asa kept a sharp eye on the female hands as they toiled in the dairy or sat upon their weaving stools; Rapp showed himself to have a good hand at carpentry and smithery, and at setting snares for birds and animals; and, each evening, Father Willibald invoked the blessing of God upon them all. Orm's only regret was that his home lay so far from the sea; for, he said, it sometimes gave him a feeling of emptiness to have no sound in his ears but the murmur of the forest on all sides, and never to hear the whisper of the summer sea or feel its salt upon his lips.

But sometimes he was visited by evil dreams, and then he would become so agitated in his sleep that Ylva would wake him to ask whether the nightmare was riding him, or whether there was any trouble on his mind. When he had awakened, and had fortified his courage with strong ale, she would hear, perhaps, that he had, in his sleep, returned to the Moorish galley, and had been rowing his heart out as the whip snaked across his shoulders and the groans of his fellows filled his ears and their wealed backs bent painfully before his eyes; and on the morning after such a dream, he loved to sit beside Rapp, who never dreamed, in the carpenter's shed, and exchange memories with him of those far-off days.

But worse than these were the two dreams that he dreamed about King Sven. For the Moorish galley was but a memory of the past, but, when he dreamed of King Sven and his wrath, he could not be sure that they might not be omens of ill-luck to come. When, therefore, he had had such a dream, a great unrest would come over him, and he would describe in great detail to Asa and Father Willibald all that he had seen in his sleep, in order that they might help him to arrive at the dream's meaning. On one occasion, he saw King Sven standing, smiling evilly, in the prow of a warlike ship which rowed nearer and nearer towards him while he, with but a few men manning his oars, strove desperately, but vainly, to flee. The second time, he was lying in the dark, unable to move a finger, listening to Ylva screaming piteously for help as men carried her away; and then, of a sudden, he saw King Sven walking towards him in the light of flames, carrying Blue-Tongue in his hand; and at this, he had awakened.

Asa and Father Willibald agreed that such dreams as these must possess some significance, and Asa wept when Orm told her of his second vision. But when she considered the matter more closely, she became less despondent.

'It may be that you have inherited from me the gift of truthful dreaming,' she said, 'though it is a gift that I would not willingly bestow on anyone, for I myself have never gained profit from it, and it has brought me nothing but anxiety and sorrow which I would not otherwise have known. One thing, however, comforts me, and that is that I myself have not had any dream which could be interpreted as a warning of evil luck to come. For any stroke of bad luck that injured you would touch me no less nearly, so that, if anything were to threaten you and your house, I, too, should receive warning of it in a dream.'

'For my part,' said Father Willibald, 'I believe that King Sven has enough to occupy him elsewhere, and has little time to spare trying to search you out in these wild forests. Besides which, do not forget that it is against me, and not you, that his anger is primarily directed, for it was my hand that flung the stone that felled him, as David, the servant of God, smote the heathen Goliath: and I have had no evil dreams. It cannot, though, be denied that the paths of evil are long and crooked, and that it is always a good thing to be prepared for the worst.'

Orm agreed with this last observation, and had the stockade on his rampart strengthened and tested, and the great gate reinforced with good cross-beams, that he might sleep the more soundly at night. Before long, the memory of these bad dreams had almost passed from his mind, and he began to think less of them than of the great christening feast which he was intending to hold in his son's honour.

He lost no sleep in trying to think of a name for the child, for he was determined that the boy should be called Harald.

'There is always the danger,' he said, 'that, by giving him a king's name, I may expose him to some grievous fate. But few men have enjoyed such luck as King Harald, or have won a greater name; and of all the chieftains I have met, only one, Almansur of Andalusia, was as wise as he. So I think I should be denying my son great possibilities if I withheld from him the name which his grandfather bore so well.'

'There is only one thing about that name that worries me,' said Ylva. 'It might cause him to become inordinately greedy for women as my father was. He could never have enough of them. It may be a good quality in a King to be so inclined, but I do not think it is to be desired in other men.'

'He will be strong and well-shaped,' said Asa. 'That I can tell already. And if he is blessed with a merry humour also, he will need no king's name for women to fall ready victims to the snares he will lay for them. My son Are was a rich man, though his talent brought him bad luck. Women could not resist him when he winked at them and took them by their plaits. I have heard them confess as much with their own lips. He had laughing eyes and a humour that was never clouded, and was the best of all my sons after Orm; and I pray that God may never allow you, Ylva, to know such grief as I knew when he came to bad luck because of his skill at love-making and went the way to Miklagard and never came back.'

'That is my wish, too,' said Ylva. 'Though, now that I think about it, I would rather that my son had his way with women than that he should stand tongue-tied in their presence and never dare to chance his luck with them.'

'You need have no fear of that,' said Orm. 'There is little bashfulness in his ancestry.'

They now began to make preparations for their son's christening feast, to which many guests were to be invited; for word of it was to be sent to all good people for miles around. It was Orm's wish that there should be no stint of anything, whether baked, brewed or slaughtered; for he was anxious that these forest people should have the opportunity to see what happened when a chieftain held open house for three whole days. All the eating and drinking was to take place in the church, because there was more room there than in any of the other buildings; then, on the third day, when all the guests were merry and replete, Father Willibald would preach them a sermon, after which, Orm doubted not, many of them would offer themselves for baptism.

At first Father Willibald flatly refused to allow a feast to be held in his church, because of the rowdiness and blasphemy that would certainly accompany such an occasion, especially since he had just completed his altar, and had carved a fine cross to stand upon it. In the end, however, the consideration that many souls might thereby be won over to the true religion overcame his scruples, and he consented. Two things troubled Ylva; firstly, she was anxious that the ale should not be brewed too strong, since their guests were, many of them, wild folk, and women as well as men would be sitting at the tables; and secondly, she could not make up her mind whether to wear her gold chain, or whether it might not perhaps be wiser to keep this hidden.

'For the last time it appeared at a feast,' she said, 'swords were bared; and the greed for gold is even greater in these parts than it was at Jellinge.'

'My advice is that you shall wear it,' said Orm. 'For I want men to see that you are superior to other women; and you will gain little joy from it if you keep it always locked in a chest.'

The whole household now began to busy itself with preparations for the feast. There was great brewing and baking, and every day Orm fingered the flesh of his slaughter-beasts and had them fattened further.

One day a man came out of the forest from the south with two pack-horses, and rode towards the house, where they welcomed him warmly and bade him enter. His name was Ole; he was an old man, and had for many years wandered from house to house throughout the forest country peddling skins and salt, for which reason he was called Salt-Ole, and was well known everywhere. No one ever offered him violence, although he always travelled alone, for he was cloven-minded and was held to be different from other men; but he knew all there was to be known about skins, and was difficult to deceive, and was always welcomed for his salt in such houses as could afford to indulge in such an extravagant luxury. The great hounds bayed as he approached; but he and his old horses paid no heed to their noise. He remained at the door, however, refusing to cross the threshold, until they had assured him that the priest was not in the house; for of him he was terrified.

'Our priest is no wolf or bear,' said Asa reprovingly, as, with her own hands, she set food before him. 'But in any case he is out to-day fishing with Rapp, so you will not have to meet him. A wise man like you ought not to be afraid of a priest of God. But you are welcome none the less; sit you here and eat, old man. You are particularly welcome with your salt just now, for our stock is nearly at an end, and we shall need more than a little to see us through this christening feast if Orm is to have everything as he wants it. It is his wish that every guest shall have a three-finger pinch of white salt to dip his food in, not merely for his meat and sausage, but for his porridge also, though most folk would say that this was going too far, even for people of our position, and that butter and honey ought to be good enough flavourings for porridge even at the greatest feast.'

The old man sat guzzling sour milk, breaking bread into it, and shaking his head at Asa's talk.

'There is nothing like salt,' he said. 'A man should eat all the salt he can. It gives health and strength and long life. It drives bad things from the body and makes the blood good and fresh. Everybody likes salt. Watch this, now!'

The twins were standing hand in hand, gazing earnestly at the old man as he ate and talked. He took two pieces of salt from his belt and held them out towards the children, making a cheerful clucking noise with his tongue. They approached him hesitantly, but at length accepted the crystals and began at once to suck them.

'You see!' cried the old man, hugely jubilant. 'Nobody can say no to salt.'

But when he had finished eating and had drunk a cup of ale, and been asked for news, and Ylva was ready to argue a price for his wares, it transpired that he had, in fact, practically no salt left in his bags; none at all of the white, which was called Emperor's salt, and which Orm wanted for his feast, and only a little of the brown.

Asa shook her fist at him.

'You should have told us this at the beginning,' she said, 'and I

267

would have given you a different welcome. But it is as I have always said: old men, trolls, and old bullocks, one gets no reward for stuffing them with food.'

Ole, however, was by now full and contented, and said that every disappointment brought consolation in its wake.

'For there are other pedlars on their way here,' he said. 'I passed them yesterday while they were resting at Gökliden; eleven men, fourteen horses and a boy. They had nails in their sacks, and cloth and salt. They had come up through the Long Stocks, they told me, and were heading for Smaland. I did not know them, though I have sometimes thought that I knew all people; but I am growing old, and new ones get born. But of this I am sure, that they will visit you, for their chieftain inquired about you, Orm.'

Orm had been taking his mid-day nap in his room, but had now come out to join the others and listen to the old man's gossip.

'About me?' said Orm. 'Who was he?'

'His name is Osten of Ore, and he comes from the Finnveding country, but has never been in these parts before. He said he had spent many years at sea, but had invested all his gains in the wares he was carrying, so as to be able to return home still richer.'

'Why did he ask about me?' said Orm.

'He had heard men speak of you as a rich and famous man, such as pedlars like to visit. He had, besides, silver ornaments in his sacks, he told me, and good arrows and bow-sinews.'

'Did he ask about anyone else?' said Orm.

'He wanted to know what other great men there were in the district who would be likely to buy his wares without haggling and complaining about the price. But most of the time he asked about you, because he had heard that you were the richest.'

Orm sat for a while in silence, looking thoughtful.

'Eleven men?' he said.

'And a boy,' replied the old man. 'A small one. Such fine wares as he carries need good men to guard them. The boy was there to help with the horses.'

'No doubt,' said Orm. 'None the less, it is a good thing to be warned in advance when strangers come in such strength.'

'I marked no evil in him,' said Ole. 'But I can tell you this, that he is a bold man, for I told him that you have a priest in your house, and he was not frightened.'

At this, they all laughed.

'Why are you afraid of the priest?' asked Orm.

But to this question the old man would give no answer: only, he shook his head, and looked cunningly at them, and mumbled beneath his breath that he was not so stupid but that he knew that sort of folk were worse than trolls. Then he got up and left, without tarrying longer.

'Seven weeks from now, I shall be holding my feast,' Orm said to him as he rode away, 'and if you are in these parts then, you will be welcome. For it may be that you have this day done me a good service.'

CHAPTER THREE

Concerning the strangers that came with salt, and how King Sven lost a head

The next evening, the strangers of whom Salt-Ole had warned Orm arrived at Gröning. It had begun to rain, and the men and their horses halted a short way from the gate while one of their number came forward and asked for Orm, adding that they would be glad of shelter for the night. The hounds had given warning of the strangers' approach, and Orm was already standing before the gate with Rapp, the priest, and five men of his household, all well armed, except for Father Willibald. The stranger who had addressed them was a tall, lean man, clad in a broad cloak. He brushed the rain from his eyes and said: 'Such rain as this is unwelcome to pedlars, for neither bales nor leathern sacks can long withstand it, and I have on my horses' backs salt and cloth which will suffer if they become damp. Therefore, although I am a stranger to you, I beg, Orm, that you will give me shelter for my wares and a roof to cover the heads of me and my men. I who address you thus am no mere vagabond, but Osen, the son of Ugge, from Orestad in Finnveden, a descendant of Long Grim; and my mother's brother was Styr the Wise, whom all men know of.'

As he spoke, Orm looked at him closely.

'You have many men with you,' he said.

'I have sometimes thought them too few,' replied Osten. 'For the wares I carry are valuable, and this is not the safest of districts for pedlars to travel in. But so far all has gone well with me, and I trust it may continue so. It may be that I have in my sacks one thing or another that you or your wife might care to buy from me.'

'Have you been baptized?' asked Father Willibald.

'Certainly not!' said Osten indignantly. 'Nor have any of my companions. We are all honourable men.'

'Your tongue led you astray there,' said Orm sternly. 'All of us are baptized men, and the man who asked you that question is a priest of Christ.'

'A stranger cannot be expected to know such things,' replied Osten humbly. 'Though, now that I remember it, a man we met on the way did tell me that there was a priest in your house. But it had slipped my memory, for most of what he had to say concerned you, Orm, and your reputation for hospitality and your fame as a warrior.'

The rain began to descend more heavily than ever, and thunder could be heard crackling in the distance. Osten glanced towards his wares, and his face began to wear a worried look. His men stood waiting beside the horses with their backs turned towards the wind and their cloaks drawn over their heads, while the rain stood like smoke about them.

Rapp smiled.

'Here is a good opportunity for us to buy salt cheaply,' he said.

But Orm said: 'Your ancestry may be good, Smalander, and I have no wish to think evil of you, but it is a great deal to ask of a man that he should take eleven armed men into his house for the night. I would not appear inhospitable, but I do not think you can blame me for being hesitant. But I give you two choices; either to depart and seek night-shelter elsewhere, or to enter my land and take shelter in my bath-house for the night with your men and your wares, having first surrendered your weapons to me here before my gate.'

'That is a hard condition,' said Osten. 'For if I accept, I place myself and all my wealth in your hands, and no man willingly takes such a risk. But I think you are too great a chieftain to contrive treachery against me, and I am so placed that I cannot but accept your condition. It shall, therefore, be as you demand.'

So saying, he unhooked his sword from his belt and handed it to Orm. Then he turned and bade his men make haste to bring his wares into the dry. They lost no time in obeying his command, but each man had to surrender his weapons at the gate before he was permitted to enter. The horses were tethered in the grass by the river, there being no danger from wolves at this season.

When all this had been done, Orm invited the strangers to take food and ale with him. After the meal, he bargained with Osten for salt and cloth and found him an honourable man to deal with, for he asked no more for his wares than what a man might reasonably be expected to pay. They drank upon the bargain as friends: then Osten said that he and his men were tired after their long day's journey, and they thanked him for the good fare he had given them and retired to rest.

Outside, the storm increased in violence, and, after a while, a noise of lowing was heard from the cattle, which were kept at night in a shed next to the house. Rapp and the old cowman went out to see if the beasts had become frightened and broken loose. It was by now quite dark, apart from an occasional flash of lightning. Rapp and the cowman went carefully round the cattle shed and found it undamaged. Then a thin voice asked from the darkness: 'Are you Red Orm?'

'I am not he,' said Rapp, 'but I am the next after him in this house. What do you want with him?'

The lightning flashed, and by its light he saw that the speaker was the little boy whom the pedlars had brought with them.

'I want to ask him how much he will give me for his head,' said the boy.

Rapp leaned swiftly down and seized him by the arm.

'What kind of pedlar are you?' he said.

'If I tell him everything I know, perhaps he will give me something for my knowledge,' said the boy eagerly. 'Osten has sold his head to King Sven, and has come here to collect it.'

'Come with me,' said Rapp.

Together they hurried into the house. Orm had gone to bed with his clothes on, for the storm and the strangers had made him uneasy, and Rapp's news at once set him wide awake. He forbade them to strike a light, but slipped on his chain-shirt.

'How did they deceive me?' he said. 'I have their weapons here.'

'They have swords and axes hidden in their bales,' replied the boy. 'They say your head is worth a deal of trouble. But I am to have no share of the reward, and they drove me out into the rain to keep a watch on the horses, so I shall not be sorry to see them get the wrong end of the bargain: for I am not of their party any more. They will be here any moment now.'

272

All Orm's men were now awake and armed. Including Orm himself and Rapp, they numbered nine; but some of them were old and could not be reckoned upon for much help when it came to fighting.

'We had better go to their place at once,' said Orm. 'With luck, we may be able to smoke them in their sleeping-quarters.'

Rapp opened the door a few inches and glanced out.

'The luck is with us,' he said. 'It is beginning to grow lighter. If they try to run, they will make good targets for our spears.'

The storm had passed, and the moon was beginning to glimmer feebly through the clouds.

Ylva watched the men as they slipped out through the door.

'I wish this business was over,' she said.

'Do not worry,' said Orm, 'but warm some ale for our return. One or another of us may find himself in need of it when we have finished this night's work.'

They walked silently across the grass towards the bath-house. A woodshed stood beside it, and they had just reached this when they saw the door of the bath-house slowly open. Through the gap they could see grey faces and the glint of arms. Orm and several of his men immediately flung their spears at the gap, but none found their mark; then the whoop of battle-cries filled the air, and the doorway became thick with figures as the pedlars swarmed forth. Orm bent down and seized hold of the great chopping-block which stood at the entrance to the woodshed. With his arms almost cracking under the strain, he lifted it from the ground, took a step forward and flung it with all his might at the open doorway. The foremost of his enemies managed to throw themselves aside in time, but several of those behind were hit and fell to the earth groaning.

'That was a useful thought,' said Rapp.

The pedlars were bold men, though things had turned out otherwise than they had expected, and such as still remained on their feet rushed at once into the attack. Fierce and confused fighting followed, for, as clouds passed across the moon, it became difficult to discern friend from foe. Orm was attacked by two men, one of whom he quickly felled; but the other, a short, thick-set, heavy-limbed man, lowered his head and charged Orm like a goat, bowling him to the ground and, at the same time, wounding him in the thigh with a long knife. Orm let go his sword and gripped the man's neck with one arm, squeezing it as tightly as he could, while in his other hand he grasped the wrist holding the knife. They rolled around in the rain for a good while, for the pedlar was short in the neck, as strong as a bear, and as slippery as a troll; but eventually they rolled up against the wall of the bath-house, and there Orm got a good purchase and slightly altered his grip. The other man began to make a sound like snoring; then something snapped in his neck, and he ceased to struggle. Orm got to his feet again, and regained his sword; but he was troubled by the knife-wound he had received, and it pained him to move a step, although he could hear two of his men calling for help in the darkness.

Then, over the clang of weapons and the screams of wounded and dying men, there arose a terrible sound of baying, and Father Willibald, with a spear clutched in his hand, came running round the corner of the house with the great Irish hounds, which he had freed from their kennel. All four of them were raging mad, with froth on their lips, and they sprang savagely at the pedlars, who were convulsed with terror at the sight of them; for hounds of the size of four-month calves were a spectacle to which they were unaccustomed. Such of them as could disengage their adversaries turned and fled towards the river, with the hounds and Orm's men at their heels. Two of them were overtaken and killed, but three managed to make good their escape through the water. Orm hobbled after them as fast as he could, for he feared Osten might be among those who were getting away; but when he came back to the house, he found Rapp seated upon a log, leaning on his axe and regarding a man who lay stretched on the ground before him.

'Here is the master pedlar himself,' said Rapp, as he saw Orm approach. 'Though, whether he is alive or not is more than I know. He was no mean fighter, though I say it myself.'

Osten was lying on his back, pale and bloody, his helmet split by a blow from Rapp's axe. Orm seated himself beside Rapp, and looked down at his defeated enemy; and the sight so cheered him that he forgot the pain from his wound. Ylva and Asa came running out of the house, with joy and anxiety mingled in their faces. They tried to persuade Orm to come indoors at once that they might dress his wounds; but he remained where he was, staring at Osten and mumbling beneath his breath. At last, he said:

'Now I know
A gift full worthy
To be sent
To Sven my brother.
Pedlar, he
Shall have his head;
But the hair on it
Shall not be red.'

Father Willibald now joined them. He examined Orm's wound and ordered him to go at once into the house, saying that if he could not walk he must allow Rapp and the women to carry him there. Then he bent down over Osten and felt with his fingers the place where Rapp's axe had made its mark.

'He is alive,' he said at last. 'But how long he will live, I cannot tell.'

'I shall send his head to King Sven,' said Orm.

But Father Willibald answered sternly that such a thing was not to be thought of, and that Osten and the other wounded pedlars who were still alive were to be carried into the house.

'This night's work will keep me busy for some time,' he said jubilantly.

Father Willibald was always a man of determination, but never more so than when there was any sick or wounded man to be dealt with; for then no man dared to say that it should be otherwise than as he commanded. So everyone who could lend a hand had to help carry the wounded men into the house and make them comfortable there.

Orm had no sooner been assisted to his room and had his wound dressed than he fainted; for he had lost a great quantity of blood. The next day, however, he felt better than he could have expected. He reflected with satisfaction on the way everything had turned out, and said that the pedlar's boy was to remain in his household for always, and was to be treated as one of the family. He learned that he had lost two men killed, and that two others had been badly wounded, as also had one of the hounds; but Father Willibald thought it likely that, with God's help, they would all eventually recover, the hound included. Orm was grieved at losing two of his men, but he comforted himself with the thought that things might easily have turned out worse. Of the pedlars, Osten and two others were still alive, apart from the three who had escaped into the river. In the bath-house, they had discovered two men who had been hit by the chopping-block. One of these was dead, and the other had a broken leg and a crushed foot. Father Willibald had had all the wounded men taken into the church, where he had bedded them in straw. They were receiving the most careful attention, and every day it became more apparent that the little priest was by no means discontented with the labour of looking after them. For of late there had been few calls upon his skill as a physician, so that time had begun to grow somewhat heavy on his hands.

Orm was soon on his feet again, with little to show for the wound he had received; and one day Father Willibald came to the dinner table with a more than usually cheerful look on his face and announced that even Osten, who had been the most gravely wounded of them all, now looked to be on the road to recovery. Rapp shook his head doubtfully at this piece of news.

'If that is so,' he said, 'my aim is less sure than it used to be.'

And Orm, too, thought it little cause for joy.

CHAPTER FOUR

How Orm preached to the salt-pedlar

The news of the fight at Gröning soon spread throughout the district, and Gudmund of Uvaberg came riding over with a flock of distant neighbours whom Orm had not seen before to learn the details of it from his own lips. They drank deeply of Orm's ale, and rejoiced exultantly as he described the battle to them. This, they vowed, was a fine thing, for it would increase still further the good name of the border country and the respect in which its inhabitants were held by the world outside. They had much, too, to say in praise of the great hounds, and begged that their own bitches might be allowed the favour of contact with them; and, when all the salt and cloth was shown to them, together with the rest of the booty that Orm had won, they sighed that such luck had not come their way. They bargained for the salt-pedlars' horses, and a satisfactory agreement was soon reached, for Orm had by now many more horses than he required, and felt that he could not honourably ask too high a price, since he had paid nothing for them himself. Then the more muscular of his guests tried their strength at lifting the chopping-block; and, although those who watched them named dead men whom they had known in their childhood and who had been able to perform more difficult feats than this, still, nobody was able to throw it as far as Orm had done. This still further improved Orm's spirits, and he told them not to take their failure too hard.

'I am not sure that even I could throw it so far again,' he said, 'without the help that great anger gives a man.'

They were all curious to see Osten, and wondered greatly that Orm had spared his life. A knife in the throat, they declared, was always the best medicine for men of that sort; and they counselled him earnestly not to stock up trouble for himself and others by allowing the man to go free. To do so, they said, would surely bring unpleasantness in its wake; of that he could be certain, for they were accustomed to the ways of Smalanders, and knew them to be a people who nursed their wrongs. Many of them wanted to go into the church to look at the man and talk to him; it would be interesting, they said, to hear whether he regarded the border country as good terrain for head-hunting. But Father Willibald bolted the door and remained deaf to their entreaties to be allowed to enter. They might, he said, be granted admission at some later date, if God so willed it, but he would not permit them to taunt a wounded man who was still hardly able to lift his head.

So they had to forgo that pleasure; but, before riding away, they agreed over their stirrup-cups that Orm must now be regarded as a chieftain even amongst the Göings, and that he was a worthy scion of Sven Rat-Nose, even though he had allowed himself to become baptized; and they swore that they would take his part in any feud which might develop as a result of all this.

Orm gave each of them his measure of salt, as a parting gift and for the maintenance of neighbourly relations. Then they rode away from Gröning at a thunderous gallop and in the best of spirits, swaying in their saddles and screeching like jays.

The boy was greatly alarmed when he heard that Osten looked likely to recover, and thought it a bad thing for him; for, he said, if Osten lived he would surely kill him in revenge as soon as he got the chance. But Orm assured him that no harm would come to him, and said that he was to lose no sleep on that score, whatever might be Osten's feelings in the matter. The boy was called Ulf, and from the first he was much cosseted by Asa and Ylva, who hardly knew how to reward him for the great service he had done them all. Asa set to work sewing him better clothes with her own fingers; and she and Father Willibald agreed that the boy was, without doubt, an instrument of God, sent to save them from the machinations of the devil. They asked him how he had come to join the pedlars. He replied that he had run away from a cruel uncle with whom he had lived down on the coast, and at whose hands he had suffered great unkindness and privation ever since his mother and father had been drowned while fishing; and that the pedlars had engaged him to look after their horses.

'But they gave me little to eat,' he continued, 'so that I was always hungry except when I could steal food from houses; and I had to stay awake each night to watch the horses, and was beaten if anything happened to them. But the worst was that I was never allowed to ride, however leg-weary I became. In spite of all this, I fared better with them than my uncle; but I never bore them any love, and am glad to be free of them. For here I have what I never knew before, food enough to eat and a bed to sleep in, so that I will gladly remain with you for ever, if you do not send me away. I am not even afraid to be baptized, if you think it necessary.'

Father Willibald said that it was, without a doubt, highly necessary, and baptized he would be as soon as he had received schooling in Christian doctrine. Ylva set him to watch Oddny and Ludmilla, who were now able to walk and found no difficulty in escaping from the house, and on two occasions had alarmed everybody by being discovered down by the river. The boy discharged this function assiduously, accompanying them wherever they went; this, he said, was better work than watching horses. He could whistle better than anyone they had ever heard, and knew many tunes, and could even imitate various birds; and both the girls loved him from the first. In time he came to be known as Glad Ulf, because of his merry temper.

Osten and his two wounded companions were, by this time, well enough to be moved; so they were taken from the church to the bath-house, where an armed man kept constant guard over them. Father Willibald now tried to give them some instruction about Christian doctrine; but before long, he came to Orm and said that the soil of their hearts was, in truth, stony and unreceptive to the seed of grace. This, though, he added, was no more than was to be expected.

'I am not a vain man,' he continued, 'and do not hanker after fame or honour. None the less, I should feel that my life's work had been well rewarded if I could become the first priest to baptize a Smalander. For there is no known instance of such a thing ever having been done before; and if it could be brought to pass, great indeed would be the rejoicing in Heaven. But whether I shall be able to prevail upon these men is, I fear, doubtful, for their obstinacy is inordinate; and it would be a good thing if you, Orm, could help me with a word of admonition to this Osten.'

Orm thought this a wise and proper suggestion, and said he would be glad to lend what help he could.

'This I promise you,' he added, 'that baptized they shall be, all three of them, before they set foot outside my gate.'

'But they cannot be baptized until they have listened to my exposition of the doctrine,' said Father Willibald, 'which they absolutely refuse to do.'

'They will listen to mine,' said Orm.

They went together to the bath-house; and there Orm and Osten met for the first time since the night of the battle. Osten was sleeping, but he opened his eyes as Orm entered. His head was swathed in bandages, which Father Willibald changed every day. He raised himself slowly into a sitting position, supporting his head between his hands, and looked unblinkingly at Orm.

'This is a good meeting for me,' said Orm, 'for my head still remains on its shoulders, rather more securely, indeed, than yours; and I owe you thanks, too, for all the wealth you have so thoughtfully brought to my door. But I think you expected things to turn out otherwise.'

'They would have been otherwise,' said Osten, 'if the boy had not served me treacherously.'

Orm laughed.

'I never thought,' he said, 'to hear you complain of treachery. But here is a question I should like you to answer. You have tried to take my head. Tell me, now, who has the best right to yours?'

Osten sat for some moments in silence. Then he said: 'The luck has gone against me in this affair. I have nothing more to say.'

'Your luck would have been much worse,' said Orm, 'if it had not been for this pious man, to whom your debt is indeed great. When I learned that King Sven wanted a head, my first thought was to send him yours, but this priest of Christ dissuaded me from carrying out my plan. He has saved your life and healed your wound, but even that has not satisfied his zeal, for he wants also to save your evil Smaland soul. So we have decided that you shall become a Christian, and your men with you. Nor have you any say in the matter, for your head belongs to me and I shall do as I please with it.'

Osten glared blackly at them both.

'My family is great and powerful,' he said, 'and no member of it sustains injury or insult without revenge. Know, therefore, that you will pay dearly for what you have already done to me, and dearer still if you force me to submit to any ignominy.'

'There is no question of anyone forcing you to do anything,' said Orm. 'You are free to make your own choice. Will you have your head sprinkled by this holy man, who wishes you nothing but good, or would you rather have it stuffed in a sack and sent to King Sven? I can promise you that it will be packed very carefully, so that it will arrive in good condition, for I want him to know whose it was. It might be best to pack it in salt; I have plenty of that now.'

'No man of my family has ever been baptized,' said Osten. 'Only our slaves are Christians.'

'You are evidently unaware,' said Orm, 'that Christ specifically commanded that all men should be baptized, including Smalanders. Father Willibald can quote you the passage.'

'His very words,' said Father Willibald. 'He said: "Go ye out into the world and preach my gospel to all men, and baptize them." He also said, on another occasion: "He that believeth and is baptized, his soul shall be saved; but he that believeth not, shall burn in Hell fire."'

'You see?' said Orm. 'The choice is yours:

> "Thou shalt to Hell
> Without thy head,
> Or else with water
> Be baptizèd."'

'Your sins are many and great,' said Father Willibald, 'and your spiritual condition most foul; but it is so with most men in this land. If though, you allow yourself to be baptized, you will be numbered among the blessed and, by Christ's mercy, stand in the ranks of the saved when He appears in the sky to judge mankind, which is due to happen very shortly.'

'One other thing,' said Orm. 'From the moment that you are baptized, God gives you His support: and you have doubtless observed, from the result of your attempt to kill me, that His hand is strong. I myself have never prospered so well as since I began to follow Christ. All that you have to do is to renounce your old gods and say: "There is no god save God, and Christ is His Prophet."'

'Not His Prophet!' said Father Willibald severely. 'His Son!'

'His Son,' said Orm quickly. 'That is what I meant to say. I know the text well; for I was not thinking, and my tongue slipped, because of the false beliefs I used to hold in the days when I served Almansur of Cordova, in the Andalusian's land. But that was long ago, and it is now four years since I was baptized by a holy bishop in England, ever since when Christ has supported me in all my enterprises. He delivers my enemies into my hand, so that not only men such as you are powerless to harm me, but King Sven also. And I have gained many other advantages besides. I was born with excellent luck, but it has increased considerably since I went over to Christ.'

'There is no denying,' said Osten, 'that your luck is better than mine.'

'But it only became as good as it is now,' said Orm, 'after I got baptized. For in former days, when I knew no religion save that of the old gods, I suffered many misfortunes, and sat for two years as a slave in Almansur's galley, chained to a bench with iron. It is true that I won this sword you see here, which is the finest weapon that was ever forged, so that Styrbjörn himself, who knew more about swords than any man, vowed when he weighed it in his hand in King Harald's hall that he had never seen a better; but even that was scant compensation for all that I underwent to secure it. Then I embraced the religion of the Andalusians, at the bidding of my master Almansur, and thereby won a necklace, a jewel of royal worth. But for that necklace's sake I was wounded almost to death in King Harald's hall, despite my good Andalusian chain-shirt, and if it had not been for this little priest and his healing skill I should have died from that wound. Then, at last, I became baptized, and came under the protection of Christ, and straightway won King Harald's daughter, whom I count the most precious jewel that I own. And now you yourself have witnessed how Christ helped me to overcome you and all the men you brought with you to kill me. If you consider the matter well, you will, being a wise man, realize that you will not lose anything by being baptized, but will, instead, gain much profit, even if you do not regard it as important that your head should remain on its shoulders.'

This was the longest sermon that anyone heard from Orm in the whole of his life, and Father Willibald told him afterwards that he had acquitted himself by no means poorly, considering his inexperience in the art.

Osten sat and pondered for a long while. Then he said: 'If all that you say is true, I must agree that you have not lost by becoming a Christian, but have rather gained; for it is no small feat to have won King Harald's daughter, nor are the wares which you have got from me to be despised. But in Smaland, where I live, there are Christian men who are thralls, and they have little to show for their religion; and I cannot be sure whether I may not have their luck instead of yours. But there is one thing I wish to know. If I do as you bid me, what do you intend to do with me then?'

'Set you free, and let you depart in peace,' replied Orm. 'And your men with you.'

Osten eyed him suspiciously; but at length he nodded.

'If you are ready to swear this before us all,' he said, 'I shall believe that you mean to keep your word. Though, what good it can do you to see me baptized is more than I can understand.'

'It is no more than just,' said Orm, 'that I should do something to please God and His Son, after all that They have done for me.'

CHAPTER FIVE

Concerning the great christening feast, and how the first Smalanders came to be baptized

When the bees had swarmed and the first hay had been garnered, Orm held his great christening feast. As he had intended from the first, it lasted for three days, and was, in every way, a feast unlike all other feasts, not least in that no weapon was blooded from beginning to end of it, despite the fact that every evening all the guests were as drunk as a man could wish to be at a great lord's banquet. The only misfortune occurred on the first evening, when, in the first flush of intoxication, two young men went to play with the great hounds in their kennel. One of them came smartly out again, having sustained nothing worse than a few gashes and the transformation of his clothes into ribbons; but the other attempted to withstand their assault, and it was only after much screaming that two women of the household, who were known to the hounds, rushed in and rescued him with his arms and legs lacerated and one ear missing. When the news of this reached the feasters it occasioned much merriment, and the hounds were praised as a credit to the district; but there were no further attempts to play with them.

Asa and Ylva had difficulty in finding room for all the guests to sleep, for more had come than had been invited, and many had brought their sons and daughters with them; and, although many of the older guests fell contentedly asleep each evening on the benches on which they had dined, or on the floor beneath, and remained there throughout the night, thereby saving much trouble, still, in spite of this, there was little room to spare. The young people managed well enough, for the girls were bedded in one barn and the boys in

284

another, in good, soft hay; and, although a surprising number of them experienced difficulty in finding their right barn, or in remaining in it once they had found it, still, no complaints were heard on this score. In the morning, the girls mumbled blushingly to their mothers of the strayings that had taken place, and of the difficulty of distinguishing one bank of hay from another, and were warned to take care that no other man stumbled over their legs on the following night, since to trip up two different men on successive nights was a thing that might damage a girl's reputation; after which, there ensued lengthy and amiable discussions between various parents, so that by the time the feast ended seven or eight marriages were as good as arranged. The news of these happenings delighted Orm and Ylva, for it was a sign that their guests, both young and old, were enjoying the feast; and only Father Willibald muttered blackly to himself, without, however, making any representations about the way things were going.

In other connections, though, Father Willibald had a great deal to say at this feast; and already on the first day, when all the guests had been fitted into their places in the church and every man and woman had received his or her cup of welcome-ale, he lit before his altar, on which his cross had been set up, three fine wax candles which he and Asa had moulded, and spoke to the gathering about the holy place in which they now found themselves.

'The God who rules in this house,' he said, 'is the only true god, and surpasses all others in wisdom, strength, and the ability to impart luck. His house, into which you have been permitted to enter, is the house of peace. For He dwelleth in peace and rejoiceth in it and giveth of it to such as come to Him for succour. You have come to this house from the regions of darkness and heresy to rest for a brief moment in His presence; and to darkness and heresy you will return when you have left it to wallow in sin and luxuriate in abomination until the span of your life is ended, when you will take your places among the regiments of the damned. But Christ offers His infinite friendship even to you, although you daily slight His name and teaching; therefore you have been permitted to enter this house. For He wants all men to be happy; that is why, when He himself was a wanderer on this earth, He turned water into good ale, that He might give joy to His friends. But the time is almost come when He will cease to be meek to such as refuse His friendship; and when they feel the whip of His anger, terrible indeed shall be their suffering, worse than that of the chieftain in the song who perished in a pit of snakes. So I think you will all agree that it will be a bad thing to be counted among His enemies. But as yet His offer still holds good, that any man or woman who wishes to do may become His servant and gain His protection merely by being baptized. Those, however, that will not do this must protect themselves as best they can.'

The guests listened with interest to Father Willibald's address, and murmured to one another that there was wisdom in a good deal of the things he had said, though some of his observations were difficult to be taken seriously. It was noticeable that the old people listened more attentively than the young, for the latter, whether boys or girls, found it difficult to take their eyes from Ylva. She was, indeed, a sight to marvel at, for she was now in the full prime of her beauty, at peace with the world and full of good-will towards everyone. She wore new garments, made from the costliest cloth that had been found in Osten's sacks, embroidered with silk and silver; and around her throat she wore the Andalusian chain. It was clear from the way so many of the guests gazed at her that such a woman and such an ornament were sights the like of which a man did not often see; and Orm was not the less happy for observing that they were properly appreciated.

When the priest had finished his speech, Orm tried to persuade one or two of the wiser among his guests to agree that a sensible man would be neglecting his own interests if he did not become a Christian; but he got no further than that two men expressed the opinion that the matter was, certainly, worth consideration; and even several hours later, when they were well on the way towards being drunk, they refused to commit themselves further.

The next day was a Sunday, and Father Willibald told the guests how God had built the world in six days, and had then rested on the seventh, which they agreed to be an excellent story; also, how, on this same day, many years later, Christ had risen from the dead, which they found more difficult to believe. Then Harald Ormsson was brought into the church to be baptized. Asa carried him to the tub, and Father Willibald performed the ceremony with the maximum of pomp and solemnity, chanting Latin prayers so loudly that they drowned the infant's bawling and caused the congregation to tremble on their benches. When the ceremony was over, toasts were drunk to the infant's luck, and to the memory of the three great heroes, Harald Blue-Tooth, Sven Rat-Nose and Ivar Broad-Hug, whose blood ran in his veins.

Then all the guests trooped out of the church to see the Smalanders baptized in the river. Osten and his two men were led from the bathhouse and were made to wade a short way into the water. There they stood in a row, bare-headed and scowling, while Father Willibald stood before them on the washing-barge, with Rapp beside him holding a couple of spears in case the men should try to offer resistance. Father Willibald read over them, his voice quivering with excitement and joy, for this was, for him, a great day; then he bade them bow their heads, and dowsed them one by one with a scoop. Having done this, he blessed each of them in order, placing his hands upon each man's head: then he leaned perilously forward from his barge and gave each of them a brotherly kiss upon the forehead.

They endured all this with no sign of expression in their faces, as though they were scarcely aware of Father Willibald's presence or of what he was doing to them, and as though the spectators on the banks did not exist at all.

When they had waded ashore again, Orm told them that they were now free to go whithersoever they pleased.

'But before you leave me,' he said, 'I wish to give you one further example of Christian behaviour. It is commanded that we, who follow Christ, shall be generous towards our enemies, even to such as have sought our life: and I do not intend to show myself less religious in my observance of this command than anyone else.'

He then ordered each of the three men to be given food for their journey, the same as the guests had enjoyed in the church on the previous evening. In addition, he presented every one of them with a horse, from those that they had brought with them in their caravan.

'Now depart in peace,' he said. 'And do not forget that you belong to Christ.'

Osten glared at him and, for the first time that day, words passed his lips.

'I am a man whose memory is long,' he said slowly; and he spoke as though he was very weary.

He said no more, but climbed upon his horse, rode out through the gate and, together with his two companions, disappeared into the forest.

Then everybody returned to the church, and the feast proceeded amid much merriment and noise, so that, when Father Willibald tried to tell them more about the Christian religion, he had difficulty in getting a hearing. They would prefer, the guests declared, to hear about the adventures that Orm had had in foreign lands, as well as about his feud with King Sven; so Orm complied with this request. There was little love lost between King Sven and the inhabitants of these parts, for it was a peculiarity of the border dwellers that they were always generous in their praise of dead kings, but seldom found anything good to say about living ones. When, therefore, Orm told them how Father Willibald had thrown a stone at King Sven and hit him in the mouth, so that blood had appeared and his teeth had been loosened, there was tremendous applause and jubilation, and all the guests made haste to fill their cups that they might drink to the honour of the little priest. Many of them swayed backwards and forwards on their benches with tears streaming from their eyes and their mouths wide open, while others were unable to swallow their ale for laughing, and snorted it out on to the table in front of them; and they all cried joyfully that they had never heard the like of such a feat by so tiny a man.

'The spirit of the Lord was upon me,' said Father Willibald humbly. 'King Sven is God's enemy, and so my weak hand brought him down.'

'We have heard it said,' remarked a man of note called Ivar the Smith who was seated near Orm, 'that King Sven hates all Christians, and their priests especially, so that he kills all he can lay his hands on. It is not difficult to guess the reason for his hatred, if he received such a blow as this from the hand of one of them. For there are few greater indignities that a king could undergo, and few that would take longer to forget.'

'Especially if he lost a tooth or two,' said another good farmer further down the table, whose name was Black Grim of the Fell. 'For, every time he bites a crust of bread, or gnaws a knuckle of sheep, he will be reminded of the incident.'

'That is true,' said a third, by name Uffe Club-Foot. 'It was so with me when I lost my foot, the time I fell out with my neighbour, Thorvald of Langaled. Midway through our argument, he aimed a blow at my leg, and I jumped too late. Long after the stump had healed and I had learned to walk with a wooden peg, I still felt tired and feeble, not only when I was standing but also when I was sitting down, and even in bed, as my woman can attest, for she was for a long time no better off than if she had been a widow. But when at last my luck changed, so that I saw Thorvald lying before me on his doorstep with my arrow in his throat, I took a great leap over him and all but broke my good leg, so full of vigour I suddenly found myself. And I have kept that vigour ever since.'

'It is not because of Father Willibald that my brother kills Christians,' said Ylva. 'He has always hated them bitterly, especially since my father took their part and allowed himself to be baptized. He could not set eyes even on the blessed Bishop Poppo, who was the mildest of men, without mumbling against him; though, more than that he dared not do as long as my father retained his power. But now, if reports are true, he kills bishops and priests of all ranks whenever he can lay his hand on them, and it will be a good thing if he does not live too long.'

'The life of evil men is often long,' said Father Willibald, 'but it is not as long as the arm of God. They shall not escape his vengeance.'

Down at the end of one of the tables, where the young people were seated and the merriment was greatest, they were now beginning to make verses; and there, on this evening, a lampoon was composed which was sung along the border for many years afterwards, at feasts, threshings and flax-strippings, and which came to be known as the Ballad of King Sven. It was a young man called Gisle, son to Black Grim, who began it. He was a shapely youth, dark-haired and fair-skinned; and, although there was nothing wrong with his head, it was a remarkable thing with him that he was shy of women, although he was often observed to cast by no means hostile glances in the direction of one or another of them. All his family regarded this as a peculiar and disturbing thing, which even the wisest among them knew no cure for; and hitherto, he had been sitting bashful and silent in his place, devoting himself solely to his food and drink, although it was well known that he had as ready a tongue as any young man there. Opposite him there sat a girl called Rannvi, a comely virgin with a snub nose and a dimple in her chin, such a woman as might easily cause a young man to cease his chatter; and ever and anon, from the time that he had taken his seat upon the bench on the first day of the feast, he had cast stealthy glances towards her, but had not dared to address her, and had become stiff with terror whenever it had so happened that their eyes had met. Once or twice she had gone so far as to chide him for his word-meanness, but without avail. Now, however, the good ale had given him better courage, and the story of King Sven's humiliation at the hand of Father Willibald had made him laugh very loudly; and of a sudden he began to rock backwards and forwards on his bench, opened his mouth wide, and roared in a high voice:

> 'You challenged a priest.
> And that was the least.
> For he toppled you into
> The mud, King Sven!'

'Here is something new!' cried those who sat nearest to him. 'Gisle has turned poet. He is making a ballad about King Sven. But this is only half a verse. Let us hear the rest.'

Many of the guests now made suggestions as to how he might finish his poem, but it was no easy thing to find words of the right length and ending; and in the end it was Gisle himself who found the answer, and completed his poem so that it might be sung to an old and well-known melody:

> 'You always were greedy for
> More, King Sven!
> You thought yourself greater than
> Thor, King Sven!
> But the priest threw a stone
> And down with a groan
> You fell on your face to the
> Floor, King Sven!'

'He is a poet! He has written a whole poem!' cried those about him; and none cried with so loud a voice as Rannvi.

'Listen to the young people,' said the old ones higher up the table. 'They have a poet there among them. Black Grim's son has wrought a ballad about King Sven. Who would have thought such a thing possible? Has he inherited the gift from you, Grim? If not from you, then from whom, pray?'

'Let us all hear this poem,' said Orm.

So Gisle was called upon to declaim his verse aloud before the whole company. At first his voice trembled somewhat; but when he saw that his audience approved his work, and that Orm himself was nodding and smiling, his fear fell from him; and now he found himself able to meet Rannvi's eyes without averting his own.

'I can write you more poems, and better,' he said to her proudly as he seated himself again.

Black Grim, Gisle's father, sat beaming with pride and satisfaction. He said that he had often felt himself to have a talent for verse-making, in his younger days, but that something had always happened which had prevented him from putting his inspirations into words.

'All the same,' he said, 'it is strange that he should have this gift; for he is folk-shy, especially when there are girls near him, although he would gladly have it otherwise.'

'Believe me, Grim,' said Ylva, 'he will not need to be shy of them any more. Trust my word for that. For, now that he has shown himself to be a poet, as many as can find space to do so will hang themselves round his neck. My father, who was full of wisdom upon all subjects, often used to say that, as flies swarm around food of any kind, but abandon it as soon as they sniff the odour of the honey-pot, so is it with young women when they sense the presence of a poet.'

Orm sat staring into his ale-cup with an anxious expression on his face, deaf to what they were saying. Asa asked him if anything was on his mind, but he only mumbled abstractedly to himself and made no reply to her question.

'If I know him aright, he is composing a verse,' said Ylva. 'He always wears that troubled look when the verse mood is upon him. It is a peculiar thing with poets that, if there are two of them in the same room and one of them composes a verse, the other cannot rest until he has composed another which he thinks is better than his rival's.'

Orm sat with his hands on his knees, rocking backwards and forwards on his bench, sighing deeply and mumbling cavernously to himself. At length, though, he found the words he wanted, gave two nods of relief, thumped his fist on the table for silence, and said:

> 'I hear you don't think
> Me your friend, King Sven!
> They tell me you drink
> To my end, King Sven!
> Wouldst catch me off my guard?
> God and my sharp-tongued sword
> Caused you to blink,
> Ay, and bend, King Sven!'

This was received with approbation by such of the company as were in a condition to appreciate the poem. Orm took a deep draught of his ale, and it could be seen that he was, once again, in excellent spirits.

'We have done well this evening,' he said, 'for we have composed a poem which has given pleasure to us all, and which will undoubtedly displease King Sven. This is a remarkable coincidence, that two poets should be found at a single feast, for they seem to be somewhat thinly sown in these parts; and, even if our quality is not fully commensurate, nevertheless, you have acquitted yourself honourably, Gisle, and I shall therefore pledge you.'

But when Orm peered down towards the end of the church through the smoke of the pitch-torches, Gisle was nowhere to be seen; nor could he be discovered among those who were asleep beneath the tables. But since Rannvi's place was also empty, their parents thought it most likely that they had both become drowsy and, as befitted well brought up children, had retired to rest without disturbing their elders.

That evening, Father Willibald, thanks partly to the good offices of Asa and Ylva, received promises from four of the women present that he might soon baptize their infants, provided that he did so in the same tub in which he had baptized Harald Ormsson, and with equal ceremony. But still none of the guests was willing to be sprinkled personally, despite the merry humour they were all in as a result of the good food and drink they had consumed. So Father Willibald had to contain himself as patiently as he might, although he had hoped for more spectacular results.

The next day, which was the concluding day of Orm's feast, the drinking reached its climax. Orm still had plenty of smoked mutton uneaten, and the greater part of a fresh ox, as well as two tubfuls of feast-ale and a small tubful of strong mead, made from lime honey, and he said that it would reflect little credit on him or his guests if any of this was left when the feast ended. All the guests were anxious to ensure that his honour, and theirs, should not thus be sullied. They therefore promised to do their best, and, from the first moment that they awoke that morning, set to with a will. It was their intention, they said, that both their host and his priest should find themselves beneath the table before the last cup was drained to its dregs.

Orm now took the priest to one side to ask his opinion on an important matter. He wanted to know, he said, whether God would regard it as lawful to baptize heathens while they were unconscious from drink.

'For, if so,' he said, 'it seems to me that a good work might be performed this evening, the way the day is beginning.'

Father Willibald replied that Orm had raised a moot point, and one that had been much debated by holy men who had devoted their whole lives to studying the craft of conversion.

'Some scholars,' he said, 'hold it to be lawful, in circumstances when the Devil shows himself particularly unwilling to yield. They support their contention by quoting the example of the great Emperor Charles who, when he desired to baptize some wild Saxons who held fast to their ancient idolatry, had the more obstinate of them stunned with a club as they were dragged forth to baptism, to quell their violence and blasphemous outpourings. It cannot be denied that such treatment must cause the Devil considerable vexation, and I do not see that there is much difference between stunning heathens with a club and befuddling them with ale. On the other hand, the blessed Bishop Piligrim of Salzburg, who lived in the time of the old Emperor Otto, held the opposite view, and expressed it in a pastoral letter of great wisdom. My good master, Bishop Poppo, always used to hold that Bishop Piligrim was right; for, he used to say, while it is true that the Devil must be discomforted by seeing his followers baptized while they are unconscious, still, such discomfiture can only be temporary, for, once they have recovered their senses and have learned what has happened to them, they lose all the feelings of reverence and love of God that the sacrament has imparted to them. They re-admit the Devil to their hearts, opening them wider than before to let him in, and rage more furiously than ever against Christ and his servants; so that no good results from the ceremony having been performed. For this reason, the holy men whom I have named to you, and many others besides, hold it inadvisable to baptize men when they are in this condition.'

Orm sighed.

'It may be as you say,' he said, 'since you have it from Bishop Poppo's own lips; for he understands the ways of God better than any man. But it is a great pity that he should be of that mind.'

'It is God's will,' replied Father Willibald, nodding sadly. 'Our task would be rendered too simple if we could enlist the assistance of ale in our endeavours to baptize the heathens. More is required than ale; eloquence, good deeds, and great patience, which last is the most difficult of all virtues to acquire and, once acquired, to retain.'

'I wish to serve God as well as I can,' said Orm. 'But how we are to further His cause among these good neighbours of mine is more than I know.'

So they left the matter at that, and the drinking proceeded merrily and apace. Later in the day, when most of the guests were still more or less upright upon their benches, the married women went in to Ylva's son to bring him name-gifts and good-luck wishes, after their ancient custom; while the men, feeling the need for air, went out on to the grass to indulge in games and tests of strength, such as finger-tug, wrestling, and flat-buttock lifting, amid shouts of encouragement and laughter; and many a good somersault was turned; while some of the more daring among them tried their hands at the difficult sport known as knot-lifting,[*]

---

[*] A sort of invitation to break one's neck, played by strong, drunken men after a feast. One (the weaker) sits on the ground, while the other (the stronger) kneels on his hands and knees. The latter is the man who risks his neck. The weaker man sits with his knees drawn up and wide apart, puts his arms outside his thighs and locks his hands under his knees. The strong man then puts his head forward between the other man's knees and into his locked hands, and tries to rise to a standing position, while the victim does his worst by pressing his knees and his locked hands round the strong man's neck. It was (says the author, in a letter to the translator), 'a frightful game, only played by drunk men.'

without, luckily, anyone overtasking his strength and breaking a limb or
dislocating his neck.

It was while these sports were in progress that the four strange
beggars arrived at Gröning.

CHAPTER SIX

Concerning four strange beggars, and how the Erin Masters came to Father Willibald's assistance

They looked as beggars usually look, trudging on foot with sack and staff, as they arrived at the house craving food and drink. Ylva was seated on the bench before the house in earnest conversation with the mothers of Gisle and Rannvi; for both these young people had come to her that morning in a state of extreme bliss to say that they were well content with each other, and to beg her to speak persuasively on their behalf to their respective parents, so that the wedding might be arranged as soon as possible; in which project Ylva had willingly undertaken to help them to the best of her ability. When news was brought her that there were beggars standing at the gate, she bade her servants request Orm to come to her, for he had ordered that no strangers were to be admitted until he had himself first carefully scrutinized them.

So he examined the travellers, who replied freely to his questions; but they did not seem to him to be like ordinary beggars. Their leader was a big man, broad of loin and well fleshed, with a grizzled beard and sharp eyes beneath his hatbrim. As he moved, he trailed one leg behind him, as though it might be somewhat stiff at the knee. He answered Orm's questions in a bold voice, and it was plain from his accent that he was a Swede. He said that they had come from Själland and were heading northwards across the border; a fisherman had brought them across the Sound, and they had begged their way up from Landöre.

'But to-day we have eaten nothing,' he concluded, 'for in these parts the houses lie far apart, and at the last house we visited we were given nothing to put in our sacks.'

'Nevertheless,' said Orm, 'you carry more flesh than I have seen on the bones of some beggars.'

'There is nourishment in Danish and Skanian pancakes,' replied the other with a sigh. 'But I fear their effect may wear somewhat thin, and I with it, before I come to the Mälar country.'

The man who stood beside him was younger, of slender build and pale of skin. His cheeks and jaw were black with a short, dense beard. Orm studied him for a few moments. Then he said: 'From your appearance, a man might suppose that you had been shaven for the priesthood.'

The slender man smiled sadly.

'My beard was burnt from my face one evening, when I was roasting pork in a wind,' he said. 'And it has not yet regained its old fullness.'

But it was at the other two beggars that Orm gazed most curiously, for of them he could make nothing. They had the appearance of being brothers, for they were both small and lean, long-eared and large-nosed, and both of them stared at him with wise brown eyes like those of squirrels. Although small, they nevertheless looked to be agile and muscular. They stood with their heads on one side, listening to the baying of the hounds; then, of a sudden, one of them placed a finger in his mouth and emitted a strange whistle, soft and vibrant. Immediately the hounds stopped howling and began to purr and pant, as they did when no strangers were about.

'Are you trolls?' asked Orm, 'or merely conjurors?'

'Neither, alas!' replied the man who had whistled, 'much as we should like to be either. For we cannot conjure food from anywhere, despite our hunger.'

Orm smiled.

'I shall not refuse you food,' he said, 'and I do not fear your witchcraft while there is yet daylight; but such beggars as you I have never before set eyes on. No other stranger has succeeded in quieting my hounds; indeed, I sometimes find it difficult to do so myself.'

'We will teach you a way,' said the second of the two small men, 'once we have got a good meal in our bellies, and food for two more in our sacks. We are wandering men who serve no master, and we understand hounds better than most men.'

Orm assured them that he would not send them away with empty sacks, and bade them enter.

'You have chosen a good time to arrive,' he said, 'for you have come in the midst of a great feast, so that there will be pancakes enough for you all, and perhaps something else besides. It is a pity for my guests that you cannot play as skilfully as you whistle.'

The two small men glanced at one another and winked, but said nothing; and they and their two companions followed Orm into the house. Orm cried to Ylva: 'Here are wayfarers, both large and small, come to crave a plate of your feast-food.'

Ylva looked up from her conversation and nodded, with her thoughts elsewhere; then, as she caught sight of the two small men, her eyes grew large with wonder, and she sprang up from the bench on which she was sitting.

'The Erin Masters!' she cried. 'Felimid and Ferdiad! My father's jesters! Are you still alive? In God's name, dear friends, what has forced you to turn beggars? Have you grown too old to practise your arts?'

The two small men stared at her in equal astonishment; then they both smiled. They dropped their staffs and beggars' sacks, took a couple of paces towards Ylva and then, in the same instant, they both sprang head over heels. One of them remained thus standing on his hands, on which he proceeded to jump to and fro, uttering small joyful cries, while the other tied himself into a ball and rolled towards her feet. Then they both leaped to their feet again and, gravely and expressionlessly, saluted her.

'We have not grown too old,' said one of them, 'as you can see for yourself, O fairest of all King Harald's daughters. For you must know that the years fear such masters as us; though it is a good while since you sat on your father's knee and saw us frolic for the first time. But we are hungrier now than we were then.'

Many of the guests, both men and women, had come running up in haste to look more closely at these marvellous men who could jump on their hands; but Ylva said that the newcomers were to eat and drink in peace, and that they were to be treated with as much honour as any guest in the church. She conducted them into the house herself, and placed before them the best of meat and drink; nor did they need any persuasion before they set to. The twins and Glad Ulf followed them in, and sat silently in a corner, in the hope that the two little men might perform further antics; meanwhile, Orm explained to his other guests who these two strange beggars were, that had so aroused their wonder.

'They were King Harald's jesters,' he said, 'though now they have no master; they come from Ireland, and are widely famed. I saw them once, when I was drinking Christmas with the King; but then they were prinked out with feathers and motley, so that I did not recognise them now. What they can be doing as wandering beggars I do not know, and it puzzles me sadly; but let us sit down to our ale again, and then, in a short while, we will hear their story.'

When all the beggars had eaten their fill, the jesters offered no objection to joining the drinkers; who, after their short rest, had now begun again in earnest. Both their companions, however, sat staring silently at their empty plates. When asked the reason for their melancholy, they replied that they were weary after the hardships of their journey and the good meal that they had just eaten. So Father Willibald led them to his room, that they might rest there undisturbed. Then he took the two jesters aside, and sat with them for some time in earnest conversation, which none dared to disturb; for they had been old friends ever since they had first met at King Harald's court, and were overjoyed to renew their acquaintance after so long an interval of time.

When, at last, all the guests had taken their places in the church, the two jesters were placed one on either side of Father Willibald. Many questions were asked concerning them, and all were anxious to see them display their skill; but the two jesters sat supping their ale in silence, as though unconscious of the excitement they were causing. Then Orm said: 'It would be ungracious of us to demand that you should show us your skill, for you have a right to be weary after your wanderings, and no guest or stranger who receives hospitality in my house is required to pay for it. But I cannot deny that we should like to take advantage of the fact that two such masters as you have arrived in the midst of my son's christening feast. For I know that you are both famous men; and I have always heard that no jesters in the world can match those of Ireland.'

'Chieftain,' replied one of the Irishmen, 'what you heard was the truth; and I can assure you that even in Ireland there are not two men more famous for their skill than I, Felimid O'Flann, and my brother Ferdiad here, who is as good as I am. My ancestors have been royal jesters ever since our great fore-father, Flann Long-Ear, performed, long ago, before King Conchobar MacNessa of Ulster and the heroes of the Red Branch in the hall of Emain Macha; and it has always been a law in our family that, once we have become proficient in our art and have earned the right to call ourselves master jesters, we display our skill only when commanded to do so by a person of royal blood. And this you must know, that we who jest before kings follow not only the most difficult calling in the world but also that which, more than any other calling, benefits mankind. For when a king is out of humour, and his fighting-men feel the itch of boredom, they are a danger to other men; but when good jesters perform for them, they rock with laughter over their ale and go contented to their beds and let their neighbours and subjects sleep in peace. After priests, therefore, we perform a more useful function than any other sort of men; for priests offer happiness in Heaven, through the influence that they have with God, while we offer happiness on earth, because of the influence we have on the humours of kings. And since there are many kings in Ireland the jesters of that land are the best in the world, and are of many different kinds: tumblers, clowns, ventriloquists, imitators of animals, men who contort their bodies, others who contort their faces, sword-swallowers, egg-dancers, and men who snort fire through their nostrils. But the true master jester is not he who can perform one or another of these arts, but he who knows them all. And it is held by wise men in Ireland that the best among us to-day are almost as good as King Conaire's three jesters were in ancient times, of whom it was said that no man who saw them could help but laugh, even though he might be sitting with his father's or his mother's corpse on the table before him.'

Everyone in the church had, by now, fallen silent, and all the guests were hanging on the Irishman's words and staring at him and at his brother, who was sitting on the other side of Father Willibald with a contented look on his face, slowly moving his large ears backwards and forwards. All agreed that the like of these men had never before been seen in these parts.

'You speak well,' said Gudmund of Uvaberg, 'and yet, it is not easy to believe that all you say is true; for, if you are both such great masters in your own land, why have you come to the north, where kings are few and live far apart?'

Felimid smiled and nodded his head.

'You may well ask that,' he said, 'for Ireland is a land that no man willingly leaves; and I will gladly tell you how we came to do so, even if what I say may sound like boasting. I must tell you all that my brother and I are exiles from our land on account of a feat which, I think, none but we could have performed. When we were young, but already expert in our art, we were jesters to the good King Domnal of Leighlin. He was a man who loved laughter and music, the word of God and legends of heroes, poetry, women's beauty, and the wisdom of old men; and he showed us great honour, rewarding our skill with silver and cattle and fine pastures in which to keep them. Because of this we loved him dearly, and were well content to be his servants; and our only worry was lest in our contentment we should grow too fat, for that is the worst thing that can happen to any man who practises our art. His neighbour was King Colla of Kilkenny, a dangerous man, very proud, and cunning at planning ways to discomfort those who lived too near him. One Whitsun, King Domnal held a great feast, and his priests, his poets and we, his jesters, were kept busier than usual; for the King was to wed Emer, the daughter of the King of Cashel. She looked as a princess should, clear-eyed, purple-mouthed and white of skin, high-breasted, slender of waist, and broad of hip, and with hair so long that she could sit upon the ends of it; so that even you, Ylva, would hardly have known which was the lovlier, you or she, if you could have seen her. This marriage was a source of great joy, not only to King Domnal, but to all his men, so that it was as merry a feast as a man could wish for. Then, on the second evening of the feast, when we were all drunk, King Colla descended upon us. King Domnal was killed as he hewed naked about him at his chamber door; many of his men fell with him; his Queen was taken from her bridal bed and carried off with the rest of the booty; and my brother and I suffered the same fate, for such was our fame. When King Colla saw Queen Emer, his lips grew moist and he leered like a hound, but us he threw into one of his dungeons until his wedding-day; for he had set his mind on marrying the woman he had stolen. Then he told us that we were to jest at his wedding-feast. At first we refused

301

to do this, for we were still heavy with grief at the death of our master; but when he swore that he would have us flogged with sharp-twigged birches unless we obeyed his bidding, we changed our tone and promised to appear before him and exhibit our finest arts. And that we kept that promise, I do not think he could well deny.'

Felimid smiled thoughtfully to himself as he drank long and slowly from his cup. All the guests drank to him, crying that he was a fine story-teller and that they were eager to hear about this great feat that he had performed. He nodded, and continued:

'There he sat on his royal throne, as we entered his presence, and already he was drunk; and never have I seen any man who looked so well at peace with himself and the world. As he saw us enter, he roared in a loud voice to his guests that the two masters from Leighlin would now display their quality as conjurors of mirth and merriment. Nor did she who sat beside him in her bridal jewels wear a sad face; for young women soon accustom themselves to a change of man, and perchance King Colla seemed to her to be an even finer match than our lord, King Domnal, had been. We began with simple jests, though we spoke them well, and with tricks that we were wont to perform on common occasions; and King Colla was in such a capital humour that he began at once to bellow with laughter. The whole hall laughed with him; and, when Ferdiad stood on his head and played the flute, while I danced the bear-dance round him, uttering growls, the applause became tremendous, and the King flung himself backwards upon his throne with his mouth wide open, splashing mead from his stoup over his lady's robe. He gasped for breath and shrieked that he had never before set eyes on jesters to compare with us. At this, we pricked up our ears and bethought ourselves, and exchanged a word in whispers; for, if he had never seen jesters like us, it was no less true that we had never before heard anyone laugh like him at the simple antics which were all that we had yet performed for him. So we turned to more diffi-cult feats, and meatier jests, and at these the King laughed like a magpie in May when the sun appears through an Irish mist. Then we began to feel merrier ourselves, and displayed our rarest arts, and told our most uproarious jests, such as contort the bellies and pain the jaws even of men who are weighed down with grief or plagued with sickness. All the while, King Colla's laughter grew louder and more breathless until it sounded like the ninth wave breaking upon the coast of Donegal when the spring tide is at its height. Then, of a sudden, his face turned black and he fell from his throne to the floor, where he remained lying; for he had burst inwardly with the violence of his laughter. When this happened, Ferdiad and I glanced at each other and nodded, remembering our master Domnal, and thinking that we had now repaid, in some measure, the gifts and kindnesses that he had showered upon us. The Queen screamed wildly with terror, and all those in the hall rushed towards him, save we, who headed for the door; but, before we reached it, we heard the cry go up that he was dead. We did not wait to hear more, but took to our heels and fled northwards across the heath as speedily as Bishop Asaph fled across the fields at Magh Slecht when the red ghosts were after him. We sought sanctuary with King Sigtrygg of Dublin, supposing we should be safe there; but Queen Emer sent armed men after us, who told King Sigtrygg that we were slaves whom she had inherited from her former husband, King Domnal, and that now, with evil and malicious intent, we had caused the death of her new husband, thereby doing great damage to her and her good name, and that she therefore wished to kill us. But we escaped in a trading ship and fled to King Harald of Denmark, into whose service we entered; and there we prospered. But never, as long as he was alive, did we tell anyone of what we had done to King Colla, for we did not want King Harald to hear of it. For it might have caused him to worry lest he might suffer a similar fate.'

When Felimid had finished telling his story, there was a tremendous uproar at the tables; for many of the guests were now beginning to be drunk, and they cried that, although the Irishman had spoken well, it was not talk that they wanted but an exhibition of the antics that had killed King Colla. Orm himself agreed with this viewpoint.

'You have already heard,' he said to the jesters, 'that our curiosity has been great from the first moment that we learned your identity; and that curiosity is now much greater, as a result of the story which you have just told us. Nor need you be alarmed lest any man or woman here should burst with laughter; for if this should happen, nobody will seek to be revenged upon you, and it will provide an excellent climax to my feast, and cause it to be long remembered throughout the border country.'

'And if it is as you say,' said Ylva, 'that you can only jest in the presence of one of royal blood, do I not count as such, as much as any small Irish king?'

'Of course you do,' said Felimid hastily, 'no one has a better right to be called royal than you, Ylva. But there is another obstacle to prevent us from performing here, and, if you will bear patiently with me, I shall tell you how the matter lies. Know, then, that my great-great-great-great-great-great-grandfather, Felimid Goatbeard, after whom I was named, was the most famous of all jesters in the days when King Finechta the Feaster was Ireland's over-king, and he was the first of our line to become a Christian. Now it so happened that on one occasion, when he was travelling, this Goatbeard met in the place where he was lodging for the night Saint Adamnan, and became inspired with a great respect and reverence for this holy man, finding him greater than any kind. So, to show his admiration for him, he jested before him, while the good man sat at his dinner table, performing the most intricate and difficult antics that he knew with such enthusiasm that, at length, he broke his neck, and lay on the floor as if dead. As soon, however, as the holy man realised his plight, he rose from his table, went over to him, touched his neck, and prayed for him, with powerful words, so that life returned to him although his head sat crooked on his neck for the rest of his days. In gratitude for this miracle, it has ever since been a tradition in our family that we may jest before the Archbishop of Cashel and the Archbishop of Armagh, the Abbot of Iona and the Abbot of Clonmacnoise, as well as before kings; and, also, that we never display our art in the presence of any man or woman who has not been baptized. For that reason, we cannot perform for you here, gladly as we would otherwise have done so.'

Orm stared at the little man in amazement when he heard these words, for, from his memory of the Christmas at King Harald's court, he knew them to be a lie; and he was on the point of saying so when he caught a warning glance from Father Willibald, which caused him to shut his mouth and remain silent.

'It may be that God himself willed it so,' said the other Irishman in a small voice, 'for, without boasting, I think it may be said that many of King Harald's best men chose to be baptized chiefly in order that they might not have to leave the hall when the time came for us to display our arts before the King.'

Ylva opened her mouth and began to speak, but Orm, Father Willibald and both the jesters immediately started talking at the same time, so that, what with their voices, the cries of disappointment, and the gurgles and snores of drunkenness that were arising from various parts of the hall, it was impossible to hear what she was saying.

Orm said: 'It is my hope that both you masters will remain here for some short while longer, so that I and my household may be able to enjoy your jests and antics when these our guests have left us; for every man and woman in my house is a good Christian.'

But at this many of the young people began to shout louder than ever that they would see the jesters perform their tricks, whatever sacrifice might be involved.

'Baptize us, if there is no other way!' cried one, 'and do not delay, but let the rite be performed at once.'

'Yes, yes!' cried the rest. 'That is the best solution. Let us all be baptized at once.'

Some of the older people laughed at this, but others looked thoughtful and glanced doubtfully at one another.

Gisle, Black Grim's son, jumped up on to his bench, and shouted: 'Let those who are not willing to be a party to this go and make themselves comfortable in the hay-barn, that they may be out of the way.'

The excitement and shouting became more and more vociferous. Father Willibald sat with his head bowed upon his chest, mumbling to himself, while the two jesters peacefully sipped their ale. Black Grim said: 'At this moment, it seems to me but a small thing to be baptized, and no cause for alarm; but that may be because I have drunk deeply of this excellent ale, and am warmed by the feast and by the wise conversation of my friends. It may be that I shall feel differently when the ale-joy has gone from me and I begin to think of the way my neighbours will laugh and jibe at me.'

'Your neighbours are all here,' said Orm, 'and who will laugh or jibe at you if everyone does as you do? It is more likely that you will all be laughing at men who are not baptized, when you all find how much you have improved your luck by submitting to the ritual.'

'It may be that you are right,' said Grim, 'for no one can deny that your luck has been as good as a man's could be.'

Father Willibald now rose to his feet and read over them in Latin, with his hands spread wide, so that all the guests sat silent and motionless beneath the sound of his words, and several of the women turned pale and began to tremble. Two of the more drunken men got up and bade their women straightway come with them and leave this witchcraft; but when those addressed remained in their seats as though they had not heard their husbands speak, with no eyes or ears for anyone save Father Willibald, both the men sat down again, with the air of men who have done all they can, and returned with glum faces to their drinking.

Everyone felt a great relief when Father Willibald came to the end of his Latin, which sounded like nothing so much as the squealing of pigs. He now began to address them in ordinary language on the subject of Christ, his power and goodness, and his willingness to take all men and women into his protection, not excluding robbers and adulterers.

'So you see,' he said, 'there is no one here unqualified to receive all the good that Christ has to offer you; for He is a chieftain who bids every man and woman welcome to His feast, and has rich gifts for every one of His guests.'

The company were greatly pleased with this speech, and many of them burst out laughing; for everyone found it an amusing and proper thing to hear his neighbours described as robbers and adulterers, comfortable in the knowledge that he himself could not be classed among those sort of people.

'It is my earnest hope,' continued Father Willibald, 'that you will be willing to follow Him for the rest of your lives, and that you will appreciate what that involves, namely, that you shall mend your ways and follow His commandments and never worship any other god.'

'Yes, yes,' cried many of them impatiently. 'We appreciate everything. And now make haste, so that we can get on with the important business.'

'One thing you must not forget,' proceeded Father Willibald, 'is that from this day forward, you must all come to me in this church of God on every Sunday, or at the least on every third Sunday, to hear the will of God and be instructed in the teaching of Christ. Will you promise me this?'

'We promise!' they roared eagerly. 'And now shut your mouth. Time is running on, and it will soon be evening.'

'It would be most beneficial to your souls, if you could all come every Sunday: but for those who live a long way off, every third week will suffice.'

'Cease gabbing, priest, and baptize us!' roared the more impatient members of the gathering.

'Quiet!' thundered Father Willibald. 'These are the ancient and cunning devils of your false beliefs that tempt you to bawl thus and interrupt my speech, hoping thereby to obstruct the will of God and so keep you for their own. But this is no superfluous information that I give you, when I speak to you of Christ and of the decrees of God, but important instruction, to which you must listen attentively and in silence. I shall now pray that all such devilry may instantly depart from you, so that you may be worthy to receive baptism.'

He then began again to read in Latin, slowly and in a stern voice, so that before long several of the older women began to wail and weep. None of the men dared utter a word; they all sat staring anxiously at him with large eyes and open mouths. Two of them, however, were seen to nod; their heads dropped nearer and nearer to their ale-cups, and, after a short while, they slid slowly beneath the table, whence lengthy snores soon began to emerge.

Father Willibald now commanded them all to come forward to the baptism-tub, in which Harald Ormsson had been baptized; and there twenty-three men and nineteen women, young and old, were duly sprinkled. Orm and Rapp pulled the two sleepers out from under the table, and tried to shake some life into them; but, finding that all their efforts failed, they carried them up to the tub and held them in position until they, too, had been sprinkled like the rest, after which they were thrown into a quiet corner to continue with their sleeping. The whole company was now in excellent spirits. They wrung the water out of their hair, went joyfully back to their places at the table, and, when Father Willibald attempted to conclude the ceremony by pronouncing a general blessing, the noise was so great that little of what he said could be heard.

'Nobody here is afraid of a little water,' they roared proudly, grinning at each other across the tables.

'Everything is ready now.'

'Up, now, jesters, and show us your skill!'

The jesters exchanged small smiles, and rose willingly from their benches. Immediately, a deep silence fell on the hall. They saluted Ylva with great courtliness, when they had come into the centre of the hall, as though she were their only spectator; then, for a long while, they held the gathering alternatively dumb with amazement and helpless with laughter. They turned somersaults both backwards and forwards, without the help of their hands, landing always on their feet; they imitated birds and beasts, played ditties on small pipes while dancing on their hands, and juggled with tankards, knives and swords. Then, out of their sacks, they produced two great dolls, clad in motley and with faces carved in the likeness of old women. These they held in their hands, Felimid taking one and Ferdiad the other, and, immediately, the dolls began to speak, at first amiably, then shaking their heads and hissing angrily, and, at the last, furiously abusing one another, vituperating tirelessly like squabbling crows. A shiver went through the gathering as the dolls began to talk; the women ground their teeth, and the men went white and reached for their swords; but Ylva and Father Willibald, who knew the Irishmen's tricks of old, calmed them with the assurance that all was the result of the jesters' skill, and that there was no witchcraft in it. Orm himself looked uncertain for a few moments, but soon recovered his mirth; and, when the jesters brought their dolls closer to one another and made them fight with their arms, while their voices cursed one another yet more shrilly, as though they might at any moment seize each other by the hair, he burst into such a bellow of laughter that Ylva leaning anxiously across to him and bade him remember who had happened to King Colla. Orm wiped the tears from his eyes, and looked at her.

'It is not easy to be prudent when one is merry,' he said. 'But I do not think God will allow any harm to befall me now, when I have just done him so great a service.'

It was, however, noticeable that he took Ylva's warning seriously; for he was never able to ignore any observation relating to his health.

At length, the jesters concluded their performance, although the guests begged them many times to continue; and the evening ended without anyone suffering the fate of King Colla. Father Willibald then thanked God for all the happiness that they had enjoyed, and for all the souls that he had been permitted to lead to Christ. So Orm's great christening feast came to a close; and the guests rode home from Gröning in the grey dawn twilight, talking of all the good ale and victuals that they had consumed and of the marvellous feats that had been performed for them by these Irish jesters.

CHAPTER SEVEN

Concerning the King of Sweden's sword-bearer, and the magister from Aachen and his sins

When all the guests, save the four beggars, had departed, and peace had returned to Gröning, Orm and all his household agreed that the feast had passed off better than any of them could have dared to hope, and that Harald Ormsson had had a christening which would, without doubt, bring much honour to himself and them. Only Asa wore a thoughtful look. She said that his sharp-toothed guests had consumed practically their entire stock of provisions, both wet and dry, so that there was scarcely enough left for their own needs.

'The bake-house is empty,' she said, 'save for one small bin; and the larder looks as though a pack of wolves had visited it. I tell you both that, if you have many sons, you will not be able to hold christening feasts like this for all of them, or it will eat up all your wealth. I do not wish to complain too loudly over so much waste on this occasion, for it is right that the first-born should be thus honoured; but now we shall all have to be content with small-beer with our meals, until the next hop-harvest.'

Orm said that he had no wish to hear any grumbling over the fact that a little extra food had been consumed.

'But I know you mean well,' he said to Asa, 'and that your grumbling arises chiefly from habit. And I have heard that small-beer is a drink that a man can be content with.'

'You must remember, Asa,' said Father Willibald, 'that this has been no ordinary feast. For it has advanced the cause of Christ, and has caused heathens to become baptized. Let us, therefore, not complain that so much has disappeared; for God will repay us tenfold.'

Asa admitted that there might be something in this argument; for she never liked to oppose Father Willibald, even when she was in her sharper moods.

Father Willibald was especially jubilant, because he had achieved so much during the feast, not only having converted all the guests but having also become the first of all Christ's servants to succeed in baptizing men from Smaland.

'No, indeed, I can truthfully say,' he said, 'that patience has earned its reward, and that I have not accompanied you to this foul land in vain. During these three feast-days, forty-five souls have received baptism at my hand. True, alas, it is that none of them can be said to have been impelled by a genuine heart-felt longing for Christ, although I told them so much about Him. Our guests were persuaded by the Irish masters, and the men from Smaland were baptized against their will. But it is my belief that, if a servant of Christ were to sit and wait for the people of this land to come to him out of the longing of their hearts, he would have to wait a long time. And I believe that much good may result from all that has happened during this feast. But the credit for all this is not mine, but belongs to these two Irish masters; and it was certainly a true miracle of God that they were sent here at the very time when their art was most needed.'

'Only God could have thought of it,' said Asa.

'But now,' said Orm to the four strangers, 'it is time for us to hear something more about you curious men, who have come to us in the guise of beggars. We should like to know why you two masters wander thus about our land, and who your two companions are, and on what errand you are bound.'

The large man with the grizzled beard glanced at his companions, and nodded his head slowly. Then he said, in a heavy voice: 'My name is Spjalle and my home is in Uppsala. I have accompanied King Erik on all his campaigns, and have stood beside him as his shield-bearer, because of my size and strength. But now I no longer perform that task; instead, it has been commanded that I shall return to Uppsala in the guise of a beggar, with a sword bound to my leg.'

He ceased speaking, and all the others stared at him in astonishment.

'Why have you a sword bound to your leg?' asked Ylva.

'There is much that I could say in reply to that question,' he replied. 'And much else besides: but perchance I have already said too much, for I know that you, woman, are King Sven's sister. But my chief news is my worst: which is that King Erik, who men called the Victorious, is dead.'

They all thought that this was news indeed, and were eager to know more.

'You need have no fear on my account,' said Ylva, 'although I am King Sven's sister. For there is no love lost between us, and the last greeting we received from him was when he sent men here to seek our lives. Was it he who killed King Erik?'

'No, no!' cried Spjalle indignantly. 'Had that been so, I should not now be here to tell the tale. King Erik died of witchcraft; of that I am sure, though whether his death was plotted by the gods, or whether by the foul Gute woman Sigrid, Skoglar-Toste's daughter and King Erik's queen – may she toss perpetually in the whirlpool of Hell amongst sword-blades and serpents' fangs! – I do not know. The King lay off the Small Islands plundering with a mighty fleet, intending shortly to sail against King Sven, who was hiding in North Själland; and good luck attended all our enterprises, so that our hearts were merry. But while we were in harbour at Falster, our luck changed; for there a madness descended upon the King, and he made it known to the whole army that he was intending to become baptized. He said that his luck against King Sven would become better if he did this, and that it would not then be long before he put an end to him for good. He had been seduced into this folly by priests who had come to him from the Saxons, and who had long been mumbling in his ear. The army liked this news but little, and wise men told him openly that it ill became the King of the Swedes to think of such foolishness, which might serve for Saxons and Danes but would be of no use to him. But he glowered fiercely at them when they counselled him thus, and answered them shortly; and, since they knew him to be the wisest of men and one, besides, who always followed his own inclinations, they said no more to him on the matter. But his queen, the crazy Gute woman, who had sailed south with us, bringing all the ships she had inherited from her father, loathed Christ and his followers with a savage loathing, and refused to let King Erik silence her; so that a terrible enmity sprang up between these two,

312

and it was rumoured among the soldiers that she had said that
there was no more pitiful object in the world than a baptized king,
and that King Erik had threatened to have her flogged if she dared
to mention the matter again. But it was too late to talk to her of
flogging; she ought to have tasted the birch long before, and many
times at that. As a result of their strife, the army became divided,
so that we Swedes and the Queen's men looked askance at each
other and exchanged sharp words, and often drew our swords
upon each other. Then the witchcraft gripped him, so that he began
to sicken and lay helpless, unable to move his limbs; and, early
one morning, while most of our men were still asleep, Skoglar-
Toste's crazy daughter sailed away with all her ships and deserted
us. Many of us thought she had sailed to join King Sven, and the
King thought so too, when he heard of her departure: but there
was nothing we could do, and the King was, by now, so weak that
he was scarcely able to speak. Then a great panic descended upon
the army, and all the ships' captains wanted to desert and return
to their homes as soon as they might; and there was much wrangling about the King's treasure-chests, and how they might best
be divided among his followers so as to prevent them from falling
into King Sven's hands. But the King called me to his bedside and
commanded me to carry his sword back to his son in Uppsala. For
this is the ancient sword of the Uppsala Kings, which was given
them by Fröj and is their dearest possession. "Take my sword home,
Spjalle," he said, "and guard it well; for in it resides the luck of
my family." Then he begged me to give him water to drink, and
from this I knew that he had not long to live. Soon afterwards,
he, whom people called the Victorious, died miserably in his bed;
and there were scarcely enough of his followers left to build his
pyre. But we performed the task as well as we could, and killed
his thralls and two of his priests and laid them on the pyre at his
feet, that he might not appear before the gods alone and unaccompanied like a man of low degree. Then, while the pyre was
yet aflame, the people of the islands fell upon us in great strength.
When I saw them coming, I straightway fled, not from fear but
for the sword's sake, and, with these three men, escaped across
the water to Skania in a fishing boat. Now I carry the sword bound
to my leg beneath my clothes, to hide it as best I can. But what
will happen in the world now that he is dead is more than I can

guess, for, of all kings, he was the greatest, although, by the foul witch's contriving, he met so mean an end and now lies far away on Falster's strand with no mound to cover his ashes.'

Such was Spjalle's story, and all his listeners stood open-eyed and silent to hear such tidings.

'These are evil times for kings,' said Orm at last. 'First Styrbjörn, who was the strongest; then King Harald, who was the wisest; and now King Erik, who was the most powerful; and not long since we heard that the great Empress Theofano had also died, she who ruled alone over the Saxons and the Lombards. Only King Sven, my wife's brother, who is more evil than other kings, does not die, but flourishes and waxes fat. It would be good to know why God does not destroy him and let better kings live.'

'God will smite him in His own good time,' said Father Willibald. 'as He smote Holofernes, who had his head hewn off by the woman Judith, or Sennacherib, the Lord of the Assyrians who was slain by his sons as he knelt praying before his idols. But it sometimes happens that evil men cling hard to life; and in these northern climes the Devil is stronger and more powerful than in more civilized regions. That this is true, has just been dreadfully testified before us; for this man Spjalle sits here telling us how he himself slew two of Christ's servants to sacrifice them on a heathen's pyre. Such devilry exists nowhere in the world save in these climes and among certain of the Wendish tribes. I do not rightly know what action I should take against the perpetrator of such a crime. Of what use would it be for me to tell you, Spjalle, that you will burn in Hell fire for this deed; for, even if you had not committed it, you would burn there just the same.'

Spjalle's gaze wandered thoughtfully around the small group in which he sat.

'In my ignorance, I have said too much,' he said, 'and I have made this priest angry. But we acted only according to our ancient custom, for we always do thus when any Swedish king sets out on his journey to the gods. And you told me, woman, that I was not among enemies here.'

'She spoke the truth,' said Orm. 'You shall suffer no harm here. But you must not be amazed that we, who are followers of Christ, hold it an evil thing to have killed a priest.'

'They are among the blessed martyrs now,' said Father Willibald.

'Are they happy there?' asked Spjalle.

'They sit on the right hand of God, and live in bliss such as no mortal man can conceive of,' replied Father Willibald.

'Then they are better off than when they were alive,' said Spjalle. 'For in King Erik's household, they were treated as thralls.'

Ylva laughed.

'You deserve more praise than blame,' she said, 'for helping to bring them to this happy state.'

Father Willibald glared angrily at her, and said that it distressed him to hear her dismiss the matter so lightly.

'Such foolish talk was pardonable in you when you were but a thoughtless girl,' he said, 'but now that you are a wise housewife with three children, and have received much Christian instruction, you should know better.'

'I am my father's child,' replied Ylva. 'And I cannot remember that he gained much spiritual profit from begetting children or from all the instruction he received from you and Bishop Poppo.'

Father Willibald nodded sorrowfully, and passed his hand gently over the crown of his head, as was his wont when anyone mentioned King Harald's name; for he still bore there the imprint of a crucifix with which the King had, in an impatient moment, struck him a violent blow.

'It cannot be denied that King Harald was a dreadful sinner,' he said. 'And, on the occasion to which you have referred, I all but joined the regiments of the blessed martyrs. In many ways, though, he was not altogether unlike King David – the resemblance is, perhaps, more noticeable if one compares him with King Sven – and I do not think he would have been pleased to hear one of his daughters jest on the subject of priest-murder.'

'We are all sinners,' said Orm. 'Even I am no exception; for I myself have more than once laid violent hands on a priest, during our campaigns in Castile and Leon, when we stormed the Christians' towns and burned their churches. Their priests fought bravely against us, with spear and sword, and it was my master Almansur's command that we should always kill them first. But that was in the days when I knew no better, so that I think God will not judge me too severely for it.'

'My luck is better than I had feared,' said Spjalle. 'For I see that I have fallen among honourable men.'

The pale young man with the short black beard, who was the fourth of these beggars, had, till now, sat silent and heavy-eyed. Now, however, he sighed and spoke.

'All men are sinners,' he said. 'Alas, it is too true! But none of you bear as heavy a burden on his soul as I carry. I am Rainald, an unworthy priest of God, canon to the good Bishop Eckard of Schleswig. But I was born at Zülpich in Lotharingia and was formerly magister in the cathedral school at Aachen, and I have come to these northern climes because I am a sinner and a most unlucky man.'

'A man would have to look far before finding more rewarding beggars than you,' said Orm, 'for not one of you but has a tale to tell. If your story is good, Rainald, let us hear it.'

'Stories about sin are always good to hear,' said Ylva.

'Only if one listens to them in a pious frame of mind, and profits from them,' said Father Willibald.

'There is, I fear, much profit to be gleaned from my story,' said the magister sadly, 'for, ever since my twelfth year, I have been the unluckiest of men. Perhaps you know that in a cave in the earth between Zülpich and Heimbach there lives a wise woman called Radla, who has the power of seeing into the future. I was taken to her by my mother, who wished to know if it would be a lucky thing for me to enter the priesthood; for I had a great longing to become a servant of Christ. The wise woman took my hands in hers and sat for a long while rocking and moaning with her eyes closed, so that I thought I would die of terror. At last, she began to speak, and said that I would be a good priest and that much of what I did would prosper. 'But one piece of bad luck you must carry with you,' she said. 'You shall commit three sins, and the second shall be worse than the first, and the third shall be the worst of all. This is your fate, and you cannot escape it.' Those were her words, and more than that she would not say. We wept bitterly, my mother and I, as we walked home from her cave, for it was our wish that I should be a holy man and free from sin. We went to our old priest to ask his advice, and he said that a man who committed only three sins in his life should be regarded as lucky; but I derived little comfort from that. So I entered the priest-school at Aachen, and none of the students was more zealous or industrious than I, or more assiduous in his avoidance of sin.

316

Both in Latin and in liturgy I was the best in the school, and, by the time I was twenty-one, I knew the gospels and the psalms by heart, as well as much of the epistles to the Thessalonians and Galatians, which were too difficult for the majority of the students, so that Dean Rumold praised me highly and took me to be his deacon. Dean Rumold was an old man with a voice like a bull and large glaring eyes. People trembled when he addressed them, and he loved two things above all else in the world, after Christ's holy church: namely, spiced wine and knowledge. He was expert in sciences so obscure and difficult that few people even knew the meaning of their names, such as astrology, mantik,* and algorism,† and it was said that he was able to converse with the Empress Theofano in her own Byzantine tongue. For in his younger days, he had been in the Eastland with the learned Bishop Liutprand of Cremona, and had rare and wonderful stories to tell of those regions. All his life he had collected books, of which he now possessed more than seventy; and often in the evenings, when I brought the hot wine to him in his chamber, he would instruct me in learned matters, or let me read aloud to him from the works of two ancient poets who were in his library. One of these was called Statius; he sang in difficult words about old wars that had been fought between the Byzantines and a town called Thebes. The other was called Ermoldus Nigellus, and he was easier to understand; he told of the blessed Emperor Ludwig, the son of the great Emperor Charles, and of the wars he had fought against the heathens in Spain. When I made errors in reading Statius, the old Dean would curse me and swipe at me with his stick saying that I ought to love him and read him with care, because he was the first poet of Rome who had turned Christian. I was anxious to please the Dean and to escape his stick, so I did my best to obey him; but I could not come to love this poet greatly, much as I tried to do so. There was, besides, a third poet whose works the Dean possessed, bound more finely than the others, and sometimes I saw him sitting mumbling over them. Whenever he did this, his mood would mellow, and he would send me to fetch more wine;

* Black sorcery.
† Counting with Arabian numerals, a science little practised at this time.

but he would never let me read to him from that book. This made me all the more curious to know what it might contain, and one evening, when he was visiting the Bishop, I went into his chamber and searched around for this book, finding it at last in a small chest that stood beneath his wall-seat. The first thing in the book was "Rules for a Magister," which is the blessed Benedict's counsel on how to lead a godly life; and after that, there came a discourse on chastity by a man from England called Aldhelmus. Following this was a long poem, beautifully and most carefully inscribed. It was called "Ars Amandi," which means The Art of Love, and was written by a poet of Ancient Rome called Ovid, who most assuredly was not a Christian.'

The magister looked sadly at Father Willibald, as he reached this point in his narrative, and Father Willibald nodded pensively.

'I have heard tell of this book,' he said, 'and know it to be highly regarded by foolish monks and learned nuns.'

'It is as Beelzebub's own brew,' said the magister, 'and yet it is sweeter than honey. It was difficult for me to understand it completely, for it was full of words that do not appear in the gospels or the epistles, nor in Statius either; but my eagerness to discover its meaning matched my fear at what it might contain. Of its content, I will say nothing, save that it was full of details concerning caresses, sweet-smelling substances, strange melodies, and every form of sensual pleasure that man and woman can indulge in. At first I feared lest it might not be a great sin to read about such matters, but then I bethought myself (it was the Devil speaking to me) and decided that what was fit matter for a wise Dean could not be sinful reading for me. This lustful Ovid was, in sooth, a great poet, though wholly of the Devil's party, and I was surprised to find that his verses remained in my head without my making any effort to memorize them – far more so than the Epistle to the Galatians, though I had struggled most assiduously to memorize that. I continued reading until I heard the Dean's footsteps outside the house; when he entered, he gave me a sharp drubbing with his stick because I had neglected to meet him with torches and help him home. But I scarcely noticed the pain, for other things were uppermost in my mind; and on two later occasions when he was absent, I stole again into his room, and so read the poem to its end. The result of this was that a great change came over me; for from that time my head was filled with sinful thoughts in most melodious verse. Shortly afterwards, because of my knowledge, I was made magister at the Cathedral school, where all went well for me until I received a summons to appear before the Bishop. He told me that the rich merchant Dudo, in the town of Maastricht, a man known for his piety, who had bestowed rich gifts upon the church, had asked for a godly and learned priest to be sent to him to instruct his son concerning the Christian virtues, and, also, to teach him to write and reckon; for which post the Bishop had chosen me, because the Dean held me to be the best of the young teachers, and the only one skilled in the difficult art of reckoning. In order that I might also conduct services for the merchant's household, the good Bishop raised me to the rank of presbyter, with the right to hear confession; and I straightway departed for the town of Maastricht, where I found the Devil awaiting me.'

He clasped his head between his hands, and groaned aloud.

'That is not much of a story, so far as it goes,' said Orm. 'But now perhaps it will get better. Let us hear what happened when you met the Devil.'

'I did not meet him in his bodily form,' said the magister, 'but it was enough as it was. The merchant Dudo lived in a large house by the river; he welcomed me warmly, and each morning and evening I led his household in prayer. I applied myself with industry to the task of teaching his son, and sometimes Dudo himself would come and listen to us, for he was, in truth, a godly man, and often bade me not to be sparing with my rod. His wife was named Alchmunda. She had a sister who lived in the house with them, a widow called Apostolica. They were both young, and fair to look on. They conducted themselves most modestly and virtuously; when they walked, they moved slowly, with their eyes directed towards their feet, and at prayer-time no one showed greater zeal than they. But since the lewd poet Ovid yet nested in my soul, I dared not glance too closely at them, and avoided speaking with them; so, all went well until the time came when the merchant had to go on a long business voyage southwards and into Lombardy. Before he set out, he confessed himself to me and vowed to give rich gifts to the Church to ensure his safe return; he delivered parting admonitions to his household, made me promise that I would pray for his safety every day and so, at last, departed with his servants and horses. His wife and her sister wept loudly as he left; but once he had gone, their weeping quickly ceased, and they now began to conduct themselves otherwise than as they had done before. At household prayers, they behaved as piously as ever; but they often came to hear me instructing my pupil at his lessons, sitting whispering together with their eyes on my face. Sometimes they expressed concern lest the child might be overstraining his mind, and suggested that he should go and play, in order, they whispered to me, that they might ask my advice on matters of serious import. They were amazed, they said, that I was such a solemn and earnest young man, in view of my youth, and Mistress Apostolica asked whether it were true that all young priests were timid of women. She said that she and her sister might both now be regarded as poor widows in mourning, and that they were in grievous need of comfort and exhortation. They told me they were both anxious to confess all their sins before Easter, and Alchmunda asked whether I had the power of granting absolution. I replied that the Bishop had given me that power, because, he had explained, this good household was known for its piety, so that its members would, in any case, have few confessions to make. At this, they clapped their hands in joy; and from that moment the Devil began to make me his plaything, so that these two women occupied more and more of my thoughts. For their good names' sake, Dudo had strictly forbidden them ever to walk alone in the town, and had commanded his steward to see that they did not disobey this order; for which reason, they often cast glances at me and so, in time, tempted me into the cave of sin. I should, alas, have been steadfast and resisted their entreaties, or else have fled from their presence, as the blessed Joseph did in the house of Potiphar; but Joseph had never read Ovid, so that his situation was less perilous than mine. When I looked at them, my mind was no longer filled with piety and chastity, but rather with lust and sinfulness, so that I trembled when they passed close to me; but I dared do nothing, being as yet youthful and innocent in such matters. But these women, who were as full of sinful thoughts as I, and far less timid, lacked not the courage. One night, when I was lying asleep in my chamber, I was awakened by a woman coming into my bed. I could not speak, being filled with great fear and joy; she whispered that it was beginning to thunder, and that she was much afraid of storms. Then she flung her arms around me and began to kiss me furiously. Suddenly a flash of lightning lit up the room, and I saw that the woman was Apostolica; and, although I, too, greatly feared the thunder, I had little time to think of such things now. A short while later, however, after I had enjoyed pleasure with her which far surpassed anything that Ovid had described, I heard the thunder clap just above the roof, and at that I became greatly frightened, for I supposed that God would strike me with his thunderbolt. This, though, did not happen; and on the following night, when Alchmunda came to me as eagerly as her sister had done, there was no thunder at all, and my lust was even greedier than before, so that I surrendered myself to the pleasures of sin with gay courage and a hard heart. These women were of a sweet and gentle temper, never upbraiding me or quarrelling with one another, and there was no evil in them, save only their great lust; nor did they ever show fear or remorse at what they had done, apart from their anxiety lest any of the servants should come to suspect what was afoot. But the Devil was strong in them; for what could be more pleasing to him than to cause the downfall of a servant of Christ? When Easter arrived, the whole household came to me in turn to confess their sins. Last of all came Alchmunda and Apostolica. Solemnly they described to me all that had taken place between them and me, and I had no alternative but to pronounce God's absolution upon them. This was, indeed, a terrible thing for me to have to do; for, although I was by now steeped in sin, yet it felt as though I had deliberately betrayed God.'

'I sincerely hope that your conduct underwent a change for the better,' said Father Willibald severely.

'I hoped it would,' replied the magister. 'But fate willed it otherwise, as the wise woman told me when she warned me about my three sins. As yet, however, the Devil had not wholly ensnared my soul, for every day I prayed for the merchant as I had promised to do, that he might be preserved from danger and return safely home; indeed, after a time I prayed for him twice and thrice a day, to soothe the remorse and terror with which my heart was filled. But my terror waxed greater every day, until, at last, on the night after the festival of Christ's resurrection, I could stand it no longer and fled secretly out of the house and the town and made my way, begging, along the weary roads until I came to my home, where my mother was yet living. She was a godly woman, and when I told her of all that had taken place, she wept bitterly; then, however, she began to comfort me, saying that it was no great wonder that women lost their prudence when they saw me, and that such things happened more often than people generally supposed. The only course for me to follow, she continued, was for me to go back to the good Dean and tell him of all that had happened; and she blessed me as I left her to obey her bidding. Dean Rumbold stared at me in amazement when I arrived at his house, and asked why I had returned; then, weeping, I gave him a truthful account of the whole matter, from beginning to end. He simmered furiously when he learned that I had read Ovid without his permission: but, when I told him what had taken place between me and the two women, he slapped his knee and broke into a thunderous bellow of laughter. He wanted, he said, to know about this business in detail, and whether I had found the women satisfactory; then he sighed, and said that there was no time in life to be compared with youth, and that no deanery in the whole of the empire was worth the loss of it. But as I proceeded further with my story, his face began to darken, and, when I had concluded, he smote the table with his fist and roared that I had behaved most scandalously, and that this was a matter for the Bishop to decide. So we went to the Bishop and told him everything; and he and the Dean agreed that I had acted most wickedly, having doubly betrayed my trust; firstly, in that I had abandoned the post to which I had been appointed, and secondly, in that I had betrayed the secrecy of the confessional by telling my mother what had occurred between me and the women. That I had committed fornication was, of course, a grievous sin, but not an uncommon one, and not to be compared with these others which I had committed, which could only be wiped out by the most rigorous penance. Since, however, I had acted out of youthful folly rather than with evil intent, they would, they said, punish me as mildly as possible; so they gave me three penances to choose from, either to spend a year as chaplain to the lepers in the great hospital at Jülich, or to make a pilgrimage to the Holy Land and bring thence to the crowning-church oil from the Mount of Olives and water from the River Jordan: or to go as a missionary to convert the Danes. Fortified by their compassion, and fired with the desire to wipe out my sin, I therefore chose the most difficult penance. So they sent me to Bishop Eckard of Hedeby. He received me warmly, and soon made me one of his canons, because of my learning; and I remained with him for two years, applying myself assiduously to the cause of piety and teaching in the school which he had founded there, until, again, my fate overtook me, and I committed my second sin.'

'You are a strange kind of priest,' said Orm, 'with your sins and your crazed women. But you still have not told us why you came here.'

'Why did you not marry, like a sensible man,' said Ylva, 'since your lust for women is so strong?'

'Some men hold that a priest should not marry,' said the magister. 'Your own priest, here, is wifeless; though it may be that he is more godly than I and so better able to resist temptation.'

'I have had more important things to bother about than women,' said Father Willibald. 'And now, God be praised, I have reached the age where such temptations no longer exist. But the blessed apostles have held differing views on this subject. St Peter himself was married, and even went so far as to take his wife with him on his travels among the heathens. St Paul, however, was of another mind, and remained unmarried throughout his life; which may be the reason why he travelled further and wrote more. For many years now, godly men have inclined to the opinion of St Paul, and St Benedict's abbots in France now hold that priests should avoid marriage and, if possible, all forms of carnal indulgence. Though it is my belief that it will be some time before all priests can be persuaded to deny themselves to that extent.'

'You speak aright,' said the magister. 'I remember that the French Abbot Odo and his pupils preached that marriage was an evil thing for a servant of Christ, and I hold their opinion to be correct on the matter. But the Devil's cunning is immeasurable, and many are his devices; so that now you see me here, an outcast and a lost wanderer in the wilderness, because I refused to enter into marriage. This was the second of the sins which the witch-woman prophesied would be my lot. And I dare not imagine what the third will be.'

They begged him earnestly to continue with his story and, after Ylva had fortified him with a strong drink, he told them about his second sin.

CHAPTER EIGHT

Concerning the sinful magister's second sin, and the penance to which he was condemned for it

'To continue with my story,' proceeded the magister in a melancholy voice, 'I must tell you that, not far from Hedeby, there dwells a woman by the name of Thordis. She is of noble birth, and is one of the richest women in those parts, with broad estates and many herds; and she was born and brought up a heathen. Because of her wealth, she has been married three times, although she is still but young; and all her husbands have died violent deaths in wars or feuds. When the third was killed, she fell into a deep melancholy, and came of her own accord to Bishop Eckard to tell him that she desired to seek help from God. The Bishop himself instructed her in the Christian doctrine, and subsequently baptized her; after which, she attended mass regularly, riding to church at the head of a large procession of followers with as much noise and clanging of weapons as any war-chieftain. Her pride was great, and her temper refractory, and at first she refused to allow her followers to divest themselves of their weapons before entering the church; for if they did so, she said, they would make a poor show as they marched down the aisle. Eventually, however, the Bishop succeeded in persuading her to consent to this; and he bade us treat her always with the utmost patience, because she was in a position to do much good to God's holy church. Nor can I deny that she came several times to the Bishop with rich gifts. But she was difficult to handle, and especially so towards me. For she had no sooner set eyes on me than she conceived a fierce passion for my body, and on one occasion after mass she waited alone for me in the porch and asked me to bless her. I did so; whereupon she allowed her eyes to roam over my body, and told me that, if I would only pay some attention to my hair and beard, as a man should do, I would be fitted for higher duties than that of conducting mass. "You are welcome to visit my house whenever you please," she added, "and I shall see to it that you do not regret your visit." Then she seized me by the ears and kissed me shamelessly, although my deacon was standing beside us: and so I was left, in great bewilderment and terror. By God's help, I had by now become strong at resisting the temptations of women, and was determined to conduct myself unimpeachably; besides which, she was not as beautiful as the two women who had led me astray in Maastricht. I had, therefore, no fears of being seduced by her; but I was alarmed lest she might act crazily, and it was a great misfortune that the good Bishop Eckard happened to be away at this time, at a church conference at Mainz. I persuaded the deacon to say nothing of what he had seen, though he laughed much about it in his ignorance and folly; and, that evening, I prayed to God to help me against this woman. When I rose from my prayers, I felt wonderfully strengthened, and decided that she must have been sent to show me how well I was now able to resist the temptations of the flesh. But the next time she came to the church, I found myself no less fearful of her than before; and, while the choir was still singing, I fled as fast as I could into the sacristy, that I might avoid meeting her. But, disdaining all modesty, she pursued me and caught me before I could leave the church, and enquired why I had not been to visit her, despite her invitation that I should do so. I replied that my time was wholly occupied with important duties. "Nothing can be more important than this," she said, "for you are the man I wish to marry, although you are one of the shaven sort; and I should have thought that you would have had better sense than to let me sit and wait for you to come to me, after the evidence I had given you of my affection." By this time, I was greatly confused, and could not at first think of any more courageous reply than that, for various reasons, I could not leave the church while the Bishop was absent. Then, however, my courage rose, and I told her in a determined manner that marriage was not a pleasure in which the servants of Christ could indulge, and that the blessed fathers of the Church would not approve of a woman entering upon marriage for the fourth time. She grew pale as I addressed her, and came menacingly nearer to me while I was yet speaking. "Are you a gelding?"

she said, "or am I too old to excite you?" She looked very dangerous in her wrath, so I seized a crucifix and held it before her, and began to pray that the evil spirit might be driven out of her; but she snatched it from my hand so violently that she fell over backwards and struck her head against the great robe-chest. But she leaped instantly to her feet, crying loudly for help; and I – I know not what I did. Then my destiny, from which there is no escape, was further fulfilled: for, in the fight which now ensued, in the church and the porch and in the square outside, between her men, who were trying to help her, and good men from the town, who were trying to help me, men were killed on both sides, including a sub-deacon, who had his head cut off by a sword, and Canon Andreas, who came rushing out of the Bishop's palace to stop the fight and received a stone on the skull, from which he died the next day. At last the woman was driven off, together with such of her followers as were still able to run; but my despair was great when I surveyed the scene of the battle, and reflected that two priests had been killed because of me. When Bishop Eckard returned and heard the news, he found that I was mostly to blame; for, he said, he had strictly ordered that the woman Thordis was to be handled with the utmost care and patience by us all, and I had disobeyed that instruction. I ought, he said, to have complied with her wishes. I begged him to condemn me to the severest possible punishment, for the thought of my sin pained me grievously, even though I knew that I could not have avoided it; I told him of the wise woman's prophecy, and how I had now committed the second of the three sins of which I was fated to be the author. The Bishop said that he would prefer that I should not be at Hedeby when the time came for me to commit the third; and at last they thought of a fit penance for me to undergo. He bade me make a pilgrimage northwards to the country of the wild Smalanders, to ransom from them God's zealous servant, Father Sebastian, who, three years ago, was sent to preach the gospel to them, ever since when he has languished there in bitter serfdom. Thither am I now bound; and this is the mission on which I have come. Now you know as much as I do about me and my misfortunes.'

With this, he ended his story. Ylva laughed, and gave him more ale.

'It seems that you are unlucky with women, whichever way you treat them,' she said, 'despite all that you have read in the book which tells everything about the art of love. And I do not think you will be likely to have better success with them in these parts.'

But magister Rainald replied that he was done with all such vanity.

'You must be a very foolish man in more respects than one,' said Orm, 'and your holy Bishop too, if you think you have any hope of ransoming your priest from the Smalanders, or even of escaping from them with your life, without the aid of silver and gold.'

The magister shook his head and smiled sorrowfully.

'I have no gold or silver,' he said, 'for I do not intend to offer metal to the Smalanders in exchange for Father Sebastian. I wish to offer myself to be their slave in place of him. I am younger than he, and stronger, so that I think they will agree to the exchange. By this means, I hope to atone in some measure for causing the deaths of the two priests.'

They were all amazed at this reply, and at first refused to believe that he could be serious in what he said. But the magister swore that this was so.

'I think I am as good a Christian as most men,' said Orm, 'but I would rather commit all manner of sins than offer myself as a thrall.'

Father Willibald said that such Christian zeal was not what every man might feel, but that the magister was acting rightly.

'Your thralldom will not last for long,' he added, 'for there are now no more than five years left before Christ shall return to the earth, according to the best calculations. If, therefore, you avoid women and meet no further misfortunes at their hands, it may be that you will succeed in baptizing many Smalanders before that day arrives, in which case you will be able to appear with a calm conscience before the judgment throne of God.'

'What you say is true,' replied the magister, 'and the same thought has occurred to me. But the worst is that I still have my third sin to commit, and the wise woman said that this would be the most heinous of all.'

None of them could think of any comfort to offer him, but Orm said that he hoped it would be some time before his third sin might be due.

'For I should not like you to commit it while you are a guest in my house,' he said. 'But be sure of this, priest, and you, too, Spjalle, and both you Irish masters, that you are welcome to stay in my house for as long as you please.'

'That is my wish also,' said Ylva.

They thanked them both for this invitation, but Spjalle said that he could not accept for more than a few days.

'For I must not loiter on my journey,' he explained, 'with the luck of the Kings of Sweden bound to my leg.'

Both the jesters said that they would go with Spjalle, since they, too, were heading for Uppsala. If they did not find things to their satisfaction there, there were other kings elsewhere who would make them welcome.

'We can go to Norway,' they said, 'where Olaf Tryggvasson is now King: for he is said to have become a zealous Christian. Or we could voyage to the Eastland, to Prince Valdemar of Gardariké, who has a great name for power and wealth, and is said to be well-disposed towards men skilful in the arts.'

'That will be a long journey for you to travel,' said Orm.

'We have no home,' they replied, 'and it is our life to wander over the earth; but where kings are, thither will we gladly journey, for all kings welcome us. Beyond Gardariké is the kingdom of Basil, he whom they call the Hammer of the Bulgars, and who is the most powerful of all the monarchs in the world, now that King Harald and King Erik are dead; though it may be that the young Emperor of Germany would be displeased to hear us say so, and King Brian, too, who rules in Ireland now. We have heard it said by far-travelled men that the jesters of the Emperor in Miklagard have a great name, and can perform marvellous feats; men speak especially of a performance they gave before the envoys of the old German Emperor, in the days when Nikeforos ruled at Miklagard. They are said to have climbed miraculously upon a pole; and this is a trick new to us, though we reckon that we know more tricks than most men. It might, therefore, be worth our while to journey there to see how skilfully they really are, and to show them what the Erin Masters can perform. It would, besides, be a great honour for us to jest before the Emperor Basil, and for him to receive a visit from us. But first we shall go to Uppsala, to the young King there, and we think it best that we should travel there in Spjalle's company. For he is a good man to go a-begging with.'

They held to this decision; and, after a few days, when he had regained his strength, Spjalle once again bound his royal sword to his leg, and he and the two masters took up their sacks and beggars' staffs. Asa and Ylva gave them fine fare for their journey; so that they said they had small hope of encountering again such hospitality as it had been their fortune to receive here at Gröning.

As they parted, Felimid said to Orm: 'If we should meet again, you may be sure that you will always have good friends in us.'

'I dearly hope that we may meet again,' said Orm. 'But, if you set forth for Miklagard, I fear my hope is not likely to be fulfilled. For I shall remain here, a man of peace, watching my children grow and my herds fatten, and shall never wander across the seas any more.'

'Who knows?' said the small, long-eared men. 'Who can tell?'

They wagged their heads, received a blessing from Father Willibald, and departed with Spjalle upon their journey.

But magister Rainald remained with Orm for a while longer, it having been decided that this was the wisest thing for him to do. They all agreed that it would be madness for him to go alone across the border to look for Father Sebastian, for, if he did so, he would be caught or killed without achieving anything. So it was decided that he should stay at Gröning until the time arrived for the border peoples to hold their great annual conference, which they called Thing, at the Kraka Stone; for the time for this was shortly due. At the Thing, said Orm, they might be able to come to some agreement with the Smalanders about the matter on which his mind was set.

CHAPTER NINE

How the magister searched for heifers and sat in a cherry-tree

So Magister Rainald remained with them over the summer. He helped Father Willibald to minister to the spiritual needs of the household, and to such of the newly baptized Christians as thought it worth their while to keep their promise to attend divine service. The magister was greatly praised by them all for his singing at Mass, which was more beautiful than anything that had been heard in these parts before. At first, the newcomers to Christianity showed some reluctance to appear on Sundays, but, as the news of the magister's singing spread, more and more people began to turn up; and tears could be seen standing in the women's eyes as he sang. Father Willibald was much gratified to receive this assistance, for he himself had an unmelodious voice.

The magister was, however, poorly qualified to do other forms of useful work. Orm wanted to give him something to occupy him during the week, and did his best to discover some task that he might be able to perform competently; but they could not find anything at which he was of the slightest use. He knew no trade, and was unable to handle any sort of tool. Orm said: 'This is a bad thing; for soon you will be a thrall in Smaland, and if you can do nothing but sing, I fear you will have a hard time of it up there. It would be best for you if you could learn to do something useful while you are staying here with me, for this will save you many stripes upon your back.'

Sighing, the magister concurred; and he tried his hand at many simple tasks, but could not succeed with any of them. When they set him to cut grass, his efforts were pathetic to see, for he could

331

not learn to swing the scythe. He was useless at carpentry, although Rapp and even Orm himself spent long hours trying to teach him the craft; and, when he tried to chop wood for the bake-oven, he hit himself in the leg, so that, when they came to fetch the wood, they found him groaning on the ground in a puddle of blood. When he had recovered from this, they sent him out with a man to watch the fishing-lines in the river; but there he was attacked by an enormous eel, which twined itself round his arm. In his terror, he upset the punt, so that all the fish they had caught fell into the water, and it was only with difficulty that he and his companion managed to reach the bank safely. So he gained the name of being a hero in church, and a good man to have in the house of an evening, when everybody would be seated at his or her handicraft and he would tell them stories about saints and emperors; but in all matters else, he was regarded as an incomparable duffer, unable to do any of the simple things that every man has to know about. Still, he was not disliked; and least of all by the women, who, from Asa and Ylva to the youngest serving-girls, fussed over him continually and, at the least excuse, spoke out manfully in his defence.

Early in the spring of that year, One-Eyed Rapp had taken himself a wife, a plump farmer's daughter called Torgunn, whom, despite his one-eyedness, he had had no difficulty in winning, on account of the great name he possessed as a widely-travelled and weapon-skilful man. Rapp having ordered her to get herself baptized, she had lost no time in doing so, and had never since failed to attend a service; she was well liked by everyone, and performed her duties industriously, and Rapp and she were well content with each other, although he was occasionally heard to mumble that she was difficult to silence and slow to bear him a child. Ylva liked her greatly, and these two often sat together exchanging confidences; nor did the flow of words from their mouths ever slacken.

It happened one day that all the people of the household had to go into the woods to look for strayed heifers; and a lengthy search ensued. Towards evening, while Rapp was on his way homewards, having found nothing, he heard a sound from a birch-copse; and, on approaching nearer, he saw Torgunn lying in the grass by the side of a great boulder, with magister Rainald arched above her. More than that he could not see, because of the height of the grass;

and both of them rose hastily to their feet as soon as they heard his footsteps. Rapp stood there without saying anything, but Torgunn immediately hopped towards him on one leg, with her mouth full of words.

'It is indeed lucky that you have come,' she said, 'for now you can help me home. I twisted my knee, falling over a root, and was lying there crying for help when this good man came to my aid. He lacked the strength to pick me up and carry me; instead, therefore, he has been reading prayers over my knee, so that it has already begun to feel better.'

'I have only one eye,' replied Rapp, 'but with that, I see clearly. Was it necessary for him to lie upon you while he prayed?'

'He was not lying upon me,' said Torgunn indignantly. 'Rapp, Rapp, what is in your mind? He was kneeling beside me, holding my knee, and praying thrice over it.'

'Thrice?' said Rapp.

'Do not make yourself more stupid than you are,' said Torgunn. 'Firstly, in the name of the Father, secondly, in the name of the Son, and lastly, in the name of the Holy Ghost. That makes three.'

Rapp looked at the priest. The latter was pale, and there was a tremble in his mouth, but otherwise, he looked as usual.

'If you had been out of breath,' said Rapp thoughtfully, 'you would, by now, be a dead man.'

'I have come to this land in search of martyrdom,' replied the magister mildly.

'You will find it, sure enough,' said Rapp. 'But first let me look at this knee of yours, woman, if you can remember which it is that is hurting you.'

Torgunn grumbled plaintively, and said that she had never been treated thus before; however, she seated herself obediently on the stone, and bared her left knee. They found difficulty in agreeing whether or not there was any swelling to be seen; but when he thumbed it, she screamed aloud.

'And it was worse a few minutes ago,' she said. 'But I think I might manage to hobble back to the house, with your help.'

Rapp stood with a dark face, thinking to himself. Then he said: 'Whether any harm has come to your knee, I do not know, for your screams mean nothing. But I do not want Orm to be able to say that I killed a guest of his without good cause. Father Willibald knows best about these things, and he will be able to tell me whether the limb is really damaged.'

They started homewards, and made fair progress, though Torgunn often had to stop and rest, because of her great pain. Over the last stretch, she was forced to support herself on both of the men, with one arm round the neck of each.

'You are hanging heavily enough upon me,' said Rapp, 'but I still do not know whether I can believe you in this matter.'

'Believe what you will,' replied Torgunn, 'but of this I am sure; that my knee will never be right again. I caught my foot between two roots, as I was jumping down from a fallen trunk; that was how it happened. I shall be lame for the rest of my days as the result of this.'

'If that is so,' replied Rapp bitterly, 'all his praying will have been to no purpose.'

They carried Torgunn to bed, and Father Willibad went to examine her. Rapp at once took Orm and Ylva aside, and told them what had happened, and what he believed to be the truth of the matter. Orm and Ylva agreed that this was a most unfortunate occurrence, and that it would be a sad thing for all of them if there should be discord between Rapp and Torgunn as a result of this.

'It is a good thing that you think before you act,' said Orm, 'otherwise, you might have killed him, which would have been a bad matter if he should turn out to be innocent. For to kill a priest would bring God's punishment down upon us all.'

'I have a better opinion than you of Torgunn, Rapp,' said Ylva. 'It is an easy thing to twist a knee when one is clambering among logs and stones. And you have admitted yourself that you saw nothing take place.'

'What I saw was bad enough,' said Rapp, 'and they were in the darkest part of the forest.'

'It is wisest not to judge too hastily in such matters,' said Orm. 'You remember the judgment delivered by our lord Almansur's magistrate in Cordova, the time when Toke Grey-Gullsson had managed, by cunning, to gain entry to the woman's room in the house of the Egyptian sugar-baker, the one that lived in the Street of Penitents, and a wind blew aside the curtain that hung across the window so that four of the sugar-baker's friends, who happened to be walking across the court, saw Toke and the sugar-baker's wife together upon her bed.'

'I remember the occasion well,' said Rapp. 'But the husband was a heathen.'

'What happened to the woman?' asked Ylva.

'The sugar-baker presented himself before the magistrate with his garments rent and with his four witnesses behind him, and begged that Toke and the woman should be stoned as adulterers. My lord Almansur had himself commanded that the case should be judged strictly according to the law, although Toke was a member of his bodyguard. The magistrate listened carefully to the evidence of the four witnesses concerning what they had seen take place, and three of them swore upon oath that they had distinctly witnessed certain things occurring; but the fourth was old, and had weak eyes, and so had not been able to see as clearly as the others. Now, the law of Mohammed, which stands written by Allah's own finger in their holy book, states that no person may be convicted of adultery, unless four pious witnesses can be found who have clearly and unmistakably seen the offence committed. So the magistrate found Toke and the woman not guilty, and sentenced the sugar-baker to the bastinado for bringing false accusation.'

'That sounds a good land for a woman to live in,' said Ylva, 'for much can take place before one is seen in the act by four witnesses. But I think the sugar-baker was unlucky.'

'He did not think so for long,' said Orm, 'for, as a result of this incident, his name became known to the whole bodyguard, and we would often visit his shop to chaff him and drink his sweet Syrian mead, so that his trade increased greatly, and he praised Allah for the magistrate's wisdom. But Toke said that, although the affair had ended well enough, he would take it as a warning, and he never again ventured to go in to the woman.'

Father Willibald now came to them and told them that Torgunn had been telling the truth when she had asserted that she had twisted her knee.

'Before long,' he said to Rapp, 'it will be swollen that even you will have no doubts upon the matter.'

They all supposed that Rapp would feel relief at this news; but he sat for some time buried in his thoughts. At length he said: 'If that is so, the magister must have lain there a good while, holding her knee with both his hands, or perhaps with one only. It is difficult for me to believe that he stopped at that, for he has himself told us that he is weak-willed where women are concerned, and that he has learned from Roman books secret methods of pleasing them. It is my belief that he did more than read over her knee; for, if he had confined himself to that, the swelling would not have arisen, if there is any virtue in his godliness.'

This was the longest speech that any one them had ever heard Rapp deliver, and none of them could persuade him that he was of a wrong opinion in the matter. Then Ylva said: 'At first you were suspicious because you could not see any swelling; now you are suspicious because you have been told that there is one. But this does not surprise me, for you men are always the same once you have an idea fixed in your head. I shall go myself to Torgunn and have the matter out with her; for she and I are close friends, and she will tell me the truth of what really happened. And if anything has taken place which she does not wish to speak of, I will know from her replies what it is that she is trying to hide. For a woman knows at once whether another woman is telling the truth or not; which is, God be praised, more than any man is capable of.'

With this, she left them; and what she and Torgunn said to one another, no man knows, for none heard their talk.

'You can put your mind at rest now, Rapp,' said Orm, 'for, in a short while, you will know the truth about this matter. There is no more cunning woman in the wide world than Ylva; of that I can promise you. I marked that the very first time I met her.'

Rapp grunted; and they began to discuss the two heifers that had escaped and had not been discovered, and where it would be best to search for them on the following day.

Ylva was absent for a long while. When at last she returned, she shook her fist under Rapp's nose.

'I have discovered the truth of this matter,' she said, 'and it was as I had supposed. You can set your mind at rest, Rapp, for nothing blameworthy took place between these two in the forest. The only one who has behaved badly is you. Torgunn does not know whether to laugh at you for your suspicions, or whether to weep at the memory of the hard words you used to her; and she tells me that she almost regrets not having seduced the priest, when she had the chance. "We could have had much pleasure before Rapp came," she told me, "and since I shall in any case have to endure his suspicions, and be looked upon as a woman of shame, I might as well have

336

got what enjoyment I could out of the affair." Those were the words she used; and, if you are as wise a man as I hold you to be, Rapp, you will never mention another word about this business; if you do, I cannot answer for her behaviour. But if you handle her tenderly, I think she will be willing to let the matter drop; and it would be a good thing if you could get her with child, for then you would not have to worry yourself any more about this poor unfortunate magister.'

Rapp scratched his scalp, and muttered something to the effect that any state she might be in was not the result of any lack of endeavour on his part. But they could see that he was much relieved by what Ylva had told him, and he thanked her for having put the matter to rights.

'And it is a good thing that I myself possess some small stock of wisdom,' he said, 'even though I am not as wise as you, Ylva. For, if I had been an impatient man, I would have killed the magister, and would now be wearing a long nose, and you and Orm would no longer be my friends. But now I will go to Torgunn, to comfort her and make things well again.'

When Orm and Ylva had gone to bed, they talked for a time about this business before falling asleep.

'All this has passed off better than I could have expected,' said Orm, 'thanks to your good offices. For, if I had been called upon to decide in this matter, I should have adjudged that they had busied themselves with more things in the forest than with this knee of hers.'

Ylva lay for a while in silence. Then she said: 'Orm, you would have judged correctly, but you must never let anyone know this. I promised her that I would not repeat what she had told me, and that I would talk Rapp into believing that nothing had taken place; and we must leave things as they now are, and nobody must know anything, not even Father Willibald; for, if the truth were to come out, it would cause great distress to both Rapp and Torgunn, as well as to this unfortunate woman-crazy magister. But to you I will tell the truth, which is that there was more done between these two than praying over her bad knee. She says that she liked him from the first, because of his beautiful singing voice and the unlucky fate to which he is condemned; besides which, she says that she could never say nay to a holy man. She says she trembled throughout her whole body like a trapped bat when he touched her knee as she lay there upon the ground, and that he did not appear embarrassed but straightway guessed what was in her mind. Before long, they were both in a state of desire; she says that she could not help this. Later, when they had become calm again, he began to groan and weep, and took up his prayers where he had left them off; but he had only had time to say a few sentences before Rapp appeared. That, doubtless, is why the swelling has become worse, for he should, properly, have repeated the prayer thrice for it to be effective. But she will thank God for the rest of her life, she says, for not allowing Rapp to arrive a few minutes earlier than he did. Now if you let Rapp or anyone else know the truth of this, you will make me exceedingly unhappy, and others also.'

This story delighted Orm hugely, and he gladly promised never to repeat a word of it, to Rapp or anyone else.

'As long as Rapp never knows that they have cuckolded him,' he said, 'no harm need result from this incident. But this magister is, indeed, a remarkable man; for in all other manly pursuits he is wholly incompetent, but his handling of women leaves nothing to be desired. It would be a bad thing if he should see any more of Torgunn without other people being present; if that were to happen, this business might end evilly, for Rapp will not allow himself to be gulled a second time. So I must think out some regular task for him to perform, which will keep him away from her, and her from him; for I cannot be sure which of the two would be the more desirous of promoting a second meeting.'

'You must not treat him too harshly,' said Ylva, 'for the poor creature has enough suffering ahead of him at the hands of the Smalanders. I myself will do what I can to keep him and Torgunn apart from one another.'

The next morning, Orm called the magister to him and told him that he had at last found him a task that he thought he would be able to perform to everyone's satisfaction.

'Hitherto,' he said, 'you have not shown much skill in any of the labours to which we have set you; but now you will have the chance to do us all a real service. Here you see this cherry-tree, which is the best of all my trees; and that is not only my opinion, but also that of the crows. You are now to climb to the top of it, and I would advise you to take food and drink with you, for you are not to come down until the crows and magpies have gone off to their night-branches. You shall sit there every day; and you shall take your place there early, for these crows awake in the grey twilight before dawn. It is my hope that you will succeed in protecting the berries for us, if you do not eat too many of them yourself.'

The magister looked gloomily up at the tree; the berries there were larger than those that are usually found on cherry-trees, and were just beginning to darken towards ripeness. All the birds were especially fond of these berries, and both Rapp and Father Willibald had tried to keep them away by shooting arrows at them, but had been able to achieve little.

'This is no more than I deserve,' said the magister, 'but I am afraid to climb so high.'

'You will have to accustom yourself to that,' said Orm.

'I easily become dizzy.'

'If you hold on tightly, the dizziness will not affect you. If you show that you have not the courage to undertake this task, everybody will laugh at you, and the women most of all.'

'I have, in truth, deserved all this,' said the magister sadly.

After some argument, he succeeded, with much difficulty, in climbing part of the way up the tree, while Orm stood on the ground below, exhorting him continually to ascend higher. At length, amid much praying, he managed to reach a fork where three branches met; it swayed beneath his weight, and, seeing this, Orm commanded him to remain there, since his rocking would make him more visible to the birds.

'You are quite safe up there,' he shouted up at the magister, 'and nearer heaven than we poor creatures who must remain on the ground. There you can eat and drink to your heart's content, and discuss your sins with God.'

So there he sat; and the crows, which came flying eagerly from all directions to peck at the good berries, fled in terror and amazement when they saw that there was a man in the tree; they circled over him, cawing with anger, and the magpies sat in the trees around him mocking him with spiteful laughter.

It was on the sixth day, on an afternoon when the heat was very great, that he fell. He had become drowsy with the heat, and swarming bees had come to the tree and had selected his head as a resting-place. Awaking in terror, he whirled his arms violently to drive them away, lost his balance and fell shrieking to the ground in a shower of bees, berries and broken branches. The twins and their playmate were the first to reach the place of the accident; they stared at him in wonder, and the boy Ulf asked him why he had fallen down. But he only lay there groaning, and saying that his last moment was at hand. The children now began joyfully to pluck the good berries that had fallen with him; but this aroused the bees, who attacked them, so that they fled shrieking. All the house-people were gathering reeds down by the river, and it was left to Ylva herself and two of her maids to rush to their help. They bore the magister into the weaving-room, and put him to bed. When the maids heard of the misfortune that had befallen him, they became so mirthful that Ylva lost patience with them and boxed their ears, and bade them go at once and fetch Father Willibald, who was down by the river with the others.

Ylva was moved with pity for the magister and did what she could to make him comfortable; she also gave him a strength-drink of her best ale. He had sustained no injury from the bees, but suspected that the fall had broken his shoulder. Ylva wondered whether this might not be God's punishment for his conduct with Torgunn in the forest; and he agreed that this might well be the case.

'But how much do you know of what happened between us in the forest?' he asked.

'Everything,' replied Ylva, 'for Torgunn has told me with her own lips; but you need not fear that anyone else will come to hear of it, for both she and I know how to keep our tongues quiet when there is need for it. And this comfort, at least, I can give you, that she had plenty to say in your praise, and that she does not regret what took place between you, although it came so near to bringing disaster on you both.'

'I regret it,' said the magister, 'although I fear there is little to be gained by that. For God has so cursed me that I cannot be alone with a young woman without straightway becoming inflamed with desire. Nor have even these days that I have spent in the tree cleansed me of this passion, for my thoughts have dwelt less upon God than upon the sins of the flesh.'

Ylva laughed.

'The bee-swarm, and your fall from the tree, have helped you now,' she said, 'for here you are, alone with me, in a place where nobody will be able to disturb us for a good while; and I think I am not less comely than Torgunn. But from this temptation, at least, I think you will be able to emerge without sin, poor foolish man.'

'You do not know,' replied the magister sadly, 'how powerful the curse is'; and he stretched his arm towards her.

What then happened between these two, nobody ever knew; and when Father Willibald came to the house to examine the magister's injuries, he found him asleep, purring contentedly, while Ylva sat working industriously on her weaving-chair.

'He is too good a man to have to climb trees,' she said to Orm and the house-folk that evening, as they were sitting at their meal, full of merriment at the manner in which the magister had ended his sojourn in the tree, 'and he shall not be forced to do it any more.'

'I know little of his goodness,' said Orm, 'but, if you mean that he is too clumsy to do so, you have my agreement. What he is fitted for is more than I know: but the Smalanders will, no doubt, be able to hit upon something. Most of the berries are ripe now, and can be picked before the birds steal them so that we shall lose little by this accident. But it is good that the time for the Thing is almost upon us.'

'Until that time arrives,' said Ylva firmly, 'I myself will keep watch over him; for I do not want him to be mocked and fare miserably during the last days that he will spend among Christians.'

'Whatever he does, women swarm to his assistance,' said Orm. 'But you may do as you think best in this matter.'

Everybody in the house laughed themselves crooked whenever any mention was made of the magister and his bee-swarms; but Asa said that this was a good omen, for she had often heard wise old people say that when bees settled on a man's head it meant that he would have a long life and many children. Father Willibald said that in his younger days he had heard the same asserted by learned men at the Emperor's court at Goslar; though, he added, he was not sure whether this was altogether applicable when the person in question was a priest.

Father Willibald could not find anything very wrong with the magister's sore shoulder; none the less, the latter preferred to remain in bed for the next few days, and, even when he felt well enough to get up, he continued to spend most of his time in his room. Ylva watched over him with care, preparing all his meals herself, and saw to it strictly that none of her servant-girls should be allowed to come near him. Orm chaffed her about this, saying that he wondered whether she, too, might not have gone crazy about the magister; besides which, he said, he could not but grudge all the good food that was taken daily into the weaving-room. But Ylva answered firmly that this was a matter for her to decide; the poor wretch, she said, needed good food to put a little flesh on his bones before he went to live among the heathens, and, as regards the servant girls, she was merely anxious to preserve him from temptation and spiteful mockery.

So Ylva had her way in this matter; and things continued thus until the time arrived for the dwellers on both sides of the border to ride to the Thing at the Kraka Stone.

CHAPTER TEN

Concerning the women's doings at the Kraka Stone, and how Blue-Tongues' edge became dented

Every third summer, at the first full moon after the heather had begun to bloom, the border peoples of Skania and Smaland met, by ancient tradition, at the stone called the Kraka Stone, in order to take vows of peace, or of war, against one another until the time of their next meeting.

To this place came chieftains and chosen men from Finnveden and Värend, and from all the districts of Göinge, and a Thing was held, which usually continued for several days. For, even when peace prevailed along the border, there were always many problems to be settled; disputes regarding hunting and pasturing rights, murders resulting from these disputes, cattle-thefts, woman-thefts, and the extradition of slaves who had escaped across the border. All such matters were duly weighed and judged, by wise men from all the various tribes, sometimes in a manner satisfactory to everyone, as when, for example, murder could be repaid by murder or rape by rape, and sometimes by an agreed fine. When, though, a difficult altercation had arisen between stubborn men, so that no agreement could be arrived at, the matter would be decided by single combat between the parties concerned on the flat grass before the Stone. This was regarded as the best entertainment of all, and any Thing during which at least three corpses had not been carried from the combat ground would be thought a poor and unworthy session. Most often, however, the Thing sustained its reputation as an occasion of much sport and displaying of wisdom, and everyone left it well contented, with fine stories to tell their wives and house-folk on their return home.

Much buying and selling also took place there, of slaves, weapons and oxen, forged iron and cloth, skins, wax and salt, so that sometimes traders came to it from as far afield as Hedeby and Gotland. In former times, the King at Uppsala and the King of the Danes had been wont to send trusted men to the Thing, partly to safeguard their rights and partly to keep an eye open for outlaws who had escaped their clutches; but the farmers had greeted these envoys by removing their heads, which they had then smoked over juniper fires and sent back to their masters, to signify to the Kings that the border peoples preferred to manage their own affairs. But stewards and ships'-chieftains from the Jarls of Skania and West Guteland still occasionally came there, to enlist the services of any good warrior who had a mind to go a-viking overseas.

Accordingly, the Thing at the Kraka Stone had come to be regarded by the border peoples as a great occasion, so that they often reckoned time from Thing to Thing.

Men said that the Stone had been set up in ancient times by Rolf Krake, during a journey that he had made through these parts; and neither kings nor border-dwellers had dared to erase this mark which he had raised to show where the country of the Danes ended and that of the Swedes began. It was a tall and mighty stone, such as only heroes of ancient times could have had the strength to raise; it stood in open ground on a hill, and was shadowed by a hawthorn tree which was held to be sacred and of equal age with the Stone. On the evening before each Thing, it was the custom of the Virds, the inhabitants of Värend, to sacrifice two goats at the Stone and perform strange rites; their blood was allowed to spread over the ground, and it was held that this blood, together with that which was spilt around the Stone during combats, gave much strength to the tree, so that it continued to flourish, despite its age, and always bloomed most richly in the year following a Thing. But few saw it bloom save the birds that nested in its branches, and eagles and kites and the wandering animals of the earth; for, all around the Kraka Stone for many miles, the land was desert and uninhabited.

As Orm was making ready to journey to the Thing, many farmers came to Gröning to accompany him thither; Gudmund of Uvaberg, Black Grim, and others. Orm left Rapp behind to guard the house, and took with him both the priests and two of his men. All the women wept because the magister was now leaving them to become a slave, but he said that there was nothing else for it, and that it was to be so. Asa and Ylva had sewn new clothes for him, a tunic and shirt and skin breeches; Orm said that it was well that they had done this, since it would make it easier for them to negotiate the exchange if he had good clothes on his back, which his new employer would be able to make use of.

'For you must not suppose,' he said, 'that he will be able to wear them for long himself.'

Torgunn brought the magister a basket of birch-bark filled with good food for his journey, which she had herself prepared specially for him. Rapp scowled when he saw it; but she insisted that the magister should have it, saying that she was giving it to him as a thanks-gift for the prayers which he had read over her knee; besides which, she said, she hoped to get a good blessing from him in return for it. The magister sat palely on his horse, and blessed her and all the others with beautiful words, so that tears appeared in all the women's eyes. Father Willibald, who was also seated high upon a horse, then offered up a prayer for a lucky journey and protection against wild beasts, robbers and all dangers that threaten men who travel. Then the company rode away to the Thing, strong in numbers and well armed.

They reached the Stone a short while before dusk, and pitched camp, together with other groups of men, upon the ground which the Göings had, by ancient custom, been used to occupy, on the bank of a brook which ran through birch-trees and thickets on the southern side of the Stone. Traces could still be seen there of camp-fires round which they and their predecessors had sat at previous Things. On the other side of the brook, the Finnvedings were encamped, and from them there came much noise and shouting. It was said to be a greater hardship for them than for other men to sit without ale around the Kraka Stone, and it was, accordingly, an ancient custom among them to arrive at the Thing already drunk. Both the Göings and the Finnvedings were encamped a short way from the brook, and only came to it to water their horses and fill their pots; for they had always thought it wisest not to crowd unnecessarily close to each other, if the peace of the Thing was to be maintained between them.

The Virds were the last to arrive at the meeting-place. Any man, looking at them, could see at once that they were a race apart, without resemblance to other peoples. They were enormously tall men with silver rings in their ears, and their swords were longer and heavier than those of other men. They had shaven chins, long cheek-beards hanging down on either side of their mouths, and eyes like the eyes of dead men. They were, moreover, short of speech. Their neighbours said that the cause of this aloofness was that they were ruled by their women-folk, and were afraid lest, if they spoke, this might be discovered; but few dared to ask them directly how much truth there was in this report.

They were encamped in a grove east of the Stone, where the brook ran broadest; there, they were apart from the other tribes, which was the way they liked it to be. They were the only men who had brought women with them to the Thing. For it was an old belief among the Virds that the best cure for a woman's barrenness was to be found at the Kraka Stone, if a man did as the wise ancients had prescribed; and young married women, who had borne no children to husbands of proved virility, were accordingly always eager to accompany their men-folk to the Thing. What they had to do would be seen to-night, under the full moon; for the whole of this evening, the Virds would be in possession of the Stone, and their concern that no stranger should see what their women did after the moon rose was well known among both the Göings and the Finnvedings. For it had happened on more than one occasion that those who, to satisfy their curiosity, had approached too near the Stone while the women were there, had seen a winging spear or a hewing sword as their last sight on earth, and this before they had had the chance to witness that for which they had come. Nevertheless, inquisitive young men of the Göings, and such of the Finnvedings as had not drunk too deeply, nursed the prospect of a fine evening's entertainment; and, as soon as the moon's glimmer could be discerned above the edge of the trees, some of them climbed up into the branches to good vantage points, while others crept forward through the thickets and undergrowth as near to the Stone as they dared.

Father Willibald was much displeased at all this, especially at the fact that young men of Orm's following, who had received baptism at the great feast and had since paid several visits to his church, were as eager as the rest to see as much as they could of witchcraft at the Stone.

'All this is the Devil's work,' he said. 'I have heard tell that it is the

346

custom of these women to run around the Stone in shameless nakedness. Every man who has received baptism should arm himself with strength from Christ against such abominations as this. You would be better employed in axing a cross for us to raise before our fire, to protect us this night from the powers of evil. I myself am too old for such work; besides which, I cannot see well in this dense wood.'

But they replied that all the crosses and all the holy water in the world would not prevent them from seeing the Vird women perform that evening.

Magister Rainald was seated beside Orm in the circle around the food-pot. He sat with his arms round his knees and his head bowed, rocking backwards and forwards; he had been given bread and smoked mutton like the rest, but showed little appetite. It was always so with him when he was contemplating his sins. But, when he heard Father Willibald's words, he stood up.

'Give me an axe,' he said, 'and I will make you a cross.'

The men round the fire laughed and expressed doubt as to whether he was capable of performing this task. But Orm said: 'It is right that you should try; and you may find it more profitable than climbing into the trees.'

They gave him an axe, and he went away to do the best he could.

Clouds now began to pass over the moon, so that at times it was quite dark; but in the intervals, the curious among them were able to see what the Virds were doing up at the Stone. Many men were assembled there. Some of these had just finished cutting a strip of turf, long and broad, and were now raising it from the ground and placing stakes beneath to hold it up. Others were collecting brushwood, which they placed in four piles at equal distances from the Stone. When these preparations had been completed, they took their weapons and walked some distance towards the ground where the Göings and the Finnvedings were encamped. There, they remained as sentries, with their backs to the Stone, some of them going down as far as the brook itself.

The noise of bleating was now heard; and, from the direction of the Vird camp, four old women appeared, leading two goats. With them came a small, bald man with a white beard, very old and bent, holding a long knife in his hand. After him followed a crowd of women, all wearing cloaks.

When they reached the Stone, the old women tied the legs of the goats together, and fastened long ropes around their backs. Then all the women helped to heave the goats up over the top of the Stone and make the rope fast, so that the goats were left hanging down one on either side of the Stone, head downwards. The little old man gesticulated and chattered petulantly until they had got them into the exact position in which he wanted them. When, at last, he was satisfied, he ordered them to lift him to the top of the Stone, which they succeeded, with difficulty, in doing. They pushed the knife up to him on a stick, and, taking it, he seated himself astride the Stone just above the goats. Then he raised his arms above his head and cried in a loud voice to the young women: 'This is the first! Go ye through earth!'

The women tittered, and nudged one another, and looked coyly hesitant. At length, however, they slipped their cloaks from their bodies, and stood naked; then they walked in a line towards the raised strip of turf, and began to creep under it, one by one. A terrific crash from the direction of the Finnvedings' camp suddenly echoed through the silence of the night; then cries and groans were heard, followed by loud laughter, for an old leaning tree, into the branches of which many of the young men had climbed, had collapsed under their weight and had crushed several of them as it fell. But the women continued to creep under the turf, until all of them had passed beneath it, whereupon the old man raised his arms again and cried: 'This is the second! Go ye through water!'

At this, the women walked down to the brook and waded out into the midst of it. They squatted down on their haunches where the water was deepest, held their hands over their faces, and, amid much shrieking, plunged their heads beneath the water, so that their hair floated on the surface, after which, without delay, they came up again.

Then the old women lit the piles of brushwood around the Stone, and, when the young women had returned from the water, the old man cried: 'This is the third! Go ye through fire!'

The women now began to run around the Stone and to leap nimbly over the fires. As they did so, the old man slit the throats of the goats, so that their blood ran down the sides of the Stone, while he mumbled words of ritual. Nine times the women had to run round the Stone, and nine times lap blood, that it might give them strength and make their wombs fruitful.

A great cloud passed over the moon, but, by the light of the fires, the women could still be seen gambolling around the Stone. Then a voice was suddenly heard to begin singing, in words which none of them could understand; and, as the moon shone forth again, the magister could be seen walking up towards the Stone. He had crossed the brook and passed the sentries without being spotted, for, in the darkness, they had turned round to watch the women dancing. He had bound two birch-rods together with osiers, so that they formed a cross, and this he held raised before him as he walked swiftly towards the Stone.

The old women began to shriek with all the force of their lungs, partly from rage and partly from fear, and the old man stood up on top of the Stone, brandishing his bloody knife like a madman, and screaming in a loud voice. The women ceased their gambolling and stood still, not knowing what to do: but the magister walked through their circle, held the cross up towards the old man, and cried: 'Get thee hence, Satan! In Jesus Christ's name, depart, thou unclean spirit!'

The old man's face became convulsed with fear as the magister threatened him with the cross; he shrank away, his foot slipped, and he toppled backwards from the Stone to the ground, where he remained lying with his neck broken.

'He has killed the priest!' shrieked the old women in confusion.

'I, too, am a priest!' cried the magister, 'and a better priest than he!'

Heavy footsteps were now heard approaching, and a powerful voice demanded to know what all this screaming might be about. A tremor passed through the magister's body, and, gripping his cross in both hands, he placed himself with his back against the Stone. Pressing the cross against his breast, he closed his eyes and began to mutter in a rapid monotone: 'I am ready! Christ and all ye holy martyrs, receive me into your blessed kingdom. I am ready! I am ready!'

The sentries remained motionless at their posts, despite the screams of the old women. They had been put there to see that no Göings or drunken Finnvedings came to meddle with or gloat at the women of their tribe, and it would have been unseemly for them to come near to other men's naked wives on open ground, lest, by doing so, they might provoke strife.

But a man now came from the Virds' camp, tall and powerfully made, who appeared not to be worried at the prospect of coming near naked women. He wore a broad-brimmed hat and a blue skirt of costly cloth, and carried a red shield by its strap, while his sword dangled from a broad belt of silver. The women looked bashful as he approached them, and tried to cover their nakedness as well as they could. Some took grass to clean the blood from their mouths; but all remained where they were.

The newcomer glanced along the line of them, and nodded.

'Have no fear,' he said, in a friendly voice. 'Such things do not bother me, save in the spring-time, and then women who take my fancy have no need to prance through fires. One thing I will not deny, now that I see you at close quarters, and that is that several of you are more comely naked than clothed. Which is as it should be; but who is this shivering fellow who stands with his eyes closed in the midst of your circle? Does the sight of you displease him?'

'He is a Christ-priest!' cried the old women. 'He has killed Styrkar!'

'It is the nature of priests to fight one another,' replied the man calmly. 'I have always said so.' He walked up to the body of the old man, and stood with his thumbs in his belt looking down at it. He rolled it over with his foot.

'Dead as a herring,' he said. 'So here you lie, Styrkar, for all your cunning and trollcraft. I do not think many people will mourn you. You were an evil-minded old snake, as I have told you more than once; though no one can deny that you were a crafty priest and full of learning. Go, now, to the trolls, to whom you belong; for the gods will kick you from their door if you try to gain admittance there. But you, my good women, why do you still stand naked in the night air? Your stomachs will surely suffer for it.'

'We have not completed the rite,' they replied. 'We still have half our laps to run around the Stone. But what shall we do, now that our priest, Styrkar, is dead? Must we depart, having gained nothing? We do not know what to do.'

'What has happened, has happened,' said the man. 'But do not grieve at it, for it is my belief that you can find better remedies for your emptiness than frolicking around this Stone. When my cows bear not, I change my bull. That usually does the trick.'

'No, no!' wailed the women sorrowfully. 'You are wrong, you are wrong! We are not so foolish as you think; this is the only remedy left to us!'

The man laughed, turned round and clapped his hand across the magister's shoulders.

'I stand here talking foolishly,' he said, 'though you all know that I am, in fact, the quickest-witted of men. Your priest Styrkar is dead, but we have here a Christ-priest to replace him. One priest is as good as another; believe me, for I have come across every variety.'

He seized the magister by one leg and the scruff of his neck, swung him up and deposited him on the top of the Stone.

'Use your tongue now,' he said, 'if you have priest-words in your mouth. Up with your chin and spout the best incantations you know. Whether we shall then kill you or let you live depends on how you acquit yourself. Spell boldly, and spell children into the wombs of these Virdwomen; if you can make it twins, so much the better.'

Standing on the Stone, the magister trembled, and his teeth were heard to chatter. But the man who stood beneath him, sword in hand, wore a dangerous and purposeful look. So the magister held the cross before him and began desperately to gabble prayers; and, once he was properly under way, his voice rang out manfully.

The newcomer stood and listened; then he nodded.

'This is a real priest,' he said. 'I have heard this sort of talk before, and there is much strength in it. Start your antics again, women, before he grows weary and the fires die to ash.'

Screwing up their courage anew, the women began again to prance around the Stone, and, once the magister had got over the worst of his fright, he acquitted himself nobly, dipping his cross over their heads as they came up to the Stone to lap the blood, and blessing them with his finest blessings. The women trembled as the cross touched them; and when the ceremony was completed they agreed unanimously that this was a good priest, and that they had been more sensible of his sacred power than they had been of Styrkar's.

'Let us not kill this man,' they said. 'He shall come with us and be our priest in Styrkar's stead.'

'If it is your wish,' said the man in the hat, 'let it be so; and may he bring you better luck than Styrkar did.'

But as he said this, a powerful voice was heard to roar from the direction of the brook: 'Give this priest to me!'

Orm and his men had seen the old priest fall down from the Stone and, a few minutes later, the magister standing there in his place, which had filled them with amazement.

'It may be that he had gone crazy,' said Father Willibald, 'or, on the other hand, it may be that God's spirit has entered into him. That is a cross he holds in his hand.'

'It does not take much to drive him to a place where women are,' said Orm darkly. 'None the less, it would be a shameful thing if we allowed him to be slaughtered like a goat.'

They took men with them and walked up from the stream. The moon was clouded over and, as Orm shouted up towards the Stone, not much could be seen. The women turned back nervously towards the camp, and the magister descended from the Stone. But the man in the broad hat strode down towards Orm, accompanied by several of the Vird sentries.

'Who is that who screams in the night?' he said.

'Give me back that priest,' said Orm grimly. 'He is mine, and has not my permission to depart.'

'What loud-mouthed fellow might you be?' asked the other.

This was a mode of address to which Orm was not accustomed, and he was seized by a fury such as seldom came over him.

'A man who is not afraid to teach you manners,' he cried, 'and that straightway.'

'Come over here,' said the other. 'And we shall see which of us is the better teacher.'

'Have I peace from your following?' said Orm.

'You have peace from us,' said the Virds calmly.

Orm drew his sword and leaped across the brook.

'You come here nimbly,' said the other. 'But you will be carried back.'

Orm charged at his adversary, and their swords met so fiercely that sparks came from them. Then the hatted man said:

> 'Dame Red-Jowl,
> Thou hardly forged one,
> Hard the fight
> When sparks fly from thee.'

Orm took a fierce slash on his shield, and his voice was changed as he replied:

> 'Friend, thy word
> Was timely spoken.
> Know, Red-Jowl
> Hath joined with Blue-Tongue.'

They lowered their swords and stood motionless.

'Welcome Orm Tostesson, chieftain of the sea. What do you among these Göing savages?'

'Welcome Toke Grey-Gullsson, warrior of Lister! What do you among the Virds?'

Both of them now began to talk eagerly and simultaneously, laughing with joy; for the friendship between them was very great, and it was several years since they had last seen each other.

'We have much to talk of,' said Toke. 'And it is fortunate that you are swift at composing verses, the way I taught you to be: for if it had not been so, we two might have hewn at each other for a while longer, and might have suffered thereby. Though, I do not think your verse was so good as mine.'

'In that, you may claim superiority without offence,' said Orm. 'I have had but little practice at making verses since last we parted.'

Toke drew his finger along Red-Jowl's edge.

'There is a dent here, where our swords met,' he said. 'She was never dented before.'

Orm likewise passed his finger along his blade.

'It is the same with mine,' he said. 'Andalusian-forged iron can only be dented by Andalusian blades.'

'It is my hope,' said Toke, 'that they will not kiss edges again.'

'That is my hope also,' said Orm.

'It would be good to know whether she who gave them to us is yet living,' said Toke. 'And how our lord Almansur now fares, and where his great war-banners now wave before him, and whether his luck still holds.'

'Who can tell?' said Orm. 'That land is far from here, and these things happened long ago; though it is true that my thoughts often turn to him. But come with me now, that we may talk alone; I wish I had ale with which to bid you welcome.'

'Have you no ale?' asked Toke in alarm. 'How can we talk without ale? Ale is the best friend of friends.'

'Nobody has brought ale to the Thing,' said Orm. 'Ale is the provoker of quarrels; which I think you know as well as the next man.'

'Our luck is good to-night,' said Toke, 'and yours is better than mine. For one man has brought ale to the Thing, and I am he. You must know that I am now a great man among the merchants of Värend, and I deal particularly in skins; and no skin-sale can be arranged without ale. I have brought five pack-horses to the Thing, all laden with ale, and I shall not be taking any of it home again, if all goes as it should; for I intend that they shall carry nothing but skins. Therefore, come with me.'

'It shall be as you wish,' said Orm. 'Perhaps I shall find my lost priest there, too.'

'The women took him with them,' said Toke. 'They said they liked the sorcery he practised, so you need not worry your head about him. He looked to me to be a bold fellow, the way he went for Styrkar with his cross. Though, what will happen to him for killing the old goat is a matter for the Thing to decide.'

'I have another priest with me here,' said Orm. 'An old friend of yours.'

Father Willibald had come across the brook to discover what had happened to the magister. Toke greeted him joyfully.

'I remember you well,' he said. 'You shall come with us and sample my ale. I owe you a great debt for the way you mended my leg in King Harald's castle, better than any other man could have done. But what are you doing here, so far from the Danish court?'

'I am God's priest to Orm's household,' said Father Willibald. 'And my mission is to christianize heathens in this wild outpost of the world, as I have already christianized him. Your turn likewise shall come, though I remember you as a man deep in godlessness; it is the finger of God that has led you here to meet us.'

'That is a point that might be argued,' said Toke. 'But what is certain is that we three shall now sit down together in friendship. *Bismillahi, er-rahmani, er-rahimi!* as we used to say when we served my lord Almansur.'

'What is that you said?' asked Father Willibald. 'What language is that? Are you, too, a victim of southern witchcraft?'

'It is the tongue of Spain,' said Toke. 'I remember it still, for my woman is from that land, and still likes to speak her own tongue, especially when she is in an ill humour. It enables me to keep in practice.'

'And I can tell you the meaning of what he said,' said Orm. 'It is: In the name of God, the Merciful, the Compassionate. The Merciful One is Christ, as everybody knows; and the Compassionate One evidently refers to the Holy Ghost, for who could be more Compassionate than He? You can see that Toke is practically a Christian already, though he pretends otherwise.'

Father Willibald mumbled doubtfully to himself; but, without more argument about the matter, they proceeded with Toke to the Vird camp.

CHAPTER ELEVEN

Concerning Toke Grey-Gullsson, and a misfortune that befell him; and of a foul gift Orm received from the Finnvedings

They sat over Toke's ale late into the night, talking of all that happened to them since they had parted. Orm told how he had gone a-viking in England under Thorkel the Tall, and of the great battle at Maldon and all the booty they had won there; how he had chanced to meet Father Willibald and had been baptized and had found again King Harald's daughter (here the little priest had a good deal to add to Orm's narrative), and of the great sum of silver which King Ethelred had elected to pay, to buy himself and his country relief from the Northmen's fury. Then he spoke of his voyage home, of his visit to Jellinge, and of his encounter with King Sven there; of what had happened at this meeting, and how he had then been forced to flee in haste to his mother's estate in the border country, in order to escape the vengeance of his brother-in-law.

'But his memory is long, like his arm,' said Orm; 'so that even in these distant parts he still pursues me, to avenge the nose-burn that this good priest gave him when last we met. This very spring I had to fight in night-darkness outside my own door with a traveller who was staying in my house as my guest, a man from Finnveden named Osten of Orestad, who had served at sea with the Danes. He had come with a strong band of followers to slay me secretly, and send my head to King Sven. But instead, he lost many men, and his horses and goods, and suffered a split skull into the bargain; which affair will, I doubt not, come up for discussion during the Thing. For as soon as his head had healed, I let him depart in peace, and two of his men with him; but first I forced him to become a Christian, because Father Willibald here, whose will I seldom oppose, preferred that they should be christianized rather than killed.'

'Even the wisest of men sometimes act foolishly,' said Toke, 'and a man who lets his enemy live has only himself to blame if he comes to regret it. I know that Christians sometimes do this, to put themselves in good odour with their god; but in these parts, the old method is still regarded as the best. Next time, you may find difficulty in killing the fellow, for he will certainly seek revenge for all he lost and for the insult you did to him by baptizing him.'

'We acted rightly,' said Father Willibald. 'Let the Devil and his minions do their worst.'

'Besides which, Toke,' said Orm, 'God's hand is stronger than you would like to think. But tell us, now, how things have gone with you since last we met.'

Toke began to tell them his story. He said that he had not undertaken any long voyage abroad, nor undergone such adventures as Orm had enjoyed; but that he had none the less had just as many troubles to contend with, if not more.

'For coming home to Lister was like tumbling into a snakepit,' he said. 'Scarcely had I reached my father's house and greeted the old people and deposited my woman and my goods inside the door than men came running to me with urgent tidings; and before long I found myself involved in a feud which embroiled the whole district.'

This was a feud which had been started by Orm's men, Ogmund, Halle, Gunne and Grinulf, as soon as they had reached home, having journeyed thither on Styrbjörn's ship from King Harald's castle, while Orm and Toke were still lying there wounded. On their return, they discovered that they were not the only ones to have come back alive from Krok's expedition. Seven years before, Berse had arrived home in one ship, with only thirty-two men at his oars but with a rich cargo, consisting of the best of all the booty from the margrave's fortress, which he had managed to bring away in his two ships after the Andalusians had surprised them.

'Berse was a man of much wisdom,' said Toke, 'even if it is true that he ate himself to death soon after his return; for in the matter of food, he was greedier than other men, and his greed proved his downfall when he found himself a rich man with no need to bestir himself. He had lost so many men in the fight with the Andalusians that he only had enough left to man one ship, and barely that; but he took all the best of the booty from the ship he had to leave behind, and managed to reach home without any further misfortunes. His men worked themselves almost to death at the oars, but did so cheerfully, knowing that, the fewer of them survived, the more each man would receive when the booty came to be shared out. Before Krok sailed forth from Lister, few of them had been fat enough to feed a louse, but when they returned there was no man in the district whose wealth could compare with theirs. And there they sat, happy in their satiety, until the time came when our men returned and discovered how things were.'

'But our men did not lack for silver or gold,' said Orm.

'They were not poor,' said Toke. 'Far from it; for they were all prudent and sensible men, so that they had brought much back with them from Spain, besides what they had received as their share of the price we got for the Andalusian rowers we sold at Jellinge. And until they reached home, they thought their luck good and felt well contented with their lot. But when they heard how Berse's men had fared, and saw them sitting fatly on their broad estates, with plump cattle and well-timbered ships, in such prosperity that even their slaves came puffing from their porridge without the appetite to scrape their platters clean, then their humour changed. Brooding and discontented, they reminded one another of all the hardships they had been forced to undergo during the seven years that they had spent in Andalusia, and so became still more inflamed with wrath against Berse's men, who had barely set foot in Spain before turning home with a shipload of gold and silver. They sat hunched on their benches, spitting on to the ground as they reflected, and thinking that the ale they drank lacked its proper flavour.

'Man is always so,' said Father Willibald, 'be he heathen or baptized; content with his lot only as long as he meets no neighbour who possesses more.'

'It is good to be rich,' said Orm. 'Nobody can deny that.'

'Gunne was the only one who had anything to smile about,' continued Toke. 'He was a married man when he sailed forth with Krok, and when Berse returned all those who did not come with him were presumed dead. So his wife married again and, by the time Gunne reappeared at her door, had already borne her new man a lapful of bawling sons. She had, to Gunne's eyes, aged, and was no longer the sort of woman that a man who had served in

Almansur's bodyguard would lust after, so that he now felt free to look for a younger and more beautiful woman on whose arms to set his fine silver bracelets. But even this consolation was soon swallowed up in the fury he felt at being cheated and, in the end, the four of them agreed that they could not honourably tolerate so ostentatious a display of wealth by their former comrades. They gathered their kinsmen, and went round the district, demanding their rightful share of all that Berse had brought home. But they received only rough answers, barred doors, and weapons bared against them. This still further increased their indignation, and they began to think that Berse's men not only owed them many marks of silver but were, besides, dishonourable traitors, who had fled like cravens from the battle, leaving Krok and ourselves to face the reckoning, and were, in short, to blame for our ship being captured.'

'There was nothing they could have done to help us,' said Orm, 'for they had lost more than half their numbers. It was our fate to be chained to slave-oars.'

'That may be,' said Toke, 'but the district was thick with Krok's kinsmen, and their minds soon began to work similarly. They demanded that his share, as chieftain, should be paid to them. Then both sides unhooked their weapons from the walls, and a feud was declared and was waged without quarter. By the time I arrived, both Halle and Grinulf were a-bed, wounded, having been surprised in an ambush; but in spite of this they were in excellent heart, and lost no time in acquainting me with the situation. Several of their enemies, they told me, had been found dead in this place or that; two had been burned in their houses by Ogmund and a brother of Krok's; and others, having grown soft with good living, had paid up in order to be allowed to grow old in peace. But others, it appeared, were more obstinate, and had demanded that Ogmund, Halle, Gunne and Grinulf should be declared outlaws; also, that the same sentence should be pronounced against me, if I should take their part.'

'One thing I can guess,' said Orm, 'and that is that you did not long remain neutral in this affair.'

Toke nodded unhappily and said that he would have liked to have settled down peacefully with his woman and avoid quarrels, for they were well content with one another, as, indeed, they had been ever since the day he had stolen her; however, he had not been able to refuse his friends help, since, if he had done so, his good name would have suffered. He therefore immediately agreed to take their part; whereupon, a short while later, at the wedding of Gunne and his new woman, he had been the victim of a fearful misfortune; a ludicrous and shameful humiliation which had caused him incalculable misery and had cost several men their lives.

'And you must know, both of you,' he said, 'that, when I tell you what happened, you may both laugh without fear that I shall draw upon you, although I have killed more than one man for twisting his mouth at this affair. What happened was as follows. On the evening of the wedding, I went drunk to the privy, and fell asleep as I sat there, as often happens to a man at a good feast: and there I was speared in the rear by two men, who had crept up secretly behind the wall. I leaped high into the air, with all my sleep and good drunkenness gone from me instantly, thinking that I had been mortally wounded; which was also the belief of the two men, for I heard them laugh with delight as they ran away. But they had fumbled their thrusts, perhaps because the spears were somewhat long in the shaft, so that I escaped with lighter injuries than I at first feared to have sustained. None the less, I had to lie a long while a-bed, and on my stomach the whole time; and it was still longer before I was able to sit comfortably upon a bench. Of all the things that have happened to me in my life, this was the worst; worse than being a galley slave among the Andalusians.'

'Then you never discovered the men who had wounded you?' asked Orm.

'I discovered them,' replied Toke. 'For they could not keep their mouths shut, but had to boast of the deed to their women; so that the story came out and became known through the whole district. They were called Alf and Steinar, insolent fellows of good family, nephews of Ossur the Braggart who was helmsman in Berse's ship, that fellow who was always boasting that on his mother's side he was descended from King Alf Woman's-Darling of Möre. I learned that they were the culprits while I was still in bed from my wounds. Then, as I lay there, I vowed that I should never enjoy ale nor woman before I had killed them both; and, whether you believe it or not, I kept that vow. As soon as I was upon my feet again, I was out after them every day; and at last, I came upon them, one day, just as they were wading ashore from fishing. I almost wept with joy when I saw them step on to the land; and there, sword in hand, the three of us fought, until I killed Steinar. Then the other fellow fled, with me at his heels. It was a beautiful race, well run by us both, through groves and fields among herds at pasture and across the meadows towards his father's house. He was a nimble-footed man, and was running for his life; but I was running for his life too, as well as to purge myself of my shame and of the great longing I had to be free of my vow. A short way from the house I caught him, as my heart seemed to be about to burst, and cleft him to the teeth in the sight of his harvesters; and never have I felt so good as when I saw him there, lying on the ground at my feet. I went home with a merry heart and drank ale for the rest of the day, and told my woman that our troubles were over. But this, as it turned out, was not the case.'

'What troubles could you have left, after such a fine revenge?' asked Orm.

'The people of the district, my friends no less than my enemies,' said Toke darkly, 'could not forget the circumstances in which I had received my wound, and there was no end to the mock they made of me. I had supposed that my revenge would put a stop to all this, seeing that I had killed both of the men single-handed in fair fight; but this seemed to make little impression on their foolish minds. More than once I and Red-Jowl had to rid men of the habit of hiding their faces behind their hands when I appeared; but even this helped but little, and soon I found myself scarcely able to endure the most solemn countenances, because I knew what lay behind their gravity. I composed an excellent poem about my slaying of Alf and Steinar, but soon discovered that there were already three poems in circulation describing the circumstances in which I had been wounded, and that in every house people were laughing themselves crooked every time they heard them. Then I realised that I would never be able to live down the shame of this incident; so I took my woman and everything else that I possessed, and journeyed up through the great forests until I came to Värend, where I have kinsmen. There I bought a house, and have dwelt contentedly ever since, being now a richer man than when I arrived first, thanks to the good skin-trade. I have three sons, all of whom promise well, and a daughter, whose suitors will be hewing hard at one another before many years have passed. But never until this evening have

361

I told anyone the reason of my leaving Lister. Only to you, Orm, and to you, little priest, have I told these things, because I know I can trust you both never to repeat them to a living soul. For should you do so, I would once again become a public butt, even though four years have now passed since this catastrophe occurred.'

Orm praised Toke for the way in which he had told his story, and assured him that he need have no fears about anyone hearing it from his lips.

'I should like,' he added, 'to hear these poems that were written about you; but no man enjoys repeating lampoons directed against himself.'

Father Willibald emptied his cup, and announced that stories of this kind, dealing with feuds and jealousies, with spear-thrusts delivered in this place or that, revenge and lampoons and the like, gave him little pleasure, whatever Orm's attitude towards them might be.

'And you can be sure of this, Toke,' he said, 'that I shall not run around gossiping to people of such matters, for I have more important things to tell them. If, though, you are a man who is willing to learn from events, you may yet gain some profit from this distressing experience. From the little I saw of you in King Harald's castle, and from what Orm has told me about you, I know you to be a bold and fearless man, sure of yourself, and merry in your disposition. But in spite of all this, you have only to undergo some misfortune which causes foolish people to laugh at you, and you at once become cowardly and downhearted, so that you had to flee from your home district as soon as you found that you could not bully your enemies into silence. We Christians are more fortunate, for we do not care what men think of us, but only what God thinks. I am an old man, and have little strength left in my bones; nevertheless, I am stronger than you, for no man can scare me with mockery, because I care not a jot for it. He who has God behind his back flinches from no man's ridicule; and all their smirks and gossipings trouble him not at all.'

'Those are wise words,' said Orm, 'and worth pondering; for, be sure of this, Toke, that this priest possesses more wisdom in his small head than we in our large ones, and it is always a good thing to mark his words.'

'I see that the ale is beginning to work on you both,' said Toke. 'For you would not address such nonsense to me if you were sober. Is it in your mind, little priest, to try to make me a Christian?'

'It is,' retorted Father Willibald purposefully.

'Then you have set yourself a difficult task,' said Toke, 'and one which will cause you more trouble than all the other religious duties you have ever performed.'

'It would be no shame for you to turn Christian,' said Orm, 'when you consider that I have been one for these five years. I am not less merry than of old, nor has my hand weakened, and I have never had cause to complain about my luck since the day I received baptism.'

'All that may be true,' said Toke. 'But you are not a skin-trader, as I am. No skin-trader can afford to be a Christian in this land; it would arouse distrust in the minds of all my customers. If he changes his gods, the Virds would say, who can rely on him in other matters? No, no. For our friendship's sake, I would do much for you, Orm, and for you too, little priest; but this I will not do. Besides which, it would drive my woman, Mirah, crazy, for she retains this characteristic of her countrymen, that she hates Christians above all things else; and to my way of thinking, her humour is brittle enough already, without whetting it with ideas such as this. It is, therefore, useless for you to try to convert me, little priest, although I am your friend and hope to remain so.'

Even Father Willibald could find no good answer to this argument; and Orm yawned, and said that the night was growing old, and that it was time to seek sleep. They parted from Toke, with many expressions of friendship; he and Orm were delighted with their luck at having once again found each other, and vowed to meet often in the future.

Orm and Father Willibald walked back to their camp. There, all was peace and stillness, and in the moonshine men lay snoring under ribbons of pale smoke from the dying fires. But one of Orm's men was sitting awake, and he lifted his head as they approached.

'A message came for you both,' he said sleepily. 'See, here, this bag; the owls have not ceased to screech since the moment I received it. I was down at the brook, drinking, when a man came from the Finnvedings' camp and asked for you, Orm. I told him that you had gone to the Virds. Then he threw his bag across the water, so that it fell at my feet, and shouted that it was a gift for Orm of Gröning and his long-nosed priest. I asked him what the bag might contain. Cabbage-heads, he replied, and laughed and went away. It is my belief that it contains something worse. Here is the bag; I have not touched the strings.'

He dropped the bag at Orm's feet, laid himself down and fell asleep at once.

Orm stared darkly at the bag, and then at the priest. Both shook their heads.

'There is devilry here,' said Father Willibald. 'It cannot but be so.'

Orm untied the strings, and shook out the contents. Two human heads rolled on to the ground, and Father Willibald fell to his knees with a groan.

'They are both shaven!' he cried. 'Priests of Christ, murdered by heathens! How can human understanding comprehend the will of God when such things are allowed to gladden Satan!'

He peered more closely at the two heads, and flung his arms towards the sky.

'I know them. I know them both!' he cried. 'This is Father Sebastian, a most pious and worthy man, whom our crazy magister was to release from his slavery. Now God has released him, and has set him high in Heaven among the blessed martyrs. And this is Brother Nithard of Rheims, who was at one time with Bishop Poppo at King Harald's court. From there, he went to Skania, since when nothing has been heard of him; he, too, must have been made a slave. I know him by his ear. He was always ardent in his zeal and passion for the true faith; and once, at the Emperor's court, he had an ear bitten off by one of the Empress Theofano's monks from Constantinople, that city which Northmen call Miklagard, during an argument concerning the nature of the Holy Ghost. He used to say that he had given his ear in the fight against heresy, and that he was ready to give his head in the fight against heathendom. And now his words have been fulfilled.'

'If he wished it to be so,' said Orm, 'we should not weep; though it is my belief that the Finnvedings did not render these god-men headless as an act of favour, however holy they may have been, but that they have done this deed and sent their heads to us as an insult, and to cause us grief. This is our reward for having baptized Osten and his two men and allowed them to go in peace, instead of killing them when we had them in our power. Perhaps you now regret, as I do, that we acted thus mercifully.'

'A good deed remains good, and should never be regretted,' replied Father Willibald, 'whatever consequences it may bring with it. These holy heads I shall bury in my churchyard, for from them much strength will come.'

'A stink is coming from them already,' said Orm darkly. 'But you may be right.'

Then, at Father Willibald's bidding, he helped to gather grass and leafy branches, with which they stuffed the bag. Among these, with great care, they placed the two heads, after which they re-fastened the strings.

CHAPTER TWELVE

Concerning the Thing at the Kraka Stone

The next morning, twelve men were chosen from each of the three border tribes, the Virds, the Göings and the Finnvedings; and these men went to the places which were traditionally reserved for them, in a half-circle facing the Stone, with each twelve seated together. The rest of the men grouped themselves behind their chosen representatives to listen to what these wise men had to say. The twelve Virds sat in the centre of the half-circle, and their chieftain rose first. His name was Ugge the Inarticulate, son of Oar; he was an old man, and had the reputation of being the wisest person in the whole of Värend. It had always been the case with him, that he was never able to speak except with great difficulty, but everyone was agreed that this was a sign of the profundity of his thinking; it was said that he had been marked out as a wise man even in his youth, when he would sometimes sit through a three-day Thing without uttering a word, only, now and then, slowly shaking his head.

He now advanced to the Stone, turned to face the assembly, and spoke.

'Wise men,' he said, 'have now gathered here. Very wise men, from Värend and Göinge and Finnveden, after the ancient custom of our fathers. This is good. I greet you all, and pronounce that our decisions shall be received peacefully. May you judge wisely, and to the advantage of us all. We have come here to talk about peace. It is the way with men that some think one thing and some another. I am old and rich in experience, and I know what I think. I think that peace is a good thing. Better than strife, better than burning, better than murder. Peace has reigned between us tribes for three whole years now, and no harm has come as a result of this. Nor will any harm come if this peace is allowed to continue. Those who have complaints to make shall be heard, and their complaints judged. Those who wish to kill one another may do so here at the Stone, for such is the law and ancient custom of the Thing. But peace is best.'

When he had finished his speech, the Virds looked this way and that, for they were proud of their chieftain and his wisdom. Then the Thing-chieftain of the Göings arose. His name was Sone the Sharp-Sighted, and he was so old that the two men who were seated next to him took hold of his arms to help him get up; but he brushed them angrily away, hobbled nimbly forward to the Stone, and took his stand beside Ugge. He was a tall and scraggy man, desiccated and bent crooked with age, with a long nose and thin wisps of mottled beard; and, although the day was fine and the late summer sun shone warmly, he wore a skin coat reaching to his knees, and a thick cap of fox-fur. He looked immeasurably wise, and had had a great reputation for as long as anyone could remember. His sharp-sightedness was famous; he could find where hidden treasure lay, and could look into the future and foretell the bad luck that lay there. In addition to all this, he had been married seven times and had twenty-three sons and eleven daughters; and it was said that he was doing his best to get round dozens of both, which made him much admired and honoured by all the Göings.

He, too, pronounced peace upon the assembly, and spoke in fine words of the peaceful intentions of the Göings; which, he said, were proved by the fact that they had undertaken no campaigns against either the Virds or the Finnvedings for four whole years. This, he continued, might be taken by foolish strangers to signify that weakness and sloth had begun to flourish among them; but if anyone thought this, he was wrong, for they were no less ready than their fathers had been to teach manners with point and blade to any man who sought to do them wrong, as could be testified by one or two people who had made the effort. It was also wrong to suppose that this peaceful attitude was the result of the good years they had enjoyed recently, with rich harvests, lush pasture and freedom from cattle sickness; for a well-fed Göing was as

367

doughty a warrior as when starvation cramped his belly, and of as proud a temper. The true cause of this desire for peace, he explained, was that men of wisdom and experience now prevailed, their counsel being accepted by the tribe.

'So long as such men are to be found, and their advice listened to,' he concluded, 'we shall prosper. But as the years pass, the number of wise men grows less, and I think that, of those men whose judgment can be fully relied upon, no more than two are alive who are likely to survive much longer. Ugge and myself. It is, therefore, more than ever necessary that you young men who have been chosen to represent your tribes, although you have not yet any streak of grey in your beards, should listen carefully to what we say and thereby glean wisdom which, as yet, you lack. For it is a good thing when old men are listened to and young men understand that they themselves have but a small measure of understanding.'

A third now joined them at the Stone. He was the chieftain of the Finnvedings, called Olof Summer-Bird; and he had already won himself a great name, although he was yet young. He was a finely proportioned man, dark-skinned, and with piercing eyes and a proud look. He had been in the Eastland, having served in the courts of both the Prince at Kiev and the Emperor at Miklagard, whence he had returned home with great wealth. The name Summer-Bird had been given him on his return because of the splendour and bright colour that he affected in his dress. He himself was well pleased with this nickname.

All the Finnvedings, both the chosen men and those who sat behind them, shouted with pride and triumph as he strode forward, for he looked in sooth like a chieftain; and when he took his place by the other two in front of the Stone, the difference between himself and them was manifest. He wore a green cloak, sewn with gold thread, and a shining helmet of polished silver.

After pronouncing peace upon the assembly, as the others had done, he said that his belief in the wisdom of old men was, perhaps, not fully commensurate with their own. Wisdom, he thought, could sometimes be found in younger heads; indeed, there were some who thought that it more often resided there. He would not disagree with the old men when they said that peace was a good thing; but everyone ought to remember that peace was nowadays becoming more and more difficult to keep. The chief cause of this, he said, was the unrest that was being aroused everywhere by the Christians, who were very evil and cunning men.

'And believe me,' he continued, 'when I speak of the Christians, I know what I am talking about. You all know that I have spent five years at Miklagard, and have served two Emperors there, Basil and Constantine. There I was able to see how the Christians behave when they are angry, even when they have only each other to vent their spite upon. They clip one another's ears and noses off with sharp tongs, as revenge for the smallest things, and sometimes geld each other. Their young women, even when they are beautiful, they often imprison in closed stone houses and forbid them to have intercourse with men; and if any woman disobeys, they wall her up alive in a hole in the stone wall, and let her die there. Sometimes it happens that they weary of their Emperor, or that his decrees displease them; and then they take him and his sons and bind them fast and hold glowing irons close to their faces until their eyes sweat and so go blind. All this they do for the glory of Christendom, for they hold it to be less of a crime to maim than to kill; from which you may gather what kind of men they are. If they behave so towards one another, what will they not do to us, who are not Christians as they are, if they should become strong enough to attack us? Everyone should, therefore, beware of this danger, that it may be met and stifled before it grows greater. Have we not all witnessed how, in this very place, a Christian priest only last night forced his way to this Stone and committed murder here, in the full sight of the Vird women? He had been brought here by the Göings, perhaps so that he might commit this foul deed. This is a matter between them and the Virds, which does not concern us Finnvedings. But it would surely be good if the Thing could declare that any Christian priest who appears among the Göings, the Virds or the Finnvedings shall instantly be killed, and shall not be kept alive as a slave, much less be permitted to practise his witchcraft undisturbed; for otherwise, much mischief may be caused, and strife be provoked.'

Thus spoke Olof Summer-Bird, and many nodded thoughtfully at his words.

He and the other two chieftains now seated themselves on the three chieftain-stones, which rested on the grass bank before the Kraka Stone, and the Thing began. It was an ancient custom that those quarrels should first be decided which had originated in the arena itself, so that the first case to be debated was that of the magister. Ugge demanded compensation for the death of Styrkar, and wished to know to whom this Christ-priest belonged, and why he had been brought to the Thing. Orm, who was among the chosen twelve of the Göings, rose, and replied that the priest might be regarded as belonging to him, although he was, in fact, no slave but a free man.

'And one would have to travel far,' he added, 'before finding a more peaceable man. He has no appetite for violence, and the only things he knows how to do are reading manuscripts and singing and winning the favours of women. And he came here on a mission which he will never, now, as things have turned out, be able to fulfil.'

Orm then told them about the magister and his mission; how he had been sent from Hedeby to offer himself in exchange for a priest who had been enslaved by the Finnvedings, but who had now been killed by them.

'Which matter,' he said, 'will doubtless be discussed later. But as regards the manner in which Styrkar met his death, those who saw it happen can testify. For my part, I do not think this priest capable of killing a grown man.'

Sone the Sharp-Sighted agreed that those who had witnessed the affair should be heard.

'But, whatever the judgment of the Thing shall be in this matter,' he said, 'it shall not result in a feud being declared between the Virds and the Göings. You, Ugge, shall judge this case alone. The man is a foreigner, good for little, and a Christian to boot, so that he will not be missed much, whatever your decision. But you cannot demand compensation from us Göings for something that has been done by a man who is a stranger to our tribe.'

The witnesses were now heard. Many men had seen Styrkar topple backwards from the Stone with a loud cry; but whether anyone might have struck him from the farther side of the Stone, none could say. Not even Toke Grey-Gullsson, who sat among the Vird twelve and who had been the first to arrive at the scene of the crime, knew for certain; but he declared that the cross which the Christ-priest had been holding in his hands, and which had been

370

his only weapon, was made of such frail twigs that it might have served as a good instrument to kill a louse with, but would have made little impression on such a tough-hided old fox as Styrkar. It was, he concluded, his belief that the old man had slipped and had broken his neck in the fall; but the people who knew best what had happened, he added, were the women, for they had been on the spot and must have seen everything; provided, he said, some means could be found of persuading them to speak the truth.

Ugge sat for a while deep in thought. At last he said that there seemed to be nothing for it but to hear what the women had to say.

'According to our ancient law,' he said, 'women can be regarded as admissible witnesses; though how such a decision ever came to be arrived at is more than a man can guess. It is not our custom to use women's evidence where we can avoid it; for, while to look for truth in a man can be like looking for a cuckoo in a dark wood, to look for the truth in a woman is like looking for the echo of the cuckoo's voice. But in this case, the women are the only persons who saw exactly what happened; and the murder of a priest on holy ground is a matter which must be investigated with care. Let them, therefore, be heard.'

The women had been waiting to be called, and now appeared, all together, the young ones who had danced round the Stone and the old women who had assisted with the ceremony. They were all wearing their finest apparel and ornaments, bracelets and neck-laces and broad finger-rings and coloured veils. At first they appeared somewhat bashful as they walked forwards into the space between the judges and the semicircle of chosen men. They had the magister with them, looking woebegone, with his hands tied and around his neck a rope, by which two of the old women led him, as they had led the goats to the Stone on the previous evening. A great shout of laughter arose from the assembly at the sight of him entering thus.

Ugge cocked his head on one side, scratched behind his ear, and looked at them with a worried expression on his face. He bade them tell him how Styrkar had met his death; whether their pris-oner had killed him, or not. They were to speak the truth, and nothing else; and it would be a good thing, he said, if no more than two or three witnesses should speak at the same time.

At first the women were afraid of the sound of their own voices, and whispered amongst themselves, and it was difficult to coax any of them to speak aloud; but, before long, they were persuaded to overcome their shyness, and began to testify vigorously. Their prisoner, they said, had gone up to the Stone and cried in a loud voice, and had then hit Styrkar over the head with his cross, causing the latter to cry also; then he had dug his cross into Styrkar's stomach and pushed him off the Stone. On this, they were all agreed; though some said that the priest had struck once, and some twice, and they began to quarrel about this.

When the magister heard them testify thus, he became white in the face with terror and astonishment. Raising his bound hands towards Heaven, he cried: 'No, no!' in a loud voice. But nobody bothered to listen to the rest of what he had to say, and the old women gave a tug on the rope to silence him.

Ugge now said that this evidence was more than sufficient, since even the speech of women could be regarded as credible when so many of them said the same thing. Whether the murderer had struck once or twice did not affect the issue: here, he said, they had before them a clear case of priest-murder committed on holy ground.

'This crime,' he proceeded, 'has been regarded ever since the most ancient times as one of the foulest that it is possible to perpetrate, and occurs so rarely that many men sit through a whole lifetime of Things without ever having to judge an instance of it. The penalty for it, which is also of ancient prescription, is, I think, known to no one here save us two old men, Sone and I; unless, perhaps, you, Olof, who reckon yourself to be wiser than us, also know it?'

It was evident that Olof Summer-Bird was displeased at this question; nevertheless, he answered boldly that he had often heard that the penalty for this crime was that the culprit should be hung by his feet from the nethermost branch of a tree, with his head resting on an ant-hill.

Ugge and Sone beamed with delight when they heard him give this answer.

'It was not to be expected that you would know the correct sentence,' said Ugge, 'so young as you are; for to attain wisdom and knowledge takes longer than you would like to think. The proper punishment is that the murderer shall be handed over to Ygg, which in former times was our fathers' name for Odin; and now Sone will tell us the manner in which the presentation is to be made.'

'Twenty good spears shall be found,' said Sone, 'with no rot in their shafts; and to each spear, just below the end of the iron shoe, a cross-piece shall be fixed. Then the spears shall be driven into the ground to half their length, close together with their points facing upwards. On to these the murderer shall be cast; and there he shall remain until his bones drop to the ground.'

'Such is the law,' said Ugge. 'The only detail you omitted to mention is that he shall be cast so as to land on the spears on his back, in order that he may lie with his face towards the sky.'

A murmur of satisfaction passed through the whole assembly as they heard this punishment, which was so ancient and rare that nobody had seen it, described. The magister had by now become calm, and stood there with his eyes closed, mumbling to himself; the women, however, received the news of his sentence much less placidly. They clamoured that this was a crazy punishment to condemn him to, and they had not intended, when testifying, that anything like that should happen; and two of them, who were related to Ugge, pushed their way through the crowd towards him, called him an old fool, and asked why he had not told them of this penalty before they had testified. They had, they said, given the evidence which he had heard because they wished to keep the Christ-priest, whom they liked, and held to be more potent than Styrkar; fearing that, if he were acquitted, he would be set free and go back to the Göings.

The most vehement protests came from one of the old women, who was Styrkar's niece. Eventually, she succeeded in quieting the others so that her voice might be heard alone. She was large and coarse-limbed, and shook with fury as she stood there before Ugge. She said that in Värend no decision was taken about anything until the women had passed judgment, and that old men there were put out to play in the woods.

'I have nursed Styrkar, troll that he was, for many years,' she shrieked, 'gaining my livelihood thereby. How shall I live now that he is dead? Are you listening to me, you crook-backed imbecile?

373

Another priest, young and beautiful, and, from his appearance, wise and tractable also, has come and killed him, and nobody can deny that it was high time that somebody did so. And what do you suggest we should now do? Throw this young man upon the points of spears! What good will that do to anybody? I tell you that he shall be handed over to me, to replace the priest I have lost. He is a fine priest, and when the dance round the Stone was finished he performed to the satisfaction of us all; in nine months, the whole of Värend will be able to testify to the efficacy of his magic. The services of such a priest will be sought by many, and all who come will bring him gifts; and I shall thereby be compensated for my loss, whether I have him as husband or as slave. What purpose will be served by throwing him upon spears! It would be better if you sat on them yourself, for it is plain that your age and learning have driven you crazy. He shall be mine, as payment for the murder he has committed, if there be any justice in the world. Do you hear that?'

She shook her clenched fist in front of Ugge's face, and appeared to be considering whether to spit in it.

'She is right, she is right! Katla is right!' cried the women. 'Give him to us in Styrkar's place! We need a priest of his mettle!'

Ugge waved his hands and shouted as loudly as he could but in an endeavour to quieten them; and, beside him, Olof Summer-Bird was near to falling backwards from his stone in his delight in the wise man's discomfiture.

But Sone the Sharp-Sighted now rose from his stone and spoke in a voice which made everyone suddenly quiet.

'Peace has been pronounced upon this assembly,' he said. 'And it is a quality of wise men to endure women patiently. It would be an ill thing if we should allow the peace to be broken, and particularly ill for you, women; for we could then sentence you to be birched before the assembly, with good switches of birch or hazel, which would be sadly ignominious for you. If that were to happen, all men would snigger at the sight of you for the rest of your days, and I think none of you would wish that to happen. Therefore, let there be an end to your screamings and vituperations. But one question I would ask of you before you depart from this place. Was Styrkar struck by the Christ-priest, or was he not?'

The women had now become calm. They replied with one accord

that he had not so much as touched Styrkar; he had merely shouted something and raised his cross, at which the old man had fallen backwards and died. This, they declared, was the pure truth; they could, they said, tell the truth as well as anyone, if only they knew what purpose it would serve.

The women, including Katla and her captive, were now ordered to leave while Ugge debated with his chosen twelve as to a suitable sentence. Several of them thought that the priest ought to be killed, since there could be no doubt that he had slain Styrkar by trollcraft, and the sooner one got rid of a Christ-priest, the better. But others opposed this argument, saying that any man who had managed to troll the life out of Styrkar was worth keeping alive. For, if he had succeeded in doing this, he must, also, have been able to perform efficaciously upon the women; besides which, there was the old woman's argument to be considered, for it was, as she had asserted, true that no compensation could be claimed from the Göings for the loss of her man. The end of it was that Ugge declared that Katla should keep the Christ-priest as a slave until the fourth Thing following this one, extracting from him as much service as she could during that period. Neither Sone nor anyone else had any fault to find with this judgment.

'I could not have judged the matter better myself,' said Orm to Father Willibald, when they were discussing the case later. 'Now he will have to get along with the old woman as best he can. He was reckoning on becoming a slave of the Smalanders anyway.'

'For all his weakness,' said Father Willibald, 'it may be that God's spirit was upon him last night, when he went up to denounce the heathen priest and his abominable practices. Perhaps he will do great works now, for the glory of God.'

'Perhaps,' said Orm. 'But the best of it is that we are now rid of him. When a man is campaigning or a-viking, it is only right that he should indulge his lust for women, even if they belong to someone else; but it seems wrong to me that a man of his mettle, a Christ-priest and a good-for-nothing, should cause women to lose all sense of decency as soon as they set eyes on him. It is not right; it is unnatural.'

'He will have plenty of opportunities to atone for his sins,' said Father Willibald, 'when that old crone Katla gets her claws into him. Certain it is that I would rather be in the hungry lions' den with the prophet Daniel, whose story you have heard me recount, than in his clothes now. But it is God's will.'

'Let us hope,' said Orm, 'that it will continue to coincide with our own.'

The Thing continued for four days, and many cases were judged. The wisdom of Ugge and Sone was praised by all, save those who received the wrong end of their decisions; and Olof Summer-Bird, too, showed himself to be a shrewd judge, rich in experience despite his youth, so that even Ugge was forced on more than one occasion to admit that he might, with the passing of the years, attain some wisdom. When difficult cases arose, in which the parties refused to come to any agreement and the representatives of the tribes involved in the dispute could not agree, the third judge was called upon to help them reach a decision, such being the ancient custom; and on two occasions, when the dispute lay between the Virds and the Göings, Olof Summer-Bird officiated as the impartial judge, and acquitted himself with great honour.

Thus far, all had gone well; but gradually the common members of the assembly began to show signs of increasing unrest, as time went on without any good fight developing. A combat had, indeed, been ordered on the second day, as the result of a dispute between a Finnveding and a Göing concerning a horse-theft, since no witnesses could be found and both parties were equally obstinate and equally cunning at prevarication; but, when they fronted each other on the combat place, they proved so unskilful that they straightway ran their swords through one another's bellies and fell dead to the ground, like two halves of a broken pitcher, so that nobody gained much pleasure from that contest. The tribesmen made wry faces at one another when this happened, thinking that this was proving a very disappointing Thing.

On the third day, however, they were cheered by the appearance of a complicated and difficult case, which promised excellent results.

Two Virds, both known men of good reputation, named Askman and Glum, came forward and told of an instance of double women-theft. Both of them had lost their daughters, buxom young women in the prime of their beauty, who had been stolen by two Göing otter-hunters in the wild country east of the Great Ox Ford. The identity of the thieves was known; one of them was called Agne of Sleven, son of Kolbjörn Burnt-in-his-House, and the other Slatte, known as Fox Slatte, nephew to Gudmund of Uvaberg, who was one of the twelve Göing representatives. The theft had taken place a year previously; the two young women were, it appeared, still in the clutches of their captors; and Askman and Glum now demanded treble bride-money for each girl, as well as reasonable compensation for the injury caused to Widow Gudny, Glum's sister, who had been with the girls when the theft had taken place and had been so affected by the incident that for a good while after it she had been out of her proper mind. This good widow, they explained, they had brought with them to the Thing; she was well known to have an honest tongue, and, since many could testify that she had by now returned to her full senses, she would, they claimed, be the best witness to tell the assembly exactly what had happened.

The Widow Gudny now came forward. She was of powerful and impressive appearance, not yet old enough to frighten men; and she described clearly and earnestly how the incident had taken place. She and the girls had gone into the wild country to gather medicinal herbs, and had had to spend the whole day there, because these herbs were rare and difficult to find. They had wandered farther afield than they had intended, and a terrible storm had suddenly broken over them with thunder and hail and pelting rain. Frightened, and drenched to the skin, they had lost their way; and, after wandering for some time without coming upon any track or landmark, they had at last arrived at a scraped-out cave in the earth, in which they had taken shelter. Here, they began to feel the effect of cold, hunger and fatigue. There were two men already in the cave, hunters who lived there while trapping otters; and she was relieved to see that they did not look dangerous. The men had given them a friendly welcome, making room for them at their fire and giving them food and hot ale; and there they had remained until the storm ceased, by which time it was night, and very dark.

Up to then, she continued, she had only worried about the storm and the ache which she was beginning to feel in her back as the result of being cold in wet clothes. But now, she began to fear for the girls; which worried her much more. For the men were now in high spirits, and were saying that this was the best thing that could have happened, for it was a long time since they had seen any women; and they were liberal with their ale, which they kept in a keg in their cave, and warmed more of it against the cold, so that the girls began to grow muzzy, being young and inexperienced. She had asked the men, in a pointed manner, to describe to her the way back to their home, and they had told her; but apart from this, they had shown no concern for the girls' safety except by sitting close to them and feeling them to see if they were dry. This went so far that, after a while, Fox Slatte picked up two small bits of wood and told the girls that they were now to draw lots to decide which man each was to sleep next to. At this, she had declared vigorously that the girls must straightway go home, finding their way as well as they might in the dark. For her own part, she was compelled to remain in the cave, because of the severe pain in her back.

'I spoke thus,' she said, 'because I thought that the men might give way and let the girls go in peace, if I undertook to remain with them. I was ready to make this sacrifice for the girls' sake, since, whatever the men might do to me, it would be less horrible for me than for them. But instead of being accommodating, the men grew angry and addressed me in the most insulting terms, and seized hold of me and threw me out of the cave, saying that they would speed me on my way with arrows if I did not instantly depart from the place. I spent the whole night wandering in the forest, in terror of wild beasts and bogeys. When I reached home, and told what had happened, people went to the cave and found it empty, with no trace of the men or the girls or the otter-skins. For a long while after this, I was sick and half crazed because of the treatment I had endured at the hands of these foul ruffians.'

Here the Widow Gudny ended her testimony, having spoken her last few sentences in a voice dimmed by weeping. Gudmund of Uvabergs now rose, and said that he would present the case of the two young men. He was, he said, doubly qualified to do this, partly because he was wiser than they, and so better able to choose his words, and partly because he had on more than one occasion heard the whole story of events, not only from Agne of Sleven and his nephew Slatte, but also from the mouths of the young women themselves. He, therefore, was as well informed about this matter as anyone, if not better; and, as regards the testimony of the Widow Gudny, to which they had just been listening, he would say this, that much of it was according to the facts, but most of it contrary to them.

'Slatte and Agne both say,' he continued, 'that they were sitting in their cave during the storm, which was so severe that they were barely able to keep their fire from blowing out, when they heard groans outside. Slatte crept out, and saw three figures moving in the rain with their skirts wrapped round their heads. At first, he feared them to be trolls; and the women supposed him to be one, when they saw his head suddenly appear from the earth, so that they quaked and screamed with terror. Realising from this that they must be mortals, he approached and calmed them. They accepted his invitation to join him in his cave, and seated themselves round the fire. The girls were very fatigued, and were snivelling with distress; but there were no tears coming from the widow, and she showed little evidence of exhaustion. She kept her eyes fixed upon them incessantly, as she sat drying herself before the fire; she wanted her back rubbed, and every part of her body warmed with otter skins; then, after she had drunk of their hot ale like a thirsty mare, she became merry and took off most of her clothes. She did this, she explained to them, so that she might feel the heat more, since heat was what she needed most.

'Now, Slatte and Agne are both young,' continued Gudmund, 'but not more foolish than the run of men; and they knew well enough what thoughts tend to enter the minds of widows when their glance falls on a man. When, therefore, she suggested that the girls should go to sleep in a corner of the cave, but said that she herself would remain awake to see that no harm came to them, the men's suspicions were aroused and they exchanged a knowing glance. Both Agne and Slatte have assured me that they would gladly have obliged the widow, had she come to them unaccompanied, but that it seemed to them an unmanly and dishonourable thing for the two of them to share a widow when there were two fair young women also present who might well be as eager for pleasure as she was; for, had they done so, they would have been laughed at by every right-thinking person to whose ears the story might have come. So they seated themselves beside the young women and spoke calmingly to them, and helped them to warm their feet at the fire. By this time, the girls were in better spirits, having swallowed food and drink and become warm; they scarcely dared, however, to glance at the men, and were shy of speech. This increased the men's respect for them, for it testified to their modesty and good upbringing; and their liking for them became so strong that, eventually, they decided to draw lots for them, so that there should be no quarrelling as to who was to have which, and so that all should be satisfied. But when they suggested this, the widow, who had been growing more and more restless because no attention was being paid to her, jumped to her feet shrieking wildly. She protested that the girls must go home at once, or terrible things would happen. They were young, she said, and able to endure the hardships of the night; but for herself, she must beg hospitality until morning, since she was too fatigued and racked with backache to undertake the journey. This suggestion astonished the men, who asked her whether it was her intention to kill the girls; for this, they swore, she would certainly do if she drove them out into the wild forest to face the darkness and rain and all the evil things that lurked there. Such cruelty and wickedness they had never before heard the like of; and they would not allow it, for they were determined to protect the girls from her mad caprices. Nor, they told her further, were they so careless of their own safety that they were prepared to allow such a murderous character as her to remain in their cave; for if they did so, they could not be sure what might not happen to them while they were asleep. So they commanded her to go; she looked, they say, as strong as an ox, so that there would be little danger for her in the forest, and if she should encounter a bear or a wolf, the animal would certainly flee at the sight of her. Seizing hold of her, therefore, they ejected her from the cave, throwing her clothes after her. The next morning, they thought it best to move on; and the girls, when they heard of this decision, volunteered to accompany them, to help them carry their traps and skins. There are witnesses present here at the Thing who have heard this from the girls' own mouths. These young women are now married to Agne and Slatte, and are well contented, and have already borne their husbands children.

'Now I do not think,' concluded Gudmund, 'that this business can properly be called woman-theft. The fact of the matter is that these men saved these young women's lives, and that not once but twice; firstly, when they took them into their cave and offered them warmth and shelter, and secondly, when they prevented them from being driven out into the forest, as the wicked widow would have done with them. The men are, therefore, willing to pay ordinary bride-money for them, but no more.'

Thus reasoned Gudmund, and his words were greeted with great acclamation by the Göings. The Virds, however, appeared to approve them somewhat less, and Askman and Glum would not relax their demand. Had the two men stolen the widow, they said, they could have had her cheaply; but virgins could not be considered as being in the same category as widows; nor would any wise man place much reliance on the defence which Gudmund had put up for them. They thought it only right that the Widow Gudny should receive compensation for the insults and injuries that had been done to her; they knew her well, and she had never shown herself to be as man-crazy as Gudmund had made her out to be. However, in this matter of her compensation they would accept whatever sum might be offered; but they were not prepared to haggle over the young women.

Witnesses were then heard for both sides, both those who had heard the story from the young women's lips, and those who had been addressed on the subject by the Widow Gudny on her return from the cave. Ugge and Sone agreed that this was a difficult case to judge; and the spirits of the assembly rose, for there appeared to be an excellent prospect of a four-handed combat, provided that no unlucky chance intervened.

Ugge said that he felt half inclined to allow Sone to judge the case alone, because of his great wisdom and for their ancient friendship's sake; but he could not persuade his chosen twelve to agree to this, and so Olof Summer-Bird was co-opted as third judge. This honour, he said, was one which gave him little joy, for much silver and several lives depended on the result of the case, so that whoever judged it would bring upon himself the hatred and abuse of many, however just his decision might be. At first he suggested, as a compromise, that the husbands should pay double bride-money instead of the treble portion that was demanded; but neither the Göings nor the Virds would have any of this. Gudmund said that Slatte was already in strained circumstances, it being impossible for those who lived by trapping otters and beavers to amass a fortune, because of the poor prices that were paid for skins nowadays; while Agne of Sleven had lost his whole inheritance through his father having been burned in his house. The most they could afford would be the ordinary bridal portion, and even that they would hardly be able to pay without assistance. The Vird representatives, on the other hand, thought that Glum and Askman were demanding no more than was reasonable.

'For,' they said, 'we Virds have, ever since ancient times, held our women in great honour; and our neighbours must not be allowed to suppose that our virgins can be picked up cheap in any forest.'

Several thought that the best solution would be for the four parties concerned to fight it out; they thought that Askman and Glum, despite their disadvantage in age, would emerge with honour from the contest.

The matter was debated this way and that for a good while; but both Sone and Ugge were reluctant to declare that it should be decided by combat.

'Nobody can say,' said Ugge, 'that either of the two stolen women has any guilt to bear in this business; and it would be a bad judgment that condemned them to the certain misfortune of having to lose either a husband or a father.'

'If we are to pass unanimous judgment on this case,' said Olof Summer-Bird, 'we must first decide whether woman-theft has been committed or not. I know my opinion; but I should prefer that those who are older should speak before me.'

Ugge said that, in his mind, there was no doubt; that which had occurred must be regarded as woman-theft.

'It is no excuse to say that the young women went with the men of their own free will,' he said. 'For they did not do so until the following morning, but which time they had spent the night with them. This we know, for it has been admitted that the men drew lots for them. And every wise man knows that a young woman is always ready to go with a man whose couch she has shared, especially if he is the first with whom she has done this.'

Sone hesitated for a considerable while before announcing his decision; but at length, he said: 'It is the duty of a judge to speak the truth, even if, in so doing, he speaks against his own people.

This is woman-theft, and I do not think anyone can deny it. For when they ejected the widow from the cave, they forcibly separated the young women from their guardian, and so stole them from her care.'

Many of the Göings complained loudly when they heard Sone speak thus; but none dared to say that he was wrong, because he had such a great name for wisdom.

'Thus far, at least, we are agreed,' said Olof Summer-Bird. 'For I, too, judge this to be woman-theft. This being so, we must also agree that greater compensation is required than the ordinary bridal portion which Gudmund offers. But still we are far from reaching any satisfactory conclusion. For how shall we get the parties to accept our decision if the fathers will not accept, nor the husbands pay, double bride-money? It is my opinion that, if either party has the right to maintain its demands, it is the Virds.'

Up to this moment, Orm had been sitting silent in his place; but he now arose and asked what the Virds reckoned to be the value of a bridal portion, either in oxen or in skins, and what would be regarded as the equivalent in silver.

Ugge replied that the men of Värend had, from ancient times, reckoned the bridal portion in skins: thirty-six martenskins for a good farmer's daughter in the prime of youth, fresh and strong and without fault or blemish; in which case, the skins must be good winter-skins, with no arrow-holes; alternatively, thirty beaver-skins, also of the first quality; in return for which, no dowry was required to accompany the bride save the clothes she wore and the shoes she walked in, together with a new linen shift for the bridal night, a horn comb, three needles with eyes, and a pair of scissors.

'Which,' he continued, 'amounts to eighteen dozen marten-skins, for two treble portions, or, alternatively, fifteen dozen beaver-skins, if my reckoning is correct. That is a great quantity, and to calculate its equivalent in silver is a problem that would tax the brain of the most skilful arithmetician.'

Several of the representatives who were experienced in calculation endeavoured to come to his assistance, among them Toke Grey-Gullsson, who was used to reckoning in skins and silver; and, after they had taxed their brains for a good while, they declared unanimously that treble bride-money for two virgins would amount to seven and a quarter marks of silver, no more, and no less.

'To reach that even figure,' explained Toke, 'we have subtracted twopence three-farthings for the shifts, which will not be needed in this instance.'

When Gudmund of Uvaberg heard this great sum named, he burst into a tremendous bellow of laughter.

'No, no!' he roared. 'I could never agree to such a sum. Do you think me mad? Let them fight it out; whatever the result, it will be the cheapest way.'

And other voices from the assembly echoed his words: 'Let them fight!'

Orm now arose, and said that a thought had occurred to him which might, perhaps, help to deliver them from this quandary; for he was of that party which felt that it would be a pity to allow the matter to be settled by blows.

'Gudmund is right,' he said, 'when he says that seven and a quarter marks of silver is a great sum, enough to alarm the richest man; and few there are who have ever held so much in their hands, save those who have gone a-viking against the Franks, or have been present when my lord Almansur of Andalusia shared out his booty, or have taken geld from King Ethelred of England, or served the great Emperor at Miklagard. But if we take a third of this sum, we find it to be two and one-third marks, plus one-twelfth of a mark; and, if we split this third into two parts, we have one and one-seventh marks, plus one-twenty-fourth. Now we have been told that Agne of Sleven and Slatte are prepared to pay ordinary bridal portions. That means that we have two-sixths of a total sum accounted for. I have been thinking that it would be no dishonour to these men's kinsmen and neighbours if they were to provide a like sum. I know Gudmund of Uvaberg, and would not like to think him less open-handed than other men; and one and one-seventh marks, plus one twenty-fourth of a mark, is not a sum that it would ruin him to pay, even if he had to do so unaided. But I am sure that there are others besides him who are willing to help Slatte, and I do not doubt that it is the same with Agne's kinsmen. If they are prepared to do this, we shall have four-sixths of the total sum already promised, and only the last third to find. As regards this final portion, I have been thinking that here among our chosen twelve there sit men who would be prepared to give something for good-neighbour's sake, and for the sake of their own good names. I could wish that I were richer than I am; nevertheless, I am prepared to give my share; and if we can but find three or four others to do likewise, the last third of the sum will be paid, and the business settled to the satisfaction of all.'

When Orm had concluded, and had seated himself again, the representatives of the three tribes glanced at one another, and several of them were heard to murmur approval. Sone the Sharp-Sighted was the first to voice his thoughts.

'It is good to hear that wisdom will not wholly depart from the border-country when Ugge and I die,' he said. 'Orm of Gröning, you have, despite your youth, spoken words of wisdom. I will not content myself with saying that your suggestion is good: I shall even offer to pay a part of the last third of the sum myself. This may surprise some of you, for you all know how many children I have to support; but there are certain advantages in having a large family. Even if I contribute as much as a quarter of this third, I shall be able to afford it; for I shall collect the sum from my sixteen grown sons, who spend most of their time wandering about the forest. So that if I take two skins from each of them, I shall be able to pay my share and have a few left over for myself; and I am prepared to do this to help Agne of Sleven, because his mother was second cousin to my fourth wife. But let no man sit here with his tongue tied; let all who wish to join with me in this speak freely, and so win honour before the whole assembly.'

Toke Grey-Gullsson arose at once, and said that it was not his custom to be close-fisted when other people were being open-handed.

'And I say this,' he said, 'although I am only a skin-merchant who has, alas, all too often been skinned himself. I possess no great wealth, and am never likely to attain to any; many of you who sit here know that well, for you have got good money from me for skins of little quality. But at least I have enough to join with Orm and Sone in contributing towards this excellent cause; so, whatever they give, I shall give the same.'

Ugge the Inarticulate now began to stutter and stammer, as he always did when anything excited him. At last, he managed to say that this solution would bring honour to both the Göings and the Virds, and that he himself was prepared to contribute as much as those who had spoken before him.

Two of the Göing representatives, Black Grim and Thorkel Hare-Ear, now cried that the Virds must not be allowed to outdo them in generosity, and that they, too, wished to give a share; and Olof Summer-Bird said that he saw no reason why other men should have all the honour, and that he therefore proposed to offer twice as much as anyone else.

'And if you take my advice,' he added, 'you will gather in the contributions at once, for money melts forth most freely when the flame of giving is still warm. Here is my helmet to collect it in; and you, Toke Grey-Gullson, being a merchant, will be able to weigh each man's contribution, to make sure that it is correct.'

Toke sent a slave to fetch his scales, and more and more of the representatives, both Virds and Göings, rose to make their offers; for they saw that they might now win honour cheaply, since, the more people contributed, the smaller each man's gift would have to be. But Olof Summer-Bird reminded them that nobody had yet heard Gudmund of Uvaberg say how much he and the other kinsmen of Slatte and Agne were prepared to give.

Gudmund rose to his feet with an uncertain expression on his face, and said that it was a matter that needed much consideration; for a sixth of the whole sum was a great amount for himself and his kinsmen to find between them.

'No man can call me mean,' he said, 'but I am, alas, only a poor farmer, and Orm of Gröning is mistaken in suggesting to you that I am anything else. There is little silver to be found in my house, and I think the same is true of Slatte's other kinsmen. Such a burden would be too heavy for us to bear. If, however, we were asked to find one-half of the sixth, I think we might manage to scrape it together. Here among us sit so many great and famous men, with their belts distended with silver, that they would hardly notice it if they gave another half-sixth, in addition to the third which has already been promised. Do this, and your honour will be increased yet more; and I shall be saved from destitution.'

But at this the judges and representatives and the whole assembly seated at their backs hooted and howled with laughter; for it was well known to all of them that Gudmund's wealth was only surpassed by his meanness. When he found that he could win no support for his suggestion, he at length yielded; and two men, acting as spokesmen for Agne's kinsmen, promised that their due share would be paid.

'It would be best,' said Sone to Gudmund, 'if you, too, could gather in your share now, since you have, I doubt not, many kinsmen and friends amongst the assembly here; and I myself will collect the sum due from Agne's kinsmen.'

By this time, Toke's silver-scales had arrived, and he was attempting to calculate how much each man would have to pay.

'Thirteen men have promised to contribute,' he said, 'and each of them is giving the same amount, except Olof Summer-Bird, who is giving a double portion. That makes fourteen lots that we have to calculate. What one-fourteenth of one-third of seven and a quarter marks of silver comes to, is not easy to say; I do not think the wisest arithmetician of Gotland would be able to tell us at once. But a man who is shrewd can find a way out of most difficulties, and if we work it out in skins the problem becomes easier. That way, each lot will be one-fourteenth of six dozen marten-skins, which is one seventh of three dozen; and each lot must be reckoned to the nearest skin, for one always loses a little in weighing, as I know from experience. By this reckoning, each man should give the equivalent in silver to six marten-skins, a small price to pay for such an honour. Here are the scales and weights, and anyone who wants to do so is welcome to test them before I begin the weighing.'

Men who knew about such things now tested the scales carefully; for merchants' scales were often cunningly adjusted, so that the test was well worth making. But the weights could only be tested by touch; and, when two men expressed doubts regarding their accuracy, Toke immediately replied that he would gladly fight any man to prove that they were correct. 'It is part of a merchant's trade,' he said, 'to fight for his weights; and anyone who is afraid to do so must be regarded as unreliable, and should not be dealt with.'

'There shall be no fighting about weights,' said Ugge sternly. 'All the silver that is collected in the helmet shall be given at once to Glum and Askman; and what good would it do Toke to weigh falsely, when his own silver is to be weighed with the rest?'

All those who had promised to contribute now took silver from their belts, and had it weighed. Some gave small silver rings, others twists of silver thread, and others yet handed over silver which had been chopped up into small squares. Most, however, gave their contribution in the form of silver coins, and these were from many different countries and the furthermost parts of the earth, some of them having been struck in lands so remote that no man knew their name. Orm paid in Andalusian coin, of which he still possessed a quantity, and Olof Summer-Bird in beautifully engraven Byzantine pieces that bore the head of the great Emperor John Zimiskes.

When all the contributions had been collected, Toke poured them into a small cloth bag, and weighed them all together; and the scales showed that his calculations had been correct, for they made up a third of the sum required. But there was also a small surplus.

'This is too little to divide up and give back to all of you,' said Toke; 'for I cannot measure such small amounts on my scales.'

'What shall be done with it?' asked Ugge. 'It seems unnecessary that Glum and Askman should receive more than they demanded.'

'Let is give it to the Widow Gudny,' said Orm. 'Then she, too, will have some compensation for the distress and disappointment that has been caused to her.'

All agreed that this was an excellent solution: and soon Sone and Gudmund came back with their respective sixths, which they had collected from their kinsmen and friends in the assembly. Sone's sixth was weighed and found correct; but Gudmund's was deficient, although he produced a pile of skins and two copper kettles to add to his silver. He bewailed the deficiency loudly, saying that he was prepared to swear upon oath that this was all that he could raise, and begging that some rich man of the chosen twelve should lend him the money that was lacking. But this nobody was willing to do, for everyone knew that lending money to Gudmund was like casting it into the sea. At length, Sone the Sharp-Sighted said: 'You are a stubborn man, Gudmund, as we all know well; but all men can be persuaded to change their attitudes, by some means or other, and I think you are no exception to this rule. I seem to remember that Orm of Gröning managed to persuade you to do so not long after he had arrived in the border country, when you were unwilling to sell him hops and cattle-fodder at a fair price. I fancy that a well entered into the story; but I forget exactly what happened, for I am beginning to grow old. While, therefore, you, Gudmund, think how you may find the rest of your share of the silver, perhaps Orm will tell us the story of how he prevailed upon you. It would be interesting to know the method he used.'

This suggestion was enthusiastically received by the assembly, so Orm rose and said that the story of what had happened was short and simple. But before he could go further, Gudmund leaped to his feet and roared that he did not wish it to be repeated.

'We made this matter up a good while ago, Orm and I,' he declared. 'And it is not a story worth listening to. Wait but a short while, for I have just remembered another man whom I might ask; and I think he will be able to supply what is lacking.'

With that, he lumbered hastily away towards his camp. As he disappeared, many shouted that they wished, nevertheless, to hear the story of how Orm had persuaded him. But Orm said that they would have to get somebody else to tell it to them.

'For what Gudmund says is true,' he said, 'that we made this matter up long ago; and why should I provoke him to no purpose, when he has already gone to fetch his silver to avoid having this story repeated? It was only to make him do this that Sone, in his wisdom, referred to the incident.'

Before anyone could say more, Gudmund returned puffing from his camp with the missing money. Toke weighed it, and found it correct; so two-thirds of the bride-money due from Slatte and Agne was handed over by Ugge to Glum and Askman, whereupon these two admitted the men who had stolen their daughters to be good and blameless sons-in-law. The remaining third, which was to be paid by Slatte and Agne themselves, they were to receive at the end of the winter, so that the young men might be able to collect the necessary amount in skins.

But, as soon as this matter was settled, Olof Summer-Bird said that he would now like to hear the story that had been promised them of how Orm had persuaded Gudmund to change his mind. All the representatives cried assent to this; and Ugge himself supported the suggestion.

'Instructive stories,' he said, 'are always worth hearing, and this is one that is new to me. It may be that Gudmund would prefer that we should not hear it; but you must remember, Gudmund, that you have caused us all a great deal of inconvenience by your attitude towards this case, and that we have paid a third of the money demanded of your kinsmen, although you were wealthy enough to have given it yourself. Seeing that you have been saved so much silver, you can put up with the shame of hearing this story repeated. If, though, you would prefer to tell it yourself, by all means do so; and Orm Tostesson will doubtless be able to refresh your memory, if any details should escape you.'

Gudmund now flew into a fury, and began to roar. This was an old habit with him when he was angry, and because of it he had come to be known as The Thunderer. He sank his head down between his shoulders and shook throughout his whole body and brandished his fists before his face and roared like a were-wolf. It was his hope that people might suppose that he was about to go berserk, and in his younger days he had often succeeded in frightening men by this means; but nobody was deceived by it any longer, and the more he roared the louder the assembly laughed. Suddenly he fell silent and glared around him.

'I am a dangerous man,' he said, 'and no man provokes me without regretting it.'

'When a representative breaks the peace of the Thing,' said Toke, 'by threat or abuse, drunken talk or malicious accusation, he shall be required to pay a fine of . . . I forget the sum, but doubtless there are men here who can remind me.'

'He shall be expelled from the precincts of the Thing by the judges and representatives,' said Sone. 'And, if he should resist, or attempt to return, he shall pay with his beard. Such is the ancient law.'

'Only twice in my life have I known a representative to be deprived of his beard,' said Ugge reflectively. 'And neither of them was able to endure life for much longer, after suffering such shame.'

Many now began to be incensed with Gudmund, not because he had howled at them, which nobody bothered much about, but because the honour which they had won by their open-handedness had cost them so much silver; and they now blamed Gudmund for this. So they roared furiously at him to depart from the Thing, swearing that otherwise they would take his beard from him. Gudmund had a very fine beard, long and luxuriant, of which he evidently took great care; he therefore yielded to their clamour and left the Thing, rather than risk exposing his beard to danger. But, as he departed, he was heard to mumble: 'No man provokes me without living to regret it.'

Orm was now commanded to tell the story of his first meeting with Gudmund, and how he had persuaded him to change his mind by holding him over his own well. This hugely delighted the assembly; but Orm himself was not greatly pleased at having to repeat the tale, and, when he had finished, said that he would now have to be prepared for some attempt by Gudmund at revenge.

So this difficult case of woman-theft was successfully concluded. Many had won honour through it; but it was the general opinion that Olof Summer-Bird and Orm of Gröning deserved the most praise for the way they had spoken.

Ever since the opening of the Thing, Orm had been expecting to hear some accusation from the Finnvedings about the way he had treated Osten of Ore, or some reference to the two heads that had been thrown across the brook on the first evening. But, since nobody mentioned either matter, he decided to find out for himself whether they felt bound as a tribe to avenge the insult inflicted upon one of their members. Accordingly, on the evening of this, the third day of the Thing, he went alone to the Finnveding camp, having first requested and obtained safe-conduct to do so, in order that he might discuss the matter privately with Olof Summer-Bird.

The latter received him in a manner befitting a chieftain. He had sheep-skins spread out for Orm to sit on, offered him fried sausage, sour milk and white bread, and commanded his servant to bring forth his feasting-cup. This was a tall clay cup with handles, narrow-necked, and terminating in a leaden stopper. It was placed carefully on flat ground between them, together with two silver mugs.

'You conduct yourself like a chieftain,' said Orm, 'here, as at the Thing.'

'It is a bad thing to sit talking without ale to drink,' said Olof Summer-Bird. 'And when chieftain entertains chieftain, they should have something better to swallow than water from the brook. You are a man who has travelled widely, as I have, and perhaps you have tasted this drink before; though it is seldom offered to guests here in the north.'

He took the stopper from the cup and poured a liquid from it into the two mugs. Orm nodded as he saw its colour.

'This is wine,' he said. 'The Roman drink. I have tasted it in Andalusia, where many people drank it secretly, although it was forbidden them by their prophet; and once again, on a later occasion, at the court of King Ethelred in England.'

'In Constantinople, which we call Miklagard,' said Olof Summer-Bird, 'it is drunk by everyone, morning and evening, especially by the priests, who thin it with water and drink it thrice as much as anyone else. They hold it to be a sacred drink, but I think that ale is better. I pledge you welcome.'

They both drank.

'Its sweetness is soothing to the throat when a man has eaten fat sausage with salt in it,' said Orm, 'though I agree with you about ale being the better drink. But it is time for me to tell you why I have come to speak with you, though I think you know the reason already. I wish to know whether the two heads which were thrown to me across the brook were sent by your kinsman Osten. They belonged to two Christian priests who had become your slaves. I also wish to know whether this Osten still seeks my life. If he does so, it is without cause, for I spared his life and gave him his freedom when he was in my power, the time he treacherously gained entry to my house to get my head, which he had promised to King Sven. You know that I am a baptized man, and a follower of Christ; and I know that you regard Christians as evil men, because of the way you saw them act in Miklagard. But I promise you that I am not that sort of Christian; and here at this Thing I have learned that you, too, are a man who hates evil and villainy. It is because I know this that I have come to you this evening; otherwise, I would have been foolish to cross the brook.'

'How you could have become a Christian,' said Olof Summer-Bird, 'is more than I can understand. Nor can I make much of your little bald priest; for I hear that he helps all members of the Thing who come to him with ailments, and refuses reward for his labour. So I hold you both to be good men, as though you had never been tainted with Christianity. Nevertheless, you must admit, Orm, that you and your priest laid a cruel burden on my kinsman, Osten, when you forced him to receive baptism. The shame of that has driven him mad; though it may be that the axe-blow he received on his head also had something to do with it. He has become folk-shy, and spends most of his time wandering in the forest or lying in his room groaning to himself. He refused to come to the Thing; but he bought these two slave-priests from their owners, paying a big price for them, and straightway hewed off their heads and sent them here by his servant, that he might give them to you and your little priest as a reminder and a greeting. He has, indeed, been well punished for his attempt against your life, for he has been baptized, and has lost all the wares you took from him, and his understanding too; but, though he is my kinsman, I will not say that he has got more than he deserved, for he was too rich a man, and too nobly born, to be a party to such a bargain as he made with King Sven. I have told him as much myself, and have said that I shall not order any feud against you to avenge him; but it is certain that he will gladly kill you, if he gets the chance. For he believes that he will become brave and merry again, as he was before, once he has killed you and your little priest.'

'I thank you for this information,' said Orm. 'Now I know how I stand. There is nothing I can do about the two priests, whose heads he took; and I shall not seek revenge for their death. But I shall be on my guard, in case his madness drives him to make some further attempt against me.'

Olof Summer-Bird nodded, and refilled their mugs with wine.

It was now quite still in the camp, and there was no sound to be heard save the breathing of sleeping men. A light breeze stirred the trees, and the aspen leaves rustled. They pledged each other again, and, as Orm drank, he heard a branch crack in the wood behind him. As he leaned forward to replace his mug on the ground, he heard a sudden gasp at his ear, as of a man fighting for breath. Olof Summer-Bird sat up alertly and gave a cry, and Orm turned half around, saw a movement in the woods, and crouched closer to the ground.

'It is a lucky thing I am sharp of hearing, and moved quickly,' he said afterwards. 'For the spear flew so close to me that it scarred the back of my neck.'

There was a howl from the woods, and a man rushed out at them whirling a sword. It was Osten of Ore; and they could see at once that he was mad, for his eyes stared stiffly out of his head like a ghost's, and there was froth upon his lips. Orm had no time to seize his sword or get to his feet. Flinging himself sideways, he managed to grip the madman's leg and throw him across his body at the same time as he received a slash across the hip from his sword. Then he heard a blow and a groan and, as he got to his feet, he saw Olof Summer-Bird standing sword in hand, and Osten lying still on the ground. His kinsman had hewed him in the neck, and he was already dead.

Men came running towards them, awakened by the noise. Olof Summer-Bird looked with a pale face at the dead man.

'I have killed him,' he said, 'although he was my kinsman. But I do not intend that any guest of mine shall be attacked, even by a madman. Besides which, his spear broke my feasting-cup; and whoever had done that, I would have killed him.'

The cup lay in fragments, and he was much grieved at its loss: for such a one he would not easily find again.

He ordered his men to carry the dead man to the marsh and sink him there, driving pointed stakes through his body: for if this is not done, madmen walk again, and are the most fearful of earth-bound spirits.

Orm had come out of this adventure with a scar on his neck and a wound in his hip; but the latter was not dangerous, for the sword-blade had struck his knife and eating-spoon, which he wore on his belt. He was, accordingly, able to walk back to his camp; and, as he said farewell to Olof Summer-Bird, they took each other by the hand.

'You have lost your cup,' said Orm, 'which is a pity. But you are the richer by a friend; if that is any consolation to you. And I should be happy if I could think that I had won as much.'

'You have,' replied Olof Summer-Bird. 'And this is no small prize that you and I have won.'

From this time, the friendship between them was very great.

On the last day of the Thing, it was agreed that peace should reign throughout the border country until the time of the next Thing. So this Thing at the Kraka Stone ended; though many thought that it had been disappointing, and nothing to boast of, because no good combat had been fought during it.

Father Willibald went to the Vird camp to look for the magister and say farewell to him, but the woman Katla had already taken him away. Orm wanted Toke to come back to Gröning with him;

but Toke refused, saying that he had to buy his skins. But they promised to entertain each other honourably in the near future, and always to keep their friendship firm.

Everyone now rode off towards their respective homes; and Orm felt much relieved that he was rid of both the magister and his enemy, Osten of Ore. When Christmas came, Toke and his Andalusian wife Mirah visited Gröning; and all that Orm and Toke had to tell each other was as nothing compared with what Ylva and Mirah had to say to one another.

At the beginning of spring, Rapp's wife, Torgunn, bore her man a boy. Rapp was much pleased at this: but, when he reckoned the months backwards, he felt somewhat suspicious, for the date of conception was not far from that time when the magister had read over Torgunn's injured knee. All the housefolk men and women alike, praised the child and his resemblance to his father; this comforted Rapp, but did not completely allay his fears. The only man whose word he wholly relied upon was Orm; so he went to him and begged him to examine the child and say whom he thought it most resembled. Orm looked at the child closely for a long while; then he said: 'There is a great difference between him and you, and nobody can fail to see it. The child has two eyes, and you have only one. But it would be churlish of you to resent this, for you, too, had two eyes when you came into the world. Apart from this disparity, I have never seen a child that more resembled its father.'

Rapp was calmed by this assurance, and became exceedingly proud of his son. He wanted Father Willibald to christen him Almansur; but the latter refused to give the child a heathen name, and he had to be content with calling him Orm instead. Orm himself carried the child to the christening.

A fortnight after this child was born, Ylva gave birth to her second son. He was black-haired and dark-skinned, and yelled little, but gazed about him with serious eyes; and, when the sword's point was offered to him, he licked it even more avidly than Harald Ormsson had done. All agreed that he was born to be a warrior, and in this they prophesied rightly. Ylva thought that he resembled Gold-Harald, King Harald's nephew, in so far as she could remember this great Viking from her childhood days; but Asa would have none of this, insisting that he bore a marked likeness to Sven

Rat-Nose, who had been similarly dark of skin. But he could not be christened Sven, and they already had one child called Harald; so in the end, Orm gave him the name of Blackhair. He behaved very quietly and solemnly during the christening, and bit Father Willibald on the thumb. He became his parents' favourite child, and, in time, the greatest warrior on the border; and, many years later, after many things had happened, there was in the court of King Canute the Mighty of Denmark and England no chieftain of greater renown than the King's cousin, Blackhair Ormsson.

PART FOUR

The Bulgar Gold

CHAPTER ONE

Concerning the end of the world, and how Orm's children grew up

At length, that year arrived in which the world was due to end. By this time, Orm was in his thirty-fifth, and Ylva in her twenty-eighth year. All good Christians believed that in this, the thousandth year after His birth, Christ would appear in the sky surrounded by hosts of shining angels and judge every man and woman, both living and dead, to decide who should go to Heaven, and who to Hell. Orm had heard Father Willibald talk about this so often that he had become resigned to it. Ylva could never make up her mind whether she really believed that it would happen, or not; but Asa was happy in the thought that she would be able to attend this great occasion as a living person, in her best clothes, and not as a corpse in a winding-sheet.

Two things, however, troubled Orm. One was that Toke still refused to be converted. The last time he had visited him Orm had striven earnestly to persuade him that he would be wise to change his faith, enumerating to him all the advantages that Christians would shortly enjoy; but Toke had remained obstinate, and had chaffed Orm for his zeal.

'The evenings will be long in Heaven if Toke is not there,' said Orm to Ylva, more than once. 'Many of the great men I have known will be elsewhere; Krok and Almansur, Styrbjörn and Olof Summer-Bird, and many other good warriors besides. Of the people who have meant most to me, I shall only have yourself, our children, Asa, Father Willibald, Rapp, and the house-folk; and also Bishop Poppo and your father, King Harald, whom it will be good to meet again. But I should have liked to have had Toke there. It is his woman who holds him back.'

'Let them do as they think best,' said Ylva. 'Things may turn out otherwise than as you anticipate. For my part, I do not think God will be in such a hurry to destroy the world, after having put himself to so much trouble to create it. Father Willibald says we shall all sprout wings, and when I picture him thus, or you, or Rapp, I cannot but laugh. I do not want any wings, but I should like to be allowed to take my gold chain with me, and Father Willibald does not think I shall be allowed to. So I am not looking forward to this event as eagerly as he is, and will believe in it when I see it happen.'

Orm's other concern was whether it would be wise to sow his crops. He was anxious to know at what season of the year Christ's advent might be expected, but Father Willibald was unable to enlighten him upon this point. Orm doubted whether it would be worth the labour, since he might never be able to reap the year's harvest, and would not be likely to need it even if it should ripen in time. Soon, however, he succeeded in solving this problem to his satisfaction.

From the very first day of this year, every young Christian woman had sought the delights of bodily pleasure more greedily than ever before; for they were uncertain whether this pleasure would be allowed them in Heaven and were, therefore, anxious to enjoy as much of it as they could while there was yet time, since, whatever form of love Heaven might have to offer them, they doubted whether it could be as agreeable as the sort practised on earth. Such of the servant-girls as were unmarried became wholly intractable, running after every man they saw; and even in the married women a certain difference was apparent, although they clung virtuously to their husbands, thinking it imprudent to do otherwise when the Judgment Day was so close upon them. The result of all this was that by the spring most of the women at Gröning were with child. When Orm discovered that Ylva, Torgunn and the rest were in this condition, his spirits perked up again, and he ordered that the sowing should take place as usual.

'No children can be born in Heaven,' he said. 'Therefore, they must all be born on earth. But this cannot be until the beginning of next year. Either the god-men have calculated wrongly, or God has changed his mind. When nine months have gone by without any woman becoming pregnant, then we shall know that the end of the world is imminent, and can begin to prepare for it; but until then, we can live our lives as usual.'

Nothing that Father Willibald said could persuade him that he was wrong in this surmise; and, as the year wore on and nothing happened, the priest himself began to have doubts about the matter. It might be, he said, that God had altered his plans, in view of the fact that there were still so many sinful men on earth to whom the Gospel had not yet penetrated.

That autumn, a band of foreigners came from the east and made their way on foot along the border. They were all soldiers, and all wounded; some of their wounds were still bleeding. There were eleven of them, and they trudged from house to house craving food and night-shelter; where this was granted them, they remained for one night, or sometimes two, and then proceeded on their way. They said they were Norwegians and were journeying homewards; but more than this they would not reveal. They conducted themselves peaceably, using no violence towards anyone; and, where night-shelter was refused them, they continued on their way without complaint, as though unconcerned whether they ate and slept or no.

At length, they arrived at Gröning, and Orm came out to speak with them, accompanied by Father Willibald. When they saw the priest, they fell on their knees, and besought him earnestly to bless them. He did so willingly, and they seemed overjoyed at having come to a Christian house and, especially, at having found a priest. They ate and drank ravenously; then, when they had consumed their fill, they sat silent and large-eyed, paying scant heed to the questions that were addressed to them, as though they had other things upper-most in their minds. Father Willibald saw to their wounds, but his blessings were what they were most eager for, and of these it seemed that they could not have enough. When they were told that the morrow was a Sunday, they begged to be allowed to stay and attend mass and to listen to the sermon. This request Orm granted them willingly, though he was vexed that they would tell him nothing about themselves, or whence they had come.

That Sunday was a fine day, and many people came riding to church, mindful of the promise they had made to Father Willibald on the evening of their baptism. The foreigners were given places on the front benches and listened earnestly to all that the priest said. As usual during this year, he took as his theme the end of the world, assuring them that it might be expected to occur very shortly, although it was difficult to say exactly when, and that every Christian must mend his

401

Eastern Europe
1000 A.D.

Denmark and Norway

Byzantine Empire

Modern Caliphate

◀━ ◀ ━ ◀━ Route of Orm's third voyage

------------ 'High Road' to Miklagard

MERIANS
• Rostov

Bolgary

GREAT
BULGARIA

R. Volga

R. Don

ATZINAKS

K A Z A R S

Tmutorokan

Sea

Caucasus Mts.

Trebizond

ARMENIA
Manzikert

Salt Sea

Aral
Sea

t s.

Aleppo
Antioch

Baghdad

N

| 0 | 200 | 400 | 600 miles |

| 0 | 500 | 1000 km |

ways, in order that he might not be found wanting when the day arrived. As he said this, several of the foreigners were seen to smile contemptuously; others, however, wept, so that the tears could be seen upon their cheeks. After Mass, they begged to be blessed again, with a great blessing; and Father Willibald did as they asked him.

After he had blessed them, they said: 'You are a good man, priest. But you do not know that the event of which you warn us has already happened. The end of the world has come; Christ has taken our King from us to live with Him, and we have been forgotten.'

Nobody could understand what they meant, and they were unwilling to say more. At length, however, they explained what had happened to them. They spoke with few words, and in voices such as dead men might have, as though nothing any longer had any meaning for them.

They said that their King, Olaf Tryggvasson of Norway, the best man who had ever lived on earth, save only Christ himself, had fallen in a great battle against the Danes and Swedes. They themselves had been captured alive by the Swedes; their ship had been boarded by great numbers and they, fatigued, had been pinned between shields, or else, because of their wounds, had been unable to resist longer. Others of their comrades, more fortunate, had followed their King to Christ. Then they had been led, together with many others, aboard one of the Swedish ships to be taken to Sweden. There had been forty of them in the ship, all told. One night, they lay in an estuary, and someone observed that this river was called The Holy River. This they took to be a sign from God, and as many of them as had the strength to do so broke their fetters and fought with the Swedes in the ship. They killed them all; but most of their comrades were slain also, so that only sixteen of them were left alive. These had then rowed the ship up the river as far as they could. Five, wounded more grievously than the rest, had died at their oars, smiling; and they, the eleven survivors, had taken weapons from the dead Swedes and abandoned the ship, thinking to march overland to the Halland border and so into Norway. For, realizing that they were the most unworthy of King Olaf's men, since they alone had been left behind when all their comrades had been permitted to accompany him, they had not dared to take their own lives, for fear lest he should refuse to know them. They believed that this was the penance demanded of them, that they should return to Norway and bring to their countrymen tidings of the death of their King. Every day, they had said all the prayers they knew, though these had been fewer than they could have wished, and had reminded one another of all the King's commandments regarding the conduct of Christian warriors. It was a great joy to them, they said, that they had at last found a priest and been permitted to attend Mass and receive God's blessing; now, however, they must continue on their journey, that they might lose no time in bringing their sad tidings to their countrymen. They believed that when they had done this, a sign would be given them, perhaps by their King himself, that they had at last been deemed worthy to join him, although they were the poorest of his men.

They thanked Orm and the priest for their kindness, and went their way; and nothing more was heard of them at Gröning, nor of the end of the world.

The year ended without the smallest sign having appeared in the sky, and there ensued a period of calm in the border country. Relations with the Smalanders continued to be peaceful, and there were no local incidents worth mentioning, apart from the usual murders at feasts and weddings, and a few men burned in their houses as the result of neighbourly disputes. At Gröning, life proceeded tranquilly. Father Willibald worked assiduously for Christ, though he was not infrequently heard to complain at the slowness with which his congregation increased, despite all his efforts; what particularly annoyed him was the number of people who came to him and said that they were willing to be baptized in return for a calf or heifer. But even he admitted that things might have been worse, and thought that some of the men and women he had converted were, perhaps, less obdurately evil than they had been before baptism. Asa did what she could to help him; and, although she was by now beginning to grow old, she was as active as ever, and had plenty to occupy her in looking after the children and the servants. She and Ylva were good friends, and seldom exchanged words, for Asa was mindful that her daughter-in-law was of royal blood; and, when they disagreed, Asa always yielded, although it could be seen that it went against her nature to do so.

'For it is certain,' said Orm to Ylva, 'that the old woman is even more obstinate than you, which is saying not a little. It is good that things have turned out as I hoped they might, and that she has never tried to challenge your authority in the house.'

Orm and Ylva still found no cause for complaint in their choice of one another. When they quarrelled, neither of them minced words; but such incidents were rare, and quickly passed, nor did either of them cherish rancour afterwards. It was a strange peculiarity of Orm's that he never birched his wife; even when a great anger came over him, he restrained his temper, so that nothing more came of it than an overturned table or a broken door. In time, he perceived a curious thing, namely, that all their quarrels always ended in the same way; he had to mend the things he had broken, and the matter about which they had quarrelled was always settled the way Ylva wanted it, although she never upturned a table or broke a door, but merely threw an occasional dish-clout in his face or smashed a plate on the floor at his feet. Having discovered this, he thought it unrewarding to have any further quarrels with her, and a whole year would sometimes pass without their harmony being threatened by hard words.

They had two more children: a son, whom they called Ivar, after Ivar of the Broad Embrace, and whom Asa hoped would, in time, become a priest, and a daughter, whom they called Sigrun. Toke Grey-Gullsson was invited as the chief guest at her christening, and it was he who chose her name, though only after a long exchange of words with Asa, who wanted the child to be given a Christian name. Toke, however, asserted that no woman's name was more beautiful than Sigrun, or more honoured in old songs; and, since Orm and Ylva wished to show him all honour, it was allowed to be as he wished it. If all went well, Toke said, she would, in good time, marry one of his sons; for he could not hope to have either of the twins as a daughter-in-law, none of his sons being old enough to be considered as future husbands for them. This, he said to himself sadly, as he sat gazing at Oddny and Ludmilla, was, in truth, a great pity.

For the two girls were, by now, beginning to grow up, and nobody could any longer doubt whether they would be pleasing to the eye. They were both red-haired and well-shaped, and men were soon glancing at them; but it was easy to perceive one difference between them. Oddny was of a mild and submissive temper: she was skilful at womanly tasks, obeyed her parents willingly, and seldom caused

Ylva or Asa any vexation. On the few occasions when she did so, her sister was chiefly to blame, for, from the first, Oddny had obeyed Ludmilla in everything, while Ludmilla, by contrast, found it irksome to obey and pleasing to command. When she was birched, she yelled more from anger than from pain, and comforted herself with the reflection that she would, before long, be big enough to give as good as she got. She disliked working at the butter-churns or on the weaving-stools, preferring to shoot with a bow, at which sport she soon became as skilful as her teacher, Glad Ulf. Orm was unable to control her, but her obstinacy and boldness pleased him; and when Ylva complained to him of her perversity and the way she played truant in the forest shooting with Glad Ulf and Harald Ormsson, he merely replied: 'What else can you expect? It is the royal blood in her veins. She has been blessed with a double measure, Oddny's as well as her own. She will be a difficult filly to tame, and let us hope that the main burden of taming her will fall on other shoulders than ours.'

In the winter evenings, when everyone was seated round the fire at his or her handicraft, she would sometimes behave peaceably and even, now and then, work at her spinning, provided that some good story was being told, by Orm of his adventures in foreign lands, or by Asa of the family in the old days, or by Father Willibald of great happenings in the days of Joshua or King David, or by Ylva of her father, King Harald. She was happiest when Toke visited Gröning, for he was a good story-teller and knew many tales of ancient heroes. Whenever he seemed to flag, it was always she who jumped to fill his ale-cup and beg him to continue, and it was seldom that he found the heart to refuse her.

For it was always so with Ludmilla Ormsdotter that, from her earliest youth, men found it difficult to gainsay her. She was pale-complexioned, with skin tightly drawn over her cheek-bones, and dark eyebrows; and, although her eyes were of the same grey as those of many other girls, it nevertheless seemed to men who studied them closely and returned their gaze that there were none to compare with them anywhere else in the whole border country.

Her first experience with men occurred in the summer after her fourteenth birthday, when Gudmund of Uvaberg came riding to Gröning with two men, whom he suggested that Orm should take into his service.

407

Gudmund had not been seen at Gröning since Orm had insulted him at the Thing, nor had he ridden to any Thing since that day. But now he came full of smiles and friendliness, and said that he wished to do Orm a kindness, so that their old quarrel might be made up.

'I have with me here,' he said, 'the two best workers that ever were; and I now offer them to you. They are not serfs, but free men, and each of them does the work of two, and sometimes more. This is, therefore, a fine service I am doing you by offering them to you, though it is equally true that you will be doing me a good one by accepting them. For they are both tremendous eaters and, though I have kept them for four months, I find myself unable to do so any longer. I am not as rich as you are, and they are eating me out of house and home. I dare not ration them, for they have told me that, if this is done, they become dangerous; unless they eat themselves full each noon and evening, a madness comes upon them. But they work willingly for anyone who will feed them full, and no man has ever seen workers to match them.'

Orm regarded this offer with suspicion, and questioned both Gudmund and the two men carefully before accepting them. The men did not attempt to conceal their shortcomings, but said honestly how things were with them and how they wished them to be; and, since Orm had good need of strong workers, he at length accepted them into his service, and Gudmund rode contentedly away.

The men were called Ullbjörn and Greip. They were young, long-faced and flaxen-haired; and a man had only to look at them to tell that they were strong; but as regards intelligence, they were less fortunately equipped. From their speech it could be heard that they came from a distant part of the country; they said they had been born in a land far beyond West Guteland, called Iron-Bearing Land, where the men were as strong as the bears, with whom they would often wrestle for amusement. But a great famine had afflicted their land, and so they had left it and journeyed southwards in the hope of reaching a country where they would be able to find enough to eat. They had worked on many farms and estates in West Guteland and Smaland. When food began to become scanty, they explained, they killed their employer and went on.

Orm thought that they must have worked for a tame lot of masters, if they had allowed themselves to be killed as easily as that;

but the men stared earnestly at him and bade him take good note of what they had said.

'For, if we become hungry, we go berserk, and no man can withstand us. But if we get enough food, we conduct ourselves peaceably and do whatever our master bids us. For we are made that way.'

'Food you shall have,' said Orm, 'as much as you want; if you are such good workers as you claim to be, you will be worth all the food you can eat. But be sure of this, that, if you enjoy going berserk, you have come to the wrong place here; for I have no patience with berserks.'

They gazed at him with thoughtful eyes and asked how long it was until the midday meal.

'We are already beginning to feel hungry,' they said.

As fortune had it, the midday meal was just due to be served. The two newcomers set to with a will, and ate so greedily that everyone watched them in amazement.

'You have both eaten enough for three men,' said Orm. 'And now I want to see each of you do two men's work, at the very least.'

'That you shall,' they replied, 'for this was a meal that suited us well.'

Orm began by setting them to dig a well, and soon had to admit that they had not exaggerated their worth, for they quickly dug a good well, broad and deep and lined from top to bottom with stone. The children stood and watched them work; the men said nothing, but it was noticeable that their eyes often turned towards Ludmilla. She showed no fear of them, and asked them how it was with men when they went berserk, but received no reply to this question.

When they had completed this task, Orm told them to build a good boat-house down by the river; and this, too, they did quickly and well. Ylva forbade her daughters to go near them while they were working there; for, she said, one could never be sure what such half-trolls as they might not suddenly do.

When the boat-house was ready, Orm set them to clean the cowshed. All the cows were at pasture, and only the bull was left in the shed, he being too evil-tempered to be allowed loose. A whole winter's droppings lay in the pens, so that Ullbjörn and Greip had several stiff days' work ahead of them.

The children and all the house-folk felt somewhat afraid of the two men, because of their strength and strangeness. Ullbjörn and Greip never had much to say to anyone; only, sometimes, when they were spoken to, they told briefly of feats of strength that they had performed, and how they had strangled men who had not given them enough to eat, or had broken their backs with their bare hands.

'Nobody can withstand us, when we are angry,' they said. 'But here we get enough to eat, and are content. So long as things continue thus, nobody has anything to fear from us.'

Ludmilla, alone, was not afraid of them, and several times went to watch them work in the cow-shed, sometimes accompanied by her brothers and sisters, and sometimes alone. When she was there, the men kept their eyes fixed on her, and, although she was young, she understood well what they were thinking.

One day, when she was there alone with them, Greip said: 'You are the sort of girl I could fancy.'

'I, too,' said Ullbjörn.

'I should like to play with you in the hay,' said Greip, 'if you are not afraid to do so with me.'

'I can play better than Greip,' said Ullbjörn.

Ludmilla laughed.

'Do you both like me?' she said. 'That is a pity. For I am a virgin, and of royal blood, and not to be bedded by any chance vagabond. But I think I prefer one of you to the other.'

'Is it me?' said Greip, throwing aside his shovel.

'Is it me?' asked Ullbjörn, dropping his broom.

'I like best,' said Ludmilla, 'whichever of you is the stronger. It would be interesting to know which that is.'

Both the men were now hot with desire. They glared silently at one another.

'I may perchance,' added Ludmilla softly, 'allow the stronger man to sit with me for a short while down by the river.'

At this, they straightway began to growl fearfully like were-wolves, and seized hold of one another. They appeared to be of equal strength, and neither could gain an ascendance. The beams and walls shook as they stumbled against them. Ludmilla went to the door to be out of their way.

As she was standing there, Orm came up.

'What is that noise?' he asked her. 'What are they doing in there?'

Ludmilla turned to him and smiled.

'Fighting,' she said.

'Fighting?' said Orm, taking a step towards her. 'What about?'

'Me,' replied Ludmilla happily. 'Perhaps this is what they call going berserk.'

Then she scampered fearfully away, for she saw a look on Orm's face that was new to her, and understood that a great anger had come over him.

An old broom was leaning against the wall. Orm wrenched the shaft out of its socket; and this was the only weapon he had as he strode in, slamming the door behind him. Then his voice was audible above the snarling of the men, and for a moment all was silence in the shed. But almost at once, the snarling broke out afresh, and with redoubled violence. The servant girls came out into the yard and stood there listening, but nobody felt inclined to open the cowshed door to see what was happening inside. Someone shouted for Rapp and his axe, but he was nowhere to be found. Then one of the doors flew open and the bull rushed forth in terror, with its halter hanging loose about its neck, and fled into the forest. Everyone shrieked aloud at this sight; and now Ludmilla began to be afraid and to cry, for she feared she had started something bigger than she had intended.

At length, the uproar ceased, and there was silence. Orm walked out, panting for breath, and wiped his arm across his brow. He was limping, his clothes were torn, and part of one of his cheek-beards had been wrenched away. The servant girls ran up to him with anxious cries and questions. He looked at them and said that they need not lay a place for Ullbjörn or Greip at supper that evening.

'Nor to-morrow, neither,' he added. 'But how it is with this leg of mine, I do not know.'

He limped into the house, to have his injury examined by Ylva and the priest.

Inside the cowshed, all was disorder, and the two berserks were lying across each other in one corner. Greip had the sharp end of the broom-shaft through his throat, and Ullbjörn's tongue was hanging out of his mouth. They were both dead.

Ludmilla was afraid that she would now be birched, and Ylva thought she had deserved it for having gone in alone to the two berserks. But Orm pleaded for her to be treated leniently, so that she escaped more lightly than she had thought possible; and she

411

described what had happened before the fight in such a manner that they agreed that no blame could be attached to her. Orm was not displeased with the incident, once Father Willibald had examined his leg and declared the injury to be slight; for, although he was now certain that Gudmund of Uvaberg had offered him the two men in the hope of gaining his revenge, he was well pleased with his feat of having overpowered two berserks single-handed and without the help of any proper weapon.

'You did wisely, Ludmilla,' he said, 'to turn them against one another when they would have molested you, for I am not sure that even I could have defeated them if they had not already tired each other somewhat. My advice, therefore, Ylva, is that she shall not be birched, although it was rash of her to go in to them alone. For she is too young to understand the thoughts that are liable to enter men's heads when they look at her.'

Ylva shook her head doubtfully at this, but allowed Orm to have his way.

'This affair has turned out well,' he said. 'Nobody can deny that these two ruffians have done good work since they arrived here. I now have a well, a boat-house, and more honour to my name, and Gudmund has been well snubbed for his pains. So everything is as it should be. But I will take care to let him know that, if he provokes me again, I shall pay him a visit that he will not forget.'

'I will come with you,' said Blackhair earnestly; he had been sitting listening to their conversation.

'You are too small to wear a sword,' said Orm.

'I have the axe Rapp forged for me,' he replied. 'He says there are not many axes with a sharper edge than mine.'

Orm and Ylva laughed, but Father Willibald shook his head frowningly, and said it was a bad thing to hear such talk from a Christian child.

'I must tell you again, Blackhair,' he said, 'what you have already heard me say five, if not ten times, that you should think less about weapons and more about learning the prayer called Pater Noster which I have so often explained to you and begged you to learn. Your brother Harald could recite that prayer by the time he was seven, and you are now twelve and still do not know it.'

'Harald can say it for us both,' retorted Blackhair boldly. 'I am in no hurry to learn priest-talk.'

So time passed at Gröning, and little of note occurred; and Orm felt well content to sit there peacefully until his days should end. But a year after he killed the berserks, he received tidings which sent him forth upon the third of his long voyages.

CHAPTER TWO

Concerning the man from the East

Olof Summer-Bird came riding to Gröning with ten followers, and was warmly welcomed. He stayed there three days, for the friendship between him and Orm was great. The purpose of his journey, however, was, he said, to ride down to the east coast to Kivik to buy salt from the Gotland traders who often anchored there. When Orm heard this, he decided to go with him on the same errand.

As things now were, salt was scarcely procurable, however large a price people might be willing to pay for it, thanks to King Sven Forkbeard of Denmark and the luck which attended all his enterprises. For King Sven was now ranging the sea with larger fleets than any man had heard tell of before, laying violent hands on any ship that crossed his path. He had plundered Hedeby and sacked it, and was reported to have laid waste all the country of the Frisians; it was, moreover, known that he had a mind to conquer the whole of England, and as much more as he had time for. Trade and merchandise interested him not at all, but only long ships and sworded men, and things had come to such a pass that, of late, no salt ships had come from the west, because they no longer dared to brave the northern waters. So no salt was procurable except that which the Gotlanders brought from Wendland, and this was bought up so eagerly by the coastal dwellers that little or none ever found its way inland.

Orm took eight men with him and rode with Olof Summer-Bird down to Kivik. There they waited for several days in the hope that a ship might soon arrive, while many people gathered there from all parts on the same errand. At last, two Gotland ships were

414

sighted. They were heavily laden, and dropped anchor a good way outside the harbour. For the hunger for salt had become so great that the Gotlanders now drove their trade cautiously, to avoid being killed by over-zealous customers. Their ships were large, high-gunwaled and well-manned, and anyone who wanted to buy from them had to row out in small boats, from which they were only allowed aboard two at a time.

Olof Summer-Bird and Orm hired a fishing-boat and were pulled out to the ships. They wore red cloaks and polished helmets. Olof grumbled at the smallness of the boat, for he had wanted to be rowed out in greater state. When their turn arrived, they climbed aboard the ship which bore a chieftain's standard, and, as they did so, their rowers, one of Orm's men and one of Olof's, cried out their names in a loud voice, so that the Gotlanders might understand at once that they were now being honoured by a visit from chieftains.

'Olof Styrsson the Magnificent, Chieftain of the Finnvedings, whom many call Olof Summer-Bird,' cried one.

'Orm Tostesson the Far-Travelled, Chieftain of the Sea, whom most men call Red Orm,' cried the other.

There was murmuring among the Gotlanders when these names were heard, and some of the men came forward to greet them; for there were several in the ship who had known Olof in the Eastland, and others who had sailed with Thorkel the Tall to England and remembered Orm from that campaign.

A man was seated by the gunwale, near to the point where they had come aboard. Suddenly he began to moan excitedly, and stretched out one of his arms towards them. He was a large man with a matted beard, which was beginning to grow grey; across his face he wore a broad bandage covering his eyes and, as he stretched his right arm towards Orm and Olof, they could see that the hand had been severed at the wrist.

'Look at the blind man,' said the Gotlanders. 'There is something he wishes to say.'

'He seems to know one of you,' said the ship's chieftain. 'Besides what you can see, he has lost his tongue, so that he cannot speak; nor do we know who he is. He was led aboard by a merchant from the east, while we were at anchor trading with the Kures, at the mouth of the River Dyna. The merchant told us that this man wished to go to Skania. He had silver to pay for his passage, so I accepted him. He understands what is said to him and, after much questioning, I have discovered that his family lives in Skania. But more than that I do not know, not even his name.'

'Tongue, eyes, and right hand,' said Olof Summer-Bird thoughtfully. 'Surely it is the Byzantines who have treated him thus.'

The blind man nodded eagerly.

'I am Olof Styrsson of Finnveden, and have served in the bodyguard of the Emperor Basil at Miklagard. Is it I whom you know?'

The blind man shook his head.

'Then perhaps it is I,' said Orm, 'though I cannot guess who you may be. I am Orm, the son of Toste the son of Thorgrim, who lived at Grimstad on the Mound. Do you know me?'

At this, the blind man nodded several times excitedly, and sounds came from his throat.

'Were you with us when we sailed to Spain with Krok? Or to England with Thorkel the Tall?'

But to both these questions the stranger shook his head. Orm stood deep in thought.

'Are you yourself from the Mound?' he asked.

The man nodded again, and began to tremble.

'It is a long while since I left those parts,' said Orm. 'But, if you know me, it may be that we were neighbours there. Have you been abroad for many years?'

The blind man nodded slowly, and heaved a deep sigh. He raised the hand which was left to him, spread the fingers wide, and closed his fist again. He did this five times, and then held up four fingers.

'This conversation goes better than one would have supposed possible,' said Olof Summer-Bird. 'By this, if I understand him aright, he means that he had been abroad for twenty-nine years.'

The blind man nodded.

'Twenty-nine years,' said Orm reflectively. 'That means that I was thirteen when you left. I ought to remember if anyone left our district for the East around that time.'

The blind man had risen to his feet, and was standing in front of Orm. His lips were moving, and he gestured with his hand, as though beseeching Orm to remember quickly who he was. Suddenly Orm said, in a changed voice: 'Are you my brother Are?'

Into the blind man's face there came a kind of smile. He nodded his head slowly; then he tottered on his feet, sank down upon his bench, and sat there, trembling in every limb.

Everyone in the ship was amazed at this encounter, and thought they had witnessed an incident worth recounting to other men. Orm stood staring thoughtfully at the blind man.

'I should be lying if I said that I recognize you,' he said, 'for it is a long while since last I saw you, and in the meantime you have changed cruelly. But you shall now ride home with me, and there you will find someone who will straightway recognize you if you are the man you claim to be. For our old mother is still alive, and often speaks of you. Surely it is God himself who has steered your steps, so that, despite your blindness, you have found your way home to me and her.'

Orm and Olof now began to bargain with the Gotlanders for salt. They were both amazed at the great meanness that the Gotlanders showed as soon as they turned to the question of business. Many of the crew owned shares in the ship and her cargo, and they all proved to be birds of a feather, merry and friendly when other matters were being discussed, but as sharp as knives when it came to striking a bargain.

'We force no man to act against his will,' they said, 'concerning salt or anything else; but anyone who comes to buy our wares must either pay our price or go without. We are richer than other men, and intend to grow richer still; for we Gotlanders are cleverer than the run of mankind. We do not rob or kill like most men, but increase our wealth by honourable trading; and we know better than you what salt is worth just now. All honour to Good King Sven, who has enabled us to raise our prices!'

'I should not regard any man who praises King Sven as clever,' said Orm bitterly. 'I think it would be easier to get justice from pirates and murderers than from such men as you.'

'Men often speak thus of us,' said the Gotlanders, 'but they do us injustice. Look at your unfortunate brother here, whom you found in our ship. He has silver in his belt, and not a little; but none of us has taken any of it, save only what we originally demanded for his passage and food-money. Other men would have taken his belt and flung him into the sea; but we are honourable men, though it is true that many think otherwise. But if he had been carrying gold, he would have been less safe, for no man can withstand the temptation of gold.'

'I begin to long to go to sea again,' said Orm, 'if only for the chance of encountering such a ship as yours.'

The Gotlanders laughed. 'Many men cherish that longing,' they said, 'but such as try to requite it go home, if at all, with grievous wounds to nurse. For you must know that we are strong fighters, and are not afraid to show our strength when the need arises. Styrbjörn we feared, but no man else. But enough of this talk. Let us know at once whether you wish to buy from us, or no; for there are many others waiting their turn.'

Olof Summer-Bird bought his sacks, and paid for them with few words; but when Orm reckoned up the amount he would have to pay, he began to grumble loudly. His brother touched him with his hand; opening his fist, he revealed a small heap of silver coins, which he carefully placed into the palm of Orm's right hand.

'You see!' said the Gotlanders. 'We spoke the truth. He has plenty of silver. Now you cannot doubt any longer that he is your brother.'

Orm glanced uncertainly at the silver. Then he said: 'From you, Are, I will accept this money; but you must not suppose that I am either mean or poor, for I have enough wealth for both of us. But it is always humiliating to pay money to merchants, especially when they are such men as these.'

'They outnumber us,' said Olof, 'and we must have salt, whatever the price. But it is certainly true that a man has to be rich to deal with men from Gotland.'

They bade the merchants a curt farewell, rowed their salt ashore, and started homewards; and Orm hardly knew whether to rejoice or be sad that he was bringing home a brother so fearfully maimed.

During their journey, when they had pitched camp for the night, Orm and Olof sought, by means of many questions, to learn from Are what had befallen him. Olof Summer-Bird could not remember having seen him in Miklagard; after much questioning, however, they at length gathered that he had been a chieftain in one of the Emperor's warships. He had not been maimed as a punishment, but while in captivity, after some fight; Olof had, however, been correct in guessing that it had been the Byzantines who had treated him thus. But more than this they could not discover, although they worded their questions skilfully; for all that Are could do in reply was to signify either yes or no, and they could see that it galled him bitterly that they could not find the right questions to ask him and that he could not guide their thoughts. They understood that he had been involved in some strange adventure, in which gold and treachery had played their part, and that he possessed some knowledge which he wished to impart to them; but all their efforts to discover what this might be proved vain.

'There is nothing for it but to be patient,' said Orm at length. 'It is useless for us to plague you with any more of this guessing, for it will lead us nowhere. When we reach home we will get our priest to help us, and then we may, perhaps, find a way to your secret; though how we shall manage to do so is more than I know.'

Olof Summer-Bird said: 'Nothing that he has to tell us can be more amazing than the fact of his having found his way home across so many miles of land and sea in such a state of helplessness. If so strange a thing can happen, let us hope that it may not be impossible for us to hit upon some way of discovering his secret. Certain it is that I shall not go home from Gröning until I know more of what he has to tell us.'

Are sighed, and wiped the sweat from his brow and sat rigid.

When they came to within sight of Gröning, Orm rode ahead of the others to break the news to Asa, for he feared that otherwise the joy and sorrow of seeing Are again might prove too great a shock for her. At first, she was confused by what he told her, and began to weep bitterly; then, however, she fell on her knees to the floor, beat her head against a bench, and thanked God for returning to her the son whom she had so long regarded as lost.

When they led Are to the house, she ran wailing to embrace him, and for some time would not let him go: then she began straightway to chide Orm for having doubted that this was his brother. After she had calmed herself, she said she would make a better bandage for his eyes; then, when she heard that he was hungry, she became more cheerful and went to prepare with her own hands those dishes which she remembered that he liked best. For several days, she moved as though in a dream, thinking of nothing but Are and what she might do to comfort him. When he showed a good appetite, she sat watching him happily; when, once, he placed his hand on hers to signify his thanks, she broke into tears of joy; and when she tired him with incessant prattling, so that he pressed his hand and the stump of his wrist against his ears and moaned aloud, she closed her mouth and sat humbly silent for a full minute before commencing afresh.

All the house-folk were filled with compassion towards Are, and helped him in every way they could think of. The children feared him at first, but soon came to like him. He loved especially to be led down to the river in the mornings and sit fishing on the bank, with someone to help him bait and cast his line. Blackhair was his favourite fishing companion, and Rapp, too, whenever the latter had time, perhaps because, of all the household, they most liked to sit in silence like himself.

Everyone was curious to know more of the bad luck that had befallen him, for Orm had told them all that he had been able to learn during the journey from Kivik. Olof Summer-Bird sent his men home with his salt, keeping only two of them with him at Gröning; he told Ylva that he would like, if he might, to stay until they had succeeded in discovering more of Are's secret, as he had the feeling that it might contain matter of some importance. Ylva was happy to let him stay, for she liked him and was always glad when he visited them; besides which, she observed that his eyes turned ever more frequently towards Ludmilla, who was, by now, a full-grown woman of fifteen, waxing lovelier every day.

'It is lucky for us that you are willing to stay,' said Orm, 'for we shall never learn much from Are without your help, since you are the only one of us here who knows Miklagard and the people who live in it.'

But, despite all their efforts, and those of the priest and the women, they could not elicit much more of Are's story. The only certain new fact they learned was that what had been done to him had been done on the River Dnieper, in the land of the Patzinaks, near the great portage beside the weirs. But more than that they could not discover; and Olof Summer-Bird found it difficult to imagine what Byzantines could be doing there.

Then Orm thought of a plan which might help them. Are was skilled in the use of runes; so Orm bade Rapp make a board of limewood, white and smooth, in order that Are might write on it in coal with the hand which had been left to him. Are was eager to do this, and worked hard at it for a time; but with his left hand he could write but awkwardly and, in his blindness, he blurred his runes into one another, so that nobody could make out what he wished to say. At length, he was seized with anger and flung the board and the coal away, and would try no more.

In the end, it was Rapp and the priest who thought of a better method, one day while they were sitting and scratching their heads about the matter. Rapp axed a short beam of wood, smoothed and polished it, and carved on its surface the sixteen runes, very large and clear, with a deep groove separating each from the next. They put the beam into Are's hands, bidding him feel it; and, when he understood what they intended, it could be seen that his heart was lightened. For now he was able to touch rune after rune, to make the words he wished to say, and Father Willibald sat beside him with sheepskin and pen, writing down the words as Are spelled them out. At first the work went slowly and with difficulty, but gradually Are came to learn the position of each rune, and everyone sat full of joy and expectation as intelligible sentences began to appear on the sheepskin. Each evening the priest read out to them what he had written down during the day. They listened greedily, and after three weeks the whole story lay written there. But the first part of it, which told where the treasure lay hidden, he read only to Orm.

CHAPTER THREE

Concerning the story of the Bulgar gold

I am the poorest of men, for my eyes have been taken from me, and my tongue and my right hand, and my son, whom the Emperor's treasurer killed. But I can also call myself the richest, for I know where the Bulgar gold lies hidden. I shall tell you where it lies, that I may not die with the secret still hidden in my breast, and you, priest, shall repeat it to my brother, but to no other man. He shall then decide whether he wishes it to be repeated for other ears.

In the River Dnieper, where the portage climbs beside the great weirs, just below the third weir as a man comes from the south, off the right bank between the skull-mound of the Patzinaks and the small rock in the river on which the three rose-bushes grow, under the water in the narrow channel where the rock-flat is broken, hidden beneath large stones where the rock-flat juts out and hides the bed beneath – there lies the Bulgar gold, and I alone know its hiding-place. As much gold as two strong men might carry lies drowned there, in four small chests sealed with the Emperor's seal, together with silver in five sacks of skin, and the sacks are heavy. This treasure first belonged to the Bulgars, who had stolen it from many wealthy men. Then it became the Emperor's, and from him it was stolen by his treasurer, Theofilus Lakenodrako. Then it became mine; and I hid it where it now lies.

I shall tell you how all this came about. When I first came to Miklagard, I entered the Imperial bodyguard, as many Northmen had done before me. Many Swedes serve in it, and Danes too, and men from Norway, and from Iceland also, far out in the western sea. The work is good, and the pay also, though I came too late to partake in the plundering of the palace when the Emperor John Zimiskes died, which was a fine plundering, still much talked of among those who took part in it. For it is the ancient custom there that, whenever an Emperor dies, his bodyguard is permitted to plunder his palace. There is much that I could tell you, priest, but I shall speak only of those things that it is necessary to know, for this fumbling upon a beam wearies me. I served in the bodyguard for a long while, and became a Christian and took a woman to wife. She was called Karbonosina, which means with coal-black eyebrows, and was of good family according to Byzantine reckoning, for her father was brother to the wife of the second wardrobe-master of the three royal Princesses.

You must know that in Miklagard, as well as the Emperor Basil, who is childless, there rules also Constantine his brother, who is also called Emperor. But Basil is the true Emperor. It is he who rules the land and crushes revolts and goes to war each year against the Bulgars and Arabs, while Constantine, his brother, sits at home in the palace playing with his treasure and his courtiers and the eunuchs who crowd about him. When any of them tells him that he is as good as his brother, or better, he strikes the speaker on the head with his little black staff, which bears a gold eagle on it, but the blow is always light, and the speaker is afterwards rewarded with rich gifts. He is a cruel man when his humour is darkened, and worst when he is drunk.

It is he who is father to the three Princesses. They are held to be greater than all other people in the world, save the Emperors themselves; for they are the only children of imperial blood. Their names are: Eudokia, who is hunch-backed and disfigured by the pox, and whom they keep hidden; Zoe, who is one of the fairest of women, and who has lusted eagerly after men since she was a young girl; and Theodora, who is weak-brained and pious. They are unmarried, for there is no man in the world worthy to marry them, say the Emperors; which has, for years, been a source of vexation to Zoe.

We of the bodyguard took it in turns to go to war with the Emperor Basil, and to remain in the palace with his brother. There is much that I remember and would tell you, but this telling goes slowly, and I shall now speak to you of my son.

My woman called him Georgios and had him christened thus, I

being in the field with the Emperor when he was born. For this I whipped her on my return, and called him Halvdan, a good name. When he grew up, he was known by both names. With her and others he conversed in the Greek tongue, which is the speech that women and priests use there, but with me he spoke our tongue, although the learning of it came more slowly to him. When he was seven years old, my woman ate a surfeit of mussels and died; and I took no other wife, for it is a bad thing to marry a foreign woman. The women of Miklagard are worth little. As soon as they marry, they become thoughtless and lazy, and child-bearing ages them and makes them fat and insubordinate. When their husbands try to tame them, they run shrieking to their priests and bishops. They are not like our women, who are understanding and work diligently and whom child-bearing makes wiser and more comely. This was the opinion of all of us Northmen who served in the bodyguard. Many of us changed our wives every year, and still were not satisfied.

But my son was my joy. He was shapely and swift-footed, quick-tongued and merry. He was afraid of nothing, not even of me. He was such that women in the street turned to look at him when he was little, and turned more swiftly as he grew to manhood. This was his misfortune, but there was no help for it. He is dead now, but is seldom out of my thoughts. He and the Bulgar gold are all I can think about. It could have become his, if all had gone well.

When my woman died, my son spent much time with her kins-folk, wardrobe-master Symbatios and his wife. They were old and childless, for the wardrobe-master, as befitted one who worked in the royal women's apartments, was a eunuch. He was, though, married, as Byzantine eunuchs often are. He and his wife both loved Halvdan, though they called him Georgios, and when I was away with the Emperor they took care of him. One day I returned from the wars to find the old man weeping for joy. He told me that my son had become the Princesses' playmate, especially Zoe's, and that Zoe and he had already fought and proved equally strong, she being two years older than he. Although they had fought, she had said that she much preferred him as a playmate to the Metropolitan Leo's niece, who fell on her knees and wept when anyone tore her clothes, or chamberlain Nikeforos's son, who was hare-lipped. The Empress Helena herself, he said, had clapped the boy on the head and called him a little wolf-cub and told him he must not pull her Imperial Highness Zoe's hair when she maltreated him. Gazing up at the Empress the boy had asked her when he might pull it. At this, the Empress had condescended to laugh aloud with her own mouth, which, the old man said, had been the happiest moment in his life.

These are childish things, but to remember them is one of the few joys that remain to me. In time things changed. I pass over many things, which would take too long to tell. But some five years later, when I was commanding a company of the bodyguard, Symbatios again came weeping to my chamber, but not, this time, for joy. He had that day gone to the inner-most clothing chamber, where the coronation garments were kept, and which was seldom visited, to see if there were any rats there. Instead of rats, he had found Halvdan and Zoe playing a new kind of game together, a game the sight of which had terrified him exceedingly, on a bed they had made of coronation garments which they had dragged from their chests. As he stood there speechless they had grabbed their clothes and disappeared, leaving the coronation robes, which were of purple-dyed silk from the land of the Seres,* severely crumpled, so that he knew not what to do. He had pressed them as well as he was able, and had replaced them carefully in their chests. There could, he said, be only one fate for him if this business was discovered, namely, that he would lose his head. It was lucky that the Empress was sick a-bed, for all the courtiers were in her chamber, and had no time to think of anything else, which was the reason the Princess was less carefully guarded than usual, and had been able to find this opportunity to seduce my son. There could, he said, be no doubt that the blame was wholly hers; for nobody could suspect a boy still in his thirteenth year of harbouring such ideas. But nothing could alter what had happened, and he held this to be the worst stroke of ill luck that had ever befallen him.

I laughed at his story, thinking the boy had behaved like a true son of mine, and tried to comfort the old man by telling him that Halvdan was too young to be able to present Princess Zoe with a little Emperor, however hard they might have striven to do so; and that, though the coronation robes might be crumpled, they could

* China. (The word 'China' was not used in those times.)

425

hardly have sustained any real damage. But the old man continued to weep and moan. He said all our lives were in danger, his, his wife's, my son's and my own, for the Emperor Constantine would immediately order us to be killed if he ever learned of what had happened. Nobody, he added, could suppose that Zoe had been frightened at being discovered thus with Halvdan, for she was by now a full fifteen, and of a temper more akin to that of a burning devil than of a blushing virgin, so that it could not be doubted that she would shortly start afresh with Halvdan, he being the only person she was allowed to associate with who was not a woman or a eunuch. In time, the scandal must inevitably be discovered, when Princess Zoe would receive an admonition from a bishop, and Halvdan and the rest of us would be killed.

As he spoke, I began to be afraid. I thought of all the people I had seen maimed and killed during the years I had served in the bodyguard, for offending the imperial humour. We sent for my son and remonstrated with him for what he had done, but he said that he regretted nothing. It had not been the first time, he said, and he was no child who required seducing, but knew as much about love as Zoe. I realized that nothing now could keep them apart, and that disaster would overtake us all if the affair was allowed to continue. So I shut him up in the wardrobe-master's house and went to call on the chief officer of the bodyguard.

He was called Zacharias Lakenodrako, and bore the title of Chief Sword-bearer, which is an office much honoured among the Byzantines. He was an old man, tall and venerable looking, with red and green jewels on his fingers, a wise and skilful talker, but sly and malignant, like everybody who holds high office in Miklagard. I bowed humbly before him, said that I was unhappy in the body-guard, and begged that I might spend the remaining years of my service on one of the Emperor's warships. He considered this request, and found it difficult to grant. At length, he said he thought he might be able to arrange it if I did him a small service in return. It was his wish, he said, that the Archimandrite Sophron, who was the Emperor Constantine's confessor, should receive a sound drub-bing, for the latter was his worst enemy and had, of late, been talking evil of him to the Emperor behind his back. He wanted, he said, no bloodshed, so that I must use no edged or pointed weapons against the Archimandrite, but merely stout sticks which would make his flesh smart. He said the deed would best be done beyond the palace gardens in the evening when he was riding home from the Emperor on his white mule.

I answered that I had long been a Christian, and that it would be a great sin for me to thrash a holy man. But he admonished me like a father, explaining that I was wrong in my supposition. 'For the Archimandrite,' he said, 'is a heretic, and confuses the two natures of Christ, which was the reason why we first became enemies. So it will be a pious action to thrash him. But he is a dangerous man, and you will be wise to take two men to help you. For before he became a monk he was chieftain of a band of robbers in Anatolia, and is still easily able to kill a man with a blow from his fist. Only strong men, such as serve in the bodyguard, will be able to give him the whipping he deserves. But I am sure your strength and wisdom will see the matter through. Take good sticks and strong men.'

Thus spoke sword-bearer Zacharias, deceiving me and leading me into sin. God has since punished me for striking a holy man; for, though he may have been evil, he was still holy. But I did not understand this then. I took with me two men on whom I could rely, Ospak and Skule, gave them wine and money, and told them we were going to beat a man who confused the two natures of Christ. It surprised them that three of us should be needed to beat one man, but when that evening we attacked the Archimandrite, their wonder ceased. As we rushed at him, I received a kick from his mule; and with his rosary, which he wore on his wrist and which consisted of heavy leaden beads, he gave Skule such a blow on the temples that he fell to the ground and remained there. But Ospak, a good man from Oland with the strength of a bear, dragged him from his saddle and threw him to the ground. By this time, our blood was roused, so that we beat him worse than we would otherwise have done. He bellowed curses and roared for help; but nobody came, for in Miklagard, when anyone hears a cry for help, everyone runs in the opposite direction, lest they be arrested as perpetrators of the crime. At last we heard the sound of hoofs and knew that the Kazar bowmen of the city watch were approaching; so we left the Archimandrite, who was by now unable to do anything save crawl, and departed. But we had to leave Skule there with him.

On the next day, I went back to sword-bearer Zacharias, who

was so pleased with the way everything had turned out that he acted honourably towards me. Everything, he said, leering with satisfaction, had gone better than he could have hoped. Skule had been dead when the watch had found him, and the Archimandrite was now in prison charged with street-brawling and murder. There was good hope that he would not be released before his ears had been clipped, for the Emperor Constantine feared his brother, and the Emperor Basil always meted out severe punishment to any monk convicted of disorderly behaviour and, moreover, disliked having men of his bodyguard murdered. As a reward for the success of my efforts, my request was to be granted immediately. He had, he said, already spoken with important friends of his who held high positions in the navy, and before long I would find myself a ship's chieftain in one of the red ships, which were regarded as the finest in the fleet.

Things turned out as he had promised, for even Byzantine courtiers sometimes keep their word. So I was appointed to a good ship and departed with my son from the palace and the perils it contained for us. We rowed westwards to the land of Apulia, where we fought Mahomet's servants, both those of Sicily and those who belonged to more distant lands. We stayed there a long time, and underwent many adventures which it would take long to relate. My son waxed strong and comely. I made him an archer in my ship. He liked the sea, and we were happy there. But when we were ashore, he was often foolish with women, as young people are, and this caused quarrels between us. When we anchored in the Emperor's harbours, Bari or Tarentum in Apulia, or Modon, or Nepanto, where the great shipyards are, and where we received our pay, there were always plenty of women to choose from, for wherever sailors are with booty and pay, thither women always flock eagerly. But there were also in these towns officers called strategi, and silver-booted naval chieftains, and officials called secretices and logothetes who dealt with matters of pay and booty. They had their wives with them, beautiful women with dove-like voices and white hands and painted eyes. They were full of witchcraft, and not for seafaring men, as I often told Halvdan.

But he paid small heed to my counsel. It was his fate that women's eyes always turned towards him, and he thought none but the best good enough for one who had lain with the Emperor's daughter.

The Byzantine women are fiery, and swift to cuckold their husbands once their lust is aroused. But their men dislike being cuckolded, and those in high office order the death of any young man who arouses their suspicions, and often kill their wives, too, that their minds may be set at rest and that they may marry again and be luckier. My advice to Halvdan was always to leave married women alone and to content himself with those whose virtue was their own business. If he had heeded my counsel, that which afterwards happened would never have happened. He would not be dead, and I should not be as I am. Neither should I be sitting here, telling you of the Bulgar gold. It would have been better so.

It was not for the woman's sake that he was killed, but for that of the gold. But it was the woman who caused our ways to separate, and the rest followed.

It was then that sword-bearer Zacharias Lakenodrako spat the communion bread into the face of his enemy, the Archimandrite Sophron, who had by this time returned into the Emperor's favour, crying aloud before the assembled court that the Archimandrite had poisoned it. The Archimandrite was whipped for this and exiled to a distant monastery, but Zacharias, too, was dismissed from his office, and had his ears clipped for dishonouring Christ. For it was held that, once a man had taken the body of Christ into his mouth, he ought to have the faith to swallow it, even if he knew it to be poisoned. When this news reached me from Miklagard, I laughed aloud, thinking that it would be difficult to decide which of the two men was the more evil, and that both their ambitions to have the other's ears clipped had now been satisfied.

But Zacharias had a son called Theofilus. He was already thirty years old, and was serving at the court. When his father lost his ears and his office, the son went to both Emperors and prostrated himself on the ground at their feet. He said that the sin his father had committed was, indeed, most foul, and the punishment inflicted upon him so mild that he wept for joy whenever he thought of it. In short, he praised the goodness of the two Emperors so enthusiastically that, before very long, the Emperor Basil appointed him naval treasurer. This meant that, for the future, he was to supervise the division of all booty won anywhere by the Emperor's ships, and was, besides, to be in complete charge of all matters concerning sailors' pay.

We came with the red fleet to Modon, to have our keels scraped and to be paid. Treasurer Theofilus was there, with his wife. I never saw her, but my son quickly did so, and she him. It was in church that their eyes first met and, although he was but a young archer and she a rich woman, it was not long before they met in secret and indulged their lust for each other. Of this I knew nothing until he came to me one day and told me he was weary of the sea and had hopes of a better position in the treasurer's household. The woman had told her husband that Halvdan was son to a man who had once done his father a service by spiting the Archimandrite, so that now Halvdan stood high not only in the woman's favour, but in that of her husband also.

When I heard the reasons for his appointment, I told him he might as well run a sword through his breast there and then as do what he intended to do. I also said that it was cruel of him to leave me alone and kinless for a woman's painted eyes. But he would have his way, and refused to hearken to my counsel. The woman, he said, was like a flame, and without flaw, and he would never be able to live without her. Besides which, he said, he would now grow rich and famous in the treasurer's service, and would no longer have to continue as a poor archer. There was no danger, he said, of his being found out and killed, for, he bade me remember, he was half Byzantine and therefore better able than I to understand many things, including women. When he said this, I was gripped with fury and cursed his mother's name; and so we parted.

This was a great grief for me. But I thought that, in time, the woman would tire of him, or he of her, and that then he would come back. Then, I thought, when my service is finished, he will return with me home to the north and take a wife there and forget his Byzantine blood.

So time passed, and the Emperor Basil, who is the greatest war-lord who has ever ruled in Miklagard, began a new campaign against the Bulgars. These people are bold warriors and terrible bandits, and plague their neighbours fearfully, so that they have excited the wrath of many Emperors; and now the Emperor Basil had sworn an oath to destroy their kingdom and every man of them and to hang their King in chains above his own city gate. He invaded their land with a mighty army, and his red fleet sailed up into the Black Sea to harry their coasts.

But twelve of the best ships were detailed upon a special mission, and mine was among them. We took soldiers from the army aboard, as many as the ships could hold, and sailed northwards along the coast till we reached the mouth of a river called Danube, which is the greatest of all rivers. The commander of our flotilla was named Bardas; he was in the biggest of our ships, and I heard, as we rowed up the river three abreast, that the naval treasurer was on board with him. At this, I rejoiced, hoping to see my son again, if he was still alive. But why the treasurer should be accompanying us, none could say.

We heard the trump of war-horns ahead, and, rounding a bend in the river, sighted a great fortress. It stood behind dykes and stockades on a hill not far from the river. All around was marsh and wilderness, with nothing to be seen but reeds and birds. We all marvelled that our Emperor had sent us to so desolate a place as this. We put soldiers and archers ashore to storm the fortress. The Bulgars fought valiantly on their ramparts, and it was not until the second day that we gained the upper hand. I was wounded in my shoulder by an arrow, and went back to my ship. There, they drew out the arrow and dressed the wound; and, as night fell, I sat on the deck and saw the fortress burn and the treasurer's men come back with prisoners who staggered beneath the weight of the booty they were carrying. The ship that had carried Bardas and the treasurer lay at the end of our line, nearest to the fortress; then came two other ships, then mine, and then the rest in a line up the river. A short while after darkness had fallen, we heard shouts and alarums from one of the ships below us, and men cried from other ships to ask what might be afoot. I thought some of the men had probably been trying to steal the booty, and that Bardas was teaching them a lesson. But soon the noise ceased and everything became quiet, save for the baying of wolves who had scented meat. So I sat there, sleepless, because of the pain in my arm.

Then a man came swimming towards my ship. I could hear him in the water, but could see nothing. I took a spear and bade him say who he was, for I feared the Bulgars might be upon us, but when I heard him reply my heart leaped, for the voice was that of my son. When I had pulled him aboard, he sat there panting. I said: 'It is good to see your face. I had small hope that we should meet again.' He replied in a low voice: 'Bardas has been murdered in his ship, and many others with him. The treasurer and his father have fled with the gold. More gold than anyone has ever seen. We must go after them and take it from them. Have you archers aboard?'

I gave him drink to calm him, and answered that I had some fifteen archers left aboard, the rest being ashore, but that I wished to know more about this gold, for this was the first I had heard of it.

Eagerly he replied: 'The gold belonged to the Bulgar King, who kept it hidden here. The Emperor learned of this, and sent us here with his treasurer, whom he trusted. I saw the gold as they were carrying it aboard, and helped to seal it with the Emperor's seal. But the treasurer hates the Emperor for what he did to his father. The old man is here with him, and they planned this together. All his men were bribed to help him and, when darkness fell, they killed Bardas and his officers, and the archers of his bodyguard. It was easy, for the others suspected nothing. But I thought to myself: "This was lately the Emperor's gold, and while it was his it was a crime for any man to touch it. Now it is the treasurer's; but if it should be taken from him, whose will it be then?" I reasoned thus; then, when no one was looking, I slipped overboard into the river, and swam here to you. They will not miss me for they will think I have been killed in the fighting. But now answer me this question: "Whose shall the gold be if it is taken from them?"'

I said: 'This must be the reason that the treasurer anchored his ship furthest downstream, so that they might more easily escape in the darkness. If they have already fled, the gold will belong to whoever can take it from them and keep it; for such is the unwritten law of the sea. First they will float silently downstream in silence; then, when they are out of earshot, they will unship their oars. When it begins to grow light, they will set sail, and with this wind they will soon be well out to sea. It would be good to know where they are making for. There is much here that requires thought, and I do not want to do anything before I am sure which is the wisest course to follow.'

Halvdan said: 'The treasurer told me that we should flee to Tmutorokan, beyond Krim, where we would divide up the treasure, and then proceed to the country of the Kazars, to be safe from the Emperor's wrath: after which, he said, we might go where we pleased. He said this to the others also; so it is certain he does not intend to go there. But a short while before we started on this voyage, I heard him sitting mumbling with his father, just after some message had reached them, and I heard the old man say it was a good thing for them that the great Prince of Kiev had begun again to beget children upon his concubines and no longer honoured his High Princess, our Emperor's sister, so that there was small friendship between him and the Emperor. I therefore think that they intend to flee to Kiev with the gold.'

I said: 'Halvdan, you are a wise boy, and I think you have guessed rightly. If they are heading for Kiev, they are sailing in a direction that suits us well, for they are taking it halfway home for us. If we let them reach Kiev, we shall find good men there willing to help us take it from them, if we find we cannot do so ourselves unaided. There is no need for us to start yet, for we must not let them see us following them over the sea, lest they should grow suspicious and alter their course. But for a short while before it is light, when even the best ship's watchmen are asleep, let us leave this place silently. I have grieved much that you left me, Halvdan, but perhaps what happened was for the best, for this affair looks as if it may prove most lucky for us both.'

Thus spake I, foolishly; for what known god likes to hear men praise their luck before it has come to them?

I asked him about the woman who had seduced him. He replied that the treasurer had wearied of her and imprisoned her in a nunnery, because she had taken to defending herself when he tried to birch her. 'And,' he said, 'when I found that she was lusting after other young men besides me, I, too, wearied of her.'

This pleased me, and I promised him far finer women when we should bring the gold home to the north.

As the first grey appeared in the sky, we weighed anchor and swung out into the river, with our oars shipped and our rowers asleep on their benches, and glided downstream without anyone crying to ask whither we were going. When the crew and the archers awoke, I gave them better food than that to which they were accustomed, and stronger drink; then I told them that we were pursuing thieves who had fled with the Emperor's booty. More than that, I did not tell them. It was not my intention to act dishonourably and steal one of the Emperor's ships, for I wished but to borrow it until I had achieved my purpose. I thought this not unjust, seeing that he owed me a year's pay.

We came out of the river and sailed across the sea, uncertain whether we had guessed rightly; but when we reached the mouth of the River Dnieper, we saw fishermen there and learned from them that one of the Emperor's red ships had entered the river the day before. My ship was smaller than the treasurer's, but I was not afraid, for I had Lesgian and Kazar archers aboard, good men for a fight, while he had only men of his own household.

Then there was heavy rowing with few intervals for resting, but whenever the rowers began to complain I gave them a double measure of wine, and comforted myself with the thought that the treasurer with his heavier ship, must be in a worse plight. I saw no horse-herds on the banks, and no Patzinaks, at which we were glad; for when the Patzinaks are on the warpath, or are pasturing their horses on the river banks, they regard the river and all that moves on its surface as their own, so that no sailor dares land to cook his food. They are the most arrogant of peoples, and the worst robbers, and the Emperor himself pays them friendship-money every year.

On the fourth day, the bodies of three men floated down the river. By the marks on their backs, it could be seen that they were oarsmen of the treasurer who had grown tired. This I took as an encouraging sign, and I now began to hope we might overtake him at the weirs. On the next day, more bodies floated downstream, but they did not belong to the treasurer's men. Then we found his ship, stranded on a tongue of land and empty. I realized from this that he had encountered a river-ship and captured it, that he might proceed more swiftly and take his treasure more easily across the portage when he came to the weirs. For a keeled warship is no easy thing to drag overland.

Towards the evening of the eighth day, we heard the splash of the weirs and reached the portage. There was nothing to be seen there save two oarsmen who had been left because they were too weak to row further. We gave them wine, which revived them, and they told us that the treasurer had put his new ship on rollers that very day. But he had been unable to find either horses or oxen to harness to it, for the river banks were deserted, so that he had only his oarsmen to pull it, and they were all exceedingly weary. They could not, therefore, have got far.

Halvdan and I rejoiced when we heard this. We took archers with us and followed the tracks of the ship. Between the second and third weir, we sighted them. Then we turned inland and crept swiftly forward behind the burial mound of the Patzinak chieftains, which stands on a rise there, surmounted by skulls, and waited beside it with arrows in our bows until they had almost reached the spot where we were hiding. I saw the treasurer and his father walking beside the ship in full armour, with swords in their hands. I ordered four archers to mark them, and the others to kill the men who were in charge of the harnessed rowers.

The bows sang, men fell to the ground, and we all drew our swords and charged, whooping our battle-cry. The rowers dropped their ropes and fled, and all was confusion; but the treasurer and his father fell not, because the Devil and their good armour protected them. Zacharias the sword-bearer, who had been grazed by several arrows, fled quicker than anyone, running like a youth. But I gave most of my attention to the treasurer. I saw him turn in astonishment, his face a sickly white above his black beard, as our arrows and war-whoops reached him. He gathered his men about him, roaring at them in a terrible voice, being pained at the prospect of being parted from so much gold. I wish he had stood his ground there longer.

Halvdan and I and the master of the archers, a Lesgian man named Abchar, were the first to reach them, and we fought with the men who stood protecting the treasurer. I saw him bare his teeth as he recognised Halvdan; but we could not get at him, for his men fought bravely, even though their leader was cowering behind them. Then the archers joined us, and we forced the treasurer's men back towards their ship; but when we at last broke their resistance, we found him fled and several of his men with him.

It was by now almost dusk, and I was uncertain what to do. The master of the archers was a man who always did as he was bidden without asking questions; I bade him take his men and pursue the enemy up the river as swiftly as he could, not pausing until darkness fell. I told him that the Emperor had put a price of a hundred pieces of silver upon the treasurer's head, and a like sum upon his father's, and that this would be paid in full to whoever brought me their heads. So he hastened away with his men.

So soon as Halvdan and I were left alone, we climbed up into the ship. There, in the cabin, hidden behind sacks and casks lay the treasure in four small chests and seven skin sacks, all sealed with the Emperor's seal. But sight of so much wealth caused me less joy than concern as to what we should do next, and how we should succeed in bringing it home without anyone else learning of its existence. Halvdan said: 'We must hide this before the archers return.' I said: 'Where can we find a place large enough to hide so much?' He said: 'Perhaps in the river.' 'You are right,' I said. 'Wait here, while I investigate.'

I went to the river, and there found the place of which I have spoken, with the river frothing as it coursed over. Together, we carried the treasure there, and hid it well, save two sacks of silver which, after much thought, I left in the ship.

Achbar and his men now returned. They carried three heads, but not those I most wished to see. Together, we ate and drank food and wine that we found in the ship. Then I said to him: 'Here, Abchar, you see these two sacks, sealed with the Emperor's seal. This is the treasure that the treasurer Theofilus and his father stole from the Emperor. Whether it is silver or gold, I know not, for none may break the Emperor's seal. Now we are in a sore plight, for all this must speedily be brought intact to the Emperor; but I was commanded by him not to return without the treasurer's head. This, therefore, is what we must do. I and my son will go up the river to search for the treasurer, as far as Kiev; and two of your men, volunteers, shall go with us. But you and the rest of your men shall return to our ship with this treasure and bid the helmsman convey you to Miklagard. We four shall find our own way back, when our task has been accomplished.'

Those were my words, and Abchar nodded and felt the weight of the sacks. He spoke to his men, and two Kazars volunteered to come with us. Abchar and the others departed with the silver-sacks, and I was glad that thus far all had gone well. I needed the two archers to help me in my quest for a boat, lest we should encounter robbers, or perhaps the treasurer himself, in case he had managed to rally his men. I thought he would probably continue his flight from us, but in that I was wrong.

We were tired, and that night I took the first watch myself. Then I bade one of the Kazars replace me; but he must have slept, in order, perhaps, that our fatal destiny might be fulfilled. For, during the night, while we were all asleep in the ship, the treasurer, with his father and four men whom he still had, fell upon us unawares. I was awakened by the clatter of stones as someone stumbled, and sprang to my feet with my sword drawn. Two men leaped at me; and, as I met them, I saw the treasurer fell one of the Kazars and charge at Halvdan, whirling his sword above his head. Halvdan must have been sleeping deeply, for he had barely managed to draw his sword; I would have given my life and all the gold to have come between them. The men who had engaged me fell dead, but I scarcely noticed them go down for, as I turned upon the treasurer, Halvdan was already lying at his feet. I hewed with both hands; it was my last blow, and my best. It cleaved his helmet and chain hood, and cleft his skull so deeply that I saw his teeth fall out through his throat. But, as death bit him, his sword entered my eye. I fell to the ground, and knew that I was about to die; but the thought of that did not trouble me, for I thought: 'Halvdan is dead, and I have avenged him, and everything is now finished.'

This story wearies me, and there is little more to tell. The next I knew was that I was lying bound, and that sword-bearer Zacharias was sitting beside me, laughing, with a laugh that was not that of a man. He told me how I was to be maimed, and croaked much about the gold. I spat in his face and bade him show me his ears. He had one man left, and between them they chopped off my hand and heated oil from the ship to dip the stump in, so that I should not die too quickly. But he promised me a quick death if I would tell him where the gold was. I did not oblige him, fearing no pain, for my soul was dead. I told him the gold was on its way to the Emperor, and he believed me. We spoke no more.

Then I heard a scream, and a man whimpered and began to cough, and then fell silent. Then I was lying in a boat which was being pulled across the ground. I was given drink, and knew nothing. Then the boat was floating on the water, and it seemed to me that I was dead. The man who was rowing talked much, and I understood some of what he said. He was the second Kazar. He was singing and whistling, and very merry. He had run away when we had been attacked, and had fled back to my ship, but it had gone. So he had returned and, creeping up close behind the men who were working on me, had killed them both with arrows. Why he troubled to save what remained of me no one can know;

437

he may have been a good man, as Kazars often are. Two poor peasants had come over from the other bank to plunder the dead, and he had given them the treasurer's ship with all that it contained, on condition that they gave him their small boat and helped him carry me up the portage. Thus had it happened; I know only what he said.

He laughed all the time, and praised his luck, for on the bodies of the treasurer and his father he had found much silver and gold, and the arms and weapons which he had taken from them were of the finest workmanship. On the bodies of the other men, too, he had found money and jewels, and had, besides, taken a fine gold ring from the finger of my son. He was now, he told me, intending to buy horses in Kiev, and a woman or two, after which he would return to his own people, a rich man, in armour. He cared for me as well as he could while telling me all this. I wanted to drag myself over the side of the boat and drown, but was too weak to do so.

He knew that I wanted to go to Kiev, and, when we reached the city, he handed me over to some monks. I wanted to reward him with silver, for he had left my belt untouched, but he would accept nothing. He had, he said, enough already, and had, besides, won favour with God for the way he had treated me.

I stayed with the monks, and was nursed by them, until at length, I grew better, and began again to think of the gold. The men from the north visited the monks and asked me questions. They understood that I wished to go home, and learned that I had the means wherewith to pay them. So I ascended the river, one ship passing me on to another, until at last I came aboard the Gotlanders' ship, where I met Orm.

All the time, the thought weighed heavily on me that I would never be able to tell anyone about the Bulgar gold and where it lies, even if I should, by some marvel, reach home and rejoin my kinsmen. But now, thanks to your cunning, priest, I have been enabled to tell everything, and can die happier.

As to the gold, Orm may do as he thinks best. It is a great treasure, enough for many men, and none can say what so much gold is worth, or how much blood has been spilt for its sake. It lies there, in the place I spoke of, and will not be hard to find for anyone who knows where to look for it. There is, besides, a mark nearby which shows the place; the bones, by now picked clean by crows, of the treasurer Theofilus and the sword-bearer Zacharias – may their souls wander without refuge till the end of time – and of my son, Halvdan, on whose soul God have mercy.

CHAPTER FOUR

How they planned to get the gold

As soon as he learned about the gold, Orm sent a man with a message to Toke.

'Tell him,' he said, 'that there is a question of a voyage after a great treasure in the Eastland, that he is the man whose advice I would most value on the matter, and that it would be good if he could come here quickly.'

Toke needed no further persuasion than this and, before Are and the priest had finished telling their story, he arrived at Gröning, eager to learn more of what was afoot. After he had been welcomed and had drunk a cup of ale, he said:

> 'I heard word
> Of bellied sailcloth,
> Creak of oars
> And bold in Eastland
> Then I smelled
> A smell remembered:
> Salt of spray
> And black-pitched boat's-keel.'

But Orm replied, more soberly:

> 'Two score years
> And their stored wisdom
> Curb men's lust
> For distant faring;

440

> No slight task
> By stealth to pilfer
> Far-drowned gold
> In Gardariké.'

'But the treasure is rich beyond imagination,' he added, 'and I have never needed counsel so urgently as in this affair. Ylva will not advise me; she says it is a matter that I must decide for myself, and it is not every day that she speaks thus. I have, therefore, asked you here, to counsel me what to do. Here you see Olof Summer-Bird, who has himself been in the Eastland, and who is a man of much wisdom. Three heads are better than two, when such an important matter as this has to be decided.'

Orm then told Toke of all that had happened to Are, and of the Bulgar gold; the only thing he did not tell him was where the gold lay hidden.

'That knowledge,' he said, 'I shall keep to myself until we reach the place. For gold can cause much bad luck; and if it should become known too soon where the gold lies, the information might come to the wrong ears, and other hands might touch it before mine. If this gold is ever to be lifted, it shall be lifted by my hands, and no one else's; for it has been bequeathed to me by Are, who thinks of himself as dead. But to those who help me get it, I shall, if our journey proves successful, give good shares of it. I have been restless ever since I heard of this gold, and sometimes have hardly been able to sleep for thinking of it. What troubles me most is that, if I go in search of it, I shall be away from my home here for a long while, and shall continually be plagued with anxiety for the safety of my house and family. Besides which, such a voyage will necessitate the expenditure of much money on a good ship and crew. And if, in spite of all this, I seek the gold, and then find that some thief has got there before me, I shall have wasted a great deal of money.'

Toke said unhesitatingly that, for his part, he was ready and willing to make the voyage.

'And my advice to you, Orm,' he said, 'is that you shall go in search of this gold. For if you do not, you will sit here brooding over it until you can neither sleep nor eat, and will never again be merry-hearted. Indeed, I should not be surprised if you brooded yourself out of your senses. It is your fate to go and look for this gold, and you cannot escape it; and I have known men have worse fates than that. True, it will be a long voyage, but you cannot expect to get so large a treasure as this without some trouble. As for me, the skin-trade is bad just now, and my wife pregnant, so that I have nothing to keep me from coming with you.'

'Rapp gave me the same advice,' said Orm, 'but when he did so, he supposed that he would be accompanying me. But when I told him that he would have to remain here to guard the house and my family, he changed his tone, and bade me forget the gold and stay at home. Father Willibald advised me as I had known he would, telling me that I am rich enough already, and old enough to be thinking more of heavenly than of earthly riches. But I find it difficult to be at one with him in this matter.'

'The priest is wrong,' said Toke, 'however wise he may be in other matters. For it is so with men that, the older they become, the more they hanker after goods and gold. So it was even with King Harald, my woman tells me, and he was the wisest of men, even if he was once fooled by me. I myself grow yearly more resentful of the Gotland merchants at Kalmarna, even when they pay me value for my skins, which is seldom.'

'The years affect a man in more respects than one,' said Orm, 'and I am not sure that I could endure a long voyage as well as I used to.'

'I am older than you,' said Toke, 'and the years do not weigh upon me. Besides which, it is not so long since, if reports be true, you killed two berserks with a broomstick. That may, without exaggeration, be described as a bold feat, and shows that you still retain some remnant of your youthful vigour, even though you yourself would like to believe that it is otherwise. I am told that your daughter Ludmilla was the subject of the quarrel; if that is so, she will be much envied by women and coveted by men. But let us hear what Olof Summer-Bird has to say about the matter.'

'Orm and I have discussed it deeply,' said Olof thoughtfully, 'and I have been as double-minded as he, unable to decide which will be the wisest course for him to take. I know better than most men how arduous this voyage will be, and how great the dangers

442

we shall encounter; but when a man has a ship filled with good men, much may be achieved. Orm wishes me to join him in this expedition, if he decides to undertake it. There are reasons why I should not; but it is true that my presence would be of use to you, for I know the whole long road to Miklagard, and the great river, and the perils that lie in its water and upon its banks. I have at last decided and my answer is this. Seek the gold, Orm, and I will come with you, if you will give me your daughter, Ludmilla, to be my wife.'

Orm stared at him in astonishment. Toke roared with laughter.

'What did I say?' he said. 'Here is the first of the flock.'

'You have a wife already,' said Orm.

'I have two,' said Olof, 'for such is the custom of chieftains in Finnveden. But if you give me your daughter, I will send them away.'

'I could think of worse sons-in-law,' said Orm reflectively, 'and it might be good to marry her off before more berserks come roaring around her. But this is a serious matter, which requires consideration. Have you talked with my women about it?'

'It would have been dishonourable of me to have spoken with them before I had asked your feelings in the matter,' replied Olof. 'But I think Ylva will not be unwilling to have me as a son-in-law. She knows, as you do, that I am the richest chieftain in all Finnveden, with seven score head of cattle, and heifers besides; and that I come of a very ancient line.'

'Of my own line, I shall say nothing,' said Orm, 'though some would regard it as better than most men's, for the blood of Ivar of the Broad Embrace flows in my veins, and it was after him that my youngest son was named. Do not forget that my daughter is granddaughter to King Harald Bluetooth, so that you could not find a bride of nobler blood if you were to search every great house in Smaland. You will have to drive your present wives further from your straw than to the brew-house or garden cottage if you wish to wed my daughter; and you will not find her a meek wife if you take other women to your bed once you have married her.'

'She is worthy to be accorded such an honour,' said Olof, 'and, indeed, I have already noticed that it is difficult to keep the peace in the house when a man has more wives than one.

But I am happy that you are not opposed to the match, and thank you for it.'

'Do not thank me yet,' said Orm. 'First, we must hear what Ylva has to say about it. It is I who shall decide whether or not the marriage will take place, but a wise man always allows his wife to speak when so important a matter as this has to be decided.'

So Ylva was sent for. When she heard what the matter was, she said that it did not altogether surprise her.

'And I think such a suitor should not be denied,' she said, 'for, Olof, you are both rich and of noble family, so that a better match would not easily be found in these parts. Besides which, you are a man of good sense, which has always seemed to me to be a quality worth having in a husband. It is true that you would have impressed me more with your wisdom if you had asked for Oddny, who is meek and submissive and no less well-shaped than her sister; but in matters such as this, a man must choose as his inclinations lead him, and cannot choose otherwise. It suits me well that you have chosen Ludmilla, for she is unruly and difficult to live with; but women sometimes improve when they have found a man.'

'That is true,' said Toke. 'There is no harm in the girl. Her temper is no worse than yours was, when Orm and I first met you in your father's castle. But you tamed quickly, and I have never heard Orm regret his choice.'

'You talk nonsense, Toke,' said Ylva. 'I was never tamed. We of Gorm's blood do not tame; we are as we are, and shall be so even when we appear before the judgment throne of God himself. But Orm killed Sigtrygg, you must remember, and gave me Almansur's chain; and then I knew that he belonged to me, for no other man would have acted thus. But do not speak to me of taming.'

'That chain proved useful,' said Orm. 'I do not think anyone can deny that. Perhaps we shall have another such for Ludmilla, when we have returned home with the gold. You must now speak to the girl yourself, Olof; and then she shall be regarded as your betrothed. You shall be married to her as soon as we have returned from our voyage, if you can get rid of your wives as easily as you claim to be able to.'

Olof said that such matters presented no difficulty in Finnveden;

one merely paid one's women well, and they went. This would take no time, and he saw no reason why the marriage should not take place before they started. But both Orm and Ylva opposed this suggestion, and at length he yielded.

So far, all had gone well for Olof Summer-Bird in this business, even if he had not had matters entirely as he wished them to be. Ludmilla received his suggestion amiably, and they began at once to discuss their plans. It was evident that she was well satisfied with the prospect of becoming his wife, even if she afterwards confided in Oddny and Ylva that she felt that so great a chieftain might have come with his hands full of ornaments. She asked him if he was ill-tempered when he was drunk, and whether he was merriest in the mornings or the evenings; and she wished to know exactly how the two women looked of whose company he was depriving himself for her sake, as well as details concerning his house and cattle, the number of his slaves and serving-maids, and a precise account of all that he had in his coffers. To all these questions he returned satisfactory answers.

But when Father Willibald heard what was afoot, he was by no means pleased. For, in their excitement, it had not occurred to them that Olof Summer-Bird was not a Christian; and this fact greatly troubled Father Willibald. A Christian maiden, whom he had baptized with his own hand, could not, he said, be bestowed upon a heathen; and this marriage could only take place if Olof first allowed himself to be baptized. On this point there was now a sharp exchange of opinions among the women, for Asa sided with the priest, while Ylva and Ludmilla opposed him. At length Orm told them to stop arguing and close their mouths; their immediate concern, he said, was to plan the voyage, and they would have time enough to discuss this other matter later. If Olof were prepared to allow himself to be baptized, he said, all would be well; if not, he was to have the girl none the less.

'For she will have plenty of opportunities to convert him,' he said, 'if she thinks it worth her while to try.'

Asa rebuked him sharply for this judgment; but Orm bade her think of Are and remember that his present condition was the work of Christian hands.

Father Willibald sat dejected in his chair. He said that, since the thousandth year had passed without Christ appearing in the sky, people had shown less willingness to become converted.

'If things continue the way they are going,' he added, 'the Devil will triumph after all, and you will all become heathens again.'

But Orm bad him be cheerful and not think so ill of them all.

'I am content with Christ,' he said, 'and I hope he will remain content with me, even if I marry my daughter to the suitor who pleases me best. Much will have to happen before I abandon him, for he has always helped me well.'

Toke said that this reminded him that he had news from Värend, which would interest them all.

'You doubtless remember the priest Rainald,' he said, 'the fellow who, for Christ's sake, knocked old Styrkar down from the Stone. The old woman to whom he was given as a slave is now dead, and he is a free man and much admired and respected. He is still a priest, but no longer serves Christ. For he wearied of him while he was the old woman's slave, and now he curses everything that has to do with him, and follows the old god Frej instead, and is amassing great wealth by his knowledge of witchcraft. All women obey him, whatever he commands them to do, and hold him to be the best priest there has ever been among the Virds. And I have heard it said that he has gathered a band of followers and has set himself up as a chieftain for vagabonds and outlaws.'

Father Willibald heard this news with horror. Hereafter, he said, he would no longer offer prayers for this man; he had never before heard of a Christian priest giving himself openly to the Devil.

Ylva thought that he had had good qualities, and that it was a pity that things had gone so ill with him. But Orm laughed.

'Let him and the Devil do as they please together,' he said. 'We have more important matters to worry about.'

He was now no longer doubtful whether or not to voyage after the gold. Between them, they decided that, if they managed to buy a good ship down at the coast, they would sail at midsummer.

'Our hardest task will be to find a good crew,' said Orm. 'We must have good sailors, who know the ways of ships, but there are few of them to be found here, inland, and it will be dangerous to hire men who are not known to us with such a cargo as we hope to be bringing home. It might be wise to take but a few men, for then we shall have less money to pay out; but it might be wiser to take many, for we do not know what dangers await us.'

CHAPTER FIVE

How they sailed to the Gotland Vi

Olof Summer-Bird rode home to make ready for the voyage, and to hire men whom he knew in Halland to serve as crew, while Orm, Toke and Harald Ormsson rode down to the coast in search of a ship. At the mouth of the river they found one for sale. The man who owned it was growing old, and wanted to sell it in order to have a good inheritance to leave his daughters when he died. They examined it carefully and found it in good order. It carried twenty-four pairs of oars; ships of such a size were reckoned to be large, but Orm thought it could without harm have been bigger, and Toke agreed with him.

'For great chieftains will be sailing in it,' he said, 'and thirty pairs of oars would not be too many for us.'

'When we come to the portage, which Olof Summer-Bird has told us of,' said Harald Ormsson, 'we may be glad that it is no larger.'

'You are luckier even than I had supposed you to be, Orm,' said Toke, 'for I see that wisdom does not reside in you only, but in your children also.'

'It is a bad thing when a man receives instruction from his son,' said Orm, 'and it shall not happen in my house, so long as I retain my tongue and my good right arm. But in this instance, I admit that the boy is right. This will be heavier work than when we dragged St James's bell.'

'We were young men then,' said Toke. 'Now we are great chieftains and shall not need to touch the rope ourselves. The young men will strain at the harness, while we walk beside them with our thumbs in our belts, marvelling at the paucity of their strength. But it may be that a ship such as this will be too big for them to manage.'

At length, after much bargaining, Orm bought the ship.

Around the mouth of the river, there lay great houses; and from these he bought malt, hogs and oxen and arranged with the farmers that they should brew, butcher and smoke his purchases, that the ship might be well provided with food and drink. He was astonished when he discovered how much all this was to cost him in silver; his astonishment became even greater when he sought to hire a number of young men from the houses for a year's voyage; and he rode dejectedly home with the others, mumbling that this Bulgar gold would surely bring him into poverty and wretchedness.

'One thing I have learned,' said Harald Ormsson, 'namely, that a man needs to have much silver before he can go in search of gold.'

'That is well said,' said Toke. 'If you continue as you have begun, you will, with experience, become as wise as your mother's father was. The old ones used to say that, from Odin's bracelet, a new bracelet used to issue every Wednesday, so that he came to have many; but that, if he had not had the first, he would never have had any. Never set yourself up as a Viking if you have not plenty of silver; nor as a skin-trader, neither. That is my advice to you. Only poets can win wealth with empty hands; but then they must make better songs than other poets, and competition spoils the pleasures of composition.'

On their way home, they rode in to speak with Sone the Sharp-Sighted, for Orm had a request that he wished to make to him.

Sone's house was large, with many rooms, and was everywhere full of his sons and their children. He himself was, by this time, immeasurably old, and very frozen, and spent all his time sitting by the fire mumbling to himself. Orm greeted him respectfully. After a few moments Sone recognised him, nodded amiably, asked him for news and began to talk about his health. This was less good than it had been, but nothing to grumble about; and one good thing was, he said, that he still had his understanding left to him, in prime condition, so that it was still as before, better than other men's.

A crowd of his sons had come in to greet the visitors and listen to them. They were powerful men, and of all ages. When they heard their father speak of his understanding, they cried that the old man was talking nonsense; there was, they said, nothing left of his understanding, but only his tongue and chatter. Resenting this, Sone brandished his stick and quietened them.

'They are foolish boys,' he said to Orm. 'They think that my understanding has been used up by begetting all of them, and that I have none left for myself. But that, as may easily be observed, is not the case; for little of it have they inherited from me. Sometimes it happens that I confuse their names, or forget one altogether, and that angers them, so that they talk ill of me. But the truth is that names are not a thing that it is important to remember.'

'I have come here partly to see you,' said Orm, 'and partly to see your sons. I intend to sail forth shortly on a long voyage, to Gardariké, to claim an inheritance. I have already bought a ship. It may be that I shall need good fighting-men on this voyage. Now I have always heard your sons praised as bold men, and it therefore seemed to me that it would be a good thing if I could have some of them with me in my ship. I shall pay them honourably, and, if all goes well, there may be silver to be shared out among such of us as survive the voyage.'

Sone became excited at this news. Better tidings he had not heard for many a day, he said, and he would be glad to send a flock of his sons to aid Orm. It was time that they went out into the world and learned wisdom and understanding. Besides which, he said, it would make things less crowded in the house.

'They are too many for me, now that I am old,' he said. 'Take half of them with you, and it will be to the advantage of us both. Do not take the eldest ones, nor yet the youngest, but a half score of those between. They have never been in a ship, but will serve for fighting.'

Some of his sons were immediately willing to go; others pondered the matter, and then agreed to come. They had heard tell how Orm had killed his two berserks, and thought him a chieftain after their liking. They conferred with Orm about the voyage late into the evening, and the end of it was that eleven of them agreed to come with him. They promised to be ready by midsummer, when Orm would come to collect them.

Toke thought this a good addition to their strength, for these men looked to him likely to render good service. Orm, too, was pleased, so that, when they rode away on the following morning, his dejection had left him.

When they reached home, everyone came running out to meet them with sad news. Are was dead; his body had lately been fished up out of the river. Blackhair was the only person who had seen what had happened, and he had little to tell. He and Are had been sitting together fishing, and Are had been as usual, save that he had, once and then again, stroked Blackhair across his cheeks and hair. After a short while, he had risen suddenly to his feet, made the sign of the cross thrice upon his breast, and had then strode forth into the river with bold steps until, reaching that part where the water was deepest, he had disappeared. He had not been seen again, and Blackhair had been unable to do anything to save him. It had been a long time before Rapp had found his body.

When the news of this had been brought to Asa, she had taken to her bed and prayed that she might die. Orm sat with her and comforted her as well as he could. Any man, he said, who had been treated as Are had been treated might be forgiven for wearying of life; and it was clear that he longed to escape from his wretchedness and seek peace with God, now that he had imparted to his kinsfolk his knowledge of the Bulgar gold.

'From God,' he said, 'he will by now have received back his sight, his tongue and his right hand; besides which, he has, I doubt not, also found his son again. That is no small sum of things to win, and any wise man would have done the same.'

Asa agreed with this reasoning; none the less, she found his death a hard thing to endure, and it was three days before she was able to move about again. They buried Are beside the church, near the place where Father Willibald had interred the two heads which Osten of Ore had hewn from the holy men. Asa chose a place for herself next to Are, for she thought it would not be long before she would go to join him.

Toke now rode home to make preparations for the voyage, and, shortly before midsummer, he and Olof Summer-Bird arrived at Gröning with good men accompanying them. Olof had had much to do; he had given his two wives rich compensation and driven them out of his house, though one of them had been unwilling to go and had resisted stubbornly. There was, therefore, now no obstacle to his taking Ludmilla in honourable marriage, and when he appeared at Gröning he expressed his wish that the ceremony might be performed immediately. But Orm held to his decision, finding it

451

foolish of Olof to think of marrying the girl before the voyage was completed.

'She is betrothed to you,' he said, 'and with that you must rest satisfied. A newly married man is a poor comrade to have on a long voyage. We have shaken hands upon the bargain, and you must stand by our original agreement. First, let us get the gold; then, when that is done, you shall have my daughter as reward for your good help. But it is, I think, nowhere customary to pay first and receive help afterwards.'

Olof Summer-Bird was a reasonable-minded man in all matters, and he could not deny that Orm had spoken wisely; he himself had no argument to advance but the great desire he felt for the girl, which was such that it was a source of merriment to them all. She could not come near him but his voice changed and he struggled hard for breath; he said himself that such a thing had never happened to him before. Ludmilla was as eager as he was that the marriage should take place as soon as possible, but knew that Orm was not to be persuaded from his original decision. However, Olof and she agreed that there was no reason for them to be down-hearted, seeing that they both felt the same towards each other.

Before his departure, Orm made careful plans to arrange how everything should be in the house during his absence. Rapp was to remain at home and be in charge of everything, although, up to the last moment, he grumbled in the hope that Orm might change his mind and allow him to go with the others. Orm saw to it that he had sufficient men left with him to do the work and protect the house. Ylva was to see to the house itself and all that went on inside it, and nothing important was to be done without her consent. Harald was to remain at home, for Orm was unwilling to risk his first born on so dangerous a voyage, and Harald himself showed no particular desire to go; but Glad Ulf was allowed to come with them and, at length, Blackhair also, after he had besought Orm and Ylva with many prayers. The obstinacy of his desire to go drove Ylva more than once to weep tears of grief and rage. She asked him what he thought a thirteen-year-old boy could do in a company of full-grown fighting-men; but he said that, if he was not permitted to sail in this ship, he would run away and join another, and Glad Ulf promised to take better care of Blackhair than of himself. That, thought Blackhair, was not necessary; however, he promised always to be careful, though he said that he fully intended to do his worst to men who robbed honest people of their eyes, if he should happen to encounter any of them. He now had both a sword and a spear, and regarded himself as a fully-fledged warrior. Orm was pleased at the prospect of having him with him, though he did not allow Ylva to know this.

Father Willibald preached a great sermon about people going down to the sea in ships, and blessed them all with a lengthy blessing. Toke and Olof Summer-Bird, and the heathen men they had brought with them, sat and listened to the sermon with the others, and agreed that they all felt hugely strengthened after the blessing. Many of them, after the service, went to the priest and, drawing their swords, asked for a blessing on them also.

When the time came for their departure, the women wept loudly, and among those who were going away there were not a few who felt grief. But most of them were glad at the prospect of adventure, and promised to bring fine things home with them when they returned; and Orm felt well contented to be riding at the head of so proud a company.

They came to Sone the Sharp-Sighted, to collect his sons, who speedily made themselves ready. The old man was sitting on a bench against the house-wall, warming himself in the sun. He ordered his sons, the eleven who were leaving him, to come to him one by one, that he might bid them farewell. They did so, and he gazed earnestly at them, mumbling their names and addressing each one correctly without exception. When the last of them had saluted him, he sat silent, staring straight before him; then a tremor ran through his limbs, and he laid his head back against the wall and closed his eyes. At this, his sons shifted their feet, and murmured uneasily: 'Now he sees!' After a while, he opened his eyes again, and looked around with an absent expression, as though he had just awakened from a long sleep. Then he blinked, moistened his lips, nodded to his sons, and said that they might now start on their voyage.

'What did you see?' they asked.

'Your fate,' he answered.

'Shall we come back?' they all cried eagerly.

'Seven shall come back.'

'But the four others?'

'They shall remain where they shall remain.'

All the eleven crowded round him, begging him to say which of them would not return.

'If four of us are doomed to die out there, it is best that those four should stay at home, so that no harm may come to them.'

But the old man smiled sadly.

'Now you talk foolishly,' he said, 'as you often do. I have seen the web that the Spinners are spinning, and for four of you there is but a short time left. Their thread, no man can lengthen. Four of you must die, whether they go or stay; which four, will be revealed to you in good time.'

He shook his head, and sat buried in thought. Then he said: 'It is no joy for a man to see the Spinners' fingers, and few are they who see them. But I am granted that vision, though I would gladly not see it. But the faces of the Spinners I have never seen.'

Again he sat silent. Then he looked at his sons, and nodded.

'Go, now,' he said. 'Seven of you will return. That is enough for you to know.'

His sons protested no longer, for it was as though a shyness had come over them in the old man's presence; and so it was also with Orm and all his following. But, as they rode away, the sons continued for some time to mutter bitterly against the old man and the strangeness of his ways.

'I should have liked to ask him how I should fare,' said Toke. 'But I dared not.'

'I had the same thought,' said Olof Summer-Bird, 'but I, too, lacked the courage.'

'It may be that his words were but empty talk,' said Orm, 'though it is true that the old woman at Gröning, too, sometimes sees what is to be.'

'Only a man who does not know him could think his words empty talk,' said one of Sone's sons who was riding beside them. 'It will happen as he has foretold, for so it has always been. But by telling us this, he has made it worse for us than he knows.'

'I think he is wiser than most men,' said Toke. 'But is it not a comfort to you all to know that seven of you will return safe and sound?'

'Seven,' replied the other darkly, 'but which seven? Now we brothers cannot have a merry moment until four of us are dead.'

'So much the merrier will that moment be,' said Orm; at which Sone's sons grunted doubtfully.

When they had reached the ship, and sent their horses home, Orm straightway set his men to repaint the dragon-head; for, if their ship was to enjoy good luck, it was necessary that its dragon-head should gleam as redly as blood. They carried everything aboard, and each man took his place. At first, Orm was unwilling to sacrifice a goat for luck on the voyage; but in this, everyone opposed him, so that at last he yielded.

'You may be as Christian as you will,' said Toke, 'but at sea, the old customs are still the best; and if you do not comply with them, you may as well jump head first into the sea where the water is deepest.'

Orm agreed that there might be some truth in this, though he found it hard that the price of a goat should now be added to all that he had had to pay out for this voyage before it had yet begun.

At last, all was ready; and, as soon as the goat's blood had streamed down the bows, they sailed out in fine weather with a good favourable wind. Ever since his boyhood, Toke had known the waters as far east as Gotland, and had undertaken to pilot the ship until they reached the Gotland Vi. Beyond, few knew how the waters ran; but they reckoned to be able to hire a pilot there to help them, for there were many pilots in Gotland.

Orm and Toke were both happy to be at sea again; it was as though many of the burdens which oppressed them ashore had suddenly fallen from them. When they sighted the coast of Lister in the distance, Toke said that the life of a skin-trader was, in truth, a hard one, but that now he felt once more as light of heart as when he had first sailed forth with Krok.

'I cannot understand why I have kept away from the sea for so long,' he said, 'for a well-manned ship is the best of all things. It is good to sit contented ashore, and no man need be ashamed to do so; but a voyage to a far land, with booty awaiting a man and this smell in his nostrils, is as good a lot as could be desired, and a sure cure for age and sorrow. It is strange that we Northmen, who know this and are more skilful seamen than other men, sit at home as much as we do, when we have the whole world to plunder.'

'Perhaps,' said Orm, 'some men prefer to grow old ashore rather than to risk encountering that surest of all cures for age that seafarers sometimes meet with.'

'I smell many odours,' said Blackhair, in a distressed voice, 'but think none of them good.'

'That is because you are unaccustomed to them, and know no better,' replied Orm. 'It may be that the sea-smell here is not as rich as that in the west, for there the sea is greener with salt, and so has a richer tang to it. But this smell is nothing to complain of.'

To this Blackhair made no reply, for the sea-sickness had come over him. At first, he was much ashamed of this, but his shame became less when he saw that many of the inland-dwellers were also beginning to hang over the ship's side. One and another of them were soon heard to beg in unsteady voices that the ship might be turned back at once, before they all perished.

Orm and Toke, however, stood by the steering-oar and found everything to their liking.

'They will have to grow used to it, poor wretches,' said Orm. 'I, too, once suffered thus.'

'Look at Sone's sons,' said Toke. 'Now they have something besides their father's prophecy to worry about. It takes time for landlubbers to appreciate the beauty of life at sea. With this wind, though, they can vomit to windward without it blowing back into the face of the next man, and many quarrels between irritable persons will thereby be avoided. But I doubt whether they appreciate this. Understanding does not come naturally to a man at sea, but only by experience.'

'It comes in time,' said Orm, 'however painful the process. If the wind drops, they will have to take to the oars, and I fear those who are not used to rowing will find the sport somewhat strenuous in such a sea as this. Then they will look back regretfully on the time when they were free to vomit in peace and had no need to toil.'

'Let us make Olof overseer,' said Toke. 'The task needs someone who is used to commanding obedience.'

'Obeyed, he may be,' said Orm, 'but his popularity will suffer for it. It is a hard office for a man to perform, and hardest when the rowers are free men who are not used to the whip.'

'It will occupy his mind,' said Toke. 'From his face, his thoughts would appear to be elsewhere; which I can well understand.'

Olof Summer-Bird was in a deep melancholy. He had seated himself on the deck beside them; he looked sleepy, and said little.

After a while, he mumbled that he was unsure whether it was the sea-sickness or the love-sickness that was weighing on him, and asked whether they would be putting in to land for the night. Orm and Toke agreed, however, that this would be unwise, if the wind held and the sky remained clear.

'To do so,' said Toke, 'would merely be pandering to the landlubbers, more than one of whom would, I doubt not, disappear during the night. For they would easily be able to find their way home from here, happy at having escaped further misery. But by the time we reach Gotland, they will have found their sea-legs, and there we shall be safely able to let them ashore.'

Olof Summer-Bird sighed, and said nothing.

'We shall, besides, save much food by keeping on our course,' said Orm. 'For if we went ashore, they would eat a good meal, and then vomit it up again the next day, so that it would be wasted.'

In this, he was right; for the wind remained favourable to them and barely half of the men succeeded in doing themselves justice at mealtimes before they sighted Gotland. Blackhair soon collected himself, and Glad Ulf had been used to the sea from boyhood; and they took great pleasure in munching their food and praising its quality, watched by pale men who had no stomach to eat. But as soon as they reached calmer water near Gotland the men began to find their appetite, and Orm thought he had never seen such gluttony as they now displayed.

'But I must not grudge it them,' he said, 'and now, perhaps, they will begin to be of some use.'

In the harbour of the Gotland Vi so many ships lay at anchor that Orm was at first doubtful whether it would be wise to sail in. But they took down the dragon-head, set up a shield of peace in its place, and rowed in without any ship opposing their passage. The town was very great, and full of seamen and rich merchants; and, when Orm's men came ashore, they found much to marvel at. There were houses built entirely of stone, and others erected for the sole purpose of drinking ale in; and the wealth of the town was such that whores walked the streets with rings of pure gold in their ears, and spat at any man who had not a fistful of silver to offer for their services. But one thing in this town they marvelled at most of all, and refused to believe in till they had actually seen it. This was a man from the Saxons' land who spent the whole of every day scraping the beards

457

from the chins of the rich men of the town. For this, he received a copper coin from every man he scraped, even when he had cut them so that they bled freely. Orm's men thought this a more astonishing custom than any they had ever before seen or heard tell of, and one that would be unlikely to afford a man much pleasure.

Olof Summer-Bird was now in a more cheerful humour, and he and Orm went in search of a skilful helmsman. Few men remained on board, for all wanted to stretch their legs and refresh themselves. Toke, however, stayed behind to guard the ship.

'The ale these Gotlanders brew is so good,' he said, 'that once, when I was a young man, I drank somewhat too deeply of it in this very harbour. As a result, I became miserable and killed a man, and only with difficulty managed to swim away with my life. These Gotlanders have a long memory, and it would be an ill thing if I were to be recognised and taken to task for such an old and trivial offence when we have important work ahead of us; so I shall remain on board. But I would advise such of you as go ashore to conduct yourselves peacefully, for they have little patience with strangers who cause disturbances.'

Some while later, Orm and Olof came aboard with the helmsman they had chosen. He was a small, thick-set, grizzled man, called Spof. He had been many times in the East, and knew all the routes, and would not agree to go with them until he had carefully inspected the whole ship. He said little, but nodded at most of what he saw. Finally, he asked to be allowed to sample the ship's ale. This was the ale that Orm had had specially brewed in the estuary before they had embarked, and nobody had yet found cause to complain of it. Spof tasted it, and stood thinking.

'Is this all the ale you have?' he said.

'Is it not good enough?' said Orm.

'It is good enough to drink during the voyage,' said Spof, 'and I shall not object to drinking it. Now, these men you have with you, are they meek and submissive, addicted to hard work and easily contented?'

'Easily contented?' said Orm. 'That they are not; indeed, the only time they do not complain is when the sea-sickness is upon them. Nor did I choose them for the meekness of their nature; and as for hard work, I do not think they like it better than most men.'

Spof nodded thoughtfully.

'It is as I feared,' he said. 'We shall arrive at the great portage in the worst of the summer heat, and you will need better portage-ale than this if all is to go well.'

'Portage-ale?' said Orm to Toke.

'We Gotlanders,' said Spof, 'have sailed the rivers of Gardariké more often than other men, and have penetrated them furthest. We know all their currents and hazards, even beyond the portage of the Meres, beyond which no man has voyaged in large ships save we. And it is thanks to our portage-ale that we have succeeded in making progress there, where all other men have been forced to turn back. This ale needs to be of extraordinary strength and flavour, so that it fortifies the spirit and cheers the heart; and it is to be given to the men only while they are hauling the ship across the portage. At no other time during the voyage must they be allowed to drink it. This device have we Gotlanders invented, and because of it we brew finer ales than any other people, for on the excellence of it our wealth depends.

'Unless I am much mistaken,' said Orm, 'this ale is not to be bought at a low price.'

'It is dearer than other ales,' replied Spof, 'in proportion as it is superior to them; possibly a fraction more. But it is well worth its price for, without its help, no ship can cross the portage into the hinterland of Gardariké.'

'How much shall we need?' asked Orm.

'Let me see,' said Spof. 'Twenty-four oars; sixty-six men; Kiev. That will involve seven small portages, but they will not be difficult. It is the great portage to the Dnieper that presents the problem. I think that five of our largest barrels would suffice.'

'Now I understand,' said Orm, 'why most men prefer to sail westwards.'

And when he had paid for the ale, and had given Spof half of his hire-money for the voyage, he began to wish more strongly still that Are's treasure had been buried in some river in west-over-sea instead of in Gardariké. As he reckoned out the silver, he mumbled heavily that he would never reach Kiev save as a beggar, armed only with his staff, for he would certainly have pawned his ship and weapons to the Gotlanders long before he sighted its walls.

'Still, you seem to me to be a good man, Spof,' he said, 'possessing both cunning and wisdom; and it may be that I shall not regret hiring you as my helmsman, although your price is high.'

459

'It is with me as with the portage-ale,' replied Spof, unoffended. 'I am expensive, but I am worth my price.'

They remained at anchor in the Gotland Vi for three days, and Spof ordered the men to carpenter strong cradles to hold the ale-casks firmly in position, until everything was as he wanted it. The ale occupied a deal of room, and weighted the ship heavily, but the men did not grumble at the extra labour it would cost them, for they had already sampled it in the town and knew its flavour. By the end of their first day ashore, many of them had drunk up all their silver and besought Orm to advance them part of their hire-money for the voyage; but nobody succeeded in persuading him to comply with this request. Some of the men then tried to barter their skin jackets in exchange for ale, and others their helmets, and, when the Gotlanders refused to accept them, fights were started, as the result of which law-men from the town came to the ship demanding stern compensation. Orm and Olof Summer-Bird sat arguing with them for half a day until they had reduced their original demands by half, though even that sum was, Orm thought, more than sufficiently large. Thereafter, they let no man ashore without first divesting him of his weapons.

Sone's sons were well supplied with silver of their own, and drank deeply in the town, but found it difficult, none the less, to put their father's prophecy wholly out of their minds. On the second day, ten of them returned to the ship, carrying the eleventh, who was on the point of expiring. They had, they said, warned him to control his passions, but, in spite of this, he had crept up upon a young woman whom he had seen chopping cabbages behind a cottage and had managed, by persuasive use of his tongue and hands, to put her upon her back. He had no sooner done this, however, than a crone had emerged from the house, picked up the chopper and deposited it in his head, which they had not been able to prevent.

Toke examined the wound, and said that the man had not long to live. He died during the night, and his brothers buried him sadly, and drank to a lucky death-voyage for him.

'It was his fate to die thus,' they said. 'When the old man sees, he sees the truth.'

But, although they mourned their brother and had nought but good to speak of him, it was noticeable that something of their melancholy had been lifted from them. For now, they reminded each other, there was bad luck in store for three of them only, so that a quarter of their troubles were past.

The next morning, they put out to sea and steering northwards, with Spof at the helm. Orm said that how they might fare in the future was uncertain, but that he dearly cherished one hope at least; namely that he would not soon find himself anchored in another harbour as ruinous to seafarers as the Gotland Vi.

CHAPTER SIX

How they rowed
to the Dnieper

They rounded the tip of Gotland, headed eastwards, past the island of Osel, and entered the mouth of the River Dyna. This river formed the beginning of the low road to Miklagard, which was that most used by Gotlanders. The high road, which the Swedes favoured, went along the coast of the Dead Land,* up the Voder river to Ladoga, and thence through Novgorod to the Dnieper.

'Which is the better road, no man has yet decided,' said Spof. 'I myself cannot say, though I have travelled them both. For the labour of rowing against the current always makes the road one has chosen seem the worse, whichever that may be. But it is lucky for us that we are starting late, and so will miss the spring tide.'

The men were in good heart as they entered the river, although they knew there was hard rowing ahead of them. After Orm had arranged matters so that each man should row for three days and rest for one, they proceeded upstream through the country of the Livonians and that of the Semgalls, occasionally passing small fishing villages sited on the banks, and beyond into a land deserted of men, with nothing to see save the river stretching away behind them and dense forest hugging them endlessly on both sides. The men felt awed by this country; and sometimes, when they had gone ashore for the night and were sitting around their fires, they heard a distant roaring which was like the voice of no animal they knew, and murmured to one another that this might, perhaps, be the Iron

---

* Balagard, i.e., the southern coast of Finland.

Forest, which the ancients spoke of, and where Loke's[*] progeny still roamed the earth.

One day they met three ships moving down the river abreast, heavily laden and well manned, though with only six pairs of oars out to each ship. They were Gotlanders, on their way home. The men were lean and burned black by the sun, and they glanced curiously at Orm's ship as it approached them. Some of them recognised Spof, and shouted greetings to him; and words were flung across from ship to ship, as they glided slowly past. They had come from Great Bulgaria, on the River Volga, and had rowed down the river to the Salt Sea,[†] where they had traded with the Arabs. They were carrying a good cargo home, they said: fabrics, silver bowls, slave-girls, wine and pepper; and three men in the second ship held up a naked young woman and dangled her over the side by her arms and hair, crying that she was for sale for twelve marks between friends. The woman shrieked and struggled, fearful lest she should fall into the water, and Orm's men drew deep breaths at the sight of her; but when, nobody having made an offer, the men drew her in again, she screamed foul words and thrust her tongue out at them.

The Gotland chieftains asked Orm who he was, whither he was heading, and what cargo he had aboard.

'I am no merchant,' replied Orm. 'I am going to Kiev to claim an inheritance.'

'It must be a great inheritance, if it is worth the labour of such a voyage,' said the Gotlanders sceptically. 'But if it is plunder you seek, seek it from others, for we always travel well prepared.'

Wth that, the ships passed on and grew small down the river.

'That woman was not contemptible,' said Toke thoughtfully. 'By her breasts, I adjudge her to be twenty at the most, though it is always difficult to be sure with a woman when she is hanging with her arms above her head. But only Gotlanders could ask twelve marks for a slave-girl, however young. None the less, I expected you, Olof, to make a bid for her.'

'I might have done,' said Olof Summer-Bird, 'if I were not so

---

[*] Loke was the spirit of evil and mischief in Norse mythology; it was he who contrived the death of Balder.
[†] The Caspian Sea.

463

placed as I am. But there is only one woman I long for, and I shall not forfeit my right to her maidenhood.'

Orm stood scowling darkly after the disappearing ships.

'I am surely fated to fight with Gotlanders before I die,' he said, 'although I am a peaceful man. Their arrogance is great, and I am beginning to weary of always letting them have the last word.'

'Perhaps we could fight them on our way home,' said Toke, 'if our other enterprise comes to nothing.'

But Spof said that, if those were his intentions, Orm would have to find another helmsman, for he would not take part in any fight against his own people.

In the afternoon of the same day, they had a further encounter. They heard the harsh creak of oars, and around the nearest bend there emerged a ship, rowing swiftly. They had all their oars out, and were rowing with all their strength. At the sight of Orm's ship, they slackened their pace; the ship carried twenty-four pairs of oars, as Orm's did, and was filled with armed men.

Orm shouted immediately to his rowers to continue strongly and steadily, and to the rest of his men to make ready for battle; and Toke, who was standing at the steering oar, altered course, so as to be able to grapple the other ship without being rammed, in case there should be fighting.

'What men are you?' came the cry from the strange ship.

'Men from Skania and Smaland,' replied Orm. 'And you?'

'East Gutes.'

The river was broad here, and the current weak. Toke shouted to the larboard rowers to pull, and told the starboard men to rest on their oars, so that the ship swung swiftly round towards the East Gutes until both the ships were gliding side by side downstream, so close that their oars were all but touching.

'We had you at our mercy then, if we had wished to ram you,' said Toke, pleased at the success of his manœuvre. 'And that even though you had the current with you. We have been in situations like this before.'

The East Gute, seeing their willingness to fight, spoke more humbly.

'Have you met Gotlanders on the river?' he asked.

'Three ships this morning,' replied Orm.

'Did you speak with them?'

'In friendliness. They were carrying a good cargo, and asked if we knew if there were any East Gutes near.'

'Did they speak of East Gutes? Were they afraid?'

'They said they found life tedious without them.'

'That is like them,' said the East Gute. 'Three ships, you said? What freight have you aboard?'

'Arms and men. Is there anything you want from us?'

'If what you say is true,' said the other, 'you carry the same cargo as we, and there is nothing for us to fight for. I have a suggestion to make. Come with me, and let us surprise these Gotlanders. They carry booty worth winning, and we shall share it like brothers.'

'What quarrel have you with them?' asked Spof.

'They have riches aboard, and I have none. Is not that cause enough? The luck has been against us since we started for home. We came rich from the Volga, but the Meres were waiting for us at the portage by the weirs, and ambushed us. We lost one of our ships and most of our cargo, and have no wish to return home empty-handed. Come now with me, if you are the men you look to be. Gotlanders are always worth attacking. I have heard at home that they are beginning to shoe their horses with silver shoes.'

'We have business elsewhere,' said Orm, 'and urgent business at that. But I doubt not the Gotlanders will be glad to see you. Three against one is the sort of odds they like.'

'Do as you wish,' said the other, sullenly. 'It is as I have always heard, that Skanians are swinish bladders of men with no thought save for themselves, and never stretch out a hand to a stranger.'

'It is true that we seldom think of East Gutes except when forced to,' replied Orm. 'But you have wasted our time for long enough. Farewell!'

Orm's ship was gliding slightly behind that of the Gutes, and Toke now swung her round facing upstream. While he was swinging her, the Gute chieftain's anger outgrew his patience, and of a sudden he flung his spear at Orm, crying as he did so: 'Perhaps this will help you to remember us!'

Olof Summer-Bird was standing beside Orm, and he now performed a feat which many had heard tell of, but few had ever had the good fortune to behold. As the spear winged its way towards Orm, Olof took a step forwards, caught it in its flight just below the blade, turned it in his hand and flung it back with such speed that few of those present realised immediately what had happened. The East Gute was not prepared for so swift a reply, and the spear took him in the shoulder, so that he staggered and sat down on his deck.

'That was a greeting from Finnveden,' shouted Olof, and his men roared with approval of his feat, and nodded to each other, hugely proud of their chieftain's performance. All the sailors rejoiced with them, although they doubted not that the East Gutes would now attack them. But the Gutes seemed to have lost their stomach for fighting, and proceeded downstream without further words.

'Such a throw I have never before seen,' said Orm, 'and I thank you for it.'

'I am as skilful with weapons as most men,' said Toke, 'but I could never match that feat. And you may be sure of this, Olof Styrsson, that few men have received such a tribute from Toke Grey-Gullsson.'

'It is a gift one is born with,' said Olof, 'though perhaps an unusual one. I could do it even as a boy, finding it easy, though I have never been able to teach it to anyone else.'

That evening, Olof's feat was much discussed around the camp fires on the bank, and they speculated as to what would happen when the Gutes caught up with the Gotlanders.

'They cannot attack three good ships with only one,' said Toke, 'however strong their itch for trouble. I think they will follow the Gotlanders out into the open sea, and hope they may become separated by bad weather. But the Gotlanders will not yield their cargo easily.'

'East Gutes are dangerous men,' said Orm. 'We had some of them among us when I sailed to England with Thorkel the Tall. They are good fighters, and regard themselves as the best in the world, which is perhaps the reason why they find it difficult to live peaceably with other men, and take few pains over their behaviour. They are merry when drunk, but otherwise take little pleasure in jests. But they are worst when they suspect that anyone is laughing at them behind their backs; rather than be mocked, they would run upon a spear-point. Therefore, I think it best that we should keep good watch to-night, lest they should regret their continence and decide to return.'

But nothing further came of this encounter; and, cheered by this meeting with their countrymen, they rowed on into the limitless land.

They came to a place where the water boiled around great stones. There, they hauled their ship on to the bank, and emptied her. Then they dragged her up a trodden track past the weir, and slid her back into the water. When they had brought the ship's contents up by the same path, and had replaced them in the ship, the men asked confidently if it was not now time for them to be given some of the good portage-ale. But Spof said that only novices at the work could suppose that they had yet earned it.

'This was not a portage,' he said, 'but a lift. The ale will only be served after we have passed the portage.'

Several times they came to similar weirs, and to some where the climb was longer and steeper. But Spof always gave the same reply, so that they began to wonder what the appearance of the great portage might be.

Every evening, after they had gone ashore for the night, they fished in the river, always making fine catches. So they did not lack for food, although they had, by now, eaten most of what they had brought with them. In spite of this, however, they sat dejected around their fires as they cooked their fish, longing for fresh meat and agreeing with one another that too much fish made a man distempered. They began, too, to grow weary at the heavy rowing; but Spof comforted them, saying that things would soon be different.

'For you must know,' he said, 'that the heavy rowing has not yet begun.'

Sone's sons liked the fish less than anyone, and went out each evening to hunt. They took spears and bows, and were cunning at discovering the tracks of animals, and their watering places. But, although they were tireless and always came back late to the camp, it was a long time before they found anything. At last they sighted an elk, which they managed to corner and kill, and that night, they did not return to the camp before dawn. They had lit a fire in the forest and eaten themselves full; and such meat as they brought back with them they were loth to part with.

After this, they had better success with their hunting. Glad Ulf and Blackhair joined them on their sorties, and others also; and Orm regretted that he had not brought with him two or three of his great hounds, thinking that he could now be using them to good purpose.

One evening, Blackhair came running back to the camp, exhausted and breathless, shouting for men and ropes. There was now, he said, meat for all; and at this, every man in the camp leaped quickly to his feet. They had driven five large animals into a bog, where they had killed them, and many men were needed to drag them out. All the men rushed joyfully to the spot, and they soon had the good meat on dry land. The animals looked like great bearded oxen, but oxen such as Orm had never before seen. Two of Toke's men, however, said that these were wild oxen, such as were still sometimes to be found near Lake Asnen in Värend, where they were held sacred.

'To-morrow, we shall have a holiday,' said Orm, 'and hold a feast.'

So they had a feast, at which no complaints were heard; and the wild oxen, which were praised by all for the flavour and good texture of their flesh, disappeared with what was left of the ale they had brought with them when they had started.

'It is no matter if we finish it,' said Orm, 'for it is already beginning to grow sharp.'

'When we come to the town of the Polotjans,' said Spof, 'we shall be able to buy mead. But do not let anyone tempt you to touch the portage-ale.'

When they had recovered from this meal, and had continued on their course, they had the good fortune to be favoured with a strong wind, so that, for a whole day, they were able to proceed by sail. They were now entering country where traces of man's habitation could be seen on the banks.

'This is the country of the Polotjans,' said Spof. 'But we shall not see any of them before we reach their town. Those who live in the wild country here never come near the river when word has come to them that ships are approaching, for fear lest they should be taken to serve at the oars, and then be sold as slaves in a foreign land.'

Spof told them also that these Polotjans had no gods save snakes, who lived with them in their huts; but Orm looked at Spof and said that he had been to sea before and knew how much to believe of that story.

They came to the town of the Polotjans, which was called Polotsk, and was of considerable size, with ramparts and stockades. Many men went naked there, though no women did so; for, a short while before, they had all been commanded to pay taxes, and the chieftain of the town had ordered that no man might wear clothes until he had paid what he owed to the great Prince. Some of these looked more resentful than the rest; they had, they said, paid their tax, but must still go naked, because they had no clothes left after having pawned them to raise the money. In order to be ready for the cold season, they offered their wives for a good shirt and their daughters for a pair of shoes, and found Orm's men willing customers.

The chieftain of this town was of Swedish blood, and was called Faste; he received them hospitably, and asked anxiously for news of events at home. He was aged, and had served the great Prince of Kiev for many years. He had Polotjan women in his house, and many children, and, when drunk, spoke their tongue in preference to his own. Orm bought from him mead and pork, and many other things also.

When they were ready to proceed, Faste came to bid them farewell and begged Orm to take with him his scribe, who was going to Kiev with a basket of heads. The great Prince, he explained, liked to be reminded that his town-chieftains served him zealously, and was always pleased to receive evidence of their zeal in the shape of the heads of the more dangerous criminals. Lately, it had become difficult to ensure a safe passage to Kiev, and he was reluctant to neglect so good an opportunity as this of sending his gift. The scribe was a young man, a native of Kiev; besides the heads, he carried a sheep-skin on which were written the names of the former owners of the heads, together with an account of their misdeeds.

In view of the hospitality that Faste had shown him, Orm felt unable to deny him this request, although he was unwilling to comply with it. The heads awoke unpleasant memories in him, for he had received a present in that shape once before; he recalled, also, that his own head had been sold to King Sven, although the transaction had never been completed. Accordingly, he regarded this basket as likely to bring bad luck with it, and all his men thought the same. It was, besides, noticeable in the summer heat that the heads were beginning to age, and before they had gone far the men began to complain of their stink. The scribe sat by his basket, as though smelling nothing; he understood the Northmen's tongue, however, and after a while suggested that the basket should be tied to a rope and allowed to trail in the water. This proposal won general approval; so the basket was tied firmly to a rope's end and heaved overboard. They had, by this time, set sail again and were making good speed; and, later that day, Blackhair cried that the basket had detached itself and disappeared.

'The best course for you now, scribe,' said Toke, 'is to jump overboard and fish for your treasure; for, if you arrive without it, I fear things may go somewhat ill for you.'

The scribe, though vexed at this occurrence, appeared not to be greatly alarmed by it. The sheep-skin was, he explained, more important than the heads; as long as he still had the former, he could manage without the latter. There were only nine of them, and he doubted not that he would be able to borrow substitutes from public officials in Kiev with whom he was friendly; for there were always plenty of malefactors in their custody awaiting execution.

'We are taught to be merciful, after the example of God,' he said, 'and therefore think it good to help one another when we are in distress. And one head is as good as another.'

'Then you are Christians in this land?' said Orm.

'In Kiev,' replied the scribe. 'For the great Prince has so commanded us, and we think it best to comply with his wishes.'

They reached a place where two rivers joined. Their course lay along the right-hand fork, which was called Ulla, and it was now that the hard rowing began. For here the current soon became stronger and the river narrower, and often they found themselves unable to make progress and had to haul the ship ashore and drag her forward along the bank. They had to toil long and strenuously, so that even the strongest among them felt it, and regretted the good days they had spent on the Dyna. At last they reached a place where Spof ordered them to bring the ship ashore, although they were making good progress and it was yet early in the day; for this, he said, was the great portage.

The ground here was scattered with various kinds of timber, left by travellers ascending or descending; broken planks, rollers, and a type of rough runner. Some of them were still usable, and the men axed others from fallen trees. They drew the ship up on to the bank and, after a great deal of carpentry, managed to fasten runners down both sides of the keel. While they were thus occupied, some men were seen to come out of the forest a little further up the river and stand there uncertainly watching them. Spof appeared pleased when

470

he saw them; he waved to them, held up a tankard, and shouted the two words that he knew of their language: oxen and silver. The men came nearer, and were offered drink, which they accepted; and Orm was now able to make use of Faste's scribe, who was able to interpret between him and the strangers. They had oxen they were prepared to hire out, but only ten, though Spof wanted more. These oxen were, the men explained, grazing deep in the forest where robbers and tax-collectors would be less likely to find them, but they would be back with them in three days. They asked only a small price for the use of them, and begged that they might be paid in sail-cloth instead of silver, as their women liked the striped woof; but in the event of any ox dying, they wanted to be given good compensation. Orm found their demands reasonable, and thought them the first honest people he had dealt with on this voyage.

All the men now set busily to work chopping and carpentering, and in a short time they had built a broad wagon, with strong rounds of oak to serve as wheels. Upon this they piled the portage-ale and made it fast, together with most of the other things from the ship.

The strangers then returned with the oxen, as they had promised; and, when everything was ready, two oxen were harnessed to the wagon and the rest to the ship.

'If we had six more oxen,' said Spof, 'all would be well; as things are, we shall have to help with the dragging ourselves. But we must be thankful that we have got any help at all, for to drag a ship up the great portage without oxen is the worst task that a man could be faced with.'

When the dragging began, some of the men walked ahead to lift fallen trees out of the way and smooth the track. Then came the wagon. They guided the oxen cautiously, lest anything should give way; and when the wheels began to smoke they greased the axles with pork and pitch. Then came the ship, with many men harnessed to the ropes beside the oxen. Where the track led downhill, or over grassland and moss, the oxen were able to manage without assistance; but where it led uphill, the men had to lend all their strength, and where the going was rough rollers had to be placed beneath the runners. The ox-drivers spoke to their beasts the whole time, and sometimes sang to them, so that they dragged willingly, but when Orm's men spoke to them, using the words which they used to address oxen at home, they received no response, because these oxen could not understand what they were saying. This surprised the men greatly; it showed, they said, that oxen were far wiser beasts than they had hitherto supposed, for here was evidence that they possessed a characteristic in common with men, namely, that they could not understand the speech of foreigners.

The men grew weary with the heat and toil and the business of changing the rollers; but they kept bravely on, for it was a great incentive to them to see the wagon with the portage-ale moving ahead of them, and they did all they could to keep pace with it. As soon as they pitched camp for the night, they all cried loudly for portage-ale; but Spof said that this first day's work had been light, and that Faste's mead was reward enough for it. They drank of this, grumbling, and soon fell asleep; but the next day's work proved more arduous, as Spof had told them it would. Before the afternoon was far advanced, many of the men began to flag; but Orm and Toke cheered them with words of encouragement, sometimes lending a hand themselves with the dragging so that the men might be stimulated by their example. When evening came on this day, Spof at last said that the time had come for the portage-ale to be opened. They breached a cask and gave a good measure to every man; and, although they had all tasted the same brew in the Gotland Vi, they declared unanimously that they had not, until this moment, appreciated its quality to the full, and that the labour they had undergone had been well worth while. Orm ordered that the ox-drivers, too, should have their share; they accepted this offer willingly, and at once became drunk and sang noisily, for they were only accustomed to thin mead.

On the third day, they soon came to a lake, long and narrow between asses'-backs, and here their task was lightened. The wagon and the oxen proceeded by land, but they launched the ship into the lake, with her runners still on her keel, and, favoured by a mild breeze, sailed down the water, encamping at length on the farther shore. On a hill not far from their camping ground lay a village with rich pastures below it: here they saw fat cattle being driven in from their grazing, although it was yet a good while before evening. The village, which appeared to be large, was curiously fortified, for, although it was surrounded by a high rampart of earth and stone, this was broken in places by a stockade of rough logs which did not look difficult to scale.

472

The men were in good spirits, for this was the lightest day's work they had had for a long while, and the sight of the cattle awakened in them a longing for fresh meat. Neither Orm nor Olof was prepared to pay out any more silver for food, reckoning this to be an unnecessary expenditure after all they had already been put to; but many of the men, unable to control their longing, determined, none the less, to go and fetch their supper. Faste's scribe said that the people who lived in these parts were wild men of the Dregovite tribe, who had not, as yet, paid their taxes, so that the men might act as they chose towards them. Spof said that the previous time he had been here, seven years before, this village was in the process of being built; but they had seen no cattle on that occasion, and so had not disturbed the inhabitants. Orm told the men that they must not kill anyone in the village without due cause, and must not take more cattle than would be enough to meet their needs. They promised, and set out towards the village. Sone's sons were the most anxious to go, for, ever since they had rowed in to the River Ulla, they had had no opportunity to go hunting, because of the incessant work to which they had been subjected.

Shortly afterwards, the men who had been coming by land with the wagon arrived at the camp. When the ox-drivers learned from the scribe that men had gone to the village to get cattle, they fell to the ground shaking with laughter. Orm and the others wondered what they could find in this news to be amused at, and the scribe tried to get them to explain the cause of their mirth, but in vain. They would only reply that the cause would, in a short while, become apparent, and then began again to shriek with laughter.

Suddenly shouts and screams were heard from the direction of the village, and the whole company of cattle-raiders emerged, running down the hill as fast as their legs would carry them. They whirled their arms above their heads and yelled fearfully, though nothing else was in sight, and two or three of them fell to the ground and remained there, rolling from side to side. The rest ran down to the lake, and jumped into the water.

Everyone in the camp stared at them in amazement.

'Have they devils or ghosts after them?' said Orm.

'I think bees,' said Toke.

It was evident that he was right, and all the men now began to laugh as loudly as the ox-drivers, who had known about this from the beginning.

The refugees from the bees had to sit in the lake for a good while longer, with only their noses showing above the surface, until, at length, the bees tired of their sport and flew home again. They returned slowly to the camp, greatly dejected, with swollen faces, and sat with few words in their mouths, thinking they had lost much honour in fleeing thus from bees. The worst of the business, though, was that three men were lying dead on the hill, where they had fallen: two of Olof Summer-Bird's men, and one of Sone's sons. They grieved at this, for the dead had all been good men, and Orm ordered that portage-ale should be drunk again that evening, to honour their memory and to cheer the stung survivors.

The ox-drivers now told them about the Dregovites, the scribe translating what they said.

These Dregovites, they said, were more cunning than other men, and had found a means to live peacefully in their villages. They had many swarms of bees which lived in the tree-trunks that formed part of their fortifications, and which, as soon as any stranger touched the trunks or tried to climb over them, came out and stung him. It was, they continued, fortunate for the men that they had tried to invade the village during day-light, for, if they had made the attempt by night, they would have suffered far worse. The bees could only guard the village by day, since they slept during the night; accordingly, the wise Dregovites had also equipped themselves with bears, which they trapped when young and trained and gave good treatment. If robbers came in the night, the bears were released and mauled the invaders, after which they returned to their masters to receive honey-cakes in reward for their services. Because of this, nobody dared to enter the villages of the Dregovites, not even the important men who collected taxes for the great Prince.

The next day, they remained in this place, and buried the dead. Some of the men wanted to throw fire into the village as a revenge; but Orm strictly forbade this, because no man had raised his hand against the dead men, who had only themselves to blame for their fate. Those who had been worst stung were in a sorry plight, for they were too ill to move; but the ox-drivers went up to the village and, standing at a distance from it, shouted to the inhabitants. A short while later, they returned to the camp, bringing with them three old women. These old women looked at the men who had been stung and placed a salve upon their swellings, consisting of snake's fat, woman's milk and honey, blended with the juice of healing herbs, which soon made the sick men feel better. Orm gave the women ale and silver; they drank eagerly, being careful to leave no drop in their cups, and thanked him humbly for the silver. The scribe spoke with them; they gazed curiously at him, curtseyed and returned to their village.

After a while, some men appeared from the village, bringing with them three pigs and two young oxen. The scribe went to greet them, but they brushed him aside, walked up to Orm and Olof Summer-Bird, and began to talk eagerly. The scribe stood listening, and then, of a sudden, uttered a yell and fled into the forest. Nobody could understand the villagers except the ox-drivers, and these knew but few words of the Northmen's tongue; but, by gestures, they managed to explain that the villagers wished to make Orm a gift of the pigs and oxen, if he would hand the scribe over to them; for they wished to give him to their bears, because they disliked any man connected with the great Prince. Orm found himself unable to accede to this request; however, he gave them ale and bought their beasts with silver, so that they parted on amiable terms. Later that afternoon, several more old women came to the camp with great cheeses, which they gave to the men in exchange for a good draught of ale. The men, who had already begun to roast the meat, thought that everything was turning out better than could have been expected. The only pity, they said, was that old women had come instead of young ones; but these the Dregovites would not allow out of the village.

Towards evening, the scribe slunk back into the camp from his hiding-place, tempted by the odour of the roasting meat. He begged Orm to lose no time in getting away from these wild people. The great Prince would, he said, be informed of their behaviour.

They proceeded on their way, and at length came to a lake larger than that which they had just left: then, on the seventh day of their portage, they reached a river which Spof called the Beaver River, the ox-drivers Beresina. There was great rejoicing among the men when they saw this river, and here they drank the last of the portage-ale, for the worst hardships of the voyage were now past.

'But now,' said Orm, 'we have no ale to help us on our homeward journey.'

'That is true,' said Spof, 'but we shall only need it on the way out. For it is with men as with horses; once their heads are turned homewards, they move willingly and do not need the spur.'

The ox-drivers were now paid off, and received more than they had demanded; for it was so with Orm that he often felt mean towards merchants, who for the most part seemed to him to be no better than robbers, and often worse, but never towards men who had served him well. Besides which, he now felt that he was a good deal nearer to the Bulgar gold. The ox-drivers thanked him for his generosity and, before departing, took Spof and Toke to a village, where they spoke to good men who were willing to hire out oxen for the return journey. Orm ordered his men to dig a hiding-place, where they hid the rollers and runners until they should need them again, having worn out three sets of runners during the long land drag. The wagon he took with him, thinking that it might prove useful when they reached the weirs.

They sailed down the river, past fishermen's shacks and beavers' huts and dams, rejoicing that the going was now light. The river ran black and shining between broad-leaved trees, rich with foliage, and the men thought that the fish from this river tasted more wholesome than those they had caught in the Dyna. Only a few men were needed at the oars; the rest sat in peace and contentment, telling each other stories and wondering whether the whole voyage might not be completed without any fighting.

The river broadened more and more, and at last they came out into the Dnieper. Orm and Toke agreed that even the biggest rivers in Andalusia could not be compared with this; and Olof Summer-Bird said that, of all the rivers in the world, only the Danube was greater. But Spof thought that the Volga was the biggest of them all, and had many stories to tell of the voyages he had made on its waters.

They met four ships labouring upstream, heavy-laden, and spoke with them. They were manned by merchants from Birka, who were on their way home from Krim. They were very tired, and said that trade had been good but the homeward journey bad. They had been engaged in fighting at the weirs and had lost many men; for the Patzinaks had come west, waging war against all men, and were trying to stop all traffic on

476

the river. It would, they said, be unwise for anyone to travel beyond Kiev before the Patzinaks had left the river and returned again to their eastern grazing-grounds.

This news gave Orm much to think about, and when they had parted from the merchants he sat for a long time pondering deeply.

CHAPTER SEVEN

Concerning what happened at the weirs

That evening, they went ashore for the night close to a village, where they found both sheep and mead for sale. After they had eaten, Orm sat in counsel with Toke and Olof upon the news which they had just heard, to decide what course they would be best advised to take now that they were approaching their goal. They went out to the empty ship, to be able to speak without fear of disturbance or of being overheard; and there they sat together in the evening stillness, while dragon-flies played over the surface of the water and the river chuckled slowly around the ship.

Orm thought that he had many difficult problems to decide.

'Such is our present situation,' he said, 'that we must plan wisely if we are to bring this voyage to a successful conclusion. Nobody knows anything about the treasure except you two and myself, and the two boys, who know how to keep their mouths shut; no one else. All that the men have been told is that we are going to Kiev to collect an inheritance, and I have not revealed our true purpose even to Spof. But we shall soon have to tell them that we are going beyond to the weirs, and that my inheritance lies hidden there. If, though, we tell them this, it is certain that the whole of Kiev will also know of it a short while after we have come to the town; for men who drink in a good harbour cannot keep such a secret longer than the time it takes to drink three cups of ale, even if they know they will lose their heads for it. And if the purpose of our journey comes to the ears of the great Prince and his men, it will be a sad piece of ill luck for us, for then there will be many who will wish to share our silver and gold with us, if not to kill us and keep the lot

478

for themselves. In addition to all this, we now have these Patzinaks to think about, who will be lurking in wait for us at the weirs.'

Olof and Toke agreed that there was much here for a man to scratch his head about. Toke asked how far it might be from Kiev to the weirs, and whether they would be able to find food on the river once they had passed beyond the city.

'From Kiev to the weirs is, I think, nine days' hard rowing,' said Olof, 'though Spof will be able to tell you more accurately than I. The time I voyaged there we bought food from the herdsmen on the banks, and also took much from a rich village of the Severians. But things may be different now that things are no longer peaceful on the river.'

'It would be foolish of us to come to Kiev without first telling the men that we intend to proceed,' said Toke. 'For there is much that will tempt them in the city, and it may be that many of them will refuse to go further, pleading that we misled them.'

'A worse danger,' said Olof, 'is that the great Prince himself will immediately conscript many, if not all of us into his service. I have served the great Prince Vladimir, and know how things are in Kiev. He has always given good pay, and, if he now has trouble on his hands, he will be offering more than before. It is so with him, that he can never have enough Northmen in his bodyguard; for he holds us to be the boldest and most loyal of men, as indeed we are, and loves us dearly, having done so ever since the Swedes helped him to his throne when he was a young man. He himself is of Swedish blood. He knows many ways to tempt Northmen to remain in Kiev, even if his gold should fail to seduce them.'

Orm nodded and sat pondering, staring down into the water.

'There is much to be said against our visiting the great Prince Vladimir,' he said, 'although his face is so great and his wisdom so renowned that it would be a pity to pass through his town without seeing him. It is said that, now that he is old, men worship him as holy, though it has taken him a long time to attain to that condition. He must be nearly as great a king as King Harald was. But that which is most important must come first. We have come on a particular errand, to collect the gold; then, when we have found it, we shall have another errand, namely, to bring it quickly and safely home again. I think we are all agreed that it would be wisest to proceed directly to the weirs.'

'That is so,' said Toke. 'None the less, I think we would do well to take Spof's counsel on the matter. He knows the route better than we do and, perchance, knows these Patzinaks better also.'

The others nodded, and Orm summoned Spof to him from the bank. When he had climbed aboard, Orm told him about the gold.

'I said nothing of this to you when I engaged you,' he concluded, 'because I was not yet sure of you. But now I know you to be a good man, and honest.'

'This is to be a longer journey than I had bargained for,' said Spof, 'and more dangerous. The price I asked for my services you found dear, but I must tell you that, if I had known we were going to the weirs, it would have been dearer still.'

'You need have no worry on that score,' said Orm. 'For this voyage to the weirs you may name your own price. And I promise you, and Toke Grey-Gullsson and Olof Styrsson will be your witnesses, that you shall have your share of the treasure, too, if we find it and bring it safely home. And it shall be a full helmsman's share.'

'Then I am content to go with you,' said Spof. 'We Gotlanders are happiest when we know that our services will be well rewarded.'

When he had reflected upon the matter, Spof said that he, too, thought that they would do best to proceed directly to the weirs.

'There will be no difficulty about procuring food,' he said. 'It is cheap and easy to find further down the river; I have known men get five fat pigs for a single broad-axe, with a sack of oats thrown in. We have rich villages ahead of us now, both on this side of Kiev and beyond, and shall be able to get enough food to last us to the weirs and back again. But it would be best if you could pay for it, as you have done hitherto, if your silver will stretch to it, for it is unwise to take things by force on an outward voyage, when one intends to return by the same route.'

Orm replied that he still had a little silver to jingle, although most of it had gone by now.

'Our chief problem will be the Patzinaks,' continued Spof. 'We may find ourselves forced to buy a safe conduct from them. It is, though, possible that they will not let us through at any price. It would be good if you could tell me off which bank the treasure lies, and between which weirs.'

'It lies off the eastern bank,' said Orm, 'between the second and third weir, reckoning from the south. But the hiding-place itself I shall reveal to no man until we have reached it.'

'Then it lies a good way from where we shall have to beach the ship for the portage,' said Spof. 'It would be best if we could go there by night. It would have been a good thing if we could have brought someone with us who understands the language of the Patzinaks, in case we should find them unwilling to talk peaceably with us. But that cannot be helped now.'

'That difficulty we can overcome,' said Toke, 'by taking Faste's scribe with us. He can do his business at Kiev on the way back. Nobody will complain of his lateness, for nobody will know when he started. If we should speak with the Patzinaks, there is sure to be someone among them who will understand his language, even if he cannot understand theirs.'

With that, their conference ended. The next morning, before they continued with their journey, Orm spoke to the men. He told them that they were going beyond Kiev, to a place where his inheritance from his brother lay hidden.

'There may well be fighting there,' he added, 'and, if you prove yourselves bold men, so that I win my inheritance safely, it may be that each of you will receive a share of it, besides the good money that you have already been promised for your hire.'

The men had little complaint to make, save Sone's sons, who were heard to mumble amongst themselves that two of them would surely die there and that they needed ale rather than the sweet drink which was all that this land had to offer them, if they were to fight with their full strength.

They landed several times during their passage down the river, to visit the villages of the Poljans, where wealth abounded. There Orm bought food and drink, so that they were as well furnished as when they had started. Then, late one evening, when a fog lay over the river, they rowed past Kiev, unable to discern much of the city.

Faste's scribe grew uneasy when he found that they did not intend to put him ashore here.

'I have an important message for the great Prince,' he said, 'as you all know.'

'It has been decided that you shall accompany us to the weirs,' said Orm. 'You are clever at speaking with all kinds of men and

481

may prove useful to us there. You will be put ashore here on our way back.'

At this the scribe showed great alarm; however, when he had prevailed upon Orm to swear an oath by the Holy Trinity and St Cyril that he would neither force him to row nor sell him to the Patzinaks, he calmed himself and said that the great Prince would have to wait.

Soon the villages along the bank began to grow fewer, until at last they ceased altogether, and were replaced by unending grassland, where the Patzinaks held sway. From the ship they could sometimes see herds of sheep and horses at their watering places, tended by men on horseback wearing tall skin caps and carrying long spears. Spof said that it was a good thing that they saw such herds only on the left bank of the river, and never on the right bank. The reason for this, he explained, was that there was a high tide on the river which prevented the Patzinaks from bringing their herds across to the right bank; if they attempted to do this, they would lose many animals at the fords. Henceforth, therefore, they always beached the ship on the safe bank, though they did not relax the sharp watch which they kept each night.

When they had come to within three days rowing of the weirs, they became yet more cautious, and rowed only by night. By day they kept the ship hidden among tall reeds in creeks in the right bank. On the last day, they anchored within hearing distance of the weirs and, when darkness fell, rowed over to the left bank, where the dragging-tracks began.

It had been decided that twenty men should remain in the ship. They had drawn lots to determine which these should be, and Toke found himself among them. They were to row the ship out into the centre of the stream and lie there at anchor during the night until they heard voices calling them from the land. Toke was reluctant to sit idle in the ship, but had to obey when the lot went against him. Orm would have liked to leave Blackhair with him, but in that matter he was unable to have his way.

Orm and Olof Summer-Bird now set off with the rest of their band up the long dragging-track, taking Spof with them as guide. All the men were armed with swords and bows. Spof had come this way several times before. He explained that the place to which they were going lay beyond the seventh weir, reckoning from the north.

This would be three hours' brisk marching, so that allowing for the time it would take to find and raise the treasure, they would be hard put to get back before it began to grow light. They had with them the wagon that they had used at the great portage, to put the treasure in, and also the scribe, although he was not greatly pleased at having to accompany them. They began their march in pitch darkness; but they knew that the moon would soon rise and, despite the added dangers that this would bring, Orm was glad that it was to be so, since otherwise he feared he might be unable to find the spot where the treasure lay.

But when the moon rose it straightway brought them trouble, for the first object upon which its rays shone was a rider in a pointed hat and a long coat standing motionless on a hill ahead of them. At the sight of him, they at once halted and stood silent. It was still dark in the hollow where they were, but the horseman seemed, they thought, to be peering in their direction, as though their footsteps or the creak of the wagon might have come to his ears.

One of Sone's sons touched Orm with his bow.

'It is a long carry,' he muttered, 'and moonlight is deceptive to shoot in; but we think we could mark him so that he will stay where he is, if you so wish it.'

Orm hesitated for a moment; then he muttered that hostilities were not to be opened from his side.

The horseman on the hill uttered a whistle, like a peewit's call, and another horseman appeared beside him. The first horseman stretched out his arm and said something. They both sat still for a few moments; then they suddenly wheeled their horses, rode off, and disappeared.

'Those must have been Patzinaks,' said Orm, 'and now things promise less well, for it is certain that they saw us.'

'We have already reached the fifth weir,' said Olof. 'It would be a pity to turn back when we have come so far.'

'There is little pleasure to be gained in fighting horsemen,' said Orm, 'especially when they outnumber those who oppose them on foot.'

'Perhaps they will wait till it is light before they attack us,' said Spof, 'for they like this moonlight no more than we do.'

'Let us proceed,' said Orm.

They made all the speed they could and, when they had reached and passed the seventh weir, Orm began to look about him.

'Those of you whose eyes are sharpest must help me now,' he said. 'There should be a rock in the water here with three rose-bushes on it, though there will be no flowers on them at this season.'

'There is a rock with bushes on it,' said Blackhair, 'but whether or not they are rose-bushes, I cannot tell.'

They crept down to the water's edge, and thence managed to discern three more rocks. All of these, however, appeared to be bald. Then Orm found the cleft where the rock-flat was broken and where the water boiled and bubbled, just as Are had described it.

'If we can now find a hill which is called the skull-mound of the Patzinaks,' he said, 'we shall not be far from that which we have come to seek.'

It did not take them long to find this, for, almost at once, Spof pointed towards a high mound that lay a short way from the bank.

'They have buried a chieftain there,' he said, 'I remember that I was once told so. And whenever they have been fighting here at the weirs, it is their custom to set the heads of their enemies on poles upon his mound.'

'Then let us make haste,' said Orm, 'lest they put ours there too.'

He walked out along the edge of the cleft until he came to the spot which lay directly between the rock with the rose-bushes on it and the mound with the skulls.

'This should be the place,' he said. 'Now we shall know whether we have made this long voyage in vain.'

All the men were much excited. With a spear, they measured the depth of the water beneath the cleft.

'We shall need tall men to catch these fish,' said Orm, 'but I can feel a pile of stones here against the base of the rock, and that is as it should be.'

Two brothers of Olof's following, named Long Staff and Skule, Hallanders by birth, were the tallest men in the band. They expressed their willingness to go into the water and do their best to see if anything lay there. When they stood on the bottom the water came up to their necks, and Orm bade them plunge their heads under and bring up, one by one, the stones that lay piled against the rock. They came spluttering up with huge stones, continuing thus for a good while; finding the work strenuous, they rested to regain their breath, and then continued. Suddenly Skule said that his fingers had touched something that was not stone, but that he could not pull it free.

'Be careful with it,' said Orm, 'and clear all the stones away first.'

'Here is something that is not stone,' said Long Staff, heaving an object out of the water. It was a sack, and evidently contained something heavy, so that he had to get a good grip on it. Just as he had got it halfway up the rock facing him, the sack burst in the middle, because the skin it was made of had rotted, and a broad stream of silver coins ran out and fell splashing into the water. At this sight, a great cry of fear and anguish arose from the men on the bank. Long Staff tried to stem the flow with his hands and face, and the men threw themselves over each other to get the sack up and save as much as possible, but in spite of their efforts much of its contents fell into the water.

'This is a fine beginning,' said Orm bitterly. 'Is that the way you handle silver? How much will be left for me, if you continue like that? However,' he added in a calmer voice, 'now at least we know that we have come to the right place, and that nobody has been here before us. But be careful with the rest, Hallander. There should be four sacks more.'

All the men jeered angrily at Long Staff, so that he began to sulk and swore he would remain in the water no longer. It was not his fault, he said, that the sack was rotten; if he had had as much silver as that to hide, he would have taken the trouble to store it in stronger sacks. Let others take his place and see whether they could do better.

But both Orm and Olof said that it was not his fault that this had happened. This encouraged him, and he continued with his fishing in a calmer spirit.

'Here is something else,' said Skule, pulling up something that he had caught, 'and this is heavier than stone.'

It was a small copper chest, very green and exceedingly heavy, bound many times with fine red ropes, which were sealed with lead.

'Ah, yes, the chests,' said Orm. 'I had forgotten them. There should be four small chests like that. They contain trash for women. But all the silver is in the sacks.'

With the other sacks they had better luck, managing to get them up on to the rock without spilling any of their contents. As each new find appeared, their merriment increased, and they had no thoughts now for the Patzinaks or for the fact that time was passing. They had to search for a good while before finding the last two chests, for they had sunk down into the gravel in the river bed; but at last they discovered these, too, and stacked all the treasure into the wagon.

By this time, the better part of the night was gone, and as soon as they started on their homeward journey their old fear of the Patzinaks once more came over them.

'They will come as soon as it is light,' said Spof.

'Orm's luck is better than that of most men,' said Olof Summer-Bird, 'nor is mine among the worst. It may be that we shall avoid these Patzinaks altogether. For a long time has now passed since the two horsemen saw us, and since that moment we have not seen a single man. This may mean that the Patzinaks are now waiting for us below the bottom weir, where the portage ends; for they could not know that we were only intending to come halfway before turning back. They will not pursue us until they have realized their mistake, and, if all goes well, we shall by that time have reached our ship safely.'

But in this he proved a false prophet, although his words almost came true; for, a short while after daybreak, when they were but a little way from the ship, they heard a great thunder of hoofs behind them, and turned to see the Patzinaks riding after them like Odin's storm.

Orm bade his men halt and position themselves in front of the wagon with their bows drawn. The men were in the best of spirits, and ready to fight for their silver with all the Patzinaks in the Eastland.

'No stranger shall touch this wagon, as long as four or five of us are left alive to defend it,' they said stolidly.

But the Patzinaks were cunning, and difficult to mark; for, instead of riding straight at the Northmen, they whipped their horses up to a full gallop and rode past them at the distance of a bowshot, releasing their arrows as they thundered by. Then they reassembled and, after a brief pause, repeated the manœuvre in the opposite direction. Most of Orm's men were skilled huntsmen, and expert with a bow, so that they were able to give a good account of themselves, and a great shout of triumph arose from them every time an enemy tumbled from his horse. But sometimes it happened that a Patzinak arrow, too, found its mark, and after a time Orm and Olof agreed that, if things continued in this wise, they would not be able to hold out for much longer.

Between two attacks, Orm called Blackhair and Glad Ulf to him. They had both been grazed by arrows, but were in good heart, and each proudly declared that he had killed his man. By good fortune, at the place where they had halted the rocks dropped steeply down to the river, so that they were secured against attack from that direction. Orm now bade the boys creep down the rocks and run along the bank as fast as they could to where the ship was anchored. Then they were to shout across the water to Toke and tell him to come at once to their aid, bringing with him every man on board.

'Whether this adventure will end well depends on you,' he said. 'For our arrows will not last much longer.'

Proud at being entrusted with so important a mission, the boys obeyed, and made swiftly down the rocks. Soon the Patzinaks attacked again, and during this assault Olof Summer-Bird fell with an arrow in his chest. It had penetrated his mail-shirt and was embedded in his flesh.

'That was shrewdly aimed,' he said. 'You will have to fight the rest of this battle without my assistance.'

As he spoke, his knees bent suddenly beneath him, but he managed to remain on his feet and, climbing on to the wagon, lay down upon it, resting his head on one of the sacks of silver. Other wounded men were already sprawled there among the sacks and chests of treasure.

The next time the Patzinaks swept past, Orm's men shot their last arrows at them. As they did so, however, they heard from behind them a great cry of joy.

'The old man's prophecy is fulfilled,' cried several voices. 'Finn Sonesson has fallen! There is an arrow through his throat, and he is already dead! Kolbjörn, his brother, fell but a few moments ago. Four are now gone; the rest of us cannot die, before we have returned home!'

And it turned out as they said, for, as they ceased crying, the others heard the sound of war-whoops from the direction of the ship, signifying that Toke had landed with his men. The sight of them seemed to slake the Patzinaks' thirst for battle, for, as Orm's men ran eagerly to search for spent arrows which might be used again, they heard the thunder of hoofs grow fainter instead of louder, and at last die away in the distance.

Orm ordered his men not to kill any of the men who lay wounded on the ground.

'Let them remain where they lie,' he said, 'until their kinsmen come to collect them.'

Their own wounded, those who were unable to walk, were lying in the wagon. Seven others lay dead on the ground, and these the men took up and carried with them, that they might give them honourable burial as soon as the opportunity arose. In the meantime, however, they made haste to return to the ship before the Patzinaks should return.

Faste's scribe had disappeared; but, when they went to pull the cart forward, they discovered him asleep beneath it. He was roused with a spear-shaft, and was much mocked. He said that this fight had been no concern of his, since he was a state official whose business was collecting taxes, and he had not wished to be in anyone's way, besides which, he had been tired after the night's marching. The men admitted that it testified to his calmness of mind that he had been able to sleep throughout the battle.

They soon met Toke and his men, and there was great rejoicing on both sides. Toke had disposed of the enemy without much difficulty; as soon as he had come against them with war-whoops and arrows, they had turned and fled. The men thought it possible that they, too, had used up all their arrows.

When they arrived at the ship Orm looked around him. 'Where are the two boys?' he asked Toke.

'The boys?' replied Toke. 'You had them with you.'

'I sent them along the bank to call you to our aid,' said Orm, in a changed voice.

'What can have become of them?' said Toke, scratching his beard. 'I heard hoof-beats and war-cries and saw the Patzinaks ride towards us and wheel their horses, and at once rowed ashore to help you. But I have seen nothing of the boys.'

One of Toke's men said that, just before the ship had reached the bank, he had seen three Patzinaks emerge on foot from among the rocks, dragging something along; dead men, he had supposed, or possibly prisoners. They had dragged them towards their horses; but, he said, he had not given the matter more thought, because at that moment the ship had touched land and he had started thinking about the forthcoming battle.

Orm stood speechless. He took off his helmet and let it drop to the ground; then he sat down on a stone on the bank, and stared into the river. There he sat, motionless, and none of the men dared speak to him.

The men stood muttering amongst themselves and gazed at him; and even Toke knew not what to say. Spof and Faste's scribe carried the wounded aboard.

At length Orm rose to his feet. He walked up to Toke and unclipped from his belt his sword, Blue-Tongue. All the men opened their mouths in fear as they saw him do this.

'I am going to the Patzinaks,' he said. 'Wait here with the ship for three days. If Blackhair returns, give the sword to him. If none of us returns, take it home for Harald.'

Toke took the sword.

'This is bad,' he said.

'Divide the treasure fairly,' said Orm, 'as it would have been divided had I lived. It has brought little luck to us of Toste's line.'

CHAPTER EIGHT

How Orm met an old friend

Orm took Faste's scribe with him, and went to search among the fallen Patzinaks. They found one who was wounded but not dead, a young man, who had received an arrow in the side and another in the knee. He appeared to be in good heart, for he was sitting up and gnawing a piece of dried meat, with a long wooden flask in his other hand, while his horse grazed beside him.

This man was able to understand something of what the scribe said and was pleased when he learned that they had not come to take his head. Orm bade the scribe say that they wished to help him on to his horse and accompany him back to his village. After the scribe had repeated this message several times, the Patzinak nodded and pointed at his knee. The arrow had gone right through it, just behind the knee-cap, so that the head was sticking out from the inner side of his leg. He had, he explained by gestures, tried to pull it out, but had not been able to do so. Orm cut the leg of his skin breeches, and worked the arrow a little, pushing it further into the knee until the whole of the metal head appeared, so that it might be cut off and the shaft drawn out from the other side. The Patzinak snapped his fingers as Orm did this, and whistled slowly; then, when the operation was completed, he set his flask to his mouth and drained it. The other arrow he had succeeded in extracting himself.

Orm took from his belt a fistful of silver and gave it to the man. His face lit up at the sight of it, and he seized it eagerly.

Near to them there stood other horses, waiting patiently by the bodies of their fallen masters. They moved away as Orm and the scribe approached them; but when the Patzinak called them with a special whistle they came willingly to him and allowed halters to be put round their necks.

They helped the wounded man on to his horse. He crooked his wounded leg up on the saddle, and appeared not to be troubled by it. The scribe was unwilling to go with them, but Orm told him curtly to do as he was told.

'If you protest, I shall wring your neck,' he said. 'It is I, not you, who am to become their prisoner.'

The scribe mumbled that this sort of thing was no fit occupation for a state officer whose concern was collecting taxes; he obeyed, however, and no more was said about this.

They rode away into the grassland, which was the Patzinaks' domain. Orm said afterwards that a man might search long for a worse land, and not succeed; for there were no trees or water, beasts or men to be seen there, but only grass and the empty air above it, and, occasionally, a kind of large rat that slunk away among the tussocks. Twice the Patzinak reined in his horse, pointed to the ground and said something to the scribe, who then dismounted from his horse and pulled up the plants that the Patzinak had indicated. These, which were broad-bladed, the Patzinak then wrapped round his wounded knee, and bound them fast with a bowstring. This seemed to soothe the pain of his wound, so that he was able to ride on without becoming exhausted.

When the sun had climbed to half of its midday height, they reached the Patzinak camp. It lay in a hollow on either side of a stream, along the banks of which their tents stood in their hundreds. As they approached, hounds began to bay and children to yell, and the camp suddenly became full of horses and men. The Patzinak rode proudly in with his prisoners; then, when they had helped him from his horse, he showed the silver he had received and pointed at Orm.

Orm told the scribe to say that he wished to speak with their chieftain. At first, nobody appeared to understand what he said, but at length a little, bandy-legged man appeared who understood him and was able to reply in the scribe's own tongue.

'Tell him this,' said Orm to the scribe. 'Both my sons, who are very young, were captured by you during the battle at the weirs last night. I am a chieftain, and have come to buy them free. I have come unarmed, as a proof of my peaceful intentions and good faith.'

The bandy-legged man pulled thoughtfully at his long cheek-beard, and exchanged a word or two with the wounded man who had brought them. Their talk sounded to Orm's ears more like the clucking of owls than the speech of men, but they seemed to be able to understand one another without difficulty. Many of those who stood watching grinned broadly at Orm, and took out their knives and drew them across their throats. This, said Orm afterwards, was the worst moment of his life, for he took it to mean that they had already cut the throats of their prisoners; though he hoped that it might merely signify that they intended to perform the operation on him. This seemed to him by far the lesser evil, if, by allowing this to happen, he could enable Blackhair to go free.

He said to the scribe: 'Ask him whether his two captives are still alive.'

The bandy-legged man nodded, and shouted to three men, who stepped forward. These were the men who owned the prisoners.

Orm said: 'Tell them that I wish to buy their prisoners for much silver. They are my sons.'

The three men began to jabber, but the bandy-legged man said that it would be best that Orm and the scribe should go with him to the chieftains. They came to three tents which were larger than the rest, and followed the little man into the centre one.

Three old men, wearing furs and with shaven heads, were seated on a sheep-skin on the ground, their legs crossed beneath them, eating a mess from a large clay bowl. When they had entered, the bandy-legged man halted, and signed to Orm and the scribe to remain silent. The three old men ate greedily, blowing on their spoons and smacking their lips with relish. When the bowl was empty they licked their spoons and stuffed them into holes in their furs. Then, at last, they condescended to notice that somebody had come in.

One of them nodded at the bandy-legged man. He bowed to the ground, and began to speak, while the chieftains sat listening with dull expressions, giving vent to an occasional belch.

The one who sat in the middle was smaller than the other two and had very large ears. Tilting his head to one side, he stared piercingly at Orm. At length, the bandy-legged man stopped talking, and there was a silence. Then the little chieftain croaked a few words, and the bandy-legged man bowed reverently and went out, taking the scribe with him.

When they had gone, the little chieftain said slowly: 'You are welcome here, Orm Tostesson, though it is better that we should conceal the fact that we know each other. It is a long time since we last met. Is Ylva, King Harald's daughter, who played as a child upon my knees, still alive?'

Orm drew a deep breath. He had recognised the little man as soon as he had begun to speak. It was Felimid, King Harald's Irish jester.

'She is alive,' replied Orm, 'and remembers you well. It is her son who is one of your prisoners here. This is certainly a strange meeting, and one that may prove lucky for us both. Are you a chieftain among these Patzinaks?'

Felimid nodded.

'When one is old, one must take the best that comes,' he said. 'But I cannot really complain.'

He spoke to his two fellow chieftains, turned round and shouted towards the back of the tent. A woman entered with a great drinking cup, which they passed around and which soon became empty. The woman filled it again; then, when it had again been emptied, the other two chieftains rose with difficulty to their feet and tottered out.

'They will sleep now,' said Felimid to Orm, when they were alone. 'It is so with these people that they easily become drunk, and then they at once fall asleep and remain thus for half the day. They are simple souls. Now you and I can sit and talk here undisturbed. You have had a long ride and are, perhaps, hungry?'

'You have guessed rightly,' said Orm. 'Since I recognised you my anxiety has been lightened, and the three things that I long for most are to see my son again and to eat and drink.'

'You shall see him as soon as we have decided the question of his ransom,' said Felimid. 'This will, I fear, cost you silver; for if I commanded otherwise, the whole tribe would become enraged with me. But first, you shall be my guest.'

He shouted orders, and six women entered and began to set out food on a mat which they spread on the floor of the tent.

'These are my wives,' explained Felimid. 'They may seem a lot for an old man; but such is the custom here. And I must have something to keep me amused, now that Ferdiad is dead and I can no longer practise my art.'

'This is sad news about your brother,' said Orm. 'How did he die? And how did you come here?'

'Eat, and I will tell you; I have already eaten enough. We have no ale, alas, but here is a drink we make from mare's milk. Taste it, you have drunk worse.'

It was a clear drink, with a sweet-sour taste, and Orm thought it would be difficult to find kind words to say of it; however, he soon noticed that there was good strength in it.

Felimid made Orm eat all the food that had been brought, and shouted to the women to bring more. Meanwhile, he told what had happened to him and his brother since they had trudged away from Gröning.

'We roamed widely,' he said, 'as we told you we would when last we parted; and at last we came to the great Prince in Kiev. We remained in his palace for two years, delighting all men wth our arts and earning great honour; but then we began to notice that we were putting on flesh. At this, we were greatly afraid, and determined to leave, although everybody begged us to remain, because we wished, while our skill yet remained to us, to perform before the great Emperor at Miklagard, as had been our intention from the beginning. But we never reached him, for at the weirs we were taken by the Patzinaks. They found us too old to be of any use and wanted to kill us, so as to be able to set up our heads upon poles, as is their custom. But we displayed our arts before them, the simplest that we know, until they prostrated themselves on their bellies in a circle around us and worshipped us as gods. Nevertheless, they would not let us go; and, as soon as we had learned something of their language, they made us chieftains, because of our wisdom and knowledge of witchcraft. We soon grew accustomed to our new life, for it is easier to be a chieftain than a jester; besides which, we had realised for some time that old age was, at last, beginning to stiffen our limbs. The great Archbishop Cormac MacCullenan spoke truly when he said, long ago: "A wise man, once he is past fifty, does not befuddle his senses with strong drink, nor make violent love in the cool spring night, nor dance upon his hands."'

Felimid took a draught from his cup, and nodded sadly.

'He spoke too truly,' he said, 'and my brother Ferdiad forgot this warning when one of his women produced male twins. Then he drank deeply of this yeasty mare's-milk and danced upon his hands before all the people, like the King of the Jews before God; and, in the midst of his dance, he fell and remained lying, and when we lifted him up he was dead. I mourned him deeply, and mourn him still; though nobody can deny that it was a worthy death for a master jester to die. Ever since then, I have remained here with these Patzinaks, in peace and contentment. They are like children, and venerate me deeply, and seldom oppose my will except when they go head-hunting, which is an ancient custom with them which they will not abandon. But now tell me how it has been with you and yours.'

Orm told him all that he wished to know. When, however, he came to speak of the treasure at the weirs, he thought it best to mention only the three sacks of silver; for he did not wish to pay more than need be when it came to fixing the ransom for Blackhair and Ulf. Lastly, he described the battle with the Patzinaks. When he had concluded, Felimid said: 'It is lucky that your son and foster son were taken alive. This was because of their youth; the men who captured them hoped to make a good profit by selling them to the Arabs or the Byzantines. You must, therefore, be prepared to pay a large price for them. It is lucky that you have the treasure within easy reach.'

'I shall pay whatever price you name,' said Orm. 'It is no more than right that a large sum should be demanded for King Harald's grandson.'

'I have not myself seen the boy,' said Felimid, 'for I do not bother myself with the thefts and rapes of my subjects, except where absolutely necessary. They are always capturing men and treasure at these weirs. But it is time for us to settle this matter without delay.'

They went out of the tent, and Felimid shouted orders to this man and that. The two other chieftains were awakened, and emerged sleepy-eyed; then, when they and Felimid had seated themselves on a grass slope, all the people in the camp came running to the place and grouped themselves around them in a tight circle. Then the two prisoners were led forth by their captors. They were both pale, and Blackhair had blood in his hair; but their faces lit up as they saw Orm and the first thing that Blackhair said was: 'Where is your sword?'

'I came here unarmed, to obtain your release,' said Orm. 'Because it was my fault that you were captured.'

'They came on us from behind among the rocks,' said Blackhair sadly, 'and we could offer no resistance.'

'They clubbed us,' said Glad Ulf, 'after which we knew nothing until we awoke to find ourselves bound upon horses.'

Felimid now spoke to the other chieftains, and to the boys' captors, and a long argument followed as to the amount of the ransom Orm should pay.

'It is our custom,' explained Felimid to Orm, 'that all those who have taken part in the fighting shall have their share of the ransom, while those who have actually captured the prisoners shall have a double share. I have told them that Blackhair is your son, and that you are a chieftain among your people; but I have not told them that he is a great King's grandson, for if they knew this there would be no end to their demands.'

At length, it was agreed that they should ride to the ship the next day, and that Glad Ulf should be ransomed with as much silver as could be contained in four of the Patzinaks' tall hats. For Blackhair, though, they demanded his weight in silver.

Orm thought this an exorbitant sum to demand, even for so important a person as his son. But when he remembered his feelings of the morning, after he had learned that Blackhair had been captured, he reflected that, on the whole, things had turned out better than he could have expected.

'He is sparely built,' said Felimid consolingly. 'You would have to dive deeper into those sacks of yours if you yourself had to be weighed. And a son is worth more than any amount of silver. I can see from his looks that he is Ylva's child. It is a great grief to me that I have no son. I had one, but he died young, and now I have only daughters. Ferdiad's sons will have to succeed me as chieftains.'

Later that day the Patzinaks went to the camp which the Northmen had pitched by the weirs, to fetch their wounded. Their dead they left lying where they had fallen, for it was not their custom to bury them, save when a great chieftain had died. But they were vexed that the Northmen had taken away their dead, thus depriving the men who had killed them of their heads, and declared that it was only right that Orm should pay them for robbing them of their lawful trophies.

Felimid upbraided them for making this demand, which he found unreasonable. When, however, they persisted, he said to Orm that it would be unwise to press the point too strongly, for their greed for heads was a kind of madness with them, against which no amount of reason would prevail.

Orm disliked acceding to this request, and thought that these Patzinaks looked likely to skin him to the bone; but since he was in their hands, he thought it would be unwise of him to refuse. He reflected miserably that his silver-sacks would become much lightened by the time he had paid the large sum demanded for the boys' ransom and had given each of his men their share. After he had pondered the matter for a while, he hit upon a solution of the problem.

'I shall pay them for my men's heads, since you so counsel me,' he said, 'and will give them a sum the size of which will surprise them. When we were taking the sacks out of the river, we were in a great hurry, for we feared we might be attacked and outnumbered. In our haste we burst one of the sacks, so that most of its contents ran out into the water; and it contained nothing but fair silver coins. We had no time to gather up this money, so that at least a third of it is still lying there on the river bed; and, if your men are not afraid of water, they will be able to fish themselves great wealth there.'

He described the place, and how they would easily find it by the stones lying on the rock-flats, where they had put them after dragging them out of the water. Felimid translated his words to the gathering, and before he had finished all the young men of the tribe were rushing to their horses so as to be the first to arrive at the place and dive for these unusual fish.

When these questions had been decided, Felimid suggested

that they should dine and make merry together, for old times' sake. He spoke much of King Harald and of his brother Ferdiad, and recalled the time he had visited Orm at Gröning and helped Father Willibald to convert the heathens after dinner in the church.

'But now that the Erin Masters have ceased to jest,' he said, 'there are no good jesters left in the world. For we had no brothers, but were the last of the line of O'Flann, who had jested before kings ever since the days of King Conchobar MacNessa. In my loneliness here I have tried to teach some of the young Patzinaks something of my art, but have failed. The boys can do nothing at all, and, when I turned in despair to the girls and tried to teach them to dance like a master jester, I found them too stupid to be able to follow my instructions, although I took pains with them and showed them how everything should be done. However, they were not quite so hopeless as the boys of this tribe, and one of them got as far as being able to dance reasonably on her hands, and pipe the while. But that was the most she could attain to; and neither her piping nor the movements of her legs were all that could be desired.'

He spat meditatively, and shook his head.

'Although she was but a novice in the art, and will never be more,' he said, 'she became so vain of her supposed skill that she performed incessantly, until at last I grew tired of her and packed her off as a gift to Gzak. This Gzak you have doubtless heard of, for he is one of the three mightiest men in the whole world. He is the Overlord of all the Patzinaks, and mostly grazes his flocks around Krim. Being a simple soul, who knows little about the arts, he was delighted with the girl. Then he sent her to the Emperor at Miklagard, as a thanks-gift for all the friendship-money which the Emperor had sent him. In Miklagard there must indeed be a dearth of dancers and jesters, for she danced before the Emperor himself and his court and won great praise and fame until, after a year, her vanity became such that she died for it. But my troubles are not at an end, for last winter Gzak sent messengers to me bidding me send him two new dancers of equal skill, to replace her at Miklagard; and my whole time is spent in training them. Their stupidity and clumsiness nauseate me, though I chose them carefully, and they are nothing for you to see, who have watched me and my brother display our art. If, though, you would care to look at them, I have no objection to their appearing; they may amuse your sons.'

Orm said that he would like to see them, and Felimid shouted orders. When the members of the tribe heard what he said, they began to clap and cheer.

'The whole tribe is proud of them,' said Felimid dolefully, 'and their mothers wash them in sweet milk every morning, to make their skins clear. But they will never learn to dance properly, whatever pains I may expend upon them.'

Mats were spread out on the ground in front of the chieftains, and men brought flaming torches. Then the dancers appeared, and were greeted with a great sigh of anticipation from all the tribesmen. They were well-shaped, and appeared to be about thirteen or fourteen years old. They wore red hats over their dark hair, and strings of green glass beads round their breasts, and were dressed in broad breeches of yellow silk from the land of the Seres, tied at the ankles.

'It is a long time since I last saw dancing girls,' said Orm. 'Not since I served my lord Almansur. But I do not think I ever saw any of a more engaging appearance than these.'

'It is not by their appearance, but by their dancing, that they are to be judged,' said Felimid. 'But I designed their costumes myself, and think them not displeasing.'

The dancers had with them two boys of the same age as themselves, who squatted on their haunches and began to blow upon pipes. As the music started, the girls began to hop around in the torchlight, to the time of the pipes, strutting and giving sudden leaps and bouncing backwards and twirling round on one leg, so that everybody except Felimid sat entranced. When the girls stopped, great applause broke out, and they looked gratified when they observed that the strangers, too, appeared pleased with their performance. Then they glanced timidly at Felimid. He nodded towards them, as though satisfied, and turned to Orm.

'I cannot tell them what I really feel,' he explained, 'for it would make them miserable, and the whole tribe with them. And they are doing their best this evening, with strangers present. But the pipers pain me more than the girls, although they are Kazar slaves who have been given much leisure for practice, and the

Kazars are said to be skilful pipers. But this is evidently a false reputation.'

The girls began to dance anew, but after a while Felimid shouted angrily at them, so that they ceased.

'I am glad my brother Ferdiad was spared this,' he said to Orm. 'He had a more tender ear than I.'

He said something to the pipers, and one of them came over and handed him his pipe.

As Felimid set his lips to it, it seemed as though witchcraft entered into its reeds. It was as though he piped of joy and luck, jests and laughter, the beauty of women and the gleam of swords, the shimmer of morning upon a lake and the wind blowing over spring grasses. Blackhair and Ulf sat rocking backwards and forwards, as though they had difficulty in remaining seated; the two chieftains sitting on either side of Felimid nodded piously and fell asleep; the Patzinaks stamped their feet and clapped their hands rhythmically, some laughing, others crying; and the dancing girls spun and hovered as though they had been translated into thistledown by the notes of Felimid's pipe.

At last he took the pipe from his lips, and twitched his huge ears contentedly.

'I have played worse,' he said.

'It is my belief,' said Orm, 'that there is still no master in the world who can compare with you, and it is not surprising that these men worshipped you from the moment you came among them. But it is beyond any man's power to understand how you can conjure such music as that from this simple pipe.'

'It comes from the goodness which is in the wood of the pipe, when the pipe is truly made,' said Felimid, 'and that goodness is revealed when the pipe is blown by someone who has a similar goodness in his soul, as well as patience to seek out the secrets that lie hidden within the pipe. But there must be no wood in his soul.'

Faste's scribe ran forward and, falling on his knees before Felimid, besought him to lend him the pipe. There were tears running down his cheeks.

'What do you want it for?' asked Felimid. 'Can you play a pipe?'

'No,' said the scribe. 'I am a state official, employed in the department of taxes. But I shall learn. I wish to remain with you and play a pipe.'

Felimid handed him the pipe. He set it to his mouth, and began to blow. He managed to produce a tiny squeak, but no more, and the Patzinaks contorted their bodies with laughter at his futile endeavours. But he continued to blow, his face pale and his eyes staring, while Felimid gazed earnestly at him.

'Do you see anything?' asked Felimid.

The scribe handed him back the pipe. Shaking with sobs, he replied: 'I see only that which you lately blew upon.'

Felimid nodded.

'You may stay,' he said. 'I will teach you. When I have finished training these girls, I shall make you good enough to play before the Emperor himself. You may keep the pipe.'

So the evening ended; and next morning, Felimid rode with his guests to the ship, with a great host of Patzinaks accompanying them. But before they took their leave of him, Felimid gave them all parting gifts. To Orm, Blackhair and Ulf he gave each a knife, with gold engraving on the hilts and cunningly worked silver sheaths; and for Ylva, he gave them a bale of Serean silk. They thanked him for his gifts, and thought it a bad thing that they had no fine present to give him in return as a token of friendship.

'I take pleasure in few things,' said Felimid, 'and gold and silver are not among them. So it matters little that you have nothing to give me, for I do not need gifts to be sure of your friendship. There is, though, now that I think of it, one thing that I should like to have, if you should ever find an opportunity to send it to me. Are your great hounds still alive?'

Orm said that they were, and in good health, and that there had been fourteen of them when he had left home. Then Felimid said: 'Soon, Blackhair, you will be a full-fledged warrior, and it cannot be long before you will set forth on a long voyage of your own, now that you have started so young. It may be that you will journey to Kiev, or perhaps to Miklagard. If this should happen, bring two or three of the great hounds with you, as a present for me. That would be a friendship-gift that I would cherish indeed, and I cannot think of one that would give me greater pleasure; for they come from Erin, which is my home also.'

Blackhair promised that he would do this, if he came again to the Eastland; then they broke camp, and turned their faces once again to the north. Faste's scribe nodded abstractedly at them as they rode away, his mind being otherwise occupied; for he was sitting with the Kazar slaves, practising busily upon his pipe. Both Blackhair and Ulf would have liked to have stayed longer with the Patzinaks, to watch the dancers and partake in other pleasures with them; but Orm was impatient to get back to his ship and his men, for he felt half-naked, he said, and a mean man, without Blue-Tongue at his waist.

When they reached the river, the Patzinaks halted a short way from the bank, so that there should be no trouble between them and Orm's men; but neither the men who had captured Blackhair and Ulf nor the rest of the band would release their prisoners before the ransom had been paid in full. Orm went alone towards the ship, and when the men aboard saw him they raised joyous cries and put out a boat. Toke handed him his sword and asked eagerly how he had fared. Orm told him how he had met Felimid and how they had settled the whole matter between them, including the amount of the ransom they were to pay for Blackhair and Ulf.

Toke laughed with joy.

'Our luck, too, has been nothing to complain of,' he said, 'and you need waste no silver to free the boys. We have nine Patzinaks aboard, bound hand and foot, and they will be more than sufficient ransom for our two.'

He added that Spof and Long Staff and many of the others had been unable to rest for thinking of all the silver that had been spilled into the water.

'They begged and badgered me,' he said, 'until at last I yielded. Spof went with twenty men along the right bank, where there was no danger of their being attacked. Midway between the two weirs, they crossed the river, at a place where the water was so shallow that they scarcely needed to swim, and crept stealthily through the dusk to the place where the treasure lay. Then they heard merry shouts, and saw horses grazing, and came upon these Patzinaks as they were fishing up the silver. We captured the lot of them without difficulty, for they were unarmed and we seized them before they could climb out of the water. With them, we captured all the silver that they had fished out. We were just debating whether to free one of them and send him back to his people to obtain the release of you and the boys.'

Orm said that this was, indeed, good news, although he doubted whether the Patzinaks would think so. He stood for a while pondering.

'I shall not demand ransom for these prisoners,' he said, 'and no man in the ship shall lose by this, but only I myself. But they shall not be released until the boys are freed.'

'You are a great chieftain,' said Toke, 'and must act like one. But in this, you are being generous to men who do not deserve such treatment. For it was they who attacked us, in the first place, and not we them.'

'You do not know Felimid,' said Orm. 'He is worth much generosity. This matter shall be settled the way I wish it.'

So he and Toke fetched a sack of silver and carried it between them to the waiting Patzinaks. When they saw what the sack contained, the Patzinaks ran around measuring each other's hats, to find the biggest. But Felimid grew vexed at this, and took off his own hat and ordered that the silver should be measured out in that; nor did they dare to say that it should be otherwise.

The men were sent to search among the pieces of timber which lay on the ground at the beginning of the dragging-tracks, and returned shortly with a plank. This was placed across a stone and axed so that it weighed evenly on either side. Then Blackhair sat on one end of it. The Patzinaks lay saddle-bags across the other end, and into these Toke poured silver from the sack until Blackhair's end was lifted from the ground. All the Patzinaks, said Felimid, agreed that this business of the weighing had been carried out in a chieftain-like manner, for they realised that, if Blackhair had taken his clothes off before sitting on the plank, Orm would thereby have saved silver, and nobody could have complained that he was acting dishonourably.

When the weighing was completed, Toke went back to the ship with the silver that remained, and Orm said to Felimid: 'I have enjoyed a deal of luck since I started on this voyage, and not the least of it was that I met you. When we rode from your camp, you gave us friendship-gifts, and now I have one to offer you in return. You see these men?'

Toke had freed his prisoners, and Felimid and his men stared at them in amazement.

'They are the men who rode out to fish for silver,' said Orm. 'My men went on a similar errand, and captured them at the fishing-place. But I give them back to you free of ransom, although I doubt not that many men would think me foolish to do so. But I have no wish to haggle with you, Felimid.'

'You are worth all your luck,' said Felimid, 'and that is a great deal.'

'I shall bring the great hounds with me, none the less,' said Blackhair, 'the next time I pass this way. And that may not be long hence, for now that I have been weighed in silver I consider myself a full man.'

'Be sure you have dancing-girls washed in milk ready to greet us,' said Glad Ulf, 'at least as pretty as the ones we saw to-day.'

Felimid scratched behind his ear.

'That is all you think me capable of,' he said, 'to provide dancing girls for you on your return. I shall choose the ugliest I can find, and have them steeped in horse-droppings, lest you foolish children should take it into your heads to steal them from old Felimid, after all the pains he has taken to train them.'

They said farewell to the master jester and his Patzinaks and returned to the ship. Then they weighed anchor, and started on their homeward voyage. The wounded among them seemed to be on the way to recovery, and even Olof Summer-Bird, who was the worst hurt, was in good heart. The men pulled at their oars with a will, although they knew they had a long row ahead of them against the current. Sone's seven sons were the merriest of all, although they had the bodies of their two dead brothers aboard, intending to bury them at their first camp with the men who had been killed by the bees. Toke thought that this had, indeed, been a strange voyage, for they had come a long way and won a great treasure, and yet Red-Jowl had not left her sheath. He thought, though, they might find themselves somewhat busier on the way home, with so much gold aboard. Ulf and Blackhair sat happily on the deck, telling the other men of all that had happened to them while they had been prisoners of the Patzinaks. Orm, alone, wore a thoughtful face.

504

'Do you regret having let those prisoners go without ransom?' asked Toke.

'No,' replied Orm. 'What troubles me is that my luck has been too good, so that I begin to fear that all may not be as it should be at home. It would be good to know how things are there.'

CHAPTER NINE

Concerning their journey home, and how Olof Summer-Bird vowed to become a Christian

They buried their dead, in ground where their bodies would not be disturbed, and journeyed up the great river without adventure, getting good help from wind and sail. Olof Summer-Bird remained sorely sick; he had no appetite for food, and his wound healed slowly, so that there was talk among them of putting in at Kiev in order that men skilled in medicine might examine him. But he himself would not hear of this, being as anxious as Orm and the others to reach home swiftly. The men rowed past the city without complaint, for they all now regarded themselves as rich men, and had no desire to hazard their silver among foreigners.

When they reached the Beaver River, and the rowing became hard, Blackhair took his turn with the others, saying that he was henceforth to be treated as a grown man. The work was heavy for him, but, although his hands were skinned, he did not desist until the time came for him to be relieved. For this, he won praise even from Spof, who seldom said an approving word about anyone.

At the portage they found plenty of oxen, in the village where they had bespoken them, so that, this time, they had less difficulty in dragging the ship overland. When they reached the Dregovites' village, where the bees and bears were, they rested for three days at their old camping-ground, and sent messengers to the village to beg the wise old women to come and look at Olof's wounds, which had been made worse by the bumping of the ship during the drag. They came willingly, examined the wound, opened it and dripped into it a juice made of crushed ants and wormwood, which made him scream aloud with the pain. This, the crones said, was a good sign; the worse

506

he shrieked, the better the medicine. They smeared it with a salve of beaver's fat, and gave him a bitter drink, which greatly strengthened him.

Then they returned to their village, and came back with a great quantity of fresh hay and two plump young women. The crones undressed Olof, washed him in birch-sap, and bedded him in the hay with a bear-skin under him and one of the two young women on either side of him to keep him warm; then they gave him more of the bitter drink, and covered the three of them with ox-hides. He fell asleep almost immediately, and slept thus for two nights and a day in great warmth; and, as soon as he awoke, the young women cried that his health was returning to him. The crones were richly paid for this; and the young women, too, were well rewarded, though they steadfastly refused to perform the same service for any of the other men.

Olof Summer-Bird recovered swiftly after this. By the time they reached the city of the Polotjans, his wound was healed, and he was able to eat and drink as well as the best of them. Here the chieftains visited Faste again, and told him what had happened to his scribe; but the news did not appear to trouble him greatly.

In this town, the men felt as though at home. They remained there for three days, drinking and love-making, to the profit and delight of all the people there. Then, as the leaves were beginning to fall, they rowed down at their leisure to the mouth of the Dyna, reaching the sea just as the first frost-nights came.

One morning, off Osel, they were attacked by Estonian pirates in four small ships full of howling men. Spof saw them as they emerged out of the mist, and straightway bade the men at the oars pull as hard as they could; then, as the pirates drew abreast, two off either bow, and prepared to grapple, he swung the helm smartly round and rammed one of them so that those aboard her had to pull smartly for the shore, sinking swiftly. One of the others succeeded in grappling Orm's ship, but no sooner had they done this than Sone's seven sons swarmed over into the pirate ship, shieldless and whooping triumphantly, and hewed about them so furiously with sword and axe that they cleared the ship of its occupants well nigh unaided. When the other pirates saw this happen, they realised that they had encountered berserks, and rowed hastily away.

Sone's sons were much praised for this feat, but several of them

507

climbed back over the gunwale in an ill humour, cursing the old man their father. One of them had lost two fingers, another's cheek had been split by a spear, a third had had his nose pulped, and scarcely one of them had come through unscathed. Those of them who had been wounded most severely said that the old man was to blame for this, having lured them by his prophecy into attempting too much; for they had assumed that they would suffer no hurt. But the others spoke against them, saying that the old man had promised no more than that seven of them should return home alive; he had said nothing about wounds and scratches. It looked as though there was going to be fighting between the brothers, but Orm and Toke calmed them with wise words, and they proceeded on their journey without more incident.

They had good weather all the way from Osel to the river mouth, and made the whole journey under sail. Meanwhile, Orm measured out silver to every man aboard, both their hire-money and their share of the treasure. No one was discontented, for he gave each man more than he had expected to receive.

One morning at dawn, as Toke stood at the steering-oar and the rest of the men were sleeping, Orm seated himself beside him, and it was plain from his face that he was heavy-hearted.

'Most men would be merry in your clothes,' said Toke. 'Everything has gone well, you have won a great treasure, and we shall soon be home.'

'My mind is troubled,' said Orm, 'though I cannot say why. Perhaps it is the gold that makes me uneasy.'

'How can the gold make you uneasy?' said Toke. 'You are now as rich as a king, and kings do not hang their heads because their wealth is great.'

'There is too much of it,' said Orm gloomily. 'You and Olof shall both have your good shares, but even so, too much will remain for me. I have deceived the men, telling them that the chests contain trash for women, and my lie will bring me bad luck.'

'You meet bad luck before it comes,' said Toke. 'None of us yet knows what the chests contain; it may be only silver. It was wise of you to say that they contained women's trash, and I should have done the same in your clothes; for even the best of men become crazed when they know that gold is near.'

'Before God,' said Orm, 'I now make this vow. I shall open one of

508

these chests; and, if it contains gold, I shall divide it among the men. We shall then have three chests left, one of which shall be yours, one Olof's, and the third mine. Now that I have said that, I feel better.'

'You shall do as you please,' said Toke. 'As for me, I shall no longer need to be a skin-trader.'

Orm fetched one of the small chests, set it down on the deck between them, and cut away the red ropes that were sealed with the Emperor's seal. The chest was strongly locked, but Orm drove his knife and Toke's under the lid and leaned upon them with all his weight until the lock broke. Then he lifted the lid, and the two of them stared silently into the chest.

> 'Not Fafnir*
> In time of yore
> Guarded e'er
> A brood more bonny.'

said Toke reverently; and Orm remained silent, although usually, when Toke wrought a verse, it was his habit to reply with one as good or better.

The sun had, by now, risen, and its rays struck into the chest. It was filled with gold, which the river water had not tarnished. Most of it was coins, of many different sorts and sizes, filling the chest to its rim; but among them many precious ornaments lay bedded, rings great and small, chains, necklaces, clasps, bracelets and such-like, marvellously worked – 'like lovely pieces of pork,' thought Toke, 'in a soup of good pease.'

'This trash will please our women well enough when we bring it home,' he said. 'Indeed, I fear the sight of it may make them mad.'

'It will be no easy task to share this out,' said Orm.

The men had, by now, begun to wake up. Orm told them that one of the chests of women's trash was to be shared out amongst them, and that its contents were better than he had expected them to be.

The division of the gold lasted the whole day. Each man received

---

* The dragon who guarded the Nibelungs' gold.

eighty-six coins, of varying sizes; the same amount was held back for each man who had been killed, to be given to his heirs, and Spof got a helmsman's quadruple share. Sharing out the ornaments fairly proved a more difficult task, and sometimes they had no alternative but to chop rings and bracelets into pieces, to make sure that nobody received less than the next man; though often the men bargained with one another, giving coins in order that they might have the whole of some trinket which had particularly taken their fancy. One or two arguments began, but Orm said that they would have to wait till they reached land before fighting them out. Several of the men had never seen gold coins before; and, when Spof told them how much silver went to a piece of gold, they sat gazing foolishly at the deck, with their heads in their hands, unable to calculate how rich they were, although they racked their brains to do so.

When everything had at last been shared out, and the chest was empty, many of the men set to work with needle and twine to enlarge the pockets of their belts. Others rubbed and polished their gold, to make it brighter; and there was great cheerfulness among them as they talked of their luck and the fine homecoming they would have, and the deep drinking that would then take place.

They reached the river-mouth and rowed upstream until they came to the land of a farmer whom Orm knew. There, they dragged the ship on to the bank, amid the crunch of fresh night-ice, shedded her, and went about hiring horses. Some of the men departed for their homes, but the majority remained.

Spof was uncertain what to do. It might be best for him, he told Orm, to stay with this farmer, who was said to be a good man, until the spring, when he would be able to find a ship to take him home to Gotland.

'But it will be a sleepless winter for me,' he added, shaking his head gloomily. 'For what farmer is so good that he will not instantly kill me in my sleep as soon as he discovers what I have in my belt? Besides which, all men have a tendency to kill Gotlanders without asking them questions, because of the wealth which they think we all possess.'

'You shall come with me,' said Orm, 'and be my guest for the winter. It is no more than you have deserved. Then you can return to this place when spring comes, and find a ship home.'

Spof thanked him for this offer, and said that he would gladly accept it.

They rode their horses away; and it was difficult to guess whether Orm or Olof Summer-Bird was the more anxious to see Gröning again.

They came to a place where the road forked, and one of the paths led to Sone's house. But the seven brothers stood sourly scratching their heads. Orm asked them what might be troubling them.

'We are lucky now,' they replied, 'more so than other men. For we are rich, and know that we cannot die before we reach home. But as soon as we see the old man again, the spell is broken, and we can die as easily as anyone else. Before we left home, we had no fear of death: but things are different now, when we have so much gold to live for.'

'Then you shall come with me,' said Orm, 'and join with me in my homecoming-feast. You are good men, and it may be that I can find sleeping-room for you all until the spring. Then you can ride forth on a new adventure, if you feel so inclined, and thus live as long as you want to.'

Sone's sons accepted this offer gladly, and promised each other that it would be a long while before they revisited their father. Their best plan, they thought, would be to make another voyage to Gardariké.

'If that is your intention, come as my men,' said Blackhair. 'It will not be long before Ulf and I return there.'

'You are young to use the words of a chieftain,' said Orm. 'You must wait a while yet.'

As they drew near to Gröning, Orm's impatience increased, and he and Olof rode ahead of the others. The first sight that met their eyes was that of men repairing the great gate. Then they saw that the church had been burnt. At this, so great a fear came over Orm that he scarcely dared to ride up to the house. Then the men working on the gate saw him and uttered a glad cry, and Ylva came running from the house. It was good for him to see that she, at least, was safe.

'It is good that you have come home at last,' she said. 'But it would have been better if you had returned five days earlier.'

'Has bad luck come upon the house?' asked Orm.

'Bandits attacked us during the night,' she said, 'four days ago. Harald is wounded and Rapp dead, and three others besides. They took Ludmilla, and the necklace and much else, and three of my women. Father Willibald was clubbed on the head and is lying half dead. I managed to escape with the little ones and Oddny and Asa. We spent all the next day hiding in the forest. They were Smalanders, that I know. They took the cattle too, but the hounds went after them and came back with fourteen head. Asa thinks that things might have been unluckier, and I think so too, now that you have come safe home.'

'They are unlucky enough,' said Orm. 'Rapp dead, Ludmilla stolen, and the priest wounded almost to death.'

'And the necklace,' said Ylva.

'Do not grieve for that,' said Orm. 'You shall have all the trinkets you need. It is lucky that I have so many men still with me, for this business shall not go unavenged.'

'You speak the truth, Orm,' said Olof Summer-Bird. 'It shall not go unavenged. Does anyone know where the robbers came from?'

'Nobody knows anything,' said Ylva. 'Harald was wounded in the beginning of the fight, and dragged himself to the bath-house and remained lying there. Only Father Willibald may have something to tell us, if he ever recovers sufficiently to be able to do so. The strangest thing is that they set fire to the church only: he was down there when they hit him. They stole all they could lay their hands on, and we could tell from their voices that they were Smalanders. There were very many of them. They took their dead with them; five were killed by Rapp and his men, as they fought at the gate. That is all I know.'

Orm's men had by now reached the house, and Ylva laughed with joy to see Blackhair safe. The first thing Orm did was to send men on horseback to rich neighbours to beg them to lend food, for there was little left in the store-house, and nothing at all in the brew-house, as the result of the bandits' depredations.

Then he turned his attention to the wounded. Harald had received a spear in his chest and an axe-wound in his shoulder, but was in good heart. He assured them that he would soon be strong again, and said that what he most wanted was to hear Glad Ulf and Blackhair tell him of the adventures that had befallen them.

Asa sat with the priest, nursing him like a son. His head was swathed in bandages, and he was still half senseless. When he saw Orm, his eyes lightened, and he said in a weak voice: 'Welcome home!' but then drowsed back into unconsciousness. Asa said that he often mumbled to himself as he lay there, but that nobody could understand what he was saying.

The sight of Orm greatly revived her spirits, and she straightway began to reproach him for not having returned in time to avert this calamity. But when she heard that he had Are's treasure with him, her temper softened, and she thought that this had been a trivial attack compared with some she could remember from her young days. That Ludmilla had been stolen, she said, was only what she had always said would happen, because of the unlucky name they had given her. Father Willibald would, she was sure, recover, although he had been near to death, for sometimes, now, he understood what she said to him, which was a good sign. What worried her most was the empty storehouse and all the cattle that had been stolen.

Toke, Spof and Blackhair took men and followed the tracks of the bandits to see whither they led: Sone's sons assured them that they would not be difficult to follow, since there had been no rain since the attack. While they were gone, Orm questioned the survivors of Rapp's men closely, in the hope of discovering more about the identity of the bandits; but they could add little to what he had already learned from Ylva.

The day before the attack, they told him, had been the holiday which the priest called All Saints' Day; he had preached a great sermon to them all, and in the evening they had drunk to the honour of the saints. Then they had all slept soundly until the grey dawn, when the bandits had fallen on them. The hounds had begun to bay and, almost at once, the bandits had attacked the gate with rams made of tree-trunks, and had broken it open.

Rapp and Harald had been the first to engage them, though the rest of the men had quickly joined them; they had done what they could, so that most of the women had succeeded in escaping with the children out of the back of the house and then down the river and into the forest. But they had been heavily outnumbered, and had not been able to hold the gate long. The priest, who had begun of late to grow harder of hearing, had not awakened immediately, despite the hubbub, and, when he at last came out, Rapp had been killed and the bandits were everywhere. He had seen them set fire to the church, and at the sight of this had cried in a loud voice and run down towards it, so that the hounds had not been slipped in time to achieve anything.

This, they said, was all they knew; for, on seeing Rapp fall, and others with him, they had realized they were hopelessly outnumbered, and had given up the battle and taken to their heels. Later, when the bandits had gone, the hounds had been released; the bandits had not dared to approach them. The hounds had followed their traces and, after being away for a whole day, had returned with some of the cattle.

Orm listened blackly to all this, thinking that things had been poorly handled; but there seemed little point in upbraiding them now for what could not be mended, and he did not reproach them for saving their own lives after they had seen Rapp killed and Harald wounded.

He hardly knew whether to grieve more over Ludmilla's fate, or Rapp's; but, the more he thought about the business, the greater his anger waxed, and he determined to lose no time in settling accounts with this rabble of bandits. He thought it likeliest that they were men from Värend, although there was peace between them and the Göings and he could not remember that he had enemies there.

The next day, Father Willibald was conscious again, though still very weak, and had important news to tell them.

By the time he came out of the house, he said, the bandits had already stormed the gate and the first sight that met his eyes was flames leaping from a pile of straw which the bandits had heaped against the church and ignited. Rushing towards the flames, he had cried to them to leave God's church in peace.

'Then,' he continued, 'a man with a black beard strode towards me. He laughed, and cried in a loud voice "God's church shall burn, for I have renounced God. This is my third sin. Now I can sin no more." Those were his words; then he laughed again, and I recognised him. It was Rainald, the priest who lived here long ago, and gave himself up to the Smalanders at the Thing. He it was, and none other; we had already heard, you remember, that he had turned himself over to the Devil. I cursed him, and ran to the blazing straw to pull it clear; but then a man struck me, and I knew no more.'

All those listening cried aloud with amazement at this news. Father Willibald closed his eyes and nodded.

514

'It is the truth,' he said. 'One who was God's servant has burned my church.'

Asa and Alva began to weep loudly; for it seemed to them a terrible thing that this priest should have given himself so utterly to the Devil's service.

Olof Summer-Bird ground his teeth, and drew his sword slowly from its sheath. Reversing it, he rested it hilt-downwards on the floor and crossed his hands upon its point.

'This I swear,' he said. 'I shall not sit at table, nor sleep in a bed, nor take pleasure in any thing, until my sword stands in the body of this man called Rainald, who was a priest of God, and who has stolen Ludmilla Ormsdotter. And if Christ helps me, so that I find her again, I shall follow him for the rest of my days.'

CHAPTER TEN

How they settled accounts with the crazy magister

As soon as the news spread of the attack on Gröning and of Orm's return, neighbours came flocking to the house with men and horses, anxious to help him secure a good vengeance. Such opportunities, they complained, occurred all too seldom nowadays, and they greatly looked forward to what might come of it. Those who were Christians said that they were entitled to a share in the vengeance because of what had been done to their priest and church. Orm bade them all welcome, and said that he was only waiting for the return of Toke and the others before setting forth.

On the third day, towards evening, Toke returned. They had followed the tracks of the bandits far to the north and east: and their best news was that they had with them Torgunn, Rapp's widow, whom they had found starving and half-dead in the wild country. She had escaped from the bandits, and had run and walked as far as her legs would take her. Toke's men had taken turns to carry her back, and three of them had already proposed marriage to her, which had revived her spirits; but none of them, they said sadly, had seemed to her to be as good a man as Rapp.

She had important information to give them. Father Willibald was right; the man whom they called the magister was the chieftain of the band. He had recognised her, and had spoken with her while they were returning to the bandits' village. He told her that he had renounced God, and could now do whatsoever he wished. He had burned the church in order to drive God out of the district; for, now that that was destroyed, there was no church standing within many miles.

His band, Torgunn continued, consisted of outlaws, criminals and all kinds of ne'er-do-wells, some from as far distant as West Guteland and Njudung, who had sought shelter with him and now lived by plundering. They were strong in numbers and feared no man, and the magister wielded great power over them.

Of Ludmilla she could tell them little, save that she had been in good heart and had threatened the magister and the rest of them with speedy retribution. While the bandits were taking them back to their village, the great hounds had overtaken them. Several of the bandits had been bitten, one to death, and the hounds had driven off a number of the cattle, which had greatly angered their captors. She and Ludmilla had tried to run away during the confusion, but had been recaptured.

At length, they had arrived at the bandits' village, which lay near the northern tip of a great lake, which they had had on their right hand during the final stages of the journey. The bandits called their village Priesby. There, Torgunn had been allotted to a man called Saxulf, a large, coarse churl of evil disposition. He had tied her up and thrown her on to a pile of skins in his cottage. In the evening, he had come to her, drunk. He had untied her arms and legs, but had brought neither meat nor drink for her. She had realized that she was now a widow; nevertheless, it had irked her to be forced to lie with a man who conducted himself so coarsely. Accordingly, a short while after he fell asleep, she had slipped out from under the skins and, looking round for a weapon, had happened upon a rolling pin. Strengthened by God, and also by her hatred of the man and her desire to avenge Rapp, she had hit Saxulf over the head with this pin. He had not uttered a sound, but had merely twitched his limbs. Then she had crept out into the night and escaped from the village without being observed. She had made what speed she could for a day and more, following the tracks along which they had come, terrified lest they might be after her, with nothing to eat save a few cranberries she picked from hedges; then, overcome by exhaustion, she had lain down, unable to move further, expecting death from starvation and fatigue, or possibly from the jaws of wild beasts, until Blackhair and his men found her and gave her food. She had had to ride home on the men's shoulders; now, however, she was already beginning to recover from this dreadful experience.

Such was Torgunn's story, and it told them what they most wished

517

to know, namely, where the bandits' hide-out lay. Men who had been along their track, and who knew the country, said that the great lake she spoke of was that called Asnen; and two of Olof Summer-Bird's men claimed to know those deserted parts and a way by which the place might be reached. They undertook to lead Orm and his companions there. The best plan, they said, would be to turn off after the first day's march and proceed westwards, coming upon the bandits from that direction. Orm and the others thought this a wise suggestion, for by this means they would trap them with the lake at their backs.

Orm counted his men, and found they numbered a hundred and twelve. The next day, he declared, they would set forth. Fearing for the safety of his Bulgar gold, he took Toke, Olof and Blackhair with him late that evening, when all the rest of the men were asleep, and hid the chests in a safe hiding-place in the forest, far from all paths and tracks; a spot to which no man ever came. His great hoard of silver he did not think worth hiding; for he had, he said, lost his fear of silver, and was content to let it lie in Ylva's coffers, although the house would only be guarded by the few men who were to be left behind.

The next morning, before dawn, all the men were up and ready. There was, however, some delay before they could start out, for Orm was intending to take the great hounds with him, and they had first to acquaint themselves with all the strangers in the party, so that there might be no misunderstandings and the wrong men bitten. The hounds took but a few moments to accustom themselves to most of the men, merely sniffing them two or three times; but others they were more suspicious of, and snarled fearfully at, appearing unwilling to accept them as people who ought not to be killed immediately. This caused much hilarity, for the men whom the hounds distrusted grew surly, claiming that they smelt as good as the next man, and words were exchanged upon this subject.

At length, however, everything was ready, and the band set out, the hounds being led by men whom they knew well.

They followed the track by which the bandits had gone, continuing thus the whole day, until they came near to the place where Torgunn had been found. There, they encamped for the night. Next morning, they turned off to the left, with Olof's two knowledgeable men leading them. They proceeded for three days across hard country through marshland and dense forest, broken by steep hills, without seeing a house or meeting a man. The hounds knew what they were hunting, and ignored all scent of game; it was a great virtue with them that, when they were hunting men, they uttered no sound until the moment when they were slipped from their leashes.

On the afternoon of the fourth day after their departure from Gröning, they reached a place where two paths crossed. Here, they halted, and the two guides said that the lake was now just ahead of them, and that the bandits' village lay between it and them. It had been a hard march, but both Orm and Olof Summer-Bird agreed that they should attack at once; for they were beginning to run short of food, and both of them were impatient to proceed with the business. Some of the young men in the band then climbed up into a tree upon a hill to spy out the lie of the village, and Orm divided the men into three bands. Toke was to lead one, Olof the second and Orm himself the third. He kept the hounds with him, so that they should not be slipped too soon. Toke was to attack from the north, and Olof Summer-Bird from the south. Blackhair went with Toke, accompanied also by Sone's sons, who were already beginning to reckon themselves as Blackhair's men. Orm commanded them that they should set fire to no house, and maltreat no woman, since some of them might have been stolen from good husbands. When Toke sounded his horn, both bands were to attack with all speed, though without war-whoops.

Toke and Olof moved quietly off with their men, while Orm and his band crept stealthily forward through the undergrowth until they reached the skirts of the forest a short way from the village. Here, the men seated themselves on the ground and began to gnaw at the little food they had left, while they waited for the sound of Toke's horn.

Orm took Spof with him and crept forward into a clump of elder-bushes. There they lay, scanning the village. It looked to be large, and many of the houses in it were new. People could be seen working in the spaces between them, both men and women. Spof calculated that a village of that size might be reckoned to contain a hundred and fifty men. Between them and the village, in a dip in the ground, there stood a small pool, which evidently served the village as a well. An old woman, carrying a yoke with two buckets, came down to it, drew water and trudged back again. Then two men appeared, and watered four horses. After the horses had drunk, they became restless and began to prance, and Orm thought that they must have sensed the presence of the hounds. But the hounds stood stock-still behind Orm, sniffing and trembling and making no sound.

The men at the well got their horses under control and led them back to the village. A short while elapsed, and then three women walked down to the pool carrying a bucket in either hand. There were two men with them who appeared to be their guards. Orm caught his breath, for the tallest of the women was Ludmilla. He mumbled this into Spof's ear, and Spof muttered back that they were within bowshot. Still Toke's horn did not sound, and Orm was unwilling to disclose the presence of his men prematurely; however, he signalled to two men crouching near him who had been with him in the battle at the weirs and who were reckoned to be sure marksmen. They said that they thought they could mark the men at the well, rose to their feet, each keeping himself concealed behind his tree, and set arrows to their bowstrings. But Orm bade them wait a while yet.

The women had, by now, filled their buckets, and turned to go back to the village. As they did so, Orm pursed his lips and uttered a cry like a buzzard's call, repeating it once. It was a call that he could skilfully ape, and all his children were acquainted with it. Ludmilla stiffened as she heard it. She took a few slow steps after her companions; then she stumbled, so that all the water in her buckets was spilled. She said something to the men, and turned back to the well to refill her buckets. She did this as slowly as she might; then, when they were full, she sat down on the ground and clasped her foot. The two men said something to her in stern voices, and went up to her to force her to her feet; but as they reached out their hands to her, she threw herself on to her back and began to scream.

Still no sound was heard from Toke's side; but when the hounds heard Ludmilla scream, they began to bay, and Orm knew that their presence was now revealed.

Orm muttered a word to his two archers, and their bows sang as one. Their aim was true, and their arrows found their marks; but the men they struck were wearing thick leather jackets, and remained on their feet. They pulled the arrows from their flesh, and shouted for help. Then Ludmilla leaped to her feet, struck one of them on the head with a bucket, and ran with all her might towards the forest. The two men made after her, and began rapidly to overhaul her; meanwhile, men appeared from the houses to learn the cause of all this confusion.

'Slip the hounds,' said Orm, and sprang out of the bushes. As he did so, Toke's horn wound, followed by violent whooping.

But both the horn and the whoops of the men were quickly drowned as the great hounds, slipped at last from their leashes, began to bay fearfully. As the two men chasing Ludmilla saw them, they halted in terror. One turned tail and fled screaming, until the swiftest of the hounds caught him and, leaping upon his neck, felled him to the ground; but the other, keeping his head, ran into the pool and, turning there, drew his sword and stood his ground. Three of the hounds leaped simultaneously at him; he met one of them with his sword, but the other two knocked him off his feet, so that he disappeared beneath the water; and only the hounds came up again.

Ludmilla danced for joy when she recognised Orm. She began at once to ask about Olof and the gold, and he told her. She herself had, she said, been treated as befitted a chieftain's daughter, and had not been forced to lie with any man save the crazy priest, who had treated her not unkindly, so that she might have suffered worse.

Orm sent after Spof, and bade him and two others of the older men take Ludmilla a short way into the forest and remain there with her until the fighting in the village had ceased. The other women came timidly up to them: they were, they said, the priest's women. When the hounds had appeared they had flung themselves face downwards upon the ground and remained motionless, so that the hounds had not touched them.

By the time that Orm and his men reached the village, the fighting was already fierce. Olof's men were engaging a group of bandits in a street between two houses, and his voice was heard to cry above the uproar that the man with the black beard was for his sword alone. Orm attacked the bandits from the rear, losing several men to arrows shot from the houses; but, although the bandits defended themselves valiantly, they were at length encircled and overcome. Then Orm led his men into the houses to fight with the men who were still holding out there. He saw two of his hounds lying dead with spears through their bodies, but each of them had his man under him, and the others could still be heard baying fearfully towards the lake.

Orm met Olof Summer-Bird; his face was bloody and his shield heavily scarred.

'Ludmilla is safe!' cried Orm. 'I have her in good keeping.'

'I thank Thee, Christ!' cried Olof. 'But where is the blackbeard? He is mine!'

Toke's men had met the fiercest opposition, for many of the bandits had rushed to meet them at the first sound of whooping. Orm and Olof gathered their men and led them to Toke's assistance, attacking their enemies in the rear. Here, the fighting became very violent, and many men fell on both sides, for the bandits fought like berserks. Orm pursued one, who had managed to break out, around the corner of a house, but, as he passed a doorway, a man clad in a chain-shirt and a bald man armed with an axe leaped out and attacked him. Orm hewed at the chain-shirted man so that he rolled upon the ground, and, in the same instant, leaped nimbly aside to evade the other's axe, but, as he did so, his foot slipped on a heap of dung and he fell on to his neck. As he fell, he saw the bald man raise his axe again, and, he said afterwards, his thoughts went back to the battle at Maldon long before, and the shields that had covered him there, and he felt little joy at the thought that his next night's camp would be on heavenly ground. But the bald man opened his eyes and mouth wide and let go his axe and sank on to his hands and knees and knelt there, staring; and, as Orm got to his feet again, he heard his name shouted from a house ahead of him, and saw Sone's sons sitting astride the roof, waving their bows in pride at their good marksmanship.

Orm felt strangely weary after this experience, and stood where he was for a moment looking about him. The village presented a scene of wild confusion. Women were shrieking, men were chasing each other throughout the houses, cattle and hogs ran terrified through the streets, and most of the bandits who were still alive had taken to their heels and were fleeing towards the lake. Toke and Blackhair appeared out of a doorway. Toke's sword was dripping redly, and he cried to Orm that he had not enjoyed better sport than this since his youthful days. But he had no time to say more, and rushed furiously after the fleeing men, shouting to his men to follow him. Blackhair, however, remained with Orm, calling his men down from the housetop.

Then a great howl was heard, and a black-bearded man came running towards them with an axe in his hand and Olof Summer-Bird at his heels. As the man caught sight of Orm, he changed his course, leaped over a low wall, and ran on. But Blackhair, turning, ran after him and struck him over the head so that he fell.

'He is mine! He is mine!' cried Olof breathlessly.

The man was twisting on the ground. Olof went up to him, gripped his sword with both hands, and drove it through the chain-shirt and the man's body beneath so that it stood fast in the ground.

'God! God!' screamed the nailed man, in a voice filled with pain and terror; and said no more.

'I have kept my vow,' said Olof.

'Is that the man?' said Orm. 'It is difficult to recognize him beneath that beard.'

'It is an ill thing to wear stolen goods in a battle, so that they can be seen,' said Olof, bending over the dead body. 'Look at this!'

Above the neck of the man's chain-shirt shone the glint of gold. Olof reached his hand inside, and pulled something out. It was Almansur's chain.

'It is he,' said Orm. 'And, now that I think of it, there is another proof. Who in this place but he could have called to God? I wonder what he can have wanted of Him?'

CHAPTER ELEVEN

Concerning the great hounds' chase

Some of the crazy magister's men escaped in boats; but not many, for they were hunted by men and dogs along the shore. Their wounded were killed, since they were all miscreants. Twenty-three of Orm's men had been killed, and many wounded; and all agreed that this had been a good fight, and one that would be much talked about in the years to come.

In the village, they found a great quantity of ale, and many hogs were slaughtered; then the men buried their dead together, and raised a mound over them, and drank to their death-voyage. As they had expected, they found a number of stolen women in the village. Each of these was given a cow and allowed to go whither she pleased, with as much booty as she could carry. Among these were Ylva's two servant-girls, who were both young and were greatly delighted at being thus liberated. They had been forced, they said, to endure great indignities, and had been kept indoors, closely guarded, ever since Torgunn had run away. They now wished to be wedded to reliable men.

The hounds were much praised for their part in the battle; only two of them had been killed. When all the cattle had been rounded up as booty, Orm said that the work of driving them back to Gröning could safely be left to the hounds, since they were used to this. Horses were found for all the wounded; then, as soon as these had recovered sufficiently to be able to sit on horseback, Orm rode forth from the bandits' village and headed homewards by the shortest route, which led southwards along the shore of the lake.

Ludmilla rode with the rest, and Olof kept his horse close to hers.

He had begged Orm and Toke not to mention the two women who had kept him warm at the Dregovites' village, lest she should take the matter amiss. They had both laughed at this, and had replied that he must be sick in the head with wounds or love if he supposed that they would do any such thing. But Olof had shaken his head doubtfully, saying that he was a good deal older than she, and so could not be too careful.

They rode slowly, for the sake of the wounded. Ahead of them, the hounds drove their herd at leisure; no disputes broke out between them and their charges, though, when any cow tried to change her direction or escape from the rest, they were quick to show her her mistake.

They camped early that evening, and saw to the wounded; then, next morning, they proceeded alongside the lake towards the place which old folk called Tyr's Meadows. In former times, men had lived there, and the meadows had been the scene of great battles, from which they had won their name. Men said that so much blood had been spilled on Tyr's Meadows that the grass flourished more richly there than elsewhere. But neither man nor house was to be seen there now.

As they approached these meadows, the hounds grew restless, so that the men wondered whether they had scented bear, or the smell of the old blood. Leaving their herd, they roamed into the woods and ranged this way and that, until, of a sudden, two or three of them began to bay. Others joined them, and soon the whole pack of them was snarling savagely, and driving deeper into the woods as though they had once more been slipped for battle. Orm could not understand what the cause of this might be, for none of the bandits had fled in this direction; and he and all the men ran up to the top of a heathered hill beside the track to see what was afoot.

Away on their right hand, beyond the woods, there lay open grassland. Across it the hounds were running, driving before them a great herd of cattle, but cattle such as few of the men had seen before.

Suddenly one of Toke's men cried: 'The wild ox! They are driving the wild ox!'

The hounds seemed to have taken it into their heads that these beasts belonged to their herd and were to be driven home with the rest. They spared no efforts to see that none escaped, and from the hill the men could see how they fought with the more obstinate animals to drive them along with the others. The wild oxen resented this treatment, and their bellowing could be heard even above the baying of the hounds; but at last, all but a few ceased their resistance, and the herd disappeared southwards into the wooded hills, with the hounds still gambolling behind and about them.

Realizing there was nothing they could do to stop them, the men proceeded on their way, driving the tame cattle themselves. Toke's men, who knew the ways of wild oxen, said that sometimes, in the beginning of winter, they came down from West Guteland to pasture in Tyr's Meadows. While they grazed on the war-god's land, they were held by old folk to be under his protection, and so were never disturbed there. In former times, they had, as was well known, been far more numerous in these parts, but nowadays they were only to be seen in Tyr's Meadows, and that but seldom.

They found traces of the wild oxen's flight in the country east of the Kraka Stone; but in the dense forest further south, it was clear that the hounds had found their task beyond them, for the tracks of the herd showed it to have diminished in strength mile by mile. They had, nevertheless, succeeded in keeping some of them together; and, when Orm reached home, he learned that the hounds had arrived there driving two bulls, five cows and a number of calves. Then men had done their best to halt them, but had been unable to do so; and, when the hounds saw the beasts proceeding into the country beyond their home, they appeared to have felt that they had done enough for honour and went to their food-troughs, very weary and sore-footed.

After this, wild oxen were seen in various parts of the forest country, and no event for many a year past had aroused as much amazement as their reappearance. Now that they had, with their own eyes, seen wild oxen in their district, anything, men said, could happen; and they all reminded one another of the old saying, that no king would ever be seen among them until the wild oxen returned to the land. Wise ancients shook their heads and warned their neighbours to prepare for the worst, and to keep their bows and spears ready to hand. Some baptized persons thought that Christ would come to Göinge in a great wagon drawn by wild oxen; but few men agreed with them in this surmise. Most took it to mean that King Sven would march against them; and, when certain tidings came that he had died in England, black in the face with anger at the stubbornness of the people there, there was such rejoicing in Göinge that all the ale was drunk up, and men sat hoarse and thirsty at their tables with nothing save milk to fill their cups with.

But such as lived long enough saw the old saying fulfilled, when Canute Svensson the Mighty, King of Denmark and England, sailed to the estuary with the greatest fleet that any man had ever seen or heard tell of, and fought with the Kings of Sweden and Norway on the waters of the Holy River.

And this is the end of the story of Orm Tostesson and his luck. He fared forth no more on voyages or campaigns; but his affairs prospered and he aged contentedly. The only thing he found to complain of was an ache in his back which sometimes troubled him, and which even Father Willibald was not always able to dispel.

Olof Summer-Bird wedded Ludmilla. They lived happily together, although it was rumoured that he had not fully as great a say in the management of his house as he had been wont to have. Spof besought Torgunn many times to marry him. At first, she refused, finding him short of limb and grey of beard; but when at last he threw caution aside and revealed to her what his belt contained, she found herself no longer able to resist his prayers. They sailed to Gotland, in the ship that lay in the shed by the estuary; and with them, in the same ship, sailed Blackhair, Glad Ulf and Sone's seven sons, upon a longer voyage. They took two of the hounds with them, to fulfil the promise they had made to Felimid, and stayed away for seven years.

When they returned, Glad Ulf wedded Oddny, who had steadfastly refused to look at any other man. But Blackhair sailed to England, and in the battle on the Holy River he fought in King Canute's own ship.

Toke Grey-Gullsson gained much pleasure from his chest of gold, and hung so many ornaments upon his wife and daughters that their clatter and jingle gave good warning of their approach whenever they went out in their best attire. He sold his house in Värend and built himself a larger one near Gröning. There, he and Orm found much satisfaction in one another's company, as did Ylva in Mirah's, although neither Toke nor his woman ever allowed themselves to be baptized. In good time, Orm's youngest daughter was wedded to the eldest of Toke's sons, their fathers having decided long ago that they were well suited to one another.

Both Orm and Toke lived to a ripe old age without wearying of life; and never, until the day they died, did they tire of telling of the years when they had rowed the Caliph's ship and served my lord Almansur.

THE SECOND SEX

Simone de Beauvoir was born in Paris in 1908. In 1929 she became the youngest person ever to obtain the agrégation in philosophy at the Sorbonne. She taught at the lycées at Marseille and Rouen from 1931 to 1937, and later in Paris from 1938 to 1943. After the war, she emerged as one of the leaders of the existentialist movement, working with Jean-Paul Sartre on *Les Temps Modernes*. *The Second Sex* was first published in Paris in 1949. It was a ground-breaking, risqué book that became a runaway success. Selling 20,000 copies in its first week, the book earned its author both notoriety and admiration. Since then, *The Second Sex* has been translated into forty languages and has become a landmark in the history of feminism. Beauvoir was the author of many books, including the novel *The Mandarins* (1957) which was awarded the Prix Goncourt. She died in 1986.

Translators Constance Borde and Shelia Malovany-Chevallier are both graduates of Rutgers University, New Jersey and have lived, studied and worked in Paris for over forty years. They were faculty members of the Institut d'Etudes Politiques and jointly authored and translated numerous works on subjects ranging from grammar and politics to art and social sciences.

ALSO BY SIMONE DE BEAUVOIR

Fiction

She Came to Stay
The Blood of Others
All Men are Mortal
The Mandarins
Les Belles Images
The Woman Destroyed

Non-Fiction

The Ethics of Ambiguity
Memoirs of a Dutiful Daughter
The Prime of Life
The Force of Circumstance
A Very Easy Death
All Said and Done
Adieux: A Farewell to Sartre

SIMONE DE BEAUVOIR

The Second Sex

TRANSLATED BY
Constance Borde and
Sheila Malovany-Chevallier

WITH AN INTRODUCTION BY
Sheila Rowbotham

VINTAGE BOOKS
London

Published by Vintage 2011

6 8 10 9 7 5

First published as *Le deuxième sexe* by Simone de Beauvoir © 1949 by
Éditions Gallimard, Paris
Translation copyright © 2009 by Constance Borde and Sheila
Malovany-Chevallier

Introduction copyright © 2009 Sheila Rowbotham

Constance Borde and Sheila Malovany-Chevallier have asserted
their right under the Copyright, Designs and Patents Act, 1988 to be
identified as translators of this work

First published in Great Britain in 2009 by Jonathan Cape

Vintage
Random House, 20 Vauxhall Bridge Road,
London SW1V 2SA

www.vintage-classics.info

Addresses for companies within The Random House Group Limited
can be found at: www.randomhouse.co.uk/offices.htm

The Random House Group Limited Reg. No. 954009

A CIP catalogue record for this book
is available from the British Library

ISBN 9780099595731

Ouvrage publié avec le concours du Ministère français
chargé de la culture – Centre national du livre

The new English translation of *The Second Sex* by Simone de Beauvoir
was granted a translation subsidy from the *Centre national du livre*
(French Ministry of Culture).

Printed and bound in Great Britain by
Clays Ltd, St Ives plc

Penguin Random House is committed to a sustainable future for
our business, our readers and our planet. This book is made from
Forest Stewardship Council® certified paper.

CONTENTS

VOLUME I
FACTS AND MYTHS

Part One

DESTINY

Part Two

HISTORY

Part Three

MYTHS

VOLUME II
LIVED EXPERIENCE

To Jacques Bost

There is a good principle which created
order, light, and man,
and an evil principle which created
chaos, darkness, and woman.

Pythagoras

Everything that men have written about
women should be viewed with suspicion
because they are both judge and party.

Poulain de la Barre

Foreword

Reading Simone de Beauvoir's *The Second Sex* in this new translation by Constance Borde and Sheila Malovany-Chevallier is both a return and a revelation. Like many others of my generation, I began reading Beauvoir, along with the works of Sartre, when I was at school in the late 1950s. They travelled with me through the 1960s and, as a consequence, I had assimilated so much from the two of them by the time I wrote *Woman's Consciousness, Man's World*, in the early 1970s, that I took them for granted. They permeated how my thinking was structured. Yet I was not aware how much of the French version had been abridged and altered in the 1954 translation by H. M. Parshley. In an effort to make Beauvoir's work more accessible he muffled existentialist terms and cut out historical material.[1] Beauvoir herself did not realise the extent of the adaptations and omissions, declaring to Margaret A. Simons in 1983, 'I wish with all my heart that you will be able to publish a new translation.'[2] She would have been delighted by this scrupulous and insightful new work.

In *The Second Sex* Beauvoir is at once a thinker, a scholar and a creative writer. Her writing communicates on several levels simultaneously, reasoning and seducing at the same time. Like that other great advocate of women's emancipation, Mary Wollstonecraft, she expresses concepts with beguiling irony. On the young woman who believes she is the exception and can circumnavigate male power, Beauvoir muses, '. . . she has been taught to overestimate her smile, but no one told her that all women smiled' (p.670). Abstractions become deft little cameos; when the girl making jam writes the date on the lid, '. . . she has captured the passage of time in the snare of sugar . . .'(p.493).

Her challenge to male cultural hegemony drives the book, sweeping up prejudice in its transcendent energy. Beauvoir writes with passion against the physical, psychological and intellectual confinement of women, which she believes encourages them to accept mediocrity instead of grandeur. Each acquiescence confirms servitude, '... her wings are cut and then she is blamed for not knowing how to fly' (p.660). Beauvoir, having penetrated the domain of male privilege, uses her skills to expose how the cards were stacked so unfairly against women. 'Being on the fringes of the world is not the best place for someone who intends to recreate it: here again, to go beyond the given, one must be deeply rooted in it' (p.154).

However, in *The Second Sex* the woman is not simply determined by a male defined culture. She is at once invented by men and 'exists without their invention' (p.209). Hence comes the male exasperation, as dream and reality fail to converge. For my generation the excitement of Beauvoir's thesis lay both in its exposure of the con trick of blaming women for not being in accord with men's fantasies *and* in the possibility she held out of women making themselves anew. Choice is always present, albeit from a specific situation in the famous assertion, 'One is not born, but rather becomes, woman' (p.293).

The boldness of Beauvoir's subversion remains exhilarating. It was not that she was the first to notice male hegemony or seek out ways to resist it. Both are refrains in women's writing about emancipation from the seventeenth century and indeed in a few cases even earlier. They would be reiterated and linked to a broader change in society by Mary Wollstonecraft in the late eighteenth century and disseminated far beyond Europe before *The Second Sex* was ever written. But Beauvoir's sustained critique takes 'femininity' by the throat to shake out illusion, examining women's circumstances along with the cultural sleights of hand which deceive and confuse. Nothing like it had been written before.

The scope of *The Second Sex* is dazzling indeed. Beauvoir launches herself into physiology, psychoanalysis, anthropology; ancient, medieval and modern history. She whizzes her reader through myths that define 'woman' in many cultures, demonstrating how the abstract ideal is superimposed on the actual experience of women. She then brings her argument closer to home by tracing how myths of 'the feminine' pervade nineteenth- and twentieth-century literature from Edgar Allan Poe to Henry Miller. These myths have material consequences. In one of her arch, carefully controlled asides, she remarks how, '... one of the most ardent zealots of unique, absolute, eternal love, André Breton, is forced to admit that at least in present circumstances this love can mistake its object: error or inconstancy, it is the same abandonment for the woman' (p. 520).

Exploring 'Lived Experience' in the second part, she breezes through child development, the cultural history of fashion and clothes, sociological surveys of prostitution, girls' attitudes to boys and to education, motherhood, ageing, and, of course, sexuality. Aware of the findings of the Kinsey Report and approving of the American young who were not restricted by European Catholic mores, her frankness scandalised many contemporaries. Resistant to biological reductionism, she argues that orgasm, '... can be qualified as psycho-physiological because it not only concerns the entire nervous system but also depends on the whole situation lived by the subject' (p.396). Yet heterosexual pleasure is, for Beauvoir, a precarious matter, bound up with pain and the threat of possession. Writing on the honeymoon, she quotes Nietzsche's *Gay Science*: 'To find love and shame in contradiction and to be forced to experience at the same time delight, surrender, duty, pity, terror and who knows what else, in the face of the unexpected proximity of God and beast! ... Thus a psychic knot has been tied that may have no equal' (p.498).

In contrast, and surprisingly in a text written in the late 1940s, Beauvoir remarks: 'Between women love is contemplation; caresses are meant less to appropriate the other than to recreate oneself slowly through her; separation is eliminated, there is neither fight nor victory nor defeat; each one is both subject and object ...' (p. 441). As Toril Moi observes the chapter on lesbianism is confused, perhaps revealing the difficulty in writing it.[3] Nevertheless Beauvoir presents love between women as an option, a possibility, though not an absolute alternative to heterosexuality. She says that lesbianism '... is an attitude that is *chosen in situation* ... It is one way among others for women to solve the problems posed by her condition in general and by her erotic situation in particular' (p.448).

The Second Sex shattered other taboos in its negative portrayal of marriage, its courageous defence of contraception and abortion, its references to women taking young lovers. These all provoked comment and criticism, but most disturbing to the defenders of the status quo was the *mix* of sex and philosophy. A woman theorising in sensuous language broke all the rules of containment. Beauvoir contrived to embed her theme of the woman defined by others and yet struggling for her existential freedom in the structure of the book and in her mode of communication. She merged female and male zones, and this combination disturbed as much as what she actually said.

Her own background stood her in good stead in expressing the consequences of living the double life of a woman in a man's world. She was born in 1908 into an haute bourgeois family in straitened circumstances, and her childhood was strictly controlled by her mother. She was sent to a Catholic girls' school where mothers were encouraged to attend classes, her letters were opened and censored until she was eighteen. Individual thought and autonomous privacy were thus to become precious. In contrast to her mother's dutiful propriety, her irreligious father spent his time on amateur theatricals and enjoyed a social life outside the family. The second son of a landowner, with right-wing views, he was inclined to regret that his talented daughter was not a boy. During summer holidays on her father's family estates, novels and a close friend, Elisabeth Le Coin, were her only immediate forms of escape.[4]

In the long term, the only way out of this enclosed world would be education. Despite their sharply contrasting outlooks, both parents encouraged her interest in literature, and the brilliant pupil made her way laboriously through an exacting series of examinations to the Sorbonne. Unlike Jean-Paul Sartre, she had not received an elite education; the French system, despite recent modifications, was still based on distinct corridors of gender.[5] Nevertheless, though Beauvoir observes in *The Second Sex* how women's education discourages 'the habit of independence', (p.598) she herself displayed a remarkable will towards freedom. Uncharacteristically for a young woman, she inclined to philosophy at the Sorbonne. She regarded it in heroic terms as a discipline that, '. . . went straight to essentials. I had never liked fiddling detail'. Other subjects appeared as 'poor relations'; only philosophy went 'right to the heart of truth'.[6]

At university she became friendly with a talented coterie of young men who had studied at the École Normale Supérieure, including Merleau-Ponty. In 1929 Beauvoir began an affair with the attractive married student Rene Maheu, a friend of Sartre's. When Maheu failed his exams and left Paris, a smitten Sartre began his courtship in earnest, mustering philosophy in his effort to woo her.

Sartre could not compete with the handsome Maheu in terms of looks. His trump cards were philosophy, his strength of character, which freed Beauvoir from her parents, and his encouragement of her dream of becoming a great writer. Beauvoir always insisted that the relationship that began in their early twenties was reciprocal, but she quickly instituted a division of labour, deciding Sartre possessed the original brain of a great philosopher and her destiny would be literary. Aware of her own abilities, she was less confident and assured than the charismatic and ugly young man who became her lover. Even at this stage, Sartre took his brilliance for granted while Beauvoir's was earnestly acquired. However, given the difference in their education, Beauvoir's accomplishments were actually the greater. Ironically she would find creative writing much harder than academic work, while Sartre, with her encouragement, would write novels and plays.[7] The agrégation jury of the Sorbonne were divided but eventually awarded Sartre first place and Beauvoir second.[8]

The new partnership did bring with it a certain power. Judith Okely suggests that Beauvoir's relationship with Sartre enabled her to enter Parisian intellectual circles. The alternative way in for a woman would have been the salon, and this she despised, even if she had possessed sufficient wealth.[9] Moreover the 'essential' bond with Sartre, despite all the strains of jealousy, for it was never exclusive, turned them into a formidable bloc of two. The 'contingent' lovers were thus loners and, because they were often younger, and sometimes students, were in a less powerful position.

Over the next ten years the young Sartre mapped out his philosophical belief in the existence of a material world independent of consciousness, while she struggled to write her first novel. Both continued to have affairs, in Beauvoir's case with women as well as men; their practice of confiding in one another served as a defence against the external world. Love, work and talk consumed their energy. Existentialism did not lend itself to an appreciation of the social and political traumas of depression, the rise of fascism and Stalinism, the outbreak of the Spanish Civil War. Though it did provide a philosophical basis for rejecting the conventional framework of morality, it did not indicate any alternative. In her memoir, *The Prime of Life* (1960), Beauvoir explains how, while she had gradually abandoned her sense of absolute autonomy, 'it was still my individual relationships with separate people that mattered most to me'. Her aim in life was 'happiness'. She adds: 'Then, suddenly, History burst over me and I dissolved into fragments. I woke to find myself scattered over the four quarters of the globe, linked by every nerve in me to each and every individual. All my ideas and values were turned upside down.'[10]

War changed everything, yet there are few references to it in *The Second Sex*. By the late 1940s the fear, the hunger, the uneasy compromises with the occupying Germans, the unsuccessful attempts at resistance had been set aside.[11] Much later, in *The Prime of Life*, she would record how she scrounged for cabbages and beetroots, took to wearing a turban because she could not have her hair done, gave up smoking – unlike Sartre who pursued dog-ends in the gutters.[12] She also remarked how hard it was '. . . to speak of those days to anyone who had not lived through them', explaining how she made her fictional character Anne in *The Mandarins* reflect in her stead, 'The real tragedies hadn't happened to me, and yet they haunted my life'.[13] The war taught Beauvoir that abstractions were not sufficient: '. . . it *did* make a very great difference whether one was Jew or Aryan; but it had not yet dawned on me that such a thing as a specifically feminine "condition" existed'.[14]

When Paris was liberated in 1944 life continued to be hard. Food was scarce, her room was too cold for writing. However, 'the future had been handed back to us'.[15] Briefly the left intelligentsia imagined a wider social change; on founding the journal *Les Temps Modernes*, Sartre proclaimed a commitment to 'la littératura engagée'.[16] The wily General de Gaulle left them with the literature and took political power, but the stark minimalism of existentialism resonated with the thoughtful young whose childhood and adolescence had been dominated by war. Ironically Sartre and Beauvoir became alternative celebrities and Beauvoir was forced to write in the basement of a bar to evade interruptions.[17]

From 1946 she was working on *The Ethics of Ambiguity*. The war had made her more alert to the constraints of circumstances. Prepared to engage with Marx's thought, while distrusting the teleological momentum of dialectical materialism, Beauvoir rejected the denial of the individual's autonomy demanded by the Communist Party despite the respect it had gained for its role in the Resistance.[18] Both she and Sartre struggled to create an alternative to the polarities of Soviet Communism and American capitalism through the medium of *Les Temps Modernes*. The journal brought Beauvoir into contact with the American left-wing writer Richard Wright, who was moving away from the Communist Party. Wright brought black American writing to her for the journal in 1946, introducing her to W. E. B. Dubois' idea of the 'double consciousness', which enabled African-Americans to survive racism while internalising elements of the inferiority projected on to them by white dominance.[19] In *The Ethics of Ambiguity* Beauvoir explored the concept of the complicity of the oppressed which would be important in *The Second Sex*.[20]

While colonialism, racism and anti-Semitism were very much part of left discourse in France after the war, discussion of the emancipation of women was less visible. Feminism had not been a strong force even before the war. The Vichy regime had celebrated the eternal feminine by excluding women from many jobs and giving out long prison sentences to anyone who distributed contraceptives. In 1943, Marie-Jeanne Latour had been guillotined for performing abortions.[21] While there was a Marxist legacy in the work of Engels and Bebel on the 'Woman Question', with which Beauvoir was familiar, the contemporary French Communist Party

stressed motherhood and the family. However, there did exist an awareness of the role women had played in the Resistance. This had both
political and cultural implications. French women would finally be given
the vote in 1944, and, in 1948, the historian Edith Thomas would dedicate her study of the early socialist women, *Les Femmes de 1848* to the
women of the Resistance.

Beauvoir's trajectory was, however, from her own subjectivity. Once
The Ethics of Ambiguity was finished, she began to contemplate writing
about herself. After a discussion with Sartre, she decided this involved
thinking through what it meant to be a woman – one of those fiddling
details she had contrived to ignore. This project of exploring her own
subjectivity fused into the broader project of *The Second Sex*. She was
adamant, however, that it was not a *feminist* work (p.3). Typically women
of her generation on the left wanted to surpass feminism, which was
regarded as narrow and restricted. Indeed it was right-wing writers such
as the Americans, Marynia Farnham and Ferdinand Lundberg who held
forth about 'Woman'. Beauvoir was sufficiently irritated to mention their
diatribe against emancipation, *Modern Woman: The Lost Sex* (1947) several
times in *The Second Sex* (pp.4, 283). This contretemps with the American
right contrasted with a bemused appreciation of the more radical aspects
of American mores, deepened by her passionate love affair with the
writer, Nelson Algren, while writing *The Second Sex*.

Beauvoir was intent on producing an existentialist analysis that recognised and demolished social and cultural constraints. As Judith Okely
notes in demonstrating the myriad ways in which women became the
Other in relation to men, Beauvoir's existentialism inclined her to see
knowledge as 'arising from each individual's specific circumstance'.[22]
This led her to take into account not only surveys of women's attitudes,
but sources that disclosed subjectivity such as the autobiography of
Isadora Duncan and the diaries of Sophia Tolstoy. She used novels by
women ranging from Virginia Woolf to Colette Audry. Two of her
childhood favourites also appear, Jo in *Little Women* and Maggie Tulliver
in *Mill on the Floss*. As a girl Beauvoir had grieved over Jo's compromise
and Maggie's death.

Beauvoir's charting of women's subjectivity is, however, problematic.
Not only does she treat fiction as evidence of actuality, as Okely notes, she
universalises from individual instances chosen to support her thesis. Okely
suggests an ethnographic reading – Beauvoir is the buried case study.[23] While
this is never explicit in the text, she is mirrored in the examples taken from
life and literature. Despite the range of her reading, her source material

focuses on women in her own image, including hardly any references to working-class women or to women of colour. Beauvoir is certainly alert to non-European cultures, but she plucks examples without situating them.

The modern historical material is scrappy and at times inaccurate. She has the militant suffragettes in the British Women's Social and Political Union joining with the Labour Party, when the reverse was the case (p.145). She dismisses Jeanne Deroin and the women around the 1848 journal *La Voix des Femmes* with an hauteur that denies the significance of their ideas and their understanding of solidarity (p.133). It is as if association and collective action by women in movements had never occurred. This is not simply because these were topics outside her experience or not her field of study, but because they do not fit into her theoretical approach. Patriarchy is boss; women are losers.

Beauvoir's ingenious strategy of entering male culture in order to undermine it is comparable to the difficulty John Milton encountered with his heroic Satan in *Paradise Lost*. Her dramatic construct inadvertently invests masculine culture with a depth and allure lacking in the female Other – who are assigned the less attractive parts as those ever inferior, bungling, moany women. Beauvoir's loathing of fixed ideals of femininity made it difficult for her to ascribe value to the lives and actualities of women, even though her intention was to show how women were not only 'diminished' but 'enriched' by the 'obstacles' they had to confront.[24] This partiality affected both her theoretical approach and the subject matter of *The Second Sex*. Her impatience with Romanticism's association of woman with nature blocked any questioning of the assumed virtue, in all circumstances, of control over nature, a critique present in the utopian socialist literature she mentions.

Beauvoir's abstraction 'patriarchy' occludes how differences in the degree of women's subordination are all important; it was after all preferable to be an Anglo-Saxon woman than a Norman. Space to manoeuvre, leeway to live your life, ideas of entitlement emerge from such distinctions. An historical approach would have yielded greater ambiguities in women's predicament and differing forms of male dominion instead of the intractable structure of 'patriarchy'. Some aspects of women's lived experience such as domestic labour are hardly mentioned though they had been extensively debated by feminists, women reformers and socialists, and Beauvoir makes only passing references to how children are to be cared for. Mothering did not adapt itself easily to her theoretical approach.

Within *The Second Sex* there are, however, interesting tensions between Beauvoir's abstract conceptualisation and what she observes. During the war she had met a number of women over forty who had confided in her. At the time she did not see their accounts of their 'dependence' as significant. Her interest, nevertheless, had been 'aroused'.[25] Perhaps she remembered their stories in noting a resolve among women to be mothers while also engaging in economic, political and social life. She ponders the problems this would entail (pp.582, 741, 751). She had located a contradiction in women's predicament which would become of crucial significance in the coming decades. Moreover, at times she provides a theoretical opening that negates the accumulative pessimism of the specific instances of women as the marginal Other. 'In truth, all human existence is transcendence and immanence at the same time; to go beyond itself, it must maintain itself, to thrust itself towards the future, it must integrate the past into itself, and while relating to others it must confirm itself in itself' (p.455). This observation, made in passing in relation to marriage, intimates a new balancing of human activity that could encompass not simply gender, but the social organisation of life and culture. While Beauvoir's work contained evident flaws, her mode of enquiry also suggests opposing perceptions of what might be.

Regardless of what Beauvoir did not do in *The Second Sex*, her originality and intellectual courage meant that one woman had mapped out terrains of thought and enquiry that would engage many thousands in the decades to come. The first volume of the book sold twenty-two thousand copies in the first week and the two volumes went on to sell in many countries.[26] The response to *The Second Sex* would transform its author's life. Paradoxically, Beauvoir, the solitary walker seeking existential freedom, would be constructed by others as a mythical antithesis to women's lot. To some this meant she was frigid and a nymphomaniac, to others a feminist heroine. Beauvoir's autobiographical writings navigated a way through the misunderstandings that assailed her. She sought to create herself in these books; and so, indirectly, *The Second Sex* did lead to her writing about herself after all.

If she was often uncomfortable with being the epitome of the emancipated woman, good also came from her new position. After so many years as Sartre's disciple, Beauvoir's writing inspired many. Among those who visited was a shy young woman called Sylvie Le Bon. She first arrived in 1960 and gradually a deep affection grew between the two women which lasted until Beauvoir's death. About this relationship and her attraction to other women, Beauvoir, who told so much about her life, remained warily silent.[27]

When the Women's Liberation Movement appeared in France in the early 1970s, Beauvoir was there defending abortion and thinking through the ideas that were being developed in many countries.[28] She told Alice Schwarzer that 'Women should not let themselves be conditioned exclusively to male desire any more'.[29] She became a feminist because she decided it was necessary to 'fight for the situation of women here and now', though she still believed that wider socialist changes were also needed.[30] During the 1970s she became more prepared to acknowledge that women's lack of power had resulted in positive qualities such as 'patience, sympathy, irony', which men would do well to acquire.[31] But she remained suspicious of strands in feminism which exalted women's essential difference from men. 'I find that it falls again into the masculine trap of wanting to enclose us in our differences,' she told Margaret A. Simons and Jessica Benjamin in 1979.[32]

The dilemmas raised by Beauvoir would be encountered again and again in the Women's Liberation Movements that spread around the globe. To what extent are we defined by biological difference? How is women's singularity to be at once affirmed and transcended? What makes women resist and what makes women comply with subordination? *The Second Sex* demonstrated the necessity of cultural resistance that went beyond complaint and even beyond critique. Beauvoir's left libertarian message was that new ways of being women and men would be created not simply theoretically but through human action, '. . . freedom can break the circle' and revolt 'create new situations' (p.780).

In 1949 Beauvoir could see that women would be able to shed their old skins and cut their own clothes, only 'if there is a collective change' (p.777). But what is to be done when this achieves partial successes, only to be confounded by force of circumstance? How was she to envisage that some aspects of equality would be achieved and new forms of inequality intensify? This is the conundrum facing women today. In rediscovering *The Second Sex* a new generation will find new insights and draw their own conclusions. Beauvoir's work retains its relevance, despite the changes that have occurred in women's position since the first publication in 1949. Moreover, she illuminates an ongoing process of exploration, resistance and creation, which is as exciting now as it ever was. Her voice echoes over the decades: 'The free woman is just being born'(p.767). Her prescient vision of '. . . new carnal and affective relations of which we cannot conceive' (p.781) carries hope for women – and for men.

Professor Sheila Rowbotham, August 2009

1 Margaret A. Simons, *Beauvoir and The Second Sex*, Rowman & Littlefield, Lanham, Maryland, 1999, pp.61–70.

2 Simons, *Beauvoir and The Second Sex*, p.71.

3 Toril Moi, *Simone de Beauvoir: The Making of an Intellectual Woman*, Blackwell, Oxford, 1994, p.200.

4 Kate Fullbrook and Edward Fullbrook, *Simone de Beauvoir and Jean-Paul Sartre: The Remaking of a Twentieth-Century Legend*, Harvester Wheatsheaf, New York, 1993, pp.33–35.

5 Moi, *Simone de Beauvoir*, pp.41–50.

6 Simone de Beauvoir, 'Memoirs of a Dutiful Daughter', 1987, p.158, quoted in Moi, *Simone de Beauvoir*, p.31.

7 Fullbrook and Fullbrook, *Simone de Beauvoir and Jean-Paul Sartre*, pp.62–74.

8 Ibid., pp.52–61.

9 Judith Okely, *Simone de Beauvoir*, Virago, London, 1986, p.128.

10 Simone de Beauvoir, *The Prime of Life*, Penguin, London, 1965, p.369.

11 Fullbrook and Fullbrook, *Simone de Beauvoir and Jean-Paul Sartre*, pp.128–145.

12 De Beauvoir, *The Prime of Life*, pp. 503–505.

13 Ibid., p.499

14 Ibid., p.572.

15 Ibid., p.598.

16 Fullbrook and Fullbrook, *Simone de Beauvoir and Jean-Paul Sartre*, p.156.

17 Ibid., pp.157–160.

18 Simone de Beauvoir, *Pour Une Morale de L'Ambiguité*, Gallimard, Paris 1947, pp.117, 153, 204–205, 214–220.

19 Simons, *Beauvoir and The Second Sex*, pp.177–178.

20 De Beauvoir, *Pour Une Morale de L'Ambiguité*, p.137.

21 Moi, *Simone de Beauvoir*, p.187; see also Francine Muel-Dreyfus, *Vichy et L'Éternel Feminin*, Editions du Seuil, Paris, 1996.

22 Okely, *Simone de Beauvoir*, p.159.

23 Ibid.

24 De Beauvoir, *The Prime of Life*, p.572.

25 Ibid.

26 Fullbrook and Fullbrook, *Simone de Beauvoir and Jean-Paul Sartre*, p.172.

27 Simons, *Beauvoir and The Second Sex*, pp.136–142.

28 Okely, *Simone de Beauvoir*, pp.113, 155.

29 Alice Schwarzer, *Simone de Beauvoir Today: Conversations, 1972–1982*, Chatto, London, 1984, p.113.

30 Ibid., p.32.

31 Margaret A. Simons and Jessica Benjamin, 'Beauvoir Interview (1979)', in Simons, *Beauvoir and The Second Sex*, p.19.

32 Ibid., p.18.

Translators' Note

We have spent the past three years researching *Le Deuxième sexe* and translating it into English – into *The Second Sex*. It has been a daunting task, and a splendid learning experience during which this monumental work entered our personal lives and changed the way we see the world. Questions naturally arose about the act of translating itself, about ourselves and our roles and about our responsibilities to both Simone de Beauvoir and her readers.

Translation has always been fraught with such questions, and different times have produced different conceptions of translating. Perhaps this is why, while great works of art seldom age, translations do. The job of the translator is not to simplify or readapt the text for a modern or foreign audience but to find the true voice of the original work, as it was written for its time and with its original intent. Seeking signification in another's words transports the translator into the mind of the writer. When the text is an opus like *The Second Sex*, whose impact on society was so decisive, the task of bringing into English the closest version possible of Simone de Beauvoir's voice, expression and mind is greater still.

This is not the first translation of *Le Deuxième sexe* into English, but it is the first complete one. H. M. Parshley translated it in 1953, but he abridged and edited passages and simplified some of the complex philosophical language. We have translated *Le Deuxième sexe* as it was written, unabridged and unsimplified, maintaining Beauvoir's philosophical language. The long and dense paragraphs that were changed in the 1953 translation to conform to more traditional styles of punctuation – or even eliminated – have now been translated as she wrote them, all within the confines of English. Long paragraphs (sometimes going on for pages) are a stylistic aspect of her writing that is essential, integral to the development of her arguments. Cutting her sentences, cutting her paragraphs, and using a more traditional and conventional punctuation do not render

Simone de Beauvoir's voice. Beauvoir's style expresses her reasoning. Her prose has its own consistent grammar, and that grammar follows a logic.

We did not modernise the language Beauvoir used and had access to in 1949. This decision precluded the use of the word 'gender', for example, as applied today. We also stayed close to Beauvoir's complicated syntax and punctuation as well as to certain usages of language that to us felt a bit awkward at first. One of the difficulties was her extensive use of the semi-colon, a punctuation mark that has suffered setbacks over the past decades in English and French, and has somewhat fallen into disuse.

Nor did we modernise structures such as 'if the subject attempts to assert himself, the other is nonetheless necessary for him.' Today we would say 'if the subject attempts to assert her or himself . . .' There are examples where the word 'individual' clearly refers to a woman, but Beauvoir, because of French rules of grammar, uses the masculine pronoun. We therefore do the same in English.

The reader will see some inconsistent punctuation and style, most evident in quotations and extracts. Indeed, while we were tempted to standardise it, we carried Beauvoir's style and formatting into English as much as possible. In addition, we used the same chapter headings and numbers that she did in the original two-volume gallimard edition. We also made the decision to keep close to Beauvoir's tense usage, most noticeably regarding the French use of the present tense for the historical past.

One particularly complex and compelling issue was how to translate 'la femme'. In Le deuxième sexe, the term has at least two translations: 'the woman' or 'woman' and at times, 'women', depending on the context. 'Woman' in English used alone without an article captures woman as an institution, a concept, femininity as determined and defined by society, culture, history. Thus in a French sentence such as Le problème de la femme a toujours été un problème d'hommes, we have used 'woman' without an article: 'The problem of woman has always been a problem of men.'

Beauvoir occasionally – but rarely – uses femme without an article to signify woman as determined by society as just described. In such cases, of course, we do the same. The famous sentence, On ne naît pas femme: on le devient, reads, in our translation: 'One is not born, but rather becomes, woman.' The original translation by H. M. Parshley read, 'One is not born, but rather becomes a woman.'

Another notable change we made was in the translation of la jeune fille. This is the title of an important chapter in Volume II dealing with the period in a female's life between childhood and adulthood. While it is often translated as 'the younger girl' (by Parshley and other translators of French works), we think it clearly means 'girl.'

We have included all of Beauvoir's footnotes, and we have added notes of our own when we felt an explanation was necessary. Among other things, they indicate errors in Beauvoir's text and discrepancies such as erroneous dates. We corrected misspellings of names without noting them. Beauvoir sometimes puts into quotes passages that she is partially or completely paraphrasing. We generally left them that way. The reader will notice that titles of the French books she cites are given in French, followed by their translation in English. The translation is in italics if it is in a published English-language edition; it is in roman if it is our translation. We supply the sources of the English translations of the authors Beauvoir cites at the end of the book.

We did not, however, facilitate the reading by explaining arcane references or difficult philosophical language. As an example of the former, in Part Three of Volume II, 'Justifications,' there is a reference to Cécile Sorel breaking the glass of a picture frame holding a caricature of her by an artist named Bib. The reference might have been as obscure in 1949 as it is today.

Our notes do not make for an annotated version of the translation, yet we understand the value such a guide would have for both the teacher and the individual reading it on their own. We hope one can be written now that this more precise translation exists.

These are but a few of the issues we dealt with. We had instructive discussions with generous experts about these points and listened to many (sometimes contradictory) opinions; but in the end, the final decisions as to how to treat the translation were ours.

It is generally agreed that one of the most serious absences in the first translation was Simone de Beauvoir the philosopher. Much work has been done on reclaiming, valorising, and expanding upon her role as philosopher since the 1953 publication, thanks to the scholarship of Margaret Simons, Eva Lundgren-Gothlin, Michèle Le Dœuff, Elizabeth Fallaize, Emily Grosholz, Sonia Kruks and Ingrid Galster, to mention only a few. We were keenly aware of the need to put the philosopher back into her text. To transpose her philosophical style and voice into English was the most crucial task we faced.

The first English-language translation did not always recognise the philosophical terminology in *The Second Sex*. Take the crucial word 'authentic' meaning 'to be in good faith'. As Toril Moi points out, Parshley changed it into 'real, genuine, and true'. The distinctive existentialist term *pour-soi*, usually translated as 'for-itself' (*pour-soi* referring to human consciousness), became 'her true nature in itself'. Thus, Parshley's 'being-in-itself' (*en-soi*, lacking human consciousness) is a reversal of Simone de Beauvoir's meaning. Margaret Simons and Toril Moi have unearthed and brought to light many other examples, such as the use of 'alienation', 'alterity', 'subject', the verb 'to posit', by now well documented. One particularly amusing rendition was of the title of Volume II, where '*L'Expérience Vécue*' ('Lived Experience') was translated as 'Woman's Life Today', making it sound like a ladies' magazine.

The Second Sex is a philosophical treatise and one of the most important books of the 20th century upon which much of the modern feminist movement was built. Beauvoir the philosopher is present right from the start of the book, building on the ideas of Hegel, Marx, Kant, Heidegger, Husserl and others. She developed, shared and appropriated these concepts alongside her equally brilliant contemporaries, Sartre, Merleau-Ponty and Lévi-Strauss, who were redefining philosophy to fit the times. Before it was published, Beauvoir read Lévi-Strauss's *Elementary Structures of Kinship* and learned from and used those ideas in *The Second Sex*. Although the ideas and concepts are challenging, the book was immediately accepted by a general readership. Our goal in this translation has been to conform to the same ideal in English: to say what Simone de Beauvoir said as close to the way she said it, in a both challenging and readable text.

We owe a debt of gratitude to the indomitable Anne-Solange Noble of Gallimard Editions, who for years believed in this re-translation project. Anne-Solange begged, badgered and persuaded ('I shall never surrender!') until she found the editor who was willing to take on the monumental task. That exceptional person is Ellah Allfrey of Jonathan Cape, a patient and superb editor who astutely worked with us step by step for three years, strongly supported by Katherine Murphy at Jonathan Cape and LuAnn Walther of Knopf. Anne-Solange introduced us to Sylvie Le Bon de Beauvoir, Simone de Beauvoir's adopted daughter, and our relationship has been a very special one ever since that first lunch on the rue du Bac where we four toasted the moment with, '*Vive le point-virgule*' ('Long live the semi-colon')!

Ann (Rusty) Shteir, our Douglass College friend, classmate and feminist scholar, now Professor of Humanities and Women's Studies at York University, Toronto, Canada, was always available to provide source material and to solve problematic issues, often many times a week. She, like we, felt that no task was too great to repay the debt women – and the world – owe to Simone de Beauvoir. Michael Mosher and Daniel Hoffman-Schwartz were extremely helpful with philosophical language and concepts. Gabrielle Spiegel and her generous colleagues took on the esoteric research required for the History chapter, notably the passages on the French Middle Ages of which Gaby is a leading expert. James Lawler, the distinguished professor, merits our heartfelt gratitude for re-translating, specially for this edition, the Paul Claudel extracts with such elegance and grace. Our thanks to Beverley Bie Brahic for her translations of Francis Ponge, Michel Leiris and Cécile Sauvage; Kenneth Haltman for Gaston Bachelard; Raymond MacKenzie for François Mauriac and others; Zach Rogow and Mary Ann Caws for André Breton; Gillian Spraggs for Renée Vivien. Richard Pevear and Larissa Volokhonsky allowed us the special privilege of using parts of their magnificent translation of *War and Peace* before the edition appeared in 2008; their views on translation were an inspiration to us. Donald Fanger helped us with Sophia Tolstoy's diaries.

Many writers, translators and researchers, friends, colleagues, and strangers who became friends, unfailingly contributed their expertise: Eliane Lecarme-Tabone, Mireille Perche, Claire Brisset, Mathilde Ferrer, David Tepfer, Marie-Victoire Louis, Virginia Larner, Nina de Voogd Fuller, Stephanie Baumann, Jane Couchman, Catherine Legault, Robert Lerner, Richard Sieburth, Sandra Bermann, Gérard Bonal, Lia Poorvu, Leila May-Landy, Karen Offen, Sybil Pollet, Janet Bodner, our copy-editor, Beth Humphries, and our indexer, Vicki Robinson and our two proofreaders, John Garrett and Sarah Barlow.

Our husbands, Bill Chevallier and Dominique Borde, were among our staunchest and most reliable partners, living out the difficult passages with us, helping us overcome obstacles (and exhaustion), and also sharing the joy and elation of the life-changing discoveries the text holds for us.

Very special thanks go to our expert readers. Our official reader, Mary Beth Mader, authority *par excellence* in French and the philosophical language of Simone de Beauvoir, enriched our text with her insights and corrections; Margaret Simons, showing no end to her boundless generosity, 'tested' our texts on her doctoral students and came back to us with meticulous perceptions and corrections; Marilyn Yalom, Susan Suleiman and Elizabeth Fallaize, with all of the discernment for which they are renowned, explored chapters with a fine-tooth comb and gave us a height-ened understanding of *The Second Sex* for which we will ever be grateful.

And now it is for English readers to discover, learn and live Simone de Beauvoir's message of freedom and independence.

VOLUME I
FACTS AND MYTHS

Introduction

I hesitated a long time before writing a book on woman. The subject is irritating, especially for women; and it is not new. Enough ink has flowed over the quarrel about feminism; it is now almost over: let's not talk about it any more. Yet it is still being talked about. And the volumes of idiocies churned out over this past century do not seem to have clarified the problem. Besides, is there a problem? And what is it? Are there even women? True, the theory of the eternal feminine still has its followers; they whisper, 'Even in Russia, *women* are still very much women'; but other well-informed people – and also at times those same ones – lament, 'Woman is losing herself, woman is lost.' It is hard to know any longer if women still exist, if they will always exist, if there should be women at all, what place they hold in this world, what place they should hold. 'Where are the women?' asked a short-lived magazine recently.* But first, what is a woman? *'Tota mulier in utero*: she is a womb,' some say. Yet speaking of certain women, the experts proclaim, 'They are not women', even though they have a uterus like the others. Everyone agrees there are females in the human species; today, as in the past, they make up about half of humanity; and yet we are told that 'femininity is in jeopardy'; we are urged, 'Be women, stay women, become women.' So not every female human being is necessarily a woman; she must take part in this mysterious and endangered reality known as femininity. Is femininity secreted by the ovaries? Is it enshrined in a Platonic heaven? Is a frilly petticoat enough to bring it down to earth? Although some women zealously strive to embody it, the model has never been patented. It is typically described in vague and shimmering terms borrowed from a clairvoyant's vocabulary. In St Thomas's time it was an essence defined with as much certainty as the sedative quality of a poppy. But conceptualism has lost ground: biological and social sciences no longer believe

* Out of print today, entitled *Franchise*.

there are immutably determined entities that define given characteristics like those of the woman, the Jew or the black; science considers
characteristics as secondary reactions to a *situation*. If there is no such
thing today as femininity, it is because there never was. Does the word
'woman', then, have no content? It is what advocates of Enlightenment
philosophy, rationalism or nominalism vigorously assert: women are,
among human beings, merely those who are arbitrarily designated by
the word 'woman'; American women in particular are inclined to think
that woman as such no longer exists. If some backward individual still
takes herself for a woman, her friends advise her to undergo psychoanalysis to get rid of this obsession. Referring to a book – a very irritating
one at that – *Modern Woman: The Lost Sex*, Dorothy Parker wrote: 'I
cannot be fair about books that treat women as women. My idea is that
all of us, men as well as women, whoever we are, should be considered
as human beings.' But nominalism is a doctrine that falls a bit short; and
it is easy for anti-feminists to show that women *are* not men. Certainly
woman like man is a human being; but such an assertion is abstract; the
fact is that every concrete human being is always uniquely situated.
Rejecting the notions of the eternal feminine, the black soul or the Jewish
character is not to deny that there are today Jews, blacks or women: this
denial is not a liberation for those concerned, but an inauthentic flight.
Clearly, no woman can claim without bad faith to be situated beyond
her sex. A few years ago, a well-known woman writer refused to have
her portrait appear in a series of photographs devoted specifically to
women writers. She wanted to be included in the men's category; but
to get this privilege, she used her husband's influence. Women who assert
they are men still claim masculine consideration and respect. I also
remember a young Trotskyite standing on a platform during a stormy
meeting, about to come to blows in spite of her obvious fragility. She
was denying her feminine frailty; but it was for the love of a militant
man she wanted to be equal to. The defiant position that American
women occupy proves they are haunted by the feeling of their own
femininity. And the truth is that anyone can clearly see that humanity is
split into two categories of individuals with manifestly different clothes,
faces, bodies, smiles, movements, interests and occupations; these differences are perhaps superficial; perhaps they are destined to disappear.
What is certain is that for the moment they exist in a strikingly obvious
way.

If the female function is not enough to define woman, and if we also
reject the explanation of the 'eternal feminine', but if we accept, even

temporarily, that there are women on the earth, we then have to ask: what is a woman?

Merely stating the problem suggests an immediate answer to me. It is significant that I pose it. It would never occur to a man to write a book on the singular situation of males in humanity.* If I want to define myself, I first have to say, 'I am a woman'; all other assertions will arise from this basic truth. A man never begins by positing himself as an individual of a certain sex: that he is a man is obvious. The categories 'masculine' and 'feminine' appear as symmetrical in a formal way on town hall records or identification papers. The relation of the two sexes is not that of two electrical poles: the man represents both the positive and the neuter to such an extent that in French *hommes* designates human beings, the particular meaning of the word *vir* being assimilated into the general meaning of the word 'homo'. Woman is the negative, to such a point that any determination is imputed to her as a limitation, without reciprocity. I used to get annoyed in abstract discussions to hear men tell me: 'You think such and such a thing because you're a woman.' But I know my only defence is to answer, 'I think it because it is true,' thereby eliminating my subjectivity; it was out of the question to answer, 'And you think the contrary because you are a man,' because it is understood that being a man is not a particularity; a man is in his right by virtue of being man; it is the woman who is in the wrong. In fact, just as for the ancients there was an absolute vertical that defined the oblique, there is an absolute human type that is masculine. Woman has ovaries and a uterus; such are the particular conditions that lock her in her subjectivity; some even say she thinks with her hormones. Man vainly forgets that his anatomy also includes hormones and testicles. He grasps his body as a direct and normal link with the world that he believes he apprehends in all objectivity, whereas he considers woman's body an obstacle, a prison, burdened by everything that particularises it. 'The female is female by virtue of a certain *lack* of qualities,' Aristotle said. 'We should regard women's nature as suffering from natural defectiveness.' And St Thomas in his turn decreed that woman was an 'incomplete man', an 'incidental' being. This is what the Genesis story symbolises, where Eve appears as if drawn from Adam's 'supernumerary' bone, in Bossuet's words. Humanity is male, and man defines woman, not in herself, but in relation to himself; she is not considered an autonomous

---

* The Kinsey Report, for example, confines itself to defining the sexual characteristics of the American man, which is completely different.

being. 'Woman, the relative being,' writes Michelet. Thus Monsieur Benda declares in *Uriel's Report*:[1] 'A man's body has meaning by itself, disregarding the body of the woman, whereas the woman's body seems devoid of meaning without reference to the male. Man thinks himself without woman. Woman does not think herself without man.' And she is nothing other than what man decides; she is thus called 'the sex', meaning that the male sees her essentially as a sexed being; for him she is sex, so she is it in the absolute. She determines and differentiates herself in relation to man, and he does not in relation to her; she is the inessential in front of the essential. He is the Subject; he is the Absolute. She is the Other.[*2]

The category of *Other* is as original as consciousness itself. The duality between Self and Other can be found in the most primitive societies, in the most ancient mythologies; this division did not always fall into the category of the division of the sexes, it was not based on any empirical given: this comes out in works like Granet's on Chinese thought, and Dumézil's on India and Rome. In couples such as Varuna–Mitra, Uranos–Zeus, Sun–Moon, Day–Night, no feminine element is involved at the outset; neither in Good–Evil, auspicious and inauspicious, left and right, God and Lucifer; alterity is the fundamental category of human thought. No group ever defines itself as One without immediately setting up the Other opposite itself. It only takes three travellers brought together by chance in the same train compartment for the rest of the travellers to become vaguely hostile 'others'. Village people view anyone not belonging to the village as suspicious 'others'. For the native

---

* This idea has been expressed in its most explicit form by E. Levinas in his essay on *Time and the Other*. He expresses it like this: 'Is there not a situation where alterity would be borne by a being in a positive sense, as essence? What is the alterity that does not purely and simply enter into the opposition of two species of the same genus? I think that the absolutely contrary contrary, whose contrariety is in no way affected by the relationship that can be established between it and its correlative, the contrariety that permits its terms to remain absolutely other, is the feminine. Sex is not some specific difference . . . Neither is the difference between the sexes a contradiction . . . Neither is the difference between the sexes the duality of two complementary terms, for two complementary terms presuppose a preexisting whole . . . [A]lterity is accomplished in the feminine. The term is on the same level as, but in meaning opposed to, consciousness.' I suppose Mr Levinas is not forgetting that woman also is consciousness for herself. But it is striking that he deliberately adopts a man's point of view, disregarding the reciprocity of the subject and the object. When he writes that woman is mystery, he assumes that she is mystery for man. So this apparently objective description, is in fact an affirmation of masculine privilege.

of a country, inhabitants of other countries are viewed as 'foreigners'; Jews are the 'others' for anti-Semites, blacks for racist Americans, indigenous people for colonists, proletarians for the propertied classes. After studying the diverse forms of primitive society in depth, Lévi-Strauss could conclude: 'The passage from the state of Nature to the state of Culture is defined by man's ability to think biological relations as systems of oppositions; duality, alternation, opposition, and symmetry, whether occurring in defined or less clear form, are not so much phenomena to explain as fundamental and immediate givens of social reality.'*³ These phenomena could not be understood if human reality were solely a *Mitsein*⁴ based on solidarity and friendship. On the contrary, they become clear if, following Hegel, a fundamental hostility to any other consciousness is found in consciousness itself; the subject posits itself only in opposition; it asserts itself as the essential and sets up the other as inessential, as the object.

But the other consciousness has an opposing reciprocal claim: travelling, a local is shocked to realise that in neighbouring countries locals view him as a foreigner; between villages, clans, nations and classes there are wars, potlatches, agreements, treaties and struggles that remove the absolute meaning from the idea of the Other and bring out its relativity; whether one likes it or not, individuals and groups have no choice but to recognise the reciprocity of their relation. How is it, then, that between the sexes this reciprocity has not been put forward, that one of the terms has been asserted as the only essential one, denying any relativity in regard to its correlative, defining the latter as pure alterity? Why do women not contest male sovereignty? No subject posits itself spontaneously and at once as the inessential from the outset; it is not the Other who, defining itself as Other, defines the One; the Other is posited as Other by the One positing itself as One. But in order for the Other not to turn into the One, the Other has to submit to this foreign point of view. Where does this submission in woman come from?

There are other cases where, for a shorter or longer time, one category has managed to dominate another absolutely. It is often numerical inequality that confers this privilege: the majority imposes its law on or persecutes the minority. But women are not a minority like American blacks, or like Jews: there are as many women as men on the earth. Often,

* See Claude Lévi-Strauss, *The Elementary Structures of Kinship*. I thank Claude Lévi-Strauss for sharing the proofs of his thesis that I drew on heavily, particularly in the second part, pp. 78–92.

the two opposing groups concerned were once independent of each other; either they were not aware of each other in the past or they accepted each other's autonomy; and some historical event subordinated the weaker to the stronger: the Jewish diaspora, slavery in America, or the colonial conquests are facts with dates. In these cases, for the oppressed there was a *before*: they share a past, a tradition, sometimes a religion, or a culture. In this sense, the parallel Bebel draws between women and the proletariat would be the best founded: proletarians are not a numerical minority either and yet they have never formed a separate group. However, not *one* event but a whole historical development explains their existence as a class and accounts for the distribution of *these* individuals in this class. There have not always been proletarians: there have always been women; they are women by their physiological structure; as far back as history can be traced, they have always been subordinate to men; their dependence is not the consequence of an event or a becoming, it did not *happen*. Alterity here appears to be an absolute, partly because it falls outside the accidental nature of historical fact. A situation created over time can come undone at another time – blacks in Haiti for one are a good example; on the contrary, a natural condition seems to defy change. In truth, nature is no more an immutable given than is historical reality. If woman discovers herself as the inessential, and never turns into the essential, it is because she does not bring about this transformation herself. Proletarians say 'we'. So do blacks. Positing themselves as subjects, they thus transform the bourgeois or whites into 'others'. Women – except in certain abstract gatherings such as conferences – do not use 'we'; men say 'women' and women adopt this word to refer to themselves; but they do not posit themselves authentically as Subjects. The proletarians made the revolution in Russia, the blacks in Haiti, the Indo-Chinese are fighting in Indochina. Women's actions have never been more than symbolic agitation; they have won only what men have been willing to concede to them; they have taken nothing; they have received.* It is that they lack the concrete means to organise themselves into a unit that could posit itself in opposition. They have no past, no history, no religion of their own; and unlike the proletariat, they have no solidarity of labour or interests; they even lack their own space that makes communities of American blacks, or the Jews in ghettos, or the workers in Saint-Denis or Renault factories. They live dispersed among men, tied by homes, work, economic interests and social

* See second part, p. 128

conditions to certain men – fathers or husbands – more closely than to
other women. As bourgeois women, they are in solidarity with bourgeois
men and not with women proletarians; as white women, they are in solidarity with white men and not with black women. The proletariat could
plan to massacre the whole ruling class; a fanatic Jew or black could dream
of seizing the secret of the atomic bomb and turning all of humanity
entirely Jewish or entirely black: but a woman could not even dream of
exterminating males. The tie that binds her to her oppressors is unlike
any other. The division of the sexes is a biological given, not a moment
in human history. Their opposition took shape within an original *Mitsein*
and she has not broken it. The couple is a fundamental unit with the two
halves riveted to each other: cleavage of society by sex is not possible.
This is the fundamental characteristic of woman: she is the Other at the
heart of a whole whose two components are necessary to each other.

One might think that this reciprocity would have facilitated her liberation; when Hercules spins wool at Omphale's feet, his desire enchains
him. Why was Omphale unable to acquire long-lasting power? Medea,
in revenge against Jason, kills her children: this brutal legend suggests
that the bond attaching the woman to her child could have given her a
formidable upper hand. In *Lysistrata*, Aristophanes light-heartedly imagined a group of women who, uniting together for the social good, tried
to take advantage of men's need for them: but it is only a comedy. The
legend that claims that the ravished Sabine women resisted their ravishers
with obstinate sterility also recounts that by whipping them with leather
straps, the men magically won them over into submission. Biological
need – sexual desire and desire for posterity – which makes the male
dependent on the female, has not liberated women socially. Master and
slave are also linked by a reciprocal economic need that does not free
the slave. That is, in the master–slave relation, the master does not *posit*
the need he has for the other; he holds the power to satisfy this need
and does not mediate it; the slave, on the other hand, out of dependence, hope or fear, internalises his need for the master; however equally
compelling the need may be to them both, it always plays in favour of
the oppressor over the oppressed: this explains the slow pace of working-
class liberation, for example. Now woman has always been, if not man's
slave, at least his vassal; the two sexes have never divided the world up
equally; and still today, even though her condition is changing, woman
is heavily handicapped. In no country is her legal status identical to man's,
and often it puts her at a considerable disadvantage. Even when her
rights are recognised abstractly, long-standing habit keeps them from

being concretely manifested in customs. Economically, men and women almost form two castes; all things being equal, the former have better jobs, higher wages and greater chances to succeed than their new female competitors; they occupy many more places in industry, in politics, and so on, and they hold the most important positions. In addition to their concrete power they are invested with a prestige whose tradition is reinforced by the child's whole education: the present incorporates the past, and in the past all history was made by males. At the moment that women are beginning to share in the making of the world, this world still belongs to men: men have no doubt about this, and women barely doubt it. Refusing to be the Other, refusing complicity with man, would mean renouncing all the advantages an alliance with the superior caste confers on them. Lord-man will materially protect liege-woman and will be in charge of justifying her existence: along with the economic risk, she eludes the metaphysical risk of a freedom that must invent its goals without help. Indeed, beside every individual's claim to assert himself as subject – an ethical claim – lies the temptation to flee freedom and to make himself into a thing: it is a pernicious path because the individual, passive, alienated and lost, is prey to a foreign will, cut off from his transcendence, robbed of all worth. But it is an easy path: the anguish and stress of authentically assumed existence are thus avoided. The man who sets the woman up as an *Other* will thus find in her a deep complicity. Hence woman makes no claim for herself as subject because she lacks the concrete means, because she senses the necessary link connecting her to man without positing its reciprocity, and because she often derives satisfaction from her role as *Other*.

But a question immediately arises: how did this whole story begin? It is understandable that the duality of the sexes, like all duality, be expressed in conflict. It is understandable that if one of the two succeeded in imposing its superiority, it had to establish itself as absolute. It remains to be explained how it was that man won at the outset. It seems possible that women might have carried off the victory, or that the battle might never be resolved. Why is it that this world has always belonged to men and that only today things are beginning to change? Is this change a good thing? Will it bring about an equal sharing of the world between men and women or not?

These questions are far from new; they have already had many answers; but the very fact that woman is *Other* challenges all the justifications that men have ever given: these were only too clearly dictated by their own interest. 'Everything that men have written about women should be viewed with suspicion, because they are both judge and party,' wrote Poulain de la Barre, a little-known seventeenth-century feminist. Males have always and everywhere paraded their satisfaction of feeling they are kings of creation. 'Blessed be the Lord our God, and the Lord of all worlds that has not made me a woman,' Jews say in their morning prayers; meanwhile their wives resignedly murmur: 'Blessed be the Lord for creating me according to His will.' Among the blessings Plato thanked the gods for was, first, being born free and not a slave, and second, a man and not a woman. But males could not have enjoyed this privilege so fully had they not considered it as founded in the absolute and in eternity: they sought to make the fact of their supremacy a right. 'Those who made and compiled the laws, being men, favoured their own sex, and the jurisconsults have turned the laws into principles,' Poulain de la Barre continues. Lawmakers, priests, philosophers, writers and scholars have gone to great lengths to prove that women's subordinate condition was willed in heaven and profitable on earth. Religions forged by men reflect this will for domination: they found ammunition in the legends of Eve and Pandora. They have put philosophy and theology in their service, as seen in the previously cited words of Aristotle and St Thomas. Since ancient times, satirists and moralists have delighted in depicting women's weaknesses. The violent indictments brought against them all through French literature are well known: Montherlant, with less verve, picks up the tradition from Jean de Meung. This hostility seems sometimes founded but is often gratuitous; in truth, it covers up a more or less skilfully camouflaged will to self-justification. 'It is much easier to accuse one sex than to excuse the other,' says Montaigne. In certain cases, the process is transparent. It is striking, for example, that the Roman code limiting a wife's rights invokes 'the imbecility and fragility of the sex' just when a weakening family structure makes her a threat to male heirs. It is striking that in the sixteenth century, to keep a married woman under wardship, the authority of St Augustine affirming 'the wife is an animal neither reliable nor stable' is called on, whereas the unmarried woman is recognised as capable of managing her own affairs. Montaigne well understood the arbitrariness and injustice of the lot assigned to women: 'Women are not wrong at all when they reject the rules of life that have been introduced into the world, inasmuch as it is the men who have made these without them.' There is a natural plotting and scheming between them and us.' But he does not go so far as to champion their cause. It is only in the eighteenth century that deeply democratic men begin to consider the issue objectively. Diderot, for one, tries to prove that, like man, woman is a human being. A bit later, John Stuart Mill ardently defends women. But these philosophers are exceptional in their impartiality. In the nineteenth century the feminist quarrel once again becomes a partisan quarrel; one of the consequences of the Industrial Revolution is that women enter the labour force: at that point, women's demands leave the realm of the theoretical and find economic grounds; their adversaries become all the more aggressive; even though landed property is partially discredited, the bourgeoisie clings to the old values where family solidity guarantees private property: it insists all the more fiercely that woman's place should be in the home as her emancipation becomes a real threat; even within the working class, men tried to thwart women's liberation because women were becoming dangerous competitors – especially as women were used to working for low salaries.*

To prove women's inferiority, antifeminists began to draw not only, as before, on religion, philosophy and theology, but also on science: biology, experimental psychology, and so forth. At most they were willing to grant 'separate but equal status'[5] to the *other* sex. That winning formula is most significant: it is exactly that formula the Jim Crow laws put into practice with regard to black Americans; this so-called egalitarian segregation served only to introduce the most extreme forms of discrimination. This convergence is in no way pure chance: whether it is race, caste, class or sex reduced to an inferior condition, the justification process is the same. 'The eternal feminine' corresponds to 'the black soul' or 'the Jewish character'. However, the Jewish problem on the whole is very different from the two others: for the anti-Semite, the Jew is more an enemy than an inferior and no place on this earth is recognised as his own; it would be preferable to see him annihilated. But there are deep analogies between the situations of women and blacks: both are liberated today from the same paternalism, and the former master caste wants to keep them 'in their place', that is, the place chosen for them; in both cases, they praise, more or less sincerely, the virtues of the 'good black', the carefree, childlike, merry soul of the resigned black, and the woman who is a 'true woman' – frivolous, infantile, irresponsible, the woman subjugated to man. In both cases, the ruling caste bases its argument on the state of affairs it created itself. The familiar line from George Bernard Shaw sums it up: 'The white American relegates the black to the rank of shoe-shine boy, and then concludes that blacks are only good for shining shoes.' The same vicious circle can be found in all analogous

* See Part Two, pp. 136-137

circumstances: when an individual or a group of individuals is kept in a situation of inferiority, the fact is that he or they *are* inferior. But the scope of the verb *to be* must be understood; bad faith means giving it a substantive value, when in fact it has the sense of the Hegelian dynamic: *to be* is to have become, to have been made as one manifests oneself. Yes, women in general *are* today inferior to men; that is, their situation provides them with fewer possibilities: the question is whether this state of affairs must be perpetuated.

Many men wish it would be: not all men have yet laid down their arms. The conservative bourgeoisie continues to view women's liberation as a danger threatening their morality and their interests. Some men feel threatened by women's competition. In *Hebdo-Latin* the other day, a student declared: 'Every woman student who takes a position as a doctor or lawyer is *stealing* a place from us.' That student never questioned his rights over this world. Economic interests are not the only ones in play. One of the benefits that oppression secures for the oppressor is that the humblest among them feels *superior*: in the United States, a 'poor white' from the South can console himself for not being a 'dirty nigger'; and more prosperous whites cleverly exploit this pride. Likewise, the most mediocre of males believes himself a demigod next to women. It was easier for M. de Montherlant to think himself a hero in front of women (handpicked, by the way) than to act the man among men, a role that many women assumed better than he did. Thus, in one of his articles in *Le Figaro Littéraire* in September 1948, M. Claude Mauriac – whom everyone admires for his powerful originality – could* write about women: '*We* listen in a tone [*sic!*] of polite indifference . . . to the most brilliant one among them, knowing that her intelligence, in a more or less dazzling way, reflects ideas that come from *us*.' Clearly his female interlocutor does not reflect M. Mauriac's own ideas, since he is known not to have any; that she reflects ideas originating with men is possible: among males themselves, more than one of them takes as his own opinions he did not invent; one might wonder if it would not be in M. Claude Mauriac's interest to converse with a good reflection of Descartes, Marx or Gide rather than with himself; what is remarkable is that with the ambiguous '*we*', he identifies with St Paul, Hegel, Lenin and Nietzsche, and from their heights he looks down on the herd of women who dare to speak to him on an equal footing; frankly, I know of more than one woman who would not put up with M. Mauriac's 'tone of polite indifference'.

* At least he thought he could.

I have stressed this example because of its disarming masculine naïvety. Men profit in many other more subtle ways from woman's alterity. For all those suffering from an inferiority complex, this is a miraculous liniment; no one is more arrogant towards women, more aggressive or more disdainful, than a man anxious about his own virility. Those who are not threatened by their fellow men are far more likely to recognise woman as a counterpart; but even for them the myth of the Woman, of the Other, remains precious for many reasons;* they can hardly be blamed for not wanting to light-heartedly sacrifice all the benefits they derive from the myth: they know what they lose by relinquishing the woman of their dreams, but they do not know what the woman of tomorrow will bring them. It takes great abnegation to refuse to posit oneself as unique and absolute Subject. Besides, the vast majority of men do not explicitly make this position their own. They do not *posit* woman as inferior: they are too imbued today with the democratic ideal not to recognise all human beings as equals. Within the family, the male child and then the young man sees the woman as having the same social dignity as the adult male; afterwards, he experiences in desire and love the resistance and independence of the desired and loved woman; married, he respects in his wife the spouse and the mother, and in the concrete experience of married life she affirms herself opposite him as a freedom. He can thus convince himself that there is no longer a social hierarchy between the sexes and that on the whole, in spite of their differences, woman is an equal. As he nevertheless recognises some points of inferiority – professional incapacity being the predominant one – he attributes them to nature. When he has an attitude of benevolence and partnership towards a woman, he applies the principle of abstract equality; and he does not *posit* the concrete inequality he recognises. But as soon as he clashes with her, the situation is reversed. He will apply the concrete inequality theme and will even allow himself to disavow abstract equality.†

* The article by Michel Carrouges on this theme in *Cahiers du Sud*, no. 292, is significant. He writes with indignation: 'If only there were no feminine myth but only bands of cooks, matrons, prostitutes and blue-stockings with functions of pleasure or utility!' So, according to him, woman has no existence for herself; he only takes into account her *function* in the male world. Her finality is in man; in fact, it is possible to prefer her poetic 'function' to all others. The exact question is why she should be defined in relation to the man.

† For example, man declares that he does not find his wife in any way diminished just because she does not have a profession: work in the home is just as noble, etc. Yet, at the first argument he remonstrates, 'You wouldn't be able to earn a living without me.'

This is how many men affirm, with quasi-good faith, that women *are* equal to man and have no demands to make, and *at the same time* that women will never be equal to men and that their demands are in vain. It is difficult for men to measure the enormous extent of social discrimination that seems insignificant from the outside and whose moral and intellectual repercussions are so deep in woman that they appear to spring from an original nature.* The man most sympathetic to women never knows her concrete situation fully. So there is no good reason to believe men when they try to defend privileges whose scope they cannot even fathom. We will not let ourselves be intimidated by the number and violence of attacks against women; nor be fooled by the self-serving praise showered on the 'real woman'; nor be won over by men's enthusiasm for her destiny, a destiny they would not for the world want to share.

We must not, however, be any less mistrustful of feminists' arguments: very often their attempt to polemicise robs them of all value. If the 'question of women' is so trivial, it is because masculine arrogance turned it into a 'quarrel'; when people quarrel, they no longer reason well. What people have endlessly sought to prove is that woman is superior, inferior or equal to man: created after Adam, she is obviously a secondary being, some say; on the contrary, say others, Adam was only a rough draft, and God perfected the human being when he created Eve; her brain is smaller, but relatively bigger; Christ was made man: but perhaps out of humility. Every argument has its opposite and both are often misleading. To see clearly, one needs to get out of these ruts; these vague notions of superiority, inferiority and equality that have distorted all discussions must be discarded in order to start anew.

But how, then, will we ask the question? And in the first place, who are we to ask it? Men are judge and party: so are women. Can an angel be found? In fact, an angel would be ill qualified to speak, would not understand all the givens of the problem; as for the hermaphrodite, it is a case of its own: it is not both a man and a woman, but neither man nor woman. I think certain women are still best suited to elucidate the situation of women. It is a sophism to claim that Epimenides should be enclosed within the concept of Cretan and all Cretans within the concept of liar: it is not a mysterious essence that dictates good or bad faith to men and women; it is their situation that disposes them to seek the truth to a greater or lesser extent. Many women today, fortunate to have had all the privileges of the human being restored to them, can afford the

* Describing this very process will be the object of Volume II of this study.

luxury of impartiality: we even feel the necessity of it. We are no longer like our militant predecessors; we have more or less won the game; in the latest discussions on women's status, the UN has not ceased to imperiously demand equality of the sexes, and indeed many of us have never felt our femaleness to be a difficulty or an obstacle; many other problems seem more essential than those that concern us uniquely: this very detachment makes it possible to hope our attitude will be objective. Yet we know the feminine world more intimately than men do because our roots are in it; we grasp more immediately what the fact of being female means for a human being, and we care more about knowing it. I said that there are more essential problems; but this one still has a certain importance from our point of view: how will the fact of being women have affected our lives? What precise opportunities have been given us and which ones have been denied? What destiny awaits our younger sisters, and in which direction should we point them? It is striking that most feminine literature is driven today by an attempt at lucidity more than by a will to make demands; coming out of an era of muddled controversy, this book is one attempt among others to take stock of the current state.

But it is no doubt impossible to approach any human problem without partiality: even the way of asking the questions, of adopting perspectives, presupposes hierarchies of interests; all characteristics comprise values; every so-called objective description is set against an ethical background. Instead of trying to conceal those principles that are more or less explicitly implied, we would be better off stating them from the start; then it would not be necessary to specify on each page the meaning given to the words 'superior', 'inferior', 'better', 'worse', 'progress', 'regression', and so on. If we examine some of the books on women, we see that one of the most frequently held points of view is that of public good or general interest: in reality, this is taken to mean the interest of society as each one wishes to maintain or establish it. In our opinion, there is no public good other than one that assures the citizens' private good; we judge institutions from the point of view of the concrete opportunities they give to individuals. But neither do we confuse the idea of private interest with happiness: that is another frequently encountered point of view; are women in a harem not happier than a woman voter? Is a housewife not happier than a woman worker? We cannot really know what the word 'happiness' means, and still less what authentic values it covers; there is no way to measure the happiness of others, and it is always easy to call a situation that one would like to impose on others happy: in particular, we declare happy those condemned to stagnation, under the pretext that happiness is immobility. This is a notion, then, we will not refer to. The perspective we have adopted is one of existentialist morality. Every subject posits itself as a transcendence concretely, through projects; it accomplishes its freedom only by perpetual surpassing towards other freedoms; there is no other justification for present existence than its expansion towards an indefinitely open future. Every time transcendence lapses into immanence, there is degradation of existence into 'in-itself', of freedom into facticity; this fall is a moral fault if the subject consents to it; if this fall is inflicted on the subject, it takes the form of frustration and oppression; in both cases it is an absolute evil. Every individual concerned with justifying his existence experiences his existence as an indefinite need to transcend himself. But what singularly defines the situation of woman is that being, like all humans, an autonomous freedom, she discovers and chooses herself in a world where men force her to assume herself as Other: an attempt is made to freeze her as an object and doom her to immanence, since her transcendence will be forever transcended by another essential and sovereign consciousness. Woman's drama lies in this conflict between the fundamental claim of every subject, which always posits itself as essential, and the demands of a situation that constitutes her as inessential. How, in the feminine condition, can a human being accomplish herself? What paths are open to her? Which ones lead to dead ends? How can she find independence within dependence? What circumstances limit women's freedom and can she overcome them? These are the fundamental questions we would like to elucidate. This means that in focusing on the individual's possibilities, we will define these possibilities not in terms of happiness but in terms of freedom.

Clearly this problem would have no meaning if we thought that a physiological, psychological or economic destiny weighed on woman. So we will begin by discussing woman from a biological, psychoanalytical and historical materialistic point of view. We will then attempt to positively demonstrate how 'feminine reality' has been constituted, why woman has been defined as Other, and what the consequences have been from men's point of view. Then we will describe the world from the woman's point of view such as it is offered to her,* and we will see the difficulties women are up against just when, trying to escape the sphere they have been assigned until now, they seek to be part of the human *Mitsein*.

* This will be the subject of a second volume.

Part One
DESTINY

Biological Data

Woman? Very simple, say those who like simple answers: she is a womb, an ovary; she is a female: this word is enough to define her. From a man's mouth, the epithet 'female' sounds like an insult; but he, not ashamed of his animality, is proud to hear: 'He's a male!' The term 'female' is pejorative not because it roots woman in nature, but because it confines her in her sex, and if this sex, even in an innocent animal, seems despicable and an enemy to man, it is obviously because of the disquieting hostility woman triggers in him. Nevertheless, he wants to find a justification in biology for this feeling. The word 'female' evokes a saraband of images: an enormous round egg snatching and castrating the agile sperm; monstrous and stuffed, the queen termite reigning over the servile males; the praying mantis and the spider, gorged on love, crushing their partners and gobbling them up; the dog in heat running through back alleys, leaving perverse smells in her wake; the monkey showing herself off brazenly, sneaking away with flirtatious hypocrisy. And the most splendid wildcats, the tigress, lioness and panther, lie down slavishly under the male's imperial embrace, inert, impatient, shrewd, stupid, insensitive, lewd, fierce and humiliated. Man projects all females at once on to woman. And the fact is that she is a female. But if one wants to stop thinking in commonplaces, two questions arise. What does the female represent in the animal kingdom? And what unique kind of female is realised in woman?

Males and females are two types of individuals who are differentiated within one species for the purposes of reproduction; they can be defined only correlatively. But it has to be pointed out first that the very meaning of *division* of the species into two sexes is not clear.

It does not occur universally in nature. In one-celled animals, infusorians, amoebas, bacilli, and so on, multiplication is fundamentally distinct from sexuality, with cells dividing and subdividing individually. For some metazoans, reproduction occurs by schizogenesis, that is dividing the individual whose origin is also asexual, or by blastogenesis, that is dividing the individual itself produced by a sexual phenomenon: the phenomena of budding or segmentation observed in fresh-water hydras, coelenterates, sponges, worms and tunicates are well-known examples. In parthenogenesis, the virgin egg develops in embryonic form without male intervention. The male plays no role or only a secondary one: unfertilised honeybee eggs subdivide and produce drones; in the case of aphids, males are absent for a number of generations, and the unfertilised eggs produce females. Parthenogenesis in the sea urchin, the starfish and the toad have been artificially reproduced. However, sometimes in the protozoa, two cells can merge, forming what is called a zygote; fertilisation is necessary for honeybee eggs to engender females and aphid eggs, males. Some biologists have thus concluded that even in species capable of perpetuating themselves unilaterally, the renewal of genetic diversity through mixing of parental chromosomes would benefit the line's rejuvenation and vigour; in this view, then, in the more complex forms of life, sexuality is an indispensable function; only elementary organisms could multiply without sexes, and even so they would exhaust their vitality. But today this hypothesis is most inexact; observations have proved that asexual multiplication can occur indefinitely without any noticeable degeneration; this is particularly striking in bacilli; more and more – and bolder and even bolder – parthenogenetic experiments have been carried out, and in many species the male seems radically useless. Moreover, even if the value of intercellular exchange could be demonstrated, it would be a purely ungrounded fact. Biology attests to sexual differentiation, but even if biology were imbued with finalism, the differentiation of sexes could not be deduced from cellular structure, laws of cellular multiplication, or from any elementary phenomenon.

The existence of heterogenetic gametes* alone does not necessarily mean there are two distinct sexes; the differentiation of reproductive cells often does not bring about a division of the species into two types: both can belong to the same individual. This is true of hermaphroditic species, so common in plants, and also in many invertebrates, among which are the annulates and molluscs. Reproduction takes place either by self-fertilisation or by cross-fertilisation. Some biologists use this fact to claim the justification of the established order. They consider gonochorism – that is, the system in which the different gonads† belong

---

* Gametes are reproductive cells whose fusion produces an egg.
† Gonads are glands that produce gametes.

to distinct individuals – as an improvement on hermaphroditism, realised by evolution; others, by contrast, consider gonochorism primitive: for those biologists, hermaphroditism would thus be its degeneration. In any case, these notions of superiority of one system over another involve highly contestable theories concerning evolution. All that can be affirmed with certainty is that these two means of reproduction coexist in nature, that they both perpetuate species, and that the heterogeneity of both gametes and gonad-producing organisms seems to be accidental. The differentiation of individuals into males and females thus occurs as an irreducible and contingent fact.

Most philosophies have taken sexual differentiation for granted without attempting to explain it. The Platonic myth has it that in the beginning there were men, women and androgynes; each individual had a double face, four arms, four legs and two bodies joined together; one day they were split into two 'as one would split eggs in two', and ever since then each half seeks to recover its other half: the gods decided later that new human beings would be created by the coupling of two unlike halves. This story only tries to explain love: the differentiation of sexes is taken as a given from the start. Aristotle offers no better account: for if cooperation of matter and form is necessary for any action, it is not necessary that active and passive principles be distributed into two categories of heterogenic individuals. St Thomas declared that woman was an 'inessential' being, which, from a masculine point of view, is a way of positing the accidental character of sexuality. Hegel, however, would have been untrue to his rationalist passion had he not attempted to justify it logically. According to him, sexuality is the mediation by which the subject concretely achieves itself as a genus. 'The genus is therefore present in the individual as a straining against the inadequacy of its single actuality, as the urge to obtain its self-feeling in the other of its genus, to integrate itself through union with it and through this mediation to close the genus with itself and bring it into existence – *copulation*.'*[1] And a little further along, 'the process consists in this, that they become in reality what they are in themselves, namely, one genus, the same subjective vitality.' And Hegel then declares that in order for the process of union to occur, there has to be differentiation of the two sexes. But his demonstration is not convincing: the preconceived idea of locating the three moments of the syllogism in any operation is too obvious here. The surpassing of the individual towards the species, by which individual

---

* Hegel, *Philosophy of Nature*, Part 3, section 369.

and species accomplish themselves in their own truth, could occur without the third element, by the simple relation of genitor to child: reproduction could be asexual. Or the relation to each other could be that of two of the same kind, with differentiation occurring in the singularity of individuals of the same type, as in hermaphroditic species. Hegel's description brings out a very important significance of sexuality: but he always makes the same error of equating significance with reason. It is through sexual activity that men define the sexes and their relations, just as they create the meaning and value of all the functions they accomplish: but sexual activity is not necessarily implied in the human being's nature. In *Phenomenology of Perception*, Merleau-Ponty[2] points out that human existence calls for revision of the notions of necessity and contingency. 'Existence has no fortuitous attributes, no content which does not contribute towards giving it its form; it does not give admittance to any pure fact because it is the process by which facts are drawn up.' This is true. But it is also true that there are conditions without which the very fact of existence would seem to be impossible. Presence in the world vigorously implies the positing of a body that is both a thing of the world and a point of view on this world: but this body need not possess this or that particular structure. In *Being and Nothingness*,[3] Sartre disputes Heidegger's affirmation that human reality is doomed to death because of its finitude; he establishes that a finite and temporally limitless existence could be conceivable; nevertheless, if human life were not inhabited by death, the relationship of human beings to the world and to themselves would be so deeply upset that the statement 'man is mortal' would be anything but an empirical truth: immortal, an existent would no longer be what we call a man. One of the essential features of man's destiny is that the movement of his temporal life creates behind and ahead of him the infinity of the past and the future: the perpetuation of the species appears thus as the correlative of individual limitation, so the phenomenon of reproduction can be considered as ontologically grounded. But this is where one must stop; the perpetuation of the species does not entail sexual differentiation. That it is taken on by existents in such a way that it thereby enters into the concrete definition of existence, so be it. Nevertheless, a consciousness without a body or an immortal human being is rigorously inconceivable, whereas a society can be imagined that reproduces itself by parthenogenesis or is composed of hermaphrodites.

Opinions about the respective roles of the two sexes have varied greatly; they were initially devoid of any scientific basis and only reflected social myths. It was thought for a long time, and is still thought in some primitive societies based on matrilineal filiation, that the father has no part in the child's conception: ancestral larvae were supposed to infiltrate the womb in the form of living germs. With the advent of patriarchy, the male resolutely claimed his posterity; the mother had to be granted a role in procreation even though she merely carried and fattened the living seed: the father alone was the creator. Artistotle imagined that the foetus was produced by the meeting of the sperm and the menses: in this symbiosis, woman just provided passive material while the male principle is strength, activity, movement and life. Hippocrates' doctrine also recognised two types of seed, a weak or female one, and a strong one, which was male. Artistotelian theory was perpetuated throughout the Middle Ages and down to the modern period. In the middle of the seventeenth century, Harvey, slaughtering female deer shortly after they had mated, found vesicles in the uterine horns that he thought were eggs but which were really embryos. The Danish scientist Steno coined the term 'ovaries' for the female genital glands that had until then been called 'feminine testicles', and he noted the existence of vesicles on their surface that Graaf, in 1672, had erroneously identified as eggs and to which he gave his name. The ovary was still regarded as a homologue of the male gland. That same year, though, 'spermatic animalcules' were discovered penetrating the feminine womb. But it was thought that they went there for nourishment only, and that the individual was already prefigured in them; in 1694, the Dutchman Hartsoeker drew an image of the homunculus hidden in the sperm, and in 1699 another scientist declared he had seen the sperm cast off a kind of slough under which there was a little man, which he also drew. In these hypotheses woman merely fattened a living and active, and perfectly constituted, principle. These theories were not universally accepted and discussion continued until the nineteenth century. The invention of the microscope led to the study of the animal egg; in 1827, Baer identified the mammal's egg: an element contained inside Graaf's follicle. Soon its structure could be studied; in 1835, the sarcode – that is, the protoplasm – and then the cell were discovered; in 1877 the sperm was observed penetrating the starfish egg. From that the symmetry of the two gametes' nuclei was established; their fusion was analysed in detail for the first time in 1883 by a Belgian zoologist.

But Aristotle's ideas have not lost all validity. Hegel thought the two sexes must be different: one is active and the other passive, and it goes without saying that passivity will be the female's lot. 'Because of this differentiation, man is thus the active principle while woman is the passive principle because she resides in her non-developed unity.'* And even when the ovum was recognised as an active principle, men continued to pit its inertia against the agility of the sperm. Today, there is a tendency to see the contrary: the discoveries of parthenogenesis have led some scientists to reduce the role of the male to that of a simple physico-chemical agent. In some species the action of an acid or a mechanical stimulation has been shown to trigger the division of the egg and the development of the embryo; and from that it was boldly assumed that the male gamete was not necessary for generation; it would be at most a ferment; perhaps man's co-operation in procreation would one day become useless: that seems to be many women's desire. But nothing warrants such a bold expectation because nothing warrants universal-ising life's specific processes. The phenomena of asexual multiplication and parthenogenesis are neither more nor less fundamental than those of sexual reproduction. And it has already been noted that this form is not a priori favoured: but no fact proves it is reducible to a more elemen-tary mechanism.

Rejecting any a priori doctrine, any implausible theory, we find ourselves before a fact that has neither ontological nor empirical basis and whose impact cannot a priori be understood. By examining it in its concrete reality, we can hope to extract its significance: thus perhaps the content of the word 'female' will come to light.

The idea here is not to propose a philosophy of life or to take sides too hastily in the quarrel between finalism and mechanism. Yet it is note-worthy that physiologists and biologists all use a more or less finalistic language merely because they ascribe meaning to vital phenomena. We will use their vocabulary. Without coming to any conclusion about life and consciousness, we can affirm that any living fact indicates transcen-dence, and that a project is in the making in every function: these descrip-tions do not suggest more than this.

In most species, male and female organisms cooperate for reproduc-tion. They are basically defined by the gametes they produce. In some algae and fungi, the cells that fuse to produce the egg are identical; these cases of isogamy are significant in that they manifest the basal equiva-lence of the usually differentiated gametes: but their analogy remains striking. Sperm and ova result from a basically identical cellular evolution:

* Ibid.

the development of primitive female cells into oocytes differs from that of spermatocytes by protoplasmic phenomena, but the nuclear phenomena are approximately the same. The idea the biologist Ancel expressed in 1903 is still considered valid today: 'An undifferentiated prog-erminating cell becomes male or female depending on the conditions in the genital gland at the moment of its appearance, conditions deter-mined by the transformation of some epithelial cells into nourishing elements, developers of a special material.'[4] This primary kinship is expressed in the structure of the two gametes that carry the same number of chromosomes inside each species. During fertilisation, the two nuclei merge their substance and the chromosomes in each are reduced to half their original number: this reduction takes place in both of them in a similar way; the last two divisions of the ovum result in the formation of polar globules equivalent to the last divisions of the sperm. It is thought today that, depending on the species, the male or female gamete determines the sex: for mammals, the sperm possesses a chromosome that is heterogenic to the others and potentially either male or female. According to Mendel's statistical laws, transmission of hereditary char-acteristics takes place equally from the father and the mother. What is important to see is that in this meeting neither gamete takes precedence over the other: they both sacrifice their individuality; the egg absorbs the totality of their substance. There are thus two strong current biases that – at least at this basic biological level – prove false: the first one is the female's passivity; the living spark is not enclosed within either of the two gametes. It springs forth from their meeting; the nucleus of the ovum is a vital principle perfectly symmetrical to the sperm's. The second bias contradicts the first, which does not exclude the fact that they often coexist: the permanence of the species is guaranteed by the female since the male principle has an explosive and fleeting existence. In reality, the embryo equally perpetuates the germ cells of the father and the mother and retransmits them together to its descendants, sometimes in a male and sometimes a female form. One might say that an androgynous germ cell survives the individual metamorphoses of the soma from genera-tion to generation.

That being said, there are highly interesting secondary differences to be observed between the ovum and the sperm; the essential singularity of the ovum is that it is supplied with material destined to nourish and protect the embryo; it stocks up on reserves from which the foetus will build its tissues, reserves that are not a living substance but an inert mater-ial; the result is a massive, relatively voluminous, spherical or ellipsoidal form. The bird's egg's dimensions are well known. The woman's egg measures 0.13 mm while the human semen contains 60,000 sperm per cubic millimetre: their mass is extremely small. The sperm has a thread-like tail, a little elongated head; no foreign substance weighs it down. It is entirely life; this structure destines it for mobility; the ovum, on the contrary, where the future of the foetus is stored, is a fixed element: enclosed in the female organism or suspended in an exterior environment, it waits passively for fertilisation. The male gamete seeks it out; the sperm is always a naked cell, while the ovum is, according to the species, protected or not by a membrane; but in any case, the sperm bumps into the ovum when it comes into contact with it, makes it waver and infiltrates it; the male gamete loses its tail; its head swells, and, twisting, it reaches the nucleus. Meanwhile, the egg immediately forms a membrane that keeps other sperm from entering. For echinoderms where fertilisation is external, it is easy to observe the rush of the sperm that surround the floating and inert egg like a halo. This competition is also another important phenomenon found in most species; much smaller than the ovum, the sperm are generally produced in considerable quantities and each ovum has many suitors.

Thus, the ovum, active in the nucleus, its essential principle, is super-ficially passive; its mass, closed upon itself, compact in itself, evokes the nocturnal heaviness and repose of the in-itself: the ancients visualised the closed world in the form of a sphere or opaque atom; immobile, the ovum waits; by contrast, the open sperm, tiny and agile, embodies the impatience and worry of existence. One should not get carried away with the pleasure of allegories: the ovum has sometimes been likened to immanence and the sperm to transcendence. By giving up its tran-scendence and mobility, the sperm penetrates the female element: it is grabbed and castrated by the inert mass that absorbs it after cutting off its tail; like all passive actions, this one is magical and disturbing; the male gamete activity is rational, a measurable movement in terms of time and space. In truth, these are merely ramblings. Male and female gametes merge together in the egg; together they cancel each other out in their totality. It is false to claim that the egg voraciously absorbs the male gamete and just as false to say that the latter victoriously appro-priates the female cell's reserves because in the act that merges them, their individuality disappears. And to a mechanistic philosophy, the move-ment undoubtedly looks like a rational phenomenon par excellence; but for modern physics the idea is no clearer than that of action at a distance; besides, the details of the physicochemical interactions leading to fertilisation are not known. It is possible, however, to come away with a valuable indication from this meeting. There are two movements that come together in life, and life maintains itself only by surpassing itself. It does not surpass itself without maintaining itself; these two moments are always accomplished together. It is academic to claim to separate them: nevertheless, it is either one or the other that dominates. The two unified gametes go beyond and are perpetuated; but the ovum's structure anticipates future needs; it is constituted to nourish the life that will awaken in it, while the sperm is in no way equipped to ensure the development of the germ it gives rise to. In contrast, whereas the sperm moves around, the ovum is incapable of triggering the change that will bring about a new explosion of life. Without the egg's prescience, the sperm's action would be useless; but without the latter's initiative, the egg would not accomplish its vital potential. The conclusion is thus that fundamentally the role of the two gametes is identical; together they create a living being in which both of them lose and surpass themselves. But in the secondary and superficial phenomena that condition fertilisation, it is through the male element that the change in situation occurs for the new eclosion of life; it is through the female element that this eclosion is established in a stable element.

It would be rash to deduce from such an observation that woman's place is in the home: but there are rash people. In his book *Nature and Character According to Individuals, Sex and Race*,[5] Alfred Fouillée claimed he could define woman entirely from the ovum and man from the sperm; many so-called deep theories are based on this game of dubious analogies. It is never clear what philosophy of nature this pseudo-thinking refers to. If one considers laws of heredity, men and women come equally from a sperm and an ovum. I suppose that vestiges of the old medieval philosophy – that the cosmos was the exact reflection of a microcosm – are floating around in these foggy minds: it was imagined that the ovum is a female homunculus and woman a giant ovum. These reveries dismissed since the days of alchemy make a weird contrast with the scientific precision of descriptions being used at this very moment: modern biology does not mesh with medieval symbolism; but our people do not look all that closely. If one is a bit scrupulous, one has to agree that it is a long way from ovum to woman. The ovum does not yet even contain the very notion of female. Hegel rightly notes that the sexual relationship cannot be reduced to that of two gametes. Thus, the female organism has to be studied in its totality.

It has already been pointed out that for many vegetables and some primitive animals, among them molluscs, gamete specification does not lead to individual specification, as they produce both ova and sperm. Even when the sexes separate, the barriers between them are not tight like those that separate species; just as gametes are defined from an originally undifferentiated tissue, males and females develop more as variations on a common base. For certain animals – *Bonellia viridis*[6] is the most typical case – the embryo is first asexual and its eventual sexuality is determined by the incertitudes of its development. It is accepted today that in most species sex determination depends on the genotypical constitution of the egg. The virgin egg of the honeybee reproducing itself by parthenogenesis yields males exclusively; that of fruit flies in the exact same conditions yields females exclusively. When eggs are fertilised, it is to be noted that – except for some spiders – an approximately equal number of male and female individuals is procreated; differentiation comes from the heterogeneity of one of the two types of gametes: for mammals sperm possess either a male or a female potentiality. It is not really known what determines the singular character of heterogenic gametes during spermatogenesis or oogenesis; in any case, Mendel's statistical laws are sufficient to explain their regular distribution. For both sexes, fertilisation and the beginning of embryonic development occur in an identical way; the epithelial tissue destined to evolve into a gonad is undifferentiated at the outset; at a certain stage of maturation testicles take shape or later the ovary takes form. This explains why there are many intermediaries between hermaphroditism and gonochorism; very often one of the sexes possesses certain organs characteristic of the complementary sex: the toad is the most striking case of that; the male has an atrophied ovary called Bidder's organ that can be made to produce eggs artificially. Mammals also have vestiges of this sexual bipotentiality: for example the pedicled and sessile hydra, the *uterus masculinus*, mammary glands in the male, Gartner's duct in the female, and the clitoris. Even in species where sexual division is the most clear-cut, there are individuals that are both male and female simultaneously: cases of intersexuality are numerous in animals and human beings; and in butterflies and crustaceans there are examples of gynandromorphism in which male and female characteristics are juxtaposed in a kind of mosaic. Genotypically defined, the foetus is nevertheless deeply influenced by the milieu from which it draws its nourishment: for ants, honeybees and termites, how nutrition occurs makes the larva a realised female or thwarts its sexual maturation, reducing it to the rank of worker; the influence in this case pervades the whole organism: for insects the soma is sexually defined very early on and does not depend on gonads. For vertebrates, it is essentially the gonadic hormones that play a regulatory role. Many experiments have demonstrated that varying the endocrine milieu makes it possible to act on sex determination; other grafting and castration experiments carried out on adult animals have led to the modern theory of sexuality: in male and female vertebrates, the soma is identical and can be considered a neutral element; the action of the gonad gives it its sexual characteristics; some of the secreted hormones act as stimulants and others as inhibitors; the genital tract itself is somatic, and embryology shows that it takes shape under the influence of hormones from bisexual precursors. Intersexuality exists when hormonal balance has not been realised and when neither of the two sexual potentialities has been clearly accomplished.

Equally distributed in the species, and evolved analogously from identical roots, male and female organisms seem profoundly symmetrical once they are formed. Both are characterised by the presence of gamete-producing glands, ovaries or testicles, with the analogous processes of spermatogenesis and ovogenesis, as was seen earlier; these glands deliver their secretion in a more or less complex canal according to the hierarchy of the species: the female drops the egg directly by the oviduct, holds it in the cloaca or in a differentiated uterus before expelling it; the male either lets go of the semen outside or is equipped with a copulating organ that allows it to penetrate the female. Statistically, the male and female thus look like two complementary types. They have to be envisaged from a functional point of view to grasp their singularity.

It is very difficult to give a generally valid description of the notion of female; defining her as a carrier of ova and the male as a carrier of sperm is insufficient because the relation of organism to gonads is extremely variable; inversely, the differentiation of the gametes does not directly affect the organism as a whole: it was sometimes claimed that as the ovum was bigger, it consumed more living force than the sperm; but the latter is secreted in infinitely greater quantity so that in the two sexes the expenditure balances out. Spermatogenesis was taken as an example of prodigality and ovulation a model of economy: but in this phenomenon there is also an absurd profusion; the immense majority of eggs are never fertilised. In any case, gametes and gonads are not microcosms of the whole organism. This is what has to be studied directly.

One of the most noteworthy features when surveying the steps of the animal ladder is that, from bottom to top, life becomes more individual; at the bottom it concentrates on the maintenance of the species, and at the top it puts its energies into single individuals. In lower species, the organism is reduced to barely more than the reproductive apparatus; in this case, the ovum – and therefore, the female – takes precedence over everything else, since it is above all the ovum that is dedicated to the sheer repetition of life; but it is barely more than an abdomen and its existence is entirely devoured by the work of a monstrous ovulation. It reaches gigantic dimensions compared with the male; but its members are often just stumps, its body a formless bag; all the organs have degenerated to nourish the eggs. In truth, although they constitute two distinct organisms, males and females can hardly be thought of as individuals; they form one whole with elements that are inextricably linked: these are intermediary cases between hermaphroditism and gonochorism. For the entoniscid, parasites that live off the crab, the female is a kind of whitish sausage surrounded by incubating slivers harbouring thousands of eggs; in their midst are minuscule males as well as larvae destined to provide replacement males. The enslavement of the dwarf male is even more total in the *Edriolydnus*: it is attached beneath the female's operculum and is without a digestive tube of its own; it is solely devoted to reproduction. In all these cases the female is just as enslaved as the male: she is a slave to the species; while the male is fastened to his spouse, his spouse is also fastened, either to a living organism on which she feeds as a parasite, or to a mineral substratum; she is consumed by producing eggs the minuscule male fertilises. As life takes on more complex forms, individual autonomy develops with the loosening of the link uniting the sexes; but insects of both sexes remain tightly subordinate to the eggs. In the case of ephemerals, both spouses often die after coitus and laying; and in the case of rotifers and mosquitoes, the male, lacking a digestive apparatus, sometimes perishes after fertilisation, while the female can feed herself and survive: egg formation and laying take time; the mother dies as soon as the next generation's future has been assured. The privilege of many female insects comes from the fact that fertilisation is generally a rapid process while ovulation and incubation of the eggs demand a long period of time. For termites, the enormous mush-stuffed queen that lays an egg a second until she is sterile – and then is pitilessly massacred – is no less a slave than the dwarf male attached to her abdomen that fertilises the eggs as they are expelled. In bee and ant matriarchies, males are intruders that are massacred each season: at the time of the wedding flight, all the male ants escape from the anthill and fly toward the females; if they reach and fertilise them, they die immediately, exhausted; if not, the female workers refuse them entry. They kill them in front of the entrances or let them starve to death; but the fertilised female has a sad fate: she digs herself into the earth alone and often dies from exhaustion while laying the first eggs; if she manages to reconstitute a colony, she is imprisoned for twelve years laying eggs ceaselessly; the female workers whose sexuality has been atrophied live for four years, but their whole life is devoted to raising the larvae. Likewise for the bees: the drone that catches the queen in her wedding flight crashes to the ground eviscerated; the other drones return to their colony, where they are unproductive and in the way; at the beginning of the winter, they are killed. But the sterile worker bees trade their right to life for incessant work; the queen is really the hive's slave: she lays eggs ceaselessly; and the old queen dies; some larvae are nourished so they can try to succeed her. The first one hatched kills the others in the cradle. The female giant spider carries her eggs in a bag until they reach maturity: she is bigger and stronger than the male, and she sometimes devours him after coupling; the same practices can be seen in the praying mantis, which has taken shape as the myth of devouring femininity: the egg castrates the sperm and the praying mantis assassinates her spouse; these facts prefigure a woman's dream of castration. But in truth, the praying mantis only manifests such cruelty in captivity: free and with rich enough food around, she rarely makes a meal out of the male; if she does, it is like the solitary ant that often eats some of her own eggs in order to have the strength to lay eggs and perpetuate the species. Seeing in these facts the harbinger of the 'battle of the sexes' that sets individuals as such against each other is just rambling. Neither for the ants, nor the honeybees, nor the termites, nor the spider, nor the praying mantis can one say that the female enslaves and devours the male: it is the species that devours both of them in different ways. The female lives longer and seems to have more importance; but she has no autonomy; laying, incubation, and care of the larvae make up her whole destiny; her other functions are totally or partially atrophied. By contrast, an individual existence takes shape in the male. He very often takes more initiative than the female in fertilisation; it is he who seeks her out, who attacks, palpates, seizes her and imposes coitus on her; sometimes he has to fight off other males. Accordingly, the organs of locomotion, touch and prehension are also often more developed; many female butterflies are apterous whereas their males have wings; males have more developed colours, elytrons, feet and claws; and sometimes this profusion can also be seen in a luxurious vanity of gorgeous colours. Aside from the fleeting coitus, the male's life is useless, gratuitous: next to the diligence of worker females, the laziness of drones is a privilege worth noting. But this privilege is outrageous; the male often pays with his life for this useless-ness that contains the germ of independence. A species that enslaves the female punishes the male attempting to escape: it eliminates him brutally.

In the higher forms of life, reproduction becomes the production of differentiated organisms; it has a twofold face: maintenance of the species and creation of new individuals; this innovative aspect asserts itself as the singularity of the individual is confirmed. It is thus striking that these two moments of perpetuation and creation divide; this break, already marked at the time of the egg's fertilisation, is present in the generating phenomenon as a whole. The structure of the egg itself does not order this division; the female, like the male, possesses a certain autonomy and her link with the egg loosens; the female fish, amphibian and bird are much more than an abdomen; the weaker the mother-to-egg link, the less labour parturition involves, and the more undifferentiated is the rela-tion between parents and their offspring. Sometimes, the newly hatched lives are the father's responsibility; this is often the case with fish. Water is an element that can carry eggs and sperm and enables their meeting; fertilisation in the aquatic milieu is almost always external; fish do not mate: at best some rub against each other for stimulation. The mother expels the ova and the father the sperm: they have identical roles. There is no more reason for the mother to recognise the eggs as her own than the father. In some species, parents abandon the eggs, which develop without help; sometimes the mother has prepared a nest for them; some-times she watches over them after fertilisation; but very often the father takes charge of them: as soon as he has fertilised them, he chases away the female, who tries to devour them; he fiercely defends them from anything that approaches; there are those that put up a kind of protec-tive nest by emitting air bubbles covered with an isolating substance; they also often incubate the eggs in their mouths or, like the sea horse, in the folds of the stomach. Analogous phenomena can be seen in toads: they do not have real coitus; the male embraces the female and this embrace stimulates the laying: while the eggs are coming out of the cloaca, the male lets out his sperm. Very often – and in particular in the toad known as the midwife toad – the father winds the strings of eggs around his feet and carries them around to guarantee their hatching. As for birds, the egg forms rather slowly within the female; the egg is both relatively big and hard to expel; it has much closer relations with the mother than the father that fertilised it during a quick coitus; the female is the one who usually sits on it and then looks after the young; but very frequently the father participates in the nest's construction and the protection and nutrition of the young; there are rare cases – for example the passerine – where the male sits on the eggs and then raises the young. Male and female pigeons secrete a kind of milk in their crop that they feed to the fledglings. What is noteworthy in all these cases in which fathers play a nurturing role is that spermatogenesis stops during the period they devote to their offspring; busy with maintaining life, the father has no impetus to bring forth new life-forms.

The most complex and concretely individualised life is found in mammals. The split of the two vital moments, maintaining and creating, takes place definitively in the separation of the sexes. In this branching out – and considering vertebrates only – the mother has the closest connection to her offspring, whereas the father is more uninterested; the whole organism of the female is adapted to and determined by the servitude of maternity, while the sexual initiative is the prerogative of the male. The female is the prey of the species; for one or two seasons, depending on the case, her whole life is regulated by a sexual cycle – the oestrous cycle – whose length and periodicity vary from one species to another. This cycle has two phases: during the first one the ova mature (the number varies according to the species) and a nidification process occurs in the womb; in the second phase a fat necrosis is produced, ending in the elimination of the structure, that is a whitish discharge. The oestrus corresponds to the period of heat; but heat in the female is rather passive; she is ready to receive the male, she waits for him; for mammals – and some birds – she might invite him; but she limits herself to calling him by noises, displays or exhibitions; she could never impose coitus. That decision is up to him in the end. Even for insects where the female has major privileges and consents to total sacrifice for the species, it is usually the male that provokes fertilisation; male fish often invite the female to spawn by their presence or by touching; for amphibians, the male acts as a stimulator. But for birds and above all mammals, the male imposes himself on her; very often she submits to him with indifference or even resists him. Whether she is provocative or consensual, it is he in any case who *takes* her: she is *taken*. The word often has a very precise meaning: either because he has specific organs or because he is stronger, the male grabs and immobilises her; he is the one that actively makes the coitus movements; for many insects, birds and mammals, he penetrates her. In that regard, she is like a raped interiority. The male does not do violence to the species, because the species can only perpetuate itself by renewal; it would perish if ova and sperm did not meet; but the female whose job it is to protect the egg encloses it in herself, and her body that constitutes a shelter for the egg removes it from the male's fertilising action; there is thus a resistance that has to be broken down, and so by penetrating the egg the male realises himself as activity. His domination is expressed by the coital position of almost all animals; the male is *on* the female. And the organ he uses is incontestably material too, but it is seen in an animated state: it is a tool, while the female organ in this operation is merely an inert receptacle. The male deposits his sperm: the female receives it. Thus, although she plays a fundamentally active role in procreation, she endures coitus, which alienates her from herself by penetration and internal fertilisation; although she feels the sexual need as an individual need – since in heat she might seek out the male – she nevertheless experiences the sexual adventure in its immediacy as an interior story and not in relation to the world and to others. But the fundamental difference between male and female mammals is that in the same quick instant, the sperm, by which the male's life transcends into another, becomes foreign to it and is separated from its body; thus the male, at the very moment it goes beyond its individuality, encloses itself once again in it. By contrast, the ovum began to separate itself from the female when, ripe, it released itself from the follicle to fall into the oviduct; penetrated by a foreign gamete, it implants itself in the uterus: first violated, the female is then alienated; she carries the foetus in her womb for varying stages of maturation depending on the species: the guinea pig is born almost adult; the dog close to a foetal state; inhabited by another who is nourished by her substance, the female is both herself and other than herself during the whole gestation period; after delivery, she feeds the newborn with milk from her breasts. This makes it difficult to know when it can be considered autonomous: at fertilisation, birth, or weaning? It is noteworthy that the more the female becomes a separate individual, the more imperiously the living continuity is affirmed beyond any separation. The fish or the bird that expels the virgin ovum or the fertilised egg is less prey to its offspring than the female mammal. The female mammal recovers her autonomy after the birth of the young: a distance is thus established between her and them; and starting from this separation, she devotes herself to them; she takes care of them, showing initiative and invention; she fights to defend them against other animals and even becomes aggressive. But she does not usually seek to affirm her individuality; she does not oppose either males or females; she does not have a fighting instinct;* in spite of Darwin's assertions, disparaged today, the female in general accepts the male that presents himself. It is not that she lacks individual qualities – far from it; in periods when she escapes the servitude of maternity, she can sometimes be the male's equal: the mare is as quick as the stallion, the female hound has as keen a nose as the male, female monkeys show as much intelligence as males when tested. But this individuality is not asserted: the female abdicates it for the benefit of the species that demands this abdication.

The male's destiny is very different; it has just been shown that in his very surpassing, he separates himself and is confirmed in himself. This feature is constant from insects to higher animals. Even fish and cetaceans that live in schools, loosely gathered within the group, tear themselves away when in heat; they isolate themselves and become aggressive towards other males. While sexuality is immediate for the female, it is indirect in the male: he actively bridges the distance between desire and its satisfaction; he moves, seeks, feels the female, caresses her, immobilises her before penetrating; the organs for the functions of relation, locomotion and prehension are often better developed in the male. It is noteworthy that the active impulsion that produces his sperm's multiplication is accompanied by brilliant feathers, shiny scales, horns, antlers, a crest, song, exuberance; neither the 'wedding attire' he puts on in heat nor the displays of seduction are now thought to have a selective finality; but they are witness to the power of life that flourishes in him with gratuitous and magnificent splendour. This vital generosity, the activity deployed in mating and in coitus itself, the dominating affirmation of his power over the female – all of this contributes to positing the individual as such at the moment he surpasses himself. Hegel is right to see the subjective element in the male while the female remains enclosed in the species. Subjectivity and separateness immediately mean conflict. Aggressiveness is one of the characteristics of the male in heat. It cannot be explained by competition, since there are about the same number of females as males; it is rather competition that is explained by this combative will. It is as if before procreating, the male, claiming as his very own the act that perpetuates the species, confirms the reality of his individuality in his fight against his fellow creatures. The species inhabits

* Some chickens fight in the barnyard for a pecking order. Cows too become head of the herd if there are no males.

the female and absorbs much of her individual life; the male, by contrast, integrates specific living forces in his individual life. He is undoubtedly also subject to laws that surpass him; he experiences spermatogenesis and periodic heats; but these processes affect the organism as a whole much less than the oestrus cycle; neither sperm production nor ovogenesis as such is tiring: the absorbing job for the female is the development of the egg into an adult animal. Coitus is a rapid operation that does not reduce the male's vitality. He manifests almost no paternal instinct. He very often abandons the female after mating. When he remains near her as head of a family group (monogamic family, harem, or herd), he plays a protective and nurturing role vis-à-vis the whole community; it is rare for him to take a direct interest in the children. In those species that are favourable to the flourishing of individual life, the male's effort at autonomy – which, in the lower animals, leads to its ruin – is crowned with success. He is usually bigger than the female, stronger, quicker, more adventurous; he leads a more independent life whose activities are more gratuitous; he is more conquering, more imperious: in animal societies, it is he who commands.

In nature nothing is ever completely clear: the two types, male and female, are not always sharply distinguished; there is often a dimorphism – the colour of the coat, the placement of the mottling – that seems absolutely contingent; it does happen though that the two types are not distinguishable, their functions barely differentiated, as was seen with fish. However, as a whole and especially at the top of the animal scale, the two sexes represent two diverse aspects of the species' life. Their opposition is not, as has been claimed, one of passivity and activity: not only is the ovum nucleus active, but the development of the embryo is also a living process and not a mechanical one. It would be too simple to define this opposition as one of change and permanence: the sperm creates only because its vitality is maintained in the egg; the ovum can only exist by surpassing itself or else it regresses and degenerates. But it is true that in both these active operations – maintenance and creation – the synthesis of becoming is not realised in the same way. Maintaining means denying the dispersion of instants, thereby affirming continuity in the course of their outpouring; creating means exploding an irreducible and separate present within a temporal unity, and it is also true that for the female it is the continuity of life that seeks to realise itself in spite of separation, while separation into new and individualised forces is brought about by male initiative; he can affirm himself in his autonomy; he integrates the specific energy into his own life; by contrast, female individuality is fought by the interest of the species; she seems possessed by outside forces: alienated. This explains why sexual opposition increases rather than abates when the individuality of organisms asserts itself. The male finds more and more ways to use the forces of which he is master; the female feels her subjugation more and more; the conflict between her own interests and those of the generating forces that inhabit her exasperate her. Giving birth for cows and mares is far more painful and dangerous than for female mice and rabbits. Woman, the most individual-ised of females, is also the most fragile, the one who experiences her destiny the most dramatically and who distinguishes herself the most significantly from her male.

In the human species as in most others, almost as many individuals of both sexes are born (100 girls for 104 boys); embryonic evolution is analogous; however, the original epithelium remains neuter longer in the female foetus; as a result it is subjected to hormonal influence over a longer period and its development is more often inverted; most hermaphrodites are thought to be genotypically female subjects who are masculinised later: it could be said that the male organism is immedi-ately defined as male, whereas the female embryo is reluctant to accept its femaleness; but these tentative beginnings of foetal life are not yet well enough understood for them to be assigned a meaning. Once formed, the genital apparatus is symmetrical in both sexes; the hormones of each type belong to the same chemical family, the sterols, and when all things are considered, all of them derive from cholesterol; they order the secondary differentiation of the soma. Neither their formula nor their anatomical singularities define the human female as such. Her functional evolution is what distinguishes her from the male. Man's development is comparatively simple. From birth to puberty, he grows more or less regularly; at around fifteen or sixteen years old, spermatogenesis begins and continues until old age; hormone production occurs at the same time and marks the male constitution of the soma. When that happens, the male's sex life is normally integrated into his individual existence: in terms of desire and coitus, his surpassing towards the species is an inte-gral part of the subjective moment of his transcendence: he *is* his body. Woman's history is much more complex. At the beginning of embry-onic life, the supply of ovocytes is definitively formed; the ovary contains about fifty thousand ova and each one is enclosed in a follicle with about four hundred reaching maturity. At the moment of birth the species has taken possession of her and seeks to affirm itself; on coming into the world, the woman goes through a kind of first puberty; ovocytes suddenly grow bigger; then the ovary reduces by about one-fifth. One could say that the child was granted a reprieve; while its organism develops, its genital system remains more or less stationary. Some follicles swell up without reaching maturity; the girl's growth is analogous to the boy's: at the same age she is often bigger and heavier than he. But at puberty the species reasserts its rights: influenced by ovarian secretions, the number of growing follicles increases, the ovary becomes congested and grows, one of the ova reaches maturity and the menstrual cycle begins; the genital system attains its definitive size and form, the soma becomes feminised, and the endocrine balance is set up. It is worth noting that this event has all the characteristics of a crisis; the woman's body does not accept the species's installation in her without a fight; and this fight weakens and endangers her; before puberty, about the same number of girls die for every 100 boys: from fourteen to eighteen, 128 girls die for every 100 boys, and from eighteen to twenty-two, 105 girls for every 100 boys. This is the period when chlorosis, tuberculosis, scoliosis, osteomyelitis, and such strike. Puberty is abnormally early for some subjects: it can occur at four or five years of age. For others, it does not begin at all: the subject is infantile, suffering from amenorrhoea or dysmenorrhoea. Some women manifest virile characteristics: too many secretions from the adrenal glands give them masculine characteristics. These anomalies are absolutely not a victory of the individual over the tyranny of the species: there is no way to escape that tyranny because it enslaves individual life at the same time that it nourishes it; this duality can be seen in the ovarian functions; the woman's vitality takes root in the ovary, that of the man in the testicles: in both cases the castrated individual is not only sterile: it regresses and degenerates; un-'formed' and badly formed, the whole organism is impoverished and out of balance; it can only flourish with the flourishing of the genital system; and yet many genital phenomena are not in the interest of the subject's individual life and even put it in danger. The mammary glands that develop at puberty have no role in the woman's individual economy: they can be removed at any moment in her life. The finality of many ovarian secretions is in the egg, in its maturity, in the adaptation of the uterus for its needs: for the organism as a whole, they are a factor of imbalance more than regulation; the woman is more adapted to the egg's needs than to herself. From puberty to menopause she is the principal site of a story that takes place in her and does not concern her personally. Anglo-Saxons call menstruation 'the curse', and it is true that there is no individual finality in the menstrual cycle. It was thought in Aristotle's time that the blood that flowed each month, if fertilisation occurred, was to constitute the flesh and blood of the child; the truth of this old theory is that women endlessly start up the labour of gestation. For other mammals, this oestrus cycle plays itself out during one season; there is no bloody flow: only in higher monkeys and women does this cycle take place in pain and blood.* For about fourteen days one of the Graafian follicles that envelops the eggs increases in volume and ripens at the same time that the ovary secretes the hormone folliculine at the level of the follicle. Ovulation takes place on the fourteenth day: the walls of the follicle disintegrate (sometimes causing a slight haemorrhage); the egg falls into the fallopian tubes while the opening evolves into the yellow body. Then begins the second or corpus luteum phase characterised by the secretion of the hormone progestin that acts on the uterus. The uterus changes in that the wall's capillary system swells, creases and waffles, forming a kind of lacework; this is the construction of a cradle in the womb meant to receive the fertilised egg. As these cellular transformations are irreversible, this construction is not reabsorbed in cases where there is no fertilisation: in other mammals the useless debris is possibly carried off by the lymph vessels. But for woman when the endometrial lace collapses, there is an exfoliation of the lining, the capillaries open up and a bloody mass seeps out. Then, while the corpus luteum is reconstituted, a new follicular phase begins. This complex process, whose details are still quite mysterious, sets the whole body in motion as it is accompanied by hormonal secretions that act on the thyroid and pituitary glands, the central and peripheral nervous systems and thus on all the organs. Almost all women – more than 85 per cent – show signs of distress during this period. Blood pressure rises before the beginning of the flow of blood and then falls; the pulse rate and often the temperature increase; there are frequent cases of fever; the abdomen is painful; there is often constipation and then diarrhoea, an increase in the liver volume, urea retention, albumin deficiency, or micro albumin; many women have hyperaemia of the pituitary gland (sore throat), and others complain of auditory and visual problems; there is a rise in perspiration secretions accompanied by a sometimes strong sui generis odour at the beginning of and often throughout the menstrual

* The analysis of these phenomena has been advanced in the last few years by comparing the phenomena occurring in women with those in the higher monkeys, especially for the Rhesus factor. 'It is obviously easier to experiment on the latter animals,' writes Louis Gallien (*La sexualité* [*Sexual Reproduction*]).

period. Basal metabolism increases. The number of red blood cells decreases; however, the blood carries substances usually kept in reserve in the tissues, in particular calcium salts; these salts act on the ovary, on the thyroid that is overactive, and on the pituitary gland that regulates the metamorphosis of the activated uterine tissue; this glandular instability weakens the nervous system: the central nervous system is affected, often causing headaches, and the peripheral nervous system overreacts: the automatic control by the central nervous system is reduced, which relaxes the reflexes and the convulsive complexes and is manifested in great mood changes: woman is more emotional, nervous and irritable than usual and can manifest serious psychological problems. This is when she feels most acutely that her body is an alienated opaque thing; it is the prey of a stubborn and foreign life that makes and unmakes a crib in her every month; every month a child is prepared to be born and is aborted in the flow of the crimson tide; woman *is* her body as man *is* his,* but her body is something other than her.

Woman experiences an even stronger alienation when the fertilised egg drops into the uterus and develops there; gestation is, of course, a normal phenomenon that is not harmful to the mother if normal conditions of health and nutrition prevail: certain beneficial interactions develop between her and the foetus; however, contrary to an optimistic theory that is so obviously useful socially, gestation is tiring work that offers woman no benefit as an individual but that demands serious sacrifices.† In the early months, it often brings with it appetite loss and vomiting that is not observed in any other domestic female and shows the body's revolt against the species taking possession of it; the body loses phosphorus, calcium and iron, the last of these losses being very hard to overcome later; the metabolic hyperactivity excites the endocrine system; the negative nervous system is in a heightened state of excitability; the specific weight of the blood decreases and it is anaemic, like 'that of people who fast, who are starving, or who have been bled many times, and convalescents'.‡ All that a healthy and well-nourished woman can hope for after child-

---

* 'I am thus my body, at least inasmuch as I have experience, and reciprocally, my body is like a natural subject, like a tentative draft of my total being' (Merleau-Ponty, *Phenomenology of Perception*).

† I am taking here an exclusively physiological point of view. It is evident that maternity can be very advantageous psychologically for a woman, just as it can also be a disaster.

‡ Cf. H. Vignes in *Traité de physiologie normale et pathologique* (*Treatise on Normal and Pathological Physiology*) volume II, edited by Roger and Binet.

birth is to recoup her losses without too much trouble; but often serious accidents or at least dangerous disorders occur during pregnancy; and if the woman is not sturdy, if she is not careful in her personal hygiene, she will be prematurely misshapen and aged by her pregnancies: it is well known how frequent this is in the countryside. Childbirth itself is painful; it is dangerous. This crisis shows clearly that the body does not always meet the needs of both the species and the individual; the child sometimes dies, or while coming into life, it kills the mother; or its birth can cause her a chronic illness. Breastfeeding is also an exhausting servitude; a set of factors – the main one undoubtedly being the appearance of a hormone, progestin – brings milk secretion into the mammary glands; the arrival of the milk is painful and is often accompanied by fever, and the breastfeeder feeds the newborn to the detriment of her own strength. The conflict between the species and the individual can have dramatic consequences in childbirth, making the woman's body distressingly fragile. One often hears that women 'have bellyaches'; true indeed, a hostile element is locked inside them: the species is eating away at them. Many of their illnesses are the result not of an external infection but of an internal disorder: false metritis occurs from a reaction of the uterine lining to an abnormal ovarian excitation; if the yellow body persists instead of being reabsorbed after menstruation, it provokes salpingitis and endometritis, and so on.

Woman escapes from the grip of the species by one more difficult crisis; between forty-five and fifty, the phenomena of menopause, the opposite of those of puberty, occur. Ovarian activity decreases and even disappears: this disappearance brings about a vital impoverishment of the individual. It is thought that the catabolic glands, thyroid and pituitary, attempt to compensate for the ovary's deficiencies; thus alongside the change-of-life depression there are phenomena of surges: hot flushes, high blood pressure, nervousness; there is sometimes an increase in the sex drive. Some women retain fat in their tissues; others acquire male traits. For many there is a new endocrine balance. So woman finds herself freed from the servitudes of the female; she is not comparable to a eunuch, because her vitality is intact; however, she is no longer prey to powers that submerge her: she is consistent with herself. It is sometimes said that older women form 'a third sex'; it is true they are not males, but they are no longer female either; and often this physiological autonomy is matched by a health, balance and vigour they did not previously have.

Overlapping women's specifically sexual differentiations are the singularities, more or less the consequences of these differentiations; these are the hormonal actions that determine her soma. On average, she is smaller than man, lighter; her skeleton is thinner; the pelvis is wider, adapted to gestation and birth; her connective tissue retains fats, and her forms are rounder than man's; the overall look: morphology, skin, hair system, and so on is clearly different in the two sexes. Woman has much less muscular force: about two-thirds that of man; she has less respiratory capacity: lungs, trachea and larynx are smaller in woman; the difference in the larynx brings about that of the voice. Women's specific blood weight is less than men's: there is less haemoglobin retention; women are less robust, more apt to be anaemic. Their pulse rate is quicker, their vascular system is less stable: they blush easily. Instability is a striking characteristic of their bodies in general; for example, man's calcium metabolism is stable; women both retain less calcium salt and eliminate it during menstruation and pregnancy; the ovaries seem to have a catabolic action concerning calcium; this instability leads to disorders in the ovaries and in the thyroid, which is more developed in a woman than in a man: and the irregularity of endocrine secretions acts on the peripheral nervous system; muscles and nerves are not perfectly controlled. More instability and less control make them more emotional, which is directly linked to vascular variations: palpitations, redness, and so on; and they are thus subject to convulsive attacks: tears, nervous laughter and hysterics.

Many of these characteristics are due to woman's subordination to the species. This is the most striking conclusion of this study: she is the most deeply alienated of all the female mammals, and she is the one that refuses this alienation the most violently; in no other is the subordination of the organism to the reproductive function more imperious nor accepted with greater difficulty. Crises of puberty and of the menopause, monthly 'curse', long and often troubled pregnancy, illnesses and accidents are characteristic of the human female: her destiny appears even more fraught the more she rebels against it by affirming herself as an individual. The male, by comparison, is infinitely more privileged: his genital life does not thwart his personal existence; it unfolds seamlessly, without crises and generally without accident. Women live, on average, as long as men, but are often sick and indisposed.

These biological data are of extreme importance: they play an all-important role and are an essential element of woman's situation: we will be referring to them in all further accounts. Because the body is the instrument of our hold on the world, the world appears different to us depending on how it is grasped, which explains why we have studied these data so deeply; they are one of the keys to enable us to understand woman. But we refuse the idea that they form a fixed destiny for her. They do not suffice to constitute the basis for a sexual hierarchy; they do not explain why woman is the Other; they do not condemn her for ever after to this subjugated role.

It has often been claimed that physiology alone provides answers to these questions: does individual success have the same chances in the two sexes? Which of the two in the species plays the greater role? But the first question does not apply to woman and other females in the same way, because animals constitute given species and it is possible to provide static descriptions of them: it is simply a question of collating observations to decide if the mare is as quick as the stallion, if male chimpanzees do as well on intelligence tests as their female counterparts; but humanity is constantly in the making. Materialist scholars have claimed to posit the problem in a purely static way; full of the theory of psychophysiological parallelism, they sought to make mathematical comparisons between male and female organisms: and they imagined that these measurements directly defined their functional abilities. I will mention one example of these senseless discussions that this method prompted. As it was supposed, in some mysterious way, that the brain secreted thinking, it seemed very important to decide if the average weight of the female brain was larger or smaller than that of the male. It was found that the former weighs, on average, 1,220 grams, and the latter 1,360, the weight of the female brain varying from 1,000 to 1,500 grams and that of the male from 1,150 to 1,700. But the absolute weight is not significant; it was thus decided that the relative weight should be taken into account. It is $\frac{1}{48.4}$ for the man and $\frac{1}{44.2}$ for the woman. She is thus supposed to be advantaged. No. This still has to be corrected: in such comparisons, the smallest organism always seems to be favoured; to compare two individuals correctly while not taking into account the body, one must divide the weight of the brain by the power of 0.56 of the body weight if they belong to the same species. It is considered that men and women are of two different types, with the following results:

For man: $W0.56 = 498$ $\dfrac{1,360}{498} = 2.73$

For woman: $W0.56 = 446$ $\dfrac{1,220}{446} = 2.74$

Equality is the result. But what removes much of the interest of these careful debates is that no relation has been established between brain weight and the development of intelligence. Nor could one give a psychic interpretation of chemical formulas defining male and female hormones. We categorically reject the idea of a psychophysiological parallelism; the bases of this doctrine have definitively and long been weakened. I mention it because although it is philosophically and scientifically ruined, it still haunts a large number of minds: it has already been shown here that some people are carrying around antique vestiges of it. We also repudiate any frame of reference that presupposes the existence of a *natural* hierarchy of values – for example, that of an evolutionary hierarchy; it is pointless to wonder if the female body is more infantile than the male, if it is closer to or further from that of the higher primates, and so forth. All these studies that confuse a vague naturalism with an even vaguer ethic or aesthetic are pure verbiage. Only within a human perspective can the female and the male be compared in the human species. But the definition of man is that he is a being who is not given, who makes himself what he is. As Merleau-Ponty rightly said, man is not a natural species: he is an historical idea. Woman is not a fixed reality but a becoming; she has to be compared with man in her becoming, that is, her *possibilities* have to be defined: what skews the issues so much is that she is being reduced to what she was, to what she is today, while the question concerns her capacities; the fact is that her capacities manifest themselves clearly only when they have been realised: but the fact is also that when one considers a being who is transcendence and surpassing, it is never possible to close the books.

However, one might say, in the position I adopt – that of Heidegger, Sartre and Merleau-Ponty – that if the body is not a *thing*, it is a situation: it is our grasp on the world and the outline for our projects. Woman is weaker than man; she has less muscular strength, fewer red blood cells, a lesser respiratory capacity; she runs less quickly, lifts less heavy weights – there is practically no sport in which she can compete with him; she cannot enter into a fight with the male. Added to that are the instability, lack of control and fragility that have been discussed: these are facts. Her grasp of the world is thus more limited; she has less firm-ness and perseverance in projects that she is also less able to carry out. This means that her individual life is not as rich as man's.

In truth these facts cannot be denied: but they do not carry their meaning in themselves. As soon as we accept a human perspective, defining the body starting from existence, biology becomes an abstract science; when the physiological given (muscular inferiority) takes on meaning, this meaning immediately becomes dependent on a whole context; 'weakness' is weakness only in light of the aims man sets for himself, the instruments at his disposal and the laws he imposes. If he did not want to apprehend the world, the very idea of a *grasp* on things would have no meaning; when, in this apprehension, the full use of body force – above the usable minimum – is not required, the differences cancel each other out; where customs forbid violence, muscular energy cannot be the basis for domination: existential, economic and moral reference points are necessary to define the notion of *weakness* concretely. It has been said that the human species was an antiphysis; the expres-sion is not really exact because man cannot possibly contradict the given; but it is in how he takes it on that he constitutes its truth; nature only has reality for him insofar as it is taken on by his action: his own nature is no exception. It is not possible to measure in the abstract the burden of the generative function for woman, just as it is not possible to measure her grasp on the world: the relation of maternity to individual life is naturally regulated in animals by the cycle of heat and seasons; it is un-defined for woman; only society can decide; woman's enslavement to the species is tighter or looser depending on how many births the society demands and the hygienic conditions in which pregnancy and birth occur. So if it can be said that among the higher animals individual existence is affirmed more imperiously in the male than in the female, in humanity individual 'possibilities' depend on the economic and social situation.

In any case, it is not always true that the male's individual privileges confer upon him superiority in the species; the female regains another kind of autonomy in maternity. Sometimes he imposes his domination: this is the case in the monkeys studied by Zuckermann; but often the two halves of the couple lead separate lives; the lion and the lioness share the care of the habitat equally. Here again, the case of the human species cannot be reduced to any other; men do not define themselves first as individuals; men and women have never challenged each other in individual fights; the couple is an original *Mitsein*; and it is always a fixed or transitory element of a wider collectivity; within these societies, who, the male or the female, is the more necessary for the species? In terms of gametes, in terms of the biological functions of coitus and gestation, the male principle creates to maintain and the female principle maintains to create: what becomes of this division in social life? For species attached to foreign bodies or to the substrata, for those to whom nature grants food abundantly and effortlessly, the role of the male is limited to fertilisation; when it is necessary to search, chase or fight to provide food needed for offspring, the male often helps with their maintenance; this help becomes absolutely indispensable in a species where children remain incapable of taking care of their own needs for a long period after the mother stops nursing them: the male's work then takes on an extreme importance; the lives he brought forth could not maintain themselves without him. One male is enough to fertilise many females each year: but males are necessary for the survival of children after birth, to defend them against enemies, to extract from nature everything they need. The balance of productive and reproductive forces is different depending on the different economic moments of human history and they condition the relation of the male and the female to children and later among them. But we are going beyond the field of biology: in purely biological terms, it would not be possible to posit the primacy of one sex concerning the role it plays in perpetuating the species.

But a society is not a species: the species realises itself as existence in a society; it transcends itself towards the world and the future; its customs cannot be deduced from biology; individuals are never left to their nature; they obey this second nature, that is, customs in which the desires and fears that express their ontological attitude are reflected. It is not as a body but as a body subjected to taboos and laws that the subject gains consciousness of and accomplishes himself. He valorises himself in the name of certain values. And once again, physiology cannot ground values: rather, biological data take on those values the existent confers on them. If the respect or fear woman inspires prohibits man from using violence against her, the male's muscular superiority is not a source of power. If customs desire – as in some Indian tribes – that girls choose husbands, or if it is the father who decides on marriages, the male's sexual aggressiveness does not grant him any initiative, any privilege. The mother's intimate link to the child will be a source of dignity or indignity for her, depending on the very variable value given to the child; this very link, as has already been said, will be recognised or not according to social biases.

Thus we will clarify the biological data by examining them in the light of ontological, economic, social and psychological contexts. Woman's enslavement to the species and the limits of her individual abilities are facts of extreme importance; the woman's body is one of the essential elements of the situation she occupies in this world. But her body is not enough to define her; it has a lived reality only as taken on by consciousness through actions and within a society; biology alone cannot provide an answer to the question that concerns us: why is woman the *Other*? The question is how, in her, nature has been taken on in the course of history; the question is what humanity has made of the human female.

CHAPTER 2

The Psychoanalytical Point of View

The enormous advance psychoanalysis made over psychophysiology is in its consideration that no factor intervenes in psychic life without having taken on human meaning; it is not the body-object described by scientists that exists concretely but the body lived by the subject. The female is a woman, insofar as she feels herself as such. Some essential biological givens are not part of her lived situation: for example, the structure of the ovum is not reflected in it; by contrast, an organ of slight biological importance like the clitoris plays a primary role in it. Nature does not define woman: it is she who defines herself by reclaiming nature for herself in her affectivity.

An entire system has been erected based on this outlook: we do not intend here to criticise it as a whole, but only to examine its contribution to the study of woman. Discussing psychoanalysis as such is not an easy undertaking. Like all religions – Christianity or Marxism – it displays an unsettling flexibility against a background of rigid concepts. Sometimes words are taken in their narrowest meanings, the term 'phallus', for example, designating very precisely the fleshy growth that is the male sex organ; at other times, infinitely broadened, they take on a symbolic value: the phallus would express all of the virile character and situation as a whole. If one criticises the doctrine to the letter, the psychoanalyst maintains that its spirit has been misunderstood; if one approves of the spirit, he immediately wants to limit you to the letter. The doctrine is unimportant, he says: psychoanalysis is a method; but the success of the method strengthens the doctrinaire in his faith. After all, where would the true features of psychoanalysis be found if not with psychoanalysts themselves? But among them, as among Christians and Marxists, there are heretics: more than one psychoanalyst has declared that 'the worst enemies of psychoanalysis are psychoanalysts themselves'. Many ambiguities remain to be dissolved, in spite of an often-pedantic scholastic precision. As Sartre and Merleau-Ponty have observed, the proposition 'sexuality is coextensive with existence' can be understood in two very different ways; it could mean that every avatar of the existent has a sexual signification, or that every sexual phenomenon has an existential meaning: these two affirmations can be reconciled; but often one tends to slip from one to the other. Besides, as soon as 'sexual' and 'genital' are distinguished, the notion of sexuality becomes blurred. 'The sexual for Freud is the intrinsic aptitude to trigger the genital,' says Dalbiez.[7] But nothing is murkier than the notion of 'aptitude', or of possibility: only reality can indubitably prove possibility. Not being a philosopher, Freud refused to justify his system philosophically; his disciples maintain that he thus eludes any attacks of a metaphysical sort. There are, however, metaphysical postulates behind all of his affirmations: to use his language is to adopt a philosophy. It is this very confusion that, while making criticism awkward, demands it.

Freud was not very concerned with woman's destiny; it is clear that he modelled his description of it on that of masculine destiny, merely modifying some of the traits. Before him, the sexologist Marañón had declared: 'As differentiated energy, the libido is, one might say, a force of virile significance. We can say as much for the orgasm.' According to him, women who attain orgasm are 'viriloid' women; sexual fulfilment is a 'one-way street' and woman is only at the halfway point.* Freud does not go that far; he accepts that woman's sexuality is as developed as man's; but he barely studies it in itself. He writes: 'The libido is constantly and regularly male in essence, whether in man or in woman.' He refuses to posit the feminine libido in its originality: he will thus necessarily see it as a complex deviation from the human libido in general. And this, he thinks, develops first identically in both sexes: all children go through an oral phase that fixes them upon their mother's breast, then an anal phase and finally they reach the genital phase; it is then that they become differentiated. Freud brought out a fact whose importance had not previously been recognised: male eroticism is definitively centred on the penis, while the woman has two distinct erotic systems, one that is clitoral and develops in infancy and another that is vaginal and develops only after puberty; when the boy gets to the genital phase, he completes his development; he has to move from the autoerotic attitude, where subjective pleasure is sought, to an hetero-erotic attitude that will link pleasure to

* Curiously, this theory is found in D. H. Lawrence. In *The Plumed Serpent*, Don Cipriano sees to it that his mistress never reaches orgasm: she must vibrate along with the man, and not find individualised pleasure.

an object, usually a woman; this passage will occur at puberty through a narcissistic phase: but the penis will remain, as in infancy, the favoured erotic organ. Woman, also passing through a narcissistic phase, must make man the object of her libido; but the process will be far more complex as she must pass from clitoral to vaginal pleasure. There is but one genital step for man, while there are two for woman; she runs a greater risk of not completing her sexual development, and of remaining at the infantile stage, and consequently of developing neuroses.

At the autoerotic stage, the child is already more or less strongly attached to an object: a boy is fixated on his mother and wants to identify with his father; he is afraid of this ambition and fears that his father will punish him for it by mutilating him; the castration complex emanates from the Oedipus complex; so he develops aggressive feelings towards his father, while at the same time interiorising his father's authority: thus develops the superego that censures incestuous tendencies; these tendencies are repressed, the complex is liquidated, and the son is freed from the father, whom he in fact has installed in himself in the form of moral precepts. The more defined and strongly fought the Oedipus complex is, the stronger the superego. Freud first described the history of the girl in a completely symmetrical way; later he named the feminine form of the infant complex the Electra complex; but clearly he defined it less in itself than based on a masculine model; yet he accepts a very important difference between the two: the little girl first has a maternal fixation, while the boy is at no time sexually attracted by the father; this fixation is a carryover from the oral phase; the infant then identifies with the father; but around the age of five, she discovers the anatomical difference between the sexes and she reacts to the absence of a penis by a castration complex: she imagines having been mutilated, and suffers from it; she must therefore renounce her virile pretensions; she identifies with her mother and tries to seduce her father. The castration complex and the Electra complex reinforce each other; the feeling of frustration for girls is all the more painful as, loving her father, the girl would like to resemble him; and inversely regret strengthens her love: through the tenderness she inspires in her father, she can compensate for her inferiority. The girl experiences feelings of rivalry and hostility towards her mother. Then her superego is constituted as well, repressing her incestuous tendencies; but her superego is more fragile: the Electra complex is less clear than the Oedipus complex, because her first fixation was maternal; and since the father was himself the object of this love that he condemned, his prohibitions had less force than in the case of the rival son. It can be seen that, as with her genital development, the little girl's overall sexual drama is more complex than her brother's: she might be tempted to react to the castration complex by rejecting her femininity, obstinately coveting a penis and identifying with her father; this attitude will lead her to remain at the clitoral stage, to become frigid or to turn to homosexuality.

The two essential objections to this description stem from the fact that Freud copied it from a masculine model. He assumes that a woman feels like a mutilated man; but the notion of mutilation implies comparison and valorisation; many psychoanalysts accept today that girls miss having a penis without assuming they were ever stripped of one; this regret is not even generalised among all girls; and it could not arise from a simple anatomical encounter; many little girls discover the masculine constitution very late; and if they do discover it, it is only by seeing it; the boy has a living experience from his penis that allows him to take pride in it, but this pride has no immediate correlation with the humiliation of his sisters since they only know the masculine organ in its exteriority; this growth, this delicate stalk of skin can only inspire their indifference and even disgust; the girl's envy, when it appears, is the result of a prior valorisation of virility: Freud takes this for granted when instead he should account for it.* Besides, because there is no original description of the feminine libido, the notion of the Electra complex is very vague. Even the presence of a specifically genital Oedipus complex in boys is by no means general; but, apart from very rare exceptions, it cannot be stated that the father is a source of genital excitation for his daughter; one of the great problems of female eroticism is that clitoral pleasure is localised: it is only in puberty, in connection with vaginal eroticism, that many erogenous zones develop in the woman's body; to say that in a child of ten a father's kisses and caresses have an 'intrinsic aptitude' to arouse clitoral pleasure is an assertion that in most cases makes no sense. If it is accepted that the 'Electra complex' has only a very diffuse and affective nature, then the whole question of affectivity is raised, a question that Freudianism does not provide the means to define, once it is distinguished from sexuality. In any case, it is not the feminine libido that deifies the father: the mother is not deified by the desire she arouses in her son; the fact that feminine desire is focused on a sovereign being gives it a unique character; but the girl is not constitutive of her object, she submits to it. The father's sovereignty is a fact

* This discussion will be taken up again in more detail in Vol. II, Chapter 1.

of social order: and Freud fails to account for this; he himself admits that it is impossible to know what authority decided at what moment in history that the father would prevail over the mother: according to him, this decision represents progress, but its causes are unknown. '[In this case] it cannot be the father himself, since it is only this progress that raises him to the rank of an authority,' he writes in his last work.*[8]

Adler departed from Freud because he understood the inadequacies of a system that bases the development of human life on sexuality alone: he means to reintegrate sexuality into the total personality; while for Freud all behaviour is driven by desire, that is, by seeking pleasure, Adler sees man as aiming at certain goals; he replaces drives with motives, finality and plans; he raises intelligence to such heights that for him sexuality often has only symbolic value. According to his theories, the human drama is divided into three steps: each individual has a will to power but along with it an inferiority complex; this conflict leads him to use countless ruses rather than confront real-life obstacles that he fears may be insurmountable; the subject establishes a distance between himself and the society he fears: thus develop neuroses that are disturbances of the social sense. As for woman, her inferiority complex manifests itself in a rejection out of shame of her femininity: it is not the absence of a penis that unleashes this complex but the total situation; the girl envies the phallus only as a symbol of the privileges granted to boys; the father's place in the family, the universal predominance of males, and upbringing all confirm her idea of masculine superiority. Later on, in the course of sexual relations, even the coital posture that places the woman underneath the man is an added humiliation. She reacts by a 'masculine protest'; she either tries to masculinise herself, or uses her feminine wiles to go into battle against man. Through motherhood she can find in her child the equivalent of the penis. But this supposes that she must first accept herself completely as woman, and thus accept her inferiority. She is far more deeply divided against herself than is man.

It is unnecessary to underline here the theoretical differences between Adler and Freud or the possibilities of reconciliation: neither the explanation based on drive nor the one based on motive is ever sufficient: all drives posit a motive, but motive is never grasped except through drives; a synthesis of Adlerism and Freudianism thus seems possible. In fact, while bringing in notions of aim and finality, Adler retains in full the idea of psychic causality; his relation to Freud resembles somewhat the

* Cf. *Moses and Monotheism*.

relation of energeticism to mechanism: whether it is a question of impact or force of attraction, the physicist always recognises determinism. This is the postulate common to all psychoanalysts: for them, human history is explained by an interplay of determined elements. They all allot the same destiny to woman. Her drama is summed up in a conflict between her 'viriloid' and her 'feminine' tendencies; the former are expressed in the clitoral system, the latter in vaginal eroticism; as a very young girl, she identifies with her father; she then experiences feelings of inferiority relative to man and is faced with the alternative of either maintaining her autonomy, becoming virilised – which, with an underlying inferiority complex, provokes a tension that risks bringing on neuroses – or else finding happy self-fulfilment in amorous submission, a solution facilitated by the love she felt for her sovereign father; it is he whom she is looking for in her lover or husband, and her sexual love is mingled with her desire to be dominated. Maternity will be her reward, restoring to her a new kind of autonomy. This drama seems to be endowed with its own dynamism; it continues to work itself out through all the mishaps that distort it, and every woman passively endures it.

Psychoanalysts have no trouble finding empirical confirmations of their theories: it is known that if Ptolemy's system is subtly complicated, his version of the position of the planets could be upheld for a long time; if an inverse Oedipus complex is superimposed on to the Oedipus complex and by showing a desire in every anxiety, the very facts that contradicted Freudianism will be successfully integrated into it. For a figure to be perceived, it must stand out from its background, and how the figure is perceived brings out the ground behind it in positive delineation; thus if one is determined to describe a particular case from a Freudian perspective, one will find the Freudian schema as the background behind it; but when a doctrine demands the multiplication of secondary explanations in an indefinite and arbitrary way, when observation uncovers as many anomalies as normal cases, it is better to give up the old frameworks. Today as well, every psychoanalyst works at adapting Freudian concepts to suit himself; he attempts compromises; for example, a contemporary psychoanalyst writes: 'Whenever there is a complex, there are by definition several components . . . The complex consists in grouping these disparate elements and not in representing one of them by the others.'*⁹ But the idea of a simple grouping of elements is unacceptable: psychic life is not a mosaic; it is altogether

---

* Baudouin, *The Child's Soul and Psychoanalysis*.

complete in every one of its moments and this unity must be respected. This is possible only by recovering the original intentionality of existence through the disparate facts. Without going back to this source, man appears a battlefield of drives and prohibitions equally devoid of meaning and contingent. All psychoanalysts systematically refuse the idea of choice and its corollary, the notion of value; and herein lies the intrinsic weakness of the system. Cutting out drives and prohibitions from existential choice, Freud fails to explain their origin: he takes them as givens. He tried to replace the notion of value with that of authority; but he admits in *Moses and Monotheism* that he has no way to account for this authority. Incest, for example, is forbidden because the father forbade it: but why did he forbid it? It is a mystery. The superego interiorises orders and prohibitions emanating from an arbitrary tyranny; instinctive tendencies exist, but we do not know why; these two realities are heterogeneous because morality is posited as foreign to sexuality; human unity appears as shattered, there is no passage from the individual to the society: Freud is forced to invent strange fictions to reunite them.* Adler saw clearly that the castration complex could be explained only in a social context; he approached the problem of valorisation, but he did not go back to the ontological source of values recognised by society, and he did not understand that values were involved in sexuality itself, which led him to misunderstand their importance.

Sexuality certainly plays a considerable role in human life: it could be said to penetrate it completely; physiology has already demonstrated how the activity of testes and ovaries is intermixed with that of the soma. The existent is a sexed body; in its relations with other existents that are also sexed bodies, sexuality is thus always involved; but as the body and sexuality are concrete expressions of existence, it is also from here that their significance can be ascertained: without this perspective, psychoanalysis takes unexplained facts for granted. For example, a young girl is said to be 'ashamed' of urinating in a squatting position, with her bottom exposed; but what is shame? Likewise, before asking if the male is proud because he has a penis or if his penis is the expression of his pride, we need to know what pride is and how the subject's aspirations can be embodied in an object. Sexuality must not be taken as an irreducible given; the existent possesses a more primary 'quest for being'; sexuality is only one of these aspects. Sartre demonstrates this in *Being and Nothingness*; Bachelard also says it in his works on Earth, Air and

* Freud, *Totem and Taboo*.

Water: psychoanalysts believe that man's quintessential truth lies in his relation to his own body and that of others like him within society; but man has a primordial interest in the substance of the natural world surrounding him that he attempts to discover in work, play and in all experiences of the 'dynamic imagination'; man seeks to connect concretely with existence through the whole world, grasped in all possible ways. Working the soil and digging a hole are activities as primal as an embrace or coitus: it is an error to see them only as sexual symbols; a hole, slime, a gash, hardness or wholeness are primary realities; man's interest in them is not dictated by libido; instead the libido will be influenced by the way these realities were revealed to him. Man is not fascinated by wholeness because it symbolises feminine virginity: rather his love for wholeness makes virginity precious. Work, war, play and art define ways of being in the world that cannot be reduced to any others; they bring to light features that impinge on those that sexuality reveals; it is both through them and through these erotic experiences that the individual chooses himself. But only an ontological point of view can restore the unity of this choice.

Psychoanalysts vehemently reject this notion of choice in the name of determinism and 'the collective unconscious'; this unconscious would provide man with ready-made imagery and universal symbolism; it would explain analogies found in dreams, lapses, delusions, allegories and human destinies; to speak of freedom would be to reject the possibility of explaining these disturbing concordances. But the idea of freedom is not incompatible with the existence of certain constants. If the psychoanalytic method is often productive in spite of errors in theory, it is because there are givens in every individual case so generalised that no one would dream of denying them: situations and behaviour patterns recur; the moment of decision springs out of generality and repetition. 'Anatomy is destiny,' said Freud; and this phrase is echoed by Merleau-Ponty: 'The body is generality.' Existence is one, across and through the separation of existents, manifesting itself in analogous organisms; so there will be constants in the relationship between the ontological and the sexual. At any given period, technology and the economic and social structure of a group reveal an identical world for all its members: there will also be a constant relation of sexuality to social forms; analogous individuals, placed in analogous conditions, will grasp analogous significations in the given; this analogy is not the basis of a rigorous universality, but it can account for finding general types in individual cases. A symbol does not emerge as an allegory worked out by a mysterious unconscious: it is the apprehension of a signification through an analogue of the signifying object; because of the identity of the existential situation cutting across all existents and the identity of the facticity they have to cope with, significations are revealed to many individuals in the same way; symbolism did not fall out of heaven or rise out of subterranean depths: it was elaborated like language, by the human reality that is at once *Mitsein* and separation; and this explains that singular invention also has its place: in practice the psychoanalytical method must accept this whether or not doctrine authorises it. This approach enables us to understand, for example, the value generally given to the penis.* It is impossible to account for this without starting from an existential fact: the subject's tendency towards *alienation;* the anxiety of his freedom leads the subject to search for himself in things, which is a way to flee from himself; it is so fundamental a tendency that as soon as he is weaned and separated from the Whole, the infant endeavours to grasp his alienated existence in the mirror, in his parents' gaze. Primitive people alienate themselves in their mana, their totem; civilised people in their individual souls, their egos, their names, their possessions and their work: and here is the first temptation of inauthenticity. The penis is singularly adapted to play this role of 'double' for the little boy: for him it is both a foreign object and himself; it is a plaything, a doll, and it is his own flesh; parents and nurses treat it like a little person. So, clearly, it becomes for the child 'an alter ego usually craftier, more intelligent and more clever than the individual'†;[10] because the urinary function and later the erection are midway between voluntary processes and spontaneous processes, because it is the impulsive, quasi-foreign source of subjectively experienced pleasure, the penis is posited by the subject as himself and other than himself; specific transcendence is embodied in it in a graspable way and it is a source of pride; because the phallus is set apart, man can integrate into his personality the life that flows from it. This is why, then, the length of the penis, the force of the urine stream, the erection and the ejaculation become for him the measure of his own worth.‡ It is thus a constant that the phallus is the fleshly incarnation of transcendence; since it is also a constant that

* We will come back to this subject in more detail in Vol. II, Chapter 1.
† Alice Bálint, *The Psychoanalysis of the Nursery.*
‡ The case of little peasant boys who entertain themselves by having excrement contests has been brought to my attention: the one producing the biggest and most solid faeces enjoys a prestige that no other success, in games or even in fighting, could replace. Faecal matter here played the same role as the penis: it was a matter of alienation in both cases.

the child feels transcended, that is, frustrated in his transcendence by his father, the Freudian idea of the castration complex will persist. Deprived of this alter ego, the little girl does not alienate herself in a graspable thing, does not reclaim herself: she is thus led to make her entire self an object, to posit herself as the Other; the question of knowing whether or not she has compared herself with boys is secondary; what is important is that, even without her knowing it, the absence of a penis keeps her from being aware of herself as a sex; many consequences result from this. But these constants we point out nevertheless do not define a destiny: the phallus takes on such importance because it symbolises a sovereignty that is realised in other areas. If woman succeeded in affirming herself as subject, she would invent equivalents of the phallus: the doll that embodies the promise of the child may become a more precious possession than a penis.* There are matrilineal societies where the women possess the masks in which the collectivity alienates itself; the penis then loses much of its glory. Only within the situation grasped in its totality does anatomical privilege found a truly human privilege. Psychoanalysis could only find its truth within an historical context.

Likewise, woman can no more be defined by the consciousness of her own femininity than by merely saying that woman is a female: she finds this consciousness within the society of which she is a member. Interiorising the unconscious and all psychic life, the very language of psychoanalysis suggests that the drama of the individual unfolds within him: the terms 'complex', 'tendencies', and so forth imply this. But a life is a relation with the world; the individual defines himself by choosing himself through the world; we must turn to the world to answer the questions that preoccupy us. In particular, psychoanalysis fails to explain why woman is the *Other*. Even Freud accepts that the prestige of the penis is explained by the father's sovereignty, and he admits that he does not know the source of male supremacy.

Without wholly rejecting the contributions of psychoanalysis, some of which are productive, we will nevertheless not accept its method. First of all, we will not limit ourselves to taking sexuality as a given: that this view falls short is demonstrated by the poverty of the descriptions touching on the feminine libido; I have already said that psychoanalysts have never studied it head-on, but only based on the male libido; they seem to ignore the fundamental ambivalence of the attraction that the male exercises

* We will come back to these ideas in Volume Two; mention is made here for the sake of methodology.

over the female. Freudians and Adlerians explain woman's anxiety before male genitalia as an inversion of frustrated desire. Stekel[11] rightly saw this as an original reaction; but he accounts for it only superficially: the woman would fear defloration, penetration, pregnancy and pain, and this fear would stifle her desire; this explanation is too rational. Instead of accepting that desire is disguised as anxiety or is overcome by fear, we should consider this sort of pressing and frightened appeal that is female desire as a basic given; it is characterised by the indissoluble synthesis of attraction and repulsion. It is noteworthy that many female animals flee from coitus at the very moment they solicit it: they are accused of coquetry or hypocrisy; but it is absurd to attempt to explain primitive behaviours by assimilating them to complex ones: they are, on the contrary, at the source of attitudes called coquetry and hypocrisy in women. The idea of a passive libido is disconcerting because the libido has been defined as a drive, as energy based on the male; but one could no more conceive a priori of a light being both yellow and blue: the intuition of green is needed. Reality would be better delineated if, instead of defining the libido in vague terms of 'energy', the significance of sexuality were juxtaposed with that of other human attitudes: taking, catching, eating, doing, undergoing, and so on; for sexuality is one of the singular modes of apprehending an object; the characteristics of the erotic object as it is shown not only in the sexual act but in perception in general would also have to be studied. This examination goes beyond the psychoanalytic framework that posits eroticism as irreducible.

In addition, we will pose the problem of feminine destiny quite differently: we will situate woman in a world of values and we will lend her behaviour a dimension of freedom. We think she has to choose between the affirmation of her transcendence and her alienation as object; she is not the plaything of contradictory drives; she devises solutions that have an ethical hierarchy among them. Replacing value with authority, choice with drives, psychoanalysis proposes an ersatz morality: the idea of normality. This idea is indeed highly useful from a therapeutic point of view; but it has reached a disturbing extent in psychoanalysis in general. The descriptive schema is proposed as a law; and assuredly, a mechanistic psychology could not accept the notion of moral invention; at best it can recognise *less* but never more; at best it acknowledges failures, but never creations. If a subject does not wholly replicate a development considered normal, his development will be seen as being interrupted, and this will be interpreted as a lack and a negation and never a positive decision. That, among other things, is what renders the psychoanalysis of great men so shocking: we are told that this transference or that sublimation was not successfully carried out in them; it is never supposed that perhaps they could have rejected it, and perhaps for good reasons; it is never considered that their behaviour might have been motivated by freely posited aims; the individual is always explained through his link to the past and not with respect to a future towards which he projects himself. Therefore, we are never given more than an inauthentic picture, and in this inauthenticity, no criterion other than normality can possibly be found. The description of feminine destiny is, from this point of view, altogether striking. The way psychoanalysts understand it, 'to identify' with the mother or the father is to *alienate oneself* in a model, it is to prefer a foreign image to a spontaneous movement of one's own existence, it is to play at being. We are shown woman solicited by two kinds of alienations; it is very clear that to play at being a man will be a recipe for failure; but to play at being a woman is also a trap: being a woman would mean being an object, the Other; and at the heart of its abdication, the Other remains a subject. The real problem for the woman refusing these evasions is to accomplish herself as transcendence: this means seeing which possibilities are opened to her by what are called virile and feminine attitudes; when a child follows the path indicated by one or another of his parents, it could be because he freely takes on their projects: his behaviour could be the result of a choice motivated by ends. Even for Adler, the will to power is only a sort of absurd energy; he calls any project that incarnates transcendence a 'masculine protest'; when a girl climbs trees, it is, according to him, to be the equal of boys: he does not imagine that she likes to climb trees; for the mother, the child is anything but a 'penis substitute'; painting, writing or engaging in politics are not only 'good sublimations': they are ends desired in themselves. To deny this is to falsify all of human history. Parallels can be noted between our descriptions and those of psychoanalysts. From man's point of view – adopted by both male and female psychoanalysts – behaviour of alienation is considered feminine, and behaviour where the subject posits his transcendence is considered masculine. Donaldson,[12] an historian of woman, observed that the definitions 'the man is a male human being, the woman is a female human being' were asymmetrically mutilated; psychoanalysts in particular define man as a human being and woman as a female: every time she acts like a human being, she is said to be imitating the male. The psychoanalyst describes the child and the young girl as required to identify with the father and the mother, torn between 'viriloid' and 'feminine' tendencies, whereas we conceive her as hesitating between the role of *object*, of *Other* that is proposed to her and her claim for freedom; thus it is possible to agree on certain points: in particular when we consider the paths of inauthentic flight offered to women. But we do not give them the same Freudian or Adlerian signification. For us woman is defined as a human being in search of values within a world of values, a world where it is indispensable to understand the economic and social structure; we will study her from an existential point of view, taking into account her total situation.

CHAPTER 3

The Point of View of Historical Materialism

The theory of historical materialism has brought to light some very important truths. Humanity is not an animal species: it is an historical reality. Human society is an anti-physis: it does not passively submit to the presence of nature, but rather appropriates it. This appropriation is not an interior, subjective operation: it is carried out objectively in praxis. Thus woman cannot simply be considered a sexed organism: among biological data, only those with concrete value in action have any importance; woman's consciousness of herself is not defined by her sexuality alone: it reflects a situation that depends on society's economic structure, a structure that indicates the degree of technical evolution humanity has attained. We have seen that two essential traits characterise woman biologically: her grasp on the world is narrower than man's; and she is more closely subjugated to the species. But these facts have a totally different value depending on the economic and social context. Throughout human history, grasp on the world is not defined by the naked body: the hand, with its prehensile thumb, moves beyond itself towards instruments that increase its power; from prehistory's earliest documents, man is always seen as armed. In the past, when it was a question of carrying heavy clubs and of keeping wild beasts at bay, woman's physical weakness constituted a flagrant inferiority: if the instrument requires slightly more strength than the woman can muster, it is enough to make her seem radically powerless. But on the other hand, technical developments can cancel out the muscular inequality separating man and woman: abundance only creates superiority relative to a need; having too much is not better than having enough. Thus operating many modern machines requires only a part of masculine resources; if the necessary minimum is not superior to woman's capacities, she becomes man's work equal. Today enormous deployments of energy can be commanded at the touch of a switch. The burdens that come with maternity vary greatly depending on customs: they are overwhelming if numerous pregnancies are imposed on the woman and if she must feed and raise her children without help; if she procreates as she wishes and if society helps her during her pregnancies and provides childcare, maternal duties are lighter and can be easily compensated for in the realm of work.

Engels retraces woman's history from this point of view in *The Origin of the Family**;[13] this family history depends principally on the history of technology. In the Stone Age, when the land belonged to all members of the clan, the rudimentary nature of the primitive spade and hoe limited agricultural possibilities: feminine strength was at the level of work needed for gardening. In this primitive division of labour, the two sexes already constitute two classes in a way; there is equality between these classes; while the man hunts and fishes, the woman stays at home; but the domestic tasks include productive work: pottery making, weaving, gardening; and in this way, she has an important role in economic life. With the discovery of copper, tin, bronze and iron, and with the advent of the plough, agriculture expands its reach: intensive labour is necessary to clear the forests and cultivate the fields. So man has recourse to the service of other men, reducing them to slavery. Private property appears: master of slaves and land, man also becomes the proprietor of the woman. This is the 'great historical defeat of the female sex'. It is explained by the disruption of the division of labour brought about by the invention of new tools. 'The same cause that had assured woman her previous authority in the home, her restriction to housework, this same cause now assured the domination of the man; domestic work thence faded in importance next to man's productive work; the latter was everything, the former an insignificant addition.' So paternal right replaces maternal right: transmission of property is from father to son and no longer from woman to her clan. This is the advent of the patriarchal family founded on private property. In such a family woman is oppressed. Man reigning sovereign permits himself, among other things, his sexual whims: he sleeps with slaves or courtesans, he is polygamous. As soon as customs make reciprocity possible, woman takes revenge through infidelity: adultery becomes a natural part of marriage. This is the only defence woman has against the domestic slavery she is bound to: her social oppression is the consequence of her economic oppression. Equality can only be reestablished when both sexes have equal legal

* Friedrich Engels, *The Origin of the Family, Private Property, and the State.*

rights; but this enfranchisement demands that the whole of the feminine sex enter public industry. 'Woman cannot be emancipated unless she takes part in production on a large social scale and is only incidentally bound to domestic work. And this has become possible only within a large modern industry that not only accepts women's work on a grand scale but formally requires it.'

Thus woman's fate is intimately bound to the fate of socialism as seen also in Bebel's vast work on women. 'Women and the proletariat', he writes, 'are both oppressed.' And both must be set free by the same economic development resulting from the upheaval caused by the invention of machines. The problem of woman can be reduced to that of her capacity for work. Powerful when technology matched her possibilities, dethroned when she became incapable of benefiting from them, she finds again equality with man in the modern world. Resistance put up by the old capitalist paternalism prevents this equality from being concretely achieved: it will be achieved the day this resistance is broken down. It already has broken down in the USSR, Soviet propaganda affirms. And when socialist society is realised throughout the whole world, there will no longer be men nor women, but only workers, equal among themselves.

Although the synthesis outlined by Engels marks an advance over those we have already examined, it is still disappointing: the most serious problems are dodged. The whole account pivots around the transition from a communitarian regime to one of private property: there is absolutely no indication of how it was able to occur; Engels even admits that 'for now we know nothing about it';* not only is he unaware of its historical details, but he offers no interpretation of it. Similarly, it is unclear if private property necessarily led to the enslavement of woman. Historical materialism takes for granted facts it should explain: it posits the *interest* that attaches man to property without discussing it; but where does this interest, the source of social institutions, have its own source? This is why Engels's account remains superficial, and the truths he uncovers appear contingent. It is impossible to go deeper into them without going beyond historical materialism. It cannot provide solutions to the problems we indicated because they concern the whole man and not this abstraction, *Homo economicus*.

It is clear, for example, that the very idea of individual possession can acquire meaning only on the basis of the original condition of the existent.

* Ibid.

For that idea to appear, it is first necessary that there be in the subject a tendency to posit himself in his radical singularity, an affirmation of his existence as autonomous and separate. Obviously this claim remained subjective, interior and without truth as long as the individual lacked the practical means to satisfy it objectively: for lack of the right tools, at first he could not experience his power over the world, he felt lost in nature and in the group, passive, threatened, the plaything of obscure forces; it was only in identifying with the whole clan that he dared to think himself: the totem, the mana and the earth were collective realities. The discovery of bronze enabled man, tested by hard and productive work, to find himself as creator, dominating nature; no longer afraid of nature, having overcome resistance, he dares to grasp himself as autonomous activity and to accomplish himself in his singularity.*[14] But this accomplishment would never have been realised if man had not originally wanted it; the lesson of labour is not inscribed in a passive subject: the subject forged and conquered himself in forging his tools and conquering the earth. On the other hand, the affirmation of the subject is not enough to explain ownership: in challenges, struggles and individual combat, every consciousness can try to rise to sovereignty. For the challenge to have taken the form of the potlatch, that is, of economic rivalry, and from there first for the chief and then for the clan members to have laid claim to private goods, there had to be another original tendency in man: in the preceding chapter we said that the existent can only succeed in grasping himself by alienating himself; he searches for himself through the world, in the guise of a foreign figure he makes his own. The clan encounters its own alienated existence in the totem, the mana and the territory it occupies; when the individual separates from the community, he demands a singular embodiment: the mana is individualised in the chief, then in each individual; and at the same time each one tries to appropriate a piece of land, tools, or crops. In these riches of his, man finds himself because he lost himself in them: it is understandable then that he can attribute to them an importance as basic as that of his life itself. Thus man's *interest* in his property becomes an intelligible relationship. But clearly the tool alone is not enough to explain it; the whole attitude of

* Gaston Bachelard in *Earth and Reveries of Will* carries out, among others, an interesting study of the blacksmith's work. He shows how man asserts and separates himself from himself by the hammer and anvil. 'The temporal existence of the blacksmith is both highly particular and larger than life. Through momentary violence, the worker, uplifted, gains mastery over time'; and further on: 'Those who forge take on the challenge of the universe rising against them.'

the tool-armed man must be grasped, an attitude that implies an onto-logical infrastructure.

Similarly, it is impossible to *deduce* woman's oppression from private property. Here again, the shortcomings of Engels's point of view are obvious. While he clearly understood that woman's muscular weakness was a concrete inferiority only in relation to bronze and iron tools, he failed to see that limits to her work capacity constituted in themselves a concrete disadvantage only from a certain perspective. Because man is transcendence and ambition, he projects new demands with each new tool: after having invented bronze instruments, he was no longer satis-fied with developing gardens and wanted instead to clear and cultivate vast fields. This will did not spring from bronze itself. Woman's power-lessness brought about her ruin because man apprehended her through a project of enrichment and expansion. And this project is still not enough to explain her oppression: the division of labour by sex might have been a friendly association. If the original relation between man and his peers had been exclusively one of friendship, one could not account for any kind of enslavement: this phenomenon is a consequence of the imperi-alism of human consciousness, which seeks to match its sovereignty objectively. Had there not been in human consciousness both the orig-inal category of the Other and an original claim to domination over the Other, the discovery of the bronze tool could not have brought about woman's oppression. Nor does Engels account for the specific character of this oppression. He tried to reduce the opposition of the sexes to a class conflict: in fact, he did it without real conviction; this thesis is inde-fensible. True, the division of labour by sex and the oppression resulting from it brings to mind class division in some ways: but they should not be confused; there is no biological basis for division by class; in work the slave becomes conscious of himself against the master; the prole-tariat has always experienced its condition in revolt, thus returning to the essential, constituting a threat to its exploiters; and the goal of the proletariat is to cease to exist as a class. We have said in the introduc-tion how different woman's situation is, specifically because of the community of life and interests that create her solidarity with man and due to the complicity he encounters in her: she harbours no desire for revolution, she would not think of eliminating herself as a sex: she simply asks that certain consequences of sexual differentiation be abolished. And more serious still, woman cannot in good faith be regarded only as a worker; her reproductive function is as important as her productive capacity, both in the social economy and in her personal life; there are periods in history when it is more useful to have children than till the soil. Engels sidestepped the problem; he limits himself to declaring that the socialist community will abolish the family, quite an abstract solution; everyone knows how often and how radically the USSR has had to change its family policy to balance out production needs of the moment with the needs of repopulation; besides, eliminating the family does not necessarily liberate woman: the example of Sparta and that of the Nazi regime prove that notwithstanding her direct attachment to the state, she might still be no less oppressed by males. A truly socialist ethic – one that seeks justice without restraining liberty, one that imposes responsibilities on individuals but without abolishing individual freedom – will find itself most uncomfortable with problems posed by woman's condition. It is impossible to simply assimilate gestation to a *job* or *service* like the military service. A deeper breach is created in a woman's life by requiring her to have children than by regulating citizens' occupations: no state has ever dared institute compulsory coitus. In the sexual act and in maternity, woman engages not only time and energy but also essential values. Rationalist materialism tries in vain to ignore this powerful aspect of sexuality: sexual instinct cannot be regulated; according to Freud, it might even possess an inherent denial of its own satisfaction; what is certain is that it cannot be integrated into the social sphere, because there is in eroticism a revolt of the instant against time, of the individual against the universal: to try to channel and exploit it risks killing it, because live spontaneity cannot be disposed of like inert matter; nor can it be compelled in the way a freedom can be. There is no way to directly oblige a woman to give birth: all that can be done is to enclose her in situations where motherhood is her only option: laws or customs impose marriage on her, anticonception measures and abortion are banned, divorce is forbidden. These old patriarchal constraints are exactly the ones the USSR has brought back to life today; it has revived paternalistic theories about marriage; and in doing so, it has asked woman to become an erotic object again: a recent speech asked Soviet women citizens to pay attention to their clothes, to use makeup and to become flirtatious to hold on to their husbands and stimulate their desire. Examples like this prove how impossible it is to consider the woman as a solely productive force: for man she is a sexual partner, a reproducer, an erotic object, an Other through whom he seeks himself. Although totalitarian or authoritarian regimes may all try to ban psychoanalysis and declare that personal emotional conflicts have no place for citizens loyally integrated into the community, eroticism is an experience where individuality always prevails over generality. And for democratic socialism where classes would be abolished but not individuals, the question of individual destiny would still retain all its importance: sexual different-iation would retain all its importance. The sexual relation that unites woman with man is not the same as the one he maintains with her; the bond that attaches her to the child is irreducible to any other. She was not created by the bronze tool alone: the machine is not sufficient to abolish her. To demand for woman all the rights, all the possibilities of the human being in general does not mean one must be blind to her singular situation. To know this situation, it is necessary to go beyond historical materialism, which only sees man and woman as economic entities.

So we reject Freud's sexual monism and Engels's economic monism for the same reason. A psychoanalyst will interpret all woman's social claims as a phenomenon of 'masculine protest'; for the Marxist, on the other hand, her sexuality only expresses her economic situation, in a rather complex, roundabout way; but the categories clitoral or vaginal, like the categories bourgeois or proletarian, are equally inadequate to encompass a concrete woman. Underlying the personal emotional conflicts as well as the economic history of humanity there is an exis-tential infrastructure that alone makes it possible to understand in its unity the unique form that is a life. Freudianism's value derives from the fact that the existent is a body: the way he experiences himself as a body in the presence of other bodies concretely translates his existential situ-ation. Likewise, what is true in the Marxist thesis is that the existent's ontological claims take on a concrete form based on the material possi-bilities offered to him, particularly based on those that technology opens to him. But if they are not incorporated into the whole of human reality, sexuality and technology of themselves will fail to explain anything. This is why in Freud prohibitions imposed by the superego and the drives of the ego appear as contingent facts; and in Engels's account of the history of the family, the most important events seem to arise unexpectedly through the whims of mysterious chance. To discover woman, we will not reject certain contributions of biology, psychoanalysis or historical materialism: but we will consider that the body, sexual life and tech-nology exist concretely for man only insofar as he grasps them from the overall perspective of his existence. The value of muscular strength, the phallus and the tool can only be defined in a world of values: it is driven by the fundamental project of the existent transcending itself towards being.

Part Two
HISTORY

This world has always belonged to males, and none of the reasons given for this have ever seemed sufficient. By reviewing prehistoric and ethnographic data in the light of existentialist philosophy, we can understand how the hierarchy of the sexes came to be. We have already posited that when two human categories find themselves face-to-face, each one wants to impose its sovereignty on the other; if both hold to this claim equally, a reciprocal relationship is created, either hostile or friendly, but always tense. If one of the two has an advantage over the other, that one prevails and works to maintain the relationship by oppression. It is thus understandable that man might have had the will to dominate woman: but what advantage enabled him to accomplish this will?

Ethnologists give extremely contradictory information about primitive forms of human society, even more so when they are well informed and less systematic. It is especially difficult to formulate an idea about woman's situation in the pre-agricultural period. We do not even know if, in such different living conditions from today's, woman's musculature or her respiratory system were not as developed as man's. She was given hard work, and in particular it was she who carried heavy loads; yet this latter fact is ambiguous: probably if she was assigned this function, it is because within the convoy men kept their hands free to defend against possible aggressors, animals or humans; so their role was the more dangerous one and demanded more strength. But it seems that in many cases women were robust and resilient enough to participate in warrior expeditions. According to the accounts by Herodotus and the traditions of the Amazons from Dahomey as well as ancient and modern testimonies, women were known to take part in bloody wars or vendettas; they showed as much courage and cruelty as males: there are references to women who bit their teeth into their enemies' livers. In spite of this, it is likely that then as now men had the advantage of physical force; in the age of clubs and wild animals, in the age when resistance to nature was at its greatest and tools were at their most rudimentary, this superiority must have been of extreme importance. In any case, as robust as women may have been at that time, the burdens of reproduction represented for them a severe handicap in the fight against a hostile world: Amazons were said to mutilate their breasts, which meant that at least during the period of their warrior lives they rejected maternity. As for ordinary women, pregnancy, giving birth and menstruation diminished their work capacity and condemned them to long periods of impotence; to defend themselves against enemies or to take care of themselves and their children, they needed the protection of warriors and the catch from hunting and fishing provided by the males. As there obviously was no birth control, and as nature does not provide woman with sterile periods as it does for other female mammals, frequent pregnancies must have absorbed the greater part of their strength and their time; they were unable to provide for the lives of the children they brought into the world. This is a primary fact fraught with great consequence: the human species's beginnings were difficult; hunter, gatherer and fishing peoples reaped meagre bounty from the soil, and at great cost in effort; too many children were born for the group's resources; the woman's absurd fertility kept her from participating actively in the growth of these resources, while it was constantly creating new needs. Indispensable to the perpetuation of the species, she perpetuated it too abundantly: so it was man who controlled the balance between reproduction and production. Thus woman did not even have the privilege of maintaining life that the creator male had; she did not play the role of ovum to his spermatozoid or womb to his phallus; she played only one part in the human species's effort to persist in being, and it was thanks to man that this effort had a concrete result.

Nonetheless, as the production-reproduction balance always finds a way of stabilising itself – even at the price of infanticide, sacrifices, or wars – men and women are equally indispensable from the point of view of group survival; it could even be supposed that at certain periods when food was plentiful, his protective and nourishing role might have subordinated the male to the wife-mother. There are female animals that derive total autonomy from motherhood; so why has woman not been able to make a pedestal for herself from it? Even in those moments when humanity most desperately needed births – since the need for manual labour prevailed over the need for raw materials to exploit – and even in those times when motherhood was the most venerated, maternity was not enough for women to conquer the highest rank.* The reason for this is that humanity is not a simple natural species: it does not seek to survive as a species; its project is not stagnation: it seeks to surpass itself.

The primitive hordes were barely interested in their posterity. Connected to no territory, owning nothing, embodied in nothing stable, they could formulate no concrete idea of permanence; they were unconcerned with survival and did not recognise themselves in their descendants; they did not fear death and did not seek heirs; children were a burden and not of great value for them; the proof is that infanticide has always been frequent in nomadic peoples; and many newborns who are not massacred die for lack of hygiene in a climate of total indifference. So the woman who gives birth does not take pride in her creation; she feels like the passive plaything of obscure forces, and painful childbirth a useless and even bothersome accident. Later, more value was attached to children. But in any case, to give birth and to breast-feed are not *activities*, but natural functions; they do not involve a project, which is why the woman finds no motive there to claim a higher meaning for her existence; she passively submits to her biological destiny. Because housework alone is compatible with the duties of motherhood, she is condemned to domestic labour, which locks her into repetition and immanence; day after day it repeats itself in identical form from century to century; it produces nothing new. Man's case is radically different. He does not provide for the group in the way worker bees do, by a simple vital process, but rather by acts that transcend his animal condition. *Homo faber* has been an inventor since the beginning of time: even the stick or the club he armed himself with to knock down fruit from a tree or to slaughter animals is an instrument that expands his grasp of the world; bringing home freshly caught fish is not enough for him: he first has to conquer the seas by constructing dugout canoes; to appropriate the world's treasures, he annexes the world itself. Through such actions he tests his own power; he posits ends and projects paths to them: he realises himself as existent. To maintain himself, he creates; he spills over the present and opens up the future. This is the reason fishing and hunting expeditions have a sacred quality. Their success is greeted by celebration and triumph, man recognises his humanity in them. This pride is still apparent today when he builds a dam, a skyscraper, or an atomic reactor.

* Sociology no longer gives credit to Bachofen's lucubrations.

He has not only worked to preserve the given world: he has burst its borders, he has laid the ground for a new future.

His activity has another dimension that endows him with supreme dignity: it is often dangerous. If blood were only a food, it would not be worth more than milk: but the hunter is not a butcher: he runs risks in the struggle against wild animals. The warrior risks his own life to raise the prestige of the horde – his clan. This is how he brilliantly proves that life is not the supreme value for man but that it must serve ends far greater than itself. The worst curse on woman is her exclusion from warrior expeditions; it is not in giving life but in risking his life that man raises himself above the animal; this is why throughout humanity, superiority has been granted not to the sex that gives birth, but to the one that kills.

Here we hold the key to the whole mystery. On a biological level, a species maintains itself only by re-creating itself; but this creation is nothing but a repetition of the same Life in different forms. By transcending Life through Existence, man guarantees the repetition of Life: by this surpassing, he creates values that deny any value to pure repetition. With an animal, the gratuitousness and variety of male activities are useless because no project is involved; what it does is worthless when it is not serving the species; but in serving the species, the human male shapes the face of the earth, creates new instruments, invents and forges the future. Positing himself as sovereign, he encounters the complicity of woman herself: because she herself is also an existent, because transcendence also inhabits her and her project is not repetition but surpassing herself towards another future; she finds the confirmation of masculine claims in the core of her being. She participates with men in festivals that celebrate the success and victories of males. Her misfortune is to have been biologically destined to repeat Life, while in her own eyes Life in itself does not provide her reasons for being, and these reasons are more important than life itself.

Certain passages where Hegel's dialectic describes the relationship of master to slave would apply far better to the relationship of man to woman. The Master's privilege, he states, arises from the affirmation of Spirit over Life in the fact of risking his life: but in fact the vanquished slave has experienced this same risk, whereas the woman is originally an existent who gives *Life* and does not risk *her* life; there has never been combat between the male and her; Hegel's definition applies singularly to her. 'The other [consciousness] is the dependent consciousness for which essential reality is animal life, that is, life given by another entity.'

But this relationship differs from the relationship of oppression because woman herself aspires to and recognises the values concretely attained by males. It is the male who opens up the future towards which she also transcends; in reality, women have never pitted female values against male ones: it is men wanting to maintain masculine prerogatives who invented this division; they wanted to create a feminine domain – a rule of life, of immanence – only to lock woman in it. But it is above and beyond all sexual specification that the existent seeks self-justification in the movement of his transcendence: the very submission of women proves this. Today what women claim is to be recognised as existents just like men, and not to subordinate existence to life or the man to his animality.

Thus an existential perspective has enabled us to understand how the biological and economic situation of primitive hordes led to male supremacy. The female, more than the male, is prey to the species; humanity has always tried to escape from its species's destiny; with the invention of the tool, maintenance of life became activity and project for man, while motherhood left woman riveted to her body like the animal. It is because humanity puts itself into question in its being – that is, values reasons for living over life – that man has set himself as master over woman; man's project is not to repeat himself in time: it is to reign over the instant and to forge the future. Male activity, creating values, has constituted existence itself as a value; it has prevailed over the indistinct forces of life; and it has subjugated Nature and Woman. We must now see how this situation has continued and evolved through the centuries. What place has humanity allotted to this part of itself that has been defined in its core as Other? What rights have been conceded to it? How have men defined it?

CHAPTER 2

We have just seen that women's fate is very harsh in primitive hordes; in female animals the reproductive function is limited naturally and when it occurs, the particular animal is more or less released from other toil; only domestic females are sometimes exploited to the point of exhaustion of their forces as reproducers and in their individual capacities by a demanding master. This was undoubtedly the case of woman at a time when the struggle against a hostile world demanded the full employment of community resources; added to the fatigues of incessant and unregulated procreation were those of hard domestic duties. Nevertheless, some historians maintain that precisely at that time, male superiority was the least marked; which means that this superiority is lived in an immediate form, not yet posited and willed; no one tries to compensate for the cruel disadvantages that handicap woman; but neither does anyone try to break her down, as will later happen in paternalistic regimes. No institution actually ratifies the inequality of the sexes; in fact, there are no institutions: no property, no inheritance, no legal system. Religion is neutral; the totems that are worshipped are asexual.

It is when nomads settled the land and became farmers that institutions and law appeared. Man no longer has to limit himself to combating hostile forces; he begins to express himself concretely through the figure he imposes on the world, thinking the world and thinking himself; at that juncture, sexual differentiation is reflected in the group structure, and it takes on a particular character: in agricultural communities, woman is often vested with extraordinary prestige. This prestige is explained essentially by the new importance that children assume in a civilisation based upon working the land; by settling a territory, men begin to appropriate it. Property appears in a collective form; it demands posterity from its owners; motherhood becomes a sacred function. Many tribes live under a communal regime: this does not mean that women belong to all the men in the community; it is no longer thought today that promiscuous marriage was ever practised; but men and women only have a religious, social and economic existence as a group: their individuality remains a purely biological fact; marriage, whatever its form – monogamy, polygamy, polyandry – is itself nothing but a secular incident that does not create a mystical link. For the wife it is in no way a source of servitude, as she remains an integral part of her clan. The clan as a whole, gathered under the same totem, mystically shares the same mana and materially shares the common enjoyment of a territory. But in the alienation process mentioned before, the clan grasps itself in this territory in the guise of an objective and concrete figure; through the permanence of the land, the clan thus realises itself as a unity whose identity persists throughout the passage of time. Only this existential process makes it possible to understand the identification that has survived to this day among the clan, the gens, the family and property. In the thinking of nomadic tribes, only the moment exists; the agricultural community replaces this thinking with the concept of a life rooted in the past and incorporating the future: the totem ancestor who gives his name to the clan members is venerated; and the clan takes an abiding interest in its descendants: it will survive through the land he bequeaths to them and that they will exploit. The community conceives of its unity and wills its existence beyond the present: it sees itself in its children, it recognises them as its own, and it accomplishes and surpasses itself through them.

But many primitives are unaware of the father's role in the procreation of children who are thought to be the reincarnation of ancestral larvae floating around certain trees, certain rocks, in certain sacred places, and descending into the woman's body; in some cases, they believe she must not be a virgin if this infiltration is to take place; but other peoples believe that it also takes place through the nostrils or mouth; at any rate, defloration is secondary here and for mystical reasons the prerogative is rarely the husband's. The mother is clearly necessary for the birth of the child; she is the one who keeps and nourishes the germ within her and so the life of the clan is propagated in the visible world through her. This is how she finds herself playing the principal role. Very often, children belong to their mother's clan, bear her name and share her rights, particularly the use of the land belonging to the clan. So communal property is transmitted through women: through them the fields and their harvests are reserved to members of the clan, and inversely it is through their mothers that members are destined to a given piece of land. The land can thus be considered as mystically belonging to women:

their hold on the soil and its fruits is both religious and legal. The tie that binds them is stronger than one of ownership; maternal right is characterised by a true assimilation of woman to the land; in each, through its avatars, the permanence of life is achieved, life that is essentially generation. For nomads, procreation seems only an accident, and the riches of the earth are still unknown; but the farmer admires the mystery of fertilisation that burgeons in the furrows and in the maternal womb. He knows that he was conceived like the cattle and the harvests, and he wants his clan to conceive other humans who will perpetuate it in perpetuating the fertility of the fields; nature as a whole seems like a mother to him; the earth is woman, and the woman is inhabited by the same obscure forces as the earth.* This is part of the reason agricultural work is entrusted to woman: able to call up the ancestral larvae within her, she also has the power to make fruit and wheat spring from the sowed fields. In both cases it is a question of a magic conjuration, not of a creative act. At this stage, man no longer limits himself to gathering the products of the earth: but he does not yet understand his power; he hesitates between technical skill and magic; he feels passive, dependent on Nature that doles out existence and death by chance. To be sure, he recognises more or less the function of the sexual act as well as the techniques for cultivating the soil: but children and crops still seem like supernatural gifts; and the mysterious emanations flowing from the feminine body bring forth into this world the riches latent in the mysterious sources of life. Such beliefs are still alive today among numerous Indian, Australian and Polynesian tribes, and become all the more important as they match the practical interests of the collectivity.† Motherhood relegates woman to a sedentary existence; it is natural for her to stay at home while men hunt, fish and go to war. But primitive people rarely

---

* 'Hail, Earth, mother of all men, may you be fertile in the arms of God and filled with fruits for the use of man,' says an old Anglo-Saxon incantation.

† For the Bhantas of India, or in Uganda, a sterile woman is considered dangerous for gardens. In Nicobar, it is believed that the harvest will be better if it is brought in by a pregnant woman. In Borneo, seeds are chosen and preserved by women. 'One seems to feel in women a natural affinity with the seeds that are said by the women to be in a state of pregnancy. Sometimes women will spend the night in the rice fields during its growth period' (Hose and MacDougall). In India of yore, naked women pushed the plough through the field at night. Indians along the Orinoco left the sowing and planting to women because 'women knew how to conceive seed and bear children, so the seeds and roots planted by them bore fruit far more abundantly than if they had been planted by male hands' (Frazer). Many similar examples can be found in Frazer.

cultivate more than a modest garden contained within their own village limits and its cultivation is a domestic task; Stone Age instruments require little effort; economics and mystical belief agree to leave agricultural work to women. Domestic work, as it is taking shape, is also their lot: they weave rugs and blankets, they shape pottery. And they are often in charge of barter; commerce is in their hands. The life of the clan is thus maintained and extended through them; children, herds, harvests, tools and the whole prosperity of the group of which they are the soul depend on their work and their magic virtues. Such strength inspires in men a respect mingled with fear, reflected in their worship. It is in women that the whole of foreign Nature is concentrated.

It has already been said here that man never thinks himself without thinking the Other; he grasps the world under the emblem of duality, which is not initially sexual. But being naturally different from man who posits himself as the same, woman is consigned to the category of Other; the Other encompasses woman; at first she is not important enough to incarnate the Other alone, so a subdivision at the heart of the Other develops: in ancient cosmographies, a single element often has both male and female incarnations; thus for the Babylonians, the Ocean and the Sea were the double incarnation of cosmic chaos. When the woman's role grows, she comes to occupy nearly the whole region of the Other. Then appear the feminine divinities through whom fertility is worshipped. A discovery made in Susa shows the oldest representation of the Great Goddess, the Great Mother in a long robe and high coiffure, which other statues show crowned with towers; excavations in Crete have yielded several effigies of her. She can be steatopygous and crouched, or thin and standing, sometimes clothed, and often naked, her arms pressed beneath her swollen breasts. She is the queen of heaven, a dove is her symbol; she is also the empress of Hades, she comes out slithering, symbolised by a serpent. She can be seen in mountains, woods, the sea and in springs. She creates life everywhere; if she kills, she resurrects. Fickle, lascivious and cruel like Nature, propitious and yet dangerous, she reigns over all of Asia Minor, over Phrygia, Syria, Anatolia, and over all of western Asia. She is known as Ishtar in Babylon, Astarte to Semitic peoples, and Gaea, Rhea, or Cybele to the Greeks; she is found in Egypt in the form of Isis; male divinities are subordinated to her. Supreme idol in faraway regions of heaven and Hades, woman on earth is surrounded by taboos like all sacred beings – she is herself taboo; because of the powers she holds, she is seen as a magician or a sorceress; she is included in prayers, and she can be at times a priestess like the druids among the ancient Celts; in certain cases she participates in the government of the tribe, and at times she even governs on her own. These distant ages have left us no literature. But the great patriarchal periods conserve in their mythology, monuments and traditions the memory of times when women occupied very high positions. From a feminine point of view, the Brahman period is a regression from that of Rig-Veda, and the latter a regression from the primitive stage that preceded it. The pre-Islamic Bedouin women had a much higher status than that accorded them by the Koran. The great figures of Niobe and Medea evoke an era when mothers, considering their children to be their own property, took pride in them. And in the Homeric poems, Andromache and Hecuba have an importance that classic Greece no longer granted to women hidden in the shadows of the gynaeceum.

These facts all lead to the supposition that in primitive times a veritable reign of women existed; this hypothesis, proposed by Bachofen, was adopted by Engels; the passage from matriarchy to patriarchy seems to him to be 'the great historical defeat of the feminine sex'. But in reality this golden age of Woman is only a myth. To say that woman was the *Other* is to say that a relationship of reciprocity between the sexes did not exist: whether Earth, Mother or Goddess, she was never a peer for man; her power asserted itself *beyond* human rule: she was thus *outside* of this rule. Society has always been male; political power has always been in men's hands. 'Political authority, or simply social authority, always belongs to men,' Lévi-Strauss affirms at the close of his study of primitive societies. For men, the counterpart – or the other – who is also the same, with whom reciprocal relationships are established, is always another male individual. The duality that can be seen in one form or another at the heart of society pits one group of men against another; and women are part of the goods men possess and a means of exchange among themselves: the mistake comes from confusing two forms of mutually exclusive alterity. Insofar as woman is considered the absolute Other, that is – whatever magic powers she has – as the inessential, it is precisely impossible to regard her as another subject.* Women have thus never constituted a separate

---

* It will be seen that this distinction has been perpetuated. Periods that regard woman as *Other* are those that refuse most harshly to integrate her into society as a human being. Today she only becomes an *other* peer by losing her mystical aura. Antifeminists have always played on this ambiguity. They readily agree to exalt the woman as Other in order to make her alterity absolute and irreducible, and to refuse her access to the human *Mitsein*.

group that posited itself *for-itself* before a male group; they have never had a direct or autonomous relationship with men. 'The relationship of reciprocity which is the basis of marriage is not established between men and women, but between men by means of women, who are merely the occasion of this relationship,' said Lévi-Strauss.*[1] Woman's concrete condition is not affected by the type of lineage that prevails in the society to which she belongs; whether the regime is patrilineal, matrilineal, bilateral, or undifferentiated (undifferentiation never being precise), she is always under men's guardianship; the only question is if, after marriage, she is still subjected to the authority of her father or her oldest brother – authority that will also extend to her children – or of her husband. In any case: 'The woman is never anything more than the symbol of her lineage. Matrilineal descent is the authority of the woman's father or brother extended to the brother-in-law's village.'[†] She only mediates the law; she does not possess it. In fact, it is the relationship of two masculine groups that is defined by the system of filiation, and not the relation of the two sexes. In practice, woman's concrete condition is not consistently linked to any given type of law. It may happen that in a matrilineal system she has a very high position: but – beware – the presence of a woman chief or a queen at the head of a tribe absolutely does not mean that women are sovereign: the reign of Catherine the Great changed nothing in the fate of Russian peasant women; and they lived no less frequently in a state of abjection. And cases where a woman remains in her clan and her husband makes rapid, even clandestine visits to her are very rare. She almost always goes to live under her husband's roof: this fact is proof enough of male domination. 'Behind the variations in the type of descent,' writes Lévi-Strauss, 'the permanence of patrilocal residence attests to the basic asymmetrical relationship between the sexes which is characteristic of human society.' Since she keeps her children with her, the result is that the territorial organisation of the tribe does not correspond to its totemic organisation: the former is contingent, the latter rigorously constructed; but in practice, the first was the more important because the place where people work and live counts more than their mystical connection. In the more widespread transitional regimes, there are two kinds of rights, one based on religion and the other on the occupation and labour on the land, and they overlap. Though only

* Lévi-Strauss, *The Elementary Structures of Kinship*.
† Ibid.

a secular institution, marriage nevertheless has great social importance, and the conjugal family, though stripped of religious signification, is very alive on a human level. Even within groups where great sexual freedom is found, it is considered conventional for a woman who brings a child into the world to be married; alone with an offspring, she cannot constitute an autonomous group; and her brother's religious protection does not suffice; a husband's presence is required. He often has many heavy responsibilities for the children; they do not belong to his clan, but it is nonetheless he who feeds and raises them; between husband and wife, and father and son, bonds of cohabitation, work, common interest and tenderness are formed. Relations between this secular family and the totemic clan are extremely complex, as the diversity of marriage rites attests. In primitive times, a husband buys a wife from a foreign clan, or at least there is an exchange of goods from one clan to another, the first giving over one of its members and the second delivering cattle, fruits, or work in return. But as husbands take charge of wives and their children, it also happens that they receive remuneration from their brides' brothers. The balance between mystical and economic realities is an unstable one. Men often have a closer attachment to their sons than to their nephews; it is as a father that a man will choose to affirm himself when such affirmation becomes possible. And this is why every society tends towards a patriarchal form as its development leads man to gain awareness of himself and to impose his will. But it is important to emphasise that even at times when he was still confused by the mysteries of Life, Nature and Woman, he never relinquished his power; when, terrified by the dangerous magic woman possesses, he posits her as the essential, it is he who posits her, and he who realises himself thereby as the essential in this alienation he grants; in spite of the fecund virtues that infuse her, man remains her master, just as he is master of the fertile earth; she is destined to be subordinated, possessed and exploited, as is also Nature, whose magic fertility she incarnates. The prestige she enjoys in the eyes of men comes from them; they kneel before the Other, they worship the Goddess Mother. But as powerful as she may appear, she is defined through notions created by the male consciousness. All of the idols invented by man, however terrifying he may have made them, are in fact dependent upon him, and this is why he is able to destroy them. In primitive societies, this dependence is not acknowledged and posited, but its existence is implicit, in itself: and it will readily become mediatory as soon as man develops a clearer consciousness of self, as soon as he dares to assert himself and stand in opposition. And in fact, even when man grasps himself as given, passive and subject to the vagaries of rain and sun, he still realises himself as transcendence, as project; already, spirit and will assert themselves within him against life's confusion and contingencies. The totem ancestor, of which woman assumes multiple incarnations, is more or less distinctly a male principle under its animal or tree name; woman perpetuates carnal existence, but her role is only that of nourisher, not of creator; in no domain whatsoever does she create; she maintains the life of the tribe by providing children and bread, nothing more; she lives condemned to immanence; she incarnates only the static aspect of society, closed in on itself. Meanwhile, man continues to monopolise the functions that open this society to nature and to the whole of humanity; the only efforts worthy of him are war, hunting or fishing; he conquers foreign prey and annexes it to the tribe; war, hunting and fishing represent an expansion of existence, his going beyond into the world; the male is still the only incarnation of transcendence. He does not yet have the practical means to totally dominate Woman-Earth, he does not yet dare stand up to her: but already he wants to tear himself away from her. I think the profound reason for the well-known custom of exogamy, so widespread in matrilineal societies, is to be found in this determination. Even though man is unaware of the role he plays in procreation, marriage has great importance for him; this is where he attains adult dignity and receives his share of a piece of the world; through his mother he is bound to the clan, his ancestors, and everything that constitutes his own subsistence; but in all of these secular functions – work or marriage – he aspires to escape this circle and assert transcendence against immanence, to open up a future different from the past where he is rooted; depending on the types of relations recognised in different societies, the banning of incest takes on different forms, but from primitive times to our days it has remained the same: man wishes to possess that which he *is* not; he unites himself to what appears to him to be Other than himself. The wife must not be part of the husband's mana, she must be foreign to him: thus foreign to his clan. Primitive marriage is sometimes founded on abduction, real or symbolic: because violence done to another is the clearest affirmation of another's alterity. Taking his wife by force, the warrior proves he is able to annex the riches of others and burst through the bounds of the destiny assigned to him at birth; purchasing her under various forms – paying tribute, rendering services – has, less dramatically, the same signification.*

Little by little, man mediated his experience, and in his representations, as in his practical existence, the male principle triumphed. Spirit prevailed over Life, transcendence over immanence, technology over magic, and reason over superstition. The devaluation of woman represents a necessary stage in the history of humanity: for she derived her prestige not from her positive value but from man's weakness; she incarnated disturbing natural mysteries: man escapes her grasp when he frees himself from nature. In passing from stone to bronze he is able to conquer the land through his work and conquer himself as well. The farmer is subjected to the vagaries of the soil, of germination and of seasons; he is passive, he beseeches and he waits: this explains why totem spirits peopled the human world; the peasant endured the whims of these forces that took possession of him. On the contrary, the worker fashions a tool according to his own design; he imposes on it the form that fits his project; facing an inert nature that defies him but that he overcomes, he asserts himself as sovereign will; if he quickens his strokes on the anvil, he quickens the completion of the tool, whereas nothing can hasten the ripening of grain; his responsibility develops with what he makes: his movement, adroit or maladroit, makes it or breaks it; careful, skilful, he brings it to a point of perfection he can be proud of: his success depends not on the favour of the gods but on himself; he challenges his fellow workers, he takes pride in his success; and while he still leaves some

---

* In Lévi-Strauss's thesis already cited, there is, in a slightly different form, a confirmation of this idea. What comes out of this study is that the prohibition of incest is in no way the primal factor underlying exogamy; but it reflects the positive desire for exogamy in a negative form. There is no intrinsic reason that it be improper for a woman to have intercourse with men in her clan; but it is socially useful that she be part of the goods by which each clan, instead of closing in on itself, establishes a reciprocal relationship with another clan: 'Exogamy has a value less negative than positive... it prohibits endogamous marriage... certainly not because a biological danger is attached to consanguineous marriage, but because exogamous marriage results in a social benefit.' The group should not for its own private purposes consume women who constitute one of its possessions, but should use them as an instrument of communication; if marriage with a woman of the same clan is forbidden, 'the sole reason is that she is *same* whereas she must (and therefore can) become *other*... the same women that were originally offered can be exchanged in return. All that is necessary on either side is the *sign of otherness*, which is the outcome of a certain position in a structure and not of any innate characteristic.'

place for rituals, applied techniques seem far more important to him; mystical values become secondary, and practical interests take precedence; he is not entirely liberated from the gods, but he distances himself by distancing them from himself; he relegates them to their Olympian heaven and keeps the terrestrial domain for himself; the great Pan begins to fade at the first sound of his hammer, and man's reign begins. He discovers his power. He finds cause and effect in the relationship between his creating arm and the object of his creation: the seed planted germinates or not, while metal always reacts in the same way to fire, to tempering and to mechanical treatment; this world of tools can be framed in clear concepts: rational thinking, logic and mathematics are thus able to emerge. The whole representation of the universe is overturned. Woman's religion is bound to the reign of agriculture, a reign of irreducible duration, contingencies, chance, anticipation and mystery; the reign of *Homo faber* is the reign of time that can be conquered like space, the reign of necessity, project, action and reason. Even when he contends with the earth, he will henceforth contend with it as a worker; he discovers that the soil can be fertilised, that it is good to let it lie fallow, that certain seeds should be treated certain ways: it is he who makes the crops grow; he digs canals, he irrigates or drains the land, he lays out roads, he builds temples: he creates the world anew. The peoples who remained under the heel of the Mother Goddess where matrilineal filiation was perpetuated were also those arrested in a primitive state of civilisation. Woman was venerated only inasmuch as man was a slave to his own fears, a party to his own impotence: it was out of fear and not love that he worshipped her. Before he could accomplish himself, he had to begin by dethroning her.* It is the male principle of creative force, light, intelligence and order that he will henceforth recognise as a sovereign. Standing beside the Mother Goddess emerges a god, a son, or a lover who is still inferior to her, but who looks exactly like her, and who is associated with her. He also incarnates the fertility principle: he is a bull, the Minotaur, or the Nile fertilising the plains of Egypt. He dies in autumn and is reborn in spring after the spouse-mother, invulnerable yet tearful, has devoted her forces to searching for his body and bringing him back to life. Appearing in Crete, this couple can also be found all

---

* Of course, this condition is necessary but not sufficient: there are patrilineal civilisations immobilised in a primitive stage; others, like the Mayas, regressed. There is no absolute hierarchy between societies of maternal right and those of paternal right: but only the latter have evolved technically and ideologically.

along the banks of the Mediterranean: Isis and Horus in Egypt, Astarte and Adonis in Phoenicia, Cybele and Attis in Asia Minor, and Rhea and Zeus in Hellenic Greece. And then the Great Mother was dethroned. In Egypt, where woman's condition is exceptionally favourable, the goddess Nout, incarnating the sky, and Isis, the fertile land, wife of the Nile, Osiris, continue to be extremely important; but it is nonetheless Ra, the sun god, virile light and energy, who is the supreme king. In Babylon, Ishtar is only the wife of Bel-Marduk; and it is he who created things and guaranteed harmony. The god of the Semites is male. When Zeus reigns in heaven, Gaea, Rhea and Cybele have to abdicate: all that is left to Demeter is a still imposing but secondary divinity. The Vedic gods have wives, but these are not worshipped as they are. The Roman Jupiter has no equal.*

Thus, the triumph of patriarchy was neither an accident nor the result of a violent revolution. From the origins of humanity, their biological privilege enabled men to affirm themselves alone as sovereign subjects; they never abdicated this privilege; they alienated part of their existence in Nature and in Woman; but they won it back afterwards; condemned to play the role of the Other, woman was thus condemned to possess no more than precarious power: slave or idol, it was never she who chose her lot. 'Men make gods and women worship them,' said Frazer; it is men who decide if their supreme divinities will be females or males; the place of woman in society is always the one they assign her; at no time has she imposed her own law.

Perhaps, however, if productive work had remained at the level of her strength, woman would have achieved the conquest of nature *with* man; the human species affirmed itself against the gods through male and female individuals; but she could not obtain the benefits of tools for herself. Engels only incompletely explained her decline: it is insufficient to say that the invention of bronze and iron profoundly modified the balance of productive forces and brought about women's inferiority; this

---

* It is interesting to note (according to H. Bégouën, *Journal of Psychology*, 1934) that in the Aurignacian period there were numerous statuettes representing women with overly emphasised sexual attributes: they are noteworthy for their plumpness and the size accorded to their vulvas. Moreover, grossly sketched vulvas on their own were also found in caves. In the Solutrean and Magdalenian epochs, these effigies disappear. In the Aurignacian, masculine statuettes are very rare, and there are never any representations of the male organ. In the Magdalenian epoch, some representations of vulvas are still found, though in small quantities, but a great quantity of phalluses was discovered.

inferiority is not in itself sufficient to account for the oppression she has suffered. What was harmful for her was that, not becoming a labour partner for the worker, she was excluded from the human *Mitsein*: that woman is weak and has a lower productive capacity does not explain this exclusion; rather, it is because she did not participate in his way of working and thinking and because she remained enslaved to the mysteries of life that the male did not recognise in her an equal; by not accepting her, once she kept in his eyes the dimension of *other*, man could only become her oppressor. The male will for expansion and domination transformed feminine incapacity into a curse. Man wanted to exhaust the new possibilities opened up by new technology: he called upon a servile workforce and he reduced his fellow man to slavery. Slave labour being far more efficient than work that woman could supply, she lost the economic role she played within the tribe. And in his relationship with the slave, the master found a far more radical confirmation of his sovereignty than the tempered authority he exercised on woman. Venerated and revered for her fertility, being *other* than man, and sharing the disquieting character of the *other*, woman, in a certain way, kept man dependent on her even while she was dependent on him; the reciprocity of the master–slave relationship existed *in the present* for her and it was how she escaped slavery. As for the slave, he had no taboo to protect him, being nothing but a servile man, not just different, but inferior: the dialectic of the slave–master relationship will take centuries to be actualised; within the organised patriarchal society, the slave is only a beast of burden with a human face: the master exercises tyrannical authority over him; this exalts his pride: and he turns it against the woman. Everything he wins, he wins against her; the more powerful he becomes, the more she declines. In particular, when he acquires ownership of land,* he also claims woman as property. Formerly he was possessed by *the* mana, by *the* earth: now he has *a* soul, *property*; freed from *Woman*, he now lays claim to *a* woman and a posterity of his own. He wants the family labour he uses for the benefit of his fields to be totally *his*, and for this to happen, the workers must belong to him: he subjugates his wife and his children. He must have heirs who will extend his life on earth because he bequeaths them his possessions, and who will give him in turn, beyond the tomb, the necessary honours for the repose of his soul. The cult of the domestic gods is superimposed on the constitution of private property, and the function of heirs is both economic and

* See Part One, Chapter 3.

mystical. Thus, the day agriculture ceases to be an essentially magic operation and becomes creative labour, man finds himself to be a generative force; he lays claim to his children and his crops at the same time.*

There is no ideological revolution more important in the primitive period than the one replacing matrilineal descent with agnation; from that time on, the mother is lowered to the rank of wet nurse or servant, and the father's sovereignty is exalted; he is the one who holds rights and transmits them. Apollo, in Aeschylus's *Eumenides*, proclaims these new truths: 'The mother is no parent of that which is called her child, but only nurse of the new-planted seed that grows. The parent is he who mounts. A stranger she preserves a stranger's seed, if no god interfere.'² It is clear that these affirmations are not the results of scientific discoveries; they are acts of faith. Undoubtedly, the experience of technical cause and effect from which man draws the assurance of his creative powers makes him recognise he is as necessary to procreation as the mother. Idea guided observation; but the latter is restricted to granting the father a role equal to that of the mother: it led to the supposition that, as for nature, the condition for conception was the encounter of sperm and menses; Aristotle's idea that woman is merely matter, and 'the principle of movement which is male in all living beings is better and more divine,' is an idea that expresses a will to power that goes beyond all of what is known. In attributing his posterity exclusively to himself, man frees himself definitively from subjugation by women, and he triumphs over woman in the domination of the world. Doomed to procreation and secondary tasks, stripped of her practical importance and her mystical prestige, woman becomes no more than a servant.

Men represented this triumph as the outcome of a violent struggle. One of the most ancient cosmologies, belonging to the Assyro-Babylonians, tells of their victory in a text that dates from the seventh century but that recounts an even older legend. The Sun and the Sea, Aton and Tiamat, gave birth to the celestial world, the terrestrial world and the great gods; but finding them too turbulent, they decided to destroy them; and Tiamat, the woman-mother, led the struggle against

---

* In the same way that woman was identified with furrows, the phallus was identified with the plough, and vice versa. In a drawing representing a plough from the Kassite period, there are traces of the symbols of the generative act; afterwards, the phallus-plough identity was frequently reproduced in art forms. The word *lak* in some Austro-Asian languages designates both phallus and plough. An Assyrian prayer addresses a god whose 'plough fertilised the earth'.

the strongest and most fine-looking of her descendants, Bel-Marduk; he, having challenged her in combat, killed her and slashed her body in two after a frightful battle; with one half he made the vault of heaven, and with the other the foundation for the terrestrial world; then he gave order to the universe and created humanity. In the *Eumenides* drama, which illustrated the triumph of patriarchy over maternal right, Orestes also assassinates Clytemnestra. Through these bloody victories, the virile force and the solar forces of order and light win over feminine chaos. By absolving Orestes, the tribunal of the gods proclaims he was the son of Agamemnon before being the son of Clytemnestra. The old maternal right is dead: the audacious male revolt killed it. But we have seen that in reality, the passage to paternal rights took place through gradual transitions. Masculine conquest was a reconquest: man only took possession of that which he already possessed; he put law into harmony with reality. There was neither struggle, nor victory, nor defeat. Nevertheless, these legends have profound meaning. At the moment when man asserts himself as subject and freedom, the idea of the Other becomes mediatory. From this day on, the relationship with the Other is a drama; the existence of the Other is a threat and a danger. The ancient Greek philosophy, which Plato, on this point, does not deny, showed that alterity is the same as negation, thus Evil. To posit the Other is to define Manichaeism. This is why religions and their codes treat woman with such hostility. By the time humankind reaches the stage of writing its mythology and laws, patriarchy is definitively established: it is males who write the codes. It is natural for them to give woman a subordinate situation; one might imagine, however, that they would consider her with the same benevolence as children and animals. But no. Afraid of woman, legislators organise her oppression. Only the harmful aspects of the ambivalent virtues attributed to her are retained: from sacred she becomes unclean. Eve, given to Adam to be his companion, lost humankind; to punish men, the pagan gods invent women, and Pandora, the firstborn of these female creatures, is the one who unleashes all the evil humanity endures. The Other is passivity confronting activity, diversity breaking down unity, matter opposing form, disorder resisting order. Woman is thus doomed to Evil. 'There is a good principle that created order, light and man and a bad principle that created chaos, darkness and woman,' says Pythagoras. The Laws of Manu define her as a vile being to be held in slavery. Leviticus assimilates her to beasts of burden, owned by the patriarch. The laws of Solon confer no rights on her. The Roman Code puts her in guardianship and proclaims her 'imbecility'. Canon law considers her 'the devil's gateway'. The Koran treats her with the most absolute contempt.

And yet Evil needs Good, matter needs the idea and night needs light. Man knows that to satisfy his desires, to perpetuate his existence, woman is indispensable to him; he has to integrate her in society: as long as she submits to the order established by males, she is cleansed of her original stain. This idea is forcefully expressed in the Laws of Manu: 'Whatever be the qualities of the man with whom a woman is united according to the law, such qualities even she assumes, like a river united with the ocean, and she is admitted after death to the same celestial paradise.' The Bible too praises the 'virtuous woman'. Christianity, in spite of its loathing of the flesh, respects the devoted virgin and the chaste and docile wife. Within a religious group, woman can even hold an important religious position: Brahmani in India and Flaminia in Rome are as holy as their husbands; in a couple, the man is dominant, but both male and female principles remain essential to the childbearing function, to life and to the social order.

This very ambivalence of the Other, of the Female, will be reflected in the rest of her history; until our times she will be subordinated to men's will. But this will is ambiguous: by total annexation, woman will be lowered to the rank of a thing; of course, man attempts to cover with his own dignity what he conquers and possesses; in his eyes the Other retains some of her primitive magic; one of the problems he will seek to solve is how to make his wife both a servant and a companion; his attitude will evolve throughout the centuries, and this will also entail an evolution in woman's destiny.*

---

* We will examine this evolution in the Western world. The history of the woman in the East, in India and in China was one of long and immutable slavery. From the Middle Ages to today, we will centre this study on France, where the situation is typical.

Once woman is dethroned by the advent of private property, her fate is linked to it for centuries: in large part, her history is intertwined with the history of inheritance. The fundamental importance of this institution becomes clear if we keep in mind that the owner alienated his existence in property; it was more important to him than life itself; it goes beyond the strict limits of a mortal lifetime, it lives on after the body is gone, an earthly and tangible incarnation of the immortal soul; but this continued survival can occur only if property remains in the owner's hands: it can remain his after death only if it belongs to individuals who are extensions of himself and recognised, who are *his own*. Cultivating paternal lands and worshipping the father's spirit are one and the same obligation for the heir: to assure the survival of ancestors on earth and in the underworld. Man will not, therefore, agree to share his property or his children with woman. He will never really be able to go that far, but at a time when patriarchy is powerful, he strips woman of all her rights to hold and transmit property. It seems logical, in fact, to deny her these rights. If it is accepted that a woman's children do not belong to her, they inevitably have no link with the group the woman comes from. Woman is no longer passed from one clan to another through marriage: she is radically abducted from the group she is born into and annexed to her husband's; he buys her like a head of cattle or a slave, he imposes his domestic divinities on her: and the children she conceives belong to her spouse's family. If she could inherit, she would thus wrongly transmit her paternal family's riches to that of her husband: she is carefully excluded from the succession. But inversely, because she owns nothing, woman is not raised to the dignity of a person; she herself is part of man's patrimony, first her father's and then her husband's. Under a strictly patriarchal regime, a father can condemn to death his male and female children at birth; but in the case of a male child, society most often puts limits on this power: a normally constituted newborn male is allowed to live; whereas the custom of exposure is very wide-spread for girls; there was massive infanticide among Arabs: as soon as they were born, girls were thrown into ditches. Accepting a female child is an act of generosity on the father's part; the woman enters such societies only through a kind of grace bestowed on her, and not legitimately like males. In any case, the stain of birth is far more serious for the mother when a girl is born: among Hebrews, Leviticus demands twice as much cleansing as for a newborn boy. In societies where 'blood money' exists, only a small sum is required when the victim is of the feminine sex or a girl: her value compared with a male's is like a slave's with a free man's. When she is a young girl, the father has total power over her; on her marriage he transmits it entirely to her spouse. Since she is his property like the slave, the beast of burden, or the thing, it is natural for a man to have as many wives as he wishes; only economic reasons put limits on polygamy; the husband can disown his wives at whim, and society barely accords them any guarantees. In return, woman is subjected to rigorous chastity. In spite of the taboos, matriarchal societies allow great freedom of behaviour; prenuptial chastity is rarely demanded; and adultery not judged severely. On the contrary, when woman becomes man's property, he wants a virgin, and he demands total fidelity at the risk of severe penalty; it would be the worst of crimes to risk giving heritage rights to a foreign offspring: this is why the paterfamilias has the right to put a guilty wife to death. As long as private property lasts, conjugal infidelity on the part of a woman is considered a crime of high treason. All codes up to our time have perpetuated inequality in issues concerning adultery, arguing the seriousness of the fault committed by the woman who might bring an illegitimate child into the family. And though the right to take the law into one's own hands has been abolished since Augustus, the Napoleonic Code still holds out the promise of the jury's leniency for a husband who avenges himself. When woman belonged to both a patrilineal clan and a conjugal family, she was able to preserve a good amount of freedom, as the two series of bonds over-lapped and even conflicted with each other and as each system served to support her against the other: for example, she could often choose the husband of her fancy, since marriage was only a secular event and had no effect on society's deep structure. But under the patriarchal regime, she was the property of a father who married her off as he saw fit; then attached to her husband's household, she was no more than his thing and the thing of the family (*genos*) in which she was placed.

When family and private patrimony incontestably remain the bases of society, woman also remains totally alienated. This is what has happened in the Muslim world. The structure is feudal in that there has never been a state strong enough to unify and dominate the numerous tribes: no power holds in check that of the patriarch chief. The religion that was created when the Arab people were warriors and conquerors professed the utmost disdain towards women. 'Men are superior to women on account of the qualities with which God has gifted the one above the other, and on account of the outlay they make from their substance for them,' says the Koran; the woman has never held real power or mystic prestige. The Bedouin woman works hard, she ploughs and carries burdens: this is how she sets up a reciprocal bond with her husband; she moves around freely, her face uncovered. The Muslim woman, veiled and shut in, is still today a kind of slave in most levels of society. I recall an underground cave in a troglodyte village in Tunisia where four women were squatting: the old, one-eyed and toothless wife, her face ravaged, was cooking dough on a small brazier surrounded by acrid smoke; two slightly younger but equally disfigured wives were rocking children in their arms; one was breast-feeding; seated before a weaver's loom was a young idol, magnificently dressed in silk, gold and silver, knotting strands of wool. Leaving this gloomy den – realm of immanence, womb and tomb – in the corridor leading up towards the light, I met the male, dressed in white, sparklingly clean, smiling, sunny. He was returning from the market, where he had bantered about world affairs with other men; he would spend a few hours in this retreat of his own, in the heart of this vast universe to which he belonged and from which he was not separated. For the old withered creatures, for the young bride doomed to the same degeneration, there was no other universe but the murky cave from which they would emerge only at night, silent and veiled.

The Jews of biblical times have more or less the same customs as the Arabs. The patriarchs are polygamous and can renounce their wives almost at whim; at the risk of harsh punishment, the young bride has to be delivered to her spouse as a virgin; in cases of adultery, she is stoned; she is confined to domestic labour, as the image of virtuous women demonstrates: 'She seeketh wool and flax . . . she riseth also while it is yet night . . . her candle goeth not off at night . . . she eateth not the bread of idleness.' Even chaste and industrious, she is impure and burdened with taboos; she cannot testify in court. Ecclesiastes treats her with the deepest disgust: 'And I find more bitter than death the woman, whose heart is snares and nets, and her hands as bands . . . one man among a thousand have I found; but a woman among all those have I not found.'[3] When her husband dies, custom and even law require her to marry a brother of the deceased.

This custom called levirate is found among many oriental peoples. In all regimes where woman is under guardianship, one of the problems is what to do with widows. The most radical solution is to sacrifice them on their husbands' tombs. But it is not true that even in India the law imposes such holocausts; the Laws of Manu permit a wife to survive a husband; spectacular suicides have never been more than an aristocratic fashion. It is far more frequent for the widow to be handed over to her husband's heirs. The levirate sometimes takes the form of polyandry; to avoid the ambiguities of widowhood, all the brothers in the family become the husbands of the woman, a custom that serves to preserve the clan against the possible infertility of the husband. According to a text of Caesar's, in Brittany all the men of one family had a certain number of women in common.

This form of radical patriarchy was not established everywhere. In Babylon, Hammurabi's Code recognised certain rights of woman: she receives a share of the paternal inheritance, and when she marries, her father provides her with a dowry. In Persia, polygamy is customary; woman is bound to absolute obedience to the husband her father chooses for her as soon as she is nubile; but she is more respected than among most Oriental peoples; incest is not forbidden, and marriage takes place frequently among sisters and brothers; she is in charge of educating the children up to the age of seven for boys and until marriage for girls. Woman can share in her husband's estate if the son proves himself unworthy; if she is a 'privileged wife', she is entrusted with the guardianship of minor children in the case of her husband's death and with the business management in the absence of an adult son. The rules of marriage clearly point out the importance posterity has for the head of a family. It is likely that there were five forms of marriage:* (1) The woman married with the consent of her parents; she was then called the 'privileged wife'; her children belonged to her husband. (2) When the woman was an only child, her firstborn would be given up to her parents to replace their daughter; then she would become a 'privileged wife'. (3) If a man died unmarried, his family would take a woman from outside, give her a dowry and marry her: she was called an 'adopted wife'; half of her children

* This account is taken from Clement Huart, *La Perse antique et la civilisation iranienne* (*Ancient Persia and Iranian Civilization*).

belonged to the deceased and the other half to the living husband. (4) A widow without children who remarried was called a servant wife: she owed half of the children of her second marriage to her deceased husband. (5) The woman who married without the consent of her parents could not inherit from them until the oldest son, coming of age, would give her to his father as a 'privileged wife'; if her husband died before, she was considered to be a minor and put under guardianship. The status of the adopted wife and the servant wife establishes the right of every man to be survived by descendants who are not necessarily connected by a blood relationship. This confirms what was said above; this relationship was in a way invented by man when he sought to annex for himself – beyond his finite life – immortality in this world and in the underworld.

In Egypt, woman's condition was the most favourable. When Goddess Mothers married, they maintained their standing; social and religious unity resides in the couple; woman is an ally, a complement to man. Her magic is so unthreatening that even the fear of incest is overcome, and no differentiation is made between a sister and a spouse.* She has the same rights as men, the same legal power; she inherits, and she owns property. This uniquely fortunate situation is in no way haphazard: it stems from the fact that in ancient Egypt the land belonged to the king and the higher castes of priests and warriors; for private individuals, landed property was only usufructuary; the land was inalienable, property transmitted by inheritance had little value, and there was no problem about sharing it. Because of this absence of personal patrimony, woman maintained the dignity of a person. She married whom she wanted, and as a widow she could remarry as she wished. The male practised polygamy, but although all of his children were legitimate, he had only one real wife, the only one associated with religion and linked to him legally: the others were mere slaves, deprived of all rights. The chief wife did not change status by marrying: she remained mistress of her possessions and was free to engage in contracts. When the pharaoh Bocchoris established private property, woman's position was too strong to be dislodged; Bocchoris opened the era of contracts, and marriage itself became contractual. There were three types of contract: one dealt with servile marriage; woman became man's thing, but she could specify that he would not have a concubine other than her; nonetheless, the legal spouse was considered equal to man and all their property was held in common; the husband would often agree to pay her a sum of money

* In some cases the brother *had to* marry his sister.

in the case of divorce. Later, this custom led to a type of contract remark-ably favourable to women; the husband agreed to absolve her of her debt. There were serious punishments for adultery, but divorce was fairly open for the two spouses. The presence of contracts soundly restrained polygamy; women got possession of the wealth and transmitted it to their children, which brought about the creation of a plutocratic class. Ptolemy Philopator decreed that women could no longer alienate their property without marital authorisation, which kept them as eternal minors. But even in times when they had a privileged status, unique in the ancient world, they were not socially equal to men; taking part in religion and government, they could have the role of regent, but the pharaoh was male; priests and warriors were males; woman's role in public life was a secondary one; and in private life, fidelity was required of her without reciprocity.

The customs of the Greeks are very similar to oriental ones; yet they do not practise polygamy. No one knows exactly why. Maintaining a harem always entails heavy costs: only the ostentatious Solomon, the sultans from *The Thousand and One Nights*, kings, chiefs or rich property owners could afford the luxury of a vast seraglio; an ordinary man had to be satisfied with three or four women; a peasant rarely possessed more than two. Besides – except in Egypt where there was no specific landed property – the concern for preserving the patrimony intact led to granting the oldest son special rights on paternal inheritance; from this stemmed a hierarchy among women, the mother of the principal heir invested with dignity far superior to that of his other wives. If the wife herself has property of her own or if she is dowered, she is consid-ered a person by her husband: he is joined to her by both a religious and an exclusive bond. From there on, the custom that only recognises one wife was undoubtedly established: but the reality was that the Greek citizen continued to be comfortably 'polygamous' since he could find the satisfaction of his desires from street prostitutes or gynaeceum servants. 'We have hetarias for spiritual pleasures,' says Demosthenes, 'concubines *(pallakes)* for sensual pleasure, and wives to give us sons.' The *pallakis* replaced the wife in the master's bed if she was ill, indis-posed, pregnant or recovering from childbirth; so there was no great difference between a gynaeceum and a harem. In Athens, the wife is shut up in her quarters, held by law under severe constraint and watched over by special magistrates. She spends her whole life as a minor; she is under the control of her guardian: either her father, or her husband, or her husband's heir or, by default, the state, represented by public officials;

here are her masters, and they use her like merchandise, the guardian's control extending over both her person and her property; the guardian can transmit her rights as he wishes: the father gives his daughter up for adoption or in marriage; the husband can repudiate his wife and hand her over to another husband. But Greek law assures woman of a dowry used to support her and that must be restored in full to her if the marriage is dissolved; the law also authorises the woman to file for divorce in certain rare cases; but these are the only guarantees that society grants. Of course, all inheritance is bequeathed to the male children, and the dowry is not considered acquired property but a kind of duty imposed on the guardian. However, thanks to this dowry custom, the widow no longer passes for a hereditary possession in the hands of her husband's heirs: she returns to her family's guardianship.

One of the problems arising from societies based on agnation is the fate of inheritance in the absence of any male descendants. The Greeks had instituted the custom of *epiklerate*: the female heir had to marry her oldest relative in the paternal family *(genos)*; thus the property her father bequeathed to her would be transmitted to children belonging to the same group, and the estate remained the property of the paternal *genos*; the *epikleros* was not a female heir but only a machine to procreate a male heir; this custom placed her entirely at man's mercy as she was automatically handed over to the firstborn of her family's men, who most often turned out to be an old man.

Since the cause of women's oppression is found in the resolve to perpetuate the family and keep the patrimony intact, if she escapes the family, she escapes this total dependence as well; if society rejects the family by denying private property, woman's condition improves considerably. Sparta, where community property prevailed, was the only city-state where the woman was treated almost as the equal of man. Girls were brought up like boys; the wife was not confined to her husband's household; he was only allowed furtive nocturnal visits; and his wife belonged to him so loosely that another man could claim a union with her in the name of eugenics: the very notion of adultery disappears when inheritance disappears; as all the children belonged to the city as a whole, women were not jealously enslaved to a master: or it can be explained inversely, that possessing neither personal wealth nor individual ancestry, the citizen does not possess a woman either. Women underwent the burdens of maternity as men did war: but except for this civic duty, no restraints were put on their freedom.

Along with the free women just discussed and slaves living within

the *genos* – unconditionally owned by the family head – are the prostitutes found in Greece. Primitive people were familiar with hospitality
prostitution, turning over a woman to a guest passing through, which
undoubtedly had mystical explanations; and with sacred prostitution,
intended for the common good by releasing the mysterious forces of
fertility. These customs existed in classical antiquity. Herodotus reports
that in the fifth century BC, every woman in Babylon had to give herself
once in her life to a stranger in the Temple of Mylitta for a coin she
contributed to the temple's coffers; she then returned home to live in
chastity. Religious prostitution has continued to our day among Egyptian
almahs and Indian *bayadères* who make up respectable castes of musicians and dancers. But most often, in Egypt, India and western Asia,
sacred prostitution slipped into legal prostitution, the priestly class finding
this trade profitable. There were venal prostitutes even among the
Hebrews. In Greece, especially along the coast or in the islands where
many foreigners stopped off, temples of 'young girls hospitable to
strangers', as Pindar called them, could be found: the money they earned
was intended for religious establishments, that is, for priests and indirectly for their maintenance. In reality, in a hypocritical way, sailors' and
travellers' sexual needs – in Corinth and other places – were exploited;
and this was already venal prostitution. Solon was the one who turned
this into an institution. He bought Asian slaves and shut them up in
dicterions located in Athens near the temple of Venus, not far from the
port, under the management of *pornotropos* in charge of the financial
administration of the establishment; each girl received wages, and the
net profit went to the state. After that, *kapaileia*, private establishments,
were opened: a red Priapus served as their display sign. Soon, in
addition to slaves, poor Greek women were taken in as residents. The
dicterions were considered so necessary that they were recognised as in-
violable places of asylum. Nonetheless, courtesans were marked with
infamy, they had no social rights, and their children were exempted from
providing for them; they had to wear specific outfits made of multi-
coloured cloth decorated with flower bouquets, and their hair was dyed
with saffron. Besides the women shut up in *dicterions*, there were free
courtesans, who could be placed in three categories: *dicteriads*, much like
today's registered prostitutes; *auletrids*, who were dancers and flute
players, and hetaeras, demimondaines who often came from Corinth
having had official liaisons with high-ranking Greek men and who played
the social role of modern-day 'worldly women'. The first ones were
found among freed women or lower-class Greek girls; exploited by

procurers, they led a pitiful life. The second type succeeded in getting rich thanks to their musical talent: the most famous of all was Lamia, mistress of Ptolemy of Egypt, then of his vanquisher, the king of Macedonia, Demetrius Poliorcetes. As for the last category, many were well known for sharing in the glory of their lovers. Disposing of themselves and their fortunes freely, intelligent, cultivated and artistic, they were treated like persons by the men who were captivated by their charms. And because they escaped from their families, because they lived on the margins of society, they also escaped men: they could seem to be their counterparts, almost their equals. In Aspasia, in Phryne and in Lais, the superiority of the free woman asserted itself over the virtuous mother of a family.

These brilliant exceptions aside, the Greek woman is reduced to semi-slavery; she does not even have the freedom to complain: Aspasia and the more passionate Sappho are barely able to make a few grievances heard. In Homer, there are still remnants of the heroic period when women had some power: still, the warriors roundly send them off to their chambers. The same scorn is found in Hesiod: 'He who confides in a woman confides in a thief.' In the great classical period, woman is resolutely confined to the gynaeceum. 'The best woman is she of whom men speak the least,' said Pericles. Plato, who proposed admitting a council of matrons to the Republic's administration and giving girls a liberal education, is an exception; he provoked Aristophanes' raillery; to a woman who questions him about public affairs, a husband responds, in *Lysistrata*: 'This is none of your business. Shut up, or you'll be beaten . . . go back to your weaving.' Aristotle expresses the common point of view in declaring that woman is woman because of a deficiency, that she must live closed up at home and obey man. 'The slave is entirely deprived of the freedom to deliberate; woman does have it, but she is weak and powerless,' he states. According to Xenophon, a woman and her spouse are complete strangers to each other: 'Are there people you communicate with less than your wife? – There are not many'; all that is required of a woman in *Oeconomicus* is to be an attentive, prudent, economical housewife, busy as a bee, a model of organisation. The modest status to which women are reduced does not keep the Greeks from being deeply misogynous. In the seventh century BC, Archilochus writes biting epigrams against women; Simonides of Amorgos says, 'Women are the greatest evil God ever created: if they sometimes seem useful, they soon change into trouble for their masters.' For Hipponax: 'There are but two days in life when your wife brings you joy: her wedding day and her funeral.' But it is the Ionians who, in Miletus's stories, are the most spiteful: for example, the tale of the matron of Ephesus. Mostly women are attacked for being lazy, shrewish or spendthrift, in fact precisely the absence of the qualities demanded of them. 'There are many monsters on the earth and in the sea, but the greatest is still woman,' wrote Menander. 'Woman is a pain that never goes away.' When the institution of the dowry brought a certain importance to women, it was her arrogance that was deplored; this is one of Aristophanes' – and notably Menander's – familiar themes. 'I married a witch with a dowry. I took her for her fields and her house, and that, O Apollo, is the worst of evils . . . !' 'Damn him who invented marriage and then the second, the third, the fourth and the rest who followed them.' 'If you are poor and you marry a rich woman, you will be reduced to being both a slave and poor.' The Greek woman was too closely controlled to be attacked for her conduct; and it was not the flesh in her that was vilified. It was more the responsibilities and duties of marriage that weighed on men; this leads to the supposition that in spite of her rigorous conditions, and although she had almost no recognised rights, she must have held an important place in the household and enjoyed some authority; doomed to obedience, she could disobey; she could bombard her husband with tantrums, tears, nagging and insults; marriage, meant to enslave woman, was a ball and chain for the husband as well. In the character of Xanthippe are embodied all the grievances of the Greek citizen against the shrewish wife and the adversities of conjugal life.

The conflict between family and state defines the history of the Roman woman. The Etruscans constituted a matrilineal filiation society and it is probable that at the time of the monarchy Rome still practised exogamy linked to a matriarchal regime: the Latin kings did not transmit power through heredity. What is certain is that after Tarquinius's death, patriarchy asserts itself: agricultural property and the private estate – thus the family – become society's nucleus. Woman will be strictly subservient to the patrimony and thus to the family group: laws deprive her of even those guarantees accorded to Greek women; she lives her life in powerlessness and servitude. She is, of course, excluded from public affairs and prohibited from any 'masculine office'; she is a perpetual minor in civil life. She is not directly deprived of her paternal inheritance but, through circuitous means, is kept from using it: she is put under the authority of a guardian. 'Guardianship was established in the interest of the guardians themselves,' said Gaius, 'so that woman – of whom they are the presumptive heirs – could not rob them of their inheritance with a will, nor diminish the inheritance by alienations or debts.' Woman's first guardian is her father; in his absence, paternal male relatives fulfil that function. When the woman marries, she passes 'into the hands' of her husband; there are three types of marriage: the *confarreatio*, where the spouses offer a spelt cake to the Capitoline Jupiter in the presence of the *flamen dialis*; the *coemptio*, a fictitious sale in which the plebeian father 'mancipated' his daughter to her husband; and the *usus*, the result of a cohabitation of one year; all three were with *manu*, meaning that the male spouse replaces the father or his male relatives; his wife is considered one of his daughters, and he thenceforth has complete power over her person and her property. But from the time of the Law of the Twelve Tables, because the Roman woman belonged to both paternal and conjugal clans, conflicts arose, giving rise to her legal emancipation. As a result, the *manu* marriage dispossesses her male agnates. To defend the paternal relatives' interests, *sine manu* marriage comes into being; in this case, the woman's property remains under the guardians' control, and the husband's rights are only over her person; and even this power is shared with the paterfamilias, who keeps his daughter under his absolute authority. The family court is in charge of settling disputes arising between father and husband: such an institution gives the woman recourse from her father to her husband or from her husband to her father; she is not one individual's thing. Moreover, although a gens is very powerful – as the existence of this court proves – independent of public courts, the father, as head of the family, is above all a citizen: his authority is unlimited, he rules absolutely over wife and children; but they are not his property; rather he administers their existence for the public good; the woman, who brings his children into the world and whose domestic duties often extend to agricultural tasks, is very useful to the country and deeply respected. Here is an important fact that recurs throughout history: abstract rights cannot sufficiently define the concrete situation of woman; this situation depends in great part on the economic role she plays; and very often, abstract freedom and concrete powers vary inversely. Legally more enslaved than the Greek woman, the Roman is more deeply integrated in society; at home she sits in the atrium which is the centre of the domicile, rather than being relegated to the gynaeceum; it is she who presides over the slaves' work; she oversees the children's education, and her influence on them often extends to an advanced age; she shares her husband's work and his concerns, she is considered a co-owner of his property; the marriage formula: '*Ubi tu Gaius, ego*

Gaia'[4] is not an empty formula; the matron is called 'domina'; she is mistress of the home, associate in religion, not a slave but man's companion; the tie that unites her to him is so sacred that in five centuries not one divorce is recorded. She is not confined to her quarters: she is present at meals and celebrations, she goes to the theatre; men give her right-of-way on the street, consuls and lictors stand aside for her. Legend accords her an eminent role in history: those of the Sabine women, Lucretia, and Virginia are well known; Coriolanus yields to the suppli-cations of his mother's and wife's pleas; the law of Licinius consecrating the triumph of Roman democracy is said to have been inspired by his wife; Cornelia forges the soul of the Gracchi. 'Everywhere men govern women,' said Cato, 'and we who govern all men are governed by our women.'

Little by little the legal situation of Roman women adapts to their practical situation. During the patrician oligarchy, each paterfamilias is an independent ruler within the Republic; but when state power becomes established, it opposes the concentration of wealth and the arrogance of powerful families. Family courts bow to public justice. And woman acquires ever greater rights. Four powers originally limited her freedom: the father and the husband controlled her person, her guardian and *manus* her property. The state takes authority over the opposition of father and husband to restrict their rights: the state court will now rule over adul-tery cases, divorce, and so on. In the same way, guardians and *manus* destroy each other. In the interest of the guardian, the *manus* had already been separated from marriage; later, the *manus* becomes an expedient that women use to escape their guardians, either by contracting ficti-tious marriages or by securing obliging guardians from their father or from the state. Under imperial legislation, guardianship will be entirely abolished. Woman simultaneously gains a positive guarantee of her inde-pendence: her father is obliged to provide her with a dowry; and it will not go back to the agnates after the marriage's dissolution, nor does it ever belong to her husband; a woman can at any moment demand resti-tution by a sudden divorce, which puts man at her mercy. 'In accepting the dowry, he sold his power,' said Plautus. From the end of the Republic on, the mother's right to her children's respect was recognised as equal to the father's; she is granted custody of her children in case of guardian-ship or of the husband's bad conduct. When she had three children and the deceased had no heirs, a Senate decree, under Hadrian, entitled her to an *ab intestat* succession right for each of them. And under Marcus Aurelius the Roman family's evolution was completed: from 178 on, the mother's children become her heirs, over her male relatives; from then on, the family is based on *coniunctio sanguinis* and the mother is equal to the father; the daughter inherits like her brothers.

Nevertheless, the history of Roman law shows a tendency that contradicts the one just described: rendering the woman independent of the family, the central power takes her back under its guardianship and subjects her to various legal restraints.

In fact, she would assume an unsettling importance if she could be both rich and independent; so what is conceded with one hand is taken away from her with the other. The Oppian law that banned luxury was voted when Hannibal threatened Rome; when the danger passed, women demanded its abrogation; in a famous speech, Cato asked that it be upheld: but a demonstration by matrons assembled in the public square carried the repeal against him. More severe laws were proposed as mores loosened, but without great success: they did little more than give rise to fraud. Only the Velleian Senate decree triumphed, forbidding woman to 'intercede' for others,* depriving her of nearly every legal capacity. It is when woman is probably the most emancipated that the inferiority of her sex is proclaimed, a remarkable example of the male justification process already discussed: when her rights as girl, wife or sister are no longer limited, she is refused equality with men because of her sex; the pretext for persecuting her becomes 'imbecility and fragility of the sex'.

The fact is that matrons did not put their newfound freedom to the best use; but it is also true that they were forbidden to take the best advantage of it. These two contradictory strains – an individualistic strain that tears woman from the family and a state-controlled strain that abuses her as an individual – result in an unbalanced situation for her. She can inherit, she has equal rights with the father concerning the children, she can will her property thanks to the institution of the dowry, she escapes conjugal restraints, she can divorce and remarry as she wishes: but she is emancipated only in a negative way because she is offered no employment for her vital forces. Economic independence remains abstract since it yields no political capacity; therefore, lacking the power to *act*, Roman women *demonstrate*: they cause a ruckus in towns, they besiege the courts, they brew, they foment plots, they lay down prescriptions, they inflame civil wars, they march along the Tiber carrying the statue of the Mother of the Gods, thus introducing Oriental divinities to Rome; in the year 114

* That is, to enter into contracts with another.

the scandal of the vestal virgins breaks out, and their college is then disbanded. As public life and virtue are out of reach, and when the dissolution of the family renders the former private virtues useless and outdated, there is no longer any moral code for women. They have two choices: either to respect the same values as their grandmothers; or to no longer recognise any. The end of the first century and beginning of the second see numerous women living as companions and partners of their spouses, as in the time of the Republic: Plotina shares the glory and responsibilities of Trajan; Sabina becomes so famous for her good deeds that statues deify her while she is still alive; under Tiberius, Sextia refuses to live on after Aemilius Scaurus and Pascea to live on after Pomponius Labeus; Paulina opens her veins at the same time as Seneca; Pliny the Younger makes Arria's 'Paete, non dolet' famous; Martial admires the irreproachable wives and devoted mothers Claudia Rufina, Virginia and Sulpicia. But numerous women refuse motherhood, and many women divorce; laws continue to ban adultery: some matrons even go so far as to register as prostitutes to avoid being constrained in their debaucheries.* Until then, Latin literature had always respected women: then satirists went wild against them. They attacked, in fact, not women in general but mainly contemporary women. Juvenal reproaches their hedonism and gluttony; he accuses them of aspiring to men's professions: they take an interest in politics, they immerse themselves in court cases, debate with grammarians and rhetoricians, develop passions for hunting, chariot racing, fencing and wrestling. But in fact they rival men mainly because of their own taste for amusement and vice; they lack sufficient education for higher aims; and besides, no objective is even proposed to them; action remains forbidden to them. The Roman woman of the ancient Republic has a place on earth, but she is still chained to it by lack of abstract rights and economic independence; the Roman woman of the decline is typical of false emancipation, possessing, in a world where men are still the only masters, nothing but empty freedom: she is free 'for nothing'.

---

* Rome, like Greece, officially tolerated prostitution. There were two categories of courtesans: those living closed up in brothels, and others, *bonae meretrices,* freely exercising their profession. They did not have the right to wear the clothing of matrons; they had a certain influence on fashion, customs and art, but they never held a position as lofty as the hetaeras of Athens.

CHAPTER 4

The evolution of the feminine condition was not a continuous process. With the great invasions, all of civilisation is put into question. Roman law itself is under the influence of a new ideology, Christianity; and in the centuries that follow, barbarians impose their laws. The economic, social and political situation is overturned: and women's situation suffers the consequences.

Christian ideology played no little role in women's oppression. Without a doubt, there is a breath of charity in the Gospels that spread to women as well as to lepers; poor people, slaves and women are the ones who adhere most passionately to the new law. In the very early days of Christianity, women who submitted to the yoke of the Church were relatively respected; they testified along with men as martyrs; but they could nonetheless worship only in secondary roles; deaconesses were authorised only to do lay work: caring for the sick or helping the poor. And although marriage is considered an institution demanding mutual fidelity, it seems clear that the wife must be totally subordinate to the husband: through St Paul the fiercely antifeminist Jewish tradition is affirmed. St Paul commands self-effacement and reserve from women; he bases the principle of subordination of women to man on the Old and New Testaments. 'The man is not of the woman; but the woman of the man'; and 'Neither was man created for the woman; but the woman for the man.' And elsewhere: 'For the husband is the head of the wife, even as Christ is the head of the church.' In a religion where the flesh is cursed, the woman becomes the devil's most fearsome temptation. Tertullian writes: 'Woman! You are the devil's gateway. You have convinced the one the devil did not dare to confront directly. It is your fault that God's Son had to die. You should always dress in mourning and rags.' St Ambrose: 'Adam was led to sin by Eve and not Eve by Adam. It is right and just that he whom she led into sin, she shall receive as master.' And St John Chrysostom: 'Of all the wild animals, none can

be found as harmful as woman.' When canon law is written in the fourth
century, marriage is treated as a concession to human failings, incompatible with Christian perfection. 'Take up the hatchet and cut the roots
of the sterile tree of marriage,' writes St Jerome. In the time of Gregory
VI, when celibacy was imposed on priests, woman's dangerous character
was more harshly asserted: all the Fathers of the Church proclaim her
wretchedness. St Thomas will remain true to this tradition, declaring
that woman is only an 'occasional' and incomplete being, a sort of failed
man. 'Man is the head of woman just as Christ is the head of man,' he
writes. 'It is a constant that woman is destined to live under the authority
of man and has no authority of her own.' Thus, the only marriage
regime canon law recognises is by dowry, rendering woman helpless and
powerless. Not only is she prohibited from male functions, but she is
also barred from making court depositions, and her testimony holds no
weight. The emperors are more or less under the influence of the Church
Fathers; Justinian's legislation honours woman as spouse and mother
but subjugates her to those functions; her helplessness is not due to her
sex but to her situation within the family. Divorce is prohibited and
marriage has to be a public event; the mother has the same authority
over her children as the father and she has equal rights to their inheritance; if her husband dies, she becomes their legal tutor. The Velleian
Senate decree is modified: from that time on she can intercede for the
benefit of a third party; but she cannot contract for her husband; her
dowry becomes inalienable; it is her children's patrimony and she is
forbidden to dispose of it.

In barbarian-occupied territories, these laws are juxtaposed with
Germanic traditions. The German customs were unique. They had chiefs
only in wartime; in peacetime the family was an autonomous society;
it seemed to be midway between matrilineal filiation clans and patriarchal gens; the mother's brother had the same power as the father and
the same authority over their niece and daughter as her husband. In a
society where all capacity was rooted in brute force, woman was entirely
powerless; but the rights that were guaranteed to her by the twofold
domestic powers on which she depended were recognised; subjugated,
she was nonetheless respected; her husband purchased her, but the price
of this purchase constituted a dowry that belonged to her; and besides,
her father dowered her; she received her portion of the paternal inheritance and, in the case of parents being murdered, a portion of the fine
paid by the murderer. The family was monogamous, adultery being
severely punished and marriage respected. The woman still lived under

wardship, but she was a close partner of her husband. 'In peace and in war, she shares his lot; she lives with him, she dies with him,' says Tacitus. She went to war with him, brought food to the soldiers and encouraged them by her presence. As a widow, part of her deceased husband's power was transmitted to her. Since her incapacity was rooted in her physical frailty, it was not considered an expression of moral inferiority. Some women were priestesses and prophets, so it could be assumed that their education was superior to men's. Among the objects that legally reverted to women in questions of inheritance were, later, jewellery and books.

This is the tradition that continues into the Middle Ages. The woman is absolutely dependent on her father and husband: during Clovis's time, the *mundium*[5] weighs on her throughout her life; but the Franks rejected Germanic chastity: under the Merovingians and Carolingians polygamy reigns; the woman is married without her consent and can be repudiated by her husband, who holds the right of life or death over her according to his whim. She is treated like a servant. Laws protect her but only inasmuch as she is the man's property and the mother of his children. Calling her a prostitute without having proof is considered an insult liable to a fine fifteen times more than any insult to a man; kidnapping a married woman is equivalent to a free man's murder; taking a married woman's hand or arm is liable to a fine of 15 to 35 sous; abortion is forbidden under threat of a 100-sou fine; murder of a pregnant woman costs four times that of a free man; a woman who has proved herself fertile is worth three times a free man; but she loses all worth when she can no longer be a mother; if she marries a slave, she becomes an outlaw and her parents have the right to kill her. She has no rights as an individual. But while the state is becoming powerful, the shift that had occurred in Rome occurs here as well: the wardship of the disabled, children and women no longer belongs to family law but becomes a public office; starting from Charlemagne, the *mundium* that weighs down the woman belongs to the king; he only intervenes at first in cases in which the woman is deprived of her natural guardians; then, little by little, he confiscates the family powers; but this change does not bring about the Frank woman's emancipation. The *mundium* becomes the guardian's responsibility; his duty is to protect his ward: this protection brings about the same slavery for woman as in the past.

When feudalism emerges out of the convulsions of the early Middle Ages, woman's condition looks very uncertain. What characterises feudal law is the confusion between sovereign and property law, between public and private rights. This explains why woman is both put down and raised up by this system. She first finds herself denied all private rights because she lacks political capacity. Until the eleventh century, order is based on force alone and property on armed power. A fief, legal experts say, is 'property held against military service'; woman cannot hold feudal property because she is incapable of defending it. Her situation changes when fiefs become hereditary and patrimonial; in Germanic law some aspects of maternal law survived, as has already been shown: if there were no male heirs, the daughter could inherit. This leads, around the eleventh century, to the feudal system's acceptance of female succession. However, military service is still required of the vassals; and woman's lot does not improve with her ability to inherit; she still needs a male guardian; the husband plays that role: he is invested with the title, holds the fief and has the usufruct of the goods. Like the Greek *epikleros*, woman is the instrument and not the bearer through which the domain is transmitted; that does not emancipate her; in a way she is absorbed by the fief, she is part of the real property. The domain is no longer the family's thing as it was for Roman gens: it is the lord's property, and the woman also belongs to the lord. He is the one who chooses a spouse for her; when she has children, she gives them to him rather than to her husband: they will be vassals who will defend his property. She is therefore a slave of the domain and of its master through the 'protection' of a husband who was imposed on her: few periods of history seem harsher for woman's lot. An heiress means land and a château: suitors fight over this prey and the girl is sometimes not even twelve years old when her father or his lord gives her to some baron as a gift. The more marriages, the more domains for a man; and thus the more repudiations; the Church hypocritically authorises them; as marriage was forbidden between relatives up to the seventh degree, and as kinship was defined by spiritual relations such as godmother and godfather as well as by blood relations, some pretext or other can always be found for an annulment; many women in the eleventh century were repudiated four or five times. Once widowed, the woman immediately has to accept a new master. In the *chansons de geste* Charlemagne has, all at once, the widows of his barons who had died in Spain remarry; in *Girard de Vienne*, the Burgundy duchess goes herself to the king to demand a new spouse. 'My husband has just died, but what good is mourning? Find me a powerful husband because I need to defend my land'; many epics show the king or lord dealing tyrannically with girls and widows. One also sees the husband treating the woman given to him as a gift without any respect; he abuses and slaps her, drags her by her hair and beats her; all that Beaumanoir in

Coutumes de Beauvaisis (*Customs of Beauvaisis*) asks is that the husband 'punish his wife reasonably'. This warlike civilisation has only scorn for women. The knight is not interested in women: his horse is a treasure of much higher value to him; in the epics, girls are always the ones to make the first step towards young men; once married, they alone are expected to be faithful; the man dissociates them from his life. 'Cursed be the knight who takes counsel from a lady on when to joust.' And in Renaud de Montauban, there is this diatribe: 'Go back into your painted and golden quarters, sit ye down in the shade, drink, eat, embroider, dye silk, but do not busy yourself with our affairs. Our business is to fight with the sword and steel. Silence!' The woman sometimes shares the males' harsh life. As a girl, she excels in all physical exercises, she rides, hunts, hawks; she barely receives any education and is raised with no regard for modesty: she welcomes the château's guests, takes care of their meals and baths, and she 'pleasures' them to sleep; as a woman, she sometimes has to hunt wild animals, undertake long and difficult pilgrimages; when her husband is far away, it is she who defends the seigneury. These ladies of the manor, called viragoes, are admired because they behave exactly like men: they are greedy, treacherous, cruel, and they tyrannise their vassals. History and legend have bequeathed the memory of several of them: the chatelaine Aubie, after having a tower built higher than any donjon, then had the architect's head cut off so her secret would be kept; she chased her husband from his domain: he stole back and killed her. Mabel, Roger de Montgomerie's wife, delighted in reducing her seigneury's nobles to begging: their revenge was to decapitate her. Juliane, bastard daughter of Henry I of England, defended the château of Breteuil against him, luring him into an ambush for which he punished her severely. Such acts remain exceptional, however. Ordinarily, the lady spent her time spinning, praying for the dead, waiting for her spouse, and being bored.

It has often been claimed that courtly love, born in the twelfth century in the Mediterranean south of France, brought about an improvement in woman's lot. There are several opposing hypotheses as to its origins: according to some people, 'courtliness' comes from the lord's relations with his young vassals; others link it to Cathar heresies and the cult of the Virgin; still others say that profane love derives from the love of God in general. It is not so sure that courts of love ever existed. What is sure is that faced with Eve the sinner, the Church comes to glorify the Mother of the Redeemer: she has such a large following that in the thirteenth century it can be said that God was made woman; a mysticism of woman thus develops in religion. Moreover, leisure in château life enables the noble ladies to promote and nurture the luxury of conversation, polite-ness and poetry; women of letters such as Béatrice de Valentinois, Eleanor of Aquitaine and her daughter Marie de France, Blanche de Navarre and many others attract and patronise poets; first in the Midi and then in the North culture thrives, giving women new prestige. Courtly love was often described as platonic; Chrétien de Troyes, probably to please his protector, banishes adultery from his novels: the only guilty love he depicts is that of Lancelot and Guinevere; but in fact, as the feudal husband was both a guardian and a tyrant, the wife sought a lover outside of marriage; courtly love was a compensation for the barbarity of official customs. 'Love in the modern sense does not exist in antiquity except outside of official society,' notes Engels: at the very point where an-tiquity broke off its penchant for sexual love, the Middle Ages took it up again with adultery. And this is the form that love will take as long as the institution of marriage lasts.

While courtly love might ease woman's lot, it does not modify it substantially. Ideologies like religion and poetry do not lead to female liberation; woman gains a little ground at the end of the feudal age for other reasons entirely. When the supremacy of royal power is imposed on feudatories, the lord loses a large part of his rights: his right, in particu-lar, to decide on his vassals' marriages is progressively suppressed; at the same time, the feudal lord loses the use of his ward's property; the benefits attached to wardship fall into disuse; and when the service of the fief is converted to a monetary fee, wardship itself disappears; woman was unable to perform military service, but she was as capable as a man of paying the financial obligations; the fief is then little more than a simple patrimony and there is no longer any reason for the two sexes not to be placed on an equal footing. In fact, women in Germany, Switzerland and Italy remain subjected to a perpetual wardship; but France accepts, in Beaumanoir's words, that 'a girl is worth a man'. Germanic tradition gave women a defender as a guardian; when she no longer needs a defender, she goes without a guardian; as a sex, she is no longer taxed with incapacity. Unmarried or widowed, she has all the rights of man; property grants her sovereignty: she governs the fief that she owns, meaning she dispenses justice, signs treaties and decrees laws. She is even seen playing a military role, commanding troops, taking part in fighting; before Joan of Arc there were women soldiers and, however surprising La Pucelle is, she is not shocking.

Nonetheless, so many factors converge to thwart woman's independ-ence that they are never all abolished simultaneously; physical weakness is no longer an issue; but feminine subordination remains useful to society in cases where the woman is married. Thus marital power outlives the feudal regime. The paradox still being perpetuated today is established: the woman most fully integrated into society is the one with the fewest privileges in the society. In civil feudality, marriage has the same features as in military feudality: the husband remains the wife's guardian. When the bourgeoisie is formed, it observes the same laws. In common law as in feudal law, the only emancipation is outside marriage; the daughter and the widow have the same capacities as the man; but by marrying, the woman falls under the husband's guardianship and administration; he can beat her; he watches over her behaviour, relations and correspondence, and disposes of her fortune, not through a contract, but by the very fact of marriage. 'As soon as the marriage is consummated,' Beaumanoir says, 'the possessions of each party are held in common by virtue of the marriage and the man is the guardian of them.' It is in the interest of property that the nobility and the bourgeoisie demand one master to administer it. The wife is not subordinated to the husband because she is judged basically incapable: when nothing else prevents it, woman's full capacities are recognised. From feudality to today, the married woman is deliberately sacrificed to private property. It is important to see that the greater the property owned by the husband, the greater this servitude: the propertied classes are those in which woman's dependence has always been the most concrete; even today, the patriarchal family survives among rich landowners; the more socially and economically powerful man feels, the more he plays the paterfamilias with authority. On the contrary, shared destitution makes the conjugal link reciprocal. Neither feudality nor the Church enfranchised woman. Rather, it was from a position of servitude that the patriarchal family moved to an authentically conjugal one. The serf and his wife owned nothing; they simply had the common use of their house, furniture and utensils: man had no reason to want to become master of woman who owned nothing; but the bonds of work and interest that joined them raised the spouse to the rank of companion. When serfdom is abolished, poverty remains; in small rural communities and among artisans, spouses live on an equal footing; woman is neither a thing nor a servant: those are the luxuries of a rich man; the poor man experiences the reciprocity of the bond that attaches him to his other half; in freely contracted work, woman wins concrete autonomy because she has an economic and social role. The farces and *fabliaux* of the Middle Ages reflect a society of artisans, small merchants and peasants in which the husband's only privilege over his wife is to be able to beat her: but she pits craftiness against force to reestablish equality. However, the rich woman pays for her idleness with submission.

In the Middle Ages, the woman still retained some privileges: she took part in local meetings in the villages, she participated in the primary meetings for the deputies' election to the Estates-General; her husband could exercise his own authority only over movables: his wife's consent was necessary to alienate real estate. The sixteenth century sees the codification of the laws perpetuated throughout the ancien régime; by that time feudal habits and customs had totally disappeared, and nothing protects women from men's claims that they should be chained to the household. The influence of Roman law, so condescending for women, can be perceived here; as in Roman times, the violent diatribes against the stupidity and fragility of the sex were not at the root of the code but are used as justifications; it is after the fact that men find reasons to act as it suits them. 'Among all the bad characteristics that women possess,' one reads in the *Songe du verger*,[6]

> I find that there are nine principal ones: To begin with, a woman hurts herself as a result of her own nature; second, women are by nature extremely stingy; third, they are driven by sudden whims; fourth, they are bad by their own volition; fifth, they are impostors. Women are known to be false and according to civil law a woman may not be accepted as a witness to a will. A woman always does the opposite of what she is commanded to do ... Women accuse themselves willingly and announce their own vituperation and shame. They are crafty and malicious. St Augustine said that 'A woman is a beast who is neither firm nor stable'; she is hateful, to the confusion of her husband; she nourishes wrongdoing and stands at the beginning of all the pleas and tensions; and is the path and road of all iniquity.

Similar texts abound around this time. The interest of this one is that each accusation is meant to justify one of the provisions of the code against women and the inferior situation in which they are kept. Naturally, any 'male office' is forbidden to them; the Velleian decree of the Senate is reinstated, depriving them of all civil capacity; birthright and masculine privilege place them second in line for the paternal inheritance. Unmarried, the daughter remains under the father's guardianship; if he does not marry her off, he generally sends her to a convent. An unwed mother has the right to seek out the father, but such a right merely provides for the costs of lying-in and the infant's food; a married woman becomes subject to the husband's authority: he determines the place of residence, directs the household, repudiates the adulteress wife, shuts her up in a monastery, or later obtains a *lettre de cachet*[7] to send her to the Bastille; no deed is valid without his authorisation; everything the wife brings to the marriage becomes part of the dowry in the Roman meaning of the word; but as marriage is indissoluble, the husband has to die before the wife can recover her property, giving rise to the adage: *Uxor non est proprie socia sed speratur fore.*[8] As she does not manage her capital, although she has rights to it, she does not have the responsibility for it; it does not provide any substance to her action: she has no concrete grasp on the world. Even her children belong to the father rather than to her, as in the time of the *Eumenides*: she 'gives' them to her spouse, whose authority is far greater than hers and who is the real master of her posterity; even Napoleon will use this argument, declaring that just as a pear tree is the property of the owner of the pears, the wife is the property of the man to whom she provides children. The status of the French wife remains as such throughout the ancien régime; little by little jurisprudence will abolish the Velleian decree, but not until the Napoleonic Code does it disappear definitively. The husband is responsible for the wife's debts as well as her behaviour, and she is accountable to him alone; she has almost no direct relations with public authorities or autonomous relations with anyone outside her family. She looks more like a servant in work and motherhood than an associate: objects, values and human beings that she creates are not her own property but her family's, that is, man's, as he is the head. Her situation is far from being more liberal in other countries – it is, on the contrary, less liberal; some maintained guardianship; and in all of them, the married woman's capacities are nonexistent and moral standards strict. All the European codes were drafted on the basis of canon, Roman and Germanic law, all were unfavourable to the woman, and all the countries recognised private property and the family, deferring to the demands of these institutions.

In all these countries, one of the consequences of the 'honest wife's' servitude to the family is prostitution. Hypocritically kept on society's fringes, prostitutes fill a highly important role. Christianity pours scorn on them but accepts them as a necessary evil. 'Getting rid of the prostitutes', said St Augustine, 'will trouble society by dissoluteness.' Later, St Thomas – or at least the theologian that signed his name to Book IV of *De regimine principium* – asserted: 'Remove public women from society and debauchery will disrupt it by disorder of all kinds. Prostitutes are to a city what a cesspool is to a palace: get rid of the cesspool and the palace will become an unsavoury and loathsome place.' In the early Middle Ages, moral licence was such that women of pleasure were hardly necessary; but when the bourgeois family became institutionalised and monogamy rigorous, man obviously had to go outside the home for his pleasure.

In vain did one of Charlemagne's capitularies vigorously forbid it, in vain did St Louis order prostitutes to be chased out of the city in 1254 and brothels to be destroyed in 1269: in the town of Damietta, Joinville tells us, prostitutes' tents were adjacent to the king's. Later, attempts by Charles IX of France and Marie-Thérèse of Austria in the eighteenth century also failed. The organisation of society made prostitution necessary. 'Prostitutes', Schopenhauer would pompously say later, 'are human sacrifices on the altar of monogamy.' And Lecky, a historian of European morality, expressed the same idea: 'Supreme type of vice, prostitutes are the most active guardians of virtue.' Their situation and the Jews' were often rightly compared:* usury and money lending were forbidden by the Church exactly as extra-conjugal sex was; but society can no more do without financial speculators than free love, so these functions fell to the damned castes: they were relegated to ghettos or reserved neighbourhoods. In Paris, loose women worked in pens where they arrived in the morning and left after the curfew had tolled; they lived on special streets and did not have the right to stray, and in most other cities brothels were outside town walls. Like Jews, they had to wear distinctive signs on their clothes. In France the most common one was a specific-coloured aiguillette hung on the shoulder; silk, fur, and honest women's apparel were often prohibited. They were *by law* taxed with infamy, had no recourse whatsoever to the police and the courts, and could be thrown out of their lodgings on a neighbour's simple claim. For most of them, life was difficult and wretched. Some were closed up in public houses. Antoine de Lalaing, a French traveller, left a description of a Spanish establishment in Valencia in the late fifteenth century. 'The place', he said, was

about the size of a small city, surrounded by walls with only one door. And in front of it there were gallows for criminals that might be inside; at the door, a man appointed to this task takes the canes

* 'Those coming to Sisteron by the Peipin passage, like the Jews, owed a toll of five sols to the ladies of Sainte-Claire' (Bahutaud).

of those wishing to enter and tells them that if they want to hand over their money, and if they have the money, he will give it to the porter. If it is stolen overnight, the porter will not answer for it. In this place there are three or four streets full of small houses, in each of which are prettily and cleanly dressed girls in velvet and satin. There are almost three hundred of them; their houses are well kept and decorated with good linens. The decreed price is four pennies of their money, which is the equivalent of our gros . . . There are taverns and cabarets. It is not easy to recognise these houses by daylight, while at night or in the evening the girls are seated at their doorways, with pretty lamps hanging near them in order to make it easier to see them at leisure. There are two doctors appointed and paid by the town to visit the girls every week in order to discover if they have any disease or intimate illness. If the town is stricken with any sickness, the lords of the place are required to maintain the girls at their expense and the foreigners are sent away to any place they wish to go.*[9]

The author even marvels at such effective policing. Many prostitutes lived freely; some of them earned their living well. As in the period of the courtesans, high gallantry provided more possibilities for feminine individualism than the life of an 'honest woman'.

A condition unique to France is that of the unmarried woman; legal independence is in stark and shocking contrast to the wife's servitude; she is an oddity and so customs hasten to withdraw everything law grants her; she has total civil capacity: but those laws are abstract and empty; she has no economic autonomy, no social dignity, and generally the spinster remains hidden in the shadow of the paternal family or finds others like her behind convent walls: there she knows no other form of freedom but disobedience and sin – just as decadent Roman women were emancipated only by vice. Negativity continues to be women's lot as long as their emancipation remains negative.

In such conditions it is clear how rare it was for a wife to act or merely to make her presence felt: among the working classes, economic oppression cancels out sexual inequality; but it deprives the individual of opportunities; among the nobility and bourgeoisie, the wife is abused because of her sex; she has a parasitic existence; she is poorly educated; she needs exceptional circumstances if she is to envisage and carry out any concrete

* De Reiffenberg, *Dictionary of Conversation*. 'Women and Girls of the Low Life'.

project. Queens and regents have that rare good fortune: their sovereignty exalts them above their sex; French Salic law denies women the right of access to the throne; but they sometimes play a great role beside their husbands or after their deaths: for example, St Clotilda, St Radegunda and Blanche de Castille. Convent life makes woman independent of man: some abbesses wield great power; Héloïse gained fame as an abbess as much as a lover. In the mystical, thus autonomous, relation that binds them to God, feminine souls draw their inspiration and force from a virile soul; and the respect society grants them enables them to undertake difficult projects. Joan of Arc's adventure is something of a miracle: and it is, moreover, a very brief adventure. But St Catherine of Siena's story is meaningful; she creates a great reputation in Siena for charitable activity and for the visions that testify to her intense inner life within a very normal existence; she thus acquires the necessary authority for success generally lacking in women; her influence is invoked to hearten those condemned to death, to bring back to the fold those who are lost, to appease quarrels between families and towns. She is supported by the community that recognises itself in her, which is how she is able to fulfil her pacifying mission, preaching submission to the pope from city to city, carrying on a vast correspondence with bishops and sovereigns, and finally chosen by Florence as ambassador to go and find the pope in Avignon. Queens, by divine right, and saints, by their shining virtues, are assured of support in the society that allows them to be men's equal. Of others, a silent modesty is required. The success of a Christine de Pizan is due to exceptional luck: even so, she had to be widowed and burdened with children for her to decide to earn her living by her pen.

Altogether, men's opinion in the Middle Ages is not favourable to women. Courtly poets did exalt love; many codes of courtly love appear, such as André le Chapelain's poem and the famous *Roman de la Rose*,[10] in which Guillaume de Lorris encourages young men to devote themselves to the service of ladies. But against this troubadour-inspired literature are pitted bourgeois-inspired writings that cruelly attack women: fabliaux, farces and plays criticise women for their laziness, coquetry and lust. Their worst enemies are the clergy. They incriminate marriage. The Church made it a sacrament and yet prohibited it for the Christian elite: this is the source of the contradiction of the *querelle des femmes*.[11] It is denounced with singular vigour in *The Lamentations of Matheolus*, famous in its time, published fifteen years after the first part of the *Roman de la Rose*, and translated into French one hundred years later.

Matthew lost his 'clergy' by taking a wife; he cursed his marriage, cursed women and marriage in general. Why did God create woman if there is this incompatibility between marriage and clergy? Peace cannot exist in marriage: it had to be the devil's work; or else God did not know what he was doing. Matthew hopes that woman will not rise on Judgment Day. But God responds to him that marriage is a purgatory thanks to which heaven is reached; and carried to the heavens in a dream, Matthew sees a legion of husbands welcoming him to the shouts of 'Here, here the true martyr!' Jean de Meung, another cleric, is similarly inspired; he enjoins young men to get out from under the yoke of women; first he attacks love:

> Love is hateful country
> Love is amorous hate.

He attacks marriage that reduces man to slavery, that dooms him to be cuckolded; and he directs a violent diatribe against woman. In return, woman's champions strive to demonstrate her superiority. Here are some of the arguments apologists for the weaker sex drew on until the seventeenth century:

> Mulier perfetur viro scilicet. Materia: quia Adam factus est de limo terrae, Eva de costa Adae. Loco: quia Adam factus est extra paradisum, Eva in paradiso. In conceptione: quia mulier concepit Deum, quid homo non potuit. Apparicione: quia Christus apparuit mulieri post mortem resurrectionem, scilicet Magdalene. Exaltatione: quia mulier exaltata est super chorus angelorum, scilicet beata Maria . . .*

To which their opponents replied that if Christ first appeared to women, it is because he knew they were talkative and he was in a hurry to make his resurrection known.

The quarrel continues throughout the fifteenth century. The author of *Fifteen Joys of Marriage* indulgently describes the misfortunes of poor husbands. Eustache Deschamps writes an interminable poem on the

---

* 'Woman is superior to man, namely: *Materially:* because Adam was made of clay, Eve from one of Adam's ribs. *In terms of place:* because Adam was created outside of paradise, Eve in paradise. *In terms of conception:* because woman conceived God, something man couldn't do. *In terms of appearance:* because Christ after his death appeared to a woman, namely Magdalene. *In terms of glorification:* because a woman was glorified above the choir of angels, namely blessed Mary.'

same theme. It is here that the 'quarrel of the *Roman de la Rose*' begins. This is the first time a woman takes up her pen to defend her sex: Christine de Pizan attacks the clerics energetically in *The Epistle to the God of Love*. The clerics rise up immediately to defend Jean de Meung; but Gerson, chancellor of the University of Paris, takes Christine's side; he writes his treatise in French to reach a wide public. Martin le Franc throws the indigestible *Ladies' Chaperon* – still being read two hundred years later – on to the battlefield. And Christine intervenes once again. Her main demand is for women's right to education: 'If the custom were to put little girls in school and they were normally taught sciences like the boys, they would learn as perfectly and would understand the subtleties of all the arts and sciences as they do.'

In truth this dispute concerns women only indirectly. No one dreams of demanding a social role for them other than what they are assigned. It is more a question of comparing the life of the cleric to the state of marriage; it is a masculine problem brought up by the Church's ambiguous attitude to marriage. Luther settles this conflict by rejecting the celibacy of priests. Woman's condition is not influenced by this literary war. While railing against society as it is, the satire of farces and fabliaux does not claim to change it: it mocks women but does not plot against them. Courtly poetry glorifies femininity: but such a cult does not in any way imply the assimilation of the sexes. The *querelle* is a secondary phenomenon in which society's attitude is reflected but which does not modify it.

It has already been said that the wife's legal status remained practically unchanged from the early fifteenth century to the nineteenth century; but in the privileged classes her concrete condition does change. The Italian Renaissance is a period of individualism propitious to the burgeoning of strong personalities, regardless of sex. There were some women at that time who were powerful sovereigns, like Jean d'Aragon, Joan of Naples and Isabella d'Este; others were adventurer *condottieri* who took up arms like men: thus Girolamo Riario's wife fought for Forli's freedom; Hippolyta Fioramenti commanded the Duke of Milan's troops and during the siege of Pavia led a company of noblewomen to the ramparts. To defend their city against Montluc, Sienese women marshalled three thousand troops commanded by women. Other Italian women became famous thanks to their culture or talents: for example, Isotta Nogarola, Veronica Gambara, Gaspara Stampa, Vittoria Colonna who was Michelangelo's friend, and especially Lucrezia Tornabuoni, mother of Lorenzo and Giuliano de' Medici, who wrote, among other things, hymns and a life of St John the Baptist and the Virgin. A majority of these distinguished women were courtesans; joining free moral behaviour with freethinking, ensuring their economic autonomy through their profession, many were treated by men with deferential admiration; they protected the arts and were interested in literature and philosophy, and they themselves often wrote or painted: Isabella da Luna, Catarina di San Celso, and Imperia, who was a poet and musician, took up the tradition of Aspasia and Phryne. For many of them, though, freedom still takes the form of licence: the orgies and crimes of these great Italian ladies and courtesans remain legendary.

This licence is also the main freedom found in the following centuries for women whose rank or fortune liberates them from common morality; in general, it remains as strict as in the Middle Ages. As for positive accomplishments, they are possible only for a very few. Queens are always privileged: Catherine de Medici, Elizabeth of England and Isabella the Catholic are great sovereigns. A few great saintly figures are also worshipped. The astonishing destiny of St Teresa of Avila is explained approximately in the same way as St Catherine's: her self-confidence is inspired by her confidence in God; by carrying the virtues connected with her status to the highest, she garners the support of her confessors and the Christian world: she is able to emerge beyond a nun's ordinary condition; she founds and runs monasteries, she travels, takes initiatives, and perseveres with a man's adventurous courage; society does not thwart her; even writing is not effrontery: her confessors order her to do it. She brilliantly shows that a woman can raise herself as high as a man when, by an astonishing chance, a man's possibilities are granted to her.

But in reality such possibilities are very unequal; in the sixteenth century, women are still poorly educated. Anne of Brittany summons many women to the court, where previously only men had been seen; she strives to form a retinue of girls of honour: but she is more interested in their upbringing than in their culture. Among women who a little later distinguish themselves by their minds, intellectual influence and writings, most are noblewomen: the duchess of Retz, Mme de Lignerolle, the Duchess of Rohan and her daughter Anne; the most famous were princesses: Queen Margot and Margaret de Navarre. Pernette du Guillet seems to have been a bourgeois; but Louise Labé is undoubtedly a courtesan: in any case, she felt free to behave unconventionally.

Women in the seventeenth century will continue to distinguish themselves essentially in intellectual spheres; social life and culture are spreading; women play a considerable role in salons; by the very fact they are not involved in the construction of the world, they have the leisure to indulge in conversation, the arts and literature; they are not formally educated, but through discussions, readings and instruction by private preceptors or public lectures, they succeed in acquiring greater knowledge than their husbands: Mlle de Gournay, Mme de Rambouillet, Mlle de Scudéry, Mme de La Fayette and Mme de Sévigné enjoy great reputations in France; and outside France similar renown is associated with the names of Princess Elisabeth, Queen Christine and Mlle de Schurman who corresponded with the whole scholarly world. Thanks to this culture and the ensuing prestige, women manage to encroach on the masculine universe; from literature and amorous casuistry many ambitious women slide towards political intrigue. In 1623 the papal nuncio wrote: 'In France all the major events, all the important plots, most often depend on women.' The princesse de Condé foments the 'women's conspiracy'; Anne of Austria readily takes the advice of the women surrounding her; Richelieu lends an indulgent ear to the duchesse d'Aiguillon; the roles played by Mme de Montbazon, the duchesse de Chevreuse, Mlle de Montpensier, the duchesse de Longueville, Anne de Gonzague and many others in the Fronde are well known. Lastly, Mme de Maintenon is a brilliant example of the influence a skilful woman adviser could wield on state affairs. Organisers, advisers and schemers, women assure themselves of a highly effective role by oblique means: the princesse des Ursins in Spain governs with more authority but her career is brief. Alongside these great noblewomen, a few personalities assert themselves in a world that escapes bourgeois constraints; a hitherto unknown species appears: the actress. The presence of a woman on stage is noted for the first time in 1545; in 1592 there is still only one; at the beginning of the sixteenth century most of them are actors' wives; they then become more and more independent both onstage and in their private lives. As far as the courtesan is concerned, after being Phryne or Imperia, she finds her highest incarnation in Ninon de Lenclos: from capitalising on her femininity, she surpasses it; from living among men, she takes on virile qualities; her independent moral behaviour disposes her to independent thinking: Ninon de Lenclos brought freedom to the highest point a woman could at that time.

In the eighteenth century, woman's freedom and independence continue to grow. Customs remained strict in principle: girls receive no more than a cursory education; they are married off or sent to a convent without being consulted. The bourgeoisie, the rising class that is being consolidated, imposes a strict morality on the wife. But on the other hand, with the nobility breaking up, the greatest freedom of behaviour is possible for women of the world, and even the *haute bourgeoisie* is contaminated by these examples; neither convent nor conjugal home can contain the woman. Once again, for the majority of women, this freedom remains negative and abstract: they limit themselves to the pursuit of pleasure. But those who are intelligent and ambitious create avenues for action for themselves. Salon life once again blossoms: the roles played by Mme Geoffrin, Mme du Deffand, Mlle de Lespinasse, Mme d'Epinay, and Mme de Tencin are well known; protectors and inspiration, women make up the writer's favourite audience; they are personally interested in literature, philosophy and sciences: like Mme du Châtelet, for example, they have their own physics workshops or chemistry laboratory; they experiment; they dissect; they intervene more actively than ever before in political life: one after the other, Mme de Prie, Mme de Mailly, Mme de Châteauneuf, Mme de Pompadour and Mme du Barry govern Louis XV; there is barely a minister without his Egeria, to such a point that Montesquieu thinks that in France everything is done by women; they constitute, he says, 'a new state within the state'; and Collé writes on the eve of 1789: 'They have so taken over Frenchmen, they have subjugated them so greatly that they think about and feel only for themselves.' Alongside society women there are also actresses and prostitutes who enjoy great fame: Sophie Arnould, Julie Talma and Adrienne Lecouvreur.

Throughout the ancien régime the cultural domain is the most accessible to women who try to assert themselves. Yet none reached the summits of a Dante or a Shakespeare; this can be explained by the general mediocrity of their condition. Culture has never been the privilege of any but the feminine elite, never of the masses; and masculine geniuses often come from the masses; even privileged women encountered obstacles that barred their access to the heights. Nothing stopped the ascent of a St Teresa, a Catherine of Russia, but a thousand circumstances conspired against the woman writer. In her small book, *A Room of One's Own*, Virginia Woolf enjoyed inventing the destiny of Shakespeare's supposed sister; while he learned a little Latin, grammar and logic in school, she was closed up at home in total ignorance; while he poached, ran around in the countryside and slept with local women, she was mending kitchen towels under her parents' watchful eyes; if, like him, she bravely left to seek her fortune in London, she could not become an actress earning her living freely: either she would be brought back to her family and married off by force; or, seduced, abandoned and dishonoured, she would commit suicide out of despair. She could also be imagined as a happy prostitute, a Moll Flanders, as Daniel Defoe portrayed her: but she would never have run a theatre and written plays. In England, Virginia Woolf notes, women writers always engender hostility. Dr Johnson compared them to 'a dog's walking on his hinder legs. It is not done well; but you are surprised to find it done at all.' Artists care about what people think more than anyone else; women narrowly depend on it: it is easy to imagine how much strength it takes for a woman artist simply to dare to carry on regardless; she often succumbs in the fight. At the end of the seventeenth century, Lady Winchilsea, a childless noblewoman, attempts the feat of writing; some passages of her work show she had a sensitive and poetic nature; but she was consumed by hatred, anger and fear:

> *Alas! A woman that attempts the pen,*
> *Such an intruder on the rights of men,*
> *Such a presumptuous creature is esteemed,*
> *The fault can by no virtue be redeemed.*[12]

Almost all her work is filled with indignation about woman's condition. The Duchess of Newcastle's case is similar; also a noblewoman, she creates a scandal by writing. 'Women live like cockroaches or owls, they die like worms,' she furiously writes. Insulted and ridiculed, she had to shut herself up in her domain; and in spite of a generous temperament and going half-mad, she produced nothing more than wild imaginings. It is not until the eighteenth century that a bourgeois widow, Mrs Aphra Behn,[13] lived by her pen like a man; others followed her example, but even in the nineteenth century they were often obliged to hide; they did not even have a 'room of their own'; that is, they did not enjoy material independence, one of the essential conditions for inner freedom.

As has already been seen, because of the development of social life and its close link to intellectual life, French women's situation is a little more favourable. Nevertheless, people are largely hostile to the bluestockings. During the Renaissance, noblewomen and intellectuals inspire a movement in favour of their sex; Platonic doctrines imported from Italy spiritualise love and woman. Many well-read men strive to defend her. *The Ship of Virtuous Ladies,*[14] *The Ladies' Chevalier,* and so on were published. Erasmus in *The Little Senate* gives the floor to Cornelia who unabashedly details the grievances of her sex. 'Men are tyrants . . . They treat us like toys . . . they make us their launderers and cooks.' Erasmus demands that women be allowed to have an education. Cornelius Agrippa, in a very famous work, *Declamation on the Nobility and Preeminence of the Female Sex*,[15] devotes himself to showing feminine superiority. He takes up the old cabbalistic arguments: Eve means Life and Adam Earth. Created after man, woman is more finished then he. She is born in paradise, he outside. When she falls into the water, she floats; man sinks. She is made from Adam's rib and not from earth. Her monthly cycles cure all illnesses. Eve merely wandered in her ignorance, whereas Adam sinned, which is why God made Himself a man: moreover, after his resurrection He appeared to women. Then Agrippa declares that women are more virtuous than men. He lists 'virtuous women' that the sex can take pride in, which is also a commonplace of these praises. Lastly, he mounts an indictment of male tyranny: 'Acting against divine right and violating natural law with impunity, the tyranny of men has deprived women of the freedom they receive at birth.' Yet she engenders children; she is as intelligent and even subtler than man; it is scandalous that her activities are limited, 'undoubtedly done not by God's order, nor by necessity or reason, but by the force of usage, by education, work and principally by violence and oppression'. He does not, of course, demand sexual equality, but wants woman to be treated with respect. The work was immensely successful; there is also *The Impregnable Fort*,[16] another in praise of woman; and *The Perfect Friend*[17] by Héroët, imbued with Platonic mysticism. In a curious book introducing Saint-Simonian doctrine, Postel announces the coming of a new Eve, the regenerating mother of humankind: he thinks he has even met her; she is dead and she is perhaps reincarnated in him. With more moderation, Marguerite de Valois, in her *Learned and Subtle Discourse*[18] proclaims that there is something divine in woman. But the writer who best served the cause of her sex was Margaret de Navarre, who proposed an ideal of sentimental mysticism and chastity without prudery to counter licentiousness, attempting to reconcile marriage and love for women's honour with happiness. Women's opponents do not, of course, give up. Among others, *Controversies over the Masculine and Feminine Sexes*,[19] in response to Agrippa, puts forward the old medieval arguments. Rabelais has a good time in *The Third Book*[20] satirising marriage in the tradition of Mathieu and Deschamps: however, it is women who lay down the law in the privileged abbey of Thélème. Antifeminism becomes virulent once again in 1617, with the *A Discourse*

of Women, Shewing Their Imperfections Alphabetically,[21] by Jacques Olivier;
the cover pictures an engraving of a woman with a harpy's hands, covered
with the feathers of lust and perched on her feet, because, like a hen,
she is a bad housewife: under every letter of the alphabet is one of her
defects. Once more it was a man of the Church who rekindled the old
quarrel; Mlle de Gournay answered back with *Equality of Men and Women*.[22]
This is followed by a quantity of libertine literature, including *Parnassus
and Satyrical Cabinets*,[23] that attacks women's moral behaviour, while the
holier-than-thous quoting Paul, the Church Fathers and Ecclesiastes drag
them down. Woman provided an inexhaustible theme for the satires of
Mathurin Régnier and his friends. In the other camp, the apologists outdo
themselves in taking up and commenting on Agrippa's arguments. Father
du Boscq in *The Honest Woman*[24] calls for women to be allowed to be
educated. The *Astrée* and a great quantity of courtly literature praise their
merits in rondeaux, sonnets, elegies, and such.

Even the successes women achieved were cause for new attacks; *The
Pretentious Young Ladies* set public opinion against them; and a bit later
The Learned Ladies[25] are applauded. Molière is not, however, woman's
enemy: he vigorously attacks arranged marriages, he demands freedom
for young girls in their love lives and respect and independence for the
wife. On the other hand, Bossuet does not spare them in his sermons.
The first woman, he preaches, is 'only a part of Adam and a kind of
diminutive. Her mind is about the same size.' Boileau's satire against
women is not much more than an exercise in rhetoric but it raises an
outcry: Pradon, Regnard and Perrault counterattack violently. La Bruyère
and Saint-Evremond take the part of women. The period's most determined feminist is Poulain de la Barre who in 1673 publishes a Cartesian-
inspired work, *On the Equality of the Two Sexes*.[26] He thinks that since
men are stronger, they favour their sex and women accept this dependence out of custom. They never had their chances: in either freedom or
education. Thus they cannot be judged by what they did in the past.
Nothing indicates their inferiority to men. Anatomy reveals differences,
but none of them constitutes a privilege for the male. And Poulain de
la Barre concludes with a demand for a solid education for women.
Fontenelle writes the *Conversations on the Plurality of Worlds*[27] for women.
And while Fénelon, following Mme de Maintenon and Abbot Fleury,
puts forward a very limited educational programme, the Jansenist
academic Rollin wants women to undertake serious studies.

The eighteenth century is also divided. In 1744, the author of the
Controversy over Woman's Soul[28] declares that 'woman created uniquely for

man will cease to be at the end of the world because she will cease to be useful for the object for which she had been created, from which follows necessarily that her soul is not immortal.' In a slightly less radical way, Rousseau is the spokesman of the bourgeoisie and dooms woman to her husband and motherhood. 'All the education of women should be relative to men . . . Woman is made to yield to man and to bear his injustices,' he asserts. However, the democratic and individualist ideal of the eighteenth century is favourable to women; for most philosophers they are human beings equal to those of the strong sex. Voltaire denounces the injustice of their lot. Diderot considers their inferiority largely *made* by society. 'Women, I pity you!' he writes. He thinks that 'In all customs the cruelty of civil laws makes common cause with the cruelty of nature against women. They have been treated as idiot beings.' Montesquieu, paradoxically, believes that women should be subordinate to man in the home but that everything predisposes them to political action. 'It is against reason and against nature for women to be mistresses in the house . . . but not for them to govern an empire.' Helvétius shows that woman's inferiority is created by the absurdity of her education; d'Alembert is of the same opinion. Economic feminism timidly makes its appearance through a woman, Mme de Ciray.* But it is Mercier almost alone in his *Tableau de Paris* who rises up against the destitution of women workers and tackles the fundamental question of women's work. Condorcet wants women to enter political life. He considers them man's equals and defends them against classic attacks: 'Women are said . . . not to have their own feeling of justice, that they listen to their feelings more than to their conscience . . . [But] it is not nature, it is education, it is the social existence that causes this difference.' And elsewhere: 'The more women have been enslaved by laws, the more dangerous their empire has been . . . It would lessen if women had less interest in keeping it, if it ceased being for them the sole means of defending themselves and escaping oppression.'

* The name Ciray is untraceable. Emilie Du Châtelet and Voltaire lived and worked in the Château de Cirey from 1734 to 1749, giving rise to some speculation about the possibility of a misspelling or an erroneous transcription from the original manuscript of the name Ciray. But there is no conclusive evidence of this.

The Revolution might have been expected to change the fate of woman. It did nothing of the kind. This bourgeois revolution respected bourgeois institutions and values; and it was waged almost exclusively by men. It must be pointed out that during the entire ancien régime working-class women as a sex enjoyed the most independence. A woman had the right to run a business and she possessed all the necessary capacities to exercise her trade autonomously. She shared in production as linen maid, laundress, burnisher, shopgirl, and so on; she worked either at home or in small businesses; her material independence allowed her great freedom of behaviour: a woman of modest means could go out, go to taverns, and control her own body almost like a man; she is her husband's partner and his equal. She is oppressed on an economic and not on a sexual level. In the countryside, the peasant woman plays a considerable role in rural labour; she is treated like a servant; often she does not eat at the same table as her husband and sons; she toils harder and the burdens of maternity add to her fatigue. But as in old farming societies, since she is necessary to man, he respects her for it; their goods, interests and concerns are shared; she enjoys great authority in the home. From within their difficult lives, these women could have asserted themselves as individuals and demanded their rights; but a tradition of timidity and submission weighed on them: the Estates-General *cahiers* record an insignificant number of feminine claims, limited to: 'Men should not engage in trades that are the prerogative of women.' And it is true that women are found alongside their men in demonstrations and riots: they are the ones who go to Versailles to find 'the baker, the baker's wife, and the baker's little boy'.[29] But it is not the people who led the Revolution and reaped its fruits. As for bourgeois women, a few rallied ardently to the cause of freedom: Mme Roland, Lucile Desmoulins and Théroigne de Méricourt; one of them, Charlotte Corday, significantly influenced the outcome when she assassinated Marat. There were a few feminist movements. In 1791, Olympe de Gouges proposed a 'Declaration of the Rights of Woman and the Female Citizen' equivalent to the 'Declaration of the Rights of Man', demanding that all masculine privileges be abolished. In 1790 the same ideas are found in *Poor Javotte's Motion*[30] and in other similar lampoons; but in spite of Condorcet's support, these efforts are abortive and Olympe perishes on the scaffold. In addition to *L'Impatient*, the newspaper she founded, a few other short-lived papers appear. Women's clubs merge for the most part with men's and are taken over by them. On 28 Brumaire 1793, when actress Rose Lacombe, president of the Society of Republican and Revolutionary Women, along with a delegation of women, forces the doors of the Conseil Général, the prosecutor Chaumette pronounces words in the assembly that could be inspired by St Paul and St Thomas: 'Since when are women allowed to renounce their sex and become men? . . . [Nature] has told woman: Be a woman. Childcare, household tasks, sundry motherhood cares, those are your tasks.' Women are banned from entering the Conseil and soon even from the clubs where they had learned their politics. In 1790, the rights of the firstborn and of masculine privilege were eliminated; girls and boys became equals regarding succession; in 1792 divorce law was established, relaxing strict marital ties; but these were feeble conquests. Bourgeois women were too integrated into the family to find concrete grounds for solidarity with each other; they did not constitute a separate caste capable of forcing their demands: on an economic level, they existed as parasites. Thus, while women could have participated in events in spite of their sex, they were prevented by their class, and those from the agitating class were condemned to stand aside because they were women. When economic power falls into the hands of the workers, it will then be possible for the working woman to gain the capacities that the parasitic woman, noble or bourgeois, never obtained.

During the liquidation of the Revolution woman enjoys an anarchic freedom. But when society is reorganised, she is rigidly enslaved again. From the feminist point of view, France was ahead of other countries; but for the unfortunate modern French woman, her status was determined during a military dictatorship; the Napoleonic Code, which sealed her fate for a century, greatly held back her emancipation. Like all military leaders, Napoleon wants to see woman solely as a mother; but, heir to a bourgeois revolution, he does not intend to demolish the social structure by giving the mother priority over the wife: he prohibits the querying of paternity; he sets down harsh conditions for the unwed mother and the illegitimate child. Yet the married woman herself does

not find recourse in her dignity as mother; the feudal paradox is perpetuated. Girls and wives are deprived of citizens' rights, prohibiting them
from functions such as the practice of law or wardship. But the unmarried woman enjoys her civil role fully while marriage preserves the
mundium. Woman owes *obedience* to her husband; he can have her confined
in cases of adultery and obtain a divorce from her; if he kills the guilty
wife when caught in the act, he is excusable in the eyes of the law; the
husband, on the other hand, receives an infraction only if he brings a
concubine into the home, and this is the only ground that would allow
his wife to divorce him. Man decides where they will live, and he has
many more rights over the children than the mother; and – except in
cases where the woman manages a business – his authorisation is necessary for her contracts. Marital power is rigorously exercised, both over
the wife herself as a person, and over her possessions.

Throughout the nineteenth century, the legal system continues to reinforce the code's severity, depriving, among other things, the woman of
all rights of alienation. In 1826[31] the Restoration abolishes divorce and the
1848 Constitutional Assembly refuses to reestablish it; it does not reappear
until 1884: and then it is still difficult to obtain. The bourgeoisie was never
more powerful, yet they recognise the dangers implicit in the Industrial
Revolution; they assert themselves with nervous authority. The freedom
of ideas inherited from the eighteenth century never makes inroads
into family moral principles; these remain as they are defined by the
early-nineteenth-century reactionary thinkers Joseph de Maistre and
Bonald. They base the value of order on divine will and demand a
strictly hierarchical society; the family, the indissoluble social cell, will
be the microcosm of society. 'Man is to woman what woman is to the
child'; or 'power is to the minister what the minister is to the people,'
says Bonald. Thus the husband governs, the wife administers and the children obey. Divorce is, of course, forbidden; and woman is confined to
the home. 'Women belong to the family and not to politics, and nature
made them for housework and not for public service,' adds Bonald.
These hierarchies were respected in the family as described by Le Play
in the middle of the century.

In a slightly different way, Auguste Comte also demands a hierarchy
of the sexes; between men and women there are 'radical differences,
both physical and moral, profoundly separating one from the other, in
every species of animal and *especially in the human race*'. Femininity is a
kind of 'prolonged childhood' that sets women apart from the 'ideal
type of the race'. This biological infantilism expresses an intellectual

weakness; the role of this purely affective being is that of spouse and housewife, no match for man: 'neither instruction nor education is suitable for her'. As with Bonald, woman is confined to the family, and within this miniature society the father governs because woman is 'inept in all government even domestic'; she only administers and advises. Her instruction has to be limited. 'Women and the proletariat cannot and must not become originators, nor do they wish to.' And Comte foresees society's evolution as totally eliminating woman's work outside the family. In the second part of his work, Comte, swayed by his love for Clotilde de Vaux, exalts woman to the point of almost making her a divinity, the emanation of the Great Being; in the Temple of Humanity, positivist religion will propose her for the adoration of the people, but only for her morality; man acts while she loves: she is more deeply altruistic than he. But according to the positivist system, she is still no less confined to the family; divorce is still forbidden for her, and it would even be preferable for her widowhood to last for ever; she has no economic or political rights; she is only a wife and an educator.

Balzac expresses the same ideal in more cynical ways: woman's destiny, and her only glory, is to make the hearts of men beat, he writes in *The Physiology of Marriage*.[32] 'Woman is a possession acquired by contract; she is personal property, and the possession of her is as good as security – indeed properly speaking, woman is only man's annexe.' Here he is speaking for the bourgeoisie which intensified its antifeminism in reaction to eighteenth-century licence and threatening progressive ideas. Having brilliantly presented the idea at the beginning of *The Physiology of Marriage* that this loveless institution forcibly leads the wife to adultery, Balzac exhorts husbands to rein wives into total subjugation if they want to avoid the ridicule of dishonour. They must be denied training and culture, forbidden to develop their individuality, forced to wear uncomfortable clothing, and encouraged to follow a debilitating dietary regime. The bourgeoisie follows this programme exactly, confining women to the kitchen and to housework, jealously watching their behaviour; they are enclosed in daily life rituals that hindered all attempts at independence. In return, they are honoured and endowed with the most exquisite respect. 'The married woman is a slave who must be seated on a throne,' says Balzac; of course men must give in to women in all irrelevant circumstances, yielding them first place; women must not carry heavy burdens as in primitive societies; they are readily spared all painful tasks and worries: at the same time this relieves them of all responsibility. It is hoped that, thus duped, seduced by the ease of their condition, they will accept the role of mother and housewife to which they are being confined. And in fact, most bourgeois women capitulate. As their education and their parasitic situation make them dependent on men, they never dare to voice their claims: those who do are hardly heard. It is easier to put people in chains than to remove them if the chains bring prestige, said George Bernard Shaw. The bourgeois woman clings to the chains because she clings to her class privileges. It is drilled into her and she believes that women's liberation would weaken bourgeois society; liberated from the male, she would be condemned to work; while she might regret having her rights to private property subordinated to her husband's, she would deplore even more having this property abolished; she feels no solidarity with working-class women: she feels closer to her husband than to a woman textile worker. She makes his interests her own.

Yet these obstinate examples of resistance cannot stop the march of history; the advent of the machine ruins landed property and brings about working-class emancipation and concomitantly that of woman. All forms of socialism, wresting woman from the family, favour her liberation: Plato, aspiring to a communal regime, promised women a similar autonomy to that enjoyed in Sparta. With the utopian socialism of Saint-Simon, Fourier and Cabet is born the utopia of the 'free woman'. The Saint-Simonian idea of universal association demands the abolition of all slavery: that of the worker and that of the woman; and it is because women like men are human beings that Saint-Simon, and Leroux, Pecqueur and Carnot after him, demand their freedom. Unfortunately, this reasonable theory has no credibility in the Saint-Simonian school. Instead, woman is exalted in the name of femininity, the surest way to disserve her. Under the pretext of considering the couple as the basis of social unity, Père Enfantin tries to introduce a woman into each 'director-couple' called the priest-couple; he awaits a better world from a woman messiah, and the Compagnons de la Femme embark for the East in search of this female saviour. He is influenced by Fourier, who confuses the liberation of woman with the restoration of the flesh; Fourier demands the right of all individuals to follow their passionate attractions; he wants to replace marriage with love; he considers the woman not as a person, but only in her amorous functions. And Cabet promises that Icarian communism will bring about complete equality of the sexes, though he accords women a limited participation in politics. In fact, women hold second place in the Saint-Simonian movement: only Claire Bazard, founder and main support for a brief period of the magazine *La Femme nouvelle* (The New Woman), plays a relatively important role. Many other minor publications appear later, but their claims are timid; they demand education rather than emancipation for women; Carnot, and later Legouvé, is committed to raising the level of education for women. The idea of the woman partner or the woman as a regenerating force persists throughout the nineteenth century in Victor Hugo. But woman's cause is discredited by these doctrines that, instead of assimilating her, oppose her to man, emphasising intuition and emotion instead of reason. The cause is also discredited by some of its partisans' mistakes. In 1848 women founded clubs and journals; Eugénie Niboyet published *La Voix des femmes* (Women's Voice), a magazine that Cabet worked on. A female delegation went to the city hall to demand 'women's rights' but obtained nothing. In 1849, Jeanne Deroin ran for deputy and her campaign foundered in ridicule. Ridicule also killed the 'Vesuvians' movement and the Bloomerists, who paraded in extravagant costumes. The most intelligent women of the period took no part in these movements: Mme de Staël fought for her own cause rather than her sisters'; George Sand demanded the right for free love but refused to collaborate on *La Voix des femmes*; her claims are primarily sentimental. Flora Tristan believed in the people's redemption through woman; but she is more interested in the emancipation of the working class than that of her own sex. Daniel Stern and Mme de Girardin, however, joined the feminist movement.

On the whole, the reform movement that develops in the nineteenth century seeks justice in equality, and is thus generally favourable to feminism. There is one notable exception: Proudhon. Undoubtedly because of his peasant roots, he reacts violently against Saint-Simonian mysticism; he supports small property owners and at the same time believes in confining woman to the home. 'Housewife or courtesan' is the dilemma he locks her in. Until then, attacks against women had been led by conservatives, bitterly combating socialism as well: *Le Charivari* was one of the inexhaustible sources of jokes; it is Proudhon who breaks the alliance between feminism and socialism; he protests against the socialist women's banquet presided over by Leroux and he fulminates against Jeanne Deroin. In his work, *Justice*,[33] he posits that woman should be dependent on man; he alone counts as a social individual; a couple is not a partnership, which would suppose equality, but a union; woman is inferior to man first because her physical force is only two-thirds that of the male, then because she is intellectually and morally inferior to the same degree: she is worth 2 x 2 x 2 against 3 x 3 x 3 or $^8/_{27}$ of the stronger sex. When two women, Mme Adam and Mme d'Héricourt, respond to him – one quite firmly, the other less effusively – Proudhon retorts with *Pornocracy, or Women in Modern Times.*[34] But, like all anti-feminists, he addresses ardent litanies to the 'real woman', slave and mirror to the male; in spite of this devotion, he has to recognise himself that the life he gave his own wife never made her happy: Mme Proudhon's letters are one long lament.

But it is not these theoretical debates that influenced the course of events; they only timidly reflected them. Woman regains the economic importance lost since prehistoric times because she escapes the home and plays a new role in industrial production. The machine makes this upheaval possible because the difference in physical force between male and female workers is cancelled out in a great number of cases. As this abrupt industrial expansion demands a bigger labour market than male workers can provide, women's collaboration is necessary. This is the great nineteenth-century revolution that transforms the lot of woman and opens a new era to her. Marx and Engels understand the full impact this will have on women, promising them a liberation brought about by that of the proletariat. In fact, 'women and workers both have oppression in common,' says Bebel. And both will escape oppression thanks to the importance their productive work will take on through technological development. Engels shows that woman's lot is closely linked to the history of private property; a catastrophe substituted patriarchy for matriarchy and enslaved woman to the patrimony; but the Industrial Revolution is the counterpart of that loss and will lead to feminine emancipation. He writes: 'Woman cannot be emancipated unless she takes part in production on a large social scale and is only incidentally bound to domestic work. And this has become possible only within a large modern industry that not only accepts women's work on a grand scale but formally requires it.'

At the beginning of the nineteenth century, woman was more shamefully exploited than workers of the opposite sex. Domestic labour constituted what the English termed the 'sweating system'; in spite of constant work, the worker did not earn enough to make ends meet. Jules Simon in *The Woman Worker*[35] and even the conservative Leroy-Beaulieu in *Women's Work in the Nineteenth Century,*[36] published in 1873, denounce loathsome abuses; the latter declares that more than 200,000 French workers earn less than 50 centimes a day. It is clear why they hasten to migrate to the factories; in fact, it is not long before nothing is left outside workshops except needlework, laundering and housework, all slave labour paying famine wages; even lacemaking, millinery, and such are taken over by the factories; in return, job offers are massive in the cotton, wool and silk industries; women are mainly used in spinning and weaving mills. Employers often prefer them to men. 'They do better work for less pay.' This cynical formula clearly shows the drama of feminine labour. It is through labour that woman won her dignity as a human being; but it was a singularly difficult and slow conquest. Spinning and weaving are done under lamentable hygienic conditions. 'In Lyon,' writes Blanqui, 'in the trimmings workshops, some women are obliged to work almost hanging in a kind of harness in order to use both their feet and hands.' In 1831, silk workers work in the summer from three o'clock in the morning to eleven at night, or seventeen[37] hours a day, 'in often unhealthy workshops where sunlight never enters', says Norbert Truquin. 'Half of the young girls develop consumption before the end of their apprenticeship. When they complain, they are accused of dissimulating.'*[38] In addition, the male assistants take advantage of the young women workers. 'To get what they wanted they used the most revolting means, hunger and want,' says the anonymous author of *The Truth about the Events of Lyon*.[39] Some of the women work on farms as well as in factories. They are cynically exploited. Marx relates in a footnote of *Das Kapital*: 'Mr E——, manufacturer, let me know that he employed only women on his mechanical weaving looms, and that he gave preference to married women, and among them, women who had a family to care for at home, because they were far more docile and attentive than unmarried women, and had to work until ready to drop from exhaustion to provide indispensable means of subsistence to support their families. This is how', adds Marx, 'the qualities proper to woman are misrepresented to her disadvantage, and all the delicate and moral elements of her nature become means to enslave her and make her suffer.' Summarising *Das Kapital* and commenting on Bebel, G. Derville writes: 'Beast of luxury or beast of burden, such is woman almost exclusively today. Kept by man when she does not work, she is still kept by him when she works herself to death.' The situation of the woman worker was so lamentable that Sismondi and Blanqui called for women to be denied access to workshops. The reason is in part that women did not at first know how to defend themselves and organise unions. Feminine 'associations' date from 1848 and are originally production associations. The movement progressed extremely slowly, as the following figures show:

* N. Truquin, *Memoirs and Adventures of a Proletarian in Times of Revolution*. Cited from E. Dolléans, *History of the Working Class Movement*, vol. I.

in 1905, out of 781,392 union members, 69,405 are women;

in 1908, out of 957,120 union members, 88,906 are women;

in 1912, out of 1,064,413 union members, 92,336 are women.

In 1920, out of 1,580,967 workers, 239,016 are women and unionised female employees, and among 1,083,957 farmworkers, only 36,193 women are unionised; in all, 292,000 women are unionised out of a total of 3,076,585 union workers.[40] A tradition of resignation and submission as well as a lack of solidarity and collective consciousness leaves them disarmed in front of the new possibilities available to them.

The result of this attitude is that women's work was regulated slowly and late. Legislation does not intervene until 1874, and in spite of the campaigns waged under the Empire, only two provisions affect women: one banning minors from night work, requiring a day off on Sundays and holidays, and limiting the work day to twelve hours; as for women over twenty-one, all that is done is to prohibit underground mine and quarry work. The first feminine work charter, dated 2 November 1892, bans night work and limits the work day in factories; it leaves the door open for all kinds of fraud. In 1900 the work day is limited to ten hours; in 1905 a weekly day of rest becomes obligatory; in 1907 the woman worker is granted free disposal of her income; in 1909 maternity leave is granted; in 1911 the 1892 provisions are reinforced; in 1913 laws are passed for rest periods before and after childbirth, and dangerous and excessive work is prohibited. Little by little, social legislation takes shape and health guarantees are set up for women's work; seats are required for salesgirls, long shifts at outdoor display counters are prohibited, and so on. The International Labour Office succeeded in getting international agreements on sanitary conditions for women's work, maternity leave, and such.

A second consequence of the resigned inertia of women workers was the salaries they were forced to accept. Various explanations with multiple factors have been given for the phenomenon of low female salaries. It is insufficient to say that women have fewer needs than men: that is only a subsequent justification. Rather, women, as we have seen, did not know how to defend themselves against exploitation; they had to compete with prisons that dumped products without labour costs on the market; they competed with each other. Besides, in a society based on the marital community, woman seeks emancipation through work: bound to her father's or husband's household, she is most often satisfied just to bring home some extra money; she works outside the family, but for it; and since the working woman does not have to support herself completely, she ends up accepting remuneration far inferior to that which a man demands. With a significant number of women accepting bargain wages, the whole female salary scale is, of course, set up to the advantage of the employer.

In France, according to an 1889–93 survey, for a day of work equal to a man's, a woman worker received only half the male's wages. A 1908 survey showed that the highest hourly rates for women working from home never rose above 20 centimes an hour and dropped as low as 5 centimes: it was impossible for a woman so exploited to live without charity or a protector. In America in 1918, women earned half men's salary. Around this period, for the same amount of coal mined in Germany, a woman earned approximately 25 per cent less than a man. Between 1911 and 1943 women's salaries in France rose a bit more rapidly than men's, but they nonetheless remained clearly inferior.

While employers warmly welcomed women because of the low wages they accepted, this provoked resistance on the part of the male workers. Between the cause of the proletariat and that of women there was no such direct solidarity as Bebel and Engels claimed. The problem was similar to that of the black labour force in the United States. The most oppressed minorities in a society are readily used by the oppressors as a weapon against the class they belong to; thus they at first become enemies, and a deeper consciousness of the situation is necessary so that blacks and whites, women and male workers, form coalitions rather than opposition. It is understandable that male workers at first viewed this cheap competition as an alarming threat and became hostile. It is only when women were integrated into unions that they could defend their own interests and cease endangering those of the working class as a whole.

In spite of all these difficulties, progress in women's work continued. In 1900, in France, 900,000 women worked from home making clothes, leather goods, funeral wreaths, purses, beadwork and Paris souvenirs, but this number diminished considerably. In 1906, 42 per cent of working-age women (between eighteen and sixty) worked in farming, industry, business, banks, insurance, offices and liberal professions. This movement spread to the whole world because of the 1914–18 labour crisis and the world war. The lower middle class and the middle class were determined to follow this movement, and women also invaded the liberal professions. According to one of the last prewar censuses, in France 42 per cent of all women between eighteen and sixty worked; in Finland 37 per cent; in Germany 34.2 per cent; in India 27.7 per cent; in England 26.9 per cent; in the Netherlands 19.2 per cent; and in the United States,

17.7 per cent. But in France and in India the high figures reflect the extent of rural labour. Excluding the peasantry, France had in 1940 approximately 500,000 heads of establishments, one million female employees, two million women workers and 1.5 million women working alone or unemployed women. Among women workers, 650,000 were domestic workers; 1.2 million worked in light industry including 440,000 in textiles, 315,000 in clothing, and 380,000 at home in dressmaking.[41] For commerce, liberal professions and public service, France, England and the USA ranked about the same.

One of the basic problems for women, as has been seen, is reconciling the reproductive role and productive work. The fundamental reason that woman, since the beginning of history, has been consigned to domestic labour and prohibited from taking part in shaping the world is her enslavement to the generative function. In female animals there is a rhythm of heat and seasons that assures the economy of their energies; nature, on the contrary, between puberty and menopause, places no limits on women's gestation. Some civilisations prohibit early marriage; Indian tribes are cited where women are guaranteed a two-year rest period between births; but in general over the centuries, women's fertility has not been regulated. Contraceptives have existed since antiquity,* generally for women's use – potions, suppositories or vaginal tampons – but they remained the secrets of prostitutes and doctors; maybe the secret was available to women of the Roman decadence whose sterility satirists reproached. But the Middle Ages knew nothing of them; no trace is found until the eighteenth century. For many women in these times, life was an uninterrupted series of pregnancies; even women of easy virtue paid for their licentious love lives with frequent births. At certain periods, humanity felt the need to reduce the size of the population; but at the same time, nations worried about becoming weak; in periods of crisis and great poverty, postponing marriage lowered the birthrates. The general rule was to marry young and have as many children as the woman could carry, infant mortality alone reducing the

---

*"The earliest known reference to birth-control methods appears to be an Egyptian papyrus from the second millennium BC, recommending the vaginal application of a bizarre mixture composed of crocodile excrement, honey, natron, and a rubbery substance' (P. Ariès, *Histoire des populations françaises* [*History of French Populations*]). Medieval Persian physicians knew of thirty-one recipes, of which only nine were intended for men. Soranus, in the Hadrian era, explains that at the moment of ejaculation, if the woman does not want a child, she should 'hold her breath, pull back her body a little so that the sperm cannot penetrate the *os uteri*, get up immediately, squat down and make herself sneeze'.

number of living children. Already in the seventeenth century, the abbé de Pure*[42] protests against the 'amorous dropsy' to which women are condemned; and Mme de Sévigné urges her daughter to avoid frequent pregnancies. But it is in the eighteenth century that the Malthusian movement develops in France. First the well-to-do class, then the population in general deem it reasonable to limit the number of children according to parents' resources, and anticonception procedures begin to enter into social practices. In 1778 Moreau, the demographer, writes, 'Rich women are not the only ones who considered the propagation of the species the greatest old-fashioned dupe; these dark secrets, unknown to all animals except man, have already made their way into the countryside; nature is confounded even in the villages.' The practice of coitus interruptus spreads first among the bourgeoisie, then among rural populations and workers; the prophylactic, which already existed as an antivenereal device, becomes a contraceptive device, widespread after the discovery of vulcanisation, towards 1840.† In Anglo-Saxon countries, birth control is official and numerous methods have been discovered to dissociate these two formerly inseparable functions: the sexual and the reproductive. Viennese medical research, precisely establishing the mechanism of conception and the conditions favourable to it, has also suggested methods for avoiding it. In France contraception propaganda and the sale of pessaries, vaginal tampons, and such are prohibited; but birth control is no less widespread.

As for abortion, it is nowhere officially authorised by law. Roman law granted no special protection to embryonic life; the *nasciturus* was not considered a human being, but part of the woman's body. '*Partus antequam edatur mulieris portio est vel viscerum.*'‡ In the era of decadence, abortion seems to have been a normal practice, and even a legislator who wanted to encourage birthrates would never dare to prohibit it. If the woman refused a child against her husband's will, he could have her punished; but her crime was her disobedience. Generally, in Oriental and Graeco-Roman civilisation, abortion was allowed by law.

It was Christianity that overturned moral ideas on this point by endowing the embryo with a soul; so abortion became a crime against the foetus itself. 'Any woman who does what she can so as not to give

---

* In *La Précieuse* (1656).
† 'Around 1930 an American firm sold twenty million prophylactics in one year. Fifteen American factories produced a million and a half of them per day' (P. Ariès, *History*).
‡ 'The infant, before being born, is a part of the woman, a kind of organ.'

birth to as many children as she is capable of is guilty of that many homicides, just as is a woman who tries to injure herself after conception,' says St Augustine. In Byzantium, abortion led only to a temporary relegation; for the barbarians who practised infanticide, it was punishable only if it was carried out by violence, against the mother's will: it was redeemed by paying blood money. But the first councils issued edicts for the severest penalties against this 'homicide', whatever the presumed age of the foetus. Nonetheless, one question arises that has been the object of infinite discussion: at what moment does the soul enter the body? St Thomas and most other writers settled on life beginning towards the fortieth day for males and the eightieth for females; thus was established a distinction between the animated and non-animated foetus. A Middle Ages penitential book declares: 'If a pregnant woman destroys her fruit before forty-five days, she is subject to a penitence of one year. For sixty days, three years. And finally, if the infant is already animated, she should be tried for homicide.' The book, however, adds: 'There is a great difference between a poor woman who destroys her infant for the pain she has to feed it and the one who has no other reason but to hide a crime of fornication.' In 1556, Henri II published a well-known edict on concealing pregnancy; since the death penalty was applied for simple concealment, it followed that the penalty should also apply to abortion manoeuvres; in fact, the edict was aimed at infanticide, but it was used to authorise the death penalty for practitioners and accomplices of abortion. The distinction between the quickened and non-quickened foetus disappeared around the eighteenth century. At the end of the century, Beccaria, a man of considerable influence in France, pleaded in favour of the woman who refuses to have a child. The 1791 Code excuses the woman but punishes her accomplices with 'twenty years of irons'. The idea that abortion is homicide disappeared in the nineteenth century: it is considered rather to be a crime against the state. The Law of 1810 prohibits it absolutely under pain of imprisonment and forced labour for the woman who aborts and her accomplices; but doctors practise abortion whenever it is a question of saving the mother's life. Because the law is so strict, juries at the end of the century stopped applying it and few arrests were made, with four-fifths of the accused acquitted. In 1923 a new law is passed, again with forced labour for the accomplices and the practitioner of the operation, but punishing the woman having the abortion with only prison or a fine; in 1939 a new decree specifically targets the technicians: no reprieve would be granted. In 1941 abortion was decreed a crime against state security. In other countries, it is a misdemeanour punishable by a short prison sentence; in England, it is a crime – a felony – punishable by prison or forced labour. Overall, codes and courts are more lenient with the woman having the abortion than with her accomplices. The Church, however, has never relaxed its severity. The 27 March 1917 code of canon law declares: 'Those who procure abortions, the mother not excepted, incur excommunication *latae sententiae*, once the result has been obtained, reserved to the Ordinary.' No reason can be invoked, even the danger of the mother's death. The Pope again declared recently that between the mother's life and the child's the former must be sacrificed: the fact is, the mother, being baptised, can enter heaven – curiously, hell never enters into these calculations – while the foetus is condemned to perpetual limbo.*

Abortion was officially recognised, but only for a short time, in Germany before Nazism and in the Soviet Union before 1936. But in spite of religion and laws, it has been practised in all countries to a large extent. In France, every year 800,000 to one million abortions are performed – as many as births – and two-thirds of the women are married, many already having one or two children. In spite of the prejudices, resistance and an outdated morality, unregulated fertility has given way to fertility controlled by the state or individuals. Progress in obstetrics has considerably decreased the dangers of childbirth; childbirth pain is disappearing; at this time – March 1949 – legislation has been passed in England requiring the use of certain anaesthetic methods; they are already generally applied in the United States and are beginning to spread in France. With artificial insemination, the evolution that will permit humanity to master the reproductive function comes to completion. These changes have tremendous importance for woman in particular; she can reduce the number of pregnancies and rationally integrate them into her life, instead of being their slave. During the nineteenth century, woman in her turn is freed from nature; she wins control

* In volume II, we will return to the discussion of this view. Let it just be said here that Catholics are far from keeping to the letter of St Augustine's doctrine. The confessor whispers to the young fiancée, on the eve of her wedding, that she can do anything with her husband, as long as 'proper' coitus is achieved; positive birth-control practices – including coitus interruptus – are forbidden; but the calendar established by Viennese sexologists can be used, where the act whose only recognised aim is reproduction is carried out on the days conception is impossible for the woman. There are spiritual advisers who even indicate this calendar to their flocks. In fact, there are ample 'Christian mothers' who only have two or three children and have nonetheless not interrupted their conjugal relations after the last delivery.

of her body. Relieved of a great number of reproductive servitudes, she can take on the economic roles open to her, roles that would assure her control over her own person.

The convergence of these two factors – participation in production and freedom from reproductive slavery – explains the evolution of woman's condition. As Engels predicted, her social and political status necessarily had to change. The feminist movement begun in France by Condorcet, in England by Mary Wollstonecraft in *Vindication of the Rights of Woman*, and followed up at the beginning of the century by the Saint-Simonians, never succeeded for lack of a concrete base. But now, women's claims would have ample weight. They would be heard even within the heart of the bourgeoisie. With the rapid development of industrial civilisation, landed property is falling behind in relation to personal property: the principle of family group unity is losing force. The mobility of capital allows its holder to own and dispose of his wealth without reciprocity instead of being held by it. Through patrimony, woman was substantially attached to her husband: with patrimony abolished, they are only juxtaposed, and even children do not constitute as strong a bond as interest. Thus, the individual will assert himself against the group; this evolution is particularly striking in America where modern capitalism has triumphed: divorce is going to flourish, and husbands and wives are no more than provisional associates. In France, where the rural population is large and where the Napoleonic Code placed the married woman under guardianship, evolution will be slow. In 1884, divorce was restored and a wife could obtain it if the husband committed adultery; nonetheless, in the penal area, sexual difference was maintained: adultery was an offence only when perpetrated by the wife. The right of guardianship, granted with restrictions in 1907, was fully granted only in 1917. In 1912, the right to determine natural paternity was authorised. It was not until 1938 and 1942 that the married woman's status was modified: the duty of obedience was then abrogated, although the father remains the family head; he determines the place of residence, but the wife can oppose his choice if she advances valid arguments; her powers are increasing; but the formula is still confused: 'The married woman has full legal powers. These powers are only limited by the marriage contract and law'; the last part of the article contradicts the first. The equality of spouses has not yet been achieved.

As for political rights, they have not easily been won in France, England or the United States. In 1867, John Stuart Mill pleaded the first case ever officially pronounced before Parliament in favour of the vote for women.

In his writings he imperiously demanded equality of men and women in the family and society: 'The principle which regulates the existing social relations between the two sexes – the legal subordination of one sex to the other – is wrong in itself, and now one of the hindrances to human improvement; and . . . it ought to be replaced by a principle of perfect equality.'[43] After that, English women organised politically under Mrs Fawcett's leadership; French women rallied behind Maria Deraismes, who between 1868 and 1871 dealt with women's issues in a series of public lectures; she joined in the lively controversy against Alexandre Dumas *fils* who advised the husband of an unfaithful wife, 'Kill her.' Léon Richer was the true founder of feminism; in 1869 he launched *Le Droit des Femmes* (*The Rights of Women*) and organised the International Congress of Women's Rights, held in 1878. The question of the right to vote was not yet dealt with; women limited themselves to claiming civil rights; for thirty years the movement remained timid in France and in England. Nonetheless, a woman, Hubertine Auclert, started a suffragette campaign; she created a group called Women's Suffrage and a newspaper, *La Citoyenne*. Many groups were organised under her influence, but they accomplished little. This weakness of feminism stemmed from its internal division; as already pointed out, women as a sex lack solidarity: they are linked to their classes first; bourgeois and proletarian interests do not intersect. Revolutionary feminism adhered to the Saint-Simonian and Marxist tradition; it is noteworthy, moreover, that a certain Louise Michel spoke against feminism because it diverted the energy that should be used entirely for class struggle; with the abolition of capital the lot of woman will be resolved.

The Socialist Congress of 1879 proclaimed the equality of the sexes, and as of that time the feminist–socialist alliance would no longer be denounced, but since women hope for their liberty through the emancipation of workers in general, their attachment to their own cause is secondary. The bourgeoisie, on the contrary, claim new rights within existing society and they refuse to be revolutionary; they want to introduce virtuous reforms into rules of behaviour: elimination of alcohol, pornographic literature and prostitution. In 1892, the Feminist Congress convenes and gives its name to the movement, but nothing comes of it. However, in 1897 a law is passed permitting women to testify in court, but the request of a woman doctor of law to become a member of the bar is denied. In 1898, women are allowed to vote for the Commercial Court, to vote and be eligible for the National Council on Labour and Employment, to be admitted to the National Council for Public Health Services and the Ecole des Beaux-Arts. In 1900, feminists hold a new congress, again without significant results. But in 1901, for the first time, Viviani presents the question of the woman's vote to the French parliament; he proposes limiting suffrage to unmarried and divorced women. The feminist movement gains importance at this time. In 1909 the French Union for Women's Suffrage is formed, headed by Mme Brunschvicg; she organises lectures, meetings, congresses and demonstrations. In 1909, Buisson presents a report on Dussaussoy's bill allowing women to vote in local assemblies. In 1910, Thomas presents a bill in favour of women's suffrage; presented again in 1918, it passes the Chamber in 1919; but it fails to pass the Senate in 1922. The situation is quite complex. Christian feminism joins forces with revolutionary feminism and Mme Brunschvicg's so-called independent feminism: in 1919, Benedict XV declares himself in favour of the women's vote, and Monsignor Baudrillart and Père Sertillanges follow his lead with ardent propaganda; Catholics believe in fact that women in France constitute a conservative and religious element; this is just what the radicals fear: the real reason for their opposition is their fear of the swing votes that women represented. In the Senate, numerous Catholics, the Union Republican group, as well as extreme left parties are for the women's vote: but the majority of the assembly is against it. Until 1932 delaying procedures are used by the majority, which refuses to discuss bills concerning women's suffrage; nevertheless, in 1932, the Chamber having voted the women's voting and eligibility amendment, 319 votes to 1, the Senate opens a debate extending over several sessions: the amendment is voted down. The record in *L'officiel* is of great importance; all the antifeminist arguments developed over half a century are found in the report, which fastidiously lists all the works in which they are mentioned. First of all come these types of gallantry arguments: we love women too much to let them vote; the 'real woman' who accepts the 'housewife or courtesan' dilemma is exalted in true Proudhon fashion; woman would lose her charm by voting; she is on a pedestal and should not step down from it; she has everything to lose and nothing to gain in becoming a voter; she governs men without needing a ballot; and so on. More serious objections concern the family's interest: woman's place is in the home; political discussions would bring about disagreement between spouses. Some admit to moderate antifeminism. Women are different from men. They do not serve in the military. Will prostitutes vote? And others arrogantly affirm male superiority: voting is a duty and not a right; women are not worthy of it. They are less intelligent and educated than men. If women voted, men would become effeminate. Women lacked political education. They would vote according to their husbands' wishes. If they want to be free, they should first free themselves from their dressmakers. Also proposed is that superbly naive argument: there are more women in France than men. In spite of the flimsiness of all these objections, French women would have to wait until 1945 to acquire political power.

New Zealand gave woman full rights in 1893. Australia followed in 1908. But in England and America victory was difficult. Victorian England imperiously isolated woman in her home; Jane Austen wrote in secret; it took great courage or an exceptional destiny to become George Eliot or Emily Brontë; in 1888 an English scholar wrote: 'Women are not only not part of the race, they are not even half of the race but a sub-species destined uniquely for reproduction.' Mrs Fawcett founded a suffragist movement towards the end of the century, but as in France the movement was hesitant. Around 1903, feminist claims took a singular turn. In London, the Pankhurst family created the Women's Social and Political Union, which joined with the Labour Party and embarked on resolutely militant activities. It was the first time in history that women took on a cause as women: this is what gave particular interest to the suffragettes in England and America. For fifteen years, they carried out a policy recalling in some respects a Ghandi-like attitude: refusing violence, they invented more or less ingenious symbolic actions. They marched on the Albert Hall during Liberal Party meetings, carrying banners with the words 'Vote for Women'; they forced their way into Lord Asquith's office, held meetings in Hyde Park or Trafalgar Square, marched in the streets carrying signs and held lectures; during demonstrations they insulted the police or threw stones at them, provoking their arrest; in prison they adopted the hunger strike tactic; they raised money and rallied millions of women and men; they influenced opinion so well that in 1907 two hundred members of Parliament made up a committee for women's suffrage; every year from then on some of them would propose a law in favour of women's suffrage, a law that would be rejected every year with the same arguments. In 1907 the WSPU organised the first march on Parliament with workers covered in shawls, and a few aristocratic women; the police pushed them back; but the following year, as married women were threatened with a ban on work in certain mines, the Lancashire women workers were called by the WSPU to hold a grand meeting. There were new arrests and the imprisoned suffragettes responded with a long hunger strike. Released, they organised new parades: one of the women rode a horse painted with the head of Queen Elizabeth. On 18 July 1910, the day the women's suffrage law went to the

Chamber, a nine-kilometre-long column paraded through London; the law rejected, there were more meetings and new arrests. In 1912, they adopted a more violent tactic: they burned empty houses, slashed pictures, trampled flower beds, threw stones at the police; at the same time, they sent delegation upon delegation to Lloyd·George and Sir Edward Grey; they hid in the Albert Hall and noisily disrupted Lloyd George's speeches. The war interrupted their activities. It is difficult to know how much these actions hastened events. The vote was granted to English women first in 1918 in a restricted form, and then in 1928 without restriction: their success was in large part due to the services they had rendered during the war.

The American woman found herself at first more emancipated than the European. Early in the nineteenth century, pioneer women had to share the hard work done by men and they fought by their sides; they were far fewer than men and thus a high value was placed on them. But little by little, their condition came to resemble that of women in the Old World; gallantry towards them was maintained; they kept their cultural privileges and a dominant position within the family; laws granted them a religious and moral role; but the command of society resided in the males' hands. Some women began to claim their political rights around 1830. They undertook a campaign in favour of blacks. As the antislavery congress held in 1840 in London was closed to them, the Quaker Lucretia Mott founded a feminist association. On 18 July 1840,[44] at the Seneca Falls Convention, they drafted a Quaker-inspired declaration, which set the tone for all of American feminism: 'that all men and women are created equal; that they are endowed by their Creator with certain inalienable rights ... that to secure these rights governments are instituted ... He [Man] has made her, if married, in the eye of the law, civilly dead ... He has usurped the prerogative of Jehovah himself, claiming it as his right to assign for her a sphere of action, when that belongs to her conscience and her God.' Three years later, Harriet Beecher Stowe wrote *Uncle Tom's Cabin*, arousing the public in favour of blacks. Emerson and Lincoln supported the feminist movement. When the Civil War broke out, women ardently participated; but in vain they demanded that the amendment giving blacks the right to vote be drafted as follows: 'The right ... to vote shall not be denied or abridged ... on account of race, color, *sex*.' Seizing on the ambiguity of one of the articles to the amendment, the great feminist leader Susan B. Anthony voted in Rochester with fourteen comrades; she was fined a hundred dollars. In 1869, she founded what later came to be called the National American

Woman Suffrage Association, and that same year the state of Wyoming gave women the right to vote. But it was only in 1893 that Colorado, then in 1896 Idaho and Utah, followed this example. Progress was slow afterwards. But women succeeded better economically than in Europe. In 1900, 5 million women worked, 1.3 million in industry, 500,000 in business; a large number worked in business, industry and liberal professions. There were lawyers, doctors and 3,373 women pastors. The famous Mary Baker Eddy founded the Christian Science Church. Women formed clubs; in 1900, they totalled about two million members.

Nonetheless, only nine states had given women the vote. In 1913, the suffrage movement was organised on the militant English model. Two women led it: Doris Stevens and a young Quaker, Alice Paul. From Wilson[45] they obtained the right to march with banners and signs; they then organised a campaign of lectures, meetings, marches and manifestations of all sorts. From the nine states where women voted, women voters went with great pomp and circumstance to the Capitol, demanding the feminine vote for the whole nation. In Chicago, the first group of women assembled in a party to liberate their sex; this assembly became the Women's Party. In 1917, suffragettes invented a new tactic: they stationed themselves at the doors of the White House, banners in hand, and often chained to the gates so they could not be driven away. After six months, they were stopped and sent to the Occuquan penitentiary; they went on hunger strike and were finally released. New demonstrations led to the beginning of riots. The government finally consented to naming a House Committee on Woman Suffrage. The executive committee of the Women's Party held a conference in Washington, and an amendment favouring the woman's vote went to the House and was voted on 10 January 1918. The vote still had to go to the Senate. Wilson would not promise to exert enough pressure, so the suffragettes began to demonstrate again. They held a rally at the White House doors. The president decided to address an appeal to the Senate, but the amendment was rejected by two votes. A Republican Congress voted for the amendment in June 1919. The battle for complete equality of the sexes went on for the next ten years. At the sixth International Conference of American States held in Havana in 1928, women obtained the creation of the Inter-American Commission of Women. In 1933, the Montevideo treaties elevated women's status by international convention. Nineteen American republics signed the convention giving women equality in all rights.

Sweden also had a very sizeable feminist movement. Invoking old traditions, Swedish women demanded the right 'to education, work and liberty'. It was largely women writers who led the fight, and it was the moral aspect of the problem that interested them at first; then, grouped in powerful associations, they won over the liberals but ran up against the hostility of the conservatives. Norwegian women in 1907 and Finnish women in 1906 obtained the suffrage that Swedish women would have to wait years to attain.

In Latin and Eastern countries woman was oppressed by customs more than by laws. In Italy, fascism systematically hindered feminism's progress. Seeking the alliance of the Church, which continued to uphold family tradition and a tradition of feminine slavery, fascist Italy held woman in double bondage: to public authority and to her husband. The situation was very different in Germany. In 1790, Hippel, a student, launched the first German feminist manifesto. Sentimental feminism analogous to that of George Sand flourished at the beginning of the nineteenth century. In 1848, the first German woman feminist, Louise Otto, demanded the right for women to assist in the transformation of their country: her feminism was largely nationalistic. She founded the General German Women's Association in 1865. German socialists, along with Bebel, advocated the abolition of the inequality of the sexes. In 1892, Clara Zetkin joined the party's council. Women workers and women socialists grouped together in a federation. German women failed in 1914 to establish a women's national army, but they took an active part in the war. After the German defeat, they obtained the right to vote and participated in political life: Rosa Luxemburg fought next to Liebknecht in the Spartacus group and was assassinated in 1919. The majority of German women chose the party of order; several took seats in the Reichstag. It was thus upon emancipated women that Hitler imposed the new Napoleonic ideal: 'Kinder, Küche, Kirche'. 'Woman's presence dishonours the Reichstag,' he declared. As Nazism was anti-Catholic and antibourgeois, he gave the mother a privileged place; protection granted to unmarried mothers and illegitimate children greatly freed woman from marriage; as in Sparta, she was more dependent on the state than on any individual, giving her both more and less autonomy than a bourgeois woman living under a capitalist regime.

In Soviet Russia the feminist movement made the greatest advances. It began at the end of the nineteenth century among women students of the intelligentsia; they were less attached to their personal cause than to revolutionary action in general; they 'went to the people' and used nihilistic methods against the Okhrana: in 1878 Vera Zasulich shot the police chief Trepov. During the Russo-Japanese War, women replaced men in many areas of work; their consciousness raised, the Russian Union for Women's Rights demanded political equality of the sexes; in the first Duma, a parliamentary women's rights group was created, but it was powerless. Women workers' emancipation would come from the revolution. Already in 1905, they were actively participating in the mass political strikes that broke out in the country, and they mounted the barricades. On 8 March 1917, International Women's Day and a few days before the revolution, they massively demonstrated in the streets of St Petersburg[46] demanding bread, peace and their husbands' return. They took part in the October insurrection; between 1918 and 1920, they played an important economic and even military role in the USSR's fight against the invaders. True to Marxist tradition, Lenin linked women's liberation to that of the workers; he gave them political and economic equality.

Article 122 of the 1936 constitution stipulates: 'In the USSR, woman enjoys the same rights as man in all aspects of economic, official, cultural, public and political life.' And these principles were spelled out by the Communist International. It demands 'social equality of man and woman before the law and in daily life. Radical transformation in conjugal rights and in the family code. Recognition of maternity as a social function. Entrusting society with the care and education of children and adolescents. Organisation of a civil effort against ideology and traditions that make woman a slave.' In the economic area, woman's conquests were stunning. She obtained equal wages with male workers, and she took on a highly active role in production; thereby gaining considerable political and social importance. The brochure recently published by the Association France-USSR reports that in the 1939 general elections there were 457,000 women deputies in the regional, district, town and village soviets; 1,480 in the socialist republics of higher soviets, and 227 seated in the Supreme Soviet of the USSR. Close to 10 million are members of unions. They constitute 40 per cent of the population of USSR workers and employees, and a great number of workers among the Stakhanovites are women. The role of Russian women in the last war is well-known; they provided an enormous labour force even in production branches where masculine professions are dominant: metallurgy and mining, timber rafting and railways and so forth. They distinguished themselves as pilots and parachutists, and they formed partisan armies.

This participation of woman in public life has raised a difficult problem: her role in family life. For a long while, means were sought to free her from her domestic constraints: on 16 November 1942, the plenary assembly of the Comintern proclaimed, 'The revolution is impotent as long as the notion of family and family relations subsists.' Respect for free unions, liberalisation of divorce and legalisation of abortion ensured woman's liberty relative to men; laws for maternity leave, child-care centres, kindergartens, and so on lightened the burdens of motherhood. From passionate and contradictory witness reports, it is difficult to discern what woman's concrete situation really was; what is sure is that today the demands of repopulation have given rise to a different family policy: the family has become the elementary social cell and woman is both worker and house-keeper.* Sexual morality is at its strictest; since the law of June 1936, reinforced by that of 7 June 1941, abortion has been banned and divorce almost suppressed; adultery is condemned by moral standards. Strictly subordinated to the state like all workers, strictly bound to the home, but with access to political life and the dignity that productive work gives, the Russian woman is in a singular situation that would be worth studying in its singularity; circumstances unfortunately prevent me from doing this.

The recent session of the United Nations Commission on the Status of Women demanded that equal rights for both sexes be recognised in all nations, and several motions were passed to make this legal status a concrete reality. It would seem, then, that the match is won. The future can only bring greater and greater assimilation of women in a hitherto masculine society.

★

Several conclusions come to the fore when taking a look at this history as a whole. And first of all this one: women's entire history has been written by men. Just as in America there is no black problem but a white one;[†] just as 'anti-Semitism is not a Jewish problem, it's our problem',[‡][47] so the problem of woman has always been a problem of men. Why they had moral prestige at the outset along with physical strength has been discussed; they created the values, customs and religions; never did women attempt to vie for that empire. A few isolated women – Sappho, Christine de Pizan, Mary Wollstonecraft, Olympe de Gouges – protested

---

* Olga Michakova, secretary of the Central Committee of the Communist Youth Organisation, stated in 1944 in an interview: 'Soviet women should try to make themselves as attractive as nature and good taste permit. After the war, they should dress like women and act feminine . . . Girls will be told to act and walk like girls and that is why they will wear skirts that will probably be very tight, making them carry themselves gracefully.'

† Cf. Myrdal, *An American Dilemma*.

‡ J. P. Sartre, *Anti-Semite and Jew*.

against their harsh destiny; and there were some collective demonstrations: but Roman matrons in league against the Oppian law or Anglo-Saxon suffragettes only managed to wield pressure because men were willing to submit to it. Men always held woman's lot in their hands; and they did not decide on it based on her interest; it is their own projects, fears and needs that counted. When they revered the Mother Goddess, it is because Nature frightened them, and as soon as the bronze tool enabled them to assert themselves against Nature, they instituted patriarchy; henceforth it was the family–state conflict that has defined woman's status; it is the attitude of the Christian before God, the world and his own flesh that is reflected in the condition he assigned to her; what was called the *querelle des femmes* in the Middle Ages was a quarrel between clergy and laity about marriage and celibacy; it is the social regime founded on private property that brought about the married woman's wardship, and it is the technical revolution realised by men that enfranchised today's women. It is an evolution of the masculine ethic that led to the decrease in family size by birth control and partially freed woman from the servitude of motherhood. Feminism itself has never been an autonomous movement: it was partially an instrument in the hands of politicians and partially an epiphenomenon reflecting a deeper social drama. Never did women form a separate caste: and in reality they never sought to play a role in history as a sex. The doctrines that call for the advent of woman as flesh, life, immanence, or the Other are masculine ideologies that do not in any way express feminine claims. For the most part, women resign themselves to their lot without attempting any action; those who did try to change attempted to overcome their singularity and not to confine themselves in it triumphantly. When they intervened in world affairs, it was in concert with men and from a masculine point of view.

This intervention, in general, was secondary and occasional. The women who enjoyed a certain economic autonomy and took part in production were the oppressed classes, and as workers they were even more enslaved than male workers. In the ruling classes woman was a parasite and as such was subjugated to masculine laws: in both cases, it was almost impossible for her to act. Law and custom did not always coincide: and a balance was set up between them so that woman was never concretely free. In the ancient Roman Republic, economic conditions give the matron concrete powers: but she has no legal independence; the same is often true in peasant civilisations and among lower-middle-class tradesmen; mistress-servant inside the home, woman is socially a minor. Inversely, in periods when society fragments, woman becomes freer, but she loses her fief when she ceases to be man's vassal; she has nothing but a negative freedom that is expressed only in licence and dissipation, as, for example, during the Roman decadence, the Renaissance, the eighteenth century, and the Directoire. Either she finds work but is enslaved; or she is enfranchised but can do nothing else with herself. It is worth noting among other points that the married woman had her place in society but without benefiting from any rights, while the single woman, honest girl or prostitute, had all man's capacities; but until this century she was more or less excluded from social life. The opposition between law and custom produced this among other curious paradoxes: free love is not prohibited by law, but adultery is a crime; the girl that 'falls', however, is often dishonoured, while the wife's shocking behaviour is treated indulgently: from the eighteenth century to today many young girls got married so that they could freely have lovers. This ingenious system kept the great mass of women under guardianship: it takes exceptional circumstances for a feminine personality to be able to affirm itself between these two series of constraints, abstract or concrete. Women who have accomplished works comparable to men's are those whom the force of social institutions had exalted beyond any sexual differentiation. Isabella the Catholic, Elizabeth of England and Catherine of Russia were neither male nor female: they were sovereigns. It is remarkable that once socially abolished, their femininity no longer constituted inferiority: there were infinitely more queens with great reigns than kings. Religion undergoes the same transformation: Catherine of Siena and St Teresa are saintly souls, beyond any physiological condition; their lay life and their mystical life, their actions and their writings, rise to heights that few men ever attain. It is legitimate to think that if other women failed to mark the world deeply, it is because they were trapped by their conditions. They were only able to intervene in a negative or indirect way. Judith, Charlotte Corday and Vera Zasulich assassinate; the Frondeuses conspire; during the Revolution and the Commune, women fight alongside men against the established order; intransigent refusal and revolt against a freedom without rights and power are permitted, whereas it is forbidden for a woman to participate in positive construction; at best she will manage to insinuate herself into masculine enterprises by indirect means. Aspasia, Mme de Maintenon and the princesse des Ursins were precious advisers: but someone still had to consent to listen to them. Men tend to exaggerate the scope of this influence when trying to convince woman she has the greater role; but in fact feminine voices are silenced when concrete action begins; they might foment wars, not suggest battle tactics; they oriented politics only inasmuch as politics was limited to intrigue: the real reins of the world have never been in women's hands; they had no role either in technology or in economy, they neither made nor unmade states, they did not discover worlds. They did set off some events: but they were pretexts more than agents. Lucretia's suicide had no more than a symbolic value. Martyrdom remains allowed for the oppressed; during Christian persecutions and in the aftermath of social or national defeats, women played this role of witness; but a martyr has never changed the face of the world. Even feminine demonstrations and initiatives were only worth something if a masculine decision positively prolonged them. The American women united around Harriet Beecher Stowe aroused public opinion to fever pitch against slavery; but the real reasons for the Civil War were not sentimental. The 8 March 1917 'woman's day' might have triggered the Russian Revolution: but it was nonetheless merely a signal. Most feminine heroines are extravagant: adventurers or eccentrics notable less for their actions than for their unique destinies; take Joan of Arc, Mme Roland and Flora Tristan: if they are compared with Richelieu, Danton, or Lenin, it is clear their greatness is mainly subjective; they are exemplary figures more than historical agents. A great man springs from the mass and is carried by circumstances: the mass of women is at the fringes of history, and for each of them, circumstances are an obstacle and not a springboard. To change the face of the world, one has first to be firmly anchored to it; but women firmly rooted in society are those subjugated by it; unless they are designated for action by divine right – and in this case they are shown to be as capable as men – the ambitious woman and the heroine are strange monsters. Only since women have begun to feel at home on this earth has a Rosa Luxemburg or a Mme Curie emerged. They brilliantly demonstrate that it is not women's inferiority that has determined their historical insignificance: it is their historical insignificance that has doomed them to inferiority.*

This fact is striking in the cultural field, the area in which they have

---

* It is worth noting that out of one thousand statues in Paris (not counting the queens that compose the corbel of the Luxembourg and fulfil a purely architectural role) there are only ten raised to women. Three are devoted to Joan of Arc. The others are Mme de Ségur, George Sand, Sarah Bernhardt, Mme Boucicaut and the Baronne de Hirsch, Maria Deraismes and Rosa Bonheur.

been the most successful in asserting themselves. Their lot has been closely linked to literature and the arts; among the ancient Germans, the roles of prophetess and priestess fell to women; because they are marginal to the world, men will look to them when they strive, through culture, to bridge the limits of their universe and reach what is other. Courtly mysticism, humanist curiosity, and the taste for beauty that thrives in the Italian Renaissance, the preciousness of the seventeenth century, and the progressive ideal of the eighteenth century bring about an exaltation of femininity in diverse forms. Woman is thus the main pole of poetry and the substance of works of art; her leisure allows her to devote herself to the pleasures of the mind: inspiration, critic, writer's audience, she emulates the writer; she can often impose a type of sensitivity, an ethic that feeds men's hearts, which is how she intervenes in her own destiny: women's education is mainly a feminine conquest. And yet as important as this collective role played by intellectual women is, their individual contributions are, on the whole, of a lesser order. Woman holds a privileged place in the fields of the mind and art because she is not involved in action; but art and thinking derive their impetus in action. Being on the fringes of the world is not the best place for someone who intends to re-create it: here again, to go beyond the given, one must be deeply rooted in it. Personal accomplishments are almost impossible in human categories collectively kept in an inferior situation. 'Where can one go in skirts?' asked Marie Bashkirtseff. And Stendhal: 'All the geniuses who are born *women* are lost for the public good.' If truth be told, one is not born, but becomes, a genius; and the feminine condition has, until now, rendered this becoming impossible.

Antifeminists draw two contradictory arguments from examining history: (1) women have never created anything grand; (2) woman's situation has never prevented great women personalities from blossoming. There is bad faith in both of these assertions; the successes of some few privileged women neither compensate for nor excuse the systematic degrading of the collective level; and the very fact that these successes are so rare and limited is proof of their unfavourable circumstances. As Christine de Pizan, Poulain de la Barre, Condorcet, John Stuart Mill, and Stendhal stated, women have never been given their chances in any area. This explains why many of them today demand a new status; and once again, their demand is not to be exalted in their femininity: they want transcendence to prevail over immanence in themselves as in all of humanity; they want abstract rights and concrete possibilities to be granted to them, without which freedom is merely mystification.*

This will is being fulfilled. But this is in a period of transition; this world that has always belonged to men is still in their hands; patriarchal civilisation's institutions and values are still, to a great extent, alive. Abstract rights are far from being wholly granted to women: in Switzerland, women still cannot vote; in France, the 1942 law upholds the husband's prerogatives in a weaker form. And abstract rights, as has just been said, have never been sufficient to guarantee woman a concrete hold on the world: there is not yet real equality today between the two sexes.

First, the burdens of marriage are still much heavier for woman than for man. We have seen that the constraints of pregnancy have been limited by the overt or clandestine use of birth control, but the practice is neither universally disseminated nor rigorously applied; as abortion is officially forbidden, many women either jeopardise their health by resorting to unregulated abortion methods or are overwhelmed by the number of their pregnancies. Child care, like housekeeping, is still almost exclusively the woman's burden. In France in particular, the antifeminist tradition is so tenacious that a man would think it demeaning to participate in chores previously reserved for women. The result is that woman has a harder time reconciling her family and work life. In cases where society demands this effort from her, her existence is much more difficult than her spouse's.

Take, for example, the lot of peasant women. In France they make up the majority of the women involved in productive labour, and they are generally married. The single woman most often remains a servant in the father's, brother's or sister's household; she only becomes mistress of a home by accepting a husband's domination; depending on the region, customs and traditions impose various roles on her: the Norman peasant woman presides over the meal, while the Corsican woman does not sit at the same table as the men; but in any case, as she plays one of the most important roles in the domestic economy, she shares the man's responsibilities, his interests and his property; she is respected and it is often she who really governs: her situation is reminiscent of the place she held in ancient agricultural communities. She often has as much moral prestige

* Here too the antifeminists are equivocal. At times, holding abstract liberty to be nothing, they glorify the great concrete role the enslaved woman can play in this world: what more does she want? And other times, they underestimate the fact that negative licence does not open any concrete possibilities and they blame abstractly enfranchised women for not having proven themselves.

as her husband and sometimes even more; but her concrete condition is much harsher. The care of the garden, barnyard, sheepfold and pigpen falls on her alone; she takes part in the heavy work: cleaning the cowshed, spreading the manure, sowing, ploughing, hoeing and hay making; she digs, weeds, harvests, picks grapes and sometimes helps load and unload wagons of straw, hay, wood and sticks, litter and so on. In addition, she prepares the meals and manages the household: washing, mending and such. She assumes the heavy burdens of pregnancies and child care. She rises at dawn, feeds the barnyard and small animals, serves the first meal to the men, takes care of the children and goes out to the fields or the woods or the kitchen garden; she draws water from the well, serves the second meal, washes the dishes, works in the fields again until dinner, and after the last meal she occupies her evening by mending, cleaning, husking the corn and so forth. As she has no time to take care of her health, even during her pregnancies, she loses her shape quickly and is prematurely withered and worn out, sapped by illnesses. She is denied the few occasional compensations man finds in his social life: he goes to the city on Sundays and fair days, meets other men, goes to the café, drinks, plays cards, hunts and fishes. She stays on the farm and has no leisure. Only the rich peasant women helped by servants or dispensed from field work lead a pleasantly balanced life: they are socially honoured and enjoy greater authority in the home without being crushed by labour. But most of the time rural work reduces woman to the condition of a beast of burden.

The woman shopkeeper, the small-business owner, have always been privileged; they are the only ones since the Middle Ages whose civil capacities have been recognised by the code; women grocers, hoteliers, or tobacconists and dairy women have positions equal to man's; single or widowed, they have a legal identity of their own; married, they possess the same autonomy as their husbands. They are fortunate in working and living in the same place, and the work is not generally too consuming.

The situation of the woman worker, employee, secretary or saleswoman working outside the home is totally different. It is much more difficult to reconcile her job with managing the household (errands, preparation of meals, cleaning, and upkeep of her wardrobe take at least three and a half hours of work a day and six on Sunday; this adds a lot of time to factory or office hours). As for the learned professions, even if women lawyers, doctors and teachers manage to have some help in their households, the home and children still entail responsibilities and cares that are a serious handicap for them. In America, ingenious technology has simplified housework; but the appearance and elegance demanded of the working woman impose another constraint on her; and she maintains responsibility for the house and children. In addition, the woman who seeks her independence through work has far fewer possibilities than her masculine competitors. Her salary is inferior to man's in many fields; her job is less specialised and hence doesn't pay as well as that of a skilled worker; and for the same job, the woman is paid less. Because she is new to the world of males, she has fewer chances of success than they. Men and women alike are loath to work under a woman's orders; they always give more confidence to a man; if being a woman is not a defect, it is at least a pecularity. To 'get ahead', it is useful for a woman to make sure she has a man's support. Men are the ones who take the best places, who hold the most important jobs. It must be emphasised that in economic terms men and women constitute two castes.*

What determines women's present situation is the stubborn survival of the most ancient traditions in the new emerging civilisation. Hasty observers are wrong to think woman is not up to the possibilities offered her today or even to see only dangerous temptations in these possibilities. The truth is that her situation is tenuous, which makes it very difficult for her to adapt. Factories, offices and universities are open to women, but marriage is still considered a more honourable career, exempting her from any other participation in collective life. As in primitive civilisations, the amorous act is a service she has the right to be paid for more or less directly. Everywhere but in the USSR,† the modern woman is allowed to use her body as capital. Prostitution is tolerated,‡

---

* In America, great business fortunes often end up in women's hands: younger than their husbands, women outlive and inherit from them; but they are then older and rarely take the initiative of new investments; they act as usufructuaries rather than owners. It is men who *dispose* of the capital. In any case, these rich privileged women make up a small minority. In America more than in Europe, it is almost impossible for a woman to reach a top position as a lawyer or doctor.

† At least according to official doctrine.

‡ In Anglo-Saxon countries prostitution has never been controlled. Until 1900, American and English common law did not deem it a crime unless it was scandalous and disturbed the peace. Since then, there has been more or less repression, applied with varying degrees of harshness and of success in England and America, whose legislation on this point varies a great deal from one state to the other. In France after a long abolitionist campaign, the 13 April 1946 law ordered brothels to be closed and the fight against procurement to be reinforced: 'Considering that the existence of these brothels is incompatible with the essential principles of human dignity and the role granted to woman in modern society . . .' Prostitution nevertheless still continues to be practised. Negative and hypocritical measures are obviously not the way the situation can be modified.

seduction encouraged. And the married woman can legally make her husband support her; in addition, she is cloaked in much greater social dignity than the unmarried woman. Social customs are far from granting her sexual possibilities on a par with those of the single male, in particular, the unwed mother is an object of scandal, as motherhood is more or less forbidden to her. How could the Cinderella myth not retain its validity? Everything still encourages the girl to expect fortune and happiness from a 'Prince Charming' instead of attempting the difficult and uncertain conquest alone. For example, she can hope to attain a higher caste through him, a miracle her whole life's work will not bring her. But such a hope is harmful because it divides her strength and interests;* this split is perhaps the most serious handicap for woman. Parents still raise their daughters for marriage rather than promoting their personal development; and the daughter sees so many advantages that she desires it herself; the result is that she is often less specialised, less solidly trained than her brothers, she is less totally committed to her profession; as such, she is doomed to remain inferior in it; and the vicious circle is knotted: this inferiority reinforces her desire to find a husband. Every benefit always has a burden; but if the burden is too heavy, the benefit is no more than a servitude; for most workers today, work is a thankless task: for woman, the chore is not offset by a concrete conquest of her social dignity, freedom of behaviour and economic autonomy; it is understandable that many women workers and employees see no more than an obligation in the right to work from which marriage would deliver them. However, because she has become conscious of self and can emancipate herself from marriage through work, a woman no longer accepts her subjection docilely. What she would hope for is to reconcile family life and profession, something that does not require exhausting acrobatics. Even then, as long as the temptations of facility remain – from the economic inequality that favours certain individuals and the woman's right to sell herself to one of these privileged people – she needs to expend a greater moral effort than the male to choose the path of independence. It has not been well enough understood that temptation is also an obstacle, and even one of the most dangerous. It is amplified here by a mystification since there will be one winner out of the thousands in the lucky marriage lottery. Today's period invites, even obliges women to work; but it lures

---

*Cf. Philip Wylie, *Generation of Vipers*.

them with an idyllic and delightful paradise: it raises up the happy few far above those still riveted to this earthly world.

Men's economic privilege, their social value, the prestige of marriage, the usefulness of masculine support – all these encourage women to ardently want to please men. They are on the whole still in a state of serfdom. It follows that woman knows and chooses herself not as she exists for herself but as man defines her. She thus has to be described first as men dream of her since her being-for-men is one of the essential factors of her concrete condition.

Part Three
MYTHS

CHAPTER I

History has shown that men have always held all the concrete powers; from patriarchy's earliest times they have deemed it useful to keep woman in a state of dependence; their codes were set up against her; she was thus concretely established as the Other. This condition served males' economic interests; but it also suited their ontological and moral ambitions. Once the subject attempts to assert himself, the Other, who limits and denies him, is nonetheless necessary for him: he attains himself only through the reality that he is not. That is why man's life is never plenitude and rest, it is lack and movement, it is combat. Facing himself, man encounters Nature; he has a hold on it, he tries to appropriate it for himself. But it cannot satisfy him. Either it realises itself as a purely abstract opposition – it is an obstacle and remains foreign – or it passively submits to man's desire and allows itself to be assimilated by him; he possesses it only in consuming it, that is, in destroying it. In both cases, he remains alone; he is alone when touching a stone, alone when digesting a piece of fruit. The other is present only if the other is himself present to himself: that is, true alterity is a consciousness separated from my own and identical to it. It is the existence of other men that wrests each man from his immanence and enables him to accomplish the truth of his being, to accomplish himself as transcendence, as flight towards the object, as a project. But this foreign freedom, which confirms my freedom, also enters into conflict with it: this is the tragedy of the unhappy consciousness; each consciousness seeks to posit itself alone as sovereign subject. Each one tries to accomplish itself by reducing the other to slavery. But in work and fear the slave experiences himself as essential, and by a dialectical reversal the master appears the inessential one. The conflict can be overcome by the free recognition of each individual in the other, each one positing both itself and the other as object and as subject in a reciprocal movement. But friendship and generosity, which accomplish this recognition of freedoms concretely, are not easy virtues;

they are undoubtedly man's highest accomplishment; this is where he is in his truth: but this truth is a struggle endlessly begun, endlessly abolished; it demands that man surpass himself at each instant. Put into other words, man attains an authentically moral attitude when he renounces *being* in order to assume his existence; through this conversion he also renounces all possession, because possession is a way of searching for being; but the conversion by which he attains true wisdom is never finished, it has to be made ceaselessly, it demands constant effort. So much so that, unable to accomplish himself in solitude, man is ceaselessly in jeopardy in his relations with his peers: his life is a difficult enterprise whose success is never assured.

But he does not like difficulty; he is afraid of danger. He has contradictory aspirations to both life and rest, existence and being; he knows very well that 'a restless spirit' is the ransom for his development, that his distance from the object is the ransom for his being present to himself; but he dreams of restfulness in restlessness and of an opaque plenitude that his consciousness would nevertheless still inhabit. This embodied dream is, precisely, woman; she is the perfect intermediary between nature that is foreign to man and the peer who is too identical to him.*[1] She pits neither the hostile silence of nature nor the hard demand of a reciprocal recognition against him; by a unique privilege she is a consciousness and yet it seems possible to possess her in the flesh. Thanks to her, there is a way to escape the inexorable dialectic of the master and the slave that springs from the reciprocity of freedoms.

It has been pointed out that there were not at first free women whom the males then enslaved and that the sexual division has never founded a division into castes. Assimilating the woman to the slave is a mistake; among slaves there were women, but free women have always existed, that is, women invested with religious and social dignity: they accepted man's sovereignty, and he did not feel threatened by a revolt that could transform him in turn into an object. Woman thus emerged as the inessential who never returned to the essential, as the absolute Other, without reciprocity. All the creation myths express this conviction that is precious to the male, for example, the Genesis legend, which, through Christianity, has spanned Western civilisation. Eve was not formed at the same time

---

* 'Woman is not the useless repetition of man but the enchanted space where the living alliance of man and nature occurs. If she disappeared, men would be alone, foreigners without passports in a glacial world. She is earth itself carried to life's summit, the earth become sensitive and joyful; and without her, for man, earth is mute and dead,' wrote Michel Carrouges in 'Woman's Powers', *Cahiers du Sud*, no. 292 (1948).

as man; she was not made either from a different substance or from the same clay that Adam was modelled from: she was drawn from the first male's flank. Even her birth was not autonomous; God did not spontaneously choose to create her for herself and to be directly worshipped in turn: he destined her for man; he gave her to Adam to save him from loneliness, her spouse is her origin and her finality; she is his complement in the inessential mode. Thus, she appears a privileged prey. She is nature raised to the transparency of consciousness, she is a naturally submissive consciousness. And therein lies the marvellous hope that man has often placed in woman: he hopes to accomplish himself as being through carnally possessing a being while making himself confirmed in his freedom by a docile freedom. No man would consent to being a woman, but all want there to be women. 'Thank God for creating woman.' 'Nature is good because it gave men woman.' In these and other similar phrases, man once more asserts arrogantly and naively that his presence in this world is an inevitable fact and a right, that of woman is a simple accident – but a fortunate one. Appearing as the Other, woman appears at the same time as a plenitude of being by opposition to the nothingness of existence that man experiences in itself; the Other, posited as object in the subject's eyes, is posited as in-itself, thus as being. Woman embodies positively the lack the existent carries in his heart, and man hopes to realise himself by finding himself through her.

But she has not represented for him the only incarnation of the Other, and she has not always had the same importance throughout history. In various periods, she has been eclipsed by other idols. When the city or the state devours the citizen, he is no longer in any position to deal with his personal destiny. Dedicated to the state, the Spartan woman has a higher station than that of other Greek women. But she is not transfigured by any masculine dream. The cult of the chief, be it Napoleon, Mussolini or Hitler, excludes any other. In military dictatorships and totalitarian regimes, woman is no longer a privileged object. It is understandable that woman is divinised in a country that is rich and where the citizens are uncertain about what meaning to give to their lives: this is what is happening in America. In contrast, socialist ideologies, which call for the assimilation of all human beings, reject the notion that any human category be object or idol, now and for the future: in the authentically democratic society that Marx heralded, there is no place for the Other. Few men, however, correspond exactly to the soldier or the militant that they have chosen to be; as long as these men remain individuals, woman retains a singular value in their eyes. I have seen letters written by German soldiers to French prostitutes in which, in spite of Nazism, the tradition of sentimentality proved to be naively alive. Communist writers like Aragon in France and Vittorini in Italy give a front row place in their works to woman as lover and mother. Perhaps the myth of woman will be phased out one day: the more women assert themselves as human beings, the more the marvellous quality of Other dies in them. But today it still exists in the hearts of all men.

Any myth implies a Subject who projects its hopes and fears of a transcendent heaven. Not positing themselves as Subject, women have not created the virile myth that would reflect their projects; they have neither religion nor poetry that belongs to them alone: they still dream through men's dreams. They worship the gods made by males. And males have shaped the great virile figures for their own exaltation: Hercules, Prometheus, Parsifal; in the destiny of these heroes, woman has merely a secondary role. Undoubtedly, there are stylised images of man as he is in his relations with woman: father, seducer, husband, the jealous one, the good son, the bad son; but men are the ones who have established them, and they have not attained the dignity of myth; they are barely more than clichés, while woman is exclusively defined in her relation to man. The asymmetry of the two categories, male and female, can be seen in the unilateral constitution of sexual myths. Woman is sometimes designated as 'sex'; it is she who is the flesh, its delights and its dangers. That for woman it is man who is sexed and carnal is a truth that has never been proclaimed because there is no one to proclaim it. The representation of the world as the world itself is the work of men; they describe it from a point of view that is their own and that they confound with the absolute truth.

It is always difficult to describe a myth; it does not lend itself to being grasped or defined; it haunts consciousnesses without ever being posited opposite them as a fixed object. The object fluctuates so much and is so contradictory that its unity is not at first discerned: Delilah and Judith, Aspasia and Lucretia, Pandora and Athena, woman is both Eve and the Virgin Mary. She is an idol, a servant, source of life, power of darkness; she is the elementary silence of truth, she is artifice, gossip and lies; she is the medicine woman and witch; she is man's prey; she is his downfall, she is everything he is not and wants to have, his negation and his raison d'être.

'To be a woman,' says Kierkegaard, 'is something so strange, so confused and so complicated that no one predicate can express it, and the multiple predicates that might be used contradict each other in such a way that only a woman could put up with it.'*² This comes from being considered not positively, as she is for herself: but negatively, such as she appears to man. Because if there are other *Others* than the woman, she is still always defined as Other. And her ambiguity is that of the very idea of Other: it is that of the human condition as defined in its relation with the Other. It has already been said that the Other is Evil; but as it is necessary for the Good, it reverts to the Good; through the Other I accede to the Whole, but it separates me from the Whole; it is the door to infinity and the measure of my finitude. And this is why woman embodies no set concept; through her the passage from hope to failure, hatred to love, good to bad, bad to good takes place ceaselessly. However she is considered, it is this ambivalence that is the most striking.

Man seeks the Other in woman as Nature and as his peer. But Nature inspires ambivalent feelings in man, as has been seen. He exploits it but it crushes him; he is born from and he dies in it; it is the source of his being and the kingdom he bends to his will; it is a material envelope in which the soul is held prisoner, and it is the supreme reality; it is contingency and Idea, finitude and totality; it is that which opposes Spirit and himself. Both ally and enemy, it appears as the dark chaos from which life springs forth, as this very life, and as the beyond it reaches for: woman embodies nature as Mother, Spouse and Idea; these figures are sometimes confounded and sometimes in opposition, and each has a double face.

Man sinks his roots in Nature; he was engendered, like animals and plants; he is well aware that he exists only inasmuch as he lives. But since the coming of patriarchy, life in man's eyes has taken on a dual aspect: it is consciousness, will, transcendence, it is intellect; and it is matter, passivity, immanence, it is flesh. Aeschylus, Aristotle and Hippocrates proclaimed that on earth as on Mount Olympus it is the male principle that is the true creator: form, number and movement come from him; Demeter makes corn multiply but the origin of corn and its truth are in Zeus; woman's fertility is considered merely a passive virtue. She is earth and man seed, she is water and he is fire. Creation has often been imagined as a marriage of fire and water; hot humidity gives birth to living beings; the Sun is the spouse of the Sea; Sun and Fire are male divinities; and the Sea is one of the most universally widespread maternal

* *Stages on Life's Way.*

symbols. Inert, water submits to the flamboyant rays that fertilise it. Likewise, the still earth, furrowed by the labourer's toil, receives the seeds in its rows. But its role is necessary: it is the soil that nourishes the seed, shelters it and provides its substance. Man thus continued to worship fertility goddesses, even once the Great Mother was dethroned;* he owes his harvests, herds and prosperity to Cybele. He owes her his very life. He exalts water and fire equally. 'Glory to the sea! Glory to its waves encircled by sacred fire! Glory to the wave! Glory to the fire! Glory to the strange adventure,' wrote Goethe in *Faust, Part Two*. He venerated earth: 'The matron Clay', as Blake called it. An Indian prophet advised his disciples not to dig up the earth because 'it is a sin to hurt or cut, to tear our common mother in agricultural works . . . Do I take a knife to drive into my mother's breast? . . . Do I mutilate her flesh so as to reach her bones? . . . How could I dare to cut my mother's hair?' In central India the Baidya also thought that it was a sin to 'rip the breast of their earth mother with the plough'. Inversely, Aeschylus says of Oedipus that he 'dared to sow the sacred furrow where he was formed'. Sophocles spoke of 'paternal furrows' and of the 'labourer, master of a remote field that he visited only once during the sowing'. The beloved in an Egyptian song declares: 'I am the earth!' In Islamic texts, woman is called 'field . . . grapevine'. In one of his hymns, St Francis of Assisi speaks of 'our sister, the earth, our mother, who preserves and cares for us, who produces the most varied fruits with many-coloured flowers and with grass'. Michelet, taking mud baths in Acqui, exclaims: 'Dear common mother! We are one. I come from you, I return to you!' And there are even periods of vitalistic romanticism that affirm the triumph of Life over Spirit: so the earth's and woman's magic fertility appear to be even more marvellous than the male's concerted works; so the man dreams of once again losing himself in maternal darkness to find the true sources of his being. The mother is the root driven into the depths of the cosmos that taps its vital juices; she is the fountain from which springs forth sweet water that is also mother's milk, a warm spring, a mud formed of earth and water, rich in regenerating forces.[†]

* 'Of Gaea sing I, Mother firm of all, the eldest one, who feedeth life on earth, whichever walk on land or swim the seas, or fly,' says a Homeric hymn. Aeschylus also glorifies the earth that 'gives birth to all beings, nourishes them, and then receives the fertilised germ once again.'

[†] 'To the letter the woman is Isis, fertile nature. She is the river and the bed of the river, the root and the rose, the earth and the cherry tree, the vine and the grape' (M. Carrouges, 'Woman's Powers').

But man's revolt against his carnal condition is more general; he considers himself a fallen god: his curse is to have fallen from a luminous and orderly heaven into the chaotic obscurity of the mother's womb. He desires to see himself in this fire, this active and pure breath, and it is woman who imprisons him in the mud of the earth. He would like himself to be as necessary as pure Idea, as One, All, absolute Spirit; and he finds himself enclosed in a limited body, in a place and time he did not choose, to which he was not called, useless, awkward, absurd. His very being is carnal contingence to which he is subjected in his isolation, in his unjustifiable gratuitousness. It also dooms him to death. This quivering gelatine that forms in the womb (the womb, secret and sealed like a tomb) is too reminiscent of the soft viscosity of carrion for him not to turn away from it with a shudder. Wherever life is in the process of being made – germination and fermentation – it provokes disgust because it is being made only when it is being unmade; the viscous glandular embryo opens the cycle that ends in the rotting of death. Horrified by death's gratuitousness, man is horrified at having been engendered; he would like to rescind his animal attachments; because of his birth, murderous Nature has a grip on him. For the primitives, childbirth is surrounded by strict taboos; in particular, the placenta must be carefully burned or thrown into the sea, because whoever might get hold of it would hold the newborn's fate in his hands; this envelope in which the foetus is formed is the sign of its dependence; in annihilating it, the individual is able to detach himself from the living magma and to realise himself as an autonomous being. The stain of childbirth falls back on the mother. Leviticus and all the ancient codes impose purification rites on the new mother; and often in the countryside the postpartum ceremony maintains that tradition. Everyone knows that young boys and girls and men feel a spontaneous embarrassment, one often camouflaged by sneering, at seeing a pregnant woman's stomach or the swollen breasts of the wet nurse. In Dupuytren's museums, the curious contemplate the wax embryos and the preserved foetuses with the morbid interest they would show in a defiled grave. Notwithstanding all the respect that society surrounds it with, the function of gestation inspires spontaneous repulsion. And while the little boy in early childhood remains sensually attached to the mother's flesh, when he grows up, when he is socialised and becomes aware of his individual existence, this flesh frightens him; he wants to ignore it and to see his mother as institution only; if he wants to think of her as pure and chaste, it is less from amorous jealousy than from the refusal to acknowledge her as a body. An adolescent boy becomes embarrassed, blushes if he meets his mother, sisters or women in his family when he is out with his friends: their presence recalls the regions of immanence from which he wants to escape; she reveals the roots that he wants to pull himself away from. The boy's irritation when his mother kisses and caresses him has the same significance; he gives up his family, mother, and mother's breast. He would like to have emerged, like Athena, into the adult world, armed from head to toe, invulnerable.* Being conceived and born is the curse weighing on his destiny, the blemish on his being. And it is the warning of his death. The cult of germination has always been associated with the cult of the dead. Mother Earth engulfs the bones of its children within it. Women – the Parcae and Moirai – weave human destiny; but they also cut the threads. In most folk representations, Death is woman and women mourn the dead because death is their work.†

Thus, Mother Earth has a face of darkness: she is chaos, where everything comes from and must return to one day; she is Nothingness. The many aspects of the world that the day uncovers commingle in the night: night of spirit locked up in the generality and opacity of matter, night of sleep and nothing. At the heart of the sea, it is night: woman is the *Mare tenebrarum* dreaded by ancient navigators; it is night in the bowels of the earth. Man is threatened with being engulfed in this night, the reverse of fertility, and it horrifies him. He aspires to the sky, to light, to sunny heights, to the pure and crystal-clear cold of blue; and underfoot is a moist, hot and dark gulf ready to swallow him; many legends have the hero falling and for ever lost in maternal darkness: a cave, an abyss, hell.

But once again ambivalence is at work here: while germination is always associated with death, death is also associated with fertility. Detested death is like a new birth and so it is blessed. The dead hero, like Osiris is resurrected every springtime, and he is regenerated by a new birth. Man's supreme hope, says Jung, 'is that the dark waters of death become the waters of life, that death and its cold embrace are the mother's lap, just as the sea, while engulfing the sun, re-births in the depths.'‡ The theme of the burial of the sun god within the sea and its

---

* See our study on Montherlant, the epitome of this attitude, a little further on.

† Demeter is the archetype of the *mater dolorosa*. But other goddesses – Ishtar and Artemis – are cruel. Kali is holding a blood-filled skull. 'The heads of your newly killed sons hang from your neck like a necklace ... Your figure is beautiful like rain clouds, your feet are soiled with blood,' says a Hindu poem.

‡ *Metamorphoses of the Libido and its Symbols.*

dazzling re-emergence is common to many mythologies. And man wants to live but he also hopes for rest, sleep, for nothingness. He does not wish for immortality for himself, and thus he can learn to love death. 'Inorganic matter is the mother's breast,' Nietzsche wrote. 'Being delivered from life means becoming real again, completing oneself. Anyone who understands that would consider returning to unfeeling dust as a holiday.' Chaucer puts this prayer into the mouth of an old man who cannot die:

> 'Thus restless I my wretched way must make
> And on the ground, which is my mother's gate,
> I knock with my staff early, aye, and late
> And cry: "Oh dear mother, let me in!"'

Man wants to assert his individual existence and proudly rest on his 'essential difference', but he also wants to break the barriers of the self and commingle with water, earth, night, Nothingness, with the Whole. Woman who condemns man to finitude also enables him to surpass his own limits: that is where the equivocal magic surrounding her comes from.

In all civilisations and still today, she inspires horror in man: the horror of his own carnal contingence that he projects on her. The girl who has not yet gone through puberty does not pose a threat; she is not the object of any taboo and has no sacred characteristics. In many primitive societies her sex even seems innocent: erotic games between boys and girls are allowed in childhood. Woman becomes impure the day she might be able to procreate. In primitive societies the strict taboos concerning girls on the day of their first period have often been described; even in Egypt, where the woman is treated with particular respect, she remains confined during her whole menstrual period.* She is often put on a rooftop or relegated to a shack on the outskirts of the town; she can be neither seen nor touched: what's more, she must not even touch herself with her own hand; for peoples that practise daily flea removal, she is given a stick with which she is able to scratch herself; she must not touch food with her fingers; sometimes she is strictly forbidden to eat; in other cases, her mother

---

* The difference between mystical and mythical beliefs and individuals' lived convictions is apparent in the following fact: Lévi-Strauss points out that 'young Winnebago Indians visit their mistresses and take advantage of the privacy of the prescribed isolation of these women during their menstrual period'.

and sister are permitted to feed her with an instrument; but all objects that come in contact with her during this period must be burned. After this first test, the menstrual taboos are a little less strict, but they remain harsh. In particular, in Leviticus: 'And if a woman have an issue, and her issue in her flesh be blood, she shall be put apart seven days: and whosoever toucheth her shall be unclean until the even. And every thing that she lieth upon in her separation shall be unclean: every thing also that she sitteth upon shall be unclean. And whosoever toucheth her bed shall wash his clothes, and bathe himself in water, and be unclean until the even.' This text is perfectly symmetrical with one concerning gonorrhoea-provoked impurity in man. And the purifying sacrifice is identical in the two cases. Seven days after she has been purified of her flow, two turtledoves or two young pigeons have to be brought to the sacrificer, who offers them to the Eternal. Even in matriarchal societies, the virtues connected to menstruation are ambivalent. On one hand, it brings social activities to a halt, destroys the vital force, withers flowers, causes fruit to fall; but it also has beneficial effects: menses are used in love philtres, in remedies, and in particular in healing cuts and bruises. Still today, when some Indians go off to fight spectral monsters haunting their rivers, they place a fibre wad filled with menstrual blood on the bow of their boat: its emanations are harmful to their supernatural enemies. In some Greek cities, young girls pay homage to the Temple of Astarte by wearing linens stained by their first menstrual blood. But since patriarchy, only harmful powers have been attributed to the bizarre liquor flowing from the feminine sex. Pliny in his *Natural History* says: 'The menstruating woman spoils harvests, devastates gardens, kills seeds, makes fruit fall, kills bees; if she touches the wine, it turns to vinegar; milk sours . . .'

An old English poet expresses the same thought:

> *Oh! Menstruating woman, thou'rt a fiend*
> *From whom all nature should be closely screened!*

These beliefs have been vigorously perpetuated right up to today. In 1878, a member of the British Medical Association wrote in the *British Medical Journal*: 'It is an indisputable fact that meat goes bad when touched by menstruating women.' He said that he personally knew of two cases of hams spoiling in such circumstances. In the refineries of the North at the beginning of this century, women were prohibited by

law from going into the factory when they were afflicted by what the
Anglo-Saxons call the 'curse' because the sugar turned black. And in
Saigon, women are not employed in opium factories: because of their
periods, the opium goes bad and becomes bitter. These beliefs survive
in many areas of the French countryside. Any cook knows how impossible it is to make mayonnaise if she is indisposed or simply in the presence of another woman who is indisposed. In Anjou, recently, an old
gardener who had stocked that year's cider harvest in the cellar wrote
to the master of the house: 'Don't let the young women of the household and their female guests go through the cellar on certain days of
the month: they would prevent the cider from fermenting.' When the
cook heard about this letter, she shrugged her shoulders: 'That never
prevented cider from fermenting,' she said, 'it is only bad for bacon
fat: it cannot be salted in the presence of an indisposed woman; it
would rot.'*

Putting this repulsion in the same category as that provoked by
blood is most inadequate: more imbued with the mysterious mana
that is both life and death than anything else, blood, of course, is in
itself a sacred element. But menstrual blood's baleful powers are more
particular. Menstrual blood embodies the essence of femininity, which
is why its flow endangers woman herself, whose mana is thus materialised. During the Chaga initiation rites, girls are urged to carefully
conceal their menstrual blood. 'Do not show it to your mother, for
she would die! Do not show it to your age-mates, for there may be a
wicked one among them, who will take away the cloth with which
you have cleaned yourself, and you will be barren in your marriage.
Do not show it to a bad woman, who will take the cloth to place it
in the top of her hut . . . with the result that you cannot bear children.
Do not throw the cloth on the path or in the bush. A wicked person
might do evil things with it. Bury it in the ground. Protect the blood
from the gaze of your father, brothers and sisters. It is a sin to let

---

*A doctor from the Cher region told me that women in that situation are banned from
going into the mushroom beds. The question as to whether there is any basis for these
preconceived ideas is still discussed today. Dr Binet's only fact supporting them is an
observation by Schink (cited by Vignes). Schink supposedly saw flowers wilt in an indisposed servant's hands; yeast cakes made by this woman supposedly rose only three
centimetres instead of the five they usually rose. In any case, these facts are pretty feeble
and poorly established when considering the importance and universality of the obviously mystical beliefs they come from.

them see it.'* For the Aleuts, if the father sees his daughter during her first menstruation, she could go blind or deaf. It is thought that during this period woman is possessed by a spirit and invested with a dangerous power. Some primitives believe that the flow is provoked by snakebite, as woman has suspicious affinities with snakes and lizards; it is supposed to be similar to crawling animals' venom. Leviticus compares it to gonorrhoea; the bleeding feminine sex is not only a wound but a suspicious sore. And Vigny associates the notion of soiling with illness: 'Woman, sick child and impure twelve times.' The result of interior alchemic troubles, the periodic haemorrhage woman suffers from is bizarrely aligned with the moon's cycle: the moon also has dangerous whims.†* Woman is part of the formidable workings that order the course of planets and the sun, she is prey to the cosmic forces that determine the destiny of stars and tides, while men are subjected to their worrisome radiation. But it is especially striking that menstrual blood's effects are linked to the ideas of cream going sour, mayonnaise that does not take, fermentation and decomposition; it is also claimed that it is apt to cause fragile objects to break; to spring violin and harp strings; but above all it influences organic substances that are midway between matter and life; this is less because it is blood than because it emanates from genital organs; even without knowing its exact function, people understood it to be linked to the germination of life: ignorant of the existence of the ovary, the ancients saw in menstruation the complement of the sperm. In fact, it is not this blood that makes woman impure, but rather, this blood is a manifestation of her impurity; it appears when the woman can be fertile; when it disappears, she becomes sterile again; it pours forth from this womb where the foetus is made. The horror of feminine fertility that man experiences is expressed through it.

The strictest taboo of all concerning woman in her impure state is the prohibition of sexual intercourse with her. Leviticus condemns man to seven days of impurity if he transgresses this rule. The Laws of Manu are even

† Quoted in Lévi-Strauss, *The Elementary Structures of Kinship*.

† The moon is a source of fertility; it is seen as the 'master of women'; it is often believed that the moon, in the form of a man or a snake, couples with women. The snake is an epiphany of the moon; it moults and regenerates, it is immortal, it is a power that distributes fertility and science; it watches over holy sources, the Tree of Life, the Fountain of Youth, and so on., but it is also the snake that takes immortality away from man. It is said that it couples with women. Persian and rabbinical traditions claim that menstruation is due to the first woman's intercourse with the snake.

harsher: 'The wisdom, energy, strength, and vitality of a man coming near a woman stained by menstrual excretions perish definitively.' Priests ordered fifty days of penance for men who had sexual relations during menstruation. Since the feminine principle is then considered as reaching its highest power, it is feared that it would triumph over the male principle in intimate contact. Less specifically, man shies away from finding the mother's feared essence in the woman he possesses; he works at dissociating these two aspects of femininity: that explains why incest is prohibited by exogamy or more modern forms and is a universal law; that explains why man distances himself from woman sexually when she is particularly destined for her reproductive role: during her period, when she is pregnant, or when she is nursing. Not only does the Oedipus complex – whose description, incidentally, has to be revised – not contradict this attitude: on the contrary, it even implies it. Man guards himself against woman to the extent that she is the confused source of the world and disorder become organic.

However, this representation of woman also allows the society that has been separated from the cosmos and the gods to remain in communication with them. She still assures the fertility of the fields for the Bedouins and the Iroquois; in ancient Greece, she heard subterranean voices; she understood the language of the wind and the trees: she was the Pythia, Sibyl and prophetess. The dead and the gods spoke through her mouth. Still today, she has these powers of divination: she is medium, palmist, card reader, clairvoyant, inspired; she hears voices and has visions. When men feel the need to delve into vegetable and animal life – like Antaeus, who touched earth to recoup his strength – they call upon woman. Throughout the Greek and Roman rationalist civilisations, chthonian cults subsisted. They could usually be found on the periphery of official religious life; they even ended up, as in Eleusis, taking the form of mysteries: they had the opposite meaning of sun cults, where man asserted his will for separation and spirituality; but they complemented them; man sought to overcome his solitude by ecstasy: that is the goal of mysteries, orgies and bacchanals. In the world reconquered by males, the male god Dionysus usurped Ishtar's and Astarte's magic and wild virtues; but yet it was women who went wild over his image: the maenads, thyades and bacchantes led men to religious drunkenness and sacred madness. The role of sacred prostitution is similar: both to unleash and to channel the powers of fertility. Even today, popular holidays are exemplified by outbreaks of eroticism; woman is not just an object of pleasure but a means of reaching this *hubris* in which the individual surpasses himself. 'What a being possesses in the deepest part of himself, what is lost and tragic, the "blinding wonder" can no longer be found anywhere but on a bed,' wrote Georges Bataille.

In sexual release, man in his lover's embrace seeks to lose himself in the infinite mystery of the flesh. But it has already been seen that his normal sexuality, on the contrary, dissociates Mother from Wife. He finds the mysterious alchemies of life repugnant, while his own life is nourished and enchanted by the tasty fruits of the earth; he desires to appropriate them for himself; he covets Venus freshly emerging from the waters. Woman first discovers herself in patriarchy as wife since the supreme creator is male. Before being the mother of humankind, Eve is Adam's companion; she was given to man for him to possess and fertilise as he possesses and fertilises the soil; and through her, he makes his kingdom out of all nature. Man does not merely seek in the sexual act subjective and ephemeral pleasure. He wants to conquer, take and possess; to have a woman is to conquer her; he penetrates her as the ploughshare in the furrows; he makes her his as he makes his the earth he is working: he ploughs, he plants, he sows: these images are as old as writing; from antiquity to today a thousand examples can be mentioned: 'Woman is like the field and man like the seeds,' say the Laws of Manu. In an André Masson drawing there is a man, shovel in hand, tilling the garden of a feminine sex organ.* Woman is her husband's prey, his property.

Man's hesitation between fear and desire, between the terror of being possessed by uncontrollable forces and the will to overcome them, is grippingly reflected in the virginity myths. Dreaded or desired or even demanded by the male, virginity is the highest form of the feminine mystery; this aspect is simultaneously the most troubling and the most fascinating. Depending on whether man feels crushed by the powers encircling him or arrogantly believes he is able to make them his, he refuses or demands that his wife be delivered to him as a virgin. In the most primitive societies, where woman's power is exalted, it is fear that dominates; woman has to be deflowered the night before the wedding. Marco Polo asserted that for the Tibetans, 'none of them wanted to take a virgin girl as wife'. A rational explanation has some-times been given for this refusal: man does not want a wife who has not yet aroused masculine desires. Al-Bakri, the Arab geographer, speaking of the Slavic peoples, notes that 'if a man gets married and

* Rabelais called the male sex organ 'the worker of nature'. The religious and histor-ical origin of the phallus-ploughshare–woman-furrow association has already been pointed out.

finds that his wife is a virgin, he says: "If you were worth something, men would have loved you and one of them would have taken your virginity."' He then chases her out and repudiates her. It is also claimed that some primitives refuse to marry a woman unless she has already given birth, thus proving her fertility. But the real reasons for the very widespread deflowering customs are mystical. Certain peoples imagine the presence of a serpent in the vagina that would bite the spouse during the breaking of the hymen; terrifying virtues are given to virginal blood, linked to menstrual blood and capable of ruining the male's vigour. These images express the idea that the feminine principle is so powerful and threatening because it is intact.* Sometimes the deflowering issue is not raised; for example, Malinowski describes an indigenous population in which, because sexual games are allowed from childhood on, girls are never virgins. Sometimes, the mother, older sister or some other matron systematically deflowers the girl and throughout her childhood widens the vaginal opening. Deflowering can also be carried out by women during puberty using a stick, a bone or a stone and this is not considered a surgical operation. In other tribes, the girl at puberty is subjected to savage initiation rites: men drag her out of the village and deflower her with instruments or by raping her. Giving over virgins to passersby is one of the most common rites; either these strangers are not thought to be sensitive to this mana dangerous only for the tribes' males or it does not matter what evils befall them. Even more often, the priest, medicine man, boss or head of the tribe deflowers the fiancée the night before the wedding; on the Malabar coast, the Brahmans have to carry out this act, apparently without joy, for which they demand high wages. All holy objects are known to be dangerous for the outsider, but consecrated individuals can handle them without risk; that explains why priests and chiefs are able to tame the malefic forces against which the spouse has to protect himself. In Rome all that was left of these customs was a symbolic ceremony: the fiancée was seated on a stone Priapus phallus, with the double aim of increasing her fertility and absorbing the over-powerful and therefore harmful fluids within her. The husband defends himself in yet another way: he himself deflowers the virgin but during ceremonies that render him invulnerable at this critical juncture; for example he does it in front of the whole village

---

* The power in combat attributed to the virgin comes from this: the Valkyries and Joan of Arc, for example.

with a stick or bone. In Samoa, he uses his finger covered in a white cloth and distributes bloodstained shreds to the spectators. There is also the case of the man allowed to deflower his wife normally but he has to wait three days to ejaculate in her so that the generating seed is not soiled by hymenal blood.

In a classic reversal in the area of sacred things, virginal blood in less primitive societies is a propitious symbol. There are still villages in France where the bloody sheet is displayed to parents and friends the morning after the wedding. In the patriarchal regime, man became woman's master; and the same characteristics that are frightening in animals or untamed elements become precious qualities for the owner who knows how to subdue them. Man took the ardour of the wild horse and the violence of lightning and waterfalls as the instruments of his prosperity. Therefore, he wants to annex woman to him with all her riches intact. The order of virtue imposed on the girl certainly obeys rational motives: like chastity for the wife, the fiancée's inno-cence is necessary to protect the father from incurring any risk of bequeathing his goods to a foreign child. But woman's virginity is demanded more imperiously when man considers the wife as his personal property. First of all, the idea of possession is always impos-sible to realise positively; the truth is that one never has anything or anyone; one attempts to accomplish it in a negative way; the surest way to assert that a good is mine is to prevent another from using it. And then nothing seems as desirable to man as what has never belonged to any other human: thus conquest is a unique and absolute event. Virgin land has always fascinated explorers; alpinists kill them-selves every year attempting to assault an untouched mountain or even trying to open up a new trail; and the curious risk their lives to descend underground to the bottom of unprobed caves. An object that men have already mastered has become a tool; cut off from its natural bonds, it loses its deepest attributes; there is more promise in the wild water of torrents than in that of public fountains. A virgin body has the freshness of secret springs, the morning bloom of a closed corolla, the orient of the pearl the sun has never yet caressed. Cave, temple, sanctuary or secret garden: like the child, man is fasci-nated by these shadowy and closed places never yet touched by animating consciousness, waiting to be lent a soul: it seems to him that he in fact created what he is the only one to grasp and pene-trate. Moreover, every desire pursues the aim of consuming the desired object, entailing its destruction. By breaking the hymen, man possesses the feminine body more intimately than by a penetration that leaves it intact; in this irreversible operation, he unequivocally makes it a passive object, asserting his hold on it. This exactly expresses the meaning in the legend of the knight who hacks his way through thorny bushes to pick a rose never before inhaled; not only does he uncover it, but he breaks its stem, thereby conquering it. The image is so clear that in popular language, 'taking a woman's flower' means destroying her virginity, giving the origin of the word 'deflowering'.

But virginity only has this sexual attraction when allied with youth; otherwise, its mystery reverts to disquiet. Many men today are sexually repulsed by older virgins; psychological reasons alone do not explain why 'old maids' are regarded as bitter and mean matrons. The curse is in their very flesh, this flesh that is object for no subject, that no desire has made desirable, that has bloomed and wilted without finding a place in the world of men; turned away from her destination, the old maid becomes an eccentric object, as troubling as the incommunicable thinking of a madman. Of a forty-year-old, still beautiful, woman presumed to be a virgin, I heard a man say with great vulgarity: 'It's full of cobwebs in there . . .' It is true that deserted and unused cellars and attics are full of unsavoury mystery; they fill up with ghosts; abandoned by humanity, houses become the dwellings of spirits. If feminine virginity has not been consecrated to a god, it is easily then thought to imply marriage with the devil. Virgins that men have not subjugated, old women who have escaped their power, are more easily looked upon as witches than other women; as woman's destiny is to be doomed to another, if she does not submit to a man's yoke, she is available for the devil's.

Exorcised by deflowering rites or on the contrary purified by her virginity, the wife could thus be desirable prey. Taking her gives the lover all the riches of life he desires to possess. She is all the fauna, all the earthly flora: gazelle, doe, lilies and roses, downy peaches, fragrant raspberries; she is precious stones, mother-of-pearl, agate, pearls, silk, the blue of the sky, the freshness of springs, air, flame, earth and water. All the poets of East and West have metamorphosed woman's body into flowers, fruits and birds. Here again, throughout antiquity, the Middle Ages and the modern period, it would be necessary to quote a thick anthology. The Song of Songs is well known, in which the male loved one says to the female loved one:

> *Thou hast doves' eyes . . .*
> *thy hair is as a flock of goats . . .*
> *Thy teeth are like a flock of sheep that are even shorn . . .*
> *thy temples are like a piece of a pomegranate . . .*
> *Thy two breasts are like two young roes that are twins . . .*
> *Honey and milk are under thy tongue.*

In *Arcanum 17*, André Breton took up this eternal song: 'Melusina at the instant of her second scream: she sprang up off her globeless haunches, her belly is the whole August harvest, her torso bursts into fireworks from her arched back, modelled on a swallow's two wings, her breasts are two ermines caught in their own scream, blinding because they are lit by scorching coals of their howling mouth. And her arms are the soul of streams that sing and float perfumes.'[4]

Man finds shining stars and the moody moon, sunlight, and the darkness of caves on woman; wildflowers from hedgerows and the garden's proud rose are also woman. Nymphs, dryads, mermaids, water sprites and fairies haunt the countryside, the woods, lakes, seas and moors. This animism is profoundly anchored in men. For the sailor, the sea is a dangerous woman, perfidious and difficult to conquer but that he cherishes by dint of taming it. Proud, rebellious, virginal and wicked, the mountain is woman for the mountain climber who wants to take it, even at risk of life. It is often said that these comparisons manifest sexual sublimation; rather, they express an affinity between woman and the elements as primal as sexuality itself. Man expects more from possessing woman than the satisfaction of an instinct; she is the special object through which he subjugates Nature. Other objects can also play this role. Sometimes it is on young boys' bodies that man seeks the sand of beaches, the velvet of nights, the fragrance of honeysuckle. But sexual penetration is not the only way to realise this carnal appropriation of the earth. In his novel *To a God Unknown*, Steinbeck shows a man who chooses a mossy rock as mediator between him and nature; in *The Cat*, Colette describes a young husband who settles his love on his favourite female cat because this gentle wild animal enables him to have a grasp on the sensual universe that his woman companion cannot give. The Other can be embodied in the sea and the mountain just as well as in the woman; they provide man with the same passive and unexpected resistance that allows him to accomplish himself; they are a refusal to conquer, a prey to possess.

If the sea and the mountain are woman, it is because woman is also the sea and the mountain for the lover.*

But not just any woman can play the role of mediator between man and the world; man is not satisfied with finding sexual organs complementary to his own in his partner. She must embody the wondrous blossoming of life while concealing its mysterious disturbances at the same time. First of all, she has to have youth and health, for man cannot be enraptured in his embrace of a living thing unless he forgets that all life is inhabited by death. And he desires still more: that his beloved be beautiful. The ideal of feminine beauty is variable; but some requirements remain constant; one of them is that since woman is destined to be possessed, her body has to provide the inert and passive qualities of an object. Virile beauty is the body's adaptation to active functions such as strength, agility, flexibility, and the manifestation of a transcendence animating a flesh that must never collapse into itself. The only symmetry to be found in the feminine ideal is in Sparta, Fascist Italy and Nazi Germany, societies that destined woman for the state and not for the individual and that considered her exclusively as mother, with no place for eroticism. But when woman is delivered to the male as his property, he claims that her flesh be presented in its pure facticity. Her body is grasped not as the emanation of a subjectivity but as a thing weighted in its immanence; this body must not radiate to the rest of the world, it must not promise anything but itself: its desire has to be stopped. The most naive form of

* The sentence by Samivel, quoted by Bachelard in *Earth and Reveries of Will*, is telling: 'I had ceased, little by little, to regard the mountains crouching in a circle at my feet as foes to vanquish, as female to trample underfoot, or trophies to provide myself and others proof of my own worth.' The mountain / woman ambivalence comes across in the common idea of 'foes to vanquish', and 'proof of my own worth'.

This reciprocity can be seen, for example, in these two poems by Senghor:[5]

> Naked woman, dark woman
> Ripe fruit with firm flesh, dark raptures of black wine,
> Mouth that gives music to my mouth
> Savanna of clear horizons, savanna quivering to the fervent caress
> Of the East Wind . . .

And:

> Oho! Congo, lying on your bed of forests, queen of subdued Africa.
> May the mountain phalluses hold high your pavilion
> For you are woman by my head, by my tongue,
> You are woman by my belly.

this requirement is the Hottentot ideal of the steatopygous Venus, as the buttocks are the part of the body with the fewest nerve endings, where the flesh appears as a given without purpose. The taste of people from the East for fleshy women is similar; they love the absurd luxury of this fatty proliferation that is not enlivened by any project, that has no other meaning than to be there.* Even in civilisations of a more subtle sensibility, where notions of form and harmony come into play, breasts and buttocks were prized objects because of the gratuitousness and contingency of their development. Customs and fashions were often applied to cut the feminine body from its transcendence: the Chinese woman with bound feet could barely walk, the Hollywood star's painted nails deprived her of her hands; high heels, corsets, hoops, farthingales and crinolines were meant less to accentuate the woman's body's curves than to increase the body's powerlessness. Weighted down by fat or on the contrary so diaphanous that any effort is forbidden to it, paralysed by uncomfortable clothes and rites of propriety, the body thus appeared to man as his thing. Makeup and jewels were also used for this petrification of the body and face. The function of dress and ornaments is highly complex; for some primitives, it had a sacred character; but its most usual role was to complete woman's metamorphosis into an idol. An equivocal idol: man wanted her erotic, for her beauty to be part of that of flowers and fruits; but she also had to be smooth, hard, eternal like a stone. The role of dress is both to link the body more closely to and to wrest it away from nature, to give a necessarily set artifice to palpitating life. Woman was turned into plant, panther, diamond or mother-of-pearl by mingling flowers, furs, precious stones, shells and feathers on her body; she perfumed herself so as to smell of roses and lilies: but feathers, silk, pearls and perfumes also worked to hide the animal rawness from its flesh and odour. She painted her mouth and her cheeks to acquire a mask's immobile solidity; her gaze was imprisoned in the thickness of kohl and mascara, it was no longer anything but her eyes' shimmering ornamentation; braided, curled or sculpted, her hair lost its troublesome vegetal mystery. In the embellished woman, Nature was present but

* 'Hottentot women, in whom steatopygia is neither as developed nor as consistent as in Bushman women, think this body type is aesthetically pleasing and starting in childhood massage their daughters' buttocks to develop them. Likewise, the artificial fattening of women, a real stuffing by two means, immobility and abundant ingestion of specific foods, especially milk, is found in various regions of Africa. It is still practised by rich Arab and Jewish city dwellers in Algeria, Tunisia and Morocco' (Luquet, 'Les Vénus des cavernes', *Journal de psychologie*, 1934).

captive, shaped by a human will in accordance with man's desire. Woman was even more desirable when nature was shown off to full advantage and more rigorously subjugated: the sophisticated woman has always been the ideal erotic object. And the taste for a more natural beauty is often a specious form of sophistication. Rémy de Gourmont wanted women's hair to be loose, free as the streams and prairie grass: but it is on Veronica Lake's hair that the waves of water and wheat could be caressed, not on a mop of hair totally left to nature. The younger and healthier a woman is and the more her new and glossy body seems destined for eternal freshness, the less useful is artifice; but the carnal weakness of this prey that man takes and its ominous deterioration always have to be hidden from him. It is also because he fears contingent destiny, because he dreams her immutable and necessary, that man looks for the idea's exactitude on woman's face, body and legs. In primitive people, this idea is the perfection of the popular type: a thick-lipped race with a flat nose forged a thick-lipped Venus with a flat nose; later on, the canons of a more complex aesthetics would be applied to women. But in any case, the more the traits and proportions of a woman seemed contrived, the more she delighted the heart of man because she seemed to escape the metamorphosis of natural things. The result is this strange paradox that by desiring to grasp nature, but transfigured, in woman, man destines her to artifice. She is not only physis but just as much antiphysis; and not only in the civilisation of electric permanents, hair waxing, latex girdles, but also in the country of African lip-disk women, in China and everywhere on earth. Swift denounced this mystification in his famous ode to Celia; he railed against the coquette's paraphernalia, pointing out with disgust her body's animal servitudes; he was doubly wrong to become indignant; because man wants woman at the same time to be animal and plant and that she hide behind a fabricated armature; he loves her emerging from the waves and from a high-fashion house, naked and dressed, naked beneath her clothes, exactly as he finds her in the human universe. The city dweller seeks animality in woman; but for the young peasant doing his military service, the brothel embodies the magic of the city. Woman is field and pasture but also Babylonia.

However, here is the first lie, the first betrayal of woman: of life itself, which, even clothed in the most attractive forms, is still inhabited by the ferments of old age and death. The very use man makes of her destroys her most precious qualities; weighed down by childbirth, she loses her sexual attraction; even sterile, the passage of time is enough to alter her charms. Disabled, ugly or old, woman repels. She is said to be withered, faded, like a plant. Man's decrepitude is obviously also frightful; but normal man does not experience other men as flesh; he has only an abstract solidarity with these autonomous and foreign bodies. It is on woman's body, this body meant for him, that man significantly feels the flesh's deterioration. It is through the male's hostile eyes that Villon's 'once beautiful courtesan' contemplates her body's degradation. Old and ugly women not only are objects without assets but also provoke hatred mixed with fear. They embody the disturbing figure of Mother, while the charms of the Wife have faded away.

But even the Wife was a dangerous prey. Demeter survives in Venus emerging from the waters, fresh foam, the blonde harvest; appropriating woman for himself through the pleasure he derives from her, man awakens in her the suspicious powers of fertility; it is the same organ he penetrates that produces the child. This explains why man in all societies is protected against the feminine sex's threats by so many taboos. There is no reciprocity as woman has nothing to fear from the male; his sex is considered secular, profane. The phallus can be raised to the dignity of a god: there is no element of terror in worshipping it, and in daily life woman does not have to be defended against it mystically; it is simply propitious for her. It also has to be pointed out that in many matriarchies, sexuality is very free; but this is only during woman's childhood, in her early youth, when coitus is not linked to the idea of generation. Malinowski is surprised that young people who sleep together freely in the 'house of the unmarried' show off their love lives so readily; the explanation is that an unmarried daughter is considered unable to bear a child and the sexual act is merely a quiet and ordinary pleasure. On the contrary, once married, her spouse cannot give her any public sign of affection, nor touch her, and any allusion to their intimate relations is sacrilegious; she then has to be part of the formidable essence of mother, and coitus becomes a sacred act. From then on it is surrounded by taboos and precautions. Intercourse is forbidden when cultivating the earth, sowing and planting: in this case fertilising forces necessary for the harvests' prosperity cannot be wasted in inter-individual relations; respect for powers associated with fertility enjoins such relations to be economised. But on most occasions, chastity protects the spouse's virility; it is demanded when man goes off fishing or hunting and above all when he is preparing for war; in the union with woman, the male principle weakens and he has to avoid intercourse whenever he needs the totality of his forces. It has been wondered if the horror man feels for woman comes from that inspired by sexuality in general, or vice versa. We have seen that in Leviticus, in particular, wet dreams are considered a stain even though woman has nothing to do with them. And in our modern societies, masturbation is considered a danger and a sin; many children and young boys who indulge in it suffer terrible anxieties because of it. Society and parents above all make solitary pleasure a vice; but more than one young boy has been spontaneously frightened by his first ejaculations: blood or sperm, any flow of one's own substance seems worrying; it is one's life, one's mana, that is running out. However, even if subjectively man can go through erotic experiences where woman is not present, she is objectively involved in his sexuality: as Plato said in the myth of the androgynes, the male organism presupposes the woman's. He discovers woman in discovering his own sex, even if she is not given to him in flesh and blood, nor in image; and inversely, woman is fearsome inasmuch as she embodies sexuality. The immanent and transcendent aspects of living experience can never be separated: what I fear or desire is always an avatar of my own existence, but nothing comes to me except through what is not my self. The nonself is involved in wet dreams, in erection, and if not in the precise figure of woman, at least in Nature and Life: the individual feels possessed by a foreign magic. Likewise, his ambivalence towards women is seen in his attitude towards his own sex organ; he is proud, he laughs about it, he is embarrassed by it. The little boy defiantly compares his penis with his friends'; his first erection fills him with pride and frightens him at the same time. The adult man looks upon his sex organ as a symbol of transcendence and power; he is as proud of it as a muscle and at the same time as a magical grace: it is a freedom rich with the whole contingence of the given, a given freely desired; this is the contradictory aspect that enchants him; but he suspects the trap in it; this sex organ by which he claims to assert himself does not obey him; full of unassuaged desires, arising unexpectedly, sometimes relieving itself in dreams, it manifests a suspicious and capricious vitality. Man claims to make Spirit triumph over Life, activity over passivity; his consciousness keeps nature at a distance, his will shapes it, but in the figure of his sex organ he rediscovers life, nature and passivity in himself. 'The sexual parts are the real centre of the will and the opposite pole is the brain,' wrote Schopenhauer. What he called will is attachment to life, which is suffering and death, while the brain is thought that separates itself from life while representing it: sexual shame according to him is what we feel about our stupid carnal stubbornness. Even if the pessimism of his theories is rejected, he is right to see the expression of man's duality in the sex–brain opposition. As a subject he posits the

world, and, remaining outside the universe he posits, he makes himself
the lord of it; if he grasps himself as flesh, as sex, he is no longer
autonomous consciousness, transparent freedom: he is engaged in the
world, a limited and perishable object; and it is undoubtedly true that
the generative act goes beyond the body's limits: but he constitutes them
at the very same instant. The penis, father of generations, is symmetrical to the maternal womb; grown from a fattened germ in woman's
womb, man is the bearer of germs himself, and by this seed that gives
life, it is also his own life that is disavowed. 'The birth of children is the
death of parents,' said Hegel. Ejaculation is the promise of death, it
affirms the species over the individual; the existence of the sex organ
and its activity negate the subject's proud singularity. The sex organ is
a focus of scandal because of this contestation of spirit over life. Man
exalts the phallus in that he grasps it as transcendence and activity, as a
means of appropriation of the other; but he is ashamed when he sees
in it only passive flesh through which he is the plaything of Life's obscure
forces. This shame is often disguised as irony. The sex organ of others
draws laughter easily; but because the erection looks like a planned movement and yet is undergone, it often looks ridiculous; and the simple
mention of genital organs provokes glee. Malinowski says that for the
wild people among whom he lived, just mentioning the word for these
'shameful parts' made them laugh uncontrollably; many crude or saucy
jokes are not much more than rudimentary puns on these words. For
some primitive peoples, during the days devoted to weeding out gardens,
women had the right to brutally rape any stranger that dared to come
into the village; attacking him all together, they often left him half-dead:
the tribesmen laughed at this exploit; by this rape, the victim was constituted as passive and dependent flesh; he was possessed by the women
and through them by their husbands, while in normal coitus man wants
to affirm himself as possessor.

But this is where he will experience the ambiguity of his carnal condition most obviously. He takes pride in his sexuality only to the extent
that it is a means of appropriation of the Other: and this dream of
possession only ends in failure. In authentic possession, the other as
such is abolished, it is consumed and destroyed: only the sultan of *The
Thousand and One Nights* has the power to cut off his mistresses' heads
when dawn withdraws them from his bed; woman survives man's
embraces and she is thus able to escape from him; as soon as he opens
his arms, his prey once again becomes foreign to him; here she is new,
intact, completely ready to be possessed by a new lover in just as

ephemeral a way. One of the male's dreams is to 'brand' woman so that she remains his for ever; but even the most arrogant male knows only too well that he will never leave her anything more than memories, and the most passionate images are cold compared with real sensation. A whole literature has denounced this failure. It is made objective in the woman, who is called fickle and treacherous because her body destines her to man in general and not to a particular man. Her betrayal is even more perfidious: it is she who turns the lover into a prey. Only a body can touch another body; the male masters the desired flesh only by becoming flesh himself; Eve is given to Adam for him to accomplish his transcendence in her and she draws him into the night of immanence; the mother forges the obscure wrapping for her son from which he now wants to escape, while the mistress encloses him in this opaque clay through the vertigo of pleasure. He wanted to possess: but here he is, possessed himself. Odour, damp, fatigue, boredom: a whole literature describes this dreary passion of a consciousness become flesh. Desire often contains an element of disgust and returns to disgust when it is assuaged. 'Post coitum homo animal triste.'[6] 'The flesh is sad.' And yet, man has not even found definitive reassurance in his lover's arms. Soon his desire is reborn; and often it is the desire not only for woman in general but for this specific woman. She wields a singularly troubling power. Because in his own body man does not feel the sexual need except as a general one similar to hunger or thirst without a particular object, the bond that links him to this specific feminine body is therefore forged by the Other. The link is mysterious like the foul and fertile womb of his roots, a sort of passive force: it is magic. The hackneyed vocabulary of serialised novels where the woman is described as an enchantress or a mermaid who fascinates man and bewitches him reflects the oldest and most universal of myths. Woman is devoted to magic. Magic, said Alain, is the spirit lurking in things; an action is magic when it emanates from a passivity instead of being produced by an agent; men have always considered woman precisely as the immanence of the given; if she produces harvests and children, it is not because she wills it; she is not subject, transcendence, or creative power, but an object charged with fluids. In societies where man worships such mysteries, woman, because of these qualities, is associated with religion and venerated as a priestess; but when he struggles to make society triumph over nature, reason over life, will over inert fact, woman is regarded as a sorceress. The difference between the priest and the magician is well known: the former dominates and directs the forces he has mastered in keeping with the gods and laws, for the good of the community, on behalf of all its members, while the magician operates outside society, against the gods and laws, according to his own passions. But woman is not fully integrated into the world of men; as other, she counters them; it is natural for her to use the strengths she possesses, not to spread the hold of transcendence across the community of men and into the future, but, being separate and opposed, to draw males into the solitude of separation, into the darkness of immanence. She is the mermaid whose songs dashed the sailors against the rocks; she is Circe, who turned her lovers into animals, the water sprite that attracted the fisherman to the depths of the pools. The man captivated by her spell loses his will, his project, his future; he is no longer a citizen but flesh, slave to his desires, he is crossed out of the community, enclosed in the instant, thrown passively from torture to pleasure; the perverse magician pits passion against duty, the present against the unity of time, she keeps the traveller far from home, she spreads forgetfulness. In attempting to appropriate the Other, man must remain himself; but with the failure of impossible possession, he tries to become this other with whom he fails to unite; so he alienates himself, he loses himself, he drinks the potion that turns him into a stranger to himself, he falls to the bottom of deadly and roiling waters. The Mother dooms her son to death in giving him life; the woman lover draws her lover into relinquishing life and giving himself up to the supreme sleep. This link between Love and Death was pathetically illuminated in the Tristan legend, but it has a more primary truth. Born of flesh, man accomplishes himself in love as flesh, and flesh is destined to the grave. The alliance between Woman and Death is thus confirmed; the great reaper is the inverted figure of corn-growing fertility. But it is also the frightening wife whose skeleton appears under deceitful and tender flesh.*

What man thus cherishes and detests first in woman, lover as well as mother, is the fixed image of her animal destiny, the life essential to her existence, but that condemns her to finitude and death. From the day of birth, man begins to die: this is the truth that the mother embodies. In procreating, he guarantees the species against himself: this is what he learns in his wife's arms; in arousal and in pleasure, even before engendering, he forgets his singular self. Should he try to differentiate them, he still finds in both one fact alone, that of his carnal condition. He wants to accom-

---

* For example in Prévert's ballet, *Le Rendez-vous* and in Cocteau's *Le Jeune homme et la mort* (*The Young Man and Death*), Death is represented as a beloved young girl.

plish it: he venerates his mother; he desires his mistress. But at the same time, he rebels against them in disgust, in fear.

An important text where we will find a synthesis of almost all these myths is Jean-Richard Bloch's *A Night in Kurdistan*,[7] in which he describes young Saad's embraces of a much older but still beautiful woman during the plundering of a city:

The night abolished the contours of things and feelings alike. He was no longer clasping a woman to him. He was at last nearing the end of an interminable voyage that had been pursued since the beginning of the world. Little by little he dissolved into an immensity that cradled him round without shape or end. All women were confused into one giant land, folded upon him, suave as desire burning in summer . . .

He, meanwhile, recognised with a fearful admiration the power that is enclosed within woman, the long, stretched, satin thighs, the knees like two ivory hills. When he traced the polished arch of the back, from the waist to the shoulders, he seemed to be feeling the vault that supports the world. But the belly ceaselessly drew him, a tender and elastic ocean, whence all life is born, and whither it returns, asylum of asylums, with its tides, horizons, illimitable surfaces.

Then he was seized with a rage to pierce that delightful envelope, and at last win to the very source of all this beauty. A simultaneous urge wrapped them one within the other. The woman now only lived to be cleaved by the share, to open to him her vitals, to gorge herself with the humours of the beloved. Their ecstasy was murderous. They came together as if with stabbing daggers . . .

He, man, the isolated, the separated, the cut off, was going to gush forth from out of his own substance, he, the first, would come forth from his fleshly prison and at last go free, matter and soul, into the universal matrix. To him was reserved the unheard of happiness of overpassing the limits of the creature, of dissolving into the one exaltation object and subject, question and answer, of annexing to being all that is not being, and of embracing, in an unextinguishable river, the empire of the unattainable . . .

But each coming and going of the bow awoke, in the precious instrument it held at its mercy, vibrations more and more piercing. Suddenly, a last spasm unloosed him from the zenith, and cast him down again to earth, to the mire.

As the woman's desire is not quenched, she imprisons her lover between her legs and he feels in spite of himself his desire returning: she is thus an enemy power who grabs his virility and while possessing her again, he bites her throat so deeply that he kills her. The cycle from mother to woman-lover to death meanders to a complex close.

There are many possible attitudes here for man depending on which aspect of the carnal drama he stresses. If a man does not think life is unique, if he is not concerned with his singular destiny, if he does not fear death, he will joyously accept his animality. For Muslims, woman is reduced to a state of abjection because of the feudal structure of society that does not allow recourse to the state against the family and because of religion, expressing this civilisation's warrior ideal, that has destined man to death and stripped woman of her magic: What would anyone on earth, ready to dive without any hesitation into the voluptuous orgies of the Muhammadan paradise, fear? Man can thus enjoy woman without worrying or having to defend himself against himself or her. *The Thousand and One Nights* looks on her as a source of creamy delights much like fruits, jams, rich desserts and perfumed oils. This sensual benevolence can be found today among many Mediterranean peoples: replete, not seeking immortality, the man from the Midi grasps Nature in its luxurious aspect, relishes women; by tradition he scorns them sufficiently so as not to grasp them as individuals: between the enjoyment of their bodies and that of sand and water there is not much difference for him; he does not experience the horror of the flesh either in them or in himself. In *Conversations in Sicily*, Vittorini recounts, with quiet amazement, having discovered the naked body of woman at the age of seven. Greek and Roman rationalist thought confirms this spontaneous attitude. Greek optimist philosophy went beyond Pythagorean Manichaeism; the inferior is subordinate to the superior and as such is useful to him: these harmonious ideologies show no hostility whatsoever to the flesh. Turned towards the heaven of Ideas or in towards the City or State, the individual thinking himself as nous or as a citizen thinks he has overcome his animal condition: whether he gives himself up to voluptuousness or practises asceticism, a woman firmly integrated into male society is only of secondary importance. It is true that rationalism has never triumphed totally and erotic experience remains ambivalent in these civilisations: rites, mythologies and literature are testimony to that. But femininity's attractions and dangers manifest themselves there only in attenuated form. Christianity is what drapes woman anew with frightening pres-

tige: one of the forms the rending of the unhappy consciousness takes for man is fear of the other sex. The Christian is separated from himself; the division of body and soul, of life and spirit, is consumed: original sin turns the body into the soul's enemy; all carnal links appear bad.*
Man can be saved by being redeemed by Christ and turning towards the celestial kingdom; but at the beginning, he is no more than rottenness; his birth dooms him not only to death but to damnation; divine grace can open heaven to him, but all avatars of his natural existence are cursed. Evil is an absolute reality; and flesh is sin. Since woman never stopped being Other, of course, male and female are never reciprocally considered flesh: the flesh for the Christian male is the enemy Other and is not distinguished from woman. The temptations of the earth, sex and the devil are incarnated in her. All the Church Fathers emphasise the fact that she led Adam to sin. Once again, Tertullian has to be quoted: 'Woman! You are the devil's gateway. You have convinced the one the devil did not dare to confront directly. It is your fault that God's Son had to die. You should always dress in mourning and rags.' All Christian literature endeavours to exacerbate man's disgust for woman. Tertullian defines her as 'Templum aedificatum super cloacam'.[8] St Augustine points out in horror the proximity of the sexual and excretory organs: 'Inter faeces et urinam nascimur'.[9] Christianity's repugnance for the feminine body is such that it consents to doom its God to an ignominious death but spares him the stain of birth: the Council of Ephesus in the Eastern Church and the Lateran Council in the West affirm the virgin birth of Christ. The first Church Fathers – Origen, Tertullian and Jerome – thought that Mary had given birth in blood and filth like other women; but the opinions of St Ambrose and St Augustine prevail. The Virgin's womb remained closed. Since the Middle Ages, the fact of having a body was considered an ignominy for woman. Science itself was paralysed for a long time by this disgust. Linnaeus, in his treatise on nature, dismissed the study of woman's genital organs as 'abominable'. Des Laurens, the French doctor, dared to ask how 'this divine animal full of reason and judgement that is called man can be attracted by these obscene parts of the woman, tainted by humours and placed

---

* Until the end of the twelfth century theologians – except St Anselm – thought, according to St Augustine's doctrine, that original sin was implied in the law of generation itself. 'Concupiscence is a vice . . . human flesh born from it is sinful flesh,' wrote St Augustine. And St Thomas: 'Since sin, the union of the sexes, when accompanied by concupiscence, transmits original sin to the child.'

shamefully at the lowest part of the trunk'. Many other influences come
into play along with Christian thought; and even this has more than one
side; but in the puritan world, for example, hatred of the flesh still obtains;
it is expressed in *Light in August*, by Faulkner; the hero's first sexual experiences are highly traumatic. In all literature, a young man's first sexual
intercourse is often upsetting to the point of inducing vomiting; and if,
in truth, such a reaction is very rare, it is not by chance that it is so often
described. In puritan Anglo-Saxon countries in particular, woman stirs
up more or less avowed terror in most adolescents and many men. This
is quite true in France. Michel Leiris wrote in *L'âge d'homme (Manhood)*:
'I have a tendency to consider the feminine organ as a dirty thing or a
wound, not less attractive though for that, but dangerous in itself, as
everything that is bloody, viscous, and contaminated.' The idea of venereal maladies expresses these frights; woman is feared not because she
gives these illnesses; it is the illnesses that seem abominable because they
come from woman: I have been told about young men who thought
that too frequent sexual relations caused gonorrhoea. People also readily
think that sexual intercourse makes man lose his muscular strength and
mental lucidity, consumes his phosphorus and coarsens his sensitivity.
The same dangers threaten in masturbation; and for moral reasons society
considers it even more harmful than the normal sexual function.
Legitimate marriage and the desire to have children guard against the
evil spells of eroticism. I have already said that the Other is implied in
all sexual acts; and its face is usually woman's. Man experiences his own
flesh's passivity the most strongly in front of her. Woman is vampire,
ghoul, eater, drinker; her sex organ feeds gluttonously on the male sex
organ. Some psychoanalysts have tried to give these imaginings scientific foundations: the pleasure woman derives from coitus is supposed
to come from the fact that she symbolically castrates the male and appropriates his sex organ. But it would seem that these theories themselves
need to be psychoanalysed and that the doctors who invented them have
projected on to them ancestral terrors.*

The source of these terrors is that in the Other, beyond any annexation, alterity remains. In patriarchal societies, woman kept many of the
disquieting virtues she held in primitive societies. That explains why she
is never left to Nature, why she is surrounded by taboos, purified by
rites, and placed under the control of priests; man is taught never to
approach her in her original nudity but through ceremonies and sacra-

* We demonstrated that the myth of the praying mantis has no biological basis.

ments that wrest her from the earth and flesh and metamorphose her into a human creature: thus the magic she possesses is channelled as lightning has been since the invention of lightning rods and electric power plants. It is even possible to use her in the group's interests: this is another phase of the oscillatory movement defining man's relationship to his female. He loves her because she is his, he fears her because she remains other; but it is as the feared other that he seeks to make her most deeply his: this is what will lead him to raise her to the dignity of a person and to recognise her as his peer.

★

Feminine magic was profoundly domesticated in the patriarchal family. Woman gave society the opportunity to integrate cosmic forces into it. In his work, *Mitra-Varuna*, Dumézil points out that in India as in Rome, masculine power asserts itself in two ways: in Varuna and Romulus, and in the Gandharvas and the Luperci, it is aggression, abduction, disorder and hubris; thus, woman is the being to be ravished and violated; if the ravished Sabine women are sterile, they are whipped with goatskin straps, compensating for violence with more violence. But on the contrary, Mitra, Numa, the Brahmin women and the Flamen wives represent reasonable law and order in the city: so the woman is bound to her husband by a ritualistic marriage, and she collaborates with him to ensure his domination over all female forces of nature; in Rome, the *flamen dialis* resigns from his position if his wife dies. In Egypt as well, Isis, having lost her supreme power as Mother Goddess, remains nonetheless generous, smiling, benevolent and obedient, Osiris's magnificent spouse. But when woman is thus man's partner, his complement, his other half, she is necessarily endowed with a consciousness and a soul; he could not so deeply depend on a being who would not participate in the human essence. It has already been seen that the Laws of Manu promised a legal wife the same paradise as her spouse. The more the male becomes individualised and claims his individuality, the more he will recognise an individual and a freedom in his companion. The Oriental man who is unconcerned with his own destiny is satisfied with a female who is his pleasure object; but Western man's dream, once elevated to consciousness of the singularity of his being, is to be recognised by a foreign and docile freedom. The Greek man cannot find the peer he wants in a woman who was prisoner of the gynaeceum: so he confers his love on male companions whose flesh, like his own, is endowed with a consciousness and a freedom, or else he gives his love to hetaeras whose independence, culture and spirit made them near equals. But when circumstances permit, the wife best satisfies man's demands. The Roman citizen recognises a person in the matron; in Cornelia or in Arria, he possesses his double. Paradoxically, it was Christianity that was to proclaim the equality of man and woman on a certain level. Christianity detests the flesh in her; if she rejects the flesh, she is, like him, a creature of God, redeemed by the Saviour: here she can take her place beside males, among those souls guaranteed celestial happiness. Men and women are God's servants, almost as asexual as the angels, who, together with the help of grace, reject earth's temptations. If she agrees to renounce her animality, woman, from the very fact that she incarnated sin, will also be the most radiant incarnation of the triumph of the elect who have conquered sin.* Of course, the divine Saviour who brings about Redemption is male; but humanity must cooperate in its own salvation, and perversely it will be called upon to manifest its submissive good will in its most humiliated figure. Christ is God; but it is a woman, the Virgin Mother, who reigns over all human creatures. Yet only marginal sects restore the great goddesses' ancient privileges to the woman. The Church expresses and serves a patriarchal civilisation where it is befitting for woman to remain annexed to man. As his docile servant she will also be a blessed saint. Thus the image of the most perfected woman, propitious to men, lies at the heart of the Middle Ages: the face of the Mother of Christ is encircled in glory. She is the inverse figure of the sinner Eve; she crushes the serpent under her foot; she is the mediator of salvation, as Eve was of damnation.

It is as Mother that the woman was held in awe; through motherhood she has to be transfigured and subjugated. Mary's virginity has above all a negative value: she by whom the flesh has been redeemed is not carnal; she has been neither touched nor possessed. Neither was the Asiatic Great Mother assumed to have a husband: she had engendered the world and reigned over it alone; she could be lascivious by impulse, but her greatness as Mother was not diminished by imposed wifely servitudes. Likewise, Mary never experienced the stain connected with sexuality. Related to the woman warrior Minerva, she is an ivory tower, a citadel, an impregnable fortress. Like most Christian saints, the priestesses of antiquity were virgins: the woman devoted to good should be devoted with the splendour of her strength intact; she must conserve the principle of her femininity in its unbroken wholeness. One rejects in Mary her character as

* This explains the privileged place she holds, for example, in Claudel's work (see pp. 245–254).

wife in order to more fully exalt in her the Woman-Mother. But she will be glorified only by accepting the subservient role assigned to her. 'I am the handmaiden of the Lord.' For the first time in the history of humanity, the mother kneels before her son; she freely recognises her inferiority. The supreme masculine victory is consummated in the worship of Mary: it is the rehabilitation of woman by the achievement of her defeat. Ishtar, Astarte and Cybele were cruel, capricious and lustful; they were powerful; the source of death as well as life, in giving birth to men, they made them their slaves. With Christianity, life and death now depended on God alone, so man, born of the maternal breast, escaped it for ever, and the earth gets only his bones; his soul's destiny is played out in regions where the mother's powers are abolished; the sacrament of baptism makes ceremonies that burned or drowned the placenta insignificant. There is no longer any place on earth for magic: God alone is king. Nature is originally bad, but powerless when countered with grace. Motherhood as a natural phenomenon confers no power. If woman wishes to overcome the original stain in herself, her only alternative is to bow before God, whose will subordinates her to man. And by this submission she can assume a new role in masculine mythology. As a vassal she will be honoured, whereas she was beaten and trampled underfoot when she saw herself as dominator or as long as she did not explicitly abdicate. She loses none of her primitive attributes; but their meanings change; from calamitous they become auspicious; black magic turns to white magic. As a servant, woman is entitled to the most splendid apotheosis.

And since she was subjugated as Mother, she will, as Mother first, be cherished and respected. Of the two ancient faces of maternity, modern man recognises only the benevolent one. Limited in time and space, possessing only one body and one finite life, man is but one individual in the middle of a foreign Nature and History. Limited like him, similarly inhabited by the spirit, woman belongs to Nature, she is traversed by the infinite current of Life, she thus appears as the mediator between the individual and the cosmos. When the mother image became reassuring and holy, it is understandable that the man turned to her with love. Lost in nature, he seeks escape, but separated from her, he aspires to return to her. Solidly settled in the family and society, in accord with laws and customs, the mother is the very incarnation of the Good: the nature in which she participates becomes Good; she is no longer the spirit's enemy; and though she remains mysterious, it is a smiling mystery, like Leonardo da Vinci's Madonnas. Man does not wish to be woman, but he longs to wrap himself in everything that is, including this woman he is not: in worshipping his mother, he tries to appropriate her riches so foreign to him. To recognise himself as his mother's son, he recognises the mother in him, integrating femininity in so far as it is a connection to the earth, to life and to the past. In Vittorini's *Conversations in Sicily*, that is what the hero goes to find from his mother: his native land, its scents and its fruits, his childhood, his ancestors' past, traditions and the roots from which his individual existence separated him. It is this very rootedness that exalts man's pride in going beyond; he likes to admire himself breaking away from his mother's arms to leave for adventure, the future, and war; this departure would be less moving if there were no one to try to hold him back: it would look like an accident, not a hard-won victory. And he also likes to know that these arms are ready to welcome him back. After the tension of action, the hero likes to taste the restfulness of immanence again, by his mother's side: she is refuge, slumber; by her hand's caress he sinks into the bosom of nature, lets himself be lulled by the vast flow of life as peacefully as in the womb or in the tomb. And if tradition has him die calling on his mother, it is because under the maternal gaze death itself, like birth, is tamed, symmetrical with birth, indissolubly linked with his whole carnal life. The mother remains connected to death as in ancient Parcae mythology; it is she who buries the dead, who mourns. But her role is precisely to integrate death with life, with society, with the good. And so the cult of 'heroic mothers' is systematically encouraged: if society persuades mothers to surrender their sons to death, then it thinks it can claim the right to assassinate them. Because of the mother's hold on her sons, it is useful for society to make her part of it: this is why the mother is showered with signs of respect, why she is endowed with all virtues, why a religion is created around her from which it is forbidden to stray under severe risk of sacrilege and blasphemy; she is made the guardian of morality; servant of man, servant of the powers that be, she fondly guides her children along fixed paths. The more resolutely optimistic the collectivity and the more docilely it accepts this loving authority, the more transfigured the mother will be. The American 'Mom' has become the idol described by Philip Wylie in *Generation of Vipers*, because the official American ideology is the most stubbornly optimistic. To glorify the mother is to accept birth, life and death in both their animal and social forms and to proclaim the harmony of nature and society. Auguste Comte makes the woman the divinity of future Humanity because he dreams of achieving this synthesis. But this is also why all rebels assail the figure of the mother; in holding her up to ridicule, they reject the given claims supposedly imposed on them through the female guardian of morals and laws.*[10]

The aura of respect around the Mother and the taboos that surround her repress the hostile disgust that mingles spontaneously with the carnal tenderness she inspires. However, lurking below the surface, the latent horror of motherhood survives. In particular, it is interesting that in France since the Middle Ages, a secondary myth has been forged, freely expressing this repugnance: that of the Mother-in-Law. From fabliau to vaudeville, there are no taboos on man's ridicule of motherhood in general through his wife's mother. He hates the idea that the woman he loves was conceived: the mother-in-law is the clear image of the decrepitude that she doomed her daughter to by giving her life, and her obesity and her wrinkles forecast the obesity and wrinkles that the future so sadly prefigures for the young bride; at her mother's side she is no longer an individual but an example of a species; she is no longer the desired prey or the cherished companion, because her individual

---

* One ought to quote Michel Leiris's poem 'The Mother' in its entirety. Here are some typical passages:

The mother in black, mauve, violet – robber of nights – that's the sorceress whose hidden industry brings you into the world, the one who rocks you, coddles you, coffins you, when she doesn't abandon her curled-up body – one last little toy – into your hands, that lay it nicely into the coffin . . .

The mother – blind statue, fate set up in the middle of the inviolate sanctuary – she's nature caressing you, the wind censing you, the whole world that penetrates you, lifts you sky-high (borne on multiple spires) and rots you. . . .

The mother – young or old, beautiful or ugly, merciful or obstinate – it's the caricature, the monster jealous woman, the fallen Prototype – assuming the Idea (a wrinkled Pythia perched on the tripod of her austere capital letter) – is but a parody of quick, light, iridescent thoughts . . .

The mother – hip round or dry, breast atremble or firm – is the decline promised to all women right from the start, the progressive crumbling of the rock that sparkles beneath the menstrual flood, the slow burying – under the sand of the old desert – of the luxuriant caravan heaped with beauty.

The mother – angel of spying death, of the embracing universe, of the love time's wave throws back – she's the shell with its senseless graphics (a sure sign of poison) to toss into the deep pools, generator of circles for the oblivious waters.

The mother – sombre puddle, eternally in mourning for everything and ourselves – she is the misty pestilence that shimmers and bursts, expanding its great bestial shadow (shame of flesh and milk) bubble by bubble, a stiff veil that a bolt of lightning as yet unborn ought to rend . . .

Will it ever occur to any of these innocent bitches to drag themselves barefoot through the centuries as pardon for this crime: having given birth to us?

existence dissolves into universality. Her individuality is mockingly
contested by generalities, her spirit's autonomy by her being rooted in
the past and in the flesh: this is the derision man objectifies as a grotesque
character; but through the rancour of his laughter, he knows that the
fate of his wife is the same for all human beings; it is his own. In every
country, legends and tales have also personified the cruel side of motherhood in the stepmother. She is the cruel mother who tries to kill Snow
White. The ancient Kali with the necklace of severed heads lives on in
the mean stepmother – Mme Fichini whipping Sophie throughout Mme
de Ségur's books.

Yet behind the sainted Mother crowds the coterie of white witches
who provide man with herbal juices and stars' rays: grandmothers, old
women with kind eyes, good-hearted servants, sisters of charity, nurses
with magical hands, the sort of mistress Verlaine dreamed of:

> Sweet, pensive and dark and surprised at nothing
> And who will at times kiss you on the forehead like a child.

They are ascribed the pure mystery of knotted vines, of fresh water;
they dress and heal wounds; their wisdom is life's silent wisdom, they
understand without words. In their presence man forgets his pride; he
understands the sweetness of yielding and becoming a child, because
between him and her there is no struggle for prestige: he could not resent
the inhuman virtues of nature; and in their devotion, the wise initiates
who care for him recognise they are his servants; he submits to their
benevolent powers because he knows that while submitting to them, he
remains their master. Sisters, childhood girlfriends, pure girls and all
future mothers belong to this blessed troupe. And the wife herself, when
her erotic magic fades, is regarded by many men less as a lover than as
the mother of their children. Once the mother is sanctified and servile,
she can safely be with a woman friend, she being also sanctified and
submissive. To redeem the mother is to redeem the flesh, and thus carnal
union and the wife.

Deprived of her magic weapons by nuptial rites, economically and
socially dependent on her husband, the 'good wife' is man's most
precious treasure. She belongs to him so profoundly that she shares the
same nature with him: 'Ubi tu Gaius, ego Gaia'; she has his name and
his gods and she is his responsibility: he calls her his other half. He takes
pride in his wife as in his home, his land, his flocks and his wealth, and
sometimes even more; through her he displays his power to the rest of

the world: she is his yardstick and his earthly share. For Orientals, a wife should be fat: everyone sees that she is well fed and brings respect to her master.* A Muslim is all the more respected if he possesses a large number of flourishing wives. In bourgeois society, one of woman's assigned roles is *to represent*: her beauty, her charm, her intelligence and her elegance are outward signs of her husband's fortune, as is the body of his car. If he is rich, he covers her with furs and jewels. If he is poorer, he boasts of her moral qualities and her housekeeping talents; most deprived, he feels he owns something earthly if he has a wife to serve him; the hero of *The Taming of the Shrew* summons all his neighbours to show them his authority in taming his wife. A sort of King Candaules resides in all men: he exhibits his wife because he believes she displays his own worth.

But woman does more than flatter man's social vanity; she allows him a more intimate pride; he delights in his domination over her; superimposed on the naturalistic images of the ploughshare cutting furrows are more spiritual symbols concerning the wife as a person; the husband 'forms' his wife not only erotically but also spiritually and intellectually; he educates her, impresses her, puts his imprint on her. One of the daydreams he enjoys is the impregnation of things by his will, shaping their form, penetrating their substance: the woman is par excellence the 'clay in his hands' that passively lets itself be worked and shaped, resistant while yielding, permitting masculine activity to go on. A too-plastic material wears out by its softness; what is precious in woman is that something in her always escapes all embraces; so man is master of a reality that is all the more worthy of being mastered as it surpasses him. She awakens in him a being heretofore ignored whom he recognises with pride as himself; in their safe marital orgies he discovers the splendour of his animality: he is the Male; and woman, correlatively, the female, but this word sometimes takes on the most flattering implications: the female who broods, who nurses, who licks her young, who defends them and who risks her life to save them is an example for humans; with emotion, man demands this patience and devotion from his companion; again it is Nature, but imbued with all of the virtues useful to society, family and the head of the family, virtues he knows how to keep locked in his home. A common desire of children and men is to uncover the secret hidden inside things; but in this, the matter can be deceptive: a doll ripped apart with her stomach outside

* See p. 182.

has no more interiority; the interior of living things is more impenetrable; the female womb is the symbol of immanence, of depth; it delivers its secrets in part as when, for example, pleasure shows on a woman's face, but it also holds them in; man catches life's obscure palpitations in his house without the mystery being destroyed by possession. In the human world, woman transposes the female animal's functions: she maintains life, she reigns over the zones of immanence; she transports the warmth and the intimacy of the womb into the home; she watches over and enlivens the dwelling where the past is kept, where the future is presaged; she engenders the future generation and she nourishes the children already born; thanks to her, the existence that man expends throughout the world by his work and his activity is re-centred by delving into her immanence: when he comes home at night, he is anchored to the earth; the wife assures the days' continuity; whatever risks he faces in the outside world, she guarantees the stability of his meals and sleep; she repairs whatever has been damaged or worn out by activity: she prepares the tired worker's food, she cares for him if he is ill, she mends and washes. And within the conjugal universe that she sets up and perpetuates, she brings in the whole vast world: she lights the fires, puts flowers in vases and domesticates the emanations of sun, water and earth. A bourgeois writer cited by Bebel summarises this ideal in all seriousness as follows: 'Man wants not only someone whose heart beats for him, but whose hand wipes his brow, who radiates peace, order and tranquillity, a silent control over himself and those things he finds when he comes home every day; he wants someone who can spread over everything the indescribable perfume of woman who is the vivifying warmth of home life.'

It is clear how spiritualised the figure of woman became with the birth of Christianity; the beauty, warmth and intimacy that man wishes to grasp through her are no longer tangible qualities; instead of being the summation of the pleasurable quality of things, she becomes their soul; deeper than carnal mystery, her heart holds a secret and pure presence that reflects truth in the world. She is the soul of the house, the family and the home, as well as larger groups: the town, province or nation. Jung observes that cities have always been compared to the Mother because they hold their citizens in their bosoms: this is why Cybele was depicted crowned with towers; for the same reason the term 'mother country' is used and not only because of the nourishing soil; rather, a more subtle reality found its symbol in the woman. In the Old Testament and in the Apocalypse, Jerusalem and Babylon are not only mothers: they are also wives. There are virgin cities and prostitute cities such as Babel and Tyre. France too has been called 'the eldest daughter' of the Church; France and Italy are Latin sisters. Woman's function is not specified, but femininity is, in statues that represent France, Rome and Germany and those on the Place de la Concorde that evoke Strasbourg and Lyon. This assimilation is not only allegoric: it is affectively practised by many men.* Many a traveller would ask woman for the key to the countries he visits: when he holds an Italian or Spanish woman in his arms, he feels he possesses the fragrant essence of Italy or Spain. 'When I come to a new city, the first thing I do is visit a brothel,' said a journalist. If a cinnamon hot chocolate can make Gide discover the whole of Spain, all the more reason kisses from exotic lips will bring to a lover a country with its flora and fauna, its traditions and its culture. Woman is the summation neither of its political institutions nor its economic resources; but she is the incarnation of carnal flesh and mystical mana. From Lamartine's *Graziella* to Loti's novels and Morand's short stories, the foreigner is seen as trying to appropriate the soul of a region through women. Mignon, Sylvie, Mireille, Colomba and Carmen uncover the most intimate truth about Italy, Valois, Provence, Corsica or Andalusia. When the Alsatian Frédérique falls in love with Goethë, the Germans take it as a symbol of Germany's annexation; likewise when Colette Baudoche refuses to marry a German, Barrès sees it as Alsace refusing Germany. He personifies Aigues-Mortes and a whole refined and frivolous civilisation in the sole person of Berenice; she represents the sensibility of the writer himself. Man recognises his own mysterious double in her, she who is the soul of nature, cities and the universe; man's soul is Psyche, a woman.

Psyche has feminine traits in Edgar Allan Poe's 'Ulalume':

---

* It is allegoric in Claudel's shameful recent poem, where Indochina is called 'That yellow girl'; it is affectionate, by contrast, in the verses of the black poet [Guy Tyrolien]:

> Soul of the black country where the elders sleep
> Live and speak
> tonight
> in the uneasy strength along your hollow loins
> Here once, through an alley Titanic,
> Of cypress, I roamed with my Soul –
> Of cypress, with Psyche, my soul . . .
> Thus I pacified Psyche and kissed her . . .
> And I said – 'What is written, sweet sister,
> On the door of this legended tomb?'

> *Here once, through an alley Titanic,*
> *Of cypress, I roamed with my Soul –*
> *Of cypress, with Psyche, my Soul . . .*
> *Thus I pacified Psyche and kissed her . . .*
> *And I said – "What is written, sweet sister,*
> *On the door of this legended tomb?"*

And Mallarmé, at the theatre, in a dialogue with 'a soul, or else our idea' (that is, divinity present in man's spirit) called it 'a most exquisite abnormal lady [*sic*]'.*

> *Thing of harmony, ME, a dream,*
> *Firm, flexible feminine, whose silences lead*
> *To pure acts! . . .*
> *Thing of mystery, ME . . .*[11]

Such is Valéry's way of hailing her. The Christian world substituted less carnal presences for nymphs and fairies; but homes, landscapes, cities and individuals themselves are still haunted by an impalpable femininity.

This truth buried in the night of things also shines in the heavens; perfect immanence, the Soul is at the same time the transcendent, the Idea. Not only cities and nations but also entities and abstract institutions are cloaked in feminine traits: the Church, the Synagogue, the Republic and Humanity are women, as well as Peace, War, Liberty, the Revolution, Victory. Man feminises the ideal that he posits before him as the essential Other, because woman is the tangible figure of alterity; this is why almost all the allegories in language and in iconography are women.† Soul and Idea, woman is also the mediator between them: she is the Grace that leads the Christian to God, she is Beatrice guiding Dante to the beyond, Laura beckoning Petrarch to the highest peaks of poetry. She appears in all doctrines assimilating Nature to Spirit as Harmony, Reason and Truth. Gnostic sects made Wisdom a woman, Sophia; they attributed the world's redemption to her, and even its creation. So woman is no longer flesh, she is glorious body; rather than trying to possess her, men venerate her for her untouched splendour;

---

* Jotted down at the theatre.

† Philology is rather mysterious on this question; all linguists recognise that the distribution of concrete words into gender is purely accidental. Yet in French most entities are feminine: beauty and loyalty, for example. And in German, most imported foreign words, *others*, are feminine: die Bar, for example.

the pale dead of Edgar Allan Poe are as fluid as water, wind or memory; for courtly love, for *les précieux*, and in all of the gallant tradition, woman is no longer an animal creature but rather an ethereal being, a breath, a radiance. Thus it is that the feminine Night's opacity is converted into transparence and obscurity into purity, as in Novalis's texts:

> Thou, Night-inspiration, heavenly Slumber, didst come upon me – the region gently upheaved itself; over it hovered my unbound, newborn spirit. The mound became a cloud of dust – and through the cloud I saw the glorified face of my beloved.
>
> Dost thou also take a pleasure in us, dark Night? . . . Precious balm drips from thy hand out of its bundle of poppies. Thou upliftest the heavy-laden wings of the soul. Darkly and inexpressibly are we moved – joy-startled, I see a grave face that, tender and worshipful, inclines toward me, and, amid manifold entangled locks, reveals the youthful loveliness of the Mother . . . More heavenly than those glittering stars we hold the eternal eyes which the Night hath opened within us.

The downward attraction exercised by woman is inverted; she beckons man no longer earthward, but towards heaven.

> *The Eternal Feminine*
> *Leads us upwards,*

proclaimed Goethe at the end of *Faust, Part Two*.

As the Virgin Mary is the most perfected image, the most widely venerated image of the regenerated woman devoted to the Good, it is interesting to see how she appears through literature and iconography. Here are passages from medieval litanies showing how fervent Christians addressed her:

> Most high Virgin, thou art the fertile Dew, the Fountain of Joy, the Channel of mercy, the Well of living waters that cools our passions.
>
> Thou art the Breast from which God nurses orphans.
>
> Thou art the Marrow, the Inside, the Core of all good.
>
> Thou art the guileless Woman whose love never changes.
>
> Thou art the Probatic Pool, the Remedy of lepers, the subtle Physician whose like is found neither in Salerno nor Montpellier.
>
> Thou art the Lady of healing hands, whose fingers so beautiful, so white, so long, restore noses and mouths, give new eyes and

ears. Thou calmest passions, givest life to the paralysed, givest
strength to the weak, risest the dead.

Most of the feminine attributes we have referred to are found in these
invocations. The Virgin is fertility, dew and the source of life; many of the
images show her at the well, the spring or the fountain; the expression
'Fountain of Life' was one of the most common; she was not a creator,
but she nourishes, she brings to the light of day what was hidden in the
earth. She is the deep reality hidden under the appearance of things: the
Core, the Marrow. Through her, passions are tempered; she is what is given
to man to satiate him. Wherever life is threatened, she saves and restores
it: she heals and strengthens. And because life emanates from God, she as
the intermediary between man and life is likewise the intermediary between
humanity and God. 'The devil's gateway,' said Tertullian. But transfigured,
she is heaven's portal; paintings represent her opening the gate or the
window onto paradise or raising a ladder from earth to the heavens. More
straightforward, she becomes an advocate, pleading beside her Son for the
salvation of men: many tableaux of the Last Judgment have her baring her
breast in supplication to Christ in the name of her glorious motherhood.
She protects men's children in the folds of her cloak; her merciful love
follows them through dangers over oceans and battlefields. She moves
Divine Justice in the name of charity: the 'Virgins of the Scales' are seen,
smiling, tilting the balance where souls are weighed to the side of the Good.

This merciful and tender role is one of the most important of all those
granted to woman. Even integrated into society, the woman subtly exceeds
its boundaries because she possesses the insidious generosity of Life. This
distance between the males' intended constructions and nature's contingency seems troubling in some cases; but it becomes beneficial when the
woman, too docile to threaten men's work, limits herself to enriching and
softening their too sharp edges. Male gods represent Destiny; on the
goddesses' side are found arbitrary benevolence and capricious favour. The
Christian God has the rigours of Justice; the Virgin has gentleness and
charity. On earth, men are the defenders of laws, reason and necessity;
woman knows the original contingency of man himself and of the necessity he believes in; from this comes her supple generosity and the mysterious irony that touches her lips. She gives birth in pain, she heals males'
wounds, she nurses the newborn and buries the dead; of man she knows
all that offends his pride and humiliates his will. While inclining before
him and submitting flesh to spirit, she remains on the carnal borders of
the spirit; and she contests the sharpness of hard masculine architecture

by softening the angles; she introduces free luxury and unforeseen grace. Her power over men comes from her tenderly recalling a modest consciousness of their authentic condition; it is the secret of her illusionless, painful, ironic and loving wisdom. Even frivolity, whimsy and ignorance are charming virtues in her because they thrive beneath and beyond the world where man chooses to live but where he does not want to feel confined. Confronted with arrested meaning and utilitarian instruments, she upholds the mystery of intact things; she brings the breath of poetry into city streets and ploughed fields. Poetry attempts to capture that which exists above everyday prose: woman is an eminently poetic reality since man projects onto her everything he is not resolved to be. She incarnates the Dream; for man, the dream is the most intimate and the most foreign presence, what he does not want, what he does not do, which he aspires to but cannot attain; the mysterious Other who is profound immanence and far-off transcendence will lend him her traits. Thus it is that Aurélia visits Nerval in a dream and gives him the whole world in a dream. 'She began to grow in a bright ray of light so that little by little the garden took on her form, and the flower beds and the trees became the rosettes and festoons of her dress; while her face and her arms impressed their shape upon the reddened clouds in the sky. I was losing sight of her as she was being transfigured, for she seemed to be vanishing into her own grandeur. "Oh flee not from me!" I cried; "for nature dies with you."'

Being the very substance of man's poetic activities, woman is understandably his inspiration: the Muses are women. The Muse is the conduit between the creator and the natural springs he draws from. It is through woman's spirit deeply connected to nature that man will explore the depths of silence and the fertile night. The Muse creates nothing on her own; she is a wise sibyl making herself the docile servant of a master. Even in concrete and practical spheres, her counsel will be useful. Man wishes to attain the goals he sets without the help of his peers, and he would find another man's opinion inopportune; but he supposes that the woman speaks to him in the name of other values, in the name of a wisdom that he does not claim to have, more instinctive than his own, more immediately in accord with the real; these are the 'intuitions' that Egeria uses to counsel and guide; he consults her without fear for his self-esteem as he consults the stars. This 'intuition' even enters into business or politics: Aspasia and Mme de Maintenon still have flourishing careers today.*

---

* It goes without saying that they, of course, demonstrate intellectual qualities perfectly identical to those of men.

There is another function that man willingly entrusts to woman: being the purpose behind men's activities and the source of their decisions, she is also the judge of values. She is revealed as a privileged judge. Man dreams of an Other not only to possess her, but also to be validated by her; to be validated by men who are his peers entails constant tension on his part: that is why he wants an outside view conferring absolute value on his life, on his undertakings, on himself. God's gaze is hidden, foreign, disquieting: even in periods of faith, only a few mystics felt its intensity. This divine role often devolved on the woman. Close to the man, dominated by him, she does not posit values that are foreign to him: and yet, as she is other, she remains exterior to the world of men and can thus grasp it objectively. It is she who will denounce the presence or absence of courage, of strength and of beauty, while confirming from the outside their universal value. Men are too busy in their cooperative or combative relations to be an audience for each other: they do not think about each other. Woman is removed from their activities and does not take part in their jousts and combats: her entire situation predestines her to play this role of onlooker. The chevalier jousts in tournaments for his lady; poets seek woman's approval. When Rastignac sets out to conquer Paris, he thinks first of *having* women, less about possessing their bodies than enjoying that reputation that only they are capable of creating for a man. Balzac projected the story of his own youth onto his young heroes: his education began with older mistresses; and the woman played the role of educator not only in *The Lily in the Valley*;[12] she was also assigned this role in [Flaubert's] *Sentimental Education*,[13] in Stendhal's novels and in numerous other coming-of-age novels. It has already been observed that the woman is both physis and anti-physis; she personifies Society as well as Nature; through her the civilisation of a period and its culture is summed up, as can be seen in courtly poetry, in the *Decameron* and in *L'Astrée*; she launches fashions, presides over salons, directs and reflects opinion. Fame and glory are women. 'The crowd is woman,' said Mallarmé. In the company of women the young man is initiated into the 'world', and into this complex reality called 'life'. She is one of the privileged prizes promised to heroes, adventurers and individualists. In ancient times, Perseus saved Andromeda, Orpheus went to rescue Eurydice from Hades and Troy fought to keep the beautiful Helen. Novels of chivalry recount barely any prowess other than delivering captive princesses. What would Prince Charming do if he did not wake up Sleeping Beauty, or lavish gifts on Donkey Skin? The myth of the king marrying a shepherdess flatters the man as much as the woman. The rich man needs to give or else his useless wealth remains an abstract object: he needs someone to give to. The Cinderella myth, indulgently described by Philip Wylie in *Generation of Vipers*, thrives in prosperous countries; it is more powerful in America than anywhere else because men are more embarrassed by their wealth: how would they spend this money for which they work their whole lives if they did not dedicate it to a woman? Orson Welles, among others, personifies the imperialism of this kind of generosity in *Citizen Kane*: Kane chooses to smother an obscure singer with gifts and impose her on the public as a great opera singer all for his own affirmation of power; in France there are plenty of small-time Citizen Kanes. In another film, *The Razor's Edge*, when the hero returns from India having acquired absolute wisdom, the only use he finds for it is to rescue a prostitute. Clearly man wants woman's enslavement when fantasising himself as a benefactor, liberator or redeemer; if Sleeping Beauty is to be awakened, she must be sleeping; to have a captive princess, there must be ogres and dragons. And the greater man's taste for difficult undertakings, the greater his pleasure in granting woman independence. Conquering is more fascinating than rescuing or giving. The average Western male's ideal is a woman who freely submits to his domination, who does not accept his ideas without some discussion, but who yields to his reasoning, who intelligently resists but yields in the end. The tougher his pride, the more he relishes dangerous adventure; it is far better to tame Penthesilea than to marry a consenting Cinderella. The 'warrior' loves danger and play, said Nietzsche. 'For that reason he wants woman as the most dangerous plaything.' The man who loves danger and play is not displeased to see woman change into an Amazon as long as he keeps the hope of subjugating her:* what he demands in his heart of hearts is that this struggle remain a game for him, while for woman it involves her very destiny: therein lies the true victory for man, liberator, or conqueror – that woman freely recognise him as her destiny.

Thus the expression 'to have a woman' conceals a double meaning: the object's functions are not dissociated from those of the judge. The moment woman is viewed as a person, she can only be conquered with her consent; she must be won. Sleeping Beauty's smile fulfils Prince Charming: the captive princesses' tears of happiness and gratitude give

---

* American detective novels – or American-style ones – are a striking example. Peter Cheyney's heroes, for instance, are always grappling with an extremely dangerous woman, unmanageable for anyone but them: after a duel that unfolds all through the novel, she is finally overcome by Campion or Callaghan and falls into his arms.

meaning to the knights' prowess. On the other hand, her gaze is not a masculine, abstract, severe one – it allows itself to be charmed. Thus heroism and poetry are modes of seduction: but in letting herself be seduced, the woman exalts heroism and poetry. She holds an even more essential privilege for the individualist: she appears to him not as the measure of universally recognised values but as the revelation of his particular merits and of his very being. A man is judged by his fellow men by what he does, objectively and according to general standards. But certain of his qualities, and among others his vital qualities, can only interest woman; his virility, charm, seduction, tenderness and cruelty only pertain to her: if he sets a value on these most secret virtues, he has an absolute need of her; through her he will experience the miracle of appearing as an other, an other who is also his deepest self. Malraux admirably expresses what the individualist expects from the woman he loves in one of his texts. Kyo wonders:

'We hear the voices of others with our ears, our own voices with our throats.' Yes. 'One hears his own life, too, with his throat, and those of others? . . . To others, I am what I have done.' To May alone, he was not what he had done; to him alone, she was something altogether different from her biography. The embrace by which love holds beings together against solitude did not bring its relief to man; it brought relief only to the madman, to the incomparable monster, dear above all things, that every being is to himself and that he cherishes in his heart. Since his mother had died, May was the only being for whom he was not Kyo Gisors, but an intimate partner . . . Men are not my kind, they are those who look at me and judge me; my kind are those who love me and do not look at me, who love me in spite of everything, degradation, baseness, treason – me, and not what I have done or shall do – who would love me as long as I would love myself – even to suicide.*[14]

What makes Kyo's attitude human and moving is that it implies reciprocity and that he asks May to love him in his authenticity, not to send back an indulgent reflection of himself. For many men, this demand is diluted: instead of a truthful revelation, they seek a glowing image of admiration and gratitude, deified in the depths of a woman's two eyes. Woman

* Man's Fate.

has often been compared to water, in part because it is the mirror where the male Narcissus contemplates himself: he leans towards her, with good or bad faith. But in any case, what he wants from her is to be, outside of him, all that he cannot grasp in himself, because the interiority of the existent is only nothingness, and to reach himself, he must project himself on to object. Woman is the supreme reward for him since she is his own apotheosis, a foreign form he can possess in the flesh. It is this 'incomparable monster', himself, that he embraces when he holds in his arms this being who sums up the World and onto whom he has imposed his values and his laws. Uniting himself, then, with this other whom he makes his own, he hopes to reach himself. Treasure, prey, game and risk, muse, guide, judge, mediator, mirror, the woman is the Other in which the subject surpasses himself without being limited, who opposes him without negating him; she is the Other who lets herself be annexed to him without ceasing to be the Other. And for this she is so necessary to man's joy and his triumph that if she did not exist, men would have had to invent her.

They did invent her.* But she also exists without their invention. This is why she is the failure of their dream at the same time as its incarnation. There is no image of woman that does not invoke the opposite figure as well: she is Life and Death, Nature and Artifice, Light and Night. Whatever the point of view, the same fluctuation is always found, because the inessential necessarily returns to the essential. In the figures of the Virgin Mother and of Beatrice lie Eve and Circe.

'Through woman', wrote Kierkegaard, 'ideality enters into life and what would man be without her? Many a man has become a genius through a girl, . . . but none has become a genius through the girl he married . . .

'It is only by a negative relation to her that man is rendered productive in his ideal endeavours. Negative relations with woman can make us infinite . . . positive relations with woman make the man finite to a far greater extent.'† This means that woman is necessary as long as she remains an Idea into which man projects his own transcendence; but she is detrimental as objective reality, existing for herself and limited to herself. In refusing to marry his fiancée, Kierkegaard believes he has established the only valid relation with woman. And he is right in the

---

* 'Man created woman – but what out of? Out of a rib of his God, of his ideal' (Nietzsche, *Twilight of the Idols*).
† *In Vino Veritas*.

sense that the myth of woman posited as infinite Other immediately entails its opposite.

Because she is faux Infinite, Ideal without truth, she is revealed as finitude and mediocrity and thus as falsehood. That is how she appears in Laforgue: throughout his work he expresses rancour against a mystification he blames on man as much as woman. Ophelia and Salome are nothing but 'little women'. Hamlet might think: 'Thus would Ophelia have loved me as her "possession" and because I was socially and morally superior to her girlish friends' possessions. And those little remarks about comfort and well-being that slipped out of her at lamp-lighting time!' Woman makes man dream, yet she is concerned with comfort and stews; one speaks to her about her soul but she is only a body. And the lover, believing he is pursuing the Ideal, is the plaything of nature that uses all these mystifications for the ends of reproduction. She represents in reality the everydayness of life; she is foolishness, prudence, mediocrity and ennui. Here is an example of how this is expressed, in a poem entitled 'Our Little Companion':

> . . . I have the talent of every school
> I have souls for all tastes
> Pick the flower of my faces
> Drink my mouth and not my voice
> And do not look for more:
> Not even I can see clearly
> Our loves are not equal
> For me to hold out my hand
> You are merely naive males
> I am the eternal feminine!
> My fate loses itself in the Stars!
> I am the Great Isis!
> No one has lifted my veil
> Dream only of my oases . . .[15]

Man succeeded in enslaving woman, but in doing so, he robbed her of what made possession desirable. Integrated into the family and society, woman's magic fades rather than transfigures itself; reduced to a servant's condition, she is no longer the wild prey incarnating all of nature's treasures. Since the birth of courtly love, it has been a commonplace that marriage kills love. Either too scorned, too respected or too quotidian, the wife is no longer a sex object. Marriage rites were originally intended

to protect man against woman; she becomes his property: but everything we possess in turn possesses us; marriage is a servitude for the
man as well; he is thus caught in the trap laid by nature: to have desired
a lovely girl, the male must spend his whole life feeding a heavy matron,
a dried-out old woman; the delicate jewel intended to embellish his existence becomes an odious burden: Xanthippe is one of those types of
women that men have always referred to with the greatest horror.* But
even when the woman is young, there is mystification in marriage because
trying to socialise eroticism only succeeds in killing it. Eroticism implies
a claim of the instant against time, of the individual against the collectivity; it affirms separation against communication; it rebels against all
regulation; it contains a principle hostile to society. Social customs are
never bent to fit the rigour of institutions and laws: love has forever
asserted itself against them. In its sensual form it addresses young people
and courtesans in Greece and Rome; both carnal and platonic, courtly
love is always directed at another's wife. *Tristan* is the epic of adultery.
The period around 1900 that re-creates the myth of the woman is one
where adultery becomes the theme of all literature. Certain writers, like
Bernstein, in the supreme defence of bourgeois institutions, struggle to
reintegrate eroticism and love into marriage; but there is more truth in
Porto-Riche's *A Loving Wife*,[16] which shows the incompatibility of these
two types of values. Adultery can disappear only with marriage itself.
For the aim of marriage is to immunise man against *his* own wife: but
other women still have a dizzying effect on him; it is to them he will
turn. Women are accomplices. For they rebel against an order that tries
to deprive them of their weapons. So as to tear woman from nature, so
as to subjugate her to man through ceremonies and contracts, she was
elevated to the dignity of a human person; she was granted freedom.
But freedom is precisely what escapes all servitude; and if it is bestowed
on a being originally possessed by malevolent forces, it becomes
dangerous. And all the more so as man stopped at half measures; he
accepted woman into the masculine world only by making her a servant,
in thwarting her transcendence; the freedom she was granted could only
have a negative use; it only manifests itself in refusal. Woman became
free only in becoming captive; she renounces this human privilege to
recover her power as natural object. By day she treacherously plays her
role of docile servant, but by night she changes into a kitten, a doe; she

* As we have seen, it was the theme of many lamentations in Greece and during the
Middle Ages.

slips back into a siren's skin, or riding on her broomstick, she makes her satanic rounds. Sometimes she exercises her nocturnal magic on her own husband; but it is wiser to conceal her metamorphoses from her master; she chooses strangers as her prey; they have no rights over her, and she remains for them a plant, wellspring, star or sorceress. So there she is, fated to infidelity: it is the only concrete form her freedom could assume. She is unfaithful over and above her own desires, her thoughts or her consciousness; because she is seen as an object, she is given up to any subjectivity that chooses to take her; it is still not sure that locked in harems, hidden behind veils, she does not arouse desire in some person: to inspire desire in a stranger is already to fail her husband and society. But worse, she is often an accomplice in this fate; it is only through lies and adultery that she can prove that she is nobody's thing, that she refutes male claims on her. This is why man's jealousy is so quick to awaken, and in legends woman can be suspected without reason, condemned on the least suspicion, as were Geneviève de Brabant and Desdemona; even before any suspicion, Griselda is subjected to the worst trials; this tale would be absurd if the woman were not suspected beforehand; there is no case presented against her: it is up to her to prove her innocence. This is also why jealousy can be insatiable; it has already been shown that possession can never be positively realised; even if all others are forbidden to draw from the spring, no one possesses the thirst-quenching spring: the jealous one knows this well. In essence, woman is inconstant, just as water is fluid; and no human force can contradict a natural truth. Throughout all literature, in *The Thousand and One Nights* as in the *Decameron*, woman's ruses triumph over man's prudence. But it is more than simply individualistic will that makes him a jailer: society itself, in the form of father, brother and husband, makes him responsible for the woman's behaviour. Chastity is imposed upon her for economic and religious reasons, every citizen having to be authenticated as the son of his own father. But it is also very important to compel woman to conform exactly to the role society devolves on her. Man's double demand condemns woman to duplicity: he wants the woman to be his own and yet to remain foreign to him; he imagines her as servant and sorceress at the same time. But he admits publicly only to the former desire; the latter is a deceitful demand hidden in the depths of his heart and flesh; it goes against morality and society; it is evil like the Other, like rebel Nature, like the 'bad woman'. Man is not wholly devoted to the Good he constructs and attempts to impose; he maintains a shameful connivance with the Bad. But whenever the Bad imprudently dares to show its face openly, he goes to war against it. In the darkness of night, man invites woman to sin. But in the light of day, he rejects sin and her, the sinner. And women, sinners themselves in the mysteries of the bed, show all the more passion for the public worship of virtue. Just as in primitive society the male sex is secular and woman's is laden with religious and magic qualities, today's modern societies consider man's failings harmless peccadilloes; they are often lightly dismissed; even if he disobeys community laws, the man continues to belong to it; he is merely an *enfant terrible*, not a profound threat to the collective order. If, on the other hand, the woman deviates from society, she returns to Nature and the devil, she triggers uncontrollable and evil forces within the group. Fear has always been mixed with the blame for licentious behaviour. If the husband cannot keep his wife virtuous, he shares her fault; his misfortune is, in society's eyes, a dishonour, and there are civilisations so strict that it is necessary to kill the criminal to dissociate him from her crime. In others, the complaisant husband will be punished by noisy demonstrations or led around naked on a donkey. And the community will take it upon itself to punish the guilty woman in his place: because she offended the group as a whole and not only her husband. These customs were particularly brutal in superstitious and mystical Spain, sensual and terrorised by the flesh. Calderón, Lorca and Valle-Inclán made it the theme of many plays. In Lorca's *La casa de Bernarda Alba* (*The House of Bernard Alba*) the village gossips want to punish the seduced girl by burning her with live coal 'in the place where she sinned'. In Valle-Inclán's *Divine Words*, the adulteress appears as a witch who dances with the devil: her fault discovered, the whole village assembles to tear off her clothes and drown her. Many traditions reported that the sinner was stripped; then she was stoned, as told in the Gospel, and she was buried alive, drowned or burned. The meaning of these tortures is that she was thus returned to Nature after being deprived of her social dignity; by her sin she had released bad natural emanations: the expiation was carried out as a kind of sacred orgy where the women stripped, beat and massacred the guilty one, releasing in turn their mysterious but beneficial fluids since they were acting in accordance with society.

This savage severity fades as superstitions diminish and fear dissipates. But in the countryside, godless and homeless bohemian women are still regarded with suspicion. The woman who freely exercises her charms – adventuress, vamp, *femme fatale* – remains a disquieting type. In Hollywood films the Circe image survives as the bad woman. Women were burned as witches simply because they were beautiful. And in the prudish intimidation of provincial virtues, the old spectre of dissolute women is perpetuated.

These very dangers make woman captivating game for an adventurous man. Disregarding his rights as a husband, refusing to uphold society's laws, he will try to conquer her in single combat. He tries to annex the woman, including her resistance; he pursues in her the same freedom through which she escapes him. In vain. Freedom cannot be carved up: the free woman will often be free at the expense of man. Sleeping Beauty might wake up with displeasure, she might not recognise her Prince Charming in the one who awakens her, she might not smile. This is precisely the case of Citizen Kane, whose protégée is seen to be oppressed and whose generosity is revealed to be a will for power and tyranny; the hero's wife listens to his exploits indifferently, the Muse yawns, listening to the verses of the poet who dreams of her. Out of boredom, the Amazon can refuse combat; and she can also emerge victorious. Roman women of the decadence, and many American women today, impose their whims or their law on men. Where is Cinderella? The man wanted to give and here is the woman taking. No longer a game, it is a question of self-defence. From the moment the woman is free, her only destiny is one she freely creates for herself. So the relation between the two sexes is a relation of struggle. Having become a peer to man, she seems as formidable as when she faced him as foreign Nature. The female nurturer, devoted and patient, turns into an avid and devouring beast. The bad woman also sets her roots in the earth, in Life; but the earth is a grave, and life a bitter combat: so the myth of the industrious honeybee or mother hen is replaced by the devouring insect, the praying mantis, the spider; the woman is no longer the one who nurses her young but the one who eats the male; the egg is no longer the storehouse of abundance but a trap of inert matter drowning the mutilated spermatozoid; the womb, that warm, peaceful and safe haven, becomes the rank octopus, the carnivorous plant, abyss of convulsive darkness; within it lives a serpent who insatiably swallows the male's strength. Such a dialectic turns the erotic object into female black magic, turns the female servant into a traitor, Cinderella into a witch, and changes all women into the enemy: here is the ransom man pays for having posited himself in bad faith as the sole essential.

But this enemy face is not woman's definitive form either. Instead, Manichaeism is introduced within the feminine kind. Pythagoras linked the good principle to man and the bad principle to woman; men have tried to overcome the bad by annexing woman; they have been partially successful; but just as Christianity, by introducing the ideas of redemption and salvation, gave its full sense to the word 'damnation', in the same way the bad woman stands out in opposition to the sanctified woman. In the course of this *querelle des femmes*, which has endured from the Middle Ages to our times, some men want only to see the blessed woman they dream of, while others want the cursed woman who belies their dreams. But in fact, if man can find *everything* in woman, it is because she has both faces. In a carnal and living way, she represents all the values and anti-values that give life meaning. Here, clear-cut, we have the Good and the Bad, in opposition to each other in the guise of devoted Mother and perfidious Lover; in the old English ballad, 'Lord Randal, My Son', a young knight dies in his mother's arms, poisoned by his mistress. Richepin's *The Leech*[17] takes up the same theme, but with more pathos and bad taste. Angelic Michaela is contrasted with dark Carmen. The mother, the faithful fiancée and the patient wife provide healing to the wounds inflicted on men's hearts by vamps and witches. Between these clearly fixed poles a multitude of ambiguous figures were yet to be defined, the pitiful, the detestable, sinners, victims, coquettes, the weak, the angelic, the devilish. A multitude of behaviours and feelings thereby solicit man and enrich him.

The very complexity of woman enchants him: here is a wonderful servant who can excite him at little expense. Is she angel or devil? Uncertainty makes her a sphinx. One of the most famous brothels of Paris was placed under its aegis. In the grand epoch of Femininity, in the time of corsets, of Paul Bourget, of Henri Bataille and of the French cancan, the Sphinx theme is all the rage in comedies, poems and songs: 'Who are you, where do you come from, strange Sphinx?' And dreams and queries about the feminine mystery continue still. To preserve this mystery, men have long implored women not to give up their long dresses, petticoats, veils, long gloves and high boots: whatever accentuates difference in the Other makes them more desirable, since it is the Other as such that man wants to possess. In his letters, Alain-Fournier reproaches English women for their boyish handshake: French women's modest reserve flusters him. Woman must remain secret, unknown, to be adored as a faraway princess; Fournier seems not to have been terribly deferential to the women who entered his life, but it is in a woman, whose main virtue was to seem inaccessible, that he incarnates all the wonder of childhood, of youth, the nostalgia for a lost paradise. In Yvonne de Galais he traced a white and gold image. But men cherish even feminine defects if they create mystery. 'A woman must have her caprices,' said a man authoritatively to a reasonable woman. Caprices are unpredictable; they lend woman the grace of undulating water; lying embellishes her with glittering reflections; coquetry, even perversity, is her intoxicating perfume. Deceitful, evasive, misunderstood, duplicitous, it is thus that she best lends herself to men's contradictory desires; she is Maya of the innumerable metamorphoses. It is a commonplace to represent the Sphinx as a young woman: virginity is one of the secrets that men – and all the more so if they are libertines – find the most disconcerting; a girl's purity gives hope for all kinds of licence and no one knows what perversities are concealed beneath her innocence; still close to animal and plant, already compliant with social rites, she is neither child nor adult; her timid femininity does not inspire fear, but mild unrest. It is understandable that she is one of the privileged figures of the feminine mystery. But as the 'real young lady' fades, worshipping her has become a bit outdated. On the other hand, the prostitute's character that Gantillon, in his triumphantly successful play, gave to Maya still has a great deal of prestige. She is one of the most flexible of feminine types, one that best allows the great game of vices and virtues. For the timorous puritan, she embodies evil, shame, disease and damnation; she inspires horror and disgust; she belongs to no man, but gives herself to all of them and lives on the trade; therein she regains the fearsome independence of lewd primitive Goddess Mothers and she embodies the Femininity that masculine society has not sanctified, that remains rife with malevolent powers; in the sexual act, the male cannot imagine that he possesses her, he is only given over to demons of the flesh, a humiliation, a stain particularly felt by Anglo-Saxons in whose eyes the flesh is more or less reviled. On the other hand, a man who is not frightened by the flesh will love the prostitute's generous and rudimentary affirmation; in her he will see exalted femininity that no morality has diminished; he will find in her body again those magic virtues that in the past made the woman kin to the stars and the sea: a Henry Miller, sleeping with a prostitute, feels he has dived into the very depths of life, death, the cosmos; he meets God in the moist shadows of the receptive vagina. Because she is on the margins of a hypocritically moral world, a sort of pariah, the 'lost girl' can be regarded as the challenger of all official virtues; her indignity relates her to authentic saints; for the oppressed shall be exalted; Christ looked upon Mary Magdalene with favour; sin opens the gates of heaven more easily than hypocritical virtue. Thus Raskolnikov sacrificed, at Sonya's feet, the arrogant masculine pride that led him to crime; murder exacerbated this will for separation that is in all men: resigned, abandoned by all, a humble prostitute is best suited to receive his vow of abdication.*[18] The words 'lost girl' awaken disturbing echoes; many men dream of losing themselves: it is not so easy, one does not easily attain Evil in a positive form; and even the demoniac is frightened by excessive crimes; the woman enables the celebration of the black masses, where Satan is evoked without exactly being invited; she is on the margin of the masculine world: acts that concern her are really without consequence; yet she is a human being and through her, dark revolts against human laws can be carried out. From Musset to Georges Bataille, visiting 'girls' was hideous and fascinating debauchery. Sade and Sacher-Masoch satisfied their haunting desires; their disciples, and most men who had to satisfy their 'vices', commonly turned to prostitutes. Of all women, they were the ones who were the most subjected to the male, and yet the ones who best escaped him; this is what makes them likely to take on numerous meanings. There is, however, no feminine figure – virgin, mother, wife, sister, servant, lover, fierce virtue, smiling odalisque – capable of encapsulating the inconstant yearnings of men.

It is for psychology – specifically psychoanalysis – to discover why an individual is drawn more particularly to one aspect or another of the multi-faceted Myth and why he incarnates it in any one particular form. But this myth is involved in all complexes, obsessions and psychoses. In particular, many neuroses are rooted in the vertigo of prohibition: and this vertigo can only emerge if taboos have previously been established; external social pressure is not enough to explain its presence; in fact, social prohibitions are not simply conventions; they have – among other significations – an ontological meaning that each individual experiences in his own way. For example, it is interesting to examine the Oedipus complex; it is too often considered as being produced by a struggle

---

* Marcel Schwob poetically renders this myth in the *Book of Monelle*:
  I will speak to you of the Little Women of Pleasure that you may know of the beginning . . . For you see, these little women call out to you . . . they utter a cry of compassion, and they hold your hand in their emaciated hands. They only understand you when you are unhappy; they can cry with you and console you . . . None of them may stay long with you. They would be too sad and too ashamed to remain. When you no longer weep, you have no need of them. They teach you the lesson they have learned from you, then they flee. They come through the cold and the rain to kiss your brow, to brush their lips across your eyes, to drive from you the terror and the sadness that you know . . . You must not think of what they do in the shadows.

between instinctive tendencies and social directives; but it is first of all an interior conflict within the subject himself. The infant's attachment to the mother's breast is first an attachment to Life in its immediate form, in its generality and its immanence; the rejection of weaning is the rejection of the abandonment to which the individual is condemned once he is separated from the Whole; from then on, and as he becomes more individualised and separated, the taste he retains for the mother's flesh now torn from his own can be termed 'sexual'; his sensuality is thus mediated, it has become transcendence towards a foreign object. But the sooner and more decidedly the child assumes itself as subject, the more the carnal bond that challenges his autonomy will become problematic for him. So he shuns his mother's caresses; his mother's authority, the rights she has over him, even her very presence, inspires a kind of shame in him. Particularly he finds it embarrassing and obscene to be aware of her as flesh, and he avoids thinking of her body; in the horror that he feels towards his father or a second husband or a lover, there is less jealousy than scandal; to be reminded that his mother is a carnal being is to be reminded of his own birth, an event he repudiates with all his force; or at least he wishes to give it the majesty of a great cosmic phenomenon; he thinks that Nature, which invests all individuals but belongs to none, should be contained in his mother; he hates her to become prey, not – as it is often presumed – because he wants to possess her himself, but because he wants her to exist above all possession: she must not have the ordinary features of wife or mistress. When in adolescence, however, his sexuality becomes virile, his mother's body begins to disturb him; but it is because he grasps femininity in general in her; and often the desire aroused by the sight of her thigh or her breast disappears as soon as the young boy realises that this flesh is maternal flesh. There are many cases of perversion, since adolescence, being the age of confusion, is the age of perversion where disgust leads to sacrilege, where temptation is born from the forbidden. But it must not be thought that the son naively wishes to sleep with his mother and that exterior prohibitions interfere and oppress him; on the contrary, desire is born because this prohibition is constituted within the heart of the individual himself. This censure is the most normal, the most general reaction. But there again, it does not arise from social regulation masking instinctive desires. Rather, respect is the sublimation of an original disgust; the young man refuses to regard his mother as carnal; he transfigures her, he associates her with one of the pure images of the sacred woman society offers. This is how he helps strengthen the image of the ideal

Mother who will save the next generation. But this image has such force only because it emanates from an individual dialectic. And since every woman is inhabited by the general essence of Woman, thus Mother, it is certain that the attitude to the Mother will have repercussions in his relations with wife and mistress; but less simply than is often imagined. The adolescent who has concretely and sensually desired his mother may have desired woman in general in her: and the fervour of his temperament will be appeased with any woman, no matter who; he is not doomed to incestuous nostalgia.* On the other hand, a young man who has had a tender but platonic respect for his mother may in every case wish for woman to be part of maternal purity.

The importance of sexuality, and therefore ordinarily of woman, in both pathological and normal behaviour is well known. Other objects can also be feminised; because since woman is certainly to a large extent man's invention, he could also invent her in the male body: in homosexuality, sexual division is maintained. But ordinarily Woman is sought in feminine beings. Through her, through the best and the worst of her, man learns happiness, suffering, vice and virtue, lust, renunciation, devotion and tyranny, and learns about himself; she is play and adventure, but also contest; she is the triumph of victory and more bitter, of failure overcome; she is the giddiness of loss, the fascination of damnation, of death. There is a world of significations that exist only through woman; she is the substance of men's actions and feelings, the embodiment of all the values that seek their freedom. It is understandable that even if he were condemned to the cruellest disavowals, man would not want to relinquish a dream containing all other dreams.

Here, then, is why woman has a double and deceptive image: she is everything he craves and everything he does not attain. She is the wise mediator between auspicious Nature and man; and she is the temptation of Nature, untamed against all reason. She is the carnal embodiment of all moral values and their opposites, from good to bad; she is the stuff of action and its obstacle, man's grasp on the world and his failure; as such she is the source of all man's reflection on his existence and all expression he can give of it; however, she works to divert him from himself, to make him sink into silence and death. As his servant and companion, man expects her also to be his public and his judge, to confirm him in his being; but she opposes him with her indifference, even with her mockery and her laughter. He projects onto her what he

* Stendhal is a striking example.

desires and fears, what he loves and what he hates. And if it is difficult to say anything about her, it is because man seeks himself entirely in her and because she is All. But she is All in that which is inessential: she is wholly the *Other*. And as other she is also other than herself, other than what is expected of her. Being all, she is never exactly *this* that she should be; she is everlasting disappointment, the very disappointment of existence that never successfully attains or reconciles itself with the totality of existents.

CHAPTER 2

In order to confirm this analysis of the feminine myth, as it is collectively presented, we will look at the singular and syncretic form it takes on in certain writers. The attitude to women seems typical in, among others, Montherlant, D. H. Lawrence, Claudel, Breton and Stendhal.

I
MONTHERLANT OR THE BREAD OF DISGUST

Montherlant belongs to the long male tradition of adopting the arrogant Manichaeism of Pythagoras. Following Nietzsche, he believes that the Eternal Feminine was exalted only during periods of weakness and that the hero has to rise up against the Magna Mater. As a specialist in heroism, he has undertaken the task of dislodging her. Woman is night, disorder and immanence. 'These convulsive shadows are nothing more than "the feminine in its pure state",'*[19] he writes about Mme Tolstoy. The stupidity and baseness of men today, he thinks, give a positive image of feminine deficiencies: the feminine instinct, feminine intuition, and women's clairvoyance are spoken about, while their absence of logic, stubborn ignorance and inability to grasp the real should be denounced; they are neither good observers nor psychologists; they neither know how to see things nor understand human beings; their mystery is a trap, their unfathomable treasures have the depth of nothingness; they have nothing to give man and can only harm him. For Montherlant the mother is the first major enemy; in *Exile*,[20] an early play of his, he depicts a mother who keeps her son from enlisting; in *Les Olympiques*, the teenager who wants to devote himself to sport is barred by his mother's fearful egotism; in *The Bachelors*[21] and in *The Girls*,[22] the mother is vilified. Her crime is to want to keep her son locked up for ever in her womb's depths; she mutilates him to make him her own and thus to

* *Pity for Women.*

fill up the sterile vacuum of her being; she is the worst educator; she cuts the child's wings; she pulls him back from the heights he aspires to; she turns him into a moron and diminishes him. These reproaches are not without some basis. But it is clear from the explicit criticisms that Montherlant addresses to woman-mother that what he hates in her is his own birth. He thinks he is God; he wants to be God: because he is male, because he is a 'superior man', because he is Montherlant. A god is not engendered; his body, if he has one, is a will moulded in hard and disciplined muscles, not in flesh mutely inhabited by life and death; this flesh that he repudiates is perishable, contingent and vulnerable and is his mother's fault. 'The only part of Achilles' body that was vulnerable was the part his mother had held.'* Montherlant never wanted to assume the human condition; what he calls his pride is, from the beginning, a panicked flight from the risks contained in a freedom engaged in the world through flesh; he claims to affirm freedom but to refuse engagement; without ties, without roots, he dreams he is a subjectivity majestically withdrawn upon itself; the memory of his carnal origins disturbs this dream and he resorts to a familiar process: instead of prevailing over it, he repudiates it.

For Montherlant, the woman lover is just as harmful as the mother; she prevents man from resurrecting the god in himself; woman's lot, he says, is life in its most immediate form, woman lives on feelings, she wallows in immanence; she has a mania for happiness: she wants to trap man in it; she does not experience the élan of her transcendence, she does not have the sense of grandeur; she loves her lover in his weakness and not in his strength, in his troubles and not in his joys; she would like him defenceless, so unhappy as to try to convince him of his misery regardless of any proof to the contrary. He surpasses and thus escapes her: she means to reduce him to her size to take him over. Because she needs him, she is not self-sufficient; she is a parasite. Through Dominique's eyes, Montherlant portrayed the promenading women of Ranelagh, women 'hanging on their lovers' arms like beings without backbones, like big disguised slugs';[†23] except for sportswomen, women are incomplete beings, doomed to slavery; soft and lacking muscle, they have no grasp on the world; thus they fiercely work to annex a lover or, even better, a husband. Montherlant, to my knowledge, did not use the praying mantis myth, but the content is there: for woman, to love is to

* Ibid.
† *The Dream.*

devour; she pretends to give of herself, and she takes. He quotes Mme
Tolstoy's cry: 'I live through him, for him; I demand the same thing for
myself,' and he denounces the dangers of such a furious love; he finds
a terrible truth in Ecclesiastes:[24] A man who wants to hurt you is better
than a woman who wants to help you. He invokes Lyautey's experience:
'A man of mine who marries is reduced to half a man.' He deems marriage
to be even worse for a 'superior man'; it is a ridiculous conformism to
bourgeois values; could you imagine saying: 'Mrs Aeschylus', or 'I'm
having dinner at the Dantes"'? A great man's prestige is weakened; and
even more, marriage shatters the hero's magnificent solitude; he 'needs
not to be distracted from his own self'.* I have already said that
Montherlant has chosen a freedom *without object*; that is, he prefers an
illusion of autonomy to an authentic freedom engaged in the world; it
is this availability that he means to use against woman; she is heavy, she
is a burden. 'It was a harsh symbol that a man could not walk straight
because the woman he loved was on his arm.'† 'I was burning, she puts
out the fire. I was walking on water, she takes my arm, I sink.'‡ How
does she have so much power since she is only lack, poverty and negativity and her magic is illusory? Montherlant does not explain it. He
simply and proudly says that 'the lion rightly fears the mosquito.'§ But
the answer is obvious: it is easy to believe one is sovereign when alone,
to believe oneself strong when carefully refusing to bear any burden.
Montherlant has chosen ease; he claims to worship difficult values: but
he seeks to attain them easily. 'The crowns we give ourselves are the
only ones worth being worn,' said the king of *Pasiphaé*. How easy.
Montherlant overloaded his brow, draping it with purple, but an outsider's
look was enough to show that his diadems were papier-mâché and that,
like Hans Christian Andersen's emperor, he was naked. Walking on water
in a dream was far less tiring than moving forward on earthly land in
reality. And this is why Montherlant the lion avoided the feminine
mosquito with terror: he is afraid to be tested by the real.◊

* *Pity for Women.*
† *The Girls.*
‡ Ibid.
§ Ibid.
◊ Adler considered this process the classic origin of psychoses. The individual, divided
between a 'will for power' and an 'inferiority complex', sets up the greatest distance
possible between society and himself so as to avoid the test of reality. He knows it
would undermine the claims he can maintain only if they are hidden by bad faith.

If Montherlant had really deflated the Eternal Feminine myth, he would have to be congratulated: women can be helped to assume themselves as human beings by denying the Woman. But he did not smash the idol, as has been shown: he converted it into a monster. He too believed in this obscure and irreducible essence: femininity; like Aristotle and St Thomas, he believed it was defined negatively; woman was woman through a lack of virility; that is the destiny any female individual has to undergo without being able to modify it. Whoever claims to escape it places herself on the lowest rung of the human ladder: she does not manage to become man, she gives up being woman; she is merely a pathetic caricature, a sham; that she might be a body and a consciousness does not provide her with any reality: Platonist when it suited him, Montherlant seems to believe that only the Ideas of femininity and virility possessed being; the individual who partakes of neither has only an appearance of existence. He irrevocably condemns these 'vampires' who dare to posit themselves as autonomous subjects, dare to think and act. And he intends to prove through his depiction of Andrée Hacquebaut that any woman endeavouring to make herself a person would be changed into a grimacing marionette. Andrée is, of course, ugly, ungainly, badly dressed, and even dirty, with dubious nails and forearms: the little culture she is granted is enough to kill all her femininity; Costals assures us she is intelligent, but with every page devoted to her, Montherlant convinces us of her stupidity; Costals claims he feels sympathy for her; Montherlant renders her obnoxious. Through this clever equivocation, the idiocy of feminine intelligence is proven, and an original fall perverting all the virile qualities to which women aspire is established.

Montherlant is willing to make an exception for sportswomen; they can acquire a spirit, a soul, thanks to the autonomous exercise of their body; yet it was easy to bring them down from these heights; he delicately moves away from the 1,000-metre winner to whom he devoted an enthusiastic hymn; knowing he could easily seduce her, he wanted to spare her this disgrace. Alban calls her to the top, but Dominique does not remain there; she falls in love with him: 'She who had been all spirit and all soul sweated, gave off body odours, and out of breath, she cleared her throat.'* Alban chases her away, indignant. If a woman kills the flesh in her through the discipline of sports, she can still be

* The Dream.

esteemed; but an autonomous existence moulded in a woman's flesh is a repulsive scandal; feminine flesh is abhorrent the moment a consciousness inhabits it. What is suitable for woman is to be purely flesh. Montherlant approves the Oriental attitude: as an object of pleasure, the weak sex has a place – modest, of course, but worthwhile – on earth; the pleasure it gives man justifies it, and that pleasure alone. The ideal woman is totally stupid and totally subjugated; she is always willing to welcome the man and never ask anything of him. Such was Douce, and Alban likes her when it is convenient: 'Douce, admirably silly and always lusted after the sillier she is . . . useless outside of love and thus firmly but sweetly avoided'.* Such is Rhadidja, the little Arab woman, a quiet beast of love who docilely accepts pleasure and money. This 'feminine beast' met on a Spanish train can thus be imagined: 'She looked so idiotic that I began to desire her.'†²⁵ The author explains: 'What is irritating in women is their claim to reason; if they exaggerate their animality, they border on the superhuman.'‡

However, Montherlant is in no way an Oriental sultan; in the first place, he does not have the sensuality. He is far from delighting in 'feminine beasts' without ulterior motives; they are 'sick, nasty, never really clean';‡‡ Costals admits that young boys' hair smelled stronger and better than women's; Solange sometimes makes him feel sick, her 'cloying, almost disgusting, smell, and this body without muscles, without nerves, like a white slug'.§ He dreams of more worthy embraces, between equals, where gentleness was born of vanquished strength . . . The Oriental relishes woman voluptuously, thereby bringing about carnal reciprocity between lovers: the ardent invocations of the Song of Songs, the tales of The Thousand and One Nights and so much other Arab poetry attest to the glory of the beloved; naturally, there are bad women; but there are also delicious ones, and sensual man lets himself go into their arms confidently, without feeling humiliated. But Montherlant's hero is always on the defensive: 'Take without being taken, the only acceptable formula between superior man and woman.'§§ He speaks readily about the moment of desire, an aggressive moment, a virile one; he avoids the moment of pleasure; he might find that he risks discovering he also

* Ibid.
† The Little Infanta of Castile.
‡ Ibid.
‡‡ The Girls.
§ Ibid.
§§ Ibid.

sweated, panted, 'gave off body odours'; but no, who would dare breathe in his odour, feel his dampness? His defenceless flesh exists for no one, because there is no one opposite him: his is the only consciousness, a pure transparent and sovereign presence; and if pleasure exists for his own consciousness, he does not take it into account: it would have power over him. He speaks complacently of the pleasure he gave, never what he receives: receiving means dependence. 'What I want from a woman is to give her pleasure';* the living warmth of voluptuousness would imply complicity: he accepts none whatsoever; he prefers the haughty solitude of domination. He seeks cerebral, not sensual, satisfactions in women.

And the first of these is an arrogance that aspires to express itself, but without running any risks. Facing the woman, 'we have the same feeling as facing the horse or the bull: the same uncertainty and the same taste *for testing one's strength*.'† Testing it against other men would be risky; they would be involved in the test; they would impose unpredictable rankings, they would return an outside verdict; with a bull or a horse, one remains one's own judge, which is infinitely safer. A woman also, if she is well chosen, remains alone opposite the man. 'I don't love in equality because I seek the child in the woman.' This truism does not explain anything: why does he seek the child and not the equal? Montherlant would be more sincere if he declared that he, Montherlant, does not have any equal; and more precisely that he does not want to have one: his fellow man frightens him. He admires the rigours of the Olympic Games that create hierarchies in which cheating is not possible; but he has not himself learned the lesson; in the rest of his work and life, his heroes, like him, steer clear of all confrontation: they deal with animals, landscapes, children, women-children, and never with equals. In love with the hard clarity of sports, Montherlant accepts as mistresses only those women from whom his fearful pride risks no judgement. He chooses them 'passive and vegetal', infantile, stupid and venal. He systematically avoids granting them a consciousness: if he finds traces of one, he balks, he leaves; there is never question of setting up any intersubjective relationship with woman: she has to be a simple animated object in man's kingdom; she can never be envisaged as subject; her point of view can never be taken into account. Montherlant's hero has a supposedly arrogant morality but it is merely

* Ibid.
† *The Little Infanta of Castile.*

convenient: he is only concerned with his relations with himself. He is attached to woman – or rather he attaches woman – not to take pleasure in her but to take pleasure in himself: as she is absolutely inferior, woman's existence shows up the substantial, the essential and the indestructible superiority of the male; risk-free.

So Douce's foolishness enables Alban to 'reconstruct in some way the sensations of the *ancient demigod* marrying a fabulous Goose'.* At Solange's first touch, Costals changes into a mighty lion: 'They had barely sat down next to each other when he put his hand on the girl's thigh (on top of her dress), then placed it in the middle of her body *as a lion* holds his paw spread out on the piece of meat he has won . . .'† This gesture made daily by so many men in the darkness of cinemas is for Costals the 'primitive gesture of the *Lord*'.‡ If, like him, they had the sense of grandeur, lovers and husbands who kiss their mistresses before taking them would experience these powerful metamorphoses at low cost. 'He vaguely sniffed this woman's face, *like a lion* who, tearing at the meat he held between his paws, stops to lick it.'‡‡ This carnivorous arrogance is not the only pleasure the male gets out of his female; she is his pretext for him to experience his heart freely, spuriously, and always without risk. One night, Costals takes such pleasure in suffering that, sated with the taste of his own pain, he joyfully attacks a chicken leg. Rarely can one indulge in such a whim. But there are other powerful or subtle joys. For example, condescension; Costals condescends to answer some women's letters, and he even sometimes does it with care; to an unimportant, enthusiastic peasant, he writes at the end of a pedantic dissertation, 'I doubt that you can understand me, but that is better than if I *abase* myself to you.'§ He likes sometimes to shape a woman to his image: 'I want you to be like an Arab scarf for me . . . I did not *raise* you up to me for you to be anything else but me.'§§ It amuses him to manufacture some happy memories for Solange. But it is above all when he sleeps with a woman that he drunkenly feels his prodigality. Giver of joy, giver of peace, heat, strength and pleasure: these riches he doles out

* *The Dream.*
† *The Girls.*
‡ Ibid.
‡‡ Ibid.
§ Ibid.
§§ Ibid.

fill him with satisfaction. He owes nothing to his mistresses; to be absolutely sure of that, he often pays them; but even when intercourse is an equal exchange, the woman is obliged to him without reciprocity: she gives nothing, he takes. He thinks nothing of sending Solange to the bathroom the day he deflowers her; even if a woman is dearly cherished, it would be out of the question for a man to go out of his way for her; he is male by divine right, she by divine right is doomed to the douche and bidet. Costals's pride is such a faithful copy of caddishness that it is hard to tell him apart from a boorish travelling salesman.

Woman's first duty is to yield to his generosity's demands; when he imagines Solange does not appreciate his caresses, Costals turns white with rage. He cherishes Rhadidja because her face lights up with joy when he enters her. So he takes pleasure in feeling both like a beast of prey and a magnificent prince. One may be perplexed, however, by where this fever to take and to satisfy comes from if the woman taken and satisfied is just a poor thing, some tasteless flesh faintly palpitating with an ersatz consciousness. How can Costals waste so much time with these futile creatures?

These contradictions show the scope of a pride that is nothing but vanity.

A more subtle delectation belonging to the strong, the generous, the master, is pity for the unfortunate race. Costals from time to time is moved to feel such fraternal gravity, so much sympathy in his heart for the humble, so much 'pity for women'. What can be more touching than the unexpected gentleness of tough beings? He brings back to life this noble postcard image when deigning to consider these sick animals that are women. He even likes to see sportswomen beaten, wounded, exhausted and bruised; as for the others, he wants them as helpless as possible. Their monthly misery disgusts him and yet Costals confides that 'he had always preferred women on those days when he knew them to be affected'.* He even yields to this pity sometimes; he goes so far as to make promises, if not to keep them: he promises to help Andrée, to marry Solange. When pity retreats from his soul, these promises die: doesn't he have the right to change his mind? He makes the rules of the game that he plays with himself as the only partner.

Inferior and pitiful, that is not enough. Montherlant wants woman

* Ibid.

to be despicable. He sometimes claims that the conflict of desire and scorn is a pathetic tragedy: 'Oh! To desire what one disdains: what a tragedy! . . . To have to attract and repel in virtually the same gesture, to light and quickly put out as one does with a match, such is the tragedy of our relations with women!'* In truth, the only tragedy is from the match's point of view, that is, a negligible point of view. For the match lighter, careful not to burn his fingers, it is too obvious that this exercise delights him. If his pleasure were not to 'desire what he disdains', he would not systematically refuse to desire what he esteems: Alban would not repel Dominique; he would choose what he desires: after all, what is so despicable about a little Spanish dancer, young, pretty, passionate and simple; is it that she is poor, from a low social class, and without culture? In Montherlant's eyes, these would seem to be defects. But above all he scorns her as a woman, by decree; he says in fact that it is not the feminine mystery that arouses males' dreams but these dreams that create mystery; but he also projects onto the object what his subjectivity demands: it is not because they are despicable that he disdains women but because he wants to disdain them that they seem abject to him. He feels that the lofty heights he is perched on are all the higher as the distance between them and her is great; that explains why his heroes choose such pathetic sweethearts: against Costals, the great writer, he pits an old provincial virgin tortured by sex and boredom, and a little far-right bourgeois, vacuous and calculating; this is measuring a superior individual with humble gauges: the result is that he comes across as very small to the reader through this awkward caution. But that does not matter as Costals thinks himself grand. The humblest weaknesses of woman are sufficient to feed his pride. A passage in *The Girls* is particularly telling. Before sleeping with Costals, Solange is preparing herself for the night. 'She has to go to the toilet, and Costals remembers this mare he had, so proud, so delicate that she neither urinated nor defecated when he was riding her.' Here can be seen the hatred of the flesh (Swift comes to mind: Celia shits), the desire to see woman as a domestic animal, the refusal to grant her any autonomy, even that of urinating; but Costals's annoyance shows above all that he has forgotten he too has a bladder and intestines; likewise, when he is disgusted by a woman bathed in sweat and body odour, he abolishes all his own secretions: he is a pure spirit served by muscles and a sex organ of steel. 'Disdain is nobler than desire,'

---

* *The Little Infanta of Castile.*

Montherlant declares in *At the Fountains of Desire*[26] and Alvaro: 'My bread is disgust.'[*27] What an alibi scorn is when it wallows in itself! Because one contemplates and judges, one feels totally other than the other that one condemns, and one dismisses the defects one is accused of free of charge. With what headiness has Montherlant exhaled his scorn for human beings throughout his whole life! It is sufficient for him to denounce their foolishness to believe he is intelligent, to denounce their cowardice to believe himself brave. At the beginning of the Occupation, he indulged in an orgy of scorn for his vanquished fellow countrymen: he who is neither French nor vanquished; he is above it all. Incidentally, all things considered, Montherlant, the accuser, did no more than the others to prevent the defeat; he did not even consent to being an officer; but he quickly and furiously resumed his accusations that take him well beyond himself.[†28] He affects to be distressed by his disgust so as to feel it is more sincere and to take more delight in it. The truth is that he finds so many advantages in it that he systematically seeks to drag the woman into abjection. He amuses himself by tempting poor girls with money and jewels: he exults when they accept his malicious gifts. He plays a sadistic game with Andrée, for the pleasure not of making her suffer but of seeing her debase herself. He encourages Solange in infanticide; she welcomes this possibility and Costals's senses are aroused: he takes this potential murderess in a ravishment of scorn.

The apologue of the caterpillars provides the key to this attitude: whatever his hidden intention, it is significant in itself.[‡] Pissing on caterpillars, Montherlant takes pleasure in sparing some and exterminating others; he takes a laughing pity on those that are determined to live and generally lets them off; he is delighted by this game. Without the caterpillars, the urinary stream would have been just an excretion; it becomes an instrument of life and death; in front of the crawling insect, man relieves himself and experiences God's despotic solitude, without running the risk of reciprocity. Likewise, faced with female animals, the male, from the top of his pedestal, sometimes cruel, sometimes tender, sometimes fair, sometimes unpredictable, gives, takes back, satisfies, pities or gets irritated; he defers to nothing but his own pleasure; he is sovereign, free and unique. But these

---

* *The Master of Santiago.*
† *June Solstice.*
‡ Ibid.

animals must not be anything but animals; they would be chosen on purpose, their weaknesses would be flattered; they would be treated as animals with such determination that they would end up accepting their condition. In similar fashion, the blacks' petty robberies and lies charmed the whites of Louisiana and Georgia, confirming the superiority of their own skin colour; and if one of these Negroes persists in being honest, he is treated even worse. In similar fashion the debasement of man was systematically practised in the concentration camps: the ruling race found proof in this abjection that it was of superhuman essence.

This was no chance meeting. Montherlant is known to have admired Nazi ideology. He loved seeing the swastika and the sun wheel triumph in a celebration of the sun. 'The victory of the sun wheel is not just a victory of the Sun, of paganism. It is the victory of the sun principle, which is that everything changes . . . I see today the triumph of the principle I am imbued with, that I praised, that with a full consciousness I feel governs my life.'* It is also known with what a relevant sense of grandeur he presented these Germans who 'breathe the great style of strength' as an example to the French during the Occupation.† The same panicky taste for facility that makes him run when facing his equals brings him to his knees when facing the winners: kneeling to them is his way of identifying with them; so now he is a winner, which is what he always wanted, be it against a bull, caterpillars or women, against life itself and freedom. It must be said that even before the victory, he was flattering the 'totalitarian magicians'.‡[29] Like them, he has always been a nihilist, he has always hated humanity. 'People aren't even worth being led (and humanity does not have to have done something to you [for you] to detest it to this extent)';‡‡ like them, he thinks that certain beings – race, nation, or he, Montherlant, himself – are in possession of an absolute privilege that grants them full rights over others. His morality justifies and calls for war and persecution. To judge his attitude regarding women, this ethic we must scrutinise, because after all it is important to know *in the name of what* they are condemned.

Nazi mythology had a historical infrastructure: nihilism expressed German despair; the cult of the hero served positive aims for which millions of soldiers lost their lives. Montherlant's attitude has no

* Ibid.
† Ibid.
‡ *September Equinox.*
‡‡ *At the Fountains of Desire.*

positive counterweight and it expresses nothing but his own existential choice. In fact, this hero chooses fear. There is a claim to sovereignty in every consciousness: but it can only be confirmed by risking itself; no superiority is ever given since man is nothing when reduced to his subjectivity; hierarchies can only be established among men's acts and works; merit must be ceaselessly won: Montherlant knows it himself. 'One only has rights over what one is willing to risk.' But he never wants to risk *himself* amid his peers. And because he does not dare confront humanity, he abolishes it. 'Infuriating obstacle that of beings,' says the king in *The Dead Queen*.[30] They give the lie to the complacent 'fairyland' the conceited creates around himself. They have to be negated. It is noteworthy that *none* of Montherlant's works depicts a conflict between man and man; coexistence is the great living drama: he eludes it. His hero always rises up alone facing animals, children, women, landscapes; he is prey to his own desires (like the queen of *Pasiphaé*) or his own demands (like the master of Santiago), but *no person* is ever beside him. Even Alban in *The Dream* does not have a friend: when Prinet was alive, he disdained him; he only exalts him over his dead body. Montherlant's works, like his life, recognise only *one* consciousness.

With this, all feeling disappears from this universe; there can be no intersubjective relation if there is only one subject. Love is derisory; but it is not in the name of friendship that it is worthy of scorn, because 'friendship lacks guts.'* And all human solidarity is haughtily rejected. The hero was not engendered; he is not limited by space and time: 'I do not see any reasonable reason to be interested in exterior things that are of my time more than any others of any past year.'†[31] Nothing that happens to others counts for him: 'In truth events never counted for me. I only liked them for the rays they made in me by going through me . . . Let them be what they want to be . . .'‡ Action is impossible: 'Having had passion, energy, and boldness and not being able to put them to any use through lack of faith in anything human!'‡‡ That means that any *transcendence* is forbidden. Montherlant recognises that. Love and friendship are twaddle, scorn prevents action; he does not believe in art for art's sake, and he does not believe in God. All that is left is

* Ibid.
† *The Possession of Oneself.*
‡ *June Solstice.*
‡‡ *At the Fountains of Desire.*

the immanence of pleasure. 'My one ambition is to use my senses better than others,' he writes in 1925.* And again: 'In fact, what do I want? To possess beings that please me in peace and poetry.'† And in 1941: 'But I who accuse, what have I done with these twenty years? They have been a dream filled with my pleasure. I have lived high and wide, drunk on what I love: what a mouth-to-mouth with life!'‡ So be it. But is it not precisely because she wallows in immanence that woman is trodden upon? What higher aims, what great designs does Montherlant set against the mother's or lover's possessive love? He also seeks 'possession'; and as for the 'mouth-to-mouth with life', many women can give that back in kind. He does partake of unusual pleasures: those that can be had from animals, boys and preadolescent girls; he is indignant that a passionate mistress would not dream of putting her twelve-year-old daughter in his bed: this indignation is not very solar. Can he not be aware that women's sensuality is no less tormented than men's? If that were the criterion for ranking the sexes, women would perhaps be first. Montherlant's inconsistencies are truly abominable. In the name of 'alternation' he declares that since nothing is worth anything, everything is equal; he accepts everything, he wants to embrace everything and it pleases him that mothers with children are frightened by his broad-mindedness; but he is the one who demanded an 'inquisition'§ during the Occupation that would censure films and newspapers; American girls' thighs disgust him, the bull's gleaming penis exalts him: to each his own; everyone re-creates his own 'phantasm'; in the name of what values does this great orgiast spit with disgust on the orgies of others? Because they are not his own? So can all morality be reduced to being Montherlant?

He would obviously answer that pleasure is not everything: style matters. Pleasure should be the other side of renunciation; the voluptuary also has to feel he is made of the stuff of heroes and saints. But many women are expert in reconciling their pleasures with the high image they have of themselves. Why should we think that Montherlant's narcissistic dreams are worth more than theirs?

---

* Ibid.

† Ibid.

‡ *June Solstice.*

§ 'We ask for a body that would have discretionary power to stop anything it deems to be harmful to the essence of French human values. Some sort of an inquisition in the name of French human values' (ibid.).

Because, in truth, this is a question of dreams. Because he denies
them any objective content, the words Montherlant juggles with –
'grandeur', 'holiness' and 'heroism' – are merely eye-catchers. Montherlant
is afraid of risking his own superiority among men; to be intoxicated
on this exalting wine, he retreats into the clouds: the Unique is obviously supreme. He closes himself up in a museum of mirages: mirrors
reflect his own image infinitely, and he thinks that he can thus populate the earth; but he is no more than a reclusive prisoner of himself.
He thinks he is free; but he alienates his liberty in the interests of his
ego; he models the Montherlant statue on postcard-imagery standards.
Alban repelling Dominique because he sees a fool in the mirror illustrates this enslavement: it is in the eyes of others that one is a fool.
The arrogant Alban subjects his heart to this collective consciousness
that he despises. Montherlant's liberty is an attitude, not a reality.
Without an aim, action is impossible, so he consoles himself with
gestures: it is mimicry. Women are convenient partners; they give him
his lines, he takes the leading role, he crowns himself with laurels and
drapes himself in purple: but everything takes place on his private stage;
thrown onto the public square, in real light, under a real sky, the actor
no longer sees clearly, cannot stand, staggers, and falls. In a moment
of lucidity, Costals cries out: 'Deep down, these "victories" over women
are some farce!'* Yes. Montherlant's values and exploits are a sad farce.
The noble deeds that intoxicate him are also merely gestures, never
undertakings: he is touched by Peregrinus's suicide, Pasiphaé's boldness, and the elegance of the Japanese who shelters his opponent under
his umbrella before taking his life in a duel. But he declares that 'the
adversary's specificity and the ideas he is supposedly representing are
not all that important'.† This declaration had a particular resonance in
1941. Every war is beautiful, he also says, whatever its aims; force is
always admirable, whatever it serves. 'Combat without faith is the
formula we necessarily end up with to maintain the only acceptable
idea of man: one where he is the hero and the sage.'‡ But it is curious
that Montherlant's noble indifference regarding all causes inclines him
not towards resistance but towards national revolution, that his sovereign freedom chooses submission and that he looks for the secret of
heroic wisdom not in the Maquis but in the conquerors. This is not by

* *The Girls.*
† *June Solstice.*
‡ Ibid.

chance either. The pseudo-sublime of *The Dead Queen* and *The Master of Santiago* is where these mystifications lead. In these plays that are all the more significant for their ambition, two imperious males sacrifice women guilty of simply being human beings to their hollow pride; they desire love and earthly happiness: as punishment, one loses her life and the other her soul. If once again one asks, what for? the author answers haughtily: for nothing. He does not want the king's reasons for killing Inès to be too imperious: the murder should be a banal political crime. 'Why do I kill her? There is probably a reason, but I cannot see it,' he says. The reason is that the solar principle triumphs over earthly banality; but this principle does not inform any aim: it calls for destruction, nothing more, as has already been seen. As for Alvaro, Montherlant says in a preface that he is interested in certain men of this period in 'their clear-cut faith, their scorn for the outside reality, their taste for destruction, their passion for nothing'. This is the passion to which the master of Santiago sacrifices his daughter. She will be arrayed in the beautiful shimmer of words mystical. Is it not boring to prefer happiness to mysticism? Sacrifices and renunciations have meaning only in the light of an aim, a human aim; and aims that go beyond singular love or personal happiness can only exist in a world that recognises the price of both love and happiness; the 'shopgirl's morality' is more authentic than hollow phantasms because it is rooted in life and reality, where great aspirations can spring forth. Inès de Castro can easily be pictured in Buchenwald, with the king hurrying to the German Embassy for reasons of state. Many shopgirls were worthy of a respect that we would not grant to Montherlant during the Occupation. The empty words he crams himself with are dangerous for their very hollowness: this superhuman mysticism justifies all kinds of temporal devastations. The fact is that in the plays under discussion, this mystique is attested to by two murders, one physical and the other moral; Alvaro does not have far to go to become a grand inquisitor: wild, solitary, unrecognisable; nor the king – misunderstood, rejected – to become a Himmler. They kill women, they kill Jews, they kill effeminate men and 'Jewed' Christians, they kill everything they want or like to kill in the name of these lofty ideas. Only by negations can negative mysticisms be affirmed. True surpassing is a positive step towards the future, towards humanity's future. The false hero, to convince himself he goes far and flies high, always looks back, at his feet; he despises, he accuses, he oppresses, he persecutes, he tortures, he massacres. It is through the evil he does to his neighbour that he measures his superiority over him. Such are Montherlant's summits that he points out with an arrogant finger when he interrupts his 'mouth-to-mouth with life'.

'Like the donkey at an Arab waterwheel, I turn, I turn, blind and endlessly retracing my steps. But I don't bring up freshwater.' There is not much to add to this avowal that Montherlant signed in 1927. Freshwater never sprang forth. Maybe Montherlant should have lit Peregrinus's pyre: that would have been the most logical solution. He preferred to take refuge in his own cult. Instead of giving himself to this world, which he did not know how to nourish, he settled for seeing himself in it; and he organised his life in the interest of this mirage visible to his eyes alone. 'Princes are at ease in all situations, even in defeat,'* he writes; and because he delighted in defeat, he believes he is king. He learns from Nietzsche that 'woman is the hero's amusement' and he thinks that it is enough to get pleasure from women to be anointed hero. The rest is the same. As Costals might say: 'Deep down, what a farce!'

II
D. H. LAWRENCE OR PHALLIC PRIDE

Lawrence is the very antipode of Montherlant. His objective is not to define the special relations of woman and man but to situate them both in the truth of Life. This truth is neither representation nor will: it envelops the animality in which human beings have their roots. Lawrence passionately rejects the antithesis sex versus brain; he has a cosmic optimism radically opposed to Schopenhauer's pessimism, the will to live expressed in the phallus is joy: thought and action must derive their source from this or else it would be an empty concept and a sterile mechanism. The sexual cycle alone is not sufficient, because it falls back into immanence: it is synonymous with death; but better this mutilated reality – sex and death – than an existence cut off from carnal humus. Unlike Antaeus, man needs more than to renew contact with the earth from time to time; his life as a male has to be wholly the expression of his virility, which posits and requires woman in its immediacy; she is thus neither diversion nor prey, she is not an object confronting a subject but a pole necessary for the existence of the pole of the opposite sign. Men who have misunderstood this truth – a Napoleon for example – have missed their destiny as men: they are fail-

* Ibid.

ures. It is by fulfilling his generality as intensely as possible, and not by affirming his singularity, that the individual can save himself: whether male or female, an individual should never seek the triumph of pride or the exaltation of his self in erotic relations; to use one's sex as a tool of one's will is the irreparable error; it is essential to break the barriers of the ego, transcend the very limits of consciousness and renounce all personal sovereignty. Nothing could be more beautiful than that little statue of a woman giving birth: 'A terrible face, void, peaked, abstracted almost into meaninglessness by the weight of sensation beneath.'* This ecstasy is neither sacrifice nor abandon; there is no question of either sex letting itself be swallowed up by the other; neither the man nor the woman should be like a broken fragment of a couple; one's sex is not a wound; each one is a complete being, perfectly polarised; when one is assured in his virility, the other in her femininity, 'each acknowledges the perfection of the polarised sex circuit';† the sexual act is without annexation, without surrender of either partner, the marvellous fulfilment of each other. When Ursula and Birkin finally found each other, they would give each other this star-equilibrium which alone is freedom . . . 'For she was to him what he was to her, the immemorial magnificence of mystic, palpable real otherness.'‡ Attaining each other in the generous wrenching of passion, two lovers together attain the Other, the All. So it is for Paul and Clara in the moment of their love:‡‡ she is for him 'a strong, strange, wild life, that breathed with his in the darkness through this hour. It was so much bigger than themselves, that he was hushed. They had met, and included in their meeting the thrust of the manifold grass stems, the cry of the peewit, the wheel of the stars.' Lady Chatterley and Mellors attain the same cosmic joys: blending into each other, they blend into the trees, the light and the rain. Lawrence develops this doctrine extensively in *A propos of 'Lady Chatterley's Lover'*: 'Marriage is no marriage that is not basically and permanently phallic, and that is not linked up with the sun and the earth, the moon and the fixed stars and the planets, in the rhythm of days, in the rhythm of months, in the rhythm of quarters, of years, of decades and of centuries. Marriage is no marriage that is not a correspondence of blood. For the blood is

* *Women in Love.*
† Ibid.
‡ Ibid.
‡‡ *Sons and Lovers.*

the substance of the soul.' 'The blood of man and the blood of woman are two eternally different streams, that can never be mingled.' This is why these two streams encircle the whole of life in their meanderings. 'The phallus is a column of blood, that fills the valley of blood of a woman. The great river of male blood touches to its depth the great river of female blood, yet neither breaks its bounds. It is the deepest of all communions . . . And it is one of the greatest mysteries.' This communion is a miraculous enrichment; but it requires that claims to 'personality' be abolished. When personalities seek to reach each other without surrendering themselves, as usually happens in modern civilisation, their attempt is doomed to failure. There is a personal, blank, cold, nervous, poetic sexuality that dissolves each one's vital stream. Lovers treat each other like instruments, breeding hate between them: so it is with Lady Chatterley and Michaelis; they remain locked in their subjectivity; they can experience a fever analogous to that procured by alcohol or opium, but it is without object: they fail to discover the reality of the other; they attain nothing. Lawrence would have condemned Costals summarily. He depicted Gerald* as one of those proud and egotistical males; and Gerald is in large part responsible for this hell he and Gudrun hurl themselves into. Cerebral and wilful, he delights in the empty assertion of his self and hardens himself against life: for the pleasure of mastering a spirited mare, he holds her firm against a fence where a train thunders past, bloodying her rebellious flanks and intoxicating himself with his power. This will to dominate debases the woman against whom it is directed; physically weak, she is thus transformed into a slave. Gerald leans over Pussum: 'Her inchoate look of a violated slave, whose fulfilment lies in her further and further violation, made his nerves quiver . . . his was the only will, she was the passive substance of his will.' Here is pitiful domination; if the woman is merely a passive substance, the male dominates nothing. He thinks he is taking, enriching himself: it is a delusion. Gerald embraces Gudrun tightly in his arms: 'She was the rich lovely substance of his being . . . So she was passed away and gone in him, and he was perfected.' But as soon as he leaves her, he finds himself alone and empty; and the next day, she fails to appear at their rendezvous. If the woman is strong, the male claim arouses a symmetrical claim in her; fascinated and rebellious, she becomes masochistic and sadistic in turn. Gudrun is greatly disturbed when she sees Gerald press the frightened mare's flanks

* *Women in Love.*

between his thighs; but she is also disturbed when Gerald's wet nurse tells her how in the past she used to 'pinch his little bottom'. Masculine arrogance provokes feminine resistance. While Ursula is won over and saved by Birkin's sexual purity, as Lady Chatterley was by the game-keeper, Gerald drags Gudrun into a struggle with no way out. One night, unhappy, shattered by a death, he abandons himself in her arms. 'She was the great bath of life, he worshipped her. Mother and substance of all life she was . . . But the miraculous, soft effluence of her breast suffused over him, over his seared, damaged brain, like a healing lymph, like a soft, soothing flow of life itself, perfect as if he were bathed in the womb again.' That night he senses what communion with woman might be; but it is too late; his happiness is vitiated because Gudrun is not really present; she lets Gerald sleep on her shoulder, but she stays awake, impatient, apart. It is the punishment of the individual who is his own prey: alone he cannot end his solitude; in erecting barriers around his self, he erected those around the *Other*: he will never connect to it. In the end, Gerald dies, killed by Gudrun and by himself.

Thus it would seem at first that neither of the two sexes is privileged. Neither is subject. Woman is neither a prey nor a simple pretext. As Malraux notes,* Lawrence thinks that it is not enough, unlike Hindus, for woman to be merely the occasion for a contact with the infinite, as would be a landscape: that would be another way of making her an object. She is as real as the man; a real communion has to be reached. This is why Lawrence's heroes demand much more from their mistresses than the gift of their bodies: Paul does not want Miriam to give herself to him as a tender sacrifice; Birkin does not want Ursula to limit herself to seeking pleasure in his arms; cold or burning, the woman who remains closed within herself leaves the man to his solitude: he must reject her. Both have to give themselves to each other, body and soul. If this giving is accomplished, they have to remain forever faithful to each other. Lawrence believed in monogamous marriage. There is only a quest for variety if one is interested in the uniqueness of beings: but phallic marriage is founded on generality. When the virility–femininity circuit is established, desire for change is inconceivable: it is a perfect circuit, closed on itself and definitive.

Reciprocal gift, reciprocal fidelity: is it really the reign of mutual recognition? Far from it. Lawrence passionately believes in male supremacy. The very expression 'phallic marriage', the equivalence he

* Preface to *L'amant de Lady Chatterly*.

establishes between the sexual and the phallic, is proof enough. Of the two bloodstreams that mysteriously marry, the phallic stream is favoured. 'The phallus is the connecting link between the two rivers, that establishes the two streams in a oneness.' Thus man is not only one of the terms of the couple, but also their relationship; he is their surpassing: 'The bridge to the future is the phallus.' Lawrence wants to substitute the cult of the phallic for that of the Goddess Mother; when he wants to highlight the sexual nature of the cosmos, it is through man's virility rather than woman's womb. He almost never shows a man excited by a woman: but over and over he shows woman secretly overwhelmed by the vibrant, subtle, insinuating appeal of the male; his heroines are beautiful and healthy, but not sensuous, while his heroes are troubled wild animals. It is male animals that embody the troubling and powerful mystery of Life; women are subjugated by their spell: this one is affected by the fox, that one is taken with a stallion, Gudrun feverishly challenges a herd of young oxen; she is overwhelmed by the rebellious vigour of a rabbit. A social privilege is connected to this cosmic one. Because the phallic stream is impetuous and aggressive and bestrides the future – Lawrence does not make himself perfectly clear on this point – it is up to man to 'carry forward the banner of life';* he reaches for goals, he incarnates transcendence; woman is absorbed by her sentiments, she is all interiority; she is doomed to immanence. Not only does man play the active role in sexual life, but it is through him that this life is transcended; he is rooted in the sexual world, but he escapes from it; she remains locked up in it. Thought and action have their roots in the phallus; lacking the phallus, woman has no rights to either: she can play the man's role, and brilliantly at that, but it is a game without truth. 'Woman is really polarised downwards, towards the centre of the earth. Her deep positivity is in the downward flow, the moon-pull. And man is polarised upwards, towards the sun and the day's activity.'† For woman, 'her deepest consciousness is in the loins and the belly'.‡ If she turns upward, the moment comes when everything collapses.' In the domain of action, man must be the initiator, the positive; woman is the positive on the emotional level. Thus Lawrence goes back to the traditional bourgeois conception of Bonald, Auguste Comte and Clément Vautel. Woman must subordinate

---

* *Fantasia of the Unconscious.*
† Ibid.
‡ Ibid.

her existence to that of man. 'She's got to believe in you . . . and in the
deep purpose you stand for.'* Then man will owe her tenderness and
infinite gratitude. 'Ah, how good it is to come home to your wife when
she *believes* in you and submits to your purpose that is beyond her . . .
You feel unfathomable gratitude to the woman who loves you.'†
Lawrence adds that to merit this devotion, man must be authentically
invested with a higher purpose; if his project is but a sham, the couple
sinks into insignificant mystification; better still to enclose one's self
in the feminine cycle – love and death – like Anna Karenina and Vronsky
or Carmen and Don José, than to lie to each other like Pierre and
Natasha. But subject to this reserve, Lawrence, like Proudhon and
Rousseau, advocates monogamous marriage where woman derives the
justification for her existence from her husband. Lawrence was just as
vituperative as Montherlant concerning the woman who wants to
reverse the roles. She should cease playing at the Magna Mater, claiming
to be in possession of the truth of life; dominating and devouring, she
mutilates the male, she forces him to fall back into immanence and
she leads him astray from his goals. Lawrence was far from disparaging
motherhood: on the contrary; he rejoices in being flesh, he accepts his
birth, he cherishes his mother; mothers appear in his work as magnificent examples of real femininity; they are pure renunciation, absolute
generosity, and all their human warmth is devoted to their children;
they accept them becoming men, they are proud of it. But the egois-
tical lover who tries to bring the man back to his childhood must be
feared; she cuts man down in his flight. 'The moon, the planet of
women, sways us back.'‡ She speaks incessantly about love: but to love
for her is to take, to fill the void she feels in herself; this love is close
to hate; so it is that Hermione, who suffers from a horrible deficiency
because she has never been able to give herself, wants to annex Birkin;
she fails; she tries to kill him and the voluptuous ecstasy she feels in
striking him is identical to the egotistic spasm of pleasure.‡‡ Lawrence
detests modern women, celluloid and rubber creatures who claim a
consciousness. When the woman has become sexually conscious, 'there
she is functioning away from her own head and her own consciousness of herself and her own automatic self-will'.§ He forbids her to

* Ibid.
† Ibid.
‡ Ibid.
‡‡ *Women in Love.*
§ *Fantasia of the Unconscious.*

have an autonomous sensuality; she is made to give, not to take. Putting words in Mellors's mouth, Lawrence cries out his horror of lesbians. But he also blames the woman who has a detached or aggressive attitude to the male; Paul feels wounded and irritated when Miriam caresses his loins, telling him: 'You are so fine!' Gudrun, like Miriam, is at fault when she feels enchanted with her lover's beauty: this contemplation separates them, as much as the irony of icy women intellectuals who consider the penis pitiful or male gymnastics ridiculous; the intense quest for pleasure is no less blameworthy: there is an acute, solitary pleasure that also separates, and woman should not aim for it. Lawrence sketched many portraits of these independent, dominating women who have missed their feminine vocation. Ursula and Gudrun are of this type. At first Ursula is a dominator. 'Man must render himself up to her. He must be quaffed to the dregs by her.'* She will learn to overcome her will. But Gudrun is stubborn; cerebral, artistic, she fiercely envies men their independence and their potential for activity; she persists in keeping her individuality intact; she wants to live for herself; ironic and possessive, she will remain forever shut up in her subjectivity. The most significant figure is Miriam† because she is the least sophisticated. Gerald is partially responsible for Gudrun's failure; but vis-à-vis Paul, Miriam alone bears the full weight of her ill fate. She also would like to be a man, and she hates men; she does not accept herself in her generality; she wants to 'distinguish herself'; because the great stream of life does not pass through her, she can be like a sorceress or a priestess, but never a bacchante; she is moved by things only when she has re-created them in her soul, giving them a religious value: this fervour itself separates her from life; she is poetic, mystical, maladapted. 'She was not clumsy, and yet none of her movements seemed quite THE movement . . . she put too much strength into the effort.' She seeks interior joys, and reality frightens her; sexuality frightens her; when she sleeps with Paul, her heart stands aside in a kind of horror; she is always consciousness, never life: she is not a companion; she does not consent to meld with her lover; she wants to absorb him into herself. He is irritated by this will; he becomes violently angry when he sees her caressing flowers: she seems to want to tear their hearts out; he insults her: 'You're always begging things to love you . . . as if you were a beggar for love . . . You don't want to love – your eternal

---

* *Women in Love.*
† *Sons and Lovers.*

and abnormal craving is to be loved. You aren't positive, you are negative. You absorb, absorb, as if you must fill yourself up with love,
because you've got a shortage somewhere.' Sexuality does not exist to
fill a void; it must be the expression of a whole being. What women
call love is their greed before the virile force they want to grab. Paul's
mother lucidly thinks about Miriam: 'She wants to absorb him. She
wants to draw him out and absorb him till there is nothing left of him,
even for himself. He will never be a man on his own feet – she will
suck him up.' The young girl is happy when her friend is ill because
she can take care of him: she attempts to serve him, but it is a way of
imposing her will on him. Because she lives apart from him, she excites
in Paul 'an intensity like madness. Which fascinated him, as drug taking
might.' But she is incapable of bringing him joy and peace; from the
depth of her love, in her secret self 'she hated him because she loved
him and he dominated her'. And Paul distances himself from her. He
seeks his balance with Clara; beautiful, lively, animal, she gives herself
unreservedly; and the lovers reach moments of ecstasy that surpass
them both; but Clara does not understand this revelation. She believes
that she owes this joy to Paul himself, to his uniqueness, and she wants
to appropriate him: she fails to keep him precisely because she wants
him for herself. As soon as love is individualised, it changes into avid
egotism and the miracle of eroticism vanishes.

The woman must renounce personal love: neither Mellors nor Don
Cipriano consents to saying words of love to his mistress. Teresa, the
model wife, becomes indignant when Kate asks her if she loves Don
Ramón.* 'He is my life,' she replies; the gift she concedes to him is something quite different from love. Woman must, like man, abdicate all pride
and all will; if she embodies life for the man, he embodies it for her as
well; Lady Chatterley only finds peace and joy because she recognises
this truth: 'She would give up her own hard, bright female power. She
was weary of it, stiffened with it. She would sink in the new bath of life,
in the depths of her womb and her bowels, that sang the voiceless song
of adoration': so she is called to the rapture of the bacchantes; blindly
obeying her lover, not seeking herself in his arms, she forms with him
a harmonious couple, in tune with the rain, the trees and the spring
flowers. Likewise, Ursula renounces her individuality in Birkin's hands
and they attain a 'star equilibrium'. But it is *The Plumed Serpent* above all
that reflects in its entirety Lawrence's ideal. For Don Cipriano is one of

* *The Plumed Serpent.*

those men who 'carry forward the banner of life'; he has a mission and is entirely given over to it to such an extent that virility in him is surpassed and exalted to the point of divinity: if he anoints himself god, it is not a mystification; every man who is fully man is a god; he thus deserves the absolute devotion of a woman. Imbued with Western prejudices, Kate at first refuses this dependence; she is attached to her personality and her limited existence; but little by little letting herself be penetrated by the great stream of life, she gives her body and soul to Cipriano. It is not a slave's surrender: before deciding to stay with him, she insists that he recognise his need for her; he recognises it, since in fact woman is necessary for man; so she consents to never being anything other than his companion; she adopts his goals, his values, his universe. This submission expresses itself even in eroticism; Lawrence does not want the woman to be tense in the search for pleasure, separated from the male by the spasm that jolts her; he deliberately refuses to bring her to orgasm; Don Cipriano withdraws from Kate when he feels her close to this nervous pleasure; she renounces even this sexual autonomy. 'Her strange seething feminine will and desire subsided in her and swept away, leaving her soft and powerfully potent, like the hot springs of water that gushed up so noiseless, so soft, yet so powerful, with a sort of secret potency.'

We can see why Lawrence's novels are first and foremost 'guidebooks for women'. It is infinitely more difficult for the woman than for the man to submit to the cosmic order, because he submits in an autonomous fashion, whereas she needs the mediation of the male. When the Other takes on the form of a foreign consciousness and will, there is real surrender; on the contrary, an autonomous submission strangely resembles a sovereign decision. Lawrence's heroes are either condemned from the start or else from the start they hold the secret of wisdom;* their submission to the cosmos was consummated so long ago and they derive such interior certitude from it that they seem as arrogant as a self-important individualist; there is a god who speaks through their mouths: Lawrence himself. But the woman must bow to their divinity. Even if the man is a phallus and not a brain, the virile individual keeps his privileges; woman is not evil, she is even good: but subordinated. Once again, it is the ideal of the 'real woman' that Lawrence offers us, that is, of the woman who unhesitatingly assents to defining herself as the Other.

---

* With the exception of Paul in *Sons and Lovers*, who is the most vibrant of all. But that is the only novel that shows us a masculine learning experience.

III

CLAUDEL OR THE HANDMAIDEN OF THE LORD

The originality of Claudel's Catholicism is of such an obstinate optimism that evil itself turns to good.

> *Evil itself*
> *Abides its own share of good which must not be wasted.**32

Adopting the point of view that can only be that of the Creator –
since we assume the Creator to be all-powerful, omniscient and benevolent – Claudel subscribes to creation entirely; without hell and sin,
there could be no free will, no salvation; when he brought forth the
world from nothing, God foresaw the Fall and the Redemption. In the
eyes of Jews and Christians, Eve's disobedience had put her daughters
in a very bad position: we see how badly the Fathers of the Church
have mistreated women. But here, on the contrary, she is justified if
one accepts that she has served divine purposes. 'Woman! that service
she once by her disobedience rendered to God in the earthly Paradise;
that deep agreement reached between her and Him; that flesh she put
at the disposal of Redemption by way of the fault!'†33 There is no doubt
she is the source of sin, and through her man lost paradise. But man's
sins have been redeemed, and this world is blessed anew: 'We have not
left the paradise of delight in which God first put us!'‡34

'Every Land is the Promised Land.'‡‡35

Nothing that has come from God's hands, nothing that is given, can
be in itself bad: 'We pray to God with the entirety of His work! Nothing
He made is in vain, nothing is alien to anything else.'§36 And furthermore there is nothing that is unnecessary. 'All things that He has created
commune together, all at one and the same time are necessary each to
each.'§§37 Thus it is that woman has her place in the harmony of the
universe; but it is not just an ordinary place; there is a 'strange and, in
Lucifer's eyes, scandalous passion that binds the Eternal to this momentary flower of Nothingness.'◊

---

* *Break of Noon.*
† *The Adventures of Sophie.*
‡ *Cantata for Three Voices.*
‡‡ *Conversations in the Loir-et-Cher.*
§ *The Satin Slipper.*
§§ *The Tidings Brought to Mary.*
◊ *The Adventures of Sophie.*

Of course, woman can be destructive: In Lechy*[38] Claudel incarnated the bad woman who drives man to his destruction; in *Break of Noon*, Ysé ruins the life of those trapped by her love. But if there were not this risk of loss, there would not be salvation either. Woman 'is the element of risk He deliberately introduced into the midst of His marvellous construction'.[†] It is good that man should know the temptations of the flesh. 'It is this enemy within us that gives our lives their dramatic element, their poignant salt. If our souls were not so brutally assailed, they would continue to sleep, yet here they leap up . . . This struggle is the apprenticeship of victory.'[‡][39] Man is summoned to become aware of his soul not only by the spiritual path but also by that of the flesh. 'And what flesh speaks more forcefully to man than the flesh of a woman?'[‡‡] Whatever wrenches him from sleep, from security, is useful: love in whatever form it presents has the virtue of appearing in 'our small personal worlds, ordered by our conventional reasoning, as a deeply perturbing element'.[§][40] Often woman is but a deceptive giver of illusions:

> I am the promise that cannot be kept, and my grace consists of that very thing. I am the sweetness of what is, with the regret for what is not. I am the truth that has the countenance of error, and he who loves me does not bother to disentangle each from each.[§§][41]

But there is also usefulness in illusion; this is what the Guardian Angel announces to Donna Prouhèze:

> *Even sin! Sin also serves.*
> *So it was good for him to love me?*
> *It was good for you to teach him desire.*
> *Desire for an illusion? For a shadow that forever escapes him?*
> *Desire is for what is, illusion is for what is not. Desire pursued to the furthermost point of illusion*
> *Is desire pursued to the furthermost point of what is not?*[◊]

* *The Trade.*
† *The Adventures of Sophie.*
‡ *The Black Bird in the Rising Sun.*
‡‡ *The Satin Slipper.*
§ *Positions and Propositions.*
§§ *The City.*
◊ *The Satin Slipper.*

By God's will, what Prouhèze was for Rodrigo is 'a sword through his heart'.*

But woman in God's hands is not only this blade, this burn; the riches of this world are not meant to be always refused: they are also nourishment; man must take them with him and make them his own. The loved one will embody for him all the recognisable beauty in the universe; she will be a chant of adoration on his lips.

'How lovely you are, Violaine, and how lovely is the world where you are.'†

'Who is she who stands before me, gentler than the breeze, like the moon among the young foliage? . . . Here she is like the fresh honeybee unfolding its newborn wings, like a lanky doe, and like a flower that does not even know it is beautiful.'‡42

'Let me breathe your scent like that of the earth, when it glows and is washed like an altar, and brings forth blue and yellow flowers.

'And let me breathe the summer's aroma that smells of grass and hay, and is like the autumn's fragrance . . .'‡‡

She is the sum of all nature: the rose and the lily, the star, the fruit, the bird, the wind, the moon, the sun, the fountain, 'the peaceful tumult, in noon's light, of a great port'.§ And she is still more: a peer.

'Now, this time for me, that luminous point of night's living sands is something quite different from a star,

'Someone human like me . . .'§§

'You will be alone no more, and I will be in you and with you, with you for ever, the devoted one. Someone yours for ever who will never be absent, your wife.'◊

'Someone to listen to what I say and trust in me.

'A soft-voiced companion who takes us in her arms and attests she is a woman.'◊◊43

Body and soul, in taking her into his heart, man finds his roots in this earth and accomplishes himself.

---

* Ibid.
† *The Tidings Brought to Mary.*
‡ *The Young Violaine.*
‡‡ *The City.*
§ *The Satin Slipper.*
§§ Ibid.
◊ *The City.*
◊◊ *The Hard Crusts.*

'I took this woman, and she is my measure and my earthly allotment.'[*]
She is a burden, and man is not made to be burdened.

'And the foolish man finds himself surprised by this absurd person,
this great heavy and cumbersome thing.

'So many dresses, so much hair, what can he do?

'He is no longer able, he no longer wants to be rid of her.'[†]

This burden is also a treasure. 'I am a great treasure,' says Violaine.

Reciprocally, woman achieves her earthly destiny by giving herself
to man.

'For what is the use of being a woman, unless to be gathered?

'And being this rose, if not to be devoured? And of being born,

'Unless to belong to another and to be the prey of a powerful lion?'[‡]

'What shall we do, who can only be a woman in his arms, and in
his heart a cup of wine?'[‡‡]

'But you my soul say: I have not been created in vain and he who
is called to gather me is alive!'

'The heart that was waiting for me, ah! what joy for me to fill it.'[§]

Of course this union of man and woman is to be consummated in
the presence of God; it is holy and belongs in the eternal; it should be
consented to by a deep movement of the will and *cannot* be broken by
an individual caprice. 'Love, the consent that two free people grant
each other, seemed to God so great a thing that he made it a sacrament. In this as in all other matters the sacrament gives reality to that
which was but the heart's supreme desire.'[§§] And further:

'Marriage is not pleasure but the sacrifice of pleasure, it is the study made
by two souls who for ever, henceforth, and to end beyond themselves,

'Must be content with one another.'[◊]

It is not only joy that man and woman will bring to each other
through this union; each will take possession of the other's being. 'He
it was who knew how to find that soul within my soul! . . . He it was
who came to me and held out his hand. He was my calling! How can
I describe it? He was my origin: it was he by whom and for whom I
came into the world.'[◊◊][44]

* *The City.*
† *Break of Noon.*
‡ *Cantata for Three Voices.*
‡‡ Ibid.
§ Ibid.
§§ *Positions and Propositions.*
◊ *The Satin Slipper.*
◊◊ *Book of Toby and Sara.*

'A whole part of myself which I thought did not exist because I was busy elsewhere and not thinking of it. Ah! My God, it exists, it does exist, terribly.'*[45]

And this being appears as justified, necessary for the one it completes. 'It is in him that you were necessary,' says Prouhèze's Angel. And Rodrigo:

'For what is it to die but to stop being necessary?

'When was she able to do without me? When shall I cease to be for her that without which she could not have been herself?'[†]

'They say that no soul was made except in a life and in a mysterious relationship with other lives.

'But for us it is still more than that. For I exist as I speak; one single thing resonating between two people.

'When we were being fashioned, Orion, I think that a bit of your substance was left over and that I am made of what you lack.'[‡]

In the marvellous necessity of this union, paradise is regained, death conquered:

'At last the being who existed in paradise is here remade of a man and woman.'‡‡[46]

'We will never manage to do away with death unless it be by one another.

'As purple mixed with orange gives pure red.'[§]

Finally, in the form of another, each one attains the Other, that is God, in his plenitude.

'What we give one another is God in different guises.'[§§]

'Would your desire for heaven have been so great if you had not glimpsed it once in my eyes?'[◊]

'Ah! Stop being a woman and let me at last see on your face the God you are powerless to hide.'[◊◊]

'The love of God calls in us the same faculty as the love of His creatures, it calls on our feeling that we are not complete in ourselves and

* *The Humiliation of the Father.*

† *The Satin Slipper.*

‡ *The Humiliation of the Father.*

‡‡ *Leaves of Saints.*

§ *The Satin Slipper.*

§§ *Leaves of Saints.*

◊ Ibid.

◊◊ *The Satin Slipper.*

that the supreme God in which we are consummated is someone outside ourselves.'*

Thus each finds in the other the meaning of his earthly life and also irrefutable proof of the insufficiency of this life:

'Since I cannot grant him heaven, at least I can tear him from the earth. I alone can give him need in the measure of his desire.'†

'What I was asking from you, and what I wanted to give you, is not compatible with time but with eternity.'‡

Yet woman's and man's roles are not exactly symmetrical. On the social level, man's primacy is evident. Claudel believes in hierarchies and, among others, the family's: the husband is the head. Anne Vercors rules over her home. Don Pelagio sees himself as the gardener entrusted with the care of this delicate plant, Doña Prouhèze; he gives her a mission she does not dream of refusing. The fact alone of being a male confers privilege. 'Who am I, poor girl, to compare myself to the male of my race?' asks Sygne.‡‡47 It is man who labours in the fields, who builds cathedrals, who fights with the sword, explores the world, who acts, who undertakes. God's plans are accomplished on earth through him. Woman is merely an auxiliary. She is the one who stays in place, who waits and who, like Sygne, maintains: 'I am she who remains and who am always there.'

She defends the heritage of Coûfontaine, keeps his accounts in order while he is far away fighting for the cause. The woman brings the relief of hope to the fighter: 'I bring irresistible hope.'§ And that of pity.

'I had pity on him. For where was he to turn, when he sought his mother, but to his own humiliated mother,

'In a spirit of confession and shame.'§§

And Tête d'Or dying murmurs:

'That is the wounded man's courage, the crippled man's support,

'The dying man's company . . .'

Claudel does not hold it against man that woman knows him in his weakest moments; on the contrary: he would find man's arrogance as

* Positions and Propositions.
† The Satin Slipper.
‡ The Humiliation of the Father
‡‡ The Hostage.
§ The City.
§§ The Trade.

displayed in Montherlant and Lawrence sacrilege. It is good that man knows he is carnal and lowly, that he forgets neither his origin nor his death, which is symmetrical to it. Every wife could say the same words as Marthe:

'It is true, it was not I who gave you life.

'But I am here to ask you for life once more. And a man's confusion in the presence of a woman comes from this very question

'Like conscience in the presence of a creditor.'*

And yet this weakness has to yield to force. In marriage, the wife *gives herself* to the husband, who takes care of her: Lâla lies down on the ground before Coeuvre, who places his foot on her. The relation of woman to husband, of daughter to father, of sister to brother, is a relation of vassalage. In George's hands, Sygne takes the vow of the knight to his sovereign.

'You are the lord and I the poor sibyl who keeps the fire.'†

'Let me take an oath like a new knight! O my lord! O my elder, let me swear in your hands

'After the fashion of a nun who makes her profession,

'O male of my race!'‡

Fidelity and loyalty are the greatest of the female vassal's human virtues. Sweet, humble, resigned as a woman, she is, in the name of her race and her lineage, proud and invincible; such is the proud Sygne de Coûfontaine and Tête d'Or's princess, who carries on her shoulder the corpse of her assassinated father, who accepts the misery of a lonely and wild life, the suffering of a crucifixion, and who assists Tête d'Or in his agony before he dies at her side. Conciliator and mediator is thus how woman often appears: she is docile Esther accountable to Mordecai, Judith obeying the priests; she can overcome her weakness, her faint-heartedness and her modesty through loyalty to the cause that is hers since it is that of her masters; she draws strength from her devotion which makes her a precious instrument.

So on the human level she is seen as drawing her greatness from her very subordination. But in God's eyes, she is a perfectly autonomous person. The fact that for man existence surpasses itself while for woman it maintains itself only establishes a difference between them on earth:

* Ibid.
† *The Hostage.*
‡ Ibid.

in any case, transcendence is accomplished not on earth but in God. And woman has just as direct a connection with Him as her companion does; perhaps hers is even more intimate and secret. It is through a man's voice – what is more, a priest's – that God speaks to Sygne; but Violaine hears his voice in the solitude of her heart, and Prouhèze only deals with the Guardian Angel. Claudel's most sublime figures are women: Sygne, Violaine, Prouhèze. This is partly because saintliness for him lies in renunciation. And woman is less involved in human projects; she has less personal will: made to give and not to take, she is closer to perfect devotion. It is through her that the earthly joys that are permissible and good will be surpassed, but their sacrifice is still better. Sygne accomplishes this for a definite reason: to save the Pope. Prouhèze resigns herself to it first because she loves Rodrigo with a forbidden love:

'Would you then have wanted me to put an adulteress into your hands? . . . I would have been only a woman who soon dies on your heart and not that eternal star that you thirst for.'*

But when this love could become legitimate, she makes no attempt to accomplish it in this world. For the Angel whispers to her:

'Prouhèze, my sister, luminous child of God whom I salute,

'Prouhèze whom the angels see and who does not know that he is watching, she it is whom you made so as to give her to him.'†

She is human, she is woman, and she does not resign herself without revolt: 'He will not know how I taste!'‡

But she knows that her true marriage with Rodrigo is only consummated by her denial:

'When will there no longer be any way to escape, when he will be attached to me for ever in an impossible marriage, when he will no longer find a way to wrench himself from the cry of my powerful flesh and that pitiless void, when I will have proved to him his nothingness and the nothingness of myself, when there will no longer be in his nothingness a secret that my secret cannot confirm.

'It is then that I shall give him to God, naked and torn, so that he may be filled in a blast of thunder, it is then that I will have a husband and clasp a god in my arms.'‡‡

Violaine's resolution is more mysterious and gratuitous still; for she

---

* *The Satin Slipper.*
† Ibid.
‡ Ibid.
‡‡ Ibid.

chose leprosy and blindness when a legitimate bond could have united her to the man she loved and who loved her.

'Jacques, perhaps we loved each other too much for it to be right for us to belong to each other, for it to be good to be each other's.'*

But if women are so singularly devoted to saintly heroism, it is above all because Claudel still grasps them from a masculine perspective. To be certain, each of the sexes embodies the *Other* in the eyes of the complementary sex; but to his man's eyes it is, in spite of everything, the woman who is often regarded as an *absolute other*. There is a mystical surpassing insofar as 'we know that in and of ourselves we are insufficient, hence the power of woman over us, like the power of Grace.'‡ The 'we' here represents only males and not the human species, and faced with their imperfection, woman is the appeal of infinity. In a way, there is a new principle of subordination here: by the communion of saints each individual is an instrument for all others; but woman is more precisely the instrument of salvation for man, without any reciprocity. *The Satin Slipper* is the epic of Rodrigo's salvation. The drama opens with a prayer his brother addresses to God on his behalf; it closes with the death of Rodrigo, whom Prouhèze has brought to saintliness. But, in another sense, the woman thereby gains the fullest autonomy: for her mission is interiorised in her, and in saving the man, or in serving as an example to him, she saves herself in solitude. Pierre de Craon prophesies Violaine's destiny to her, and he receives in his heart the wonderful fruits of her sacrifice; he will exalt her before mankind in the stones of cathedrals. But Violaine accomplished it without help. In Claudel there is a mystique of woman akin to Dante's for Beatrice, to that of the Gnostics, and even to that of the Saint-Simonian tradition which called woman a regenerator. But because men and women are equally God's creatures, he also attributed an autonomous destiny to her. So that for him it is in becoming *other* – I am the Servant of the Lord – that woman realises herself as subject; and it is in her for-itself that she appears as the Other.

There is a passage from *The Adventures of Sophie* that more or less sums up the whole Claudelian concept. God, we read, has entrusted to woman 'this face which, however remote and deformed it may be, is a certain image of His perfection. He has rendered her desirable. He

* *The Young Violaine.*
‡ *The Satin Slipper*

has joined the end and the beginning. He has made her the keeper of
His projects and capable of restoring to man that creative slumber in
which even she was conceived. She is the foundation of destiny. She is
the gift. She is the possibility of possession . . . She is the connection
in this affectionate link that ever unites the Creator to His work. She
understands Him. She is the soul that sees and acts. She shares with
Him in some way the patience and power of creation.'

In a way, it seems that woman could not be more exalted. But deep
down Claudel is only expressing in a poetic way a slightly modernised
Catholic tradition. We have seen that the earthly vocation of woman
does not cancel out any of her supernatural autonomy; on the contrary,
in recognising this, the Catholic feels authorised to maintain male prerogatives in this world. If the woman is venerated *in God*, she will be treated
like a servant in this world: and further, the more total submission is
demanded of her, the more surely will she move forward on the road
to her salvation. Her lot, the lot the bourgeoisie has always assigned to
her, is to devote herself to her children, her husband, her home, her
realm, to country and to church; man gives activity, woman her person;
to sanctify this hierarchy in the name of divine will does not modify it
in the least, but on the contrary attempts to fix it in the eternal.

IV
BRETON OR POETRY

In spite of the gulf separating Claudel's religious world and Breton's
poetic universe, there is an analogy in the role they assign to women:
she is an element that perturbs; she wrests man from the sleep of
immanence; mouth, key, door, bridge, it is Beatrice initiating Dante
into the beyond. 'The love of man for woman, if we think for a
moment about the palpable world, continues to fill the sky with
gigantic and wild flowers. It is the most awful stumbling block for
the mind that always feels the need to believe itself on safe ground.'
The love for an other, a woman, leads to the love of the Other. 'It is
at the height of elective love for a particular being that the floodgates
of love for humanity open wide.' But for Breton the beyond is not a
foreign heaven: it is right here; it unveils itself if one knows how to
lift the veils of everyday banality; eroticism, for one, dissipates the
lure of false knowledge. 'The sexual world, nowadays . . . has not
stopped pitting its unbreakable core of night against our will to penetrate the universe.' Colliding with the mystery is the only way of

discovering it. Woman is enigma and poses enigmas; the addition of her multiple faces composes 'the unique being in which we are granted the possibility of seeing the last metamorphosis of the Sphinx'; and that is why she is revelation. 'You were the very image of secrecy,' says Breton to a woman he loved. And a little farther: 'That revelation you brought me: before I even knew what it consisted of, I knew it was a revelation.' This means that woman is poetry. She plays that role in Gérard de Nerval as well: but in *Sylvie* and *Aurélia* she has the consistency of a memory or a phantom because the dream, more real than the real, does not exactly coincide with it; the coincidence is perfect for Breton: there is only one world; poetry is objectively present in things, and woman is unequivocally a being of flesh and bones. She can be found wide-awake and not in a half dream, in the middle of an ordinary day on a date like any other day on the calendar – 5 April, 12 April, 4 October, 29 May – in an ordinary setting: a café, a street corner. But she always stands out through some unusual feature. Nadja 'carried her head high, unlike everyone else on the pavement . . . she was curiously made up . . . I had never seen such eyes.' Breton approaches her. 'She smiles, but quite mysteriously and somehow knowingly.'[48] In *Mad Love*: 'This young woman who just entered appeared to be swathed in mist – clothed in fire? . . . And I can certainly say that here, on the twenty-ninth of May 1934, this woman was *scandalously* beautiful.'*[49] The poet immediately admits she has a role to play in his destiny; at times this is a fleeting, secondary role, such as the child with Delilah's eyes in *Communicating Vessels*;[50] even when tiny miracles emerge around her: the same day Breton has a rendezvous with this Delilah, he reads a good review written by a friend called Samson with whom he had not been in touch for a long time. Sometimes wonders occur; the unknown woman of 29 May, Ondine, who had a swimming piece in her music-hall act, was presaged by a pun heard in a restaurant: 'Ondine, one dines'; and her first long date with the poet had been described in great detail in a poem he wrote eleven years earlier. Nadja is the most extraordinary of these sorceresses: she predicts the future and from her lips spring forth words and images her friend has in mind at the very same instant; her dreams and drawings are oracles: 'I am a soul in limbo,' she says; she went forward in life with 'behaviour based as it was on the purest intuition alone and ceaselessly relying on miracle'; around her, objective

* Breton's italics.

chance spreads strange events; she is so marvellously liberated from appearances that she scorns laws and reason: she ends up in an asylum. She is a 'free genius, something like one of those spirits of the air which certain magical practices momentarily permit us to entertain but which we can never overcome'. This prevents her from fulfilling her feminine role completely. Medium, prophetess, inspiration, she remains too close to the unreal creatures that visited Nerval; she opens the doors to the surreal world: but she is unable to give it because she could not give herself. Woman accomplishes herself and is really transformed in love; unique, accepting a unique destiny – and not floating rootless through the universe – so she is the sum of all. The moment her beauty reaches its highest point is at night when 'she is the perfect mirror in which everything that has been and everything that is destined to be is suffused adorably in what is going to be *this time*'. For Breton 'finding the place and the formula'[51] is one with 'possessing the truth within one soul and one body'.[52] And this possession is only possible in reciprocal love, carnal love, of course. 'The portrait of the woman one loves must be not only an image one smiles at but even more an oracle one questions'; but oracle only if this very woman is something other than an idea or an image; she must be the 'keystone of the material world'; for the seer this is the same world as Poetry and in this world he has to really possess Beatrice. 'Reciprocal love alone is what conditions total magnetic attraction which nothing can affect, which makes flesh sun and splendid impression on the flesh, which makes spirit a forever-flowing stream, inalterable and alive whose water moves once and for all between marigold and wild thyme.'

This indestructible love can only be unique. It is the paradox of Breton's attitude that, from *Communicating Vessels* to *Arcanum 17*, he is determined to promise love both unique and eternal to different women. But, according to him, it is social circumstances, thwarting the freedom of his choice, that lead man into erroneous choices; in fact, through these errors, he is really looking for *one* woman. And if he remembers the faces he has loved, he 'will discover at the same time in all these women's faces one face only: the *last* face* loved. How many times, moreover, have I noticed that under extremely dissimilar appearances one exceptional trait was developing.' 'How many times, moreover, have I noticed that under extremely dissimilar appearances one exceptional trait was developing.' He asks Ondine in *Mad Love*: 'Are you at last this

* Breton's italics.

woman, is it only today you were to come?' But in *Arcanum 17*: 'You know very well that when I first laid eyes on you I recognised you without the slightest hesitation.'[53] In a completed, renewed world, the couple would be indissoluble, through an absolute and reciprocal gift: since the beloved is all, how could there be any room for another? She is also this other; and all the more fully as she is more her self. 'The unusual is inseparable from love. Because you are unique you can't help being for me always another, another you. Across the diversity of these inconceivable flowers over there, it is you over there changing whom I love in a red blouse, naked, in a grey blouse.' And about a different but equally unique woman, Breton wrote: 'Reciprocal love, such as I envisage it, is a system of mirrors which reflects for me, under the thousand angles that the unknown can take for me, the faithful image of the one I love, always more surprising in her divining of my own desire and more gilded with life.'[54]

This unique woman, both carnal and artificial, natural and human, casts the same spell as the equivocal objects loved by the surrealists: she is like the spoon-shoe, the table-magnifying glass, the sugar cube of marble that the poet discovers at the flea market or invents in a dream; she shares in the secret of familiar objects suddenly discovered in their truth; and the secret of plants and stones. She is all things:

> *My love whose hair is woodfire*
> *Her thoughts heat lightning*
> *Her hourglass waist . . .*
> *My love whose sex is*
> *Algae and sweets of yore . . .*
> *My love of savannah eyes*[55]

But she is Beauty, above and beyond every other thing. Beauty for Breton is not an idea one contemplates but a reality that reveals itself – and therefore exists – only through passion; only through woman does beauty exist in the world.

'And it is there – right in the depths of the human crucible, in this paradoxical region where the fusion of two beings who have really chosen each other renders to all things the lost colours of the times of ancient suns, where, however, loneliness rages also, in one of nature's fantasies which, around the Alaskan craters, demands that under the ashes there remain snow – it is there that years ago I asked that we look for a new beauty, a beauty "envisaged exclusively to produce passion."'

'Convulsive beauty will be veiled-erotic, fixed-explosive, magic-circumstantial, or it will not be.'

It is from woman that everything that is derives meaning. 'Love and love alone is precisely what the fusion of essence and existence realises to the highest degree.' It is accomplished for lovers and thus throughout the whole world. 'The recreation, the perpetual recoloration of the world in a single being, such as they are accomplished through love, light up with a thousand rays the advance of the earth ahead.' For all poets – or almost all – woman embodies nature; but for Breton, she not only expresses it: she delivers it. Because nature does not speak in a clear language, its mysteries have to be penetrated in order to grasp its truth, which is the same thing as its beauty: poetry is not simply the reflection of it but rather its key; and woman here cannot be differentiated from poetry. That is why she is the indispensable mediator without whom the whole earth would be silenced: 'Nature is likely to light up and to fade out, to serve and not to serve me, only to the extent that I feel the rise and the fall of the fire of a hearth which is love, the only love, that for a single being... It was only lacking for a great iris of fire to emerge from me to give its value to what exists... I contemplate to the point of dizziness your hands opened above the fire of twigs which we just kindled and which is now raging, your enchanting hands, your transparent hands hovering over the fire of my life.' Every woman loved is a natural wonder for Breton: 'a tiny, unforgettable fern climbing the inside wall of an ancient well.' 'Something so blinding and serious that she could not but bring to mind . . . the great natural physical necessity while at the same time tenderly dreaming of the nonchalance of some tall flowers beginning to blossom.' But inversely: every natural wonder merges with the beloved; he exalts her when he waxes emotional about a grotto, a flower, a mountain. Between the woman who warms his hands on a landing of Teide and Teide itself, all distance is abolished. The poet invokes both in one prayer: 'Wonderful Teide, take my life! Mouth of the heavens and yet mouth of hell, I prefer you thus in your enigma, able to send natural beauty to the skies and to swallow up everything.'

Beauty is even more than beauty; it fuses with 'the deep night of knowledge'; it is truth and eternity, the absolute; woman does not deliver a temporal and contingent aspect of the world, she is the necessary essence of it, not a fixed essence as Plato imagined it but a 'fixed-explosive' one. 'The only treasure I find in myself is the key that opens this limitless field since I have known you, this field made of the repetition of one plant, taller and taller, swinging in a wider and wider arc and leading

me to death . . . Because one woman and one man, who until the end
of time must be you and me, will drift in their turn without ever turning
back as far as the path goes, in the optical glow, at the edges of life and
of the oblivion of life . . . The greatest hope, I mean the one encom-
passing all the others, is that this be for all people, and that for all people
this lasts, that the absolute gift of one being to another who cannot exist
without his reciprocity be in the eyes of all the only natural and supernatural bridge spanning life.'

Through the love she inspires and shares, woman is thus the only
possible salvation for each man. In *Arcanum 17*, her mission spreads
and takes shape: she has to save humanity. Breton has always been
part of the Fourier tradition that, demanding rehabilitation of the
flesh, exalts woman as erotic object; it is logical that he should come
to the Saint-Simonian idea of the regenerating woman. In today's
society, the male dominates to such an extent that it is an insult for
someone like Gourmont to say of Rimbaud: 'a girl's temperament'.
However, 'the time has come to value the ideas of woman at the
expense of those of man, whose bankruptcy is coming to pass fairly
tumultuously today.'[56] 'Yes, it is always the lost woman, she who sings
in man's imagination, but after such trials for her and for him, it must
also be the woman retrieved. And first of all, woman has to retrieve
herself; she has to learn to recognise herself through the hells she is
destined to by the more than problematic view that man, in general,
carries of her.'

The role she should fill is above all that of pacifier. 'I've always been
stupefied that she didn't make her voice heard, that she didn't think of
taking every possible advantage, the immense advantage of the two
irresistible and priceless inflexions given to her, one for talking to men
during love, the other that commands all of a child's trust . . . What
clout, what future would this great cry of warning and refusal from
woman have had . . . When will we see a woman simply as woman
perform quite a different *miracle* of extending her arms between those
who are about to grapple to say: You are brothers.' If woman today
looks ill adapted or off balance, it is due to the treatment masculine
tyranny has inflicted on her; but she maintains a miraculous power
because her roots plunge deep into the wellspring of life whose secrets
males have lost. 'Melusina, half reclaimed by panic-stricken life,
Melusina with lower joints of broken stones, aquatic plants or the down
of a nest, she's the one I invoke, she's the only one I can see who could
redeem this savage epoch. She's all of woman and yet woman as she

exists today, woman deprived of her human base, prisoner of her mobile roots, if you will, but also through them in providential communication with nature's elemental forces. Woman deprived of her human base, legend has it, by the impatience and jealousy of man.'

So today one has to be on woman's side; while waiting for her real worth to be restored to her, 'those of us in the arts must pronounce ourselves unequivocally against man and for woman'. 'The child-woman. Systematically art must prepare her advent into the empire of tangible things.' Why child-woman? Breton explains: 'I choose the child-woman not in order to oppose her to other women, but because it seems to me that in her and in her alone exists in a state of absolute transparency the *other* prism of vision.'*

Insofar as woman is merely assimilated to a human being, she will be as unable as male human beings to save the doomed world; it is femininity as such that introduces this *other* element – the truth of life and poetry – into civilisation, and that alone can free humanity.

As Breton's view is exclusively poetic, it is exclusively as poetry and thus as *Other* that woman is envisaged. If one were to ask about her own destiny, the response would be implied in the ideal of reciprocal love: her only vocation is love; this is in no way inferiority, since man's vocation is also love. However, one would like to know whether for her as well, love is the key to the world, the revelation of beauty; will she find this beauty in her lover? Or in her own image? Will she be capable of the poetic activity that makes poetry happen through a sentient being: or will she be limited to approving her male's work? She is poetry itself, in the immediate that is, for man; we are not told whether she is poetry for herself too. Breton does not speak of woman as subject. Nor does he ever evoke the image of the bad woman. In his work as a whole – in spite of a few manifestos and pamphlets in which he vilifies the human herd – he focuses not on categorising the world's superficial resistances but on revealing the secret truth: woman interests him only because she is a privileged 'mouth'. Deeply anchored in nature, very close to the earth, she also appears to be the key to the beyond. One finds in Breton the same esoteric naturalism as in the Gnostics who saw in Sophia the principle of redemption and even of creation, as in Dante choosing Beatrice for guide, or Petrarch illuminated by Laura's love. That is why the being most rooted in nature, the closest to the earth, is also the key to the beyond. Truth, Beauty,

* Breton's italics.

Poetry, she is All: once more all in the figure of the other, All except herself.

V

STENDHAL OR ROMANCING THE REAL

If now, leaving the present period, I return to Stendhal, it is because, leaving behind these carnivals where Woman is disguised as shrew, nymph, morning star or mermaid, I find it reassuring to approach a man who lives among flesh-and-blood women.

Stendhal loved women sensually from childhood; he projected the hopes of his adolescence onto them: he readily imagined himself saving a beautiful stranger and winning her love. Once he was in Paris, what he wanted the most ardently was a 'charming wife; we will adore each other, she will know my soul'. Grown old, he writes the initials of the women he loved the most in the dust. 'I believe that dreaming was what I preferred above all,' he admits. And his dreams are nourished by images of women; his memories of them enliven the countryside. 'The line of rocks when approaching Arbois and coming from Dôle by the main road was, I believe, a touching and clear image for me of Métilde's soul.' Music, painting, architecture, everything he cherished, he cherished it with an unlucky lover's soul; while he is walking around Rome, a woman emerges at every turn of the page; by the regrets, desires, sadnesses and joys women awakened in him, he came to know the nature of his own heart; it is women he wants as judges: he frequents their salons, he wants to shine; he owes them his greatest joys, his greatest pain, they were his main occupation; he prefers their love to any friendship, their friendship to that of men; women inspire his books, women figures populate them; he writes in great part for them. 'I might be lucky enough to be read in 1900 by the souls I love, the Mme Rolands, the Mélanie Guilberts . . .' They were the very substance of his life. Where did this privilege come from?

This tender friend of women – and precisely because he loves them in their truth – does not believe in feminine mystery; there is no essence that defines woman once and for all; the idea of an eternal feminine seems pedantic and ridiculous to him. 'Pedants have been repeating for two thousand years that women have quicker minds and men more solidity; that women have more subtlety in ideas and men more attention span. A Parisian passerby walking around the Versailles gardens once concluded that from everything he saw, the trees are born pruned.'

The differences that one notices between men and women reflect those of their situation. For example, how could women not be more romantic than their lovers? 'A woman at her embroidery frame, insipid work that only involves her hands, dreams of her lover, who, galloping around the countryside with his troop, is put under arrest if he makes one false move.' Likewise, women are accused of lacking common sense. 'Women prefer emotions to reason; this is so simple: as they are not given responsibility for any family affair by virtue of our pedestrian customs, *reason is never useful to them* . . . Let your wife settle your affairs with the farmers on two of your lands, and I wager that the books are better kept than by you.' If so few female geniuses are found in history, it is because society denies them any means of expression. 'All the geniuses who are born *women** are lost for the public good; when chance offers them the means to prove themselves, watch them attain the most difficult skills.' The worst handicap they have to bear is the deadening education they are given; the oppressor always attempts to diminish those he oppresses; man intentionally refuses women their chances. 'We allow their most brilliant qualities and the ones richest in happiness for themselves and for us to remain idle.' At ten years of age, the girl is quicker, subtler than her brother; at twenty, the scamp is a quick-witted adult and the girl 'a big awkward idiot, shy and afraid of a spider'; at fault is the training she has received. Women should be given exactly as much education as boys. Antifeminists object that cultured and intelligent women are monsters: the whole problem comes from the fact that they are still exceptional; if all women had equal access to culture as naturally as men, they would just as naturally take advantage of it. After having been mutilated, they are then subjected to laws against nature: married against their hearts, they are supposed to be faithful, and even divorce is reproached as wild behaviour. A great number of them are destined to idleness when the fact is that there is no happiness without work. This condition scandalises Stendhal and therein he finds the source of all the faults blamed on women. They are neither angels nor demons nor sphinx: but human beings reduced to semi-slavery by idiotic customs.

It is precisely because they are oppressed that the best of them will avoid the faults that tarnish their oppressors; in themselves they are neither inferior nor superior to man: but by a curious reversal, their unfortunate situation works in their favour. It is well known that Stendhal

* Stendhal's emphasis.

hates the spirit of seriousness:[57] money, honours, rank and power are
the saddest of idols to him; the immense majority of men alienate themselves in their pursuit; the pedant, the self-important man, the bourgeois and the husband stifle in themselves any spark of life and truth;
armed with preconceived ideas and learned feelings, obeying social
routines, they are inhabited only by emptiness; a world populated with
these creatures without a soul is a desert of boredom. There are unfortunately many women who stagnate in these dismal swamps; they are
dolls with 'narrow and Parisian ideas' or else self-righteous hypocrites;
Stendhal experiences 'a mortal disgust for decent women and the
hypocrisy that is indispensable to them'; they bring to their frivolous
occupations the same seriousness that represses their husbands; stupid
through education, envious, vain, talkative, mean through idleness, cold,
emotionless, pretentious, harmful, they populate Paris and the provinces;
they can be seen swarming about behind the noble figure of a Mme de
Rênal or a Mme de Chasteller. The one Stendhal depicted with the most
bitter care is undoubtedly Mme Grandet, the exact negative of a Mme
Roland or a Métilde. Beautiful but expressionless, condescending and
without charm, she intimidates by her 'famous virtue' but does not
know real modesty, which comes from the soul; full of admiration for
self, imbued with her own personage, she only knows how to copy
grandeur from the outside; deep down inside she is vulgar and inferior;
'she has no character . . . she bores me,' thinks M. Leuwen. 'Perfectly
reasonable, concerned by the success of her projects', she focuses all of
her ambition on making her husband a minister; 'her mind was arid';
careful and conformist, she always kept herself from love, she is incapable of a generous movement; when passion sets into this dry soul, it
burns without illuminating her.

It is only necessary to reverse this image to discover what Stendhal
asks of women: first, not to fall prey to the traps of seriousness; because
the supposedly important things are out of their reach, women risk alienating themselves in them less than men; they have a better chance of
preserving this natural side, this naïveté, this generosity that Stendhal
places higher than any other merit; what he appreciates in them is what
we would call today their authenticity: that is the common trait of all
the women he loved or invented with love; all are free and true beings.
For some, their freedom is strikingly visible: Angela Pietragrua, 'sublime
whore, Italian style, à la Lucrezia Borgia', or Mme Azur, 'whore à la du
Barry . . . one of the least doll-like French women that I have met', oppose
social custom openly. Lamiel laughs at conventions, customs and laws;

Sanseverina throws herself ardently into the intrigue and does not stop at crime. Others rise above the vulgar through the vigour of their minds: like Menta or Mathilde de la Mole, who criticises, denigrates, and scorns the society that surrounds her and wants to stand apart from it. For others, freedom takes a wholly negative form; what is remarkable in Mme de Chasteller is her indifference to everything secondary; subjected to her father's will and even his opinions, she still manages to contest bourgeois values by means of the indifference she is criticised for as childish, and that is the source of her carefree gaiety; Clélia Conti also stands apart by her reserve; balls and other traditional entertainments for girls leave her cold; she always seems distant 'either out of scorn for what surrounds her or out of regret for some missing chimera'; she judges the world, she takes offence at its indignities. Mme de Rênal is the one whose soul's independence is the most deeply hidden; she herself does not know she is not really resigned to her lot; her extreme delicacy and acute sensitivity show her repugnance for her milieu's vulgarity; she is without hypocrisy; she has kept a generous heart, capable of violent emotions, and she has the taste for happiness; the fire that smoulders barely gives off any heat, but only a breath is needed for it to be fully kindled. These women are, simply, *living*; they know the source of real values is not in exterior things but in the heart; that is what makes the charm of the world they inhabit: they chase away boredom merely by being present with their dreams, desires, pleasures, emotions and inventions. Sanseverina, that 'active soul', dreads boredom more than death. Stagnating in boredom 'is preventing one from dying, she said, it is not living'; she is 'always totally involved in something, always active, always gay'. Foolhardy, childish or deep, gay or serious, reckless or secretive, they all refuse the heavy sleep in which humanity sinks. And these women who have been able to preserve their freedom, albeit unfulfilled, will rise up by passion to heroism as soon as they meet an object worthy of them; their force of soul and their energy attest to the fierce purity of total commitment.

But freedom alone would not be sufficient to endow them with so many romantic attractions: a pure freedom inspires esteem but not emotion; what is touching is their effort to accomplish themselves in spite of the obstacles that beleaguer them; it creates even more pathos in women because the struggle is more difficult. The victory over exterior constraints is sufficient to enchant Stendhal; in *Three Italian Chronicles*[38] he cloisters his heroines in remote convents, he locks them up in a jealous spouse's palace: they have to invent a thousand tricks to meet their lovers; secret doors, rope ladders, bloody chests, kidnappings, sequestrations and assassinations, the unleashing of passion and disobedience is served by an ingenuity in which all the mind's resources are displayed; death and the threat of tortures highlight even more the daringness of the deranged souls he depicts. Even in his more mature work, Stendhal remains sympathetic to this external expression of the romantic: it is the manifestation of the one born from the heart; they cannot be distinguished from each other just as a mouth cannot be separated from its smile. Clélia invents love anew by inventing the alphabet that allows her to correspond with Fabrice; Sanseverina is described to us as 'a soul always sincere who never acts with caution, who totally gives herself over to the impression of the moment'; it is when she schemes, when she poisons the prince and floods Parma, that this soul is revealed to us: she is no other than the sublime and mad escapade that she has chosen to live. The ladder that Mathilde de la Mole leans against her window is much more than a prop: her proud recklessness, her penchant for the extraordinary, and her provocative courage take a tangible form. The qualities of these souls would not be revealed were they not surrounded by enemies: prison walls, a lord's will and a family's harshness.

But the most difficult constraints to overcome are those that one finds in oneself: then the adventure of freedom is the most uncertain, the most poignant and the most piquant. Clearly, the more often Stendhal's heroines are prisoners, the greater his sympathy for them. Yes, he enjoys whores – sublime or not – who have once and for all trampled on the conventions; but he cherishes Métilde more tenderly, restrained by her scruples and modesty. Lucien Leuwen is happy when near Mme de Hocquincourt, that liberated person: but it is Mme de Chasteller, chaste, reserved and hesitant, that he loves passionately; Fabrice admires the undivided soul of Sanseverina that stops at nothing; but he prefers Clélia and it is the young girl who wins his heart. And Mme de Rênal, bound by her pride, her prejudices and her ignorance is perhaps the most astonishing of all the women Stendhal created. He readily places his heroines in the provinces, in a confined milieu, under the authority of a husband or a foolish father; it pleases him that they are uneducated and even full of false ideas. Mme de Rênal and Mme de Chasteller are both obstinately legitimist; the former is a timid mind and without experience, the latter is a brilliant intelligence but she underestimates its worth; they are therefore not responsible for their errors, but they are the victims of them as much as of institutions and social customs; and it is from error that romance springs forth, as poetry is born from failure. A lucid mind that decides on its actions in full knowledge is approved or blamed coldly, whereas the courage and ruses of a generous heart seeking its way in the shadows is admired with fear, pity, irony or love. It is because women are mystified that useless and charming qualities such as their modesty, pride and extreme delicacy flourish; in one sense, these are defects: they lead to lies, susceptibilities and anger, but they can be explained by the situation in which women are placed; it leads them to take pride in little things or at least in 'things determined by feeling' because all the 'supposedly important' objects are out of their reach; their modesty results from the dependence they suffer: because it is forbidden to them to show their worth in action, it is their very being that they put in question; it seems to them that the other's consciousness, and particularly that of their lover, reveals them in their truth: they are afraid, they try to escape it; in their evasions, their hesitations, their revolts, and even their lies an authentic concern for worth is expressed; that is what makes them respectable; but it is expressed awkwardly, even with bad faith, and that makes them touching and even discreetly comic. When freedom is hoist by its own petard and cheats on itself, it is at the most deeply human and so in Stendhal's eyes at its most endearing. Stendhal's women are imbued with pathos when their hearts pose unexpected problems for them: no outside law, recipe, reasoning or example can then guide them; they have to decide alone: this abandon is the extreme moment of freedom. Clélia is brought up with liberal ideas, she is lucid and reasonable: but learned opinions, whether right or wrong, are of no help in a moral conflict; Mme de Rênal loves Julien in spite of his morality, Clélia saves Fabrice in spite of herself: in both cases there is the same surpassing of all accepted values. This daring is what exalts Stendhal; but it is even more moving because it barely dares to declare itself: it is all the more natural, spontaneous and authentic. In Mme de Rênal, boldness is hidden by innocence: because she does not know love, she does not recognise it and yields to it without resistance; one could say that having lived in darkness, she is defenceless against the violent light of passion; she welcomes it, blinded, even against God, against hell; when this fire goes out, she falls back in the shadows that husbands and priests govern; she does not trust her own judgement, but the evidence overwhelms her; as soon as she sees Julien again, she once more unburdens her soul to him; her remorse and the letter her confessor wrests from her show the distance this ardent and sincere

soul had to span to tear herself away from the prison society enclosed
her in and accede to the heaven of happiness. The conflict is more
conscious for Clélia; she hesitates between her loyalty to her father and
pity inspired by love; she is searching for a rationale; the triumph of
the values in which Stendhal believes are all the more striking to him
in that this triumph is experienced as a defeat by the victims of a hypocritical civilisation; and he delights in seeing them use ruses and bad
faith to make the truth of passion and happiness prevail against the
lies in which they believe: Clélia, promising the Madonna to no longer
see Fabrice, and accepting his kisses and his embraces for two years,
providing she closes her eyes, is both laughable and heartbreaking.
Stendhal considers Mme de Chasteller's hesitations and Mathilde de la
Mole's inconsistencies with the same tender irony; so many detours,
changes of mind, scruples, victories and hidden defeats in order to
reach simple and legitimate ends is for him the most delightful of
comedies; there is drollery in these dramas because the actress is both
judge and party, because she is her own dupe, and because she burdens
herself with complicated paths where a decree would suffice for the
Gordian knot to be cut; but they nonetheless show the most respectable
concern that could torture a noble soul: she wants to remain worthy
of her own esteem; she places her own approbation higher than that
of others and thus she realises herself as an absolute. These solitary
debates without reverberation have more gravity than a ministerial
crisis; when she wonders if she is going to respond to Lucien Leuwen's
love or not, Mme de Chasteller decides for herself and the world: can
one have confidence in others? Can one trust one's own heart? What
is the value of love and human vows? Is it mad or generous to believe
and to love? These questions challenge the very meaning of life, that
of each and every one. The so-called important man is futile, in fact,
because he accepts ready-made justifications of his life, while a
passionate and deep woman revises established values at each instant;
she knows the constant tension of an unassisted freedom; thus she feels
herself in constant danger: she can win or lose everything in a second.
It is this risk, accepted with apprehension, that gives her story the
colour of a heroic adventure. And the stakes are the highest that can
be: the very meaning of this existence of which everyone has a share,
his only part. Mina de Vanghel's escapade can seem absurd in one sense;
but she brings to it a whole ethic. 'Was her life a false calculation? Her
happiness lasted eight months. She had too ardent a soul to settle for
the real life.' Mathilde de la Mole is less sincere than Clélia or Mme

de Chasteller; she orders her acts on the idea she has of herself rather than on the evidence of love and happiness: is it more arrogant, grander to keep oneself than to lose oneself, to humiliate oneself before one's beloved than to resist him? She is alone with her doubts, and she risks this self-esteem that is more important to her than life itself. It is the ardent quest for the real reasons to live through the shadows of ignorance, prejudice and mystifications, in the wavering and feverish light of passion, it is the infinite risk of happiness or death, of grandeur or shame that gives romantic glory to these women's destinies.

The woman is of course unaware of the seduction she radiates; self-contemplation and playacting are always inauthentic attitudes; by the mere fact of comparing herself to Mme Roland, Mme Grandet proves she does not resemble her; if Mathilde de la Mole continues to be endearing, it is because she gets confused in her playacting and is often prey to her heart just when she thinks she governs it; she moves us insofar as she is not ruled by her will. But the purest of heroines lack consciousness of themselves. Mme de Rênal is unaware of her grace just as Mme de Chasteller is of her intelligence. It is one of the deep joys of the lover with whom the author and the reader identify: he is the witness through whom these secret riches are revealed; the vivacity Mme Rênal deploys out of everyone's sight, the 'bright wit, changing and deep', unknown to Mme de Chasteller's milieu, he alone admires them; and even if others appreciate Sanseverina's wit, he is the one who penetrates the deepest into her soul. Faced with the woman, the man tastes the pleasure of contemplation; she intoxicates him like a landscape or a painting; she sings in his heart and lights up the sky. This revelation reveals him to himself: one cannot understand women's delicacy, their sensibilities and their ardour without developing a delicate, sensitive and ardent soul oneself; female feelings create a world of nuances and requirements whose discovery enriches the lover: when with Mme de Rênal, Julien becomes someone other than the ambitious man he had decided to be; he chooses himself anew. If the man has only a superficial desire for the woman, he will find seducing her amusing. But it is real love that will transfigure his life. 'Love à la Werther opens the soul ... to feeling and pleasure in the *beautiful* in whatever form it takes, even in a hair shirt. It makes happiness attainable even without wealth ...' 'It is a new aim in life to which everything is connected and that changes the appearance of everything. Love-as-passion throws in man's eyes all of nature with its sublime aspects as if it were a novelty invented yesterday.' Love shatters daily routine, chases away boredom, the boredom in which Stendhal sees such a deep evil because it is the absence of all the reasons for living or dying; the lover has an aim and that is enough for each day to become an adventure: what a pleasure for Stendhal to spend three days hidden in Menta's cellar! Rope ladders and bloody chests represent this taste for the extraordinary in his novels. Love, that is woman, reveals the real ends of existence: beauty, happiness, the freshness of feelings and of the world. It tears man's soul out and thus gives him possession of it; the lover experiences the same tension, the same risks, as his mistress and feels himself more authentically than during a planned career. When Julien hesitates at the base of the ladder Mathilde has set up, he puts his whole destiny into question: in that very moment, he demonstrates his true worth. It is through women, under their influence, in reaction to their behaviour, that Julien, Fabrice and Lucien learn about the world and themselves. Test, reward, judge or friend, the woman in Stendhal is really what Hegel was once tempted to make of her: that other consciousness that, in reciprocal recognition, gives to the other subject the same truth it receives from it. The happy couple that recognises each other in love defies the universe and time; it is sufficient in itself, it realises the absolute.

But this supposes that woman is not pure alterity: she is subject herself. Stendhal never describes his heroines as a function of his heroes: he provides them with their own destinies. He undertook something rarer and that no other novelist, I think, has ever done: he projected himself into a female character. He does not examine Lamiel as Marivaux does Marianne, or Richardson does Clarissa Harlowe: he shares her destiny as he had shared that of Julien. Precisely because of that, the character of Lamiel is singularly significant, if somewhat theoretical. Stendhal sets up all imaginable obstacles around the girl: she is a peasant, poor, ignorant, and brought up harshly by people imbued with every prejudice; but she eliminates from her path all the moral barriers the day she understands the scope of these little words: 'it's stupid.' Her mind's freedom enables her to take responsibility for all the movements of her curiosity, her ambition, her gaiety; faced with such a resolute heart, material obstacles cannot fail to decrease; her only problem will be to carve out a destiny worthy of her in a mediocre world. That destiny accomplishes itself in crime and death: but that is also Julien's lot. There is no place for great souls in society as it is: men and women are in the same boat.

It is remarkable that Stendhal is both so profoundly romantic and

so decidedly feminist; feminists are usually rational minds that adopt
a universal point of view in all things; but it is not only in the name
of freedom in general but also in the name of individual happiness
that Stendhal calls for women's emancipation. Love, he thinks, will
have nothing to lose; on the contrary, it will be all the truer that woman,
as the equal of man, will be able to understand him more completely.
Undoubtedly, some of the qualities one enjoys in woman will disappear: but their value comes from the freedom that is expressed in them
and that will show in other guises; and the romantic will not fade out
of this world. Two separate beings, placed in different situations,
confronting each other in their freedom and seeking the justification
of existence through each other, will always live an adventure full of
risks and promises. Stendhal trusts the truth; as soon as one flees it,
one dies a living death; but where it shines, so shine beauty, happiness,
love, and a joy that carries in it its own justification. That is why he
rejects the false poetry of myths as much as the mystifications of seriousness. Human reality is sufficient for him. Woman, according to
him, is simply a human being: dreams could not invent anything more
intoxicating.

VI

These examples show that the great collective myths are reflected in
each singular writer: woman appears to us as *flesh*; male flesh is engendered by the maternal womb and re-created in the woman lover's
embrace: thus, woman is akin to *nature*, she embodies it: animal, little
vale of blood, rose in bloom, siren, curve of a hill, she gives humus,
sap, tangible beauty and the world's soul to man; she can hold the keys
to *poetry*; she can be *mediator* between this world and the beyond: grace
or Pythia, star or witch, she opens the door to the supernatural, the
surreal; she is destined to *immanence*; and through her passivity she
doles out peace and harmony: but should she refuse this role, she
becomes praying mantis or ogress. In any case, she appears as the *privileged Other* through whom the subject accomplishes himself: one of
the measures of man, his balance, his salvation, his adventure and his
happiness.

But these myths are orchestrated differently for each individual. The
Other is singularly defined according to the singular way the *One* chooses
to posit himself. All men assert themselves as freedom and transcendence: but they do not all give the same meaning to these words. For

Montherlant transcendence is a state: he is the transcendent, he soars in the sky of heroes; the woman crouches on the ground, under his feet; he enjoys measuring the distance separating him from her; from time to time, he raises her to him, takes and then rejects her; never does he lower himself towards her sphere of viscous darkness. Lawrence situates transcendence in the phallus; the phallus is life and power only thanks to woman; immanence is thus good and necessary; the false hero who deigns not to touch the earth, far from being a demigod, fails to be a man; woman is not despicable, she is deep wealth, hot spring; but she must renounce all personal transcendence and settle for nourishing that of her male. Claudel demands the same devotion: woman is also for him the one who maintains life, while man prolongs the vital momentum by his activity; but for the Catholic everything that occurs on earth is steeped in vain immanence: the only transcendent is God; in God's eyes the active man and the woman who serves him are exactly equal; each one has to surpass his earthly condition: salvation in any case is an autonomous undertaking. For Breton sexual hierarchy is inverted; action and conscious thought in which the male situates his transcendence are for him a banal mystification that engenders war, stupidity, bureaucracy and negation of the human; it is immanence, the pure opaque presence of the real, that is the truth; true transcendence would be accomplished by the return to immanence. His attitude is the exact opposite of Montherlant's: the latter likes war because women are banished from it, Breton venerates woman because she brings peace; one confuses mind and subjectivity, he rejects the given universe; the other thinks the mind is objectively present in the heart of the world; woman compromises Montherlant because she shatters his solitude; she is, for Breton, revelation because she wrests him from subjectivity. As for Stendhal, we saw that woman barely takes on a mythical value for him: he considers her as also being a transcendence; for this humanist, it is in their reciprocal relations that freedoms are accomplished; and it is sufficient that the *Other* is simply another for life to have, according to him, a little spice; he does not seek a stellar equilibrium, he does not nourish himself with the bread of disgust; he does not expect miracles; he does not wish to concern himself with the cosmos or poetry but with freedoms.

That is, he also experiences himself as a translucent freedom. The others – and this is one of the most important points – posit themselves as transcendences but feel they are prisoners of an opaque presence in their own hearts: they project onto woman this 'unbreakable core of night'. In Montherlant there is an Adlerian complex where heavy bad faith is born: these pretensions and fears are what he incarnates in woman; the disgust he feels for her is what he fears to feel for himself; he intends to trample in her the ever possible proof of his own insufficiency; he asks scorn to save him; woman is the ditch in which he throws all the monsters that inhabit him.* Lawrence's life shows us that he suffered from an analogous complex but more purely sexual: woman in his work has the value of a compensatory myth; through her is found an exalted virility of which the writer was not very sure; when he describes Kate at Don Cipriano's feet, he believes he has won a male triumph over Frieda; nor does he accept that his female companion challenges him: if she contested his aims, he would probably lose confidence in them; her role is to reassure him. He asks for peace, rest and faith from her, just as Montherlant asks for the certitude of his superiority: they demand what they lack. Self-confidence is not lacking in Claudel: if he is shy, it is only the secret of God. Thus, there is no trace of the battle of the sexes. Man bravely takes on the weight of woman: she is the possibility of temptation or of salvation. For Breton it seems that man is only true through the mystery that inhabits him; it pleases him that Nadja sees that star he is going towards and that is like 'a heartless flower'; his dreams, intuitions and the spontaneous unfolding of his inner language: it is in these activities that are out of the control of will and reason that he recognises himself: woman is the tangible figure of this veiled presence infinitely more essential than her conscious personality.

As for Stendhal, he quietly coincides with himself; but he needs woman as she does him so that his dispersed existence is gathered in the unity of a figure and a destiny; it is as for-another that the human being reaches being; but another still has to lend him his consciousness: other men are too indifferent to their peers; only the woman in love opens her heart to her lover and shelters it in its entirety. Except for Claudel, who finds a perfect witness in God, all the writers we have considered expect, in Malraux's words, woman to cherish in them this 'incomparable monster' known to themselves alone. In collaboration or combat, men come up against each other in their generality. Montherlant, for his peers, is a writer, Lawrence a doctrinaire, Breton

---

* Stendhal judged in advance the cruelties with which Montherlant amuses himself: 'In indifference, what should be done? Love-taste, but without the horrors. The horrors always come from a little soul that needs reassurance of its own merits.'

a leader of a school, Stendhal a diplomat or a man of wit; it is women who reveal in one a magnificent and cruel prince, in another a disturbing animal, in still another a god or a sun or a being 'black and cold . . . like a man struck by lightning, lying at the feet of the Sphinx',* and in the other, a seducer, a charmer, a lover.

For each of them, the ideal woman will be she who embodies the most exactly the *Other* able to reveal him to himself. Montherlant, the solar spirit, looks for pure animality in her; Lawrence, the phallic, demands that she sum up the female sex in its generality; Claudel defines her as a soul sister; Breton cherishes Melusina rooted in nature, he puts his hopes in the child-woman; Stendhal wants his mistress intelligent, cultivated, free of spirit and morals: an equal. But the only earthly destiny reserved to the woman equal, child-woman, soul sister, woman-sex and female animal is always man. Regardless of the ego looking for itself through her, it can only attain itself if she consents to be his crucible. In any case, what is demanded of her is self-forgetting and love. Montherlant consents to be moved by the woman who enables him to measure his virile power; Lawrence addresses an ardent hymn to the woman who renounces herself for him; Claudel exalts the vassal, servant and devoted woman who submits herself to God by submitting herself to the male; Breton puts his hopes in woman for humanity's salvation because she is capable of the most total love for her child and her lover; and even in Stendhal the heroines are more moving than the masculine heroes because they give themselves over to their passion with a more ardent violence; they help man to accomplish his destiny as Prouhèze contributes to Rodrigo's salvation; in Stendhal's novels, women often save their lovers from ruin, prison or death. Feminine devotion is demanded as a duty by Montherlant and Lawrence; less arrogant, Claudel, Breton and Stendhal admire it as a generous choice; they desire it without claiming to deserve it; but – except for the astonishing *Lamiel* – all their works show they expect from woman this altruism that Comte admired in and imposed on her, and which, according to him, also constituted both a flagrant inferiority and an equivocal superiority.

We could find many more examples: they would always lead to the same conclusions. In defining woman, each writer defines his general ethic and the singular idea he has of himself: it is also in her that he often registers the distance between his view of the world and his

* *Nadja.*

egotistical dreams. The absence or insignificance of the female element in a body of work in general is itself symptomatic; it has an extreme importance when it sums up in its totality all the aspects of the Other, as it does for Lawrence; it remains important if woman is grasped simply as another but the writer is interested in her life's individual adventure, which is Stendhal's case; it loses importance in a period like ours in which each individual's particular problems are of secondary import. However, woman as other still plays a role inasmuch as even to transcend himself, each man still needs to take consciousness of himself.

CHAPTER 3

The myth of woman plays a significant role in literature; but what is its importance in everyday life? To what extent does it affect individual social customs and behaviour? To reply to this question, it will be necessary to specify the relation of this myth to reality.

There are different kinds of myths. This one, sublimating an immutable aspect of the human condition, that is, the 'division' of humanity into two categories of individuals, is a static myth; it projects into a Platonic heaven a reality grasped through experience or conceptualised from experience; for fact, value, significance, notion and empirical law, it substitutes a transcendent Idea, timeless, immutable and necessary. This idea escapes all contention because it is situated beyond the given; it is endowed with an absolute truth. Thus, to the dispersed, contingent and multiple existence of *women*, mythic thinking opposes the Eternal Feminine, unique and fixed; if the definition given is contradicted by the behaviour of real flesh-and-blood women, it is women who are wrong: it is said not that Femininity is an entity but that women are not feminine. Experiential denials cannot do anything against myth. Though in a way, its source is in experience. It is thus true that woman is other than man, and this alterity is concretely felt in desire, embrace and love; but the real relation is one of reciprocity; as such, it gives rise to authentic dramas: through eroticism, love, friendship and their alternatives of disappointment, hatred and rivalry, the relation is a struggle of consciousnesses, each of which wants to be essential, it is the recognition of freedoms that confirm each other, it is the undefined passage from enmity to complicity. To posit the Woman is to posit the absolute Other, without reciprocity, refusing, against experience, that she could be a subject, a peer.

In concrete reality, women manifest themselves in many different ways; but each of the myths built around woman tries to summarise her as a whole; each is supposed to be unique; the consequence of this is a multiplicity of incompatible myths, and men are perplexed before the strange inconsistencies of the idea of Femininity; as every woman enters into many of these archetypes, each of which claims to incarnate its Truth alone, men also find the same old confusion before their companions as did the Sophists, who had difficulty understanding how a person could be light and dark at the same time. The transition to the absolute shows up in social representations: relations are quickly fixed in classes and roles in types, just as, for the childlike mentality, relations are fixed in things. For example, patriarchal society, focused on preserving the patrimony, necessarily implies, in addition to individuals who hold and transmit goods, the existence of men and women who wrest them from their owners and circulate them; men – adventurers, crooks, thieves, speculators – are generally repudiated by the group; women using their sexual attraction can lure young people and even family men into dissipating their patrimony, all within the law; they appropriate men's fortunes or seize their inheritance; this role being considered bad, women who play it are called 'bad women'. But in other families – those of their fathers, brothers, husbands or lovers – they can in fact seem like guardian angels; the courtesan who swindles rich financiers is a patroness of painters and writers. The ambiguity of personalities like Aspasia and Mme de Pompadour is easy to understand as a concrete experience. But if woman is posited as the Praying Mantis, the Mandrake or the Demon, then the mind reels to discover in her the Muse, the Goddess Mother and Beatrice as well.

As group representation and social types are generally defined by pairs of opposite terms, ambivalence will appear to be an intrinsic property of the Eternal Feminine. The saintly mother has its correlation in the cruel stepmother, the angelic young girl has the perverse virgin: so Mother will be said sometimes to equal Life and sometimes Death, and every virgin is either a pure spirit or flesh possessed by the devil.

It is obviously not reality that dictates to society or individuals their choices between the two opposing principles of unification; in every period, in every case, society and individual decide according to their needs. Very often they project the values and institutions to which they adhere onto the myth they adopt. Thus paternalism that calls for woman to stay at home defines her as sentiment, interiority and immanence; in fact, every existent is simultaneously immanence and transcendence; when he is offered no goal, or is prevented from reaching any goal, or denied the victory of it, his transcendence falls uselessly into the past, that is, it falls into immanence; this is the lot assigned to women in patriarchy; but this is in no way a vocation, any more than slavery is the slave's vocation. The development of this mythology is all too clear in Auguste Comte. To identify Woman with Altruism is to guarantee man absolute rights to her devotion; it is to impose on women a categorical must-be.

The myth must not be confused with the grasp of a signification; signification is immanent in the object; it is revealed to consciousness in a living experience, whereas the myth is a transcendent Idea that escapes any act of consciousness. When Michel Leiris in *Manhood*[59] describes his vision of female organs, he provides significations and does not develop a myth. Wonder at the feminine body or disgust for menstrual blood are apprehensions of a concrete reality. There is nothing mythical in the experience of discovering the voluptuous qualities of feminine flesh, and expressing these qualities by comparisons with flowers or pebbles does not turn them into myth. But to say that Woman is Flesh, to say that Flesh is Night and Death, or that she is the splendour of the cosmos, is to leave terrestrial truth behind and spin off into an empty sky. After all, man is also flesh for woman; and woman is other than a carnal object; and for each person and in each experience the flesh takes on singular significations. It is likewise perfectly true that woman – like man – is a being rooted in nature; she is more enslaved to the species than the male is, her animality is more manifest; but in her as in him, the given is taken on by existence; she also belongs to the human realm. Assimilating her with Nature is simply a prejudice.

Few myths have been more advantageous to the ruling master caste than this one: it justifies all its privileges and even authorises taking advantage of them. Men do not have to care about alleviating the suffering and burdens that are physiologically women's lot since they are 'intended by Nature'; they take this as a pretext to increase the misery of the woman's condition – for example by denying woman the right to sexual pleasure, or making her work like a beast of burden.*

Of all these myths, none is more anchored in masculine hearts than the feminine 'mystery'. It has numerous advantages. And first it allows an easy explanation for anything that is inexplicable; the man who does not 'understand' a woman is happy to replace his subjective deficiency

---

* Cf. Balzac, *Physiology of Marriage*: 'Do not trouble yourself in any way about her mumurings, her cries, her pains; nature has made her for your use, made her to bear all: the children, the wor ries, the blows, and the sorrows of man. But do not accuse us of harshness. In the codes of all the so-called civilised nations, man has written the laws which rule the destiny of woman beneath this blood inscription: *Vae Victis!* Woe to the vanquished.'

with an objective resistance; instead of admitting his ignorance, he recognises the presence of a mystery exterior to himself: here is an excuse that flatters his laziness and vanity at the same time. An infatuated heart thus avoids many disappointments: if the loved one's behaviour is capricious, her remarks stupid, the mystery serves as an excuse. And thanks to the mystery, this negative relation that seemed to Kierkegaard infinitely preferable to positive possession is perpetuated; faced with a living enigma, man remains alone: alone with his dreams, hopes, fears, love, vanity; this subjective game that can range from vice to mystical ecstasy is for many a more attractive experience than an authentic relation with a human being. Upon what bases does such a profitable illusion rest?

Surely, in a way, woman is mysterious, 'mysterious like everyone', according to Maeterlinck. Each one is subject only for himself; each one can grasp only his own self in his immanence; from this point of view, the other is always mystery. In men's view, the opacity of the for-itself is more flagrant in the feminine other; they are unable to penetrate her unique experience by any effect of sympathy; they are condemned to ignorance about the quality of woman's sexual pleasure, the discomforts of menstruation and the pains of childbirth. The truth is that mystery is reciprocal: as another, and as a masculine other, there is also a presence closed on itself and impenetrable to woman in the heart of every man; she is without knowledge of male eroticism. But according to a universal rule already mentioned, the categories in which men think the world are constituted from *their point of view as absolutes*: they fail to understand reciprocity here as everywhere. As she is mystery for man, woman is regarded as mystery in herself.

It is true that her situation especially disposes her to be seen in this image. Her physiological destiny is very complex; she herself endures it as a foreign story; her body is not for her a clear expression of herself; she feels alienated from it; the link that for every individual joins physiological to psychic life – in other words, the relation between the facticity of an individual and the freedom that assumes it – is the most difficult enigma brought about by the human condition: for woman, this enigma is posed in the most disturbing way.

But what is called mystery is not the subjective solitude of consciousness, or the secret of organic life. The word's true meaning is found at the level of communication: it cannot be reduced to pure silence, to obscurity, to absence; it implies an emerging presence that fails to appear. To say that woman is mystery is to say not that she is silent but that her language is not heard; she is there, but hidden beneath veils; she exists beyond these uncertain appearances. Who is she? An angel, a demon, an inspiration, an actress? One supposes that either there are answers impossible to uncover, or that none is adequate because a fundamental ambiguity affects the feminine being; in her heart she is indefinable for herself: a sphinx.

The fact is, deciding *who* she *is* would be quite awkward for her; the question has no answer; but it is not that the hidden truth is too fluctuating to be circumscribed: in this area there is no truth. An existent *is* nothing other than what he does; the possible does not exceed the real, essence does not precede existence: in his pure subjectivity, the human being *is nothing*. He is measured by his acts. It can be said that a peasant woman is a good or bad worker, that an actress has or does not have talent: but if a woman is considered in her immanent presence, absolutely nothing can be said about that, she is outside of the realm of qualification. Now, in amorous or conjugal relations and in all relations where woman is the vassal, the Other, she is grasped in her immanence. It is striking that the woman friend, colleague or associate is without mystery; on the other hand, if the vassal is male and if, in front of an older and richer man or woman, a young man, for example, appears as the inessential object, he also is surrounded in mystery. And this uncovers for us an infrastructure of feminine mystery that is economic. A sentiment cannot *be* something, either. 'In the domain of feeling, what is real is indistinguishable from what is imaginary,' writes Gide. 'And it is sufficient to imagine one loves, in order to love, so it is sufficient to say to oneself that when one loves one imagines one loves, in order to love a little less.' There is no discriminating between the imaginary and the real except through behaviour. As man holds a privileged place in this world, he is the one who is able actively to display his love; very often he keeps the woman, or at least he helps her out; in marrying her, he gives her social status; he gives her gifts; his economic and social independence permits his endeavours and innovations: separated from Mme de Villeparisis, M. de Norpois takes twenty-four-hour trips to be with her; very often he is busy and she is idle: he *gives* her the time he spends with her; she takes it: with pleasure, passion or simply for entertainment? Does she accept these benefits out of love or out of one interest? Does she love husband or marriage? Of course, even the proof man gives is ambiguous: is such a gift given out of love or pity? But while normally woman finds numerous advantages in commerce with man, commerce with woman is profitable to man only inasmuch as he loves her. Thus, the degree of his attachment to her can be roughly estimated by his general attitude, while woman barely has the means to sound out her own heart; according to her moods she will take different points of view about her own feelings, and as long as she submits to them passively, no one interpretation will be truer than another. In the very rare cases where it is she who holds the economic and social privileges, the mystery is reversed: this proves that it is not linked to *this* sex rather than to the other, but to a situation. For many women, the roads to transcendence are blocked: because they *do* nothing, they do not make themselves *be* anything; they wonder indefinitely what they *could have* become, which leads them to wonder what they *are*: it is a useless questioning; if man fails to find that secret essence, it is simply because it does not exist. Kept at the margins of the world, woman cannot be defined objectively through this world and her mystery conceals nothing but emptiness.

Furthermore, like all oppressed people, woman deliberately dissimulates her objective image; slave, servant, indigent, all those who depend upon a master's whims have learned to present him with an immutable smile or an enigmatic impassivity; they carefully hide their real feelings and behaviour. Woman is also taught from adolescence to lie to men, to outsmart, to sidestep them. She approaches them with artificial expressions; she is prudent, hypocritical, playacting.

But feminine Mystery as recognised by mythical thinking is a more profound reality. In fact, it is immediately implied in the mythology of the absolute Other. If one grants that the inessential consciousness is also a transparent subjectivity, capable of carrying out the cogito, one grants that it is truly sovereign and reverts to the essential; for all reciprocity to seem impossible, it is necessary that the Other be another for itself, that its very subjectivity be affected by alterity; this consciousness, which would be alienated as consciousness, in its pure immanent presence, would obviously be a Mystery; it would be a Mystery in itself because it would be it for itself; it would be absolute Mystery. It is thus that, beyond the secrecy their dissimulation creates, there is a mystery of the Black, of the Yellow, insofar as they are considered absolutely as the inessential Other. It must be noted that the American citizen who deeply confounds the average European is nonetheless not considered 'mysterious': one more modestly claims not to understand him; likewise, woman does not always 'understand' man, but there is no masculine mystery; the fact is that rich America and the male are on the side of the Master, and Mystery belongs to the slave.

Of course, one can only dream about the positive reality of the Mystery in the twilight of bad faith; like certain marginal hallucinations, it dissolves once one tries to pin it down. Literature always fails to depict 'mysterious' women; they can only appear at the beginning of a novel as strange and enigmatic; but unless the story remains unfinished, they give up their secret in the end and become consistent and translucent characters. The heroes in Peter Cheyney's books, for example, never cease to be amazed by women's unpredictable caprices; one can never guess how they will behave, they confound all calculations; in truth, as soon as the workings of their actions are exposed to the reader, they are seen as very simple mechanisms: this one is a spy or that one a thief; however clever the intrigue, there is always a key, and it could not be otherwise, even if the author had all the talent, all the imagination possible. Mystery is never more than a mirage; it vanishes as soon as one tries to approach it.

Thus we see that myths are explained in large part by the use man makes of them. The myth of the woman is a luxury. It can appear only if man escapes the imperious influence of his needs; the more relations are lived concretely, the less idealised they are. The fellah in ancient Egypt, the bedouin peasant, the medieval artisan and the worker of today, in their work needs and their poverty, have relations with the particular woman who is their companion that are too basic for them to embellish her with an auspicious or fatal aura. Eras and social classes that had the leisure to daydream were the ones who created the black-and-white statues of femininity. But luxury also has its usefulness; these dreams were imperiously guided by interest. Yes, most myths have their roots in man's spontaneous attitude to his own existence and the world that invests it: but the move to surpass experience towards the transcendent Idea was deliberately effected by patriarchal society for the end of self-justification; through myths, this society imposed its laws and customs on individuals in an imagistic and sensible way; it is in a mythical form that the group imperative insinuated itself into each consciousness. By way of religions, traditions, language, tales, songs and film, myths penetrate even into the existence of those most harshly subjected to material realities. Everyone can draw on myth to sublimate their own modest experiences: betrayed by a woman he loves, one man calls her a slut; another is obsessed by his own virile impotence: this woman is a praying mantis; yet another takes pleasure in his wife's company: here we have Harmony, Repose, Mother Earth. The taste for eternity at bargain prices and for a handy, pocket-sized absolute, seen in most men, is satisfied by myths. The least emotion, a small disagreement, become the reflection of a timeless Idea; this illusion comfortably flatters one's vanity.

The myth is one of those traps of false objectivity into which the spirit of seriousness falls headlong. It is once again a matter of replacing lived experience and the free judgements of experience it requires by a static idol. The myth of Woman substitutes for an authentic relationship with an autonomous existent the immobile contemplation of a mirage. 'Mirage! Mirage! Kill them since we cannot seize them; or else reassure them, instruct them, help them give up their taste for jewellery, make them real equal companions, our intimate friends, associates in the here and now, dress them differently, cut their hair, tell them everything,' cried Laforgue. Man would have nothing to lose, quite the contrary, if he stopped disguising woman as a symbol. Dreams, when collective and controlled – clichés – are so poor and monotonous compared to living reality: for the real dreamer, for the poet, living reality is a far more generous resource than a worn-out fantasy. The times when women were the most sincerely cherished were not courtly feudal ones, nor the gallant nineteenth century; they were the times – the eighteenth century, for example – when men regarded women as their peers; this is when women looked truly romantic: only read *Dangerous Liaisons*,[60] *The Red and the Black*[61] or *A Farewell to Arms* to realise this. Laclos' heroines like Stendhal's and Hemingway's are without mystery: and they are no less engaging for it. To recognise a human being in a woman is not to impoverish man's experience: that experience would lose none of its diversity, its richness or its intensity if it was taken on in its inter-subjectivity; to reject myths is not to destroy all dramatic relations between the sexes, it is not to deny the significations authentically revealed to man through feminine reality; it is not to eliminate poetry, love, adventure, happiness and dreams: it is only to ask that behaviour, feelings and passion be grounded in truth.*

'Woman is lost. Where are the women? Today's women are not women'; we have seen what these mysterious slogans mean. In the eyes of men – and of the legions of women who see through these eyes – it is not enough to have a woman's body or to take on the female function as lover and mother to be a 'real woman'; it is possible for the subject to claim autonomy through sexuality and maternity; the 'real woman' is one who accepts herself as Other. The duplicitous attitude

* Laforgue goes on to say about woman: 'As she has been left in slavery, idleness, without arms other than her sex, she has overdeveloped it and has become the Feminine . . . we have permitted her to overdevelop; she is on the earth for us . . . Well, that is all wrong . . . we have played doll with the woman until now. This has gone on too long!'

of men today creates a painful split for women; men accept, for the most part, that woman be a peer, an equal; and yet they continue to oblige her to remain the inessential; for her, these two destinies are not reconcilable; she hesitates between them without being exactly suited to either, and that is the source of her lack of balance. For man, there is no hiatus between public and private life: the more he asserts his grasp on the world through action and work, the more virile he looks; human and vital characteristics are merged in him; but women's own successes are in contradiction with her femininity since the 'real woman' is required to make herself object, to be the Other. It is very possible that on this point even men's sensibility and sexuality are changing. A new aesthetic has already been born. Although the fashion for flat chests and narrow hips – the boyish woman – only lasted a short while, the opulent ideal of past centuries has nevertheless not returned. The feminine body is expected to be flesh, but discreetly so; it must be slim and not burdened with fat; toned, supple, robust, it has to suggest transcendence; it is preferred tanned, having been bared to a universal sun like a worker's torso, not white like a hothouse plant. Woman's clothes, in becoming more practical, have not made her look asexual: on the contrary, short skirts have shown off her legs and thighs more than before. There is no reason for work to deprive her of her erotic appeal. To see woman as both a social person and carnal prey can be disturbing: in a recent series of drawings by Peynet,* there is a young fiancé deserting his fiancée because he was seduced by the pretty mayoress about to celebrate the marriage; that a woman could hold a 'man's office' and still be desirable has long been a subject of more or less dirty jokes; little by little, scandal and irony have lost their bite and a new form of eroticism seems to be coming about: perhaps it will produce new myths.

What is certain is that today it is very difficult for women to assume both their status of autonomous individual and their feminine destiny; here is the source of the awkwardness and discomfort that sometimes leads them to be considered 'a lost sex'. And without doubt it is more comfortable to endure blind bondage than to work for one's liberation; the dead, too, are better suited to the earth than the living. In any case, turning back is no more possible than desirable. What must be hoped is that men will assume, without reserve, the situation being created; only then can women experience it without being torn. Then will Laforgue's wish be fulfilled: 'O, young women, when will you be our

* November 1948.

brothers, our closest brothers without ulterior motives of exploitation? When will we give to each other a true handshake?' Then 'Melusina, no longer under the burden of the fate unleashed on her by man alone, Melusina rescued,' will find 'her human base'.* Then will she fully be a human being, 'when woman's infinite servitude is broken, when she lives for herself and by herself, man – abominable until now –giving her her freedom'.†

* Breton, *Arcanum 17*.
† Rimbaud, *Lettre à Demeny*, 15 May 1871.

II

LIVED EXPERIENCE

What a curse to be a woman! And yet the very worst curse when one is a woman is, in fact, not to understand that it is one.

Kierkegaard

Half victim, half accomplice, like everyone.

J. P. Sartre

Introduction

Women of today are overthrowing the myth of femininity; they are beginning to affirm their independence concretely; but their success in living their human condition completely does not come easily. As they are brought up by women, in the heart of a feminine world, their normal destiny is marriage, which still subordinates them to man from a practical point of view; virile prestige is far from being eradicated: it still stands on solid economic and social bases. It is thus necessary to study woman's traditional destiny carefully. What I will try to describe is how woman is taught to assume her condition, how she experiences this, what universe she finds herself enclosed in and what escape mechanisms are permitted her. Only then can we understand what problems women – heirs to a weighty past, striving to forge a new future – are faced with. When I use the words 'woman' or 'feminine' I obviously refer to no archetype, to no immutable essence; 'in the present state of education and customs' must be understood to follow most of my affirmations. There is no question of expressing eternal truths here, but of describing the common ground from which all singular feminine existence stems.

Part One

FORMATIVE YEARS

CHAPTER I

Childhood

One is not born, but rather becomes, woman. No biological, psychical or economic destiny defines the figure that the human female takes on in society; it is civilisation as a whole that elaborates this intermediary product between the male and the eunuch that is called feminine. Only the mediation of another can constitute an individual as an *Other*. Inasmuch as he exists for himself, the child would not grasp himself as sexually differentiated. For girls and boys, the body is first the radiation of a subjectivity, the instrument that brings about the comprehension of the world: they apprehend the universe through their eyes and hands, and not through their sexual parts. The drama of birth and weaning takes place in the same way for infants of both sexes; they have the same interests and pleasures; sucking is the first source of their most pleasurable sensations; they then go through an anal phase in which they get their greatest satisfactions from excretory functions common to both; their genital development is similar; they explore their bodies with the same curiosity and the same indifference; they derive the same uncertain pleasure from the clitoris and the penis; insofar as their sensibility already needs an object, it turns towards the mother: it is the soft, smooth, supple feminine flesh that arouses sexual desires and these desires are prehensile; the girl like the boy kisses, touches and caresses her mother in an aggressive manner; they feel the same jealousy at the birth of a new child; they show it with the same behaviour: anger, sulking, urinary problems; they have recourse to the same coquetry to gain the love of adults. Up to twelve, the girl is just as sturdy as her brothers; she shows the same intellectual aptitudes; she is not barred from competing with them in any area. If well before puberty and sometimes even starting from early childhood she already appears sexually specified, it is not because mysterious instincts immediately destine her to passivity, coquetry or motherhood but because the intervention of others in the infant's life is almost originary, and her vocation is imperiously breathed into her from the first years of her life.

The world is first present to the newborn only in the form of immanent sensations; he is still immersed within the Whole as he was when
he was living in the darkness of a womb; whether raised on the breast
or on a bottle, he is invested with the warmth of maternal flesh. Little
by little he learns to perceive objects as distinct from himself: he separates himself from them; at the same time, more or less suddenly, he
is removed from the nourishing body; sometimes he reacts to this separation with a violent fit;* in any case, when it is consummated – around
six months – he begins to manifest the desire to seduce others by
mimicking, which then turns into a real display. Of course, this attitude is not defined by a reflective choice; but it is not necessary to
think a situation to *exist* it. In an immediate way the newborn lives the
primeval drama of every existent – that is, the drama of one's relation
to the Other. Man experiences his abandonment in anguish. Fleeing
his freedom and subjectivity, he would like to lose himself within the
Whole: here is the origin of his cosmic and pantheistic reveries, of his
desire for oblivion, sleep, ecstasy and death. He never manages to
abolish his separated self: at the least he wishes to achieve the solidity
of the in-itself, to be petrified in thing; it is uniquely when he is fixed
by the gaze of others that he appears to himself as a being. It is in this
vein that the child's behaviour has to be interpreted: in a bodily form
he discovers finitude, solitude and abandonment in an alien world; he
tries to compensate for this catastrophe by alienating his existence in
an image whose reality and value will be established by others. It would
seem that from the time he recognises his reflection in a mirror – a
time that coincides with weaning – he begins to affirm his identity:†
his self merges with this reflection in such a way that it is formed only
by alienating itself. Whether the mirror as such plays a more or less
considerable role, what is sure is that the child at about six months of
age begins to understand his parents' miming and to grasp himself
under their gaze as an object. He is already an autonomous subject
transcending himself towards the world: but it is only in an alienated
form that he will encounter himself.

---

* Judith Gautier says in her accounts of her memories that she cried and wasted away
so terribly when she was pulled away from her wet nurse that she had to be reunited
with her. She was weaned much later.
† This is Dr Lacan's theory in *Family Complexes in the Formation of the Individual*. This
fundamental fact would explain that during its development 'the self keeps the ambiguous
form of spectacle'.

When the child grows up, he fights against his original abandonment in two ways. He tries to deny the separation: he crushes himself in his mother's arms, he seeks her loving warmth, he wants her caresses. And he tries to win the approbation of others in order to justify himself. Adults are to him as gods: they have the power to confer being on him. He experiences the magic of the gaze that metamorphoses him now into a delicious little angel and now into a monster. These two modes of defence are not mutually exclusive: on the contrary, they complete and infuse each other. When seduction is successful, the feeling of justification finds physical confirmation in the kisses and caresses received: it is the same contented passivity that the child experiences in his mother's lap and under her benevolent eyes. During the first three or four years of life, there is no difference between girls' and boys' attitudes; they all try to perpetuate the happy state preceding weaning; both boys and girls show the same behaviour of seduction and display. Boys are just as desirous as their sisters to please, to be smiled at, to be admired.

It is more satisfying to deny brutal separation than to overcome it, more radical to be lost in the heart of the Whole than to be petrified by the consciousness of others: carnal fusion creates a deeper alienation than any abdication under the gaze of another. Seduction and display represent a more complex and less easy stage than the simple abandonment in maternal arms. The magic of the adult gaze is capricious; the child pretends to be invisible, his parents play the game, grope around for him, they laugh and then suddenly they declare: 'You are bothersome, you are not invisible at all.' A child's phrase amuses, then he repeats it: this time, they shrug their shoulders. In this world as unsure and unpredictable as Kafka's universe, one stumbles at every step.*² That is why so many children are afraid of growing up; they desperately want their parents to continue taking them on their laps, taking them into

* In *The Blue Orange,* Yassu Gauclère says about her father: 'His good mood seemed as fearsome as his impatiences because nothing explained to me what could bring it about . . . As uncertain of the changes in his mood as I would have been of a god's whims, I revered him with anxiety . . . I threw out my words as I might have played heads or tails, wondering how they would be received.' And further on, she tells the following anecdote: 'For example, one day, after being scolded, I began my litany: old table, floor brush, stove, large bowl, milk bottle, casserole, and so on. My mother heard me and burst out laughing . . . A few days later, I tried to use my litany to soften my grandmother who once again had scolded me: I should have known better this time. Instead of making her laugh, I made her angrier and got an extra punishment. I told myself that adults' behaviour was truly incomprehensible.'

their bed: through physical frustration they experience ever more cruelly that abandonment of which the human being never becomes aware without anguish.

It is here that little girls first appear privileged. A second weaning, less brutal and slower than the first one, withdraws the mother's body from the child's embraces; but little by little boys are the ones who are denied kisses and caresses; the little girl continues to be doted upon, she is allowed to hide behind her mother's skirts, her father takes her on his knees and pats her hair; she is dressed in dresses as lovely as kisses, her tears and whims are treated indulgently, her hair is done carefully, her expressions and affectations amuse: physical contact and complaisant looks protect her against the anxiety of solitude. For the little boy, on the other hand, even affectations are forbidden; his attempts at seduction, his games irritate. 'A man doesn't ask for kisses . . . A man doesn't look at himself in the mirror . . . A man doesn't cry,' he is told. He has to be 'a little man'; he obtains adults' approbation by freeing himself from them. He will please by not seeming to seek to please.

Many boys, frightened by the harsh independence they are condemned to, thus desire to be girls; in times when they were first dressed as girls, they cried when they had to give dresses up for long trousers and had to have their curls cut. Some obstinately would choose femininity, which is one of the ways of gravitating towards homosexuality: 'I wanted passionately to be a girl, and I was unconscious of the grandeur of being a man to the point of trying to urinate sitting down,' Maurice Sachs*[3] recounts. However, if the boy at first seems less favoured than his sisters, it is because there are greater designs for him. The requirements he is subjected to immediately imply a higher estimation. In his memoirs, Maurras recounts that he was jealous of a younger son his mother and grandmother doted upon: his father took him by the hand and out of the room: 'We are men; let's leave these women,' he told him. The child is persuaded that more is demanded of boys because of their superiority; the pride of his virility is breathed into him in order to encourage him in this difficult path; this abstract notion takes on a concrete form for him: it is embodied in the penis; he does not experience pride spontaneously in his little indolent sex organ; but he feels it through the attitude of those around him. Mothers and wet nurses perpetuate the tradition that assimilates phallus and maleness; whether they recognise

* *Witches' Sabbath.*

its prestige in amorous gratitude or in submission, or whether they gain revenge by seeing it in the baby in a reduced form, they treat the child's penis with a singular deference. Rabelais[4] reports on Garguanta's* wet nurses' games and words; history has recorded those of Louis XIII's wet nurses. Less daring women, however, give a friendly name to the little boy's sex organ, they speak to him about it as of a little person who is both himself and other than himself; they make of it, according to the words already cited, 'an *alter ego* usually craftier, more intelligent and more clever than the individual'.[†5] Anatomically, the penis is totally apt to play this role; considered apart from the body, it looks like a little natural plaything, a kind of doll. The child is esteemed by esteeming his double. A father told me that one of his sons at the age of three was still urinating sitting down; surrounded by sisters and girl cousins, he was a shy and sad child; one day his father took him with him to the toilet and said: 'I will show you how men do it.' From then on, the child, proud to be urinating standing up, scorned the girls 'who urinated through a hole'; his scorn came originally not from the fact that they were lacking an organ but that they had not like him been singled out and initiated by the father. So, far from the penis being discovered as an immediate privilege from which the boy would draw a feeling of superiority, its value seems, on the contrary, like a compensation – invented by adults and fervently accepted by the child – for the hardships of the last weaning: in that way he is protected against regret that he is no longer a breast-feeding baby or a girl. From then on, he will embody his transcendence and his arrogant sovereignty in his sex.[‡]

The girl's lot is very different. Mothers and wet nurses have neither reverence nor tenderness for her genital parts; they do not focus attention on this secret organ of which only the outside envelope can be seen and that cannot be taken hold of; in one sense, she does not have a sex. She does not experience this absence as a lack; her body is evidently a plenitude for her; but she finds herself in the world differently from the

---

* 'And already beginning to exercise his codpiece, which each and every day his nurses would adorn with lovely bouquets, fine ribbons, beautiful flowers, pretty tufts, and they spent their time bringing it back and forth between their hands like a cylinder of salve, then they laughed their heads off when it raised its ears, as if they liked the game. One would call it my little spigot, another my ninepin, another my coral branch, another my stopper, my cork, my gimlet, my ramrod, my awl, my pendant.'

† Cited by A. Bàlint, *The Psychoanalysis of the Nursery.*

‡ See Vol. I, Chapter 2.

boy; and a group of factors can transform this difference into inferiority in her eyes.

Few questions are as much discussed by psychoanalysts as the famous 'female castration complex'. Most accept today that penis envy manifests itself in very different ways depending on the individual case.* First, many girls are ignorant of male anatomy until an advanced age. The child accepts naturally that there are men and women as there are a sun and a moon: he believes in essences contained in words and his curiosity is at first not analytical. For many others, this little piece of flesh hanging between boys' legs is insignificant or even derisory; it is a particularity like that of clothes and hair style; often the female child discovers it at a younger brother's birth, and 'when the little girl is very young,' says Helene Deutsch,[6] 'she is not impressed by her younger brother's penis'; she cites the example of an eighteen-month-old girl who remained absolutely indifferent to the discovery of the penis and did not give it any value until much later, in connection with her personal preoccupations. The penis can even be considered an anomaly: it is a growth, a vague hanging thing like nodules, teats and warts; it can inspire disgust. Lastly, the fact is that there are many cases of the little girl being interested in a brother's or a friend's penis; but that does not mean she experiences a specifically sexual jealousy and even less that she feels deeply moved by the absence of this organ; she desires to appropriate it for herself as she desires to appropriate any object; but this desire may remain superficial.

It is certain that the excretory function and particularly the urinary one interest children passionately: wetting the bed is often a protest against the parents' marked preference for another child. There are countries where men urinate sitting down and there are women who urinate standing up: this is the way among many women peasants; but in contemporary Western society, custom generally has it that they squat, while the standing position is reserved to males. This is the most striking sexual difference for the little girl. To urinate she has to squat down, remove some clothes and above all hide, a shameful and uncomfortable servitude.

---

* Besides Freud's and Adler's works, there is today an abundant literature on the subject. Abraham was the first one to put forward the idea that the girl considered her sex a wound resulting from a mutilation. Karen Horney, Ernest Jones, Jeanne Lampl de Groot, H. Deutsch and A. Bálint studied the question from a psychoanalytical point of view. Saussure tries to reconcile psychoanalysis with Piaget's and Lucquet's ideas. See also Pollack, *Children's Ideas on Sex Differences*.

Shame increases in the frequent cases in which she suffers from involuntary urinary emissions, when bursting out laughing, for example; control is worse than for boys. For them, the urinary function is like a free game with the attraction of all games in which freedom is exercised; the penis can be handled, through it one can act, which is one of the child's deep interests. A little girl seeing a boy urinate declared admiringly: 'How practical!'* The stream can be aimed at will, the urine directed far away: the boy draws a feeling of omnipotence from it. Freud spoke of 'the burning ambition of early diuretics'; Stekel discussed this formula sensibly, but it is true that, as Karen Horney says, 'fantasies of omnipotence, especially of a sadistic character, are as a matter of fact more easily associated with the jet of urine passed by the male';† there are many such fantasies in children and they survive in some men.‡ Abraham speaks of 'the great pleasure women experience watering the garden with a hose'; I think, in agreement with Sartre's and Bachelard's theories,‡‡ that it is not necessarily the assimilation of the hose with the penis that is the source of pleasure;§ every stream of water seems like a miracle, a defiance of gravity: directing or governing it means carrying off a little victory over natural laws; in any case, for the little boy there is a daily amusement that is impossible for his sisters. He is also able to establish many relations with things through the urinary stream, especially in the countryside: water, earth, moss, snow. There are little girls who lie on their backs and try to practise urinating 'in the air' or who try to urinate standing up in order to have these experiences. According to Karen Horney, they also envy the opportunity to exhibit which the boy is granted. 'A sick woman suddenly exclaimed, after seeing a man urinating in the street: "If I might ask a gift of Povidence, it would be to be able to just for once to urinate like a man,"' Karen Horney reports. It seems to girls that the boy, having the right to touch his penis, can use it as a plaything, while their organs are taboo. That these factors make the possession of a male sex organ desirable for many of them is a fact confirmed by many studies and confidences gathered by psychiatrists. Havelock Ellis§§ 7 quotes the words of a patient he calls Zenia: 'The noise

* Cited by A. Bálint.

† 'On the Genesis of the Castration Complex in Women', *International Journal of Psychoanalysis*, 1923–24.

‡ Montherlant ('The Caterpillars', *June Solstice*).

‡‡ See Vol. I, Part One, Chapter 2.

§ It is clear, though, in some cases.

§§ Cf. Havelock Ellis, *Ondinism*.

14. Cf. Ellis [discussion of "undinism" in *Studies in the Psychology of Sex*. – TRANS.].

of a jet of water, especially coming out of a long hose, has always been very stimulating for me, recalling the noise of the stream of urine observed in childhood in my brother and even in other people.' Another woman, Mme R. S., recounts that as a child she absolutely loved holding a little friend's penis in her hands; one day she was given a hose: 'It seemed delicious to hold that as if I was holding a penis.' She emphasised that the penis had no sexual meaning for her; she only knew its urinary usage. The most interesting case, that of Florrie, is reported by Havelock Ellis*[8] and analysed by Stekel later on. Here is a detailed account from it:

> The woman concerned is very intelligent, artistic, active, biologically normal, and not homosexual. She says that the urinary function played a great role in her childhood; she played urinary games with her brothers, and they wet their hands without feeling disgust. 'My earliest ideas of the superiority of the male were connected with urination. I felt aggrieved with nature because I lacked so useful and ornamental an organ. No teapot without a spout felt so forlorn. It required no one to instil into me the theory of male predominance and superiority. Constant proof was before me.' She took great pleasure in urinating in the country. 'Nothing could come up to the entrancing sound as the stream descended on crackling leaves in the depth of a wood and she watched its absorption. Most of all she was fascinated by the idea of doing it into water' [as are many little boys]. There is a quantity of childish and vulgar imagery showing little boys urinating in ponds and brooks. Florrie complains that the style of her knickers prevented her from trying various desired experiments, but often during country walks she would hold back as long as she could and then suddenly relieve herself standing. 'I can distinctly remember the strange and delicious sensation of this forbidden delight, and also my puzzled feeling that it came standing.' In her opinion, the style of children's clothing has great importance for feminine psychology in general. 'It was not only a source of annoyance to me that I had to unfasten my drawers and then squat down for fear of wetting them in front, but the flap at the back, which must be removed to uncover the posterior parts during the act, accounts for my early impression that in girls this function is connected with those parts. The first distinction in sex that impressed me – the one great difference in sex – was that boys

* H. Ellis, *Studies in the Psychology of Sex*, Vol. fl¾¾¾.

urinated standing and that girls had to sit down . . . The fact that my earliest feelings of shyness were more associated with the back than the front may have thus originated.' All these impressions were of great importance in Florrie's case because her father often whipped her until the blood came and also a governess had once spanked her to make her urinate; she was obsessed by masochistic dreams and fancies in which she saw herself whipped by a school mistress under the eyes of all and having to urinate against her will, 'an idea that gives one a curious sense of gratification'. At the age of fifteen it happened that under urgent need she urinated standing in a deserted street. 'In trying to analyse my sensations I think the most prominent lay in the shame that came from standing, and the consequently greater distance the stream had to descend. It seemed to make the affair important and conspicuous, even though clothing hid it. In the ordinary attitude there is a kind of privacy. As a small child, too, the stream had not far to go, but at the age of fifteen I was tall and it seemed to give one a glow of shame to think of this stream falling unchecked such a distance. (I am sure that the ladies who fled in horror from the urinette at Portsmouth* thought it most indecent for a woman to stand, legs apart, and to pull up her clothes and make a stream which descended unabashed all that way.)' She renewed this experience at twenty and frequently thereafter. She felt a mixture of shame and pleasure at the idea that she might be surprised and that she would be incapable of stopping. 'The stream seemed to be drawn from me without my consent, and *yet with even more pleasure than if I were doing it freely.*† This curious feeling – that it is being drawn away by some unseen power which is determined that one shall do it – is an entirely feminine pleasure and a subtle charm . . . There is a fierce charm in the torrent that binds one to its will by a mighty force.' Later Florrie developed a flagellatory eroticism always combined with urinary obsessions.

This case is very interesting because it throws light on several elements of the child's experience. But of course there are particular circumstances

---

* In an allusion to an episode she related previously: at Portsmouth a modern urinette for ladies was opened which called for the standing position; all the clients were seen to depart hastily as soon as they entered.

† Florrie's italics.

that confer such a great importance upon them. For normally raised little girls, the boy's urinary privilege is too secondary a thing to engender a feeling of inferiority directly. Psychoanalysts following Freud who think that the mere discovery of the penis would be sufficient to produce a trauma seriously misunderstand the child's mentality; it is much less rational than they seem to think, it does not establish clear-cut categories and is not bothered by contradictions. When the little girl seeing a penis declares: 'I had one too' or 'I'll have one too', or even 'I have one too', this is not a defence in bad faith; presence and absence are not mutually exclusive; the child – as his drawings prove – believes much less in what he *sees* with his eyes than in the signifying *types* that he has determined once and for all: he often draws without looking and in any case he finds in his perceptions only what he puts there. Saussure,*[9] who emphasises this point, quotes this very important observation of Luquet: 'Once a line is considered wrong, it is as if inexistent, *the child literally no longer sees it*, hypnotised in a way by the new line that replaces it, nor does he take into account lines that can be accidentally found on his paper.' Male anatomy constitutes a strong form that is often imposed on the little girl; and *literally she no longer sees* her own body. Saussure brings up the example of a four-year-old girl who, trying to urinate like a boy between the bars of a fence, said she wanted 'a little long thing that runs'. She affirmed at the same time that she had a penis and that she did not have one, which goes along with the thinking by 'participation' that Piaget described in children. The little girl takes it for granted that all children are born with a penis but that the parents then cut some of them off to make girls; this idea satisfies the artificialism of the child who glorifies his parents and 'conceives of them as the cause of everything he possesses', says Piaget; he does not see punishment in castration right away. For it to become a frustration, the little girl has to be unhappy with her situation for some reason; as Deutsch justly points out, an exterior event like the sight of a penis could not lead to an internal development. 'The sight of the male organ can have a traumatic effect,' she says, 'but only if a chain of prior experiences that would create that effect had preceded it.' If the little girl feels powerless to satisfy her desires of masturbation or exhibition, if her parents repress her onanism, if she feels less loved or less valued than her brothers, then she will project her dissatisfaction onto the male organ. 'The little girl's discovery of the anatomical difference with the boy confirms a previously felt need;

* 'Genetic Psychology and Psychoanalysis', *Revue française de psychanalyse*, 1933.

it is her rationalization, so to speak.'* And Adler also insisted on the fact that it is the validation by the parents and others that gives the boy prestige, and that the penis becomes the explanation and symbol in the little girl's eyes. Her brother is considered superior; he himself takes pride in his maleness; so she envies him and feels frustrated. Sometimes she resents her mother and less often her father; either she accuses herself of being mutilated or she consoles herself by thinking that the penis is hidden in her body and that one day it will come out.

It is sure that the absence of a penis will play an important role in the little girl's destiny, even if she does not really envy those who possess one. The great privilege that the boy gets from it is that as he is bestowed with an organ that can be seen and held, he can at least partially alienate himself in it. He projects the mystery of his body and its dangers outside himself, which permits him to keep them at a distance: of course, he feels endangered through his penis, he fears castration, but this fear is easier to dominate than the pervasive overall fear the girl feels concerning her 'insides', a fear that will often be perpetuated throughout her whole life as a woman. She has a deep concern about everything happening inside her; from the start, she is far more opaque to herself and more profoundly inhabited by the worrying mystery of life than the male. Because he recognises himself in an alter ego, the little boy can boldly assume his subjectivity; the very object in which he alienates himself becomes a symbol of autonomy, transcendence and power: he measures the size of his penis; he compares his urinary stream with that of his friends; later, erection and ejaculation will be sources of satisfaction and challenge. But a little girl cannot incarnate herself in any part of her own body. As compensation, and to fill the role of alter ego for her, she is handed a foreign object: a doll. Note that the bandage wrapped on an injured finger is also called a *poupée* ('doll' in French): a finger dressed and separate from the others is looked on with amusement and a kind of pride with which the child initiates the process of its alienation. But it is a figurine with a human face – or a corn husk or even a piece of wood – that will most satisfyingly replace this double, this natural toy, this penis.

The great difference is that, on one hand, the doll represents the whole body and, on the other hand, it is a passive thing. As such, the little girl will be encouraged to alienate herself in her person as a whole and to

* H. Deutsch, *The Psychology of Women*. She also cites the authority of K. Abraham and J. H. W. van Ophuijsen.

consider it as an inert given. While the boy seeks himself in his penis as an autonomous subject, the little girl pampers her doll and dresses her as she dreams of being dressed and pampered; inversely, she thinks of herself as a marvellous doll.* Through compliments and admonishments, through images and words, she discovers the meaning of the words 'pretty' and 'ugly'; she soon knows that to please she has to be 'pretty as a picture'; she tries to resemble an image, she disguises herself, she looks at herself in the mirror, she compares herself to princesses and fairies from tales. Marie Bashkirtseff[10] gives a striking example of this infantile coquetry. It is certainly not by chance that, weaned late – she was three and a half – she fervently felt the need at the age of four or five to be admired and to exist for others: the shock must have been violent in a more mature child and she had to struggle even harder to overcome the inflicted separation. 'At five years old,' she writes in her diary, 'I would dress in Mummy's lace, with flowers in my hair and I would go and dance in the living room. I was Petipa, the great dancer, and the whole house was there to *look at me*.'

This narcissism appears so precociously for the little girl and will play so fundamental a part in her life that it is readily considered as emanating from a mysterious feminine instinct. But we have just seen that in reality it is not an anatomical destiny that dictates her attitude. The difference that distinguishes her from boys is a fact that she could assume in many ways. Having a penis is certainly a privilege, but one whose value naturally diminishes when the child loses interest in his excretory functions and becomes socialised: if he retains interest in it past the age of eight or nine years, it is because the penis has become the symbol of a socially valorised virility. The fact is that the influence of education and society is enormous here. All children try to compensate for the separation of weaning by seductive and attention-seeking behaviour; the boy is forced to go beyond this stage, he is saved from his narcissism by turning his attention to his penis, whereas the girl is reinforced in this tendency to make herself object, which is common to all children. The doll helps her, but it does not have a determining role; the boy can also treasure a teddy bear or a rag doll on whom he can project himself; it is in their life's overall form that each factor – penis, doll – takes on its importance.

* The analogy between the woman and the doll remains until the adult age; in French, a woman is vulgarly called a doll; in English, a dressed-up woman is said to be 'dolled up'.

Thus, the passivity that essentially characterises the 'feminine' woman is a trait that develops in her from her earliest years. But it is false to claim that therein lies a biological given; in fact, it is a destiny imposed on her by her teachers and by society. The great advantage for the boy is that his way of existing for others leads him to posit himself for himself. He carries out the apprenticeship of his existence as free movement towards the world; he rivals other boys in toughness and independence; he looks down on girls. Climbing trees, fighting with his companions, confronting them in violent games, he grasps his body as a means to dominate nature and as a fighting tool; he is proud of his muscles, as he is of his sex organ; through games, sports, fights, challenges and exploits, he finds a balanced use of his strength; at the same time, he learns the severe lessons of violence; he learns to take blows, to deride pain, to hold back tears from the earliest age. He undertakes, he invents, he dares. Granted, he also experiences himself as if 'for others'; he tests his own virility, and consequently, trouble ensues with adults and friends. But what is very important is that there is no fundamental opposition between this objective figure that is his and his will for self-affirmation in concrete projects. It is by doing that he makes himself be, in one single movement. On the contrary, for the woman there is, from the start, a conflict between her autonomous existence and her 'being-other'; she is taught that to please, she must try to please, must make herself object; she must therefore renounce her autonomy. She is treated like a living doll and freedom is denied her; thus a vicious circle is closed; for the less she exercises her freedom to understand, grasp and discover the world around her, the less she will find its resources, and the less she will dare to affirm herself as subject; if she were encouraged, she could show the same vibrant exuberance, the same curiosity, the same spirit of initiative, and the same intrepidness as the boy. Sometimes this does happen when she is given a male upbringing; she is thus spared many problems.* Interestingly, this is the kind of education that a father habitually gives his daughter; women brought up by a man escape many of the defects of femininity. But customs oppose treating girls exactly like boys. I knew a village where girls of three and four years old were persecuted because their father made them wear trousers: 'Are they girls or boys?' And the other children tried to find out; the result was their pleading to wear dresses. Unless she leads a very solitary life, even if parents allow her to

---

* At least in her early childhood. In today's society, adolescent conflicts could, on the contrary, be exacerbated.

have boyish manners, the girl's companions, her friends and her teachers will be shocked. There will always be aunts, grandmothers and girl cousins to counterbalance the father's influence. Normally, his role regarding his daughters is secondary. One of the woman's curses – as Michelet has justly pointed out – is that in her childhood she is left in the hands of women. The boy is also brought up by his mother in the beginning; but she respects his maleness and he escapes from her relatively quickly,* whereas the mother wants to integrate the girl into the feminine world.

We will see later how complex the relation is between the mother and the daughter: for the mother, the daughter is both her double and an other, the mother cherishes her and at the same time is hostile to her; she imposes her own destiny on her child: it is a way to proudly claim her own femininity and also to take revenge on it. The same process is found with pederasts, gamblers, drug addicts, and all those who are flattered to belong to a certain community, and are also humiliated by it: they try through ardent proselytism to win over converts. Thus, women given the care of a little girl are bent on transforming her into women like themselves with zeal and arrogance mixed with resentment. And even a generous mother who sincerely wants the best for her child will, as a rule, think it wiser to make a 'true woman' of her, as that is the way she will be best accepted by society. So she is given other little girls as friends, she is entrusted to female teachers, she lives among matrons as in the days of the gynaeceum, books and games are chosen for her that introduce her to her destiny, her ears are filled with the treasures of feminine wisdom, feminine virtues are presented to her, she is taught cooking, sewing and housework as well as how to dress, how to take care of her personal appearance, charm and modesty; she is dressed in uncomfortable and fancy clothes that she has to take care of, her hair is done in complicated styles, posture is imposed on her: stand up straight, don't walk like a duck; to be graceful she has to repress spontaneous movements, she is told not to look like a tomboy, strenuous exercise is banned, she is forbidden to fight; in short, she is committed to becoming, like her elders, a servant and an idol. Today, thanks to feminism's breakthroughs, it is becoming more and more normal to encourage her to pursue her education, to devote herself to sports; but she is more easily excused for not succeeding; success is made more difficult for her as another kind of

---

* There are, of course, many exceptions: but the mother's role in bringing up a boy cannot be studied here.

accomplishment is demanded of her: she must at least *also* be a woman, she must not *lose* her femininity.

In her early years she resigns herself to this lot without much difficulty. The child inhabits the level of play and dream, he plays at being, he plays at doing; doing and being are not clearly distinguishable when it is a question of imaginary accomplishments. The little girl can compensate for boys' superiority of the moment by those promises inherent in her woman's destiny, which she already achieves in her play. Because she still only knows her childhood universe, her mother seems endowed with more authority than her father; she imagines the world as a sort of matriarchy; she imitates her mother, she identifies with her; often she even inverses the roles: 'When I am big and you are little . . . ,' she often says. The doll is not only her double: it is also her child, functions that are not mutually exclusive insofar as the real child is also an alter ego for the mother; when she scolds, punishes and then consoles her doll, she is defending herself against her mother, and she assumes a mother's dignity: she sums up both elements of the couple as she entrusts herself to her doll, educates her, asserts her sovereign authority over her and sometimes even tears off her arms, beats her, tortures her; that is to say, through her she accomplishes the experience of subjective affirmation and alienation. Often the mother is associated with this imaginary life: in playing with the doll and the mother, the child plays both the father and the mother, a couple where the man is excluded. No 'maternal instinct', innate and mysterious, lies therein either. The little girl observes that child care falls to the mother, that is what she is taught; stories told, books read, all her little experience confirms it; she is encouraged to feel delight for these future riches, she is given dolls so she will already feel the tangible aspect of those riches. Her 'vocation' is determined imperiously. Because her lot seems to be the child, and also because she is more interested in her 'insides' than the boy, the little girl is particularly curious about the mystery of procreation; she quickly ceases to believe that babies are born in cabbages or delivered by the stork; especially in cases where the mother gives her brothers or sisters, she soon learns that babies are formed in their mother's body. Besides, parents today make less of a mystery of it than before; she is generally more amazed than frightened because the phenomenon seems like magic to her; she does not yet grasp all of the physiological implications. First of all, she is unaware of the father's role and supposes that the woman gets pregnant by eating certain foods, a legendary theme (queens in fairy tales give birth to a little girl or a handsome boy after eating this fruit, that fish) and one that later leads some women to link the idea of gestation and the digestive system. Together these problems and these discoveries absorb a great part of the little girl's interests and feed her imagination. I will cite a typical example from Jung,* which bears remarkable analogies with that of little Hans, analysed by Freud around the same time:

When Anna was about three years old she began to question her parents about where babies come from; Anna had heard that children are 'little angels'. She first seemed to think that when people die, they go to heaven and are reincarnated as babies. At age four she had a little brother; she hadn't seemed to notice her mother's pregnancy but when she saw her the day after the birth, she looked at her 'with something like a mixture of embarrassment and suspicion' and finally asked her, 'Aren't you going to die now?' She was sent to her grandmother's for some time; when she came back, a nurse had arrived and was installed near the bed; she at first hated her but then she amused herself playing nurse; she was jealous of her brother: she sniggered, made up stories, disobeyed and threatened to go back to her grandmother's; she often accused her mother of not telling the truth, because she suspected her of lying about the infant's birth; feeling obscurely that there was a difference between 'having' a child as a nurse and having one as a mother, she asked her mother: 'shall I be a different woman from you?' She got into the habit of yelling for her parents during the night; and as the earthquake of Messina was much talked about she made it the pretext of her anxieties; she constantly asked questions about it. One day, she asked outright: 'Why is Sophie younger than I? Where was Freddie before? Was he in heaven and what was he doing there?' Her mother decided she ought to explain that the little brother grew inside her stomach like plants in the earth. Anna was enchanted with this idea. Then she asked: 'But did he come all by himself?' 'Yes.' 'But he can't walk yet!' 'He crawled out.' 'Did he come out here (pointing to her chest), or did he come out of your mouth?' Without waiting for an answer, she said she knew it was the stork that had brought it; but in the evening she suddenly said: 'My brother is in Italy;† he has a house made of cloth and glass and it doesn't fall down'; and she was no longer interested in

---

* Jung, 'Psychic Conflicts of a Child'.

† This was a made-up older brother who played a big role in her games.

the earthquake or asked to see photos of the eruption. She spoke again of the stork to her dolls but without much conviction. Soon however, she had new curiosities. Seeing her father in bed: 'Why are you in bed? Have you got a plant in your inside too?' She had a dream; she dreamed of Noah's Ark: 'And underneath, there was a lid which opened and all the little animals fell out'; in fact, her Noah's Ark opened by the roof: At this time, she again had nightmares: one could guess that she was wondering about the father's role. A pregnant woman having visited her mother, the next day her mother saw Anna put a doll under her skirts and take it out slowly, saying: 'Look, the baby is coming out, now it is all out.' Some time later, eating an orange, she said: 'I'll swallow it all down into my stomach, and then I shall get a baby.' One morning, her father was in the bathroom, she jumped on his bed, lay flat on her face, and flailed with her legs, crying out, 'Look, is that what Papa does?' For five months she seemed to forget her preoccupations and then she began to mistrust her father: she thought he wanted to drown her, etc. One day she was happily sowing seeds in the earth with the gardener, and she asked her father: 'How did the eyes grow into the head? And the hair?' The father explained that they were already there from the beginning and grew with the head. Then, she asked: 'But how did Fritz get into Mama? Who stuck him in? And who stuck you into your mama? Where did he come out?' Her father said, smiling, 'What do you think?' So she pointed to his sexual organs: 'Did he come out from there?' 'Well, yes.' 'But how did he get into Mama? Did someone sow the seed?' So the father explained that it is the father who gives the seed. She seemed totally satisfied and the next day she teased her mother: 'Papa told me that Fritz was a little angel and was brought down from heaven by the stork.' She was much calmer than before; she had, though, a dream in which she saw gardeners urinating, her father among them; she also dreamed, after seeing the gardener plane a drawer, that he was planing her genitals; she was obviously preoccupied with knowing the father's exact role. It seems that, almost completely enlightened at the age of five, she did not experience any other disturbance.[11]

This story is characteristic, although very often the little girl is less precisely inquisitive about the role played by the father, or the parents are much more evasive on this point. Many little girls hide cushions under their pinafores to play at being pregnant, or else they walk around with their doll in the folds of their skirts and let it fall into the cradle, or they give it their breast. Boys, like girls, admire the mystery of motherhood; all children have an 'in depth' imagination that makes them sense secret riches inside things; they are all sensitive to the miracle of 'nesting', dolls that contain other, smaller dolls, boxes containing other boxes, vignettes identically reproduced in reduced form; they are all enchanted when a bud is unfolded before their eyes, when they are shown a chick in its shell or the surprise of 'Japanese flowers' in a bowl of water. One little boy, upon opening an Easter egg full of little sugar eggs, exclaimed with delight: 'Oh! A mummy!' Having a child emerge from a woman's stomach is beautiful, like a magic trick. The mother seems endowed with wonderful fairy powers. Many boys bemoan that such a privilege is denied them; if, later, they take eggs from nests, stamp on young plants, if they destroy life around them with a kind of rage, it is out of revenge at not being able to hatch life, while the little girl is enchanted with the thought of creating it one day.

In addition to this hope made concrete by playing with dolls, a housewife's life also provides the little girl with possibilities of affirming herself. A great part of housework can be accomplished by a very young child; a boy is usually exempted from it; but his sister is allowed, even asked, to sweep, dust, peel vegetables, wash a newborn, watch the stew. In particular, the older sister often participates in maternal chores; either for convenience or because of hostility and sadism, the mother unloads many of her functions onto her; she is then prematurely integrated into the universe of the serious; feeling her importance will help her assume her femininity; but she is deprived of the happy gratuitousness, the carefree childhood; a woman before her time, she understands too soon what limits this specificity imposes on a human being; she enters adolescence as an adult, which gives her story a unique character. The overburdened child can prematurely be a slave, condemned to a joyless existence. But, if no more than an effort equal to her is demanded, she experiences the pride of feeling efficient like a grown person and is delighted to feel solidarity with adults. This solidarity is possible for the child because there is not much distance between the child and the housewife. A man specialised in his profession is separated from the infant stage by years of training; paternal activities are profoundly mysterious for the little boy; the man he will be later is barely sketched in him. On the contrary, the mother's activities are accessible to the little girl. 'She's already a little woman,' say her parents, and often she is considered more precocious than the boy: in fact, if she is closer to the adult stage, it is because this stage traditionally remains more infantile for the majority of women. The fact is that she feels precocious, she is flattered to play the role of 'little mother' to the younger ones; she easily becomes important, she speaks reason, she gives orders, she takes on superior airs with her brothers, who are still closed in the baby circle, she talks to her mother on an equal footing.

In spite of these compensations, she does not accept her assigned destiny without regret; growing up, she envies boys their virility. Sometimes parents and grandparents poorly hide the fact that they would have preferred a male offspring to a female; or else they show more affection to the brother than to the sister: research shows that the majority of parents wish to have sons rather than daughters. Boys are spoken to with more seriousness and more esteem, and more rights are granted them; they themselves treat girls with contempt, they play among themselves and exclude girls from their group, they insult them: they call them names like 'piss pots', thus evoking girls' secret childhood humiliations. In France, in coeducational schools, the boys' caste deliberately oppresses and persecutes the girls'. But girls are reprimanded if they want to compete or fight with them. They doubly envy singularly boyish activities: they have a spontaneous desire to affirm their power over the world and they protest against the inferior situation they are condemned to. They suffer in being forbidden to climb trees, ladders and roofs, among other activities. Adler observes that the notions of high and low have great importance, the idea of spatial elevation implying a spiritual superiority, as can be seen in numerous heroic myths; to attain a peak or a summit is to emerge beyond the given world as sovereign subject; between boys, it is frequently a pretext for challenge. The little girl, to whom exploits are forbidden and who sits under a tree or by a cliff and sees the triumphant boys above her, feels herself, body and soul, inferior. And the same is true if she is left *behind* in a race or a jumping competition, or if she is thrown *to the ground* in a fight or simply pushed to the side.

The more the child matures, the more his universe expands and masculine superiority asserts itself. Very often, identification with the mother no longer seems a satisfactory solution. If the little girl at first accepts her feminine vocation, it is not that she means to abdicate: on the contrary, it is to rule; she wants to be a matron because matrons' society seems privileged to her; but when her acquaintances, studies, amusements and reading material tear her away from the maternal circle, she realises that it is not women but men who are the masters of the world.

It is this revelation – far more than the discovery of the penis – that imperiously modifies her consciousness of herself.

She first discovers the hierarchy of the sexes in the family experience; little by little she understands that the father's authority is not the one felt most in daily life, but it is the sovereign one; it has all the more impact for not being wasted on trifling matters; even though the mother reigns over the household, she is clever enough to put the father's will first; at important moments, she makes demands, rewards and punishes in his name. The father's life is surrounded by mysterious prestige: the hours he spends in the home, the room where he works, the objects around him, his occupations, his habits, have a sacred character. It is he who feeds the family, is the one in charge and the head. Usually he works outside the home and it is through him that the household communicates with the rest of the world: he is the embodiment of this adventurous, immense, difficult and marvellous world; he is transcendence, he is God.* This is what the child feels physically in the power of his arms that lift her, in the strength of his body that she huddles against. The mother loses her place of honour to him just as Isis once did to Ra and the earth to the sun. But for the child, her situation is deeply altered: she was intended one day to become a woman like her all-powerful mother – she will never be the sovereign father; the bond that attached her to her mother was an active emulation; from her father she can only passively expect esteem. The boy grasps paternal superiority through a feeling of rivalry, whereas the girl endures it with impotent admiration. I have already stated that what Freud called the 'Electra complex' is not, as he maintains, a sexual desire; it is a deep abdication of the subject who consents to be object in submission and adoration. If the father shows tenderness for his daughter, she feels her existence magnificently justified; she is endowed with all the merits that others have to acquire the hard way; she is fulfilled and deified. It may be that she nostalgically searches for this plenitude and peace her whole life. If she is refused love, she can feel guilty and condemned for ever; or else she can seek self-esteem elsewhere and become indifferent – even hostile – to her father. Besides, the father is not the only one to hold the keys to the world: all men normally share virile prestige; there is no reason to consider them father 'substitutes'. It is implicitly as men

* 'His generous person inspired in me a great love and an extreme fear,' says Mme de Noailles, speaking of her father. 'First of all, he astounded me. The first man astounds a little girl. I well understood that everything depended on him.'

that grandfathers, older brothers, uncles, girlfriends' fathers, friends of the family, professors, priests or doctors fascinate a little girl. The emotional consideration that adult women show the Man would be enough to perch him on a pedestal.*

Everything helps to confirm this hierarchy in the little girl's eyes. Her historical and literary culture, the songs and legends she is raised on, are an exaltation of the man. Men made Greece, the Roman Empire, France and all countries, they discovered the earth and invented the tools to develop it, they governed it, peopled it with statues, paintings and books. Children's literature, mythology, tales and stories reflect the myths created by men's pride and desires: the little girl discovers the world and reads her destiny through the eyes of men. Male superiority is overwhelming: Perseus, Hercules, David, Achilles, Lancelot, du Guesclin, Bayard, Napoleon – so many men for one Joan of Arc; and behind her stands the great male figure of St Michael the archangel! Nothing is more boring than books retracing the lives of famous women: they are very pale figures next to those of the great men; and most are immersed in the shadows of some male hero. Eve was not created for herself but as Adam's companion and drawn from his side; in the Bible few women are noteworthy for their actions: Ruth merely found herself a husband. Esther gained the Jews' grace by kneeling before Ahasuerus, and even then she was only a docile instrument in Mordecai's hands; Judith was bolder but she too obeyed the priests and her exploit has a dubious after-taste: it could not be compared to the pure and shining triumph of young David. Mythology's goddesses are frivolous or capricious and they all tremble before Jupiter; while Prometheus magnificently steals the fire from the sky, Pandora opens the box of catastrophes. There are a few sorceresses, some old women who wield formidable power in stories. Among them is 'The Garden of Paradise' by Andersen, in which the figure of the mother of the winds recalls that of the primitive Great

* It is worth noting that the cult of the father is most prevalent with the oldest child: the man is more involved in his first paternal experience; it is often he who consoles his daughter, as he consoles his son, when the mother is occupied with newborns, and the daughter becomes ardently attached to him. On the contrary, the younger child never has her father to herself; she is ordinarily jealous both of him and her older sister; she attaches herself to that same sister whom the devoted father invests with great prestige, or she turns to her mother, or she revolts against her family and looks for relief somewhere else. In large families, the youngest girl child finds other ways to have a special place. Of course, many circumstances can motivate the father to have special preferences. But almost all of the cases I know confirm this observation on the contrasting attitudes of the oldest and the youngest sisters.

Goddess: her four enormous sons fearfully obey her; she beats and encloses them in bags when they behave badly. But they are not attractive characters. More seductive are the fairies, mermaids and nymphs who escape male domination; but their existence is dubious and barely individualised; they are involved in the human world without having their own destiny: the day Andersen's little mermaid becomes a woman, she experiences the yoke of love and suffering that is her lot. In contemporary accounts as in ancient legends, the man is the privileged hero. Mme de Ségur's books are a curious exception: they describe a matriarchal society where the husband plays a ridiculous character when he is not absent; but usually the image of the father is, as in the real world, surrounded by glory. It is under the aegis of the father sanctified by his absence that the feminine dramas of *Little Women* take place. In adventure stories it is boys who go around the world, travel as sailors on boats, subsist on breadfruit in the jungle. All important events happen because of men. Reality confirms these novels and legends. If the little girl reads the newspapers, if she listens to adult conversation, she notices that today, as in the past, men lead the world. The heads of state, generals, explorers, musicians and painters she admires are men; it is men who make her heart beat with enthusiasm.

That prestige is reflected in the supernatural world. Generally, as a result of the role religion plays in women's lives, the little girl, more dominated by the mother than the boy, is also more subjected to religious influences. And in Western religions, God the Father is a man, an old man endowed with a specifically virile attribute, a luxuriant white beard.* For Christians, Christ is even more concretely a man of flesh and blood with a long blond beard. Angels have no sex, according to theologians; but they have masculine names and are shown as handsome young men. God's emissaries on earth – the Pope, the bishop whose ring is kissed, the priest who says Mass, the preacher, the person one kneels before in the secrecy of the confessional – these are men. For a pious little girl, relations with the eternal Father are analogous to those she maintains with her earthly father; as they take place on an imaginary level, she experiences an even more total surrender. The

---

* 'Moreover, I was no longer suffering from my inability to *see* God, because I had recently managed to imagine him in the form of my dead grandfather; this image in truth was rather human; but I had quickly glorified it by separating my grandfather's head from his bust and mentally putting it on a sky blue background where white clouds made him a collar,' Yassu Gauclère says in *The Blue Orange*.

Catholic religion, among others, exercises on her the most troubling of influences.* The Virgin welcomes the angel's words on her knees. 'I am the *handmaiden* of the Lord,' she answers. Mary Magdalene is prostrate at Christ's feet and she washes them with her long womanly hair. Women saints declare their love to a radiant Christ on their knees. On his knees, surrounded by the odour of incense, the child gives himself up to God's and the angels' gaze: a man's gaze. There are many analogies between erotic and mystical language as spoken by women; for example, St Thérèse writes of the child Jesus:

> Oh, my beloved, by your love I accept not to see on earth the sweetness of your gaze, not to feel the inexpressible kiss from your mouth but I beg of you to embrace me with your love . . .

> > *My beloved, of your first smile*
> > *Let me soon glimpse the sweetness.*
> > *Ah! Leave me in my burning deliriousness,*
> > *Yes, let me hide myself in your heart!*

> I want to be mesmerised by your divine gaze; I want to become prey to your love. One day, I have hope, you will melt on me carrying me to love's hearth; you will put me into this burning chasm to make me become, once and for all, the lucky victim.

But it must not be concluded from this that these effusions are always sexual; rather, when female sexuality develops, it is penetrated with the religious feeling that woman has devoted to man since childhood. It is true that the little girl experiences a thrill in the confessional and even at the foot of the altar close to what she will later feel in her lover's arms: woman's love is one of the forms of experience in which a consciousness makes itself an object for a being that transcends it; and these are also the passive delights that the young pious girl tastes in the shadows of the church.

Prostrate, her face buried in her hands, she experiences the miracle of renunciation: on her knees she climbs to heaven; her abandon in God's

* There is no doubt that women are infinitely more passive, given to man, servile and humiliated in Catholic countries, Italy, Spain and France, than in the Protestant Scandinavian and Anglo-Saxon ones. And this comes in great part from their own attitude: the cult of the Virgin, confession, and so on invites them to masochism.

arms assures her an assumption lined with clouds and angels. She models
her earthly future on this marvellous experience. The child can also
discover it in other ways: everything encourages her to abandon herself
in dreams to the arms of men to be transported to a sky of glory. She
learns that to be happy she has to be loved; to be loved, she has to await
love. Woman is Sleeping Beauty, Donkey Skin, Cinderella, Snow White,
the one who receives and endures. In songs and tales, the young man
sets off to seek the woman; he fights against dragons, he combats giants;
she is locked up in a tower, a palace, a garden, a cave, chained to a rock,
captive, put to sleep: she is waiting. *One day my prince will come . . . Some
day he'll come along, the man I love* . . . the popular refrains breathe dreams
of patience and hope in her. The supreme necessity for woman is to
charm a masculine heart; this is the recompense all heroines aspire to,
even if they are intrepid, adventuresome; and only their beauty is asked
of them in most cases. It is thus understandable that attention to her
physical appearance can become a real obsession for the little girl;
princesses or shepherds, one must always be pretty to conquer love and
happiness; ugliness is cruelly associated with meanness and when one
sees the misfortunes that befall ugly girls, one does not know if it is their
crimes or their disgrace that destiny punishes. Young beauties promised
a glorious future often start out in the role of victim; the stories of
Genevieve de Brabant or of Griselda are not as innocent as it would seem;
love and suffering are intertwined in a troubling way; woman is assured
of the most delicious triumphs when falling to the bottom of abjection;
whether it be a question of God or a man, the little girl learns that by
consenting to the most serious renunciations, she will become all-powerful:
she takes pleasure in a masochism that promises her supreme conquests.
St Blandine, white and bloody in the paws of lions, Snow White lying as
if dead in a glass coffin, Sleeping Beauty, Atala fainting, a whole cohort
of tender heroines beaten, passive, wounded, on their knees, humiliated,
teach their younger sisters the fascinating prestige of martyred, abandoned and resigned beauty. It is not surprising that, while her brother
plays at the hero, the little girl plays so easily at the martyr: the pagans
throw her to the lions, Bluebeard drags her by her hair, the king, her
husband, exiles her to the depth of the forests; she resigns herself, she
suffers, she dies and her brow is haloed with glory. 'While still a little girl,
I wanted to draw men's attention, trouble them, be saved by them, die
in their arms,' Mme de Noailles writes. A remarkable example of these
masochistic musings is found in *The Black Sail*[12] by Marie Le Hardouin.

At seven, from I don't know which rib, I made my first man. He was tall, thin, very young, dressed in a suit of black satin with long sleeves touching the ground. His beautiful blond hair cascaded in heavy curls onto his shoulders . . . I called him Edmond . . . Then a day came when I gave him two brothers . . . These three brothers, Edmond, Charles and Cedric, all three dressed in black satin, all three blond and slim, procured for me strange blessings. Their feet shod in silk were so beautiful and their hands so fragile that I felt all sorts of movements in my soul . . . I became their sister Marguerite . . . I loved to represent myself as subjected to the whims of my brothers and totally at their mercy. I dreamed that my oldest brother, Edmond, had the right of life and death over me. I never had permission to raise my eyes to his face. He had me whipped under the slightest pretext. When he addressed himself to me, I was so overwhelmed by fear and respect that I found nothing else to answer him and mumbled constantly, 'Yes, my lordship', 'No, my lordship' and I savoured the strange delight of feeling like an idiot . . . When the suffering he imposed on me was too great, I murmured, 'Thank you, my lordship,' and there came a moment when, almost faltering from suffering, I placed, so as not to shout, my lips on his hand, while, some movement finally breaking my heart, I reached one of these states in which one desires to die from too much happiness.

At an early age, the little girl already dreams she has reached the age of love; at nine or ten, she loves to make herself up, she pads her blouse, she disguises herself as a lady. She does not, however, look for any erotic experience with little boys: if she does go with them into the corner to play 'doctor', it is only out of sexual curiosity. But the partner of her amorous dreaming is an adult, either purely imaginary or based on real individuals: in the latter case, the child is satisfied to love him from afar. In Colette Audry's memoirs*[13] there is a very good example of a child's dreaming; she recounts that she discovered love at five years of age:

This naturally had nothing to do with the little sexual pleasures of childhood, the satisfaction I felt, for example, straddling a certain chair in the dining room or caressing myself before falling asleep . . .

*In the Eyes of Memory.

The only common characteristic between the feeling and the pleasure is that I carefully hid them both from those around me . . . My love for this young man consisted of thinking of him before falling asleep and imagining marvellous stories . . . In Privas, I was in love with all the department heads of my father's office . . . I was never very deeply hurt by their departure, because they were barely more than a pretext for my amorous musings . . . In the evening in bed I got my revenge for too much youth and shyness. I prepared everything very carefully, I did not have any trouble making him present to me, but it was a question of transforming myself, me, so that I could see myself from the interior because I became her, and stopped being I. First, I was pretty and eighteen years old. A tin of sweets helped me a lot: a long tin of rectangular and flat sweets that depicted two girls surrounded by doves. I was the dark, curly-headed one, dressed in a long muslin dress. A ten-year absence had separated us. He returned scarcely aged and the sight of this marvellous creature overwhelmed him. She seemed to barely remember him, she was unaffected, indifferent and witty. I composed truly brilliant conversations for this first meeting. They were followed by misunderstandings, a whole difficult conquest, cruel hours of discouragement and jealousy for him. Finally, pushed to the limit, he admitted his love. She listened to him in silence and just at the moment he thought all was lost, she told him she had never stopped loving him and they embraced a little. The scene normally took place on a park bench, in the evening. I saw the two forms close together, I heard the murmur of voices, I felt at the same time the warm body contact. But then everything came loose . . . never did I broach marriage* . . . The next day I thought of it a little while washing. I don't know why the soapy face I was looking at in the mirror delighted me (the rest of the time I didn't find myself beautiful) and filled me with hope. I would have considered for hours this misty, tilted face that seemed to be waiting for me from afar on the road to the future. But I had to hurry; once I dried my face, everything was over, and I got back my banal child's face, which no longer interested me.

---

* Unlike Le Hardouin's masochistic imagination, Audry's is sadistic. She wants the beloved to be wounded, in danger, for her to save him heroically, not without humiliating him. This is a personal note, characteristic of a woman who will never accept passivity and will attempt to conquer her autonomy as a human being.

Games and dreams orient the girl towards passivity; but she is a human being before becoming a woman; and she already knows that accepting herself as woman means resigning and mutilating herself, while renunciation might be tempting, mutilation is abhorrent. Man and Love are still far away in the mist of the future; in the present, the little girl seeks activity, autonomy, like her brothers. The burden of freedom is not heavy for children because it does not involve responsibility; they know they are safe in the shelter of adults: they are not tempted to flee from themselves. The girl's spontaneous zest for life, her taste for games, laughter and adventure, make her consider the maternal circle narrow and stultifying. She wants to escape her mother's authority, an authority that is wielded in a more routine and intimate manner than the one that boys have to accept. Rare are the cases in which she is as understanding and discreet as in this Sido that Colette painted with love. Not to mention the almost pathological cases – there are many*[14] – where the mother is a kind of executioner, satisfying her domineering and sadistic instincts on the child; her daughter is the privileged object opposite whom she attempts to affirm herself as sovereign subject; this attempt makes the child balk in revolt. Colette Audry described this rebellion of a normal girl against a normal mother:

I wouldn't have known how to answer the truth, however innocent it was, because I never felt innocent in front of Mama. She was the essential adult and I resented her for it as long as I was not yet cured. There was deep inside me a kind of tumultuous and fierce sore that I was sure of always finding raw . . . I didn't think she was too strict; nor that she hadn't the right. I thought: no, no, no with all my strength. I didn't even blame her for her authority or for her orders or arbitrary defences but for *wanting to subjugate me*. She said it sometimes: when she didn't say it, her eyes and voice did. Or else she told ladies that children are much more docile after a punishment. These words stuck in my throat, unforgettable: I couldn't vomit them; I couldn't swallow them. This anger was my guilt in front of her and also my shame in front of me (because in reality she frightened me, and all I had on my side in the form of retaliation were a few violent words or acts of insolence) but also my glory, nevertheless: as long as the sore was there, and living the silent madness that made me only repeat: 'subjugate, docile, punishment, humiliation', I wouldn't be subjugated.

* Cf. V. Leduc, *In the Prison of Her Skin*; S. de Tervagne, *Maternal Hatred*; H. Bazin, *Viper in the Fist*.

Rebellion is even more violent in the frequent cases when the mother has lost her prestige. She appears as the one who waits, endures, complains, cries and makes scenes: and in daily reality this thankless role does not lead to any apotheosis; victim, she is scorned; shrew, she is detested; her destiny appears to be the prototype of bland *repetition*: with her, life only repeats itself stupidly without going anywhere; blocked in her housewifely role, she stops the expansion of her existence, she is obstacle and negation. Her daughter wants *not* to take after her. She dedicates a cult to women who have escaped feminine servitude: actresses, writers and professors; she gives herself enthusiastically to sports and to studies, she climbs trees, tears her clothes, tries to compete with boys. Very often she has a best friend in whom she confides; it is an exclusive friendship like a love affair that usually includes sharing sexual secrets: the little girls exchange information they have succeeded in getting and talk about it. Often there is a triangle, one of the girls falling in love with her girlfriend's brother: thus Sonia in *War and Peace* is in love with her best friend Natasha's brother. In any case, this friendship is shrouded in mystery, and in general at this period the child loves to have secrets; she makes a secret of the most insignificant thing: thus does she react against the secrecies that thwart her curiosity; it is also a way of giving herself importance; she tries by all means to acquire it; she tries to be part of adults' lives, she makes up stories about them that she only half believes and in which she plays a major role. With her friends, she feigns returning boys' scorn with scorn; they form a closed group, they sneer and mock them. But in fact, she is flattered when they treat her as an equal; she seeks their approbation. She would like to belong to the privileged caste. The same movement that in primitive hordes subjects woman to male supremacy is manifested in each new 'arrival' by a refusal of her lot: in her, transcendence condemns the absurdity of immanence. She is annoyed at being oppressed by rules of decency, bothered by her clothes, enslaved to cleaning tasks, held back in all her enthusiasms; on this point there have been many studies that have almost all given the same result:* all the boys – like Plato in the past – say they would have hated to be girls; almost all the girls are sorry not to be boys. According to Havelock Ellis's statistics, one boy out of a hundred wanted to be a

---

* There is an exception, for example, in a Swiss school where boys and girls participating in the same coeducation, in privileged conditions of comfort and freedom, all declared themselves satisfied; but such circumstances are exceptional. Obviously, the girls *could be* as happy as the boys, but in present society the fact is that they are not.

girl; more than 75 per cent of the girls would have preferred to change sex. According to a study by Karl Pipal (cited by Baudouin in his work on *The Mind of the Child*),[15] out of twenty boys of twelve to fourteen years of age, eighteen said they would rather be anything in the whole world than a girl; out of twenty-two girls, ten wished to be boys and gave the following reasons: 'Boys are better: they do not have to suffer like women . . . My mother would love me more . . . A boy does more interesting work . . . A boy has more aptitude for school . . . I would have fun frightening girls . . . I would not fear boys any more . . . They are freer . . . Boys' games are more fun . . . They are not held back by their clothes.' This last observation is recurrent: almost all the girls complain of being bothered by their clothes, of not being free in their movements, of having to watch their skirts or light-coloured outfits that get dirty so easily. At about ten or twelve years of age, most little girls are really tomboys, that is, children who lack the licence to be boys. Not only do they suffer from it as a privation and an injustice but the regime they are condemned to is unhealthy. The exuberance of life is prohibited to them, their stunted vigour turns into nervousness; their goody-goody occupations do not exhaust their brimming energy; they are bored: out of boredom and to compensate for the inferiority from which they suffer, they indulge in morose and romantic daydreams; they begin to have a taste for these facile escapes and lose the sense of reality; they succumb to their emotions with a confused exaltation; since they cannot act, they talk, readily mixing up serious words with totally meaningless ones; abandoned, 'misunderstood', they go looking for consolation in narcissistic sentiments: they look on themselves as heroines in novels, admire themselves and complain; it is natural for them to become keen on their appearance and to playact: these defects will grow during puberty. Their malaise expresses itself in impatience, tantrums, tears; they indulge in tears – an indulgence many women keep later – largely because they love to play the victim: it is both a protest against the harshness of their destiny and a way of endearing themselves to others. 'Little girls love to cry so much that I have known them to cry in front of a mirror in order to double the pleasure,' says Monseigneur Dupanloup. Most of their dramas concern relations with their family; they try to break their bonds with their mothers: either they are hostile to them or they continue to feel a profound need for protection; they would like to monopolise their fathers' love for themselves; they are jealous, touchy, demanding. They often make up stories; they imagine they are adopted, that their parents are not really theirs; they attribute a secret life to them; they dream about their sexual relations; they love to imagine that their father is misunderstood, unhappy, that he is not finding in his wife the ideal companion that his daughter would be for him; or, on the contrary, that the mother rightly finds him rough and brutal, that she is appalled by any physical relations with him. Fantasies, acting out, childish tragedies, false enthusiasms, strange things: the reason must be sought not in a mysterious feminine soul but in the child's situation.

It is a strange experience for an individual recognising himself as subject, autonomy and transcendence, as an absolute, to discover inferiority – as a given essence – in his self: it is a strange experience for one who posits himself for himself as One to be revealed to himself as alterity. That is what happens to the little girl when, learning about the world, she grasps herself as a woman in it. The sphere she belongs to is closed everywhere, limited, dominated by the male universe: as high as she climbs, as far as she dares go, there will always be a ceiling over her head, walls that block her path. Man's gods are in such a faraway heaven that in truth, for him, there are no gods: the little girl lives among gods with a human face.

This is not a unique situation. American blacks, partially integrated into a civilisation that nevertheless considers them as an inferior caste, live it; what Bigger Thomas experiences with so much bitterness at the dawn of his life is this definitive inferiority, this cursed alterity inscribed in the colour of his skin: he watches planes pass and knows that because he is black the sky is out of bounds for him.* Because she is woman, the girl knows that the sea and the poles, a thousand adventures, a thousand joys, are forbidden to her: she is born on the wrong side. The great difference is that the blacks endure their lot in revolt – no privilege compensates for its severity – while for the woman her complicity is invited. Earlier I recalled that in addition to the authentic claim of the subject who claims sovereign freedom, there is an inauthentic desire for renunciation and escape in the existent;† these are the delights of passivity that parents and educators, books and myths, women and men dangle before the little girl's eyes; in early childhood she is already taught to taste them; temptation becomes more and more insidious; and she yields to it even more fatally as the thrust of her transcendence comes up against harsher and harsher resistance. But in accepting her passivity, she also accepts without resistance enduring a destiny that is going to be imposed on her

* Richard Wright, *Native Son*.
† See Vol. I, Introduction.

from the exterior, and this fatality frightens her. Whether ambitious, scatterbrained or shy, the young boy leaps towards an open future; he will be a sailor or an engineer, he will stay in the fields or will leave for the city, he will see the world, he will become rich; he feels free faced with a future where unexpected opportunities await him. The girl will be wife, mother, grandmother; she will take care of her house exactly as her mother does, she will take care of her children as she was taken care of: she is twelve years old and her story is already written in the heavens; she will discover it day after day without shaping it; she is curious but frightened when she thinks about this life whose every step is planned in advance and towards which each day irrevocably moves her.

This is why the little girl, even more so than her brothers, is preoccupied with sexual mysteries; of course boys are interested as well, just as passionately; but in their future, their role of husband and father is not what concerns them the most; marriage and motherhood put in question the little girl's whole destiny; and as soon as she begins to perceive their secrets, her body seems odiously threatened to her. The magic of motherhood has faded: whether she has been informed early or not, she knows, in a more or less coherent manner, that a baby does not appear by chance in the mother's belly and does not come out at the wave of a magic wand; she questions herself anxiously. Often it seems not extraordinary at all but rather horrible that a parasitic body should proliferate inside her body; the idea of this monstrous swelling frightens her. And how will the baby get out? Even if she was never told about the cries and suffering of childbirth, she has overheard things, she has read the words in the Bible: 'In sorrow thou shalt bring forth children'; she has the presentiment of tortures she cannot even imagine; she invents strange operations around her navel; she is no less reassured if she supposes that the foetus will be expelled by her anus: little girls have been seen to have nervous constipation attacks when they thought they had discovered the birthing process. Accurate explanations will not bring much relief: images of swelling, tearing and haemorrhaging will haunt her. The more imaginative she is, the more sensitive the little girl will be to these visions; but no girl could look at them without shuddering. Colette relates how her mother found her in a faint after reading Zola's description of a birth:

> [The author depicted the birth] with a rough-and-ready, crude wealth of detail, an anatomical precision, and a lingering over colours, postures and cries, in which I recognised none of the tranquil,

knowing experience on which I as a country girl could draw. I felt credulous, startled and vulnerable in my nascent femininity ... Other words, right in front of my eyes, depicted flesh splitting open, excrement and sullied blood ... The lawn rose to welcome me ... like one of those little hares that poachers sometimes brought, freshly killed, into the kitchen.[16]

The reassurance offered by grown-ups leaves the child worried; growing up she learns not to trust the word of adults; often it is on the very mysteries of her conception that she has caught them in lies; and she also knows that they consider the most frightening things normal; if she has ever experienced a violent physical shock – tonsils removed, tooth pulled, whitlow lanced – she will project the remembered anxiety onto childbirth.

The physical nature of pregnancy and childbirth suggests as well that 'something physical' takes place between the spouses. The often-encountered word 'blood' in expressions like 'same-blood children', 'pure blood', 'mixed blood' sometimes orients the childish imagination; it is supposed that marriage is accompanied by some solemn transfusion. But more often the 'physical thing' seems to be linked to the urinary and excremental systems; in particular, children think that the man urinates into the woman. This sexual operation is thought of as *dirty*. This is what overwhelms the child for whom 'dirty' things have been rife with the strictest taboos: how then can it be that they are integrated into adults' lives? The child is first of all protected from scandal by the very absurdity he discovers: he finds there is no sense to what he hears around him, what he reads, what he writes; everything seems unreal to him. In Carson McCullers's charming book *The Member of the Wedding*, the young heroine surprises two neighbours in bed nude; the very anomaly of the story keeps her from giving it too much importance.

It was a summer Sunday and the hall door of the Marlowes' room was open. She could see only a portion of the room, part of the dresser and only the footpiece of the bed with Mrs Marlowe's corset on it. But there was a sound in the quiet room she could not place, and when she stepped over the threshold she was startled by a sight that, after a single glance, sent her running to the kitchen, crying: Mr Marlowe is having a fit! Berenice had hurried through the hall, but when she looked into the front room, she merely bunched her lips and banged the door ... Frankie had tried to question Berenice and find out what was the matter. But Berenice had only said that they were common people and added that with a certain party in the house they ought at least to know enough to shut a door. Though Frankie knew she was the certain party, still she did not understand. What kind of a fit was it? she asked. But Berenice would only answer: Baby, just a common fit. And Frankie knew from the voice's tones that there was more to it than she was told. Later she only remembered the Marlowes as common people . . .[17]

When children are warned against strangers, when a sexual incident is described to them, it is often explained in terms of sickness, maniacs or madmen; it is a convenient explanation; the little girl fondled by her neighbour at the cinema or the girl who sees a man expose himself thinks that she is dealing with a crazy man; of course, encountering madness is unpleasant: an epileptic attack, hysteria or a violent quarrel upsets the adult world order, and the child who witnesses it feels in danger; but after all, just as there are homeless, beggars and injured people with hideous sores in harmonious society, there can also be some abnormal ones without its base disintegrating. It is when parents, friends and teachers are suspected of celebrating black masses that the child really becomes afraid.

When I was first told about sexual relations between man and woman, I declared that such things were impossible since my parents would have had to do likewise, and I thought too highly of them to believe it. I said that it was much too disgusting for me ever to do it. Unfortunately I was to be disabused shortly after when I heard what my parents were doing . . . that was a fearful moment; I hid my face under the bedcovers, stopped my ears and wished I were a thousand miles from there.*[18]

How to go from the image of dressed and dignified people, these people who teach decency, reserve and reason, to that of naked beasts confronting each other? Here is a contradiction that shakes their pedestal, darkens the sky. Often the child stubbornly refuses the odious revelation: 'My parents don't do that,' he declares. Or he tries to give coitus a decent image: 'When you want a child,' said a little girl, 'you go to the doctor; you undress, you cover your eyes, because you mustn't watch; the doctor ties the parents together and helps them so that it works right'; she had changed the act of love into a surgical operation, rather unpleasant at that, but as

---

* Cited by Dr W. Liepmann, *Youth and Sexuality*.

honourable as going to the dentist. But despite denial and escape, embarrassment and doubt creep into the child's heart; a phenomenon as painful as weaning occurs: it is no longer separating the child from the maternal flesh, but the protective universe that surrounds him falls apart; he finds himself without a roof over his head, abandoned, absolutely alone before a future as dark as night. What adds to the little girl's anxiety is that she cannot discern the exact shape of the equivocal curse that weighs on her. The information she gets is inconsistent, books are contradictory; even technical explanations do not dissipate the heavy shadow; a hundred questions arise: is the sexual act painful? Or delicious? How long does it last? Five minutes or all night? Sometimes you read that a woman became a mother with one embrace, and sometimes you remain sterile after hours of sexual activity. Do people 'do that' every day? Or rarely? The child tries to learn more by reading the Bible, consulting dictionaries, asking friends, and he gropes in darkness and disgust. An interesting document on this point is the study made by Dr Liepmann; here are a few responses given to him by young girls about their sexual initiation:

I continued to stray among my nebulous and twisted ideas. No one broached the subject, neither my mother nor my schoolteacher; no book treated the subject fully. Little by little a sort of perilous and ugly mystery was woven around the act, which at first had seemed so natural to me. The older girls of twelve used crude jokes to bridge the gap between themselves and our classmates. All that was still so vague and disgusting; we argued about where the baby was formed, if perhaps the thing only took place once for the man since marriage was the occasion for so much fuss. My period at fifteen was another new surprise. It was my turn to be caught up, in a way, in the round.

Sexual initiation! An expression never to be mentioned in our parents' house! . . . I searched in books, but I agonised and wore myself out looking for the road to follow . . . I went to a boys' school: for my schoolteacher the question did not even seem to exist . . . Horlam's work, *Little Boy and Little Girl*,[19] finally brought me the truth. My tense state and unbearable overexcitement disappeared, although I was very unhappy and took a long time to recognise and understand that eroticism and sexuality alone constitute real love.

Stages of my initiation: (1) First questions and a few vague notions (totally unsatisfactory). From three and a half to eleven years old . . .

No answers to the questions I had in the following years. When I was seven, right there feeding my rabbit, I suddenly saw little naked ones underneath her ... My mother told me that in animals and people little ones grow in their mother's belly and come out through the loins. This birth through the loins seemed unreasonable to me ... a nursemaid told me about pregnancy, birth and menstruation ... Finally, my father replied to my last question about his true function with obscure stories about pollen and pistil. (2) Some attempts at personal experimentation (eleven to thirteen years old). I dug out an encyclopaedia and a medical book ... It was only theoretical information in strange gigantic words. (3) Testing of acquired knowledge (thirteen to twenty): *(a)* in daily life, *(b)* in scientific works.

At eight, I often played with a boy my age. One day we broached the subject. I already knew, because my mother had already told me, that a woman has many eggs inside her ... and that a child was born from one of these eggs whenever the mother strongly desired it ... Giving this same answer to my friend, I received this reply: 'You are completely stupid! When our butcher and his wife want a baby, they go to bed and do dirty things.' I was indignant ... We had then (around twelve and a half) a maid who told me all sorts of scandalous tales. I never said a word to Mama, as I was ashamed; but I asked her if sitting on a man's knees could give you a baby. She explained everything as best she could.

At school I learned where babies emerged, and I had the feeling that it was something horrible. But how did they come into the world? We both formed a rather monstrous idea about the thing, especially since one winter morning on the way to school together in the darkness we met a certain man who showed us his sexual parts and asked us, 'Don't they seem good enough to eat?' Our disgust was inconceivable and we were literally nauseated. Until I was twenty-one, I thought babies were born through the navel.

A little girl took me aside and asked me: 'Do you know where babies come from?' Finally she decided to speak out: 'Goodness! How foolish you are! Kids come out of women's stomachs, and for them to be born, women have to do completely disgusting things with men!' Then she went into details about how disgusting. But I had become totally transformed, absolutely unable to believe that such things could be possible. We slept in the same room as our parents . . . One night later I heard take place what I had thought was impossible, and, yes, I was ashamed, I was ashamed of my parents. All of this made of me another being. I went through horrible moral suffering. I considered myself a deeply depraved creature because I was now aware of these things.

It should be said that even coherent instruction would not resolve the problem; in spite of the best will of parents and teachers, the sexual experience could not be put into words and concepts; it could only be understood by living it; all analysis, however serious, will have a comic side and will fail to deliver the truth. When, from the poetic loves of flowers to the nuptials of fish, by way of the chick, the cat or the kid, one reaches the human species, the mystery of conception can be theoretically elucidated: that of voluptuousness and sexual love remains total. How would one explain the pleasure of a caress or a kiss to a dispassionate child? Kisses are given and received in a family way, sometimes even on the lips: why do these mucus exchanges in certain encounters provoke dizziness? It is like describing colours to the blind. As long as there is no intuition of the excitement and desire that give the sexual function its meaning and unity, the different elements seem shocking and monstrous. In particular, the little girl is revolted when she understands that she is virgin and sealed, and that to change into a woman a man's sex must penetrate her. Since exhibitionism is a widespread perversion, many little girls have seen the penis in an erection; in any case, they have observed the sexual organs of animals, and it is unfortunate that the horse's so often draws their attention; one imagines that they would be frightened by it. Fear of childbirth, fear of the male sex organ, fear of the 'crises' that threaten married couples, disgust for dirty practices, derision for actions devoid of signification, all of this often leads a young girl to declare: 'I will never marry.'*

---

* 'Filled with repugnance, I implored God to grant me a religious vocation that would allow me to escape the laws of maternity. And after having long reflected on the repugnant mysteries that I hid in spite of myself, reinforced by such repulsion as by a divine sign, I concluded: chastity is certainly my vocation,' writes Yassu Gauclère in *The Blue Orange*. Among others, the idea of perforation horrified her. 'Here, then, is what makes the wedding night so terrible! This discovery overwhelmed me, adding the physical terror of this operation that I imagined to be extremely painful to the disgust I previously felt. My terror would have been all the worse if I had supposed that birth came about through the same channel; but having known for a long time that children were born from their mother's belly, I believed that they were detached by segmentation.'

Therein lies the surest defence against pain, folly and obscenity. It is useless to try to explain that when the day comes, neither deflowering nor childbirth would seem so terrible, that millions of women resign themselves to it and are none the worse for it. When a child fears an outside occurrence, he is relieved of the fear, but not by predicting that, later, he will accept it naturally: it is himself he fears meeting in the far-off future, alienated and lost. The metamorphosis of the caterpillar, through chrysalis and into butterfly, brings about a deep uneasiness: is it still the same caterpillar after this long sleep? Does she recognise herself beneath these brilliant wings? I knew little girls who were plunged into an alarming reverie at the sight of a chrysalis.

And yet the metamorphosis takes place. The little girl herself does not understand the meaning, but she realises that in her relations with the world and her own body something is changing subtly: she is sensitive to contacts, tastes and odours that previously left her indifferent; baroque images pass through her head; she barely recognises herself in mirrors; she feels 'funny', things seem 'funny'; such is the case of little Emily described by Richard Hughes in A High Wind in Jamaica:[20]

Emily, for coolness, sat up to her chin in water and hundreds of infant fish were tickling with their inquisitive mouths every inch of her body, a sort of expressionless light kissing. Anyhow she had lately come to hate being touched – but this was abominable. At last, when she could stand it no longer, she clambered out and dressed.

Even Margaret Kennedy's serene Tessa feels this strange disturbance:

Suddenly she had become intensely miserable. She stared down into the darkness of the hall, cut in two by the moonlight which streamed in through the open door. She could not bear it. She jumped up with a little cry of exasperation. 'Oh!' she exclaimed. 'How I hate it all!' . . . She ran out to hide herself in the mountains, frightened and furious, pursued by a desolate foreboding which seemed to fill the quiet house. As she stumbled up towards the pass she kept murmuring to herself: 'I wish I could die! I wish I were dead!'

She knew that she did not mean this; she was not in the least anxious to die. But the violence of such a statement seemed to satisfy her . . .[21]

This disturbing moment is described at length in Carson McCullers's previously mentioned book, *The Member of the Wedding*.

This was the summer when Frankie was sick and tired of being Frankie. She hated herself, and had become a loafer and a big no-good who hung around the summer kitchen: dirty and greedy and mean and sad. Besides being too mean to live, she was criminal . . . Then the spring of that year had been a long queer season. Things began to change . . . There was something about the green trees and the flowers of April that made Frankie sad. She did not know why she was sad, but because of this peculiar sadness, she began to realise that she ought to leave the town . . . She ought to leave the town and go to some place far away. For the late spring, that year, was lazy and too sweet. The long afternoons flowered and lasted and the green sweetness sickened her . . . Many things made Frankie suddenly wish to cry. Very early in the morning she would sometimes go out into the yard and stand for a long time looking at the sunrise sky. And it was as though a question came into her heart, and the sky did not answer. Things she had never noticed much before began to hurt her: home lights watched from the evening sidewalks, an unknown voice from an alley. She would stare at the lights and listen to the voice, and something inside her stiffened and waited. But the lights would darken, the voice fall silent, and though she waited, that was all. She was afraid of these things that made her suddenly wonder who she was, and what she was going to be in the world, and why she was standing at that minute, seeing a light, or listening, or staring up into the sky: alone. She was afraid, and there was a queer tightness in her chest . . .

She went around town, and the things she saw and heard seemed to be left somehow unfinished, and there was the tightness in her that would not break. She would hurry to do something, but what she did was always wrong . . . After the long twilights of this season, when Frankie had walked around the sidewalks of the town, a jazz sadness quivered her nerves and her heart stiffened and almost stopped.

What is happening in this troubled period is that the child's body is becoming a woman's body and being made flesh. Except in the case of glandular deficiency where the subject remains fixed in the infantile stage, the puberty crisis begins around the age of twelve or thirteen.* This crisis begins much earlier for girls than for boys and it brings about far greater changes. The little girl approaches it with worry and displeasure. As her breasts and body hair develop, a feeling is born that sometimes changes into pride, but begins as shame; suddenly the child displays modesty, she refuses to show herself nude, even to her sisters or her mother, she inspects herself with surprise mixed with horror and she observes with anxiety the swelling of this hard core, somewhat painful, appearing under nipples that until recently were as inoffensive as a navel. She is worried to discover a vulnerable spot in herself: undoubtedly this pain is slight compared to a burn or a toothache; but in an accident or illness, pain was always abnormal, while the youthful breast is normally the centre of who knows what indefinable resentment. Something is happening, something that is not an illness, but that involves the very law of existence and is yet struggle and suffering. Of course, from birth to puberty the little girl grew up, but she never felt growth; day after day, her body was present like an exact finished thing; now she is 'developing': the very word horrifies her; vital phenomena are only reassuring when they have found a balance and taken on the stable aspect of a fresh flower, a lustrous animal; but in the blossoming of her breasts, the little girl feels the ambiguity of the word 'living'. She is neither gold nor diamond, but a strange matter, moving and uncertain, inside of which impure chemistries develop. She is used to a free-flowing head of hair that falls like a silken skein; but this new growth under her arms, beneath her belly, metamorphoses her into an animal or alga. Whether she is more or less prepared for it, she foresees in these changes a finality that rips her from her self; thus hurled into a vital cycle that goes beyond the moment of her own existence, she senses a dependence that dooms her to man, child and tomb. In themselves, her breasts seem to be a useless and indiscreet proliferation. Arms, legs, skin, muscles, and even the round buttocks she sits on, all have had until now a clear usefulness; only the sex organ defined as urinary was a bit dubious, though secret and invisible to others. Her breasts show through her sweater or blouse, and this body that the little girl identified with self appears to her as flesh; it is an object that others look at and see. 'For two years I wore capes to hide my chest, I was so ashamed of it,' a woman told me. And another: 'I still remember the strange confusion I felt when a friend of my age, but more developed than I was, stooped to pick up a ball, I noticed by the

---

* These purely physiological processes have already been described in Vol. I, Chapter 1. [In Part One, 'Destiny'.]

opening in her blouse two already heavy breasts: this body so similar to mine, on which my body would be modelled, made me blush for myself.' 'At thirteen, I walked around bare-legged, in a short dress,' another woman told me. 'A man, sniggering, made a comment about my fat calves. The next day, my mother made me wear stockings and lengthen my skirt, but I will never forget the shock I suddenly felt in seeing myself *seen*.' The little girl feels that her body is escaping her, that it is no longer the clear expression of her individuality; it becomes foreign to her; and at the same moment, she is grasped by others as a thing: on the street, eyes follow her, her body is subject to comments; she would like to become invisible; she is afraid of becoming flesh and afraid to show her flesh.

This disgust is expressed in many young girls by the desire to lose weight: they do not want to eat any more; if they are forced, they vomit; they watch their weight incessantly. Others become pathologically shy; entering a room or going out on the street becomes a torture. From these experiences, psychoses sometimes develop. A typical example is Nadia, the patient from *Obsessions and Psychasthenia* (*Les obsessions et la psychasthénie*), described by Pierre Janet[22]:

Nadia, a girl from a wealthy and remarkably intelligent family, was stylish, artistic, and above all an excellent musician; but from infancy she was obstinate and irritable . . . 'She demanded excessive affection from everyone, her parents, sisters and servants, but she was so demanding and dominating that she soon alienated people; horribly susceptible, when her cousins used mockery to try to change her character, she acquired a sense of shame fixed on her body.' Then, too, her need for affection made her wish to remain a child, to remain a little girl to be petted, one whose every whim is indulged, and in short made her fear growing up . . . A precocious puberty worsened her troubles, mixing fears of modesty with fears of growing up: 'Since men like plump women, I want to remain extremely thin.' Pubic hair and growing breasts added to her fears. From the age of eleven, as she wore short skirts, it seemed to her that everyone eyed her; she was given long skirts and was then ashamed of her feet, her hips, etc. The appearance of menstruation drove her half mad; believing that she was the only one in the world having the monstrosity of pubic hair, she laboured up to the age of twenty 'to rid herself of this savage decoration by depilation'. The development of breasts exacerbated these obsessions because she had always had a horror of obesity; she did not detest it in others; but for herself she considered it a defect. 'I don't care about being pretty, but I would be too *ashamed* if I became bloated, that would horrify me; if by bad luck I became fat, I wouldn't dare let anyone see me.' So she tried every means, all kinds of prayers and conjurations, to prevent normal growth: she swore to repeat prayers five or ten times, to hop five times on one foot. 'If I touch one piano note four times in the same piece, I accept growing and not being loved by anyone.' Finally she decided not to eat. 'I did not want to get fat, nor to grow up, nor resemble a woman because I always wanted to remain a little girl.' She solemnly promised to accept no food at all; when she yielded to her mother's pleas to take some food and broke her vow, she knelt for hours writing out vows and tearing them up. Her mother died when she was eighteen, and she then imposed a strict regime on herself: two clear bouillon soups, an egg yolk, a spoonful of vinegar, a cup of tea with the juice of a whole lemon, was all she would take in a day. Hunger devoured her. 'Sometimes I spent hours thinking of food, I was so hungry: I swallowed my saliva, gnawed on my handkerchief and rolled on the floor from wanting to eat.' But she resisted temptations. She was pretty, but believed that her face was puffy and covered with pimples; if her doctor stated that he did not see them, she said he didn't understand anything, that he couldn't see the pimples between the skin and the flesh. She left her family in the end and hid in a small apartment, seeing only a guardian and the doctor; she never went out; she accepted her father's visit, but only with difficulty; he brought about a serious relapse by telling her that she looked well; she dreaded having a fat face, healthy complexion, big muscles. She lived most of the time in darkness, so intolerable it was for her to be seen or even *visible*.

Very often the parents' attitude contributes to inculcating shame in the little girl for her physical appearance. A woman's testimony:*

I suffered from a very keen sense of physical inferiority, which was accentuated by continual nagging at home ... Mother, in her excessive pride, wanted me to appear at my best, and she always found many faults which required 'covering up' to point out to the dressmaker; for instance, drooping shoulders! Heavy hips! Too flat in

* Wilhelm Stekel, *Frigidity in Woman*.

the back! Bust too prominent! Having had a swollen neck for years, it was not possible for me to have an open neck. And so on. I was particularly worried on account of the appearance of my feet . . . and I was nagged on account of my gait . . . There was some truth in every criticism . . . but sometimes I was so embarrassed, particularly during my 'backfisch' stage, that at times I was at a loss to know how to move about. If I met someone, my first thought was: 'If I could only hide my feet!'

This shame makes the girl act awkwardly, blush at the drop of a hat; this blushing increases her timidity and itself becomes the object of a phobia. Stekel recounts among others a woman who 'as a young girl blushed so pathologically and violently that for a year she wore bandages around her face with the excuse of toothaches'.*

Sometimes, in prepuberty preceding the arrival of her period, the girl does not yet feel disgust for her body; she is proud of becoming a woman, she eagerly awaits her maturing breasts, she pads her blouse with handkerchiefs and brags around her older sisters; she does not yet grasp the meaning of the phenomena taking place in her. Her first period exposes this meaning and feelings of shame appear. If they existed already, they are confirmed and magnified from this moment on. All the accounts agree: whether or not the child has been warned, the event always appears repugnant and humiliating. The mother very often neglected to warn her; it has been noted† that mothers explain the mysteries of pregnancy, childbirth and even sexual relations to their daughters more easily than that of menstruation; they themselves hate this feminine servitude, a hatred that reflects men's old mystical terrors and one that they transmit to their offspring. When the girl finds suspicious stains on her underwear, she thinks she has diarrhoea, a fatal haemorrhage, a venereal disease. According to a survey that Havelock Ellis cited in 1896, out of 125 American high school students 36 at the time of their first period knew absolutely nothing on the question, 39 had vague ideas; that is, more than half of the girls were unaware. And according to Helene Deutsch, things had not changed much by 1946. Ellis cites the case of a young girl who threw herself into the Seine in Saint-Ouen because she thought she had an 'unknown disease'. Stekel, in *Letters to a Mother*,[23]

---

* Ibid.
† Cf. the works of Daly and Chadwick, cited by H. Deutsch, in *The Psychology of Women*, 1946.

tells the story of a little girl who tried to commit suicide, seeing in the menstrual flow the sign of and punishment for the impurities that sullied her soul. It is natural for the young girl to be afraid: it seems to her that her life is seeping out of her. According to Klein and the English psycho-analytic school, blood is for the young girl the manifestation of a wound of the internal organs. Even if cautious advice saves her from excessive anxiety, she is ashamed, she feels dirty: she rushes to the sink, she tries to wash or hide her dirtied underwear. There is a typical account of the experience in Colette Audry's book, *In the Eyes of Memory*:²⁴

At the heart of this exaltation, the brutal and finished drama. One evening while getting undressed, I thought I was sick; it did not frighten me and I kept myself from saying anything in the hope that it would disappear the next day . . . Four weeks later, the illness occurred again, but more violently. I was quietly going to throw my knickers into the hamper behind the bathroom door. It was so hot that the diamond-shaped tiles of the hallway were warm under my naked feet. When I then got into bed, Mamma opened my bedroom door: she came to explain things to me. I am unable to remember the effect her words had on me at that time but while she was whispering, Kaki poked her head in. The sight of this round and curious face drove me crazy. I screamed at her to get out of there and she disappeared in fright. I begged Mama to go and beat her because she hadn't knocked before entering. My mother's calmness, her knowing and quietly happy air, were all it took to make me lose my head. When she left, I dug myself in for a stormy night.

Two memories all of a sudden come back: a few months earlier, coming back from a walk with Kaki, Mama and I had met the old doctor from Privas, built like a logger with a full white beard. 'Your daughter is growing up, madam,' he said while looking at me; and I hated him right then and there without understanding anything. A little later, coming back from Paris, Mama put away some new little towels in the chest of drawers. 'What is that?' Kaki asked. Mamma had this natural air of adults who reveal one part of the truth while omitting the other three: 'It's for Colette soon.' Speechless, unable to utter one question, I hated my mother.

That whole night I tossed and turned in my bed. It was not possible. I was going to wake up. Mama was mistaken, it would go away and not come back again . . . The next day, secretly changed and stained, I had to confront the others. I looked at my sister with hatred because she did not yet know, because all of a sudden she found herself, unknown to her, endowed with an overwhelming superiority over me. Then I began to hate men, who would never experience this, and who knew. And then I also hated women who accepted it so calmly. I was sure that if they had been warned of what was happening to me, they would all be overjoyed. 'So it's your turn now,' they would have thought. That one too, I said to myself when I saw one. And this one too. I was had by the world. I had trouble walking and didn't dare run. The earth, the sun-hot greenery, even the food, seemed to give off a suspicious smell . . . The crisis passed and I began to hope against hope that it would not come back again. One month later, I had to face the facts and accept the evil definitively, in a heavy stupor this time. There was now in my memory a 'before'. All the rest of my existence would no longer be anything but an 'after'.

Things happen in a similar way for most little girls. Many of them are horrified at the idea of sharing their secret with those around them. A friend told me that, motherless, she lived between her father and a primary school teacher and spent three months in fear and shame, hiding her stained underwear before it was discovered that she had begun menstruating. Even peasant women who might be expected to be hardened by their knowledge of the harshest sides of animal life are horrified by this malediction, which in the countryside is still taboo: I knew a young woman farmer who washed her underwear in secret in the frozen brook, putting her soaking garment directly back on her naked skin to hide her unspeakable secret. I could cite a hundred similar facts. Even admitting this astonishing misfortune offers no relief. Undoubtedly, the mother who slapped her daughter brutally, saying: 'Stupid! You're much too young,' is exceptional. But this is not only about being in a bad mood; most mothers fail to give the child the necessary explanations and so she is full of anxiety before this new state brought about by the first menstruation crisis: she wonders if the future does not hold other painful surprises for her; or else she imagines that from now on she could become pregnant by the simple presence or contact with a man, and she feels real terror of males. Even if she is spared these anxieties by intelligent explanations, she is not so easily granted peace of mind. Prior to this, the girl could, with a little bad faith, still think herself an asexual being, she could just not think herself; she even dreams of waking up one morning changed into a man; these days, mothers and aunts flatter and whisper to each other: 'She's a big girl now'; the brotherhood of matrons has won: she belongs to them. Here she takes her place on the women's side without recourse. Sometimes, she is proud of it; she thinks she has now become an adult and an upheaval will occur in her existence. As Thyde Monnier recounts:[25]

> Some of us had become 'big girls' during vacation; others would while at school, and then, one after the other in the toilets in the courtyard, where they were sitting on their 'thrones' like queens receiving their subjects, we would go and 'see the blood'.*

But the girl is soon disappointed because she sees that she has not gained any privilege and that life follows its normal course. The only novelty is the disgusting event repeated monthly; there are children that cry for hours when they learn they are condemned to this destiny; what adds to their revolt is that this shameful defect is known by men as well: what they would like is that the humiliating feminine condition at least be shrouded in mystery for them. But no, father, brothers, cousins, men know and even joke about it sometimes. This is when the shame of her too carnal body is born or exacerbated. And once the first surprise has passed, the monthly unpleasantness does not fade away at all: each time, the girl finds the same disgust when faced by this unappetising and stagnant odour that comes from herself – a smell of swamps and wilted violets – this less red and more suspicious blood than that flowing from children's cuts and scratches. Day and night she has to think of changing her protection, watching her underwear, her sheets, and solving a thousand little practical and repugnant problems; in thrifty families sanitary napkins are washed each month and take their place among the piles of handkerchiefs; this waste coming out of oneself has to be delivered to those handling the laundry: the laundress, servant, mother or older sister. The types of bandages pharmacies sell in boxes named after flowers, Camellia or Edelweiss, are thrown out after use; but while travelling, on vacation or on a trip it is not so easy to get rid of them, the toilet bowl being specifically prohibited. The young heroine of the *Psychoanalytical Journal*† described her horror of the sanitary napkin; she did not even consent to undress in front of

---

* Me.

† Translated by Clara Malraux.

her sister except in the dark during these times. This bothersome, annoying object can come loose during violent exercise; it is a worse humiliation than losing one's knickers in the middle of the street: this horrid possibility sometimes brings about fits of psychasthenia. By a kind of ill will of nature, indisposition and pain often do not begin until the initial bleeding – often hardly noticed – has passed; young girls are often irregular: they might be surprised during a walk, in the street, at friends'; they risk – like Mme de Chevreuse* – dirtying their clothes or their seat; such a possibility makes one live in constant anxiety. The greater the young girl's feeling of revulsion towards this feminine defect, the greater her obligation to pay careful attention to it so as not to expose herself to the awful humiliation of an accident or a little word of warning.

Here is the series of answers that Dr Liepmann obtained during his study of juvenile sexuality:†

At sixteen years of age, when I was indisposed for the first time, I was very frightened in seeing it one morning. In truth, I knew it was going to happen, but I was so ashamed of it that I remained in bed for a whole half day and had one answer to all questions: I cannot get up.

I was speechless in astonishment when, not yet twelve, I was indisposed for the first time. I was struck by horror, and as my mother limited herself to telling me drily that this would happen every month, I considered it as something disgusting and refused to accept that this did not also happen to men.

This adventure made my mother decide to initiate me, without forgetting menstruation at the same time. I then had my second disappointment because as soon as I was indisposed, I ran joyfully to my mother, who was still sleeping, and I woke her up, shouting, 'Mother, I have it!' 'And that is why you woke me up?' she managed to say in response. In spite of everything, I considered this thing as a real upheaval in my existence.

---

* Disguised as a man during the Fronde, Mme de Chevreuse, after a long excursion on horseback, was unmasked because of bloodstains seen on the saddle.
† Dr W. Liepmann, *Youth and Sexuality*.

And so I felt the most intense horror when I was indisposed for the first time seeing that the bleeding did not stop after a few minutes. Nevertheless, I did not whisper a word to anyone, not to my mother either. I had just reached the age of fifteen. In addition I suffered very little. Only one time was I taken with such terrifying pain that I fainted and stayed on the floor in my room for almost three hours. But I still did not say anything to anyone.

When for the first time this indisposition occurred, I was about thirteen. My school friends and I had already talked about it and I was proud to finally become one of the big girls. With great importance I explained to the gym teacher that it was impossible today for me to take part in the lesson because I was indisposed.

It was not my mother who initiated me. It was not until the age of nineteen that she had her period, and for fear of being scolded for dirtying her underwear, she buried it in a field.

I reached the age of eighteen and I then had my period for the first time.* I was totally unprepared for what was happening . . . At night, I had violent bleeding accompanied by heavy diarrhoea and I could not rest for one second. In the morning, my heart racing, I ran to my mother and weeping constantly asked her advice. But I only obtained this harsh reprimand: 'You should have been aware of it sooner and not have dirtied the sheets and bed.' That was all as far as explanation was concerned. Naturally, I tried very hard to know what crime I might have committed, and I suffered terrible anguish.

I already knew what it was. I was waiting for it impatiently because I was hoping my mother would reveal to me how children were made. The celebrated day arrived, but my mother remained silent. Nevertheless, I was joyous. 'From now on,' I said to myself, 'you can make children: you are a lady.'

This crisis takes place at a still tender age; the boy only reaches adolescence at about fifteen or sixteen; the girl changes into a woman at thirteen or fourteen. But the essential difference in their experience does not stem from there; nor does it lie in the physiological manifestations

* She was a girl from a very poor Berlin family.

that give it its awful shock in the case of the girl: puberty has a radically different meaning for the two sexes because it does not announce
the same future to them.

Granted, boys too at puberty feel their body as an embarrassing presence, but because they have been proud of their virility from childhood,
it is towards that virility that they proudly transcend the moment of
their development; they proudly exhibit the hair growing between their
legs and that makes men of them; more than ever, their sex is an object
of comparison and challenge. Becoming adults is an intimidating metamorphosis: many adolescents react with anxiety to a demanding freedom;
but they accede to the dignified status of male with joy. On the contrary,
to become a grown-up, the girl must confine herself within the limits
that her femininity imposes on her. The boy admires undefined promises in the growing hair: she remains confused before the 'brutal and
finished drama' that limits her destiny. Just as the penis gets its privileged value from the social context, the social context makes menstruation a malediction. One symbolises virility and the other femininity: it
is because femininity means alterity and inferiority that its revelation is
met with shame. The girl's life has always appeared to her to be determined by this impalpable essence to which the absence of the penis has
not managed to give a positive image: it is this essence that is revealed
in the red flow that escapes from between her thighs. If she has already
assumed her condition, she welcomes the event with joy: 'Now you are
a lady.' If she has always refused it, the bloody verdict strikes her like
lightning; most often, she hesitates: the menstrual stain inclines her
towards disgust and fear. 'So this is what these words mean: being a
woman!' The fate that until now has weighed on her ambivalently and
from the outside is lodged in her belly; there is no escape; she feels
trapped. In a sexually egalitarian society, she would envisage menstruation only as her unique way of acceding to an adult life; the human
body has many other more repugnant servitudes in men and women:
they make the best of them because as they are common to all they do
not represent a flaw for anyone; menstrual periods inspire horror in
adolescent girls because they thrust them into an inferior and damaged
category. This feeling of degradation will weigh on her heavily. She would
retain the pride of her bleeding body if she did not lose her self-respect
as a human being. And if she succeeds in preserving her self-respect, she
will feel the humiliation of her flesh much less vividly: the girl who
opens paths of transcendence in sports, social, intellectual and mystical
activities will not see a mutilation in her specificity, and she will over-

come it easily. If the young girl often develops psychoses in this period, it is because she feels defenceless in front of a deaf fate that condemns her to unimaginable trials; her femininity signifies illness, suffering and death in her eyes and she is transfixed by this destiny.

One example that vividly illustrates these anxieties is that of the patient called Molly described by Helene Deutsch.

Molly was fourteen when she began to suffer from psychic disorders; she was the fourth child in a family of five siblings. Her father is described as extremely strict and narrow-minded. He criticised the appearance and behaviour of his children at every meal. The mother was worried and unhappy; and every so often the parents were not on speaking terms; one brother ran away from home. The patient was a gifted youngster, a good tap dancer; but she was shy, took the family troubles seriously, and was afraid of boys. Her older sister got married against her mother's wishes and Molly was very interested in her pregnancy: she had a difficult delivery and forceps were necessary and she heard that women often die in childbirth. She took care of the baby for two months; when the sister left the house, there was a terrible scene and the mother fainted. Molly fainted too. She had seen classmates faint in class and her thoughts were much concerned with death and fainting. When she got her period, she told her mother with an embarrassed air: 'That thing is here.' She went with her sister to buy some menstrual pads; on meeting a man in the street, she hung her head. In general she acted 'disgusted with herself'. She never had pain during her periods, but tried to hide them from her mother, even when the latter saw stains on the sheets. She told her sister: 'Anything might happen to me now. I might have a baby.' When told, 'You have to live with a man for that to happen', she replied: 'Well, I am living with two men – my father and your husband.'

The father did not permit his daughters to go out . . . because one heard stories of rape: these fears helped to give Molly the idea of men being redoubtable creatures. From her first menstruation her anxiety about becoming pregnant and dying in childbirth became so severe that after a time she refused to leave her room, and now she sometimes stays in bed all day; if she has to go out of the house, she has an attack and faints. She is afraid of cars and taxis and she cannot sleep, she fears that someone is trying to enter the house at night, she screams and cries. She has eating spells; sometimes she eats too much to keep herself from fainting; she is also afraid when she feels closed in. She cannot go to school any more or lead a normal life.

A similar story not linked to the crisis of menstruation but which shows the girl's anxiety about her insides is Nancy's.*

Toward the age of thirteen the little girl was on intimate terms with her older sister, and she had been proud to be in her confidence when the sister was secretly engaged and then married: to share the secret of a grown-up was to be accepted among the adults. She lived for a time with her sister; but when the latter told her that she was going 'to buy' a baby, Nancy got jealous of her brother-in-law and of the coming child: to be treated again as a child to whom one made little mysteries of things was unbearable. She began to experience internal troubles and wanted to be operated on for appendicitis. The operation was a success, but during her stay at the hospital Nancy lived in a state of severe agitation; she made violent scenes with a nurse she disliked; she tried to seduce the doctor, making dates with him, being provocative and demanding throughout her crises to be treated as a woman. She accused herself of being to blame for the death of a little brother some years before. And in particular she felt sure that they had not removed her appendix or had left a part of it inside her; her claim that she had swallowed a penny was probably intended to make sure an X-ray would be taken.

This desire for an operation – and in particular for the removal of the appendix – is often seen at this age; girls thus express their fear of rape, pregnancy or having a baby. They feel in their womb obscure perils and hope that the surgeon will save them from this unknown and threatening danger.

It is not only the arrival of her period that signals to the girl her destiny as a woman. Other dubious phenomena occur in her. Until then her eroticism was clitoral. It is difficult to know if solitary sexual practices are less widespread in girls than in boys; the girl indulges in them in her first two years, and perhaps even in the first months of her life; it seems that she stops at about two before taking them up again later;

* Cited also by H. Deutsch, *The Psychology of Women* (1946).

because of his anatomical makeup, this stem planted in the male flesh asks to be touched more than a secret mucous membrane: but the chances of rubbing – the child climbing on gym apparatus or on trees or onto a bicycle – of contact with clothes, or in a game or even initiation by friends, older friends or adults, frequently make the girl discover sensations she tries to renew. In any case, pleasure, when reached, is an autonomous sensation: it has the lightness and innocence of all childish amusements.* As a child, she hardly established a relation between these intimate delights and her destiny as a woman; her sexual relations with boys, if there were any, were essentially based on curiosity. And all of a sudden she experiences emotional confusion in which she does not recognise herself. Sensitivity of the erogenous zones is developing and they are so numerous in the woman that her whole body can be considered erogenous: this is what comes across from familial caresses, innocent kisses, the casual touching of a dressmaker, a doctor, a hairdresser, or a friendly hand on her hair or neck; she learns and often deliberately seeks a deeper excitement in her relations of play and fighting with boys or girls: thus Gilberte fighting on the Champs-Elysées with Proust; in the arms of her dancing partners, under her mother's naive eyes, she experiences a strange lassitude. And then, even a well-protected young woman is exposed to more specific experiences; in conventional circles regrettable incidents are hushed up by common agreement; but it often happens that some of the caresses of friends of the household, uncles, cousins, not to mention grandfathers and fathers, are much less inoffensive than the mother thinks; a professor, a priest, a doctor was bold, indiscreet. Such experiences are found in *In the Prison of Her Skin* by Violette Leduc, in *Maternal Hatred* by Simone de Tervagne and in *The Blue Orange* by Yassu Gauclère. Stekel thinks that grandfathers in particular are often very dangerous.

I was fifteen. The night before the funeral, my grandfather came to sleep at our house. The next day, my mother was already up, he asked me if he could get into bed with me to play; I got up immediately without answering him . . . I began to be afraid of men, a woman recounted.

Another girl recalled receiving a serious shock at eight or ten

* Except, of course, in numerous cases where the direct or indirect intervention of the parents, or religious scruples, make a sin of it. Little girls have sometimes been subjected to abominable persecutions, under the pretext of saving them from 'bad habits'.

years of age when her grandfather, an old man of sixty, had groped
her genitals. He had taken her on his lap while sliding his finger
into her vagina. The child had felt an immense anxiety but yet did
not dare talk about it. Since that time she has been very afraid of
everything sexual.*

Such incidents are usually endured in silence for the little girl because
of the shame they cause. Moreover, if she does reveal them to her parents,
their reaction is often to reprimand her. 'Don't say such stupid things . . .
you've got an evil mind.' She is also silent about bizarre activities of
some strangers. A little girl told Dr Liepmann:

> We had rented a room from the shoemaker in the basement. Often
> when our landlord was alone, he came to get me, took me in his
> arms and kissed me for a long time all the while wiggling back and
> forth. His kiss wasn't superficial besides, since he stuck his tongue
> into my mouth. I detested him because of his ways. But I never
> whispered a word, as I was very fearful.†

In addition to enterprising companions and perverse girlfriends, there
is this knee in the cinema pressed against the girl's, this hand at night
in the train, sliding along her leg, these boys who sniggered when she
passed, these men who followed her in the street, these embraces, these
furtive touches. She does not really understand the meaning of these
adventures. In the fifteen-year-old head, there is often a strange confusion because theoretical knowledge and concrete experiences do not
match. She has already felt all the burnings of excitement and desire,
but she imagines – like Clara d'Ellébeuse invented by Francis Jammes
– that a male kiss is enough to make her a mother; she has a clear idea
of the genital anatomy but when her dancing partner embraces her,
she thinks the agitation she feels is a migraine. It is certain that girls
are better informed today than in the past. However, some psychiatrists
affirm that there is more than one adolescent girl who does not know
that sexual organs have a use other than urinary.‡ In any case, girls do
not draw much connection between their sexual agitation and the existence of their genital organs, since there is no sign as precise as the
male erection indicating this correlation. There is such a gap between

* *Frigidity in Woman.*

† Liepmann, *Youth and Sexuality.*

‡ Cf. H. Deutsch, *The Psychology of Women,* 1946.

their romantic musings concerning man and love and the crudeness of certain facts that are revealed to them that they do not create any link between them. Thyde Monnier* relates that she had made the pledge with a few girlfriends to see how a man was made and to tell it to the others:

Having entered my father's room on purpose without knocking, I described it: 'It looks like a leg of lamb, that is, it is like a rolling pin and then there is a round thing.' It was difficult to explain. I drew it. I even did it three times and each one took hers away hidden in her blouse and from time to time she burst out laughing while looking at it and then went all dreamy . . . How could innocent girls like us set up a connection between these objects and sentimental songs, pretty little romantic stories where love as a whole – respect, shyness, sighs and kissing of the hand – is sublimated to the point of making a eunuch?

Nevertheless, through reading, conversations, theatre and words she has overheard, the girl gives meaning to the disturbances of her flesh; she becomes appeal and desire. In her fevers, shivers, dampness and uncertain states, her body takes on a new and unsettling dimension. The young man is proud of his sexual propensities because he assumes his virility joyfully; sexual desire is aggressive and prehensile for him; there is an affirmation of his subjectivity and transcendence in it; he boasts of it to his friends; his sex organ is for him a disturbance he takes pride in; the drive that sends him towards the female is of the same nature as that which throws him towards the world, and so he recognises himself in it. On the contrary, the girl's sexual life has always been hidden; when her eroticism is transformed and invades her whole flesh, the mystery becomes agonising: she undergoes the disturbance as a shameful illness; it is not active: it is a state, and even in imagination she cannot get rid of it by any autonomous decision; she does not dream of taking, pressing, violating: she is wait and appeal; she feels dependent; she feels herself at risk in her alienated flesh.

Her diffuse hope and her dream of happy passivity clearly reveal her body as an object destined for another; she seeks to know sexual experience only in its immanence; it is the contact of the hand, mouth or another flesh that she desires; the image of her partner is left in the

* Me.

shadows or she drowns it in an idealised haze; however, she cannot prevent his presence from haunting her. Her terrors and juvenile revulsions regarding man have assumed a more equivocal character than before and because of that they are more agonising. Before, they stemmed from a profound divorce between the child's organism and her future as an adult; now they come from this very complexity that the girl feels in her flesh. She understands that she is destined for possession because she wants it: and she revolts against her desires. She at once wishes for and fears the shameful passivity of the consenting prey. She is overwhelmed with confusion at the idea of baring herself before a man; but she also senses that she will then be given over to his gaze without recourse. The hand that takes and that touches has an even more imperious presence than do eyes: it is more frightening. But the most obvious and detestable symbol of physical possession is penetration by the male's sex organ. The girl hates the idea that this body she identifies with may be perforated as one perforates leather, that it can be torn as one tears a piece of fabric. But the girl refuses more than the wound and the accompanying pain; she refuses that these be *inflicted*. 'The idea of being *pierced* by a man is horrible,' a girl told me one day. It is not fear of the virile member that engenders horror of the man, but this fear is the confirmation and symbol; the idea of penetration acquires its obscene and humiliating meaning within a more generalised form, of which it is in turn an essential element.

The girl's anxiety shows itself in nightmares that torment her and fantasies that haunt her: just when she feels an insidious complaisance in herself, the idea of rape becomes obsessive in many cases. It manifests itself in dreams and behaviour in the form of many more or less obvious symbols. The girl explores her room before going to bed for fear of finding some robber with shady intentions; she thinks she hears thieves in the house; an aggressor comes in through the window armed with a knife and he stabs her. In a more or less acute way, men inspire terror in her. She begins to feel a certain disgust for her father; she can no longer stand the smell of his tobacco, she detests going into the bathroom after him; even if she continues to cherish him, this physical revulsion is frequent; it takes on an intensified form if the child was already hostile to her father, as often happens in the youngest children. A dream often encountered by psychiatrists in their young female patients is that they imagine being raped by a man in front of an older woman and with her consent. It is clear that they are symbolically asking their mother for permission to give in to their desires. That is because one of the most detestable constraints weighing on them is that of hypocrisy.

The girl is dedicated to 'purity', to innocence, at precisely the moment she discovers in and around her the mysterious disturbances of life and sex. She has to be white like an ermine, transparent like crystal, she is dressed in vaporous organdie, her room is decorated with candy-coloured hangings, people lower their voice when she approaches, she is prohibited from seeing indecent books; yet there is not one child on earth who does not relish 'abominable' images and desires. She tries to hide them from her best friend, even from herself; she only wants to live or to think by the rules; her self-defiance gives her a devious, unhappy and sickly look; and later, nothing will be harder than combating these inhibitions. But in spite of all these repressions, she feels oppressed by the weight of unspeakable faults. Her metamorphosis into a woman takes place not only in shame but in remorse for suffering that shame.

We understand that the awkward age is a period of painful distress for the girl. She does not want to remain a child. But the adult world seems frightening or boring to her. Colette Audry says:

So I wanted to grow up but never did I seriously dream of leading the life I saw adults lead . . . And thus the desire to grow up without ever assuming an adult state, without ever feeling solidarity with parents, mistresses of the house, housewives, or heads of family, was forming in me.

She would like to free herself from her mother's yoke; but she also has an ardent need for her protection. The faults that weigh on her consciousness – solitary sexual practices, dubious friendships, improper books – make this refuge necessary. The following letter, written to a girlfriend by a fifteen-year-old girl, is typical:*

Mother wants me to wear a long dress at the big dance party at W.'s – my first long dress. She is surprised that I do not want to. I begged her to let me wear my short pink dress for the last time . . . I am so afraid. This long dress makes me feel as if Mummy were going on a long trip and I did not know when she would return. Isn't that silly? And sometimes she looks at me as though I were still a little girl. Ah, if she knew! She would tie my hands to the bed and despise me.

* Quoted by H. Deutsch, *Psychology of Women*.

Stekel's book, *Frigidity in Woman*, is a remarkable document on female childhood. In it a Viennese *süsse Mädel*[26] wrote a detailed confession at about the age of twenty-one. It is a concrete synthesis of all the moments we have studied separately.

'At the age of five I chose for my playmate Richard, a boy of six or seven . . . For a long time I had wanted to know how one can tell whether a child is a girl or a boy. I was told: by the earrings . . . or by the nose. This seemed to satisfy me, though I had a feeling that they were keeping something from me. Suddenly Richard expressed a desire to urinate . . . Then the thought came to me of lending him my chamber pot . . . When I saw his organ, which was something entirely new to me, I went into highest raptures: "What have you there? My, isn't that nice! I'd like to have something like that, too." Whereupon I took hold of the membrum and held it enthusiastically . . . My great-aunt's cough awoke us . . . and from that day on our doings and games were carefully watched.'

At nine she played 'marriage' and 'doctor' with two other boys of eight and ten; they touched her parts and one day one of the boys touched her with his organ, saying that her parents had done just the same thing when they got married. 'This aroused my indignation: "Oh, no! They never did such a nasty thing!"' She kept up these games for a long time in a strong sexual friendship with the two boys. One day her aunt caught her and there was a frightful scene with threats to put her in the reformatory. She was prevented from seeing Arthur, whom she preferred, and she suffered a good deal from it; her work went badly, her writing was deformed, and she became cross-eyed. She started another intimacy with Walter and Franz. 'Walter became the goal of all thoughts and feeling. I permitted him very submissively to reach under my dress while I sat or stood in front of him at the table, pretending to be busy with a writing exercise; whenever my mother . . . opened the door, he withdrew his hand on the instant; I, of course, was busy writing . . . In the course of time, we also behaved as husband and wife; but I never allowed him to stay long; whenever he thought he was inside me, I tore myself away saying that somebody was coming . . . I did not reflect that this was "sinful" . . .

'My childhood boy friendships were now over. All I had left were girl friends. I attached myself to Emmy, a highly refined, well-educated girl. One Christmas we exchanged gilded heart-shaped lockets with our initials engraved on them – we were, I believe, about twelve years of age at the time – and we looked upon this as a token of "engagement"; we swore eternal faithfulness "until death do us part". I owe to Emmy a goodly part of my training. She taught me also a few things regarding sexual matters. As far back as during my fifth grade at school I began seriously to doubt the veracity of the stork story. I thought that children developed within the body and that the abdomen must be cut open before a child can be brought out. She filled me with particular horror of self-abuse. In school the Gospels contributed a share towards opening our eyes with regard to certain sexual matters. For instance, when Mary came to Elizabeth, the child is said to have "leaped in her womb"; and we read other similarly remarkable Bible passages. We underscored these words; and when this was discovered the whole class barely escaped a "black mark" in deportment. My girl friend told me also about the "ninth month reminder" to which there is a reference in Schiller's *The Robbers* [*Die Räuber*]. . . Emmy's father moved from our locality and I was again alone. We corresponded, using for the purpose a cryptic alphabet which we had devised between ourselves; but I was lonesome and finally I attached myself to Hedl, a Jewish girl. Once Emmy caught me leaving school in Hedl's company; she created a scene on account of her jealousy . . . I kept up my friendship with Hedl until I entered the commercial school. We became close friends. We both dreamed of becoming sisters-in-law sometimes, because I was fond of one of her brothers. He was a student. Whenever he spoke to me I became so confused that I gave him an irrelevant answer. At dusk we sat in the music room, huddled together on the little divan, and often tears rolled down my cheek for no particular reason as he played the piano.

'Before I befriended Hedl, I went to school for a number of weeks with a certain girl, Ella, the daughter of poor people. Once she caught her parents in a "tête-à-tête". The creaking of the bed had awakened her . . . She came and told me that her father had crawled on top of her mother, and that the mother had cried out terribly; and then the father said to her mother: "Go quickly and wash so that nothing will happen!" After this I was angry at her father and avoided him on the street, while for her mother I felt the greatest sympathy. (He must have hurt her terribly if she cried out so!)

'Again with another girl I discussed the possible length of the male membrum; I had heard that it was 12 to 15 cm long. During the fancy-work period (at school) we took the tape-measure and indicated the stated length on our stomachs, naturally reaching to the navel. This horrified us; if we should ever marry we would be literally impaled.'

She saw a male dog excited by the proximity of a female, and felt strange stirrings inside herself. 'If I saw a horse urinate in the street, my eyes were always glued to the wet spot in the road; I believe the length of time (urinating) is what always impressed me.' She watched flies in copulation and in the country domesticated animals doing the same.

'At twelve I suffered a severe attack of tonsillitis. A friendly physician was called in. He seated himself on my bed and presently he stuck his hand under the covers, almost touching me on the genitalia. I exclaimed: "Don't be so rude!" My mother hurried in; the doctor was much embarrassed. He declared I was a horrid monkey, saying he merely wanted to pinch me on the calf. I was compelled to ask his forgiveness . . . When I finally began to menstruate and my father came across the blood-stained cloths on one occasion, there was a terrible scene. How did it happen that he, so clean a man, had to live among such dirty females? . . . I felt the injustice of being put in the wrong on account of my menstruation.' At fifteen she communicated with another girl in shorthand 'so that no one else could decipher our missives. There was much to report about conquests. She copied for me a vast number of verses from the walls of lavatories; I took particular notice of one. It seemed to me that love, which ranged so high in my fantasy, was being dragged in the mud by it. The verse read: "What is love's highest aim? Four buttocks on a stem." I decided I would never get into that situation; a man who loves a young girl would be unable to ask such a thing of her.

'At fifteen and a half I had a new brother. I was tremendously jealous, for I had always been the only child in the family. My friend reminded me to observe "how the baby boy was constructed", but with the best intentions I was unable to give her the desired information . . . I could not look there. At about this time another girl described to me a bridal night scene . . . I think that then I made up my mind to marry after all, for I was very curious; only the "panting like a horse", as mentioned in the description, offended my aesthetic sense . . . Which one of us girls would not have gladly

married then to undress before the beloved and be carried to bed
in his arms? It seemed so thrilling!'

It will perhaps be said – even though this is a normal and not a
pathological case – that this child was exceptionally 'perverse'; she was
only less watched over than others. If the curiosities and desires of
'well-bred' girls do not manifest themselves in acts, they nonetheless
exist in the form of fantasies and games. I once knew a very pious and
disconcertingly innocent girl – who became an accomplished woman,
devoted to maternity and religion – who one evening confided all trembling to an older woman: 'How marvellous it must be to get undressed
in front of a man! Let's suppose you are my husband'; and she began
to undress, all trembling with emotion. No upbringing can prevent the
girl from becoming aware of her body and dreaming of her destiny;
the most one can do is to impose strict repression that will then weigh
on her for her whole sexual life. What would be desirable is that she
be taught, on the contrary, to accept herself without excuses and
without shame.

One understands now the drama that rends the adolescent girl at
puberty: she cannot become 'a grown-up' without accepting her femininity; she already knew her sex condemned her to a mutilated and frozen
existence; she now discovers it in the form of an impure illness and an
obscure crime. Her inferiority was at first understood as a privation: the
absence of a penis was converted to a stain and fault. She makes her
way towards the future wounded, shamed, worried and guilty.

CHAPTER 2

The Girl

Throughout her childhood, the little girl was bullied and mutilated; but she nonetheless grasped herself as an autonomous individual; in her relations with her family and friends, in her studies and games, she saw herself in the present as a transcendence: her future passivity was something she only imagined. Once she enters puberty, the future not only moves closer: it settles into her body; it becomes the most concrete reality. It retains the fateful quality it always had; while the adolescent boy is actively routed towards adulthood, the girl looks forward to the opening of this new and unforeseeable period where the plot is already hatched and towards which time is drawing her. As she is already detached from her childhood past, the present is for her only a transition; she sees no valid ends in it, only occupations. In a more or less disguised way, her youth is consumed by waiting. She is waiting for Man.

Surely the adolescent boy also dreams of woman, he desires her; but she will never be more than one element in his life: she does not encapsulate his destiny; from childhood, the little girl, whether wishing to realise herself as woman or overcome the limits of her femininity, has awaited the male for accomplishment and escape; he has the dazzling face of Perseus or St George; he is the liberator; he is also rich and powerful, he holds the keys to happiness, he is Prince Charming. She anticipates that in his caress she will feel carried away by the great current of life as when she rested in her mother's bosom; subjected to his gentle authority, she will find the same security as in her father's arms: the magic of embraces and gazes will petrify her back into an idol. She has always been convinced of male superiority; this male prestige is not a childish mirage; it has economic and social foundations; men are, without any question, the masters of the world; everything convinces the adolescent girl that it is in her interest to be their vassal; her parents prod her on; the father is proud of his daughter's success, the mother sees the promise of a prosperous future, friends envy and admire the one among them who gets the most masculine admiration; in American colleges, the student's status is based on the number of dates she has. Marriage is not only an honourable and less strenuous career than many others; it alone enables woman to attain her complete social dignity and also to realise herself sexually as lover and mother. This is the role her entourage thus envisages for her future, as she envisages it herself. Everyone unanimously agrees that catching a husband – or a protector in some cases – is for her the most important of undertakings. In her eyes, man embodies the Other, as she does for man; but for her this *Other* appears in the essential mode and she grasps herself as the inessential opposite him. She will free herself from her parents' home, from her mother's hold; she will open up her future not by an active conquest but by passively and docilely delivering herself into the hands of a new master.

It has often been declared that if she resigns herself to this surrender, it is because physically and morally she has become inferior to boys and incapable of competing with them: forsaking hopeless competition, she entrusts the assurance of her happiness to a member of the superior caste. In fact, her humility does not stem from a given inferiority: on the contrary, her humility engenders all her failings; its source is in the adolescent girl's past, in the society around her, and precisely in this future that is proposed to her.

True, puberty transforms the girl's body. It is more fragile than before; female organs are vulnerable, their functioning delicate; strange and uncomfortable, breasts are a burden; they remind her of their presence during strenuous exercise, they quiver, they ache. From here on, woman's muscle force, endurance and suppleness are inferior to man's. Hormonal imbalances create nervous and vasomotor instability. Menstrual periods are painful: headaches, stiffness and abdominal cramps make normal activities painful and even impossible; added to these discomforts are psychic problems; nervous and irritable, the woman frequently undergoes a state of semi-alienation each month; central control of the nervous and sympathetic systems is no longer assured; circulation problems and some auto-intoxications turn the body into a screen between the woman and the world, a burning fog that weighs on her, stifling her and separating her: experienced through this suffering and passive flesh, the entire universe is a burden too heavy to bear. Oppressed and submerged, she becomes a stranger to herself because she is a stranger to the rest of the world. Syntheses disintegrate, instants are no longer connected, others are recognised but only abstractly; and if reasoning and logic do remain intact, as in melancholic delirium, they are subordinated to passions that surge out of organic disorder. These facts are extremely important; but the way the woman becomes conscious of them gives them their weight.

At about thirteen, boys serve a veritable apprenticeship in violence, developing their aggressiveness, their will for power and taste for competition; it is exactly at this moment that the little girl renounces rough games. Some sports remain accessible to her, but sport that is specialisation, submission to artificial rules, does not offer the equivalent of a spontaneous and habitual recourse to force; it is marginal to life; it does not teach about the world and about one's self as intimately as does an unruly fight or an impulsive rock climb. The sportswoman never feels the conqueror's pride of the boy who pins down his comrade. In fact, in many countries, most girls have no athletic training; like fights, climbing is forbidden to them, they only submit to their bodies passively; far more clearly than in their early years, they must forgo *emerging* beyond the given world, affirming themselves *above* the rest of humanity: they are banned from exploring, daring, pushing back the limits of the possible. In particular, the attitude of defiance, so important for boys, is unknown to them; true, women compare themselves with each other, but defiance is something other than these passive confrontations: two freedoms confront each other as having a hold on the world whose limits they intend to push; climbing higher than a friend or getting the better in arm wrestling is affirming one's sovereignty over the world. These conquering actions are not permitted to the girl, and violence in particular is not permitted to her. Undoubtedly, in the adult world brute force plays no great role in normal times; but it nonetheless haunts the world; much of masculine behaviour arises in a setting of potential violence: on every street corner skirmishes are waiting to happen; in most cases they are aborted; but it is enough for the man to feel in his fists his will for self-affirmation for him to feel confirmed in his sovereignty. The male has recourse to his fists and fighting when he encounters any affront or attempt to reduce him to an object: he does not let himself be transcended by others; he finds himself again in the heart of his subjectivity. Violence is the authentic test of every person's attachment to himself, his passions and his own will; to radically reject it is to reject all objective truth, it is to isolate one's self in an abstract subjectivity; an anger or a revolt that does not exert itself in muscles remains imaginary. It is a terrible frustration not to be able to imprint the movements of one's heart on the face of the earth. In the South of the United States, it is strictly impossible for a black person to use violence against whites; this rule is the key to the mysterious 'black soul'; the way the black experiences himself in the white world, his behaviour in adjusting to it, the compensations he seeks, his whole way of feeling and acting, are explained on the basis of the passivity to which he is condemned. During the Occupation, the French who had decided not to let themselves resort to violent gestures against the occupants even in cases of provocation (whether out of egotistical prudence or because they had overriding duties) felt their situation in the world profoundly overturned: depending upon the whims of others, they could be changed into objects, their subjectivity no longer had the means to express itself concretely, it was merely a secondary phenomenon. In the same way, for the adolescent boy who is allowed to manifest himself imperiously, the universe has a totally different face from what it has for the adolescent girl whose feelings are deprived of immediate effectiveness; the former ceaselessly calls the world into question, he can at every instance revolt against the given and thus has the impression of actively conforming it when he accepts it; the latter only submits to it; the world is defined without her and its face is immutable. This lack of physical power expresses itself as a more general timidity: she does not believe in a force she has not felt in her body, she does not dare to be enterprising, to revolt, to invent; doomed to docility, to resignation, she can only accept a place that society has already made for her. She accepts the order of things as a given. A woman told me that all through her youth, she denied her physical weakness with fierce bad faith; to accept it would have been to lose her taste and courage to undertake anything, even in intellectual or political fields. I knew a girl, brought up as a tomboy and exceptionally vigorous, who thought she was as strong as a man; though she was very pretty, though she had painful periods every month, she was completely unconscious of her femininity; she had a boy's toughness, exuberance of life and initiative; she had a boy's boldness: on the street she would not hesitate to jump into a fistfight if she saw a child or a woman harassed. One or two bad experiences revealed to her that brute force is on the male's side. When she became aware of her weakness, a great part of her assurance crumbled; this was the beginning of an evolution that led her to feminise herself, to realise herself as passivity, to accept dependence. To lose confidence in one's body is to lose confidence in one's self. One needs only to see the importance that young men give to their muscles to understand that every subject grasps his body as his objective expression.

The young man's erotic drives only go to confirm the pride that he obtains from his body: he discovers in it the sign of transcendence and its power. The girl can succeed in accepting her desires: but most often they retain a shameful nature. Her whole body is experienced as embarrassment. The defiance she felt as a child regarding her 'insides' contributes to giving the menstrual crisis the dubious nature that renders it loathsome. The psychic attitude evoked by menstrual servitude constitutes a heavy handicap. The threat that weighs on the girl during certain periods can seem so intolerable for her that she will give up expeditions and pleasures out of fear of her disgrace becoming known. The horror that this inspires has repercussions on her organism and increases her disorders and pains. It has been seen that one of the characteristics of female physiology is the tight link between endocrinal secretions and the nervous system: there is reciprocal action; a woman's body – and specifically the girl's – is a 'hysterical' body in the sense that there is, so to speak, no distance between psychic life and its physiological realisation. The turmoil brought about by the girl's discovery of the problems of puberty exacerbates them. Because her body is suspect to her, she scrutinises it with anxiety and sees it as sick: it is sick. It has been seen that indeed this body is fragile and real organic disorders arise; but gynaecologists concur that nine-tenths of their patients have imaginary illnesses; that is, either their illnesses have no physiological reality or the organic disorder itself stems from a psychic attitude. To a great extent, the anguish of being a woman eats away at the female body.

It is clear that if woman's biological situation constitutes a handicap for her, it is because of the perspective from which it is grasped. Nervous frailty and vasomotor instability, when they do not become pathological, do not keep her from any profession: among males themselves, there is a great diversity of temperament. A one- or two-day indisposition per month, even painful, is not an obstacle either; in fact, many women accommodate themselves to it, particularly women for whom the monthly 'curse' could be most bothersome: athletes, travellers and women who do strenuous work. Most professions demand no more energy than women can provide. And in sports, the goal is not to succeed independently of physical aptitudes: it is the accomplishment of perfection proper to each organism; the lightweight champion is as worthy as the heavyweight; a female ski champion is no less a champion than the male who is more rapid than she: they belong to two different categories. It is precisely athletes who, positively concerned with their own accomplishments, feel the least handicapped in comparison to men. But nonetheless her physical weakness does not allow the woman to learn the lessons of violence: if it were possible to assert herself in her body and be part of the world in some other way, this deficiency would be easily compensated. If she could swim, scale rocks, pilot a plane, battle the elements, take risks and venture out, she would not feel the timidity towards the world that I spoke about. It is within the whole context of a situation that leaves her few outlets that these singularities take on their importance, and not immediately but by confirming the inferiority complex that was developed in her by her childhood.

It is this complex as well that will weigh on her intellectual accomplishments. It has often been noted that from puberty, the girl loses ground in intellectual and artistic fields. There are many reasons for this. One of the most common is that the adolescent girl does not receive the same encouragement accorded to her brothers; on the contrary, she is expected to be a *woman as well* and she must add to her professional work the duties that femininity implies. The headmistress of a professional school made these comments on the subject:

> The girl suddenly becomes a being who earns her living by working. She has new desires that have nothing to do with the family. It very often happens that she must make quite a considerable effort . . . she gets home at night exhausted, her head stuffed with the day's events . . . How will she be received? Her mother sends her right out to do an errand. There are home chores left unfinished to do, and she still has to take care of her own clothes. It is impossible to disconnect from the personal thoughts that continue to preoccupy her. She feels unhappy and compares her situation to that of her brother, who has no duties at home, and she revolts.*[27]

Housework or everyday chores that the mother does not hesitate to impose on the girl student or trainee completely exhaust her. During the war I saw my students in Sèvres worn out by family tasks added on top of their schoolwork: one developed Pott's disease, the other meningitis. Mothers – we will see – are blindly hostile to freeing their daughters and, more or less deliberately, work at bullying them even more; for the adolescent boy, his effort to become a man is respected and he is already granted great freedom. The girl is required to stay home; her outside activities are watched over: she is never encouraged to organise her own fun and pleasure. It is rare to see women organise a long hike on their

* Cited by Liepmann, *Youth and Sexuality*.

own, a walking or biking trip, or take part in games such as billiards
and bowling. Beyond a lack of initiative that comes from their education, customs make their independence difficult. If they wander the
streets, they are stared at, accosted. I know some girls, far from shy, who
get no enjoyment strolling through Paris alone because, incessantly
bothered, they are incessantly on their guard: all their pleasure is ruined.
If girl students run through the streets in happy groups as boys do, they
attract attention; striding along, singing, talking and laughing loudly or
eating an apple are provocations, and they will be insulted or followed
or approached. Light-heartedness immediately becomes a lack of
decorum. This self-control imposed on the woman becomes second
nature for 'the well-bred girl' and kills spontaneity; lively exuberance is
crushed. The result is tension and boredom. This boredom is contagious:
girls tire of each other quickly; being in the same prison does not create
solidarity among them, and this is one of the reasons the company of
boys becomes so necessary. This inability to be self-sufficient brings on
a shyness that extends over their whole lives and even marks their work.
They think that brilliant triumphs are reserved for men; they do not dare
aim too high. It has already been observed that fifteen-year-old girls,
comparing themselves to boys, declare, 'Boys are better.' This conviction is debilitating. It encourages laziness and mediocrity. A girl – who
had no particular deference for the stronger sex – reproached a man for
his cowardice; when she was told that she herself was a coward, she
complacently declared: 'Oh! It's not the same thing for a woman.'

The fundamental reason for this defeatism is that the adolescent girl
does not consider herself responsible for her future; she judges it useless
to demand much of herself since her lot in the end will not depend on
her. Far from destining herself to man because she thinks she is inferior
to him, it is because she is destined for him that, in accepting the idea
of her inferiority, she constitutes it.

In fact, she will gain value in the eyes of males not by increasing her
human worth but by modelling herself on their dreams. When she is
inexperienced, she is not always aware of this. She sometimes acts as
aggressively as boys; she tries to conquer them with a brusque authority,
a proud frankness: this attitude is almost surely doomed to failure. From
the most servile to the haughtiest, girls all learn that to please, they must
give in to them. Their mothers urge them not to treat boys like companions, not to make advances to them, to assume a passive role. If they
want to flirt or initiate a friendship, they should carefully avoid giving
the impression they are taking the initiative; men do not like tomboys,

nor bluestockings, nor thinking women; too much audacity, culture, intelligence or character frightens them. In most novels, as George Eliot observes, it is the dumb, blonde heroine who outshines the virile brunette; and in *The Mill on the Floss*, Maggie tries in vain to reverse the roles; in the end she dies and it is blonde Lucy who marries Stephen. In *The Last of the Mohicans*, vapid Alice wins the hero's heart and not valiant Clara; in *Little Women* kindly Jo is only a childhood friend for Laurie; he vows his love to curly-haired and insipid Amy. To be feminine is to show oneself as weak, futile, passive and docile. The girl is supposed not only to primp and dress herself up but also to repress her spontaneity and substitute for it the grace and charm she has been taught by her elder sisters. Any self-assertion will take away from her femininity and her seductiveness. A young man's venture into existence is relatively easy, as his vocations of human being and male are not contradictory; his childhood already predicted this happy fate. It is in accomplishing himself as independence and freedom that he acquires his social value and, concurrently, his manly prestige: the ambitious man, like Rastignac, targets money, glory and women all at once; one of the stereotypes that stimulates him is that of the powerful and famous man adored by women. For the girl, on the contrary, there is a divorce between her properly human condition and her feminine vocation. This is why adolescence is such a difficult and decisive moment for woman. Until then she was an autonomous individual: she now has to renounce her sovereignty. Not only is she torn like her brothers, and more acutely, between past and future, but in addition a conflict breaks out between her originary claim to be subject, activity and freedom, on the one hand and, on the other, her erotic tendencies and the social pressure to assume herself as a passive object. She spontaneously grasps herself as the essential: how will she decide to become the inessential? If I can accomplish myself only as the *Other*, how will I renounce my *Self*? Such is the agonising dilemma the woman-to-be must struggle with. Wavering from desire to disgust, from hope to fear, rebuffing what she invites, she is still suspended between the moment of childish independence and that of feminine submission: this is the incertitude that, as she grows out of the awkward age, gives her the bitter taste of unripe fruit.

The girl reacts to her situation differently depending on her earlier choices. The 'little woman', the matron-to-be, can easily resign herself to her metamorphosis; but she may also have drawn a taste for authority from her condition as 'little woman' that lets her rebel against the masculine yoke: she is ready to establish a matriarchy, not to become an erotic object and servant. This will often be the case of those older sisters who took on important responsibilities at a young age. The 'tomboy', upon becoming a woman, often feels a burning disappointment that can drive her directly to homosexuality; but what she was looking for in independence and intensity was to possess the world: she may not want to renounce the power of her femininity, the experiences of maternity, a whole part of her destiny. Generally, with some resistance, the girl consents to her femininity: already at the stage of childish coquetry, in front of her father, in her erotic fantasies, she understood the charm of passivity; she discovers the power in it; vanity is soon mixed with the shame that her flesh inspires. That hand that moves her, that glance that excites her, they are an appeal, an invitation; her body seems endowed with magic virtues; it is a treasure, a weapon; she is proud of it. Her coquetry, which often has disappeared during her years of childhood autonomy, is revived. She tries makeup, hairstyles; instead of hiding her breasts, she massages them to make them bigger, she studies her smile in the mirror. The link is so tight between arousal and seduction that in all cases where erotic sensibility lies dormant, no desire to please is observed in the subject. Experiments have shown that patients suffering from a thyroid deficiency, and thus apathetic and sullen, can be transformed by an injection of glandular extracts: they begin to smile; they become gay and simpering. Psychologists imbued with materialistic metaphysics have boldly declared flirtatiousness an 'instinct' secreted by the thyroid gland; but this obscure explanation is no more valid here than for early childhood. The fact is that in all cases of organic deficiency – lymphatism, anaemia, and such – the body is endured as a burden; foreign, hostile, it neither hopes for nor promises anything; when it recovers its equilibrium and vitality, the subject at once recognises it as his and through it he transcends towards others.

For the girl, erotic transcendence consists in making herself prey in order to make a catch. She becomes an object; and she grasps herself as object; she is surprised to discover this new aspect of her being: it seems to her that she has been doubled; instead of coinciding exactly with her self, here she is existing *outside* of her self. Thus in Rosamond Lehmann's *Invitation to the Waltz*, Olivia discovers an unknown face in the mirror: it is she-object suddenly rising up opposite herself; she experiences a quickly fading but upsetting emotion:

Nowadays a peculiar emotion accompanied the moment of looking into the mirror: fitfully, rarely a stranger might emerge: a new self.

It had happened two or three times already . . . She looked in
the glass and saw herself . . . Well, what was it? . . . But this was
something else. This was a mysterious face; both dark and glowing;
hair tumbling down, pushed back and upwards, as if in currents of
fierce energy. Was it the frock that did it? Her body seemed to
assemble itself harmoniously within it, to become centralised, to
expand, both static and fluid; alive. It was the portrait of a young
girl in pink. All the room's reflected objects seemed to frame, to
present her, whispering: Here are You . . .[28]

What astonishes Olivia are the promises she thinks she reads in this
image in which she recognises her childish dreams and which is herself;
but the girl also cherishes in her carnal presence this body that fascinates her as if it were someone else's. She caresses herself, she embraces
the curve of her shoulder, the bend of her elbow, she contemplates her
bosom, her legs; solitary pleasure becomes a pretext for reverie, in it she
seeks a tender self-possession. For the boy adolescent, there is an opposition between love of one's self and the erotic movement that thrusts
him towards the object to be possessed: his narcissism generally disappears at the moment of sexual maturity. Instead of the woman being a
passive object for the lover as for herself, there is a primitive blurring in
her eroticism. In one complex step, she aims for her body's glorification
through the homage of men for whom this body is intended; and it
would be a simplification to say that she wants to be beautiful in order
to charm, or that she seeks to charm to assure herself that she is beautiful: in the solitude of her room, in salons where she tries to attract the
gaze of others, she does not separate man's desire from the love of her
own self. This confusion is manifest in Marie Bashkirtseff.[29] It has already
been seen that late weaning disposed her more deeply than any other
child to wanting to be gazed at and valorised by others; from the age of
five until the end of adolescence, she devotes all her love to her image;
she madly admires her hands, her face, her grace, and she writes: 'I am
my own heroine.' She wants to become an opera singer to be *gazed
at* by a dazzled public so as to *look back* with a proud gaze; but this
'autism' expresses itself through romantic dreams; from the age of twelve,
she is in love: she wants to be loved, and the adoration that she seeks
to inspire only confirms that which she devotes to herself. She dreams
that the Duke of H., with whom she is in love without having ever
spoken to him, prostrates himself at her feet: 'You will be dazzled by
my splendour and you will love me . . . You are worthy only of such a

woman as I intend to be.' The same ambivalence is found in Natasha in *War and Peace*:[30]

> 'Even mama doesn't understand. It's astonishing how intelligent I am and how . . . sweet she is,' she went on, speaking of herself in the third person and imagining that it was some very intelligent man saying it about her, the most intelligent and best of men . . . 'There's everything in her, everything,' this man went on, 'she's extraordinarily intelligent, sweet, and then, too, pretty, extraordinarily pretty, nimble – she swims, she's an excellent horsewoman, and the voice! One may say, an astonishing voice!' . . .
>
> That morning she returned again to her favorite state of love and admiration for herself. 'How lovely that Natasha is!' she said of herself again in the words of some collective male third person. 'Pretty, a good voice, young, and doesn't bother anybody, only leave her in peace.'

Katherine Mansfield (in 'Prelude') has also described, in the character of Beryl, a case in which narcissism and the romantic desire for a woman's destiny are closely intermingled:

> In the dining-room, by the flicker of a wood fire, Beryl sat on a hassock playing the guitar . . . She played and sang half to herself, for she was watching herself playing and singing. The firelight gleamed on her shoes, on the ruddy belly of the guitar, and on her white fingers . . .
>
> 'If I were outside the window and looked in and saw myself I really would be rather struck,' thought she. Still more softly she played the accompaniment – not singing now but listening . . .
>
> '. . . The first time that I ever saw you, little girl – oh, you had no idea that you were not alone – you were sitting with your little feet upon a hassock, playing the guitar. God, I can never forget . . .' Beryl flung up her head and began to sing again:
>
> *Even the moon is aweary . . .*
>
> But there came a loud bang at the door. The servant girl's crimson face popped through . . . But no, she could not stand that fool of a girl. She ran into the dark drawing-room and began walking up and down . . . Oh, she was restless, restless. There was a mirror over the

mantel. She leaned her arms along and looked at her pale shadow in it. How beautiful she looked, but there was nobody to see, nobody . . .

Beryl smiled, and really her smile *was* so adorable that she smiled again.[31]

This cult of the self is not only expressed by the girl as the adoration of her physical person; she wishes to possess and praise her entire self. This is the purpose of these diaries into which she freely pours her whole soul: Marie Bashkirtseff's is famous and it is a model of the genre. The girl speaks to her notebook the way she used to speak to her dolls, as a friend, a confidante, and addresses it as if it were a person. Recorded in its pages is a truth hidden from parents, friends and teachers, and which enraptures the author when she is all alone. A twelve-year-old girl, who kept a diary until she was twenty, wrote the inscription:

> I am the little notebook
> Nice, pretty and discreet
> Tell me all your secrets
> I am the little notebook.*[32]

Others announce: 'To be read after my death' or 'To be burned when I die'. The little girl's sense of secrecy that developed at prepuberty only grows in importance. She closes herself up in fierce solitude: she refuses to reveal to those around her the hidden self that she considers to be her real self and that is in fact an imaginary character: she plays at being a dancer like Tolstoy's Natasha, or a saint like Marie Lenéru, or simply that singular wonder that is herself. There is still an enormous difference between this heroine and the objective face that her parents and friends recognise in her. She is also convinced that she is misunderstood: her relationship with herself becomes even more passionate: she becomes intoxicated with her isolation, feels different, superior, exceptional: she promises that the future will take revenge on the mediocrity of her present life. From this narrow and petty existence she escapes by dreams. She has always loved to dream: she gives herself up to this penchant more than ever; she uses poetic clichés to mask a universe that intimidates her, she sanctifies the male sex with moonlight, rose-coloured clouds, velvet nights; she turns her body into a marble, jasper or mother-of-pearl temple; she tells herself foolish fairy tales. She sinks so often

---

* Cited by Debesse in *The Adolescent Identity Crisis*.

into such nonsense because she has no grasp on the world; if she had to *act*, she would be forced to see clearly, whereas she can *wait* in the fog. The young man dreams as well: he dreams especially of adventures where he plays an active role. The girl prefers wonderment to adventure; she spreads a vague magic light on things and people. The idea of magic is that of a passive force; because she is doomed to passivity and yet wants power, the adolescent girl must believe in magic: her body's magic that will bring men under her yoke, the magic of destiny in general that will fulfil her without her having *to do* anything. As for the real world, she tries to forget it.

'In school I sometimes escape, I know not how, the subject being explained and fly away to dreamland . . .' writes a young girl.*[33] 'I am thus so absorbed in delightful chimeras that I completely lose the notion of reality. I am nailed to my bench and, when I awake, I am amazed to find myself within four walls.'

'I like to daydream much more than doing my verses,' writes another, 'to dream up nice, nonsensical stories or make up fairy tales when looking at mountains in the starlight. This is much more lovely because it is *more vague* and leaves the impression of repose, of refreshment.'

Daydreaming can take on a morbid form and invade the whole existence, as in the following case:†[34]

Marie B. . . . an intelligent and dreamy child, entering puberty at fourteen, had a psychic crisis with delusions of grandeur. 'She suddenly announces to her parents that she is the queen of Spain, assumes haughty airs, wraps herself in a curtain, laughs, sings, commands and orders.' For two years, this state is repeated during her periods, then for eight years she leads a normal life but is dreamy, loves luxury and often says bitterly, 'I'm an employee's daughter.' Toward twenty-three she grows apathetic, hateful of her surroundings and manifests ambitious ideas; she gets worse to the point of being interned in Sainte-Anne asylum, where she spends eight months; she returns to her family, where, for three years she remains in bed,

* Cited by Marguerite Evard, *The Adolescent Girl.*
† From Borel and Robin, *Morbid Reveries.* Cited by Minkowski in *Schizophrenia.*

'disagreeable, mean, violent, capricious, unoccupied and a burden to all those around her'. She is taken back to Sainte-Anne for good and does not come out again. She remains in bed, interested in nothing. At certain periods – seeming to correspond to menstrual periods – she gets up, drapes herself in her bedcovers, strikes theatrical attitudes, poses, smiles at doctors or looks at them ironically . . . Her comments often express a certain eroticism and her regal attitude expresses megalomaniac concepts. She sinks further and further into her dreamworld, where smiles of satisfaction appear on her face; she is careless of her appearance and even dirties her bed. 'She adorns herself with bizarre ornaments, shirtless, often naked, with a tinfoil diadem on her head and string or ribbon bracelets on her arms, her wrists, her shoulders, her ankles. Similar rings adorn her fingers.' Yet at times she makes lucid comments on her condition. 'I recall the crisis I had before. I knew deep down that it was not real. I was like a child who plays with dolls and who knows that her doll is not alive but wants to convince herself . . . I fixed my hair; I draped myself. I was having fun and then little by little, as if in spite of myself, I became bewitched; it was like a dream I was living . . . I was like an actress who would play a role. I was in an imaginary world. I lived several lives at a time and *in each life, I was the principal player* . . . Ah! I had so many different lives; once I married a handsome American who wore golden glasses . . . We had a grand hotel and a room for each of us. What parties I gave! . . . I lived in the days of cavemen . . . I was wild in those days. I couldn't count how many men I slept with. Here people are a little backward. They don't understand why I go naked with a gold bracelet on my thigh. I used to have friends that I liked a lot. We had parties at my house. There were flowers, perfume, ermine fur. My friends gave me art objects, statues, cars . . . When I get into my sheets naked, it reminds me of old times. *I admired myself in mirrors*, as an artist . . . In my bewitched state, I was anything I wanted. I was even foolish. I took morphine, cocaine. I had lovers . . . They came to my house at night. They came two at a time. They brought hairdressers and we looked at postcards.' She was also the mistress of two of her doctors. She says she had a three-year-old daughter. She has another six-year-old, very rich, who travels. Their father is a very chic man. 'There are ten other similar stories. Every one is a feigned existence that she lives in her imagination.'

Clearly this morbid daydreaming was essentially to satiate the girl's narcissism, as she feels that her life was inadequate and is afraid to confront the reality of her existence. Marie B. merely carried to the extreme a compensation process common to many adolescents.

Nonetheless, this self-provided solitary cult is not enough for the girl. To fulfil herself, she needs to exist in another consciousness. She often turns to her friends for help. When she was younger, her best girlfriend provided support for her to escape the maternal circle, to explore the world and in particular the sexual world; now her friend is both an object wrenching her to the limits of her self and a witness who restores that self to her. Some girls exhibit their nudity to each other, they compare their breasts: an example would be the scene in *Girls in Uniform*[35] that shows the daring games of boarding-school girls; they exchange random or particular caresses. As Colette recounts in *Claudine at School*[36] and Rosamond Lehmann less frankly in *Dusty Answer*,[37] nearly all girls have lesbian tendencies; these tendencies are barely distinguishable from narcissistic delights: in the other, it is the sweetness of her own skin, the form of her own curves that each of them covets; and vice versa, implicit in her self-adoration is the cult of femininity in general. Sexually, man is subject; men are thus normally separated by the desire that drives them towards an object different from themselves; but woman is an absolute object of desire; this is why 'special friendships' flourish in lycées, schools, boarding schools and workshops; some are purely spiritual and others deeply carnal. In the first case, it is mainly a matter of friends opening their hearts to each other, exchanging confidences; the most passionate proof of confidence is to show one's intimate diary to the chosen one; short of sexual embraces, friends exchange extreme signs of tenderness and often give to each other, in indirect ways, a physical token of their feelings: thus Natasha burns her arm with a red-hot ruler to prove her love for Sonia; mostly they call each other thousands of affectionate names and exchange ardent letters. Here is an example of a letter written by Emily Dickinson, a young New England Puritan, to a beloved female friend:

> I think of you all day, and dreamed of you last night . . . I was walking with you in the most wonderful garden, and helping you pick roses, and although we gathered with all our might, the basket was never full. And so all day I pray I may walk with you, and gather roses again, and as night draws on, it pleases me, and I count

impatiently the hours 'tween me and the darkness, and the dream
of you and the roses, and the basket never full . . .

In his work on the adolescent girl's soul,[38] Mendousse cites a great
number of similar letters:

My Dear Suzanne . . . I would have liked to copy here a few verses
from Song of Songs: how beautiful you are, my friend, how beautiful you are! Like the mystical bride, you were like the rose of
Sharon, the lily of the valley, and like her, you have been for me
more than an ordinary girl; you have been a symbol, the symbol
of all things beautiful and lofty . . . and because of this, pure
Suzanne, I love you with a pure and unselfish love that hints of the
religious.

Another confesses less lofty emotions in her diary:

I was there, my waist encircled by this little white hand, my hand
resting on her round shoulder, my arm on her bare, warm arm,
pressed against the softness of her breast, with her lovely mouth
before me, parted on her dainty teeth . . . I trembled and felt my
face burning.*

In her book *The Adolescent Girl*, Mme Evard also collected a great
number of these intimate effusions:

To my beloved fairy, my dearest darling. My lovely fairy. Oh! Tell
me that you still love me, tell me that for you I am still the devoted
friend. I am sad, I love you so, oh my L. . . . and I cannot speak to
you, tell you enough of my affection for you; there are no words
to describe my love. *Idolise* is a poor way to say what I feel; sometimes it seems that my heart will burst. To be loved by you is too
beautiful, I cannot believe it. *Oh my dear*, tell, will you love me
longer still?

It is easy to slip from these exalted affections into guilty juvenile
crushes; sometimes one of the two girlfriends dominates and exercises her power sadistically over the other; but often, they are reciprocal

* Cited by Mendousse, *The Adolescent Girl's Soul*.

loves without humiliation or struggle; the pleasure given and received remains as innocent as it was at the time when each one loved alone, without being doubled in a couple. But this very innocence is bland; when the adolescent girl decides to enter into life and becomes the Other, she hopes to rekindle the magic of the paternal gaze to her advantage; she demands the love and caresses of a divinity. She will turn to a woman less foreign and less fearsome than the male, but one who will possess male prestige: a woman who has a profession, who earns her living, who has a certain social base, will easily be as fascinating as a man: we know how many 'flames' are lit in schoolgirls' hearts for professors and tutors. In *Regiment of Women*,[39] Clemence Dane uses a chaste style to describe ardently burning passions. Sometimes the girl confides her great passion to her best friend; they even share it, adding spice to their experience. A schoolgirl writes to her best friend:

> I'm in bed with a cold, and can think only of Mlle X. . . . I never loved a teacher to this point. I already loved her a lot in my first year, but now it is real love. I think that I'm more passionate than you. I imagine kissing her; I half faint and thrill at the idea of seeing her when school begins.*

More often, she even dares admit her feeling to her idol herself:

> Dear Mademoiselle, I am in an indescribable state over you. When I do not see you, I would give the world to meet you; I think of you every moment. If I spot you, my eyes fill up with tears, I want to hide; I am so small, so ignorant in front of you. When you chat with me, I am embarrassed, moved, I seem to hear the sweet voice of a fairy and the humming of loving things, impossible to translate; I watch your slightest moves; I lose track of the conversation and mumble something stupid: you must admit, dear Mademoiselle, that this is all mixed up. I do see one thing clearly, that I love you from the depths of my soul.†

The headmistress of a professional school recounts:

---

* Cited by Marguerite Evard, *The Adolescent Girl*.
† Ibid.

I recall that, in my own youth, we fought over one of our young professors' lunch papers and paid up to twenty pfennigs to have it. Her used metro tickets were also objects of our collectors' rage.

Since she must play a masculine role, it is preferable for the loved woman not to be married; marriage does not always discourage the young admirer, but it interferes; she detests the idea that the object of her adoration could be under the control of a spouse or a lover. Her passions often unfold in secret, or at least on a purely platonic level; but the passage to a concrete eroticism is much easier here than if the loved object is masculine; even if she has had difficult experiences with friends her age, the feminine body does not frighten the girl; with her sisters or her mother, she has often experienced an intimacy where tenderness was subtly penetrated with sensuality, and when she is with the loved one she admires, slipping from tenderness to pleasure will take place just as subtly. When Dorothea Wieck kisses Herta Thiele on the lips in *Girls in Uniform*, this kiss is both maternal and sexual. Between women there is a complicity that disarms modesty; the excitement one arouses in the other is generally without violence; homosexual embraces involve neither defloration nor penetration: they satisfy infantile clitoral eroticism without demanding new and disquieting metamorphoses. The girl can realise her vocation as passive object without feeling deeply alienated. This is what Renée Vivien expresses in her verses, where she describes the relation of 'damned women' and their lovers:

> *Our bodies to theirs are a kindred mirror . . .*
> *Our lunar kisses have a pallid softness,*
> *Our fingers do not ruffle the down on a cheek,*
> *And we are able, when the sash becomes untied,*
> *To be at the same time lovers and sisters.*[*40]

And in these verses:

> *For we love gracefulness and delicacy,*
> *And my possession does not bruise your breasts . . .*
> *My mouth would not know how to bite your mouth roughly.*

> *My mouth will not bitterly bite your mouth.*[†41]

* *At the Sweet Hour of Hand in Hand.*
† *Sea Wakes.*

Through the poetic impropriety of the words 'breasts' and 'mouth', she clearly promises her friend not to brutalise her. And it is in part out of fear of violence and of rape that the adolescent girl often gives her first love to an older girl rather than to a man. The masculine woman reincarnates for her both the father and the mother: from the father she has authority and transcendence, she is the source and standard of values, she rises beyond the given world, she is divine; but she remains woman: whether she was too abruptly weaned from her mother's caresses or if, on the contrary, her mother pampered her too long, the adolescent girl, like her brothers, dreams of the warmth of the breast; in this flesh similar to hers she loses herself again in that immediate fusion with life that weaning destroyed; and through this foreign enveloping gaze, she overcomes the separation that individualises her. Of course, all human relationships entail conflicts; all love entails jealousies. But many of the difficulties that arise between the virgin and her first male love are smoothed away here. The homosexual experience can take the shape of a true love; it can bring to the girl so happy a balance that she will want to continue it, repeat it, and will keep a nostalgic memory of it; it can awaken or give rise to a lesbian vocation.* But most often, it will only represent a stage: its very facility condemns it. In the love that she declares to a woman older than herself, the girl covets her own future: she is identifying with an idol; unless this idol is exceptionally superior, she loses her aura quickly; when she begins to assert herself, the younger one judges and compares: the other, who was chosen precisely because she was close and unintimidating, is not *other* enough to impose herself for very long; the male gods are more firmly in place because their heaven is more distant. Her curiosity and her sensuality incite the girl to desire more aggressive embraces. Very often, she has envisaged, from the start, a homosexual adventure just as a transition, an initiation, a temporary situation; she acts out jealousy, anger, pride, joy and pain with the more or less admitted idea that she is imitating, without great risk, the adventures of which she dreams but that she does not yet dare, nor has had the occasion, to live. She is destined for man, she knows it, and she wants a normal and complete woman's destiny.

Man dazzles yet frightens her. To reconcile the contradictory feelings she has about him, she will dissociate in him the male that frightens her from the shining divinity whom she piously adores. Abrupt, awkward with her masculine acquaintances, she idolises distant Prince Charmings:

* See Chapter 4 of this volume.

movie actors whose pictures she pastes over her bed, heroes, living or dead but inaccessible, an unknown glimpsed by chance and whom she knows she will never meet again. Such loves raise no problems. Very often she approaches a socially prestigious or intellectual man who is physically unexciting: for example, an old slightly ridiculous professor; these older men emerge from a world beyond the world where the adolescent girl is enclosed, and she can secretly devote herself to them, consecrate herself to them as one consecrates oneself to God: such a gift is in no way humiliating, it is freely given since the desire is not carnal. The romantic woman in love freely accepts that the chosen one be unassuming, ugly, a little foolish: she then feels all the more secure. She pretends to deplore the obstacles that separate her from him; but in reality she has chosen him precisely because no real rapport between them is possible. Thus she can make of love an abstract and purely subjective experience, unthreatening to her integrity; her heart beats, she feels the pain of absence, the pangs of presence, vexation, hope, bitterness, enthusiasm, but not authentically; no part of her is engaged. It is amusing to observe that the idol chosen is all the more dazzling the more distant it is: it is convenient for the everyday piano teacher to be ridiculous and ugly; but if one falls in love with a stranger who moves in inaccessible spheres, it is preferable that he be handsome and masculine. The important thing is that, in one way or another, the sexual issue not be raised. These make-believe loves prolong and confirm the narcissistic attitude where eroticism appears only in its immanence, without real presence of the Other. Finding a pretext that permits her to elude concrete experiences, the adolescent girl often develops an intense imaginary life. She chooses to confuse her fantasies with reality. Among other examples, Helene Deutsch[*42] describes a particularly significant one: a pretty and seductive girl, who could have easily been courted, refused all relations with young people around her; but at the age of thirteen, in her secret heart, she had chosen to idolise a rather ugly seventeen-year-old boy who had never spoken to her. She got hold of a picture of him, wrote a dedication to herself on it, and for three years kept a diary recounting her imaginary experiences: they exchanged kisses and passionate embraces; there were sometimes crying scenes where she left with her eyes all red and swollen; then they were reconciled, and she sent herself flowers, and so on. When a move separated her from him, she wrote him letters she never sent him but that she answered herself.

* *The Psychology of Women.*

This story was most obviously a defence against real experiences that she feared.

This case is almost pathological. But it illustrates a normal process by magnifying it. Marie Bashkirtseff gives a gripping example of an imaginary sentimental existence. The Duke of H., with whom she claims to be in love, is someone to whom she has never spoken. What she really desires is to exalt herself; but being a woman, and especially in the period and class she belongs to, she had no chance of achieving success through an independent existence. At eighteen years of age, she lucidly notes: 'I write to C. that I would like to be a man. I know that I could be someone; but where can one go in skirts? Marriage is women's only career; men have thirty-six chances, women have but one, zero, like in the bank.' She thus needs a man's love; but to be able to confer a sovereign value on her, he must himself be a sovereign consciousness. 'Never will a man beneath my position be able to please me,' she writes. 'A rich and independent man carries pride and a certain comfortable air with him. Self-assurance has a certain triumphant aura. I love H.'s capricious air, conceited and cruel: something of Nero in him.' And further: 'This annihilation of the woman before the superiority of the loved man must be the greatest thrill of self-love that the superior woman can experience.' Thus narcissism leads to masochism: this liaison has already been seen in the child who dreams of Bluebeard, of Griselda, of the martyred saints. The self is constituted as for others, by others: the more powerful others are, the more riches and power the self has; captivating its master, it envelops in itself the virtues possessed by him; loved by Nero, Marie Bashkirtseff *would be* Nero; to annihilate oneself before others is to realise others at once in oneself and for oneself; in reality this dream of nothingness is an arrogant will to be. In fact, Bashkirtseff never met a man superb enough to alienate herself through him. It is one thing to kneel before a far-off god shaped by one's self and another thing to give one's self over to a flesh-and-blood man. Many girls long persist in stubbornly following their dream throughout the real world: they seek a male who seems superior to all others in his position, his merits, his intelligence; they want him to be older than themselves, already having carved out a place for himself in the world, enjoying authority and prestige; fortune and fame fascinate them: the chosen one appears as the absolute Subject who by his love will convey to them his splendour and his indispensability. His superiority idealises the love that the girl brings to him: it is not only because he is a male that she wants to give herself to him, it is because he is *this* elite being. 'I would like giants and all I find is men,' a friend once said to me. In the name of these high standards, the girl disdains too-ordinary suitors and eludes the problem of sexuality. In her dreams and without risk, she cherishes an image of herself that enchants her as an image, though she has no intention of conforming to it. Thus, Maria Le Hardouin explains that she gets pleasure from seeing herself as a victim, ever devoted to a man, when she is really authoritarian.*[43]

Out of a kind of modesty, I could never in reality express my nature's hidden tendencies that I lived so deeply in my dreams. As I learned to know myself, I am in fact authoritarian, violent and deeply incapable of flexibility.

Always obeying a need to suppress myself, I sometimes imagined that I was an admirable woman, living only by duty, madly in love with a man whose every wish I endeavoured to anticipate. We struggled within an ugly world of needs. He killed himself working and came home at night pale and undone. I lost my sight mending his clothes next to a lightless window. In a narrow smoky kitchen, I cooked some miserable meals. Sickness ceaselessly threatened our only child with death. Yet a sweet, crucified smile was always on my lips and my eyes always showed that unbearable expression of silent courage that in reality I could never stand without disgust.

Beyond these narcissistic gratifications, some girls do concretely find the need for a guide, a master. From the time they escape their parents' hold, they find themselves encumbered by an autonomy that they are not used to; they only know how to make negative use of it; they fall into caprice and extravagance; they want to give up their freedom. The story of the young and capricious girl, rebellious and spoiled, who is tamed by the love of a sensible man, is a standard of cheap literature and cinema: it is a cliché that flatters both men and women. It is the story, among others, told by Mme de Ségur in *Such an Adorable Child!*[44] As a child, Gisèle, disappointed by her overly indulgent father, becomes attached to a severe old aunt; as a girl, she comes under the influence of an irritable young man, Julien, who judges her harshly, humiliates her and tries to reform her; she marries a rich, characterless duke with whom she is extremely unhappy, and when, as a widow, she accepts the demanding love of her mentor, she finally finds joy and wisdom. In Louisa

* *The Black Sail.*

May Alcott's *Good Wives,* independent Jo begins to fall in love with her future husband because he seriously reproaches her for an imprudent act; he also scolds her, and she rushes to excuse herself and submit to him. In spite of the edgy pride of American women, Hollywood films have hundreds of times presented *enfants terribles* tamed by the healthy brutality of a lover or husband: a couple of slaps, even a good spanking, seem to be a good means of seduction. But in reality, the passage from ideal love to sexual love is not so simple. Many women carefully avoid approaching the object of their passion through more or less admitted fear of disappointment. If the hero, the giant or the demigod responds to the love he inspires and transforms it into a real-life experience, the girl panics; her idol becomes a male she shies away from, disgusted. There are flirtatious adolescents who do everything in their power to seduce a seemingly 'interesting' or 'fascinating' man, but paradoxically they recoil if he manifests too vivid an emotion in return; he was attractive because he seemed inaccessible: in love, he becomes commonplace. 'He's just a man like the others.' The young woman blames him for her disgrace; she uses this pretext to refuse physical contacts that shock her virgin sensibilities. If the girl gives in to her 'Ideal one', she remains unmoved in his arms and 'it happens', says Stekel,*[45] 'that obsessed girls commit suicide after such scenes where the whole construction of amorous imagination collapses because the Ideal one is seen in the form of a "brutal animal".' The taste for the impossible often leads the girl to fall in love with a man when he begins to court one of her friends, and very often she chooses a married man. She is readily fascinated by a Don Juan; she dreams of submitting and attaching herself to this seducer that no woman has ever held on to, and she kindles the hope of reforming him: but in fact, she knows she will fail in her undertaking and this is the reason for her choice. Some girls end up for ever incapable of knowing real and complete love. They will search all their lives for an ideal impossible to reach.

But there is a conflict between the girl's narcissism and the experiences for which her sexuality destines her. The woman only accepts herself as the inessential on the condition of finding herself the essential once again by abdicating. In making herself object, suddenly she has become an idol in which she proudly recognises herself; but she refuses the implacable dialectic that makes her return to the inessential. She wants to be a fascinating treasure, not a thing to be taken. She loves to

* *Frigidity in Woman.*

seem like a marvellous fetish, charged with magic emanations, not to see herself as flesh that lets herself be seen, touched, bruised: thus man prizes the woman prey, but flees the ogress Demeter.

Proud to capture masculine interest and to arouse admiration, woman is revolted by being captured in return. With puberty she learned shame: and shame is mixed with her coquetry and vanity, men's gazes flatter and hurt her at the same time; she would only like to be seen to the extent that she shows herself: eyes are always too penetrating. Hence the inconsistency disconcerting to men: she displays her décolletage and her legs, but she blushes and becomes vexed when someone looks at her. She enjoys provoking the male, but if she sees she has aroused his desire, she backs off in disgust: masculine desire is an offence as much as a tribute; in so far as she feels responsible for her charm, as she feels she is using it freely, she is enchanted with her victories: but while her features, her forms, her flesh are given and endured, she wants to keep them from this foreign and indiscreet freedom that covets them. Here is the deep meaning of this primal modesty, which interferes in a disconcerting way with the boldest coquetry. A little girl can be surprisingly audacious because she does not realise that her initiatives reveal her in her passivity: as soon as she sees this, she becomes indignant and angry. Nothing is more ambiguous than a look; it exists at a distance, and that distance makes it seem respectable: but insidiously it takes hold of the perceived image. The unripe woman struggles with these traps. She begins to let herself go, but just as quickly she tenses up and kills the desire in herself. In her as yet uncertain body, the caress is felt at times as an unpleasant tickling, at times as a delicate pleasure; a kiss moves her first, and then abruptly makes her laugh; she follows each surrender with a revolt; she lets herself be kissed, but then she wipes her mouth noticeably; she is smiling and caring, then suddenly ironic and hostile; she makes promises and deliberately forgets them. In such a way, Mathilde de La Mole is seduced by Julien's beauty and rare qualities, desirous to reach an exceptional destiny through her love, but fiercely refusing the domination of her own senses and that of a foreign consciousness; she goes from servility to arrogance, from supplication to scorn; she demands an immediate payback for everything she gives. Such is also Monique whose profile is drawn by Marcel Arland, who confuses excitement with sin, for whom love is a shameful abdication, whose blood is hot but who detests this ardour and who, while bridling, submits to it.

The 'unripe fruit' defends herself against man by exhibiting a childish and perverse nature. This is often how the girl has been described:

half-wild, half-dutiful. Colette, for one, depicted her in *Claudine at School* and also in *Green Wheat*[46] in the guise of the seductive Vinca. She maintains an interest in the world around her, over which she reigns sovereign; but she is also curious and feels a sensual and romantic desire for man. Vinca gets scratched by brambles, fishes for prawns and climbs trees and yet she quivers when her friend Phil touches her hand; she knows the agitation of the body becoming flesh, the first revelation of woman as woman; aroused, she begins to want to be pretty: at times she does her hair, she uses makeup, dresses in gauzy organdie, she takes pleasure in appearing attractive and seductive; she also wants to exist *for herself* and not only *for others*, at other times, she throws on old formless dresses, unbecoming trousers; there is a whole part of her that criticises seduction and considers it as giving in: so she purposely lets herself be seen with ink-stained fingers, messy hair, dirty. This rebelliousness gives her a clumsiness she resents: she is annoyed by it, blushes, becomes even more awkward and is horrified by these aborted attempts at seduction. At this point, the girl no longer wants to be a child, but she does not accept becoming an adult, and she blames herself for her childishness and then for her female resignation. She is in a state of constant denial.

This is the characteristic trait of the girl and gives the key to most of her behaviour; she does not accept the destiny nature and society assign to her; and yet, she does not actively repudiate it: she is too divided internally to enter into combat with the world; she confines herself to escaping reality or to contesting it symbolically. Each of her desires is matched by an anxiety: she is eager to take possession of her future, but she fears breaking with her past; she would like 'to have' a man, she balks at being his prey. And behind each fear hides a desire: rape is abhorrent to her but she aspires to passivity. Thus she is doomed to bad faith and all its ruses; she is predisposed to all sorts of negative obsessions that express the ambivalence of desire and anxiety.

One of the most common forms of adolescent contestation is giggling. High school girls and shopgirls burst into laughter while recounting love or risqué stories, while talking about their flirtations, meeting men, or seeing lovers kiss; I have known schoolgirls going to lovers' lane in the Luxembourg Gardens just to laugh; and others going to the Turkish baths to make fun of the fat women with sagging stomachs and hanging breasts they saw there; scoffing at the female body, ridiculing men, laughing at love, are ways of disavowing sexuality: this laughter that defies adults is a way of overcoming one's own embarrassment; one plays with images and words to kill the dangerous magic of them: for example, I saw twelve-year-old students burst out laughing when they saw a Latin text with the word *femur*. If in addition the girl lets herself be kissed and petted, she will get her revenge in laughing outright at her partner or with friends. I remember in a train compartment one night two girls being fondled one after the other by a travelling salesman overjoyed with his good luck: between each session they laughed hysterically, reverting to the behaviour of the awkward age in a mixture of sexuality and shame. Girls giggle and they also resort to language to help them: some use words whose coarseness would make their brothers blush; half ignorant, they are even less shocked by those expressions that do not evoke very precise images; the aim, of course, is to prevent these images from taking shape, at least to defuse them; the dirty stories high school girls tell each other are less to satisfy sexual instincts than to deny sexuality: they only want to consider the humorous side, like a mechanical or almost surgical operation. But like laughter, the use of obscene language is not only a protest: it is also a defiance of adults, a sort of sacrilege, a deliberately perverse kind of behaviour. Rebuffing nature and society, the girl nettles and challenges them by many oddities. She often has food manias: she eats pencil lead, sealing wax, bits of wood, live prawns, she swallows dozens of aspirins at a time, or she even ingests flies or spiders; I knew a girl – very obedient otherwise – who made horrible mixtures of coffee and white wine that she forced herself to swallow; other times she ate sugar soaked in vinegar; I saw another chewing determinedly into a white worm found in lettuce. All children endeavour to experience the world with their eyes, their hands and more intimately their mouths and stomachs: but at the awkward age, the girl takes particular pleasure in exploring what is indigestible and repugnant. Very often, she is attracted by what is 'disgusting'. One of them, quite pretty and attractive when she wanted to be and carefully dressed, proved really fascinated by everything that seemed 'dirty' to her: she touched insects, looked at dirty sanitary napkins, sucked the blood of her cuts. Playing with dirty things is obviously a way of overcoming disgust; this feeling becomes much more important at puberty: the girl is disgusted by her too-carnal body, by menstrual blood, by adults' sexual practices, by the male she is destined for; she denies it by indulging herself specifically in the familiarity of everything that disgusts her. 'Since I have to bleed each month, I prove that my blood does not scare me by drinking that of my cuts. Since I will have to submit myself to a revolting test, why not eat a white worm?' This attitude is affirmed more clearly in self-mutilation, so frequent at this age. The girl gashes her thigh with a razor, burns herself with cigarettes, cuts and scratches herself; so as not to go to a boring garden party, a girl during my youth cut her foot with an axe and had to spend six weeks in bed. These sadomasochistic practices are both an anticipation of the sexual experience and a revolt against it; girls have to undergo these tests, hardening themselves to all possible ordeals and rendering them harmless, including the wedding night. When she puts a slug on her chest, when she swallows a bottle of aspirin, when she wounds herself, the girl is defying her future lover: you will never inflict on me anything more horrible than I inflict on myself. These are morose and haughty initiations in sexual adventure. Destined to be a passive prey, she claims her freedom right up to submitting to pain and disgust. When she inflicts the cut of the knife, the burning of a coal on herself, she is protesting against the penetration that deflowers her: she protests by nullifying it. Masochistic, since she welcomes the pain caused by her behaviour, she is above all sadistic: as autonomous subject, she beats, scorns and tortures this dependent flesh, this flesh condemned to submission that she detests but from which she does not want to separate herself. Because, in all these situations, she does not choose authentically to reject her destiny. Sadomasochistic crazes imply a fundamental bad faith: if the girl indulges in them, it means she accepts, through her rejections, her future as woman; she would not mutilate her flesh with hatred if first she did not recognise herself as flesh. Even her violent outbursts arise from a situation of resignation. When a boy revolts against his father or against the world, he engages in effective violence; he picks a quarrel with a friend, he fights, he affirms himself as subject with his fists: he imposes himself on the world, he goes beyond it. But affirming herself, imposing herself, are forbidden to the adolescent girl, and that is what fills her heart with revolt: she hopes neither to change the world nor to emerge from it; she knows or at least believes, and perhaps even wishes, herself tied up: she can only destroy; there is despair in her rage; during a frustrating evening, she breaks glasses, windows, vases: it is not to overcome her lot; it is only a symbolic protest. The girl rebels against her future enslavement through her present powerlessness; and her vain outbursts, far from freeing her from her bonds, often merely restrict her even more. Violence against herself or the universe around her always has a negative character: it is more spectacular than effective. The boy who climbs rocks or fights with his friends regards physical pain, the injuries and the bumps, as an insignificant consequence of the positive activities he indulges in; he neither seeks nor flees them for themselves (except if an inferiority complex puts him in a situation similar to women's). The girl watches herself suffer: she seeks in her own heart the taste of violence and revolt rather than being concerned with their results. Her perversity stems from the fact that she remains stuck in the childish universe from which she cannot or does not really want to escape; she struggles in her cage rather than seeking to get out of it; her attitudes are negative, reflexive and symbolic. This perversity can take disturbing forms. Many young virgins are kleptomaniacs; kleptomania is a very ambiguous 'sexual sublimation'; the desire to transgress laws, to violate a taboo, the giddiness of the dangerous and forbidden act are certainly essential in the girl thief: but there is a double face. Taking objects without having the right is affirming one's autonomy arrogantly, it is putting oneself forward as subject facing the things stolen and the society that condemns stealing, and it is rejecting the established order as well as defying its guardians; but this defiance also has a masochistic side; the thief is fascinated by the risk she runs, by the abyss she will be thrown into if she is caught; it is the danger of being caught that gives such a voluptuous attraction to the act of taking; thus looked at with blame, or with a hand placed on her shoulder in shame, she can realise herself as object totally and without recourse. Taking without being taken in the anguish of becoming prey is the dangerous game of adolescent feminine sexuality. All perverse or illegal conduct found in girls has the same meaning. Some specialise in sending anonymous letters, others find pleasure in mystifying those around them: one fourteen-year-old persuaded a whole village that a house was haunted by spirits. They simultaneously enjoy the clandestine exercise of their power, disobedience, defiance of society, and the risk of being exposed; this is such an important element of their pleasure that they often unmask themselves, and they even sometimes accuse themselves of faults or crimes they have not committed. It is not surprising that the refusal to become object leads to constituting oneself as object: this process is common to all negative obsessions. It is in a single movement that in a hysterical paralysis the ill person fears paralysis, desires it and brings it on: he is cured from it only by no longer thinking about it; likewise with psychasthenic tics. The depth of the girl's bad faith is what links her to these types of neuroses: manias, tics, conspiracies, perversities; many neurotic symptoms are found in her due to this ambivalence of desire and anxiety that has been pointed out. It is quite common, for example, for her to 'run away'; she goes away at random, she wanders far from her father's house and two or three days later she comes back by herself. It is not a real departure or a real act of rupture with the family; it is mere playacting and the girl is often totally disconcerted if it is suggested that she leave her circle definitively: she wants to leave while not wanting to at the same time. Running away is sometimes linked to fantasies of prostitution: the girl dreams she is a prostitute, she plays this role more or less timidly; she wears excessive makeup, she leans out the window and winks at passersby; in some cases, she leaves the house and carries the drama so far that it becomes confused with reality. Such conduct often expresses a disgust with sexual desire, a feeling of guilt: since I have these thoughts, these appetites, I am no better than a prostitute, I am one, thinks a girl. Sometimes, she attempts to free herself: let's get it over with, let's go to the limit, she says to herself; she wants to prove to herself that sexuality is of little importance by giving herself to the first one. At the same time, such an attitude is often a manifestation of hostility to the mother, either that the girl is horrified by her austere virtue or that she suspects her mother of being, herself, of easy morality; or she holds a grudge against her father who has shown himself too indifferent. In any case, in this obsession – as in the fantasies of pregnancy about which we have already spoken and that are often associated with it – there is the meeting of this inextricable confusion of revolt and complicity, characterised by psychasthenic dizziness. It is noteworthy that in all these behaviours the girl does not seek to go beyond the natural and social order, she does not attempt to push back the limits of the possible or to effectuate a transmutation of values; she settles for manifesting her revolt within an established world where boundaries and laws are preserved; this is the often-defined 'devilish' attitude, implying a basic deception: the good is recognised so that it can be trampled upon, the rule is set so that it can be violated, the sacred is respected so that it is possible to perpetrate the sacrileges. The girl's attitude is defined essentially by the fact that in the agonising shadows of bad faith, she refuses the world and her own destiny at the same time as she accepts them.

However, she does not confine herself to contesting negatively the situation imposed on her; she also tries to compensate for its insufficiencies. Although the future frightens her, the present dissatisfies her; she hesitates to become woman; she frets at still being only a child; she has already left her past; she is not yet committed to a new life. She is occupied but she does not *do* anything; because she does not do anything, she *has* nothing, she *is nothing*. She tries to fill this void by playacting and mystifications. She is criticised for being devious, a liar, and troublesome. The truth is she is doomed to secrets and lies. At sixteen, a woman has already gone through disturbing experiences: puberty, menstrual periods, awakening of sexuality, first arousals, first passions, fears, disgust and ambiguous experiences: she has hidden all these things in her heart; she has learned to guard her secrets preciously. The mere fact of having to hide her sanitary napkins and of concealing her periods inclines her to lies. In the short story 'Old Mortality', Katherine Anne Porter recounts that young American women from the South, around 1900, made themselves ill by swallowing mixtures of salt and lemon to stop their periods when going to balls: they were afraid that the young men would recognise their state by the bags under their eyes, by contact with their hands, by a smell perhaps, and this idea upset them. It is difficult to play the idol, the fairy or the remote princess when one feels a bloody piece of material between one's legs and more generally, when one knows the primal misery of being a body. Modesty, a spontaneous refusal to let oneself be grasped as flesh, comes close to hypocrisy. But above all, the adolescent girl is condemned to the lie of pretending to be object, and a prestigious one, while she experiences herself as an uncertain, dispersed existence, knowing her failings. Makeup, false curls, corsets, padded bras, are lies; the face itself becomes a mask: spontaneous expressions are produced artfully, a wondrous passivity is imitated; there is nothing more surprising than suddenly discovering in the exercise of one's feminine functions a physiognomy with which one is familiar; its transcendence denies itself and imitates immanence; one's eyes no longer perceive, they reflect; one's body no longer lives: it waits; every gesture and smile becomes an appeal; disarmed, available, the girl is nothing but a flower offered, a fruit to be picked. Man encourages her in these lures by demanding to be lured: then he gets irritated, he accuses. But for the guileless girl, he has nothing but indifference and even hostility. He is seduced only by the one who sets traps for him; offered, she is still she who stalks her prey; her passivity takes the form of an undertaking, she makes her weakness a tool of her strength; since she is forbidden to attack outright, she is reduced to manoeuvres and calculations; and it is in her interest to appear freely given; therefore, she will be criticised for being perfidious and treacherous, and she is. But it is true that she is obliged to offer man the myth of her submission because he insists on dominating. And can one demand that she stifle her most essential claims? Her complaisance can only be perverted right from the outset. Besides, she cheats not only out of concerted, deliberate ruse. Because all roads are barred to her, because she cannot *do*, because she must *be*, a curse weighs on her. As a child, she played at being a dancer or a saint; later, she plays at being herself; what is really the truth? In the area in which she has been shut up, this is a word without sense. Truth is reality unveiled, and unveiling occurs through acts: but she does not act. The romances she tells herself about herself – and that she also often tells others – seem better ways of expressing the possibilities she feels in herself than the plain account of her daily life. She is unable to take stock of herself: so she consoles herself by playacting; she embodies a character she seeks to give importance to; she tries to stand out by extravagant behaviour because she does not have the right to distinguish herself in specific activities. She knows she is without responsibilities, insignificant in this world of men: she makes trouble because she has nothing else important to do. Giraudoux's Electra is a woman who makes trouble, because it is up to Orestes alone to accomplish a real murder with a real sword. Like the child, the girl wears herself out in scenes and rages, she makes herself ill, she manifests signs of hysteria to try to attract attention and be someone who *counts*. She interferes in the destiny of others so that she can count; she uses any weapon she can; she tells secrets, she invents others, she betrays, she calumniates; she needs tragedy around her to feel alive since she finds no support in her own life. She is unpredictable for the same reason; the fantasies we form and the images by which we are lulled are contradictory: only action unifies the diversity of time. The girl does not have a real will but has desires, and she jumps from one to the other at random. What makes her flightiness sometimes dangerous is that at every moment, committing herself in dream only, she commits herself wholly. She puts herself on a level of intransigence and perfection; she has a taste for the definitive and absolute: if she cannot control the future, she wants to attain the eternal. 'I will never give up. I want everything always. I need to prefer my life in order to accept it,' writes Marie Lenéru. So echoes Anouilh's Antigone: 'I want everything, immediately.' This childish imperialism can only be found in an individual who dreams his destiny: dreams abolish time and obstacles, they need to be exaggerated to compensate for the small amount of reality; whoever has authentic projects knows a finitude that is the gauge of one's concrete power. The girl wants to receive *everything* because there is *nothing* that depends on her. That is where her character of *enfant terrible* comes from, faced with adults and man in particular. She does not accept the limitations an individual's insertion in the real world imposes; she defies him to go beyond them. Thus Hilda* expects Solness to give her a kingdom: as she is not the one who has to conquer it, she wants it without limits; she demands

* See Ibsen, *The Master Builder*.

that he build the highest tower ever built and that he 'climb as high as he builds': he hesitates to climb, because he is afraid of heights; she who remains on the ground and looks on denies contingency and human weakness; she does not accept that reality imposes a limit on her dreams of grandeur. Adults always seem mean and cautious to the girl who stops at nothing because she has nothing to lose; imagining herself taking the boldest risks, she dares them to match her in reality. Unable to put herself to the test, she invests herself with the most astonishing qualities without fear of being contradicted.

However, her uncertainty also stems from this lack of control; she dreams she is infinite; she is nevertheless alienated in the character she offers for the admiration of others; it depends on these foreign consciousnesses: this double she identifies with herself but to whose presence she passively submits is dangerous for her. This explains why she is touchy and vain. The slightest criticism or gibe destabilises her. Her worth does not derive from her own effort but from a fickle approbation. This is not defined by individual activities but by general reputation; it seems to be quantitatively measurable; the price of merchandise decreases when it becomes too common: thus the girl is only rare, exceptional, remarkable or extraordinary if no other one is. Her female companions are rivals or enemies; she tries to denigrate, to deny them; she is jealous and hostile.

It is clear that all the faults for which the adolescent girl is reproached merely express her situation. It is a painful condition to know one is passive and dependent at the age of hope and ambition, at the age where the will to live and to take a place in the world intensifies; woman learns at this conquering age that no conquest is allowed her, that she must disavow herself, that her future depends on men's good offices. New social and sexual aspirations are awakened but they are condemned to remain unsatisfied; all her vital or spiritual impulses are immediately barred. It is understandable that she should have trouble establishing her balance. Her erratic mood, her tears and her nervous crises are less the result of a physiological fragility than the sign of her deep maladjustment.

However, this situation that the girl flees by a thousand inauthentic paths is also one that she sometimes assumes authentically. Her shortcomings make her irritating: but her unique virtues sometimes make her astonishing. Both have the same origin. From her rejection of the world, from her unsettled waiting, and from her nothingness, she can create a springboard for herself and emerge then in her solitude and her freedom.

The girl is secretive, tormented, in the throes of difficult conflicts. This complexity enriches her; her interior life develops more deeply than her brothers'; she is more attentive to her heart's desires that thus become more subtle, more varied; she has more psychological sense than boys turned towards external goals. She is able to give weight to these revolts that oppose her to the world. She avoids the traps of seriousness and conformism. The concerted lies of her circle meet with her irony and clear-sightedness. She tests her situation's ambiguity on a daily basis: beyond sterile protest, she can have the courage to throw into question established optimism, preconceived values, and hypocritical and re-assuring morality. Such is Maggie, the moving example given in *The Mill on the Floss*, in which George Eliot embodied the doubts and courageous rebellions of her youth against Victorian England; the heroes – particularly Tom, Maggie's brother – stubbornly affirm conventional wisdom, immobilising morality in formal rules: Maggie tries to reintroduce a breath of life, she overturns them, she goes to the limits of her solitude and emerges as a pure freedom beyond the fossilised male universe.

The adolescent girl barely finds anything but a negative use of this freedom. But her openness can engender a precious faculty of recep-tivity; she will prove to be devoted, attentive, understanding and loving. Rosamond Lehmann's heroines are marked by this docile generosity. In *Invitation to the Waltz*, Olivia, still shy and gauche, and barely interested in her appearance, is seen scrutinising this world she will enter tomorrow with excited curiosity. She listens with all her heart to her succession of dancers, she endeavours to answer them according to their wishes, she is their echo, she vibrates, she accepts everything that is offered. Judy, the heroine of *Dusty Answer*, has the same endearing quality. She has not relinquished childhood joys; she likes to bathe naked at night in the park river; she loves nature, books, beauty and life; she does not cultivate a narcissistic cult; without lies, without egotism, she does not look for an exaltation of self through men: her love is a gift. She bestows it on any being who seduces her, man or woman, Jennifer or Roddy. She gives herself without losing herself: she leads an independent student life; she has her own world, her own projects. But what distinguishes her from a boy is her attitude of expectation, her tender docility. In a subtle way, she is, in spite of everything, destined to the Other: the Other has a marvellous dimension in her eyes to the point that she is in love with all the young men of the neighbouring family, their house, their sister and their universe, all at the same time; it is not as a friend, it is as Other that Jennifer fascinates her. And she charms Roddy and his cousins by her capacity to yield to them, to shape herself to their desires; she is patience, sweetness, acceptance and silent suffering.

Different but also captivating in the way she welcomes into her heart those she cherishes, Tessa, in Margaret Kennedy's *The Constant Nymph*, is simultaneously spontaneous, wild and giving. She refuses to abdicate anything of herself: finery, makeup, disguises, hypocrisy, acquired charms, caution and female submission are repugnant to her; she desires to be loved but not behind a mask; she yields to Lewis's moods, but without servility; she understands him, she vibrates in unison with him; but if they ever argue, Lewis knows that caresses will not subdue her: while authoritarian and vain Florence lets herself be conquered by kisses, Tessa succeeds in the extraordinary accomplishment of remaining free in her love, allowing her to love without either hostility or pride. Her nature has all the lures of artifice; to please, she never degrades herself, never lowers herself or locks herself in as object. Surrounded by artists who have committed their whole existence to musical creation, she does not feel this devouring demon within her; she wholly endeavours to love, understand and help them: she does it effortlessly, out of a tender and spontaneous generosity, which is why she remains perfectly autonomous even in the instances in which she forgets herself in favour of others. Thanks to this pure authenticity, she is spared the conflicts of adolescence; she can suffer from the world's harshness, she is not divided within herself; she is harmonious both as a carefree child and as a very wise woman. The sensitive and generous girl, receptive and ardent, is very ready to become a great lover.

When not encountering love, she may encounter poetry. Because she does not act, she watches, she feels, she records; she responds deeply to a colour or a smile; because her destiny is scattered outside her, in cities already built, on mature men's faces, she touches and tastes both passionately and more gratuitously than the young man. As she is poorly integrated into the human universe, and has trouble adapting to it, she is, like the child, able to see it; instead of being interested only in her grasp of things, she focuses on their meaning; she perceives particular profiles, unexpected metamorphoses. She rarely feels a creative urge and all too often she lacks the techniques that would allow her to express herself; but in conversations, letters, literary essays and rough drafts, she does show an original sensibility. The girl throws herself passionately into things, because she is not yet mutilated in her transcendence; and the fact that she does not accomplish anything, that she is nothing, will make her drive even more fervent: empty and unlimited, what she will seek to reach from within her nothingness is All. That is why she will devote a special love to Nature: more than the adolescent boy, she worships it. Untamed and inhuman, Nature encompasses most obviously the totality of what is. The adolescent girl has not yet annexed any part of the universe: thanks to this impoverishment, the whole universe is her kingdom; when she takes possession of it, she also proudly takes possession of herself. Colette often recounted these youthful orgies:*

> For even then I so loved the dawn that my mother granted it to me as a reward. She used to agree to wake me at half-past three and off I would go, an empty basket on each arm, towards the kitchen-gardens that sheltered in the narrow bend of the river, in search of strawberries, blackcurrants, and hairy gooseberries.
>
> At half-past three everything slumbered still in a primal blue, blurred and dewy, and as I went down the sandy road the mist, grounded by its own weight, bathed first my legs, then my well-built little body, reaching at last my mouth and ears, and finally to that most sensitive part of all, my nostrils . . . It was on that road and at that hour that I first became aware of my own self, experienced an inexpressible state of grace, and felt one with the first breath of air that stirred, the first bird, and the sun so newly born that it still looked not quite round . . . I came back when the bell rang for the first Mass. But not before I had eaten my fill, not before I had described a great circle in the woods, like a dog out hunting on its own, and tasted the water of the two hidden springs which I worshipped.[47]

Mary Webb describes in *The House in Dormer Forest* the intense joys a girl can know in communion with a familiar landscape:

> When the atmosphere of the house became too thunderous and Amber's nerves were strained to breaking-point, she crept away to the upper woods . . . It seemed to her that while Dormer lived by law, the forest lived by impulse. Through a gradual awakening to natural beauty, she reached a perception of beauty peculiar to herself. She began to perceive analogies. Nature became for her, not a fortuitous assemblage of pretty things, but a harmony, a poem

---

* *Sido.*

solemn and austere . . . Beauty breathed there, light shone there that was not of the flower or the star. A tremor, mysterious and thrilling, seemed to run with the light . . . through the whispering forest . . . So her going out into the green world had in it something of a religious rite . . . On a still morning . . . she went up to the Birds' Orchard. She often did this before the day of petty irritation began . . . she found some comfort in the absurd inconsequence of the bird people . . . she came at last to the upper wood, and was instantly at grips with beauty. There was for her literally something of wrestling, of the mood which says: 'I will not let thee go until thou bless me' . . . Leaning against a wild pear tree, she was aware, by her inward hearing, of the tidal wave of sap that rose so full and strong that she could almost imagine it roaring like the sea. Then a tremor of wind shook the flowering tree-tops, and she awoke again to the senses, to the strangeness of these utterances of the leaves . . . Every petal, every leaf, seemed to be conning some memory of profundities whence it had come. Every curving flower seemed full of echoes too majestic for its fragility . . . A breath of scented air came from the hilltops and stole among the branches. That which had form, and knew the mortality which is in form, trembled before that which passed, formless and immortal . . . Because of it the place became no mere congregation of trees, but a thing fierce as stellar space . . . For it possesses itself forever in a vitality withheld, immutable. It was this that drew Amber with breathless curiosity into the secret haunts of nature. It was this that struck her now into a kind of ecstasy . . . [48]

Women as different as Emily Brontë and Anna de Noailles experienced similar fervour in their youth – and it continued throughout their lives.

The texts I have cited convincingly show the comfort the adolescent girl finds in fields and woods. In the paternal house reign mother, laws, custom and routine, and she wants to wrest herself from this past; she wants to become a sovereign subject in her own turn: but socially she only accedes to her adult life by becoming woman; she pays for her liberation with an abdication; but in the midst of plants and animals she is a human being; a subject, a freedom, she is freed both from her family and from males. She finds an image of the solitude of her soul in the secrecy of forests and the tangible figure of transcendence in the vast horizons of the plains; she is herself this limitless land, this summit jutting towards the sky; she can follow, she will follow, these roads that leave for an unknown future; sitting on the hilltop she dominates the riches of the world spread out at her feet, given to her; through the water's palpitations, the shimmering of the light, she anticipates the joys, tears and ecstasies that she does not yet know; the adventures of her own heart are confusedly promised her by ripples on the pond and patches of sun. Smells and colours speak a mysterious language but one word stands out with triumphant clarity: 'life'. Existence is not only an abstract destiny inscribed in town hall registers; it is future and carnal richness. Having a body no longer seems like a shameful failing; in these desires that the adolescent girl repudiates under the maternal gaze, she recognises the sap mounting in the trees; she is no longer cursed, she proudly claims her kinship with leaves and flowers; she rumples a corolla and she knows that a living prey will fill her empty hands one day. Flesh is no longer filth: it is joy and beauty. Merged with sky and heath, the girl is this vague breath that stirs up and kindles the universe, and she is every sprig of heather; an individual rooted in the soil and infinite consciousness, she is both spirit and life; her presence is imperious and triumphant like that of the earth itself.

Beyond Nature she sometimes seeks an even more remote and stunning reality; she is willing to lose herself in mystical ecstasies; in periods of faith many young female souls demanded that God fill the emptiness of their being; the vocations of Catherine of Siena and Teresa of Avila were revealed to them at a young age.* Joan of Arc was a girl. In other periods, humanity appears the supreme end; so the mystical impulse flows into defined projects; but it is also a youthful desire for the absolute that gave birth to the flame that nourished the lives of Mme Roland or Rosa Luxemburg. From her subjugation, her impoverishment, and the depths of her refusal, the girl can extract the most daring courage. She finds poetry; she finds heroism too. One of the ways of assuming the fact that she is poorly integrated into society is to go beyond its restricting horizons.

The richness and strength of their nature and fortunate circumstances have enabled some women to continue in their adult lives their passionate projects from adolescence. But these are exceptions. George Eliot had Maggie Tulliver and Margaret Kennedy had Tessa die for good reason. It was a bitter destiny that the Brontë sisters had. The girl is touching because she rises up against the world, weak and alone; but the world is too powerful; she persists in refusing it, she is broken. Belle de Zuylen,

---

* We will return to the specific characteristics of the feminine mystic.

who overwhelmed all of Europe with her mind's originality and caustic power, frightened all her suitors: her refusal to make concessions condemned her to long years of celibacy that weighed on her since she declared that the expression 'virgin and martyr' was a pleonasm. This stubbornness is rare. In the immense majority of cases, the girl is aware that the fight is much too unequal, and she ends up yielding. 'You will all die at fifteen,' writes Diderot to Sophie Volland. When the fight has only been – as happens most often – a symbolic revolt, defeat is certain. Demanding in dreams, full of hope but passive, the girl makes adults smile with pity; they doom her to resignation. And in fact, the rebellious and eccentric girl that we left is found two years later, calmer, ready to consent to her woman's life. This is the future Colette predicted for Vinca; this is how the heroines of Mauriac's early novels appear. The adolescent crisis is a type of 'work' similar to what Dr Lagache calls 'the work of mourning'. The girl buries her childhood slowly – this autonomous and imperious individual she has been – and she enters adult existence submissively.

Of course, it is not possible to establish defined categories based on age alone. Some women remain infantile their whole lives; the behaviours we have described are sometimes perpetuated to an advanced age. Nevertheless, on the whole, there is a big difference between the girlish fifteen-year-old and an older girl. The latter is adapted to reality; she scarcely advances on the imaginary level; she is less divided within herself than before. At about eighteen, Marie Bashkirtseff writes:

The more I advance in age towards the end of my youth, the more I am covered with indifference. Little agitates me and everything used to agitate me.

Irène Reweliotty comments:

To be accepted by men you have to think and act like them; if you don't they treat you like a black sheep and solitude becomes your lot. And I, now, I'm fed up with solitude and I want people not only around me but with me . . . Living now and no longer existing and waiting and dreaming and telling yourself everything within yourself, your mouth shut and your body motionless.

And further along:

> With so much flattery, wooing, and such, I become terribly ambitious. This is no longer the trembling, marvellous happiness of the fifteen-year-old. It is a kind of cold and hard intoxication to take my revenge on life, to climb. I flirt; I play at loving. I do not love . . . I gain in intelligence, in sangfroid, in ordinary lucidity. I lose my heart. It was as if it cracked . . . In two months, I left childhood behind.

Approximately the same sound comes from these secrets of a nineteen-year-old girl:*

> In the old days Oh! What a conflict against a mentality that seemed incompatible with this century and the appeals of this century itself! I now have a peaceful feeling. Each new big idea that enters me, instead of provoking a painful upheaval, a destruction, and an incessant reconstruction, adapts marvellously to what is already in me . . . Now I go seamlessly from theoretical thinking to daily life without attempting continuity.

The girl – unless she is particularly graceless – accepts her femininity in the end; and she is often happy to enjoy gratuitously the pleasures and triumphs she gets from settling definitively into her destiny; as she is not yet bound to any duty, irresponsible, available, for her the present seems neither empty nor disappointing since it is just one step; dressing and flirting still have the lightness of a game and her dreams of the future disguise their futility. This is how Virginia Woolf describes the impressions of a young coquette during a party:

> I feel myself shining in the dark. Silk is on my knee. My silk legs rub smoothly together. The stones of a necklace lie cold on my throat . . . I am arrayed, I am prepared . . . My hair is swept in one curve. My lips are precisely red. I am ready now to join men and women on the stairs, my peers. I pass them, exposed to their gaze, as they are to mine . . . I now begin to unfurl, in this scent, in this radiance, as a fern when its curled leaves unfurl . . . I feel a thousand capacities spring up in me. I am arch, gay, languid, melancholy

---

* Cited by Debesse in *Adolescent Identity Crisis*.

by turns; I am rooted, but I flow. All gold, flowing that way, I say to this one, 'Come' . . . He approaches. He makes towards me. This is the most exciting moment I have ever known. I flutter. I ripple . . . Are we not lovely sitting together here, I in my satin; he in black and white? My peers may look at me now. I look straight back at you, men and women. I am one of you. This is my world . . . The door opens. The door goes on opening. Now I think, next time it opens the whole of my life will be changed . . . The door opens. Come, I say to this one, rippling gold from head to heels. 'Come,' and he comes towards me.*[49]

But the more the girl matures, the more maternal authority weighs on her. If she leads a housekeeper's life at home, she suffers from being only an assistant, she would like to devote her work to her own home, to her own children. Often the rivalry with her mother worsens: in particular, the older daughter is irritated if younger brothers and sisters are born; she feels her mother 'has done her time' and it is up to her now to bear children, to reign. If she works outside the house, she suffers when she returns home from still being treated as a simple member of the family and not as an autonomous individual.

Less romantic than before, she begins to think much more of marriage than love. She no longer embellishes her future spouse with a prestigious halo: what she wishes for is to have a stable position in this world and to begin to lead her life as a woman. This is how Virginia Woolf describes the imaginings of a rich country girl:

For soon in the hot midday when the bees hum round the hollyhocks my lover will come. He will stand under the cedar tree. To his one word I shall answer my one word. What has formed in me I shall give him. I shall have children; I shall have maids in aprons; men with pitchforks; a kitchen where they bring the ailing lambs to warm in baskets, where the hams hang and the onions glisten. I shall be like my mother, silent in a blue apron locking up the cupboards.

A similar dream dwells in poor Prue Sarn:†

* *The Waves.*
† Mary Webb, *Precious Bane.*

It seemed such a terrible thing never to marry. All girls got married . . . And when girls got married, they had a cottage, and a lamp, maybe, to light when their man came home, or if it was only candles it was all one, for they could put them in the window, and he'd think 'There's my missus now, lit the candles!' And then one day Mrs Beguildy would be making a cot of rushes for 'em, and one day there'd be a babe in it, grand and solemn, and bidding letters sent round for the christening, and the neighbours coming round the babe's mother like bees round the queen. Often when things went wrong, I'd say to myself, 'N'er mind, Prue Sarn! There'll come a day when you'll be queen in your own skep.'[50]

For most older girls, whether they have a laborious or frivolous life, whether they be confined to the paternal household or partially get away from it, the conquest of a husband – or at the least a serious lover – turns into a more and more pressing enterprise. This concern is often harmful for feminine friendships. The 'best friend' loses her privileged place. The girl sees rivals more than partners in her companions. I knew one such girl, intelligent and talented but who had chosen to think herself a 'faraway princess': this is how she described herself in poems and literary essays; she sincerely admitted she did not remain attached to her childhood friends: if they were ugly and stupid, she did not like them; if seductive, she feared them. The impatient wait for a man, often involving manoeuvres, ruses and humiliations, blocks the girl's horizon; she becomes egotistical and hard. And if Prince Charming takes his time appearing, disgust and bitterness set in.

The girl's character and behaviour express her situation: if it changes, the adolescent girl's attitude also changes. Today, it is becoming possible for her to take her future in her hands, instead of putting it in those of the man. If she is absorbed by studies, sports, a professional training, or a social and political activity, she frees herself of the male obsession; she is less preoccupied by love and sexual conflicts. However, she has a harder time than the young man in accomplishing herself as an autonomous individual. I have said that neither her family nor customs assist her attempts. Besides, even if she chooses independence, she still makes a place in her life for the man, for love. She will often be afraid of missing her destiny as a woman if she gives herself over entirely to any undertaking. She does not admit this feeling to herself: but it is there, it distorts all her best efforts, it sets up limits. In any case, the woman who works wants to reconcile her success with purely feminine successes; that not only requires devoting considerable time to her appearance and beauty but also, what is more serious, implies that her vital interests are divided. Outside of his regular studies, the male student amuses himself by freely exercising his mind and from there emerge his best discoveries; the woman's daydreams are oriented in a different direction: she will think of her physical appearance, of man, of love, she will give the bare minimum to her studies, to her career, whereas in these areas nothing is as necessary as the superfluous. It is not a question of mental weakness, of a lack of concentration, but of a split in her interests that do not coincide well. A vicious circle is knotted here: people are often surprised to see how easily a woman gives up music, studies, or a job as soon as she has found a husband; this is because she had committed too little of herself to her projects to derive benefit from their accomplishment. Everything converges to hold back her personal ambition while enormous social pressure encourages her to find a social position and justification in marriage. It is natural that she should not seek to create her place in this world by and for herself or that she should seek it timidly. As long as perfect economic equality is not realised in society and as long as customs allow the woman to profit as wife and mistress from the privileges held by certain men, the dream of passive success will be maintained in her and will hold back her own accomplishments.

However the girl approaches her existence as an adult, her apprenticeship is not yet over. By small increments or bluntly, she has to undergo her sexual initiation. There are girls who refuse. If sexually difficult incidents marked their childhood, if an awkward upbringing has gradually rooted a horror of sexuality in them, they carry over their adolescent repugnance of men. There are also circumstances that cause some women to have an extended virginity in spite of themselves. But in most cases, the girl accomplishes her sexual destiny at a more or less advanced age. How she braves it is obviously closely linked to her whole past. But this is also a novel experience that presents itself in unforeseen circumstances and to which she freely reacts. This is the new stage we must now consider.

CHAPTER 3

Sexual Initiation

In a sense, woman's sexual initiation, like man's, begins in infancy. There is a theoretical and practical initiation period that follows continuously from the oral, anal and genital phases up to adulthood. But the young girl's erotic experiences are not a simple extension of her previous sexual activities; they are very often unexpected and brutal; they always constitute a new occurrence that creates a rupture with the past. While she is going through them, all the problems the girl faces are concentrated in an urgent and acute form. In some cases, the crisis is easily resolved; there are tragic situations where the crisis can only be resolved through suicide or madness. In any case, the way woman reacts to the experiences strongly affects her destiny. All psychiatrists agree on the extreme importance her erotic beginnings have for her: their repercussions will be felt for the rest of her life.

The situation is profoundly different here for man and woman from the biological, social and psychological points of view. For man, the passage from childhood sexuality to maturity is relatively simple: erotic pleasure is objectified; now, instead of being realised in his immanent presence, this erotic pleasure is intended for a transcendent being. The erection is the expression of this need; with penis, hands, mouth, with his whole body, the man reaches out to his partner, but he remains at the heart of this activity, as the subject generally does before the objects he perceives and the instruments he manipulates; he projects himself towards the other without losing his autonomy; feminine flesh is a prey for him and he seizes in woman the attributes his sensuality requires of any object; of course he does not succeed in appropriating them: at least he holds them; the embrace and the kiss imply a partial failure: but this very failure is a stimulant and a joy. The act of love finds its unity in its natural culmination: orgasm. Coitus has a specific physiological aim; in ejaculation the male releases burdensome secretions; after orgasm, the male feels complete relief regularly accompanied by pleasure. And, of

course, pleasure is not the only aim; it is often followed by disappointment: the need has disappeared rather than having been satisfied. In any
case, a definite act is consummated and the man's body remains intact:
the service he has rendered to the species becomes one with his own
pleasure. Woman's eroticism is far more complex and reflects the
complexity of her situation. It has been seen* that instead of integrating
forces of the species into her individual life, the female is prey to the
species, whose interests diverge from her own ends; this antinomy reaches
its height in woman; one of its manifestations is the opposition of two
organs: the clitoris and the vagina. At the infant stage, the former is the
centre of feminine eroticism: some psychiatrists uphold the existence of
vaginal sensitivity in little girls, but this is a very inaccurate opinion; at
any rate, it would have only secondary importance. The clitoral system
does not change with adulthood† and woman preserves this erotic
autonomy her whole life; like the male orgasm, the clitoral spasm is a
kind of detumescence that occurs quasi-mechanically; but it is only indirectly linked to normal coitus, it plays no role whatsoever in procreation.
The woman is penetrated and impregnated through the vagina; it
becomes an erotic centre uniquely through the intervention of the male,
and this always constitutes a kind of rape. In the past, a woman was
snatched from her childhood universe and thrown into her life as a wife
by a real or simulated rape; this was an act of violence that changed the
girl into a woman: it is also referred to as 'ravishing' a girl's virginity, or
'taking' her flower. This deflowering is not the harmonious outcome of
a continuous development; it is an abrupt rupture with the past, the
beginning of a new cycle. Pleasure is then reached by contractions of
the inside surface of the vagina; do these contractions result in a precise
and definitive orgasm? This point is still being debated. The anatomical
data are vague. 'There is a great deal of anatomic and clinical evidence
that most of the interior of the vagina is without nerves,' states, among
other things, the Kinsey Report. 'A considerable amount of surgery may
be performed inside the vagina without need for anesthetics. Nerves
have been demonstrated inside the vagina only in an area in the anter-
ior wall, proximate to the base of the clitoris.' However, in addition to
the stimulation of this innervated zone, 'the female may be conscious
of the intrusion of an object into the vagina, particularly if vaginal
muscles are tightened; but the satisfaction so obtained is probably related

---

* Vol. I, Chapter 1.

† Unless excision is practised, which is the rule in some primitive cultures.

more to muscle tonus than it is to erotic nerve stimulation.'[51] Yet, it is beyond doubt that vaginal pleasure exists; and even vaginal masturbation – for adult women – seems to be more widespread than Kinsey says.* But what is certain is that the vaginal reaction is very complex and can be qualified as psychophysiological because it not only concerns the entire nervous system but also depends on the whole situation lived by the subject: it requires profound consent of the individual as a whole; to establish itself, the new erotic cycle launched by the first coitus demands a kind of 'preparation' of the nervous system, the elaboration of a totally new form that has to include the clitoral system as well; it takes a long time to be put in place, and sometimes it never succeeds in being created. It is striking that woman has the choice between two cycles, one of which perpetuates youthful independence, while the other destines her to man and children. The normal sexual act effectively makes woman dependent on the male and the species. It is he – as for most animals – who has the aggressive role, and she who submits to his embrace. Ordinarily she can be taken at any time by man, while he can take her only when he is in the state of erection; feminine refusal can be overcome except in the case of a rejection as profound as vaginismus, sealing woman more securely than the hymen; still vaginismus leaves the male the means to relieve himself on a body that his muscular force permits him to reduce to his mercy. Since she is object, her inertia does not profoundly alter her natural role: to the extent that many men are not interested in whether the woman who shares their bed wants coitus or only submits to it. One can even go to bed with a dead woman. Coitus cannot take place without male consent, and male satisfaction is its natural end result. Fertilisation can occur without the woman deriving any pleasure. On the other hand, fertilisation is far from representing the completion of the sexual process for her; by contrast, it is at this moment

---

* 'The use of an artificial penis in solitary sexual gratification may be traced down from classic times, and doubtless prevailed in the very earliest human civilization . . . in more recent years the following are a few of the objects found in the vagina or bladder whence they could only be removed by surgical interference: Pencils, sticks of sealing-wax, cotton-reels, hair-pins (and in Italy very commonly the bone-pins used in the hair), bodkins, knitting-needles, crochet-needles, needle-cases, compasses, glass stoppers, candles, corks, tumblers, forks, tooth-picks, toothbrushes, pomade-pots (in a case recorded by Schroeder with a cockchafer inside, a makeshift substitute for the Japanese *rin-no-tama*, while in one recent English case a full-sized hen's egg was removed from the vagina of a middle-aged married woman . . . the large objects, naturally, are found chiefly in the vagina, and in the married woman' (Havelock Ellis, *Studies in the Psychology of Sex*, Volume I).

that the service demanded of her by the species begins: it takes place slowly and painfully in pregnancy, birth and breast-feeding.

Man's 'anatomical destiny' is profoundly different from woman's. Their moral and social situations are no less different. Patriarchal civilisation condemned woman to chastity; the right of man to relieve his sexual desires is more or less openly recognised, whereas woman is confined within marriage: for her the act of the flesh, if not sanctified by the code, by a sacrament, is a fault, a fall, a defeat, a weakness; she is obliged to defend her virtue, her honour; if she 'gives in' or if she 'falls', she arouses disdain, whereas even the blame inflicted on her vanquisher brings him admiration. From primitive civilisations to our times, the bed has always been accepted as a 'service' for a woman for which the male thanks her with gifts or guarantees her keep: but to serve is to give herself up to a master; there is no reciprocity at all in this relationship. The marriage structure, like the existence of prostitutes, proves it: the woman *gives herself*; the man remunerates her and takes her. Nothing forbids the male to act the master, to take inferior creatures: ancillary loves have always been tolerated, whereas the bourgeois woman who gives herself to a chauffeur or a gardener is socially degraded. Fiercely racist American men in the South have always been permitted by custom to sleep with black women, before the Civil War as today, and they exploit this right with a lordly arrogance; a white woman who had relations with a black man in the time of slavery would have been put to death, and today she would be lynched. To say he slept with a woman, a man says he 'possessed' her, that he 'had' her; on the contrary, 'to have' someone is sometimes vulgarly expressed as 'to fuck someone'; the Greeks called a woman who did not have sexual relations with the male *Parthenos adamatos*, an untaken virgin; the Romans called Messalina *invicta* because none of her lovers gave her satisfaction. So for the male lover, the love act is conquest and victory. While, in another man, the erection often seems like a ridiculous parody of voluntary action, each one nonetheless considers it in his own case with a certain pride. Males' erotic vocabulary is inspired by military vocabulary: the lover has the ardour of a soldier, his sexual organ stiffens like a bow, when he ejaculates, he 'discharges', it is a machine gun, a cannon; he speaks of attack, assault, of victory. In his arousal there is a certain flavour of the heroic. 'The generative act, consisting in the occupation of one being by another,' writes Benda,[52] 'imposes, on the one hand, the idea of a conqueror, on

* Uriel's Report.

the other of something conquered. Thus when they refer to their most civilised love relationships, they talk of conquest, attack, assault, siege and defence, defeat, and capitulation, clearly copying the idea of love from that of war. This act, involving the pollution of one being by another, imposes a certain pride on the polluter and some humiliation on the polluted, even when she is consenting.' This last phrase introduces a new myth: that man inflicts a stain on woman. In fact, sperm is not excrement; one speaks of 'nocturnal pollution' because the sperm does not serve its natural purpose; while coffee can stain a light-coloured dress, it is not said to be waste that defiles the stomach. Other men maintain, by contrast, that woman is impure because it is she who is 'soiled by discharges' and that she pollutes the male. In any case, being the one who pollutes confers a dubious superiority. In fact, man's privileged situation comes from the integration of his biologically aggressive role into his social function of chief and master; it is through this function that physiological differences take on all their full meaning. Because man is sovereign in this world, he claims the violence of his desires as a sign of his sovereignty; it is said of a man endowed with great erotic capacities that he is strong and powerful: epithets that describe him as an activity and a transcendence; on the contrary, woman being only an object is considered *hot* or *cold*; that is, she will never manifest any qualities other than passive ones.

So the climate in which feminine sexuality awakens is nothing like the one surrounding the adolescent boy. Besides, when woman faces the male for the first time, her erotic attitude is very complex. It is not true, as has been held at times, that the virgin does not know desire and that the male awakens her sensuality; this legend once again betrays the male's taste for domination, never wanting his companion to be autonomous, even in the desire that she has for him; in fact, for man as well, desire is often aroused through contact with woman, and, on the contrary, most girls feverishly long for caresses before a hand ever touches them. Isadora Duncan in *My Life*[53] says,

> My hips, which had been like a boy's, took on another undulation, and through my whole being I felt one great surging, longing, unmistakable urge, so that I could no longer sleep at night but tossed and turned in feverish, painful unrest.

In a long confession of her life to Stekel, a young woman recounts:

I began vigorously to flirt. I had to have 'my nerves tickler [sic].' I was a passionate dancer, and while dancing I always shut my eyes the better to enjoy it . . . During dancing, I was somewhat exhibitionistic; my sensuality seemed to overcome my feeling of shame. During the first year, I danced with avidity and great enjoyment. I slept many hours, masturbated daily, often keeping it up for an hour . . . I masturbated often until I was covered with sweat, too fatigued to continue, I fell asleep . . . I was burning and I would have taken anyone who would relieve me. I wasn't looking for a person, just a man.*[54]

The issue here is rather that virginal agitation is not expressed as a precise need: the virgin does not know exactly what she wants. Aggressive childhood eroticism still survives in her; her first impulses were prehensile and she still has the desire to embrace, to possess; she wants the prey that she covets to be endowed with the qualities which through taste, smell and touch have been shown to her as values; for sexuality is not an isolated domain, it extends the dreams and joys of sensuality; children and adolescents of both sexes like what is smooth, creamy, satiny, soft, elastic: that which yields to pressure without collapsing or decomposing and slips under the gaze or the fingers; like man, woman is charmed by the warm softness of sand dunes, so often compared to breasts, or the light touch of silk, of the fluffy softness of an eiderdown, the velvet feeling of a flower or fruit; and the young girl especially cherishes the pale colours of pastels, froths of tulle and muslin. She has no taste for rough fabrics, gravel, rocks, bitter flavours, acrid odours; like her brothers, it was her mother's flesh that she first caressed and cherished; in her narcissism, in her diffuse or precise homosexual experiences, she posited herself as a subject and she sought the possession of a female body. When she faces the male, she has, in the palms of her hands and on her lips, the desire to actively caress a prey. But man, with his hard muscles, his scratchy and often hairy skin, his crude odour and his coarse features, does not seem desirable to her, and he even stirs her repulsion. Renée Vivien expresses it this way:

> I am a woman, I have no right to beauty
> They have condemned me to the ugliness of men . . .
> They have forbidden me your hair, your eyes
> Because your hair is long and scented with odours[55]

* Frigidity in Woman.

If the prehensile, possessive tendency exists in woman more strongly, her orientation, like that of Renée Vivien, will be towards homosexuality. Or she will become attached only to males she can treat like women: thus the heroine of Rachilde's *Monsieur Vénus* buys herself a young lover whom she enjoys caressing passionately, but will not let herself be deflowered by him. There are women who love to caress young boys of thirteen or fourteen years old or even children, and who reject grown men. But we have seen that passive sexuality has also been developed since childhood in the majority of women: the woman loves to be hugged and caressed, and especially from puberty she wishes to be flesh in the arms of a man; the role of subject is normally his; she knows it; 'A man does not need to be handsome,' she has been told over and over; she should not look for the inert qualities of an object in him but for strength and virile force. She thus becomes divided within herself: she wants a strong embrace that will turn her into a trembling thing; but brutality and force are also hostile obstacles that wound her. Her sensuality is located both in her skin and in her hand: and their exigencies are in opposition to each other. Whenever possible, she chooses a compromise; she gives herself to a man who is virile but young and seductive enough to be an object of desire; she will be able to find all the traits she desires in a handsome adolescent; in the Song of Songs, there is a symmetry between the delights of the wife and those of the husband; she grasps in him what he seeks in her: earthly fauna and flora, precious stones, streams, stars. But she does not have the means to *take* these treasures; her anatomy condemns her to remaining awkward and impotent, like a eunuch: the desire for possession is thwarted for lack of an organ to incarnate it. And man refuses the passive role. Often, besides, circumstances lead the young girl to become the prey of a male whose caresses move her, but whom she has no pleasure to look at or caress in return. Not enough has been said not only about the fear of masculine aggressiveness but also about a deep feeling of frustration at the disgust that is mixed with her desires: sexual satisfaction must be achieved against the spontaneous thrust of her sensuality, while for the man the joy of touching and seeing merges with the sexual experience as such.

Even the elements of passive eroticism are ambiguous. Nothing is murkier than *contact*. Many men who triturate all sorts of material in their hands without disgust hate it when grass or animals touch them; women's flesh can tremble pleasantly or bristle at the touch of silk or velvet: I recall a childhood friend who had gooseflesh simply at the sight of a peach; the transition is easy from agitation to titillation, from irritation to pleasure; arms enlacing a body can be a refuge and protection, but they also imprison and suffocate. For the virgin, this ambiguity is perpetuated because of her paradoxical situation: the organ that will bring about her metamorphosis is sealed. Her flesh's uncertain and burning longing spreads through her whole body except in the very place where coitus should occur. No organ permits the virgin to satisfy her active eroticism; and she does not have the lived experience of he who dooms her to passivity.

However, this passivity is not pure inertia. For the woman to be aroused, positive phenomena must be produced in her organism: stimulation in erogenous zones, swelling of certain erectile tissue, secretions, temperature rise, pulse and breathing acceleration. Desire and sexual pleasure demand a vital expenditure for her as for the male; receptive, the female need is in one sense active and is manifested in an increase of nervous and muscular energy. Apathetic and languid women are always cold; there is a question as to whether constitutional frigidity exists, and surely psychic factors play a preponderant role in the erotic capacities of woman; but it is certain that physiological insufficiencies and a depleted vitality are manifested in part by sexual indifference. If, on the other hand, vital energy is spent in voluntary activities – sports, for example – it is not invested in sex. Scandinavians are healthy, strong and cold. 'Fiery' women are those who combine their languor with 'fire', like Italian or Spanish women, that is to say, women whose ardent vitality flows from their flesh. To *make* oneself object, to *make* oneself passive, is very different from *being* a passive object: a woman in love is neither asleep nor a corpse; there is a surge in her that ceaselessly falls and rises: it is this surge that creates the spell that perpetuates desire. But the balance between ardour and abandon is easy to destroy. Male desire is tension; it can invade a body where nerves and muscles are taut: positions and movements that demand a voluntary participation of the organism do not work against it, and instead often serve it. On the contrary, every voluntary effort keeps female flesh from being 'taken'; this is why the woman spontaneously* refuses forms of coitus that demand work and tension from her; too many and too abrupt changes in position, the demands of consciously directed activities – actions or words – break the spell. The violence of uncontrolled tendencies can

---

* We will see further on that there can be psychological reasons that modify her immediate attitude.

bring about tightening, contraction or tension: some women scratch or bite, their bodies arching, infused with an unaccustomed force; but these phenomena are only produced when a certain paroxysm is attained, and it is attained only if first the absence of all inhibition – physical as well as moral – permits a concentration of all living energy into the sexual act. This means that it is not enough for the young girl to *let it happen*; if she is docile, languid or removed, she satisfies neither her partner nor herself. She must participate actively in an adventure that neither her virgin body nor her consciousness – laden with taboos, prohibitions, prejudices and exigencies – desire positively.

In the conditions we have just described, it is understandable that woman's erotic beginnings are not easy. Quite frequently, incidents that occur in childhood and youth provoke deep resistance in her, as has been seen; sometimes it is insurmountable; most often, the girl tries to overcome it, but violent conflicts build up in her. Her strict education, the fear of sinning and feelings of guilt toward her mother all create powerful blocks. Virginity is valued so highly in many circles that to lose it outside marriage seems a veritable disaster. The girl who surrenders by coercion or by surprise thinks she dishonours herself. The 'wedding night', which delivers the virgin to a man whom she has ordinarily not even chosen, and which attempts to condense into a few hours – or instants – the entire sexual initiation, is not a simple experience. In general, any 'passage' is distressing because of its definitive and irreversible character: becoming a woman is breaking with the past, without recourse; but this particular passage is more dramatic than any other; it creates not only a hiatus between yesterday and tomorrow; it tears the girl from the imaginary world where a great part of her existence took place and hurls her into the real world. By analogy with a bullfight, Michel Leiris calls the nuptial bed 'a moment of truth'; for the virgin, this expression takes on its fullest and most fearsome meaning. During the engagement, dating or courtship period, however basic it may have been, she continued to live in her familiar universe of ceremony and dreams; the suitor spoke a romantic, or at least courteous, language; it was still possible to make believe. And suddenly there she is, gazed upon by real eyes, handled by real hands: it is the implacable reality of this gazing and grasping that terrifies her.

Both anatomy and customs confer the role of initiator on the man. Without doubt, for the young male virgin, his first mistress also provides his initiation; but he possesses an erotic autonomy clearly manifested in

the erection; his mistress only delivers to him the object in its reality
that he already desires: a woman's body. The girl needs a man to make
her discover her own body: her dependence is much greater. From his
very first experiences, man is ordinarily active and decisive, whether he
pays his partner or courts and solicits her. By contrast, in most cases,
the young girl *is* courted and solicited; even if it is she who first flirts
with the man, he is the one who takes their relationship in hand; he is
often older and more experienced, and it is accepted that he has the
responsibility for this adventure that is new for her; his desire is more
aggressive and imperious. Lover or husband, he is the one who leads her
to the bed, where her only choice is to let go of herself and obey. Even
if she had accepted this authority in her mind, she is panic-stricken the
moment she must concretely submit to it. She first of all fears this gaze
that engulfs her. Her modesty may have been taught her, but it has deep
roots; men and women all know the shame of their flesh; in its pure,
immobile presence, its unjustified immanence, the flesh exists in the gaze
of another as the absurd contingence of facticity and yet flesh is *oneself*:
we want to prevent it from existing for others; we want to deny it. There
are men who say they cannot stand to be naked in front of a woman,
except in the state of erection; through the erection, the flesh becomes
activity, force, the penis is no longer an inert object but, like the hand
or the face, the imperious expression of a subjectivity. This is one reason
why modesty paralyses young men much less than young women; their
aggressive role exposes them less to being gazed at; and if they are,
they do not fear being judged because it is not inert qualities that their
mistresses demand of them: it is rather their amorous potency and
their skill at giving pleasure that will give rise to complexes; at least they
can defend themselves and try to win their match. Woman does not
have the option of transforming her flesh into will: when she stops hiding
it, she gives it up without defences; even if she longs for caresses, she
recoils from the idea of being seen and felt; all the more so as her breasts
and buttocks are particularly fleshy; many adult women cannot bear to
be seen from the rear even when they are dressed; imagine the resistance a naive girl in love has to overcome to consent to showing herself. A
Phryne undoubtedly does not fear being gazed at; she bares herself, on
the contrary, superbly. Her beauty clothes her. But even if she is the
equal of Phryne, a young girl never feels it with certainty; she cannot
have arrogant pride in her body as long as male approval has not
confirmed her young vanity. And this is just what frightens her; the lover
is even more terrifying than a gaze: he is a judge; he is going to reveal

her to herself in her truth; even passionately taken with her own image, every young girl doubts herself at the moment of the masculine verdict; this is why she demands darkness, she hides in the sheets; when she admired herself in the mirror, she was only dreaming: she was dreaming through man's eyes; now the eyes are really there; impossible to cheat; impossible to fight: a mysterious freedom decides, and this decision is final. In the real ordeal of the erotic experience, the obsessions of child-hood and adolescence will finally fade or be confirmed for ever; many young girls suffer from muscular calves, breasts that are too little or too big, narrow hips, a wart; or else they fear some secret malformation. Stekel writes,*

Every young girl carries in her all sorts of ridiculous fears that she barely dares to admit to herself. One would not believe how many young girls suffer from the obsession of being physically abnormal and torment themselves secretly because they cannot be sure of being normally constructed. One young girl, for example, believed that her 'lower opening' was not in the right place. She thought that sexual intercourse took place through the navel. She was unhappy because her navel was closed and she could not stick her finger in it. Another thought she was a hermaphrodite. And another thought she was crippled and would never be able to have sexual relations.

Even if they are unfamiliar with these obsessions, they are terrified by the idea that certain regions of their bodies that did not exist for them or for anyone, that absolutely did not exist, will suddenly be seen. Will this unknown figure that the young girl must assume as her own provoke disgust? Indifference? Irony? She can only submit to male judgement: the die is cast. This is why man's attitude will have such deep resonance. His ardour and tenderness can give woman a confidence in herself that will stand up to every rejection: until she is eighty years old, she will believe she is this flower, this exotic bird that made man's desire bloom one night. On the contrary, if the lover or husband is clumsy, he will arouse an infer-iority complex in her that is sometimes compounded by long-lasting neuroses; and she will hold a grudge that will be expressed in a stubborn frigidity. Stekel describes striking examples:

* *Frigidity in Woman.*

A woman of 36 years of age suffers from such back pain across 'the small of her back' for the past 14 years. These pains are so unbearable that she is forced to stay in bed for weeks . . . she felt the great pains for the first time during her wedding night. On that occasion, during the defloration, which caused her considerable pain, her husband exclaimed: 'You have deceived me! You are not a virgin!' Her pains in the back represent the fixation of this painful episode. Her illness is her vengeance on the man. The various cures have cost him considerable money for her innumerable treatments . . . This woman was anaesthetic during her wedding night and she remained in this condition throughout her marital experience . . . The wedding night was for her a terrible mental shock that has influenced her whole life.

A woman consults me for various nervous troubles and particularly on account of her complete sexual frigidity . . . During her wedding night, her husband, after uncovering her, exclaimed: 'Oh, how stubby and thick your limbs are!' Then he tried to carry out intercourse. She felt only pain and remained wholly frigid . . . She knows very well that the slightest remark he made about her during the wedding night was responsible for her sexual frigidity.

Another frigid woman says that 'during her wedding night, her husband deeply insulted her' seeing her get undressed, he allegedly said: 'My God, how thin you are!' Then he nevertheless decided to caress her. For her this moment was unforgettable and horrible. What brutality!

Mme. Z. W. is also completely frigid. The great traumatism of her wedding night was that her husband supposedly said after the first intercourse: 'You have a big hole, you tricked me.'

The gaze is danger; hands are another threat. Woman does not usually have access to the universe of violence; she has never gone through the ordeal the young man overcame in childhood and adolescent fights: to be a thing of flesh on which others have a hold; and now that she is grasped, she is swept away in a body-to-body clasp where man is the stronger; she is no longer free to dream, to withdraw, to manoeuvre: she is given over to the male; he disposes of her. These wrestling-like embraces terrorise her, she who has never wrestled. She had let herself go to the caresses of a fiancé, a fellow student, a colleague, a civilised and courteous man: but he has assumed an unfamiliar, selfish and stubborn attitude; she no longer has recourse against this stranger. It is not uncommon that the young girl's first experience is a real rape and that man's behaviour is odiously brutal; particularly in the countryside, where customs are harsh, it often happens that a young peasant woman, half-consenting, half-outraged, in shame and fright, loses her virginity at the bottom of some ditch. What is in any case extremely frequent in all societies and classes is that the virgin is rushed by an egotistical lover seeking his own pleasure quickly, or by a husband convinced of his conjugal rights who takes his wife's resistance as an insult, to the point of becoming furious if the defloration is difficult.

In any case, however deferential and courteous a man might be, the first penetration is always a rape. While she desires caresses on her lips and breasts and perhaps yearns for a familiar or anticipated orgasm, here is a male sex organ tearing the girl and introducing itself into regions where it was not invited. The painful surprise of a swooning virgin – who thinks she has finally reached the accomplishment of her voluptuous dreams and who feels in the secret of her sex an unexpected pain – in a husband's or lover's arms has often been described; the dreams faint away, the excitement dissipates, and love takes on the appearance of a surgical operation.

In the confessions gathered by Dr Liepmann,* there is the following typical account. It concerns a very sexually unaware girl from a modest background.

'I often imagined that one could have a child just by the exchange of a kiss. During my eighteenth year, I made the acquaintance of a man with whom I really fell madly in love.' She often went out with him and during their conversations he explained to her that when a young girl loves a man, she must give herself to him because men cannot live without sexual relations and that as long as they cannot afford to get married, they have to have relations with young girls. She resisted. One day, he organised an excursion so that they could spend the night together. She wrote him a letter to repeat that 'it would harm her too much'. The morning of the arranged day, she gave him the letter but he put it in his pocket without reading it and took her to the hotel; he dominated her morally, she loved him, she followed him. 'I was as if hypnotised. As we were going along, I begged him to spare me . . . How I arrived at the hotel, I do not know at all. The only memory that remained is that

* Published in French under the title *Jeunesse et sexualité* [*Youth and Sexuality*].

my whole body trembled violently. My companion tried to calm me; but he succeeded only after much resistance. I was no longer mistress of my will and in spite of myself I let myself go. When I found myself later in the street, it seemed to me that everything had only been a dream I had just awakened from.' She refused to repeat the experience and for nine years did not have sexual relations with any other man. She then met one who asked her to marry him and she agreed.

In this case, the defloration was a kind of rape. But even if it is consensual, it can be painful. Look at the fevers that tormented young Isadora Duncan. She met an admirably handsome actor with whom she fell in love at first sight and who courted her ardently.*

I myself felt ill and dizzy, while an irresistible longing to press him closer and closer surged in me, until, losing all control and falling into a fury, he carried me into the room. Frightened but ecstatic, the realisation was made clear to me. I confess my first impressions were a horrible fright, but a great pity for what he seemed to be suffering prevented me from running away from what was at first sheer torture . . . [The next day], what had been for me only a painful experience began again amid my martyr's sobs and cries.[56]

She was soon to know the paradise she lyrically described, first with this lover and then with others.

However, in actual experience, as previously in one's virginal imagination, it is not pain that plays the greatest role: the fact of penetration counts far more. In intercourse the man introduces only an exterior organ: woman is affected in her deepest interior. Undoubtedly, there are many young men who tread with anguish in the secret darkness of woman; their childhood terrors resurface at the threshold of caves and graves and so does their fright in front of jaws, scythes and wolf traps: they imagine that their swollen penis will be caught in the mucous sheath; the woman, once penetrated, does not have this feeling of danger; but she does feel carnally alienated. The property owner affirms his rights over his lands, the housewife over her house by proclaiming 'no trespassing'; because of their frustrated transcendence, women, in

* My Life.

particular, jealously defend their privacy: their room, their wardrobe and their chests are sacred. Colette tells of an old prostitute who told her one day: 'In my room, Madame, no man has ever set foot; for what I have to do with men, Paris is quite big enough.' If not her body, at least she possessed a plot of land where entry was prohibited. The young girl, though, possesses little of her own except her body: it is her most precious treasure; the man who enters her *takes* it from her; the familiar word is confirmed by her lived experience. She experiences concretely the humiliation she had felt: she is dominated, subjugated, conquered. Like almost all females, she is *under* the man during inter-course.* Adler emphasised the feeling of inferiority resulting from this. Right from infancy, the notions of superior and inferior are extremely important; climbing trees is a prestigious act; heaven is above the earth; hell is underneath; to fall or to descend is to degrade oneself and to climb is to exalt oneself; in wrestling, victory belongs to the one who pins his opponent down, whereas the woman lies on the bed in a posi-tion of defeat; it is even worse if the man straddles her like an animal subjugated by reins and a bit. In any case, she feels passive: she *is* caressed, penetrated, she undergoes intercourse, whereas the man spends himself actively. It is true that the male sex organ is not a stri-ated muscle commanded by will; it is neither ploughshare nor sword but merely flesh; but it is a voluntary movement that man imprints on her; he goes, he comes, stops, resumes while the woman receives him submissively; it is the man – especially when the woman is a novice – who chooses the amorous positions, who decides the length and frequency of intercourse. She feels herself to be an instrument: all the freedom is in the other. This is what is poetically expressed by saying that woman is comparable to a violin and man to the bow that makes her vibrate. 'In love,' says Balzac,† 'leaving the soul out of consider-ation, woman is a lyre which only yields up its secrets to the man who can play upon it skillfully.'[57] He *takes* his pleasure with her; he *gives* her pleasure; the words themselves do not imply reciprocity. Woman is imbued with collective images of the glorious aura of masculine sexual

---

* The position can undoubtedly be reversed. But in the first experiences, it is extremely rare for the man not to practise the so-called normal coitus.

† *Physiology of Marriage.* In *Bréviaire de l'amour expérimental (A Ritual for Married Lovers)*, Jules Guyot also says of the husband: 'He is the minstrel who produces harmony or cacophony with his hand and bow. From this point of view woman is really a many-stringed instrument producing harmonious or discordant sounds depending on how she is tuned.'

excitement that make feminine arousal a shameful abdication: her intimate experience confirms this asymmetry. It must not be forgotten
that boy and girl adolescents experience their bodies differently: the
former tranquilly takes his body for granted and proudly takes charge
of his desires; for the latter, in spite of her narcissism, it is a strange
and disturbing burden. Man's sex organ is neat and simple, like a finger;
it can be innocently exhibited, and boys often show it off to their friends
proudly and defiantly; the feminine sex organ is mysterious to the
woman herself, hidden, tormented, mucous and humid; it bleeds each
month, it is sometimes soiled with bodily fluids, it has a secret and
dangerous life. It is largely because woman does not recognise herself
in it that she does not recognise her own desires. They are expressed
in a shameful manner. While the man has a 'hard-on', the woman 'gets
wet'; there are in the very word infantile memories of the wet bed, of the
guilty and involuntary desire to urinate; man has the same disgust for
his nocturnal unconscious wet dreams; projecting a liquid, urine or
sperm, is not humiliating: it is an active operation; but there is humiliation if the liquid escapes passively since the body then is no longer
an organism, muscles, sphincters and nerves, commanded by the brain
and expressing the conscious subject, but a vase, a receptacle made of
inert matter and the plaything of mechanical caprices. If the flesh oozes
– like an old wall or a dead body – it does not seem to be emitting
liquid but deliquescing: a decomposition process that horrifies. Feminine
heat is the flaccid palpitation of a shellfish; where man has impetuousness, woman merely has impatience; her desire can become ardent
without ceasing to be passive; the man dives on his prey like the eagle
and the hawk; she, like a carnivorous plant, waits for and watches the
swamp where insects and children bog down; she is sucking, suction,
sniffer, she is pitch and glue, immobile appeal, insinuating and viscous:
at least this is the way she indefinably feels. Thus, there is not only
resistance against the male who attempts to subjugate her but also
internal conflict. Superimposed on the taboos and inhibitions that arise
from her education and society are disgust and refusals that stem from
the erotic experience itself: they all reinforce each other to such an
extent that often after the first coitus the woman is more in revolt
against her sexual destiny than before.

Lastly, there is another factor that often gives man a hostile look and
changes the sexual act into a grave danger: the danger of a child. An
illegitimate child in most civilisations is such a social and economic handicap for the unmarried woman that one sees young girls committing

suicide when they know they are pregnant and unwed mothers cutting the throats of their newborns; such a risk constitutes a quite powerful sexual brake, making many young girls observe the prenuptial chastity prescribed by customs. When the brake is insufficient, the young girl, while yielding to the lover, is horrified by the terrible danger he possesses in his loins. Stekel cites, among others, a young girl who for the entire duration of intercourse shouted: 'Don't let anything happen! Don't let anything happen!' Even in marriage, the woman often does not want a child, her health is not good enough, or a child would be too great a burden on the young household. Whether he is lover or husband, if she does not have absolute confidence in her partner, her eroticism will be paralysed by caution. Either she will anxiously watch the man's behaviour, or else, once intercourse is over, she will run to the bathroom to chase the living germ from her belly, put there in spite of herself. This hygienic operation brutally contradicts the sensual magic of the caresses; she undergoes an absolute separation of the bodies that were merged in one single joy; thus the male sperm becomes a harmful germ, a soiling; she cleans herself as one cleans a dirty vase, while the man reclines on his bed in his superb wholeness. A young divorcee told me how horrified she was when – after a dubiously pleasurable wedding night – she had to shut herself in the bathroom and her husband nonchalantly lit a cigarette: it seems that the ruin of the couple was decided at that instant. The repugnance of the douche, the beaker and the bidet is one of the frequent causes of feminine frigidity. The existence of surer and more convenient contraceptive devices is helping woman's sexual freedom a great deal; in a country like America where these practices are widespread, the number of young girls still virgins at marriage is much lower than in France; such practices make for far greater abandon during the love act. But there again, the young woman has to overcome her repugnance before treating her body as a thing: she can no more resign herself to being 'corked' to satisfy a man's desires than she can to being 'pierced' by him. Whether she has her uterus sealed or introduces some sperm-killing tampon, a woman who is conscious of the ambiguities of the body and sex will be bridled by cold premeditation: besides, many men consider the use of condoms repugnant. It is sexual behaviour as a whole that justifies its various moments: conduct that when analysed would seem repugnant seems natural when bodies are transfigured by the erotic virtues they possess; but inversely, when bodies and behaviours are decomposed into separate elements and deprived of meaning, these elements become disgusting and obscene. The surgical and dirty perception that penetration had in the eyes of the child returns if it is not carried out with the arousal, desire and pleasure a woman in love will joyfully experience as union and fusion with the beloved: this is what happens with the concerted use of prophylactics. In any case, these precautions are not at the disposal of all women; many young girls do not know of any defence against the threats of pregnancy and they feel great anguish that their lot depends on the good will of the man they give themselves up to.

It is understandable that an ordeal experienced through so much resistance, fraught with such weighty implications, often creates serious traumas. A latent precocious dementia has often been revealed by the first experience. Stekel gives several examples:

Mlle M. G. . . . suddenly developed an acute delirium in her 19th year. I found her storming in her room, shouting repeatedly: 'I won't! No! I won't!' She tore off her clothes and wanted to flee into the street naked . . . she had to be taken to the psychiatric clinic. There her delirium gradually abated and she passed into a catatonic state . . . This girl . . . was a clerk in an office, in love with the head clerk in the company . . . She had gone to the country with a girl friend . . . and a couple of young men who worked in the same office . . . she went to her room with one of the men [who] promised not to touch her and that 'it was merely a prank'. He roused her to slight tenderness for three nights without touching her virginity . . . She apparently remained 'as cold as a dog's muzzle' and declared that it was disgraceful. For a few fleeting minutes her mind seemed confused and she exclaimed: 'Alfred, Alfred.' (Alfred was the head clerk's first name.) She was reproaching herself for what she had done (What would mother say about this if she knew?). Once she returned home, she took to her bed, complaining of a migraine.

Mlle L. X.[58] . . . very depressed . . . She cried often and could not sleep; she had begun to have hallucinations and failed to recognise her environment. She had jumped to the windows and tried to throw herself out . . . She was taken to the sanitarium. I found this twenty-three-year-old girl sitting up in bed; she paid no attention to me when I entered . . . Her face depicted abject fear and horror; her limbs were crossed and they twitched vigorously. She was shouting. 'No! No! No! You villain! Men such as you ought to be locked up! It hurts! Oh!' Then there followed some unintelligible mumbling. Suddenly her whole facial expression changed. Her eyes lit up, her lips pursed in the manner of kissing someone, her limbs ceased twitching and she gave forth outcries which suggested delight and rapture and love . . . Finally the attack ended in a subdued but persistent weeping . . . The patient kept pushing down her night-gown as if it were a dress, at the same time continually repeating the exclamation, 'Don't!' It was known that a married colleague had often come to see her when she was ill, that she was first happy about it, but that later on she had had hallucinations and attempted suicide.[59] She got better but keeps all men at a distance and has rejected an earnest marriage offer.

In other cases the illness triggered is less serious. Here is an example where regret for lost virginity plays the main role in the problems following the first coitus:

A young twenty-three-year-old girl suffers from various phobias. The illness began at Franzensbad out of fear of catching a pregnancy by a kiss or a contact in a toilet . . . Perhaps a man had left some sperm in the water after masturbation; she insisted that the bathtub be cleaned three times in her presence and did not dare to move her bowels in the normal position. Some time afterwards she developed a phobia of tearing her hymen, she did not dare to dance, jump, cross a fence or even walk except with very little steps; if she saw a post, she feared being deflowered by a clumsy movement and went around it, trembling all the way. Another of her phobias in a train or in the middle of a crowd was that a man could introduce his member from behind, deflower her and provoke a pregnancy . . . During the last phase of the illness, she feared finding pins in her bed or on her shirt that could enter her vagina. Each evening the sick girl stayed naked in the middle of her room while her unfortunate mother was forced to go through a difficult examination of the bedclothes . . . She had always affirmed her love for her fiancé. An examination revealed that she was no longer a virgin and was putting off marriage because she feared her fiancé's disastrous observations. She admitted to him that she had been seduced by a tenor, married him and was cured.*

* Stekel, *Frigidity in Woman*.

In another case, remorse – uncompensated by voluptuous satisfaction – provoked psychic troubles:

Mlle. H. B., twenty years old, after a trip to Italy with a girl friend, went into a serious depression. She refused to leave her room and did not utter one word. She was taken to a nursing home, where her situation got worse. She heard voices that were insulting her, everyone made fun of her, etc. She was brought back to her parents' where she stayed in a corner without moving. She asked the doctor: 'Why didn't I come before the crime was committed?' She was dead. Everything was killed, destroyed. She was dirty. She could not sing one note, bridges with the world were burnt . . . The fiancé admitted having followed her to Rome where she gave herself to him after resisting a long time; she had crying fits . . . She admitted never having pleasure with her fiancé. She was cured when she found a lover who satisfied her and married her.

The 'sweet Viennese girl' whose childish confessions I summarised also gave a detailed and gripping account of her first adult experiences. It will be noticed that – in spite of the very advanced nature of her previous adventures – her 'initiation' still has an absolutely new character.

'At sixteen, I began working in an office. At seventeen and a half, I had my first holiday; it was a great period for me. I was courted on all sides . . . I was in love with a young office colleague . . . We went to the park. It was 15 April 1909. He made me sit next to him on a bench. He kissed me, begging me: open your lips; but I closed them convulsively. Then he began to unbutton my jacket. I would have let him when I remembered that I did not have any breasts; I gave up the voluptuous sensation I would have had if he had touched me . . . On 7 April a married colleague invited me to go to an exhibition with him. We drank wine at dinner. I lost some of my reserve and began telling him some ambiguous jokes. In spite of my begging, he hailed a cab, pushed me into it and hardly had the horses started than he kissed me. He became more and more intimate, he pushed his hand farther and farther; I defended myself with all my strength and I do not remember if he got his way. The next day I went to the office rather flustered. He showed me his hands covered with the scratches I had given him . . . He asked me to come see him more often . . . I yielded, not very comfortable but still full of curiosity ... As soon as he came near my sex I pulled away and returned to my place; but once, more clever than I, he overcame me and probably put his finger into my vagina. I cried with pain. It was June 1909 and I left on vacation. I took a trip with my girl friend. Two tourists arrived. They invited us to accompany them. My companion wanted to kiss my friend, she punched him. He came towards, grabbed me from behind, bent me to him, and kissed me. I did not resist ... He invited me to come with him. I gave him my hand and we went into the middle of the forest. He kissed me ... he kissed my sex, to my great indignation. I said to him: "How can you do such a disgusting thing?" He put his penis in my hand ... I caressed it ... all of a sudden he pulled away my hand and threw a handkerchief over it to keep me from seeing what was happening ... Two days later we went to Liesing. All of a sudden in a deserted field he took off his coat and put it on the grass ... he threw me down in such a way that one of his legs was placed between mine. I still did not think how serious the situation was. I begged him to kill me rather than deprive me of "my most beautiful finery". He became very rough, swore at me and threatened me with the police. He covered my mouth with his hand and introduced his penis. I thought my last hour had arrived. I had the feeling my stomach was turning. When he was finally finished, I began to be able to put up with him. He had to pick me up because I was still stretched out. He covered my eyes and face with kisses. I did not see or hear anything. If he had not held me back, I would have fallen blindly in front of the traffic ... We were alone in a second-class compartment; he opened his trousers again to come towards me. I screamed and ran quickly through the whole train until the last running board ... Finally he left me with a vulgar and strident laugh that I will never forget, calling me a stupid goose who does not know what is good. He let me return to Vienna alone. I went quickly to the bathroom because I had felt something warm running along my thigh. Frightened, I saw traces of blood. How could I hide this at home? I went to bed as early as possible and cried for hours. I still felt the pressure on my stomach caused by the pushing of his penis. My strange attitude and lack of appetite told my mother something had happened. I admitted everything to her. She did not see anything so terrible in it ... My colleague did what he could to console me. He took advantage of dark evenings to take walks with me in the park and caress me under my skirts. I let him; but as soon as I felt my vagina become wet I pulled myself away because I was terribly ashamed.'

She goes to a hotel with him sometimes but without sleeping with him. She makes the acquaintance of a very rich young man that she would like to marry. She sleeps with him but without feeling anything and with disgust. She resumes her relations with her colleague but she misses the other one and begins to be cross-eyed and to lose weight. She is sent to a sanatorium where she almost sleeps with a young Russian, but she chases him from her bed at the last minute. She begins affairs with a doctor and an officer but without consenting to complete sexual relations. Then she became mortally ill and decided to go to a doctor. After her treatment she consented to give herself to a man who loved her and then married her. In marriage her frigidity disappeared.

In these few examples chosen from many similar ones, the partner's brutality or at least the abruptness of the event is the determining factor in the traumatism or disgust. The best situation for sexual initiation is one in which the girl learns to overcome her modesty, to get to know her partner, and to enjoy his caresses without violence or surprise, without fixed rules or a precise time frame. In this respect, the freedom of behaviour appreciated by young American girls and more and more by French girls today can only be endorsed: they slip almost without noticing from necking and petting to complete sexual relations. The less tabooed it is, the smoother the initiation, and the freer the girl feels with her partner and the more the domination aspect of the male fades; if her lover is also young, a novice, shy, and an equal, the girl's defences are not as strong; but her metamorphosis into a woman will also be less of a transformation. In *Green Wheat*,[60] Colette's Vinca, the day after a rather brutal defloration, displays surprising placidity to her friend Phil: she did not feel 'possessed', on the contrary, she took pride in freeing herself of her virginity; she did not feel an overwhelming mental turmoil; in truth, Phil is wrong to be surprised as his girlfriend did not really know the male. Claudine was less unaffected after a turn on the dance floor in Renaud's arms. I was told of a French high school student still stuck in the 'green fruit' stage, who, having spent a night with a male school-friend, ran to a girlfriend's the next morning to announce: 'I slept with C. . . . it was a lot of fun.' An American high school teacher told me his students stopped being virgins long before becoming women; their partners respect them too much to offend their modesty; the boys themselves are too young and too prudish to awaken any demon in the girls. There are girls who throw themselves into many erotic experiences in order to escape sexual anxiety; they hope to rid themselves of their curiosity and obsessions, but their acts often have a theoretical cast, rendering such behaviour as unreal as the fantasies through which others anticipate the future. Giving oneself out of defiance, fear or puritan rationalism is not achieving an authentic erotic experience: one merely reaches a pseudo-experience without danger and without much flavour; the sexual act is not accompanied by either anguish or shame, because arousal remains superficial and pleasure has not permeated the flesh. These deflowered virgins are still young girls; and it is likely that the day they find themselves in the grip of a sensual and imperious man, they will put up virginal resistance to him. Meanwhile, they remain in a kind of awkward age; caresses tickle them, kisses sometimes make them laugh: they look on physical love as a game and if they are not in the mood to have fun, the lover's demands quickly seem importunate and abusive; they hold on to the disgusts, phobias and prudishness of the adolescent girl. If they never go beyond this stage – which is, according to American males, the case with many American girls – they spend their life in a state of semi-frigidity. Real sexual maturity for the woman who consents to becoming flesh can only occur in arousal and pleasure.

But it must not be thought that all difficulties subside in women with a passionate temperament. On the contrary, they sometimes worsen. Feminine arousal can reach an intensity unknown by man. Male desire is violent but localised, and he comes out of it – except perhaps in the instant of ejaculation – conscious of himself; woman, by contrast, undergoes a real alienation; for many, this metamorphosis is the most voluptuous and definitive moment of love; but it also has a magical and frightening side. The woman he is holding in his arms appears so absent from herself, so much in the throes of turmoil, that the man may feel afraid of her. The upheaval she feels is a far more radical transmutation than the male's aggressive frenzy. This fever frees her from shame; but when she awakes, it in turn makes her feel ashamed and horrified; for her to accept it happily – or even proudly – she has at least to be sexually and sensually fulfilled; she can admit to her desires if she has gloriously satisfied them: if not, she repudiates them angrily.

Here we reach the crucial problem of feminine eroticism: at the beginning of her erotic life, woman's abdication is not rewarded by a wild and confident sensual pleasure. She would readily sacrifice modesty and pride if it meant opening up the gates of paradise. But it has been seen that defloration is not a successful accomplishment of youthful eroticism; it is on the contrary an unusual phenomenon; vaginal pleasure is not attained immediately; according to Stekel's statistics – confirmed by many sexologists and psychologists – barely 4 per cent of women experience pleasure at the first coitus; 50 per cent do not reach vaginal pleasure for weeks, months, or even years. Psychic factors play an essential role in this. Woman's body is singularly 'hysterical' in that there is often no distance between conscious facts and their organic expression; her moral inhibitions prevent the emergence of pleasure; as they are not counterbalanced by anything, they are often perpetuated and form a more and more powerful barrier. In many cases, a vicious circle is created: the lover's first clumsiness – a word, an awkward gesture, or an arrogant smile – will resonate throughout the whole honeymoon or even married life; disappointed by not experiencing pleasure immediately, the young woman feels a resentment that badly prepares her for a happier experience. It is true that if the man cannot give her normal satisfaction, he can always give her clitoral pleasure that, in spite of moralising legends, can provide her with relaxation and contentment. But many women reject it because it seems to be *inflicted* even more than vaginal pleasure; because if women suffer from the egotism of men concerned only with their own satisfaction, they are also offended by too obvious a determination to give them pleasure. 'Making the other come,' says Stekel, 'means dominating him; giving oneself to someone is abdicating one's will.' Woman will accept pleasure more easily if it seems to flow naturally from man's own pleasure, as happens in normal and successful coitus. 'Women submit themselves joyously as soon as they understand that the partner does not *want* to subjugate them,' continues Stekel; inversely, if they feel this desire, they resist. Many shy away from being caressed by the hand because it is an instrument that does not participate in the pleasure it gives, it is activity and not flesh; and if sex itself does not come across as flesh penetrated with desire but as a cleverly used tool, woman will feel the same repulsion. Besides, anything else will seem to confirm the woman's failure to experience a normal woman's feelings. Stekel notes, after many, many observations, that all the desire of so-called frigid women aims at the norm. 'They want to reach orgasm like a normal woman; no other process satisfies them morally.'

Man's attitude is thus of extreme importance. If his desire is violent and brutal, his partner feels changed into a mere thing in his arms; but if he is too self-controlled, too detached, he does not constitute himself as flesh; he asks woman to make herself object without her being able to have a hold on him in return. In both cases, her pride rebels; to reconcile her metamorphosis into a carnal object with the demands of her subjectivity, she must make him her prey as she makes herself his. This is often why the woman obstinately remains frigid. If the lover lacks seductive techniques, if he is cold, negligent or clumsy, he fails to awaken her sexuality or he leaves her unsatisfied; but if he is virile and skilful, he can provoke reactions of rejection; woman fears his domination: some can find pleasure only with timid, inept, or even almost impotent men, ones who do not scare them away. It is easy for a man to awaken hostility and resentment in his mistress. Resentment is the most common source of feminine frigidity; in bed, the woman makes the male pay for all the affronts she considers she has been subjected to by an insulting coldness; her attitude is often one of an aggressive inferiority complex: since you do not love me, since I have flaws preventing me from being liked and since I am despicable, I will not surrender to love, desire and pleasure either. This is how she exacts vengeance both on him and on herself if he has humiliated her by his negligence, if he has aroused her jealousy, if he has declared himself too slowly, if he has made her his mistress whereas she desired marriage; the complaint can appear suddenly and set off this reaction even during a relationship that began happily. The man who caused this hostility can rarely succeed in undoing it: a persuasive testimony of love or appreciation may, however, sometimes modify the situation. It also happens that women who are defiant or stiff in their lovers' arms can be transformed by a ring on their finger: happy, flattered, their conscience at peace, they let all their defences fall. But a newcomer, respectful, in love and delicate can best transform the disenchanted woman into a happy mistress or wife; if he frees her from her inferiority complex she will give herself to him ardently.

Stekel's work *Frigidity in Woman* essentially focuses on demonstrating the role of psychic factors in feminine frigidity. The following examples clearly show that it is often an act of resentment of the husband or lover:

Mlle G. S. . . . had given herself to a man while waiting for him to marry her, while insisting on the fact 'that she did not care about marriage', that she did not want 'to be attached'. She played the free woman. In truth, she was a slave to morality like her whole family. But her lover believed her and never spoke of marriage. Her stubbornness increased more and more until she became apathetic.

When he finally did ask her to marry him, she took her revenge by admitting her numbness and no longer wanting to hear anything about a union. She no longer wanted to be happy. She had waited too long . . . She was consumed by jealousy and waited anxiously for the day he proposed so she could refuse it proudly. Then she wanted to commit suicide just to punish her lover in style.

A very jealous woman who until then had found pleasure with her husband imagines that her husband is cheating on her while she was ill. Coming home, she decides to be cold to her husband. She would never be aroused by him again because he did not appreciate her and used her only when in need. Since her return she has been frigid. At first she used little tricks not to be aroused. She pictured to herself that her husband was flirting with her girl friend. But soon orgasm was replaced by pain.

A young seventeen-year-old had an affair with a man and derived intense pleasure from it. Pregnant at nineteen, she asked her lover to marry her; he was ambivalent and advised her to get an abortion, which she refused to do. Three weeks later, he declared he was ready to marry her and she became his wife. But she never forgave those three tormented weeks and became frigid. Later on, a talk with her husband overcame her frigidity.

Mme N. M . . . learns that two days after the wedding, her husband went to see a former mistress. The orgasm she had had previously disappeared forever. She was obsessed by the thought that she no longer pleased her husband whom she thought she had disappointed; that is the cause of frigidity for her.

Even when a woman overcomes her resistance and eventually experiences vaginal pleasure, not all her problems are eliminated: the rhythm of her sexuality and that of the male do not coincide. She is much slower to reach orgasm than the man. The Kinsey Report states:

For perhaps three-quarters of all males, orgasm is reached within two minutes after the initiation of the sexual relation . . . Considering the many upper level females who are so adversely conditioned to sexual situations that they may require ten to fifteen minutes of the most careful stimulation to bring them to climax, and considering the fair number of females who never come to climax in their whole lives, it is, of course, demanding that the male be quite abnormal in his ability to prolong sexual activity without ejaculation if he is required to match the female partner.

It is said that in India the husband, while fulfilling his conjugal duties, smokes his pipe to distract himself from his own pleasure and to make his wife's last; in the West, it is more the number of 'times' that a Casanova boasts of; and his supreme pride is to have a woman beg for mercy: according to erotic tradition, this is not often a successful feat; men often complain of their partners' exacting demands: she is a wild uterus, an ogre, insatiable; she is never assuaged. Montaigne demonstrates this point of view in the third book of his *Essays*:[61]

They are incomparably more capable and ardent than we in the acts of love – and that priest of antiquity so testified, who had been once a man and then a woman ... and besides, we have learned from their own mouth the proof that was once given in different centuries by an emperor and an empress of Rome, master workmen and famous in this task: he indeed deflowered in one night ten captive Sarmatian virgins; but she actually in one night was good for twenty-five encounters, changing company according to her need and liking,

> *Adhuc ardens rigidae tentigine vulvo*
> *Et lassata viris, necdum satiata recessite*[*62]

We know about the dispute that occurred in Catalonia from a woman complaining of the over-assiduous efforts of her husband: not so much, in my opinion, that she was bothered by them (for I believe in miracles only in matters of faith) ... There intervened that notable sentence of the Queen of Aragon, by which, after mature deliberation with her council, this good queen ... ordained as the legitimate and necessary limit the number of six a day, relinquishing and giving up much of the need and desire of her sex, in order, she said, to establish an easy and consequently permanent and immutable formula.

* Juvenal.

It is true that sexual pleasure for woman is not at all the same as for man. I have already said that it is not known exactly if vaginal pleasure ever results in a definite orgasm: feminine confidences on this point are rare and even when they try to be precise, they remain extremely vague; reactions seem to vary greatly according to the subject. What is certain is that coitus for man has a precise biological end: ejaculation. And certainly many other very complex intentions are involved in aiming at this end; but once obtained, it is seen as an achievement, and if not as the satisfaction of desire, at least as its suppression. On the other hand, the aim for woman is uncertain in the beginning and more psychic than physiological; she desires arousal and sexual pleasure in general, but her body does not project any clear conclusion of the love act: and thus for her coitus is never fully completed: it does not include any finality. Male pleasure soars; when it reaches a certain threshold it fulfils itself and dies abruptly in the orgasm; the structure of the sexual act is finite and discontinuous. Feminine pleasure radiates through the whole body; it is not always centred in the genital system; vaginal contractions then even more than a true orgasm constitute a system of undulations that rhythmically arise, subside, re-form, reach for some instants a paroxysm, then blur and dissolve without ever completely dying. Because no fixed goal is assigned to it, pleasure aims at infinity: nervous or cardiac fatigue or psychic satiety often limit the woman's erotic possibilities rather than precise satisfaction; even fully fulfilled, even exhausted, she is never totally relieved: *Lassata necdum satiata*, according to Juvenal.

Man commits a grave error when he attempts to impose his own rhythm on his partner and when he is determined to give her an orgasm: often he only manages to destroy the form of pleasure she was experiencing in her own way.* This form is malleable enough to give itself a conclusion: spasms localised in the vagina, in the whole genital system or coming from the whole body can constitute a resolution; for certain women, they are produced fairly regularly and with sufficient violence to be likened to an orgasm; but a woman lover can also find a conclusion in the masculine orgasm that calms and satisfies her. And it is also possible that in a gradual and gentle way, the erotic phase dissolves calmly. Success requires not a mathematical synchronisation of pleasure, what-

---

* Lawrence clearly saw the opposition of these two erotic forms. But it is arbitrary to declare as he does that the woman *must* not experience orgasm. It might be an error to try to provoke it at all costs, but it is also an error to reject it in all cases, as Don Cipriano does in *The Plumed Serpent*.

ever many meticulous but simplistic men believe, but the establishment of a complex erotic form. Many think that 'making a woman come' is a question of time and technique, therefore of violence; they disregard the extent to which woman's sexuality is conditioned by the situation as a whole. Sexual pleasure for her, we have said, is a kind of spell; it demands total abandon; if words or gestures contest the magic of caresses, the spell vanishes. This is one of the reasons that the woman often closes her eyes: physiologically there is a reflex that compensates for the dilation of the pupil; but even in the dark she still lowers her eyelids; she wants to do away with the setting, the singularity of the moment, herself and her lover; she wants to lose herself within the carnal night as indistinct as the maternal breast. And even more particularly, she wants to abolish this separation that sets the male in front of her; she wants to merge with him. We have said already that she desires to remain a subject while making herself an object. More deeply alienated than man, as her whole body is desire and arousal, she remains a subject only through union with her partner; receiving and giving have to merge for both of them; if the man just takes without giving or if he gives pleasure without taking, she feels used; as soon as she realises herself as Other, she is the inessential other; she has to invalidate alterity. Thus the moment of the separation of bodies is almost always painful for her. Man, after coitus, whether he feels sad or joyous, duped by nature or conqueror of woman, whatever the case, he repudiates the flesh; he becomes a whole body; he wants to sleep, take a bath, smoke a cigarette, get a breath of fresh air. She would like to prolong the bodily contact until the spell that made her flesh dissipates completely; separation is a painful wrenching like a new weaning; she resents the lover who pulls away from her too abruptly. But what wounds her even more are the words that contest the fusion in which she believed for a moment. The 'wife of Gilles', whose story Madeleine Bourdouxhe told, pulls back when her husband asks her: 'Did you come?' She puts her hand on his mouth; many women hate this word because it reduces the pleasure to an immanent and separated sensation. 'Is it enough? Do you want more? Was it good?' The very fact of asking the question points out the separation and changes the love act into a mechanical operation assumed and controlled by the male. And this is precisely the reason he asks it. Much more than fusion and reciprocity, he seeks domination; when the unity of the couple is undone, he becomes the sole subject: a great deal of love or generosity is necessary to give up this privilege; he likes the woman to feel humiliated, possessed in spite of herself; he always wants to take her a little more than she gives herself. Woman would be spared many difficulties were man not to trail behind him so many complexes making him consider the love act a battle: then it would be possible for her not to consider the bed as an arena.

However, along with narcissism and pride, one observes in the girl a desire to be dominated. According to some psychoanalysts, masochism is a characteristic of women, by means of which they can adapt to their erotic destiny. But the notion of masochism is very confused and has to be considered attentively.

Freudian psychoanalysts distinguish three forms of masochism: one is the link between pain and sexual pleasure, another is the feminine acceptance of erotic dependence, and the last resides in a mechanism of self-punishment. Woman is masochistic because pleasure and pain in her are linked through defloration and birth, and because she consents to her passive role.

It must first be pointed out that attributing erotic value to pain does not in any way constitute behaviour of passive submission. Pain often serves to raise the tonus of the individual who experiences it, to awaken a sensitivity numbed by the very violence of arousal and pleasure; it is a sharp light bursting out in the carnal night, it removes the lover from the limbo where he is swooning so that he might once more be thrown into it. Pain is normally part of erotic frenzy; bodies that delight in being bodies for their reciprocal joy seek to find each other, unite with each other, and confront each other in every possible way. There is a wrenching from oneself in eroticism, a transport, an ecstasy: suffering also destroys the limits of the self, it is a going beyond and a paroxysm; pain has always played a big role in orgies; and it is well known that the exquisite and the painful converge: a caress can become torture, torment gives pleasure. Embracing easily leads to biting, pinching, scratching; such behaviour is not generally sadistic; it expresses a desire to merge and not to destroy; and the subject that submits to it does not seek to disavow and humiliate himself but to unite; besides, it is far from being specifically masculine. In fact, pain has a masochistic meaning only when it is grasped and desired as the manifestation of enslavement. As for the pain of defloration, it is specifically not accompanied by pleasure; and all women fear the suffering of giving birth and they are happy that modern methods free them from it. Pain has neither more nor less place in their sexuality than in that of man.

Feminine docility is, moreover, a very equivocal notion. We have seen that most of the time the young girl accepts in her *imagination*

the domination of a demigod, a hero, a male, but it is still only a narcissistic game. She is in no way disposed to submit to the carnal expression
of this authority in reality. By contrast, she often refuses to give herself
to a man she admires and respects, giving herself to an ordinary man
instead. It is an error to seek the key to concrete behaviour in fantasy,
because fantasies are created and cherished as fantasies. The little girl
who dreams of rape with a mixture of horror and complicity does not
desire to be raped and the event, if it occurred, would be a loathsome
catastrophe. We have already seen in Marie Le Hardouin a typical
example of this dissociation. She writes:

> But there remained an area on the path of abolition that I only
> entered with pinched nostrils and a beating heart. This was the
> path that beyond amorous sensuality led me to sensuality itself . . .
> there was no deceitful infamy that I did not commit in dreams. I
> suffered from the need to affirm myself in every possible way.*[63]

The case of Marie Bashkirtseff should also be recalled:

> All my life I have tried to place myself *voluntarily* under some kind
> of *illusory domination*, but all the people I tried were so ordinary in
> comparison with me that all I felt for them was disgust.

Moreover, it is true that the woman's sexual role is largely passive; but
to live this passive situation in its immediacy is no more masochistic than
the male's normal aggressiveness is sadistic; woman can transcend caresses,
arousal and penetration towards achieving her own pleasure, thus maintaining the affirmation of her subjectivity; she can also seek union with
the lover and give herself to him, which signifies a surpassing of herself
and not an abdication. Masochism exists when the individual chooses to
constitute himself as a pure thing through the consciousness of the other,
to represent oneself to oneself as a thing, to play at being a thing.
'Masochism is an attempt not to fascinate the other by my objectivity
but to make myself be fascinated by my objectivity for others.'[†64] Sade's
Juliette or the young virgin from *Philosophy in the Boudoir*,[65] who both
give themselves to the male in all possible ways, but for their own pleasure,
are not in any way masochists. Lady Chatterley and Kate, in the total

---

* *The Black Sail.*
† J. P. Sartre, *Being and Nothingness.*

abandon they consent to, are not masochists. To speak of masochism, one has to posit the *self* and this alienated double has to be considered as founded on the other's freedom.

In this sense, true masochism can be found in some women. The girl is susceptible to it since she is easily narcissistic and narcissism consists in alienating one's self in one's ego. If she experienced arousal and violent desire right from the beginning of her erotic initiation, she would live her experiences authentically and stop projecting them towards this ideal pole that she calls self; but in frigidity, the self continues to affirm itself; making it the thing of a male seems then like a fault. But 'masochism, like sadism, is an assumption of guilt. I am guilty due to the very fact that I am an object.'[66] This idea of Sartre's fits in with the Freudian notion of self-punishment. The young girl considers herself guilty of delivering her self to another and she punishes herself for it by willingly increasing humiliation and subjugation; we have seen that virgins defied their future lovers and punished themselves for their future submission by inflicting various tortures on themselves. When the lover is real and present, they persist in this attitude. Frigidity itself can be seen as a punishment that woman imposes as much on herself as on her partner: wounded in her vanity, she resents him and herself, and she does not permit herself pleasure. In masochism, she will wildly enslave herself to the male, she will tell him words of adoration, she will wish to be humiliated, beaten; she will alienate herself more and more deeply out of fury for having agreed to the alienation. This is quite obviously Mathilde de La Mole's behaviour, for example; she regrets having given herself to Julien; which is why she sometimes falls at his feet, bends over backwards to indulge each of his whims, sacrifices her hair; but at the same time, she is in revolt against him as much as against herself; one imagines that she is icy in his arms. The fake abandon of the masochistic woman creates new barriers that keep her from pleasure; and at the same time, she is taking vengeance against herself for this inability to experience pleasure. The vicious circle from frigidity to masochism can establish itself for ever, bringing sadistic behaviour along with it as compensation. Becoming erotically mature can also deliver woman from her frigidity and her narcissism, and assuming her sexual passivity, she lives it immediately instead of playing the role. Because the paradox of masochism is that the subject reaffirms itself constantly even in its attempt to abdicate itself, it is in the gratuitous gift, in the spontaneous movement towards the other, that he succeeds in forgetting himself. It is thus true that woman will be more prone than man to masochistic temptation; her erotic situation as passive object commits her to playing passivity; this game is the self-punishment to which her narcissistic revolts and consequent frigidity lead her; the fact is that many women and in particular young girls are masochists. Colette, speaking of her first amorous experiences, confides to us in *My Apprenticeship*:

> Ridden by youth and ignorance, I had known intoxication – a guilty rapture, an atrocious, impure, adolescent impulse. There are many scarcely nubile girls who dream of becoming the show, the plaything, the licentious masterpiece of some middle-aged man. It is an ugly dream that is punished by its fulfilment, a morbid thing, akin to the neuroses of puberty, the habit of eating chalk and coal, of drinking mouthwash, of reading dirty books and sticking pins into the palm of the hand.[67]

This perfectly expresses the fact that masochism is part of juvenile perversions, that it is not an authentic solution of the conflict created by woman's sexual destiny, but a way of escaping it by wallowing in it. In no way does it represent the normal and happy blossoming of feminine eroticism.

This blossoming supposes that – in love, tenderness and sensuality – woman succeeds in overcoming her passivity and establishing a relationship of reciprocity with her partner. The asymmetry of male and female eroticism creates insoluble problems as long as there is a battle of the sexes; they can easily be settled when a woman feels both desire and respect in a man; if he covets her in her flesh while recognising her freedom, she recovers her essentialness at the moment she becomes object, she remains free in the submission to which she consents. Thus, the lovers can experience shared pleasure each in their own way; each partner feels pleasure as being his own while at the same time having its source in the other. The words 'receive' and 'give' exchange meanings, joy is gratitude, pleasure is tenderness. In a concrete and sexual form the reciprocal recognition of the self and the other is accomplished in the keenest consciousness of the other and the self. Some women say they feel the masculine sex organ in themselves as a part of their own body; some men think they *are* the woman they penetrate; these expressions are obviously inaccurate; the dimension of the *other* remains; but the fact is that alterity no longer has a hostile character; this consciousness of the union of the bodies in their separation is what makes the sexual act moving; it is all the more overwhelming that the two beings who together passionately negate and affirm their limits are fellow creatures and yet are different. This difference that all too often isolates them becomes the source of their marvelling when they join together; woman recognises the virile passion in man's force as the reverse of the fever that burns within her, and this is the power she wields over him; this sex organ swollen with life belongs to her just as her smile belongs to the man who gives her pleasure. All the treasures of virility and femininity reflecting off and reappropriating each other make a moving and ecstatic unity. What is necessary for such harmony is not technical refinements but rather, on the basis of an immediate erotic attraction, a reciprocal generosity of body and soul.

This generosity is often hampered in man by his vanity and in woman by her timidity; if she does not overcome her inhibitions, she will not be able to make it thrive. This is why full sexual blossoming in woman arrives rather late: she reaches her erotic peak at about thirty-five. Unfortunately, if she is married, her husband is too used to her frigidity; she can still seduce new lovers, but she is beginning to fade: time is running out. At the very moment they cease to be desirable, many women finally decide to assume their desires.

The conditions under which woman's sexual life unfolds depend not only on these facts but also on her whole social and economic situation. It would be too vague to attempt to study this further without this context. But several generally valid conclusions emerge from our examination. The erotic experience is one that most poignantly reveals to human beings their ambiguous condition; they experience it as flesh and as spirit, as the other and as subject. Woman experiences this conflict at its most dramatic because she assumes herself first as object and does not immediately find a confident autonomy in pleasure; she has to reconquer her dignity as transcendent and free subject while assuming her carnal condition: this is a delicate and risky enterprise that often fails. But the very difficulty of her situation protects her from the mystifications by which the male lets himself be duped; he is easily deceived by the fallacious privileges that his aggressive role and satisfied solitude of orgasm imply; he hesitates to recognise himself fully as flesh. Woman has a more authentic experience of herself.

Even if woman accommodates herself more or less exactly to her passive role, she is still frustrated as an active individual. She does not envy man his organ of possession: she envies in him his prey. It is a curious paradox that man lives in a sensual world of sweetness, tenderness, softness – a feminine world – while woman moves in the hard and harsh male universe; her hands still long for the embrace of smooth skin and soft flesh: adolescent boy, woman, flowers, furs, child; a whole part of herself remains available and wishes to possess a treasure similar to the one she gives the male. This explains why there subsists in many women, in a more or less latent form, a tendency towards homosexuality. For a set of complex reasons, there are those for whom this tendency asserts itself with particular authority. Not all women agree to give their sexual problems the one classic solution officially accepted by society. Thus must we envisage those who choose forbidden paths.

CHAPTER 4

The Lesbian

People are always ready to see the lesbian as wearing a felt hat, her hair short and a necktie; her mannishness is seen as an abnormality indicating a hormonal imbalance. Nothing could be more erroneous than this confusion of the homosexual and the virago. There are many homosexual women among odalisques, courtesans and the most deliberately 'feminine' women; by contrast, a great number of 'masculine' women are heterosexual. Sexologists and psychiatrists confirm what ordinary observation suggests: the immense majority of 'cursed women' are constituted exactly like other women. Their sexuality is not determined by anatomical 'destiny'.

There are certainly cases where physiological givens create particular situations. There is no rigorous biological distinction between the two sexes; an identical soma is modified by hormonal activity whose orientation is genotypically defined, but can be diverted in the course of the foetus's development; this results in individuals halfway between male and female. Some men take on a feminine appearance because of late development of their male organs, and sometimes girls as well – athletic ones in particular – change into boys. Helene Deutsch tells of a young girl who ardently courted a married woman, wanted to run off and live with her: she realised one day that she was in fact a man, so she was able to marry her beloved and have children. But it must not be concluded that every homosexual woman is a 'hidden man' in false guise. The hermaphrodite who has elements of two genital systems often has a female sexuality: I knew of one, exiled by the Nazis from Vienna, who greatly regretted her inability to appeal to either heterosexuals or homosexuals as she loved only men. Under the influence of male hormones, 'viriloid' women present masculine secondary sexual characteristics; in infantile women, female hormones are deficient and their development remains incomplete. These particularities can more or less directly trigger a lesbian orientation. A person with a vigorous, aggressive and exuberant vitality wishes to exert himself actively and usually rejects passivity; an unattractive and malformed woman may try to compensate for her inferiority by acquiring virile attributes; if her erogenous sensitivity is undeveloped, she does not desire masculine caresses. But anatomy and hormones never define anything but a situation and do not posit the object towards which the situation will be transcended. Deutsch also cites the case of a wounded Polish legionnaire she treated during World War I, who was, in fact, a young girl with marked viriloid characteristics; she had joined the army as a nurse, then succeeded in wearing the uniform; she nevertheless fell in love with a soldier – whom she later married – which caused her to be regarded as a male homosexual. Her masculine behaviour did not contradict a feminine type of eroticism. Man himself does not exclusively desire woman; the fact that the male homosexual body can be perfectly virile implies that a woman's virility does not necessarily destine her to homosexuality.

Even in woman physiologically normal themselves, it has sometimes been asserted that there is a distinction between 'clitoral' and 'vaginal' women, the former being destined to sapphic love; but it has been seen that all childhood eroticism is clitoral; whether it remains fixed at this stage or is transformed has nothing to do with anatomical facts; nor is it true, as has often been maintained, that infant masturbation explains the ulterior primacy of the clitoral system: a child's masturbation is recognised today by sexologists as an absolutely normal and generally widespread phenomenon. The development of feminine eroticism is – we have seen – a psychological situation in which physiological factors are included, but which depends on the subject's overall attitude to existence. Marañón considered sexuality to be 'one-way', and that man attains a completed form of it, while for woman, it remains 'halfway'; only the lesbian could possess a libido as rich as a male's and would thus be a 'superior' feminine type. In fact, feminine sexuality has its own structure, and the idea of a hierarchy in male and female libidos is absurd; the choice of sexual object in no way depends on the amount of energy woman might have.

Psychoanalysts have had the great merit of seeing a psychic phenomenon and not an organic one in inversion; to them, nonetheless, it still seems determined by external circumstances. But in fact they have not studied it very much. According to Freud, female erotic maturation requires the passage from the clitoral to the vaginal stage, symmetrical with the change transferring the love the little girl felt first for her mother to her father; various factors may hinder this development; the woman is not resigned to castration, hides the absence of the penis from herself, or remains fixated on her mother, for whom she seeks substitutes. For Adler, this fixation is not a passively endured accident: it is desired by the subject who, in her will for power, deliberately denies her mutilation and seeks to identify with the man whose domination she refuses. Whether from infantile fixation or masculine protest, homosexuality would appear in any case as unfinished development. In truth, the lesbian is no more a 'failed' woman than a 'superior' woman. The individual's history is not an inevitable progression: at every step, the past is grasped anew by a new choice, and the 'normality' of the choice confers no privileged value on it: it must be judged by its authenticity. Homosexuality can be a way for woman to flee her condition or a way to assume it. Psychoanalysts' great error, through moralising conformity, is that they never envisage it as anything but an inauthentic attitude.

Woman is an existent who is asked to make herself object; as subject she has an aggressive sensuality that does not find satisfaction in the masculine body: from this are born the conflicts her eroticism must overcome. The system is considered normal that, delivering her as prey to a male, restores her sovereignty by putting a baby in her arms: but this 'naturalism' is determined by a more or less well understood social interest. Even heterosexuality permits other solutions. Homosexuality for woman is one attempt among others to reconcile her autonomy with the passivity of her flesh. And if nature is invoked, it could be said that every woman is naturally homosexual. The lesbian is characterised simply by her refusal of the male and her preference for feminine flesh; but every adolescent female fears penetration and masculine domination, and she feels a certain repulsion for the man's body; on the contrary, the feminine body is for her, as for man, an object of desire. As I have already said: men posit themselves as subjects and at the same time they posit themselves as separate; to consider the other as a thing to take is to attack the virile ideal in the other and thus jointly in one's self as well; by contrast, the woman who regards herself as object sees herself and her fellow creatures as prey. The homosexual man inspires hostility from male and female heterosexuals as they both demand that man be a dominating subject;* by contrast, both sexes spontaneously view lesbians with

---

* A heterosexual woman can easily have a friendship with certain homosexual men, because she finds security and amusement in these asexual relations. But on the whole, she feels hostile towards these men who in themselves or in others degrade the sovereign male into a passive thing.

indulgence. 'I swear,' says the comte de Tilly, 'it is a rivalry that in no way bothers me; on the contrary, I find it amusing and I am immoral enough to laugh at it.' Colette attributed this same amused indifference to Renaud faced with the couple Claudine and Rézi.* A man is more irritated by an active and autonomous heterosexual woman than by a non-aggressive homosexual one; only the former challenges masculine prerogatives; sapphic loves in no way contradict the traditional model of the division of the sexes: in most cases, they are an assumption of femininity and not a rejection of it. We have seen that they often appear in the adolescent girl as an ersatz form of heterosexual relations she has not yet had the opportunity or the audacity to experience: it is a stage, an apprenticeship, and the one who most ardently engages in such loves may tomorrow be the most ardent of wives, lovers and mothers. What must be explained in the female homosexual is thus not the positive aspect of her choice but the negative side: she is not characterised by her preference for women but by the exclusiveness of this preference.

According to Jones and Hesnard, lesbians mostly fall into two categories: 'masculine lesbians', who 'try to act like men', and 'feminine' ones, who 'are afraid of men'. It is a fact that one can, on the whole, observe two tendencies in homosexual women; some refuse passivity, while others choose to lose themselves passively in feminine arms; but these two attitudes react upon each other reciprocally; relations to the chosen object and to the rejected one are explained by each other reciprocally. For numerous reasons, as we shall see, the distinction given seems quite arbitrary.

To define the lesbian as 'virile' because of her desire to 'imitate man' is to doom her to inauthenticity. I have already said how psychoanalysts create ambiguities by accepting masculine-feminine categories as currently defined by society. Thus, man today represents the positive and the neuter – that is, the male and the human being – while woman represents the negative, the female. Every time she behaves like a human being, she is declared to be identifying with the male. Her sports, her political and intellectual activities, and her desire for other women are interpreted as 'masculine protest'; there is a refusal to take into account the values towards which she is transcending, which inevitably leads to the belief that she is making the inauthentic choice of a subjective attitude. The great misunderstanding upon which this system of interpretation rests is to hold that it is *natural* for the human female to make a *feminine* woman

---

* It is noteworthy that English law punishes homosexuality in men while not considering it a crime for women.

of herself: being a heterosexual or even a mother is not enough to realise this ideal; the 'real woman' is an artificial product that civilisation produces the way eunuchs were produced in the past; these supposed 'instincts' of coquetry or docility are inculcated in her just as phallic pride is for man; he does not always accept his virile vocation; she has good reasons to accept even less docilely the vocation assigned to her. The notions of inferiority complex and masculinity complex remind me of the anecdote that Denis de Rougemont recounts in *The Devil's Share*:[68] a woman imagined that birds were attacking her when she went walking in the country; after several months of psychoanalytical treatment that failed to cure her of her obsession, the doctor accompanied her to the clinic garden and realised that *the birds were attacking her*. Woman feels undermined because in fact the restrictions of femininity undermine her. She spontaneously chooses to be a complete individual, a subject and a freedom before whom the world and future open: if this choice amounts to the choice of virility, it does so to the extent that femininity today means mutilation. Homosexuals' confessions collected by Havelock Ellis and Stekel – platonic in the first case and openly declared in the second – clearly show that feminine *specificity* is what outrages the two subjects.

> Ever since I can remember anything at all I could never think of myself as a girl and I was in perpetual trouble, with this as the real reason. When I was 5 or 6 years old I began to say to myself that, whatever anyone said, if I was not a boy at any rate I was not a girl . . . I regarded the conformation of my body as a mysterious accident . . . When I could only crawl my absorbing interest was hammers and carpet-nails. Before I could walk I begged to be put on horses' backs . . . By the time I was 7 it seemed to me that everything I liked was called wrong for a girl . . . I was not at all a happy little child and often cried and was made irritable; I was so confused by the talk about boys and girls . . . Every half-holiday I went out with the boys from my brothers' school . . . When I was about 11 my parents got more mortified at my behaviour and perpetually threatened me with boarding school . . . My going was finally announced to me as a punishment to me for being what I was . . . In whatever direction my thoughts ran I always surveyed them from the point of view of a boy . . . A consideration of social matters led me to feel very sorry for women, whom I regarded as made by a deliberate process of manufacture into the fools I thought they were, and by the same process that I myself was being made one.

I felt more and more that men were to be envied and women pitied. I lay stress on this for it started in me a deliberate interest in women as women, I began to feel protective and kindly toward women.

As for Stekel's transvestite:

Until her sixth year, in spite of assertions of those around her, she thought she was a boy, dressed like a girl for reasons unknown to her . . . At 6, she told herself, 'I'll be a lieutenant, and if God wills it, a marshal.' She often dreamed of mounting a horse and riding out of town at the head of an army. Though very intelligent, she was miserable to be transferred from an ordinary school to a lycée . . . *she was afraid of becoming effeminate.*

This revolt by no means implies a sapphic predestination; most little girls feel the same indignation and despair when they learn that the accidental conformation of their bodies condemns their tastes and aspirations; Colette Audry*[69] angrily discovered at the age of twelve that she could never become a sailor; the future woman naturally feels indignant about the limitations her sex imposes on her. The question is not why she rejects them: the real problem is rather to understand why she accepts them. Her conformism comes from her docility and timidity; but this resignation will easily turn to revolt if society's compensations are judged inadequate. This is what will happen in cases where the adolescent girl feels unattractive as a woman: anatomical configurations become particularly important when this happens; if she is, or believes she is, ugly or has a bad figure, woman rejects a feminine destiny for which she feels ill adapted; but it would be wrong to say that she acquires a mannish attitude to compensate for a lack of femininity: rather, the opportunities offered to the adolescent girl in exchange for the masculine advantages she is asked to sacrifice seem too meagre to her. All little girls envy boys' practical clothes; it is their reflection in the mirror and the promises of things to come that make their furbelows little by little all the more precious; if the mirror harshly reflects an ordinary face, if it offers no promise, then lace and ribbons are an embarrassing, even ridiculous, livery, and the 'tomboy' obstinately wishes to remain a boy.

Even if she has a good figure and is pretty, the woman who is involved in her own projects or who claims her freedom in general refuses to

---

* *In the Eyes of Memory.*

abdicate in favour of another human being; she recognises herself in her acts, not in her immanent presence: male desire reducing her to the limits of her body shocks her as much as it shocks a young boy; she feels the same disgust for her submissive female companions as the virile man feels for the passive homosexual. She adopts a masculine attitude in part to repudiate any involvement with them; she disguises her clothes, her looks and her language, she forms a couple with a female friend where she assumes the male role: this playacting is in fact a 'masculine protest'; but it is a secondary phenomenon; what is spontaneous is the conquering and sovereign subject's shame at the idea of changing into a carnal prey. Many women athletes are homosexual; they do not perceive this body that is muscle, movement, extension and momentum as passive flesh; it does not magically beckon caresses, it is a hold on the world, not a thing of the world: the gap between the body for-itself and the body for-others seems in this case to be unbreachable. Analogous resistance is found in women of action, 'brainy' types for whom even carnal submission is impossible. Were equality of the sexes concretely realised, this obstacle would be in large part eradicated; but man is still imbued with his own sense of superiority, which is a disturbing conviction for the woman who does not share it. It should be noted, however, that the most wilful and domineering women seldom hesitate to confront the male: the woman considered 'virile' is often clearly heterosexual. She does not want to renounce her claims as a human being; but she has no intention of mutilating her femininity either; she chooses to enter the masculine world, even to annex it for herself. Her robust sensuality has no fear of male roughness; she has fewer defences to overcome than the timid virgin in finding joy in a man's body. A rude and animal nature will not feel the humiliation of coitus; an intellectual with an intrepid mind will challenge it; sure of herself and in a fighting mood, a woman will gladly engage in a duel she is sure to win. George Sand had a predilection for young and 'feminine' men; but Mme de Staël looked for youth and beauty only in her later life: dominating men by her sharp mind and proudly accepting their admiration, she could hardly have felt a prey in their arms. A sovereign such as Catherine the Great could even allow herself masochistic ecstasies: she alone remained the master in these games. Isabelle Eberhardt, who dressed as a man and traversed the Sahara on horseback, felt no less diminished when she gave herself to some vigorous sharpshooter. The woman who refuses to be the man's vassal is far from always fleeing him; rather she tries to make him the instrument of her pleasure. In certain favourable circumstances – mainly dependent on her partner – the very notion of competition will disappear and she will enjoy experiencing her woman's condition just as man experiences his.

But this arrangement between her active personality and her role as passive female is nevertheless more difficult for her than for man; rather than wear themselves out in this effort, many women will give up trying. There are numerous lesbians among women artists and writers. It is not because their sexual specificity is the source of creative energy or a manifestation of the existence of this superior energy; it is rather that being absorbed in serious work, they do not intend to waste their time playing the woman's role or struggling against men. Not admitting male superiority, they do not wish to pretend to accept it or tire themselves contesting it; they seek release, peace and diversion in sexual pleasure: they could spend their time more profitably without a partner who acts like an adversary; and so they free themselves from the chains attached to femininity. Of course, the nature of her heterosexual experiences will often lead the 'virile' woman to choose between assuming or repudiating her sex. Masculine disdain confirms the feeling of unattractiveness in an ugly woman; a lover's arrogance will wound a proud woman. All the motives for frigidity we have envisaged are found here: resentment, spite, fear of pregnancy, abortion trauma, and so on. They become all the weightier the more woman defies man.

However, homosexuality is not always an entirely satisfactory solution for a domineering woman; since she seeks to affirm herself, it vexes her not to fully realise her feminine possibilities; heterosexual relations seem to her at once an impoverishment and an enrichment; in repudiating the limitations implied by her sex, she may limit herself in another way. Just as the frigid woman desires pleasure even while rejecting it, the lesbian would often like to be a normal and complete woman, while at the same time not wanting it. This hesitation is evident in the case of the transvestite studied by Stekel.

We have seen that she was only comfortable with boys and did not want to 'become effeminate'. At sixteen years of age, she formed her first relations with young girls; she had a profound contempt for them, which gave her eroticism a sadistic quality; she ardently, but platonically, courted a friend she respected: she felt disgust for those she possessed. She threw herself fiercely into difficult studies. Disappointed by her first serious Sapphic love affair, she frenetically indulged in purely sensual experiences and began to drink.

At seventeen, she met the young man she married: but she thought of him as her wife; she dressed in a masculine way, and she continued to drink and study. At first she only had vaginismus and intercourse never produced an orgasm. She considered her position 'humiliating'; she was always the one to take the aggressive and active role. She left her husband even while being 'madly in love with him' and took up relations with women again. She met a male artist to whom she gave herself, but still without an orgasm. Her life was divided into clearly defined periods; for a while she wrote, worked creatively and felt completely male; she episodically and sadistically slept with women during these periods. Then she would have a female period. She underwent analysis because she wanted to reach orgasm.

The lesbian would easily be able to consent to the loss of her femininity if in doing so she gained triumphant masculinity. But no. She obviously remains deprived of the virile organ; she can deflower her girl-friend with her hand or use an artificial penis to imitate possession; but she is still a eunuch. She may suffer acutely from this. Because she is incomplete as a woman, impotent as a man, her malaise sometimes manifests itself in psychoses. A patient told Roland Dalbiez,*[70] 'It would be better if I had a thing to penetrate with.' Another wished that her breasts were rigid. The lesbian will often try to compensate for her virile inferiority by arrogance or exhibitionism, which in fact reveals inner imbalance. Sometimes, also, she will succeed in establishing with other women a type of relation completely analogous to those a 'feminine' man or an adolescent still unsure of his virility might have with them. A striking case of such a destiny is that of Sandor reported by Krafft-Ebing. She used this means to attain a perfect balance destroyed only by the intervention of society:

Sarolta came of a titled Hungarian family known for its eccentricities. Her father had her reared as a boy, calling her Sandor; she rode horseback, hunted and so on. She was under such influences until, at thirteen, she was placed in an institution. A little later she fell in love with an English girl, pretending to be a boy, and ran away with her. At home again, she resumed the name Sandor and wore boys' clothing, while being carefully educated. She went on long trips with her father, always in male attire; she was addicted to sports, drank, and visited brothels. She felt particularly drawn

* *Psychoanalytical Method and the Doctrine of Freud.*

toward actresses and other such detached women, preferably not too young but 'feminine in nature'. 'It delighted me,' she related, 'if the passion of a lady was disclosed under a poetic veil. All immodesty in a woman was disgusting to me. I had an indescribable aversion to female attire – indeed, for everything feminine. But only insofar as it concerned me; for, on the other hand, I was all enthusiasm for the beautiful Sex.' She had numerous affairs with women and spent a good deal of money on them. At the same time, she was a valued contributor to two important journals.

She lived for three years in 'marriage' with a woman ten years older than herself, from whom she broke away only with great difficulty. She was able to inspire violent passions. Falling in love with a young teacher, she was married to her in an elaborate ceremony, the girl and her family believing her to be a man; her father-in-law on one occasion noticed what seemed to be an erection (probably a priapus); she shaved as a matter of form, but servants in the hotel room suspected the truth from seeing blood on her bedclothes and from spying through the keyhole.

Thus unmasked, Sandor was put in prison and later acquitted, after thorough investigation. She was greatly saddened by her enforced separation from her beloved Marie, to whom she wrote long and impassioned letters from her cell.

The examination showed that her conformation was not wholly feminine: her pelvis was small and she had no waist. Her breasts were developed, her sexual parts quite feminine but not maturely formed. Her menstruation appeared late, at seventeen, and she felt a profound horror of the function. She was equally horrified at the thought of sexual relations with the male; her sense of modesty was developed only in regard to women and to the point that she would feel less shyness in going to bed with a man than with a woman. It was very embarrassing for her to be treated as a woman, and she was truly in anguish at having to wear feminine clothes. She felt that she was 'drawn as by a magnetic force toward women of twenty-four to thirty'. She found sexual satisfaction exclusively in caressing her loved one, never in being caressed. At times she made use of a stocking stuffed with oakum as a priapus. She detested men. She was very sensitive to the moral esteem of others, and she had much literary talent, wide culture, and a colossal memory.[71]

Sandor was not psychoanalysed but several salient points emerge just from the presentation of the facts. It seems that most spontaneously and 'without a masculine protest', she always thought of herself as a man, thanks to the way she was brought up and her body's constitution; the way her father included her in his trips and his life obviously had a decisive influence on her; her virility was so confirmed that she did not show the slightest ambivalence towards women: she loved them like a man, without feeling compromised by them; she loved them in a purely dominating and active way, without accepting reciprocity. However, it is striking that she 'detested men' and that she particularly cherished older women. This suggests that Sandor had a *masculine* Oedipus complex vis-à-vis her mother; she perpetuated the infantile attitude of the very young girl who, forming a couple with her mother, nourished the hope of one day protecting and dominating her. Very often the maternal tenderness a child has been deprived of haunts her whole adult life: raised by her father, Sandor must have dreamed of a loving and treasured mother, whom she sought afterwards in other women; this explains her deep jealousy of other men, linked to her respect and 'poetic' love for 'isolated' and older women who were endowed in her eyes with a sacred quality. Her attitude was exactly that of Rousseau with Mme de Warens and the young Benjamin Constant concerning Mme de Charrière: sensitive, 'feminine' adolescent boys also turn to maternal mistresses. This type of lesbian is found in more or less pronounced forms, one who has never identified with her mother – because she either admired or detested her too much – but who, refusing to be a woman, desires the softness of feminine protection around her. From the bosom of this warm womb she can emerge into the world with boyish daring; she acts like a man but as a man she has a fragility that makes her desire the love of an older mistress; the couple will reproduce the classic heterosexual couple: matron and adolescent boy.

Psychoanalysts have clearly noted the importance of the relationship a homosexual woman had earlier with her mother. There are two cases where the adolescent girl has difficulty escaping her influence: if she has been overly protected by an anxious mother; or if she was mistreated by a 'bad mother' who inculcated a deep feeling of guilt in her. In the first case, their relations often bordered on homosexuality: they slept together, caressed or kissed each other's breasts; the young girl will seek this same pleasure in new arms. In the second case, she will feel an ardent need of a 'good mother' who protects her against her own mother, who removes the curse she feels weighing on her. One of the stories Havelock Ellis recounts concerns a subject who detested her mother throughout her childhood; she describes the love she felt at sixteen for an older woman:

> I felt like an orphan child who had suddenly acquired a mother, and through her I began to feel less antagonistic to grown people and to feel . . . respect [for them] . . . My love for her was perfectly pure, and I thought of hers as simply maternal . . . I liked her to touch me and she sometimes held me in her arms or let me sit on her lap. At bedtime she used to come and say good-night and kiss me upon the mouth.[72]

If the older woman is willing, the younger one will joyfully abandon herself to more ardent embraces. She will usually assume the passive role because she desires to be dominated, protected, rocked and caressed like a child. Whether these relations remain platonic or become carnal, they often have the characteristics of a truly passionate love. However, the very fact that they appear as a classic stage in the adolescent girl's development means that they cannot suffice to explain a determined choice of homosexuality. The young girl seeks in it both a liberation and a security she can also find in masculine arms. Once the period of amorous enthusiasm has passed, the younger one often experiences the ambivalent feeling for her older partner she felt towards her mother; she falls under her influence while at the same time wishing to extricate herself from it; if the other persists in holding her back, she will remain her 'prisoner'* for a time; but either in violent scenes or amicably, she will manage to escape; having succeeded in expunging her adolescence, she feels ready to face a normal woman's life. For her lesbian vocation to affirm itself she either has to reject her femininity – like Sandor – or her femininity has to flourish more happily in feminine arms. Thus, fixation on the mother is clearly not enough to explain homosexuality. And it can be chosen for completely different reasons. A woman may discover or sense through complete or tentative experiences that she will not derive pleasure from heterosexual relations, that only another woman is able to satisfy her: in particular, for the woman who worships her femininity, the sapphic embrace turns out to be the most satisfying.

It is very important to emphasise this: the refusal to make oneself an object is not always what leads a woman to homosexuality; most lesbians, on the contrary, seek to claim the treasures of their femininity. Consenting

---

* As in Dorothy Baker's novel, *Trio*, which is, moreover, very superficial.

to metamorphose oneself into a passive thing does not mean renouncing all claims to subjectivity: the woman thereby hopes to realise herself as the in-itself; but she will then seek to grasp herself in her alterity. Alone, she does not succeed in separating herself in reality; she might caress her breasts but she does not know how they would seem to a foreign hand, nor how they would come to life under the foreign hand; a man can reveal to her the existence *for itself* of her flesh, but not what it is *for an other*. It is only when her fingers caress a woman's body whose fingers in turn caress her body that the miracle of the mirror takes place. Between man and woman love is an act; each one torn from self becomes other: what delights the woman in love is that the passive listlessness of her flesh is reflected in the man's ardour; but the narcissistic woman is clearly baffled by the charms of the erect sex organ. Between women, love is contemplation; caresses are meant less to appropriate the other than to re-create oneself slowly through her; separation is eliminated, there is neither fight nor victory nor defeat; each one is both subject and object, sovereign and slave in exact reciprocity; this duality is complicity. 'The close resemblance,' says Colette,*[73] 'validates even sensual pleasure. The woman friend basks in the certitude of caressing a body whose secrets she knows and whose own body tells her what she prefers.' And Renée Vivien:

> Our heart is alike in our woman's breast,[74]
> Dearest! Our body is identically formed.
> The same heavy fate was laid on our soul
> I translate your smile and the shadow on your face.
> My softness is equal to your immense softness,
> At times it even seems we are of the same race
> I love in you my child, my friend and my sister.†[75]

This uncoupling can occur in a maternal form; the mother who recognises and alienates herself in her daughter often has a sexual attachment to her; the desire to protect and rock in her arms a soft object made of flesh is shared with the lesbian. Colette emphasises this analogy, writing in *Tender Shoot*:[76] 'You will give me pleasure, bent over me, your eyes full of maternal concern, you who seek, through your passionate woman friend, the child you never had.'

* *The Pure and the Impure.*
† *Sortilèges.*

And Renée Vivien expresses the same feeling:

> *Come, I shall carry you off like a child who is sick,*
> *Like a child who is plaintive and fearful and sick.*
> *Within my firm arms I clasp your slight body,*
> *You shall see that I know how to heal and protect,*
> *And my arms are strong, the better to protect you.*[77]

And again:

> *I love you to be weak and calm in my arms . . .*
> *Like a warm cradle where you will take your rest.*[78]

In all love – sexual or maternal – there is both greed and generosity, the desire to possess the other and to give the other everything; but when both women are narcissists, caressing an extension of themselves or their reflection in the child or the lover, the mother and the lesbian are notably similar.

However, narcissism does not always lead to homosexuality either, as Marie Bashkirtseff's example shows; there is not the slightest trace of affection for women in her writings; intellectual rather than sensual, extremely vain, she dreams from childhood of being validated by man: nothing interests her unless it contributes to her glory. A woman who idolises only herself and who strives for abstract success is incapable of a warm complicity with other women; for her, they are only rivals and enemies.

In truth, there is never only one determining factor; it is always a question of a choice made from a complex whole, contingent on a free decision; no sexual destiny governs an individual's life: on the contrary, his eroticism expresses his general attitude to existence.

Circumstances, however, also have an important part in this choice. Today, the two sexes still live mostly separated: in boarding schools and in girls' schools the passage from intimacy to sexuality is quick; there are far fewer lesbians in circles where girl and boy camaraderie encourages heterosexual experiences. Many women who work among women in workshops and offices and who have little opportunity to be around men will form amorous friendships with women: it will be materially and morally practical to join their lives. The absence or failure of heterosexual relations will destine them to inversion. It is difficult to determine

* *At the Sweet Hour of Hand in Hand.*

the boundary between resignation and predilection: a woman can devote herself to women because a man has disappointed her, but sometimes he disappoints her because she was looking for a woman in him. For all these reasons, it is wrong to establish a radical distinction between heterosexual and homosexual. Once the indecisive time of adolescence has passed, the normal male no longer allows himself homosexual peccadilloes; but the normal woman often returns to the loves – platonic or not – that enchanted her youth. Disappointed by men, she will seek in feminine arms the male lover who betrayed her; in *The Vagabond*, Colette wrote about this consoling role that forbidden sexual pleasures often play in the lives of women: some of them can spend their whole existence consoling each other. Even a woman fulfilled by male embraces might not refuse calmer sexual pleasures. Passive and sensual, a woman friend's caresses will not shock her since all she has to do is let herself go, let herself be fulfilled. Active and ardent, she will seem 'androgynous', not because of a mysterious combination of hormones, but simply because aggressiveness and the taste for possession are looked on as virile attributes; Claudine in love with Renaud still covets Rézi's charms; as fully woman as she is, she still continues to desire to take and caress. Of course, these 'perverse' desires are carefully repressed in 'nice women'; they nonetheless manifest themselves as pure but passionate friendships or in the guise of maternal tenderness; sometimes they are suddenly revealed during a psychosis or a menopausal crisis.

So it is all the more useless to try to place lesbians in two definitive categories. Because social role-playing is sometimes superimposed on their real relations – taking pleasure in imitating a bisexual couple – they themselves suggest the division into 'virile' and 'feminine'. But the fact that one wears an austere suit and the other a flowing dress must not create an illusion. Looking more closely, one can ascertain – except in special cases – that their sexuality is ambiguous. A woman who becomes lesbian because she rejects male domination often experiences the joy of recognising the same proud Amazon in another; not long ago many guilty loves flourished among the women students of Sèvres who lived together far from men; they were proud to belong to a feminine elite and wanted to remain autonomous subjects; this complexity that united them against the privileged caste enabled each one to admire in a friend this prestigious being she cherished in herself; embracing each other, each one was both man and woman and was enchanted with the other's androgynous virtues. Inversely, a woman who wants to enjoy the pleasures of her femininity in feminine arms also knows the pride of obeying no master. Renée Vivien ardently loved feminine beauty and she wanted to be beautiful; she took great care of her appearance, she was proud of her long hair; but she also liked to feel free and intact; in her poems she expresses scorn for those women who through marriage consent to become serfs of a male. Her taste for hard liquor and her sometimes obscene language manifested her desire for virility. The truth is that for most couples caresses are reciprocal. Thus it follows that the roles are distributed in very uncertain ways: the most infantile woman can play an adolescent boy towards a protective matron, or a mistress leaning on her lover's arm. They can love each other as equals. Because her partners are counterparts, all combinations, transpositions, exchanges and scenarios are possible. Relations balance each other out depending on the psychological tendencies of each woman friend and on the situation as a whole. If there is one who helps or keeps the other, she assumes the male's functions: tyrannical protector, exploited dupe, respected lord or even sometimes a pimp; a moral, social and intellectual superiority will often confer authority on her; however, the one more loved will enjoy the privileges that the more loving one's passionate attachment invests her with. Like that of a man and a woman, the association of two women can take many different forms; it is based on feeling, interest or habit; it is conjugal or romantic; it has room for sadism, masochism, generosity, faithfulness, devotion, caprice, egotism and betrayal; there are prostitutes as well as great lovers among lesbians.

There are, however, certain circumstances that give these relations particular characteristics. They are not established by an institution or customs, nor regulated by conventions: they are lived more sincerely because of this. Men and women – even husband and wife – more or less play roles with each other, and woman, on whom the male always imposes some kind of directive, does so even more: exemplary virtue, charm, coquetry, childishness or austerity; never in the presence of the husband and the lover does she feel fully herself; she does not show off to a woman friend, she has nothing to feign, they are too similar not to show themselves as they are. This similarity gives rise to the most complete intimacy. Eroticism often has only a very small part in these unions; sexual pleasure has a less striking character, less dizzying than between man and woman, it does not lead to such overwhelming metamorphoses; but when male and female lovers have separated into their individual flesh, they become strangers again; and even the male body is repulsive to the woman; and the man sometimes feels a kind of bland distaste for the woman's body; between women, carnal tenderness is more equal, continuous, they are not transported in frenetic ecstasy but they never fall into hostile indifference; seeing and touching each other are calm pleasures discreetly prolonging those of the bed. Sarah Ponsonby's union with her beloved lasted for almost fifty years without a cloud: they seem to have been able to create a peaceful Eden on the fringes of the world. But sincerity also has a price. Because they show themselves freely, without caring either to hide or control themselves, women incite each other to incredible violence. Man and woman intimidate each other because they are different: he feels pity and apprehension towards her; he strives to treat her courteously, indulgently and circumspectly; she respects him and somewhat fears him, she tries to control herself in front of him; each one tries to spare the mysterious other whose feelings and reactions are hard to discern. Women among themselves are pitiless; they foil, provoke, chase, attack and lead each other on to the limits of abjection. Masculine calm – be it indifference or self-control – is a barrier feminine emotions come up against: but between two women friends, there is escalation of tears and convulsions; their patience in endlessly going over criticisms and explanations is insatiable. Demands, recriminations, jealousy, tyranny – all these plagues of conjugal life pour out in heightened form. If such love is often stormy, it is also usually more threatened than heterosexual love. It is criticised by the society into which it cannot always integrate. A woman who assumes the masculine attitude – by her character, situation and the force of her passion – will regret not giving her woman friend a normal and respectable life, not being able to marry her, leading her along unusual paths: these are the feelings Radclyffe Hall attributes to her heroine in The Well of Loneliness;[79] this remorse is conveyed by a morbid anxiety and an even greater torturous jealousy. The more passive or less infatuated woman will suffer from society's censure; she will think herself degraded, perverted, frustrated, she will resent the one who has imposed this lot on her. It might be that one of the two women desires a child; either she sadly resigns herself to her childlessness or both adopt a child or the one who desires motherhood asks a man for his services; the child is sometimes a link, sometimes also a new source of friction.

What gives women enclosed in homosexuality a masculine character is not their erotic life, which, on the contrary, confines them to a feminine universe: it is all the responsibilities they have to assume because they do without men. Their situation is the opposite of that of the courtesan who sometimes has a male mind by dint of living among males – like Ninon de Lenclos – but who depends on them. The particular atmosphere around lesbians stems from the contrast between the gynae-ceum character of their private life and the masculine independence of their public existence. They behave like men in a world without men. A woman alone always seems a little unusual; it is not true that men respect women: they respect each other through their women – wives, mistresses, 'kept' women; when masculine protection no longer extends over her, woman is disarmed before a superior caste that is aggressive, sneering or hostile. As an 'erotic perversion', feminine homosexuality elicits smiles; but inasmuch as it implies a way of life, it provokes scorn or scandal. If there is an affectation in lesbians' attitudes, it is because they have no way of living their situation naturally: natural implies that one does not reflect on self, that one acts without representing one's acts to oneself; but people's behaviour constantly makes the lesbian conscious of herself. She can only follow her path with calm indiffer-ence if she is older or secure in her social prestige.

It is difficult to determine, for example, if it is by taste or by defence mechanism that she so often dresses in a masculine way. It certainly comes in large part from a spontaneous choice. Nothing is less *natural* than dressing like a woman; no doubt masculine clothes are also artifi-cial, but they are more comfortable and simple and made to favour action rather than impede it; George Sand and Isabelle Eberhardt wore men's suits; Thyde Monnier in her last book*[80] spoke of her predilection for wearing trousers; all active women like flat shoes and sturdy clothes. The meaning of feminine attire is clear: it is a question of decoration, and decorating oneself is offering oneself; heterosexual feminists were formerly as intransigent as lesbians on this point: they refused to make themselves merchandise on display, they wore suits and felt hats; fancy low-cut dresses seemed to them the symbol of the social order they were fighting. Today they have succeeded in mastering reality and the symbolic has less importance in their eyes. But it remains for the lesbian insofar as she must still assert her claim. It might also be – if physical particu-larities have motivated her vocation – that austere clothes suit her better. It must be added that one of the roles clothing plays is to gratify woman's tactile sensuality; but the lesbian disdains the consolations of velvet and silk: like Sandor she will appreciate them on her woman friend, or her friend's body may even replace them. This is why a lesbian often likes hard liquor, smokes strong tobacco, uses rough language and imposes rigorous exercise on herself: erotically, she shares in feminine softness;

* *Me.*

by contrast, she likes an intense environment. This aspect can make her enjoy men's company. But a new factor enters here: the often ambiguous relationship she has with them. A woman who is very sure of her masculinity will want only men as friends and associates: this assurance is rarely seen except in a woman who shares interests with men, who – in business, action or art – works and succeeds like a man. When Gertrude Stein entertained, she only talked with the men and left to Alice Toklas the job of talking with their women companions.* It is towards women that the very masculine homosexual woman will have an ambivalent attitude: she scorns them but she has an inferiority complex in relation to them both as a woman and as a man; she fears being perceived by them as a tomboy, an incomplete man, which leads her either to display a haughty superiority or to manifest – like Stekel's transvestite – a sadistic aggressiveness towards them. But this case is rather rare. We have seen that most lesbians partially reject men. For them as well as for the frigid woman, there is disgust, resentment, shyness or pride; they do not really feel similar to men; to their feminine resentment is added a masculine inferiority complex; they are rivals, better armed to seduce, possess and keep their prey; they detest their power over women, they detest the 'soiling' to which they subject women. They also take exception to seeing men hold social privileges and to feeling that men are stronger than they: it is a crushing humiliation not to be able to fight with a rival, to know he can knock you down with one blow. This complex hostility is one of the reasons some homosexual women declare themselves as homosexuals; they see only other homosexual women; they group together to show they do not need men either socially or sexually. From there one easily slides into useless boastfulness and all the playacting of inauthenticity. The lesbian first plays at being a man; then being lesbian itself becomes a game; a transvestite goes from disguise to livery; and the woman under the pretext of freeing herself from man's oppression makes herself the slave of her personage; she did not want to confine herself in a woman's situation, but she imprisons herself in that of the lesbian. Nothing gives a worse impression of small-mindedness and mutilation than these clans of liberated women. It must be added that many women only declare themselves homosexual out of self-interest: they adopt equivocal appearances with exaggerated consciousness, hoping to catch men

* A heterosexual woman who believes – or wants to persuade herself – that she transcends the difference of the sexes by her own worth will often have the same attitude; for example, Mme de Staël.

who like 'perverts'. These show-off zealots – who are obviously those one notices most – contribute to throwing discredit on what public opinion considers a vice and a pose.

In truth, homosexuality is no more a deliberate perversion than a fatal curse.* It is an attitude that is *chosen in situation*; it is both motivated and freely adopted. None of the factors the subject accepts in this choice – physiological facts, psychological history or social circumstances – is determining, although all contribute to explaining it. It is one way among others for woman to solve the problems posed by her condition in general and by her erotic situation in particular. Like all human behaviour, this will involve playacting, imbalance, failure or lies, or, on the other hand, it will be the source of fruitful experiences, depending on whether it is lived in bad faith, laziness and inauthenticity or in lucidity, generosity and freedom.

---

* *The Well of Loneliness* presents a heroine marked by a psychophysiological inevitability. But the documentary value of this novel is very insubstantial in spite of its reputation.

Part Two
SITUATION

CHAPTER 5

The Married Woman

The destiny that society traditionally offers women is marriage. Even today, most women are, were, or plan to be married, or they suffer from not being so. Marriage is the reference by which the single woman is defined, whether she is frustrated by, disgusted at, or even indifferent to this institution. Thus we must continue this study by analysing marriage.

The economic evolution of woman's condition is in the process of upsetting the institution of marriage: it is becoming a union freely entered into by two autonomous individuals; the commitments of the two parties are personal and reciprocal; adultery is a breach of contract for both parties; either of them can obtain a divorce on the same grounds. Woman is no longer limited to the reproductive function: it has lost, in large part, its character of natural servitude and has come to be regarded as a freely assumed responsibility;* and it is considered productive work since, in many cases, maternity leave necessitated by pregnancy must be paid to the mother by the state or the employer. For a few years in the USSR, marriage was a contract between individuals based on complete freedom of the spouses; today it seems to be a duty the state imposes on them both. Which of these tendencies prevails in tomorrow's world depends on the general structure of society: but in any case, masculine guardianship is becoming extinct. Yet, from a feminist point of view, the period we are living through is still a period of transition. Only a part of the female population participates in production, and those same women belong to a society where ancient structures and values still survive. Modern marriage can be understood only in light of the past it perpetuates.

Marriage has always been presented in radically different ways for men and for women. The two sexes are necessary for each other, but this necessity has never fostered reciprocity; women have never constituted

* See Vol. I.

a caste establishing exchanges and contracts on an equal footing with men. Man is a socially autonomous and complete individual; he is regarded above all as a producer and his existence is justified by the work he provides for the group; we have already seen* the reasons why the reproductive and domestic role to which woman is confined has not guaranteed her an equal dignity. Of course, the male needs her; with some primitive peoples, a bachelor, unable to support himself alone, may become a sort of pariah; in agricultural societies, a woman partner-worker is indispensable to the peasant; and for most men, it is advantageous to unload some of the chores onto a woman; the man himself wishes to have a stable sexual life, he desires posterity, and society requires him to contribute to its perpetuation. But man does not address his appeal to woman herself: it is men's society that allows each of its members to accomplish himself as husband and father; woman, integrated as slave or vassal into the family group dominated by fathers and brothers, has always been given in marriage to males by other males. In primitive times, the clan, the paternal gens, treats her almost like a thing: she is part of payments to which two groups mutually consent; her condition was not deeply modified when marriage evolved† into a contractual form; dowered or receiving her share of an inheritance, woman becomes a civil person: but a dowry or an inheritance still enslaves her to her family; for a long period, the contracts were signed between father-in-law and son-in-law, not between husband and wife; in those times, only the widow benefited from an economic independence.‡ A girl's free choice was always highly restricted; and celibacy – except in rare cases where it bears a sacred connotation – ranked her as a parasite and pariah; marriage was her only means of survival and the only justification of her existence. It was doubly imposed on her: she must give children to the community; but rare are the cases where – as in Sparta and to some extent under the Nazi regime – the state takes her under its guardianship and asks only that she be a mother. Even civilisations that ignore the father's generative role demand that she be under the protection of a husband; and she also has the function of satisfying the male's sexual needs and caring for the home. The charge society imposes on her is considered as a *service* rendered to the husband: and he owes his wife gifts or a marriage

---

* See Vol. I.

† This evolution took place in a discontinuous manner. It was repeated in Egypt, Rome and in modern civilisation; see Vol. I.

‡ Hence the special character of the young widow in erotic literature.

dowry and agrees to support her; using him as an intermediary, the community acquits itself of its responsibilities to the woman. The rights the wife acquires by fulfilling her duties have their counterpart in the obligations the male submits to. He cannot break the conjugal bond at whim; repudiation and divorce can only be granted by public authority, and then sometimes the husband owes a monetary compensation: the practice even becomes abusive in Bocchoris's Egypt, as it is today with alimony in the United States. Polygamy was always more or less tolerated: a man can have slaves, *pallakès*, concubines, mistresses and prostitutes in his bed; but he is required to respect certain privileges of his legitimate wife. If she thinks she is maltreated or wronged, she has the option – more or less concretely guaranteed – to return to her family and to obtain a separation or divorce in her own right. Thus for both parties marriage is a charge and a benefit at the same time; but their situations are not symmetrical; for girls, marriage is the only way to be integrated into the group, and if they are 'rejects', they are social waste. This is why mothers have always at all costs tried to marry them off. Among the bourgeoisie of the last century, girls were barely consulted. They were offered to possible suitors through 'interviews' set up in advance. Zola describes this custom in *Pot-Bouille.*[1]

'A failure, it's a failure,' said Mme Josserand, falling into her chair.

'Ah!' M. Josserand simply said.

'But you don't seem to understand,' continued Mme Josserand in a shrill voice. 'I'm telling you that here's another marriage gone down the river, and it's the fourth to fall through!

'Listen,' went on Mme Josserand, advancing toward her daughter. 'How did you spoil *this* marriage too?'

Bertha realised that her turn had come.

'I don't know, Mamma,' she murmured.

'An assistant department head,' continued her mother, 'not yet thirty, a superb future. Every month it brings you money: solid, that's all that counts . . . You did something stupid, as you did with the others?'

'I swear I didn't, Mamma.'

'When you were dancing, you slipped into the small parlour.'

Bertha was unnerved: 'Yes, Mamma . . . and as soon as we were alone, he wanted to do disgraceful things, he kissed me and grabbed me like this. So I got scared and pushed him against the furniture!'

Her mother interrupted her: 'Pushed him against the furniture!
Ah, you foolish girl, pushed him against the furniture!'

'But, Mamma, he was holding on to me.'

'And what? He was holding on to you . . . how bad is that! Putting
you idiots in boarding school! What do they teach you there, tell
me! . . . For a kiss behind a door! Should you really even tell us
about this, us, your parents? And you push people against furniture and you ruin your chances of getting married!'

Assuming a pontificating air, she continued:

'It's over, I give up, you are just stupid, my dear . . . Since you
have no fortune, just understand that you have to catch men
some other way. By being pleasant, gazing tenderly, forgetting
your hand, allowing little indulgences without seeming to; in
short, you have to fish a husband . . . And what bothers me is
that she is not too bad when she wants,' continued Mme
Josserand. 'Come now, dry your eyes, look at me as if I were a
gentleman courting you. You see, you drop your fan so that when
the gentleman picks it up he'll touch your fingers . . . And don't
be stiff, let your waist bend. Men don't like boards. And above
all, don't be a simpleton if they go too far. A man who goes too
far is caught, my dear.'

The clock in the parlour rang two o'clock; and in the excitement
of the long evening, fired by her desire for an immediate marriage,
the mother let herself think aloud, twisting and turning her daughter
like a paper doll. The girl, docile and dispirited, gave in, but her
heart was heavy and fear and shame wrung her breast.

This shows the girl becoming absolutely passive; she is *married, given*
in marriage by her parents. Boys *marry*, they *take* a wife. In marriage
they seek an expansion, a confirmation of their existence but not the
very right to exist; it is a charge they assume freely. So they can question its advantages and disadvantages just as the Greek and medieval
satirists did; for them it is simply a way of life, not a destiny. They are
just as free to prefer a celibate's solitude or to marry late or not at all.

In marrying, the woman receives a piece of the world as property;
legal guaranties protect her from man's caprices; but she becomes his
vassal. He is economically the head of the community, and he thus
embodies it in society's eyes. She takes his name; she joins his religion,
integrates into his class, his world; she belongs to his family, she becomes
his other 'half'. She follows him where his work calls him: where he

works essentially determines where they live; she breaks with her past more or less brutally, she is annexed to her husband's universe; she gives him her person: she owes him her virginity and strict fidelity. She loses part of the legal rights of the unmarried woman. Roman law placed the woman in the hands of her husband *loco filiae*; at the beginning of the nineteenth century, Bonald declared that the woman is to her husband what the child is to the mother; until the 1942 law, French law demanded a wife's obedience to her husband; law and customs still confer great authority on him: it is suggested by her very situation within the conjugal society. Since he is the producer, it is he who goes beyond family interest to the interest of society and who opens a future to her by cooperating in the construction of the collective future: it is he who embodies transcendence. Woman is destined to maintain the species and care for the home, which is to say, to immanence.* In truth, all human existence is transcendence and immanence at the same time; to go beyond itself, it must maintain itself; to thrust itself towards the future, it must integrate the past into itself; and while relating to others, it must confirm itself in itself. These two moments are implied in every living movement: for *man,* marriage provides the perfect synthesis of them; in his work and political life, he finds change and progress, he experiences his dispersion through time and the universe; and when he tires of this wandering, he establishes a home, he settles down, he anchors himself in the world; in the evening he restores himself in the house, where his wife cares for the furniture and children and safeguards the past she keeps in store. But the wife has no other task save the one of maintaining and caring for life in its pure and identical generality; she perpetuates the immutable species, she assures the even rhythm of the days and the permanence of the home she guards with locked doors; she is given no direct grasp on the future, nor on the universe; she goes beyond herself towards the group only through her husband as mouthpiece.

Marriage today still retains this traditional form. And, first of all, it is imposed far more imperiously on the girl than on the young man. There are still many social strata where she is offered no other perspective; for peasants, an unmarried woman is a pariah; she remains the servant of her father, her brothers and her brother-in-law; moving to the city is

* Cf. Vol. I. This thesis is found in St Paul, the Church Fathers, Rousseau, Proudhon, Auguste Comte, D. H. Lawrence, and others.

virtually impossible for her; marriage chains her to a man and makes her mistress of a home. In some bourgeois classes, a girl is still left incapable of earning a living; she can only vegetate as a parasite in her father's home or accept some lowly position in a stranger's home. Even when she is more emancipated, the economic advantage held by males forces her to prefer marriage over a career: she will look for a husband whose situation is superior to her own, a husband she hopes will 'get ahead' faster and further than she could. It is still accepted that the love act is a *service* she renders to the man; he *takes* his pleasure and he owes compensation in return. The woman's body is an object to be purchased; for her it represents capital she has the right to exploit. Sometimes she brings a dowry to her husband; she often agrees to provide some domestic work: she will keep the house, raise the children. In any case, she has the right to let herself be supported, and traditional morality even exhorts it. It is understandable that she is tempted by this easy solution, especially as women's professions are so unrewarding and badly paid; marriage is a more beneficial career than many others. Mores still make sexual enfranchisement for a single woman difficult; in France a wife's adultery was a crime until recent times, while no law forbade a woman free love; however, if she wanted to take a lover, she had to be married first. Many strictly controlled young bourgeois girls still marry 'to be free'. A good number of American women have won their sexual freedom; but their experiences are like those of the young primitive people described by Malinowski in 'The Bachelors' House'[2] – girls who engage in pleasures without consequences; they are expected to marry, and only then will they be fully considered adults. A woman alone, in America even more than in France, is a socially incomplete being, even if she earns her living; she needs a ring on her finger to achieve the total dignity of a person and her full rights. Motherhood in particular is respected only in the married woman; the unwed mother remains an object of scandal, and a child is a severe handicap for her. For all these reasons, many Old and New World adolescent girls, when interviewed about their future projects, respond today just as they did in former times: 'I want to get married.' No young man, however, considers marriage as his fundamental project. Economic success is what will bring him to respectable adulthood: it may involve marriage – particularly for the peasant – but it may also exclude it. Modern life's conditions – less stable, more uncertain than in the past – make marriage's responsibilities particularly heavy for the young man; the benefits, on the other hand, have decreased since he can easily live on his own and sexual satisfaction is generally available.

Without doubt, marriage brings material conveniences ('Eating home is better than eating out') and erotic ones ('This way we have a brothel at home'), and it frees the person from loneliness, it establishes him in space and time by providing him with a home and children; it is a definitive accomplishment of his existence. In spite of this, overall there is still less masculine demand than feminine supply. The father does not so much give his daughter as get rid of her; the girl seeking a husband does not respond to a masculine call: she provokes it.

Arranged marriages have not disappeared; there is still a right-minded bourgeoisie perpetuating them. In France, near Napoleon's tomb, at the Opera, at balls, on the beach or at a tea, the young hopeful with every hair in place, in a new dress, shyly exhibits her physical grace and modest conversation; her parents nag her: 'You've already cost me enough in meeting people; make up your mind. The next time it's your sister's turn.' The unhappy candidate knows her chances diminish the older she gets; there are not many suitors: she has no more freedom of choice than the young bedouin girl exchanged for a flock of sheep. As Colette says,[*3] 'A young girl without a fortune or a trade, who is dependent on her brothers for everything, has only one choice: shut up, be grateful for her good luck, and thank God!'

In a less crude way, high society permits young people to meet under mothers' watchful eyes. Somewhat more liberated, girls go out more, attend university, take jobs that give them the chance to meet men. Between 1945 and 1947, Claire Leplae conducted a survey on the Belgian bourgeoisie, about the problem of matrimonial choice.[†4] The author conducted interviews; I will cite some questions she asked and the responses given:

Q: *Are arranged marriages common?*
A: There are no more arranged marriages (51%).
   Arranged marriages are very rare, 1% at most (16%).
   1 to 3% of marriages are arranged (28%).
   5 to 10% of marriages are arranged (5%).

The people interviewed point out that arranged marriages, frequent before 1945, have almost disappeared. Nonetheless, 'specific interests,

* *Claudine's House.*
† Cf. Claire Leplae, *The Engagement.*

poor relations, self-interest, not much family, shyness, age and the desire to make a good match are motives for some arranged marriages'. These marriages are often conducted by priests; sometimes the girl marries by correspondence. 'They describe themselves in writing, and it is put on a special sheet with a number. This sheet is sent to all persons described. It includes, for example, two hundred female and an equal number of male candidates. They also write their own profiles. They can all freely choose a correspondent to whom they write through the agency.'

Q: *How did young people meet their fiancées or fiancés over the past ten years?*
A: Social events (48%).
   School or clubs (22%).
   Personal acquaintances, travel (30%).

Everyone agrees that 'marriages between childhood friends are very rare. Love is found in unexpected places.'

Q: *Is money a primary factor in the choice of a spouse?*
A: 30% of marriages are based on money (48%).
   50% of marriages are based on money (35%).
   70% of marriages are based on money (17%).

Q: *Are parents anxious to marry their daughters?*
A: Parents are anxious to marry their daughters (58%).
   Parents are eager to marry their daughters (24%).
   Parents wish to keep their daughters at home (18%).

Q: *Are girls anxious to marry?*
A: Girls are anxious to marry (36%).
   Girls are eager to marry (38%).
   Girls prefer not to marry than to have a bad marriage (26%).

'Girls besiege boys. Girls marry the first boy to come along simply to get married. They all hope to marry and work at doing so. A girl is humiliated if she is not sought after: to escape this, she will often marry her first prospect. Girls marry to get married. Girls marry to be married. Girls settle down because marriage assures them more freedom.' Almost all the interviews concur on this point.

Q: *Are girls more active than boys in seeking marriage?*
A: Girls declare their intentions to boys and ask them to marry
them (43%).
Girls are more active than boys in seeking marriage (43%).
Girls are discreet (14%).

Here again the response is nearly unanimous: it is the girls who usually take the initiative in pursuing marriage. 'Girls realise they are not equipped to get along on their own; not knowing how they can work to make a living, they seek a lifeline in marriage. Girls make declarations, throw themselves at boys. They are frightening! Girls use all their resources to get married . . . it's the woman who pursues the man,' and so forth.

No such document exists in France; but as the situation of the bourgeoisie is similar in France and Belgium, the conclusions would probably be comparable; 'arranged' marriages have always been more numerous in France than in any other country, and the famous 'Green Ribbon Club',[5] whose members have parties for the purpose of bringing people of both sexes together, is still flourishing; matrimonial announcements take up columns in many newspapers.

In France, as in America, mothers, older sisters and women's magazines cynically teach girls the art of 'catching' a husband like flypaper catching flies; this is 'fishing' and 'hunting', demanding great skill: do not aim too high or too low; be realistic, not romantic; mix coquetry with modesty; do not ask for too much or too little. Young men mistrust women who 'want to get married'. A young Belgian man* declares, 'There is nothing more unpleasant for a man than to feel himself pursued, to realise that a woman wants to get her hooks into him.' They try to avoid their traps. A girl's choice is often very limited: it would be truly free only if she felt free enough not to marry. Her decision is usually accompanied by calculation, distaste and resignation rather than enthusiasm. 'If the young man who proposes to her is more or less suitable (background, health, career), she accepts him without loving him. She will accept him without passion even if there are "buts".'

At the same as she desires it, however, a girl is often apprehensive of marriage. It represents a more considerable benefit for her than for the man, which is why she desires it more fervently; but it demands weighty sacrifices as well; in particular, it implies a more brutal rupture with the past. We have seen that many adolescent girls are anguished by the idea

* Ibid.

of leaving the paternal home: when the event draws near, this anxiety is heightened. This is the moment when many neuroses develop; the same thing is true for young men who are frightened by the new responsibilities they are assuming, but such neuroses are much more widespread in girls for the reasons we have already seen and they become even more serious in this crisis. I will cite only one example, taken from Stekel.[6] He treated a girl from a good family who manifested several neurotic symptoms.

When Stekel meets her, she is suffering from vomiting, takes morphine every night, has fits of temper, refuses to wash, eats in bed, refuses to leave her room. She is engaged to be married and affirms that she loves her fiancé. She admits to Stekel that she gave herself to him. Later she says that she derived no pleasure from it: the memory of his kisses was even repugnant to her and they are the cause of her vomiting. It is discovered that, in fact, she succumbed to him to punish her mother, who she felt never loved her enough; as a child, she spied on her parents at night because she was afraid they might give her a brother or sister; she adored her mother. 'And now she had to get married, leave [her parents'] home, abandon her parents' bedroom? It was impossible.' She lets herself grow fat, scratches and hurts her hands, deteriorates, falls ill, tries to offend her fiancé in all ways. The doctor heals her, but she pleads with her mother to give up this idea of marriage: 'She wanted to stay home, to remain a child for ever.' Her mother insists that she marry. A week before the wedding day, she is found in her bed, dead; she shot herself with a revolver.

In other cases, the girl wilfully falls into a protracted illness; she becomes desperate because her state keeps her from marrying the man 'she adores'; in fact, she makes herself ill to avoid marrying him and finds her balance only by breaking her engagement. Sometimes the fear of marriage originates in former erotic experiences that have left their mark on her; in particular, she might dread that her loss of virginity will be discovered. But frequently the idea of submitting to a male stranger is unbearable because of her ardent feelings for her father and mother or a sister, or her attachment to her family home in general. And many of those who decide to marry because it is what they should do, because of the pressure on them, because they know it is the only reasonable solution, because they want a normal existence of wife and mother, nonetheless keep a secret and obstinate resistance in their deepest hearts, making the early days of their married lives difficult and even keeping themselves from ever finding a happy balance.

Marriages, then, are generally not based on love. 'The husband is, so to speak, never more than a substitute for the loved man, and not that man himself,' said Freud. This dissociation is not accidental. It is implicit in the very nature of the institution. The economic and sexual union of man and woman is a matter of transcending towards the collective interest and not of individual happiness. In patriarchal regimes, a fiancé chosen by parents had often never seen his future wife's face before the wedding day – and this still happens today with some Muslims. There would be no question of founding a lifelong enterprise, considered in its social aspect, on sentimental or erotic caprice. Montaigne says:

> In this sober contract the appetites are not so wanton; they are dull and more blunted. Love hates people to be attached to each other except by himself, and takes a laggard part in relations that are set up and maintained under another title, as marriage is. Connections and means have, with reason, as much weight in it as graces and beauty, or more. We do not marry for ourselves, whatever we say; we marry just as much or more for our posterity, for our family.[7]

Because it is the man who 'takes' the woman – and especially when there is a good supply of women – he has rather more possibilities for choosing. But since the sexual act is considered to be a *service* imposed on the woman and upon which are founded the advantages conceded to her, it is logical to ignore her own preferences. Marriage is intended to defend her against man's freedom: but as there is neither love nor individuality without freedom, she must renounce the love of a particular individual to ensure the protection of a male for life. I heard a mother of a family teach her daughters that 'love is a vulgar sentiment reserved for men and unknown to women of good standing'. In a naïve form, this was the very doctrine Hegel professed in *Phenomenology of the Spirit*:[8]

> The relationships of mother and wife, however, are those of particular individuals, partly in the form of something natural pertaining to desire, partly in the form of something negative which sees in those relationships only something evanescent and also, again, the particular individual is for that very reason a contingent element which can be replaced by another individual. In the ethical household, it is not a question of *this* particular husband, *this* particular child, but simply of husband and children generally; the relationships of the woman

are based, not on feeling, but on the universal. The difference between the ethical life of the woman and that of the man consists just in this, that in her vocation as an individual and in her pleasure, her interest is centred on the universal and remains alien to the particularity of desire; whereas in the husband these two sides are separated; and since he possesses as a citizen the self-conscious power of universality, he thereby acquires the right of desire and, at the same time, preserves his freedom in regard to it. Since, then, in this relationship of the wife there is an admixture of particularity, her ethical life is not pure; but in so far as it *is* ethical, the particularity is a matter of indifference, and the wife is without the moment of knowing herself as *this* particular self in the other partner.

This points out that for a woman it is not at all a question of establishing individual relations with a chosen husband, but rather of justifying the exercise of her feminine functions in their generality; she should have sexual pleasure only in a generic form and not an individualised one; this results in two essential consequences that touch upon her erotic destiny. First, she has no right to sexual activity outside marriage; for both spouses, sexual congress becoming an institution, desire and pleasure are superseded by the interest of society; but man, as worker and citizen transcending towards the universal, can savour contingent pleasures prior to marriage and outside of married life: in any case, he finds satisfaction in other ways; but in a world where woman is essentially defined as female, she must be justified wholly as a female. Second, it has been seen that the connection between the general and the particular is biologically different for the male and the female: in accomplishing his specific task as husband and reproducer, the male unfailingly finds his sexual pleasure;* on the contrary, very often for the woman, there is a dissociation between the reproductive function and sexual pleasure. This is so to the extent that in claiming to give ethical dignity to her erotic life, marriage, in fact, means to suppress it.

Woman's sexual frustration has been deliberately accepted by men; it has been seen that men rely on an optimistic naturalism to tolerate her frustrations: it is her lot; the biblical curse confirms men's convenient

---

* Of course, the adage 'A hole is always a hole' is vulgarly humorous; man does seek something other than brute pleasure; nonetheless, the success of certain 'slaughterhouses' is enough to prove a man can find some satisfaction with the first available woman.

opinion. Pregnancy's pains – the heavy ransom inflicted on the woman in exchange for a brief and uncertain pleasure – are often the object of various jokes. 'Five minutes of pleasure: nine months of pain . . . It goes in more easily than it comes out.' This contrast often makes them laugh. It is part of this sadistic philosophy: many men relish feminine misery and are repulsed by the idea of reducing it.* One can understand, then, that males have no scruples about denying their companion sexual happiness; and it even seems advantageous to them to deny woman the temptations of desire along with the autonomy of pleasure.†

This is what Montaigne expresses with a charming cynicism:

And so it is a kind of incest to employ in this venerable and sacred alliance the efforts and extravagances of amorous license, as it seems to me I have said elsewhere. A man, says Aristotle, should touch his wife prudently and soberly, lest if he caresses her too lasciviously the pleasure should transport her outside the bounds of reason . . . I see no marriages that sooner are troubled and fail than those that progress by means of beauty and amorous desires. It needs more

* There are some, for example, who support the idea that painful childbirth is necessary to awaken the maternal instinct: those who deliver under anaesthesia have been known to abandon their fawns. Such alleged facts are at best vague; and a woman is in no way a doe. The truth is that some males are shocked that the burdens of womanhood might be lightened.

† Still, in our times, woman's claim to pleasure incites male anger; a striking document on this subject is Dr Grémillon's treatise, 'The Truth about the Genital Orgasm of the Woman' (La vérité sur l'orgasme vénérien de la femme). The preface informs us that the author, a World War I hero who saved the lives of fifty-five German prisoners, is a man of the highest moral standing. Taking serious issue with Stekel in Frigidity in Woman, he declares, 'The normal and fertile woman does not have a genital orgasm. Many are the mothers (and the best of them) who have never experienced these wondrous spasms . . . the most latent erogenous zones are not natural but artificial. They are delighted to have them, but they are stigmas of decadence . . . Tell all that to a man seeking pleasure and he does not care. He wants his depraved partner to have a genital orgasm, and she will have it. If it does not exist, it will be made to exist. Modern woman wants a man to make her vibrate. To her we answer: Madam, we don't have the time and hygiene forbids it! . . . The creator of erogenous zones works against himself: he creates insatiable women. The female ghoul can tirelessly exhaust innumerable husbands . . . the "zoned" one becomes a new woman with a new spirit, sometimes a terrible woman capable of crime . . . there would be no neuroses, no psychoses if we understood that the "two-backed beast" is an act as indifferent as eating, urinating, defecating or sleeping.'

solid and stable foundations, and we need to go at it circumspectly; this ebullient ardor is no good for it. . . . A good marriage, if such there be, rejects the company and conditions of love.[9]

He also says:

Even the pleasures they get in making love to their wives are condemned, unless moderation is observed; and . . . it is possible to err through licentiousness and debauchery, just as in an illicit affair. Those shameless excesses that our first heat suggests to us in this sport are not only indecently but detrimentally practiced on our wives. Let them at least learn shamelessness from another hand. They are always aroused enough for our need . . . Marriage is a religious and holy bond. That is why the pleasure we derive from it should be a restrained pleasure, serious, and mixed with some austerity; it should be a somewhat discreet and conscientious voluptuousness.

In fact, if the husband awakens feminine sensuality, he awakens it in its general form, since he was not singularly chosen by her; he is preparing his wife to seek pleasure in other arms; 'to love one's wife too well,' says Montaigne, is to 'shit in your hat and then put it on your head'. He admits in good faith that masculine prudence puts the woman in a thankless situation:

Women are not wrong at all when they reject the rules of life that have been introduced into the world, inasmuch as it is the men who have made these without them. There is naturally strife and wrangling between them and us . . . we treat them inconsiderately in the following way. We have discovered . . . that they are incomparably more capable and ardent than we in the acts of love . . . we have gone and given women continence as their particular share, and upon utmost and extreme penalties . . . We, on the contrary, want them to be healthy, vigorous, plump, well-nourished, and chaste at the same time: that is to say, both hot and cold. For marriage, which we say has the function of keeping them from burning, brings them but little cooling off, according to our ways.

Proudhon is less scrupulous: according to him, separating love from marriage conforms to justice:

Love must be buried in justice . . . all love conversations, even between people who are engaged, even between husband and wife, are unsuitable, destructive of domestic respect, of the love of work and of the practice of one's social duty . . . (once the function of love has been fulfilled) . . . we have to discard it like the shepherd who removes the rennet once the milk has coagulated.

Yet, during the nineteenth century, conceptions of the bourgeoisie changed somewhat; it ardently strove to defend and maintain marriage; and besides, the progress of individualism made it impossible to stifle feminine claims; Saint-Simon, Fourier, George Sand and all the Romantics had too intensely proclaimed the right to love. The problem arose of integrating into marriage those individual feelings that had previously and carelessly been excluded. It was thus that the ambiguous notion of conjugal love was invented, miraculous fruit of the traditional marriage of convenience. Balzac expresses the ideas of the conservative bourgeoisie in all their inconsequence. He recognises that the principle of marriage has nothing to do with love; but he finds it repugnant to assimilate a respectable institution with a simple business deal where the woman is treated like a thing; and he ends up with the disconcerting inconsistencies in *The Physiology of Marriage*,[10] where we read:

Marriage can be considered politically, civilly, or morally, as a law, a contract, or an institution . . .

Thus marriage ought to be an object of general respect. Society has only considered it under these three heads – they dominate the marriage question.

Most men who get married have only in view reproduction, propriety, or what is due to the child; yet neither reproduction, propriety, nor the child constitute happiness. 'Crescite et multiplicamini' [increase and multiply] does not imply love. To ask a girl whom one has seen fourteen times in a fortnight for her love on behalf of the law, the king and justice, is an absurdity only worthy of the fore-ordained!

This is as clear as Hegelian theory. But Balzac continues without any transition:

Love is the union of desire and tenderness, and happiness in marriage comes from a perfect understanding between two souls.

And from this it follows that to be happy a man is obliged to bind himself by certain rules of honour and delicacy. After having enjoyed the privilege of the social laws which consecrate desire, he should obey the secret laws of nature which bring to birth the affections. If his happiness depends on being loved, he himself must love sincerely; nothing can withstand true passion.

But to be passionate is always to desire.

Can one always desire one's wife?

Yes.

After that, Balzac exposes the science of marriage. But one quickly sees that for the husband it is not a question of being loved but of not being deceived: he will not hesitate to inflict a debilitating regime on his wife, to keep her uncultured, and to stultify her solely to safeguard his honour. Is this still about love? If one wants to find a meaning in these murky and incoherent ideas, it seems man has the right to choose a wife through whom he can satisfy his needs in their generality, a generality that is the guarantee of his faithfulness: then it is up to him to waken his wife's love by applying certain recipes. But is he really *in love* if he marries for his property or for his posterity? And if he is not, how can his passion be irresistible enough to bring about a reciprocal passion? And does Balzac really not know that an unshared love, on the contrary, annoys and disgusts? His bad faith is clearly visible in *Letters of Two Brides*,[11] an epistolary novel with a message. Louise de Chaulieu believes that marriage is based on love: in a fit of passion, she kills her first husband; she dies from the jealous fixation she feels for her second. Renée de l'Estorade sacrifices her feelings to reason: but the joys of motherhood mostly compensate her and she builds a stable happiness. One wonders first what curse – except the author's own decree – deprives the amorous Louise of the motherhood she desires: love has never prevented conception; and one also thinks that to accept her husband's embraces joyfully, Renée had to accept this 'hypocrisy' Stendhal hated in 'honest women'. Balzac describes the wedding night in these words:

'The animal that we call a husband,' to quote your words, disappeared, and one balmy evening I discovered in his stead a lover, whose words thrilled me and on whose arm I leant with pleasure beyond words . . . I felt a fluttering of curiosity in my heart . . . [Know that] nothing was lacking either of satisfaction for the most fastidious sentiment, or of that unexpectedness which brings, in a sense, its own sanction. Every witchery of imagination, of passion, of reluctance overcome, of the ideal passing into reality, played its part.

This beautiful miracle must not have occurred too often, since, several letters later, we find Renée in tears: 'Formerly I was a person, now I am a chattel'; and she consoles herself after her nights 'of conjugal love' by reading Bonald. But one would nevertheless like to know what recipe was used for the husband to change into an enchanter, during the most difficult moment of feminine initiation; those Balzac gives in *The Physiology of Marriage* are succinct: 'Never begin marriage by rape,' – or vague: 'The genius of the husband lies in deftly handling the various shades of pleasure, in developing them, and endowing them with a new style, an original expression.' He quickly goes on to say, moreover, that 'between two people who do not love one another, this genius is wanton'; then, precisely, Renée does not love Louis; and as he is depicted, where does this 'genius' come from? In truth, Balzac has cynically skirted the problem. He underestimates the fact that there are no neutral feelings and that in the absence of love, constraints, together with boredom, engender tender friendship less easily than resentment, impatience and hostility. He is more sincere in *The Lily in the Valley*[12] and the destiny of the unfortunate Mme de Mortsauf seems to be far less instructive.

Reconciling marriage and love is such a feat that at the very least divine intervention is necessary; this is the solution Kierkegaard adopts after complicated detours. He likes to denounce the paradox of marriage:

Indeed, what a passing strange device is marriage! And what makes it all the stranger is that it could be a step taken without thought. And yet no step is more decisive ... And such an important step as marriage ought to be taken without reflection!*

This is the difficulty: love and falling in love are spontaneous, marriage is a decision; yet falling in love should be awakened by marriage or by decision: wanting to marry; this means that what is the most spontaneous must at the same time be the freest decision, and what is, because of the spontaneity, so inexplicable that

* *In Vino Veritas.*

it must be attributed to a divinity, must at the same time take place because of reflection and such exhausting reflection that a decision results from it. Besides, these things must not follow each other, the decision must not come sneaking up behind; everything must occur simultaneously, the two things have to come together at the moment of dénouement.*[13]

This underlines that loving is not marrying and it is quite difficult to understand how love can become duty. But paradoxes do not faze Kierkegaard: his whole essay on marriage is an attempt to elucidate this mystery. It is true, he agrees: 'Reflection is the angel of death for spontaneity ... If it were true that reflection must take precedence over falling in love, there would never be marriage.' But 'decision is a new spontaneity obtained through reflection, experienced in a purely ideal way, a spontaneity that precisely corresponds to that of falling in love. Decision is a religious view of life constructed upon ethical presuppositions, and must, so to speak, pave the way for falling in love and securing it against any danger, exterior or interior.' This is why 'a husband, a real husband, is himself a miracle! ... Being able to keep the pleasure of love while existence focuses all the power of seriousness on him and his beloved!'

As for the wife, reason is not her lot, she is without 'reflection'; so 'she goes from the immediacy of love to the immediacy of the religious'. Expressed in simple language, this doctrine means a man in love chooses marriage by an act of faith in God that guarantees him the accord of both feelings and duty; and the woman wishes to marry as soon as she is in love. I knew an old Catholic woman who, most naively, believed in a 'sacramental falling in love'; she asserted that at the moment the couple pronounce the definitive 'I do' at the altar, they feel their hearts burst into flame. Kierkegaard does admit there must previously be an 'inclination', but that it be thought to last a whole lifetime is no less miraculous.

However, in France, late nineteenth-century novelists and playwrights, less confident in the value of the holy vows, try to ensure conjugal happiness by more human means; more boldly than Balzac, they envisage the possibility of integrating eroticism with legitimate love. Porto-Riche affirms, in the play A Loving Wife,[14] the incompatibility of sexual love and home life: the husband, worn out by his wife's

---

* 'Some Reflections on Marriage'.

ardour, seeks peace with his more temperate mistress. But at Paul Hervieu's instigation, 'love' between spouses is a legal duty. Marcel Prévost preaches to the young husband that he must treat his wife like a mistress, alluding to conjugal pleasures in a discreetly libidinous way. Bernstein is the playwright of legitimate love: the husband is put forward as a wise and generous being next to the amoral, lying, sensual, fickle and mean wife; and he is also understood to be a virile and expert lover. Much romantic defence of marriage comes out in reaction to novels of adultery. Even Colette yields to this moralising wave in *The Innocent Libertine*,[15] when, after describing the cynical experiences of a clumsily deflowered young bride, she has her experience sexual pleasure in her husband's arms. Likewise, Martin Maurice, in a somewhat controversial book, brings the young woman, after a brief incursion into the bed of an experienced lover, to that of her husband, who benefits from her experience. For other reasons and in a different way, Americans today, who are both respectful of the institution of marriage and individualistic, endeavour to integrate sexuality into marriage. Many books on initiation into married life come out every year aimed at teaching couples to adapt to each other, and in particular teaching man how to create harmony with his wife. Psychoanalysts and doctors play the role of 'marriage counsellors'; it is accepted that the wife too has the right to pleasure and that the man must know the right techniques to provide her with it. But we have seen that sexual success is not merely a technical question. The young man, even if he has memorised twenty textbooks such as *What Every Husband Should Know, The Secret of Conjugal Happiness* and *Love without Fear*,[16] is still not sure he will know how to make his new wife love him. She reacts to the psychological situation as a whole. And traditional marriage is far from creating the most propitious conditions for the awakening and blossoming of feminine eroticism.

In the past, in matriarchal communities, virginity was not demanded of the new wife, and for mystical reasons she was normally supposed to be deflowered before the wedding. In some French regions, these ancient prerogatives can still be observed; prenuptial chastity is not required of girls; and even girls who have 'sinned' or unmarried mothers sometimes find a husband more easily than others. Moreover, in circles that accept woman's liberation, girls are granted the same sexual freedom as boys. However, paternalistic ethics imperiously demand that the bride be delivered to her husband as a virgin; he wants to be sure she does not carry within her a foreign germ; he wants the entire and exclusive property of this flesh he makes his own;* virginity has taken on a moral, religious and mystical value, and this value is still widely recognised today. In France, there are regions where friends of the husband stay outside the door of the bridal suite, laughing and singing until the husband comes out triumphantly showing them the bloodstained sheet; or else the parents display it in the morning to the neighbours.† The custom of the 'wedding night' is still widespread, albeit in a less brutal form. It is no coincidence that it has spawned a whole body of ribald literature: the separation of the social and the animal necessarily produces obscenity. A humanist morality demands that all living experience have a human meaning, that it be invested with freedom; in an authentically moral erotic life, there is the free assumption of desire and pleasure, or at least a deeply felt fight to regain freedom within sexuality: but this is only possible if a *singular* recognition of the other is accomplished in love or in desire. When sexuality is no longer redeemed by the individual, but God or society claims to justify it, the relationship of the two partners is no more than a bestial one. It is understandable that right-thinking matrons spurn adventures of the flesh: they have reduced them to the level of scatological functions. This is also why one hears so many sniggers at wedding parties. There is an obscene paradox in the super-imposing of a pompous ceremony on a brutally real animal function. The wedding presents its universal and abstract meaning: a man and a woman are united publicly according to symbolic rites; but in the secrecy of the bed it is concrete and singular individuals who confront each other face to face and all gazes turn away from their embraces. Colette, attending a peasant wedding at the age of thirteen, was terribly consternated when a girlfriend took her to see the wedding chamber:

> The young couple's bedroom . . . Under its curtains of Adrianople red, the tall, narrow bed, the bed stuffed with down and crammed with goose-down pillows, the bed that is to be the final scene of this wedding day all steaming with sweat, incense, the breath of cattle, the aroma of different sauces . . . Shortly the young couple will be arriving here. I hadn't thought of that. They will dive into that deep mound of feathers . . . They will embark on that obscure struggle

---

* See Vol. I, 'Myths'.
† 'Today, in certain regions of the United States, first-generation immigrants still send the bloody sheet back to the family in Europe as proof of the consummation of the marriage,' says the Kinsey Report.

about which my mother's bold and direct language and the life of animals have taught me both too much and too little . . . And then? . . . I'm afraid of that bedroom, afraid of that bed which I hadn't thought of.*[17]

In her childish distress, the girl felt the contrast between the pomp of the family feast and the animal mystery of the enclosed double bed. Marriage's comic and lewd side is scarcely found in civilisations that do not individualise woman: in the East, in Greece, in Rome; the animal function appears there in as generalised a form as do the social rites; but today in the West, men and women are grasped as individuals and wedding guests snigger because it is this particular man and this particular woman who, in an altogether individual experience, are going to consummate the act that we disguise in rites, speeches and flowers. It is true that there is also a macabre contrast between the pomp of great funerals and the rot of the tomb. But the dead person does not awaken when he is put into the ground, while the bride is terribly surprised when she discovers the singularity and contingence of the *real* experience to which the mayor's tricoloured sash and church organ pledged her. It is not only in vaudeville that one sees young women returning in tears to their mothers on their wedding night: psychiatric books are full of this type of account; several have been told to me directly: they concern girls, too well brought up, without any sexual education and whose sudden discovery of eroticism overwhelmed them. Last century, Mme Adam thought it was her duty to marry a man who had kissed her on the mouth because she believed that was the completed form of sexual union. More recently, Stekel writes about a young bride: 'When during the honeymoon, her husband deflowered her, she thought he was of unsound mind and did not dare say a word for fear of dealing with an insane person.'†[18] It even happens that the girl is so innocent she marries a woman invert and lives with her pseudo-husband for a long time without doubting that she is dealing with a man.

If on your marriage day, returning home, you set your wife in a well to soak for the night, she will be dumbfounded. No comfort to her now that she has always had a vague uneasiness . . .

---

* *Claudine's House.*
† *Conditions of Nervous Anxiety and Their Treatment.*

'Well now!' she will say, 'so that's what marriage is. That's why they keep it all so secret. I've let myself be taken in.'

But being annoyed, she will say nothing. That is why you will be able to dip her for long periods and often, without causing any scandal in the neighbourhood.

This fragment of a poem by Michaux,* called 'Bridal Night',[19] accurately conveys the situation. Today, many girls are better informed; but their consent remains abstract; and their defloration has the characteristics of a rape. 'There are certainly more rapes committed in marriage than outside of marriage,' says Havelock Ellis. In his work, *Monatsschrift für Geburtshülfe*, 1889, Vol. IX, Neugebauer found more than 150 cases of injuries inflicted on women by the penis during coitus; the causes were brutality, drunkenness, false position, and a disproportion of the organs. In England, Havelock Ellis reports, a woman asked six intelligent, married, middle-class women about their reactions on their wedding night: for all of them intercourse was a shock; two of them had been ignorant of everything; the others thought they knew but were no less psychically wounded. Adler also emphasised the psychic importance of the act of defloration.

The first moment man acquires his full rights often decides his whole life. The inexperienced and over-aroused husband can sow the germ of feminine insensitivity and through his continual clumsiness and brutality transform it into permanent desensitisation.

Many examples of these unfortunate initiations were given in the previous chapter. Here is another case reported by Stekel:

Mme H. N. . . ., raised very prudishly, trembled at the idea of her wedding night. Her husband undressed her almost violently without allowing her to get into bed. He undressed, asking her to look at him nude and to admire his penis. She hid her face in her hands. And so he exclaimed: 'Why didn't you stay at home, you halfwit!' Then he threw her on the bed and brutally deflowered her. Naturally, she remained frigid for ever.

* In *Night Moves*.

We have, thus far, seen all the resistance the virgin has to overcome to accomplish her sexual destiny: her initiation demands 'labour', both physiological and psychic. It is stupid and barbaric to want to put it all into one night; it is absurd to transform an operation as difficult as the first coitus into a duty. The woman is all the more terrorised by the fact that the strange operation she is subjected to is sacred, and that society, religion, family and friends delivered her solemnly to the husband as to a master; and in addition, that the act seems to engage her whole future, because marriage still has a definitive character. This is when she feels truly revealed in the absolute: this man to whom she is pledged to the end of time embodies all of Man in her eyes; and he is revealed to her, too, as a figure she has not heretofore known, which is of immense importance since he will be her lifelong companion. However, the man himself is anguished by the duty weighing on him; he has his own difficulties and his own complexes that make him shy and clumsy or on the contrary brutal; many men are impotent on their wedding night because of the very solemnity of marriage. Janet writes in *Obsessions and Psychasthenia*:[20]

Who has not known these young grooms ashamed of their bad fortune in not succeeding in accomplishing the conjugal act and who are plagued by it with an obsession of shame and despair? We witnessed a very curious tragi-comic scene last year when a furious father-in-law dragged his humble and resigned son-in-law to Salpêtrière: the father-in-law demanded a medical attestation enabling him to ask for a divorce. The poor boy explained that in the past he had been potent, but since his wedding a feeling of awkwardness and shame had made everything impossible.

Too much impetuousness frightens the virgin, too much respect humiliates her; women forever hate the man who has taken his pleasure at the expense of their suffering; but they feel an eternal resentment against the one who seems to disdain them,* and often against the one who has not attempted to deflower them the first night or who was unable to do it. Helene Deutsch points out† that some timid or clumsy husbands ask the doctor to deflower their wife surgically on the pretext that she is not normally constituted; the reason is not usually valid. Women, she

* See Stekel's observations quoted in the previous chapter.
† *Psychology of Women.*

says, harbour scorn and resentment for the husband unable to penetrate them normally. One of Freud's* observations shows that the husband's impotence can traumatise the woman:

> One patient would run from one room to another in which there was a table in the middle. She put on the tablecloth in a certain way, rang for the maid who was supposed to go towards the table and then sent her away ... When she tried to explain this obsession, she recalled that this cloth had a bad stain and that she arranged it each time so that the stain should jump out at the maid ... The whole thing was a reproduction of the wedding night in which the husband had not shown himself as virile. He ran from his room to hers a thousand times to try again. Being ashamed in front of the maid who had to make the beds, he poured some red ink on the sheet to make her think there was blood.

The 'wedding night' transforms the erotic experience into an ordeal that neither partner is able to surmount, too involved with personal problems to think generously of each other; it is invested with a solemnity that makes it formidable; and it is not surprising that it often dooms the woman to frigidity forever. The difficult problem facing the husband is this: if he 'titillates his wife too lasciviously', she might be scandalised or outraged; it seems this fear paralyses American husbands, among others, especially in college-educated couples, says the Kinsey Report, because wives, more conscious of themselves, are more deeply inhibited. But if he 'respects' her, he fails to waken her sensuality. This dilemma is created by the ambiguity of the feminine attitude: the young woman both wants and rejects pleasure; she demands a delicateness from which she suffers. Unless he is exceptionally lucky, the husband will necessarily appear as either clumsy or a libertine. It is thus not surprising that 'conjugal duties' are often only a repugnant chore for the wife. According to Diderot,†

> Submission to a master she dislikes is a torture to her. I have seen a virtuous wife shiver with horror at her husband's approach. I have seen her plunge into a bath and never think herself properly cleansed from the soilure of her duty. This sort of repugnance is almost

* We summarise it following Stekel in *Frigidity in Woman*.
† 'On Women'.

unknown with us. Our organ is more indulgent. Many women die without having experienced the extreme of pleasure. This sensation which I am willing to consider a passing attack of epilepsy is rare with them, but never fails to come when we call for it. The sovereign happiness escapes them in the arms of the man they adore. We experience it with an easy woman we dislike. Less mistresses of their *sensations* than we are, their reward is less prompt and certain. A hundred times their expectation is deceived.[21]

Many women, indeed, become mothers and grandmothers without ever having experienced pleasure or even arousal; they try to get out of their soilure of duty by getting medical certificates or using other pretexts. The Kinsey Report says that, in America, many wives 'report that they consider their coital frequencies already too high and wish that their husbands did not desire intercourse so often. A very few wives wish for more frequent coitus.' We have seen, though, that woman's erotic possibilities are almost indefinite. This contradiction points up the fact that marriage, claiming to regulate feminine eroticism, kills it.

In *Thérèse Desqueyroux*, Mauriac described the reactions of a young 'reasonably married' woman to marriage in general and conjugal duties in particular:

Perhaps she was seeking less a dominion or a possession out of this marriage than a refuge. What finally pushed her into it, after all – wasn't it a kind of panic? A practical girl, a child housewife, she was in a hurry to take up her station in life, to find her definitive place; she wanted assurance against some peril that she could not name. She was never so rational and determined as she had been during the engagement period; she embedded herself in the family bloc, 'she settled down,' she entered into an order of life. She saved herself . . .

The suffocating wedding day in the narrow Saint-Clair church, where the women's cackling drowned out the wheezing harmonium, and the body odor overpowered the incense – this was the day when Thérèse realised she was lost. She had entered the cage like a sleepwalker and, as the heavy door groaned shut, the miserable child in her reawakened. Nothing had changed, but she had the sensation that she would never again be able to be alone. In the thick of a family, she would smolder, like a hidden fire that leaps up on to a branch, lights up a pine tree, then another, then step by step creates a whole forest of torches . . .

On the evening of that half-peasant, half-bourgeois wedding day, groups of the guests crowded around their car, forcing it to slow down; the girls' dresses fluttered in the crowd . . . Thérèse, thinking of the night that was coming, murmured, 'It was horrible . . .' but then caught herself and said, 'no – not so horrible.' On their trip to the Italian lakes, had she suffered so much? No – she played the game; don't lie . . . Thérèse knew how to bend her body to these charades, and she took a bitter pleasure in the accomplishment. This unknown world of sensual pleasure into which the man forced her – her imagination helped her conceive that there was a real pleasure there for her too, a possible happiness – but what happiness? As when, before a country scene pouring with rain, we imagine to ourselves what it looks like in the sunshine – thus it was that Thérèse looked upon sensuality.

Bernard, the boy with the vacant stare, . . . what an easy dupe! He was as sunk in his pleasure as those sweet little pigs you can watch through the fence, snorting with happiness in their trough ('and I was the trough,' thought Thérèse) . . . Where had he learned it, this ability to classify everything relating to the flesh, to distinguish the honorable caress from that of the sadist? Never a moment's hesitation . . .

'Poor Bernard! He's no worse than others. But desire transforms the one who approaches us into a monster, a different being. . . . I played dead, as if the slightest movement on my part could make this madman, this epileptic, strangle me.'[22]

Here is a blunter account. Stekel obtained this confession from which I quote the passage about married life. It concerns a twenty-eight-year-old woman, brought up in a refined and cultivated home:

I was a happy fiancée; I finally had the feeling I was safe, all at once I was the focus of attention. I was spoiled, my fiancé admired me, all this was new for me . . . our kisses (my fiancé had never attempted any other caresses) had aroused me to such a point that I could not wait for the wedding day . . . The morning of the wedding I was in such a state of excitation that my camisole was soaking with sweat: Just the idea that I was finally going to know the stranger I had so desired. I had the infantile image that the man was supposed to urinate in the woman's vagina . . . In our room, there was already a little disappointment when my husband asked me if he should move away. I asked him to do that because I was really ashamed in front of him. The undressing scene had played such a role in my imagination. He came back, very embarrassed, when I was in bed. Later on, he admitted that my appearance had intimidated him: I was the incarnation of radiant and eager youth. Barely had he undressed than he shut out the light. Barely kissing me, he immediately tried to take me. I was frightened and asked him to let me alone. I wanted to be very far from him. I was horrified at this attempt without prior caresses. I found him brutal and often criticised him for it later. It was not brutality but very great clumsiness and a lack of sensitivity. All the attempts that night were in vain. I began to be very unhappy, I was ashamed of my stupidity, I thought I was at fault and badly formed . . . Finally, I settled for his kisses. Ten days later he succeeded in deflowering me, I had felt nothing. It was a major disappointment! Then I felt a little joy during coitus but success was very disturbing, my husband labouring hard to reach his goal . . . In Prague in my brother-in-law's bachelor apartment I imagined my brother-in-law's feelings learning I had slept in his bed. That is when I had my first orgasm, making me very happy. My husband made love with me every day during the first weeks. I was still reaching orgasm but I was not satisfied because it was too short and I was excited to the point of crying . . . After two births . . . coitus became less and less satisfying. It rarely led to orgasm, my husband always reaching it before me; I followed each session anxiously (how long is it going to continue?). If he was satisfied leaving me at halfway, I hated him. Sometimes, I imagined my cousin during coitus or the doctor who had delivered me. My husband tried to excite me with his finger . . . I was very aroused but, at the same time, I found this means shameful and abnormal and experienced no pleasure . . . During the whole time of our marriage, he never caressed even one part of my body. One day he told me that he did not dare do anything with me . . . He never saw me naked because we always kept on our night-clothes, he performed coitus only at night.

This very sensual woman was perfectly happy in the arms of a lover later on.

Engagements are specifically meant to create gradations in the young girl's initiation; but mores often impose extreme chastity on the engaged couple. When the virgin 'knows' her future husband during this period, her situation is not very different from that of the young bride; she yields only because her engagement already seems to her as definitive as marriage and the first coitus has the characteristics of a test; once she has given herself – even if she is not pregnant, which would keep her in chains – it is very rare for her to assert herself again.

The difficulties of the first experiences are easily overcome if love or desire generates total consent from the two partners; physical love draws its strength and dignity from the joy lovers give each other and take in the reciprocal consciousness of their freedom; thus there are no degrading practices since, for both of them, their practices are not submitted to but generously desired. But the principle of marriage is obscene because it transforms an exchange that should be founded on a spontaneous impulse into rights and duties; it gives bodies an instrumental, thus degrading, side by dooming them to grasp themselves in their generality; the husband is often frozen by the idea that he is accomplishing a duty, and the wife is ashamed to feel delivered to someone who exercises a right over her. Of course, relations can become individualised at the beginning of married life; sexual apprenticeship is sometimes accomplished in slow gradations; as of the first night, a happy physical attraction can be discovered between the spouses. Marriage facilitates the wife's abandon by suppressing the notion of sin still so often attached to the flesh; regular and frequent cohabitation engenders carnal intimacy that is favourable to sexual maturity: there are wives fully satisfied in their first years of marriage. It is to be noted that they remain grateful to their husbands, which makes it possible to pardon them later for the wrongs they might be responsible for. 'Women who cannot get out of an unhappy home life have always been satisfied by their husbands,' says Stekel. It remains that the girl runs a terrible risk in promising to sleep exclusively and for her whole life with a man she does not know sexually, whereas her erotic destiny essentially depends on her partner's personality: this is the paradox Léon Blum rightfully denounced in his work, *Marriage*.

To claim that a union founded on convention has much chance of engendering love is hypocritical; to ask two spouses bound by practical, social and moral ties to satisfy each other sexually for their whole lives is pure absurdity. Yet advocates of marriages of reason have no trouble showing that marriages of love do not have much more chance of assuring the spouses' happiness. In the first place, ideal love, which is often what the girl knows, does not always dispose her to sexual love; her platonic adorations, her daydreaming, and the passions into which she projects her infantile or juvenile obsessions are not meant to resist the tests of daily life nor to last for a long time. Even if there is a sincere and violent erotic attraction between her and her fiancé, that is not a solid basis on which to construct the enterprise of a life. Colette writes:*

> But voluptuous pleasure is not the only thing. In the limitless desert of love it holds a very small place, so flaming that at first one sees nothing else ... All about this flickering hearth there lies the unknown, there lies danger ... After we have risen from a short embrace, or even from a long night, we shall have to begin to live at close quarters to each other, and in dependence on each other.[23]

Moreover, even in cases where carnal love exists before marriage or awakens at the beginning of the marriage, it is very rare for it to last many long years. Certainly fidelity is necessary for sexual love, since the two lovers' desire encompasses their singularity; they do not want it contested by outside experiences, they want to be irreplaceable for each other; but this fidelity has meaning only as long as it is spontaneous; and spontaneously, erotic magic dissolves rather quickly. The miracle is that it gives to each of the lovers, in the instant and in their carnal presence, a being whose existence is an unlimited transcendence: and *possession* of this being is undoubtedly impossible, but at least each of them is reached in a privileged and poignant way. But when individuals no longer want to reach each other because of hostility, disgust or indifference between them, erotic attraction disappears; and it dies almost as surely in esteem and friendship: two human beings who come together in the very movement of their transcendence through the world and their common projects no longer need carnal union; and further, because this union has lost its meaning, they are repelled by it. The word 'incest' that Montaigne pronounces is very significant. Eroticism is a movement towards the *Other*, and this is its essential character; but within the couple, spouses become, for each other, the *Same*; no exchange is possible between them anymore, no giving, no conquest. If they remain lovers, it is often in embarrassment: they feel the sexual act is no longer an intersubjective experience where each one goes beyond himself, but rather a kind of mutual masturbation. That they consider each other a necessary tool for the satisfaction of their needs is a fact conjugal politeness disguises but

* *The Vagabond.*

which bursts out when this politeness is rejected, for example in observations reported by Dr Lagache in his work *The Nature and Forms of Jealousy*:[24] the wife regards the male member as a certain source of pleasure that belongs to her, and she guards it in as miserly a way as the preserves she stores in the cupboard: if the man gives some away to a woman neighbour, there will be no more for her; she looks at his underwear to see if he has not wasted the precious semen. In *The Bold Chronicle of a Strange Marriage*,[25] Jouhandeau notes this 'daily censure practised by the legitimate wife who scrutinises your shirt and your sleep to discover the sign of ignominy'. For his part, the man satisfies his desires on her without asking her opinion.

This brutal satisfaction of need is, in fact, not enough to satisfy human sexuality. That is why there is often an aftertaste of vice in these seemingly most legitimate embraces. The woman often helps herself along with erotic imaginings. Stekel cites a twenty-five-year-old woman who 'could reach a slight orgasm with her husband by imagining that a strong, older man is taking her by force, so she cannot defend herself'. She sees herself as being raped, beaten, and her husband is not himself but an Other. He indulges in the same dream: in his wife's body he possesses the legs of a dancer seen in a music hall, the breasts of this pin-up whose photo he has dwelled on, a memory, an image; or else he imagines his wife desired, possessed or raped, which is a way to give her back her lost alterity. 'Marriage,' says Stekel, 'creates gross transpositions and inversions, refined actors, scenarios played out between the two partners who risk destroying the limits between appearance and reality.' Pushed to the limit, real vices appear. The husband becomes a voyeur: he needs to see his wife, or know she is sleeping with a lover to feel a little of her magic again; or he sadistically strives to provoke her to refuse him, so her consciousness and freedom show through, assuring it is really a human being he is possessing. Inversely, masochistic behaviour can develop in the wife who seeks to bring out in the man the master and tyrant he is not; I knew an extremely pious woman, brought up in a convent, who was authoritarian and dominating during the day and who, at night, begged her husband to whip her, which, though horrified, he consented to do. In marriage, vice itself takes on an organised and cold aspect, a sombre aspect that makes it the saddest of possible choices.

The truth is that physical love can be treated neither as an absolute end in itself nor as a simple means; it cannot justify an existence: but it can receive no outside justification. It means it must play an episodic and autonomous role in all human life. This means it must above all be free.

Love, then, is not what bourgeois optimism promises the young bride: the ideal held up to her is happiness, that is, a peaceful equilibrium within immanence and repetition. At certain prosperous and secure times, this ideal was that of the whole bourgeoisie and specifically of landed property owners; their aim was not the conquest of the future and the world but the peaceful conservation of the past, the status quo. A gilded mediocrity with neither passion nor ambition, days leading nowhere, repeating themselves indefinitely, a life that slips towards death without looking for answers, this is what the author of 'Sonnet to Happiness' prescribes; this pseudo-wisdom loosely inspired by Epicurus and Zenon has lost currency today: to conserve and repeat the world as it is seems neither desirable nor possible. The male's vocation is action; he needs to produce, fight, create, progress, go beyond himself towards the totality of the universe and the infinity of the future; but traditional marriage does not invite woman to transcend herself with him; it confines her in immanence. She has no choice but to build a stable life where the present, prolonging the past, escapes the threats of tomorrow, that is, precisely to create a happiness. In the place of love, she will feel for her husband a tender and respectful sentiment called conjugal love; within the walls of her home she will be in charge of managing, she will enclose the world; she will perpetuate the human species into the future. Yet no existent ever renounces his transcendence, especially when he stubbornly disavows it. The bourgeois of yesterday thought that by conserving the established order, displaying its virtue by his prosperity, he was serving God, his country, a regime, a civilisation: to be happy was to fulfil his function as man. For woman as well, the harmonious home life has to be transcended towards other ends: it is man who will act as intermediary between woman's individuality and the universe; it is he who will imbue her contingent facticity with human worth. Finding in his wife the force to undertake, to act, to fight, he justifies her: she has only to put her existence in his hands, and he will give it its meaning. This presupposes humble renunciation on her end; but she is rewarded because guided and protected by male force, she will escape original abandonment; she will become necessary. Queen of her hive, tranquilly resting on herself within her domain, but carried by man's mediation through the universe and limitless time, wife, mother and mistress of the house, woman finds in marriage both the force to live and life's meaning. We must see how this ideal is expressed in reality.

The home has always been the material realisation of the ideal of happiness, be it a cottage or a château; it embodies permanence and separation. Inside its walls, the family constitutes an isolated cell and affirms its identity beyond the passage of generations; the past, preserved in the form of furniture and ancestral portraits, prefigures a risk-free future; in the garden, seasons mark their reassuring cycle with edible vegetables; every year the same spring adorned with the same flowers promises the summer's immutable return and autumn's fruits, identical to those of every autumn: neither time nor space escapes into infinity, but instead quietly go round and round. In every civilisation founded on landed property, an abundant literature sings of the poetry and virtues of the home; in Henry Bordeaux's novel precisely entitled *The Home*,[26] the home encapsulates all the bourgeois values: faithfulness to the past, patience, economy, caution, love of family, of native soil, and so forth; the home's champions are often women, since it is their task to assure the happiness of the familial group; as in the days when the *domina* sat in the atrium, their role is to be 'mistress of the house'. Today the home has lost its patriarchal splendour; for most men, it is simply a place to live, no longer overrun by memories of deceased generations and no longer imprisoning the centuries to come. But woman still tries to give her 'interior' the meaning and value a true home possessed. In *Cannery Row*, Steinbeck describes a woman hobo determined to decorate with rugs and curtains the old abandoned boiler she lives in with her husband: he objects in vain that not having windows makes curtains useless.

This concern is specifically feminine. A normal man considers objects around him as instruments; he arranges them according to the purpose for which they are intended; his 'order' – where woman will often only see disorder – is to have his cigarettes, his papers and his tools within reach. Artists – sculptors and painters, among others – whose work it is to recreate the world through material, are completely insensitive to the surroundings in which they live. Rilke writes about Rodin:

> When I first came to Rodin . . . I knew that his house was nothing to him, a paltry little necessity perhaps, a roof for time of rain and sleep; and that it was no care to him and no weight upon his solitude and composure. Deep in himself he bore the darkness, shelter, and peace of a house, and he himself had become sky above it, and wood around it, and distance and great stream always flowing by.[27]

But to find a home in oneself, one must first have realised oneself in works or acts. Man has only a middling interest in his domestic interior because he has access to the entire universe and because he can affirm himself in his projects. Woman, instead, is locked into the conjugal community: she has to change this prison into a kingdom. Her attitude to her home is dictated by this same dialectic that generally defines her condition: she takes by becoming prey, she liberates herself by abdicating; by renouncing the world, she means to conquer a world.

She regrets closing the doors of her home behind herself; as a girl, the whole world was her kingdom; the forests belonged to her. Now she is confined to a restricted space; Nature is reduced to the size of a geranium pot; walls block out the horizon. One of Virginia Woolf's heroines murmurs:

> Whether it is summer, whether it is winter, I no longer know by the moor grass and the heath flower; only by the steam on the window-pane, or the frost on the window-pane . . . I, who used to walk through beech woods noting the jay's feather turning blue as it falls, past the shepherd and the tramp, . . . go from room to room with a duster.*28

But she is going to make every attempt to refuse this limitation. She encloses faraway countries and past times within her four walls in the form of more or less expensive earthly flora and fauna; she encloses her husband, who personifies human society for her, and the child who gives her the whole future in a portable form. The home becomes the centre of the world and even its own one truth; as Bachelard appropriately notes, it is 'a sort of counter- or exclusionary universe';29 refuge, retreat, grotto, womb, it protects against outside dangers: it is this confused exteriority that becomes unreal. Especially at evening time, when the shutters are closed, woman feels like a queen; the light shed at noon by the universal sun disturbs her; at night she is no longer dispossessed because she does away with that which she does not possess; from under the lampshade she sees a light that is her own and that illuminates her abode alone: nothing else exists. Another text by Virginia Woolf shows us reality concentrated in the house, while the outside space collapses.

---

* *The Waves.*

The night was now shut off by panes of glass, which, far from giving any accurate view of the outside world, rippled it so strangely that here, inside the room, seemed to be order and dry land; there, outside, a reflection in which things wavered and vanished, waterily.[30]

Thanks to the velvets, silks and china with which she surrounds herself, woman can in part assuage this grasping sensuality that her erotic life cannot usually satisfy; she will also find in this decor an expression of her personality; it is she who has chosen, made and 'hunted down' furniture and knick-knacks, who has aesthetically arranged them in a way where symmetry is important; they reflect her individuality while bearing social witness to her standard of living. Her home is thus her earthly lot, the expression of her social worth and her intimate truth. Because she *does* nothing, she avidly seeks herself in what she *has*.

It is through housework that the wife comes to make her 'nest' her own; this is why, even if she has 'help', she insists on doing things herself; at least by watching over, controlling and criticising, she endeavours to make her servants' results her own. By administrating her home, she achieves her social justification; her job is also to oversee the food, clothing and care of the familial society in general. Thus she too realises herself as an activity. But, as we will see, it is an activity that brings her no escape from her immanence and allows her no individual affirmation of herself.

The poetry of housework has been highly praised. It is true that housework makes the woman grapple with matter, and she finds an intimacy in objects that is the revelation of being and that consequently enriches her. In *Marie*, Madeleine Bourdouxhe describes her heroine's pleasure in spreading the cleaning paste on her stove. In her fingertips she feels the freedom and power that the brilliant image from scrubbed cast iron reflects back to her:

When she comes up from the cellar, she enjoys the weight of the full coal-buckets, even though they seem heavier with every step. She has always felt affection for simple things that have their own particular smell, their own particular roughness, and she's always known how to handle them. Without fear or hesitation her hands plunge into dead fires or into soapy water, they rub the rust off a piece of metal and grease it, spread polish, and after a meal, sweep the scraps from a table in one great circular movement. It's a perfect harmony, a mutual understanding between the palms of her hands and the objects they touch.[31]

Numerous women writers have lovingly spoken of freshly ironed linens, of the whitening agents of soapy water, of white sheets, of shining copper. When the housewife cleans and polishes furniture, 'dreams of saturating penetration nourish the gentle patience of the hand striving to bring out the beauty of the wood with wax', says Bachelard. Once the job is finished, the housewife experiences the joy of contemplation. But for the precious qualities to show themselves – the polish of a table, the shine of a chandelier, the icy whiteness and starch of the laundry – a negative action must first be applied; all foul causes must be expelled. There, writes Bachelard, is the essential reverie to which the housewife surrenders: the dream of active cleanliness, that is, cleanliness conquering dirt. He describes it this way:

> It would seem that in imagination the struggle for tidiness requires provocation. The imagination needs to work itself up into a cunning rage. With a nasty grin and dirty greasy rag one smears the copper faucet with a thick paste of scouring powder. Bitterness and hostility build up in the worker's heart. Why does the chore have to be so foul? But the moment for the dry cloth arrives and, along with it, a lighter-hearted malice, vigorous and talkative: faucet, you'll soon be like a mirror; kettle, you'll soon be like a sun! In the end, when the copper shines and laughs with the churlishness of an amiable fellow, peace is made. The housewife contemplates her gleaming victories.*[32]

Ponge has evoked the struggle, in the heart of the laundrywoman, between uncleanliness and purity:†

> Whoever has not lived for at least one winter in the company of a wash boiler[33] knows nothing of a certain order of highly touching qualities and emotions.
>   It is necessary – wincing – to have heaved it, brimful with soiled fabrics, off the ground and carried it over to the stove – where one

---

*Gaston Bachelard, *Earth and Reveries of Repose*.
†Ponge, 'The Wash Boiler', in *Sheaf*.

must then drag it in a particular way so as to sit it right on top of the burner.

Beneath it one needs to have stirred up the fire, to set the boiler in motion gradually, touched its warm or burning sides often; next listened to the deep internal hum, from that point onwards to have lifted the lid several times to check the tension of the spurts and the regularity of the wettings.

Finally, it is necessary to have embraced it once again, boiling hot, so as to set it back down on the ground . . .

The wash boiler is so conceived that, filled with a heap of disgusting rags, the inner emotion, the boiling indignation it feels, conducted towards the higher part of its being, rains back down on this heap of disgusting rags that turns its stomach – and this virtually endlessly – and that the outcome is a purification . . .

True, the linens, when the boiler received them, had already been soaked free of the worst of their filth.

Nonetheless it has an idea or a feeling of the diffuse dirtiness of things inside it, which by dint of emotion, seethings and exertions, it manages to get the best of – to remove the spots from the fabrics: so that these, rinsed in a catastrophe of cool water, will appear white to an extreme . . .

And here in effect the miracle takes place:

Thousands of white flags are all at once deployed – which mark, not a capitulation, but a victory – and are perhaps not merely the sign of the bodily cleanness of this place's inhabitants.[34]

These dialectics can give housework the charm of a game: the little girl readily enjoys shining the silver, polishing doorknobs. But for a woman to find positive satisfaction, she must devote her efforts to an interior she can be proud of; if not, she will never know the pleasure of contemplation, the only pleasure that can repay her efforts. An American reporter,* who lived several months among American Southern 'poor whites', has described the pathetic destiny of one of these women, overwhelmed with burdens, who laboured in vain to make a hovel livable. She lived with her husband and seven children in a wooden shack, the walls covered with soot, crawling with cockroaches; she had tried to 'make the house pretty'; in the main room, the fireplace covered with bluish plaster, a table and a few pictures hanging on the wall suggested

* James Agee, *Let Us Now Praise Famous Men.*

a sort of altar. But the hovel remained a hovel, and Mrs G. said with tears in her eyes, 'Oh, I hate this house. It seems there is nothing that can be done to make it pretty!' Legions of women have in common only endlessly recurrent fatigue in a battle that never leads to victory. Even in the most privileged cases, this victory is never final. Few tasks are more similar to the torment of Sisyphus than those of the housewife; day after day, one must wash dishes, dust furniture, mend clothes that will be dirty, dusty and torn again. The housewife wears herself out running on the spot; she does nothing; she only perpetuates the present; she never gains the sense that she is conquering a positive Good, but struggles indefinitely against Evil. It is a struggle that begins again every day. We know the story of the valet who despondently refused to polish his master's boots. 'What's the point?' he asked. 'You have to begin again the next day.' Many still unresigned girls share this discouragement. I recall an essay of a sixteen-year-old student that opened with words like these: 'Today is housecleaning day. I hear the noise of the vacuum Mama walks through the living room. I would like to run away. I swear when I grow up, there will never be a housecleaning day in my house.' The child thinks of the future as an indefinite ascent towards some unidentified summit. Suddenly in the kitchen, where her mother is washing dishes, the little girl realises that over the years, every afternoon at the same time, these hands have plunged into greasy water and wiped the china with a rough dish towel. And until death they will be subjected to these rites. Eat, sleep, clean . . . the years no longer reach towards the sky, they spread out identical and grey as a horizontal tablecloth; every day looks like the previous one; the present is eternal, useless and hopeless. In the short story 'Dust',[35] Colette Audry subtly describes the sad futility of an activity that stubbornly resists time:

The next day while cleaning the sofa with a horsehair brush, she picked up something that she first took for an old morsel of cotton or a big feather. But it was only a dust ball like those that form on high wardrobes that you forget to dust or behind furniture between the wall and the wood. She remained pensive before this curious substance. So here they were living in these rooms for eight or ten weeks and already, in spite of Juliette's vigilance, a dust ball had had the time to take form, to grow, crouching in a shadow like those grey beasts that frightened her when she was small. A fine

* *Playing a Losing Game.*

ash of dust proclaims negligence, the beginning of carelessness, it's the impalpable sediment from the air we breathe, clothes that flutter, from the wind coming through open windows; but this tuft already represented a second stage of dust, triumphant dust, a thickening that takes shape and from sediment becomes waste. It was almost pretty to look at, transparent and light like bramble puffs, but more drab.

. . . The dust had beaten out all the world's vacuum power. It had taken over the world and the vacuum cleaner was no more than a witness object destined to show everything the human race was capable of ruining in work, matter and ingenuity in struggling against all-powerful dirt. It was waste made instrument . . .

It was their life together that was the cause of everything, their little meals that left skin peelings, dust from both of them that mingled everywhere . . . Every couple secretes these little bits of litter that must be destroyed to make space for new ones . . . What a life one spends – and to be able to go out with a fresh little shirt, attractive to passersby, so your engineer husband looks good in his life. Mantras replayed in Marguerite's head: take care of the wooden floors . . . for the care of brass, use . . . she was in charge of the care of two ordinary beings for the rest of their days.

Washing, ironing, sweeping, routing out tufts of dust in the dark places behind the wardrobe, this is holding away death but also refusing life: for in one movement time is created and destroyed; the housewife only grasps the negative aspect of it. Hers is the attitude of a Manichaean. The essence of Manichaeism is not only to recognise two principles, one good and one evil: it is also to posit that good is attained by the abolition of evil and not by a positive movement; in this sense, Christianity is hardly Manichaean in spite of the existence of the devil, because it is in devoting oneself to God that one best fights the devil and not in trying to conquer him. All doctrines of transcendence and freedom subordinate the defeat of evil to progress towards good. But the wife is not called to build a better world; the house, the bedroom, the dirty laundry, the wooden floors, are fixed things: she can do no more than rout out indefinitely the foul causes that creep in; she attacks the dust, stains, mud and filth; she fights sin, she fights with Satan. But it is a sad destiny to have to repel an enemy without respite instead of being turned towards positive aims; the housewife often submits to it in rage. Bachelard uses the word 'malice' for it; psychoanalysts have written about it. For them, housekeeping mania is a form of sadomasochism; it is characteristic of mania and vice to make freedom want what it does not want; because the maniacal housewife detests having negativity, dirt and evil as her lot, she furiously pursues dust, accepting a condition that revolts her. She attacks life itself through the rubbish left from any living growth. Whenever a living being enters her sphere, her eye shines with a wicked fire. 'Wipe your feet; don't mess up everything; don't touch that.' She would like to stop everyone from breathing: the least breath is a threat. Every movement threatens her with more thankless work: a child's somersault is a tear to sew up. Seeing life as a promise of decomposition demanding more endless work, she loses her joie de vivre; her eyes sharpen, her face looks preoccupied and serious, always on guard; she protects herself through prudence and avarice. She closes the windows because sun would bring in insects, germs and dust; besides, the sun eats away at the silk wall coverings; the antique armchairs are hidden under loose covers and embalmed in mothballs: light would fade them. She does not even care to let her visitors see these treasures: admiration sullies. This defiance turns to bitterness and causes hostility to everything that lives. In the provinces, some bourgeois women have been known to put on white gloves to make sure no invisible dust remains on the furniture: these were the kind of women the Papin sisters murdered several years ago; their hatred of dirt was inseparable from their hatred of their servants, of the world and of each other.

Few women choose such a gloomy vice when they are young. Those who generously love life are protected from it. Colette tells us about Sido:

> The fact is that, though she was active and always on the go, she was not a sedulous housewife. She was clean and tidy, fastidious even but without a trace of that solitary, maniacal spirit that counts napkins, lumps of sugar, and full bottles. With a flannel in her hands, and one eye on the servant dawdling over her window-cleaning and smiling at the man next door, she would utter nervous exclamations like impatient cries for freedom.
> 'When I take a lot of time and trouble wiping my Chinese cups,' she would say, 'I can actually feel myself getting older.'
> But she always persevered loyally until the job was finished. Then off she would go, down the two steps that led into the garden, and at once her resentment and her nervous exasperation subsided.[36]

It is in this nervousness and resentment that frigid or frustrated women, old maids, desperate housewives, and those condemned by their husbands to a solitary and empty existence are satisfied. I knew, among others, an elderly woman who woke up every morning at five o'clock to inspect her wardrobes and begin rearranging them; it seems that at twenty she was gay and coquettish; closed up in her isolated estate, with a husband who neglected her and a single child, she took to arranging as others take to drink. For Élise in *The Bold Chronicle of a Strange Marriage*, the taste for housework stems from the exasperated desire to rule the universe, from a living exuberance and from a will for domination, which, for lack of an outlet, leads nowhere; it is also a challenge to time, the universe, life, men and everything that exists:

Since dinner from nine o'clock onwards, she has been doing the washing. It is midnight. I had been dozing, but her fortitude annoys me because it insults my rest by making it look like laziness.

Élise: 'If you want things to be clean, you shouldn't be afraid of getting your hands dirty first.'

And the house will soon be so spotless that we shall hardly dare live in it. There are divans, but you are expected to lie down beside them on the parquet floor. The cushions are too clean. You are afraid to soil or crumple them by putting your head or your feet on them, and every time I step on a carpet, I am followed with a carpet sweeper to remove the marks that I've made.

In the evening:

'It's done.'

What is the point of her moving every object and every piece of furniture and going over all the floors, the walls, and the ceilings from the time she gets up till the time she goes to bed?

For the moment, it is the housewife who is uppermost in her. Once she has dusted the insides of her cupboards, she dusts the geraniums on the windowsills.

His mother: Élise always keeps so busy she does not notice she is alive.[37]

Housework in fact allows the woman an indefinite escape far from herself. Chardonne rightly remarks:

Here is a meticulous and disordered task, with neither stops nor limits. In the home, a woman certain to please quickly reaches her breaking point, a state of distraction and mental void that effaces her . . .'[38]

This escape, this sadomasochism in which woman persists against both objects and self, is often precisely sexual. 'The kind of housecleaning that calls for bodily gymnastics amounts to a bordello for women,' says Violette Leduc.*[39] It is striking that the taste for cleanliness is of utmost importance in Holland, where women are cold, and in puritanical civilisations that juxtapose the joys of the flesh with an ideal of order and purity. If the Mediterranean Midi lives in joyous filth, it is not only because water is scarce there: love of the flesh and its animality is conducive to tolerating human odour, squalor and even vermin.

Preparing meals is more positive work and often more enjoyable than cleaning. First of all, it involves going to the market, which is for many housewives the best time of the day. The loneliness of the household weighs on the woman just as routine tasks leave her head empty. She is happy when, in Midi towns, she can sew, wash and peel vegetables while chatting on her doorstep; fetching water from the river is a grand adventure for half-cloistered Muslim women: I saw a little village in Kabyle where the women tore down the fountain an official had built on the plaza; going down every morning to the wadi flowing at the foot of the hill was their only distraction. All the time they are doing their marketing, waiting in queues, in shops, on street corners, they talk about things that affirm their 'homemaking worth' from which each one draws the sense of her own importance; they feel part of a community that – for an instant – is opposed to the society of men as the essential to the inessential. But above all, making a purchase is a profound pleasure: it is a discovery, almost an invention. Gide observes in his *Journals* that the Muslims, unfamiliar with games of chance, have replaced them with the discovery of hidden treasures; this is the poetry and adventure of mercantile civilisations. The housewife is oblivious to the gratuitousness of games: but a good firm cabbage and a ripe Camembert are treasures that must be subtly discovered in spite of the cunning shopkeeper;

* *The Starved Woman.*

between seller and buyer, relations of dealing and ruse are established: for her, winning means getting the best goods for the lowest price; concern for a restricted budget is not enough to explain the extreme importance given to being economical: winning the game is what counts. When she suspiciously inspects the stalls, the housewife is queen; the world, with its riches and traps, is at her feet, for her taking. She tastes a fleeting triumph when she empties her shopping basket on the table. She puts her canned food and nonperishables in the larder, guarding her against the future, and she contemplates with satisfaction the raw vegetables and meats she is about to submit to her power.

Gas and electricity have killed the magic of fire; but in the countryside, many women still know the joys of kindling live flames from inert wood. With the fire lit, the woman changes into a sorceress. With a simple flip of the hand – beating the eggs or kneading the dough – or by the magic of fire, she effects transmutations of substances; matter becomes food. Colette, again, describes the enchantment of this alchemy:

> All is mystery, magic, spell, all that takes place between the time the casserole, kettle, stewpot and their contents are put on the fire and the moment of sweet anxiety, of voluptuous expectation, when the dish is brought steaming to the table and its headdress removed.

Among other things, she lovingly depicts the metamorphoses that take place in the secret of hot ashes:

> Wood ash does a flavoursome job of cooking whatever it is given to cook. The apple, the pear nestling among the ashes, come out wrinkled and smoke-tanned but soft under the skin like a mole's belly, and however *bonne femme* the apple cooked in the stove might be, it is a far cry from this jam enclosed in its original robe, thick with flavour, and – if you go about it right – has oozed but a single tear of honey . . . a tall three-legged cauldron held sifted ash that never saw the fire. But stuffed with potatoes lying side by side without touching, its black claws planted in the embers, the cauldron laid tubers for us white as snow, burning hot, flaky.[40]

Women writers have particularly celebrated the poetry of making preserves: it is a grand undertaking, marrying pure solid sugar and the soft pulp of fruit in a copper preserving pan; foaming, viscous, boiling, the substance being made is dangerous: it is a bubbling lava the house-wife proudly captures and pours into jars. When she covers them with parchment paper and inscribes the date of her victory, it is a triumph over time itself: she has captured the passage of time in the snare of sugar, she has put life in jars. Cooking is more than penetrating and revealing the intimacy of substances. It reshapes and re-creates them. In working the dough she experiences her power. 'The hand as well as the eye has its reveries and poetry,' says Bachelard.*⁴¹ And he speaks of this 'suppleness that fills one's hands, rebounding endlessly from matter to hand and from hand to matter'. The hand of the cook who kneads is a 'gratified hand' and cooking lends the dough a new value still. 'Cooking is thus a great material transformation from whiteness to golden brown, from dough to crust':† women can find a special satisfaction in a successful cake or a flaky pastry because not everyone can do it: it takes a gift. 'Nothing is more complicated than the art of pastry,' writes Michelet. 'Nothing proceeds less according to rule, or is less dependent on educa-tion. One must be *born* with it. It is wholly a gift of the mother.'⁴²

Here again, it is clear that the little girl passionately enjoys imitating her female elders: with chalk and grass she plays at make-believe; she is happier still when she has a real little oven to play with, or when her mother lets her come into the kitchen and roll out the pastry with her palms or cut the hot burning caramel. But this is like housework: repe-tition soon dispels these pleasures. For Indians who get their nourishment essentially from tortillas, the women spend half their days kneading, cooking, reheating and kneading again identical tortillas, under every roof, identical throughout the centuries: they are hardly sensitive to the magic of the oven. It is not possible to transform marketing into a treasure hunt every day, nor to delight in a shiny water tap. Women and men writers can lyrically exalt these triumphs because they never or rarely do housework. Done every day, this work becomes monotonous and mechan-ical; it is laden with waiting: waiting for the water to boil, for the roast to be cooked just right, for the laundry to dry; even if different tasks are well organised, there are long moments of passivity and emptiness; most of the time, they are accomplished in boredom; between present life and the life of tomorrow, they are but an inessential intermediary. If the indi-vidual who executes them is himself a producer or creator, they are inte-grated into his existence as naturally as body functions; this is why everyday

---

* Gaston Bachelard, *Earth and Reveries of Will*.
† Ibid.

chores seem less dismal when performed by men; they represent for them only a negative and contingent moment they hurry to escape. But what makes the lot of the wife-servant ungratifying is the division of labour that dooms her wholly to the general and inessential; home and food are useful for life but do not confer any meaning on it: the housekeeper's immediate goals are only means, not real ends, and they reflect no more than anonymous projects. It is understandable that to give meaning to her work, she endeavours to give it her individuality and to attach an absolute value to the results obtained; she has her rituals, her superstitions, she has her ways of setting the table, arranging the living room, mending, cooking a dish; she persuades herself that in her place, no one could make such a good roast, or do the polishing as well; if her husband or daughter wants to help her or tries to do without her, she grabs the needle or the broom. 'You don't know how to sew a button.' Dorothy Parker* described with a pitying irony the dismay of a young woman convinced she should bring a personal note to the arrangement of her house, but not knowing how:

Mrs Ernest Weldon wandered about the orderly living-room, giving it some of those little feminine touches. She was not especially good as a touch-giver. The idea was pretty, and appealing to her. Before she was married, she had dreamed of herself as moving softly about her new dwelling, deftly moving a vase here or straightening a flower there, and thus transforming it from a house to a home. Even now, after seven years of marriage, she liked to picture herself in the gracious act.

But, though she conscientiously made a try at it every night as soon as the rose-shaded lamps were lit, she was always a bit bewildered as to how one went about performing those tiny miracles that make all the difference in the world to a room . . . Touch-giving was a wife's job. And Mrs Weldon was not one to shirk the business she had entered.

With an almost pitiable air of uncertainty, she strayed over to the mantel, lifted a small Japanese vase, and stood with it in her hand, gazing helplessly around the room . . .

Then she stepped back, and surveyed her innovations. It was amazing how little difference they made to the room.[43]

---

* 'Too Bad!'

The wife wastes a great deal of time and effort searching for originality or her individual perfection; this gives her work the characteristic of a 'meticulous and disordered task, with neither stops nor limits', as Chardonne points out, which makes it so difficult to measure the burden that household cares really mean. According to a recent report (published in 1947 by the newspaper *Combat*, written by C. Hébert), married women devote about three hours and forty-five minutes to housework (cleaning, food shopping, and so on) each working day, and eight hours on the day of rest, that is thirty hours a week, which corresponds to three-quarters of the working week of a woman worker or employee; this is enormous if it is added to a paid job; it is not much if the wife has nothing else to do (especially as woman workers and employees lose time travelling that has no equivalent here). Caring for children, if there are many, considerably adds to the wife's fatigue: a poor mother depletes her strength every one of her hectic days. By contrast, bourgeois women who have help are almost idle; and the ransom of this leisure is boredom. Because they are bored, many complicate and endlessly multiply their duties so that they become more stressful than a skilled job. A woman friend who had gone through nervous breakdowns told me that when she was in good health she took care of her house almost without thinking of it, leaving her time for much more challenging occupations; when neurasthenia prevented her from giving herself to other jobs, she allowed herself to be swallowed up by household cares, devoting whole days to them without managing to finish.

The saddest thing is that this work does not even result in a lasting creation. Woman is tempted – all the more as she is so attentive to it – to consider her work as an end in itself. Contemplating the cake she takes out of the oven, she sighs: what a pity to eat it! What a pity husband and children drag their muddy feet on the waxed floor. As soon as things are used, they are dirtied or destroyed: she is tempted, as we have already seen, to withdraw them from being used; she keeps the jam until mould invades it; she locks the living room doors. But time cannot be stopped; supplies attract rats; worms start their work. Covers, curtains and clothes are eaten by moths: the world is not a dream carved in stone, it is made of a suspicious-looking substance threatened by decomposition; edible stuff is as questionable as Dalí's meat monsters: it seemed inert and inorganic but hidden larvae have metamorphosed it into corpses. The housewife who alienates herself in things depends, like things, on the whole world: linens turn grey, the roast burns, china breaks; these are absolute disasters because when things disappear, they disappear irremediably. It is impossible to obtain permanence and security through them. Wars with their looting and bombs threaten wardrobes and the home.

Thus, the product of housework has to be consumed; constant renunciation is demanded of the wife whose work is finished only with its destruction. For her to consent to it without regret, these small holocausts must spark some joy or pleasure somewhere. But as housework is spent in maintaining the status quo, the husband – when he comes home – notices disorder and negligence but takes order and neatness for granted. He attaches more positive importance to a well-prepared meal. The triumphant moment of the cook is when she places a successful dish on the table: husband and children welcome it warmly, not only with words but also by consuming it joyously. Culinary alchemy continues with the food becoming chyle and blood. Taking care of a body is of more concrete interest, is more vital than taking care of a parquet floor; the cook's effort transcends towards the future in an obvious way. However, while it is less futile to depend on an outside freedom than to alienate oneself in things, it is no less dangerous. It is only in the guests' mouths that the cook's work finds its truth; she needs their approval; she demands that they appreciate her dishes, that they take more; she is irritated if they are no longer hungry: to the point that one does not know if the fried potatoes are destined for the husband or the husband for the fried potatoes. This ambiguity is found in the housewife's whole attitude: she keeps the house for her husband; but she also insists on his devoting all the money he earns to buying furniture or a refrigerator. She wants to make him happy: but she approves of his activities only if they fit into the framework of the happiness she has constructed.

There have been periods when these claims were generally satisfied: periods when happiness was also the man's ideal, when he was primarily attached to his house and family and when the children themselves chose to define themselves by family, their traditions and their past. Then she who ruled the home, who presided over the table, was recognised as sovereign; she still plays this glorious role as wife in relation to some landowners, or some rich farmers who occasionally still perpetuate the patriarchal civilisation. But on the whole, marriage today is the survival of obsolete customs with the wife's situation much more thankless than before since she still has the same duties while these no longer confer the same rights; she has the same chores without the rewards or honour from doing them. Today, man marries to anchor himself in immanence but not to confine himself in it; he wants a home but also to remain free to escape from it; he settles down but he often remains a vagabond in his heart; he does not scorn happiness but he does not make it an end in itself; repetition bores him; he seeks novelty, risk, resistance to overcome, camaraderie, friendships that wrest him from the solitude of the couple. Children even more than husbands want to go beyond the home's limits: their life is elsewhere, in front of them; the child always desires what is other. The wife tries to constitute a universe of permanence and continuity: husband and children want to go beyond the situation she creates and which for them is only a given. Thus, if she is loath to admit the precariousness of the activities to which her whole life is devoted, she is led to impose her services by force: from mother and housewife she becomes cruel mother and shrew.

So the wife's work within the home does not grant her autonomy; it is not directly useful to the group, it does not open on to the future, it does not produce anything. It becomes meaningful and dignified only if it is integrated into existences that go beyond themselves, towards the society in production or action: far from enfranchising the matron, it makes her dependent on her husband and children; she justifies her existence through them: she is no more than an inessential mediation in their lives. That the civil code erased 'obedience' from her duties changes nothing in her situation; her situation is not based on what the couple wants but on the very structure of the conjugal community. The wife is not allowed to *do* any positive work and consequently to have herself known as a complete person. Regardless of how well she is respected, she is subjugated, secondary, parasitic. The heavy curse weighing on her is that the very meaning of her existence is not in her hands. This is the reason the successes and failures of her conjugal life have much more importance for her than for the man: he is a citizen, a producer before being a husband; she is above all, and often exclusively, a wife; her work does not extract her from her condition; it is from her condition, on the contrary, that her work derives its price or not. Loving, generously devoted, she will carry out her tasks joyously; these chores will seem insipid to her if she accomplishes them with resentment. They will never play more than an inessential role in her destiny; in the misadventures of conjugal life they will be of no help. We thus have to see how this condition is concretely lived, one that is essentially defined by bed 'service' and housework 'service' in which the wife finds her dignity only in accepting her vassalage.

It is a crisis that pushes the girl from childhood to adolescence; an even more acute crisis thrusts her into adult life. The anxieties inherent in all passages from one condition to another are superimposed on those that a somewhat brusque sexual initiation provokes in a woman. Nietzsche writes:

And then to be hurled, as by a gruesome lightning bolt, into reality and knowledge, by marriage . . . To catch love and shame in a contradiction and to be forced to experience at the same time delight, surrender, duty, pity, terror, and who knows what else, in the face of the unexpected neighbourliness of God and beast! . . . Thus a psychic knot has been tied that may have no equal.[44]

The excitement that surrounded the traditional 'honeymoon' was meant in part to hide this confusion: thrown outside her everyday world for a few weeks, all connections with society being temporarily broken, the young woman was no longer situated in space, in time, in reality.* But sooner or later she has to take her place there again; and she finds herself in her new home, but never without apprehension. Her ties with her father's home are much stronger than her ties with the young man's. Tearing oneself away from one's family is a definitive weaning: this is when she experiences the anguish of abandon and the giddiness of freedom. The break is more or less painful, depending on the case; if she has already broken the ties connecting her to her father, brothers and sisters, and above all her mother, she can leave painlessly; if, still dominated by them, she can practically remain in their protection, she will be less affected by her change in condition; but ordinarily, even if she wanted to escape from the paternal household, she feels disconcerted when she is separated from the little society in which she was integrated, cut off from her past, her child's universe with its familiar principles and unquestioned values. Only an ardent and full erotic life could make her bathe again in the peace of immanence; but usually she is at first more upset than fulfilled; that sexual initiation is more or less successful simply adds to her confusion. The day after her wedding finds many of the same reactions she had on her first menstruation: she often experiences disgust at this supreme revelation of her femininity, horror at the idea that this experience will be renewed. She also feels the bitter disappointment of the day after; once she began menstruating, the girl sadly realised she was not an adult; deflowered, now the young woman is an adult and the last step is taken: and now what? This worrying disappointment is moreover linked as much to marriage itself as it is to defloration: a woman who had already 'known' her fiancé, or who had 'known' other men but for whom marriage represents the full accession to adult life will often

* Fin-de-siècle literature often has defloration take place in the sleeping car, which is a way of placing it 'nowhere'.

have the same reaction. Living the beginning of an enterprise is exalting; but nothing is more depressing than discovering a destiny over which one no longer has a hold. From this definitive, immutable background, freedom emerges with the most intolerable gratuitousness. Previously the girl, sheltered by her parents' authority, made use of her freedom in revolt and hope; she used it to refuse and go beyond a condition in which she nevertheless found security; her own transcendence toward marriage took place from within the warmth of the family; now she *is* married, there is no *other* future in front of her. The doors of home are closed around her: of all the earth, this will be her portion. She knows exactly what tasks lie ahead of her: the same as her mother's. Day after day, the same rites will be repeated. As a girl her hands were empty: in hope, in dreams, she possessed everything. Now she has acquired a share of the world and she thinks in anguish: there is nothing more than this, forever. Forever this husband, this home. She has nothing more to expect, nothing more to want. However, she is afraid of her new responsibilities. Even if her husband is older and has authority, the fact that she has sexual relations with him removes some of his prestige: he cannot replace a father, and even less a mother, and he cannot give her her freedom. In the solitude of the new home, tied to a man who is more or less a stranger, no longer child but wife and destined to become mother in turn, she feels numb; definitively removed from her mother's breast, lost in the middle of a world to which no aim calls her, abandoned in an icy present, she discovers the boredom and blandness of pure facticity. This is the distress so stunningly expressed in the young Countess Tolstoy's diary;[45] she enthusiastically gave her hand to the great writer she admired; after the passionate embraces she submitted to on the wooden balcony at Yasnaya Polyana, she found herself disgusted by carnal love, far from her family, cut off from her past, at the side of a man to whom she had been engaged for one week, someone who was seventeen years her senior, with a totally foreign past and interests; everything seems empty, icy to her; her life is no more than an eternal sleep. Her diary account of the first years of her marriage must be quoted.

On 23 September 1862, Sophia gets married and leaves her family in the evening:

A difficult and painful feeling gripped my throat and held me tight. I then felt that the time had come to leave forever my family and all those I loved deeply and with whom I had always lived . . . The farewells began and were ghastly . . . Now the last minutes.

I had intentionally reserved the farewells to my mother till the end . . . When I pulled myself from her embrace and without turning around I went to take my place in the car, she uttered a heart-rending cry I have never forgotten all my life. Autumn rain did not cease to fall . . . Huddled in my corner, overwhelmed with fatigue and sorrow, I let my tears flow. Leon Nikolaivitch seemed very surprised, even discontent . . . When we left the city, I felt in the depths a sentiment of fear . . . The darkness oppressed me. We barely said anything to each other until the first stop, Birioulev, if I am not mistaken. I remember that Leon Nikolaivitch was very tender and attentive to my every need. At Birioulev, we were given the rooms said to be for the tsar, big rooms with furniture uphol- stered in red rep that was not very welcoming. We were brought the samovar. Cuddled up in a corner of the couch, I kept silent as a condemned person. 'Well!', said Leon Nikolaivitch to me, 'if you did the honors.' I obeyed and served the tea. I was upset and could not free myself from a kind of fear. I did not dare address Leon Nikolaivitch in the familiar form and avoided calling him by his name. For a long time I continued to use the formal form.

Twenty-four hours later, they arrive at Yasnaya Polyana. She resumes her diary again on 8 October. She feels anxious. She suffers from the fact that her husband has a past:

I always dreamt of the man I would love as a completely whole, new, *pure*, person . . . in these childish dreams, which I still find hard to give up . . . When he kisses me I am always thinking, 'I am not the first woman he has loved.'

The following day she notes:

I feel downcast all the same. I had such a depressing dream last night, and it is weighing on me, although I do not remember it in detail. I thought of Maman today and grew dreadfully sad . . . I seem to be asleep all the time and unable to wake up . . . Something is weighing on me. I keep thinking that at any moment I might die. It is so strange to be thinking such things now that I have a husband. I can hear him in there sleeping. I am frightened of being on my own. He will not let me go into his room, which makes me very sad. All physical things disgust him.

October 11: I am terribly, terribly sad, and withdrawing further and further into myself. My husband is ill and out of sorts and doesn't love me. I expected this, yet I could never have imagined it would be so terrible. Why do people always think I am so happy? What no one seems to realise is that I cannot create happiness, either for him or for myself. Before when I was feeling miserable I would ask myself, 'What is the use of living when you make others unhappy and yourself wretched?' This thought keeps recurring to me now, and I am terrified. He grows colder and colder every day, while I, on the contrary, love him more and more . . . I keep thinking of my own family and how happy my life was with them; now, my God, it breaks my heart to think that nobody loves me. Darling Mother, Tanya – what wonderful people they were, why did I ever leave them? . . . it gnaws at my conscience . . . Lyovochka is a wonderful man . . . Now I have lost everything I once possessed, all my energy for work, life and household tasks has been wasted. Now I want only to sit in silence all day, doing nothing but think bitter thoughts. I wanted to do some work, but could not; . . . I long to play the piano but it is so awkward in this place . . . He suggested today that I stay at home while he went off to Nikolskoe. I should have agreed and set him free from my presence, but I simply could not . . . Poor man, he is always looking for something to divert him and take him away from me. What is the point of living?

November 13: It is true, I cannot find anything to occupy me. He is fortunate because he is talented and clever. I am neither . . . It is not difficult to find work, there is plenty to do, but first you have to enjoy such petty household tasks as breeding hens, tinkling on the piano, reading a lot of fourth-rate books and precious good ones, and pickling cucumbers. I am asleep now, since nothing brings me any excitement or joy – neither the trip to Moscow nor the thought of the baby. I wish I could take some remedy to refresh me and wake me up . . .

It is terrible to be alone. I am not used to it. There was so much life and love at home, and it's so lifeless here without him. He is almost always on his own . . . He . . . finds pleasure not in the company of those close to him, as I do, but in his work . . . he never had a family.

November 23: . . . Of course I am idle at present, but I am not so by nature; I simply have not discovered anything I could do . . . Sometimes I long to break free of his rather oppressive influence and stop worrying about him, but I cannot. I find his influence oppressive because I have begun thinking his thoughts and seeing with his eyes, trying to become like him, and losing myself. And I have changed too, which makes it even harder for me.

April 1: I have a very great misfortune: I have no inner resources to draw on . . . Lyova has his work and the estate to think about while I have nothing . . . What am I good for? I would like to *do* more, something *real*. At this wonderful time of year, I always used to long for things, aspire to things, dream about God knows what. But I no longer need anything, no longer have those foolish aspirations, for I know instinctively that I have all I need now and there is nothing left to strive for . . . Everything seems stupid now and I get irritable.

April 20:[46] . . . Lyova ignores me more and more. The physical side of love is very important for him. This is terrible, for me it is quite the opposite.

It is clear, during these first six months, that the young woman is suffering from her separation from her family, from solitude, and from the definitive turn her destiny has taken; she detests her physical relations with her husband and she is bored. This is the same ennui Colette's mother feels to the point of tears after the first marriage her brothers imposed on her.*

So she left the cosy Belgian house, the cellar-kitchen that smelled of gas, warm bread and coffee; she left her piano, her violin, the big Salvator Rosa she had inherited from her father, the tobacco jar and the fine long-stemmed clay pipes, the coke braziers, the books that lay open and the crumpled newspapers, and as a new bride entered the house with its flight of steps, isolated by the harsh winter of the forest lands all around . . . Here she found, to her surprise, a white and gold living room on the ground floor, but a first floor with barely even rough-cast walls, as abandoned as a loft . . .

* *Claudine's House.*

the bedrooms were icy-cold and prompted no thoughts of either love or sweet sleep . . . Sido, who longed for friends and an innocent and cheerful social life, found on her estate only servants, cunning farmers . . . She filled the big house with flowers, had the dark kitchen whitewashed, oversaw in person the preparation of the Flemish dishes, kneaded cakes with raisins and looked forward to having her first child. The savage would smile at her between two outings and then set off once more . . . When she had exhausted her tasty recipes, her patience and her furniture polish, Sido – who had grown thin with loneliness – started to cry . . .[47]

In *Letters to Françoise, Married*[48] Marcel Prévost describes the young woman's dismay upon her return from her honeymoon.

She thinks of her mother's apartment with its Napoleon III and MacMahon furniture, its plush velvet, its wardrobes in black plum wood, everything she judged so old-fashioned, so ridiculous . . . In one instant all of that is evoked in her memory as a real haven, a true *nest*, the nest where she was watched over with disinterested tenderness, sheltered from all storms and danger. This apartment with its new-carpet smell, its unadorned windows, the chairs in disarray, its whole air of improvisation and haste, no; it is not a nest. It is only the place of the nest that has to be built . . . she suddenly felt horribly sad, as if she had been abandoned in a desert.

This distress is what often causes long depressions and various psychoses in the young woman. In particular, in the guise of different psychasthenic obsessions, she feels the giddiness of her empty freedom; she develops, for example, fantasies of prostitution we have already seen in girls. Pierre Janet* cites the case of a young bride who could not stand being alone in her apartment because she was tempted to go to the window and wink at passersby. Others remain abulic faced with a universe that 'no longer seems real', peopled only with ghosts and painted cardboard sets. There are those who try to refuse their adulthood, who will obstinately persist in refusing it their whole life, like another patient† whom Janet designates with the initials Qi:[49]

* *Obsessions and Psychasthenia.*
† Ibid.

Qi, a thirty-six-year-old woman, is obsessed by the idea that she is a little ten- to twelve-year-old girl; especially when she is alone, she lets herself jump, laugh, dance; she lets her hair down, lets it loose on her shoulders, sometimes cuts it in places. She would like to lose herself completely in this dream of being a child: It is so unfortunate that she cannot play hide-and-seek, play tricks . . . in front of everyone . . . 'I would like people to think I am nice, I am afraid of being the ugly duckling, I would like to be liked, talked to, petted, to be constantly told that I am loved as one loves little children . . . A child is loved for his mischievousness, for his good little heart, for his kindness and what is asked of him in return? To love you, nothing more. That is what is good, but I cannot say that to my husband, he would not understand me. Look, I would so much like to be a little girl, have a father or a mother who would take me on their lap, caress my hair . . . but no, I am Madame, a mother; I have to keep the home, be serious, think on my own, oh, what a life!'

Marriage is often a crisis for man as well: the proof is that many masculine psychoses develop during the engagement period or the early period of conjugal life. Less attached to his family than his sisters are, the young man belongs to some group: a special school, a university, a guild, a team, something that protects him from loneliness; he leaves it behind to begin his real existence as an adult; he is apprehensive of his future solitude and it is often to exorcise it that he gets married. But he is fooled by the illusion maintained by the whole community that depicts the couple as a 'conjugal *society*'. Except in the brief fire of a passionate affair, two individuals cannot form a world that protects each of them against the world: this is what they both feel the day after the wedding. The wife, soon familiar, subjugated, does not obstruct her husband's freedom: she is a burden, not an alibi; she does not free him from the weight of his responsibilities but on the contrary she exacerbates them. The difference of the sexes often means differences in age, education and situation that do not bring about any real understanding: familiar, the spouses are still strangers. Previously, there was often a real chasm between them: the girl, raised in a state of ignorance and innocence, had no 'past', while her fiancé had 'lived'; it was up to him to initiate her into the reality of life. Some males feel flattered by this delicate role; more lucid, they warily measure the distance that separates them from their future companion. In her novel, *The Age of Innocence*,[50] Edith

Wharton describes the scruples of a young American of 1870 concerning the woman destined for him:

> With a new sense of awe he looked at the frank forehead, serious eyes and gay innocent mouth of the young creature whose soul's custodian he was to be. That terrifying product of the social system he belonged to and believed in, the young girl who knew nothing and expected everything, looked back at him like a stranger . . . What could he and she really know of each other, since it was his duty, as a 'decent' fellow, to conceal his past from her, and hers, as a marriageable girl, to have no past to conceal? . . . The young girl who was the centre of this elaborate system of mystification remained the more inscrutable for her very frankness and assurance. She was frank, poor darling, because she had nothing to conceal, assured because she knew of nothing to be on her guard against; and with no better preparation than this, she was to be plunged overnight into what people evasively called 'the facts of life' . . . But when he had gone the brief round of her he returned discouraged by the thought that all this frankness and innocence were only an artificial product . . . so cunningly manufactured by a conspiracy of mothers and aunts and grandmothers and long-dead ancestresses, because it was supposed to be what he wanted, what he had a right to, in order that he might exercise his lordly pleasure in smashing it like an image made of snow.

Today, the gap is not as wide because the girl is a less artificial being; she is better informed, better armed for life. But she is often much younger than her husband. The importance of this point has not been emphasised enough; the consequences of an unequal maturity are often taken as differences of sex; in many cases the wife is a child not because she is a woman but because she is in fact very young. The seriousness of her husband and his friends overwhelms her. Sophia Tolstoy wrote about one year after her wedding day:

> He is old and self-absorbed, whereas I feel young and long to do something wild. I'd like to turn somersaults instead of going to bed. But with whom?
> Old age hovers over me; everything here is old. I try to suppress all youthful feelings, for they would seem odd and out of place in this somber environment.[51]

As for the husband, he sees a 'baby' in his wife; for him she is not the companion he expected, and he makes her feel it; she is humiliated by it. No doubt she likes finding a guide when she leaves her father's home, but she also wants to be seen as a 'grown-up'; she wants to remain a child, she wants to become a woman; her older spouse can never treat her in a way that totally satisfies her.

Even if their age difference is slight, the fact remains that the young woman and young man have generally been brought up very differently; she is the product of a feminine universe where she was inculcated with feminine sagacity and respect for feminine values, whereas he is imbued with the male ethic. It is often very difficult for them to understand each other and conflicts soon arise.

Because marriage usually subordinates the wife to the husband, the intensity of the problem of conjugal relations rests mainly on her. The paradox of marriage is that it brings into play an erotic function as well as a social one: this ambivalence is reflected in the figure the husband presents to the young wife. He is a demigod endowed with virile prestige and destined to replace her father: protector, overseer, tutor, guide; the wife has to thrive in his shadow; he is the holder of values, the guarantor of truth, the ethical justification of the couple. But he is also a male with whom she must share an experience often shameful, bizarre, disgusting, or upsetting, and in any case, contingent; he invites his wife to wallow with him in bestiality while directing her with a strong hand towards the ideal.

One night in Paris – where they had come on their return journey – Bernard made a show of walking out of a nightclub, shocked at the revue: 'To think that foreign visitors will see that! What shame! And that's how they'll judge us . . .' Thérèse could only marvel that this so chaste man was the same one who would be making her submit, in less than an hour, to his patient inventions in the dark.*[52]

There are many hybrid forms between mentor and beast. Sometimes man is at once father and lover; the sexual act becomes a sacred orgy and the loving wife finds ultimate salvation in the arms of her husband, redeemed by total abdication. This love-passion within married life is very rare. And at times the wife will love her husband platonically but will be unable to abandon herself in the arms of a man she respects too

---

* Mauriac, *Thérèse Desqueyroux*.

much. Such is this woman whose case Stekel reports. 'Mme D. S., a great artist's widow, is now forty years old. Although she adored her husband, she was completely frigid with him.' On the contrary, she may experience pleasure with him that she suffers as a common disgrace, killing all respect and esteem she has for him. Besides, an erotic failure relegates her husband to the ranks of a brute: hated in his flesh, he will be reviled in spirit; inversely, we have seen how scorn, antipathy and rancour doomed the wife to frigidity. What often happens is that the husband remains a respected superior being after the sexual experience, excused of his animalistic weaknesses; it seems that this was the case, among others, of Adèle Hugo. Or else he is a pleasant partner, without prestige. Katherine Mansfield described one of the forms this ambivalence can take in her short story, 'Prelude':

For she really was fond of him; she loved and admired and respected him tremendously. Oh, better than anyone else in the world. She knew him through and through. He was the soul of truth and decency, and for all his practical experience he was awfully simple, easily pleased and easily hurt . . . If only he wouldn't jump at her so, and bark so loudly, and watch her with such eager, loving eyes. He was too strong for her; she had always hated things that rushed at her, from a child. There were times when he was frightening – really frightening – when she just had not screamed at the top of her voice: 'You are killing me.' And at those times she had longed to say the most coarse, hateful things . . . Yes, yes, it was true . . . For all her love and respect and admiration she hated him. It had never been so plain to her as it was at this moment. There were all her feelings for him, sharp and defined, one as true as the other. And there was this other, this hatred, just as real as the rest. She could have done her feelings up in little packets and given them to Stanley. She longed to hand him that last one, for a surprise. She could see his eyes as he opened that.[53]

The young wife rarely admits her feelings to herself with such sincerity. To love her husband and to be happy is a duty to herself and society; this is what her family expects of her; or if her parents were against the marriage, she wants to prove how wrong they were. She usually begins her conjugal life in bad faith; she easily persuades herself that she feels great love for her husband; and this passion takes on a more manic, possessive and jealous form the less sexually satisfied she is; to console herself for this disappointment that she refuses at first to admit, she has an insatiable need for her husband's presence. Stekel cites numerous examples of these pathological attachments:

A woman remained frigid for the first years of her marriage, due to childhood fixations. She then developed a hypertrophic love as is frequently found in women who cannot bear to see that their husbands are indifferent to them. She lived only for her husband, and thought only of him. She lost all will. He had to plan her day every morning, tell her what to buy, etc. She carried out everything conscientiously. If he did not tell her what to do, she stayed in her room doing nothing and worried about him. She could not let him go anywhere without accompanying him. She could not stay alone, and she liked to hold his hand . . . She was unhappy and cried for hours, trembling for her husband and if there were no reasons to tremble, she created them.

My second case concerned a woman closed up in her room as if it were a prison for fear of going out alone. I found her holding her husband's hands, pleading with him to stay near her . . . Married for seven years, he was never able to have relations with his wife.

Sophia Tolstoy's case was similar; it comes out clearly in the passage I have cited and all throughout her diaries that as soon as she was married, she realised she did not love her husband. Sexual relations with him disgusted her; she reproached him for his past, found him old and boring, had nothing but hostility for his ideas; and it seems that, greedy and brutal in bed, he neglected her and treated her harshly. To her hopeless cries, her confessions of ennui, sadness and indifference were nevertheless added Sophia's protestations of passionate love; she wanted her beloved husband near her always; as soon as he was away from her, she was tortured with jealousy. She writes:

January 11, 1863: My jealousy is a congenital illness, or it may be because in loving him I have nothing else to love; I have given myself so completely to him that my only happiness is with him and from him . . .

January 15, 1863:[54] I have been feeling [out of sorts and] angry that he should love everything and everyone, when I want him to love only me . . . The moment I think fondly of something or someone

I tell myself no, I love only Lyovochka. But I absolutely *must* learn to love something else as he loves his *work* . . . but I hate being alone without him . . . My need to be near him grows stronger every day.

October 17, 1863: I feel I don't understand him properly, that's why I am always jealously following him . . .

July 31, 1868: It makes me laugh to read my diary. What a lot of contradictions – as though I were the unhappiest of women! . . . Could any marriage be more happy and harmonious than ours? I have been married six years now, but I love him more and more . . . I still love him with the same passionate, poetic, fevered, jealous love, and his composure occasionally irritates me.

September 16, 1876:[55] I avidly search his diaries for any reference to love, and am so tormented by jealousy that I can no longer see anything clearly. I am afraid of my resentment of Lyovochka for leaving me . . . I choke back the tears, or hide away several times a day and weep with anxiety. I have a fever every day and a chill at night . . . 'What is he punishing me for?' I keep asking myself? 'Why, for loving him so much.'

These pages convey the feeling of a vain effort to compensate for the absence of a real love with moral and 'poetic' exaltation; demands, anxieties, jealousy, are expressions of the emptiness in her heart. A great deal of morbid jealousy develops in such conditions; in an indirect way, jealousy conveys a dissatisfaction that woman objectifies by inventing a rival; never feeling fulfilment with her husband, she rationalises in some way her disappointment by imagining him deceiving her.

Very often, the wife persists in her pretence through morality, hypocrisy, pride or timidity. 'Often, an aversion for the dear husband will go unnoticed for a whole life: it is called melancholia or some other name,' says Chardonne.* But the hostility is no less felt even though it is not named. It is expressed with more or less violence in the young wife's effort to refuse her husband's domination. After the honeymoon and the period of confusion that often follows, she tries to win back her autonomy. This is not an easy undertaking. The fact that her husband is often older than she is, that he possesses in any case masculine prestige

* *Eva.*

and that he is the 'head of the family' according to the law means he bears moral and social superiority; very often he also possesses – or at least appears to – an intellectual superiority. He has the advantage of culture or at least professional training over his wife; since adolescence, he has been interested in world affairs: they are his affairs; he knows a little law, he follows politics, he belongs to a party, a union, clubs; worker and citizen, his thinking is connected to action; he knows that one cannot cheat reality: that is, the average man has the technique of reasoning, the taste for facts and experience, a certain critical sense; here is what many girls lack; even if they have read, listened to lectures, touched upon the fine arts, their knowledge amassed here and there does not constitute culture; it is not because of an intellectual defect that they have not learned to reason: it is because they have not had to practise it; for them thinking is more of a game than an instrument; lacking intellectual training, even intelligent, sensitive and sincere women do not know how to present their opinions and draw conclusions from them. That is why a husband – even if far more mediocre – will easily take the lead over them; he knows how to prove himself right, even if he is wrong. Logic in masculine hands is often violence. Chardonne explained this kind of sly oppression well in *Epithalamium*. Older, more cultivated and educated than Berthe, Albert uses this pretext to deny any value to opinions of his wife that he does not share; he untiringly *proves* he is right; for her part she becomes adamant and refuses to accept that there is any substance in her husband's reasoning: he persists in his ideas, and that is the end of it. Thus a serious misunderstanding deepens between them. He does not try to understand feelings or deep-rooted reactions she cannot justify; she does not understand what lives behind her husband's pedantic and overwhelming logic. He even goes so far as to become irritated by the ignorance she never hid from him, and challenges her with questions about astronomy; he is flattered, nonetheless, to tell her what to read, to find in her a listener he can easily dominate. In a struggle where her intellectual shortcomings condemn her to losing every time, the young wife has no defence other than silence, or tears or violence:

> Her head spinning, as if overcome by blows, Berthe could no longer think when she heard that erratic and strident voice, and Albert continued to envelop her in an imperious drone to confuse her, to injure her in the distress of her humiliated spirit . . . she was defeated, disarmed before the asperities of an inconceivable argumentation, and to release herself from this unjust power, she cried:

Leave me alone! These words seemed too weak to her; she saw a crystal flask on her dressing table, and all at once threw the bottle at Albert . . .

Sometimes a wife will fight back. But often, with good or bad will, like Nora in *A Doll's House*,*[56] she lets her husband think for her; it is he who will be the couple's consciousness. Through timidity, awkwardness or laziness, she leaves it up to the man to formulate their common opinions on all general and abstract subjects. An intelligent woman, cultivated and independent but who, for fifteen years, had admired a husband she deemed superior, told me how, after his death, she was obliged, to her dismay, to have her own convictions and behaviour: she is still trying to guess what he would have thought and decided in each situation. The husband is generally comfortable in this role of mentor and chief.† In the evening after a difficult day dealing with his equals and obeying his superiors, he likes to feel absolutely superior and dispense incontestable truths.‡ Happy to find in his wife a double who shores up his self-confidence, he tells her about the day's events, tells her how he wins over his adversaries; he comments on the daily paper and the political

---

* 'When I was at home with papa, he told me his opinion about everything, and so I had the same opinions; and if I differed from him I concealed the fact, because he would not have liked it . . . I mean that I was simply transferred from papa's hands into yours. You arranged everything according to your own taste, and so I got the same tastes as yours – or else I pretended to, I am really not quite sure which – I think sometimes the one and sometimes the other . . . You and papa have committed a great sin against me. It is your fault that I have made nothing of my life.'

† Helmer says to Nora: 'But do you suppose you are any the less dear to me, because you don't understand how to act on your own responsibility? No, no; only lean on me; I will advise you and direct you. I should not be a man if this womanly helplessness did not just give you a double attractiveness in my eyes . . . Be at rest, and feel secure; I have broad wings to shelter you under . . . There is something so indescribably sweet and satisfying, to a man, in the knowledge that he has forgiven his wife . . . she has in a way become both wife and child to him. So you shall be for me after this, my little scared, helpless darling. Have no anxiety about anything, Nora; only be frank and open with me, and I will serve as will and conscience both to you.'

‡ Cf. Lawrence, *Fantasia of the Unconscious*: 'You'll have to fight to make a woman believe in you as a real man, a real pioneer. No man is a man unless to his woman he is a pioneer. You'll have to fight still harder to make her yield her goal to yours . . . ah, then, how wonderful it is! How wonderful it is to come back to her, at evening, as she sits half in fear and waits! How good it is to come home to her! . . . How rich you feel, tired, with all the burden of the day in your veins, turning home! . . . And you feel an unfathomable gratitude to the woman who loves you and believes in your purpose . . .'

news, he gladly reads aloud to his wife so that even her connection with culture should not be her own. To increase his authority, he likes to exaggerate feminine incapacity; she accepts this subordinate role with more or less docility. We have seen the surprised pleasure of women who, sincerely regretting their husbands' absence, discover in themselves at such times unsuspected possibilities; they run businesses, bring up children, decide and administer without help. They suffer when their husbands return and doom them again to incompetence.

Marriage incites man to a capricious imperialism: the temptation to dominate is the most universal and the most irresistible there is; to turn over a child to his mother or to turn over a wife to her husband is to cultivate tyranny in the world; it is often not enough for the husband to be supported and admired, to give counsel and guidance; he gives orders, he plays the sovereign; all the resentments accumulated in his childhood, throughout his life, accumulated daily among other men whose existence vexes and wounds him, he unloads at home by unleashing his authority over his wife; he acts out violence, power, intransigence; he issues orders in a severe tone, or he yells and hammers the table: this drama is a daily reality for the wife. He is so convinced of his rights that his wife's least show of autonomy seems a rebellion to him; he would keep her from breathing without his consent. She, nonetheless, rebels. Even if she started out recognising masculine prestige, her dazzlement is soon dissipated; one day the child recognises his father is but a contingent individual; the wife soon discovers she is not before the grand Suzerain, the Chief, the Master, but a man; she sees no reason to be subjugated to him; in her eyes, he merely represents unjust and unrewarding duty. Sometimes she submits with a masochistic pleasure: she takes on the role of victim and her resignation is only a long and silent reproach; but she often fights openly against her master as well, and begins tyrannising him back.

Man is being naive when he imagines he will easily make his wife bend to his wishes and 'shape' her as he pleases. 'A wife is what her husband makes her,' says Balzac; but he says the opposite a few pages further on. In the area of abstraction and logic, the wife often resigns herself to accepting male authority; but when it is a question of ideas and habits she really clings to, she opposes him with covert tenacity. The influence of her childhood and youth is deeper for her than for the man, as she remains more closely confined in her own personal history. She usually does not lose what she acquires during these periods. The husband will impose a political opinion on his wife, but he will not change her religious convictions, nor will he shake her superstitions: this is what Jean Barois saw, he who imagined having a real influence on the devout little ninny who shared his life. Overcome, he says: 'A little girl's brain, conserved in the shadows of a provincial town: all the assertions of ignorant stupidity: this can't be cleaned up.' In spite of opinions she has learned and principles she reels off like a parrot, the wife retains her own vision of the world. This resistance can render her incapable of understanding a husband smarter than herself; or, on the contrary, she will rise above masculine seriousness like the heroines in Stendhal or Ibsen. Sometimes, out of hostility towards the man – either because he has sexually disappointed her or, on the contrary, because he dominates her and she wants revenge – she will clutch on to values that are not his; she relies on the authority of her mother, father, brother, or some masculine personality who seems 'superior' to her, a confessor or a sister to prove him wrong. Or rather than opposing him with anything positive, she continues to contradict him systematically, attack him, insult him; she strives to instil in him an inferiority complex. Of course, if she has the necessary capacity, she will delight in outshining her husband, imposing her advice, opinions, directives; she will seize all moral authority. In cases where it is impossible to contest her husband's intellectual superiority, she will try to take her revenge on a sexual level. Or she will refuse him, as Halévy tells us about Mme Michelet:[57]

> She wanted to dominate everywhere; in bed because she had to do that and at the worktable. It was the table she aimed for and Michelet defended it at first while she defended the bed. For several months, the couple was chaste. Finally Michelet got the bed and Athénaïs Mialaret soon after had the table: she was born a woman of letters and it was her true place . . .

Either she stiffens in his arms and inflicts the insult of her frigidity on him; or she shows herself to be capricious and coquettish, imposing on him the attitude of suppliant; she flirts, she makes him jealous, she is unfaithful to him: in one way or another, she tries to humiliate him in his virility. While caution prevents her from pushing him too far, at least she preciously keeps in her heart the secret of her haughty coldness; she confides sometimes to her diary, more readily to her friends: many married women find it amusing to share 'tricks' they use to feign pleasure they claim not to feel; and they laugh wildly at the vain naïveté of their dupes; these confidences are perhaps another form of playacting: between frigidity and wilful frigidity, the boundaries are uncertain. In any case, they consider themselves to be unfeeling and satisfy their resentment this way. There are women – ones likened to the praying mantis – who want to triumph night and day: they are cold in embrace, contemptuous in conversations, and tyrannical in their behaviour. This is how – according to Mabel Dodge's testimony – Frieda behaved with Lawrence. Unable to deny his intellectual superiority, she attempted to impose her own vision of the world on him where only sexual values counted.[58]

He must see life through her and she had to see life from the sex center. She endorsed or repudiated experience from that angle.

One day she declared to Mabel Dodge:

'He has to get it all from me. Unless I am there, he feels nothing. Nothing. And he gets his books from me,' she continued, boastfully. 'Nobody knows that. Why, I have done pages of his books for him.'

Nonetheless, she bitterly and ceaselessly needs to prove this need he has for her; she demands he take care of her without respite: if he does not do it spontaneously, she corners him:

I discovered that Frieda would not let things slide. I mean between them. Their relationship was never allowed to become slack. When . . . they were going along smoothly . . . not noticing each other much, when the thing between them tended to slip into unconsciousness and *rest*, Frieda would burst a bombshell at him. She *never* let him forget her. What in the first days must have been the splendor of fresh and complete experience had become, when I knew them, the attack and the defense between enemies. . . . Frieda would sting him in a tender place . . . At the end of an evening when he had not particularly noticed her, she would begin insulting him.

Married life had become for them a series of scenes repeated over and over in which neither of them would give in, turning the least quarrel into a titanic duel between Man and Woman.

In a very different way, the same untamed will to dominate is found in Jouhandeau's Élise,* driving her to undermine her husband as much as possible:[59]

> *Élise*: Right from the start, around me, I undermine everything. Afterwards, I don't have anything to worry about. I don't only have to deal with monkeys or monsters.
>
> When she wakes up she calls me:
> —My ugly one.
> It is a policy.
> She wants to humiliate me.
> She went about making me give up all my illusions about myself, one after the other, with such outright pleasure. She has never missed the chance to tell me that I am this or that miserable thing, in front of my astonished friends or our embarrassed servants. So I finally ended up believing her . . . To despise me, she never misses an occasion to make me feel that my work interests her less than any of her own improvements.
>
> It is she who dried up the source of my thoughts by patiently, slowly and purposefully discouraging me, methodically humiliating me, making me renounce my pride, in spite of myself, by chipping away with a precise, imperturbable, implacable logic.
> —In the end, you earn less than a worker, she threw out at me one day in front of the polisher . . .
> She wants to belittle me to seem superior or at least equal, and this disdain keeps her in her high place over me . . . She only has esteem for me insofar as what I do serves her as a stepping-stone or piece of merchandise.

To posit themselves before the male as essential subjects, Frieda and Élise make use of a tactic men have often denounced: they try to deny them their transcendence. Men readily suppose that woman entertains dreams of castration against them; in fact, her attitude is ambiguous: she desires to humiliate the masculine sex rather than suppress it. Far more exact, she wishes to damage man in his projects, his future. She is triumphant when her husband or child is ill, tired, reduced to a bodily presence. They then appear to be no more than an object among others in the house over which she reigns; she treats them with a house-wife's skill; she bandages them like she glues together a broken dish, she

---

* *The Bold Chronicle of a Strange Marriage* and *New Marriage Chronicles*.

cleans them as one cleans a pot; nothing resists her angelic hands, friends of peelings and dishwater. In speaking about Frieda, Lawrence told Mabel Dodge, 'You cannot imagine what it is to feel the hand of that woman on you if you are sick ... The heavy, German hand of the flesh ...' Consciously, the woman imposes her hand with all its weight to make the man feel he also is no more than a being of flesh. This attitude cannot be pushed further than it is with Jouhandeau's Élise:

> I remember, for example, Tchang Tsen lice in the beginning of our marriage ... I really only became intimate with a woman thanks to it, the day Élise took me naked on her lap to shave me like a sheep, lighting me up with a candle she moved around my body down to my secret parts. Oh, her close inspection of my armpits, my chest, my navel, the skin of my testicles taut like a drum between her fingers, her prolonged pauses along my thighs, between my feet and the passage of the razor around my asshole: the final drop into the basket a tuft of blond hair where the lice were hiding, and that she burned, giving me over in one fell swoop, delivering me at the same time from the lice and their den, to a new naked-ness and to the desert of isolation.

Woman loves man to be passive flesh and not a body that expresses subjectivity. She affirms life against existence, values of the flesh against values of the spirit; she readily adopts Pascal's humorous attitude to male enterprises; she thinks as well, 'All man's miseries derive from not being able to sit quiet in a room alone'; she would gladly keep him shut up at home; all activity that does not directly benefit family life provokes her hostility; Bernard Palissy's wife is indignant when he burns the furniture to invent a new enamel without which the world had done very well until then; Mme Racine makes her husband take an interest in her red currants and refuses to read his tragedies. Jouhandeau is often peeved in the *The Bold Chronicles of a Strange Marriage* because Élise stubbornly considers his literary work merely a source of mat-erial profit.

> I said to her: My latest story was published this morning. She replied (without in any way wishing to be cynical and merely because it is the only thing that matters to her): That means we shall have at least three hundred francs extra this month.

It happens that these conflicts worsen and then provoke a rupture. But generally the woman wants to 'hold on to' her husband as well as to refuse his domination. She struggles against him to defend her autonomy, and she fights against the rest of the world to conserve the 'situation' that dooms her to dependence. This double game is difficult to play, which explains in part the worried and nervous state in which multitudes of women spend their lives. Stekel gives a very significant example:

Mme Z. T., who never had an orgasm, is married to a very culti-vated man. But she cannot bear his superiority and she began to want to be his equal by studying his speciality. As it was too diffi-cult, she gave up her studies as soon as they were engaged.

The very famous man had many students chasing after him. She decides not to partake in this ridiculous cult. In her marriage she was insensitive from the start and she remained that way. She attained an orgasm only through masturbation when her husband had finished, satisfied, and she would tell him about it. She refused his attempts to excite her by his caresses . . . Soon she began to ridicule him and undermine her husband's work. She could not 'understand these ninnies who pursued him, she who knew the behind-the-scenes of the great man's private life'. In their daily quar-rels, expressions arose such as: 'You can't put anything over on me with your scribbling!' Or: 'You think you can do what you want with me because you're a little writer.' The husband spent more and more time with his students, she surrounded herself with young men. She continued this way for years until her husband fell in love with another woman. She always stood for his little liaisons, she even made friends of his abandoned 'poor idiots' . . . But then she changed her attitude and gave in, without orgasm, to the first adolescent who came along. She admitted to her husband that she had cheated on him, which he accepted without a problem. They could peacefully separate . . . She refused the divorce. There followed a long explanation and reconciliation. She broke down in tears and experienced her first intense orgasm.

It is clear that in her struggle against her husband she never intended to leave him.

There is an art to 'catching a husband': 'keeping' him is a profession. It takes a great deal of skill. A prudent sister said to a cranky young wife: 'Be careful, making scenes with Marcel will make you lose your *situation*.'

The stakes are the highest: material and moral security, a home of one's own, wifely dignity, a more or less successful substitute for love and happiness. The wife quickly learns that her erotic attraction is the weakest of her weapons; it disappears with familiarity; and there are, alas, other desirable women in the world; so she still works at being seductive and pleasing: she is often torn between the pride that inclines her to frigidity and the notion that her sensual ardour will flatter and keep her husband. She also counts on the force of habit, on the charm he finds in a pleasant home, his taste for good food, his affection for his children; she tries to 'make him proud' by her way of entertaining, dressing and exercising authority over him with her advice and her influence; as much as she can, she will make herself indispensable, either by her social success or by her work. But, above all, a whole tradition teaches wives the art of 'how to catch a man'; one must discover and flatter his weaknesses, cunningly use flattery and disdain, docility and resistance, vigilance and indulgence. This last blend is especially subtle. One must not give a husband too much or too little freedom. If she is too indulgent, the wife finds her husband escaping her; the money and passion he spends on other women are her loss; she runs the risk of having a mistress get enough power over him to seek a divorce or at least take first place in his life. Yet, if she forbids him all adventure, if she overwhelms him by her close scrutiny, her scenes, her demands, she can seriously turn him against her. It is a question of knowing how to 'make concessions' advisedly; if the husband puts 'a few dents in the contract', she will close her eyes; but at other moments, she must open them wide; in particular the married woman mistrusts girls who would be only too happy to take over her 'position'. To tear her husband from a worrying rival, she will take him on a trip, she will try to distract him; if necessary – following Mme de Pompadour's model – she will seek out another, less dangerous rival; if nothing succeeds, she will resort to crying, nervous fits, suicide attempts, and such; but too many scenes and recriminations will chase her husband from the house; the wife will make herself unbearable just when she most needs to seduce; if she wants to win her hand, she will skilfully combine touching tears and heroic smiles, blackmail and coquetry. Dissimulate, trick, hate and fear in silence, bet on the vanity and weakness of a man, learn how to foil him, play him, manipulate him, it is all quite a sad science. The wife's great excuse is that she is forced to involve her whole self in marriage: she has no profession, no skills, no personal relations, even her name is not her own; she is nothing but her husband's 'other half'. If he abandons her, she will most often find no help, either within or outside of herself. It is easy to cast a stone at Sophia Tolstoy, as A. de Monzie and Montherlant do: but if she had refused the hypocrisy of conjugal life, where could she have gone? What destiny awaited her? True, she seems to have been a contemptible shrew: but could one ask her to love her tyrant and bless her enslavement? For there to be loyalty and friendship between spouses, the *sine qua non* is that both must be free vis-à-vis each other and concretely equal. As long as man alone possesses economic autonomy and holds – by law and custom – privileges conferred on him by his masculinity, it is natural that he should so often appear a tyrant, inciting woman to revolt and duplicity.

No one dreams of denying the tragedies and nastiness of married life: but advocates of marriage defend the idea that spouses' conflicts arise out of the bad faith of individuals and not out of the institution's. Tolstoy, among others, describes the ideal couple in the epilogue to *War and Peace*:[60] Pierre and Natasha. She was a coquettish and romantic girl; when married she astounds those who knew her by giving up her interest in her appearance, society and pastimes and devoting herself exclusively to her husband and children; she becomes the very epitome of a matron:

> In her face there was not, as formerly, that ceaselessly burning fire of animation that had constituted her charm. Now one often saw only her face and body, while her soul was not seen at all. One saw only a strong, beautiful, and fruitful female.

She demands from Pierre a love as exclusive as the one she swears to him; she is jealous of him; he gives up going out, all his old friends, and devotes himself entirely to his family as well.

> Pierre's subjection consisted in his . . . not daring to go to clubs or dinners . . . not daring to leave for long periods of time except on business, in which his wife also included his intellectual pursuits, of which she understood nothing, but to which she ascribed great importance.

Pierre is 'under the slipper of his wife', but in return:

> At home Natasha put herself on the footing of her husband's slave . . . The entire household was governed only by the imaginary orders of the husband, that is, by Pierre's wishes, which Natasha tried to guess.

When Pierre goes far away from her, Natasha impatiently greets him upon his return because she suffers from his absence; but a wonderful harmony reigns over the couple; they understand each other with barely a few words. Between her children, her home, her loved and respected husband, she savours nearly untainted happiness.

This idyllic tableau merits closer scrutiny. Natasha and Pierre are united, says Tolstoy, like soul and body; but when the soul leaves the body, only one dies; what would happen if Pierre should cease to love Natasha? Lawrence, too, rejects the hypothesis of masculine inconstancy: Don Ramón will always love the little Indian girl Teresa, who gave him her soul. Yet one of the most ardent zealots of unique, absolute, eternal love, André Breton, is forced to admit that at least in present circumstances this love can mistake its object: error or inconstancy, it is the same abandonment for the woman. Pierre, robust and sensual, will be physically attracted to other women; Natasha is jealous; soon the relationship will sour; either he will leave her, which will ruin her life, or he will lie and resent her, which will spoil his life, or they will live with compromises and half measures, which will make them both unhappy. One might object that Natasha will at least have her children: but children are a source of joy only within a well-balanced structure, where the husband is one of its peaks; for the neglected, jealous wife they become a thankless burden. Tolstoy admires Natasha's blind devotion to Pierre's ideas; but another man, Lawrence, who also demands blind devotion from women, mocks Pierre and Natasha; so in the opinion of other men, a man can be a clay idol and not a real god; in worshipping him, one loses one's life instead of saving it; how is one to know? Masculine claims compete with each other, authority no longer plays a part: the wife must judge and criticise, she cannot be but a feeble echo. Moreover, it is degrading to her to impose principles and values on her that she does not believe in with her own free will; what she might share of her husband's thinking, she can only share through her own independent judgement; she should not have to accept or refuse what is foreign to her; she cannot borrow her own reasons for existing from another.

The most radical condemnation of the Pierre-Natasha myth comes from the Leon-Sophia couple. Sophia feels repulsion for her husband, she finds him 'tedious'; he cheats on her with all the surrounding peasants, she is jealous and bored; she is frustrated by her multiple pregnancies and her children do not fill the emptiness in her heart or her days; home for her is an arid desert; for him it is hell. And it ends up with an old hysterical woman lying half-naked in the humid night of the forest, with this old hounded man fleeing, renouncing finally the 'union' of a whole life.

Of course, Tolstoy's case is exceptional; there are many marriages that 'work well', that is, where the spouses reach a compromise; they live next to each other without antagonising each other, without lying to each other too much. But there is a curse they rarely escape: boredom. Whether the husband succeeds in making his wife an echo of himself, or whether each one entrenches himself in his universe, they have nothing else to share with each other after a few months or years. The couple is a community whose members have lost their autonomy without escaping their solitude; they are statically assimilated to each other instead of sustaining a dynamic and lively relation together; this is why they can give nothing to each other, exchange nothing on a spiritual or erotic level. In one of her best short stories, 'Too Bad!', Dorothy Parker sums up the sad saga of many conjugal lives; it is night and Mr Weldon comes home:

Mrs Weldon opened the door at his ring.

'Well!' she said, cheerily.

They smiled brightly at each other.

'Hel-lo,' he said. 'Well! You home?'

They kissed, slightly. She watched with polite interest while he hung up his hat and coat, removed the evening papers from his pocket, and handed one to her.

'Bring the papers?' she said, taking it . . .

'Well, what have you been doing with yourself today?' he inquired.

She had been expecting the question. She had planned before he came in, how she would tell him all the little events of her day . . . But now, . . . it seemed to her a long, dull story . . .

'Oh, nothing,' she said, with a gay little laugh. 'Did you have a nice day?'

'Why—' he began . . . But his interest waned, even as he started to speak. Besides, she was engrossed in breaking off a loose thread from the wool fringe of one of the pillows beside her.

'Oh, pretty fair,' he said . . .

She could talk well enough to other people . . .

Ernest, too, seemed to be talkative enough when he was with others . . .

She tried to remember what they used to talk about before they were married, when they were engaged. It seemed to her that they never had had much to say to each other. But she hadn't worried about it then ... Then, besides, there had been always kissing and things, to take up your mind ... And you can't depend on kisses and all the rest of it to while away the evenings, after seven years.

You'd think that you would get used to it, in seven years, would realise that that was the way it was, and let it go at that. You don't, though. A thing like that gets on your nerves. It isn't one of those cozy, companionable silences that people occasionally fall into together. It makes you feel as if you must do something about it, as if you weren't performing your duty. You have the feeling a hostess has when her party is going badly ...

Ernest would read industriously, and along toward the middle of the paper, he would start yawning aloud. Something happened inside Mrs Weldon when he did this. She would murmur that she had to speak to Delia, and hurry to the kitchen. She would stay there rather a long time, looking vaguely into jars and inquiring half-heartedly about laundry lists, and when she returned, he would have gone in to get ready for bed.

In a year, three hundred of their evenings were like this. Seven times three hundred is more than two thousand.[61]

It is sometimes claimed this very silence is the sign of an intimacy deeper than any word; and obviously no one dreams of denying that conjugal life creates intimacy: this is true of all family relations, even those that include hatreds, jealousies and resentments. Jouhandeau strongly emphasises the difference between this intimacy and a real human fraternity, writing:

Élise is my wife and it is probable that none of my friends, none of the members of my family, not a single one of my own limbs is more intimate with me than she; but however close to me is the place that she has made for herself and that I have made for her in my own most private universe; however deeply rooted she has become in the inextricable web of my body and soul (and there lies the whole mystery and the whole drama of our indissoluble union), the unknown person, whoever he may be, who happens to pass in the street at this particular moment and whom I can barely see from my window is less of a stranger to me than she is.[62]

He says elsewhere:

> We discover that we are the victims of poisoning, but that we have grown used to it. How can we give it up without giving up ourselves?

Still more:

> When I think of her, I feel that married love has nothing to do with sympathy, with sensuality, with passion, with friendship, or with love. It alone is adequate to itself and cannot be reduced to one or other of these different feelings, it has its own nature, its particular essence, and its unique mode which depends on the couple that it brings together.

Advocates of conjugal love* readily admit it is not love, which is precisely what makes it marvellous. For in recent years the bourgeoisie has invented an epic style: routine takes on the allure of adventure, faithfulness that of sublime madness, boredom becomes wisdom and family hatreds are the deepest form of love. In truth, that two individuals hate each other without, however, being able to do without each other is not at all the truest, the most moving of all human relations, it is one of the most pitiful. The ideal would be, on the contrary, that each human being, perfectly self-sufficient, be attached to another by the free consent of their love alone. Tolstoy admires the fact that the link between Natasha and Pierre is something 'indefinable, but firm, solid, as was the union of his own soul with his body'. If one accepts the dualist hypothesis, the body represents only a pure facticity for the soul; so in the conjugal union, each one would have for the other the inevitable weight of contingent fact; one would have to assume and love the other as an absurd and unchosen presence as the necessary condition for and very matter of existence. There is a deliberate confusion between these two words – 'assuming' and 'loving' – and the mystification stems from this: one does not love what one assumes. One assumes one's body, past, and present situation: but love is a movement towards an other, towards an existence

---

* There can be love within marriage; but then one does not speak of 'conjugal love'; when these words are uttered, it means that love is missing; likewise, when one says of a man that he is 'very communist', one means that he is not a communist; 'a great gentleman' is a man who does not belong to the simple category of gentlemen, and so on.

separated from one's own, towards a finality, a future; the way to assume or take on a load or a tyranny is not to love it but to revolt. A human relation has no value if it is lived in the immediacy; children's relations with their parents, for example, only have value when they are reflected in a consciousness; one cannot admire conjugal relations that degenerate into the immediate in which the spouses squander their freedom. One claims to respect this complex mixture of attachment, resentment, hatred, rules, resignation, laziness and hypocrisy called conjugal love only because it serves as an alibi. But what is true of friendship is true of physical love: for friendship to be authentic, it must first be free. Freedom does not mean whim: a feeling is a commitment that goes beyond the instant; but it is up to the individual alone to compare his general will to his personal behaviour so as either to uphold his decision or, on the contrary, to break it; feeling is free when it does not depend on any outside command, when it is lived in sincerity without fear. The message of 'conjugal love' is an invitation, by contrast, to all kinds of repression and lies. And above all it keeps the husband and wife from genuinely knowing each other. Daily intimacy creates neither understanding nor sympathy. The husband respects his wife too much to be interested in the meta-morphoses of her psychological life: that would mean recognising in her a secret autonomy that could prove to be bothersome, dangerous; does she really get pleasure in bed? Does she really love her husband? Is she really happy to obey him? He prefers not to question himself; these ques-tions even seem shocking to him. He married a 'good woman'; by nature she is virtuous, devoted, faithful, pure and happy, and she thinks what she should think. A sick man, after thanking his friends, his family and his nurses, says to his young wife who, for six months, had not left his bedside: 'I do not have to thank you, you merely did your duty.' He gives her no credit for any of her good qualities: they are guaranteed by society, they are implied by the very institution of marriage; he does not notice that his wife does not come out of a book by Bonald, that she is an indi-vidual of flesh and blood; he takes for granted her faithfulness to the orders she imposes on herself: he takes no account of the fact that she might have temptations to overcome, that she might succumb to them, that in any case, her patience, her chastity and her decency might be difficult conquests; he ignores even more completely her dreams, her fantasies, her nostalgia, and the emotional climate in which she spends her days. Thus Chardonne shows us in *Eva* a husband who has for years kept a journal of his conjugal life: he speaks of his wife with delicate nuances; but only of his wife as he sees her, as she is for him without ever giving her dimensions as a free individual: he is stunned when he suddenly learns she does not love him, that she is leaving him. One often speaks of the naive and loyal man's disillusionment in the face of feminine perfidy: the husbands in Bernstein are scandalised to discover that the women in their lives are fickle, mean or adulterous; they take it with a virile courage but the author does not fail to make them seem generous and strong: they seem more like boors to us, without sensitivity and goodwill; man criticises women for their duplicity but he must be very complacent to let himself be duped with so much constancy. Woman is doomed to immorality because morality for her consists in embodying an inhuman entity: the strong woman, the admirable mother, the virtuous woman, and so on. As soon as she thinks, dreams, sleeps, desires and aspires without orders, she betrays the masculine ideal. This is why so many women do not let themselves 'be themselves' except in their husbands' absence. Likewise, the woman does not know her husband: she thinks she perceives his true face because she grasps it in its daily contingency: but the man is first what he *does* in the world among other men. Refusing to understand the movement of his transcendence is denaturing it. 'One marries a poet,' says Élise, 'and when one is his wife, the first thing she notices is he forgets to flush the toilet.'* He nevertheless remains a poet and the wife who is not interested in his works knows him less than a remote reader. It is often not the wife's fault that this complicity is forbidden to her: she cannot share her husband's affairs, she lacks the experience and the necessary culture to 'follow' him: she fails to join him in the projects that are far more essential for him than the monotonous repetition of everyday life. In certain privileged cases the wife can succeed in becoming a real companion for her husband: she discusses his plans, gives him advice, participates in his work. But she is deluding herself if she thinks she can accomplish work of her own like that: he alone remains the active and responsible freedom. To find joy in serving him, she must love him; if not she will experience only vexation because she will feel frustrated by the fruit of her efforts. Men – faithful to the advice given by Balzac to treat the wife as a slave while persuading her she is queen – exaggerate to the utmost the importance of the influence women wield; deep down, they know well they are lying. Georgette Leblanc was duped by this mystification when she demanded of Maeterlinck that he write their two names on the book they had, or so she thought, written together; in the preface to the

* Jouhandeau, *The Bold Chronicle of a Strange Marriage.*

singer's *Souvenirs*, Grasset bluntly explains that any man is ready to hail
the woman who shares his life as an associate and an inspiration but
that he nevertheless still regards his work as belonging to him alone;
rightfully. In any action, any work, what counts is the moment of choice
and decision. The wife generally plays the role of the crystal ball clair-
voyants use: another would do just as well. And the proof is that often
the man welcomes another adviser, another collaborator, with the same
confidence. Sophia Tolstoy copied her husband's manuscripts and put
them in order: he later gave the job to one of his daughters; she understood that even her zeal had not made her indispensable. Only
autonomous work can assure the wife an authentic autonomy.*

Conjugal life takes different forms depending on the case. But for
many wives, the day begins approximately in the same way. The husband
leaves his wife hurriedly in the morning: she is happy to hear the door
close after him; she likes to find herself free, without duties, sovereign
in her home. The children in turn leave for school: she will stay alone
all day; the baby squirming in his crib or playing in his playpen is not
company. She spends more or less time getting dressed, doing the housework; if she has a maid, she gives her instructions, lingers a little in the
kitchen while chatting; or else she will stroll in the market, exchanging
comments on the cost of living with her neighbours or shopkeepers. If
her husband and children come home for lunch, she cannot take advantage of their presence very much; she has too much to do to get the
meal ready, serve and clean up; most often, they do not come back for
lunch. In any case, she has a long, empty afternoon in front of her. She
takes her youngest children to the public park and knits or sews while
keeping an eye on them; or, sitting at the window at home, she does
her mending; her hands work, her mind is not occupied; she ruminates
over her worries; she makes plans; she daydreams, she is bored; none
of her occupations suffices in itself; her thoughts are directed towards
her husband and her children who will wear these shirts, who will eat
the meal she is preparing; she lives for them alone; and are they at all
grateful to her? Little by little her boredom changes into impatience,
she begins to wait for their return anxiously. The children come back

---

* There is sometimes a *real* collaboration between a man and a woman, in which the
two are equally autonomous: in the Joliot-Curie couple, for example. But then the wife
who is as skilled as the husband goes out of her wifely role; their relation is no longer
of a conjugal order. There are also wives who use the man to achieve personal aims;
they escape the condition of the married woman.

from school, she kisses them, questions them; but they have homework to do, they want to have fun together, they escape, they are not a distraction. And then they have bad grades, they have lost a scarf, they are noisy, messy, they fight with each other: she almost always has to scold them. Their presence annoys the mother more than it soothes her. She waits for her husband more and more urgently. What is he doing? Why is he not home already? He has worked, seen the world, chatted with people, he has not thought of her; she starts ruminating nervously that she is stupid to sacrifice her youth to him; he is not grateful to her. The husband making his way towards the house where his wife is closed up feels vaguely guilty; early in the marriage, he would bring a bunch of flowers, a little gift, as an offering; but this ritual soon loses any meaning; now he arrives empty-handed, and he is even less in a hurry when he anticipates the usual greeting. Indeed, the wife often takes revenge with a scene of boredom, of the daily wait; this is how she wards off the disappointment of a presence that does not satisfy the expectation of her waiting. Even if she does not express her grievances, her husband too is disappointed. He has not had a good time at his office, he is tired; he has a contradictory desire for stimulation and for rest. His wife's too familiar face does not free him from himself; he feels she would like to share his worries with him, that she also expects distraction and relaxation from him: her presence weighs on him without satisfying him, he does not find real abandon with her. Nor do the children bring entertainment or peace; during the meal and the evening there is a vague bad mood; reading, listening to the radio, chatting idly, each one, under the cover of intimacy, will remain alone. Yet the wife wonders with an anxious hope – or a no less anxious apprehension – if tonight – finally! again! – something will happen. She goes to sleep disappointed, irritated or relieved; she will be happy to hear the door slam shut tomorrow. The lot of wives is even harsher if they are poor and overburdened with chores; it lightens when they have both leisure and distractions. But this pattern – boredom, waiting and disappointment – is found in many cases.

There are some escapes* available to the wife; but in practice they are not available to all. The chains of marriage are heavy, particularly in the provinces; a wife has to find a way of coming to grips with a situation she cannot escape. Some, as we have seen, are puffed up with importance and become tyrannical matrons and shrews. Others take refuge in

* See Chapter 7.

the role of the victim, they make themselves their husbands' and children's pathetic slaves and find a masochistic joy in it. Others perpetuate the narcissistic behaviour we have described in relation to the young girl: they also suffer from not realising themselves in any undertaking, and, being able to do nothing, they are nothing; undefined, they feel undetermined and consider themselves misunderstood; they worship melancholy; they take refuge in dreams, playacting, illnesses, fads, scenes; they create problems around them or close themselves up in an imaginary world; the 'smiling Mme Beudet' that Amiel depicted is one of these. Shut up in provincial monotony with a boorish husband, with no chance to act or to love, she is devoured by the feeling of her life's emptiness and uselessness; she tries to find compensation in romantic musings, in the flowers she surrounds herself with, in her clothes, her person: her husband interferes even with these games. She ends up trying to kill him. The symbolic behaviour into which the wife escapes can bring about perversions, and these obsessions can lead to crime. There are conjugal crimes dictated less by interest than by pure hatred. Thus, Mauriac shows us Thérèse Desqueyroux trying to poison her husband as Mme Lafarge did previously. A forty-year-old woman who had endured an odious husband for twenty years was recently acquitted for having coldly strangled her husband with the help of her elder son. There had been no other way for her to free herself from an intolerable situation.

For a wife who wants to live her situation in lucidity, in authenticity, her only resort is often to stoic pride. Because she is totally dependent, she can only have a deeply interior and therefore abstract freedom; she refuses ready-made principles and values, she judges, she questions, and thus escapes conjugal slavery; but her haughty reserve and her acceptance of the saying 'Suffer and be still' constitute no more than a negative attitude. Confined in denial, in cynicism, she lacks a positive use of her strength; as long as she is passionate and living, she finds ways to use it: she helps others, she consoles, protects, gives, she has many interests; but she suffers from not finding any truly demanding job, from not devoting her activity to an end. Often eaten away by loneliness and sterility, she ends up by giving up, destroying herself. Mme de Charrière provides us with a notable example of such a destiny. In the sympathetic book* he devotes to her, Geoffrey Scott depicts her with 'a frond of flame; a frond of frost'. But it is not her reason that put out this flame of life which Hermenches said could 'warm the heart of a Laplander', it is

---

* Geoffrey Scott, *The Portrait of Zélide*.

marriage that slowly assassinates the brilliant Belle de Zuylen; she resigned herself and called it reason: either heroism or genius would have been necessary to invent a different outcome. That her lofty and rare qualities were not sufficient to save her is one of the most stunning condemnations of the conjugal institution found in history.

Brilliant, cultivated, intelligent and ardent, Mlle de Zuylen astonished Europe; she frightened away suitors; she rejected more than twelve of them, but others, perhaps more acceptable, backed off. Hermenches was the only man who interested her, but it was out of the question to make him her husband: she carried on a twelve-year correspondence with him; but this friendship and her studies no longer satisfied her. 'Virgin and martyr' was a pleonasm, she said; and the constraints of Zuylen's life were unbearable; she wanted to become a woman, a free being. At thirty, she married M. de Charrière; she liked the 'honesty of heart' she found in him, his 'sense of justice', and she first decided to make him 'the most tenderly loved husband in the world'. Later, Benjamin Constant recounts that 'she had tormented him greatly to impress upon him reactions equal to hers'; she did not manage to overcome his methodical impassivity; shut up in Colombier with this honest and dull husband, a senile father-in-law, two dull sisters-in-law, Mme de Charrière began to be bored; the narrow-mindedness of Neufchâtel provincial society displeased her; she killed her days in washing the household linen and playing 'Comet' in the evening. A young man briefly crossed her life and left her lonelier than before. 'Taking ennui as muse', she wrote four novels on the customs of Neufchâtel, and the circle of her friends grew narrower. In one of her works, she described the long sadness of a marriage between a lively and sensitive woman and a good but ponderous and cold man: conjugal life seemed to her like a chain of misunderstandings, disappointments, petty resentments. It was clear she herself was unhappy; she fell ill, recovered, returned to the long accompanied solitude that was her life. 'It is clear that the routine of the life at Colombier and the negative, unresisting smoothness of her husband's temperament were like a perpetual pause which no activity of Mme de Charrière's could fill,' writes her biographer. And then appears Benjamin Constant, who passionately occupied her for eight years. When, too proud to wrest him from Mme de Staël, she gave him up, her pride hardened. She wrote to him one day: 'The stay at Colombier was abhorrent to me and I never went back there without despair. I decided not to leave it any more and made it bearable for myself.' She closed herself up there and did not leave her garden for fifteen years; this is how she applied the stoic precept: seek to conquer one's heart rather than fortune. As a prisoner, she could only find freedom by choosing her prison. 'She accepted M. de Charrière at her side as she accepted the Alps,' says Scott. But she was too lucid not to understand that this resignation was, after all, only deception; she became so withdrawn, so hard, she was thought to be so despairing that she was frightening. She had opened her house to the immigrants who were pouring into Neufchâtel; she protected them, helped them, guided them; she wrote elegant and disillusioned works that Huber, a poor German philosopher, translated; she lavished advice on a circle of young women and taught Locke to her favourite one, Henriette; she loved to play the role of divine protection for the peasants of the area; avoiding Neufchâtel society more and more carefully, she preciously limited her life; she 'sought only to create routine, and to endure it. Even her infinite acts of kindness had something frightening about them, in the chill of her self-control . . . She seemed to those around her like one moving in an empty room.'* On rare occasions – a visit, for example – the flame of life awakened. But 'the years passed aridly. Ageing side by side live M. and Mme de Charrière, a whole universe apart; and often a visitor would turn from the house with relief, and hearing the gate clang behind him, would feel that he was leaving a shut tomb . . . The clock ticked; M. de Charrière sat below, alone, poring over his mathematics. Rhythmically, from the barn outside, came the sound of the threshers, it throbbed, and it ceased. Life went on, though it was threshed out . . . A life of small things, desperately compelled to fill every crevice of the day: to this Zélide, who hated littleness, had come.'

One might say M. de Charrière's life was no livelier than his wife's: at least he had chosen it; and it seems it suited his mediocrity. If one imagines a man endowed with the exceptional qualities of Belle de Zuylen, he surely would not be consumed in Colombier's arid solitude. He would have carved out a place for himself in the world where he would undertake things, fight, act and live. How many wives swallowed up in marriage have been, in Stendhal's words, 'lost to humanity'! It is said that marriage diminishes man: it is often true; but it almost always destroys woman. Marcel Prévost, advocate of marriage, admits it himself:

> How many times have I met after a few months or years of marriage a young woman I had known as a girl and been struck by the ordinariness of her character, the meaninglessness of her life.

* Ibid.

Sophia Tolstoy uses almost the same words six months after her marriage:

> My life is so mundane, and my death. But he has such a rich internal
> life, talent and immortality. (23 December 1863)[63]

A few months earlier, she had uttered another complaint:

> ... You simply cannot be happy just sitting there sewing or playing
> the piano alone, completely *alone*, and gradually realizing, or rather
> becoming convinced that even though your husband may not love
> you, you are stuck there forever and there you must sit. (9 May
> 1863)

Twelve years later, she writes these words that many women today
subscribe to:

> ... day after day, month after month, year after year – nothing ever
> changes. I wake up in the morning and just lie there wondering
> who will get me up, who is waiting for me. The cook is bound to
> come in, then the nurse, ... so then I get up, ... and sit silently
> darning holes, and then it's time for the children's grammar and
> piano lessons. Then in the evening more darning, with Auntie and
> Lyovochka playing endless ... games of patience. (22 October 1875)[64]

Mme Proudhon's complaint resonates with the same sound. 'You have
your ideas,' she said to her husband. 'And I, when you are at work, when
the children are in school, I have nothing.'

In the first years the wife often lulls herself with illusions, she tries
to admire her husband unconditionally, to love him unreservedly, to feel
she is indispensable to him and her children; and then her true feelings
emerge; she sees her husband can get along without her, that her children are made to break away from her: they are always more or less
thankless. The home no longer protects her from her empty freedom;
she finds herself alone, abandoned, a subject, and she finds nothing to
do with herself. Affections and habits can still be of great help, but not
salvation. All sincere women writers have noted this melancholy that
inhabits the heart of 'thirty-year-old women'; this is a characteristic
common to the heroines of Katherine Mansfield, Dorothy Parker
and Virginia Woolf. Cécile Sauvage who sang so gaily of marriage and
children at the beginning of her life, later expresses a subtle distress. It

is noteworthy that the number of single women who commit suicide, compared with married women, shows that the latter are solidly protected from revulsion against life between twenty and thirty years of age (especially between twenty-five and thirty) but not in the following years. 'As for marriage,' writes Halbwachs,* 'it protects provincial as well as Parisian women until thirty years of age but not after.'[65]

The drama of marriage is not that it does not guarantee the wife the promised happiness – there is no guarantee of happiness – it is that it mutilates her; it dooms her to repetition and routine. The first twenty years of a woman's life are extraordinarily rich; she experiences menstruation, sexuality, marriage and motherhood; she discovers the world and her destiny. She is mistress of a home at twenty, linked from then on to one man, a child in her arms, now her life is finished forever. Real activity, real work are the privilege of man: her only occupations are sometimes exhausting but never fulfil her. Renunciation and devotion have been extolled; but it often seems highly futile to devote herself to 'the upkeep of any two beings until the end of their lives'. It is all very grand to forget oneself, but one must know for whom and for what. Worst of all is that her devotion itself is exasperating; in her husband's eyes, it changes into a tyranny from which he tries to escape; and yet it is he who imposes his presence on woman as her supreme, one justification; by marrying her he obliges her to give herself to him completely; he does not accept the reciprocal obligation, which is to accept this gift. Sophia Tolstoy's words: 'I live through him and for him, I demand the same thing for me', are certainly revolting; but Tolstoy demanded she only live for him and through him, an attitude reciprocity alone can justify. It is the husband's duplicity that dooms the wife to a misfortune of which he later complains to be the victim. Just as he wants her both hot and cold in bed, he claims her totally given and yet weightless; he asks her to fix him to earth and to let him be free, to ensure the daily monotonous repetition and not to bother him, always to be present and never nag him; he wants her entirely for himself and not to belong to him; to live in a couple and to remain alone. Thus, as soon as he marries her, he mystifies her. She spends her life measuring the extent of this betrayal. What D. H. Lawrence says about sexual love is generally valid: the union of two human beings is doomed to failure if it requires an effort for each of them to complete each other, which supposes a primal mutilation;

---

* *The Causes of Suicide*. The comment applies to France and Switzerland but not to Hungary or Oldenburg.

marriage must combine two autonomous existences, not be a withdrawal, an annexation, an escape, a remedy. This is what Nora* understands when she decides that before being able to be a wife and mother, she has to be a person. The couple should not consider itself as a community, a closed cell: instead, the individual as individual has to be integrated into a society in which he can thrive without assistance; he will then be able to create links in pure generosity with another individual equally adapted to the group, links founded on the recognition of two freedoms.

This balanced couple is not a utopia; such couples exist sometimes even within marriage, more often outside of it; some are united by a great sexual love that leaves them free in their friendships and occupations; others are linked by a friendship that does not hamper their sexual freedom; more rarely there are still others who are both lovers and friends but without seeking in each other their exclusive reason for living. Many nuances are possible in the relations of a man and a woman: in companionship, pleasure, confidence, tenderness, complicity and love, they can be for each other the most fruitful source of joy, richness and strength offered to a human being. It is not the individuals who are responsible for the failure of marriage: it is – unlike what Bonald, Comte and Tolstoy claim – the institution that is perverted at its base. Declaring that a man and a woman who do not even choose each other *must* meet each other's needs in all respects, at once, for their whole life, is a monstrosity that necessarily gives rise to hypocrisy, hostility and unhappiness.

The traditional form of marriage is changing: but it still constitutes an oppression that both spouses feel in different ways. Considering the abstract rights they enjoy, they are almost equals; they choose each other more freely than before, they can separate much more easily, especially in America, where divorce is commonplace; there is less difference in age and culture between the spouses than previously; the husband more easily acknowledges the autonomy his wife claims; they might even share housework equally; they have the same leisure interests: camping, bicycling, swimming, and so on. She does not spend her days waiting for her spouse's return: she practises sports, she belongs to associations and clubs, she has outside occupations, sometimes she even has a little job that brings her some money. Many young couples give the impression of perfect equality. But as long as the man has economic responsibility for the couple, it is just an illusion. He is the one who determines the conjugal domicile according to the demands of his job: she *follows* him

* Ibsen, *A Doll's House*.

from the provinces to Paris, from Paris to the provinces, the colonies, abroad; the standard of living is fixed according to his income; the rhythm of the days, the weeks and the year is organised on the basis of his occupations; relations and friendships most often depend on his profession. Being more positively integrated than his wife into society, he leads the couple in intellectual, political and moral areas. Divorce is only an abstract possibility for the wife, if she does not have the means to earn her own living: while alimony in America is a heavy burden for the husband, in France the lot of the wife and mother abandoned with a derisory pension is scandalous. But the deep inequality stems from the fact that the husband finds concrete accomplishment in work or action while for the wife in her role as wife, freedom has only a negative form: the situation of American girls, among others, recalls that of the emancipated girls of the Roman decadence. We saw that they had the choice between two types of behaviour: some perpetuated the style of life and the virtues of their grandmothers; others spent their time in futile activity; likewise, many American women remain 'housewives' in conformity with the traditional model; the others mostly whittle away their energy and time. In France, even if the husband has all the goodwill in the world, the burdens of the home do not weigh on him anymore once the young wife is a mother.

It is a commonplace to say that in modern households, and especially in the United States, the wife has reduced the husband to slavery. The fact is not new. Since the Greeks, males have complained of Xanthippe's tyranny; what is true is that the wife intervenes in areas that previously were forbidden to her; I know, for example, of students' wives who contribute to the success of their man with frenetic determination; they organise their schedules, their diet, they watch over their work; they cut out all distractions, and almost keep them under lock and key. It is also true that man is more defenceless than previously against this despotism; he recognises his wife's abstract rights and he understands that she can concretise them only through him: it is at his own expense that he will compensate for the powerlessness and the sterility the wife is condemned to; to realise an apparent equality in their association, he has to give her more because he possesses more. But precisely because she receives, takes and demands, she is the poorer. The dialectic of the master and slave has its most concrete application here: in oppressing, one becomes oppressed. Males are in chains by their very sovereignty; it is because they alone earn money that the wife demands cheques, because men alone practise a profession that the wife demands that they succeed, because they alone embody transcendence that the wife wants to steal it from them by taking over their projects and successes. And inversely, the tyranny wielded by the woman only manifests her dependence: she knows the success of the couple, its future, its happiness, and its justification, reside in the hands of the other; if she bitterly seeks to subjugate him to her will, it is because she is alienated in him. She makes a weapon of her weakness; but the fact is she is weak. Conjugal slavery is ordinary and irritating for the husband; but it is deeper for the wife; the wife who keeps her husband near her for hours out of boredom irritates him and weighs on him; but in the end, he can do without her more easily than she him; if he leaves her, it is she whose life will be ruined. The big difference is that for the wife, dependence is interiorised; she *is* a slave even when she conducts herself with apparent freedom, while the husband is essentially autonomous and enchained from the outside. If he has the impression he is the victim, it is because the burdens he bears are more obvious: the wife feeds on him like a parasite; but a parasite is not a triumphant master. In reality, just as biologically males and females are never victims of each other but all together of the species, the spouses together submit to the oppression of an institution they have not created. If it is said *men* oppress *women*, the husband reacts indignantly; he feels oppressed: he is; but in fact, it is the masculine code, the society developed by males and in their interest, that has defined the feminine condition in a form that is now for both sexes a source of distress.

The situation has to be changed in their common interest by prohibiting marriage as a 'career' for the woman. Men who declare themselves anti-feminist with the excuse that 'women are already annoying enough as it is' are not very logical: it is precisely because marriage makes them 'praying mantises', 'bloodsuckers' and 'poison' that marriage has to be changed and, as a consequence, the feminine condition in general. Woman weighs so heavily on man because she is forbidden to rely on herself; he will free himself by freeing her, that is, by giving her something *to do* in this world.

There are young women who are already trying to win this positive freedom; but seldom do they persevere in their studies or their jobs for long: they know the interests of their work will most often be sacrificed to their husband's career; their salary will only 'help out' at home; they hesitate to commit themselves to undertakings that do not pull them away from conjugal enslavement. Those who do have a serious profession will not draw the same social advantages as men: lawyers' wives, for example, are entitled to a pension on their husbands' death; women lawyers are prohibited from paying a corresponding pension to their husbands in case of death. This shows that the woman who works cannot keep the couple at the same level as the man. There are women who find real independence in their profession; but many discover that work 'outside' only represents another source of fatigue within the framework of marriage. Moreover and most often, the birth of a child forces them to confine themselves to their role of matron; it is still very difficult to reconcile work and motherhood.

According to tradition, it is the child who should assure the wife a concrete autonomy that dispenses her from devoting herself to any other aim. If she is not a complete individual as a wife, she becomes it as a mother: the child is her joy and justification. She reaches sexual and social self-realisation through him; it is thus through him that the institution of marriage has meaning and reaches its aim. Let us examine this ultimate step in woman's development.

CHAPTER 6

The Mother

It is through motherhood that woman fully achieves her physiological destiny; that is her 'natural' vocation, since her whole organism is directed towards the perpetuation of the species. But we have already shown that human society is never left to nature. And in particular, for about a century, the reproductive function has no longer been controlled by biological chance alone but by design.* Some countries have officially adopted specific methods of birth control; in Catholic countries, it takes place clandestinely: either man practises coitus interruptus, or woman rids her body of the sperm after the sexual act. This is often a source of conflict or resentment between lovers or married partners; the man gets irritated at having to check his pleasure; the woman detests the chore of douching; he begrudges her too-fertile womb; she dreads these living germs he risks leaving in her. And for both of them there is consternation when, in spite of precautions, she finds herself 'caught'. This happens frequently in countries where contraceptive methods are rudimentary. Then anti-physis takes a particularly acute form: abortion. As it is even banned in countries that authorise birth control, there are many fewer occasions to have recourse to it. But in France, many women are forced to have this operation, which haunts the love lives of most of them.

There are few subjects on which bourgeois society exhibits more hypocrisy: abortion is a repugnant crime to which it is indecent to make an allusion. For an author to describe the joys and suffering of a woman giving birth is perfectly fine; if he talks about a woman who has had an abortion, he is accused of wallowing in filth and describing humanity in an abject light: meanwhile, in France every year there are as many abortions as births. It is such a widespread phenomenon that it has to

* See Vol. I, Part Two, 'History', Chapter 5, where a historical account of the question of birth control and abortion can be found.

be considered one of the risks normally involved in the feminine condition. The law persists, however, in making it a misdemeanour: it demands that this delicate operation be executed clandestinely. Nothing is more absurd than the arguments used against legislating abortion. It is claimed to be a dangerous operation. But honest doctors recognise, along with Dr Magnus Hirschfeld, that 'abortion performed by a competent specialist, in a clinic and with proper preventative measures, does not involve the serious dangers penal law asserts.' It is, on the contrary, its present form that makes it a serious risk for women. The incompetence of 'back-alley' abortionists and their operating conditions cause many accidents, some of them fatal. Forced motherhood results in bringing miserable children into the world, children whose parents cannot feed them, who become victims of public assistance or 'martyr children'. It must be pointed out that the same society so determined to defend the rights of the foetus shows no interest in children after they are born; instead of trying to reform this scandalous institution called public assistance, society prosecutes abortionists; those responsible for delivering orphans to torturers are left free; society closes its eyes to the horrible tyranny practised in 'reform schools' or in the private homes of child abusers; and while it refuses to accept that the foetus belongs to the mother carrying it, it nevertheless agrees that the child is his parents' thing; this very week, a surgeon committed suicide because he was convicted of performing abortions and a father who had beaten his son nearly to death has been condemned to three months of prison *with a suspended sentence*. Recently a father let his son die of whooping cough by not providing medical care; a mother refused to call a doctor for her daughter in the name of unconditional submission to God's will: in the cemetery, other children threw stones at her; but when some journalists showed their indignation, a group of right-thinking people protested that children belong to their parents, that outside control would be unacceptable. Today there are 'a million children in danger', says the newspaper *Ce Soir;* and *France-Soir* writes that: 'Five hundred thousand children are *reported* to be in physical or moral danger.' In North Africa, the Arab woman has no recourse to abortion: out of ten children she gives birth to, seven or eight die, and no one is disturbed because painful and absurd childbirth has killed maternal sentiments. If this is morality, then what kind of morality is it? It must be added that the men who most respect embryonic life are the same ones who do not hesitate to send adults to death in war.

The practical reasons invoked against legal abortion are completely unfounded; as with moral reasons, they are reduced to the old Catholic argument: the foetus has a soul and the gates to paradise are closed to it without baptism. It is worth noting that the Church authorises the killing of adult men in war, or when it is a question of the death penalty; but it stands on intransigent humanitarianism for the foetus. It is not redeemed by baptism: but in the times of the holy wars against the infidel, the infidels were not baptised either and massacre was still strongly encouraged. Victims of the Inquisition were undoubtedly not all in a state of grace, nor are criminals who are guillotined and soldiers killed on the battlefield. In all these cases, the Church leaves it to the grace of God; it accepts that man is only an instrument in His hands and that the soul's salvation depends on the Church and God. Why, then, keep God from welcoming the embryonic soul into His heaven? If a council authorised it, he would not protest against the pious massacre of the Indians any more than in the good old days. The truth is that this is a conflict with a stubborn old tradition that has nothing to do with morality. The masculine sadism I have already discussed also has to be taken into account. The book Dr Roy dedicated to Pétain in 1943 is a striking example; it is a monument of bad faith. In a paternalistic way it underlines the dangers of abortion; but nothing seems more hygienic to him than a Caesarean. He wants abortion to be considered a crime and not a misdemeanour; and he wishes to have it banned even in its therapeutic form, that is, when the mother's life or health are in danger: it is immoral to choose between one life and another, he declares, and bolstered by this argument, he advises sacrificing the mother. He declares that the foetus does not belong to the mother, that it is an autonomous being. But when these same 'right-thinking' doctors exalt motherhood, they affirm that the foetus is part of the mother's body, that it is not a parasite nourished at the mother's expense. This fervour on the part of some men to reject everything that might liberate women shows how alive antifeminism still is.

Besides, the law that dooms young women to death, sterility and illness is totally powerless to ensure an increase of births. A point of agreement for both partisans and enemies of legal abortion is the total failure of repression. According to Professors Doléris, Balthazard and Lacassagne, there were 500,000 abortions a year around 1933; a statistic (cited by Dr Roy) established in 1938 estimated the number at a million. In 1941, Dr Aubertin from Bordeaux hesitated between 800,000 and a million. This last figure seems closest to the truth. In a March 1948 article in *Combat*, Dr Desplas wrote:

Abortion has entered into our customs . . . Repression has practically failed . . . In the Seine district, in 1943, 1,300 investigations found 750 charged and of them, 360 women were arrested, 513 condemned to a minimum of one to five years in prison, which is low compared to the 15,000 presumed abortions in the district. There are 10,000 reported cases in the territory.

He adds:

So-called criminal abortion is as familiar to all social classes as the contraceptive policies accepted by our hypocritical society. Two-thirds of abortions are performed on married women . . . it can be roughly estimated that there are as many abortions as births in France.

Due to the fact that the operation is often carried out in disastrous conditions, many abortions end in these women's deaths.

Two bodies of women who had abortions arrive per week at the medical-legal institute in Paris; many abortions result in permanent illnesses.

It is sometimes said that abortion is a 'class crime' and this is very often true. Contraceptive practices are more prevalent in the bourgeoisie; the existence of bathrooms makes their use easier than for workers or farmers deprived of running water; young girls in the bourgeoisie are more careful than others; a child is less of a burden in these households: poverty, insufficient housing and the necessity for the wife to work outside the home are among the most common reasons for abortions. It seems that most often couples decide to limit births after two children; an ugly woman can have an abortion just as can this magnificent mother rocking her two blond angels in her arms: she is the same woman. In a document published in *Les Temps Modernes* in October 1945, under the title, 'Common Ward', Mme Geneviève Serreau describes a hospital room where she had to go once, and where many of the patients had just undergone curettages: fifteen out of eighteen had had miscarriages, half of which were induced. Number 9 was the wife of a market porter; she had had ten children in two marriages, of which only three were still living, and she had seven miscarriages, five of which were induced; she regularly used the 'coat hanger' technique that she complaisantly displayed, as well as pills whose names she shared with her companions. Number 16, sixteen years old and married, had had affairs and contracted salpingitis as the result of an abortion. Number 7, thirty-five, explained: 'I've been married twenty years. I never loved him: for twenty years I behaved properly. Three months ago I took a lover. One time, in a hotel room. I got pregnant . . . So what else could I do? I had it taken out. No one knows anything, not my husband, not . . . him. Now it's over; I'll never go through it again. I've suffered too much . . . I'm not speaking about the curettage . . . No, no, it's something else: it's . . . it's self-respect, you see.' Number 14 had had five children in five years; at forty she looked like an old woman. All of them had an air of resignation that comes from despair: 'Women are made to suffer,' they said sadly.

The seriousness of this ordeal varies a great deal depending on the circumstances. The conventionally married woman or one comfortably provided for, supported by a man, having money and relations, is better off: first, she finds ways to have a 'therapeutic' abortion much more easily; if necessary, she has the means to pay for a trip to Switzerland, where abortion is liberally tolerated; gynaecology today is such that it is a benign operation when performed by a specialist with all hygienic guarantees and, if necessary, anaesthetic resources; failing official approval, she can find unofficial help that is just as safe: she has the right addresses, she has enough money to pay for conscientious care, without waiting until her pregnancy is advanced; she will be treated respectfully; some of these privileged people even maintain that this little accident can be beneficial to one's health and improve the complexion. On the other hand, there is little distress more pathetic than that of an isolated and penniless girl who sees herself ensnared in a 'crime' to erase a 'fault' that people around her consider unpardonable: in France this is the case of approximately 300,000 women employees, secretaries, students, workers and peasants; illegitimate motherhood is still so terrible a stain that many prefer suicide or infanticide to being an unmarried mother: proof that no punishment will ever stop them from 'getting rid of the infant'. A typical case heard thousands of times is one related by Dr Liepmann.* It concerns a young Berlin woman, the natural child of a shoemaker and a maid:

I became friendly with a neighbour's son ten years older than myself . . . His caresses were so new to me that, well, I let myself go.

* *Youth and Sexuality.*

However, in no way was it a question of love. But he continued to teach me a lot of things, giving me books to read on women; and finally I gave him the gift of my virginity. When, two months later, I accepted a situation as a teacher in a nursery school in Speuze, I was pregnant. I didn't see my period for two more months. My seducer wrote to me that I absolutely had to make my period come back by drinking gasoline and eating black soap. I can no longer now describe the torments I went through . . . I had to see this misery through to the end on my own. The fear of having a child made me do the awful thing. This is how I learned to hate men.

The school pastor, having learned the story from a letter gone astray, gave her a long sermon and she left the young man; she was called a black sheep.

That was how I ended up doing eighteen months in a reformatory.

Afterwards she became a children's maid in a professor's home and stayed for four years.

At that period, I came to know a judge. I was happy to have a real man to love. I gave him all my love. Our relations were such that at twenty-four years old, I gave birth to a healthy boy. Today that child is ten. I have not seen the father for nine and a half years . . . as I found the sum of two thousand five hundred marks insufficient, and as he refused to give the child his name and denied paternity, everything was over between us. No other man has aroused my desire since.

It is often the seducer himself who convinces the woman that she should rid herself of the child. Either he has already abandoned her when she learns she is pregnant, or she altruistically wants to hide her disgrace from him, or else she finds no support from him. Sometimes it is not without regret that she refuses to have the child; either because she does not decide to abort early enough, or because she does not know where to go to do it, or because she does not have the money to hand and she has wasted her time trying ineffective drugs, she is in the third, fourth, fifth month of her pregnancy when she tries to eliminate it; the miscarriage will be infinitely more dangerous, more painful, more compromising than in the course of the first weeks. The woman knows this; in anguish and fear, she tries to find a way out. In the countryside, using a catheter is hardly known; the peasant woman who has 'sinned' accidentally lets herself fall off an attic ladder, throws herself from the top of a staircase, often hurts herself with no result; it also happens that a small strangled corpse is found in the bushes, in a ditch, or in an outhouse. In towns, women help each other out. But it is not always easy to get hold of a backstreet abortionist, and still less easy to get the money demanded; the pregnant woman requests help from a friend or she may perform the operation herself; these cut-price women surgeons are often incompetent; it does not take long to perforate oneself with a coat hanger or knitting needle; a doctor told me that an ignorant woman, trying to inject vinegar into her uterus, injected it into her bladder instead, provoking unspeakable pain. Brutally begun and poorly treated, the miscarriage, often more painful than an ordinary delivery, is accompanied by nervous disorders that can verge on epileptic fits, sometimes provoke serious internal illnesses, and bring on fatal haemorrhaging. In *Gribiche*, Colette recounts the harsh agony of a little music-hall dancer abandoned to the ignorant hands of her mother; a standard remedy, she says, is to drink a concentrated soap solution and then to run for a quarter of an hour: with such treatments, it is often by killing the mother that one gets rid of the child. I was told about a secretary who stayed in her room for four days, lying in her blood, without eating or drinking, because she did not dare call anyone. It is difficult to imagine abandonment more frightful than the kind where the threat of death converges with that of crime and shame. The ordeal is less harsh in the case of poor but married women who act in accord with their husbands and without being tormented by useless scruples: a social worker told me that in 'poor neighbourhoods' women share advice, borrow and lend instruments, and help each other out as simply as if they were removing corns. But they undergo severe physical suffering; hospitals are obliged to accept a woman whose miscarriage has already commenced; but she is sadistically *punished* by being refused sedatives during labour and during the final curettage procedure. As seen in reports by Serreau, for example, these persecutions do not even shock women all too used to suffering: but they are sensitive to the humiliations heaped on them. The fact that the operation they undergo is a clandestine and criminal one multiplies the dangers and makes it abject and anguishing. Pain, sickness and death seem like chastisement: we know what distance separates suffering from torture, accident from punishment; with the risks she assumes, the woman feels guilty, and it is this interpretation of pain and blame that is particularly distressful.

This moral aspect of the drama is more or less intensely felt depending on the circumstances. For very 'liberated' women, thanks to their financial resources, their social situation, the free milieu they belong to, or for those who have learned through poverty and misery to disdain bourgeois morality, the question hardly arises: there is a difficult moment to go through, but it must be gone through, and that is all. But many women are intimidated by a morality that maintains its prestige in their eyes, even though their behaviour cannot conform to it; inwardly, they respect the law they are breaking, and they suffer from committing a crime; they suffer even more for having to find accomplices. In the first place, they undergo the humiliation of begging: they beg for an address, a doctor's care, a midwife; they risk being haughtily snubbed; or they expose themselves to a degrading connivance. To deliberately invite another to commit a crime is a situation that most men never know and that the woman experiences with a mixture of fear and shame. This intervention she demands is one she often rejects in her own heart. She is divided inside herself. It might be that her spontaneous desire is to keep this child whose birth she is preventing; even if she does not positively want this motherhood, she feels ill at ease with the ambiguity of the act she is about to perform. For even if abortion is not murder, it cannot be assimilated to a simple contraceptive practice; an event has taken place that is an absolute commencement and whose development is being halted. Some women are haunted by the memory of this child who did not come to be. Helene Deutsch* cites the case of a psychologically normal married woman who, having twice lost third-month foetuses due to her physical condition, made them little tombs that she treated with great piety even after the birth of many other children. If the miscarriage was induced, this is all the more reason to feel she has committed a sin. The childhood remorse that follows the jealous desire for the death of a newborn little brother is revived, and the woman blames herself for really killing a child. This feeling of guilt can be expressed in pathological melancholies. In addition to women who think they tried to kill a living thing, there are many who feel they have mutilated a part of themselves; from here stems a resentment against the man who accepted or solicited this mutilation. Deutsch, once again, cites the case of a young girl who, deeply infatuated with her lover, herself insisted on eliminating

---

* *The Psychology of Women.*

a child who would have been an obstacle to their happiness; leaving the hospital, she refused to see the man she loved from then on. Even if such a definitive rupture is rare, it is, on the contrary, common for a woman to become frigid, either with all men or with the one who made her pregnant.

Men tend to take abortion lightly; they consider it one of those numerous accidents to which the malignity of nature has destined women: they do not grasp the values involved in it. The woman repudiates feminine values, her values, at the moment the male ethic is contested in the most radical way. Her whole moral future is shaken by it. Indeed, from childhood woman is repeatedly told she is made to bear children, and the praises of motherhood are sung; the disadvantages of her condition – periods, illness, and such – the boredom of household tasks, all this is justified by this marvellous privilege she holds, that of bringing children into the world. And in an instant, the man, to keep his freedom and not to handicap his future, in the interest of his job, asks the woman to renounce her female triumph. The child is no longer a priceless treasure: giving birth is no longer a sacred function: this proliferation becomes contingent and inopportune, and it is again one of femininity's defects. The monthly labour of menstruation becomes a blessing by comparison: now the return of the red flow that once plunged the girl into horror is anxiously awaited; it was in promising her the joys of childbearing that she had been consoled. Even consenting to and wanting an abortion, woman feels her femininity sacrificed: she will from now on definitively see in her sex a malediction, a kind of infirmity, a danger. Taking this denial to its extreme, some women become homosexual after the trauma of abortion. Yet when man asks woman to sacrifice her bodily possibilities for the success of his male destiny, he is denouncing the hypocrisy of the male moral code at the same time. Men universally forbid abortion; but they accept it individually as a convenient solution; they can contradict themselves with dizzying cynicism; but woman feels the contradictions in her wounded flesh; she is generally too shy to deliberately revolt against masculine bad faith; while seeing herself as a victim of an injustice that decrees her to be a criminal in spite of herself, she still feels dirtied and humiliated; it is she who embodies man's fault in a concrete and immediate form, in herself; he commits the fault, but unloads it onto her; he just says words in a pleading, threatening, reasonable or furious tone: he forgets them quickly; it is she who translates these phrases into pain and blood. Sometimes he says nothing, he just walks away; but his silence and avoidance are a far more obvious indictment of the whole moral code instituted by men. What is called 'immorality' in women, a favourite theme with misogynists, should surprise no one; how could women not feel inwardly defiant against the arrogant principles men publicly advocate and secretly denounce? Women learn to believe men no longer when they exalt women or when they exalt men; the one sure thing is the manipulated and bleeding womb, those shreds of red life, that absence of a child. With her first abortion, the woman begins to 'understand'. For many women, the world will never be the same. And yet, for lack of access to contraceptives, abortion is the only way out today in France for women who do not want to bring into the world children condemned to death and misery. Stekel* said it correctly: 'Prohibition of abortion is an immoral law, since it must be forcibly broken every day, every hour.'

Birth control and legal abortion would allow women to control their pregnancies freely. In fact, what decides woman's fecundity is in part a considered desire and in part chance. As long as artificial insemination is not widely practised, a woman might desire to become pregnant but be unable to – because either she does not have relations with men, or her husband is sterile, or she is unable to conceive. And, on the other hand, she is often forced to give birth against her will. Pregnancy and motherhood are experienced in very different ways depending on whether they take place in revolt, resignation, satisfaction or enthusiasm. One must keep in mind that the decisions and feelings the young mother expresses do not always correspond to her deep desires. An unwed mother can be overwhelmed in material terms by the burden suddenly imposed on her, be openly distressed by it, and yet find in the child the satisfaction of secretly harboured dreams; inversely, a young married woman who joyfully and proudly welcomes her pregnancy can fear it in silence, hate it with obsessions, fantasies and infantile memories that she herself refuses to recognise. This is one of the reasons why women are so secretive on this subject. Their silence comes in part from liking to surround an experience that is theirs alone in mystery; but they are also disconcerted by the contradictions and conflicts of which they themselves are the centre. 'The preoccupations of pregnancy are a dream that is forgotten as entirely as the dream of birth pains,'† one woman said. These are complex

* *Frigidity in Woman.*
† N. Hale.

truths that come to the fore in women and that they endeavour to bury in oblivion.

We have seen that in childhood and adolescence woman goes through several phases in connection with motherhood. When she is a little girl, it is a miracle and a game: she sees in the doll and she feels in the future child an object to possess and dominate. As an adolescent girl, on the contrary, she sees in it a threat to the integrity of her precious person. Either she rejects it violently, like Colette Audry's heroine who confides to us:

> Each little child playing in the sand, I loathed him for coming out of a woman . . . I loathed the adults too for lording it over the children, purging them, spanking them, dressing them, shaming them in all ways: women with their soft bodies always ready to bud out with new little ones, men who looked at all this pulp of their women and children belonging to them with a satisfied and independent air. My body was mine alone, I only liked it brown, encrusted with sea salt, scratched by the rushes. It had to stay hard and sealed.*[66]

Or else she fears it at the same time as she wishes it, which leads to pregnancy fantasies and all kinds of anxieties. Some girls enjoy exercising maternal authority but are not at all disposed to assume the responsibilities fully. Such is the case of Lydia cited by Helene Deutsch who, at sixteen, placed as a maid with foreigners, took the most extraordinarily devoted care of the children entrusted to her: it was a prolongation of her childish dreams in which she formed a couple with her mother to raise a child; suddenly she began to neglect her service, to be indifferent to the children, to go out, flirt; the time of games was finished and she was beginning to pay attention to her real life, where desire for motherhood did not hold a great place. Some women have the desire to dominate children their whole lives but they are horrified by the biological labour of parturition: they become midwives, nurses, grammar school teachers; they are devoted aunts, but they refuse to have children. Others too, without being disgusted by maternity, are too absorbed by their love lives or careers to make a place for it in their existence. Or they are afraid of the burden a child would mean for them or their husbands.

Often a woman deliberately ensures her sterility either by refusing all

* 'The Child', in *Playing a Losing Game*.

sexual relations or by birth-control practices; but there are also cases where she does not admit her fear of the infant and where conception is prevented by a psychic defence mechanism; functional problems of nervous origin occur that can be detected in a medical examination. Dr Arthus* cites a striking example, among others:

> Mme H. . . . had been poorly prepared for her life as a woman by her mother; who had always warned her of the worst catastrophes if she became pregnant . . . When Mme H. . . . was married she thought she was pregnant the following month; she realised her error; then once more after three months; new mistake. A year later she went to a gynaecologist, who did not see any cause of infertility in her or her husband. Three years later, she saw another one who told her: 'You will get pregnant when you talk less.' After five years of marriage, Mme H. . . . and her husband had accepted that they would not have a child. A baby was born after six years of marriage.

The acceptance or refusal of conception is influenced by the same factors as pregnancy in general. The subject's infantile dreams and her adolescent anxieties are revived during pregnancy; it is experienced in different ways depending on the woman's relations with her mother, her husband, and herself.

Becoming a mother in turn, woman somehow takes the place of the one who gave birth to her: this means total emancipation for her. If she sincerely desires her pregnancy, it will be of utmost importance for her to carry it out without assistance; still dominated and consenting to it, she will put herself on the contrary in her mother's hands: the newborn will seem like a brother or sister to her rather than her own offspring; if at the same time she wants and does not dare to liberate herself, she fears that the child, instead of saving her, will make her fall back under the yoke: this anguish can cause miscarriages; Deutsch cites the case of a young woman who, having to accompany her husband on a trip and leaving the child with her mother, gave birth to a stillborn child; she wondered why she had not mourned it more because she had ardently desired it; but she would have hated giving it over to her mother, who would have dominated her through this child. Guilt feelings towards one's mother are common, as was seen, in the adolescent girl; if they

* *Marriage* (*Le Mariage*).

are still strong, the wife imagines that a curse weighs on her offspring or on herself: the child, she thinks, will kill her upon coming into the world or he will die in birth. This anguish that they will not carry their pregnancy to term – so frequent in young women – is often provoked by remorse. This example reported in Deutsch shows how the relationship to the mother can have a negative importance.

Mrs Smith was the youngest in a family with many other children, one boy and several girls. After this boy had disappointed the ambitious hopes of the parents, they wanted to have another son, but instead my patient was born. Her mother never concealed her disappointment over this fact . . . the patient was saved from traumatic reactions to this attitude by two compensations – her father's deep and tender love for her, and the maternal affection of one of her sisters . . . As a little girl she had reacted to her mother's rejections with conscious hatred . . . Up to her pregnancy she had been able to disregard her mother problem; but this method no longer worked when she herself was about to become a mother . . . she gave birth one month before term to a stillborn child. Soon she was again pregnant; and her joy was now even more mixed with fear of loss than during her first pregnancy. By this time she had come into close relation with a former friend of hers who was also pregnant . . . The friend had a mother who was the opposite of her own . . . full to the brim with maternal warmth. She spread her motherly wings both over her own loving daughter and Mrs Smith. [But] her friend had conceived a whole month before her; thus during the last month she would be left to her own fate . . . to the surprise of everyone concerned, her friend did not have her child at the expected time . . . and gave birth to a boy overdue by a whole month on the very day that Mrs Smith expected her own delivery.* The two friends now consciously adjusted themselves to each other in regard to their next pregnancies and conceived in the same month. This second time, Mrs Smith had no fears or doubts. But during the third month of her pregnancy her friend told her that her husband had been offered a position in another town and that the family would probably move there. That very day Mrs Smith started on a miscarriage. This woman could not

* H. Deutsch affirms that she verified the fact that the child was really born ten months after conception.

manage to have a second child ... After her friend had failed her she could no longer chase away the shadow of the mother she had rejected.

The woman's relationship with her child's father is no less important. An already mature and independent woman can desire a child belonging wholly to herself: I knew one whose eyes lit up at the sight of a handsome male, not out of sensual desire, but because she judged his stud-like capacities; there are maternal Amazons who enthusiastically welcome the miracle of artificial insemination. Even if the child's father shares their life, they deny him any right over their offspring; they try – like Paul's mother in *Sons and Lovers* – to form a closed couple with their child. But in most cases, a woman needs masculine support to accept her new responsibilities; she will only devote herself joyously to a newborn if a man devotes himself to her.

The more infantile and shy she is, the more she needs this. Deutsch thus recounts the story of a young woman who at fifteen years of age married a sixteen-year-old boy who had got her pregnant. As a little girl, she had always loved babies and helped her mother take care of her brothers and sisters. But once she herself became a mother of two children, she panicked. She demanded that her husband constantly stay with her; he had to take a job that allowed him to remain home for long periods. She lived in a state of constant anxiety, exaggerating her children's fights, giving excessive importance to the slightest incidents of their days. Many young mothers demand so much help from their husbands that they drive them away by overburdening them with their problems. Deutsch cites other curious cases, like this one:

A young married woman thought she was pregnant and was extremely happy about it; separated from her husband by a trip, she had a very brief adventure that she accepted specifically because, delighted by her pregnancy, nothing else seemed to be of consequence; back with her husband, she learned later on that in truth, she had been mistaken about the conception date: it dated from his trip. When the child was born, she suddenly wondered if he was her husband's son or her fleeting lover's; she became incapable of feeling anything for the desired child; anguished and unhappy, she resorted to a psychiatrist and was not interested in the baby until she decided to consider her husband as the newborn's father.[67]

The woman who feels affection for her husband will often tailor her feelings to his: she will welcome pregnancy and motherhood with joy or misery depending on whether he is proud or put upon. Sometimes a child is desired to strengthen a relationship or a marriage, and the mother's attachment depends on the success or failure of her plans. If she feels hostility towards the husband, the situation is quite different: she can fiercely devote herself to the child, denying the father possession, or on the other hand, hate the offspring of the detested man. Mme H. N., whose wedding night we recounted as reported by Stekel, immediately became pregnant and she detested the little girl conceived in the horror of this brutal initiation her whole life. In Sophia Tolstoy's *Diaries* too, the ambivalence of her feelings for her husband is reflected in her first pregnancy. She writes:

> I am in an unbearable state, physically and mentally. Physically I am always ill with something, mentally there is this awful emptiness and boredom, like a dreadful depression. As far as Lyova is concerned I do not exist . . . I can do nothing to make him happy, because I am pregnant.

The only pleasure she feels in this state is masochistic: it is probably the failure of her sexual relations that gives her an infantile need for self-punishment.

> I have been ill since yesterday. I am afraid I may miscarry, yet I even take pleasure from the pain in my stomach. It is like when I did something naughty as a child, and Maman would always forgive me but I could never forgive myself, and would pinch and prick my hand. The pain would become unbearable but I would take intense pleasure in enduring it . . . I shall enjoy my new baby and also enjoy physical pleasures again – how disgusting . . . Everything here seems so depressing. Even the clock sounds melancholy when it strikes the hour; . . . everything is dead. But if Lyova . . . !

But pregnancy is above all a drama playing itself out in the woman between her and herself. She experiences it both as an enrichment and a mutilation; the foetus is part of her body and it is a parasite exploiting her; she possesses it and she is possessed by it; it encapsulates the whole future and in carrying it, she feels as vast as the world; but this very richness annihilates her, she has the impression of not being anything else. A new existence is going to manifest itself and justify her own existence, she is proud of it; but she also feels like the plaything of obscure forces, she is tossed about, assaulted. What is unique about the pregnant woman is that at the very moment her body transcends itself, it is grasped as immanent: it withdraws into itself in nausea and discomfort; it no longer exists for itself alone and then becomes bigger than it has ever been. The transcendence of an artisan or a man of action is driven by a subjectivity, but for the future mother the opposition between subject and object disappears; she and this child who swells in her form an ambivalent couple that life submerges; snared by nature, she is plant and animal, a collection of colloids, an incubator, an egg; she frightens children who are concerned with their own bodies and provokes sniggers from young men because she is a human being, consciousness and freedom, who has become a passive instrument of life. Life is usually just a condition of existence; in gestation it is creation; but it is a strange creation that takes place in contingency and facticity. For some women the joys of pregnancy and nursing are so strong they want to repeat them indefinitely; as soon as the baby is weaned, they feel frustrated. These 'breeders' rather than mothers eagerly seek the possibility of alienating their liberty to the benefit of their flesh: their existence appears to them to be tranquilly justified by the passive fertility of their body. If flesh is pure inertia, it cannot embody transcendence, even in a degraded form; it is idleness and ennui, but as soon as it burgeons, it becomes progenitor, source, flower, it goes beyond itself, it is movement towards the future while being a thickened presence at the same time. The separation woman suffered from in the past during her weaning is compensated for; it is submerged again in the current of life, reintegrated into the whole, a link in the endless chain of generations, flesh that exists for and through another flesh. When she feels the child in her heavy belly or when she presses it against her swollen breasts, the mother accomplishes the fusion she sought in the arms of the male, and that is refused as soon as it is granted. She is no longer an object subjugated by a subject; nor is she any longer a subject anguished by her freedom, she is this ambivalent reality: life. Her body is finally her own since it is the child's that belongs to her. Society recognises this possession in her and endows it with a sacred character. She can display her breast that was previously an erotic object, it is a source of life: to such an extent that pious paintings show the Virgin Mary uncovering her breast and begging her Son to save humanity. Alienated in her body and her social dignity, the mother has the pacifying illusion of feeling she is a being *in itself*, a ready-made *value*.

But this is only an illusion. Because she does not really make the child: it is made in her; her flesh only engenders flesh: she is incapable of founding an existence that will have to found itself; creations that spring from freedom posit the object as a value and endow it with a necessity: in the maternal breast, the child is unjustified, it is still only a gratuitous proliferation, a raw fact whose contingency is symmetrical with that of death. The mother can have *her* reasons for wanting *a* child, but she cannot give to *this* other – who tomorrow is going to be – his own raisons d'être; she engenders him in the generality of his body, not in the specificity of his existence. This is what Colette Audry's heroine understands when she says:

> I never thought he could give meaning to my life . . . His being
> had grown in me and I had to go through with it to term, what-
> ever happened, without being able to hasten things, even if I had
> to die from it. Then he was there, born from me; so he was like
> the work I might have done in my life . . . but after all he was
> not.*

In one sense the mystery of incarnation is repeated in each woman; every child who is born is a god who becomes man: he could not realise himself as consciousness and freedom if he did not come into the world; the mother lends herself to this mystery, but she does not control it; the supreme truth of this being taking shape in her womb escapes her. This is the ambivalence she expresses in two contradictory fantasies: all mothers have the idea that their child will be a hero; they thus express their wonderment at the idea of giving birth to a consciousness and a liberty; but they also fear giving birth to a cripple, a monster, because they know the awful contingency of flesh, and this embryo who inhabits them is merely flesh. There are cases where one of these myths wins out: but often the woman wavers between them. She is also susceptible to another ambivalence. Trapped in the great cycle of the species, she affirms life against time and death: she is thus promised to immortality; but she also experiences in her flesh the reality of Hegel's words: 'The birth of children is the death of parents.' The child, he also says, is for the parents 'the being for itself of their love that falls outside of them';

---

* 'The Child', in *Playing a Losing Game*.

and inversely, he will obtain his being for himself 'in separating from the source, a separation in which this source dries up'. Going beyond self for woman is also the prefiguration of her death. She manifests this truth in the fear she feels when imagining the birth: she fears losing her own life in it.

As the meaning of pregnancy is thus ambiguous, it is natural for the woman's attitude to be ambivalent as well: it changes moreover with the various stages of the foetus's evolution. It has to be noted first that at the beginning of the process the child is not present; he has only an imaginary existence; the mother can dream of this little individual who will be born in a few months, be busy preparing his cradle and layette: she grasps concretely only the organic and worrisome phenomena of which she is the seat. Some priests of Life and Fecundity mystically claim that woman knows the man has just made her a mother by the quality of the pleasure she experiences: this is one of the myths to be put into the trash heap. She never has a decisive intuition of the event: she deduces it from uncertain signs. Her periods stop, she thickens, her breasts become heavy and hurt, she has dizzy spells and is nauseous; sometimes she thinks she is simply ill and it is the doctor who informs her. Then she knows her body has been given a destination that transcends it; day after day a polyp born of her flesh and foreign to it is going to fatten in her; she is the prey of the species that will impose its mysterious laws on her, and generally this alienation frightens her: her fright manifests itself in vomiting. It is partially provoked by modifications in the gastric secretions then produced; but if this reaction, unknown in other female mammals, becomes more serious, it is for psychic reasons; it expresses the acute character of the conflict between species and individual in the human female.* Even if the woman deeply desires the child, her body revolts at first when it has to deliver. In *Conditions of Nervous Anxiety and Their Treatment*, Stekel asserts that the pregnant woman's vomiting always expresses a certain rejection of the child; and if the child is greeted with hostility – often for unavowed reasons – gastric troubles are exacerbated.

'Psychoanalysis has taught us that psychogenic intensification of the oral pregnancy symptom of vomiting takes place only when the oral expulsion tendencies are accompanied by unconscious and sometimes even manifest emotions of hostility to pregnancy or to the foetus,' says Deutsch. She adds, 'the psychologic content in pregnancy vomiting was

---

* See Vol. I, Chapter I.

exactly the same as that in the hysterical vomiting of young girls that is induced by an unconscious pregnancy fantasy and not by a real condition'.* In both cases, the old idea that children have of fertilisation through the mouth comes back to life. For infantile women in particular, pregnancy is, as in the past, assimilated to an illness of the digestive apparatus. Deutsch cites a woman patient who anxiously studied her vomit to see if there were not fragments of the foetus; but she *knew*, she said, that this obsession was absurd. Bulimia, lack of appetite and feeling sick signal the same hesitation between the desire to conserve and the desire to destroy the embryo. I knew a young woman who suffered from both excessive vomiting and fierce constipation; she told me that one day she had the impression both of trying to reject the foetus and of striving to keep it, corresponding exactly to her avowed desires. Dr Arthus† cites the following example, which I have summarised:

> Mme T. . . . presents serious pregnancy problems with irrepressible vomiting . . . The situation is so worrisome that an abortion is being considered . . . The young woman is disconsolate . . . The brief analysis that can be practised shows [that]: Mme T. subconsciously identifies with one of her former boarding-school friends who had played a great role in her emotional life and who died during her first pregnancy. As soon as this cause could be uncovered, the symptoms improved; vomiting continued somewhat for two weeks but does not present any more danger.

Constipation, diarrhoea and expulsion tendencies always express the same mixture of desire and anguish; the result is sometimes a miscarriage: almost all spontaneous miscarriages have a psychic origin. The more importance woman gives these malaises and the more she coddles herself, the more intense they are. In particular, pregnant women's famous 'cravings' are indulgently nurtured infantile obsessions: they are always focused on food, and have to do with the old idea of fertilisation by food; feeling distressed in her body, woman expresses, as often happens

---

* I was specifically told about the case of a man who for the first months of his wife's pregnancy – a wife he did not even love very much – presented the exact symptoms of nausea, dizziness and vomiting seen in pregnant women. They obviously express unconscious conflicts in a hysterical form.

† *Marriage.*

in psychasthenies, this feeling of strangeness through a desire that fascinates her. There is moreover a 'culture', a tradition, of these cravings as there once was a culture of hysteria; woman expects to have these cravings, she waits for them, she invents them for herself. I was told of a teenage mother who had such a frenetic craving for spinach that she ran to the market to buy it and jumped up and down in impatience watching it cook: she was thus expressing the anxiety of her solitude; knowing she could only count on herself, she was in a feverish rush to satisfy her desires. The duchesse d'Abrantès described very amusingly in her *Memoirs*[68] a case where the craving is imperiously suggested by the woman's circle of friends. She complains of having been surrounded by too much solicitude during her pregnancy:

> These cares and kind attentions increased the discomfort, nausea, nervousness and thousands of sufferings that almost always accompany first pregnancies. I found it so . . . It was my mother who started it one day when I was having dinner at her house . . . 'Good heavens,' she cried suddenly, putting down her fork and looking at me with dismay. 'Good heavens! I forgot to ask what you especially *craved*.'
>
> 'But there is nothing in particular,' I replied.
>
> 'You have no special craving,' exclaimed my mother, 'nothing! But that is unheard of. You must be wrong. You haven't noticed. I'll speak to your mother-in-law about it.'
>
> And so there were my two mothers in consultation. And there was Junot, afraid I would bear him a child with a wild boar's head . . . asking me every morning: 'Laura, what do you crave?' My sister-in-law came back from Versailles and added her voice to the choir of questions, saying that she had seen innumerable people disfigured because of unsatisfied longings . . . I finally got frightened myself . . . I tried to think of what would please me most and couldn't think of a thing. Then, one day, it occurred to me when I was eating pineapple lozenges that a pineapple had to be a very excellent thing . . . Once I persuaded myself that I had a *longing* for a pineapple I felt at first a very lively desire, increased when Corcelet declared that . . . they were not in season. Ah, then I felt that mad desire which makes you feel that you will die if it is not satisfied.

Junot, after many attempts, finally received a pineapple from Mme Bonaparte. The duchess of Abrantès welcomed it joyously and spent the night feeling and touching it as the doctor had ordered her not to eat it until morning, when Junot finally served it to her.

I pushed the plate away. 'But – I don't know what is the matter with me. I can't eat pineapple.' He put my nose into the cursed plate, which made it clear that I could not eat pineapple. They not only had to take it away but also to open the windows and perfume my room in order to remove the least traces of an odour that had become hateful to me in an instant. The strangest part of it is that since then I have never been able to eat pineapple without practically forcing myself.

Women who are too coddled or who coddle themselves too much are the ones who present the most morbid phenomena. Those that go through the ordeal of pregnancy the most easily are, on the one hand, matrons totally devoted to their function as breeders, and on the other hand, mannish women who are not fascinated by the adventures of their bodies and who do everything they can to triumph over them with ease: Mme de Staël went through pregnancy as easily as a conversation.

As the pregnancy proceeds, the relation between mother and foetus changes. It is solidly settled in the maternal womb, the two organisms adapt to each other and there are biological exchanges between them allowing the woman to regain her balance. She no longer feels possessed by the species: she herself possesses the fruit of her womb. The first months she was an ordinary woman, and diminished by the secret labour taking place in her; later she is obviously a mother and her malfunctions are the reverse of her glory. The increasing weakness she suffers from becomes an excuse. Many women then find a marvellous peace in their pregnancy: they feel justified; they always liked to observe themselves, to spy on their bodies; because of their sense of social duty, they did not dare to focus on their body with too much self-indulgence: now they have the right to; everything they do for their own well-being they also do for the child. They are not required to work or make an effort; they no longer have to pay attention to the rest of the world; the dreams of the future they cherish have meaning for the present moment; they only have to enjoy the moment: they are on vacation. The reason for their existence is there, in their womb, and gives them a perfect impression of plenitude. 'It is like a stove in winter that is always lit, that is there for you alone, entirely subject to your will. It is also like a constantly gushing cold shower in the summer, refreshing you. It is there,' says a woman quoted by Helene Deutsch. Fulfilled, woman also experiences the satisfaction of feeling 'interesting', which has been, since her adolescence, her deepest desire; as a wife, she suffered from her dependence on man; at present she is no longer sex object or servant, but she embodies the species, she is the promise of life, of eternity; her friends and family respect her; even her caprices become sacred: this is what encourages her, as we have seen, to invent 'cravings'. 'Pregnancy permits woman to rationalise performances which otherwise would appear absurd,' says Helene Deutsch. Justified by the presence within her of another, she finally fully enjoys being herself.

Colette wrote about this phase of her pregnancy in *The Evening Star*:[69]

Insidiously, unhurriedly, I was invaded by the beatitude of the woman great with child. I was no longer the prey of any malaise, any unhappiness. Euphoria, purring – what scientific or familiar name can one give to this saving grace? It must certainly have filled me to overflowing, for I haven't forgotten it . . . One grows weary of suppressing what one has never said – such as the state of pride, of banal magnificence which I savoured in ripening my fruit . . . Every evening I said a small farewell to one of the good periods of my life. I was well aware that I should regret it. But the cheerfulness, the purring, the euphoria submerged everything, and I was governed by the calm animality, the unconcern, with which I was charged by my increasing weight and the muffled call of the being I was forming.

Sixth, seventh month . . . the first strawberries, the first roses . . . Can I call pregnancy anything but a long holiday? One forgets the anguish of the term, one doesn't forget a unique long holiday; I've forgotten none of it. I particularly recall that sleep used to overwhelm me at capricious hours, and that I would be seized, as in my childhood, by the desire to sleep on the ground, on the grass, on warm straw. Unique 'craving', healthy craving . . .

Towards the end I had the air of a rat that drags a stolen egg. Uncomfortable in myself, I would be too tired to go to bed . . . Even then, the weight and the tiredness did not interrupt my long holiday. I was borne on a shield of privilege and solicitude.

This happy pregnancy was called by one of Colette's friends 'a man's pregnancy'. And she seemed to be the epitome of these women who valiantly support their state because they are not absorbed in it. She continued her work as a writer at the same time. 'The child showed signs of coming first and I screwed on the top of my pen.'

Other women are more weighed down; they mull indefinitely over their new importance. With just a little encouragement they adopt masculine myths: they juxtapose the lucidity of the mind to the fertile night of Life, clear consciousness to the mysteries of interiority, sterile freedom to the weight of this womb there in its enormous facticity; the future mother smells of humus and earth, spring and root; when she dozes, her sleep is that of chaos where worlds ferment. There are those more forgetful of self who are especially enchanted with the treasure of life growing in them. This is the joy Cécile Sauvage expresses in her poems in *The Soul in Bud*:[70]

> *You belong to me as dawn to the plain*
> *Around you my life is a warm fleece*
> *Where your chilly limbs grow in secret.*

And further on:

> *Oh you whom I fearfully cuddle in fleecy cotton*
> *Little soul in bud attached to my flower*
> *With a piece of my heart I fashion your heart*
> *Oh my cottony fruit, little moist mouth.*[71]

And in a letter to her husband:

It's funny, it seems to me I am watching the formation of a tiny planet and that I am kneading its frail globe. I have never been so close to life. I have never so felt I am sister of the earth with all vegetation and sap. My feet walk on the earth as on a living beast. I dream of the day full of flutes, of awakened bees, of dew because here he is bucking and stirring in me. If you knew what springtime freshness and what youth this soul in bud puts in my heart. And to think this is Pierrot's infant soul and that in the night of my being it is elaborating two big eyes of infinity like his.

In contrast are women who are very flirtatious, who grasp themselves essentially as erotic objects, who love themselves in the beauty of their bodies, and who suffer from seeing themselves deformed, ungainly, incapable of arousing desire. Pregnancy does not at all appear to them as a celebration or an enrichment, but as a diminishing of their self.

In *My Life* by Isadora Duncan one can read, among other observations:[72]

The child asserted itself now, more and more. It was strange to see my beautiful marble body softened and broken and stretched and deformed ... As I walked beside the sea, I sometimes felt an excess of strength and prowess, and I thought this creature would be mine, mine alone, but on other days ... I felt myself some poor animal in a mighty trap ... With alternate hope and despair, I often thought of the pilgrimage of my childhood, my youth, my wanderings ... my discoveries in Art, and they were as a misty, far-away prologue, leading up to this – the before-birth of a child. What any peasant woman could have! ... I began to be assailed with all sorts of fears. In vain I told myself that every woman had children ... It was all in the course of life, etc. I was, nevertheless, conscious of fear. Of what? Certainly not of death, nor even of pain – some unknown fear, of what I did not know ... More and more my lovely body bulged under my astonished gaze ... Where was my lovely, youthful naiad form? Where my ambition? My fame? Often, in spite of myself, I felt very miserable and defeated. This game with the giant Life was too much. But then I thought of the child to come, and all such painful thoughts ceased ... Helpless, cruel hours of waiting in the night ... With what a price we pay for the glory of motherhood.

In the last stage of pregnancy begins the separation between mother and child. Women experience his first movement differently, his kick knocking at the doors of the world, knocking against the wall of the womb that encloses him away from the world. Some women welcome and marvel at this signal announcing the presence of an autonomous life; others think of themselves with repugnance as the receptacle of a foreign individual. Once again, the union of foetus and maternal body is disturbed: the uterus descends, the woman has a feeling of pressure, tension, respiratory trouble. She is possessed this time not by the indistinct species but by this child who is going to be born; until then, he was just an image, a hope; he becomes heavily present. His reality creates new problems. Every passage is anguishing: the birth appears particularly frightening. When the woman comes close to term, all the infantile terrors come back to life; if, from a feeling of guilt, she thinks she is cursed by her mother, she persuades herself she is going to die or that the child will die. In *War and Peace*, Tolstoy painted in the character of Lise one of these infantile women who see a death sentence in birth: and she does die.

Depending on the case, the birth takes many different forms: the mother wants both to keep in her womb the treasure of her flesh that is a precious piece of her self and to get rid of an intruder; she wants finally to hold her dream in her hands but she is afraid of new responsibilities this materialisation will create: either desire can win, but she is often divided. Often, also, she does not come to the anguishing ordeal with a determined heart: she intends to prove to herself and to her family – her mother, her husband – that she is capable of surmounting it without help; but at the same time she resents the world, life and her family for the suffering inflicted on her and in protest she adopts a passive attitude. Independent women – matrons or masculine women – attach great importance to playing an active role in the period preceding and even during the birth; very infantile women let themselves passively go to the midwife, to their mother; some take pride in not crying out; others refuse to follow any recommendations. On the whole, it can be said that in this crisis they express their deepest attitude to the world in general, and to their motherhood in particular: they are stoic, resigned, demanding, imperious, revolted, inert, tense . . . These psychological dispositions have an enormous influence on the length and difficulty of the birth (which also, of course, depends on purely organic factors). What is significant is that normally woman – like some domesticated female animals – needs help to accomplish the function to which nature destines her; there are peasants in rough conditions and shamed young unmarried mothers who give birth alone: but their solitude often brings about the death of the child or for the mother incurable illnesses. At the very moment woman completes the realisation of her feminine destiny, she is still dependent: which also proves that in the human species nature can never be separated from artifice. With respect to nature, the conflict between the interest of the feminine person and that of the species is so acute it often brings about the death of either the mother or the child: human interventions by doctors and surgeons have considerably reduced – and even almost eliminated – the accidents that were previously so frequent. Anaesthetic methods are in the process of giving the lie to the biblical affirmation 'In sorrow thou shalt bring forth children'; they are commonly used in America and are beginning to spread to France; in March 1949, a decree has just made them compulsory in England.*

It is difficult to know exactly what suffering these methods save women from. The fact that delivery sometimes lasts more than twenty-four hours and sometimes is completed in two or three hours prevents any generalisation. For some women, childbirth is martyrdom. Such is the case of Isadora Duncan: she lived through her pregnancy in anxiety, and psychic resistance undoubtedly aggravated the pains of childbirth even more. She writes:

Talk about the Spanish Inquisition! No woman who has borne a child would have to fear it. It must have been a milk sport in comparison. Relentless, cruel, knowing no release, no pity, this terrible, unseen genie had me in his grip, and was, in continued spasms, tearing my bones and my sinews apart. They say such suffering is soon forgotten. All I have to reply is that I have only to shut my eyes and I hear again my shrieks and groans as they were then.

On the other hand, some women think it is a relatively easy ordeal to bear. A small number experience sensual pleasure in it.
One woman writes:†

I am so strongly sexed that even childbirth means to me a sexual act ... I had a very pretty 'madame' for a nurse. She bathed me and gave me my vaginal douches. This was enough for me – it kept me in such a high state of sexual agitation that I trembled.

---

* I have already said that some antifeminists, in the name of nature and the Bible, were indignant at the attempt to eliminate the suffering of childbirth; it is supposed to be one of the sources of the maternal 'instinct'. Helene Deutsch seems tempted by this opinion; she writes that when the mother has not felt the labour of childbirth, she does not profoundly recognise the child as her own at the moment she is presented with him; however, she agrees that the same feeling of emptiness and strangeness is encountered in women who have given birth and suffered; and she maintains all through her book that maternal love is a feeling, a conscious attitude, and not an instinct; that it is not necessarily linked to pregnancy; according to her, a woman can maternally love an adopted child or one her husband has had from a first marriage, and so on. This contradiction obviously comes from the fact that she has destined woman to masochism and her thesis demands she grant a high value to feminine suffering.

† Stekel recorded this subject's confession, which I have partially summarised.

Some women say they felt creative power during childbirth; they truly accomplished a voluntary and productive piece of work; many others feel passive, a suffering and tortured instrument.

The mother's first relations with the newborn vary as well. Some women suffer from this emptiness they now feel in their bodies: it seems to them that someone has stolen their treasure. Cécile Sauvage writes:

> I am the hive without speech
> Whose swarm has flown into the air
> No longer do I bring back the beakful
> Of my blood to your frail body
> My being is a closed-up house
> From which they have removed a body,

And more:

> No longer are you mine alone. Your head
> Already reflects other skies.

And also:

> He is born, I have lost my young beloved
> Now that he is born, I am alone, I feel
> Terrifying within me the void of my blood . . .[73]

Yet, at the same time, there is a wondrous curiosity in every young mother. It is a strange miracle to see, to hold a living being formed in and coming out of one's self. But what part has the mother really had in the extraordinary event that brings a new existence into the world? She does not know. The being would not exist without her and yet he escapes her. There is a surprising sadness in seeing him outside, cut off from herself. And there is almost always a disappointment. The woman would like to feel him *hers* as surely as her own hand: but everything he feels is closed up inside him, he is opaque, impenetrable, apart; she does not even recognise him, since she does not know him; she lived her pregnancy without him: she has no common past with this little stranger; she expected to be familiar right away; but no, he is a newcomer and she is stupefied by the indifference with which she receives him. In her pregnancy reveries he was an image, he was infinite and the mother mentally played out her future motherhood; now he is a tiny, finite individual, he is really there, contingent, fragile, demanding. The joy that he is finally here, quite real, is mingled with the regret that this is all he is.

After the initial separation, many young mothers regain an intimate animal relationship with their children through nursing; this is a more stressful fatigue than that of pregnancy, but it allows the nursing mother to prolong the 'vacation' state of peace and plenitude she relished in pregnancy. Colette Audry* says of one of her heroines:

> When the baby was suckling, there was really nothing else to do, and it could last for hours; she did not even think of what would come after. She could only wait for him to release her breast like a big bee.

But there are women who cannot nurse, and in whom the surprising indifference of the first hours continues until they regain concrete bonds with the child. This was the case, among others, with Colette, who was not able to nurse her daughter and who describes her first maternal feelings with her customary sincerity:[†]

> The outcome is the contemplation of a new person who has entered the house without coming in from outside . . . Did I devote enough love to my contemplation? I should not like to say so. True, I had the capacity – I still have – for wonder. I exercised it on that assembly of marvels which is the newborn. Her nails, resembling in their transparency the convex scale of the pink shrimp – the soles of her feet, which have reached us without touching the ground . . . The light plumage of her lashes, lowered over her cheek, interposed between the scenes of earth and the bluish dream of her eye . . . The small sex, a barely incised almond, a bivalve precisely closed, lip to lip. . . . But the meticulous admiration I devoted to my daughter – I did not call it, I did not feel it as love. I waited . . . I did not derive from these scenes, so long awaited in my life, the vigilance and emulation of besotted mothers. When, then, would be vouchsafed to me the sign that was to mark my second, more difficult, violation? I had to accept that an accumulation of warnings, of furtive, jealous outbursts, of false premonitions – and even of real ones – the pride in managing an existence of which I was

* *Playing a Losing Game.*
† *Evening Star.*

the humble creditor, the somewhat perfidious awareness of giving the other love a lesson in modesty, would eventually change me into an ordinary mother. Yet I only regained my equanimity when intelligible speech blossomed on those ravishing lips, when recognition, malice and even tenderness turned a run-of-the-mill baby into a little girl, and a little girl into my daughter!

There are also many mothers who are terrified of their new responsibilities. During pregnancy, they had only to abandon themselves to their flesh; no initiative was demanded of them. Now in front of them is a person who has rights to them. Some women happily caress their babies while they are still in the hospital, still gay and carefree, but upon returning home, they start to regard them as burdens. Even nursing brings them no joy, and, on the contrary, they worry about ruining their breasts; they resent feeling their cracked breasts, their painful glands; the baby's mouth hurts them: he seems to be sucking their strength, life and happiness from them. He inflicts a harsh servitude on them, and he is no longer part of his mother: he is like a tyrant; she feels hostility for this little individual who threatens her flesh, her freedom, her whole self.

Many other factors are involved. The woman's relations with her mother are still of great importance. Helene Deutsch cites the case of a young nursing mother whose milk dried up whenever her mother came to see her; she often solicits help, but is jealous of the care someone else gives to the baby and feels depressed about this. Her relations with the infant's father and the feelings he himself fosters also have a strong influence. A whole set of economic and sentimental considerations define the infant as a burden, a shackle, or a liberation, a jewel, a form of security. There are cases where hostility becomes outright hatred resulting in extreme neglect or bad treatment. Most often the mother, conscious of her duties, combats this hostility; she feels remorse that gives rise to anxieties prolonging the apprehensions of pregnancy. All psychoanalysts agree that mothers who are obsessed about harming their children, or who imagine horrible accidents, feel an enmity towards them they force themselves to repress. What is nonetheless remarkable and distinguishes this relationship from all other human relationships is that in the beginning the child himself does not play a part: his smiles, his babbling, have no meaning other than the one his mother gives them; it depends on her, not him, whether he seems charming, unique, bothersome, ordinary or obnoxious. This is why cold, unsatisfied, melancholic women who expect a child to be a companion, or to provide warmth and excitement that draw them out of themselves, are always deeply disappointed. Like the 'passage' into puberty, sexual initiation, and marriage, motherhood generates morose disappointment for subjects who are waiting for an external event to renew and justify their lives. This is the sentiment found in Sophia Tolstoy. She writes:

> 'These past nine months have been practically the worst in my life,' to say nothing of the tenth.[75]

She tries in vain to express a conventional joy: we are struck by her sadness and fear of responsibilities.

> It is all over, the baby has been born and my ordeal is at last at an end. I have risen from my bed and am gradually entering into life again, but with a constant feeling of fear and dread about my baby and especially my husband. Something within me seems to have collapsed, and I sense that whatever it is it will always be there to torment me; it is probably the fear of not doing my duty towards *my family* . . . I have become insincere, for I am frightened by the womb's vulgar love for its offspring, and frightened by my somewhat unnatural love for my husband . . . I sometimes comfort myself with the thought that most people see this love of one's husband and children as a virtue . . . But how strong these maternal feelings are! . . . He is Lyovochka's child, that's why I love him.

But we know very well that she only exhibits so much love for her husband because she does not love him; this antipathy marks the child conceived in embraces that disgusted her.

Katherine Mansfield describes the hesitation of a young mother who loves her husband but is repulsed by his caresses. For her children she feels tenderness and at the same time has an impression of emptiness she sadly interprets as complete indifference. Linda, resting in the garden next to her newborn, thinks about her husband, Stanley.*

> Well, she was married to him. And what was more she loved him. Not the Stanley whom everyone saw, not the everyday one; but a timid, sensitive, innocent Stanley who knelt down every night to say

*'At the Bay'.

his prayers . . . But the trouble was . . . she saw her Stanley so seldom. There were glimpses, moments, breathing spaces of calm, but all the rest of the time it was like living in a house that couldn't be cured of the habit of catching on fire, on a ship that got wrecked every day. And it was always Stanley who was in the thick of the danger. Her whole time was spent in rescuing him, and restoring him, and calming him down, and listening to his story. And what was left of her time was spent in the dread of having children . . . It was all very well to say it was the common lot of women to bear children. It wasn't true. She, for one, could prove that wrong. She was broken, made weak, her courage was gone, through child-bearing. And what made it doubly hard to bear was, she did not love her children. It was useless pretending . . . No, it was as though a cold breath had chilled her through and through on each of those awful journeys; she had no warmth left to give them. As to the boy – well, thank Heaven, mother had taken him; he was mother's, or Beryl's, or anybody's who wanted him. She had hardly held him in her arms. She was so indifferent about him that as he lay there . . . Linda glanced down . . . There was something so quaint, so unexpected about that smile that Linda smiled herself. But she checked herself and said to the boy coldly, 'I don't like babies.' 'Don't like babies?' The boy couldn't believe her. 'Don't like me?' He waved his arms foolishly at his mother. Linda dropped off her chair on to the grass. 'Why do you keep on smiling?' she said severely. 'If you knew what I was thinking about, you wouldn't' . . . Linda was so astonished at the confidence of this little creature . . . Ah no, be sincere. That was not what she felt; it was something far different, it was something so new, so . . . The tears danced in her eyes; she breathed in a small whisper to the boy, 'Hallo, my funny!'

These examples all prove that there is no such thing as maternal 'instinct': the word does not in any case apply to the human species. The mother's attitude is defined by her total situation and by the way she accepts it. It is, as we have seen, extremely variable.

But the fact is that if circumstances are not positively unfavourable, the mother will find herself enriched by a child. 'It was like a response to the reality of her own existence . . . through him she had a grasp on all things and on herself to begin with,' wrote Colette Audry about a young mother.

And she has another character say these words:

> He was heavy in my arms, and on my breast, like the heaviest thing
> in the world, to the limit of my strength. He buried me in silence
> and darkness. All at once he had put the weight of the world on
> my shoulders. That was indeed why I wanted him. I was too light
> myself. Alone, I was too light.

While some women are 'breeders' rather than mothers and lose
interest in their child as soon as it is weaned, or as soon as it is born,
and only desire another pregnancy, many others by contrast feel that it
is the separation itself that gives them the child; it is no longer an indistinct part of themselves but a piece of the world; it no longer secretly
haunts the body, but can be seen, touched; after the melancholy of
delivery, Cécile Sauvage expresses the joy of possessive motherhood:

> *Here you are my little lover*
> *On your mother's big bed*
> *I can kiss you, hold you,*
> *Feel the weight of your fine future;*
> *Good day my little statue*
> *Of blood, of joy and naked flesh,*
> *My little double, my excitement . . .*

It has been said again and again that woman happily finds an equivalent of the penis in the infant: this is completely wrong. In fact, the adult
man no longer sees his penis as a wonderful toy: his organ is valued in
relation to the desirable objects it allows him to possess; by the same
token, the adult woman envies the male for the prey he acquires, not
the instrument of this acquisition; the infant satisfies this aggressive eroticism that the male embrace does not fulfil: the infant is homologous to
this mistress that she is for the male and that he is not for her; of course
there is no exact correspondence; every relation is unique; but the mother
finds in the child – like the lover in the beloved – a carnal plenitude, not
in surrender but in domination; she grasps in the child what man seeks
in woman: an other, both nature and consciousness, who is her prey, her
double. He embodies all of nature. Audry's heroine tells us she found in
her child:

The skin that was for my fingers to touch, that fulfilled the promise
of all little kittens, all flowers . . .

His skin has that sweetness, that warm elasticity that, as a little girl,
the woman coveted in her mother's flesh and, later, everywhere in the
world. He is plant and animal, he holds rains and rivers in his eyes, the
azure of the sky and the sea, his fingernails are coral, his hair a silky
growth, he is a living doll, a bird, a kitten; my flower, my pearl, my
chick, my lamb . . . His mother murmurs words almost of a lover and
uses, like a lover, the possessive adjective; she uses the same words of
appropriation: caresses, kisses; she hugs the infant to her body, she
envelops him in the warmth of her arms, of her bed. At times these
relations have a clearly sexual cast. Thus in the confession collected by
Stekel I have already cited, we read:

> I nursed my baby but I took no particular joy in doing so because
> he did not thrive well. We were both losing ground. The act of
> nursing seemed something sexual to me. I was always ashamed
> of it . . . it was for me a majestic experience to feel the warm
> little body snuggling up to me . . . The touch of his little hands
> thrilled me . . . My whole love went out to him . . . The child
> would cling to me and did not leave my side. It was troublesome
> to try to keep him away from me . . . When he saw me in bed
> he crawled up at once – he was two years of age at the time –
> and tried to lie on top of me. At the same time his little hands
> wandered over my breasts and tried to reach down. I found this
> very pleasurable; it was not easy for me to send the child away.
> Frequently I fought against the temptation of playing with his
> genitals.

Motherhood takes on a new aspect when the child grows older; at
first he is only a 'standard baby', existing in his generality: little by little
he becomes individualised. Very dominating or very carnal women grow
cold towards him; it is then that some others – like Colette – begin to
take an interest in him. The mother's relation to the child becomes more
and more complex: he is a double and at times she is tempted to alienate
herself completely in him, but he is an autonomous subject, and therefore rebellious; today he is warmly real, but in the far-off future he is
an adolescent, an imaginary adult; he is her wealth, a treasure: but he
is also a responsibility, a tyrant. The joy the mother can find in him is

a joy of generosity; she must take pleasure in serving, giving, creating happiness, such as the mother depicted by Colette Audry:

> Thus, he had a happy storybook infancy, but his infancy was to storybook infancy as real roses were to postcard roses. And this happiness of his came out of me like the milk with which I nourished him.

Like the woman in love, the mother is delighted to feel needed; she is justified by the demands she responds to; but what makes maternal love difficult and great is that it implies no reciprocity; the woman is not before a man, a hero, a demigod, but a little stammering consciousness, lost in a fragile and contingent body; the infant possesses no value, and he can bestow none; the woman remains alone before him; she expects no compensation in exchange for her gifts, she justifies them with her own freedom. This generosity deserves the praise that men forever bestow on her; but mystification begins when the religion of Motherhood proclaims that all mothers are exemplary. For maternal devotion can be experienced in perfect authenticity; but in fact, this is rarely the case. Ordinarily, maternity is a strange compromise of narcissism, altruism, dream, sincerity, bad faith, devotion and cynicism.

The great risk our mores present for the infant is that the mother to whom he is tied and bound is almost always an unfulfilled woman: sexually she is frigid or unsatisfied; socially she feels inferior to man; she has no hold on the world or the future; she will try to compensate for her frustrations through the child; when one recognises how the present situation of woman makes her full development difficult, how many desires, revolts, pretensions and claims she secretly harbours, one is frightened that helpless little children are given over to her. Just as when she both pampered and tortured her dolls, her behaviour is symbolic: but these symbols become bitter reality for the child. A mother who beats her child does not only beat the child, and in a way she does not beat him at all: she is taking her vengeance on man, on the world, or on herself; but it is the child who receives the blows. Mouloudji expresses this painful misunderstanding in *Enrico*: Enrico well understands it is not he whom his mother beats so wildly; and waking from her delirium, she sobs with remorse and tenderness; he does not hold it against her, but he is no less disfigured by her blows. And the mother described in Violette Leduc's *In the Prison of Her Skin*, in lashing out against her daughter is in fact taking revenge on the seducer who abandoned her, on life that humiliated and defeated her. This cruel aspect of motherhood has always been known; but with hypocritical prudishness, the idea of the 'bad mother' has been defused by inventing the cruel stepmother; the father's second wife torments the child of the deceased 'good mother'. Indeed, Mme Fichini is a mother figure, the exact counterpart of the edifying Mme de Fleurville described by Mme de Ségur. Since Jules Renard's *Carrot Top*,[76] there have been more and more accusations: *Enrico, In the Prison of Her Skin*, Simone de Tervagne's *Maternal Hatred*,[77] Hervé Bazin's *Viper in the Fist*.[78] While the types sketched in these novels are somewhat exaggerated, the majority of women suppress their spontaneous impulses out of morality and decency; but these impulses flare up in scenes, slaps, anger fits, insults, punishments, and so on. In addition to frankly sadistic women, there are many who are especially capricious; what delights them is to dominate; when the baby is tiny, he is a toy: if it is a boy, they shamelessly play with his penis; if it is a girl, they treat her like a doll; later they only want a little slave who will blindly obey them: vain, they show the child off like a trained pet; jealous and exclusive, they set him apart from the rest of the world. Also, the woman often continues to expect gratitude for the care she gives the child: she shapes an imaginary being through him who will recognise her with gratitude for being an admirable mother and one in whom she recognises herself. When Cornelia, proudly showing her children, said, 'These are my jewels,' she gave an ill-fated example to posterity; too many mothers live in the hope of one day repeating this arrogant gesture; and they do not hesitate to sacrifice the little flesh-and-blood individual whose contingent and indecisive existence does not fulfil them. They force him to resemble their husbands, or on the contrary, not to resemble them, or to reincarnate a father, a mother or a venerated ancestor; they model him on someone prestigious: a German socialist deeply admired Lily Braun, recounts Helene Deutsch; the famous activist had a brilliant son who died young; her imitator was determined to treat her own son like a future genius and as a result he became a bandit. Harmful to the child, this ill-adapted tyranny is always a source of disappointment for the mother. Deutsch cites another striking example, of an Italian woman whose case history she followed for several years.

Mrs Mazzetti . . . had a number of small children . . . who caused her difficulties, all of them, one after the other. Personal contact with Mrs Mazzetti soon revealed that although she sought help it was difficult to influence her . . . Her entire bearing . . . was

consistently used only in face of the outside world, but . . . in relations with her family, she gave way to uncontrolled emotional
outbursts . . . we learned that coming from a poor, uncultured
milieu, she had always had the urge to become something 'better'.
She always attended night schools and would perhaps have achieved
something in harmony with her aspirations if she had not met her
husband. He . . . exerted an irresistible sexual attraction upon her.
At the age of sixteen she had sexual relations with him, soon became
pregnant, and found herself compelled to marry him . . . She continually tried to raise herself again . . . she went to night school, etc.
The man was a first class workman . . . Mrs Mazzetti evidently had
emphasised her superiority to him in a very aggressive way, which
drove this simple man to . . . alcoholism. He tried to devaluate his
wife's superiority by . . . making her repeatedly pregnant . . . After
her separation from her husband she turned all her emotions to
the children, and began to treat them as she had treated her
husband . . . As long as the children were small she appeared to be
attaining her goal. They were very ambitious, successful in school,
etc. When Louise, the oldest child, approached the age of sixteen,
her mother seems to have fallen into a state of anxiety that was
based upon her own past experiences. This anxiety was expressed
in heightened watchfulness and strictness, to which Louise reacted
with protests, and had an illegitimate child . . . The children
emotionally clung to their father and were against their mother
who tried to impose her moral standards on them . . . She could
never be kind to more than one of her older children at a time,
and always indulged her negative, aggressive emotions at the
expense of the others. Since the children thus alternated as objects
of her love, the child who had just been loved, was driven to rage,
jealousy and revenge . . . one daughter after another became promiscuous, they brought syphilis and illegitimate children into the home,
the little boys began to steal, and Mrs Mazzetti could not understand that ideal demands instead of tender harmony pushed them
in that direction.

This authoritarian upbringing and capricious sadism I spoke of are often
mixed together; to justify her anger, the mother uses the pretext
of wanting to 'shape' the child; and inversely, failure in her endeavour
exacerbates her hostility.

Masochistic devotion is another quite common attitude, and no less harmful for the child; some mothers make themselves slaves of their offspring to compensate for the emptiness in their hearts and to punish themselves for the hostility they do not want to admit; they endlessly cultivate a morbid anxiety, they cannot bear to let their child do anything on his own; they give up all pleasure, all personal life, enabling them to assume the role of victim; and from these sacrifices they derive the right to deny the child all independence; this renunciation is easily reconciled with a tyrannical will to domination; the *mater dolorosa* turns her suffering into a weapon she uses sadistically; her displays of resignation spur guilt feelings in the child, which he will often carry through his whole life: they are more harmful than aggressive displays. Tossed about, baffled, the child finds no defence mechanism: sometimes blows, sometimes tears, show him to be a criminal. The mother's main excuse is that the child is far from bringing her that satisfying self-accomplishment she was promised since childhood: she takes out on him the mystification of which she was a victim and that the child innocently exposes. She did what she wanted with her dolls; when she helped care for her sister's or a friend's baby, it was without responsibility. But now society, her husband, her mother and her own pride hold her responsible for this little foreign life as if it were her own composition: the husband in particular is irritated by the child's faults just as he is by a spoiled dinner or his wife's improper behaviour; his abstract demands often weigh heavily on the mother's relation to the child; an independent woman – thanks to her solitude, her carefree state or her authority in the household – will be much more serene than those carrying the weight of dominating demands in making her child obey. For the great difficulty is to contain within a fixed framework a mysterious existence like that of animals, turbulent and disorderly, like the forces of nature, but human nonetheless; one cannot train a child in silence like training a dog, nor persuade him with adult words: he plays on this ambiguity, pitting words against the animality of sobs and tantrums, and constraints against the insolence of language. Of course, the problem thus posed is challenging and, when she has time for it, the mother enjoys being an educator: peacefully settled in a park, the baby is still as good an excuse as he was when he nestled in her stomach; often still more or less infantile herself, she delights in being silly with him, reviving games, words, interests and joys of days gone by. But when she is washing, cooking, nursing another infant, shopping, entertaining callers, and mainly when she is taking care of her husband, the child is no more than a bothersome, harassing presence; she does not have the leisure time to 'train' him; she must first keep him from making trouble; he demolishes, tears, dirties, he is a constant danger to objects and to himself; he fidgets, he screams, he talks, he makes noise: he lives for himself; and this life disturbs his parents' life. Their interest and his do not converge: therein lies the drama. Forever burdened by him, parents inflict sacrifices on him for reasons he does not understand: they sacrifice him for their tranquillity and his own future. It is natural for him to rebel. He does not understand the explanations his mother tries to give him: she cannot penetrate his consciousness; his dreams, his phobias, his obsessions and his desires shape an opaque world: the mother can only gropingly control a being who sees these abstract laws as absurd violence from the outside. As the child grows older, this lack of comprehension remains: he enters a world of interests and values from which his mother is excluded; he often scorns her for it. The boy in particular, proud of his masculine prerogatives, laughs off a woman's orders: she insists on him doing his homework, but she cannot solve his problems, translate his Latin text; she cannot 'keep up' with him. The mother is sometimes driven to tears over this task whose difficulty the husband rarely appreciates: raising an individual with whom one does not communicate but who is nonetheless a human being; interfering in a foreign freedom that defines and affirms itself only by rebelling against you.

The situation differs, depending on whether the child is a boy or a girl; and while boys are more 'difficult', the mother generally gets along better with them. Because of the prestige woman attributes to men, and also the privileges they hold concretely, many women wish for a son. 'It's marvellous to bring a man into the world,' they say; as has been seen, they dream of giving birth to a 'hero', and the hero is obviously of the male sex. The son will be a chief, a leader of men, a soldier, a creator; he will impose his will on the face of the earth and his mother will share in his immortality; the houses she did not build, the countries she did not explore, the books she did not read, he will give to her. Through him she will possess the world: but on condition that she possesses her son. This is the source of her paradoxical attitude. Freud believes that the mother–son relationship contains the least ambivalence; but in fact in motherhood, as in marriage and love, woman has an ambiguous attitude to masculine transcendence; if her conjugal or love life has made her hostile to men, she will find satisfaction in dominating the male reduced to his infantile figure; she will treat the arrogantly pretentious sex organ with an ironic familiarity: at times she will frighten the child by announcing she will cut it off if he does not behave. Even if she is humble and more peaceful and respects the future hero in her son, she does what she can to reduce him to his immanent reality in order to ensure that he is really hers: just as she treats her husband like a child, she treats her child like a baby. It is too rational, too simple, to think she wishes to castrate her son; her dream is more contradictory: she wants him to be infinite and yet fit in the palm of her hand, dominating the whole world and kneeling before her. She encourages him to be soft, greedy, selfish, shy, sedentary, she forbids sports and friends and she makes him unsure of himself because she wants to have him for herself; but she is disappointed if he does not at the same time become an adventurer, a champion, a genius she can be proud of. There is no doubt that her influence is often harmful – as Montherlant maintains and as Mauriac demonstrates in *Génitrix*.[79] Luckily, boys can fairly easily escape this hold; customs and society encourage them to. And the mother herself is resigned to it: she knows very well that the struggle against man is unfair. She consoles herself by acting the *mater dolorosa* or by pondering the pride of having given birth to one of her conquerors.

The little girl is more wholly under the control of her mother; her claims on her daughter are greater. Their relations assume a much more dramatic character. The mother does not greet a daughter as a member of the chosen caste: she seeks a double in her. She projects on to her all the ambiguity of her relationship with her self; and when the alterity of this alter ego affirms itself, she feels betrayed. The conflicts we have discussed become all the more intensified between mother and daughter.

There are women who are satisfied enough with their lives to want to reincarnate themselves in a daughter, or at least welcome her without disappointment; they would like to give their child the same chances they had, as well as those they did not have: they will give her a happy youth. Colette traced the portrait of one of those well-balanced and generous mothers; Sido cherishes her daughter in her freedom; she fulfils her without ever making demands in return because her joy comes from her own heart. It can happen that in devoting herself to this double in whom she recognises and transcends herself, the mother ends up totally alienating herself in her; she renounces herself, her only care is for her child's happiness; she will even be egotistical and hard towards the rest of the world; she runs the danger of becoming annoying to the one she adores, as did Mme de Sévigné for Mme de Grignan; the disgruntled daughter will try to rid herself of such tyrannical devotion; often she is unsuccessful and she lives her whole life as a child, frightened of responsibilities because she has been too 'sheltered'. But it is especially a certain masochistic form of motherhood that risks weighing heavily on the young daughter. Some women feel their femininity as an absolute curse: they wish for or accept a daughter with the bitter pleasure of finding another victim; and at the same time they feel guilt at having brought her into the world; their remorse and the pity they feel for themselves through their daughter are manifested in endless anxieties; they will never take a step away from the child; they will sleep in the same bed for fifteen or twenty years; the little girl will be destroyed by the fire of this disquieting passion.

Most women both claim and detest their feminine condition; they experience it in resentment. The disgust they feel for their sex could incite them to give their daughters a virile education: they are rarely generous enough to do so. Irritated at having given birth to a female, the mother accepts her with this ambiguous curse: 'You will be a woman.' She hopes to redeem her inferiority by turning this person she considers a double into a superior being; and she also has a tendency to inflict on her the defect she has had to bear. At times she tries to impose exactly her own destiny on her child: 'What was good enough for me is good enough for you; this is the way I was brought up, so you will share my lot.' And at times, by contrast, she fiercely forbids her to resemble her: she wants her own experience to be useful, it is a way to get even. The courtesan will send her daughter to a convent, the ignorant woman will give her an education. In *In the Prison of Her Skin*, the mother who sees the hated consequence of a youthful error in her daughter tells her with fury:

Try to understand. If such a thing happened to you, I would disown you. I did not know a thing. Sin! A vague idea, sin! If a man calls you, don't go. Go on your way. Don't turn back. Do you hear me? You've been warned, this must not happen to you, and if it happened, I would have no pity, I would leave you in the gutter.[80]

We have seen that Mrs Mazzetti, because she wanted to spare her daughter from her own error, precipitated it. Stekel recounts a complex case of 'maternal hatred' of a daughter:

I know a mother who disliked at birth her fourth daughter, a quiet charming girl . . . She claimed that this child had inherited, in concentrated measure, all her father's unpleasant traits . . . The child was born to her during the year when this exalted, dreamy woman had fallen passionately in love with another man, a poet, who was courting her ... during her husband's embraces she permitted her mind to dwell on the poet, hoping that the child would thus become endowed with her beloved's traits – as in Goethe's *Elective Affinities*. However, the child looked so much like its father, from the moment of its birth, that its paternity was obvious ... She saw in the child a reflection of herself – a reflection of the dreamy, tender, yielding, sensual side of herself. She despised these qualities, scorned them in herself. She would have preferred to have been strong, unyielding, vigorous, prudish and energetic. Thus she hated herself even more than she hated her husband through her hatred of the child.[81]

It is when the girl grows up that real conflicts arise; we have seen that she wishes to affirm her autonomy from her mother: this is, in her mother's eyes, a mark of detestable ingratitude; she obstinately tries to 'tame' this determination that is lurking; she cannot accept that her double becomes *an other*. The pleasure man savours in women – feeling absolutely superior – is something a woman experiences only towards her children, and her daughters in particular; she feels frustration if she renounces these privileges and her authority. Whether she is a passionate or a hostile mother, her child's independence ruins her hopes. She is doubly jealous: of the world that takes her daughter, and of her daughter who, in conquering part of the world, robs her of it. This jealousy first involves the father–daughter relationship; sometimes the mother uses the child to keep her husband home: if this fails, she is vexed, but if her manoeuvre succeeds, she is sure to revive her infantile complex in an inverted form: she becomes irritated by her daughter as she was once by her own mother; she sulks, she feels abandoned and misunderstood. A French woman, married to a foreigner who loved his daughters very much, angrily said one day: 'I've had enough of living with these "wogs"!' Often the eldest daughter, the father's favourite, is the target of the mother's persecution. The mother heaps the worst chores on her, demands a seriousness beyond her age: since she is a rival, she will be treated as an adult; she too will learn that 'life is not a storybook romance, everything is not rosy, you can't do whatever you please, you're not on earth to have fun.' Very often, the mother strikes the child for no reason, simply 'to teach her a lesson'; she wants to show her she is still in charge: for what vexes her the most is that she does not have any real superiority to set against a girl of eleven or twelve; the latter can already perform household tasks perfectly well, she is 'a little woman'; she even has a liveliness, curiosity and lucidity that, in many regards, makes her superior to adult women. The mother likes to rule over her feminine universe without competition; she wants to be unique, irreplaceable; and yet here her young assistant reduces her to the pure generality of her function. She scolds her daughter sternly if, after being away for two days, she finds her household in disorder; but she goes into fits of anger if it so happens that family life continued along well without her. She cannot accept that her daughter will really become her double, a substitute of herself. Yet it is still more intolerable that she should boldly assert herself as an other. She systematically detests the girlfriends in whom her daughter seeks succour against family oppression, friends who 'spur her on'; she criticises them, prevents her daughter from seeing them too often or even uses the pretext of their 'bad influence' to radically forbid her to be with them. All influence that is not her own is bad; she has a particular animosity towards women of her own age – teachers, girlfriends' mothers – towards whom her daughter turns her affection: she declares these sentiments absurd or unhealthy. At times, gaiety, silliness or children's games and laughter are enough to exasperate her; she more readily accepts this of boys; they are exercising their male privilege, as is natural, and she has long given up this impossible competition. But why should this other woman enjoy advantages that she has been refused? Imprisoned in the snares of seriousness, she envies all occupations and amusements that wrench her daughter from the boredom of the household; this escape makes a sham of all the values to which she has sacrificed herself. The older the child gets, the more this bitterness eats at the mother's heart; every year brings the mother closer to her decline; from year to year the youthful body develops and flourishes; this future opening up to her daughter seems to be stolen from the mother; this is why some mothers become irritated when their daughters first get their period: they begrudge their consecration from now on as newly-become women. This new woman is offered still-indefinite possibilities in contrast to the repetition and routine that are the lot of the older woman: these chances are what the mother envies and detests; not able to take them herself, she tries to diminish or suppress them: she keeps her daughter home, watches over her, tyrannises her, dresses her like a frump on purpose, refuses her all pastimes, goes into rages if the adolescent puts on makeup, if she 'goes out'; she turns all her own rage towards life against this young life who is embarking on a new future; she tries to humiliate the girl, she ridicules her ventures, she bullies her. Open war is often declared between them, and it is usually the younger woman who wins as time is on her side; but victory has a guilty taste: her mother's attitude gives rise to both revolt and remorse; her mother's presence alone makes her the guilty one: we have seen how this sentiment can seriously affect her future. Willy-nilly, the mother accepts her defeat in the end; when her daughter becomes an adult, they reestablish a more or less distressed friendship. But one of them will forever be disappointed and frustrated; the other will often be haunted by a curse.

We will return later to the older woman's relations with her adult children: but it is clear that for their first twenty years they occupy a most important place in the mother's life. A dangerous misconception about two currently accepted preconceived ideas strongly emerges from the descriptions we have made. The first is that motherhood is enough in all cases to fulfil a woman: this is not at all true. Many are the mothers who are unhappy, bitter and unsatisfied. The example of Sophia Tolstoy, who gave birth more than twelve times, is significant; she never stops repeating, all through her diary, that everything seems useless and empty in the world and in herself. Children bring a kind of masochistic peace for her. 'With the children, I do not feel young anymore. I am calm and happy.' Renouncing her youth, her beauty and her personal life brings her some calm; she feels old, justified. 'The feeling of being indispensable to them is my greatest happiness.' They are weapons enabling her to reject her husband's superiority. 'My only resources, my only weapons to establish equality between us, are the children, energy, joy, health . . .' But they are absolutely not enough to give meaning to an existence worn down by boredom. On 25 January 1875, after a moment of exaltation, she writes:

*I too want and can do everything.** But as soon as this feeling goes away, I realise that I don't want and can't do anything, except care for my babies, eat, drink, sleep, love my husband and my children, which should really be happiness but which makes me sad and like yesterday makes me want to cry.

And eleven years later:

I devote myself energetically to my children's upbringing and education and have an ardent desire to do it well. But my God! How impatient and irascible I am, how I yell! . . . This eternal fighting with the children is so sad.

* S. Tolstoy's emphasis.

The mother's relation with her children is defined within the overall context of her life; it depends on her relations with her husband, her past, her occupations, herself; it is a fatal and absurd error to claim to see a child as a panacea. This is also Helene Deutsch's conclusion in the work I have often cited, where she studies phenomena of motherhood on the basis of her experience in psychiatry. She ranks this function highly; she believes woman accomplishes herself totally through it: but under the condition that it is freely assumed and sincerely desired; the young woman must be in a psychological, moral and material situation that allows her to bear the responsibility; if not, the consequences will be disastrous. In particular, it is criminal to advise having a child as a remedy for melancholia or neuroses; it causes unhappiness for mother and child. Only a balanced, healthy woman, conscious of her responsibilities, is capable of becoming a 'good mother'.

I have said that the curse weighing on marriage is that individuals too often join together in their weakness and not in their strength, that each one asks of the other rather than finding pleasure in giving. It is an even more deceptive lure to dream of attaining through a child a plenitude, warmth and value one is incapable of creating oneself; it can bring joy only to the woman capable of disinterestedly wanting the happiness of another, to the woman who seeks to transcend her own existence without any reward for her. To be sure, a child is an undertaking one can validly aspire to; but like any other undertaking, it does not represent a justification in itself; and it must be desired for itself, not for hypothetical benefits. Stekel quite rightly says:

> Children are not substitutes for one's disappointed love; they are not substitutes for one's thwarted ideal in life, children are not mere material to fill out an empty existence. Children are a responsibility and an opportunity. Children are the loftiest blossoms upon the tree of untrammeled love ... They are neither playthings, nor tools for the fulfillment of parental needs or ungratified ambitions. Children are obligations; they should be brought up so as to become happy human beings.

Such an obligation is not at all *natural*: nature could never dictate a moral choice; this implies an engagement. To have a child is to take on a commitment; if the mother shrinks from it, she commits an offence against human existence, against a freedom; but no one can impose it on her. The relation of parents to children, like that of spouses, must be freely chosen. And it is not even true that the child is a privileged accomplishment for a woman; it is often said that a woman is coquettish, or amorous, or lesbian, or ambitious as a result of 'being childless'; her sexual life, her goals and the values she pursues are deemed to be substitutes for the child. In fact, from the beginning there is indetermination: one can just as well say that lacking love, an occupation, or the power to satisfy her homosexual tendencies, a woman wants to have a child. A social and artificial morality hides behind this pseudo-naturalism. That the child is the ultimate end for woman is an affirmation worthy of an advertising slogan.

The second preconceived idea immediately following the first is that the child is sure to find happiness in his mother's arms. There is no such thing as an 'unnatural mother', since maternal love has nothing natural about it: but precisely because of that, there are bad mothers. And one of the great truths that psychoanalysis has proclaimed is the danger 'normal' parents constitute for a child. The complexes, obsessions and neuroses adults suffer from have their roots in their family past; parents who have their own conflicts, quarrels and dramas are the least desirable company for children. Deeply marked by the paternal household, they approach their own children through complexes and frustrations: and this chain of misery perpetuates itself indefinitely. In particular, maternal sadomasochism creates guilt feelings for the daughter that will express themselves in sadomasochistic behaviour towards her own children, without end. There is extravagant bad faith in the conflation of contempt for women and respect shown for mothers. It is a criminal paradox to deny women all public activity, to close masculine careers to them, to proclaim them incapable in all domains, and to nonetheless entrust to them the most delicate and most serious of all undertakings: the formation of a human being. There are many women who, out of custom and tradition, are still refused education, culture, responsibilities and activities that are the privileges of men, and in whose arms, nevertheless, babies are placed without scruple, as in earlier life they were consoled for their inferiority to boys with dolls; they are deprived of living their lives; as compensation, they are allowed to play with flesh-and-blood toys. A woman would have to be perfectly happy or a saint to resist the temptation of abusing her rights. Montesquieu was perhaps right when he said it would be better to entrust women with the government of the state than with a family; for as soon as she is given the opportunity, woman is as reasonable and efficient as man: it is in abstract thought, in concerted action that she most easily rises above her sex; it is far more difficult in this day and age to free herself from her feminine past, to find an emotional balance that nothing in her situation favours. Man is also much more balanced and rational in his work than at home; he calculates with mathematical precision: he 'lets himself go' with his wife, becoming illogical, a liar, capricious; likewise, she 'lets herself go' with her child. And this self-indulgence is more dangerous because she can better defend herself against her husband than the child can defend himself against her. It would obviously be better for the child if his mother were a complete person and not a mutilated one, a woman who finds in her work and her relations with the group a self-accomplishment she could not attain through his tyranny; and it would be preferable also for the child to be left infinitely less to his parents than he is now, that his studies and amusements take place with other children under the control of adults whose links with him are only impersonal and dispassionate.

Even in cases where the child is a treasure within a happy or at least balanced life, he cannot be the full extent of his mother's horizons. He does not wrest her from her immanence; she shapes his flesh, she supports him, she cares for him: she can do no more than create a situation that solely the child's freedom can transcend; when she invests in his future, it is again by proxy that she transcends herself through the universe and time; that is, once again she dooms herself to dependency. Not only his ingratitude but the failure of her son will refute all of her hopes: as in marriage or love, she puts the care of justifying her life in the hands of another, whereas the only authentic behaviour is to assume it freely herself. Woman's inferiority, as we have seen, originally came from the fact that she was restricted to repeating life, while man invented reasons for living, in his eyes more essential than the pure facticity of existence; confining woman to motherhood is the perpetuation of this situation. But today she demands participation in the movement by which humanity ceaselessly tries to find justification by surpassing itself; she can only consent to give life if life has meaning; she cannot try to be a mother without playing a role in economic, political or social life. It is not the same thing to produce cannon fodder, slaves, victims, as to give birth to free men. In a properly organised society where the child would in great part be taken charge of by the group, where the mother would be cared for and helped, motherhood would absolutely not be incompatible with women's work. On the contrary, a woman who works – farmer, chemist or writer – has the easiest pregnancy because she is not centred on her own person; it is the woman who has the richest personal life who will give the most to her child and who will ask for the least, she who acquires real human values through effort and struggle will be the most fit to bring up children. If too often today a woman has a hard time reconciling the interests of her children with a profession that demands long hours away from home and all her strength, it is because, on the one hand, woman's work is still too often a kind of slavery; on the other hand, no effort has been made to assure children's health, care and education outside the home. This is social neglect: but it is a sophism to justify it by pretending that a law was written in heaven or in the bowels of the earth that requires that the mother and child belong to each other exclusively; this mutual belonging in reality only constitutes a double and harmful oppression.

It is a mystification to maintain that woman becomes man's equal through motherhood. Psychoanalysts have tried hard to prove that the child provides the equivalent of the penis for her: but enviable as this attribute may be, no one believes that possessing one can justify an existence or that such possession can be a supreme end in itself. There has been an enormous amount of talk about the sacred rights of women, but being a mother is not how women gained the right to vote; the unwed mother is still scorned; it is only in marriage that the mother is glorified – in other words, as long as she is subordinate to the husband. As long as he is the economic head of the family, even though it is she who cares for the children, they depend far more on him than on her. This is why, as has been seen, the mother's relationship with her children is deeply influenced by the one she maintains with her husband.

So conjugal relations, homemaking and motherhood form a whole in which all the parts are determinant; tenderly united to her husband, the wife can cheerfully carry out the duties of the home; happy with her children, she will be understanding of her husband. But this harmony is not easy to attain, for the different functions assigned to the wife conflict with each other. Women's magazines amply advise the housewife on the art of maintaining her sexual attraction while doing the dishes, of remaining elegant throughout pregnancy, of reconciling flirtation, motherhood and economy; but if she conscientiously follows their advice, she will soon be overwhelmed and disfigured by care; it is very difficult to remain desirable with chapped hands and a body deformed by pregnancies; this is why a woman in love often feels resentment of the children who ruin her seduction and deprive her of her husband's caresses; if she is, by contrast, deeply maternal, she is jealous of the man who also claims the children as his. But then, the perfect homemaker, as has been seen, contradicts the movement of life: the child is the enemy of waxed floors. Maternal love is often lost in the reprimands and outbursts that underlie the concern for a well-kept home. It is not surprising that the woman torn between these contradictions often spends her day in a state of nervousness and bitterness; she always loses on some level, and her gains are precarious, they do not count as any sure success. She can never save herself by her work alone; it keeps her occupied, but does not constitute her justification: her justification rests on outside freedoms. The wife shut up in her home cannot establish her existence on her own; she does not have the means to affirm herself in her singularity: and this singularity is consequently not acknowledged. For Arabs or Indians, and in many rural populations, a wife is only a female servant appreciated according to the work she provides, and who is replaced without regret if she disappears. In modern civilisation, she is more or less individualised in her husband's eyes; but unless she completely renounces her self, swallowed up like Natasha in a passionate and tyrannical devotion to her family, she suffers from being reduced to pure generality. She is *the* mistress of the house, the wife, the unique and indistinct mother; Natasha delights in this supreme self-effacement, and in rejecting all confrontation, she negates others. But the modern Western woman, by contrast, wants to be noticed by others as *this* mistress of the house, *this* wife, *this* mother, *this* woman. Herein lies the satisfaction she will seek in her social life.

CHAPTER 7

Social Life

The family is not a closed community: notwithstanding its separateness, it establishes relations with other social units; the home is not only an 'interior' in which the couple is confined; it is also the expression of its living standard, its wealth, its tastes: it must be exhibited for others to see. It is essentially the woman who will organise this social life. The man is connected to the community as producer and citizen, by ties of an organic solidarity based on the division of labour; the couple is a social person, defined by the family, class, milieu and race to which it belongs, attached by ties of mechanical solidarity to groups socially similar to themselves; the woman is the one most likely to embody this most purely: the husband's professional relations often do not reflect his social level, while the wife, who does not have the obligations brought about by work, can limit herself to the company of her peers; besides, she has the leisure, through her 'visits' and 'receptions', to promote these relations, useless in practice, and that, of course, matter only in categories of people wanting to hold their rank in the social hierarchy, that is, who consider themselves superior to certain others. She delights in showing off her home and even herself, which her husband and children do not see because they have a vested interest in them. Her social duty, which is to 'represent', will become part of the pleasure she has in showing herself to others.

First, she has to represent herself; at home, going about her occupations, she merely dresses: to go out, to entertain, she 'dresses up'. Dressing has a twofold significance: it is meant to show the woman's social standing (her standard of living, her wealth, the social class she belongs to) but at the same time it concretises feminine narcissism; it is her uniform and her attire; the woman who suffers from not *doing* anything thinks she is expressing her *being* through her dress. Beauty treatments and dressing are kinds of work that allow her to appropriate her person as she appropriates her home through housework; she thus believes that she is choosing and re-creating her own self. And social customs encourage her to alienate herself in her image. Like his body, a man's clothes must convey his transcendence and not attract attention;* for him neither elegance nor beauty constitutes him as object; thus he does not usually consider his appearance as a reflection of his being. By contrast, society even requires woman to make herself an erotic object. The goal of the fashion to which she is in thrall is not to reveal her as an autonomous individual but, on the contrary, to cut her from her transcendence so as to offer her as a prey to male desires: fashion does not serve to fulfil her projects but on the contrary to thwart them. A skirt is less convenient than trousers and high-heeled shoes impede walking; the least practical dresses and high heels, the most fragile hats and stockings, are the most elegant; whether the outfit disguises, deforms or moulds the body, in any case, it delivers it to view. This explains why dressing is an enchanting game for the little girl who wants to look at herself; later on her child's autonomy rises up against the constraints of light-coloured muslin and patent-leather shoes; at the awkward age she is torn between the desire and the refusal to show herself off; once she has accepted her vocation as sex object, she enjoys adorning herself.

As we have said,[†] by adorning herself, woman is akin to nature, while attesting to nature's need for artifice; she becomes flower and jewel for man and for herself as well. Before giving him rippling water or the soft warmth of furs, she takes them for herself. More intimately than her knick-knacks, rugs, cushions and bouquets, she prizes feathers, pearls, brocade and silks that she mingles with her flesh; their shimmer and their gentle contact compensate for the harshness of the erotic universe that is her lot: the more her sensuality is unsatiated, the more importance she gives to it. If many lesbians dress in a masculine way, it is not only out of imitation of males and defiance of society: they do not need the caresses of velvet and satin because they grasp such passive qualities[‡] on a feminine body. The woman given to the harsh masculine embrace – even if she savours it and even more if she gets no pleasure from it – can embrace no carnal prey other than her own body: she

* See Vol. I. Homosexuals are an exception as they specifically grasp themselves as sexual objects; dandies also, who must be studied separately. Today, in particular, the 'zoot-suitism' of the American blacks who dress in light-coloured, noticeable suits is explained with very complex reasons.

† See Vol. I, Part Three, 'Myths', Chapter 1.

‡ Sandor, whose case Krafft-Ebing detailed, adored well-dressed women but did not 'dress up'.

perfumes it to change it into a flower, and the shine of the diamonds she puts around her neck is no different from that of her skin; in order to possess them, she identifies with all the riches of the world. She covets not only sensual treasures but sometimes also sentimental values and ideals. This jewel is a souvenir, that one is a symbol. Some women make themselves bouquets, aviaries; others are museums and still others hieroglyphs. Georgette Leblanc tells us in her memoirs, evoking her youth:

> I was always dressed like a painting. I walked around in Van Eyck, in an allegory of Rubens or in the Virgin of Memling. I still see myself crossing a street in Brussels one winter day in a dress of amethyst velvet embellished with old silver binding taken from some tunic. Dragging insouciantly my long train behind me, I was conscientiously sweeping the pavement. My folly of yellow fur framed my blond hair but the most unusual thing was the diamond placed on the frontlet on my forehead. Why all this? Simply because it pleased me and so I thought I was living outside of all convention. The more I was laughed at as I went by, the more extravagant my burlesque inventions. I would have been ashamed to change anything in my appearance just because I was being mocked. That would have seemed to me to be a degrading capitulation . . . At home it was something else again. The angels of Gozzoli, Fra Angelico, Burne Jones and Watts were my models. I was always attired in azure and aurora; my flowing dresses spread out in manifold trains around me.

The best examples of this magical appropriation of the universe are found in mental institutions. A woman who does not control her love for precious objects and symbols forgets her own appearance and risks dressing outlandishly. The very little girl thus sees in dressing a disguise that changes her into a fairy, a queen, a flower; she thinks she is beautiful as soon as she is laden with garlands and ribbons because she identifies with these flashy clothes; charmed by the colour of a piece of material, the naive young girl does not notice the wan complexion it gives her; one also finds this excessive bad taste in women artists or intellectuals more fascinated by the outside world than conscious of their own appearance: infatuated by these old materials and antique jewels, they delight in conjuring up China or the Middle Ages and give the mirror no more than a cursory or passing glance. It is sometimes surprising to see the strange getups elderly women like: tiaras, lace, bright dresses, and extravagant necklaces unfortunately draw attention to their ravaged features. Now that they have given up seduction, clothes often become once again a gratuitous game for them as in their childhood. An elegant woman by contrast can seek sensual or aesthetic pleasures in her clothes if need be, but she must reconcile them in harmony with her image: the colour of her dress will flatter her complexion, the cut will emphasise or improve her figure; arrayed, she complaisantly cherishes her adorned self and not the objects that adorn her.

Dressing is not only adornment: it expresses, as we have said, woman's social situation. Only the prostitute whose function is exclusively that of a sex object displays herself exclusively in this light; in the past it was her saffron hair and the flowers that dotted her dress; today it is her high heels, skimpy satin, harsh makeup and heavy perfume that are the signature of her profession. Any other woman is criticised for dressing 'like a strumpet'. Her erotic qualities are integrated into social life and can only appear in this toned-down form. But it must be emphasised that decency does not mean dressing with strict modesty. A woman who teases male desire too blatantly is considered vulgar; but a woman who is seen to repudiate this is disreputable as well: she is seen as wanting to look like a man: she's a lesbian; or to single herself out: she's an eccentric; refusing her role as object, she defies society: she's an anarchist. If she simply does not want to be noticed, she must still conserve her femininity. Custom dictates the compromise between exhibitionism and modesty; sometimes it is the neckline and sometimes the ankle that the 'virtuous woman' must hide; sometimes the young girl has the right to highlight her charms so as to attract suitors, while the married woman gives up all adornment: such is the usage in many peasant civilisations; sometimes young girls have to dress in flowing clothes of baby colours and modest cut, while their elders are allowed tight-fitting dresses, heavy material, rich hues and daring cuts; on a sixteen-year-old, black stands out because the rule at that age is not to wear it.* One must, of course, conform to these laws; but in any case, and even in the most austere circles, woman's sexual attributes will be emphasised: the pastor's wife curls her hair, wears some makeup, is discreetly fashion-conscious, indicating through the attention to her physical charm that she accepts her female role. This integration of eroticism into social life is particularly obvious

---

* In a film set last century – and rather a stupid one – Bette Davis created a scandal by wearing a red dress to the ball whereas white was de rigueur until marriage. Her act was considered a rebellion against the established order.

in the 'evening gown'. To mark a social gathering, that is, luxury and waste, these dresses must be costly and delicate, they must be as uncomfortable as possible; skirts are long and so wide or so complicated that they impede walking; under the jewels, ruffles, sequins, flowers, feathers and false hair, woman is changed into a flesh-doll; even this flesh is exposed; just as flowers bloom gratuitously, the woman displays her shoulders, back, bosom; except in orgies, the man must not indicate that he covets her: he only has the right to looks and the embraces of the dance; but he can take delight in being the king of a world of such tender treasures. From one man to another, the festivity takes on the appearance of a potlatch; each of them gives the vision of this body that is his property to all the others as a gift. In her evening dress, the woman is disguised as woman for all the males' pleasure and the pride of her owner.

This social significance of the toilette allows woman to express her attitude to society by the way she dresses; subject to the established order, she confers on herself a discreet and tasteful personality; many nuances are possible: she will make herself fragile, childlike, mysterious, candid, austere, gay, poised, a little daring, self-effacing, as she chooses. Or, on the contrary, she will affirm her rejection of conventions by her originality. It is striking that in many novels the 'liberated' woman distinguishes herself by an audacity in dressing that emphasises her character as sex object, and thus of dependence: so in Edith Wharton's *The Age of Innocence*, the young divorced woman with an adventuresome past and a bold heart is first presented with a plunging décolletage; the whiff of scandal she provokes becomes the tangible reflection of her scorn for conformity. Thus the girl will enjoy dressing as a woman, the older woman as a little girl, the courtesan as a sophisticated woman of the world and the woman of the world as a vamp. Even if every woman dresses according to her status, there is still play in it. Artifice like art is situated in the imagination. Not only do girdle, bra, hair dyes and makeup disguise body and face; but as soon as she is 'dressed up', the least sophisticated woman is not concerned with perception: she is like a painting, a statue, like an actor on stage, an analogon through which is suggested an absent subject who is her character but is not she. It is this confusion with an unreal object – necessary, perfect like a hero in a novel, like a portrait or a bust – that flatters her; she strives to alienate herself in it and so to appear frozen, justified to herself.

Page by page we see Marie Bashkirtseff in *Intimate Writings*[82] endlessly remaking her image. She does not spare us any of her dresses:

for each new outfit, she believes she is an other and she adores herself
anew.

> I took one of Mama's great shawls, I made a slit for my head and
> I sewed up the two sides. This shawl that falls in classic folds gives
> me an oriental, biblical, strange look.
>   I go to the Laferrières' and in just three hours Caroline makes
> me a dress in which I look as if I'm enveloped in a cloud. This is
> a piece of English crepe that she drapes over me, making me thin,
> elegant, and long.
>   Enveloped in a warm wool dress hanging in harmonious folds,
> a character out of Lefebvre who knows so well how to draw these
> lithe and young bodies in modest fabrics.

This refrain is repeated day after day: 'I was charming in black . . . In
grey, I was charming . . . I was in white, charming.'

Mme de Noailles, who also accorded much importance to her dress,
speaks sadly in her *Memoirs* of the crisis of a failed dress:

> I loved the vividness of the colours, their daring contrast, a dress
> seemed like a landscape, the beginning of adventure. Just as I was
> putting on the dress made by unsure hands, I suffered from all the
> defects I saw.

If the toilette has so much importance for many women, it is
because they are under the illusion that it provides them both with
the world and their own self. A German novel, *The Artificial Silk Girl*,*
tells the story of a poor girl's passion for a vair coat; sensually she
loved the caressing warmth of it, the furry tenderness; in precious
skins it is her transfigured self she cherishes; she finally possesses the
beauty of the world she had never embraced and the radiant destiny
that had never been hers.

> And then I saw a coat hanging from a hook, a fur so soft, so smooth,
> so tender, so grey, so shy: I felt like kissing it I loved it so much. It
> looked like consolation and All Saints' Day and total safety, like the
> sky. It was genuine vair. Silently, I took off my raincoat and put on
> the vair. This fur was like a diamond on my skin that loved it and

* By Irmgard Keun.

what one loves, one doesn't give it back once one has it. Inside, a Moroccan crepe lining, pure silk, with hand embroidery. The coat enveloped me and spoke more than I to Hubert's heart . . . I am so elegant in this fur. It is like the rare man who would make me precious through his love for me. This coat wants me and I want it: we have each other.

As woman is an object, it is obvious that how she is adorned and dressed affects her intrinsic value. It is not pure frivolousness for her to attach so much importance to silk stockings, gloves and a hat: keeping her rank is an imperious obligation. In America, a great part of the working woman's budget is devoted to beauty care and clothes; in France, this expense is lighter; nevertheless, a woman is all the more respected if she 'presents well'; the more she needs to find work, the more useful it is to look well-off: elegance is a weapon, a sign, a banner of respect, a letter of recommendation.

It is a servitude; the values it confers have a price; they sometimes have such a high price that a detective catches a socialite or an actress shoplifting perfumes, silk stockings or underwear. Many women prostitute themselves or 'get help' in order to keep themselves well dressed; it is their clothes that determine their need for money. Being well dressed also requires time and care; it is a chore that is sometimes a source of positive joy: in this area there is also the 'discovery of hidden treasures', trades, ruses, arrangements and invention; a clever woman can even be creative. Showroom days – especially the sales – are frenetic adventures. A new dress is a celebration in itself. Makeup and hair are substitutes for a work of art. Today, more than before,* woman knows the joys of shaping her body by sports, gymnastics, swimming, massage and diets; she decides on her weight, her figure and her complexion; modern beauty treatments allow her to combine beauty and activity: she has the right to toned muscles, she refuses to put on weight; in physical culture, she affirms herself as subject; this gives her a kind of liberation from her contingent flesh; but this liberation easily lapses back into dependence. The Hollywood star triumphs over nature: but she finds herself a passive object in the producer's hands.

Next to these victories in which woman rightly takes delight, taking

---

* According to recent studies, however, it seems that women's gymnasiums in France are almost empty; it was especially between 1920 and 1940 that French women indulged in physical culture. Household problems weigh too heavy on them at this time.

care of one's appearance implies – like household tasks – a fight against time, because her body too is an object eroded by time. Colette Audry describes this fight, comparable to the one the housewife engages against dust.*

Already it was no longer the compact flesh of youth; along her arms and thighs the pattern of her muscles showed through a layer of fat and slightly flabby skin. Upset, she once again changed her schedule: her day would begin with half an hour of gymnastics and in the evening, before getting into bed, a quarter of an hour of massage. She took to reading medical books and fashion magazines, to watching her waistline. She prepared fruit juices, took a laxative from time to time and did the dishes with rubber gloves. Her two concerns – rejuvenating her body and refurbishing her home – finally became one so that one day she would reach a kind of steadiness, a kind of dead centre ... the world would be as if stopped, suspended outside of ageing and decay ... At the swimming pool, she now took serious lessons to improve her style and the beauty magazines kept her breathless with infinitely renewed recipes. Ginger Rogers confides to us: 'I brush my hair 100 strokes every morning, it takes exactly two and a half minutes and I have silky hair ...' How to get thinner ankles: stand on your toes every day, thirty times in a row, without putting your heels down, this exercise only takes a minute; what is a minute in a day? Another time it is an oil bath for nails, lemon paste for hands, crushed strawberries on cheeks.

Routine, here again, turns beauty care and wardrobe maintenance into chores. The horror of degradation that all living change involves in some cold or frustrated women arouses a horror of life itself: they seek to preserve themselves as others preserve furniture or jam; this negative stubbornness makes them enemies of their own existence and hostile to others: good meals damage their figures, wine spoils their complexions, smiling too much gives you wrinkles, the sun hurts the skin, rest makes you lethargic, work wears you out, love gives you circles under your eyes, kisses make your cheeks red, caresses deform your breasts, embraces shrivel the flesh, pregnancies disfigure your face and body; you know how young mothers angrily push away the child marvelling at

* *Playing a Losing Game.*

their ball gown. 'Don't touch me, your hands are all sticky, you're going to get me dirty'; the appearance-conscious rejects her husband's or lover's ardour with the same rebuffs. Just as one covers furniture with loose covers, she would like to withdraw from men, the world, time. But none of these precautions prevents the appearance of grey hair and crow's-feet. Starting from youth, woman knows this destiny is inevitable. And, regardless of her vigilance, she is a victim of accidents: a drop of wine falls on her dress, a cigarette burns it; and so the creature of luxury and parties who smilingly struts about the living room disappears: she turns into the serious and hard housewife; suddenly one discovers that her toilette was not a bouquet of flowers, fireworks, a gratuitous and perishable splendour destined to generously light up an instant: it is an asset, capital, an investment, it demands sacrifices; its loss is an irreparable disaster. Stains, holes, dresses that are failures and ruined perms are far more serious catastrophes than a burnt roast or a broken vase: because the coquettish woman is not only alienated in things, she wants to be a thing and without an intermediary she feels insecure in the world. The relations she maintains with her dressmaker and milliner, her impatience, her demands are manifestations of her seriousness and insecurity. A successful dress creates in her the character of her dreams; but in a soiled, ruined outfit, she feels demeaned.

Marie Bashkirtseff writes: 'My mood, my manners, the expression on my face, everything depended on my dress.' And then: 'Either you have to go around naked, or you have to dress according to your body, taste and character. When they are not right, I feel gauche, common and therefore humiliated. What happens to the mood and mind? They think about clothes and so one becomes stupid, boring and one does not know what to do with oneself.'

Many women prefer to miss a party than go badly dressed, even if they are not going to be noticed.

However, although some women affirm: 'I dress for myself only,' we have seen that even in narcissism the gaze of the other is involved. Only in asylums do the fashion-conscious stubbornly keep their faith in absent gazes; normally, they demand witnesses. After ten years of marriage, Sophia Tolstoy writes:

> I want people to admire me and say how pretty I am, and I want Lyova to see and hear them too . . . I hate people who tell me I am beautiful. I never believed them . . . what would be the point of it? My darling little Petya loves his old nanny just as much as he would

love a great beauty . . . I am having my hair curled today, and have
been happily imagining how nice it will look, even though nobody
will see me and it is quite unnecessary. I adore ribbons, and I would
like a new leather belt – and now I have written this I feel like
crying . . .[83]

Husbands do not perform this role well. Here again the husband's
demands are duplicitous. If his wife is too attractive, he becomes
jealous; but every husband is more or less King Candaules; he wants
his wife to make him proud; for her to be elegant, pretty or at least
'presentable'; if not, he will humorously tell her these words of Pére
Ubu: 'You are quite ugly today! Is it because we are expecting
company?' In marriage, as we have seen, erotic and social values are
not very compatible; such antagonism is reflected in this situation.
The wife who accentuates her sexual attraction is considered vulgar
in her husband's eyes; he criticises this boldness that would seduce
him in an unknown woman and this criticism kills all desire for her;
if his wife dresses decently, he approves but coldly: he does not find
her attractive and vaguely reproaches her for it. Because of that, he
rarely looks at her on his own account: he inspects her through the
eyes of others. 'What will they say about her?' He does not see clearly
because he projects his spousal point of view onto others. Nothing
is more irritating for a woman than to see him appreciate in another
the dresses or way of dressing he criticises in her. Naturally, of course,
he is too close to her to see her; her face is immutable for him; nor
does he notice her outfits or hairstyle. Even a husband in love or an
infatuated lover is often indifferent to a woman's clothes. If they love
her ardently in her nudity, the most attractive adornments merely
disguise her; and they will cherish her whether badly dressed, tired
or dazzling. If they no longer love her, the most flattering dresses
will be of no avail. Clothes can be an instrument of conquest but not
a weapon of defence; their art is to create mirages, they offer the
viewer an imaginary object: in the erotic embrace and in daily relations mirages fade; conjugal feelings like physical love exist in the
realm of reality. Women do not dress for the loved man. Dorothy
Parker, in one of her short stories,*[84] describes a young woman who,
waiting impatiently for her husband, who is on leave, decides to make
herself beautiful to welcome him:

* 'The Lovely Eva'.

She bought a new dress; black – he liked black dresses – simple –
he liked plain dresses – and so expensive that she would not think
of its price . . .

'Do you . . . like my dress?'

'Oh yes,' he said. 'I always liked that dress on you.'

It was as if she turned to wood. 'This dress,' she said, enunciating with insulting distinctness, 'is brand new. I have never had
it on before in my life. In case you are interested, I bought it especially for this occasion.'

'I'm sorry, honey,' he said. 'Oh, sure, now I see it's not the other
one at all. I think it's great. I like you in black.'

'At moments like this,' she said, 'I almost wish I were in it for
another reason.'

It is often said that women dress to arouse jealousy in other women:
this jealousy is really a clear sign of success; but this is not its only aim.
Through envious or admiring approbation, woman seeks an absolute
affirmation of her beauty, her elegance, her taste: of herself. She dresses
to display herself; she displays herself to make herself be. She thus submits
herself to a painful dependence; the housewife's devotion is useful even
if it is not recognised; the effort of the fashion-conscious woman is in
vain unless consciousness is involved. She is looking for a definitive valorisation of herself; it is this attempt at the absolute that makes her quest
so exhausting; criticised by only one voice – this hat *is* not beautiful –
she is flattered by a compliment but a contradiction demolishes her; and
as the absolute only manifests itself in an indefinite series of appearances, she will never have entirely won; this is why the fashion-conscious
woman is sensitive; it is also why some pretty and much-admired women
can be sadly convinced they are neither beautiful nor elegant, that this
supreme approbation of an unknown judge is exactly what is missing:
they are aiming for an in-itself that is unrealisable. Rare are the gorgeous
stylish women who embody in themselves the laws of elegance, whom
no one can fault because they are the ones who define success or failure;
as long as their reign endures, they can think of themselves as an exemplary success. What is unfortunate is that this success serves nothing and
no one.

Clothes immediately imply going out and receptions, and besides,
that is their original intent. The woman parades her new outfit from
place to place and invites other women to see her reign over her 'interior'. In certain particularly important situations, the husband accompanies

her on her 'calls'; but most often she fulfils her 'social obligations' while he is at work. The implacable ennui weighing on these gatherings has been described hundreds of times. It comes from the fact that these women gathered there by 'social obligations' have nothing to say to each other. There is no common interest linking the lawyer's wife to the doctor's – and none between Dr Dupont's and Dr Durand's. It is bad taste in a general conversation to talk of one's children's pranks or problems with the help. What is left is discussion of the weather, the latest novel, and a few general ideas borrowed from their husbands. This custom of 'calling' is tending to disappear; but the chore of the 'call' in various forms survives in France. American women often replace conversation with bridge, which is an advantage only for women who enjoy this game.

However, social life has more attractive forms than carrying out this idle duty of etiquette. Entertaining is not just welcoming others into one's own home; it is changing one's home into an enchanted domain; the social event is both festivity and potlatch. The mistress of the house displays her treasures: silver, table linen, crystal; she dresses the house with flowers: ephemeral and useless, flowers exemplify the gratuitousness of occasions that mean expenses and luxury; blooming in vases, doomed to a rapid death, flowers are ceremonial bonfires, incense and myrrh, libation, sacrifice. The table is laden with fine food, precious wines; it means satisfying the guests' needs, it is a question of inventing gracious gifts that anticipate their desires; the meal becomes a mysterious cere-mony. Virginia Woolf emphasises this aspect in this passage from *Mrs Dalloway*:[85]

And so there began a soundless and exquisite passing to and fro through swing doors of aproned, white-capped maids, handmaidens not of necessity but adepts in a mystery or grand deception prac-tised by hostesses in Mayfair from one-thirty to two, when, with a wave of the hand, the traffic ceases, and there rises instead this profound illusion in the first place about the food – how it is not paid for; and then that the table spreads itself voluntarily with glass and silver, little mats, saucers of red fruit; films of brown cream mask turbot; in casseroles severed chickens swim; coloured, un-domestic, the fire burns; and with the wine and the coffee (not paid for) rise jocund visions before musing eyes; gently speculative eyes; eyes to whom life appears musical, mysterious.

The woman who presides over these mysteries is proud to feel she is the creator of a perfect moment, the dispenser of happiness and gaiety. She is the one bringing the guests together, she is the one making the event take place, she is the gratuitous source of joy and harmony.

This is exactly what Mrs Dalloway feels:

> But suppose Peter said to her, 'Yes, yes, but your parties – what's the sense of your parties?' all she could say was (and nobody could be expected to understand): They're an offering; . . . Here was So-and-so in South Kensington; someone up in Bayswater; and somebody else, say, in Mayfair. And she felt quite continuously a sense of their existence; and she felt what a waste; and she felt what a pity; and she felt if only they could be brought together; so she did it. And it was an offering; to combine, to create; but to whom? . . . An offering for the sake of offering, perhaps. Anyhow, it was her gift. Nothing else had she of the slightest importance . . . anybody could do it; yet this anybody she did a little admire, couldn't help feeling that she had, anyhow, made this happen.

If there is pure generosity in this homage to others, the party is really a party. But social routine quickly changes the potlatch into an institution, the gift into an obligation and the party hardens into a rite. All the while savouring the 'dinner out', the invited woman ponders having to return the invitation: she sometimes complains of having been entertained too well. 'The Xs . . . wanted to impress us,' she says bitterly to her husband. I have been told that during the last war in a little Portuguese city, tea parties had become the most costly of potlatches: at each gathering the mistress of the house had to serve more varied cakes and in greater number than the previous one; this burden became so heavy that one day all the women decided together not to serve anything anymore with the tea. The party loses its generous and magnificent character in such circumstances; it is one more chore; the accessories that make up a party are only a source of worry: you have to check the crystal and the tablecloth, measure the champagne and petits fours; a broken cup, the silk upholstering of a burned armchair are a disaster; tomorrow you have to clean, put away, put in order: the woman dreads this extra work. She feels this multiple dependence that defines the housewife's destiny: she is dependent on the soufflé, the roast, the butcher, the cook, the extra help; she is dependent on the husband who frowns every time something goes wrong; she is dependent on the guests who judge the furniture and wine and who decide if the evening has been a success or not. Only generous or self-confident women will go through this ordeal with a light heart. A triumph can give them a heady satisfaction. But in this respect many resemble Mrs Dalloway, about whom Woolf tells us: Although she loved these triumphs . . . and their brilliance and the excitement they brought, she also felt the hollowness, the sham. The woman can only take pleasure in it if she does not attach too much importance to it; if she does she will be tormented by a perpetually unsatisfied vanity. Besides, few women are wealthy enough to find their life's occupation in 'socialising'. Those who devote themselves to it entirely usually try not only to make a cult of it but also to go beyond this social life towards other aims: genuine salons have a literary or political side. These women try to influence men and to play a personal role. They escape from the condition of the married woman. She is not usually fulfilled by the pleasures and ephemeral triumphs rarely bestowed on her and that often mean as much fatigue as distraction. Social life demands that woman 'represent', that she show off, but does not create between her and others real communication. It does not wrest her from her solitude.

'It is painful to think,' writes Michelet, 'that woman, the relative being who can only live in a couple, is more often alone than man. He finds social life everywhere, makes new contacts. As for her, she is nothing without her family. And the family weighs her down; all weight is on her.' And, in fact, the woman kept confined, isolated, does not have the joys of a comradeship that involves pursuing aims together; her work does not occupy her mind, her education did not give her either the taste or the habit of independence, and yet she spends her days in solitude; we have seen that this is one of the miseries Sophia Tolstoy complained of. Her marriage often took her away from her father's home and the friends of her youth. In My Apprenticeships, Colette[86] described the uprooting of a bride transported from her province to Paris; only the long correspondence she exchanged with her mother provided any relief; but letters are no substitute for presence and she cannot admit her disappointments to Sido. Often, there is no longer any real closeness between the young woman and her family: neither her mother nor her sisters are her friends. Nowadays, due to a housing crisis, many young couples live with their families or in-laws; but this enforced presence is far from ever providing real companionship for the young woman.

The feminine friendships she is able to keep or make are precious for a woman; they are very different from relations men have; men relate to each other as individuals through their ideas, their own personal projects;

women, confined within the generality of their destiny as women, are united by a kind of immanent complicity. And what they seek first of all from each other is the affirmation of their common universe. They do not discuss opinions: they exchange confidences and recipes; they join together to create a kind of counter-universe whose values outweigh male values; when they meet, they find the strength to shake off their chains; they negate male sexual domination by confiding their frigidity to each other and cynically deriding the appetites or the clumsiness of their males; they also contest with irony the moral and intellectual superiority of their husbands and men in general. They compare their experiences: pregnancies, deliveries, children's illnesses, their own illnesses and housework become the essential events of human history. Their work is not technical: in transmitting recipes for cooking or housework, they give them the dignity of a secret science founded in oral traditions. Sometimes they examine moral problems together. Letters to the editor in women's magazines are a good example of these exchanges; we can hardly imagine a Lonely Hearts column reserved for men; they meet in *the* world which is *their* world, whereas women must define, measure and explore their own space; mostly they share beauty tips cooking or knitting recipes, and they ask each other for advice; real anxieties can sometimes be perceived in women's tendency to talk and show off. The woman knows the male code is not hers, that man even expects she will not observe it since he pushes her to abortion, adultery, misdeeds, betrayal, and lies he officially condemns; she then asks other women to help her to define a sort of 'parallel law', a specifically feminine moral code. It is not only out of malevolence that women comment on and criticise the conduct of their girlfriends so much: to judge them and to lead their own lives, they need much more moral invention than men.

What makes these relationships valuable is their truthfulness. When confronting man, woman is always on stage; she lies when pretending to accept herself as the inessential other, she lies when she presents to him an imaginary personage through impersonations, clothes and catch-phrases; this act demands constant tension; every woman thinks more or less, 'I am not myself' around her husband or her lover; the male world is hard, there are sharp angles, voices are too loud, lights are too bright, contacts brusque. When with other women, the wife is backstage; she sharpens her weapons, she does not enter combat; she plans her clothes, devises makeup, prepares her ruses: she lies around in slippers and robe in the wings before going on stage; she likes this lukewarm, soft, relaxed atmosphere. Colette describes the moments she spends with her girlfriend Marco like this: 'Brief confidences, the amusements of two women shut away from the world, hours that were now like those in a sewing room, now like the idle ones of convalescence.'[*87]

She enjoys playing the adviser to the older woman:

> As we sat under the balcony awning on those hot afternoons, Marco mended her underclothes. She sewed badly, but conscientiously, and I flattered my vanity by giving her pieces of advice, such as: 'You're using too coarse a thread for fine needles . . . You shouldn't put blue baby ribbon in chemises, pink is much prettier in lingerie and up against the skin.' It was not long before I gave her others, concerning her face powder, the colour of her lipstick, a hard line she pencilled around the edge of her beautifully shaped eyelids. 'D'you think so? D'you think so?' she would say. My youthful authority was adamant. I took the comb, I made a charming little gap in her tight, sponge-like fringe, I proved expert at softly shadowing her eyes and putting a faint pink glow high up on her cheekbones, near her temples.

A bit further on, she shows us Marco anxiously preparing to face a young man she wants to win over:

> She was about to wipe her wet eyes but I stopped her.
> 'Let me do it, Marco.'
> With my two thumbs, I raised her upper eyelids so that the two tears about to fall should be reabsorbed and not smudge the mascara on her lashes by wetting them.
> 'There! Wait, I haven't finished.'
> I retouched all her features. Her mouth was trembling a little. She submitted patiently, sighing as if I were dressing a wound. To complete everything, I filled the puff in her handbag with a rosier shade of powder. Neither of us uttered a word meanwhile.
> 'Whatever happens,' I told her, 'don't cry. At all costs, don't let yourself give way to tears' . . .
> She pressed her hand to her forehead, under her fringe.
> 'I *ought* to have bought that black dress last Saturday – the one I saw in the secondhand shop . . . Tell me, could you possibly lend me some very fine stockings? I've left it too late now to . . .'

* *The Kepi.*

'Yes, yes, of course.'

'Thank you. Don't you think a flower to brighten up my dress? No, *not* a flower on the bodice. Is it true that iris is a scent that's gone out of fashion? I'm sure I had heaps of other things to ask you . . . heaps of things.'

And in still another of her books, *Le toutounier*, Colette evoked this other side of women's life. Three sisters, unhappy or troubled in their loves, gather every night around the old sofa from their childhood; there they relax, pondering the worries of the day, preparing tomorrow's battles, tasting the ephemeral pleasures of a reparative rest, a good sleep, a warm bath, a crying session, they barely speak but each one creates a nesting space for the others; and everything taking place with them is real.

For some women, this frivolous and warm intimacy is more precious than the serious pomp of their relations with men. It is in another woman that the narcissist, as in the days of her adolescence, sees a favourite double; it is through her attentive and competent eyes that she can admire her well-cut dress, her elegant interior. Over and above marriage, the best friend remains her favourite witness: she can still continue to be a desirable and desired object. In almost every young girl, as we have seen, there are homosexual tendencies; the often awkward embraces of her husband do not efface these tendencies; this is the source of the sensual softness woman feels for her counterparts and that has no equal in ordinary men. Sensual attachment between two women friends can be sublimated into exalted sentimentality or expressed in diffuse or real caresses. Their embraces can also be no more than a distracting pastime – such is the case for harem women whose principal concern is to kill time – or they can become of primary importance.

It is nonetheless rare for feminine complicity to reach true friendship; women feel more spontaneous solidarity with each other than men do, but from within this solidarity they do not transcend towards each other: together they are turned towards the masculine world whose values each hopes to monopolise for herself. Their relations are not built on their singularity, but are lived immediately in their generality: and from there, the element of hostility comes into play. Natasha,* who cherished the women in her family because they could witness the births of her babies, nevertheless felt jealous of them: every one of them could embody *the*

* Tolstoy, *War and Peace.*

woman in Pierre's eyes. Women's mutual understanding lies in the fact that they identify with each other: but then each one competes with her companion. A housewife has a more intimate relationship with her maid than a man – unless he is homosexual – has with his valet or chauffeur; they tell each other secrets, and sometimes they are accomplices; but there are also hostile rivalries between them, because while freeing herself from the actual work, the mistress of the house wants to assume the responsibility and credit for the work she assigns; she wants to think of herself as irreplaceable, indispensable. 'Everything goes wrong as soon as I'm not there.' She harasses her maid in order to find fault with her; if she does her job too well, the mistress cannot be proud of feeling unique. Likewise, she systematically becomes irritated with teachers, governesses, nurses and children's maids who care for her offspring, with parents and friends who help her out; she gives the excuse that they do not respect 'her will', that they do not carry out 'her ideas'; the truth is that she has neither particular will nor ideas; what irritates her, on the contrary, is that others carry out her functions exactly as she would. This is one of the main sources of family and domestic discussions that poison the life of the home: the less able she is to show her own merits, the fiercer she is in wanting to be sovereign. But where women especially see each other as enemies is in the area of seduction and love; I have pointed out this rivalry in girls: it often continues throughout life. We have seen how they seek absolute validation in the ideal of the fashionable woman or the socialite; she suffers from not being surrounded by glory; she cannot bear to perceive the slightest halo around someone else's head; she steals all the credit others receive; and what is an absolute if not unique? A woman who truly loves is satisfied to be glorified in one heart, she will not envy her friends' superficial success; but she feels threatened in her very love. The fact is that the theme of the woman betrayed by her best friend is not only a literary cliché; the closer two women are as friends, the more their duality becomes dangerous. The confidante is invited to see through the eyes of the woman in love, to feel with her heart, with her flesh: she is attracted by the lover, fascinated by the man who seduces her friend; she feels protected enough by her loyalty to let her feelings go; she does not like playing an inessential role: soon she is ready to surrender, to offer herself. Many women prudently avoid their 'intimate girlfriends' as soon as they fall in love. This ambivalence keeps women from relying on their mutual feelings. The shadow of the male always weighs heavily on them. Even when not mentioning him, the verse of Saint-John Perse applies:

'And the sun is not named, but its presence is among us.'

Together women take revenge on him, set traps for him, malign him, insult him: but they wait for him. As long as they stagnate in the gynae-ceum, they bask in contingency, in blandness, in boredom; this limbo has retained some of the warmth of the mother's breast: but it is still limbo. Woman is content to linger there on condition that she will soon be able to emerge from it. She is thus content enough in the dampness of her bathroom imagining she will later make her entrance into the luminous salon. Women are comrades for each other in captivity, they help each other endure their prison, even prepare their escape: but their liberator will come from the masculine world.

For most women, this world keeps its glow after marriage; only the husband loses his prestige; the wife discovers that his pure manly essence tarnishes: but man still remains the truth of the universe, the supreme authority, the wonderful, adventure, master, gaze, prey, pleasure, salvation; he still embodies transcendence, he is the answer to all questions. And the most loyal wife never consents to give him up completely and close herself in a dismal tête-à-tête with a contingent individual. Her childhood left her in absolute need of a guide; when the husband fails to fulfil this role, she turns to another man. Sometimes her father, a brother, an uncle, a relative or an old friend has kept his former prestige: so she will lean on him. There are two categories of men whose professions destine them to become confidants and mentors: priests and doctors. The first have that great advantage of not having to be paid for these consultations; the confessional renders them defenceless in the face of the babbling of the pious; they avoid 'sacristy pests' and 'holy Marys' as best they can; but their duty is to lead their flock on the moral path, a most urgent duty as women gain social and political importance and the Church endeavours to make instru-ments of them. The 'spiritual guide' dictates his political opinions to his penitent and influences her vote; and many husbands are irritated by his interference in their conjugal life: it is he who defines what they do in the privacy of the bedroom as licit or illicit; he is concerned in the education of the children; he advises the woman on her conduct with her husband; she who always hailed man as a god kneels with pleasure before the male who is the earthly substitute for God. The doctor is better protected as he requires payment; and he can close his door to clients who are too indis-creet; but he is the target of more specific, more stubborn aims; three-quarters of the men harassed by nymphomaniacs are doctors; to undress in front of a man is a great exhibitionistic pleasure for many women.

Stekel says: I know some women who find satisfaction only in an examination by a doctor they like. In particular, there are among spinsters many rich women who see their doctor for 'a very careful' examination because of minor discharges or a banal problem. Others suffer from a cancer phobia or infections from toilets and these phobias provide them with the pretext to have an examination.

He cites two cases among others:

A spinster, B. V. . . ., 43 years old and rich, goes to see a doctor once a month, after her period, demanding a very careful examination because she believed that something was wrong. She changes doctors every month and plays the same game each time. The doctor asks her to undress and lie down on the table or couch. She refuses, saying that she is too modest, that she cannot do such a thing, that it is against nature! The doctor forces her or gently persuades her, and she finally undresses, explaining she is a virgin and he should not hurt her. He promises to give her a rectal exam. Her orgasm often comes as soon as the doctor examines her; it is repeated, intensified, during the rectal exam. She always uses a false name and pays right away . . . She admits to having entertained the hope of being raped by a doctor.

Mrs L. M. . . ., 38 years old, married, tells me she is completely unfeeling when with her husband. She comes to be analysed. After two sessions only, she admits to having a lover. But he cannot make her reach orgasm. She could only have one by being examined by a gynaecologist (her father was a gynaecologist!). Every two or three sessions or so, she had the urge to go to the doctor and have an examination. From time to time, she requested a treatment and those were the happiest times. The last time, a gynaecologist massaged her at length because of a supposed fallen womb. Each massage brought about several orgasms. She explains her passion for these examinations by the first touch that had caused the first orgasm of her life . . .[88]

The woman easily imagines that the man to whom she has exhibited herself is impressed by her physical charm or her soul's beauty, and she thus is persuaded, in pathological cases, that she is loved by a priest or doctor. Even if she is normal, she has the impression that a subtle bond exists between them; she basks in respectful obedience to him; in addition, she sometimes finds in him a source of security that helps her accept her life.

There are women, nonetheless, who are not content to prop up their existence with moral authority; they also need romantic exaltation in their lives. If they do not want to cheat on or leave their husbands, they will seek recourse in the same tactic as a girl who fears flesh-and-blood males: they give themselves over to imaginary passions. Stekel gives several examples of this.*

A decent married woman of the better social class suffers from 'nervous anxiety' and is predisposed to depressions. One evening during the performance at the opera she falls in love with the tenor. His singing suffuses her with a strange warmth. She becomes the singer's fanatic admirer. Thenceforth she does not miss a single performance in which he appears. She obtains his photograph, she dreams of him, and once she sent him an imposing bouquet of roses with the inscription: 'From a grateful unknown admirer!' She even goes so far as to write him a letter... This letter she also signs, 'From an unknown admirer!' but she keeps at a distance. An occasion unexpectedly arises, making it possible for her to meet this singer at a social gathering. She decides very promptly that she will not go. She does not care to become personally acquainted with him. She does not require closer contact. She is happy to be able to love so warmly and still remain a faithful wife!

I became acquainted with a woman obsessed with the most remarkable Kainz, a famous actor from Vienna. She had a special Kainz room, embellished with numerous portraits of the famous artist. There was a Kainz library in one corner. Here there was to be found everything in the shape of his books, pamphlets and clippings which she could gather bearing on her hero. She had also gathered in this library a collection of theatre programs, including, of course, Kainz festivals and premières. A particularly precious possession was the portrait of the great artist bearing his autograph. This woman wore mourning for a whole year after the artist's death. She took long journeys to attend lectures on Kainz... This Kainz cult served to preserve the woman's physical chastity, it protected her against all temptation, leaving no room for any other erotic thoughts.

* Stekel, *Frigidity in Woman*.

We recall what tears Rudolph Valentino's death brought forth. Married women and young girls alike worship cinema heroes. Women often evoke their images when engaged in solitary pleasures, or they call up such fantasies in conjugal lovemaking; these images also often revive some childhood memory in the figure of a grandfather, a brother, a teacher, and so on.

Nevertheless, there are also men of flesh and blood in women's circles; whether she is sexually fulfilled, frigid or frustrated – except in the rare case of a complete, absolute, and exclusive love – the woman places great value on their approbation. Her husband's too mundane gaze no longer nurtures her image; she needs eyes still full of mystery to discover her as mystery; she needs a sovereign consciousness before her to receive her confidences, to revive the faded photographs, to bring to life that dimple in the corner of her mouth, the fluttering eyelashes that are hers alone; she is only desirable, lovable, if she is desired, loved. While she more or less makes the best of her marriage, she looks to other men mainly to satisfy her vanity: she invites them to share in her cult; she seduces, she pleases, happy to dream about forbidden loves, to think: If I wanted to . . .; she prefers to charm many admirers than to attach herself deeply to any one; more ardent, less shy than a young girl, her coquetry needs males to confirm her in the consciousness of her worth and power; she is often all the bolder as, anchored in her home and having succeeded in conquering one man, she leads him on without great expectations and without great risks.

It happens that after a longer or shorter period of fidelity, the woman no longer confines herself to these flirtations or coquetries. Often, she decides to deceive her husband out of resentment. Adler maintains that woman's infidelity always stems from revenge; this is going too far; but the fact is that she often yields less to a lover's seduction than to a desire to defy her husband: 'He is not the only man in the world – I can attract others – I am not his slave, he thinks he is clever but he can be duped.' It may happen that the derided husband retains his primordial importance for the wife; just as the girl will sometimes take a lover to rebel against her mother or protest against her parents, disobey them, affirm herself, so a woman whose very resentment attaches her to her husband seeks a confidant in her lover, an observer who considers her a victim, an accomplice who helps her humiliate her husband; she talks to him endlessly about her husband under the pretext of subjecting him to his scorn; and if the lover does not play his role well, she moodily turns from him either to go back to her husband or to find another consoler.

But, very often, it is less resentment than disappointment that drives her into the arms of a lover; she does not find love in marriage; she resigns herself with difficulty to never knowing the sensual pleasures and joys whose expectations charmed her youth. Marriage, by frustrating women's erotic satisfaction, denies them the freedom and individuality of their feelings, drives them to adultery by way of a necessary and ironic dialectic.

Montaigne says:

> We train them from childhood to the ways of love. Their grace, their dressing up, their knowledge, their language, all their instruction, has only this end in view. Their governesses imprint in them nothing else but the idea of love, if only by continually depicting it to them in order to disgust them with it.[89]

Thus it is folly to try to bridle women's desire which is so burning and natural.

And Engels declares:

> With monogamous marriage, two constant social types, unknown hitherto, make their appearance on the scene – the wife's attendant lover and the cuckold husband ... Together with monogamous marriage and hetaerism, adultery became an unavoidable social institution – denounced, severely penalised, but impossible to suppress.[90]

If conjugal sex has excited the wife's curiosity without satisfying her senses, like in Colette's *Innocent Libertine*,[91] she tries to complete her education in the beds of strangers. If she has no singular attachment to her husband, but he has succeeded in awakening her sexuality, she will want to taste the pleasures she has discovered through him with others.

Some moralists have been outraged by the preference shown to the lover, and I have pointed out the efforts of bourgeois literature to rehabilitate the figure of the husband; but it is absurd to defend him by showing that often in the eyes of society – that is to say, other men – he is better than his rival: what is important here is what he represents for the wife. So there are two traits that make him detestable. First of all, it is he who assumes the thankless role of initiator; the contradictory demands of the virgin who dreams of being both violated and respected almost surely condemn him to failure; she remains for ever frigid in his arms; with her lover she experiences neither the torment of

defloration nor the initial humiliation of modesty overcome; she is spared
the trauma of surprise: she knows more or less what to expect; more
honest, less vulnerable, less naive than on her wedding night, she does
not confuse ideal love and physical hunger, sentiment and sexual excitement: when she takes a lover, it is a lover she wants. This lucidity is an
aspect of the freedom of her choice. For here lies the other defect
weighing on her husband: he was usually imposed and not chosen. Either
she accepted him in resignation, or she was given over to him by her
family; in any case, even if she married him for love, she makes him her
master by marrying him; their relations have become a duty and he often
takes on the figure of tyrant. Her choice of lover is doubtless limited
by circumstances, but there is an element of freedom in this relationship; to marry is an obligation, to take a lover is a luxury; it is because
he has solicited her that the woman yields to him: she is sure, if not of
his love, at least of his desire; it is not for the purpose of obeying laws
that he acts upon his desire. He also has this advantage: that his seduction and prestige are not tarnished by the frictions of everyday life; he
remains removed, an other. Thus the woman has the impression of getting
out of herself in their meetings, of finding new riches: she feels other.
This is above all what some women seek in a liaison: to be involved,
surprised, rescued from themselves by the other. A rupture leaves them
with a desperate empty feeling. Janet*[92] cites several cases of this melancholia that show us bluntly what the woman looks for and finds in her
lover:

> A thirty-nine-year-old woman, heartbroken at having been aban-
> doned by a writer with whom she worked for five years, writes to
> Janet: 'He had such a rich life and was so tyrannical that all I could
> do was take care of him, and I could not think of anything else . . .'

> Another woman, thirty-one, fell ill after breaking with a lover she
> adored. 'I wanted to be an inkwell on his desk to see him, hear
> him,' she writes. And she explains: 'Alone, I am bored, my husband
> brings me no intellectual stimulation, he knows nothing, he teaches
> me nothing, he does not *surprise* me . . . , he has nothing but
> common sense, it crushes me.' But by contrast, she writes about
> her lover: 'He is an *astonishing* man, I never saw in him a moment
> of confusion, emotion, gaiety, carelessness, always in control,

* See *Obsessions and Psychasthenia*.

mocking, cold enough to make you die of shame. In addition, an impudence, sang-froid, a sharp mind, a lively intelligence that made my head spin . . .'

There are women who savour this feeling of plenitude and joyful excitement only in the first moments of a liaison; if a lover does not give them instant pleasure – and this frequently happens the first time as the partners are intimidated and ill adapted to each other – they feel resentment and disgust towards him; these 'Messalinas' have multiple affairs and leave one lover after another. But it also happens that a woman, enlightened by the failure of her marriage, is attracted this time by a man who suits her well, and a lasting relation is created between them. Often he will appeal to her because he is of a radically different type from her husband. This is without a doubt the contrast that Sainte-Beuve, who seduced Adèle, provides with Victor Hugo. Stekel cites the following case:

> Mrs P. H. has been married for the past eight years to a man who is a member of an athletic club. She visits the gynaecologic clinic on account of a slight inflammation of the ovaries. There she complains that her husband gives her no peace . . . She perceives only pain and does not know the meaning of gratification. The man is rough and violent . . . Finally he takes a sweetheart . . . [This does not trouble her in the least.] She is happy . . . she wants a divorce and calls on an attorney. In his office she meets a clerk who is the exact opposite of her husband. The clerk is humble, delicate, weak, but he is also loving and tender. They become closely acquainted and he begins to court her. He writes her tender letters. His petty attentions flatter and please her . . . They find that they have similar intellectual interests . . . With his first kiss her anaesthesia vanishes . . . This man's relatively weak *potentia* has roused the keenest orgasm in the woman. After the divorce they married; now they live very happily together . . . He is also able to rouse this woman's orgasm with kisses and other caresses. This was the same woman whose frigidity in the embrace of a highly potent man drove her to take a lover!

Not all affairs have fairy-tale endings. It happens that just as the young girl dreams of a liberator who will wrest her from under her father's roof, the wife awaits the lover who will save her from the conjugal yoke: an often-told story is that of the ardent lover who cools off and flees when his mistress starts talking about marriage; she is often hurt by his reluctance, and from then on, their relations become distorted by resentment and hostility. If a relationship becomes a stable one, it often takes on a familiar conjugal character in the end; all the vices of marriage – boredom, jealousy, prudence, deception – can be found in it. And the woman dreams of another man who will rescue her from this routine.

Adultery, furthermore, has very different characteristics according to customs and circumstances. In our civilisation of enduring patriarchal traditions, marital infidelity is still more serious for the woman than the man. Montaigne says:

> Iniquitous appraisal of vices! . . . But we create and weigh vices not according to nature but according to our interest, whereby they assume so many unequal shapes. The severity of our decrees makes women's addiction to this vice more exacerbated and vicious than its nature calls for, and involves it in consequences that are worse than their cause.

We have seen the primary reasons for this severity: women's adultery risks introducing the child of a stranger into a family, dispossessing legitimate heirs; the husband is master, the wife his property. Social changes and the practice of birth control have taken much of the force out of these motives. But the will to keep woman in a state of dependency perpetuates the proscriptions that still surround her. She often interiorises them; she closes her eyes to the conjugal escapades that her religion, morality and her 'virtue' do not permit her to envisage with reciprocity. The control imposed by her social environment – in particular in 'small towns' in the Old as well as the New World – is far more severe for her than for her husband: he goes out more, he travels, and his dalliances are more indulgently tolerated; she risks losing her reputation and her situation as a married woman. The ruses women use to thwart this scrutiny have often been described; I know a small Portuguese town of ancient severity where young women only go out in the company of a mother-in-law or sister-in-law; but the hairdresser rents out rooms above his shop; between hair being set and combed out, lovers steal a furtive embrace. In large cities, women have far fewer wardens: but the old custom of 'afternoon dalliances' was hardly more conducive to the happy fulfilment of illicit feelings. Furtive and clandestine, adultery does not create human and free relationships; the lies it entails rob conjugal relations of what is left of their dignity.

In many circles today, women have partially gained sexual freedom. But it is still a difficult problem for them to reconcile their conjugal life with sexual satisfaction. As marriage generally does not mean physical love, it would seem reasonable to clearly differentiate one from the other. A man can admittedly make an excellent husband and still be inconstant: his sexual caprices do not in fact keep him from carrying out the enterprise of a friendly communal life with his wife; this amity will be all the purer, less ambivalent if it does not represent a shackle. One might allow that it could be the same for the wife; she often wishes to share in her husband's existence, create a home with him for their children, and still experience other embraces. It is the compromises of prudence and hypocrisy that make adultery degrading; a pact of freedom and sincerity would abolish one of the defects of marriages. It must be recognised, however, that *today* the irritating formula that inspired *Francillon* by Dumas, fils – 'It is not the same thing for women' – retains a certain truth. There is nothing *natural* about the difference. It is claimed that woman needs sexual activity less than man: nothing is less sure. Repressed women make shrewish wives, sadistic mothers, fanatical housekeepers, unhappy and dangerous creatures; in any case, even if her desires were more infrequent, there is no reason to consider it superfluous for her to satisfy them. The difference stems from the overall erotic situation of man and woman as defined by tradition and today's society. For woman, the love act is still considered a *service* woman renders to man, thus giving him the status of master; we have seen that he can always *take* an inferior woman, but she degrades herself if she *gives herself* to a male who is not her equal; her consent, in any case, is of the same nature as a surrender, a fall. A woman often graciously accepts her husband having other women: she is even flattered; Adèle Hugo apparently saw her fiery husband take his ardours to other beds without regret; some women even copy Mme de Pompadour and act as procurers.* By contrast, in lovemaking, the woman is changed into object, into prey; it seems to the husband that she is possessed by a foreign mana, that she ceases to belong to him, she is stolen from him. And the fact is that in bed the woman often feels, wants to be and, consequently, is dominated; the fact also is that because of virile prestige, she tends to approve, to imitate the male who, having possessed her, embodies in her eyes all men. The husband is irritated, not without reason, to hear in his wife's familiar

---

* I am speaking here of marriage. We will see that the attitude of the couple is reversed in a love affair.

mouth the echo of a stranger's thinking: it seems to him in a way that it is he who is possessed, violated. If Mme de Charrière broke with the young Benjamin Constant – who played the feminine role between two virile women – it was because she could not bear to feel him marked by the hated influence of Mme de Staël. As long as the woman acts like a slave and the reflection of the man to whom she 'gives herself', she must recognise the fact that her infidelities wrest her from her husband more radically than do his reciprocal infidelities.

If she does preserve her integrity, she may nonetheless fear that her husband will be compromised in her lover's consciousness. Even a woman is quick to imagine that in sleeping with a man – if only once, in haste, on a sofa – she has gained a certain superiority over the legitimate spouse; a man who believes he possesses a mistress thinks, with even more reason, that he has trumped her husband. This is why the woman is careful to choose her lover from a lower social class in Bataille's *Tenderness* or Kessel's *Belle de Nuit*;[93] she seeks sexual satisfaction from him, but she does not want to give him an advantage over her respected husband. In *Man's Fate*,[94] Malraux shows us a couple where man and woman make a pact for reciprocal freedom: yet when May tells Kyo she has slept with a friend, he grieves over the fact that this man thinks he 'had' her; he chose to respect her independence because he knows very well that one never *has* anyone; but the complaisant ideas held by another man hurt and humiliate him through May. Society confuses the free woman and the loose woman; the lover himself may not recognise the freedom from which he profits; he would rather believe his mistress has yielded, let herself go, that he has conquered her, seduced her. A proud woman might personally come to terms with her partner's vanity; but it would be detestable for her that her esteemed husband should stand such arrogance. For as long as this equality is not universally recognised and concretely realised, it is very difficult for a woman to act as an equal to a man.

In any case, adultery, friendships and social life are but diversions within married life; they can help its constraints to be endured, but they do not break them. They are only artificial escapes that in no way authentically allow the woman to take her destiny into her own hands.

CHAPTER 8

Prostitutes and Hetaeras

Marriage, as we have seen,* has an immediate corollary in prostitution. 'Hetaerism', says Morgan, 'follows mankind in civilization as a dark shadow upon the family.' Man, out of prudence, destines his wife to chastity but he does not derive satisfaction from the regime he imposes on her.

Montaigne says:

> The kings of Persia used to invite their wives to join them at their feasts; but when the wine began to heat them in good earnest and they had to give completely free rein to sensuality, they sent them back to their private rooms, so as not to make them participants in their immoderate appetites, and sent for other women in their place, to whom they did not have this obligation of respect.[95]

Sewers are necessary to guarantee the sanitation of palaces, said the Church Fathers. And Mandeville, in a very popular book, said: 'It is obvious that some women must be sacrificed to save others and to prevent an even more abject filth.' One of the arguments of American slaveholders and defenders of slavery is that, released from slavish drudgery, Southern whites could establish the most democratic and refined relations with each other; likewise, the existence of a caste of 'lost women' makes it possible to treat 'the virtuous woman' with the most chivalric respect. The prostitute is a scapegoat; man unloads his turpitude onto her and he repudiates her. Whether a legal status puts her under police surveillance or she works clandestinely, she is in any case treated as a pariah.

From the economic point of view, her situation is symmetrical to the married woman's. 'Between those who sell themselves through prostitution and those who sell themselves through marriage, the only difference

* Vol. I, Part Two.

resides in the price and length of the contract,' says Marro.*[96] For both, the sexual act is a service; the latter is engaged for life by one man; the former has several clients who pay her per item. One male against all the others protects the former; the latter is defended by all against the exclusive tyranny of each one. In any case, the advantages they derive from giving their bodies are limited by competition; the husband knows he could have had another wife: the accomplishment of his 'conjugal duties' is not a favour; it is the execution of a contract. In prostitution, masculine desire can be satisfied on any body as it is specific and not individual. Wives or courtesans do not succeed in exploiting man unless they wield a singular power over him. The main difference between them is that the legitimate woman, oppressed as a married woman, is respected as a human person; this respect begins seriously to bring a halt to oppression. However, the prostitute does not have the rights of a person; she is the sum of all types of feminine slavery at once.

It is naive to wonder what motives drive a woman to prostitution; Lombroso's theory that assimilated prostitutes with criminals and that saw them both as degenerates is no longer accepted; it is possible, as the statistics show, that in general prostitutes have a slightly below-average mental level and that some are clearly retarded: women with fewer mental faculties readily choose jobs that do not demand of them any specialisation; but most are normal and some very intelligent. No hereditary fate, no physiological defect, weighs on them. In reality, as soon as a profession opens in a world where misery and unemployment are rife, there are people to enter it; as long as there are police and prostitution, there will be policemen and prostitutes. Especially because these professions are, on average, more lucrative than many others. It is very hypocritical to be surprised by the supply masculine demand creates; this is a rudimentary and universal economic process. 'Of all the causes of prostitution,' wrote Parent-Duchâtelet in his study of 1857,[97] 'none is more active than the lack of work and the misery that is the inevitable consequence of inadequate salaries.' Right-thinking moralists respond sneeringly that the pitiful accounts of prostitutes are just stories for the naive client. It is true that in many cases a prostitute could earn her living in a different way: that the living she has chosen does not seem the worst to her does not prove she has this vice in her blood; rather, it condemns a society where this profession is still one that seems the least repellent to many women. One asks, why did she choose it? The question should be: Why

---

* 'Puberty'.

should she not choose it? It has been noted that, among other things, many 'girls' were once servants; this is what Parent-Duchâtelet established for all countries, what Lily Braun noted in Germany and Ryckère in Belgium. About 50 per cent of prostitutes were first servants. One look at 'maids' rooms' is enough to explain this fact. Exploited, enslaved, treated as an object rather than as a person, the maid or chambermaid cannot look forward to any improvement of her lot; sometimes she has to submit to the whims of the master of the house: from domestic slavery and sexual subordination to the master, she slides into a slavery that could not be more degrading and that she dreams will be better. In addition, women in domestic service are very often uprooted; it is estimated that 80 per cent of Parisian prostitutes come from the provinces or the countryside. Proximity to one's family and concern for one's reputation are thought to prevent a woman from turning to a generally discredited profession; but if she is lost in a big city, no longer integrated into society, the abstract idea of 'morality' does not provide any obstacle. While the bourgeoisie invests the sexual act – and above all virginity – with daunting taboos, the working class and peasantry treat it with indifference. Numerous studies agree on this point: many girls let themselves be deflowered by the first comer and then find it natural to give themselves to anyone who comes along. In a study of one hundred prostitutes, Dr Bizard recorded the following facts: one had been deflowered at eleven, two at twelve, two at thirteen, six at fourteen, seven at fifteen, twenty-one at sixteen, nineteen at seventeen, seventeen at eighteen, six at nineteen; the others, after twenty-one. There were thus 5 per cent who had been raped before puberty. More than half said they gave themselves out of love; the others consented out of ignorance. The first seducer is often young. Usually it is someone from the workshop, an office colleague, a childhood friend; then come soldiers, foremen, valets and students; Dr Bizard's list also included two lawyers, an architect, a doctor and a pharmacist. It is rather rare, as legend has it, for the employer himself to play this initiating role: but often it is his son or nephew or one of his friends. Commenge, in his study, also reports on forty-five girls from twelve to seventeen who were deflowered by strangers whom they never saw again; they had consented with indifference, and without experiencing pleasure. Dr Bizard recorded the following, more detailed cases, among others:

Mlle G. de Bordeaux, leaving the convent at eighteen, is persuaded, out of curiosity and without thinking of any danger, to follow a stranger from the fair into his caravan where she is deflowered.

Without thinking, a thirteen-year-old child gives herself to a man she has met in the street, whom she does not know and whom she will never see again.

M. . . . tells us explicitly that she was deflowered at seventeen by a young man she did not know . . . she let it happen out of total ignorance.

R. . . . , deflowered at seventeen and a half by a young man she had never seen whom she had met by chance at the doctor's, where she had gone to get the doctor for her sick sister; he brought her back by car so that she could get home more quickly, but in fact he left her in the middle of the street after getting what he wanted from her.

B. . . . deflowered at fifteen and a half 'without thinking about what she was doing', in our client's words, by a young man she never saw again; nine months later, she gave birth to a healthy boy.

S. . . . , deflowered at fourteen by a young man who drew her to his house under the pretext that he wanted her to meet his sister. The young man in reality did not have a sister, but he had syphilis and contaminated the girl.

R. . . . deflowered at eighteen in an old trench from the front by a married cousin with whom she was visiting the battlefields; he got her pregnant and made her leave her family.

C. . . . at seventeen, deflowered on the beach one summer evening by a young man whom she had just met at the hotel and at 100 metres from their two mothers, who were talking about trifles. Contaminated with gonorrhoea.

L. . . . deflowered at thirteen by her uncle while listening to the radio at the same time as her aunt, who liked to go to bed early, was sleeping quietly in the next room.[98]

We can be sure that these girls who gave in passively nevertheless suffered the trauma of defloration; one would like to know what psychological influence this brutal experience had on their future; but 'girls' are not psychoanalysed, they are inarticulate in describing themselves and take refuge behind clichés. For some, the facility of giving themselves to the first comer can be explained by the existence of prostitution fantasies about which we have spoken: out of family resentment, horror of their budding sexuality, the desire to act grown-up, some young girls imitate prostitutes; they use harsh makeup, see boys, act flirtatiously and provocatively; they who are still infantile, asexual and cold think they can play with fire with impunity; one day a man takes them at their word and they slip from dreams to acts.

'When a door has been broken open, it is then hard to keep it closed,' said one fourteen-year-old prostitute.* However, the girl rarely decides to be a streetwalker immediately following her defloration. In some cases, she remains attached to her first lover and continues to live with him; she takes an 'honest' job; when the lover abandons her, another consoles her; since she no longer belongs to one man, she decides she can give herself to all; sometimes it is the lover – the first, the second – who suggests this means of earning money. There are also many girls who are prostituted by their parents: in some families, like the famous American family, the Jukes, all the women are doomed to this job. Among young female vagabonds, there are also many girls abandoned by their families who begin by begging and slip from there to the streets. In 1857, out of 5,000 prostitutes, Parent-Duchâtelet found that 1,441 were influenced by poverty, 1,425 seduced and abandoned, 1,255 abandoned and left penniless by their parents. Contemporary studies suggest approximately the same conclusions. Illness often leads to prostitution as the woman has become unable to hold down a real job or has lost her place; it destroys her precarious budget, it forces the woman to come up with new resources quickly. So it is with the birth of a child. More than half the women of Saint-Lazare had at least one child; many raised from three to six children; Dr Bizard points out one who brought fourteen into the world of whom eight were still living when he knew her. Few of them, he says, abandon their children; and sometimes the unwed mother becomes a prostitute in order to feed the child. He cites this case among others:

> Deflowered in the provinces, at nineteen, by a sixty-year-old director while she was still living at home, she had to leave her family, as she was pregnant, and she gave birth to a healthy girl that she brought up well. After nursing, she went to Paris, found a job as a nanny and began to carouse at the age of twenty-nine. She has been a prostitute for thirty-three years. Weak and exhausted, she is now asking to be hospitalised in Saint-Lazare.

It is well known that there is an increase of prostitution in wars and the crises of their aftermath.

* Cited by Marro, 'Puberty'.

The author of *The Life of a Prostitute*, published in part in *Les Temps Modernes*,* tells of her beginnings:

> I got married at sixteen to a man thirteen years older than I. I did it to get out of my parents' house. My husband only thought of making me have kids. 'Like that, you'll stay at home, you won't go out,' he said. He wouldn't let me wear makeup, didn't want to take me to the movies. I had to stand my mother-in-law who came to the house every day and always took the side of her bastardly son. My first child was a boy, Jacques; fourteen months later, I gave birth to another, Pierre . . . As I was very bored, I took courses in nursing, which I liked a lot . . . I got work at a hospital on the outskirts of Paris, working with women. A nurse who was just a girl taught me things I hadn't known about before. Sleeping with my husband was mostly a chore. As for men, I didn't have a fling with anyone for six months. Then one day, a real tough guy, a cad but good-looking, came into my own room. He convinced me I could change my life, that I could go with him to Paris, that I wouldn't work any more . . . He knew how to fool me . . . I decided to go off with him . . . I was really happy for a month . . . One day he brought along a well-dressed, chic woman, saying: 'So here, this one does all right for herself.' At the beginning, I didn't go along with it. I even found a job as a nurse in a local hospital to show him that I didn't want to walk the streets, but I couldn't carry on for long. He would say: 'You don't love me. When you love a man, you work for him.' I cried. At the hospital, I was sad. Finally, I was persuaded to go to the hairdresser's . . . I began to turn tricks! Julot followed me to see if I was doing well and to be able to warn me if the cops were on to me . . .

In some ways, this story is the classic one of the girl doomed to the street by a pimp. This role might also be played by the husband. And sometimes, by a woman as well. L. Faivre made a study in 1931 of 510 young prostitutes;[†99] he found that 284 of them lived alone, 132 with a male friend, and 94 with a female friend with whom they usually had homosexual ties. He cites (with their spelling) extracts of the following letters:

* She had this story published in secret under the pseudonym Marie-Thérèse; I will refer to her by this name.
† *Young Vagabond Prostitutes in Prison.*

Suzanne, seventeen. I gave myself to prostitution, especially with women prostitutes. One of them who kept me for a long time was very jealous, and so I left that street.

Andrée, fifteen and a half. I left my parents to live with a friend I met at a dance, I understood right away that she wanted to love me like a man, I stayed with her four months, then . . .

Jeanne, fourteen. My poor sweet papa's name was X . . . he died in the hospital from war wounds in 1922. My mother got married again. I was going to school to get my primary school diploma, then having got it, I went to study sewing . . . then as I earned very little, the fights with my stepfather began . . . I had to be placed as a maid at Mme X's, on X street . . . I was alone with a girl who was probably twenty-five for about ten days; I noticed a very big change in her. Then one day, just like a boy, she admitted her great love. I hesitated, then afraid of being let go, I finally gave in; I understood then certain things . . . I worked, then finding myself without a job, I had to go to the Bois where I continued with women. I met a very generous lady, and so forth.[100]

Quite often, the woman only envisages prostitution as a temporary way of increasing her resources. But the way in which she then finds herself enslaved to it has been described many times. While cases of the 'white slave trade', where she is dragged into the spiral by violence, false promises, mystifications, and so on, are relatively rare, what happens more often is that she is kept in this career against her will. The capital necessary to get her started is provided by a pimp or a madam who acquires rights over her, who gets most of her profits and from whom she is not able to free herself. Marie-Thérèse carried on a real fight for several years before succeeding.

I finally understood that Julot[101] didn't want anything but my dough and I thought that far from him, I could save a bit of money . . . At home in the beginning, I was shy, I didn't dare go up to clients and tell them 'come on up'. The wife of one of Julot's buddies watched me closely and even counted my tricks . . . So Julot writes to me that I should give my money every evening to the madam, 'Like that, nobody will steal it from you.' When I wanted to buy a dress, the hotel manager told me that Julot had forbidden her to give my dough . . . I decided to get out of this trick house as fast as I could. When the boss lady found out I wanted to leave, she didn't give me the tampon* before the visit like the other times and I was stopped and put into the hospital . . . I had to return to the brothel to earn some money for my trip . . . but I only stayed in the house for four weeks . . . I worked a few days in Barbès like before but I was too furious at Julot to stay in Paris: we fought, he beat me, once he almost threw me out of the window . . . I made an arrangement with a go-between to go to the provinces. When I realised he knew Julot, I didn't show up at the rendezvous. The agent's two broads met me on rue Belhomme and gave me a thrashing . . . The next day, I packed my bags and left alone for the isle of T . . . Three weeks later I was fed up with the brothel, I wrote to the doctor to mark me as going out when he came for the visit . . . Julot saw me on Boulevard de Magenta and beat me . . . My face was scarred after the thrashing on Boulevard de Magenta. I was fed up with Julot. So I signed a contract to go to Germany . . .

Literature has popularised the character of the fancy man. He plays a protective role in the girl's life. He advances her money to buy outfits, then he defends her against the competition of other women and the police – sometimes he himself is a policeman – and against the clients. They would like to be able to consume without paying; there are those who would readily satisfy their sadism on a woman. In Madrid a few years ago Fascist and gilded youth amused themselves by throwing prostitutes into the river on cold nights; in France students having fun sometimes brought women into the countryside and abandoned them, entirely naked, at night; in order to get her money and avoid bad treatment, the prostitute needs a man. He also provides her with moral support: 'You work less well alone, you don't have your heart in it, you let yourself go,' some say. She often feels love for him; she takes on this job or justifies it out of love; in this milieu, man's superiority over woman is enormous: this distance favours love-religion, which explains some prostitutes' passionate abnegation. They see in their male's violence the sign of his virility and submit to him even more docilely. They experience jealousy and torment with him, but also the joys of the woman in love.

But sometimes they feel only hostility and resentment for him: it is

---

* 'A tampon to anaesthetise the gono was given to prostitutes before the doctor's visit so that he only found a woman to be sick if the madam wanted to get rid of her.'

out of fear, because he has a hold over them, that they remain under his thumb, as we just saw in the case of Marie-Thérèse. So sometimes they console themselves with a 'fling' with one of their clients. Marie-Thérèse writes:

> All the women have flings, me too, in addition to their Julot. He was a very handsome sailor. Even though he was a good lover, he didn't turn me on but we felt a lot of friendship for each other. Often he came up with me without making love, just to talk; he told me I should get out of this, that my place wasn't here.

They also find consolation with women. Many prostitutes are homosexual. We saw that there was often a homosexual adventure at the beginning of their careers and that many continued to live with a woman. According to Anna Rueling, about 20 per cent of prostitutes in Germany are homosexual. Faivre points out that in prison young women prisoners correspond with each other with pornographic and passionate letters that they sign 'United for life'. These letters are similar to those schoolgirls write to each other, feeding the 'flames' in their hearts; these girls are less aware, shyer; the prisoners carry their feelings to the limit, in both their words and their actions. We can see in the life of Marie-Thérèse – who was launched into lovemaking by a woman – what special role the female 'pal' plays in comparison to the despised male client or the authoritarian pimp:

> Julot brought around a girl, a poor drudge who didn't even have a pair of shoes to wear. At the flea market they buy what she needed and then she comes to work with me. She was sweet and in addition she liked women, so we got along well. She reminded me of everything I learned with the nurse. We had a lot of fun and instead of working we went to the movies. I was happy to have her with us.

One can see that the girlfriend plays approximately the same role that the best friend plays for the virtuous woman surrounded by women: she is the companion in pleasure, she is the one with whom she has free, gratuitous relations, that can thus be chosen; tired of men, disgusted by them or wishing for a diversion, the prostitute will often seek relief and pleasure in the arms of another woman. In any case, the complicity I spoke of and that immediately unites women exists more strongly in this case than in any other. Because their relations with half of humanity are commercial, because the whole of society treats them as pariahs, there is great solidarity among prostitutes; they might be rivals, jealous of each other, insult each other, fight with each other; but they have a great need of each other to form a 'counter-universe' in which they regain their human dignity; the friend is the confidante and the privileged witness; she is the one who approves of the dress and hairdo meant to seduce the man, but which are ends in themselves in other women's envious or admiring gazes.

As for the prostitute's relations with her clients, opinions vary and cases undoubtedly vary. It is often emphasised that she reserves kissing on the lips, the expression of real tenderness, for her true love, and she makes no connection between amorous embraces and professional ones. Men's views are dubious because their vanity incites them to let themselves be duped by simulated orgasm. It must be said that the circumstances are very different when it is a question of a 'mass turnover', often physically exhausting, a quick trick, or regular relations with a familiar client. Marie-Thérèse generally did her job indifferently, but she mentions some nights of delights; she had 'crushes' and says that all her friends did too; a woman might refuse to be paid by a client she liked, and sometimes, if he is in a difficult situation, she offers to help him. In general, however, the woman works 'cold'. Some only feel indifference tinged with scorn for their clientele. 'Oh! What saps men are! Women can put anything they want into men's heads!' writes Marie-Thérèse. But many feel a disgusted resentment of men; they are sickened, for one thing, by their perversions, either because they go to the brothel to satisfy the perversions they do not dare to admit to their wives or mistresses, or because being at a brothel incites them to invent perversions; many men demand 'fantasies' from the woman. Marie-Thérèse complained in particular that the French have an insatiable imagination. The sick women treated by Dr Bizard confided in him that 'all men are more or less perverted'. One of my female friends spoke at great length at the Beaujon hospital with a young, very intelligent prostitute who started off as a servant and who lived with a pimp she adored. 'All men are perverted,' she said, 'except mine. That's why I love him. If I ever discover he's a pervert, I'll leave him. The first time the client doesn't always dare, he seems normal; but when he comes back, he begins to want things . . . You say your husband isn't a pervert: you'll see. They all are.' Because of these perversions she detested them. Another of my female friends, in 1943 in Fresnes, became intimate with a prostitute. She emphasised that 90 per cent of her clients were perverts and about 50 per cent were self-hating pederasts. Those who showed too much imagination terrified her. A German officer asked her to walk about the room naked with flowers in her arms while he imitated the flight of a bird; in spite of her courtesy and generosity, she ran away every time she caught sight of him. Marie-Thérèse hated 'fantasy' even though it had a much higher rate than simple coitus, and was often less demanding for the woman. These three women were particularly intelligent and sensitive. They certainly understood that as soon as they were no longer protected by the routine of the job, as soon as man stopped being a client in general and became individualised, they were prey to consciousness, to a capricious freedom: it was no longer just a simple business transaction. Some prostitutes, though, specialise in 'fantasy' because it brings in more money. In their hostility to the client there is often class resentment. Helene Deutsch speaks at great length about the story of Anna, a pretty blonde prostitute, childlike, generally very gentle, but who had fierce fits of anger against some men. She was from a working-class family; her father drank, her mother was sickly: this unhappy household gave her such a horrible idea of family life that she rejected all proposals to marry, even though throughout her career she had many opportunities. The young men of the neighbourhood debauched her; she liked her job well enough; but when, ill with tuberculosis, she was sent to the hospital, she developed a fierce hatred of doctors; 'respectable' men were abhorrent to her; she could not stand gentility, her doctor's solicitude. 'Don't we know better than anyone that these men easily drop their masks of gentility, self-control, and behave like brutes?' she said. Other than that, she was mentally perfectly well balanced. She pretended to have a child that she left with a wet nurse, but otherwise she did not lie. She died of tuberculosis. Another young prostitute, Julia, who gave herself to every boy she met from the age of fifteen, only liked poor and weak men; she was gentle and nice with them; she considered the others 'wicked beasts who deserved harsh treatment'. (She had an obvious complex that manifested an unsatisfied maternal vocation: she had fits as soon as 'mother', 'child' or similar-sounding words were uttered.)

Most prostitutes are morally adapted to their condition; that does not mean they are hereditarily or congenitally immoral, but they rightly feel integrated into a society that demands their services. They know well that the edifying lecture of the policeman who puts them through an inspection is pure verbiage, and the lofty principles their clients pronounce outside the brothel do little to intimidate them. Marie-Thérèse explains to the baker woman with whom she lives in Berlin:

Myself, I like everyone. When it's a question of dough, madame . . . Yes, because sleeping with a man for free, for nothing, says the same thing about you, that one's a whore; if you get paid, they call you a whore, yes, but a smart one; because when you ask a man for money, you can be sure that he'll tell you right off: 'Oh! I didn't know you did that kind of work,' or 'Do you have a man?' There you are. Paid or not, for me it's the same thing. 'Ah, yes!' she answers. 'You're right.' Because, I tell her, you're going to stand in line for a half hour to have a ticket for shoes. Myself, for a half hour, I'll turn a trick. I get the shoes without paying, and on the contrary, if I do my thing right, I'm paid as well. So you see, I'm right.

It is not their moral and psychological situation that makes prostitutes' existence miserable. It is their material condition that is deplorable for the most part. Exploited by their pimps and hotel keepers, they have no security, and three-quarters of them are penniless. After five years in the trade, around 75 per cent of them have syphilis, says Dr Bizard, who has treated thousands; among others, inexperienced minors are frighteningly susceptible to contamination; close to 25 per cent must be operated on for complications resulting from gonorrhoea. One in twenty has tuberculosis, 60 per cent become alcoholics or drug addicts; 40 per cent die before forty. It must be added that, in spite of precautions, they do become pregnant from time to time, and they are generally operated on in bad conditions. Common prostitution is a hard job where the sexually and economically oppressed woman – subjected to the arbitrariness of the police, humiliating medical checkups, the whims of her clients, and the prospect of germs, sickness and misery – is really reduced to the level of a thing.*

There are many degrees between the common prostitute and the grand hetaera. The main difference is that the former trades in her pure generality, so that competition keeps her at a miserable level of living, while the latter tries to be recognised in her singularity: if she succeeds, she can aspire to a lofty future. Beauty, charm and sex appeal are necessary for this, but they are not sufficient: the woman must be considered

---

* Obviously, it is not through negative and hypocritical measures that this situation can be changed. For prostitution to disappear, two conditions are necessary: a decent job must be guaranteed to all women; customs must not place any obstacles to free love. Prostitution will be suppressed only by suppressing the needs to which it responds.

distinguished. Her value will often be revealed through a man's desire: but she will be 'launched' only when the man declares her price to the eyes of the world. In the last century, it was the town house, carriage and pair, and pearls that proved the influence of the cocotte on her protector and that raised her to the rank of demimondaine; her worth was confirmed as long as men continued to ruin themselves for her. Social and economic changes abolished the Blanche d'Antigny types. There is no longer a demimonde in which a reputation can be established. An ambitious woman has to try to attain fame in other ways. The most recent incarnation of the hetaera is the movie star. Flanked by her husband or serious male friend – rigorously required by Hollywood – she is no less related to Phryne, Imperia or Casque d'Or. She delivers Woman to the dreams of men who give her fortune and glory in exchange.

There has always been a vague connection between prostitution and art, because beauty and sexuality are ambiguously associated with each other. In fact, it is not Beauty that arouses desire: but the Platonic theory of love suggests hypocritical justifications for lust. Phryne baring her breast offers Areopagus the contemplation of a pure idea. Exhibiting an unveiled body becomes an art show; American burlesque has turned undressing into a stage show. 'Nudity is chaste,' proclaim those old gentlemen who collect obscene photographs in the name of 'artistic nudes'. In the brothel, the moment of choice begins as a display; if choosing is more complicated, *tableaux vivants* and 'artistic poses' are offered to the client. The prostitute who wishes to acquire a singular distinction does not limit herself to showing her flesh passively; she tries to have her own talents. Greek flute-playing women charmed men with their music and dances. The Ouled Nails performing belly dances and Spanish women dancing and singing in the Barrio Chino are simply offering themselves in a refined manner to enthusiasts. Nana goes on stage to find herself a 'protector'. Some music halls, like some concert cafés before them, are simply brothels. All occupations where a woman displays herself can be used for amatory purposes. Of course there are showgirls, taxi dancers, nude dancers, escorts, pin-ups, models, singers and actresses who do not let their sexual lives interfere with their occupations; the more skill and invention involved in their work, the more it can be taken as a goal in itself; but a woman who 'goes onstage' to earn a living is often tempted to use her charms for more intimate commercial ends. Inversely, the courtesan wishes to have an occupation that will serve as her alibi. Rare are those like Colette's Léa who, addressed by a friend as 'Dear artist', would respond: 'Artist? My lovers are truly most indiscreet.' We have said that her reputation confers a market value on her: the stage or screen where she makes a 'name' for herself will become her capital.

Cinderella does not always dream of Prince Charming: husband or lover, she fears he may change into a tyrant; she prefers to dream of her own smiling face on a movie theatre marquee. But it is more often thanks to her masculine 'protection' that she will attain her goal; and it is men – husbands, lovers, suitors – who confirm her triumph by letting her share their fortune or their fame. It is this need to *please* another or a crowd that connects the movie star to the hetaera. They play a similar role in society: I will use the word hetaera to designate women who use not only their bodies but also their entire person as exploitable capital. Their attitude is very different from that of a creator who, transcending himself in a work, goes beyond the given and appeals to a freedom in others to whom he opens up the future; the hetaera does not uncover the world, she opens no road to human transcendence:* on the contrary, she seeks to take possession of it for her profit; offering herself for the approval of her admirers, she does not disavow this passive femininity that dooms her to man: she endows it with a magic power that allows her to take males into the trap of her presence, and to feed herself on them; she engulfs them with herself in immanence.

In this way, woman succeeds in acquiring a certain independence. Giving herself to many men, she belongs to none definitively; the money she accumulates, the name she 'launches' as one launches a product, assure her economic autonomy. The freest women in Ancient Greece were neither matrons nor common prostitutes but hetaeras. Renaissance courtesans and Japanese geishas enjoy an infinitely greater freedom than their contemporaries. In France, the woman who seems to be the most virile and independent is perhaps Ninon de Lenclos. Paradoxically, those women who exploit their femininity to the extreme create a situation for themselves nearly equal to that of a man; moving from this sex that delivers them to men as objects, they become subjects. They not only earn their living like men but they live in nearly exclusively masculine company; free in their mores and speech, they can rise to the rarest intellectual freedom – like Ninon de Lenclos. The most distinguished among

---

* It may happen that she is *also* an artist and seeking to please, she invents and creates. She can either combine these two functions or go beyond the amatory level and class herself in the category of actress, opera singer, dancer, and so on, which will be discussed later.

them are often surrounded with artists and writers who find 'virtuous women' boring. Masculine myths find their most seductive incarnation in the hetaera; more than any other woman, she is flesh and consciousness, idol, inspiration, muse; painters and sculptors want her as their model; she will nourish poets' dreams; it is in her that the intellectual will explore the treasures of feminine 'intuition'; she is more readily intelligent than the matron, because she is less set in hypocrisy. Women who are extremely talented will not readily settle for the role of Egeria; they will feel the need to show autonomously the value that the admiration of others confers on them; they will try to transform their passive virtues into activities. Emerging in the world as sovereign subjects, they write poems, prose; they paint and compose music. Thus Imperia became famous among Italian courtesans. A woman might also use man as an instrument, so as to practise through him masculine functions: the 'favourite royal mistresses' participated in the government of the world through their powerful lovers.*

This liberation can be conveyed on the erotic level as well. Woman might find compensation for the feminine inferiority complex in the money and services she extorts from man; money has a purifying role; it abolishes the war of the sexes. If many nonprofessional women insist on extracting cheques and gifts from their lovers – making the man pay – and paying him, as we will see further on, it is not out of cupidity alone: it is to change him into an instrument. In that way, the woman defends herself from becoming one herself; perhaps he believes he 'has' her, but this sexual possession is illusory; it is she who *has* him on the far more solid economic ground. Her self-esteem is satisfied. She can abandon herself to her lover's embraces; she is not yielding to a foreign will; pleasure will not be 'inflicted' on her, it will become rather a supplementary benefit; she will not be 'taken' because she is paid.

Nevertheless, the courtesan has the reputation of being frigid. It is useful for her to know how to govern her heart and her sexual appetite: sentimental or sensual, she risks being under the influence of a man who will exploit or dominate her or make her suffer. Among the sexual acts she accepts, there are many – especially early in her career – that humiliate her; her revolt against male arrogance is expressed by her frigidity. Hetaeras, like matrons, freely confide 'tricks' to each other that enable

---

* Just as some women use marriage to serve their own ends, others use their lovers as means for attaining a political or economic aim. They go beyond the hetaera's situation as others go beyond the matron's.

them to 'fake' their work. This contempt, this disgust for men clearly shows they are not at all sure they have won the game of exploiter-exploited. And in fact, in the great majority of cases, dependence is still their lot.

No man is their definitive master. But they have the most urgent need of man. The courtesan loses all her means of existence if he ceases to desire her: the novice knows that her whole future is in his hands; deprived of masculine support, even the movie star sees her prestige fade: abandoned by Orson Welles, Rita Hayworth wandered over Europe like a sickly orphan until she found Ali Khan. The most beautiful woman is never sure of tomorrow because her weapons are magic, and magic is capricious; she is bound to her protector – husband or lover – nearly as tightly as a 'virtuous' wife is bound to her husband. She not only owes him bed service but also is subjected to his presence, conversation, friends and especially his vanity's demands. By paying for his steady's high heels and satin skirts, the pimp makes an investment that will bring a return; by offering his girlfriend pearls and furs, the industrialist or the producer displays his wealth and power through her: whether the woman is a means for earning money or a pretext for spending it, it is the same servitude. The gifts showered on her are chains. And are these clothes and jewels she wears really hers? The man sometimes reclaims them after they break up, as Sacha Guitry once did with elegance. To 'keep' her protector without renouncing her pleasures, the woman uses ruses, manoeuvres, lies and hypocrisy that dishonour conjugal life; even if she only feigns servility, this game is itself servile. Beautiful and famous, she can choose another if the master of the moment becomes odious. But beauty is a worry, a fragile treasure; the hetaera is totally dependent on her body, which time pitilessly degrades; the fight against ageing is most dramatic for her. If she is endowed with great prestige, she will be able to survive the ruin of her face and figure. But caring for this renown, her surest asset, subjects her to the hardest of tyrannies: that of public opinion. We know that Hollywood stars fall into slavery. Their bodies are no longer their own; the producer decides on their hair colour, weight, figure and type; teeth are pulled out to change the shape of a cheek. Diets, exercise, fittings and makeup are daily chores. Going out and flirting are part of 'personal appearances'; private life is just a moment in their public life. In France there is no written contract, but a careful and clever woman knows what 'promotion' demands of her. The star who refuses to give in to these demands will face a brutal or slow but ineluctable decline. The prostitute who only gives her body is perhaps less of a slave than the woman whose occupation it is to entertain. A woman who has 'arrived' through a real profession and whose talent is recognised – actress, opera singer, dancer – escapes the hetaera's condition; she can experience true independence; but most spend their entire lives in danger; they must seduce the public and men over and over without respite.

Very often the kept woman interiorises her dependence; subjected to public opinion, she accepts its values; she admires the 'fashionable world' and adopts its customs; she wants to be regarded according to bourgeois standards. She is a parasite of the rich bourgeoisie and she adheres to its ideas; she is 'right thinking'; in former times she would readily send her daughters to a convent school and as she got older, she even went to Mass and openly converted. She is on the conservatives' side. She is too proud to have made her place in this world to want to change. The struggle she wages to 'arrive' does not dispose her to feelings of brotherhood and human solidarity; she paid for her success with too much slavish compliance to sincerely wish for universal freedom. Zola highlights this trait in Nana:[102]

As for books and plays, Nana had very definite opinions: she wanted tender and noble works, things to make her dream and elevate her soul . . . she was riled up against the republicans. What on earth did those dirty people who never washed want? Weren't people happy, didn't the emperor do everything he could for the people? A pretty bit of filth, the people! She knew them, she could talk about them: No, you see, their republic would be a great misfortune for everyone. Oh, may God preserve the emperor as long as possible!

In times of war, no one displays a more aggressive patriotism than high-level prostitutes; they hope to rise to the level of duchess through the noble sentiments they affect. Commonplaces, clichés, prejudices and conventional feelings form the basis of their public conversations, and they have often lost all sincerity deep in their hearts. Between lies and hyperbole, language is destroyed. The hetaera's whole life is a show: her words, her gestures, are intended not to express her thoughts but to produce an effect. She plays a comedy of love for her protector: at times she plays it for herself. She plays comedies of respectability and prestige for the public: she ends up believing herself to be a paragon of virtue and a sacred idol. Stubborn bad faith governs her inner life and permits her studied lies to seem true. There are moments of spontaneity in her life: she does experience love; she has 'flings' and 'infatuations'; sometimes she is even 'mad about' someone. But the one who spends too much time on caprices, feelings or pleasure will soon lose her 'position'. Generally, she composes her fantasies with the prudence of an adulterous wife; she hides from her producer and the public; thus, she cannot give too much of herself to her 'true loves'; they can only be a distraction, a respite. Besides, she is usually too obsessed with her own success to be able to lose herself in a real love affair. As for other women, it often happens that the hetaera loves them sensually; as an enemy of men who impose their domination on her, she will find sensual relaxation as well as revenge in the arms of a woman friend: so it was with Nana and her dear Satin. Just as she wishes to play an active role in the world to put her freedom to positive use, she likes to possess other beings: very young men whom she enjoys 'helping', or young women she will willingly support and, in any case, for whom she will be a virile personage. Whether she is homosexual or not, she will have the complex relations I have discussed with women in general: she needs them as judges and witnesses, as confidantes and accomplices, to create this 'counter-universe' that every woman oppressed by man must have. But feminine rivalry reaches its paroxysm here. The prostitute who trades on her generality has competition; but if there is enough work for everyone, they feel solidarity, even with their disputes. The hetaera who seeks to 'distinguish' herself is a priori hostile to the one who, like her, lusts for a privileged place. This is where the well-known theme of feminine 'cattiness' proves true.

The greatest misfortune for the hetaera is that not only is her independence the deceptive reverse side of a thousand dependencies, but this very freedom is negative. An actress like Rachel, a dancer like Isadora Duncan, even if they are aided by men, have occupations that are demanding and justify them; they attain concrete freedom from the work they choose and love. But for the great majority of them, their art, their occupations are only a means; they are not involved in real projects. Cinema in particular, which subjects the star to the director, allows her no invention, no progress, in creative activity. *Others* exploit what she *is*; she does not create a new object. Still it is quite rare to become a star. In 'amorous adventures', properly speaking, no road opens onto transcendence. Here again, ennui accompanies the confinement of woman in immanence. Zola shows this with Nana:

However, in the midst of all this luxury, and surrounded by her courtiers, Nana was bored to tears. She had men for every minute of the night, and money all over the house, even among the brushes and combs in the drawers of her dressing-table. But all this had ceased to satisfy her; and she was conscious of a void in her existence, a gap which made her yawn. Her life dragged on without occupation, each day bringing back the same monotonous hours. The next day did not exist: she lived like a bird, sure of having enough to eat, and ready to perch on the first branch she came to. This certainty of being fed caused her to stretch out in languid ease all day, lulled to sleep in conventional idleness and submission as if she were the prisoner of her own profession. Never going out except in her carriage, she began to lose the use of her legs. She reverted to her childish habits, kissing Bijou from morning to night and killing time with stupid pleasures, as she waited for some man or other.[103]

American literature abounds with this opaque ennui that stifles Hollywood and chokes the traveller as soon as he arrives there: actors and extras are as bored as the women whose condition they share. Even in France, official events are often burdensome. The protector who rules the starlet's life is an older man whose friends are his age: their preoccupations are foreign to the young woman, their conversations weary her; there is a chasm far deeper than in bourgeois marriages between the twenty-year-old novice and the forty-five-year-old banker who spend their days and nights side by side.

The Moloch to whom the hetaera sacrifices pleasure, love and freedom is her career. The matron's ideal is static happiness that envelops her relations with her husband and children. Her 'career' stretches across time, but it is nonetheless an immanent object that is summed up in a name. The name gets bigger on billboards and on people's lips as the steps mounted up the social ladder get higher. According to her temperament, the woman administers her enterprise prudently or boldly. One woman will find satisfaction in housekeeping, folding laundry in her closet, the other in the headiness of adventure. Sometimes the woman limits herself to perpetually balancing a perpetually threatened situation that sometimes breaks down; or sometimes she endlessly builds – like a Tower of Babel aiming in vain for the sky – her renown. Some of them, mixing amorous commerce with other activities, are true adventurers: they are spies, like Mata Hari, or secret agents; they generally are not the ones who initiate the projects, they are rather instruments in men's hands. But overall, the hetaera's attitude is similar to that of the adventurer; like him, she is often halfway between the *serious* and the *adventure* as such; she seeks ready-made values – money and glory – but she attaches as much value to winning them as to possessing them; and finally, the supreme value in her eyes is subjective success. She, too, justifies this individualism by a more or less systematic nihilism, but experienced with all the more conviction as she is hostile to men and sees enemies in other women. If she is intelligent enough to feel the need for moral justification, she will invoke a more or less well assimilated Nietzscheism; she will affirm the right of the elite being over the vulgar. Her person belongs to her like a treasure whose mere existence is a gift: so much so that in being dedicated to herself, she will claim to serve the group. The destiny of the woman devoted to man is haunted by love: she who exploits the male fulfils herself in the cult of self-adoration. If she attaches such a price to her glory, it is not only for economic interest: she seeks there the apotheosis of her narcissism.

CHAPTER 9

From Maturity to Old Age

The history of woman – because she is still trapped in her female functions – depends much more than man's on her physiological destiny; and the arc of this destiny is more erratic, more discontinuous, than the masculine one. Every period of woman's life is fixed and monotonous: but the passages from one stage to another are dangerously abrupt; they reveal themselves in far more decisive crises than those of the male: puberty, sexual initiation, menopause. While the male grows older continuously, the woman is brusquely stripped of her femininity; still young, she loses sexual attraction and fertility, from which, in society's and her own eyes, she derives the justification of her existence and her chances of happiness: bereft of all future, she has approximately half of her adult life still to live.

The 'dangerous age' is characterised by certain organic troubles,* but the symbolic value they embody gives them their importance. The crisis is felt much less acutely by women who have not essentially staked everything on their femininity; those who work hard – in their home or outside – are relieved when their menstrual servitude ends; peasants and workers' wives who are constantly threatened with new pregnancies are happy when, finally, that risk no longer exists. In this situation as in many others, women's disorders come less from the body itself than from their anxious consciousness of it. The moral drama usually begins before the onset of the physiological phenomena and it does not end until long after they have been eliminated.

Well before the definitive mutilation, woman is haunted by the horror of ageing. The mature man is engaged in more important enterprises than those of love; his sexual ardour is less pressing than in his youth; and as he is not expected to have the passive qualities of an object, the alteration of his face and body do not spoil his possibilities of seduction.

* See Vol. I, Chapter I.

By contrast, woman reaches her full sexual blossoming at about thirty-five, having finally overcome all her inhibitions: this is when her desires are the most intense and when she wants to satisfy them the most ardently; she has counted on her sexual attributes far more than man has; to keep her husband, to be assured of protection and to succeed in most jobs she holds, she has to please; she has not been allowed a hold on the world except through man's mediation: what will become of her when she no longer has a hold on him? This is what she anxiously wonders while she witnesses, powerless, the degradation of this object of flesh with which she is one; she fights; but dyes, peeling and plastic surgery can never do more than prolong her dying youth. At least she can play tricks with the mirror. But when the inevitable, irreversible process starts, which is going to destroy in her the whole edifice constructed during puberty, she feels touched by the very inevitability of death.

One might think that the woman who experiences the greatest distress is the one who has been the most passionately enraptured by her beauty and youth; but no; the narcissist is too attentive to her person not to have envisaged the ineluctable moment and not to have worked out an alternative position; she will certainly suffer from her mutilation: but at least she will not be caught short and will adapt rather quickly. The woman who has forgotten, devoted and sacrificed herself will be disrupted much more by the sudden revelation. 'I had only one life to live; this was my lot, so here I am!' To the surprise of her family and friends, a radical change takes place in her: expelled from her shelter, torn away from her projects, she brusquely finds herself, without resources, face-to-face with herself. Beyond this barrier she has unexpectedly struck, she has the feeling that she will do no more than survive; her body will be without promise; the dreams and desires she has not realised will for ever remain unaccomplished; she will look back on the past from this new perspective; the time has come to draw the line, to take stock. And she is horrified by the narrow strictures inflicted on her life. Faced with this, her brief and disappointing story, she behaves like an adolescent girl on the threshold of a still inaccessible future: she denies her finitude; to the poverty of her existence she contrasts the nebulous treasures of her personality. Because as a woman she endured her destiny more or less passively, she feels that her chances were taken from her, that she was duped, that she slid from youth to maturity without being aware of it. She discovers that her husband, her milieu and her occupations were not worthy of her; she feels misunderstood. She withdraws from the surroundings to which she esteems herself superior; she shuts herself up with the secret she carries in her heart and which is the mysterious key to her unfortunate lot; she tries to see the possibilities she has not exhausted. She begins to keep a diary; if she has understanding confidantes, she pours out her heart in endless conversations; and she ruminates on her regrets, her grievances, all day and all night. Just as the girl dreams of what her future *will be*, she recalls what her past *could have been*; she remembers the missed occasions and constructs beautiful retrospective romances. Helene Deutsch cites the case of a woman who had broken off an unhappy marriage very early on and who had then spent long serene years with a second husband: at forty-five, she painfully began to miss her first husband and to sink into melancholy. The cares of childhood and puberty come back to life, the woman constantly mulls over the story of her youth, and forgotten feelings for her parents, brothers and sisters and childhood friends come alive once again. Sometimes she indulges in dreamy and passive moroseness. But more often she is jolted into saving her wasted existence. She displays, exhibits and praises the merits of this personality she has just discovered in contrast with the pettiness of her destiny. Matured by experience, she believes she is finally able to prove her worth; she would like to have another chance. And first in a pathetic effort, she tries to stop time. A maternal woman is sure she can still have a child: she passionately seeks to create life once more. A sensual woman strives to conquer a new lover. The coquette is more than ever determined to please. They all declare they have never felt so young. They want to persuade others that the passage of time has not really touched them; they begin to 'dress young', they act childishly. The ageing woman well knows that if she has ceased being a sexual object, it is not only because her flesh no longer provides man with fresh treasures: it is also that her past and her experience make a person of her whether she likes it or not; she has fought, loved, wanted, suffered and taken pleasure for herself: this autonomy is intimidating; she tries to disavow it; she exaggerates her femininity, she adorns herself, wears perfume, she becomes totally charming, gracious, pure immanence; she admires her male interlocutor with a naive eye and childish intonations; she ostentatiously brings up her memories of girlhood; instead of speaking, she chirps, she claps her hands, bursts out laughing. She plays this game with a kind of sincerity. This newfound interest in herself and her desire to wrench herself from old routines and start over again give her the impression of a new beginning.

In fact, it is not really a question of a new start; she discovers no goals in the world towards which she could project herself in a free and effective movement. Her agitation is more eccentric, incoherent and useless because it only serves as symbolic compensation for past errors and failures. Among other things and before it is too late, the woman will try to realise all her childhood and adolescent desires: this one goes back to the piano, that one begins to sculpt, to write, to travel; she takes up skiing, foreign languages. She welcomes everything she had refused until then – again before it is too late. She admits her repugnance for a husband she had previously tolerated and she becomes frigid in his arms; or by contrast, she abandons herself to the passions she repressed; she overwhelms the husband with her demands; she goes back to practising masturbation, which she had given up since childhood. Her homosexual tendencies – that are latent in almost all women – come out. The subject often carries them over to her daughter; but sometimes unusual feelings arise for a woman friend. In his work, *Sex, Life and Faith*, Rom Landau tells the following story, confided to him by the person herself:

Mrs X., a woman in the late forties, married for over twenty-five years, mother of three grown-up children, occupied a prominent position in . . . the social and charitable activities of the town in which she lived. Mrs X. met a woman in London some ten years her junior who, like herself, was a leading social worker. The two . . . became friends. Miss Y. invited Mrs X. to stay as her guest during her next visit to London, and Mrs X. . . . accepted. During the second evening of her visit – Mrs X. assured me repeatedly that she had not the least idea how it happened – she suddenly found herself passionately embracing her hostess, and subsequently she spent the whole night with her . . . she was terrified . . . and left London the same day . . . Never in her life had she read or heard anything about homosexuality and had had no idea that 'such things' existed . . . she could do nothing to stifle her ever-growing feelings for Miss Y. . . . For the first time in her life she found [her husband's] caresses unwelcome, even his routine kiss . . . Finally, she decided to revisit Miss Y. and 'clear up' the situation . . . she only found herself more deeply involved in it; . . . to be with her filled her with a delight that she had never experienced before . . . she was troubled by a profound sin-consciousness, and was anxious to discover whether there was a 'scientific explanation' of her state and any moral justification for it.[104]

In this case, the subject gave in to a spontaneous drive and was herself deeply disconcerted by it. But often the woman deliberately seeks to live the romances she has not experienced and that soon she will no longer be able to experience. She leaves her home, both because it seems unworthy of her and because she desires solitude as well as the chance to seek adventure. If she finds it, she throws herself into it greedily. Thus, in this story by Stekel:

> Mme B. Z. was forty years old, had three children and twenty years of married life behind her when she began to think she was misunderstood, that she had wasted her life; she took up various new activities among which was going skiing in the mountains; there she met a thirty-year-old man and became his mistress; but soon after, he fell in love with Mme B. Z.'s daughter . . . she agreed to their marriage so as to keep her lover near her; there was an unacknowledged but very strong homosexual love between mother and daughter, which partially explains this decision. Nevertheless, the situation soon became intolerable, the lover sometimes leaving the mother's bed during the night to be with the daughter. Mme B. Z. . . . attempted suicide. It was then – she was forty-six – that she was treated by Stekel. She decided to break it off and while her daughter gave up her marriage plans Mme B. Z. . . . then became an exemplary wife and fell into piousness.

A woman influenced by a tradition of decency and honesty does not always follow through with action. But her dreams are peopled with erotic fantasies that she calls up during waking hours as well; she manifests an exalted and sensual tenderness to her children; she cultivates incestuous obsessions with her son; she secretly falls in love with one young man after another; like an adolescent girl, she is haunted by ideas of rape; she also feels the attraction of prostitution; the ambivalence of her desires and fears produces an anxiety that sometimes leads to neuroses: she scandalises her family and friends by bizarre behaviour that in fact merely expresses her imaginary life.

The boundary between the imaginary and the real is even less distinct in this troubled period than during puberty. One of the most salient characteristics in the ageing woman is the feeling of depersonalisation that makes her lose all objective landmarks. People in good health who have come close to death also say they have felt a curious impression of doubling; when one feels oneself to be consciousness, activity and freedom, the passive object affected by fate seems necessarily like another: *I* am not the one run over by a car; *I* am not the old woman the mirror shows me. The woman who 'never felt so young' and who never saw herself so old is not able to reconcile these two aspects of herself; time passes and diminishes her in dreams. So reality fades and becomes less important: likewise, she can no longer tell herself apart from the illusion. The woman relies on interior proof rather than on this strange world where time proceeds in reverse, where her double no longer resembles her, where events have betrayed her. She is thus inclined to ecstasies, visions and deliriums. And since love is even more than ever her essential preoccupation, it is understandable that she lets herself go to the illusion that she is loved. Nine out of ten erotomaniacs are women; and they are almost all between forty and fifty years old.

However, not everyone is able to cross over the wall of reality so boldly. Deprived of all human love, even in their dreams, many women seek relief in God; the flirt, the lover and the dissolute become pious around menopause. The vague ideas of destiny, secrecy and misunderstood personality of woman in her autumn years find a rational unity in religion. The devotee considers her wasted life as a test sent by the Lord; in her unhappiness, her soul has drawn exceptional advantages from misfortune, making her worthy of being visited by the grace of God; she will readily believe that heaven sends her illuminations or even – like Mme Krüdener – that it imperiously entrusts her with a mission. As she has more or less lost the sense of reality during this crisis, the woman is open to any suggestion: any spiritual guide is in a strong position to wield power over her soul. She will also enthusiastically accept more questionable authorities; she is an obvious prey for religious sects, spirits, prophets, faith healers and any charlatan. Not only has she lost all critical sense by losing contact with the given world, but she is also desperate for a definitive truth: she has to have the remedy, the formula, the key, that will suddenly save her by saving the universe. She scorns more than ever a logic that obviously could not possibly apply to her own case; the only arguments that seem convincing to her are those that are particularly destined for her: revelations, inspirations, messages, signs or even miracles begin to appear around her. Her discoveries sometimes draw her into paths of action: she throws herself into schemes, undertakings and adventures whose idea is whispered to her by some adviser or inner voices. Sometimes, she simply deems herself the holder of the truth and absolute wisdom. Whether she is active or contemplative, her attitude is accompanied by feverish exaltation. The crisis of menopause brutally cuts feminine life into two: it is this discontinuity that gives woman the illusion of a 'new life'; it is an *other* time opening before her: she approaches it with the fervour of a convert; she is converted to love, life, God, art and humanity: she loses and magnifies herself in these entities. She is dead and resuscitated, she views the earth with a gaze that has pierced the secrets of the beyond and she thinks she is flying towards uncharted heights.

Yet the earth does not change; the summits remain out of reach; the messages received – even in blinding clarity – are hard to decipher; the inner lights go out; what remains before the mirror is a woman one day older than yesterday. Doleful hours of depression follow moments of fervour. The body determines this rhythm since a reduction in hormonal secretions is offset by a hyperactive hypophysis; but it is above all the psychological state that orders this alternation. For the agitation, illusions and fervour are merely a defence against the inevitability of what has been. Once again, anxiety grabs the throat of the one whose life is already finished even though death is not imminent. Instead of fighting against despair, she often chooses to intoxicate herself with it. She rehashes grievances, regrets and recriminations; she imagines that her neighbours and family are engaging in dark machinations; if she has a sister or woman friend of her age who is associated with her life, they may construct persecution fantasies together. But above all she becomes morbidly jealous of her husband: she is jealous of his friends, his sisters, his job; and rightly or wrongly, she accuses some rival of being responsible for all her problems. Cases of pathological jealousy mostly occur between fifty and fifty-five years of age.

The problems of menopause will last – sometimes until death – if the woman does not decide to let herself grow old; if she does not have any resources other than the use of her charms, she will fight tooth and nail to maintain them; she will also fight with rage if her sex drives remain alive. This is not unusual. Princess Metternich was asked at what age a woman stops being tormented by the flesh: 'I don't know,' she said, 'I'm only sixty-five.' Marriage, which Montaigne thought provided 'little relief' for woman, becomes a more and more inadequate solution as a woman gets older; she often pays for the resistance and coldness of her youth in maturity; when she finally begins to experience the fevers of desire, her husband has been resigned to her indifference for a long time: he has found a solution for himself. Stripped of her attraction by habit and time, the wife seldom has the opportunity to awaken the conjugal flame. Vexed, determined to 'live her life', she will have fewer scruples than before – if she ever had any – in taking lovers; but there again they have to let themselves be taken: it is a manhunt. She deploys a thousand ruses: feigning to offer herself, she imposes herself; she uses charm, friendship and gratitude as traps. It is not only out of a desire for fresh flesh that she goes after young men: they are the only ones from whom she can hope for this disinterested tenderness the adolescent male can sometimes feel for a maternal mistress; she has become aggressive and domineering: Léa is fulfilled by Chéri's docility as well as by his beauty. Once she reached her forties, Mme de Staël chose pages whom she overwhelmed with her prestige; and a shy man, a novice, is also easier to capture. When seduction and intrigue really prove useless, there is still one resource: paying. The tale of the little knife, popular in the Middle Ages, illustrates these insatiable ogresses' fate: a young woman, as thanks for her favours, asked each of her lovers for a little knife, which she kept in a cupboard; the day came when the cupboard was full: but it was then that the lovers began to demand from her a little knife after each night of love; the cupboard was soon emptied; all the little knives had been returned: others had to be bought. Some women take a cynical view of the situation: they have had their moment, now it is their turn to 'return the little knives'. Money in their eyes can even play the opposite – but equally purifying – role of the one it plays for the courtesan: it changes the male into an instrument and provides woman with the erotic freedom that her young pride used to deny her. But more romantic than lucid, the mistress-benefactress often attempts to buy a mirage of tenderness, admiration and respect; she even persuades herself that she gives for the pleasure of giving, without being asked: here too a young man is the perfect choice because a woman can pride herself on maternal generosity towards him; and then there is a little of this 'mystery' the man also asks of the woman he 'helps' so that this crude deal is thus camouflaged as enigma. But it is rare for this bad faith to be moderate for long; the battle of the sexes changes into a duel between exploiter and exploited where woman, disappointed and ridiculed, risks suffering cruel defeats. If she is prudent, she will resign herself to 'disarming', without waiting too long, even if all her passions are not yet spent.

From the day woman agrees to grow old, her situation changes. Until then, she was still young, determined to fight against an evil that mysteriously made her ugly and deformed her; now she becomes a different being, asexual but complete: an elderly woman. It may be thought that the change-of-life crisis is then finished. But one must not conclude that it will be easy to live from then on. When she has given up the fight against the inevitability of time, another combat opens: she has to keep a place on earth.

Woman frees herself from her chains in her autumn and winter years; she uses the pretext of her age to escape burdensome chores; she knows her husband too well to let herself still be intimidated by him, she avoids his embraces, she carves out – in friendship, indifference or hostility – a real life of her own alongside him; if he declines more quickly than she, she takes the lead in the couple. She can also allow herself to disdain fashion and public opinion; she refuses social obligations, diets and beauty treatment: like Léa, whom Chéri finds liberated from dressmakers, corset-makers and hairdressers, and happily settled down indulging herself in food. As for her children, they are old enough not to need her, they get married, they leave home. Relieved of her duties, she finally discovers her freedom. Unfortunately, every woman's history repeats the fact we have observed throughout the history of woman: she discovers this freedom when she can find nothing more to do with it. This repetition has nothing coincidental about it: patriarchal society has made all feminine functions servile; woman escapes slavery only when she loses all productivity. At fifty, she is in full possession of her strength, she feels rich in experience; this is the age when man rises to the highest positions, the most important jobs: and as for her, she is forced into retirement. She has only been taught to devote herself and there is no one who requires her devotion any more. Useless, unjustified, she contemplates these long years without promise she still has to live and murmurs: 'No one needs me!'

She does not resign herself right away. Sometimes, out of despair, she clings to her husband; she overwhelms him more imperiously than ever with her ministrations; but the routine of conjugal life has been too well established; either she has known for a long time that her husband does not need her, or he does not seem precious enough to her to justify her any longer. Assuring the maintenance of their shared life is as contingent a task as watching over herself alone. She turns to her children with hope: for them the die is not yet cast; the world, the future is open to them; she would like to dive into it after them. The woman who has had the chance of giving birth at an advanced age finds herself privileged: she is still a young mother when the others are becoming grandparents. But in general, between forty and fifty, the mother sees her little ones become adults. It is at the very instant they are escaping her that she passionately attempts to live through them.

Her attitude is different depending on whether she is counting on being saved by a son or a daughter; she usually puts her strongest hope in her son. Here he finally comes to her from the far past, the man whose marvellous appearance she waited to see coming over the horizon; from the first scream of the newborn she has waited for this day when he will hand out all the treasures the father was never able to satisfy her with. During that time, she has doled out slaps and purges but she has forgotten them; he whom she carried in her womb was already one of these demigods who govern the world and women's destiny: now he will recognise her in the glory of her motherhood. He will defend her against her spouse's supremacy, avenge her for the lovers she has had and those she has not had; he will be her liberator, her saviour. She will behave like the seductive and ostentatious girl waiting for Prince Charming; when she is walking beside him, elegant and still charming, she thinks she looks like his 'older sister'; she is delighted if – taking after the heroes of American films – he teases and jostles her, laughing and respectful: with proud humility she recognises the virile superiority of the one she carried in her womb. To what extent can these feelings be considered incestuous? It is sure that when she thinks of herself complaisantly on her son's arm, the expression 'older sister' prudishly expresses ambivalent fantasies; when she sleeps, when she does not control herself, her musings sometimes carry her very far; but I have already said that dreams and fantasies are far from always expressing the hidden desire of a real act: they are often sufficient, they are the completion of a desire that only requires an imaginary satisfaction. When the mother plays in a more or less veiled way at seeing her son as a lover, it is just a game. Real eroticism usually has little place in this couple. But it is a couple; it is from the depths of her femininity that the mother hails in her son the sovereign man; she puts herself in his hands with as much fervour as a lover, and in exchange for this gift, she counts on being raised to the right hand of the god. To gain this assumption, the woman in love appeals to the lover's freedom: she generously assumes a risk; her anxious demands are the ransom. The mother reckons she has acquired holy rights by the simple fact of giving birth; she does not expect her son to see himself in her in order for her to consider him her creation, her property; she is less demanding than the woman lover because she is of a more tranquil bad faith; having made a being of flesh, she makes an existence her own: she appropriates its acts, accomplishments and merits. In exalting her fruit, she is carrying her own person to the heights.

Living by proxy is always a precarious expedient. Things may not turn out as one wished. It often happens that a son is no more than a good-for-nothing, a hooligan, a failure, a lost cause, an empty promise, ungrateful. The mother has her own ideas about the hero her son is supposed to embody. Nothing is rarer than a mother who authentically respects the human person her child is, who recognises his freedom even in his failures, who assumes with him the risks implied by any engagement. One more often encounters mothers who emulate that over-glorified Spartan woman who cavalierly condemns her son to glory or death; on earth, the son has to justify his mother's existence by taking hold of values she herself respects for their mutual advantage. The mother demands that the child-god's projects conform to her own ideal and that their success be assured. Every woman wants to give birth to a hero, a genius; but all mothers of heroes and geniuses began by proclaiming they were breaking their mothers' hearts. It is in reaction to his mother that man most often wins the trophies she dreamed of displaying for herself and that she does not recognise even when he lays them at her feet. Though she may approve in principle of her son's undertakings, she is torn by a contradiction similar to one that tortures the woman in love. To justify his life – and his mother's – the son must surpass her towards his ends; and to attain them, he is led to risk his health and put himself in danger: but he contests the value of the gift she gave him when he places certain goals above the pure fact of living. She is shocked by this; she reigns sovereign over man only if this flesh she has engendered is for him the supreme good: he does not have the right to destroy this work she has produced through suffering. 'You'll tire yourself out, you'll make yourself ill, you'll be sorry,' she drones in his ears. Yet she knows very well that to live is not enough, or else procreation itself would be superfluous; she is the first to be irritated if her offspring is a loafer, a coward. She is never at rest. When he goes to war, she wants him home alive but decorated. In his career, she wishes him to 'make it' but trembles when he overworks. Whatever he does, she always worries that she will stand by powerless in the unfolding of a story that is hers but over which she has no control: she fears he will make the wrong decision, that he will not succeed, that if he succeeds, he will ruin his health. Even if she has confidence in him, differences of age and sex keep a real complicity from being established between her son and her; she is not informed about his work; no collaboration is demanded of her.

This is why the mother remains unsatisfied, even if she admires her son with inordinate pride. Believing that she has not only engendered a being of flesh but also founded an absolutely necessary existence, she feels retrospectively justified; but having rights is not an occupation: to fill her days she needs to perpetuate her beneficent activity; she wants to feel indispensable to her god; the mystification of devotion in this case is denounced in the most brutal manner: his wife will strip her of her functions. The hostility she feels to this stranger who 'steals' her child has often been described. The mother has raised the contingent facticity of parturition to the height of divine mystery: she refuses to accept that a human decision can have more weight. In her eyes, values are preestablished, they proceed from nature, from the past: she does not understand the value of a freely made engagement. Her son owes her his life; what does he owe this woman he did not know until yesterday? It is through some evil spell that she convinced him of the existence of a bond that until now did not *exist*; she is devious, calculating and dangerous. The mother impatiently waits for the imposture to be revealed; encouraged by the old myth of the good mother with healing hands who binds the wounds inflicted on him by the bad wife, she watches her son's face for signs of unhappiness: she finds them, even if he denies it; she feels sorry for him even when he complains of nothing; she spies on her daughter-in-law, she criticises her, she counters all her innovations with the past and the customs that condemn the intruder's very presence. Each woman understands the beloved's happiness in her own way: the wife wants to see in him a man through whom she will control the world; the mother tries to keep him by taking him back to his childhood; to the projects of the young wife who expects her husband to *become* rich or important, the mother counters with the laws of his unchanging essence: he *is* fragile, he must not tire himself. The conflict between the past and the future is exacerbated when it is the newcomer's turn to get pregnant. 'The birth of children is the death of parents'; here this truth is at its cruellest: the mother who had hoped to live on through her son understands he has condemned her to death. She gave life: life will continue without her; she is no longer *the* Mother: simply a link; she falls from the heaven of timeless idols; she is no more than a finished, outdated individual. It is then that in pathological cases her hatred intensifies to the point where she has a neurosis or is driven to commit a crime; it was when her daughter-in-law's pregnancy was announced that Mme Lefebvre, who had long hated her, decided to kill her.*

Normally, the grandmother overcomes her hostility; sometimes she obstinately sees the newborn as her son's alone, and she loves it tyrannically; but generally the young mother and her own mother claim it for their own; the jealous grandmother cultivates an ambiguous affection for the baby, where hostility hides in the guise of concern.

The mother's attitude to her grown daughter is very ambivalent: she seeks a god in her son; in her daughter, she finds a double. The 'double' is an ambiguous personage; it assassinates the one from which it emanates, as can be seen in the tales of Poe, in *The Picture of Dorian Gray* and in the story told by Marcel Schwob. Thus the girl condemns her mother to death by becoming a woman; and yet, she permits her to survive. The mother's behaviour depends on whether she grasps her child's healthy development as a promise of ruin or of resurrection.

Many mothers become rigid in hostility; they do not accept being supplanted by the ingrate who owes them her life; we have often pointed out the coquette's jealousy of the fresh adolescent who denounces her artifices: a woman who has detested a rival in any woman will hate the rival even in her child; she sends her away, hides her, or finds ways to deprive her of opportunities. A woman who took pride in being the Wife and the Mother in an exemplary and unique way will refuse no less fiercely to give up her throne; she continues to affirm that her daughter is merely a child, and she considers her undertakings to be childish games; she is too young to marry, too delicate to give birth; if she insists on wanting a husband, a home and children, they will never be more than look-alikes; the mother tirelessly criticises, derides or prophesies misfortune. If she can, she condemns her daughter to eternal childhood; if not, she tries to ruin this adult life the daughter is trying to lead on her own.

* In August 1925, a sixty-year-old bourgeois woman from the North, Mme Lefebvre, who lived with her husband and her children, killed her daughter-in-law, six months pregnant, during a car trip while her son was driving. Condemned to death and then pardoned, she spent the rest of her life in a reformatory where she showed no remorse; she believed God approved of her when she killed her daughter-in-law 'as one kills a weed, a bad seed, as one kills a savage beast'. The only savagery she gave as proof was that the young woman one day said to her: 'You have me now, so you now have to take me into account.' It was when she suspected her daughter-in-law's pregnancy that she bought a revolver, supposedly to defend herself against robbers. After her menopause, she was desperately attached to her maternity: for twelve years she had suffered from malaises that manifested themselves symbolically in an imaginary pregnancy.

We have seen that she often succeeds: many young women remain sterile, have miscarriages, prove incapable of nursing and raising their children or running their homes because of this evil influence. Their conjugal life becomes impossible. Unhappy and isolated, they will find refuge in the sovereign arms of their mothers. If they resist her, a perpetual conflict will pit them against each other; the frustrated mother largely transfers onto her son-in-law the irritation her insolent daughter's independence provokes in her.

The mother who passionately identifies with her daughter is no less tyrannical; what she wants, having acquired mature experience, is to relive her youth: thus will she save her past while saving herself from it; she herself will choose a son-in-law who conforms to the perfect husband she never had; flirtatious and tender, she will easily imagine somewhere in her heart that it is she he is marrying; through her daughter, she will satisfy her old desires for wealth, success and glory; such women, who ardently 'push' their children along the paths of seduction, cinema or theatre, have often been described; under the pretext of watching over them, they take over their lives: I have been told about some who go so far as to take the girl's suitor to bed with them. But it is rare for the girl to put up with this guardianship indefinitely; the day she finds a husband or a serious protector, she will rebel. The mother-in-law who had begun by cherishing her son-in-law then becomes hostile to him; she moans about human ingratitude, takes the role of victim herself; she becomes in her turn an enemy mother. Foreseeing these disappointments, many women feign indifference when they see their children grow up: but they take little joy from it. A mother must have a rare mixture of generosity and detachment to find enrichment in her children's lives without becoming a tyrant or turning them into her tormentors.

The grandmother's feelings towards her grandchildren are an extension of those she has for her daughter: she often transfers her hostility onto them. It is not only out of fear of public opinion that so many women force their seduced daughter to have an abortion, to abandon the child, to do away with it: they are only too happy to keep her from motherhood; they obstinately wish to keep the privilege for themselves. They readily advise even a legitimate mother to provoke a miscarriage, not to breast-feed the child, or to rid herself of it. They themselves will deny the existence of this impudent little being by their indifference; or else they will spend their time endlessly scolding the child, punishing him, even mistreating him. By contrast, the mother who identifies with her daughter often welcomes the children more avidly than the young woman does; the daughter is disconcerted by the arrival of the little stranger; the grandmother recognises him: she goes back twenty years in time, she becomes the young woman giving birth again; all the joys of possession and domination her children long ago ceased to give her are returned to her, all the desires of motherhood she had renounced with menopause are miraculously fulfilled; she is the real mother, she takes charge of the baby with authority, and if the baby is given over to her, she will passionately devote herself to him. Unfortunately for her, the young woman is keen to hold on to her rights: the grandmother is authorised only to play the role of assistant that her elders formerly played with her; she feels dethroned; and besides, she has to share this with her son-in-law's mother, of whom she is naturally jealous. Resentment often distorts the spontaneous love she felt at first for the child. The anxiety often observed in grandmothers expresses the ambivalence of their feelings: they cherish the baby insofar as it belongs to them, they are hostile to the little stranger that he is to them, they are ashamed of this enmity. Yet if the grandmother maintains her warm affection for her grandchildren while giving up the idea of entirely possessing them, she can play the privileged role of guardian angel in their lives: recognising neither rights nor responsibilities, she loves them out of pure generosity; she does not entertain narcissistic dreams through them, she asks nothing of them, she does not sacrifice their future in which she will not be present: what she loves are the little flesh-and-blood beings who are there today in their contingency and their gratuitousness; she is not an educator; she does not represent abstract justice or law. This is where the conflicts that at times set her in opposition to the parents will sometimes arise.

It may be that the woman has no descendants or is not interested in posterity; lacking natural bonds with children or grandchildren, she sometimes tries to create them artificially with counterparts. She offers maternal tenderness to young people; whether or not her affection remains platonic, it is not necessarily hypocrisy that makes her declare that she loves her young protégé 'like a son': the mother's feelings, inversely, are love feelings. It is true that Mme de Warens's competitors take pleasure in generously satisfying, helping and shaping a man: they want to be the source, the necessary condition and the foundation of an existence that has passed them by; they become mothers and find their identity in their lovers far more in this role than in the role of mistress. Very often also the maternal woman adopts girls: here again their relations take more or less sexual forms; but whether platonic or carnal, what she seeks in her protégées is her own double, miraculously rejuvenated. The actress, the dancer, the singer become teachers – they form pupils – and the intellectual woman – such as Mme de Charrière, alone in Colombier – indoctrinates disciples; the devotee gathers spiritual daughters around her; the seductress becomes a madam. It is never pure self-interest that brings such ardent zeal to their proselytising: they are passionately seeking to reincarnate themselves. Their tyrannical generosity gives rise to more or less the same conflicts as between mothers and daughters united by blood. It is also possible to adopt grandchildren: great-aunts and godmothers gladly play a role similar to that of grandmothers. But in any case, it is rare for a woman to find in posterity – natural or selected – a justification of her declining life: she fails to make the enterprise of these young existences her own. Either she persists in the effort to appropriate it, consumed in the struggles and dramas that leave her disappointed and broken; or she resigns herself to a modest participation. This is the most common case. The aged mother and grandmother repress their dominating desires, they conceal their resentments; they are satisfied with whatever their children choose to give them. But then they get little help from them. They remain available facing the desert of the future, prey to solitude, regret and ennui.

Here we touch upon the older woman's tragedy: she realises she is useless; all through her life, the bourgeois woman often has to resolve the derisory problem: how to kill time? For once the children are raised and the husband has become successful, or at least settled, days drag on. 'Women's handiwork' was invented to mask this horrible idleness; hands embroider, knit, they are busy hands and they move; it is not a question here of real work because the object produced is not the goal; it has little importance and it is often a problem to know what to do with it: one gets rid of it by giving it to a friend or a charitable organisation or by cluttering mantelpieces or coffee tables; neither is it a game that reveals the pure joy of existence in its gratuitousness; and it is hardly a diversion because the mind is vacant: it is an absurd distraction, as Pascal described it; with needle or hook, woman sadly weaves the very nothingness of her days. Watercolours, music or reading have the very same role; the unoccupied woman does not try to extend her grasp on the world in giving herself over to such activities, but only to relieve boredom; an activity that does not open up the future slides into the vanity of immanence; the idle woman begins a book, then puts it down, opens the piano, closes it, returns to her embroidery, yawns and ends up on the telephone. In fact, she is more likely to seek relief in social life; she goes out, makes visits, and – like Mrs Dalloway – attaches enormous importance to her parties; she goes to every wedding, every funeral; no longer having any existence of her own, she feeds on the company of others; she goes from being a coquette to a gossip: she watches, she comments; she compensates for her inaction by dispensing criticism and advice to those around her. She gives her experienced advice even to those around her who do not seek it. If she has the means, she holds a salon; in this way she hopes to appropriate undertakings and successes that are not hers; Mme du Deffand's and Mme Verdurin's despotism over their subjects is well known. To be a centre of attraction, a crossroads, an inspiration, or to create an 'atmosphere' is in itself an ersatz activity. There are other more direct ways to intervene in the course of the world; in France, there are 'charities' and a few 'clubs', but it is particularly true in America that women group together in clubs where they play bridge, hand out literary prizes, or reflect on social improvement. What characterises most of these organisations on the two continents is that they are in themselves their own reason for existence: the aims they claim to pursue serve only as a pretext. Things happen exactly as in Kafka's fable:* no one is concerned about building the Tower of Babel; a vast city is built around its ideal place, consuming all its resources for administration, growth and resolving internal dissensions. So charity women spend most of their time organising their organisation; they elect a board, discuss its statutes, dispute among themselves and struggle to keep their prestige over rival associations: no one must steal *their* poor, *their* sick, *their* wounded, *their* orphans; they would rather leave them to die than yield them to their neighbours. And they are far from wanting a regime that, in doing away with injustice and abuse, would make their dedication useless; they bless the wars and famines that transform them into benefactresses of humanity. It is clear that in their eyes the knitted hats and parcels are not intended for soldiers and the hungry: instead the soldiers and hungry are made expressly to receive knitted goods and parcels.

In spite of everything, some of these groups attain positive results. In the United States, the influence of venerated 'Moms' is strong; this is explained by the leisure time their parasitic existence leaves them: and this is why it is harmful. 'Knowing nothing about medicine, art, science, religion, law, health, sanitation . . .' says Philip Wylie,† speaking of the American Mom, 'she seldom has any special interest in *what*, exactly, she is doing as a member of any of these endless organizations,

---

* 'The City Coat of Arms'.
† *Generation of Vipers*.

so long as it is *something*.' Their effort is not integrated into a coherent and constructive plan, it does not aim at objective ends: imperiously, it tends only to show their tastes and prejudices or to serve their interests. They play a considerable role in the domain of culture, for example: it is they who buy the most books; but they read as one plays the game of solitaire; literature takes its meaning and dignity when it is addressed to individuals committed to projects, when it helps them surpass themselves towards greater horizons; it must be integrated into the movement of human transcendence; instead, woman devalues books and works of art by swallowing them into her immanence; a painting becomes a knick-knack, music an old song, a novel a reverie as useless as crocheted antimacassars. It is American women who are responsible for the degradation of best sellers: these books are only intended to please, and worse to please idle women who need escape. As for their activities in general, Philip Wylie defines them like this:

They frighten politicians into sniveling servility and they terrify pastors; they bother bank presidents and they pulverise school boards. Mom has many such organizations, the real purpose of which is to compel an abject compliance of her environs to her personal desires . . . she drives out of the town and the state, if possible, all young harlots . . . she causes bus lines to run where they are convenient for her rather than for workers . . . throws prodigious fairs and parties for charity and gives the proceeds . . . to the janitor to buy the committee some beer for its headache on the morning after . . . The clubs afford mom an infinite opportunity for nosing into other people's business.

There is much truth in this aggressive satire. Not being specialised in politics or economics or any technical discipline, old women have no concrete hold on society; they are unaware of the problems action poses; they are incapable of elaborating a constructive programme. Their morality is abstract and formal, like Kant's imperatives; they issue prohibitions instead of trying to discover the paths of progress; they do not positively try to create new situations; they attack what already exists in order to do away with the evil in it; this explains why they are always forming coalitions against something – against alcohol, prostitution or pornography – they do not understand that a purely negative effort is doomed to be unsuccessful, as evidenced by the failure of prohibition in America or the law in France voted by Marthe Richard. As long as woman remains a parasite, she cannot effectively participate in the building of a better world.

It does happen that in spite of everything, some women entirely committed to a cause truly have an impact; these women are not merely seeking to keep themselves busy, they have ends in view; autonomous producers, they escape from the parasitic category we are considering here: but this conversion is rare. In their private or public activities, most women do not aim for a goal that can be reached but for a way to keep busy: and no occupation is meaningful if it is only a pastime. Many of them suffer from this; with a life already behind them, they feel the same distress as adolescent boys whose lives have not yet opened up; nothing is calling them, around them both is a desert; faced with any action, they murmur: What's the use? But the adolescent boy is drawn, willingly or not, into a man's existence that reveals responsibilities, goals and values; he is thrown into the world, he takes a stand, he becomes committed. If it is suggested to the older woman that she begin to move towards the future, she responds sadly: it's too late. It is not that her time is limited from here on: a woman is made to retire very early; but she lacks the drive, confidence, hope and anger that would allow her to discover new goals in her own life. She takes refuge in the routine that has always been her lot; she makes repetition her system, she throws herself into household obsessions; she becomes more deeply religious; she becomes rigidly stoic, like Mme de Charrière. She becomes brittle, indifferent, egotistical.

The old woman often finds serenity towards the end of her life when she has given up the fight, when death's approach frees her from anxiety about the future. Her husband was often older than she, she witnesses his decline with silent complacency: it is her revenge; if he dies first, she cheerfully bears the mourning; it has often been observed that men are far more overwhelmed by being widowed late in life: they profit more from marriage than women do, and particularly in their old age, because then the universe is concentrated within the limits of the home; the present does not spill over into the future: it is their wife who assures their monotonous rhythm and reigns over them; when he loses his public functions, man becomes totally useless; woman continues at least to run the home; she is necessary to her husband, whereas he is only a nuisance. Women are proud of their independence, they finally begin to view the world through their own eyes; they realise they have been duped and mystified their whole lives; now lucid and wary, they often attain a delicious cynicism. In particular, the woman who 'has lived' has a knowledge of men that no man shares: for she has seen not their public image but the contingent individual that every one of them lets show in the absence of their counterparts; she also knows women, who only show themselves in their spontaneity to other women: she knows what happens behind the scenes. But even if her experience allows her to denounce mystifications and lies, it is not enough to reveal the truth to her. Whether she is amused or bitter, the old woman's wisdom still remains completely negative: it is contestation, accusation, refusal; it is sterile. In her thoughts as in her acts, the highest form of freedom a woman-parasite can have is stoic defiance or sceptical irony. At no time in her life does she succeed in being both effective and independent.

CHAPTER 10

Woman's Situation and Character

We can now understand why, from Ancient Greece to today, there are so many common features in the indictments against woman; her condition has remained the same throughout superficial changes, and this condition defines what is called the woman's 'character': she 'wallows in immanence', she is argumentative, she is cautious and petty, she does not have the sense either of truth or of accuracy, she lacks morality, she is vulgarly self-serving, selfish, she is a liar and an actress. There is some truth in all these affirmations. But the types of behaviour denounced are not dictated to woman by her hormones or predestined in her brain's compartments: they are suggested in negative form by her situation. We will attempt to take a synthetic point of view of her situation, necessarily leading to some repetition, but making it possible to grasp the Eternal Feminine in her economic, social and historical conditioning as a whole.

The 'feminine world' is sometimes contrasted with the masculine universe, but it must be reiterated that women have never formed an autonomous and closed society; they are integrated into the group governed by males, where they occupy a subordinate position; they are united by a mechanical solidarity only insofar as they are similar: they do not share that organic solidarity upon which any unified community is founded; they have always endeavoured – in the period of the Eleusinian mysteries just like today in clubs, salons and recreation rooms – to band together to assert a 'counter-universe', but it is still within the masculine universe that they frame it. And this is where the paradox of their situation comes in: they belong both to the male world and to a sphere in which this world is challenged; enclosed in this sphere, involved in the male world, they cannot peacefully establish themselves anywhere. Their docility is always accompanied by refusal, their refusal by acceptance; this is similar to the girl's attitude; but it is more difficult to maintain because it is no longer simply a question of the adult woman dreaming her life through symbols, but of living it.

The woman herself recognises that the universe as a whole is masculine; it is men who have shaped it, ruled it and who still today dominate it; as for her, she does not consider herself responsible for it; it is understood that she is inferior and dependent; she has not learned the lessons of violence, she has never emerged as a subject in front of other members of the group; enclosed in her flesh, in her home, she grasps herself as passive opposite to these human-faced gods who set goals and standards. In this sense there is truth in the saying that condemns her to remaining 'an eternal child'; it has also been said of workers, black slaves, and colonised natives that they were 'big children' as long as they were not threatening; that meant they had to accept without argument the truths and laws that other men gave them. Woman's lot is obedience and respect. She has no grasp, even in thought, on this reality that involves her. It is an opaque presence in her eyes. That means she has not learned the technology that would enable her to dominate matter; as for her, she is not fighting with matter but with life, and life cannot be mastered by tools: one can only submit to its secret laws. The world does not appear to the woman as a 'set of tools' halfway between her will and her goals, as Heidegger defines it: on the contrary, it is a stubborn, indomitable resistance; it is dominated by fate and run through with mysterious caprices. No mathematics can make an equation out of this mystery of a spot of blood that changes into a human being in the mother's womb, no machine can rush it or slow it down; she experiences the resistance of a duration that the most ingenious machines fail to divide or multiply; she experiences it in her flesh that is subjected to the rhythm of the moon, and that the years first ripen and then corrode. Daily cooking teaches her patience and passivity; it is alchemy; one must obey fire, water, 'wait for the sugar to melt', the dough to rise and also the clothes to dry, the fruit to ripen. Housework comes close to a technical activity; but it is too rudimentary, too monotonous to convince the woman of the laws of mechanical causality. Besides, even in this area, things are capricious; there is material that 'revives' and material that does not 'revive' in the wash, spots that come out and others that persist, objects that break on their own, dust that grows like plants. Woman's mentality perpetuates that of agricultural civilisations that worship the earth's magical qualities: she believes in magic. Her passive eroticism reveals her desire not as will and aggression but as an attraction similar to that which makes the dowser's pendulum quiver; the mere presence of her flesh makes the male sex swell and rise; why should hidden water not make the dowser's wand jump? She feels surrounded by waves, radiation, fluid; she believes in telepathy, astrology, divination, Mesmer's *baquet*, theosophy, table turning, mind readers and healers; she intro-duces primitive superstitions into religion – candles, ex votos, and such – she embodies ancient spirits of nature in the saints – this one protects travellers, that one women who have just given birth, another one finds lost objects – and of course no marvel surprises her. Her attitude will be that of conjuration and prayer; to obtain a certain result, she will follow certain time-tested rites. It is easy to understand why she is ruled by routine; time has no dimension of novelty for her, it is not a creative spring; because she is doomed to repetition, she does not see in the future anything but a duplication of the past; if one knows the word and the recipe, duration is allied with the powers of fecundity: but this too obeys the rhythm of months and seasons; the cycle of each preg-nancy, of each flowering, reproduces the preceding one identically; in this circular movement, time's sole becoming is slow degradation: it eats at furniture and clothes just as it disfigures the face; fertile powers are destroyed little by little by the flight of years. So the woman does not trust this force driven to destroy.

Not only is she unaware of what real action is, that is able to change the face of the world, but she is lost in the middle of this world as in the heart of an immense and confused mass. She does not know how to use masculine logic well. Stendhal noted that she handles it as skilfully as man if she has to. But it is an instrument she does not often have the occasion to use. A syllogism is not useful in making mayonnaise or calming a child's tears; masculine reasoning is not relevant to the reality she experiences. And in the man's world, since she does not *do* anything, her thinking, as it does not flow into any project, is no different from a dream; she does not have the sense of truth, because she lacks efficacy; she struggles only by means of images and words: that is why she accepts the most contradictory assertions without a problem; she does not care about clarifying the mysteries of a sphere, which in any case is beyond her scope; she settles for horribly vague knowledge when it concerns her: she confuses parties, opinions, places, people and events; there is a strange jumble in her head. But after all, seeing clearly is not her business: she was taught to accept masculine authority; she thus forgoes criticising, examining and judging for herself. She leaves it to the superior caste. This is why the masculine world seems to be a transcendent reality, an absolute to her. 'Men make gods,' says Frazer, 'and women worship them.' Men cannot kneel with total conviction in front of idols they themselves have created but when women come across these imposing statues on their path they cannot imagine any hand making them and they meekly bow down before them.*[105] They specifically like Law and Order to be embodied in a chief. In all Olympus, there is one sovereign god; the prestigious virile essence must be gathered in one archetype of which father, husband and lovers are merely vague reflections. It is somewhat humorous to say that their worship of this great totem is sexual; what is true is that women fully realise their infantile dream of abdication and prostration. In France, the generals Boulanger, Pétain and de Gaulle[†] have always had the support of women; one remembers the purple prose of *L'Humanité*'s women journalists when writing about Tito and his beautiful uniform. The general the dictator – eagle eye, prominent chin – is the celestial father the serious universe demands, the absolute guarantor of all values. The respect women grant to heroes and to the masculine world's laws stems from their powerlessness and ignorance; they acknowledge these laws not through judgement but through an act of faith: faith draws its fanatical power from the fact that it is not knowledge: it is blind, passionate, stubborn and stupid; what it puts forward is done unconditionally, against reason, against history, against all refutation. This stubborn reverence can take two forms depending on circumstances: sometimes it is the content of the law and sometimes the empty form alone that the woman passionately abides by. If she belongs to the privileged elite that profits from the given social order, she wants it unshakeable and she is seen as intransigent. The man knows he can reconstruct other institutions, another ethics, another code; grasping himself as transcendence, he also envisages history as a becoming; even the most conservative knows that some change is inevitable and that he has to adapt his action and thinking to it; as the woman does not participate in history, she does not understand its necessities; she mistrusts the future and wants to stop time. If the idols her father, brothers and husband propose are knocked down, she cannot imagine any way of repopulating the heavens; she is determined to defend them. Among the Southerners during the Civil War, no one was as

---

* Cf. J.-P. Sartre, *Dirty Hands*: 'HOEDERER: They need props, you understand, they are given ready-made ideas, then they believe in them as they do in God. We're the ones who make these ideas and we know how they are cooked up; we are never quite sure of being right.'

† 'On the general's passage, the public was made up mostly of women and children' (*Les Journaux*, about the September 1948 tour in Savoy).

'The men applauded the general's speech, but the women stood out by their enthusiasm. Some were literally in ecstasy, singling out almost every word and clapping and shouting with a fervour that made their faces turn poppy-red' (*Aux Écoutes*, 11 April 1947).

passionately in favour of slavery as the women; in England during the Boer war, and in France against the Commune, it was the women who were the most enraged; they seek to compensate for their inaction by the force of the feelings they display; in victory they are as wild as hyenas against the beaten enemy; in defeat, they bitterly refuse any arrangement; as their ideas are only attitudes, they do not mind defending the most outdated causes: they can be legitimists in 1914, tsarists in 1949. Sometimes the man smilingly encourages them: it pleases him to see his measured opinions reflected in a fanatical form; but sometimes he is also bothered by the stupid and stubborn way his own ideas are transformed.

It is only in strongly integrated civilisations and classes that the woman looks so intransigent. Generally, as her faith is blind, she respects the laws simply because they are laws; the laws may change, but they keep their prestige; in the eyes of women, power creates law since the laws they recognise in men come from their power; that is why they are the first to throw themselves at the victors' feet when a group collapses. In general, they accept what is. One of their typical features is resignation. When the ashes of Pompeii's statues were dug out, it was observed that the men were caught in movements of revolt, defying the sky or trying to flee, while the women were bent, withdrawn into themselves, turning their faces towards the earth. They know they are powerless against things: volcanoes, policemen, employers or men. 'Women are made to suffer,' they say. 'That's life; nothing can be done about it.' This resignation engenders the patience often admired in women. They withstand physical suffering much better than men; they are capable of stoic courage when circumstances demand it: without the aggressive daring of the male, many women are distinguished by the calm tenacity of their passive resistance; they deal with crises, misery and misfortune more energetically than their husbands; respectful of duration that no haste can conquer, they do not measure their time; when they apply their calm stubbornness to any undertaking, they are sometimes brilliantly successful. 'Whatever woman wants',[106] says the proverb. In a generous woman, resignation looks like indulgence: she accepts everything, she condemns no one because she thinks that neither people nor things can be different from what they are. A proud woman can make a lofty virtue of it, like Mme de Charrière, rigid in her stoicism. But she also engenders a sterile prudence; women always try to keep, to fix, to arrange rather than to destroy and reconstruct anew; they prefer compromises and exchanges to revolutions. In the nineteenth century, they constituted one of the biggest obstacles to the effort of women workers' emancipation: for every

Flora Tristan or Louise Michel, how many utterly timid housewives begged their husbands not to take any risk! They were afraid not only of strikes, unemployment and misery; they also feared that the revolt was a mistake. Submission for submission, it is understandable that they prefer routine to adventure: they eke out for themselves a more meagre happiness at home than on the streets. Their lot is one with that of perishable things: they would lose everything in losing them. Only a free subject, asserting himself beyond time, can foil destruction; this supreme recourse is forbidden to the woman. It is mainly because she has never experienced the powers of liberty that she does not believe in liberation: the world to her seems governed by an obscure destiny against which it is presumptuous to react. These dangerous paths that she is compelled to follow are ones she herself has not traced: it is understandable that she does not take them enthusiastically.[*][107] When the future is open to her, she no longer hangs on to the past. When women are concretely called to action, when they identify with the designated aims, they are as strong and brave as men.[†]

Many of the faults for which they are reproached – mediocrity, meanness, shyness, pettiness, laziness, frivolity and servility – simply express the fact that the horizon is blocked for them. Woman, it is said, is sensual, she wallows in immanence; but first she was enclosed in it. The slave imprisoned in the harem does not feel any morbid passion for rose jelly and perfumed baths: she has to kill time somehow; inasmuch as the woman is stifling in a dismal gynaeceum – brothel or bourgeois home – she will also take refuge in comfort and well-being; moreover, if she avidly pursues sexual pleasure, it is often because she is frustrated; sexually unsatisfied, destined to male brutality, 'condemned to masculine ugliness', she consoles herself with creamy sauces, heady wines, velvets, the caresses of water, sun, a woman friend or a young lover. If

---

* Cf. Gide, *Journals*: 'Creusa or Lot's wife: one tarries and the other looks back, which is a worse way of tarrying . . . There is no greater cry of passion than this:

> *And Phaedra having braved the Labyrinth with you*
> *Would have been found with you or lost with you.*

But passion blinds her; after a few steps, to tell the truth, she would have sat down, or else would have wanted to go back – or even would have made him carry her.'

† This is how the attitude of the proletarian women has changed over the century; during the recent strikes in the mines of the North, for example, they showed as much passion and energy as men, demonstrating and fighting side by side.

she appears to man as such a 'physical' being, it is because her condition incites her to attach a great deal of importance to her animality.
Carnality does not cry out any more strongly in her than in the male:
but she watches out for its slightest signs and amplifies it; sexual pleasure,
like the wrenching of suffering, is the devastating triumph of immediacy; the violence of the instant negates the future and the universe:
outside of the carnal blaze, what is there is nothing; during this brief
apotheosis, she is no longer mutilated or frustrated. But once again, she
attaches such importance to these triumphs of immanence because it is
her only lot. Her frivolity has the same cause as her 'sordid materialism'; she gives importance to little things because she lacks access to big
ones: moreover the futilities that fill her days are often of great seriousness; she owes her charm and her opportunities to her toilette and beauty.
She often seems lazy, indolent; but the occupations that are offered her
are as useless as the pure flowing of time; if she is talkative or a scribbler,
it is to while away her time: she substitutes words for impossible acts.
The fact is that when a woman is engaged in an undertaking worthy of
a human being, she knows how to be as active, effective and silent, as
ascetic, as a man. She is accused of being servile; she is always willing,
it is said, to lie at her master's feet and to kiss the hand that has beaten
her. It is true that she generally lacks real self-regard; advice to the
'lovelorn', to betrayed wives and abandoned lovers is inspired by a spirit
of abject submission; the woman exhausts herself in arrogant scenes and
in the end gathers up the crumbs the male is willing to throw her. But
what can a woman – for whom the man is both the only means and the
only reason for living – do without masculine help? She has no choice
but to endure all humiliations; a slave cannot understand the meaning
of 'human dignity'; for him it is enough if he manages to survive. Finally,
if she is 'down to earth', a homebody, simply useful, it is because she
has no choice but to devote her existence to preparing food and cleaning
nappies: she cannot draw the meaning of grandeur from this. She must
ensure the monotonous repetition of life in its contingency and facticity:
it is natural for her to repeat herself, to begin again, without ever
inventing, to feel that time seems to be going around in circles without
going anywhere; she is busy without ever *doing* anything: so she is alienated in what she *has;* this dependence on things, a consequence of the
dependence in which she is held by men, explains her cautious management, her avarice. Her life is not directed towards goals: she is absorbed
in producing or maintaining things that are never more than means –
food, clothes, lodging – these are inessential intermediaries between

animal life and free existence; the only value that is attached to inessential means is usefulness; the housewife lives at the level of utility, and she takes credit for herself only when she is useful to her family. But no existent is able to satisfy itself with an inessential role: he quickly makes ends out of means – as can be observed in politicians, among others – and in his eyes the value of the means becomes an absolute value. Thus utility reigns higher than truth, beauty and freedom in the housewife's heaven; and this is the point of view from which she envisages the whole universe; and this is why she adopts the Aristotelian morality of the golden mean, of mediocrity. How could one find daring, ardour, detachment and grandeur in her? These qualities appear only where a freedom throws itself across an open future, emerging beyond any given. A woman is shut up in a kitchen or a boudoir and one is surprised her horizon is limited; her wings are cut and then she is blamed for not knowing how to fly. Let a future be open to her and she will no longer be obliged to settle in the present.

The same foolishness is seen when, closed up in the limits of her self or her home, she is criticised for her narcissism and egotism with their corollaries: vanity, touchiness, meanness, and so forth. All possibility of concrete communication with others is removed from her; in her experience she does not recognise either the appeal or the advantages of solidarity, since, separated, she is entirely devoted to her own family; she cannot be expected therefore to go beyond herself towards the general interest. She obstinately confines herself in the only familiar area where she has the power to grasp things and where she finds a precarious sovereignty.

Although she might close the doors and cover the windows, the woman does not find absolute security in her home; this masculine universe that she respects from afar without daring to venture into it involves her; and because she is unable to grasp it through technology, sound logic or coherent knowledge, she feels like a child and a primitive surrounded with dangerous mysteries. She projects her magic conception of reality: the flow of things seems inevitable to her and yet anything can happen; she has difficulty differentiating the possible and the impossible, she is ready to believe anyone; she welcomes and spreads rumours, she sets off panics; even in calm periods she lives in worry; at night half-asleep, the inert body is frightened by the nightmare images reality acquires: so for the woman condemned to passivity, the opaque future is haunted by phantoms of war, revolution, famine and misery; not being able to act, she worries. When her husband and son embark on a job, when they are passionately involved in an event, they take their own risks: their projects and the orders they follow show them a sure way even in darkness; but the woman struggles in the blurry night; she 'worries' because she does not do anything; in imagination all possibilities are equally real: the train may derail, the operation may be unsuccessful, the affair may fail; what she vainly tries to ward off in her long, despondent ruminations is the spectre of her own powerlessness.

Worry expresses her mistrust of the given world; if it seems threatening, ready to sink into obscure catastrophes, it is because she does not feel happy in it. Most often, she is not resigned to being resigned; she knows what she is going through, she goes through it in spite of herself: she is woman without being asked; she does not dare revolt; she submits against her will; her attitude is a constant recrimination. Everyone who receives women's confidences – doctors, priests, social workers – knows that complaint is the commonest mode of expression; together, women friends groan individually about their own ills and all together about the injustice of their lot, the world and men in general. A free individual takes the blame for his failures on himself, he takes responsibility for them: but what happens to the woman comes from others, it is others who are responsible for her misfortune. Her furious despair rejects all remedies; suggesting solutions to a woman determined to complain does not help: no solution seems acceptable. She wants to live her situation exactly as she lives it: in impotent anger. If a change is suggested to her, she throws her arms up: 'That's all I need!' She knows that her malaise is deeper than the pretexts she gives for it, and that one expedient is not enough to get rid of it; she takes it out on the whole world because it was put together without her, and against her; since adolescence, since childhood, she has protested against her condition; she was promised compensations, she was assured that if she abdicated her opportunities into the hands of the man, they would be returned to her a hundred-fold and she considers herself duped; she accuses the whole masculine universe; resentment is the other side of dependence: when one gives everything, one never receives enough in return. But she also needs to respect the male universe; if she contested it entirely, she would feel in danger, and without a roof over her head: she adopts the Manichaean attitude also suggested to her by her experience as a housewife. The individual who acts accepts responsibility for good and evil just like the others, he knows that it is up to him to define ends, to see that they triumph; in action he experiences the ambiguity of all solutions; justice and injustice, gains and losses, are inextricably intermingled. But whoever is passive puts himself on the sidelines and refuses to pose, even in thought, ethical problems: good *must* be realised and if it is not, there is wrongdoing for which the guilty must be punished. Like the child, the woman imagines good and evil in simple storybook images; Manichaeism reassures the mind by eliminating the anguish of choice; deciding between one scourge and a lesser one, between a benefit today and a greater benefit tomorrow, having to define by oneself what is defeat and what is victory: this means taking terrible risks; for the Manichaean, the wheat is clearly distinguishable from the chaff, and the chaff has to be eliminated; dust condemns itself and cleanliness is the absolute absence of filth; cleaning means getting rid of waste and mud. Thus the woman thinks that 'everything is the Jews' fault' or the Masons' or the Bolsheviks' or the government's; she is always *against* someone or something; women were even more violently anti-Dreyfusard than men; they do not always know what the evil principle is; but what they expect from a 'good government' is that it get rid of it as one gets rid of dust from the house. For fervent Gaullists, de Gaulle is the king sweeper; they imagine him, dust mops and rags in hand, scrubbing and polishing to make a 'clean' France.

But these hopes are always placed in an uncertain future; meanwhile evil continues to eat away at good; and as woman does not have Jews, Masons and Bolsheviks to hand, she seeks someone against whom she can rise up concretely: the husband is the perfect victim. He embodies the masculine universe, it is through him that the male society took the woman in hand and duped her; he bears the weight of the world and if things go wrong, it is his fault. When he comes home in the evening, she complains to him about the children, the suppliers, the housework, the cost of living, her rheumatism and the weather: and she wants him to feel guilty. She often harbours specific complaints about him; but he is particularly guilty of being a man; he might well have illnesses and problems too – 'It just isn't the same thing' – he is privy to a privilege she constantly resents as an injustice. It is noteworthy that the hostility she feels for the husband or the lover binds her to him instead of moving her away from him; a man who begins to detest wife or mistress tries to get away from her: but she wants to have the man she hates nearby to make him pay. Choosing to recriminate is choosing not to get rid of one's misfortunes but to wallow in them; her supreme consolation is to set herself up as martyr. Life and men have conquered her: she will make a victory of this very defeat. Thus, as she did in childhood, she quickly gives way to the frenzy of tears and scenes.

It is surely because her life takes place against a background of powerless revolt that the woman cries so easily; she undoubtedly has less physiological control of her nervous and sympathetic systems than the man; her education taught her to let herself go: orders and instruction play a great role here since, although Diderot and Benjamin Constant shed rivers of tears, men stopped crying when custom forbade it for them. But the woman is still inclined to be defeatist vis-à-vis the world because she has never frankly assumed it. The man accepts the world; even misfortune will not change his attitude, he will cope with it, he will 'not let it get him down', while a little setback is enough for the woman to rediscover the universe's hostility and the injustice of her lot; so she throws herself into her safest refuge: herself; this moist trace on her cheeks, this burning in her eyes, are the tangible presence of her suffering soul; gentle on one's skin, barely salty on one's tongue, tears are also a tender and bitter caress; the face burns under a stream of mild water; tears are both complaint and consolation, fever and soothing coolness. They are also a supreme alibi; sudden as a storm, coming out in fits, a cyclone, shower, deluge, they metamorphose the woman into a complaining fountain, a stormy sky; her eyes can no longer see, mist blurs them: they are no longer even a gaze, they melt in rain; blinded, the woman returns to the passivity of natural things. She must be vanquished: she is lost in her defeat; she sinks, she drowns, she escapes man who contemplates her, powerless as if before a cataract. He judges this way of behaving as unfair: but she thinks that the battle has been unfair from the beginning because no effective weapon has been put into her hands. She resorts once again to magical conjuration. And the fact that these sobs exasperate the male provides her with one more reason to indulge herself in them.

If tears are not sufficient to express her revolt, she will carry on in such incoherent violence that it will disconcert the man even more. In some circles, the man might strike his wife with actual blows; in others, because he is the stronger and his fist an effective instrument, he will forgo all violence. But the woman, like the child, indulges in symbolic outbursts: she might throw herself on the man, scratch him; these are only gestures. But above all, through nervous fits in her body she attempts to express the refusals she cannot carry out concretely. It is not only for physiological reasons that she is subject to convulsive manifestations: a convulsion is an interiorisation of an energy that, thrown into the world, fails to grasp any object; it is a useless expenditure of all the powers of negation caused by the situation. The mother rarely has crying fits in front of her young children because she can beat or punish them: it is in front of her older son, her husband or her lover on whom she has no hold that the woman gives vent to furious hopelessness. Sophia Tolstoy's hysterical scenes are significant; it is true that she made the big mistake of never trying to understand her husband and in her diary she does not seem generous, sensitive or sincere, she is far from coming across as an endearing person; but whether she was right or wrong does not change the horror of her situation at all: she never did anything in her whole life but submit to the conjugal embraces, pregnancies, solitude and mode of life that her husband imposed on her while receiving constant recriminations; when new decisions of Tolstoy's worsened the conflict, she found herself weaponless against the enemy's will, which she rejected with all her powerless will; she threw herself into rejection scenes – fake suicides, false escapes, false illnesses – unpleasant to her family and friends, exhausting for herself: it is hard to see any other solution available to her since she had no positive reason to silence her feelings of revolt and no effective way of expressing them.

There is only one solution available to the woman when rejection runs its course: suicide. But it would seem that she resorts to it less than the man. The statistics are very ambiguous:*[108] if one considers successful suicides, there are many more men than women who put an end to their lives; but suicide attempts are more frequent in women. This may be because they settle more often for playacting: they *play* at suicide more often than man but they *want* it more rarely. It is also in part because such brutal means are repugnant to them: they almost never use knives or firearms. They drown themselves more readily, like Ophelia, showing woman's affinity for water, passive and full of darkness, where it seems that life might be able to dissolve passively. On the whole, this is the ambiguity I already mentioned: the woman does not sincerely seek to take leave of what she detests. She plays at rupture but in the end remains with the man who makes her suffer; she pretends to leave the life that mistreats her but it is relatively rare for her to kill herself. She does not favour definitive solutions: she protests against man, against life, against her condition, but she does not escape from it.

There is much feminine behaviour that has to be interpreted as protest. We have seen that the woman often cheats on her husband by defiance and not for pleasure; she will be absentminded and a spendthrift on purpose because he is methodical and careful. Misogynists who accuse woman of 'always being late' think she lacks 'the sense of exactitude'.

* See Halbwachs, *The Causes of Suicide*.

In truth, we have seen how docilely she adapts to the demands of time. Being late is deliberate. Some flirtatious women think that this is the way to excite the desire of the man, who will thus attach more importance to their presence; but above all, in keeping a man waiting for a few minutes, the woman protests against this long wait that is her own life. In one sense, her whole existence is a waiting since she is enclosed in the limbo of immanence and contingency and her justification is always in someone else's hands: she is waiting for a tribute, men's approval, she is waiting for love, she is waiting for gratitude and her husband's or lover's praise; she expects to gain from them her reasons to exist, her worth and her very being. She awaits her subsistence from them; whether she has her own chequebook or receives the money her husband allocates to her every week or month, he has to have been paid, obtained the raise for her to pay the grocer or buy a new dress. She awaits men's presence: her economic dependence puts her at their disposal; she is only one element of masculine life, whereas the man is her whole life; the husband has occupations outside the home, the woman endures his absence every day; it is the lover – even if passionate – who decides on the separation and meetings according to his obligations. In bed, she awaits the male's desire, she awaits – sometimes anxiously – her own pleasure. The only thing she can do is to be late for the date the lover set up; or not to be ready at the time the husband fixed; this is the way she asserts the importance of her own occupations, she claims her independence, she becomes the essential subject for a moment while the other passively submits to her will. But this is meagre revenge; no matter how determined she might be to make men stew, she will never compensate for the infinite hours she has spent being subjected to and watching out and hoping for the male's goodwill.

In general, while more or less acknowledging men's supremacy and accepting their authority, worshipping their idols, she will contest their reign tooth and nail; hence the famous 'contrariness' for which she is so often criticised; as she does not possess an autonomous domain, she cannot put forward truths or positive values different from those that males assert; she can only negate them. Her negation is more or less systematic depending on her particular balance of respect and resentment. But the fact is, she knows all the fault lines of the masculine system and she hastens to denounce them.

Women do not have a hold on the world of men because their experience does not teach them to deal with logic and technology: conversely, the power of male instruments disappears at the borders of the feminine domain. There is a whole region of human experience that the male deliberately chooses to ignore because he fails to *think* it: this experience, the woman *lives* it. The engineer, so precise when making his plans, behaves like a demigod at home: one word and his meal is served, his shirts starched, his children silenced: procreating is an act that is as quick as Moses's magic rod; he sees nothing surprising in these miracles. The notion of miracle differs from the idea of magic: from within a rationally determined world a miracle posits the radical discontinuity of an event without cause against which any thinking shatters, whereas magic phenomena are united by secret forces of which a docile consciousness can embrace the continuous becoming – without understanding it. The newborn is miraculous for the demigod father, magic for the mother who has undergone the ripening in her womb. Man's experience is intelligible but full of holes; that of the wife is, in its own limits, obscure but complete. This opacity weighs her down; the male is light in his relations with her: he has the lightness of dictators, generals, judges, bureaucrats, codes and abstract principles. This is undoubtedly what this housewife meant when, shrugging her shoulders, she murmured: 'Men, they don't think!' Women also say: 'Men, they don't know; they don't know life.' As a contrast to the myth of the praying mantis, they juxtapose the symbol of the frivolous and importunate bumblebee.

It is understandable why, from this perspective, woman objects to masculine logic. Not only does it have no bearing on her experience, but she also knows that in men's hands reason becomes an insidious form of violence; their peremptory affirmations are intended to mystify her. They want to confine her in a dilemma: either you agree or you don't; she has to agree in the name of the whole system of accepted principles: in refusing to agree, she rejects the whole system; she cannot allow herself such a dramatic move; she does not have the means to create another society: yet she does not agree with this one. Halfway between revolt and slavery, she unwillingly resigns herself to masculine authority. He continuously uses force to make her shoulder the consequences of her reluctant submission. He pursues the chimera of a freely enslaved companion: he wants her to yield to him as yielding to the proof of a theorem; but she knows he himself has chosen the postulates on which his vigorous deductions are hung; as long as she avoids questioning them, he will easily silence her; nevertheless, he will not convince her, because she senses their arbitrariness. Thus will he accuse her, with stubborn irritation, of being illogical: she refuses to play the game because she knows the dice are loaded.

The woman does not positively think that the truth is *other* than what men claim: rather, she holds that there *is* no truth. It is not only life's becoming that makes her suspicious of the principle of identity, nor the magic phenomena surrounding her that ruin the notion of causality: it is at the heart of the masculine world itself, it is in her as belonging to this world, that she grasps the ambiguity of all principles, of all values, of all that exists. She knows that when it comes to her, masculine morality is a vast mystification. The man pompously drums his code of virtue and honour into her; but secretly he invites her to disobey it: he even counts on this disobedience; the whole lovely façade he hides behind would collapse without it.

The man readily uses the pretext of the Hegelian idea that the male citizen acquires his ethical dignity by transcending himself towards the universal: as a singular individual, he has the right to desire and pleasure. His relations with woman thus lie in a contingent region where morality no longer applies, where conduct is inconsequential. His relations with other men are based on certain values; he is a freedom confronting other freedoms according to laws universally recognised by all; but with woman – she was invented for this reason – he ceases to assume his existence, he abandons himself to the mirage of the in-itself, he situates himself on an inauthentic plane; he is tyrannical, sadistic, violent or puerile, masochistic or querulous; he tries to satisfy his obsessions, his manias; he 'relaxes', he 'lets go' in the name of rights he has acquired in his public life. His wife is often surprised – like Thérèse Desqueyroux – by the contrast between the lofty tone of his remarks, of his public conduct and 'his patient inventions in the dark'.[109] He preaches population growth: but he is clever at not having more children than are convenient for him. He praises chaste and faithful wives: but he invites his neighbour's wife to commit adultery. We have seen the hypocrisy of men decreeing abortion to be criminal when every year in France a million women are put by men into the situation where they have to abort; very often the husband or lover imposes this solution on them; and often these men tacitly assume that it will be used if necessary. They openly count on the woman to consent to making herself guilty of a crime: her 'immorality' is necessary for the harmony of moral society, respected by men. The most flagrant example of this duplicity is man's attitude to prostitution: it is his demand that creates the offer; I have spoken of the disgusted scepticism with which prostitutes view respectable gentlemen who condemn vice in general but show great indulgence for their personal foibles; they consider girls who make a living with their bodies perverse and debauched, and not the men who use them. An anecdote illustrates this state of mind: at the end of the last century, the police discovered two little girls of twelve or thirteen in a bordello; a trial was held where they testified; they spoke of their clients who were important gentlemen; one of them opened her mouth to give a name. The judge abruptly stopped her: *Do not sully the name of an honest man!* A gentleman decorated with the Legion of Honour remains an honest man while deflowering a little girl; he has his weaknesses, but who does not? However, the little girl who has no access to the ethical region of the universal – who is neither judge nor general nor a great French man, nothing but a little girl – gambles her moral value in the contingent region of sexuality: she is perverted, corrupted, depraved and good only for the reformatory. In many cases, the man can commit acts with woman's complicity that degrade her without tarnishing his lofty image. She does not understand these subtleties very well; what she does understand is that the man's actions do not conform to the principles he professes and that he asks her to disobey them; he does not want what he says he wants: she therefore does not give him what she pretends to give him. She will be a chaste and faithful wife: and in secret she will give in to her desires; she will be an admirable mother: but she will carefully practise birth control and she will have an abortion if she must. Officially the man renounces her, those are the rules of the game; but he is clandestinely grateful to one for her 'easy virtue', to another for her sterility. The woman has the role of those secret agents who are left to the firing squad if they are caught, and who are covered with rewards if they succeed; it is for her to shoulder all of males' immorality: it is not only the prostitute; it is all the women who serve as the gutter to the luminous and clean palaces where respectable people live. When one speaks to these women of dignity, honour, loyalty and of all the lofty virile virtues, one should not be surprised if they refuse to 'go along'. They particularly snigger when virtuous males reproach them for being calculating, actresses, liars:* they know well that no other way is open to them. The man also is 'calculating' about money and success: but he has the means to acquire them through his work: the woman has been assigned the role of parasite: all parasites are necessarily exploiters; she needs the male to

---

* 'All these women with this little delicate and touch-me-not air accumulated by a whole past of slavery, with no other means of salvation and livelihood than this unintentional seductive air biding its time' (Jules Laforgue).

acquire human dignity, to eat, to feel pleasure, to procreate; she uses the service of sex to ensure her benefits; and since she is trapped in this function, she is entirely an instrument of exploitation. As for falsehoods, except in the case of prostitution, there is no fair arrangement between her and her protector. Man even requires her to playact: he wants her to be the *Other;* but every existent, as desperately as he may disavow himself, remains a subject; he wants her to be object: she *makes* herself object; at the moment she makes herself being, she is exercising a free activity; this is her original treason; the most docile, the most passive woman is still consciousness; and it is sometimes enough to make him feel duped by her for the male to glimpse that in giving herself to him she is watching and judging him; she should be no more than an offered thing, a prey. Nonetheless, he also demands that she surrender this thing to him freely: in bed he asks her to feel pleasure; at home, she must sincerely recognise his superiority and his strengths; at the very moment she obeys, she must also feign independence, even though she actively plays the role of passivity at other moments. She lies to keep her man and ensure her daily bread – scenes and tears, uncontrollable transports of love, hysterics – and she lies as well to escape the tyranny she accepts out of self-interest. He encourages playacting as it feeds his imperialism and vanity: she uses her powers of dissimulation against him; revenge is thus doubly delicious: for in deceiving him, she satisfies her own particular desires and she savours the pleasure of mocking him. The wife and the courtesan lie in feigning transports they do not feel; afterwards with their lovers or girlfriends, they make fun of the naive vanity of their dupe: 'Not only do they "botch it", but they want us to wear ourselves out moaning with pleasure,' they say resentfully. These conversations resemble those of servants who criticise their 'bosses' in the servants' kitchen. The woman has the same faults because she is a victim of the same paternalistic oppression; she has the same cynicism because she sees the man from head to toe as a valet sees his master. But it is clear that none of these traits manifests a perverted essence or perverted original will; they reflect a situation. 'There is duplicity wherever there is a coercive regime,' says Fourier. 'Prohibition and contraband are inseparable in love as in business.' And men know so well that the woman's faults show her condition that, careful to maintain the hierarchy of the sexes, they encourage these very traits in their companion that allow them to scorn her. Doubtless the husband or lover is irritated by the faults of the particular woman he lives with; yet, extolling the charms of femininity in general, he considers it to be inseparable from its flaws.

If the woman is not perfidious, futile, cowardly or indolent, she loses her seduction. In *A Doll's House,* Helmer explains how just, strong, understanding and indulgent man feels when he pardons his weak wife for her puerile faults. Thus Bernstein's husbands are moved – with the author's complicity – by the thieving, cruel, adulterous wife; bowing indulgently to her, they prove their virile wisdom. American racists and French colonialists wish the black man to be thieving, indolent and lying: he proves his indignity, putting the oppressors in the right; if he insists on being honest and loyal, he is regarded as quarrelsome. Woman's faults are amplified all the more to the extent that she will not try to combat them but, on the contrary, will make an ornament of them.

Rejecting logical principles and moral imperatives, sceptical about the laws of nature, woman lacks a sense of the universal; the world seems to her a confused collection of individual cases; this is why she more readily accepts a neighbour's gossip than a scientific explanation; she doubtless respects the printed book, but this respect skims along the written pages without grasping the content; by contrast, the anecdote told by an unknown person waiting in a queue or in a drawing room instantly takes on overwhelming authority; in her domain, everything is magic; outside, everything is mystery; she is ignorant of the criterion for credibility; only immediate experience convinces her: her own experience or another's, as long as it is forcefully affirmed. As for herself, she feels she is a special case because she is isolated in her home and has no active contact with other women; she always expects destiny and men to make an exception in her favour; she believes in whatever insights come her way far more than in reasoning that is valid for everyone; she readily admits that they have been sent by God or by some obscure world spirit; in relation to misfortunes or accidents, she calmly thinks, 'That can't happen to me,' or else she imagines, 'I'll be the exception': she enjoys special favours; the shopkeeper will give her a discount, the policeman will let her go to the head of the queue; she has been taught to overestimate the value of her smile, but no one told her that all women smiled. It is not that she thinks herself more special than her neighbour: it is that she does not make comparisons; for the same reason experience rarely proves her wrong: she suffers one failure, then another, but she does not add them up.

This is why women do not succeed in building a solid 'counteruniverse' where they can defy males; they sporadically rant against men in general, they tell stories about the bedroom or childbirth, they exchange horoscopes and beauty secrets. But to truly build this 'world of grievances' that their resentment calls for, they lack conviction; their attitude to man is too ambivalent. Indeed, he is a child, a contingent and vulnerable body, an innocent, an unwanted drone, a mean tyrant, an egotist, a vain man: and he is also the liberating hero, the divinity who sets the standards. His desire is a gross appetite, his embraces a degrading chore: yet his ardour and virile force are also a demiurgic energy. When a woman ecstatically utters, 'This is a man!' she is evoking both the sexual vigour and the social effectiveness of the male she admires: in both are expressed the same creative sovereignty; she does not think he can be a great artist, a grand businessman, a general or a chief without being a great lover: his social success is always a sexual attraction; inversely, she is ready to recognise genius in the man who satisfies her. She is, in fact, turning to a masculine myth here. The phallus for Lawrence and many others is both living energy and human transcendence. Thus in the pleasures of the bed, woman can see a communion with the spirit of the world. Worshipping man as in a mystical cult, she loses and finds herself in his glory. The contradiction is easily perceived here due to the different types of individual who are virile. Some – whose contingence she encounters in everyday life – are the incarnation of human misery; in others, man's grandeur is exalted. But the woman even accepts that these two figures be fused into one. 'If I become famous,' wrote a girl in love with a man she considered superior, 'R . . . will surely marry me because it will flatter his vanity; his chest will swell with me on his arm.' Yet she admired him madly. The same individual, in the eyes of the woman, may very well be stingy, mean, vain, foolish and a god; after all, gods have their weaknesses. One feels a demanding severity – the opposite of authentic esteem – for an individual who is loved in his freedom and humanity; whereas a woman kneeling before her male can very well pride herself on 'knowing how to deal with him', or 'handle him', and she complaisantly flatters his 'weaknesses' without his losing prestige; this is the proof that she does not feel friendship for his individual person as expressed in his real acts; blindly she bows to the general essence her idol is part of: virility is a sacred aura, a given fixed value, which is affirmed despite the weaknesses of the individual who bears it; this individual does not count; by contrast, the woman, jealous of his privilege, is delighted to exercise sly superiority over him.

The same ambiguity of woman's feelings for man is found in her general attitude concerning her self and the world; the domain in which she is enclosed is invested by the masculine universe; but it is haunted by obscure forces of which men themselves are the playthings; if she allies herself with these magical virtues, she will, in her turn, acquire power. Society subjugates Nature; but Nature dominates it; the Spirit affirms itself over Life; but it dies if life no longer supports it. Woman uses this ambivalence to assign more truth to a garden than a city, to an illness than an idea, to a birth than a revolution; she tries to reestablish this reign of the earth, of the Mother, imagined by Bachofen, to be able to find herself as the essential facing the inessential. But as she herself is an existent that a transcendence inhabits, she will be able to valorise this region where she is confined only by transfiguring it: she lends it a transcendent dimension. Man lives in a coherent universe that is a thought reality. Woman struggles with a magic reality that does not allow thinking: she escapes through thoughts lacking real content. Instead of assuming her existence, she contemplates in the heavens the pure Idea of her destiny; instead of acting, she erects her statue in her imagination; instead of reasoning, she dreams. From here comes the fact that while being so 'physical', she is also so artificial, while being so terrestrial, she can be so ethereal. Her life is spent scrubbing pots and pans and it is a marvellous romance; vassal to man, she believes she is his idol; debased in her flesh, she exalts Love. Because she is condemned to know only life's contingent facticity, she becomes priestess of the Ideal.

This ambivalence is marked by the way woman deals with her body. It is a burden: weakened by the species, bleeding every month, passively propagating, for her it is not the pure instrument of her grasp on the world but rather an opaque presence; it is not certain that it will give her pleasure and it creates pains that tear her apart; it contains threats: she feels danger in her 'insides'. Her body is 'hysterical' because of the close connection between endocrine secretions and nervous and sympathetic systems commanding muscles and viscera; it expresses reactions the woman refuses to accept: in sobs, convulsions and vomiting, her body escapes her, it betrays her; it is her most intimate reality, but it is a shameful reality that she keeps hidden. And yet it is her marvellous double; she contemplates it in the mirror with amazement; it is the promise of happiness, a work of art, a living statue; she shapes it, adorns it, displays it. When she smiles into the mirror she forgets her carnal contingence; in love's embrace, in motherhood, her image disappears. But often, dreaming about herself, she is surprised to be both that heroine and that flesh.

Nature symmetrically provides her with a double face: it supplies the stew and incites mystical effusions. In becoming a housewife and mother, woman gave up her free getaways into fields and woods, she preferred the calm cultivation of the kitchen garden, she tamed flowers and put them in vases: yet she is still exalted by moonlights and sunsets. In the terrestrial fauna and flora, she sees food and ornamentation before all; yet a sap flows that is generosity and magic. Life is not only immanence and repetition: it is also a dazzling face of light; in flowering meadows, it is revealed as Beauty. In tune with nature by the fertility of her womb, woman also feels swept by the breath that animates her and is spirit. And insofar as she is unsatisfied and feels like the uncompleted and unlimited girl, her soul will then rush forward on endlessly unwinding roads towards limitless horizons. Slave to her husband, children and home, she finds it intoxicating to be alone, sovereign on the hillside; she is no longer spouse, mother, housewife, but a human being; she contemplates the passive world: and she recalls that she is a whole consciousness, an irreducible freedom. In front of the mystery of water and the mountain summit's thrust, male supremacy is abolished; walking through the heather, dipping her hand in the river, she lives not for others but for herself. The woman who maintained her independence through all her servitudes will ardently love her own freedom in Nature. The others will find in it only the pretext for refined raptures and they will hesitate at twilight between the fear of catching a cold and a swooning soul.

This double belonging to the carnal world and to a 'poetic' world defines the metaphysics and wisdom to which the woman more or less explicitly adheres. She tries to combine life and transcendence; this is to say she rejects Cartesianism and all doctrines connected to it; she is comfortable in a naturalism similar to that of the Stoics or Neoplatonists of the sixteenth century: it is not surprising that women, Margaret of Navarre being the first of them, should be attached to such a philosophy, at once so material and so spiritual. Socially Manichaean, the woman has a deep need to be ontologically optimistic: the moralities of action do not suit her, since it is forbidden for her to act; she submits to the given: so the given must be Good; but a Good recognised by reason like that of Spinoza or by calculation like that of Leibniz cannot touch her. She requires a good that is a living Harmony and within which she situates herself by the mere fact of living. The notion of harmony is one of the keys of the feminine universe: it implies perfection in immobility, the immediate justification of each element as part of the whole and her passive participation in the totality. In a harmonious world, woman thus attains what man will seek in action: she has purchase on the world, she is necessary to it, she cooperates in the triumph of Good. Moments women consider as revelations are those where they discover they are in harmony with a reality based on peace with one's self. These are the moments of luminous happiness that Virginia Woolf – in *Mrs Dalloway*, in *To the Lighthouse* – that Katherine Mansfield, all through her work, grant to their heroines as a supreme recompense. The joy that is a surge of freedom is reserved for the man; what the woman knows is an impression of smiling plenitude.* One understands that simple ataraxia, in her eyes, can be of utmost importance, as she normally lives in the tension of denial, recrimination and demands; one could never reproach her for savouring a beautiful afternoon or the sweetness of an evening. But it is a delusion to try to find here the true definition of the hidden soul of the world. Good *is* not; the world is not harmony and no individual has a necessary place in it.

There is a justification, a supreme compensation that society has always been bent on dispensing to woman: religion. There must be religion for women as for the people, for exactly the same reasons: when a sex or a class is condemned to immanence, the mirage of transcendence must be offered to it. It is to man's total advantage to have God endorse the codes he creates: and specifically because he exercises sovereign authority over the woman, it is only right that this authority be conferred on him by the sovereign being. Among others, for Jews, Muslims and Christians, man is the master by divine right: fear of God will stifle the slightest inclination of revolt in the oppressed. Their credulity can be counted on. Woman adopts an attitude of respect and faith before the masculine universe: God in His heaven seems barely farther from her than a government minister, and the mystery of Genesis matches that of an electrical power station. But more important, if she throws herself so willingly into religion, it is because religion fills a profound need. In modern civilisation where freedom plays an important role – even for the woman – religion becomes less of an instrument of constraint than of mystification. The woman is less often asked to accept her inferiority in the name of God than to believe, thanks to Him,

---

* Out of reams of texts, I will cite Mabel Dodge's lines where the passage to a global vision of the world is not explicit but is clearly suggested: 'It was a still, autumn day, all yellow and crimson. Frieda and I, in a lapse of antagonism, sat on the ground together, with the red apples piled all around us. We were warmed and scented by the sun and the rich earth – and the apples were living tokens of plenitude and peace and rich living; the rich, natural flow of the earth, like the sappy blood in our veins, made us feel gay, indomitable and fruitful like orchards. We were united for a moment, Frieda and I, in a mutual assurance of self-sufficiency, made certain, as women are sometimes, of our completeness by the sheer force of our bountiful health.'

that she is equal to the male lord; even the temptation to revolt is avoided by pretending to overcome injustice. The woman is no longer robbed of her transcendence, since she will dedicate her immanence to God; souls' merits are judged only in heaven and not according to their terrestrial accomplishments; here below, as Dostoevsky would have said, they are never more than occupations: shining shoes or building a bridge is the same vanity; over and above social discriminations, equality of the sexes is reestablished. This is why the little girl and the adolescent girl throw themselves into devotion with an infinitely greater fervour than their brothers; God's gaze that transcends his transcendence humiliates the boy: he will for ever remain a child under this powerful guardianship, it is a more radical castration than that with which he feels his father's existence threatens him. But the 'eternal girl child' finds her salvation in this gaze that metamorphoses her into a sister of the angels; it cancels out the privilege of the penis. A sincere faith helps the girl avoid all inferiority complexes: she is neither male nor female, but God's creature. This is why we find a virile steadfastness in the great female saints: St Bridget and St Catherine of Siena arrogantly tried to rule the world; they recognised no male authority: Catherine even directed her directors very severely; Joan of Arc and St Teresa followed their own paths with an intrepidness surpassed by no man. The Church sees to it that God never authorises women to escape from male guardianship; it has put these powerful weapons in masculine hands only: refusal of absolution and excommunication; for her obstinate visions, Joan of Arc was burned at the stake. Nevertheless, even subjected by God's will to men's laws, the woman finds a solid recourse against them through Him. Masculine logic is refuted by mysteries; males' pride becomes a sin, their agitation is not only absurd but culpable: why remodel this world created by God Himself? The passivity to which woman is doomed is sanctified. Reciting her rosary by the fire, she knows she is closer to heaven than her husband, who is out at political meetings. There is no need to *do* anything to save her soul, it is enough to *live* without disobeying. The synthesis of life and spirit is completed: the mother not only engenders body but also gives God a soul; this is higher work than penetrating the secrets of the atom. With the complicity of the heavenly Father, woman can make a claim to the glory of her femininity against man.

Not only does God thus reestablish the dignity of the feminine sex in general, but every woman will find special support in the celestial absence; as a human person, she carries little weight; but as soon as she acts in the name of divine inspiration, her desires become sacred. Mme Guyon says that, concerning a nun's illness, she learned 'what it meant to command by the Word and obey by the same Word'; thus the devotee camouflages her authority in humble obedience; raising her children, governing a convent or organising a charity, she is but a docile tool in supernatural hands; one cannot disobey her without offending God Himself. To be sure, men do not disdain this support either; but it loses its force when they encounter other men who make equal claim to it: the conflict finishes by being solved on a human level. Woman invokes divine will to justify her authority absolutely in the eyes of those who are naturally subordinated to her, and to justify it in her own eyes. If this cooperation is useful for her, it is because she is above all concerned with her relations with herself – even when those relations interest others; it is only in these totally interior debates that the Supreme Silence can have the force of law. In truth, woman uses the pretext of religion to satisfy her desires. Frigid, masochistic or sadistic, she sanctifies herself by renouncing the flesh, playing the victim, stifling every living impulse around her; mutilating and annihilating herself, she rises in the ranks of the chosen; when she martyrs husband and children by depriving them of all terrestrial happiness, she is preparing them for a choice place in paradise; 'to punish herself for having sinned', Margaret of Cortona's pious biographers recount, she maltreated the child of her sin; she fed him only after feeding all the beggars she passed; we have seen that hatred of the unwanted child is common: it is a godsend to be able to express it in a virtuous rage. On her side, a woman whose morals are loose conveniently makes an arrangement with God; the certainty of being purified from sin by absolution tomorrow often helps the pious woman conquer her scruples now. Whether she has chosen asceticism or sensuality, pride or humility, the concern she has for her salvation encourages her to give in to this pleasure that she prefers over all others: taking care of self; she listens to her heart beat, she watches every quiver of her flesh, justified by the presence of grace within herself, like the pregnant woman with her fruit. Not only does she examine herself with tender vigilance, but she reports to her confessor; in days gone by, she could savour the headiness of public confessions. We are told that Margaret of Cortona, to punish herself for an act of vanity, climbed onto her terrace and began to cry out like a woman in labour: 'Wake up, people of Cortona, wake up and bring candles and lanterns and come out to hear the sinner!' She enumerated all her sins, proclaiming her misery to the stars. By this noisy humility, she satisfied this need for exhibitionism, found in so many examples of narcissistic women. For the woman, religion authorises self-indulgence; it gives her the guide, father, lover, titular divinity she nostalgically needs; it feeds her reveries; it fills her empty hours. But especially, it confirms the world order; it justifies resignation by bringing hope for a better future in an asexual heaven. This is why today women are still a powerful asset in the hands of the Church; it is why the Church is so hostile to any measure that might facilitate their emancipation. Women must have religion; there must be women, 'real women', to perpetuate religion.

It is clear that woman's whole 'character' – her convictions, values, wisdom, morality, tastes and behaviour – is explained by her situation. The fact that she is denied transcendence usually prohibits her from having access to the loftiest human attitudes – heroism, revolt, detachment, invention and creation – but they are not so common even in men. There are many men who are, like woman, confined within the domain of the intermediary, of inessential means; the worker escapes from it through political action, expressing a revolutionary will; but men from what we precisely call the 'middle' class settle in this sphere deliberately; destined like the woman to the repetition of daily tasks, alienated in ready-made values, respecting public opinion and only seeking vague comforts on earth, the employee, the shopkeeper and the bureaucrat hold no superiority over their women companions; cooking, washing, running her home, raising her children, the woman shows more initiative and independence than the man enslaved to orders; he must obey his superiors every day, wear a removable collar and affirm his social rank; she can lie about in a housecoat in her apartment, sing, laugh with her women neighbours; she acts as she pleases, takes small risks and efficiently tries to attain a few results. She lives much less according to convention and appearances than does her husband. The bureaucratic world described by Kafka – among others – this universe of ceremonies, absurd gestures, meaningless behaviour is essentially masculine; she has greater purchase on reality; when he lines up his figures, or converts sardine boxes into money, he grasps nothing but abstracts; the child content in his cradle, clean laundry, the roast are more tangible things; yet, just because she feels their contingence – and consequently her own contingence – in the concrete pursuit of these objectives, it often happens that she does not alienate herself in them: she remains available. Man's undertakings are both projects and escapes: he lets himself be overwhelmed by his career, his personage; he is readily self-important, serious; contesting masculine logic and morality, woman does not fall into these traps: that is what Stendhal appreciated so strongly in her; she does not resort to pride to elude the ambiguity of her condition; she does not hide behind the mask of human dignity; she reveals her undisciplined thoughts, her emotions, her spontaneous reactions with more sincerity. This is why her conversation is far less boring than her husband's whenever she speaks in her own name and not as her seigneur's loyal half; he recites so-called general ideas, meaning words and formulas found in the columns of his newspaper or in specialist works; she brings experience, limited but concrete. The famous 'feminine sensitivity' is part myth, part theatre; but the fact remains that woman is more attentive than man to herself and the world. Sexually, she lives in a crude masculine climate: she compensates by appreciating 'pretty things', which can lead to sentimentality, but also to refinement; because her sphere is limited, the objects she touches are precious to her: by not binding them in concepts or projects, she displays their splendour; her desire for escape is expressed in her taste for festiveness: she enjoys the gratuitousness of a bouquet of flowers, a cake, a well-laid table, she is pleased to transform the emptiness of her idle hours into a generous offering; loving laughter, songs, adornment and knickknacks, she is also ready to welcome everything that palpitates around her: the spectacle of the street, of the sky; an invitation or an excursion offer her new horizons; the man often refuses to participate in these pleasures; when he comes home, joyous voices become silent and the women in the family assume the bored and proper air expected of them. From the depths of solitude, of separation, the woman finds the sense of the singularity of her life: she has a more intimate experience than the man of the past, death, of time passing; she is concerned with the adventures of her heart, her flesh, her mind because she knows that on earth she has but one lot; and also, because she is passive, she bears the reality that submerges her in a more passionate manner, with more pathos than the individual absorbed by an ambition or job; she has the leisure and the tendency to abandon herself to her emotions, study her feelings and draw conclusions from them. When her imagination is not lost in vain dreams, she becomes full of sympathy: she tries to understand the other in his uniqueness and re-create him in herself; regarding her husband, her lover, she is capable of true identification: she makes his projects and his cares her own in a way he could not imitate. She watches anxiously over the whole world; it seems to be an enigma to her: each being, every object, can be a reply; she questions avidly. When she grows older, her disenchanted expectation is converted into irony and an often piquant cynicism; she refuses masculine mystifications, she sees the contingent, absurd, gratuitous reverse side of the imposing structure built by males. Her dependence prohibits detachment for her; but she draws real generosity from her imposed devotion; she forgets herself in favour of her husband, her lover, her child, she ceases to think of herself, she is pure offering, gift. Being poorly adapted to men's society, she is often forced to invent her own conduct; she is less able to settle for ready-made patterns and clichés; if she is of good will, her apprehensions are closer to authenticity than is her husband's self-confidence.

But she will only have these advantages over her husband if she rejects the mystifications he offers her. In the upper classes, women are willing accomplices to their masters because they stand to profit from the benefits they are guaranteed. We have seen that women of the high bourgeoisie and aristocracy have always defended their class interests more stubbornly than their husbands: they do not hesitate to radically sacrifice their autonomy as human beings; they stifle all thinking, all critical judgement, all spontaneity; they parrot conventional wisdom, they identify with the ideal imposed on them by the male code; in their hearts, and even on their faces, all sincerity is dead. The housewife regains independence in her work, in caring for the children: she draws a limited but concrete experience from it: a woman who is 'waited on' no longer has any grasp on the world; she lives in dreams and abstraction, in a void. She is unaware of the reach of the ideas she professes; the words she rattles off have lost all meaning in her mouth; the banker, the businessman and even at times the general take risks, accepting exhaustion and problems; they purchase their privileges in an unfair market, but at least they pay for them themselves; for all they receive, their wives give nothing, do nothing in return; and they even more righteously believe in their imprescriptible rights with a blind faith. Their vain arrogance, their radical incapability, their stubborn ignorance, turn them into the most useless beings, the most idiotic that the human species has ever produced.

It is thus as absurd to speak of 'the woman' in general as of 'the eternal man'. And we can see why all comparisons where we try to decide if the woman is superior, inferior or equal to the man are pointless: their situations are profoundly different. If these same situations are compared, it is obvious that the man's is infinitely preferable, that is to say he has far more concrete opportunities to project his freedom in the world; the inevitable result is that masculine realisations outweigh by far those of women: for women, it is practically forbidden to *do* anything. But to compare the use that, within their limits, men and women make of their freedom is a priori meaningless, precisely because they use it freely. In various forms, the traps of bad faith and the mystifications of seriousness are lying in wait for both of them; freedom is entire in each. However, because of the fact that in woman this freedom remains abstract and empty, it cannot authentically assume itself except in revolt: this is the only way open to those who have no chance to build anything; they must refuse the limits of their situation and seek to open paths to the future; resignation is only a surrender and an evasion; for woman there is no other way out than to work for her liberation.

This liberation can only be collective, and it demands above all that the economic evolution of the feminine condition be accomplished. There have been and there still are many women who do seek to attain individual salvation on their own. They try to justify their existence within their own immanence, that is, to achieve transcendence through immanence. It is this ultimate effort – sometimes ridiculous, often pathetic – of the imprisoned woman to convert her prison into a heaven of glory, her servitude into sovereign freedom, that we find in the narcissist, the woman in love and the mystic.

Part Three
JUSTIFICATIONS

CHAPTER II

The Narcissist

It has sometimes been asserted that narcissism is the fundamental attitude of all women;* but overextending this notion destroys it as La Rochefoucauld destroyed the notion of egotism. In fact, narcissism is a well-defined process of alienation: the self is posited as an absolute end and the subject escapes itself in it. There are many other – authentic or inauthentic – attitudes found in woman: we have already studied some of them. What is true is that circumstances invite woman more than man to turn towards self and to dedicate her love to herself.

All love demands the duality of a subject and an object. Woman is led to narcissism by two convergent paths. As subject, she is frustrated; as a little girl, she was deprived of this alter ego that the penis is for the boy; later on, her aggressive sexuality remained unsatisfied. Of far greater importance is that she is forbidden virile activities. She is busy but she does not *do* anything; in her functions as wife, mother and housewife, she is not recognised in her singularity. Man's truth is in the houses he builds, the forests he clears, the patients he cures: not being able to accomplish herself in projects and aims, woman attempts to grasp herself in the immanence of her person. Parodying Sieyès's words, Marie Bashkirtseff wrote: 'Who am I? Nothing. What would I like to be? All.' It is because they are nothing that many women fiercely limit their interests to their self alone, that their self becomes hypertrophied so as to be confounded with All. 'I am my own heroine,' continues Marie Bashkirtseff. A man who acts necessarily confronts himself. Inefficient and separated, woman can neither situate nor assess herself; she gives herself sovereign importance because no important object is accessible to her.

If she can put *herself* forward in her own desires, it is because since childhood she has seen herself as an object. Her education has encouraged her to alienate herself wholly in her body, puberty having revealed

---

* Cf. Helene Deutsch, *The Psychology of Women*.

this body as passive and desirable; it is a thing she can touch, that satin or velvet arouses, and that she can contemplate with a lover's gaze. In solitary pleasure, it may happen that the woman splits into a male subject and a female object; Dalbiez[*1] studied the case of Irène, who said to herself, 'I'm going to love myself', or more passionately, 'I'm going to possess myself', or in a paroxysm: 'I'm going to fecundate myself.' Marie Bashkirtseff is also both subject and object when she writes, 'It's really a pity that no one sees my arms and torso, all this freshness and youth.'

In truth, it is not possible to be *for self* positively Other and grasp oneself as object in the light of consciousness. Doubling is only dreamed. For the child, it is the doll that materialises this dream; she recognises herself in it more concretely than in her own body because there is separation between the two. Mme de Noailles expresses this need to be two so as to establish a tender dialogue between self and self in, among other works, *The Book of My Life*.[2]

I loved dolls, I endowed their immobility with the life of my own existence; I could not have slept under the warmth of a cover if they were not also wrapped in wool and feathers . . . I dreamt of truly savouring pure solitude as two . . . This need to persist intact, to be twice myself, I felt it avidly as a little child . . . Oh! How I wanted in the tragic instants where my dreamy sweetness was the plaything of hurtful tears to have another little Anna next to me who would throw her arms around my neck, who would console me, understand me . . . during my life I met her in my heart and I held her tight: she helped me not in the form of hoped-for consolation but in the form of courage.

The adolescent girl leaves her dolls dormant. But throughout her life, woman will be vigorously encouraged to leave and come back to herself by the magic of the mirror. Otto Rank brought to light the mirror-double relation in myths and dreams. It is above all in woman that the reflection allows itself to be assimilated to the self. Male beauty is a sign of transcendence, that of woman has the passivity of immanence: the latter alone is made to arrest man's gaze and can thus be caught in

---

* *Psychoanalytical Method and the Doctrine of Freud*. In her childhood, Irène liked to urinate like boys; she often sees herself in her dreams in undine form, which confirms Havelock Ellis's ideas on the relation between narcissism and what he calls 'undinism'; that is, a certain urinary eroticism.

the immobile trap of the mirror's silvering; man who feels and wants himself to be activity and subjectivity does not recognise himself in his immobile image; it does not appeal to him since the man's body does not appear to him as an object of desire; while the woman, knowing she is and making herself object, really believes she is seeing *herself* in the mirror: passive and given, the reflection is a thing like herself; and as she covets feminine flesh, her flesh, she enlivens the inert qualities she sees with her admiration and desire. Mme de Noailles, who knew about this, confides to us:

> I was less vain about the gifts of the mind, so vigorous in me that I did not doubt them, than about the image reflected by a frequently consulted mirror . . . Only physical pleasure satisfies the soul fully.

The words 'physical pleasure' are vague and inadequate here. What satisfies the soul is that, while the mind will have to prove its worth, the contemplated face is here, today, given and indubitable. The whole future is concentrated in this rectangle of light and its frame makes a universe; outside these narrow limits, things are no more than disorganised chaos; the world is reduced to this piece of glass where one image shines: the One and Only. Every woman drowned in her reflection reigns over space and time, alone, sovereign; she has total rights over men, fortune, glory and sensual pleasure. Marie Bashkirtseff was so intoxicated by her beauty that she wanted to fix it in indestructible marble; it is herself she would have thus destined to immortality:

> Coming home I get undressed, I am naked and am struck by the beauty of my body as if I had never seen it. A statue has to be made of me, but how? Without getting married, it is almost impossible. And I have to, I would only get ugly, spoiled . . . I have to take a husband, if only to have my statue made.

Cécile Sorel, preparing for an amorous rendezvous, depicts herself like this:

> I am in front of my mirror. I would like to be more beautiful. I fight with my lion's mane. Sparks fly from my comb. My head is a sun in the middle of my tresses set like golden rays.

I also recall a young woman I saw one morning in the restroom of a café; she was holding a rose and she looked a little drunk; she brought her lips to the mirror as if to drink her image and she was murmuring while smiling: 'Adorable, I find myself adorable.' Both priestess and idol, the narcissist crowned with glory hovers in the heart of eternity and on the other side of the clouds kneeling creatures worship her: she is God contemplating Himself. 'I love myself, I am my God!' said Mme Mejerowsky. To become God is to realise the impossible synthesis of the in-itself and for-itself: the moments an individual thinks he has succeeded are special times of joy, exaltation and plenitude. One day in an attic, Roussel, at nineteen, felt the aura of glory around his head: he never got over it. The girl who saw beauty, desire, love and happiness deep in her mirror, endowed with her own features – animated, so she thinks, by her own consciousness – will try her whole life to use the promises of this blinding revelation. 'It is you I love,' confides Marie Bashkirtseff to her reflection one day. Another day she writes: 'I love myself so much, I make myself so happy that I was as if crazy at dinner.' Even if the woman is not of irreproachable beauty, she will see her soul's unique riches appear on her face and that will be enough to make her drunk. In the novel where she portrayed herself as Valérie, Mme Krüdener describes herself like this:

> She has something special that I have never yet seen in any woman. One can be as graceful, much more beautiful, and be far from her. She is perhaps not admired, but she has something ideal and charming that makes one pay attention. Seeing her so delicate, so svelte that she is a thought . . .

It should not be surprising that those less advantaged might sometimes experience the ecstasy of the mirror: they are moved by the mere fact of being a thing of flesh, which is there; like man, all they need is the pure generosity of young feminine flesh; and since they grasp themselves as a singular subject, with a little bad faith they will also endow their generic qualities with an individual charm; they will discover some gracious, rare or amusing feature in their face or body; they will think they are beautiful just because they feel they are women.

Moreover, the mirror is not the only instrument of doubling, although it is the favoured one. Each person can try to create a twin brother in his inner dialogue. Alone most of the day, fed up with household tasks, woman has the leisure to shape her own figure in dreams. As a young girl, she dreamed of the future; trapped in an uncertain present, she tells her story to herself; she retouches it so as to introduce an aesthetic order, transforming her contingent life into a destiny well before her death.

We know, for example, how attached women are to their childhood memories; women's literature makes it clear; in general, childhood takes a secondary place in men's autobiographies; women, on the other hand, often go no further than recounting their early years; these are the favourite subjects of their novels and stories. A woman who confides in a woman friend or a lover almost always begins her stories with these words: 'When I was a little girl . . .' They are nostalgic for this period when they felt their father's beneficent and imposing hand on their head while tasting the joys of independence; protected and justified by adults, they were autonomous individuals with a free future opening before them: now, however, they are poorly protected by marriage and love and have become servants or objects, imprisoned in the present. They reigned over the world, conquering it day after day: and now they are separated from the universe, doomed to immanence and repetition. They feel dispossessed. But what they suffer from the most is being swallowed up in generality: a wife, mother, housewife, or one woman among millions of others; as a child, by contrast, the woman lived her condition in an individual way; she was unaware of the analogies between her apprenticeship to the world and that of her friends; through her parents, teachers and friends, she was recognised in her individuality, she thought herself incomparable to any other woman, unique, promised to unique possibilities. She returns emotionally to this younger sister whose freedom, demands and sovereignty she abdicated and whom she more or less betrayed. The woman she has become misses this human being she was; she tries to find this dead child in her deepest self. The words 'little girl' move her; but 'What a funny little girl' do even more, words that revive her lost originality.

She is not satisfied with marvelling from afar at this precious childhood: she tries to revive it in her. She tries to convince herself that her tastes, ideas and feelings have kept their exceptional freshness. Perplexed, quizzical and playing with her necklace or twisting her ring, she murmurs: 'That's funny . . . That's just how I am . . . You know? Water fascinates me . . . Oh! I adore the countryside.' Each preference seems like an eccentricity, each opinion a challenge to the world. Dorothy Parker captured this widespread true-to-life characteristic:

> She liked to think of herself as one for whom flowers would thrive, who must always have blossoms about her, if she would be truly

happy . . . She told people, in little bursts of confidence, that she loved flowers. There was something almost apologetic in her way of uttering her tender avowal, as if she would beg her listeners not to consider her too bizarre in her taste. It seemed rather as though she expected the hearer to fall back, startled, at her words, crying, 'Not really! Well, what *are* we coming to?' She had other little confessions of affection . . . always with a little hesitation, as if understandably delicate about baring her heart, she told her love for color, the country, a good time, a really interesting play, nice materials, well-made clothes, and sunshine. But it was her fondness for flowers that she acknowledged oftenest. She seemed to feel that this, even more than her other predilections, set her apart from the general.[3]

The woman eagerly tries to confirm these analyses in her behaviour; she chooses a colour: 'Green is really my colour'; she has a favourite flower, perfume, musician, superstitions and fetishes that she treats with respect; she does not have to be beautiful to express her personality in her outfits and home. The character she portrays is more or less coherent and original according to her intelligence, obstinacy and depth of alienation. Some women just randomly put together a few sparse and mismatched traits; others systematically create a figure whose role they consistently play: it has already been said that women have trouble differentiating this game from the truth. Around this heroine, life goes on like a sad or marvellous novel, always somewhat strange. Sometimes it is a novel already written. I do not know how many girls have told me they see themselves in Judy of *Dust*.[4] I remember an old, very ugly lady who used to say: 'Read *The Lily in the Valley*;[5] it's my story'; as a child I used to contemplate this wilted lily for hours. Others, more vaguely, murmur: 'My life is a novel.' A good or bad star hovers over them. 'Things like this only happen to me,' they say. Rotten luck dogs them or good luck smiles on them: in any case they have a destiny. Cécile Sorel writes with the naïveté that characterises her *Mémoires*: 'This is how I made my debut in the world. My first friends were genius and beauty.' And in *The Book of My Life*, a fabulous narcissistic monument, Mme de Noailles writes:

The governesses disappeared one day: chance took their place. It mistreated the creature both powerful and weak as much as it had satisfied it, it kept it from shipwrecks where it was like a combative Ophelia, saving her flowers and whose voice ever rises. It asked the creature to hope that this final promise be kept: the Greeks use death.

This other example of narcissistic literature must be cited:

From the sturdy little girl I was with delicate but rounded arms and legs and healthy cheeks, I acquired a more frail physique, more evanescent that made me a pathetic adolescent, in spite of the source of life that can spring forth from my desert, my famine, and my brief and mysterious deaths as strangely as Moses's rock. I will not boast of my courage as I have the right to. It is part of my strengths, my luck. I could describe it as one says: I have green eyes, black hair, a small and powerful hand.

And these lines too:

Today I can recognise that, bolstered by my soul and its harmonious powers, I have lived to the sound of my voice.

Without beauty, brilliance or happiness, woman will choose the character of a victim; she will obstinately embody the *mater dolorosa*, the misunderstood wife, she will be 'the unhappiest woman in the world'. This is the case of this melancholic woman Stekel describes:*

Each time around Christmas, Mrs H. W. appears at my office, pale-faced, clad in somber black and complains of her fate. She relates a sad story while tears stream down her face. A thwarted existence, an unfortunate marriage! . . . The first time I was moved to tears and would have almost wept with her . . . Two[6] years has since flown . . . but she is still at the threshold of her hopes, still bewailing her misspent life . . . her face begins to show the early signs of the disintegration brought on by age. She thus has an additional reason for bemoaning her fate . . . 'What has become of me! I was once so beautiful and so much admired' . . . Her complaints are cumulative; she stresses her despair. Her friends . . . are well familiar with her sad plight . . . She makes herself a nuisance to everybody with her perpetual complaints . . . this in turn again furnishes her the opportunity to feel herself lonely, abandoned, not understood . . .

* *Frigidity in Woman.*

This woman found her satisfaction in the *tragic role*. The thought that she was the unhappiest woman on earth intoxicated her . . . All attempts to awaken her interest in the active current life ended in failure.

A trait shared by young Mrs Weldon, stunning Anna de Noailles, Stekel's unfortunate patient and the multitude of women marked by an exceptional destiny is that they feel misunderstood; their family and friends do not recognise – or inadequately recognise – their singularity; they transform this ignorance, this indifference of others, into the positive idea that they hold a secret inside them. The fact is that many have silently buried childhood and youthful memories that had a great importance for them; they know their official biography is not to be confused with their real history. But above all, because she has not realised herself in her life, the heroine cherished by the narcissist is merely an imaginary character; her unity does not come from the concrete world: it is a hidden principle, a kind of 'strength', 'virtue' as obscure as phlogistonism; the woman believes in its presence but if she wanted to show it to others she would be as bothered as the psychasthenic determined to confess to intangible crimes. In both cases, the 'secret' is reduced to the empty conviction of possessing in one's deepest self a key to decipher and justify feelings and behaviour. It is their abulia and inertia that give this illusion to psychasthenics; and it is because of her inability to express herself in daily action that woman believes an inexpressible mystery inhabits her: the famous myth of the eternal feminine encourages her in this and is thus, in turn, confirmed.

Enriched by these misunderstood treasures, whether she be under a lucky or an unlucky star, woman, in her own eyes, adopts the tragic hero's need to be governed by destiny. Her whole life is transfigured into a sacred drama. In her solemnly chosen dress emerges both a priestess clothed in holy garb and an idol attired by faithful hands, offered for the adoration of devotees. Her home becomes her temple of worship. Marie Bashkirtseff gives as much care to the decoration she places around her as to her dresses:

Near the desk, an old-style armchair, so that upon entering, I need make only a small movement in the chair to find myself facing the people . . . near the pedantic-looking desk with books in the background, in between, paintings and plants, legs and feet visible instead of being cut in two as before by this black wood. Hanging above the divan are two mandolins and the guitar. Put a blond and white girl with fine small blue-veined hands in the middle of this.

When she parades in salons, when she abandons herself on the arm of a lover, the woman accomplishes her mission: she is Venus dispensing the treasures of her beauty to the world. It is not she herself, it is Beauty that Cécile Sorel defended when she broke the glass covering Bib's caricature of her; one can see in her *Mémoires* that she invited mortals to the cult of Art at each moment of her life. Likewise Isadora Duncan, as she depicts herself in *My Life*:

After a performance, in my tunic, with my hair crowned with roses, I was so lovely. Why should not this loveliness be enjoyed? . . . A man who labours all day with his brain . . . why should he not be taken in those beautiful arms and find comfort for his pain and a few hours of beauty and forgetfulness?

The narcissist's generosity is profitable to her: better than in mirrors it is in others' admiring eyes that she sees her double haloed in glory. Without a complaisant audience, she opens her heart to a confessor, doctor or psychoanalyst; she will consult chiromancers, mediums. 'It's not that I believe in it,' said an aspiring starlet, 'but I love it so much when I'm spoken about!' She talks about herself to her women friends; more avidly than in anything else, she seeks a witness in the lover. The woman in love quickly forgets herself; but many women are incapable of real love, precisely because they never forget themselves. They prefer the wider stage to the privacy of the bedroom. Thus the importance of society life for them: they need gazes to contemplate them, ears to listen to them; they need the widest possible audience for their personage. Describing her room once more, Marie Bashkirtseff reveals: 'Like this, *I am on stage* when someone enters and finds me writing.' And further on: 'I decided to buy myself a *considerable mise en scène*. I am going to build a more beautiful townhouse and grander workshops than Sarah's.'

And Mme de Noailles writes:

I loved and love the agora . . . And so I have often reassured my friends who apologised for the many guests they feared I would be importuned by with this sincere admission: I don't like *to play to empty seats.*

Dressing up and conversation largely satisfy this feminine taste for display. But an ambitious narcissist wants to exhibit herself in a more recherché and varied way. In particular, making her life a play offered to public applause, she will take delight in really staging herself. In *Corinne*, Mme de Staël recounts at length how she charmed Italian crowds by reciting poems that she accompanied on a harp. At Coppet, one of her favourite pastimes was to declaim tragic roles; playing Phaedra, she would readily make ardent declarations to young lovers whom she dressed up as Hippolytus. Mme Krüdener specialised in the dance of the shawl that she describes in *Valérie*.

Valérie required a dark blue muslin shawl, she took her hair away from her forehead; she put the shawl on her head; it went down along her temples and shoulders; her forehead appeared in an antique manner, her hair disappeared, her eyelids lowered, her usual smile faded little by little: her head bent, her shawl fell softly on her crossed arms, on her bust, and this blue piece of clothing and this pure and gentle figure seem to have been drawn by Correggio to express tranquil resignation; and when her eyes looked up, and her lips dared a smile, one could say that one was seeing, as Shakespeare described it, Patience on a monument smiling at Grief.

One has to see Valérie. She is simultaneously timid, noble and profoundly sensitive and she troubles, leads, moves, draws tears and makes the heart beat as it beats when dominated by a great ascendant; it is she who possesses this charming grace that cannot be taught but that nature secretly reveals to some superior beings.

If circumstances allow it, nothing will give the narcissist deeper satisfaction than devoting herself publicly to the theatre. 'The theatre,' says Georgette Leblanc, 'provided me what I had sought in it: a reason for exaltation. Today, it is for me the *caricature of action*, something indispensable for excessive temperaments.' The expression she uses is striking: if she cannot take action, the woman invents substitutes for action; the theatre represents a privileged subsitute for some women. The actress can have very different aims. For some, acting is a means of earning one's living, a simple profession; for others, it is access to fame that will be exploited for amorous aims; for still others, the triumph of their narcissism; the greatest – Rachel, Eleonora Duse – are authentic artists who transcend themselves in the role they create; the ham, by contrast, cares not for what she accomplishes but for the glory that will cascade over her; she seeks above all to put herself in the limelight. The stubborn narcissist will be as limited in art as in love because she does not know how to give herself.

This failing will be seriously felt in all her activities. She will be tempted by all roads leading to glory; but she will never unreservedly take any. Painting, sculpture and literature are disciplines requiring strict training and demanding solitary work; many women try such work but quickly abandon it if they are not driven by a positive desire to create; and many of those who persevere never do more than 'play' at working. Marie Bashkirtseff, so avid for glory, spent hours in front of her easel; but she loved herself too much to seriously love to paint. She admits it herself after years of bitterness. 'Yes, I don't take the trouble to paint, I watched myself today, I *cheat*.' When a woman succeeds, like Mme de Staël or Mme de Noailles, in building a body of work, it is because she is not exclusively absorbed by self-worship: but one of the burdens that weighs on many women writers is a self-indulgence that hurts their sincerity, limits and diminishes them.

Many women imbued with a feeling of superiority, however, are not able to show it to the world; their ambition will thus be to use a man whom they convince of their worth as their means of intervention; they do not aim for specific values through free projects; they want to attach ready-made values to their egos; they will thus turn – by becoming muses, inspiration and stimulation – to those who hold influence and glory in the hope of being identified with them. A striking example is Mabel Dodge in her relations with Lawrence:

> I wanted to seduce his spirit so that I could make him carry out certain things . . . It was his soul I needed for my purpose, his soul, his will, his creative imagination, and his lighted vision. The only way to obtain the ascendancy over these essential tools was by way of the blood . . . I was always trying to get things done: I didn't often even try to do anything myself. I seemed to want to use all my power upon delegates to carry out the work. This way – *perhaps a compensation for that desolate and barren feeling of having nothing to do!* – I achieved a sense of fruitfulness and activity vicariously.[7]

And further on:

> I wanted Lawrence to understand things for me. To take *my* experience, *my* material, through *my* Taos, and to formulate it all into a magnificent creation.

In a similar way, Georgette Leblanc wanted to be 'food and flame' for Maeterlinck; but she also wanted to see her name inscribed in the poet's book. This is not, here, a question of ambitious women having chosen personal aims and using men to reach them – as did Mme de Staël and the princesse des Ursins – but rather of women animated by a wholly subjective desire for *importance*, with no objective aim, trying to appropriate for themselves the transcendence of another. They do not always succeed – far from it – but they are skilful in hiding their failure and in persuading themselves that they are endowed with irresistible seduction. Knowing they are lovable, desirable and admirable, they feel certain of being loved, desired and admired. Bélise is wholly narcissistic. Even the innocent Brett, devoted to Lawrence, invents for herself a little personage she endows with weighty seduction:

> I raise my eyes and see that you are looking at me with your mischievous fawn-like air, a provocative gleam in your eyes, Pan. I stare back at you with a solemn and dignified air until the gleam goes out of your face.

These illusions can give rise to real derangement; Clérambault had good reason to consider erotomania 'a kind of professional derangement'; to feel like a woman is to feel like a desirable object, to believe oneself desired and loved. It is significant that nine out of ten patients with 'illusions of being loved' are women. They are clearly seeking in their imaginary lover the apotheosis of their narcissism. They want him to be endowed with unconditional distinction: priest, doctor, lawyer, superior man; and the unquestionable truth his behaviour reveals is that his ideal mistress is superior to all other women, that she possesses irresistible and sovereign virtues.

Erotomania can be part of various psychoses; but its content is always the same. The subject is illuminated and glorified by the love of an admirable man who was suddenly fascinated by her charms – though she expected nothing from him – and displays his feelings in a circuitous but imperious way; this relation at times remains ideal and at other times assumes a sexual form; but what characterises it essentially is that the powerful and glorious demigod loves more than he is loved and he displays his passion in bizarre and ambiguous behaviour. Among the great number of cases reported by psychiatrists, here is a typical one adapted from Ferdière.* It concerns a forty-eight-year-old woman, Marie-Yvonne, who makes the following confession:

This is about Mr. Achille, Esq., former deputy and under-secretary of state, member of the bar and the Conseil de l'Ordre. I have known him since 12 May 1920; the evening before, I tried to meet him at the courts; from afar I had noticed his strong stature, but I did not know who he was; it sent chills up my spine . . . Yes, there is an affair of feeling between us, a reciprocal feeling: our eyes, our gazes met. From the moment I saw him, I had a liking for him; it is the same for him . . . In any case, he declared his feeling first: it was early in 1922; he received me in his home, always alone; one day he even sent his son out . . . One day . . . he got up and came towards me, carrying on with his conversation. I understood right away that it was a sentimental surge . . . His words made me understand. By various kindnesses he made me understand we had reciprocal feelings. Another time, once again in his office, he approached me saying: 'It is you, it is you alone and no one else, Madam, you understand clearly.' I was so taken aback that I did not know what to answer; I simply said, 'Thank you, sir!' Then another time he accompanied me from his office to the street; he even got rid of a man who was with him, he gave him twenty sous on the staircase and told him: 'Leave me, my boy, you see I am with Madam!' All of that was to accompany me and be alone with me. He always shook my hands tightly. During his first court pleading, he made a comment to let me know he was a bachelor.

He sent a singer to my courtyard to demonstrate his love to me . . . He watched my windows; I could sing you his romance . . . He had a town band march by my door. I was foolish. I should have responded to his advances. I gave M. Achille the cold shoulder . . . he thus thought I was rejecting him and he took action; he should have spoken out openly; he took revenge on me. M. Achille thought that I had feelings for B. . . . and he was jealous . . . He made me suffer by putting a magic spell on my photograph; at

* Erotomania (L'érotomanie).

least that is what I discovered this year through studies in books and dictionaries. He worked enough on this photo: it all comes from that.

This delusion easily changes, in fact, into a persecution complex. And this process is found even in normal cases. The narcissist cannot accept that others are not passionately interested in her; if she has the clear proof she is not adored, she immediately supposes she is hated. She attributes all criticism to jealousy or spite. Her failures are the result of dark machinations: and thus they confirm her in the idea of her importance. She easily slips into megalomania or the opposite, persecution delirium: as centre of her universe and aware of no other universe except her own, she becomes the absolute centre of the world.

But narcissist drama plays itself out at the expense of real life; an imaginary personage solicits the admiration of an imaginary public; a woman tormented by her ego loses all hold on the concrete world, she does not care about establishing any real relationship with others; Mme de Staël would not have declaimed *Phaedra* so wholeheartedly if she had foreseen the mockeries her 'admirers' noted that night in their notebooks; but the narcissist refuses to accept she can be seen other than as she shows herself: this is what explains why, so busy contemplating herself, she totally fails to judge herself, and she falls so easily into ridiculousness. She no longer listens, she talks, and when she talks, she recites her lines. Marie Bashkirtseff writes: 'It amuses me. I don't speak with him, I *act* and, feeling I am in front of a receptive audience, I am excellent at childlike and fanciful intonations and attitudes.'

She looks at herself too much to see anything; she understands in others only what she recognises about them; whatever she cannot assimilate to her own case, to her own story, remains foreign to her. She likes to expand her experiences: she wants to experience the headiness and torments of being in love, the pure joys of motherhood, friendship, solitude, tears and laughter; but because she can never give herself, her sentiments and emotions are fabricated. Isadora Duncan undoubtedly cried real tears on the death of her children. But when she cast their ashes into the sea with a great theatrical gesture, she was merely being an actress; and one cannot read this passage where she evokes her sorrow in *My Life* without embarrassment:

I feel the warmth of my own body. I look down on my bare legs – stretching them out. The softness of my breasts, my arms that are never still but continually waving about in soft undulations, and I realise that for twelve years I have been weary, this breast has harboured a never-ending ache, these hands before me have been marked with sorrow, and when I am alone these eyes are seldom dry.

In the worship of self, the adolescent girl can muster the courage to face the disturbing future; but it is a stage she must go beyond quickly: if not, the future closes up. The woman in love who encloses her lover in the couple's immanence dooms him to death with herself: the narcissist, alienating herself in her imaginary double, destroys herself. Her memories become fixed, her behaviour stereotyped, she dwells on the same words, repeats gestures that have lost all meaning: this is what gives the impression of poverty found in 'secret diaries' or 'feminine autobiographies'; so occupied in flattering herself, the woman who does nothing becomes nothing and flatters a nothing.

Her misfortune is that, in spite of all her bad faith, she is aware of this nothingness. There cannot be a real relationship between an individual and his double because this double does not exist. The woman narcissist suffers a radical failure. She cannot grasp herself as a totality, as plenitude; she cannot maintain the illusion of being in itself – for itself. Her solitude, like that of every human being, is felt as contingence and abandonment. And this is why – unless there is a conversion – she is condemned to hide relentlessly from herself in crowds, noise, and others. It would be a grave error to believe that in choosing herself as the supreme end she escapes dependence: on the contrary, she dooms herself to the most severe slavery; she does not make the most of her freedom, she makes herself an endangered object in the world and in foreign consciousnesses. Not only are her body and face vulnerable flesh worn by time, but from a practical point of view it is a costly enterprise to adorn the idol, to put her on a pedestal, to erect a temple to her: we have seen that to preserve her form in immortal marble, Marie Bashkirtseff had to consent to marry for money. Masculine fortunes paid for the gold, incense and myrrh that Isadora Duncan and Cécile Sorel laid at the foot of their thrones. As it is man who incarnates destiny for woman, women usually gauge their success by the number and quality of men subjected to their power. But reciprocity comes into play again here; the 'praying mantis', attempting to make the male her instrument, does not free herself from him like this, because to catch him, she must please him. The American woman, trying to be an idol, makes herself the slave of her admirers, does not dress, live or breathe other than through the man and for him. In fact, the narcissist is as dependent as the hetaera. If she escapes an individual man's domination, it is by accepting the tyranny of public opinion. This link that rivets her to others does not imply reciprocity; if she sought recognition by others' freedom while also recognising that freedom as an end through activity, she would cease to be narcissistic. The paradox of her attitude is that she demands to be valued by a world to which she denies all value, since she alone counts in her own eyes. Outside approbation is an inhuman, mysterious and capricious force that must be tapped magically. In spite of her superficial arrogance, the narcissistic woman knows she is threatened; it is why she is uneasy, susceptible, irritable and constantly suspicious; her vanity is never satisfied; the older she grows, the more anxiously she seeks praise and success, the more she suspects plots around her; lost and obsessed, she sinks into the darkness of bad faith and often ends up by building a paranoid delirium around herself. The words 'Whosoever shall save his life will lose it' apply specifically to her.

CHAPTER 12

The Woman in Love

The word 'love' has not at all the same meaning for both sexes and this is a source of the grave misunderstandings that separate them. Byron rightly said that love is merely an occupation in the life of the man, while it is life itself for the woman. The same idea is expressed by Nietzsche in *The Gay Science*: the same word 'love', he says, means, in fact, two different things for the man and for the woman:

> What woman means by love is clear enough: total devotion (not mere surrender) with soul and body, without any consideration or reserve . . . In this absence of conditions her love is a faith; woman has no other *faith*.* Man, when he loves a woman, *wants*† precisely this love from her and is thus himself as far as can be from the presupposition of feminine love. Supposing, however, that there should also be men to whom the desire for total devotion is not alien; well, then they simply are not men.[8]

Men might be passionate lovers at certain moments of their existence, but there is not one who could be defined as 'a man in love'; in their most violent passions, they never abandon themselves completely; even if they fall on their knees before their mistresses, they still wish to possess them, annex them; at the heart of their lives, they remain sovereign subjects; the woman they love is merely one value among others; they want to integrate her into their existence, not submerge their entire existence in her. By contrast, love for the woman is a total abdication for the benefit of a master.

Cécile Sauvage writes: 'When the woman loves, she must forget her

---

* Nietzsche's emphasis.
† Also Nietzsche's emphasis.

own personality. This is a law of nature. A woman does not exist without a master. Without a master, she is a scattered bouquet.'

In reality, this has nothing to do with a law of nature. It is the difference in their situations that is reflected in the conceptions man and woman have of love. The individual who is a subject, who is himself, endeavours to extend his grasp on the world if he has the generous inclination for transcendence: he is ambitious, he acts. But an inessential being cannot discover the absolute in the heart of his subjectivity; a being doomed to immanence could not realise himself in his acts. Closed off in the sphere of the relative, destined for the male from her earliest childhood, used to seeing him as a sovereign, with whom equality is not permitted, the woman who has not suppressed her claim to be human will dream of surpassing her being towards one of those superior beings, of becoming one, of fusing with the sovereign subject; there is no other way out for her than losing herself body and soul in the one designated to her as the absolute, as the essential. Since she is, in any case, condemned to dependence, she would rather serve a god than obey tyrants – parents, husband, protector; she chooses to want her enslavement so ardently that it will seem to her to be the expression of her freedom; she will try to overcome her situation as inessential object by radically assuming it; through her flesh, her feelings and her behaviour, she will exalt as sovereign the one she loves, she will posit him as value and supreme reality: she will efface herself before him. Love becomes a religion for her.

We have seen that the adolescent girl at first wishes to identify with males; once she renounces this, she then seeks to participate in their virility by being loved by one of them; it is not the individuality of one man or another that seduces her; she is in love with man in general. 'And you, the men I will love, how I await you,' writes Irène Reweliotty. 'How I rejoice in soon knowing you. You, especially, the first one.' Of course, the man must belong to the same class and the same race as her own: the privilege of sex works only within this framework; for him to be a demigod, he must obviously be a human being first; for the daughter of a colonial officer, the native is not a man; if the young girl gives herself to an 'inferior', she is trying to degrade herself because she does not think she is worthy of love. Normally, she looks for the man who represents male superiority; she is rapidly led to discover that many individuals of the chosen sex are sadly contingent and mundane; but first she is favourably disposed towards them; they have less to prove their value than to keep from grossly disavowing it: this explains many often lamentable errors; the naive young girl is taken in by virility. According to the circumstances, male worth will appear to her as physical force, elegance, wealth, culture, intelligence, authority, social situation or a military uniform: but what she always hopes for is that her lover will be the summation of the essence of man. Familiarity often is enough to destroy his prestige; it breaks down with the first kiss, or in everyday contact, or on the wedding night. Love at a distance is nonetheless merely a fantasy, not a real experience. When it is carnally consummated, desire for love becomes passionate love. Inversely, love can arise from making love, the sexually dominated woman exalting the man who first seemed insignificant to her. But it often happens that the woman is unable to transform any of the men she knows into a god. Love holds less place in feminine life than is often believed. Husband, children, home, pleasures, social life, vanity, sexuality and career are far more important. Almost all women have dreamed of the 'great love': they have had imitations, they have come close to it; it has come to them in incomplete, bruised, trifling, imperfect and false forms; but very few have really dedicated their existence to it. The great women lovers are often those who did not waste their emotions on juvenile crushes; they first accepted the traditional feminine destiny: husband, home, children; or they lived in difficult solitude; or they counted on some venture that more or less failed; when they glimpse the chance to save their disappointing life by dedicating it to an elite being, they desperately give themselves up to this hope. Mlle Aïssé, Juliette Drouet and Mme d'Agoult were nearly thirty when they began their love lives, Julie de Lespinasse was close to forty; no goal was available to them, they were unprepared to undertake any venture that seemed worthwhile to them, love was their only way out.

Even if they are allowed independence, this road is still the one that seems the most attractive to most women; it is agonising to take responsibility for one's life endeavour; the adolescent boy too readily turns to older women, seeking a guide, a tutor, a mother in them; but his education, customs and the inner constraints he faces prevent him from definitively accepting the easy solution of abdication; he views such loves merely as a phase. It is man's luck – in adulthood as in childhood – to be made to take the most arduous roads but the surest ones; woman's misfortune is that she is surrounded by nearly irresistible temptations; everything incites her to take the easy way out: instead of being encouraged to fight on her own account, she is told that she can let herself get by and she will reach enchanted paradises; when she realises she was fooled by a mirage, it is too late; she has been worn out in this adventure.

Psychoanalysts like to claim that the woman seeks her father's image in her lover; but it is because he is man, not father, that he dazzles the child, and every man shares this magic; the woman wishes not to reincarnate one individual in another but to bring back to life a situation: one she knew as a little girl, sheltered by adults; she was an integral part of her family home life, she felt the peace of quasi-passivity; love will bring her mother as well as her father back to her, and her childhood as well; what she wishes is to find a roof over her head, walls that hide her from her abandonment within the world, laws that protect her from her freedom. This childish dream haunts many feminine loves; the woman is happy when her lover calls her 'my little girl, my dear child'; men know the words well: 'You look like a little girl' are among the words that most surely touch the hearts of women: we have seen how many of them have suffered becoming adults; many persist in 'acting like a child', and indefinitely prolonging their childhood in their attitude and dress. To become a child again in the arms of a man brings them great satisfaction. It is the theme of this popular tune:

> *I feel so small in your arms*
> *So small, o my love . . .*

a theme tirelessly repeated in lovers' conversations and correspondence. 'Baby, my baby,' murmurs the lover and the woman calls herself, 'little one, your little one'. Irène Reweliotty writes: 'When, then, will he come, the one who will be able to dominate me?' And thinking she had met him: 'I love feeling you a man and better than me.'

A psychasthenic woman studied by Janet* illustrates this attitude in the most striking way:

As far back as I can recall, all the foolish acts or all the good deeds I have done stem from the same cause, an aspiration to the perfect and ideal love where I can give myself entirely, confide all my being to another being, God, man or woman, so superior to me that I would no longer think of leading my life or watching over myself. To find someone who would love me enough to take the trouble to make me live, someone whom I would blindly and confidently obey, sure that he would keep me from all failure and would put me on the right track, very gently and with much love, towards

* *Obsessions and Psychasthenia.*

perfection. How I envy the ideal love of Mary Magdalene and Jesus: to be the ardent disciple of an adored and worthy master; to live and die for one's idol, believe in him without any possible shadow of doubt, to hold at last the final victory of the Angel over the beast, to be held in his enveloping arms, so small, so pressed in his protection and so much his that I no longer exist.[9]

Many examples have already proven to us that this dream of annihilation is in fact an avid will to be. In all religions, the adoration of God is part of the devotee's desire for his own salvation; by giving herself up entirely to the idol, the woman hopes he will give her possession both of herself and of the universe contained in him. In most cases, it is first the justification, the exaltation of her ego, she asks of her lover. Many women do not abandon themselves to love unless they are loved in return: and the love they are shown is sometimes enough to make them fall in love. The young girl has dreamed of herself as seen through the man's eyes: it is in man's eyes that the woman believes she has at last found herself.

Cécile Sauvage writes:

Walking beside you, moving my tiny little feet that you loved, feeling them so slender in their high felt-topped shoes, made me love all the love you surrounded them with. The slightest movements of my hands in my muff, of my arms, of my face, the inflections of my voice, filled me with happiness . . .[10]

The woman feels endowed with a sure and high value; at last she has the right to cherish herself through the love she inspires. She is exhilarated at finding a witness in her lover. This is what Colette's 'Vagabond' admits:

I must confess that, in allowing this man to return tomorrow, I was giving way to my desire to keep, not an admirer, not a friend, but an eager spectator of my life and my person. 'One has to get terribly old,' said Margot to me one day, 'before one can give up the vanity of living in the presence of someone else.'[11]

In one of her letters to Middleton Murry, Katherine Mansfield recounts that she has just bought a ravishing mauve corset; she quickly adds: 'What a pity there is no one to *see* it!' Nothing is more discouraging than to feel that one is the flower, the perfume, the treasure that no desire seeks: what good is an asset that does not enrich me and that no one wants as a gift? Love is the revealer that shows up in positive and clear traits the dull negative image as empty as a blank print; the woman's face, the curves of her body, her childhood memories, her dried tears, her dresses, her habits, her universe, everything she is, everything that belongs to her escapes contingence and becomes necessary: she is a marvellous gift at the foot of her god's altar.

> Before his hands were laid gently on her shoulders, before his eyes took their fill of hers, she had been a plain dull woman in a plain dull world. He kissed her, and she stood in the rose-light of immortality.*12

Thus, men endowed with social prestige and good at flattering feminine vanity will arouse passion even if they have no physical charm. Because of their lofty situation, they incarnate Law and Truth: their consciousness discloses an uncontested reality. The woman they praise feels transformed into a priceless treasure. According to Isadora Duncan,† D'Annunzio's success came from this.

> When D'Annunzio loves a woman, he lifts her spirit from this earth to the divine regions where Beatrice moves and shines. In turn he transforms each woman to a part of the divine essence, he carries her aloft until she believes herself really with Beatrice . . . he flung over each favourite in turn a shining veil. She rose above the heads of ordinary mortals and walked surrounded by a strange radiance. But when the caprice of the poet ended, this veil vanished, the radiance was eclipsed, and the woman turned again to common clay . . . To hear oneself praised with that magic peculiar to D'Annunzio is, I imagine, something like the experience of Eve when she heard the voice of the serpent in Paradise. D'Annunzio can make any woman feel that she is the centre of the universe.13

Only in love can woman harmoniously reconcile her eroticism and her narcissism; we have already seen an opposition between these two systems that makes the woman's adaptation to her sexual destiny very difficult.

---

* Mary Webb, *The House in Dormer Forest*.
† Isadora Duncan, *My Life*.

Making herself carnal object and prey contradicts her self-adoration: it seems to her that lovemaking disfigures and defiles her body or degrades her soul. Some women, therefore, choose frigidity, thinking they can thus preserve the integrity of their ego. Others dissociate animal sensuality and lofty sentiments. A very characteristic case is Mme D. S.'s, reported by Stekel and which I have already cited concerning marriage:

> Frigid, and married to a respected man, after his death, there came into her life a young man . . . he, too, was an artist and a wonderful musician . . . She became his mistress. Her love was and is to this day so great that she feels happy only in his presence. Her whole life is wrapped in her Lothar. In spite of her great love for him she has remained cool in his arms. Another man, too, crossed her path. He was a forester, a powerful, rough individual who, on finding himself alone with her one day, took possession of her without saying a word. She was so consternated that she didn't object. In his embrace she experienced the keenest orgasm. 'In his arms,' she states, 'I have regained my health for the past months. It is like a wild intoxication, but followed by an indescribable disgust when I think of my Lothar. Paul I hate; Lothar I love. Nevertheless, Paul is the one who gratifies me. Everything about Lothar holds me to him; but it seems I must act like a harlot in order to feel. As a lady I can never respond.' [She refuses to marry Paul but continues to sleep with him; in those moments][14] she becomes like a person transformed and the raw words which escape her lips she would never be guilty of using on any other occasion.

Stekel adds that 'for many women, the descent into animality is the condition for orgasm'. They see an abasement in physical love impossible to reconcile with feelings of esteem and affection. For others, by contrast, it is by the man's esteem, tenderness and admiration that this abasement can be abolished. They only consent to give themselves to a man if they believe they are deeply loved by him; a woman has to be very cynical, indifferent or proud to consider physical relations as an exchange of pleasures in which each partner equally gets something out of it. The man revolts as much as – and perhaps more than – the woman against anyone who wants to exploit* him sexually; but she is the one

---

* See, among others, *Lady Chatterley's Lover*. Through Mellors, Lawrence expresses his horror of women who make him a tool of pleasure.

who generally has the impression that her partner is using her as an instrument. Only exalted admiration can make up for the humiliation of an act she considers a defeat. We have seen that the love act requires a woman's profound alienation; she is awash in the indolence of passivity; eyes closed, anonymous, lost, she feels transported by waves, caught up in torment, buried in the night: night of flesh, of the womb, of the tomb; reduced to nothing, she reaches the Whole, her self effaced. But when the man separates himself from her, she finds herself thrown back to earth, on a bed, in the light; she has a name and a face again: she is a conquered person, a prey, an object. This is when love becomes necessary to her. Just as after being weaned the child seeks the reassuring gaze of his parents, it is in the eyes of the lover who contemplates her that the woman whose flesh has been painfully detached has to feel reunited with the Whole. She is rarely completely satisfied; even if she experienced the relief of pleasure, she is not entirely freed of the carnal spell, her arousal becomes feeling; in providing her with sensuality, the man attaches her to him and does not liberate her. He, though, no longer feels desire for her: she only forgives him for this momentary indifference if he has vowed timeless and absolute feeling to her. Then the immanence of the instant is transcended; the burning memories are no longer a regret but a treasure; as it dies down, the sensuality becomes hope and promise; sexual pleasure is justified; the woman can gloriously assume her sexuality because she transcends it; arousal, pleasure and desire are no longer a state but a gift; her body is no longer an object: it is a song, a flame. Thus she can abandon herself passionately to the magic of eroticism; night becomes light; the woman in love can open her eyes, look at the man who loves her and whose gaze glorifies her; through him nothingness becomes plenitude of being and being is transfigured into value; she no longer sinks into a sea of darkness, she is transported on wings, exalted to the sky. Abandon becomes holy ecstasy. When she *receives* the loved man, the woman is inhabited, visited like the Virgin by the Holy Spirit, like the believer by the wafer; this explains the obscene analogy between holy hymns and ribald songs: it is not that mystical love always has a sexual side; but the sexuality of the woman in love takes on a mystical tone. 'My God, my beloved, my master', the same words spill from the lips of the kneeling saint and the woman in love lying on the bed; the saint offers her flesh to Christ's arrows, she holds out her hands to receive the stigmata, she implores the burning of divine Love; the woman in love also offers and waits: darts, stinger and arrows are embodied in the male sex. In both of them there is the same dream, the infantile, mystical, love dream: to exist sovereignly by effacing oneself within the other.

It has sometimes been claimed* that this desire for effacement leads to masochism. But as I have noted concerning eroticism, one can only speak of masochism if I try 'to cause myself to be fascinated by my objectivity-for-others',†15 that is if the consciousness of the subject turns back to the ego to grasp it in its humiliated situation. But the woman in love is not only a narcissist alienated in her self: she also experiences a passionate desire to go beyond her own limits and become infinite, thanks to the intervention of another who has access to infinite reality. She abandons herself first to love to save *herself*; but the paradox of idolatrous love is that in order to save herself she ends up totally disavowing *herself*. Her feeling takes on a mystical dimension; she no longer asks God to admire her or approve her; she wants to melt into him, forget herself in his arms. 'I would have liked to be a love saint,' writes Mme d'Agoult. 'I envied the martyr in such moments of exaltation and ascetic furore.' What comes through in these words is the desire for a radical destruction of the self, abolishing the frontiers that separate her from her beloved: it is not masochism but a dream of ecstatic union. The same dream inspires these words of Georgette Leblanc: 'At that time, had I been asked what I most wanted in the world, without any hesitation I would have said: to be food and flame for his spirit.'

To achieve this union, the woman first wants to serve; she will feel necessary in responding to her lover's demands; she will be integrated into his existence, she will be a part of his value, she will be justified; even mystics like to believe, according to Angelus Silesius, that God needs man, otherwise the gift they make of themselves would be in vain. The more demands the man makes, the more fulfilled the woman feels. Although the seclusion Hugo imposed on Juliette Drouet weighed on the young woman, one feels she is happy to obey him: staying seated close to the fire is doing something for the master's happiness. She passionately tries to be positively useful to him. She prepares special dishes for him, creates a home for him: your little 'nest for two', she said sweetly; she takes care of his clothes.

She writes to him: 'I want you to stain and tear all your clothes as much as possible and that I alone should mend and clean them and nobody else.'

---

* It is, among others, H. Deutsch's theory in *The Psychology of Women*.
† Cf. Sartre, *Being and Nothingness*.

For him she reads newspapers, cuts out articles, organises letters and notes, copies manuscripts. She is upset when the poet entrusts part of this work to his daughter Léopoldine. Similar characteristics are found in all women in love. If need be she tyrannises herself in the lover's name; everything she is, everything she has, every second of her life must be devoted to him and thus find their raison d'être; she does not want to possess anything except in him; what would make her unhappy is that he demand nothing of her, and so an attentive lover invents demands. She first sought in love a confirmation of what she was, her past, her personage; but she also commits her future: to justify it she destines it to the one who possesses all values; she thus gives up her transcendence: she subordinates it to that of the essential other whose vassal and slave she makes herself. It is to find herself, to save herself that she began by losing herself in him: the fact is that little by little she loses herself; all reality is in the other. Love that was originally defined as a narcissistic apotheosis is accomplished in the bitter joys of a devotion that often leads to self-mutilation. At the outset of a consuming passion, the woman becomes prettier, more elegant than before. 'When Adèle does my hair, I look at my forehead because you love it', writes Mme d'Agoult. This face, this body, this room, this me, she has found a raison d'être for them, she cherishes them through the mediation of this beloved man who loves her. But later, she gives up all coquetry; if the lover so desires, she changes this face that had once been more precious than love itself; she loses interest in it; she makes what she is and what she has the fief of her lord; what he disdains, she disavows; she would like to devote to him each beat of her heart, each drop of blood, the marrow of her bones; this is what a dream of martyrdom expresses: to exaggerate the gift of self to the point of torture, of death, to be the ground the beloved treads on, to be nothing but that which responds to his call. She vigorously eliminates everything the beloved finds useless. If this gift she makes of self is totally accepted, there is no masochism: few traces of it are seen in Juliette Drouet. In her excessive adoration she sometimes knelt before the poet's portrait and asked him to excuse the mistakes she might have committed; she did not angrily turn against herself. But the slide from generous enthusiasm to masochistic rage is easy. The woman in love who finds herself before her lover in the same situation as the child before his parents also recovers the feeling of guilt she experienced around them; she does not choose to revolt against him as long as she loves him: she revolts against her self. If he loves her less than she desires, if she fails to interest him, to make him happy, to be sufficient to him, all her narcissism turns into disgust, humiliation and self-hatred that push her to self-punishment. During a longer or shorter crisis, sometimes for a whole life, she will be a willing victim; she will go out of her way to harm this self that has not been able to satisfy the lover. Then her atti-tude is specifically masochistic. But cases where the woman in love seeks her own suffering so as to get revenge on herself and those where she seeks confirmation of the man's freedom and power must not be confused. It is a commonplace – and seems to be a reality – that the prostitute is proud to be beaten by her man: but it is not the idea of her battered and enslaved person that exalts her, it is the strength, authority and sover-eignty of the male on whom she depends; she also likes to see him mistreat another male, she often pushes him into dangerous competi-tions: she wants her master to hold the values recognised in the milieu to which she belongs. The woman who gladly submits to masculine caprices also admires the proof of a sovereign freedom in the tyranny that is wielded over her. One must be careful to note that, if for some reason the lover's prestige is ruined, his blows and demands become odious to her: they are only worth something if they manifest the beloved's divinity. In that case, it is intoxicatingly joyous to feel oneself the prey of a foreign freedom: for any existent the most surprising adventure is to find oneself sustained by the diverse and imperious will of another; one is tired of inhabiting the same skin all the time; blind obedience is the only chance of radical change that a human being might experience. So here is the woman slave, queen, flower, doe, stained-glass window, doormat, servant, courtesan, muse, companion, mother, sister or child depending on the lover's fleeting dreams, the lover's imperious orders: she complies with delight with these metamorphoses as long as she does not recognise that she still has the same taste of submission on her lips. In love as well as in eroticism, it appears that masochism is one of the paths the unsatisfied woman takes, disappointed by the other and by herself; but this is not the natural slope of a happy resignation. Masochism perpetuates the presence of the self as a hurt, fallen figure; love aims at the forgetting of self in favour of the essential subject.

The supreme aim of human love, like mystical love, is identification with the loved one. The measure of values and the truth of the world are in his own consciousness; that is why serving him is still not enough. The woman tries to see with his eyes; she reads the books he reads, prefers the paintings and music he prefers, she is only interested in the landscapes she sees with him, in the ideas that come from him; she adopts his friends, his enemies and his opinions; when she questions herself, she endeavours to hear the answer he gives; she wants the air he has already breathed in her lungs; the fruit and flowers she has not received from his hands have neither fragrance nor taste; even her hodological space is upset: the centre of the world is no longer where she is but where the beloved is; all roads leave from and lead to his house. She uses his words, she repeats his gestures, adopts his manias and tics. 'I *am* Heathcliff,' says Catherine in *Wuthering Heights*; this is the cry of all women in love; she is another incarnation of the beloved, his reflection, his double: she is *he*. She lets her own world founder in contingence: she lives in his universe.

The supreme happiness of the woman in love is to be recognised by the beloved as part of him; when he says 'we', she is associated and identified with him, she shares his prestige and reigns with him over the rest of the world; she does not tire of saying – even if it is excessive – this delicious 'we'. Necessary to a being who is absolute necessity, who projects himself in the world towards necessary goals and who reconstitutes the world as necessity, the woman in love experiences in her resignation the magnificent possession of the absolute. It is this certitude that gives her such great joys; she feels exalted at the right hand of the god; what does it matter that she is always in second place as long as it is *her* place, forever, in a marvellously ordered world? As long as she loves, as she is loved and necessary for the beloved, she feels completely justified: she savours peace and happiness. Such was perhaps Mlle Aïssé's lot at Knight d'Aydie's side before religious scruples troubled her soul, of Juliette Drouet's in Hugo's shadow.

But this glorious felicity is seldom stable. No man is God. The relations the mystic has with the divine absence depend on his fervour alone: but the deified man – who is not God – is present. That is where the torments of the woman in love stem from. Her most ordinary destiny can be summarised in Julie de Lespinasse's famous words: 'At every instant of my life, my friend, I love you, I suffer and I await you.' Of course for men too suffering is linked to love; but their heartbreaks either do not last long or are not all consuming; Benjamin Constant wanted to die for Juliette Récamier: in one year, he was cured. Stendhal missed Métilde for years, but it was a regret that enriched his life more than destroying it. In accepting herself as the inessential and as total dependence, the woman creates a hell for herself; all women in love see themselves in Andersen's Little Mermaid, who, having exchanged her fish tail for a woman's legs out of love, walked on needles and burning coals. It is not true that the beloved man is unconditionally necessary and that she is not necessary to him; it is not up to him to justify the woman who worships him, and he does not let himself be possessed by her.

An authentic love should take on the other's contingence, that is, his lacks, limitations and originary gratuitousness; it would claim to be not a salvation but an inter-human relation. Idolatrous love confers an absolute value on the loved one: this is the first lie strikingly apparent to all outsiders: '*He* doesn't deserve so much love,' people whisper around the woman in love; posterity smiles pityingly when evoking the pale figure of Count Guibert. It is a heartrending disappointment for the woman to discover her idol's weaknesses and mediocrity. Colette – in *The Vagabond* and *Mes apprentissager (My Apprenticeships)* – often alludes to this bitter agony; this disillusion is even crueller than the child's at seeing paternal prestige crumble, because the woman herself chose the one to whom she made a gift of her whole being. Even if the chosen one is worthy of the deepest attachment, his truth is earthbound: it is not he whom the woman kneeling before a supreme being loves; she is duped by that spirit of seriousness which refuses to put values 'in parentheses', not recognising that they stem from human existence; her bad faith erects barriers between her and the one she worships. She flatters him, she bows down before him, but she is not a friend for him since she does not realise he is in danger in the world, that his projects and finalities are as fragile as he himself is; considering him the Law and Truth, she misunderstands his freedom, which is hesitation and anguish. This refusal to apply a human measure to the lover explains many feminine paradoxes. The woman demands a favour from the lover, he grants it: he is generous, rich, magnificent, he is royal, he is divine; if he refuses, he is suddenly stingy, mean and cruel, he is a devilish being or bestial. One might be tempted to counter: If a 'yes' is understood as a superb extravagance, why should one be surprised by a 'no'? If the no manifests such an abject egotism, why admire the yes so much? Between the superhuman and the inhuman is there not room for the human?

A fallen god, then, is not a man: it is an imposture; the lover has no alternative other than to prove he is really the king one adulates or to denounce himself as a usurper. When he is no longer worshipped, he has to be trampled on. In the name of this halo with which the woman in love adorns her beloved, she forbids him all weakness; she is disappointed and irritated if he does not conform to this image she put in his place; if he is tired, confused, if he is hungry or thirsty when he should not be, if he makes a mistake, if he contradicts himself, she decrees he is 'not himself' and she reproaches him for this. Likewise, she will go so far as to reproach him for all the initiatives she does not appreciate; she judges her judge, and in order for him to deserve to remain her master, she refuses him his freedom. Her adoration is sometimes better served by his absence than his presence; there are women, as we have seen, who devote themselves to dead or inaccessible heroes so that they never have to compare them with flesh-and-blood beings; the latter inevitably fail to live up to their dreams. Hence the disillusioned sayings: 'You shouldn't believe in Prince Charming. Men are just poor things.' They would not seem like dwarfs if they were not required to be giants.

This is one of the curses weighing on the passionate woman: her generosity is immediately converted into demands. Being alienated in another, she also wants to salvage herself: she has to annex this other who holds her being. She gives herself to him entirely: but he has to be totally available to receive this gift honourably. She dedicates all her moments to him: he has to be present at every moment; she only wants to live through him: but she wants to live; he has to devote himself to making her live.

Mme d'Agoult writes to Liszt: 'I love you sometimes stupidly and at such times I do not understand that I could not, would not be able to and should not be for you the same absorbing thought as you are for me.' She tries to curtail her spontaneous wish: to be everything for him. There is the same appeal in Mlle de Lespinasse's complaint:

My God! If you only knew what the days are like, what life is like without the interest and pleasure of seeing you! My friend, dissipation, occupation and movement satisfy you; and I, my happiness is you, it is only you; I would not want to live if I could not see you and love you every minute of my life.

At first, the woman in love is delighted to satisfy her lover's desire; then – like the legendary fireman who out of love for his job lights fires everywhere – she works at awakening this desire so as to have to satisfy it; if she does not succeed, she feels humiliated, useless to such an extent that the lover will feign passion he does not feel. In making herself a slave, she has found the surest means of subjugating him. This is another lie of love that many men – Lawrence, Montherlant – have resentfully denounced: he takes himself for a gift when he is a tyranny. In *Adolphe*, Benjamin Constant fiercely painted the chains the overly generous passion of a woman entwines around the man. 'She did not count her sacrifices because she was busy making me accept them,' he says cruelly about

Ellénore. Acceptance is thus a commitment that ties the lover up, without his even having the benefit of appearing to be the one who gives; the woman demands that he graciously welcome the loads she burdens him with. And her tyranny is insatiable. The man in love is authoritarian: but when he has obtained what he wanted, he is satisfied; but there are no limits to the demanding devotion of the woman. A lover who has confidence in his mistress shows no displeasure at her absences or if she is occupied when away from him: sure that she belongs to him, he prefers to possess a freedom more than a thing. By contrast, the absence of the lover is always torture for the woman: he is a gaze, a judge, as soon as he looks at something other than her, he frustrates her; everything he sees, he steals from her; far from him, she is dispossessed both of herself and of the world; even seated at her side, reading, writing, he abandons her, he betrays her. She hates his sleep. Baudelaire is touched by the sleeping woman: 'Your beautiful eyes are weary, poor lover.' Proust delights in watching Albertine* sleep; male jealousy is thus simply the desire for exclusive possession; the woman beloved, when sleep gives her back the disarming candour of childhood, belongs to no one: for the man, this certitude suffices. But the god, the master, must not abandon himself to the repose of immanence; it is with a hostile look that the woman contemplates this destroyed transcendence; she detests his animal inertia, this body that no longer exists *for her* but *in itself*, abandoned to a contingence whose ransom is her own contingence. Violette Leduc forcefully expressed this feeling:

> I hate sleepers. I lean over them with bad intent. Their submission exasperates me. I hate their unconscious serenity, their false anaesthesia, their studiously blind face, their reasonable drunkenness, their incompetent earnestness . . . I hovered, I waited for a long time for the pink bubble that would come out of my sleeper's mouth. I only wanted a bubble of presence from him. I didn't get it . . . I saw that his night eyelids were eyelids of death . . . I took refuge in his eyelids' gaiety when this man was impossible. Sleep is hard when it wants to be. He walked off with everything. I hate my sleeper who can create peace for himself with an unconsciousness that is alien to me. I hate his sweet forehead . . . He is deep down inside himself busy with his rest. He

---

* That Albertine is an Albert does not change anything; Proust's attitude here is in any case the masculine attitude.

is recapitulating who knows what . . . We had left posthaste. We wanted to leave the earth by using our personality. We had taken off, climbed up, watched out, waited, hummed, arrived, whined, won and lost together. It was a serious school for playing hooky. We had uncovered a new kind of nothingness. Now you're sleeping. Your effacement is not honest . . . If my sleeper moves, my hand touches, in spite of itself, the seed. It is the barn with fifty sacks of grain that is stifling, despotic. The scrotum of a sleeping man fell on my hand . . . I have the little bags of seed. I have in my hand the fields that will be ploughed, the orchards that will be pruned, the force of the waters that will be transformed, the four boards that will be nailed, the tarpaulins that will be lifted. I have in my hand the fruit, flowers and chosen animals. I have in my hand the lancet, the clippers, the probe, the revolver, the forceps and all that does not fill my hand. The seed of the sleeping world is only the dangling extra of the soul's prolongation . . .

You, when you sleep, I hate you.*[16]

The god must not sleep, or he becomes clay and flesh; he must not cease to be present, or his creature founders in nothingness. For woman, man's sleep is avarice and betrayal. At times the lover wakes his mistress: it is to make love to her; she wakes him simply to keep him from sleeping, to keep him nearby, thinking only of her, there, closed up in the room, in the bed, in her arms – like God in the tabernacle – this is what the woman desires: she is a gaoler.

And yet, she does not really consent to have the man be nothing else but her prisoner. Here is one of the painful paradoxes of love: captive, the god sheds his divinity. The woman preserves her transcendence by handing it over to him: but he must bring it to the whole world. If two lovers disappear into the absolute of passion together, all freedom deteriorates into immanence; only death can provide a solution: this is one of the meanings of the Tristan and Isolde myth. Two lovers who are exclusively destined for each other are already dead: they die of boredom. Marcel Arland in *Foreign Lands*[17] described this slow agony of a love that devours itself. The woman understands this danger. Except for cases of jealous frenzy, she herself demands that man be project and action: he has to accomplish exploits to remain a hero. The chevalier who embarks

* *I Hate Sleepers.*

on new feats of prowess offends his lady; but she scorns him if he stays seated at her feet. This is the torture of impossible love; woman wants to *have* man all to herself, but she demands that he go beyond all the givens he could possibly possess; one does not *have* a freedom; she wants to lock up *here* an existent who is, in Heidegger's words, a 'being from afar', she knows full well that this effort is futile. 'My friend, I love you as one should love, with excess, madness, rapture and despair,' writes Julie de Lespinasse. Idolatrous love, if lucid, can only be hopeless. For the woman in love who asks her lover to be a hero, giant, demigod, demands not to be everything for him, whereas she can find happiness only if she contains him entirely within herself.

Nietzsche says:*[18]

A woman's passion in its unconditional renunciation of rights of her own presupposes precisely that . . . there is no equal pathos, no equal will to renunciation; for if both partners felt impelled by love to renounce themselves, we should then get – I do not know what; perhaps an empty space? Woman wants to be taken . . . she wants someone who *takes*, who does not give himself or give himself away; on the contrary, he is supposed to become richer in 'himself' . . . Woman gives herself away, man acquires more.

In any case, the woman will be able to find her joy in this enrichment she brings to her loved one; she is not All for him: but she will try to believe herself indispensable; there are no degrees in necessity. If he cannot 'get along without her', she considers herself the foundation of his precious existence, and she derives her own worth from that. Her joy is to serve him: but he must gratefully recognise this service; giving becomes demand according to the customary dialectic of devotion.[†] And a woman of scrupulous mind asks herself: is it really *me* he needs? The man cherishes her, desires her with singular tenderness and desire: but would he not have just as singular feelings for another? Many women in love let themselves be deluded; they want to ignore the fact that the general is enveloped in the particular, and the man facilitates this illusion because he shares it at first; there is often in his desire a passion that seems to defy time; at the moment he desires this woman, he desires her with passion, he wants only her: and certainly, the moment is an

---

* *The Gay Science.*
† I have tried to show this in *Pyrrhus et Cinéas.*

absolute, but a momentary absolute. Duped, the woman passes into the eternal. Deified by the embrace of the master, she believes she has always been divine and destined for the god: she alone. But male desire is as fleeting as it is imperious; once satisfied, it dies rather quickly, while it is most often after love that the woman becomes his prisoner. This is the theme of a whole type of shallow literature and songs. 'A young man was passing by, a girl was singing . . . A young man was singing, a girl was crying.' And even if the man is seriously attached to the woman, it still does not mean that she is necessary to him. Yet this is what she demands: her abdication only saves her if it reinstates her empire; one cannot escape the play of reciprocity. So she must suffer or lie to herself. Most often she clutches first at the lie. She imagines the man's love as the exact counterpart of the love she bears him; with bad faith, she takes desire for love, an erection for desire, love for religion. She forces the man to lie to her. Do you love me? As much as yesterday? Will you always love me? She cleverly asks the questions just when there is not enough time to give nuanced and sincere answers or when circumstances prevent them; imperiously she asks her questions during lovemaking, at the moment of convalescence, when sobbing, or on a railway station platform; she makes trophies of the answers she extorts; and in the absence of responses, she interprets the silences; every genuine woman in love is more or less paranoid. I remember a woman friend who, when faced with the long silence from a far-off lover, declared, 'When one wants to break up, one writes to announce it'; then upon receiving an unambiguous letter: 'When one really wants to break up, one doesn't write.' It is often very difficult to decide where pathological delirium begins when hearing such confidences. Described by the panicking woman in love, the man's behaviour always seems extravagant: he's neurotic, sadistic, repressed, a masochist, a devil, unstable, cowardly or all of these together; he defies the most subtle psychological explanations. 'X. . . . adores me, he's wildly jealous, he wants me to wear a mask when I go out; but he's such a strange being and so suspicious of love that he keeps me in the hallway and doesn't invite me in when I ring his bell.' Or: 'Z. . . . adored me. But he was too proud to ask me to go to Lyon where he lives: I went there, I moved in with him. After eight days, without an argument, he threw me out. I saw him twice afterwards. The third time I called him and he hung up in the middle of the conversation. He's a neurotic.' These mysterious stories become clearer when the man explains: 'I absolutely did not love her,' or 'I liked her well enough, but I could not have lived one month with her.' Bad faith in excess leads to the mental asylum: one of the constants of erotomania is that the lover's behaviour seems enigmatic and paradoxical; from this slant, the patient's delirium always succeeds in breaking down the resistance of reality. A normal woman sometimes finally realises the truth, recognising that she is no longer loved. But as long as her back is not to the wall, she always cheats a little. Even in reciprocal love, there is a fundamental difference between the lovers' feelings that she tries to hide. The man must of course be capable of justifying himself without her since she hopes to be justified through him. If he is necessary to her, it is because she is fleeing her freedom: but if he assumes the freedom without which he would be neither a hero nor simply man, nothing and no one will be necessary for him. The dependence woman accepts comes from her weakness: how could she find a reciprocal dependence in the man she loves in his strength?

A passionately demanding soul cannot find tranquillity in love, because she sets her sights on a contradictory aim. Torn and tormented, she risks being a burden to the one for whom she dreamed of being a slave; she becomes importunate and obnoxious for want of feeling indispensable. Here is a common tragedy. Wiser and less intransigent, the woman in love resigns herself. She is not all, she is not necessary: it is enough for her to be useful; another can easily take her place: she is satisfied to be the one who is there. She recognises her servitude without asking for reciprocity. She can thus enjoy modest happiness; but even in these limits, it will not be cloudless. Far more painfully than the wife, the woman in love waits. If the wife herself is exclusively a woman in love, the responsibilities of the home, motherhood, her occupations and her pleasures will have little value in her eyes: it is the presence of her husband that lifts her out of the limbo of ennui. 'When you are not there, it seems not even worthwhile to greet the day; everything that happens to me seems lifeless, I am no more than a little empty dress thrown on a chair,' writes Cécile Sauvage early in her marriage.* And we have seen that, very often, it is outside marriage that passionate love arises and blooms. One of the most remarkable examples of a life entirely devoted to love is Juliette Drouet's: it is an endless wait. 'I must always come back to the same starting point, meaning eternally waiting for you,' she writes to Victor Hugo. 'I wait for you like a squirrel in a cage.' 'My God! How sad it is for someone with my nature to wait from one end of life to

---

* The case is different if the wife has found her autonomy in the marriage; in such a case, love between the two spouses can be a free exchange of two self-sufficient beings.

another.' 'What a day! I thought it would never end waiting for you and now I feel it went too quickly since I did not see you.' 'I find the day eternal.' 'I wait for you because after all I would rather wait than believe you are not coming at all.' It is true that Hugo, after having made her break off from her rich protector, Prince Demidoff, confined Juliette to a small apartment and forbade her to go out alone for twelve years, to prevent her from seeing her former friends. But even when her lot – she called herself 'your poor cloistered victim' – had improved, she still continued to have no other reason to live than her lover and not to see him very much. 'I love you, my dearest Victor,' she wrote in 1841, 'but my heart is sad and full of bitterness; I see you so little, so little, and the little I see you, you belong to me so little that all these littles make a whole of sadness that fills my heart and mind.' She dreams of reconciling independence and love. 'I would like to be both independent and slave, independent through a state that nourishes me and slave only to my love.' But having totally failed in her career as an actress, she had to resign herself to being no more than a lover 'from one end of life to the other'. Despite her efforts to be of service to her idol, the hours were too empty: the 17,000 letters she wrote to Hugo at the rate of three to four hundred every year are proof of this. Between visits from the master, she could only kill time. The worst horror of woman's condition in a harem is that her days are deserts of boredom: when the male is not using this object that she is for him, she is absolutely nothing. The situation of the woman in love is analogous: she only wants to be this loved woman and nothing else has value in her eyes. For her to exist, then, her lover must be by her side, taken care of by her; she awaits his return, his desire, his waking; and as soon as he leaves her, she starts again to wait for him. Such is the curse that weighs on the heroines of *Back Street*[*][19] and *The Weather in the Streets*,[†][20] priestesses and victims of pure love. It is the harsh punishment inflicted on those who have not taken their destiny in their own hands.

Waiting can be a joy; for the woman who watches for her loved one, knowing he is hurrying to her, that he loves her, the wait is a dazzling promise. But over and above the confident intoxication of love that changes absence itself into presence, the torment of worry gets confused with the emptiness of absence: the man might never return. I knew a woman who greeted her lover with surprise each time they met: 'I

* Fanny Hurst, *Back Street*.
† Rosamond Lehmann, *The Weather in the Streets*.

thought you would never return,' she would say. And if he asked her why: 'Because you *could* never return; when I wait, I always have the impression that I will never see you again.' Above all, he may cease to love her: he may love another woman. The vehemence with which she tries to fool herself by saying 'He loves me madly, he can love no one but me' does not exclude the torture of jealousy. It is characteristic of bad faith that it allows passionate and contradictory affirmations. Thus the madman who stubbornly takes himself for Napoleon does not mind admitting he is also a barber. The woman rarely consents to ask herself does he really love me? but asks herself a hundred times: Does he love another? She does not accept that her lover's fervour could have dimmed little by little, nor that he gives less value to love than she does: she immediately invents rivals. She considers love both a free feeling and a magic spell; and she assumes that 'her' male continues to love her in his freedom while being 'snared' or 'tricked' by some clever schemer. The man grasps the woman as being assimilated to him, in her immanence; here is why he easily plays the Boubouroche; he cannot imagine that she too could be someone who slips away from him; jealousy for him is ordinarily just a passing crisis, like love itself: the crisis may be violent and even murderous, but rarely does it last long in him. Jealousy for him mainly appears derivative: when things go badly for him or when he feels threatened by life, he feels derided by his wife.*[21] By contrast, a woman loving a man in his alterity and transcendence feels in danger at every moment. There is no great distance between betrayal by absence and infidelity. As soon as she feels unloved, she becomes jealous: given her demands, it is always more or less true; her reproaches and her grievances, whatever their pretexts, are converted into jealous scenes: this is how she will express her impatience, the ennui of waiting, the bitter feeling of her dependence, the regret of having only a mutilated existence. Her whole destiny is at stake in every glance her lover casts at another woman since she has alienated her entire being in him. And she becomes irritated if for one instant her lover turns his eyes to another woman; if he reminds her that she has just been dwelling on a stranger for a long time, she firmly answers: 'It's not the same thing.' She is right. A man looked at by a woman receives nothing: giving begins only at the moment when the feminine flesh becomes prey. But the coveted woman is immediately metamorphosed into a desirable and desired

* This comes to the fore, for example, in Lagache's work *The Nature and Forms of Jealousy*.

object; and the neglected woman in love 'returns to ordinary clay'. Thus she is always on the lookout. What is he doing? At whom is he looking? To whom is he talking? What one smile gave her, another smile can take back from her; an instant is enough to hurl her from 'the pearly light of immortality' to everyday dusk. She has received everything from love; she can lose everything by losing it. Vague or definite, unfounded or justified, jealousy is frightening torture for the woman because it is a radical contestation of love: if the betrayal is certain, it is necessary to either renounce making a religion of love or renounce that love; it is such a radical upheaval that one can understand how the woman in love, both doubting and deceived, can be obsessed by the desire and fear of discovering the mortal truth.

Being both arrogant and anxious, the woman is often constantly jealous but wrongly so: Juliette Drouet had pangs of suspicion towards all the women who came near Hugo, only forgetting to fear Léonie Biard, who was his mistress for eight years. When unsure, every woman is a rival and a danger. Love kills friendship insofar as the woman in love encloses herself in the universe of the loved man; jealousy exasperates her solitude, thus constricting her dependence even more. But she finds there recourse against boredom; keeping a husband is work; keeping a lover is a kind of vocation. The woman who, lost in happy adoration, neglected her personal appearance begins to worry about it again the moment she senses a threat. Dressing, caring for her home or social appearances become moments of combat. Fighting is stimulating activity; as long as she is fairly certain to win, the woman warrior finds a poignant pleasure in it. But the tormented fear of defeat transforms the generously consented gift into a humiliating servitude. The man attacks in defence. Even a proud woman is forced to be gentle and passive; manoeuvres, prudence, trickery, smiles, charm and docility are her best weapons. I still see this young woman whose bell I unexpectedly rang; I had just left her two hours before, badly made up, sloppily dressed, her eyes dull; but now she was waiting for *him*; when she saw me, she put on her ordinary face again, but for an instant I had the time to see her, prepared for him, her face contracted in fear and hypocrisy, ready for any suffering behind her breezy smile; her hair was carefully coiffed, special makeup brightened her cheeks and lips, and she was dressed up in a sparkling white lace blouse. Party clothes, fighting clothes. The masseuse, beauty consultant and 'aesthetician' know how tragically serious their women clients are about treatments that seem useless; new seductions have to be invented for the lover, she has to become that woman he wishes to meet and possess. But all effort is in vain: she will not resurrect in herself that image of the Other that first attracted him, that might attract him to another. There is the same duplicitous and impossible imperative in the lover as in the husband; he wants his mistress absolutely his and yet another; he wants her to be the answer to his dreams and still be different from anything his imagination could invent, a response to his expectations and an unexpected surprise. This contradiction tears the woman apart and dooms her to failure. She tries to model herself on her lover's desire; many women who bloomed at the beginning of a love affair that reinforced their narcissism become frightening in their maniacal servility when they feel less loved; obsessed and diminished, they irritate their lover; giving herself blindly to him, the woman loses that dimension of freedom that made her fascinating at first. He was looking for his own reflection in her: but if he finds it too faithful, he becomes bored. One of the misfortunes of the woman in love is that her love itself disfigures her, demolishes her; she is no more than this slave, this servant, this too-docile mirror, this too-faithful echo. When she realises it, her distress reduces her worth even more; she ends up losing all attraction with her tears, demands and scenes. An existent is what he does; to be, she has to put her trust in a foreign consciousness and give up doing anything. 'I only know how to love,' writes Julie de Lespinasse. *I Who Am Only Love*:[22] this title of a novel* is the motto of the woman in love; she is only love and when love is deprived of its object, she is nothing.

Often she understands her mistake; and so she tries to reaffirm her freedom, to find her alterity; she becomes flirtatious. Desired by other men, she interests her blasé lover again: such is the hackneyed theme of many awful novels, absence is sometimes enough to bring back her prestige; Albertine seems insipid when she is present and docile; from afar she becomes mysterious again and the jealous Proust appreciates her again. But these manoeuvres are delicate; if the man sees through them, they only serve to reveal to him how ridiculous his slave's servitude is. And even their success can be dangerous: because she is his the lover disdains his mistress, but he is attached to her because she is his; is it disdain or is it attachment that an infidelity will kill? It may be that, vexed, the man turns away from the indifferent one: he wants her free, yes; but he wants her given. She knows this risk: it paralyses her flirtatiousness. It is almost impossible for a woman in love to play this game skilfully; she is too afraid to be caught in her own trap. And insofar as

* By Dominique Rolin.

she still reveres her lover, she is loath to dupe him: how can he remain a god in her eyes? If she wins the match, she destroys her idol; if she loses it, she loses herself. There is no salvation.

A cautious woman in love – but these words clash – tries to convert the lover's passion into tenderness, friendship, habit; or she tries to attach him with solid ties: a child or marriage; this desire of marriage haunts many liaisons: it is one of security; the clever mistress takes advantage of the generosity of young love to take out insurance on the future: but when she gives herself over to these speculations, she no longer deserves the name of woman in love. For she madly dreams of securing the lover's freedom for ever, but not of destroying it. And this is why, except in the rare case where free commitment lasts a whole life, love-religion leads to catastrophe. With Mora, Mlle de Lespinasse was lucky enough to tire of him first: she tired of him because she had met Guibert, who in return promptly tired of her. The love between Mme d'Agoult and Liszt died of this implacable dialectic: the passion, vitality and ambition that made Liszt so easy to love destined him to other loves. The Portuguese nun could only be abandoned. The fire that made d'Annunzio so captivating* had a price: his infidelity. A rupture can deeply mark a man: but in the end, he has his life as man to live. The abandoned woman is nothing, has nothing. If she is asked 'How did you live before?' she cannot even remember. She let fall into ashes the world that was hers to adopt a new land from which she is brutally expelled; she gave up all the values she believed in, broke off her friendships; she finds herself without a roof over her head and the desert all around her. How could she begin a new life when outside her lover there is nothing? She takes refuge in delirious imaginings as in former times in the convent; or if she is too reasonable, there is nothing left but to die: very quickly, like Mlle de Lespinasse, or little by little; the agony can last a long time. When a woman has been devoted to a man body and soul for ten or twenty years, when he has remained firmly on the pedestal where she put him, being abandoned is a crushing catastrophe. 'What can I do,' asks this forty-year-old woman, 'what can I do if Jacques no longer loves me?' She dressed, fixed her hair and made herself up meticulously; but her hardened face, already undone, could barely arouse a new love; and she herself, after twenty years spent in the shadow of a man, could she ever love another? There are many years still to live at forty. I still see that other woman who kept her beautiful eyes and noble features in spite of a face swollen with

---

* According to Isadora Duncan.

suffering and who let her tears flow down her cheeks in public, blind and deaf, without even realising it. Now the god is telling another the words invented for her; dethroned queen, she no longer knows if she ever reigned over a true kingdom. If the woman is still young, she has the chance of healing; a new love will heal her; sometimes she will give herself to it with somewhat more reserve, realising that what is not unique cannot be absolute; but often she will be crushed even more violently than the first time because she will have to redeem herself for her past defeat. The failure of absolute love is a productive ordeal only if the woman is capable of taking herself in hand again; separated from Abélard, Héloïse was not a wreck, because, directing an abbey, she constructed an autonomous existence. Colette's heroines have too much pride and too many resources to let themselves be broken by an amorous disillusion; Renée Néré is saved by her work. And Sido tells her daughter that she was not too worried about her emotional destiny because she knew that Colette was much more than a woman in love. But there are few crimes that bring worse punishment than this generous mistake: to put one's self entirely in another's hands.

Authentic love must be founded on reciprocal recognition of two freedoms; each lover would then experience himself as himself and as the other; neither would abdicate his transcendence, they would not mutilate themselves; together they would both reveal values and ends in the world. For each of them, love would be the revelation of self through the gift of self and the enrichment of the universe. In his work *The Discovery of Self*, Georges Gusdorf summarises precisely what *man* demands of love:

Love reveals us to ourselves by making us come out of ourselves. We affirm ourselves by contact with that which is foreign and complementary to us. Love as a form of understanding discovers new heavens and new earths even in the very landscape where we have always lived. Here is the great secret: the world is other, *I myself am other*. And I am no longer alone in knowing it. Even better: someone taught me this. Woman therefore plays an indispensable and capital role in the consciousness man has of himself.[23]

This accounts for the importance the young man gives to love's apprenticeship;* we have seen how Stendhal and Malraux marvel at the miracle

* See Vol. I.

that 'I myself am another.' But Gusdorf is wrong to write: 'and *in the same way* man represents for the woman an indispensable intermediary of herself to herself', because today her situation is not *the same*; man is revealed in the guise of another, but he remains himself and his new face is integrated into the whole of his personality. It would only be the same for woman if she also existed essentially for-herself; this would imply that she possessed an economic independence, that she projected herself towards her own ends and surpassed herself without intermediary towards the group. Thus equal loves are possible, such as the one Malraux describes between Kyo and May. It can even happen that the woman plays the virile and dominating role like Mme de Warens with Rousseau, Léa with Chéri. But in most cases, the woman knows herself only as other: her for-others merges with her very being; love is not for her an intermediary between self and self, because she does not find herself in her subjective existence; she remains engulfed in this loving woman that man has not only revealed but also created; her salvation depends on this despotic freedom that formed her and can destroy her in an instant. She spends her life trembling in fear of the one who holds her destiny in his hands without completely realising it and without completely wanting it; she is in danger in an other, an anguished and powerless witness of her own destiny. Tyrant and executioner in spite of himself, this other wears the face of the enemy in spite of her and himself: instead of the sought-after union, the woman in love experiences the bitterest of solitudes; instead of complicity, struggle and often hate. Love, for the woman, is a supreme attempt to overcome the dependence to which she is condemned by assuming it; but even consented to, dependence can only be lived in fear and servility.

Men have rivalled each other proclaiming that love is a woman's supreme accomplishment. 'A woman who loves like a woman becomes *a more perfect woman*,'[24] says Nietzsche; and Balzac: 'In the higher order, man's life is glory, woman's is love. Woman is equal to man only in making her life a perpetual offering, as his is perpetual action.' But there again is a cruel mystification since what she offers, he cares not at all to accept. Man does not need the unconditional devotion he demands, nor the idolatrous love that flatters his vanity; he only accepts them on the condition that he does not satisfy the demands these attitudes reciprocally imply. He preaches to the woman about giving: and her gifts exasperate him; she finds herself disconcerted by her useless gifts, disconcerted by her vain existence. The day when it will be possible for the woman to love in her strength and not in her weakness, not to escape from herself but to find herself, not out of resignation but to affirm herself, love will become for her as for man the source of life and not a mortal danger. For the time being, love epitomises in its most moving form the curse that weighs on woman trapped in the feminine universe, the mutilated woman, incapable of being self-sufficient. Innumerable martyrs to love attest to the injustice of a destiny that offers them as ultimate salvation a sterile hell.

CHAPTER 13

The Mystic

Love has been assigned to woman as her supreme vocation, and when she addresses it to a man, she is seeking God in him: if circumstances deny her human love, if she is disappointed or demanding, she will choose to worship the divinity in God himself. It is true that there are also men who have burned with this flame; but they are rare and their fervour has been of a highly refined intellectual form. Women, though, who abandon themselves to the delights of celestial marriages are legion: and they experience them in a strangely affective way. Women are accustomed to living on their knees; normally, they expect their salvation to descend from heaven, where males reign; men too are enveloped in clouds: their majesty is revealed from beyond the veils of their bodily presence. The Beloved is always more or less absent; he communicates with her, his worshipper, in ambiguous signs; she only knows his heart by an act of faith; and the more superior to her he seems, the more impenetrable his behaviour seems to her. We have seen that in erotomania this faith resisted all refutations. A woman does not need to see or touch to feel the Presence at her side. Whether it be a doctor, a priest or God, she will find the same incontestable proof; she will welcome as a slave the waves of a love that falls from on high into her heart. Human love and divine love melt into one not because the latter is a sublimation of the former but because the former is also a movement towards a transcendent, towards the absolute. In any case, the woman in love has to save her contingent existence by uniting with the Whole incarnated in a sovereign Person.

This ambiguity is flagrant in many cases – pathological or normal – where the lover is deified, where God has human traits. I will only cite this one reported by Ferdière in his work on erotomania.[25] It is the patient who is speaking:

In 1923, I corresponded with a journalist from *La Presse*; every day
I read his articles about morality. I read between the lines; it seemed
to me that he was answering me, giving me advice; I wrote him
love letters; I wrote to him a lot . . . In 1924, it suddenly came to
me: it seemed to me that God was looking for a woman, that he
was going to come and speak to me; I had the impression he had
given me a mission, chosen me to found a temple; I believed myself
to be the centre of a big complex where doctors would take care
of women . . . It was then that . . . I was transferred to the Clermont
mental institution . . . There were young doctors who wanted to
change the world: in my cabin, I felt their kisses on my fingers, I
felt their sex organs in my hands; once, they told me: 'You are not
sensitive, but sensual; turn over'; I turned over and I felt them in
me: it was very pleasant . . . The head doctor, Dr D. . . ., was like a
god; I really felt there was something when he came near my bed;
he looked at me as if to say: I am all yours. He really loved me:
one day, he looked at me insistently in a truly extraordinary way . . .
his green eyes became blue as the sky; they widened intensely in
an incredible way . . . he saw the effect that produced all the while
speaking to another woman patient and he smiled . . . and I thus
remained fixated, fixated on Dr D. . . . one nail does not replace
another and in spite of all my lovers (I have had fifteen or sixteen),
I could not separate myself from him; that's why he's guilty . . .
For more than twelve years, I have been having mental conversations with him . . . when I wanted to forget him, he reappeared . . .
he was sometimes a bit mocking . . . 'You see, I frighten you,' he
said again, 'you can love others, but you always will come back to
me . . .' I often wrote him letters, even making appointments I would
keep. Last year, I went to see him; he was remote; there was no
warmth; I felt so silly and I left . . . People tell me he married another
woman, but he will always love me . . . he is my husband and yet
the act has never taken place, the act that would make the fusion . . .
'Abandon everything,' he sometimes says, 'with me you will always
rise upwards, you will not be like a being of the earth.' You see:
each time I look for God, I find a man; now I don't know what
religion I should turn to.

This is a pathological case. But there is this inextricable confusion in
many devotees between man and God. In particular, the confessor occupies an ambiguous place between heaven and earth. He listens with

carnal ears to the penitent who bares her soul, but it is a supernatural light that shines in the gaze with which he enfolds her; he is a divine man, he is God in the appearance of a man. Mme Guyon describes her meeting with Father La Combe in these terms: 'It seemed to me that an effect of grace came from him to me by the most intimate soul and returned from me to him so that he felt the same thing.' The priest's intercession pulled her out of the drought she had been suffering from for years and inflamed her soul once again with ardour. She lived by his side during her entire great mystical period. And she admits: 'There was nothing but one whole unity, so that *I could no longer tell him apart from God.*' It would be too simple to say she was really in love with a man and she feigned to love God: she also loved this man because he was something other than himself in her eyes. Like Ferdière's patient, what she was groping for was the supreme source of values. That is what every mystic is aiming for. The male intermediary is sometimes useful for her to launch herself toward heaven's desert; but he is not indispensable. Having difficulty separating reality from play, the act from magical behaviour, the object from imagination, woman is singularly likely to presentify through her body an absence. What is much less humorous is confusing mysticism with erotomania, as has sometimes been done: the erotomaniac feels glorified by the love of a sovereign being; he is the one who takes the initiative in the love relationship, he loves more passionately than he is loved; he makes his feelings known by clear but secret signs; he is jealous and irritated by the chosen woman's lack of fervour: he does not hesitate then to punish her; he almost never manifests himself in a carnal and concrete form. All these characteristics are found in mystics; in particular, God cherishes for all eternity the soul He inflames with His love, He shed His blood for her, He prepares splendid apotheoses for her; the only thing she can do is abandon herself to His flames without resistance.

It is accepted today that erotomania takes a sometimes platonic and sometimes sexual form. Likewise, the body has a greater or lesser role in the feelings the mystic devotes to God. Her effusions are modelled on those that earthly lovers experience. While Angela de Foligno contemplates an image of Christ holding St Francis in his arms, he tells her: 'This is how I will hold you tight and much more than can be seen by the body's eyes . . . I will never leave you if you love me.' Mme Guyon writes: 'Love gave me no respite. I said to him: Oh my love, enough, leave me.' 'I want the love that thrills my soul with ineffable tremors, the love that makes me swoon . . .' 'Oh my God! If You made the most sensual of women feel what I feel, they would soon quit their false pleasures to partake of such true riches.' St Teresa's vision is well known:

> In [an angel's] hands I saw a great golden spear . . . This he plunged into my heart several times so that it penetrated my entrails. When he pulled it out I felt that he took them with it, and left me utterly consumed by the great love of God. The pain was so severe that it made me utter several moans. What I am certain of is that the pain penetrates the depths of my entrails and it seems to me that they are torn when my spiritual spouse withdraws the arrow he uses to enter them.

It is sometimes piously claimed that the poverty of language makes it necessary for the mystic to borrow this erotic vocabulary; but she also has only one body and she borrows from earthly love not only words but also physical attitudes; she has the same behaviour when offering herself to God as offering herself to a man. This, however, does not at all diminish the validity of her feelings. When Angela of Foligno becomes 'pale and dry' or then 'full and flushed', according to the rhythm of her heart, when she breaks down in deluges of tears,* when she comes back to earth, it is hardly possible to consider these phenomena as purely 'spiritual'; but to explain them by her excessive 'emotivity' alone is to invoke the poppy's 'sleep-inducing virtue'; the body is never the *cause* of subjective experiences since it is the subject himself in his objective form: the subject experiences his attitudes in the unity of his existence. Both adversaries and admirers of mystics think that giving a sexual content to St Teresa's ecstasies is to reduce her to the rank of a hysteric. But what diminishes the hysterical subject is not the fact that his body actively expresses his obsessions: it is that he is obsessed, that his freedom is subjugated and annulled; the mastery a fakir acquires over his body does not make him its slave; bodily gestures can be part of the expression of a freedom. St Teresa's texts are not at all ambiguous and they justify Bernini's statue showing us the swooning saint in thrall to a stunning sensuality; it would be no less false to interpret her emotions as simple 'sexual sublimation'; there is not first an unavowed sexual desire that takes the form of divine love; the woman in love herself is not first the prey of a desire without object that then fixes itself on an individual; it

* 'Tears burned her cheeks to such an extent that she had to apply cold water,' says one of her biographers.

is the presence of the lover that arouses an excitement in her immediately intended to him; thus, in one movement, St Teresa seeks to unite with God and experiences this union in her body; she is not slave to her nerves and hormones: rather, she should be admired for the intensity of a faith that penetrates to the most intimate regions of her flesh. In truth, as St Teresa herself understood, the value of a mystical experience is measured not by how it has been subjectively experienced but by its objective scope. The phenomena of ecstasy are approximately the same for St Teresa and Marie Alacoque: the interest of their message is very different. St Teresa situates the dramatic problem of the relationship between the individual and the transcendent Being in a highly intellectual way; she lived an experience as a woman whose meaning extends beyond any sexual specification; it has to be classified along with that of St John of the Cross. But it is a striking exception. What her minor sisters provide is an essentially feminine vision of the world and of salvation; it is not transcendence they are aiming for: it is the redemption of their femininity.*

The woman first seeks in divine love what the woman asks for in man's love: the apotheosis of her narcissism; this sovereign gaze fixed on her attentively and lovingly is a miraculous chance for her. Throughout her life as a girl and young woman, Mme Guyon had always been tormented by the desire to be loved and admired. A modern Protestant mystic, Mlle Vé, writes: 'Nothing makes me unhappier than having no one interested in me in a special and sympathetic way, in what is taking place in me.' Mme Krüdener imagined that God was constantly occupied with her, to such an extent that, says Sainte-Beuve, 'in the most decisive moments with her lover she moaned: "My God how happy I am! I ask You to forgive my extreme happiness!"' One can understand the intoxication that permeates the heart of the narcissist when all of heaven becomes her mirror; her deified image is infinite like God Himself, it will never disappear; and at the same time she feels in her burning, palpitating and love-drowned breast her soul created, redeemed and cherished by the adoring Father; it is her double, it is she herself she is embracing, infinitely magnified by God's mediation. These texts of St Angela of Foligno are particularly significant. This is how Jesus speaks to her:

---

* For Catherine of Siena, theological preoccupations nevertheless remain very important. She also is of a rather virile type.

My daughter, sweeter to me than I am to you, my temple, my delight. My daughter, my beloved, *love me because you are very much loved by me;* much more than you could love me. Your whole life, your eating, drinking, your sleeping, and all that you do are pleasing to me. I will do great things in you in the sight of the nations. Through you, I shall be known and my name will be praised by many nations. My daughter and my sweet spouse, I love you so much more than any other woman.

And again:

My daughter, sweeter to me than I am to you, . . . my delight, the heart of God almighty is now upon your heart . . . God almighty has deposited much love in you, more than any woman of this city. He takes delight in you.

And once more:

Such is the love I have for you that I am totally unable to remember your faults and my eyes no longer see them. In you I have deposited a great treasure.

The chosen woman cannot fail to respond passionately to such ardent declarations falling from such a lofty place. She tries to connect with the lover using the usual technique of the woman in love: annihilation. 'I have only one concern, which is to love, to forget myself, and to annihilate myself,' writes Marie Alacoque. Ecstasy bodily mimics this abolition of self; the subject no longer sees or feels, he forgets his body, disavows it. The blinding and sovereign Presence is indirectly indicated by the intensity of this abandon, by the hopeless acceptance of passivity. Mme Guyon's quietism erected this passivity into a system: as for her, she spent a great deal of her time in a kind of catalepsy; she slept wide awake.

Most women mystics are not satisfied with abandoning themselves passively to God: they actively apply themselves to self-annihilation by the destruction of their flesh. Of course, asceticism was also practised by monks and brothers. But woman's relentlessness in violating her flesh has specific characteristics. We have seen how ambiguous the woman's attitude to her body is: it is through humiliation and suffering that she metamorphoses it into glory. Given over to a lover as a thing of pleasure, she becomes a temple, an idol; torn by the pain of childbirth, she creates heroes. The mystic will torture her flesh to have the right to claim it; reducing it to abjection, she exalts it as the instrument of her salvation. This accounts for the strange excesses of some women saints. St Angela of Foligno recounts her delectation in drinking the water in which she had just washed the lepers' hands and feet:

> This concoction filled us with such sweetness that joy followed us and brought it home with us. Never had I drunk with such delight. A piece of scaly skin from one of the lepers' wounds had stuck in my throat. Rather than spitting it out, I tried very hard to swallow it and I succeeded. It seemed to me that I had just received communion. Never will I be able to express the delights that flooded over me.

It is known that Marie Alacoque cleaned a sick person's vomit with her tongue; she describes in her autobiography her happiness when she had filled her mouth with the excrement of a man with diarrhoea; Jesus rewarded her by keeping her lips glued to his Sacred Heart for three hours. Devotion has a carnal coloration in countries of ardent sensuality like Italy and Spain: in a village in Abruzzo, even today women tear their tongues by licking the rocks on the ground along the stations of the cross. In all these practices they are only imitating the Redeemer, who saved flesh by the abasement of his own flesh: women show their sensitivity to this great mystery in a much more concrete way than males.

God appears to woman more readily in the figure of the husband; sometimes He reveals Himself in His glory, dazzlingly white and beautiful, and dominating; He clothes her in a wedding dress, He crowns her, takes her by the hand and promises her a celestial apotheosis. But most often He is a being of flesh: the wedding ring Jesus had given to St Catherine and that she wore, invisible, on her finger, was this 'ring of flesh' that circumcision had cut off. Above all, He is a mistreated and bloody body: it is in the contemplation of the Crucified that she drowns herself the most fervently; she identifies with the Virgin Mary holding the corpse of her Son in her arms, or with Magdalene standing at the foot of the cross and being sprinkled with the Beloved's blood. Thus does she satisfy her sadomasochistic fantasies. In the humiliation of God, she admires Man's fall: inert, passive, covered with sores, the crucified is the inverted image of the white and red martyr offered to wild beasts, to the knife, to males, and with whom the little girl has so often identified: she is thrown into confusion seeing that Man, Man-God, has assumed His role. It is she who is placed on the wood, promised the splendour of the Resurrection. It is she: she proves it; her forehead bleeds under the crown of thorns; her hands, her feet, her side are transpierced by an invisible iron. Out of the 321 people with stigmata recognised by the Catholic Church, only forty-seven are men; the others – including Helen of Hungary, Joan of the Cross, G. van Oosten, Osanna of Mantua, and Clare of Montefalco – are women, who are, on average, past the age of menopause. Catherine Emmerich, the most famous, was marked prematurely. At the age of twenty-four, having desired the sufferings of the crown of thorns, she saw coming towards her a dazzling young man who pushed this crown onto her head. The next day, her temples and forehead swelled and blood began to flow. Four years later, in ecstasy, she saw Christ with rays pointed like fine blades coming from his wounds, and drops of blood then sprang from the saint's hands, feet and side. She sweated blood, she spat blood. Still today, every good Friday, Therese Neumann turns a face dripping with Christ's blood towards her visitors. The mysterious alchemy that changes flesh into glory ends in the stigmata since, in the form of a bloody pain, they are the presence of divine love itself. It is quite understandable why women particularly are attached to the metamorphosis of the red flow into pure golden flame. They have a horror of this blood that runs out of the side of the King of men. St Catherine of Siena speaks of it in almost all her letters. Angela of Foligno lost herself in the contemplation of the heart of Jesus and the gaping wound in His side. Catherine Emmerich put on a red shirt so as to resemble Jesus when He was like 'a cloth soaked in blood'; she saw all things 'through Jesus's blood'. We have seen in which circumstances Marie Alacoque quenched her thirst for three hours from the Sacred Heart of Jesus. It was she who offered the enormous red clot surrounded by flamboyant darts of love to the adoration of the faithful. That is the emblem symbolising the great feminine dream: from blood to glory through love.

Ecstasies, visions and dialogues with God, this interior experience is sufficient for some women. Others feel the need to communicate it to the world through acts. The connection between action and contemplation takes two very different forms. There are women of action like St Catherine, St Teresa and Joan of Arc who are well aware of the goals they set themselves and who lucidly invent the means to reach them: their revelations merely give an objective form to their certainties; they encourage them to take the paths they have carefully planned. There are women narcissists like Mme Guyon and Mme Krüdener who, at the limit of silent fervour, feel suddenly 'in an apostolic state'.* They are not very precise concerning their tasks; and – like patronesses seeking excitement – they do not care too much what they do as long as it is *something*. Thus after displaying herself as ambassador and novelist, Mme Krüdener interiorised the conception she had of her own worth: it was not to see definite ideas triumph but to see herself confirmed in her role as God's inspired one that she took the destiny of Alexander I in hand. If a little beauty and intelligence are often enough for a woman to feel endowed with a holy character, it is even more so when she knows she is God's chosen; she feels filled with a mission: she preaches dubious doctrines, she eagerly founds sects, and this allows her to effectuate, through the members of the group she inspires, a thrilling multiplication of her personality.

Mystical fervour, like love and even narcissism, can be integrated into active and independent lives. But in themselves these attempts at individual salvation can only result in failures; either the woman establishes a relation with an unreal: her double or God; or she creates an unreal relation with a real being; in any case, she has no grasp on the world; she does not escape her subjectivity; her freedom remains mystified; there is only one way of accomplishing it authentically: it is to project it by a positive action into human society.

* Mme Guyon.

Part Four

TOWARDS LIBERATION

CHAPTER 14

The Independent Woman

French law no longer includes obedience among a wife's duties, and every woman citizen has become a voter; these civic liberties remain abstract if there is no corresponding economic autonomy; the kept woman – wife or mistress – is not freed from the male just because she has a ballot paper in her hands; while today's customs impose fewer constraints on her than in the past, such negative licences have not fundamentally changed her situation; she remains a vassal, imprisoned in her condition. It is through work that woman has been able, to a large extent, to close the gap separating her from the male; work alone can guarantee her concrete freedom. The system based on her dependence collapses as soon as she ceases to be a parasite; there is no longer need for a masculine mediator between her and the universe. The curse on the woman vassal is that she is not allowed to do anything; so she stubbornly pursues the impossible quest for being through narcissism, love or religion; when she is productive and active, she regains her transcendence; she affirms herself concretely as subject in her projects; she senses her responsibility relative to the goals she pursues and to the money and rights she appropriates. Many women are conscious of these advantages, even those with the lowest-level jobs. I heard a cleaning woman as she was washing a hotel lobby floor say, 'I never asked anyone for anything. I made it on my own.' She was as proud of being self-sufficient as a Rockefeller. However, one must not think that the simple juxtaposition of the right to vote and a job amounts to total liberation; work today is not freedom. Only in a socialist world would the woman who has one be sure of the other. Today, the majority of workers are exploited. Moreover, social structures have not been deeply modified by the changes in women's condition. This world has always belonged to men and still retains the form they have imprinted on it. It is important not to lose sight of these facts that make the question of women's work complex. An important and self-righteous woman recently carried out a study on women workers at a Renault factory: she asserts that they would rather to stay at home than work in a factory. Without a doubt, they are economically independent only within an economically oppressed class; and besides, tasks carried out in a factory do not free them from household chores.* If they had been able to choose between forty hours of weekly work in a factory *or* at home, they would undoubtedly have responded quite differently; and they might even accept both jobs eagerly if, as women workers, they would become part of a world that would be their world, that they would proudly and happily participate in building. In today's work, without even mentioning women who work on the land,† most working women do not escape the traditional feminine world; neither society nor their husbands give them the help needed to become, in concrete terms, the equals of men. Only those women with political convictions, active in trade unions, who are confident in the future, can give an ethical meaning to the thankless daily labour; but as women deprived of leisure time and inheriting a tradition of submissiveness, it is understandable that women are just beginning to develop their political and social awareness. It is understandable that since they do not receive the moral and social benefits they could legitimately expect in exchange for their work, they simply resign themselves to its constraints. It is also understandable that a shopgirl, an office worker or a secretary should not want to give up the advantages of having a male to lean on. I have already said that it is an almost irresistible temptation for a young woman to be part of a privileged caste when she can do so simply by surrendering her body; she is doomed to have love affairs because her wages are minimal for the very high standard of living society demands of her; if she settles for what she earns, she will be no more than a pariah: without decent living accommodation or clothes, all amusement and even love will be refused her. Virtuous people preach asceticism to her; in fact, her diet is often as austere as a Carmelite's; but not everyone can have God as a lover: she needs to please men to succeed in her life as a woman. So she will accept help: her employer cynically counts on this when he pays her a pittance. Sometimes this help will enable her to improve her situation and achieve real independence; but sometimes she will give up her job to become a kept woman. She often does both: she frees herself from

---

* I said in Vol. I, Part Two, 'History', chapter 5, how burdensome these are for the woman who works outside the home.
† Whose condition we examined, ibid.

her lover through work, and she escapes work thanks to her lover; but then she experiences the double servitude of a job and masculine protection. For the married woman, her salary usually only means extra income; for the 'woman who is helped' it is the man's protection that seems inessential; but neither woman buys total independence through her own efforts.

However, there are quite a lot of privileged women today who have gained economic and social autonomy in their professions. They are the ones who are at issue when the question of women's possibilities and their future is raised. While they are still only a minority, it is particularly interesting to study their situation closely; they are the subject of continuing debate between feminists and antifeminists. The latter maintain that today's emancipated women do not accomplish anything important, and that besides they have trouble finding their inner balance. The former exaggerate the emancipated women's achievements and are blind to their frustrations. In fact, there is no reason to assume that they are on the wrong track; and yet it is obvious that they are not comfortably settled in their new condition: they have come only halfway as yet. Even the woman who has emancipated herself economically from man is still not in a moral, social or psychological situation identical to his. Her commitment to and focus on her profession depend on the context of her life as a whole. And, when she starts her adult life, she does not have the same past as a boy; society does not see her with the same eyes; she has a different perspective on the universe. Being a woman poses unique problems to an autonomous human being today.

The advantage man enjoys and which manifests itself from childhood onwards is that his vocation as a human being in no way contradicts his destiny as a male. The fact that the phallus is assimilated with transcendence means that man's social and spiritual successes endow him with virile prestige. He is not divided. However, for a woman to accomplish her femininity she is required to be object and prey; that is, she must renounce her claims as a sovereign subject. This is the conflict that singularly characterises the situation of the emancipated woman. She refuses to confine herself to her role as female because she does not want to mutilate herself; but it would also be a mutilation to repudiate her sex. Man is a sexed human being; woman is a complete individual, and equal to the male, only if she too is a sexed human being. Renouncing her femininity means renouncing part of her humanity. Misogynists have often reproached intellectual women for 'letting themselves go'; but they also preach to them: if you want to be our equals, stop wearing makeup and polishing your nails. This advice is absurd. Precisely because the idea of femininity is artificially defined by customs and fashion, it is imposed on every woman from the outside; it may evolve so that its fashion standards come closer to those of men: on the beach, women now wear trousers. That does not change the core of the problem: the individual is not free to shape the idea of femininity at will. By not conforming, a woman devalues herself sexually and consequently socially because society has incorporated sexual values. Rejecting feminine attributes does not mean acquiring virile ones; even a transvestite cannot turn herself into a man: she is a transvestite. We have seen that homosexuality also constitutes a specification: neutrality is impossible. There is no negative attitude that does not imply a positive counterpart. The adolescent girl often thinks she can simply scorn convention; but by doing so, she is making a statement; she is creating a new situation involving consequences she will have to assume. Whenever one ignores an established convention, one becomes a rebel. A flamboyantly dressed woman is lying when she ingenuously claims she is simply dressing to suit herself, and that is all: she knows perfectly well that suiting herself is an absurdity. Inversely, if she does not want to look eccentric, she follows the rules. Choosing defiance is a risky tactic unless it is a positively effective action; more time and energy are spent than saved. A woman who has no desire to shock, no intention to devalue herself socially, has to live her woman's condition as a woman: very often her professional success even requires it. But while conformity is quite natural for a man – custom being based on his needs as an autonomous and active individual – the woman who is herself also subject and activity has to fit into a world that has doomed her to passivity. This servitude is even greater since women confined to the feminine sphere have magnified its importance: they have made dressing and housekeeping difficult arts. The man barely has to care about his clothes; they are comfortable, adapted to his active life, and need not be original; they are hardly part of his personality; what's more, no one expects him to take care of them himself: some woman, volunteer or paid, delivers him from this chore. The woman, on the other hand, knows that when people look at her, they do not distinguish her from her appearance: she is judged, respected or desired in relation to how she looks. Her clothes were originally meant to doom her to impotence, and they still remain fragile: stockings run; heels wear down; light-coloured blouses and dresses get dirty; pleats unpleat; but she must still repair most of these accidents herself; her peers will never volunteer to help her out, and she will have second thoughts about straining her budget for work she *can* do herself: perms, hairdos, makeup and new dresses are already expensive enough. Secretary or student, when she goes home at night, there is always a stocking to mend, a blouse to wash, a skirt to iron. The woman who earns a good living will spare herself these chores; but she will be held to a higher standard of elegance, she will waste time on shopping and dress fittings, and such. Tradition also demands that the woman, even unmarried, pay attention to her home; a government official sent to a new city thinks nothing of living in a hotel; his woman colleague will try to 'set up house'; she has to keep it spotless because her negligence will not be excused whereas a man's will be overlooked. However, public opinion is not the only concern that makes her devote so much time and care to her looks and home. She wants to feel like a real woman for her own personal satisfaction. She only succeeds in accepting herself from the perspective of both the present and the past by combining the life she has made for herself with the destiny prepared for her by her mother, her childhood games and her adolescent fantasies. She has cultivated narcissistic dreams; she continues to pit the cult of her image against the phallic pride of the male; she wants to show off, to charm. Her mother and other older women have fostered her nesting instinct: a home of her own was the earliest form of her dream of independence; she would not think of discarding it, even when she finds freedom in other ways. And not yet feeling secure in the male universe, she still needs a retreat, a symbol of that interior refuge she has been used to finding in herself. Following docilely in the feminine tradition, she will wax her floors or do her own cooking instead of going to a restaurant like her male colleague. She wants to live both like a man and like a woman; her workload and her fatigue are multiplied as a result.

If she intends to remain fully woman, it also means she intends to approach the opposite sex with the maximum of odds on her side. It is in the area of sex that the most difficult problems will arise. To be a complete individual, equal to man, woman has to have access to the male world as man does to the female one, access to the *other*; but the demands of the *other* are not symmetrical in the two cases. Once acquired, the seemingly immanent virtues of fame and fortune can enhance the woman's sexual attraction; but being an autonomous activity contradicts her femininity: she knows this. The independent woman – and especially the intellectual who thinks through her situation – will suffer from an inferiority complex as a female; she does not have as much free time for beauty care as a flirt, whose only preoccupation is to seduce; while she might follow all the experts' advice, she will never be more than an amateur in the elegance department; feminine charm demands that transcendence deteriorating into immanence no longer be anything more than a subtle carnal throb; she must be a spontaneously offered prey: the intellectual woman knows she is offering herself, she knows she is a consciousness, a subject; one cannot wilfully kill one's gaze and change one's eyes into empty pools; a body that reaches out to the world cannot be thwarted and metamorphosed into a statue animated by hidden vibrations. The more the intellectual woman fears failure, the more zealously she will try; but this conscious zeal remains an activity and falls short of its goal. She makes mistakes like those blamed on menopause: she tries to deny her intelligence as an ageing woman tries to deny her age; she dresses like a girl, she overdoes the flowers, the frills and the loud materials; she carries childish and wide-eyed mimicry too far. She romps, skips, prattles, acts overly casual, scatterbrained and impulsive. But she looks like those actors who, failing to feel the emotion that would relax certain muscles, purposely contract antagonistic ones instead, lowering their eyelids or the corners of their mouths instead of letting them drop; thus the intelligent woman, wishing to appear uninhibited, stiffens instead. She senses this, and it irritates her; suddenly an unintended piercing spark of intelligence passes over her totally naive face; her lips full of promise become pursed. If she has trouble pleasing men, it is because she is not like her little slave sisters, a pure will to please; her desire to seduce may be strong, but it has not penetrated into the marrow of her bones; as soon as she feels awkward, she gets fed up with her servility; she tries to take her revenge by playing the game with masculine weapons: she talks instead of listening, she flaunts clever ideas, unusual feelings; she contradicts her interlocutor instead of going along with him, she tries to outdo him. Mme de Staël cleverly mixed both methods with stunning triumphs: she was almost always irresistible. But defiance, so frequent, for example, among American women, irritates men more than it wins them over; it is men, however, who provoke it by their own defiance; if men were content to love a peer instead of a slave – as indeed some men do who are without either arrogance or an inferiority complex – then women would be far less obsessed with their femininity; they would become more natural and simple and would easily rediscover themselves as women, which, after all, they are.

The fact is that men are beginning to come to terms with the new condition of women; no longer feeling condemned a priori, women feel more at ease; today the working woman does not neglect her femininity, nor does she lose her sexual attraction. This success – already a step towards equality – remains, nonetheless, incomplete; it is still much harder for a woman than for a man to have the type of relationship she would like with the other sex. Many obstacles stand in the way of her sex and love life. And the vassal woman is no better off: sexually and emotionally, most wives and mistresses are radically frustrated. These difficulties are more obvious for the independent woman because she has chosen not resignation but combat. All living problems find a silent solution in death; so a woman who works at living is more torn than one who buries her will and desires; but she will not accept being offered this as an example. She will consider herself at a disadvantage only when she compares herself with man.

A woman who works hard, who has responsibilities and who knows how harsh the struggle is against the world's obstacles needs – like the male – not only to satisfy her physical desires but also to experience the relaxation and diversion provided by enjoyable sexual adventures. Now there are still some environments where it is not concretely recognised that she should have this freedom; if she avails herself of it, she risks compromising her reputation and career; at the least, a burdensome hypocrisy is demanded of her. The more she has succeeded in making her mark socially, the more willingly will people close their eyes; but she is severely scrutinised, especially in the provinces. Even in the most favourable circumstances – when fear of public opinion is not an issue – her situation is not the same in this area as the man's. Differences stem from both tradition and the problems posed by the particular nature of feminine sexuality.

The man can easily engage in casual sex that at least calms his physical needs and is good for his morale. There have been women – a small number – who have demanded the opening of bordellos for women; in a novel entitled *Number 17*,[1] a woman proposed creating houses where women could go and find 'sexual relief' with a sort of 'taxi-boy'.* It seems that such an establishment once existed in San Francisco; it was frequented only by the girls from the bordellos, amused by the idea of paying instead of being paid: their pimps had them closed. Besides the fact that this solution is utopian and undesirable, it would also probably have little success: we have seen that woman does not attain 'relief' as mechanically as man;

---

* The author – whose name I have forgotten, but it is unimportant – explains at length how they could be trained to satisfy any client, what kind of life should be imposed on them, and so forth.

most women would hardly consider this solution favourable to sexual
abandon. In any case, the fact is that this recourse is not open to them
today. The solution of women picking up a partner for a night or an hour
– assuming that the woman, endowed with a strong temperament and
having overcome all her inhibitions, can consider it without disgust – is
far more dangerous for her than for the male. The risk of venereal disease
is more serious for her in that it is up to him to take precautions to avoid
contamination; and, however prudent she may be, she is never completely
covered against the threat of becoming pregnant. But the difference in
physical strength is also very significant, especially in relations between
strangers – relations that take place on a physical level. A man has little
to fear from the woman he takes home; a little vigilance is enough. It is
not the same for the woman who lets a man into her house. I have been
told of two young women, newly arrived in Paris and avid to 'see life',
who, after doing the town, invited two seductive Montmartre pimps to
a late supper: in the morning they found themselves robbed, brutalised
and threatened with blackmail. A worse case is that of a divorced woman
of about forty who worked hard all day to feed her three grown children
and elderly parents. Still beautiful and attractive, she had absolutely no
leisure time to have a social life, to flirt or to make any of the usual efforts
necessary for seduction, which in any case would have bored her. Yet she
had strong physical desires; and she felt that, like a man, she had the right
to satisfy them. Some evenings she went out to roam the streets and
managed to pick up a man. But one night, after an hour or two spent in
a thicket in the Bois de Boulogne, her lover refused to let her leave: he
wanted her name, her address, to see her again, to live with her; when
she refused, he beat her violently and only left her when she was wounded
and terrorised. As for taking on a lover by supporting him or helping him
out, as men often take on a mistress, it is possible only for wealthy women.
There are some for whom this deal works: by paying the male, they make
an instrument of him, permitting them to use him with disdainful
abandon. But women must usually be older to dissociate eroticism from
sentiment so crudely, because in feminine adolescence this connection is,
as we have seen, so deep. There are also many men who never accept
this division between flesh and consciousness. For even more reasons, the
majority of women will refuse to consider it. Besides, there is an element
of deception they are more aware of than men: the paying client is an
instrument as well, used by the partner as a livelihood. Virile arrogance
hides the ambiguities of the erotic drama from the male: he spontaneously lies to himself; the woman is more easily humiliated, more suscep-

tible, and also more lucid; she will succeed in blinding herself only at the price of a more cunning bad faith. Even supposing she has the means, she will not find it generally satisfying to buy a man.

For most women – and also for some men – it is a question not only of satisfying their desires but of maintaining their dignity as human beings while satisfying them. When the male gets sexual satisfaction from the woman, or when he satisfies her, he posits himself as the unique subject: imperious victor, generous donor, or both. She wants to affirm reciprocally that she submits her partner to her pleasure and covers him with her gifts. Thus when she convinces the man of her worth, either by the benefits she promises him or by relying on his courtesy or by skilfully arousing his desire in its pure generality, she easily persuades herself that she is satisfying him. Thanks to this beneficial conviction, she can solicit him without feeling humiliated since she claims she is acting out of generosity. Thus in *Green Wheat*,[2] the 'woman in white' who lusts for Phil's caresses archly tells him: 'I only like beggars and the hungry.' In fact, she is cleverly angling for him to act imploringly. So, says Colette, 'she rushed toward the narrow and dark kingdom where her pride could believe that a moan is a confession of distress and where the aggressive beggars of her sort drink the illusion of generosity.' Mme de Warens exemplifies these women who choose their lovers young, unhappy or of a lower social class to make their appetite look like generosity. But there are also fearless women who take on the challenge of the most robust males and who are delighted to have satisfied them even though they may have succumbed only out of politeness or fear.

On the other hand, while the woman who traps the man likes to imagine herself giving, the woman who gives herself wants it understood that she takes. 'As for me, I am a woman who takes,' a young woman journalist told me one day. The truth in these cases is that, except for rape, no one really takes the other; but the woman is lying doubly to herself. For the fact is that man does often seduce by his passion and aggressiveness, thereby actively gaining his partner's consent. Except in special cases – like Mme de Staël, to whom I have already referred – it is otherwise for the woman: she can do little else than offer herself; for most males are fiercely jealous of their role; they want to awaken a personal sexual response in the woman, not to be selected to satisfy her need in its generality: chosen, they feel exploited.* 'A woman who is not

---

* This feeling corresponds to the one we have pointed out in the girl. Only she resigns herself to her destiny in the end.

afraid of men frightens them,' a young man told me. And I have often heard adults declare: 'I am horrified by a woman who takes the initiative.' If the woman proposes herself too boldly, the man flees: he insists on conquering. The woman can thus take only when she is prey: she must become a passive thing, a promise of submission. If she succeeds, she will think she has willingly performed this magic conjuration; she will see herself become subject again. But she runs the risk of being turned into a fixed and useless object by the male's disdain. This is why she is so deeply humiliated if he rejects her advances. The man also sometimes gets angry when he feels he has been taken in; nonetheless, he has only failed in an enterprise, nothing more. The woman, on the other hand, has consented to make herself flesh through her sexual arousal, anticipation and promise; she could only win by losing: she remains lost. One must be particularly blind or exceptionally lucid to choose such a defeat. And even when seduction succeeds, victory remains ambiguous; thus, according to public opinion, it is the man who conquers, who *has* the woman. It does not accept that she can, like the man, assume her desires: she is their prey. It is understood that the male has integrated the forces of the species into his individuality, whereas the woman is the slave of the species.* She is represented alternately as pure passivity: she is a 'slut; open for business'; ready and willing, she is a utensil; she limply gives in to the spell of arousal, she is fascinated by the male who picks her like a fruit. Or else she is seen as an alienated activity: there is a devil raging in her womb, a serpent lurks in her vagina, craving to devour male sperm. In any case, it is out of the question to think of her as simply free. In France especially, the free woman and the easy woman are stubbornly confused, as the idea of easy implies an absence of resistance and control, a lack, the very negation of freedom. Women authors try to combat this prejudice: for example, in *Portrait of Grisela*,[3] Clara Malraux emphasises that her heroine does not let herself be drawn in, but accomplishes an act for which she accepts full responsibility. In America, a freedom is recognised in woman's sexual activity, which is very favourable to her. But in France, men's disdain for women who 'sleep around', the very men who profit from their favours, paralyses many women. They fear the remonstrances they would incite, the remarks they would provoke.

---

* We have seen in Vol. I, Chapter 1 that there is a certain truth in this opinion. But it is precisely not at the moment of desire that this asymmetry appears: it is in procreation. In desire man and woman assume their natural function identically.

Even if the woman scorns anonymous rumours, she has concrete difficulties in her relations with her partner, for public opinion is embodied in him. Very often, he considers the bed the terrain for asserting his aggressive superiority. He wants to take and not receive, not exchange but ravish. He seeks to possess the woman beyond that which she gives him; he demands that her consent be a defeat, and that the words she murmurs be avowals that he extracts from her; if she admits her pleasure, she is acknowledging her submission. When Claudine defies Renaud by her promptness in submitting to him, he anticipates her: he rushes to rape her when she was going to offer herself; he forces her to keep her eyes open to contemplate his triumph in their torment. Thus, in *Man's Fate*,[4] the overbearing Ferral insists on switching on the lamp Valérie wants to put out. Proud and demanding, the woman faces the male as an adversary; she is far less well armed in this battle than he; first of all, he has physical force and it is easier for him to impose his desires; we have also noted that tension and activity correspond to his eroticism, whereas the woman who refuses passivity breaks the spell that brings her sexual satisfaction; if she mimics domination in her attitudes and movements, she fails to reach a climax: most women who surrender to their pride become frigid. Rare are those lovers who allow their mistresses to satisfy their dominating or sadistic tendencies; and even rarer still are those women who derive full erotic satisfaction from this male docility.

There is a road that seems much less thorny for the woman, that of masochism. When one works, struggles and takes responsibilities and risks during the day, it is relaxing to abandon oneself at night to vigorous caprices. In love or naive, the woman in fact is often happy to annihilate herself for the benefit of a tyrannical will. But she still has to feel truly dominated. It is not easy for a woman who lives daily among men to believe in the unconditional supremacy of males. I have been told about the case of a not really masochistic but very 'feminine' woman, that is, one who deeply appreciated the pleasure of abdication in masculine arms; from the age of seventeen, she had had several husbands and numerous lovers, all of whom gave her great satisfaction; having successfully carried out a difficult project where she managed men, she complained of having become frigid: her once-blissful submission became impossible for her because she had become used to dominating males and because their prestige had vanished. When the woman begins to doubt men's superiority, their claims can only diminish her esteem for them. In bed, at moments where the man feels he is most fiercely male, the very fact of his miming virility makes him look infantile to knowing eyes: he is merely warding off the old castration complex, the shadow of his father, or some other fantasy. It is not always out of pride that the mistress refuses to give in to her lover's caprices: she wants to interact with an adult who is living a real moment of his life, not a little boy fooling himself. The masochistic woman is particularly disappointed: a maternal, exasperated or indulgent complaisance is not the abdication she dreams of. Either she herself will also have to make do with meaningless games, pretending to be dominated and subjugated, or she will run after men considered 'superior' in the hope of coming across a master, or else she will become frigid.

We have seen that it is possible to escape the temptations of sadism and masochism when both partners recognise each other as equals; as soon as there is a little modesty and some generosity between men and women, ideas of victory and defeat are abolished: the act of love becomes a free exchange. But, paradoxically, it is harder for woman than for man to recognise an individual of the opposite sex as her equal. Precisely because the male caste enjoys superiority, man can hold many individual women in affectionate esteem: a woman is easy to love; she has, first of all, the privilege of introducing her lover to a world different from his own and one that he is pleased to explore at her side; she fascinates, she amuses, at least for a little while; and then, because her situation is limited and subordinate, all her qualities seem like conquests while her errors are excusable. Stendhal admires Mme de Rênal and Mme de Chasteller in spite of their detestable prejudices; the man does not hold a woman responsible for not being very intelligent, clear-sighted or courageous: she is a victim, he thinks – often rightly – of her situation; he dreams of what she could have been, of what she will perhaps be: she can be given credit, one can grant her a great deal because she *is* nothing definite in particular; this lack is what will cause the lover to grow tired of her quickly: but it is the source of her mystery, the charm that seduces him and inclines him to feel superficial tenderness for her. It is far less easy to show friendship for a man: for he is what he made himself be, without help; he must be loved in his presence and his reality, not in his promises and uncertain possibilities; he is responsible for his behaviour, his ideas; he has no excuse. There is fraternity with him only if his acts, goals and opinions are approved; Julien can love a legitimist; a Lamiel could not cherish a man whose ideas she detests. Even ready to compromise, the woman has trouble adopting a tolerant attitude. For the man does not offer her a green paradise of childhood, she meets him in this world that is common to both of them: he brings only himself. Closed in on himself, defined, decided, he does not inspire dreams; when he speaks, one must listen; he takes himself seriously: if he does not prove interesting, he becomes bothersome, his presence weighs heavily. Only very young men allow themselves to appear adorned by the marvellous; one can seek mystery and promise in them, find excuses for them, take them lightly: this is one of the reasons mature women find them so seductive. But they themselves prefer young women in most cases. The thirty-year-old woman has no choice but to turn to adult males. And she will undoubtedly meet some who deserve both her esteem and her friendship; but she will be lucky if they do not then display arrogance. The problem she has when looking for an affair or an adventure involving her heart as well as her body is meeting a man she can consider her equal, without his seeing himself as superior.

One might say that in general women do not make such a fuss; they seize the occasion without much questioning, and then they make do with their pride and sensuality. That is true. But it is also true that they bury in the secret of their hearts many disappointments, humiliations, regrets and grievances whose equivalents are unknown – on the whole – to men. The man will almost surely get the benefit of pleasure from a more or less unsuccessful affair; the woman might well not profit from it at all; even if indifferent, she politely lends herself to lovemaking when the decisive moment arrives. The lover might prove to be impotent, and she will suffer from having compromised herself in a ludicrous escapade; if she does not reach arousal, then she feels 'had', deceived; if she is satisfied, she will want to hold on to her lover for a longer time. She is rarely completely sincere when she claims to envisage nothing more than a short-term adventure just for pleasure, because pleasure, far from freeing her, binds her; separation, even a so-called friendly one, wounds her. It is far more rare to hear a woman talk good-naturedly about a former lover than a man about his mistresses.

The nature of her eroticism and the difficulties of a free sexual life push the woman towards monogamy. Nonetheless, a liaison or marriage is far less easily reconciled with a career for her than for the man. The lover or husband may ask her to give up her career: she hesitates, like Colette's Vagabond, who ardently wishes to have a man's warmth at her side but who dreads the conjugal shackles; if she gives in, she is once again a vassal; if she refuses, she condemns herself to a withering solitude. Today, the man generally accepts the idea that his partner should continue working; novels by Colette Yver that show young women cornered into sacrificing their professions to maintain peace at home are somewhat outdated; living together is an enrichment for two free beings, who find a guarantee of their own independence in the partner's occupations; the self-sufficient wife frees her husband from the conjugal slavery that was the price of her own. If the man is scrupulously well intentioned, lovers and spouses can attain perfect equality in undemanding generosity.* Sometimes the man himself plays the role of devoted servant; thus did Lewes create for George Eliot the favourable atmosphere the wife usually creates around the lord-husband. But most of the time, it is still the woman who pays the price for harmony at home. It seems natural to the man that she run the house and oversee the care and raising of the children alone. The woman herself believes that her personal life does not dispense her from the duties she assumed in marrying; she does not want her husband to be deprived of the advantages he would have had in marrying a 'real woman': she wants to be elegant, a good housekeeper and devoted mother as wives traditionally are. It is a task that easily becomes overwhelming. She assumes it out of both consideration for her partner and fidelity to herself: for she insists, as we have seen, on fulfilling every aspect of her destiny as woman. She will be a double for her husband at the same time as being herself; she will take charge of his worries, she will participate in his successes just as much as taking care of her own lot, and sometimes even more so. Taught to respect male superiority, she may still believe that man takes first place; and sometimes she fears that claiming it would ruin her family; split between the desire to affirm herself and self-effacement, she is divided and torn.

There is nonetheless one advantage woman can gain from her very inferiority: since from the start she has fewer chances than man, she does not feel a priori guilty towards him; it is not up to her to compensate for social injustice, and she is not called upon to do so. A man of goodwill feels it his duty to 'help' women because he is more favoured than they are; he will let himself be caught up in scruples or pity, and he risks being the prey of 'clinging' or 'devouring' women because they are at a disadvantage. The woman who achieves a virile independence has the great privilege of dealing sexually with autonomous and active individuals who – generally – will not play a parasite's role in her life, who will not bind her by their weaknesses and the demands of their needs. But women who know how to create a free relation with their partners are

---

* Clara and Robert Schumann's life seems to have had this kind of success for a certain time.

in truth rare; they themselves forge the chains with which men do not wish to burden them: they adopt towards their partner the attitude of the woman in love. For twenty years of waiting, dreaming and hoping, the young girl has embraced the myth of the liberating hero and saviour: independence won through work is not enough to abolish her desire for a glorious abdication. She would have had to be brought up exactly like a boy* to be able to comfortably overcome adolescent narcissism: but in her adult life she perpetuates this cult of self towards which her whole youth has predisposed her; she uses the merits of her professional success to enrich her image; she needs a gaze from above to reveal and consecrate her worth. Even if she is severe on men whom she judges daily, she reveres Man nonetheless and if she encounters him, she is ready to fall on her knees. To be justified by a god is easier than to be justified by her own effort; the world encourages her to believe in the possibility of a *given* salvation: she chooses to believe in it. At times she entirely renounces her autonomy, she is no more than a woman in love; more often she tries conciliation; but adoring love, the love of abdication, is devastating: it takes up all thoughts, all instants, it is obsessive, tyrannical. If she encounters a professional disappointment, the woman passionately seeks refuge in love: her failures find expression in scenes and demands at the lover's expense. But her heartbreaks in no way have the effect of increasing her professional zeal: generally she becomes irritated, on the contrary, by the kind of life that keeps her from the royal road of the great love. A woman who worked ten years ago for a political magazine run by women told me that in the office people talked rarely about politics but incessantly about love: one would complain that she was loved only for her body, ignoring her fine intelligence; another would whine that she was only appreciated for her mind and no one ever appreciated her physical charms. Here again, for the woman to be in love like a man – that is to say, without putting her very *being* into question, freely – she would have to think herself his equal, and be his equal concretely: she would have to commit herself with the same decisiveness to her enterprises, which, as we will see, is still not common.

There is one female function that is still almost impossible to undertake in complete freedom, and that is motherhood; in England and in America, the woman can at least refuse it at will, thanks to the practice of birth control; we have seen that in France she is often compelled to

---

* That is, not only with the same methods, but in the same climate, which today is impossible in spite of all the efforts of educators.

have painful and costly abortions; she often finds herself burdened with a child she did not want, ruining her professional life. If this burden is a heavy one, it is because, inversely, social norms do not allow the woman to procreate as she pleases: the unwed mother causes scandal and for the child an illegitimate birth is a stain; it is rare for a woman to become a mother without accepting the chains of marriage or lowering herself. If the idea of artificial insemination interests women so much, it is not because they wish to avoid male lovemaking: it is because they hope that voluntary motherhood will finally be accepted by society. It must be added that given the lack of well-organised day nurseries and kindergartens, even one child is enough to entirely paralyse a woman's activity; she can continue to work only by abandoning the child to her parents, friends or servants. She has to choose between sterility, often experienced as a painful frustration, and burdens hardly compatible with a career.

Thus the independent woman today is divided between her professional interests and the concerns of her sexual vocation; she has trouble finding her balance; if she does, it is at the price of concessions, sacrifices and juggling that keep her in constant tension. More than in physiological facts, it is here that one must seek the reason for the nervousness and frailty often observed in her. It is difficult to decide how much woman's physical makeup in itself represents a handicap. The obstacle created by menstruation, for example, has often been examined. Women known for their work or activities seem to attach little importance to it: is this because they owe their success to the fact that their monthly problems are so mild? One may ask if it is not on the contrary the choice of an active and ambitious life that confers this privilege on them: the attention women pay to their ailments exacerbates them; athletic women and women of action suffer less than the others because they pass over their sufferings. It is clear that menstrual pain does have organic causes, and I have seen the most energetic women spend twenty-four hours in bed every month in the throes of pitiless tortures; but their enterprises were never hindered by them. I am convinced that most ailments and illnesses that weigh women down have psychic causes: this is in fact what gynaecologists have told me. Women are constantly overwhelmed by the psychological tension I have spoken about, because of all the tasks they take on and the contradictions they struggle against; this does not mean that their ills are imaginary: they are as real and devouring as the situation they convey. But a situation does not depend on the body, it is rather the body that depends on it. So woman's health will not detract from her work when the working woman has the place she deserves in society; on the contrary, work will strongly reinforce her physical balance by keeping her from being endlessly preoccupied with it.

When we judge the professional accomplishments of women and try to speculate on their future on that basis, we must not lose sight of all these facts. The woman embarks on a career in the context of a highly problematic situation, subjugated still by the burdens traditionally implied by her femininity. Objective circumstances are no more favourable to her either. It is always hard to be a newcomer trying to make one's way in a hostile society, or at least a mistrustful one. Richard Wright showed in *Black Boy* how blocked from the start the ambitions of a young American black man are and what struggle he has to endure merely to raise himself to the level where whites begin to have problems; the blacks who came to France from Africa also have – within themselves as well as from outside – difficulties similar to those encountered by women.

The woman first finds herself in a state of inferiority during her period of apprenticeship: I have already pointed this out in relation to the period of girlhood, but it must be dealt with in more detail. During her studies and in the early decisive years of her career, it is rare for the woman to be able to make full use of her possibilities: many will later be handicapped by a bad start. In fact, the conflicts I have discussed will reach their greatest intensity between the ages of eighteen and thirty: and this is when their professional future is determined. Whether the woman lives with her family or is married, her friends and family will rarely respect her efforts as they respect a man's; they will impose duties and chores on her, and curtail her freedom; she herself is still profoundly marked by her upbringing, respectful of the values the older women around her represent, haunted by childhood and adolescent dreams; she has difficulty reconciling the inheritance of her past with the interest of her future. Sometimes she rejects her femininity, she hesitates between chastity, homosexuality or a provocative virago attitude, she dresses badly or like a man: she wastes a lot of time and energy in defiance, scenes and anger. More often she wants, on the contrary, to assert her femininity: she dresses up, goes out and flirts, she is in love, wavering between masochism and aggressiveness. In all cases, she questions herself, is agitated and scattered. By the very fact that she is in thrall to outside preoccupations, she does not commit herself entirely to her enterprise; thus she profits from it less, and is more tempted to give it up. What is extremely demoralising for the woman trying to be self-sufficient is the existence of other women of her class, having from the start the same situation and chances, and who live as parasites; the man might resent privileged people: but he feels solidarity with his class; on the whole, those who begin on an equal footing with equal chances arrive at approximately the same standard of living, while women in similar situations have greatly differing fortunes because of man's mediation; the woman friend who is married or comfortably kept is a temptation for the woman who has to ensure her success alone; she feels she is arbitrarily condemning herself to the most difficult paths: at each obstacle she wonders if it would not be better to choose a different way. 'When I think I have to get everything from my brain!' a young, poor student told me indignantly. The man obeys an imperious necessity: the woman must constantly renew her decision; she goes forward, not with her eye fixed on a goal directly in front of her, but letting her attention wander all around her; thus her progress is timid and uncertain. And moreover – as I have already said – it seems to her that the farther she advances, the more she renounces her other chances; in becoming a bluestocking, a cerebral woman, she will either displease men in general or humiliate her husband or lover by being too dazzling a success. Not only will she apply herself all the more to appearing elegant and frivolous, but she will also hold herself back. The hope of one day being free from looking after herself and the fear of having to give up this hope by coping with this anxiety come together to prevent her from devoting herself single-mindedly to her studies and career.

Inasmuch as the woman wants to be woman, her independent status produces an inferiority complex; inversely, her femininity leads her to doubt her professional opportunities. This is a most important point. A study showed that fourteen-year-old girls believed: 'Boys are better; they find it easier to work.' The girl is convinced that she has limited capacities. Because parents and teachers accept that the girl's level is lower than the boy's, students readily accept it too; and in truth, in spite of the fact that the curricula are identical, girls' intellectual growth in secondary schools is given less importance. With few exceptions, the students in a female philosophy class overall have a markedly lower achievement level than a class of boys: many female students do not intend to continue their studies, they work superficially and others suffer from a lack of competitiveness. As long as the exams are fairly easy, their inadequacy will not be noticed too much; but when serious competitive exams are in question, the female student will become aware of her weaknesses; she will attribute them to the unjust curse of femaleness and not to the mediocrity of her education; resigning herself to this inequality, she exacerbates it; she persuades herself that her chances of success are related to her patience and assiduity; she decides to use her strength sparingly: this is a bad calculation. Above all, in studies and professions requiring a degree of inventiveness, originality and some small discoveries, a utilitarian attitude is disastrous; conversations, reading outside the syllabus, or a walk that allows the mind to wander freely can be far more profitable even for the translation of a Greek text than the dreary compilation of complex syntaxes. Crushed by respect for those in authority and the weight of erudition, her vision blocked by blinkers, the overly conscientious female student kills her critical sense and even her intelligence. Her methodical determination gives rise to tension and ennui: in classes where female secondary school students prepare for the Sèvres examination, there is a stifling atmosphere that discourages even slightly spirited individuality. Having created her own jail, the female examination candidate wants nothing more than to escape from it; as soon as she closes her books, she thinks about any other subject. She does not experience those rich moments where study and amusement merge, where adventures of the mind acquire living warmth. Overwhelmed by the thanklessness of her chores, she feels less and less able to carry them out. I remember a female student doing the *agrégation* who said, at the time when there was a coed competitive exam in philosophy: 'Boys can succeed in one or two years; we need at least four.' Another – who was recommended a book on Kant, a writer on the curriculum – commented: 'This book is too difficult: It's for Normalians!'[5] She seemed to think that women could take easier exams; beaten before even trying, she was in effect giving all chances of success to the men.

Because of this defeatist attitude, the woman easily settles for a mediocre success; she does not dare to aim higher. Starting out in her job with a superficial education, she very quickly curtails her ambitions. She often considers the very fact of earning her own living a great enough feat; like so many others, she could have entrusted her future to a man; to continue to want her independence she needs to take pride in her effort but it exhausts her. It seems to her she has done enough just in choosing to do something. 'That's not so bad for a woman,' she thinks. A woman in an unusual profession said: 'If I were a man, I would feel obliged to be in the top rank; but I am the only woman in France holding such a position: that's enough for me.' There is prudence in her modesty. In trying to go further, the woman is afraid of failing miserably. She is bothered, and rightly so, by the idea that no one has confidence in her. In general, the superior caste is hostile to the parvenus of the inferior caste: whites will not go to see a black doctor, nor men a woman doctor; but individuals from the lower caste, imbued with the feeling of their generic inferiority and often full of resentment of someone who has prevailed over destiny, will also prefer to turn to the masters; in particular, most women, steeped in the adoration of the male, avidly seek him in the doctor, lawyer, office manager. Neither men nor women like working under a woman's orders. Even if her superiors appreciate her, they will always be somewhat condescending; to be a woman is, if not a defect, at least a peculiarity. The woman must ceaselessly earn a confidence not initially granted to her: at the outset she is suspect; she has to prove herself. If she is any good, she will, people say. But worth is not a given essence: it is the result of a favourable development. Feeling a negative judgement weighing on one rarely helps one to overcome it. The initial inferiority complex most usually leads to the defensive reaction of an exaggerated affectation of authority. Most women doctors, for example, have too much or too little. If they are natural, they are not intimidating because their life as a whole disposes them more to seduce than to command; the patient who likes to be dominated will be disappointed by advice simply given; conscious of this, the woman doctor uses a low voice, a decisive tone, but then she does not have the cheerful simplicity that is so seductive in the confident doctor. The man is used to being imposing; his clients believe in his competence; he can let himself go: he is sure to impress. The woman does not inspire the same feeling of security; she stiffens, exaggerates, overdoes it. In business, in the office, she is scrupulous, a stickler and easily aggressive. Just as she is in her studies, she lacks confidence, inspiration and daring. In an effort to succeed she becomes tense. Her behaviour is a series of provocations and abstract self-affirmations. The greatest failure a lack of self-assurance brings about is that the subject cannot forget himself. He does not generously aim for a goal: he tries to prove he is worth what is demanded of him. Throwing oneself boldly towards goals risks setbacks: but one also attains unexpected results; prudence necessarily leads to mediocrity. It is rare to see in the woman a taste for adventure, gratuitous experience or disinterested curiosity; she seeks 'to build a career' the way others construct a happy life; she remains dominated, invested by the male universe, she lacks the audacity to break through the ceiling, she does not passionately lose herself in her projects; she still considers her life an immanent enterprise: she aims not for an object, but through an object for her subjective success. This is a very striking attitude in, among others, American women; it pleases them to have a job and to prove to themselves they are able to carry it out properly: but they do not become passionate about the *content* of their tasks. Likewise, the woman has a tendency to attach too much importance to minor failures and modest successes; she either gets discouraged or she swells with vanity; when success is expected, it is welcomed with simplicity; but it becomes an intoxicating triumph if one doubted obtaining it; that is the excuse of women who get carried away with their own importance and who ostentatiously display their least accomplishments. They constantly look back to see how far they have come: this curbs their drive. They can have honourable careers with such methods, but will not accomplish great things. It should be said that many men too are only able to build mediocre careers. It is only in relation to the best of them that the woman – with very rare exceptions – seems to us still to be bringing up the rear. The reasons I have given sufficiently explain this and do not in any way compromise the future. To do great things, today's woman needs above all forgetfulness of self: but to forget oneself one must first be solidly sure that one has already found oneself. Newly arrived in the world of men, barely supported by them, the woman is still much too busy looking for herself.

There is one category of women to whom these remarks do not apply because their careers, far from harming the affirmation of their femininity, reinforce it; through artistic expression they seek to go beyond the very given they constitute: actresses, dancers and singers. For three centuries they have almost been the only ones to possess concrete independence in society, and today they still hold a privileged place in it. In the past, actresses were cursed by the Church: this excessive severity allowed them great freedom of behaviour; they are often involved in seduction, and like courtesans they spend much of their days in the company of men: but as they earn their living themselves, finding the meaning of their existence in their work, they escape men's yoke. Their great advantage is that their professional successes contribute – as for males – to their sexual worth; by realising themselves as human beings, they accomplish themselves as women: they are not torn between contradictory aspirations; on the contrary, they find in their jobs a justification for their narcissism: clothes, beauty care and charm are part of their professional duties; a woman infatuated with her image finds great satisfaction in *doing* something simply by exhibiting what she *is*; and this exhibition requires sufficient amounts of both artifice and study if it is to be, in Georgette Leblanc's words, a substitute for action. A great actress will aim even higher: she will go beyond the given in the way she expresses it, she will really be an artist, a creator who gives meaning to her life by lending meaning to the world.

But these rare advantages also conceal traps: instead of integrating her narcissistic indulgence and the sexual freedom she enjoys into her artistic life, the actress often falls into self-worship or seduction; I have already spoken of these pseudo-artists who seek only 'to make a name for themselves' in the cinema or theatre by representing capital to exploit in a man's arms; the comfort of masculine support is very tempting compared with the risks of a career and the harshness any real work involves. The desire for a feminine destiny – a husband, a home, children – and the spell of love are not always easily reconcilable with the desire to succeed. But above all, the admiration she feels for herself limits the actress's talent in many cases; she deludes herself as to the value of her mere presence to the extent that serious work seems useless to her; more than anything else, she prefers to place herself in the limelight and sacrifices the character she is interpreting to ham acting; she, like others, does not have the generosity to forget herself, which keeps her from going beyond herself: rare are the Rachels or the Duses who overcome this risk and who make of their person the instrument of their art instead of seeing in art a servant of their self. In her private life, though, the ham will exaggerate all her narcissistic defects: she will appear vain, touchy and a phoney; she will treat the whole world as a stage.

Today the expressive arts are not the only ones open to women: many try their hand at creative activities. Woman's situation encourages her to seek salvation in literature and in art. Living on the margin of the masculine world, she does not grasp it in its universal guise but through a particular vision; for her it is not a group of implements and concepts but a source of feelings and emotions; she is interested in the qualities of things inasmuch as they are gratuitous and secret; taking on a negative attitude, one of refusal, she does not lose herself in the real: she protests against it, with words; she looks for the image of her soul in nature, she abandons herself to her reveries, she wants to reach her *being*: she is doomed to failure; she can only recover it in the realm of imagination. So as not to allow an inner life that does not *serve* any purpose to sink into nothingness, so as to assert herself against the given that she endures in revolt, so as to create a world other than the one in which she cannot succeed in reaching herself, she needs *to express herself*. Thus it is well known that she is talkative and a scribbler; she pours out her feelings in conversations, letters and diaries. If she is at all ambitious, she will be writing her memoirs, transposing her biography into a novel, breathing her feelings into poems. She enjoys vast leisure time that favours these activities.

But the very circumstances that orient the woman towards creation also constitute obstacles she will often be unable to overcome. When she decides to paint or write just to fill the emptiness of her days, paintings and essays will be treated as 'ladies' work'; she will devote little time or care to them and they will be worth about as much. To compensate for the flaws in her existence, often the woman at menopause feverishly takes up the brush or pen: it is late; without serious training, she will never be more than an amateur. But even if she begins quite young, she rarely envisages art as serious work; used to idleness, never having experienced in her life the austere necessity of a discipline, she will not be capable of a steady and persevering effort, she will not compel herself to acquire a solid technique; she balks at the thankless and solitary trials and errors of work that is never exhibited, that has to be destroyed and done over again a hundred times; and as from childhood she was taught to cheat in order to please, she hopes to get by with a few ruses. This is what Marie Bashkirtseff admits. 'Yes, I don't take the trouble to paint. I watched myself today, *I cheat.*' The woman easily *plays* at working but she does not work; believing in the magic virtues of passivity, she confuses conjurations and acts, symbolic gestures and effective behaviour; she disguises herself as a Beaux-Arts student, she arms herself with her arsenal of brushes; planted in front of her easel, her gaze wanders from the blank canvas to her mirror; but the bouquet of flowers, the bowl of apples, do not appear on their own on the canvas. Seated at her desk, musing over vague stories, the woman acquires a peaceful alibi in imagining she is a writer: but she must at some point make signs on the blank page; they have to have a meaning in the eyes of others. So the trickery is exposed. To please one needs only to create mirages: but a work of art is not a mirage, it is a solid object; to construct it, one must know one's craft. It is not only thanks to her gifts or personality that Colette became a great writer; her pen was often her livelihood and she demanded of it the careful work that a good artisan demands of his tool; from *Claudine* to *Break of Day*,[6] the amateur became professional: the progress brilliantly shows the advantages of a strict apprenticeship. Most women, though, do not understand the problems that their desire for communication poses: and this is what largely explains their laziness. They have always considered themselves as givens; they believe their worth comes from an inner grace and they do not imagine that value can be acquired;

to seduce, they know only how to display themselves: their charm works or does not work, they have no grasp on its success or failure; they suppose that, in a similar way, to express oneself, one needs only show what one is; instead of constituting their work by a thoughtful effort, they put their confidence in spontaneity; writing or smiling is all one to them: they try their luck, success will come or will not. Sure of themselves, they reckon that the book or painting will be successful without effort; timid, they are discouraged by the least criticism; they do not know that error can open the road to progress, they take it for an irreparable catastrophe, like a malformation. This is why they often over-react, which is harmful to themselves: they become irritated and discouraged when recognising their errors rather than drawing valuable lessons from them. Unfortunately, spontaneity is not as simple as it appears: the paradox of the commonplace – as Paulhan explains in *The Flowers of Tarbes*[7] – is that it is nothing more than the immediate translation of the subjective impression. Thus, when the woman produces the image she creates without taking others into account, she thinks she is most unusual, but she is merely reinventing a banal cliché; if she is told, she is surprised and vexed and throws down her pen; she is not aware that the public reads with its own eyes and its own mind and that a brand-new epithet can awaken in it many old memories; of course, it is a precious gift to be able to dig down into oneself and bring up vibrant impressions to the surface of language; one admires Colette for a spontaneity not found in any male writer; but – although these two terms seem to contradict each other – hers is a thoughtful spontaneity: she refuses some of its contributions and accepts others as she sees fit; the amateur, rather than seizing words as an interindividual relation, an appeal to the other, sees in them the direct revelation of her feelings; editing or crossing out for her means repudiating a part of self; she does not want to sacrifice anything both because she delights in what she *is* and because she hopes not to become other. Her sterile vanity comes from the fact that she cherishes herself without daring to construct herself.

Thus, very few of the legions of women who attempt to dabble in literature and art persevere; those who overcome this first obstacle very often remain divided between their narcissism and an inferiority complex. Not being able to forget oneself is a failure that will weigh on them more heavily than in any other career; if their essential goal is an abstract self-affirmation, the formal satisfaction of success, they will not abandon themselves to the contemplation of the world: they will be incapable of creating it anew. Marie Bashkirtseff decided to paint because she wanted to become famous; the obsession with glory comes between her and reality; she does not really like to paint: art is merely a means; it is not her ambitious and empty dreams that will reveal to her the meaning of a colour or face. Instead of giving herself generously to the work she undertakes, the woman all too often considers it a simple ornament of her life; books and paintings are only an inessential intermediary allowing her to exhibit this essential reality publicly: her own person. Thus it is her person that is the main – sometimes only – subject that interests her: Mme Vigée-Lebrun does not tire of putting her smiling maternity on her canvases. Even if she speaks of general themes, the woman writer will still speak of herself: one cannot read such and such theatre reviews without being informed of the size and corpulence of their author, the colour of her hair and the peculiarities of her personality. Of course, the self is not always detestable. Few books are as fascinating as certain confessions: but they have to be sincere and the author has to have something to confess. Instead of enriching the woman, her narcissism impoverishes her; involved in nothing but self-contemplation, she eliminates herself; even the love she bestows on herself becomes stereotyped: she does not discover in her writings her authentic experience but an imaginary idol constructed from clichés. She cannot be criticised for projecting herself in her novels as Benjamin Constant and Stendhal did: but unfortunately she sees her story too often as a silly fairy tale; the young girl hides the brutal and frightening reality from herself with good doses of fantasising: it is a pity that once she is an adult, she still buries the world, its characters, and herself in the fogginess of poetry. When the truth emerges from this travesty, there are sometimes charming successes, but next to *Dusty Answer*[8] or *The Constant Nymph*,[9] how many bland and dull escapist novels there are!

It is natural for women to try to escape this world where they often feel unrecognised and misunderstood; what is regrettable is that they do not dare the bold flights of a Gérard de Nerval or a Poe. Many reasons excuse woman's timidity. Her great concern is to please; and as a woman she is often already afraid of displeasing just because she writes: the term 'bluestocking', albeit a bit overused, still has a disagreeable connotation; she lacks the courage to displease even more as a writer. The writer who is original, as long as he is not dead, is always scandalous; what is new disturbs and antagonises; women are still astonished and flattered to be accepted into the world of thinking and art, a masculine world: the woman watches her manners; she does not dare to irritate, explore, explode; she thinks she has to excuse her literary pretensions by her modesty and good taste; she relies on the proven values of conformism; she introduces just the personal note that is expected of her into her literature: she points out that she is a woman with some well chosen affectations, simpering and preciosities; so she will excel at producing 'bestsellers' but she cannot be counted on to blaze new trails. Women do not lack originality in their behaviour and feelings: there are some so singular that they have to be locked up; on the whole, many of them are more baroque and eccentric than the men whose strictures they reject. But they put their bizarre genius into their lives, conversation and correspondence; if they try to write, they feel crushed by the universe of culture because it is a universe of men: they just babble. Inversely, the woman who chooses to reason, to express herself using masculine techniques, will do her best to stifle an originality she distrusts; like a female student, she will be assiduous and pedantic; she will imitate rigour and virile vigour. She may become an excellent theoretician and acquire a solid talent; but she will make herself repudiate everything in her that is 'different'. There are women who are mad and there are women of talent: none of them has this madness in talent called genius.

This reasonable modesty is what has above all defined the limits of feminine talent until now. Many women have eluded – and they increasingly elude – the traps of narcissism and faux wonderment; but no woman has ever thrown prudence to the wind to try to *emerge* beyond the given world. In the first place, there are, of course, many who accept society just as it is; they are par excellence the champions of the bourgeoisie since they represent the most conservative element of this threatened class; with well-chosen adjectives, they evoke the refinements of a civilisation 'of quality'; they extol the bourgeois ideal of happiness and disguise their class interests under the banner of poetry; they orchestrate the mystification intended to persuade women to 'remain women'; old houses, parks and kitchen gardens, picturesque grandparents, mischievous children, laundry, jams and jellies, family gatherings, clothes, salons, balls, suffering but exemplary wives, the beauty of devotion and sacrifice, small disappointments and great joys of conjugal love, dreams of youth, mature resignation – women novelists from England, France, America, Canada and Scandinavia have exploited these themes to the utmost; they have attained glory and wealth but have not enriched our vision of the world. Far more interesting are the women insurgents who have indicted this unjust society; protest literature can give rise to strong and sincere works; George Eliot drew from her revolt a detailed and dramatic vision of Victorian England; however, as Virginia Woolf shows,

Jane Austen, the Brontë sisters and George Eliot had to spend so much negative energy freeing themselves from external constraints that they arrived out of breath at the point where the major masculine writers were starting out; they have little strength left to benefit from their victory and break all the ties that bind them: for example, they lack the irony, the nonchalance, of a Stendhal or his calm sincerity. Nor have they had the wealth of experience of a Dostoevsky, a Tolstoy: it is why the great book *Middlemarch* does not equal *War and Peace*; *Wuthering Heights*, in spite of its stature, does not have the scope of *The Brothers Karamazov.* Today, women already have less trouble asserting themselves; but they have not totally overcome the age-old specification that confines them in their femininity. Lucidity, for example, is a conquest they are justly proud of but with which they are a little too quickly satisfied. The fact is that the traditional woman is a mystified consciousness and an instrument of mystification; she tries to conceal her dependence from herself, which is a way of consenting to it; to denounce this dependence is already a liberation; cynicism is a defence against humiliation and shame: it is the first stage of assuming responsibility. In trying to be lucid, women writers render the greatest service to the cause of women; but – without generally realising it – they remain too attached to serving this cause to adopt, in front of the whole world, the disinterested attitude that opens up wider horizons. When they pull away the veils of illusion and lies, they think they have done enough: nonetheless, this negative daring still leaves us with an enigma; for truth itself is ambiguity, depth, mystery: after its presence is acknowledged, it must be thought, re-created. It is all well and good not to be duped: but this is where it all begins; the woman exhausts her courage in dissipating mirages and she stops in fear at the threshold of reality. This is why, for example, there are sincere and endearing women's autobiographies: but none can compare with *Confessions* or *Memoirs of an Egotist*.[10] We women are still too preoccupied with seeing clearly to try to penetrate other shadows beyond that clarity.

'Women never go beyond the pretext,' a writer told me. This is true enough. Still amazed at having had permission to explore the world, they take its inventory without trying to discover its meaning. Where they sometimes excel is in the observation of facts: they make remarkable reporters; no male journalist has outdone Andrée Viollis's eyewitness reports on Indochina and India. They know how to describe atmosphere and people, to show the subtle relations between them, and let us share in the secret workings of their souls: Willa Cather, Edith Wharton,

Dorothy Parker and Katherine Mansfield have sharply and sensitively brought to life individuals, climates and civilisations. They have rarely succeeded in creating as convincing a masculine hero as Heathcliff: they grasp little more than the male in man; but they often describe their own interior lives, experiences and universe very well; attached to the secret side of objects, fascinated by the uniqueness of their own sensations, they convey their fresh experience through the use of savoury adjectives and sensual images; their vocabulary is usually more noticeable than their syntax because they are interested in things more than their relations; they do not aim for abstract elegance; instead, their words speak to the senses. One area they have most lovingly explored is Nature; for the girl or the woman who has not completely abdicated, nature represents what woman represents for man: herself and her negation, a kingdom and a place of exile; she is all in the guise of the other. The woman writer will most intimately reveal her experience and dreams in speaking of moors or kitchen gardens. There are many who enclose the miracles of sap and seasons in pots, vases and flower beds; others, without imprisoning plants and animals, nonetheless try to appropriate them by the attentive love they dispense to them: so it is with Colette and Katherine Mansfield; very rare are those who approach nature in its inhuman freedom, who try to decipher its foreign meanings and lose themselves in order to unite with this other presence: hardly any women venture down these roads Rousseau invented, except for Emily Brontë, Virginia Woolf and sometimes Mary Webb. And to an even greater extent we can count on the fingers of one hand the women who have traversed the given in search of its secret dimension: Emily Brontë explored death, Virginia Woolf life, and Katherine Mansfield sometimes – not very often – daily contingence and suffering. No woman ever wrote *The Trial*, *Moby-Dick*, *Ulysses*, or *The Seven Pillars of Wisdom*. Women do not challenge the human condition because they have barely begun to be able to assume it entirely. This explains why their works generally lack metaphysical resonance and black humour as well; they do not set the world apart, they do not question it, they do not denounce its contradictions: they take it seriously. The fact is that most men have the same limitations as well; it is when she is compared with the few rare artists who deserve to be called 'great' that woman comes out as mediocre. Destiny is not what limits her: it is easy to understand why it has not been possible for her to reach the highest summits, and why it will perhaps not be possible for some time.

Art, literature and philosophy are attempts to found the world anew on a human freedom: that of the creator; to foster such an aim, one must first unequivocally posit oneself as a freedom. The restrictions that education and custom impose on woman limit her grasp of the universe; when the struggle to claim a place in this world gets too rough, there can be no question of tearing oneself away from it; one must first emerge within it in sovereign solitude if one wants to try to grasp it anew: what woman primarily lacks is learning from the practice of abandonment and transcendence, in anguish and pride. Marie Bashkirtseff writes:

> What I want is the freedom to walk around alone, come and go, sit on park benches in the Tuileries Gardens. Without this freedom you cannot become a true artist. You think you can profit from what you see when you are being accompanied or when you must wait for your car, your nursemaid, your family to go to the Louvre! . . . This is the freedom that is missing and without which one cannot seriously become something. *Thinking is imprisoned by this stupid and incessant constraint . . . That is all it takes to clip one's wings.* This is one of the reasons there are no women artists.

Indeed, for one to become a creator, it is not enough to be cultivated, that is, to make going to shows and meeting people part of one's life; culture must be apprehended through the free movement of a transcendence; the spirit with all its riches must project itself in an empty sky that is its to fill; but if a thousand fine bonds tie it to the earth, its surge is broken. The girl today can certainly go out alone, stroll in the Tuileries; but I have already said how hostile the street is: eyes everywhere, hands waiting; if she wanders absentmindedly, her thoughts elsewhere, if she lights a cigarette in a café, if she goes to the cinema alone, an unpleasant incident can quickly occur; she must inspire respect by the way she dresses and behaves: this concern rivets her to the ground and to self. 'Her wings are clipped.' At eighteen, T. E. Lawrence went on a grand tour through France by bicycle; a young girl would never be permitted to take on such an adventure: still less would it be possible for her to take off on foot for a half-desert and dangerous country as Lawrence did. Yet, such experiences have an inestimable impact: this is how an individual in the headiness of freedom and discovery learns to look at the entire world as his fief. The woman is already naturally deprived of the lessons of violence: I have said how physical weakness disposes her to passivity; when a boy settles a fight with punches, he feels he can rely on himself in his own interest; at least the girl should be allowed to compensate by sports, adventure and the pride of obstacles overcome. But no. She may feel alone *within* the world: she never stands up *in front* of it, unique and sovereign. Everything encourages her to be invested and dominated by foreign existences: and particularly in love, she disavows rather than asserts herself. Misfortune and distress are often learning experiences in this sense: it was isolation that enabled Emily Brontë to write a powerful and unbridled book; in the face of nature, death and destiny, she relied on no one's help but her own. Rosa Luxemburg was ugly; she was never tempted to wallow in the cult of her image, to make herself object, prey and trap: from her youth she was wholly mind and freedom. Even then, it is rare for a woman to fully assume the agonising tête-à-tête with the given world. The constraints that surround her and the whole tradition that weighs on her keep her from feeling responsible for the universe: this is the profound reason for her mediocrity.

Men we call great are those who – in one way or another – take the weight of the world on their shoulders; they have done more or less well, they have succeeded in re-creating it or they have failed; but they took on this enormous burden in the first place. This is what no woman has ever done, what no woman has ever been *able* to do. It takes belonging to the privileged caste to view the universe as one's own, to consider oneself as guilty of its faults and take pride in its progress; those alone who are at the controls have the opportunity to justify it by changing, thinking and revealing it; only they can identify with it and try to leave their imprint on it. Until now it has only been possible for Man to be incarnated in the man, not the woman. Moreover, individuals who appear exceptional to us, the ones we honour with the name of genius, are those who tried to work out the fate of all humanity in their particular lives. No woman has thought herself authorised to do that. How could van Gogh have been born woman? A woman would not have been sent on mission to Borinage, she would not have felt men's misery as her own crime, she would not have sought redemption; so she would never have painted van Gogh's sunflowers. And this is without taking into account that the painter's kind of life – the solitude in Arles, going to cafés, whorehouses, everything that fed into van Gogh's art by feeding his sensibility – would have been prohibited to her. A woman could never have become Kafka: in her doubts and anxieties, she would never have recognised the anguish of Man driven from paradise. St Teresa is one of the only women to have lived the human condition for herself, in total abandonment: we have seen why. Placing herself beyond earthly hierarchies, she, like St John of the Cross, felt no reassuring sky over her head. For both of them it was the same night, the same flashes of light, in each the same nothingness, in God the same plenitude. When finally it is possible for every human being to place his pride above sexual differences in the difficult glory of his free existence, only then will woman be able to make her history, her problems, her doubts and her hopes those of humanity; only then will she be able to attempt to discover in her life and her works all of reality and not only her own person. As long as she still has to fight to become a human being, she cannot be a creator.

Once again, to explain her limits, we must refer to her situation and not to a mysterious essence: the future remains wide open. The idea that woman has no 'creative genius' has been defended ad nauseam; Mme Marthe Borély, a noted antifeminist of former times, defends this thesis, among others: but it looks as if she tried to make her books the living proof of incoherence and feminine silliness, and so they contradict themselves. Besides, the idea of a given creative 'instinct' must be rejected like that of the 'eternal feminine' and put away in the attic of entities. Some misogynists affirm a bit more concretely that because women are neurotic, they will never create anything of value: but these same people often declare that genius is a neurosis. In any case, the example of Proust shows clearly enough that psychophysiological imbalance does not mean powerlessness or mediocrity. As for the argument drawn from history, we have just seen what we should think of it; the historical past cannot be considered as defining an eternal truth; it merely translates a situation that is showing itself to be historical precisely in that it is in the process of changing. How could women ever have had genius when all possibility of accomplishing a work of genius – or just a work – was refused them? Old Europe formerly heaped its contempt on barbarian Americans for possessing neither artists nor writers: 'Let us live before asking us to justify our existence,' Jefferson wrote, in essence. Blacks give the same answers to racists who reproach them for not having produced a Whitman or Melville. Neither can the French proletariat invoke a name like Racine or Mallarmé. The free woman is just being born; when she conquers herself, she will perhaps justify Rimbaud's prophecy: 'Poets will be. When woman's infinite servitude is broken, when she lives for herself and by herself, man – abominable until now – giving her her freedom, she too will be a poet! Woman will find the unknown! Will her worlds of ideas differ from ours? She will find strange, unfathomable, repugnant, delicious things, we will take them, we will understand them.'* Her 'worlds of ideas' are not necessarily different from men's, because she will free herself by assimilating them; to know how singular she will remain and how important these singularities will continue to be, one would have to make some foolhardy predictions. What is beyond doubt is that until now women's possibilities have been stifled and lost to humanity, and in her and everyone's interest it is high time she be left to take her own chances.

* Rimbaud to Paul Demeny, 15 May 1871.

Conclusion

'No, woman is not our brother; through negligence and corruption, we have made her a being apart, unknown, having no weapon but her sex, which is not only perpetual war but in addition an unfair weapon – adoring or hating, but not a frank companion or a being with *esprit de corps* and freemasonry – of the eternal little slave's defiances.'

Many men would still subscribe to these words of Jules Laforgue; many think that there will always be Sturm und Drang between the two sexes and that fraternity will never be possible for them. The fact is that neither men nor women are satisfied with each other today. But the question is whether it is an original curse that condemns them to tear each other apart or whether the conflicts that pit them against each other express a transitory moment in human history.

We have seen that in spite of legends, no physiological destiny imposes eternal hostility on the Male and Female as such; even the notorious praying mantis devours her male only for lack of other food and for the good of the species: in the animal kingdom, from the top of the ladder to the bottom, all individuals are subordinated to the species. Moreover, humanity is something other than a species: it is an historical becoming; it is defined by the way it assumes natural facticity. Indeed, even with the greatest bad faith in the world, it is impossible to detect a rivalry between the male and the female human that is specifically physiological. And so their hostility is located on that ground that is intermediate between biology and psychology, namely, psychoanalysis. Woman, it is said, envies man's penis and desires to castrate him, but the infantile desire for the penis only has importance in the adult woman's life if she experiences her femininity as a mutilation; and it is only to the extent that the penis embodies all the privileges of virility that she wishes to appropriate the male organ for herself. It is generally agreed that her dream of castration has a symbolic significance: she wishes, so it is thought, to deprive the male of his transcendence. Her wish, as we have seen, is much more ambiguous: she wishes, in a contradictory way, *to have* this transcendence, which presupposes that she both respects and denies it, and that she intends both to throw herself into it and to keep it within herself. This means that the drama does not unfold on a sexual level; sexuality, moreover, has never seemed to us to define a destiny or to provide in itself the key to human behaviour, but to express the totality of a situation it helps define. The battle of the sexes is not immediately implied by the anatomy of man and woman. In fact, when it is mentioned, it is taken for granted that in the timeless heaven of Ideas a battle rages between these uncertain essences: the Eternal Feminine and the Eternal Masculine; and it is not noticed that this titanic combat assumes two totally different forms on earth, corresponding to different historical moments.

The woman confined to immanence tries to keep man in this prison as well; thus the prison will merge with the world and she will no longer suffer from being shut up in it: the mother, the wife, the lover are the gaolers; society codified by men decrees that woman is inferior: she can only abolish this inferiority by destroying male superiority. She does her utmost to mutilate, to dominate man, she contradicts him, she denies his truth and values. But in doing that, she is only defending herself; neither immutable essence nor flawed choice has doomed her to immanence and inferiority. They were imposed on her. All oppression creates a state of war. This particular case is no exception. The existent considered as inessential cannot fail to attempt to reestablish his sovereignty.

Today, the combat is taking another form; instead of wanting to put man in prison, woman is trying to escape from it; she no longer seeks to drag him into the realms of immanence but to emerge into the light of transcendence. And the male attitude here creates a new conflict: the man petulantly 'dumps' the woman. He is pleased to remain the sovereign subject, the absolute superior, the essential being; he refuses to consider his companion concretely as an equal; she responds to his defiance by an aggressive attitude. It is no longer a war between individuals imprisoned in their respective spheres: a caste claiming its rights lays siege but is held in check by the privileged caste. Two transcendences confront each other; instead of mutually recognising each other, each freedom wants to dominate the other.

This difference in attitude is manifest on the sexual as well as the spiritual level; the 'feminine' woman, by becoming a passive prey, tries to reduce the male to carnal passivity as well; she works at entrapping him, at imprisoning him, by the desire she arouses, docilely making herself a thing; the 'emancipated' woman, on the contrary, wants to be active and prehensile and refuses the passivity the man attempts to impose on her. Likewise, Élise[1] and her followers do not accord any value to virile activities; they place flesh above spirit, contingence above freedom, conventional wisdom above creative daring. But the 'modern' woman accepts masculine values: she prides herself on thinking, acting, working and creating on the same basis as males; instead of trying to belittle them, she declares herself their equal.

This claim is legitimate insofar as it is expressed in concrete ways; and it is men's insolence that is then reprehensible. But in their defence it must be said that women themselves tend to confuse the issue. A Mabel Dodge attempted to enslave Lawrence by her feminine wiles in order to then dominate him spiritually; to show by their successes that they equal a man, many women strive to secure masculine support through sex; they play both sides, demanding both old-fashioned respect and modern esteem, relying on their old magic and their fledgling rights; it is understandable that the irritated man should go on the defensive, but he too is duplicitous when he demands that the woman play the game loyally whereas he, in his hostility and distrust, refuses to grant her indispensable trump cards. In reality, the struggle between them cannot be clear-cut, since woman's very being is opacity; she does not stand in front of man as a subject but as an object paradoxically endowed with subjectivity; she assumes herself as both *self* and *other*, which is a contradiction with disconcerting consequences. When she makes a weapon of both her weakness and her strength, it is not a deliberate calculation: she is spontaneously seeking her salvation in the path imposed on her, that of passivity, at the same time as she is actively demanding her sovereignty; and this process is undoubtedly not 'fair play', but it is dictated by the ambiguous situation assigned to her. Man, though, when he treats her like a freedom, is indignant that she is still a trap for him; while he flatters and satisfies her in her role as his prey, he gets annoyed at her claims to autonomy; whatever he does, he feels duped and she feels wronged.

The conflict will last as long as men and women do not recognise each other as peers, that is, as long as femininity is perpetuated as such; which of them is the most determined to maintain it? The woman who frees herself from it nevertheless wants to conserve its prerogatives; and the man then demands that she assume its limitations. 'It is easier to accuse one sex than to excuse the other,' says Montaigne. Meting out blame and approbation is useless. In fact, the vicious circle is so difficult to break here because each sex is victim both of the other and of itself; between two adversaries confronting each other in their pure freedom, an agreement could easily be found, especially as this war does not benefit anyone; but the complexity of this whole business comes from the fact that each camp is its enemy's accomplice; the woman pursues a dream of resignation, the man a dream of alienation; inauthenticity does not pay: each one blames the other for the unhappiness brought on himself by taking the easy way out; what the man and the woman hate in each other is the striking failure of their own bad faith or their own cowardice.

We have seen why men originally enslaved women; the devaluation of femininity was a necessary step in human development; but this step could have brought about a collaboration between the two sexes; oppression is explained by the tendency of the existent to flee from himself by alienating himself in the other that he oppresses for that purpose; this tendency can be found in each individual man today: and the vast majority give in to it; a husband looks for himself in his wife, a lover in his mistress, in the guise of a stone statue; he seeks in her the myth of his virility, sovereignty, his unmediated reality. 'My husband never goes to the movies,' says the woman, and the dubious masculine pronouncement is engraved in the marble of eternity. But he himself is a slave to his double: what effort to build up an image in which he is always in danger! After all, it is founded on the capricious freedom of women: it must constantly be made favourable; man is consumed by the concern to appear male, important, superior; he playacts so that others will playact with him; he is also aggressive and nervous; he feels hostility for women because he is afraid of them, and he is afraid of them because he is afraid of the character with whom he is assimilated. What time and energy he wastes in getting rid of, idealising and transposing complexes, in speaking about women, seducing and fearing them! He would be liberated with their liberation. But that is exactly what he fears. And he persists in the mystifications meant to maintain woman in her chains.

That she is mystified is something of which many men are conscious. 'What a curse to be a woman! And yet the very worst curse when one is a woman is, in fact, not to understand that it is one,' says Kierkegaard.* Attempts have been made to disguise this misfortune for a long time.

---

* *In Vino Veritas*. He also says: 'Gallantry is essentially woman's due; and the fact that she unconsciously accepts it may be explained by the solicitude of nature for the weak and the disadvantaged, those who feel more than recompensed by an illusion. But this illusion is precisely fatal . . . Is it not an even worse mockery to feel freed from misery – thanks to one's imagination, to be the dupe of imagination? Woman certainly is far from being *verwahrlost* [abandoned]; but inasmuch as she never can free herself from the illusion with which nature consoles her, she is.'

Guardianship, for example, was eliminated: the woman was given 'protectors' and if they were endowed with the rights of the old guardians, it
was in her best interest. Forbidding her to work and keeping her at home
is intended to defend her against herself and ensure her happiness. We
have seen the poetic veils used to hide the monotonous burdens she
bears: housework and maternity; in exchange for her freedom she was
given fallacious treasures of 'femininity' as a gift. Balzac described this
manoeuvre very well in advising a man to treat her as a slave while
persuading her she is a queen. Less cynical, many men endeavour to
convince themselves she is truly privileged. There are American sociol-
ogists seriously teaching today the theory of 'low-class gain', that is, the
'advantages of the lower castes'. In France as well it has often been
proclaimed – albeit less scientifically – that workers are indeed lucky not
to be obliged to 'present well', and, even more so tramps who could
dress in rags and sleep on the streets, pleasures that were forbidden to
the conte de Beaumont and those poor Wendel gentlemen. Like the
filthy carefree souls cheerfully scratching their vermin, like the joyful
Negroes laughing while being lashed, and like these gay Arabs of Sousse
with a smile on their lips, burying their children who starved to death,
the woman enjoys this incomparable privilege: irresponsibility. Without
difficulties, without responsibility, without cares, she obviously has 'the
best part'. What is troubling is that by a stubborn perversity – undoubtedly linked to original sin – across centuries and countries, the people
who have the best part always shout to their benefactors: It's too much!
I'll settle for yours! But the magnanimous capitalists, the generous colonialists, the superb males persist: Keep the best part, keep it!

The fact is that men encounter more complicity in their woman
companions than the oppressor usually finds in the oppressed; and in bad
faith they use it as a pretext to declare that woman *wanted* the destiny
they imposed on her. We have seen that in reality her whole education
conspires to bar her from paths of revolt and adventure; all of society –
beginning with her respected parents – lies to her in extolling the high
value of love, devotion and the gift of self and in concealing the fact that
neither lover, husband nor children will be disposed to bear the burdensome responsibility of it. She cheerfully accepts these lies because they
invite her to take the easy slope: and that is the worst of the crimes
committed against her; from her childhood and throughout her life, she
is spoiled, she is corrupted by the fact that this resignation, tempting to
any existent anxious about her freedom, is meant to be her vocation; if
one encourages a child to be lazy by entertaining him all day, without

giving him the occasion to study, without showing him its value, no one will say when he reaches the age of man that he chose to be incapable and ignorant; this is how the woman is raised, without ever being taught the necessity of assuming her own existence; she readily lets herself count on the protection, love, help and guidance of others; she lets herself be fascinated by the hope of being able to realise her being without *doing* anything. She is wrong to yield to this temptation; but the man is ill advised to reproach her for it since it is he himself who tempted her. When a conflict breaks out between them, each one will blame the other for the situation; she will blame him for creating it: no one taught me to reason, to earn my living . . . He will blame her for accepting it: you know nothing, you are incompetent . . . Each sex thinks it can justify itself by taking the offensive: but the wrongs of one do not absolve the other.

The innumerable conflicts that set men and women against each other stem from the fact that neither sex assumes all the consequences of this situation that one proposes and the other undergoes: this problematic notion of 'equality in inequality' that one uses to hide his despotism and the other her cowardice does not withstand the test of experience: in their exchanges, woman counts on the abstract equality she was guaranteed, and man the concrete inequality he observes. From there ensues the endless debate on the ambiguity of the words 'give' and 'take' in all relationships: she complains of giving everything; he protests that she takes everything from him. The woman has to understand that an exchange – a basic law of political economy – is negotiated according to the value the proposed merchandise has for the buyer and not for the seller: she was duped by being persuaded she was priceless; in reality she is merely a distraction, a pleasure, company, an inessential article for the man; for her he is the meaning, the justification of her existence; the two objects exchanged are thus not of the same quality; this inequality will be particularly noticeable because the time they spend together – and that fallaciously seems to be the same time – does not have the same value for both partners; during the evening the lover spends with his mistress, he might be doing something useful for his career, seeing friends, cultivating relations, entertaining himself; for a man normally integrated into his society, time is a positive asset: money, reputation, pleasure. By contrast, for the idle and bored woman time is a burden she aspires to get rid of; she considers it a benefit to succeed in killing time: the man's presence is pure profit; in many cases, what interests man the most in a relationship is the sexual gain he draws from it: he can, at worst, settle for spending just enough time with his mistress to perform the sex act, but what she herself wants – with rare exceptions – is to 'dispose of' all this excess time she has on her hands: and – like the shopkeeper who will not sell his potatoes if one does not 'take' his turnips – she only gives her body if the lover 'takes' hours of conversation and outings into the bargain. Balance can be established if the cost of the whole matter does not seem too high to the man: that depends, of course, on how intense is his desire and how important to him the occupations he sacrifices; but if the woman demands – offers – too much time, she becomes completely importunate, like the river that overflows its banks, and the man will choose to have nothing rather than to have too much. So she moderates her demands; but very often a balance is found at the price of a twofold tension: she believes that the man *has* her at a bargain price; he thinks he is paying too much. Of course this explanation is somewhat humorous; but – except in cases of jealous and exclusive passion where the man wants the woman in her entirety – this conflict, in tenderness, desire, even love, is always present; the man always has 'something else to do' with his time, whereas she is trying to get rid of hers; and he does not consider the hours she devotes to him as a gift but as a burden. Generally, he consents to tolerate it because he knows he is on the privileged side, he has a 'guilty conscience'; and if he has any goodwill, he tries to compensate for the unequal conditions with generosity; however, he gives himself credit for being compassionate and at the first clash he treats the woman as ungrateful, he gets irritated: I am too generous. She feels she is acting like a beggar while she is convinced of the high value of her gifts, and this humiliates her. This explains the cruelty of which the woman often shows herself capable; she feels 'self-righteous' because she has the bad role; she does not feel any obligation to accommodate the privileged caste, she thinks only of defending herself; she will even be very happy if she has the opportunity to display her resentment to the lover who has not been able to satisfy her: since he does not give enough, she will take everything back with fierce pleasure. Then the wounded man discovers the total price of the relationship whose every minute he disdained: he agrees to all the promises, even if it means he will again consider himself exploited when he has to honour them; he accuses his mistress of blackmailing him: she blames him for his stinginess; both consider themselves frustrated. Here too it is useless to allocate excuses and criticism: justice can never be created within injustice. It is impossible for a colonial administrator to conduct himself well with the indigenous population, or a general with his soldiers; the only solution is to be neither colonialist nor military leader; but a man cannot prevent himself from being a man.

So here he is, thus guilty in spite of himself and oppressed by this fault that he has not committed himself; likewise she is a victim and a shrew in spite of herself; sometimes he revolts, he chooses cruelty, but then he makes himself an accomplice of injustice, and the fault really becomes his; sometimes he allows himself to be destroyed, devoured, by his protesting victim: but then he feels duped; often he settles for a compromise that both diminishes him and puts him ill at ease. A man of goodwill will be more torn by the situation than the woman herself: in one sense, one is always better off being on the side of the defeated; but if she is also of goodwill, unable to be self-sufficient, unwilling to crush the man with the weight of her destiny, she struggles with herself in an inextricable confusion. One meets so many of these cases in daily life for which there are no satisfactory solutions because they are defined by unsatisfactory conditions: a man who sees himself as obligated to maintain a woman he no longer loves materially and morally feels he is a victim; but if he abandoned without resources the one who has committed her whole life to him, she would be a victim in an equally unjust manner. The wrong does not come from individual perversity – and bad faith arises when each person attacks the other – it comes from a situation in the face of which all individual behaviour is powerless. Women are 'clingy', they are a burden and they suffer from it; their lot is that of a parasite that sucks the life from a foreign organism; were they endowed with an autonomous organism, were they able to fight against the world and wrest their subsistence from it, their dependence would be abolished: the man's also. Both would undoubtedly be much better off for it.

A world where men and women would be equal is easy to imagine because it is exactly the one the Soviet revolution *promised*: women raised and educated exactly like men would work under the same conditions* and for the same salaries; erotic freedom would be accepted by custom, but the sexual act would no longer be considered a remunerable 'service'; women would be *obliged* to provide another livelihood for themselves; marriage would be based on a free engagement that the spouses could break when they wanted to; motherhood would be freely chosen – that is, birth control and abortion would be allowed – and in return all mothers and their children would be given the same rights; maternity

* That some arduous professions are prohibited to them does not contradict this idea: even men are seeking professional training more and more; their physical and intellectual capacities limit their choices; in any case, what is demanded is that no boundaries of sex or caste be drawn.

leave would be paid for by the society that would have responsibility for the children, which does not mean that they would be *taken* from their parents but that they would not be *abandoned* to them.

But is it enough to change laws, institutions, customs, public opinion and the whole social context for men and women to really become peers? 'Women will always be women,' say the sceptics; other seers prophesy that in shedding their femininity, they will not succeed in changing into men and will become monsters. This would mean that today's woman is nature's creation; it must be repeated again that within the human collectivity nothing is natural, and woman, among others, is a product developed by civilisation; the intervention of others in her destiny is originary: if this process were driven in another way, it would produce a very different result. Woman is defined neither by her hormones nor by mysterious instincts but by the way she grasps, through foreign consciousnesses, her body and her relation to the world; the abyss that separates adolescent girls from adolescent boys was purposely dug out from early infancy; later, it would be impossible to keep woman from being what she *was made*, and she will always trail this past behind her; if the weight of this past is accurately measured, it is obvious that her destiny is not fixed in eternity. One must certainly not think that modifying her economic situation is enough to transform woman: this factor has been and remains the primordial factor of her development, but until it brings about the moral, social and cultural consequences it heralds and requires, the new woman cannot appear; as of now, these consequences have been realised nowhere: in the USSR no more than in France or the United States; and this is why today's woman is torn between the past and the present; most often, she appears as a 'real woman' disguised as a man, and she feels as awkward in her woman's body as in her masculine garb. She has to shed her old skin and cut her own clothes. She will only be able to do this if there is a collective change. No one teacher can today shape a 'female human being' that would be an exact homologue to the 'male human being': if raised like a boy, the girl feels she is an exception and that subjects her to a new kind of specification. Stendhal understood this, saying: 'The forest must be planted all at once.' But if we suppose, by contrast, a society where sexual equality is concretely realised, this equality would newly assert itself in each individual.

If, from the earliest age, the little girl were raised with the same demands and honours, the same severity and freedom, as her brothers, taking part in the same studies and games, promised the same future, surrounded by women and men who are unambiguously equal to her, the meanings of the 'castration complex' and the 'Oedipus complex' would be profoundly modified. The mother would enjoy the same lasting prestige as the father if she assumed equal material and moral responsibility for the couple; the child would feel an androgynous world around her and not a masculine world; were she more affectively attracted to her father – which is not even certain – her love for him would be nuanced by a will to emulate him and not a feeling of weakness: she would not turn to passivity; if she were allowed to prove her worth in work and sports, actively rivalling boys, the absence of a penis – compensated for by the promise of a child – would not suffice to cause an 'inferiority complex'; correlatively, the boy would not have a natural 'superiority complex' if it were not instilled in him and if he held women in the same esteem as men.* The little girl would not seek sterile compensations in narcissism and dreams, she would not take herself as given, she would be interested in what she does, she would throw herself into her pursuits. I have said how much easier puberty would be if she surpassed it, like the boy, towards a free adult future; menstruation horrifies her only because it signifies a brutal descent into femininity; she would also assume her youthful eroticism more peacefully if she did not feel a frightening disgust for the rest of her destiny; a coherent sexual education would greatly help her to surmount this crisis. And thanks to coeducation, the august mystery of Man would have no occasion to arise: it would be killed by everyday familiarity and open competition. Objections to this system always imply respect for sexual taboos; but it is useless to try to inhibit curiosity and pleasure in children; this only results in creating repression, obsessions and neuroses; exalted sentimentality, homosexual fervour and the platonic passions of adolescent girls along with the whole procession of nonsense and dissipation are far more harmful than a few childish games and actual experiences. What would really be profitable for the girl is that, not seeking in the male a demigod – but only a pal, a friend, a partner – she not be diverted from assuming her own existence; eroticism and love would be a free surpassing and not a resignation; she could experience them in a relationship of equal to equal. Of course, there is no question of writing off all the difficulties a child must overcome to become an adult; the most intelligent, tolerant education could not free her from having her own experi-

---

* I know a little boy of eight who lives with a mother, aunt and grandmother, all three independent and active, and a grandfather who is half-senile. He has a crushing inferiority complex in relation to the female sex, though his mother tries to combat it. In his lycée he scorns his friends and professors because they are poor males.

ences at her own expense; what one would want is that obstacles should not accumulate gratuitously on her path. It is already an improvement that 'depraved' little girls are no longer cauterised with red-hot irons; psychoanalysis has enlightened parents somewhat; yet the conditions in which woman's sexual education and initiation take place today are so deplorable that none of the objections to the idea of a radical change are valid. It is not a question of abolishing the contingencies and miseries of the human condition in her but of giving her the means to go beyond them.

Woman is the victim of no mysterious fate; the singularities that make her different derive their importance from the meaning applied to them; they can be overcome as soon as they are grasped from new perspectives; we have seen that in her erotic experience, the woman feels – and often detests – male domination: it must not be concluded that her ovaries condemn her to living on her knees eternally. Virile aggressiveness is a lordly privilege only within a system where everything conspires to affirm masculine sovereignty; and woman *feels* so deeply passive in the love act only because she already *thinks* herself that way. Many modern women who claim their dignity as human beings still grasp their sexual lives by referring back to a tradition of slavery: so it seems humiliating to them to lie under the man and be penetrated by him, and they tense up into frigidity; but if reality were different, the meaning sexual gestures and postures symbolically express would be different as well: a woman who pays, who dominates her lover, can for example feel proud of her superb inertia and think that she is enslaving the male who is actively exerting himself; and today there are already many sexually balanced couples for whom notions of victory and defeat yield to an idea of exchange. In fact, man is, like woman, a flesh, thus a passivity, the plaything of his hormones and the species, uneasy prey to his desire; and she, like him, in the heart of carnal fever, is consent, voluntary gift and activity; each of them lives the strange ambiguity of existence made body in his or her own way. In these combats where they believe they are tackling each other, they are fighting their own self, projecting onto their partner the part of themselves they repudiate; instead of living the ambiguity of their condition, each one tries to make the other accept the abjection of this condition and reserves the honour of it for one's self. If, however, both assumed it with lucid modesty, as the correlate of authentic pride, they would recognise each other as peers and live the erotic drama in harmony. The fact of being a human being is infinitely more important than all the singularities that distinguish human beings; it is never the given that confers superiority: 'virtue', as the Ancients called it, is defined at the level of 'what depends on us'. The same drama of flesh and spirit, and of finitude and transcendence, plays itself out in both sexes; both are eaten away by time, stalked by death, they have the same essential need of the other; and they can take the same glory from their freedom; if they knew how to savour it, they would no longer be tempted to contend for false privileges; and fraternity could then be born between them.

People will say that all these considerations are merely utopian because to 'remake woman', society would have had to have already made her *really* man's equal; conservatives have never missed the chance to denounce this vicious circle in all analogous circumstances: yet history does not go round in circles. Without a doubt, if a caste is maintained in an inferior position, it remains inferior: but freedom can break the circle; let blacks vote and they become worthy of the vote; give woman responsibilities and she knows how to assume them; the fact is, one would not think of expecting gratuitous generosity from oppressors; but the revolt of the oppressed at times and changes in the privileged caste at other times create new situations; and this is how men, in their own interest, have been led to partially emancipate women: women need only pursue their rise and the success they obtain encourages them; it seems most certain that they will sooner or later attain perfect economic and social equality, which will bring about an inner metamorphosis.

In any case, some will object that if such a world is possible, it is not desirable. When woman is 'the same' as her male, life will lose 'its spice'. This argument is not new either: those who have an interest in perpetuating the present always shed tears for the marvellous past about to disappear without casting a smile on the young future. It is true that by doing away with slave markets, we destroyed those great plantations lined with azaleas and camellias, we dismantled the whole delicate Southern civilisation; old lace was put away in the attics of time along with the pure timbres of the Sistine castrati, and there is a certain 'feminine charm' that risks turning to dust as well. I grant that only a barbarian would not appreciate rare flowers, lace, the crystal-clear voice of a eunuch or feminine charm. When shown in her splendour, the 'charming woman' is a far more exalting object than 'the idiotic paintings, over-doors, décors, circus backdrops, sideboards or popular illuminations' that maddened Rimbaud; adorned with the most modern of artifices, worked on with the newest techniques, she comes from the remotest ages, from Thebes, Minos, Chichén Itzá; and she is also the totem planted in the heart of the African jungle; she is a helicopter and she is a bird; and here is the greatest wonder: beneath her painted hair, the rustling of leaves becomes a thought and words escape from her breasts. Men reach out their eager hands to the marvel; but as soon as they grasp it, it vanishes; the wife and the mistress speak like everyone else, with their mouths: their words are worth exactly what they are worth; their breasts as well. Does such a fleeting miracle – and one so rare – justify perpetuating a situation that is so damaging for both sexes? The beauty of flowers and women's charms can be appreciated for what they are worth; if these treasures are paid for with blood or misery, one must be willing to sacrifice them.

The fact is that this sacrifice appears particularly heavy to men; few of them really wish in their hearts to see women accomplish themselves; those who scorn woman do not see what they would have to gain, and those who cherish her see too well what they have to lose; and it is true that present-day developments not only threaten feminine charm: in deciding to live for herself, woman will abdicate the functions as double and mediator that provide her with her privileged place within the masculine universe; for the man caught between the silence of nature and the demanding presence of other freedoms, a being who is both his peer and a passive thing appears as a great treasure; he may well perceive his companion in a mythical form, but the experiences of which she is the source or pretext are no less real: and there are hardly more precious, intimate or urgent ones; it cannot be denied that feminine dependence, inferiority and misfortune give women their unique character; assuredly, women's autonomy, even if it spares men a good number of problems, will also deny them many conveniences; assuredly, there are certain ways of living the sexual adventure that will be lost in the world of tomorrow: but this does not mean that love, happiness, poetry and dreams will be banished from it. Let us beware lest our lack of imagination impoverish the future; the future is only an abstraction for us; each of us secretly laments the absence in it of what was; but tomorrow's humankind will live the future in its flesh and in its freedom; that future will be its present and humankind will in turn prefer it; new carnal and affective relations of which we cannot conceive will be born between the sexes: friendships, rivalries, complicities, chaste or sexual companionships that past centuries would not have dreamed of are already appearing. For example, nothing seems more questionable to me than a catchphrase that dooms the new world to uniformity and then to boredom. I do not see an absence of boredom in this world of ours nor that freedom has ever created uniformity. First of all, certain differences between man and woman will always exist; her eroticism, and thus her sexual world, possessing a singular form, cannot fail to engender in her a sensuality, a singular sensitivity: her relation to her body, to the male body and to the child will never be the same as those man has with his body, with the female body and with the child; those who talk so much about 'equality in difference' would be hard put not to grant me that there are differences in equality. Besides, it is institutions that create monotony: young and pretty, slaves of the harem are all the same in the sultan's arms; Christianity gave eroticism its flavour of sin and legend by endowing the human female with a soul; restoring woman's singular sovereignty will not remove the emotional value from amorous embraces. It is absurd to contend that orgies, vice, ecstasy and passion would become impossible if man and woman were concretely peers; the contradictions opposing flesh to spirit, instant to time, the vertigo of immanence to the appeal of transcendence, the absolute of pleasure to the nothingness of oblivion will never disappear; tension, suffering, joy and the failure and triumph of existence will always be materialised in sexuality. To emancipate woman is to refuse to enclose her in the relations she sustains with man, but not to deny them; while she posits herself for herself, she will nonetheless continue to exist for him *as well*: recognising each other as subject, each will remain an *other* for the other; reciprocity in their relations will not do away with the miracles that the division of human beings into two separate categories engenders: desire, possession, love, dreams, adventure; and the words that move us: 'to give', 'to conquer', and 'to unite' will keep their meaning; on the contrary, it is when the slavery of half of humanity is abolished and with it the whole hypocritical system it implies that the 'division' of humanity will reveal its authentic meaning and the human couple will discover its true form.

'The direct, natural, and necessary relation of person to person is the *relation of man to woman*,' said Marx.* From the character of this relationship follows how much man as *a species-being*, as man, has come to be himself and to comprehend himself; the relation of man to woman is the most natural relation of human being to human being. It therefore reveals the extent to which man's *natural* behaviour has become *human*, or the extent to which the *human* essence in him has become a *natural* essence – the extent to which his *human nature* has come to be *natural* to him.[2]

This could not be better said. Within the given world, it is up to man to make the reign of freedom triumph; to carry off this supreme victory, men and women must, among other things and above and beyond their natural differentiations, unequivocally affirm their brotherhood.

* *Philosophical Works*, Vol. VI. Marx's italics.

Notes

These translators' notes do not in any way constitute an annotated version of *The Second Sex*. They provide the translated versions of books and works to which Beauvoir makes reference and which we used in our translation. Where published translations do not exist, we give the title of the work in French only. When a translation into English exists, we have provided both French and English titles and bibliographic information for the title in English. Despite our best efforts, we were not able to find all of them. In addition we have noted a few discrepancies between the original text and our research.

Vol I: Introduction

1. Julien Benda, *Le rapport d'Uriel*.
2. Emmanuel Levinas, *Le Temps et l'autre. Time and the Other*, trans. Richard Cohen, Duquesne University Press, 1987.
3. Claude Lévi-Strauss, *Les structures élémentaires de la parenté. The Elementary Structures of Kinship*, trans. James Harle Bell, Rodney Needham and John Richard von Sturmer, Beacon Press, 1969.
4. *Mitsein* can be translated as 'being with'. The French term *réalité humaine* has been erroneously used to translate Heidegger's *Dasein*.
5. '*L'égalité dans la différence*' in the French text. Literal translation: 'different but equal'.

Vol I: Part One
Chapter 1 Biological Data

1. G. W. F. Hegel, *The Philosophy of Nature*, trans. J. N. Findlay and A. V. Miller, Oxford University Press, 1979.
2. Maurice Merleau-Ponty, *Phénoménologie de la perception. Phenomenology of Perception*, trans. Colin Smith, Routledge, 2005.
3. Jean-Paul Sartre, *L'Etre et le Néant. Being and Nothingness*, trans. Hazel Barnes, Citadel Press, 2001.

4. Paul Ancel, 'Histogenèse et structure de la glande hermaphrodite d'Helix pomatia (Linn.)', in *Archives de Biologie*, tome XIX, 1903.

5. Alfred Fouillée, *Tempérament et caractère selon les individus, les sexes et les races*.

6. *Bonellia viridis* is a sandworm that has no sex chromosomes.

Chapter 2 The Psychoanalytical Point of View

7. Roland Dalbiez, *La méthode psychanalytique et la doctrine freudienne. Psychoanalytical Method and the Doctrine of Freud*, Longmans, Green, & Co., 1941.

8. Sigmund Freud, *Moses and Monotheism*, trans. Katherine Jones, Knopf, 1939.

9. Charles Baudouin, *L'âme enfantine et la psychanalyse*.

10. Alice Bálint, *The Psychoanalysis of the Nursery*, Routledge and Kegan Paul, 1953.

11. Wilhelm Stekel, *Frigidity in Woman*, trans. James S. Van Teslaar, Liveright Publishing Corporation, 1943. *Frigidity in Woman* was published in French translation by Gallimard in 1937.

12. Sir James Donaldson, *Woman, Her Position and Influence in Ancient Greece and Rome, and Among the Early Christians*, Elibron Classics, 1906.

Chapter 3 The Point of View of Historical Materialism

13. Friedrich Engels, *The Origin of the Family, Private Property and the State*, trans. Alick West and Dona Torr, Marxist-Leninist Library, 1942.

14. Gaston Bachelard, *La Terre et les rêveries de la volonté. Earth and Reveries of Will*, trans. Kenneth Haltman, Dallas Institute of Humanities and Culture, 2002.

Vol I: Part Two, History
Chapter 2

1. Lévi-Strauss, *Les structures élémentaires de la parenté. The Elementary Structures of Kinship*.

2. Aeschylus, *Eumenides*, trans. Richard Lattimore, University of Chicago Press, 1969.

Chapter 3

3. King James Bible (Authorised Version).

4. '*Ubi tu Gaius, ego Gaia*': 'Where you are Gaius, I am Gaia.'

Chapter 4

5. *Mundium*: almost total legal guardianship over women by father and husband.

6. *Songe du verger*: treatise of political doctrine, written first in Latin (1370) and then in French (1378). Title usually kept in French.

7. *Lettre de cachet*: letter with a seal. It carries an official seal, usually signed by the king of France, authorising the imprisonment without trial of a named person.

8. *Uxor non est proprie socia sed speratur fore*: the wife is not exactly a partner, but it is hoped she will become one.

9. *Dictionnaire de la conversation*, 'Femmes et filles de folles vie'. Translation of Old French by Gabrielle Spiegel.

10. The title *Roman de la Rose* is usually kept in French.

11. *Querelle des femmes*: a literary quarrel traced to Christine de Pizan's objection to the portrayal of women in the *Roman de la Rose*, voiced in her *Epître au dieu d'amour* (*Epistle to the God of Love*), 1399, a debate that helped nurture literary production throughout the early modern period.

12. The original is from Lady Winchilsea's poem 'The Introduction'. Beauvoir shortened and paraphrased the quote when she translated it.

13. Discrepancy: In fact Mrs Aphra Behn, dramatist and novelist, lived from 1640 to 1689.

14. *La Nef des dames vertueuses*, *Le Chevalier des dames* and *Le Petit Sénat*.

15. *Déclamation de la noblesse et de l'excellence du sexe féminin. Declamation on the Nobility and Preeminence of the Female Sex*, ed. and trans. Albert Rabil, Jr; repr. University of Chicago Press, 1996.

16. *Le fort inexpugnable*.

17. *La parfaite amye*.

18. *Docte et subtil discours*.

19. *Les controverses des sexes masculin et féminin*.

20. Rabelais, *Tiers livre*.

21. *Alphabet de l'imperfection et malice des femmes*.

22. *Egalité des hommes et des femmes*.

23. *Parnasse et cabinets satyriques*. This title might be a confusion and combination of *Le cabinet satyrique* (1618) and *Le parnasse des poètes sartyriques* (1622).

24. *L'honneste femme*.

25. Molière, *Les précieuses ridicules* and *Les femmes savants*.

26. *De l'égalité des deux sexes*.

27. *Entretiens sur la pluralité des mondes.*
28. *Controverse sur l'âme de la femme.*

Chapter 5

29. The 'baker, the baker's wife and the baker's little boy' refer to King Louis XVI, the queen and the dauphin, forced by the starving people to leave Versailles for Paris, October 1789.
30. *Motion de la pauvre Javotte.*
31. Divorce was in fact abolished in 1816.
32. Balzac, Honoré de, *La Physiologie du mariage. The Physiology of Marriage.* trans. Sharon Maras, Johns Hopkins University Press, 1997.
33. Proudhon, Pierre-Joseph, *La Justice.*
34. Proudhon, *La pornocratie, ou Les femmes dans les temps modernes.*
35. *L'ouvrière.*
36. *Le travail des femmes au XIXe siècle.*
37. Beauvoir's calculations. 3 a.m. to 11 p.m adds up to twenty hours.
38. *Mémoires et aventures d'un prolétaire.* Cited from E. Dolléans, *Histoire du mouvement ouvrier,* vol. I.
39. *La verité sur les événements de Lyon.*
40. Discrepancy in Beauvoir's calculations. The totals are 2,664,924 unionised workers, and 275,209 women.
41. Discrepancy in Beauvoir's calculations. The totals are 1.850 million.
42. *La Précieuse, l'abbé de Pure.* Usually kept in French. Literally 'the precious woman', i.e. sophisticated, refined.
43. From John Stuart Mill, 'The Subjection of Women', reprinted in *Philosophy of Women,* ed. Mary Briody Mahowald.
44. The convention actually took place 19–20 July, 1848.
45. President Woodrow Wilson.
46. The name of the city was Petrograd from 1914–24.
47. Jean-Paul Sartre, *Réflexions sur la question juive. Anti-Semite and Jew,* trans. George J. Becker, Schocken, 1948.

Vol I: Part Three, Myths
Chapter 1

1. Michel Carrouges, 'Les pouvoirs de la femme' (Chapter 1), *Cahiers du Sud,* no. 292 (1948).
2. Søren Kierkegaard, *Stages on Life's Way,* trans. H. V. Hong, Princeton University Press, 1989.
3. Carl Jung, *Metamorphoses of the Libido and its Symbols,* in *Collected Works of C. G. Jung,* trans. R. F. C. Hull, Princeton University Press, 1967.

4. André Breton, *Arcanum 17*, trans. Zach Rogow, Green Integer, 2004.

5. Leopold Sédar Senghor, *Oeuvres Poetiques Completes. The Collected Poetry*, trans. Melvin Dixon, University of Virginia Press, 1991.

6. Most likely: '*Post coitum omne animal triste.*' All animals are sad after sex.

7. Jean-Richard Bloch, *La Nuit kurde. A Night in Kurdistan*, trans. Stephen Haden Guest, Victor Gollancz Ltd, 1930.

8. 'A temple built over a sewer.'

9. 'We are born between shit and piss.'

10. Michel Leiris, *La mère. 'The Mother'*, trans. Beverley Bie Brahic.

11. Paul Valéry. Poem translated by James Lawler.

12. Honoré de Balzac, *Le lys dans la vallée. The Lily in the Valley*, trans. Lucienne Hill, Carroll & Graf Publishers, Inc., 1997.

13. Gustave Flaubert, *L'education sentimentale. Sentimental Education*, trans. Robert Baldick, Penguin, 1964.

14. André Malraux, *La condition humaine. Man's Fate*, trans. Haakon M. Chevalier, The Modern Library, 1934.

15. 'Notre petite campagne'. No source for this poem is provided by Simone de Beauvoir.

16. Georges de Porto-Riche, *Amoureuse*, 1891.

17. *La Glu*, a play by Jean Richepin, 1883.

18. Schwob, Marcel, *Le Livre de Monelle. The Book of Monelle*, trans. William Brown-Maloney, Bobbs-Merrill Company, 1929.

Chapter 2
Montherlant or the Bread of Disgust

19. Henry de Montherlant, *Pitié pour les femmes. Pity for Women*, Knopf, 1937.

20. Montherlant, *L'exil*.

21. Montherlant, *Les Célibataires. The Bachelors*, trans. Terence Kilmartin, Greenwood Press, 1977.

22. Montherlant, *Les Jeunes Filles. The Girls*, trans. Terence Kilmartin, Harper & Row, 1968.

23. Montherlant, *Le Songe. The Dream*, trans. Terence Kilmartin, Macmillan, 1963.

24. Quotation from Ecclesiastes not found.

25. Montherlant, *La Petite Infante de Castille. The Little Infanta of Castile*, French & European Pubns, 1973.

26. *Aux Fontaines du désir.*

27. *Le Maitre de Santiago. The Master of Santiago*, trans. Jonathan Griffen, Knopf, 1951.

28. *Le solstice de juin.*
29. *L'equinoxe de septembre.*
30. *La reine morte.*
31. *La possession de soi-même.*

Claudel or the Handmaiden of the Lord

32. *Partage de midi*, trans. Wallace Fowlie. All other Claudel translations are by James Lawler.
33. *Les aventures de Sophie.*
34. *La cantate à trois voix.*
35. *Conversations dans le Loir-et-Cher.*
36. *Le soulier de satin.*
37. *L'annonce faite à Marie.*
38. *L'échange.*
39. *L'oiseau noir dans le soleil levant.*
40. *Positions et propositions.*
41. *La ville.*
42. *La jeune fille Violaine.*
43. *Le pain dur.*
44. *Livre de Tobie et de Sara.*
45. *Le père humilié.*
46. *Feuilles de saints.*
47. *L'otage.*

Breton or Poetry

48. *Nadja*, trans. Richard Howard, Grove Press, 1994.
49. *L'amour fou. Mad Love*, trans. Mary Ann Caws, University of Nebraska Press, 1988.
50. *Les vases communicants. Communicating Vessels*, trans. Mary Ann Caws and Geoffrey Harris, University of Nebraska Press, 1990.
51. Arthur Rimbaud, 'Vagabonds' in *Illuminations:* trans. Helen Rootham, New Directions, 1943.
52. Arthur Rimbaud, 'Adieu (Farewell) in *Une saison en enfer, A Season in Hell*, Part III: trans. Delmore Schwartz, New Directions, 1939.
53. Breton, *Arcanum 17.*
54. *Poems of André Breton: A Bilingual Anthology*, trans. Mary Ann Caws, University of Texas Press, 1982.
55. Ibid.
56. Ibid.

Stendhal or Romancing the Real

57. 'L'esprit de sérieux': conventional thinking.
58. *Chroniques italiennes.*

Chapter 3

59. *L'âge d'homme.*
60. Choderlos de Laclos, *Les liaisons dangereuses. Dangerous Liaisons*, trans. P. W. K. Stone, Penguin, 1961.
61. Stendhal, *Le rouge et le noir. The Red and the Black*, trans. Roger Gard, Penguin, 2002.

Vol. II: Part One
Chapter 1 Childhood

1. Jacques Lacan, *Les complexes familiaux dans la formation de l'individu.*
2. Yassu Gauclère, *L'orange bleue.*
3. Maurice Sachs, *Le Sabbat. Witches' Sabbath*, trans. Richard Howard, Jonathan Cape, 1965.
4. François Rabelais, *The Complete Works*, trans. Donald M. Frame, University of California Press, 1991.
5. Bàlint, *The Psychoanalysis of the Nursery.*
6. Helene Deutsch, *The Psychology of Women*, Bantam, 1973.
7. Havelock Ellis, *Ondinism*, Random House.
8. Havelock Ellis, *Studies in the Psychology of Sex*, vol. XIII, The Minerva Group Inc., 2001.
9. Raymond de Saussure, 'Psycholgie génétique et psychanalyse'. 'Psychogenesis and Psychoanalysis'.
10. Marie Bashkirtseff, *Mon Journal. I am the Most Interesting Book of All.*
11. Carl Jung, *The Development of Personality*, 'Psychic Conflicts of a Child', trans. R. F. C. Hull, Princeton University Press, 1970.
12. Marie Le Hardouin, *La voile noire.*
13. Colette Audry, *Aux yeux du souvenir.*
14. Violette Leduc, *L'asphyxie*; S. de Tervagne, *La haine maternelle*; H. Bazin, *Vipère au poing*, trans. W. J. Strachan, Prentice Hall, 1951.
15. Charles Baudouin, *l'âme enfantine.*
16. Colette, *La maison de Claudine, Claudine's House*, trans. Andrew Brown, Hesperus Press, 2006.
17. Carson McCullers, *The Member of the Wedding*, Penguin Classics, 1962.
18. Wilhelm Liepmann, *Jeunesse et sexualité.*
19. Horlam, *Garçonnet et fillette.*

20. Richard Hughes, *A High Wind in Jamaica*, Harper & Brothers, 1925.
21. Margaret Kennedy, *The Constant Nymph*, Doubleday, Page, 1925.
22. Stekel, *Frigidity in Woman*.
23. Wilhelm Stekel, *Lettres à une mère*.
24. Colette Audry, *Aux yeux du souvenir*.
25. Thyde Monnier, *Moi*, du Rocher, Monaco, 1949.
26. 'Sweet girl'.

Chapter 2 The Girl

27. Wilhelm Liepmann, *Jeunesse et sexualité*.
28. Rosamond Lehmann, *Invitation to the Waltz*, Virago, 2006.
29. Marie Bashkirtseff, *I Am the Most Interesting Book of All*.
30. Leo Tolstoy, *War and Peace*, trans. Richard Pevear and Larissa Volokhonsky, Knopf, 2008.
31. Katherine Mansfield, 'Prelude', in *The Short Stories of Katherine Mansfield*, Knopf, 1937.
32. Maurice Debesse, *La crise d'originalité juvénile*. This is cited by de Beauvoir as *La Crise d'originalité de l'adolescent*.
33. Marguerite Evard, *L'adolescente*.
34. From Borel and Robin, *Les reveries morbides*. Cited by Minkowski in *La schizophrénie*. Borel and Robin wrote *Les rêveurs éveillés* (Daydreamers). Minkowski wrote an article, 'De la rêverie morbide au délire d'influence' (From Morbid Reverie to Delusions of Grandeur).
35. *Mädchen in Uniform* (German film), 1931.
36. Colette, *Claudine à l'école. Claudine at School*, trans. Antonia White, Farrar, Straus & Giroux, 2001.
37. Rosamond Lehmann, *Dusty Answer*, Virago Press, 2008.
38. P. Mendousse, *L'âme de l'adolescente*.
39. Clemence Dane, *Regiment of Women*, Virago Press, 1995.
40. Renée Vivien, 'Psappha revit', in *A l'heure des mains jointes*, trans. Gillian Spraggs.
41. Renée Vivien, 'Pareilles', in *Sillages*, trans. Gillian Spraggs.
42. Deutsch, *The Psychology of Women*.
43. Le Hardouin, *La voile noire*.
44. Mme de Ségur, *Quel amour d'enfant!*
45. Stekel, *Frigidity in Woman*.
46. Colette, *Le blé en herbe. Green Wheat*, trans. Zach Rogow, Sarabande Books, 2004.
47. Colette, *Sido*, trans. Una Vicenzo Troubridge and Enid McLeod, Farrar, Straus & Giroux, 2002.

48. Mary Webb, *The House in Dormer Forest*, Kessinger Publishing, 1945.
49. Virginia Woolf, *The Waves*, Hogarth Press, 1931.
50. Mary Webb, *Precious Bane*, E. P. Dutton, New York, 1926.

Chapter 3 Sexual Initiation

51. The Kinsey Reports are two books on human sexual behaviour: *Sexual Behavior in the Human Male*, 1948, and *Sexual Behavior in the Human Female*, 1953, by Alfred Kinsey, Wardell Pomeroy and others.
52. Benda, *Le rapport d'Uriel*.
53. Isadora Duncan, *My Life*, Boni & Liveright, 1955.
54. Stekel, *Frigidity in Woman*.
55. Renée Vivien, *At the Sweet Hour of Hand in Hand*, trans. Gillian Spraggs.
56. Duncan, *My Life*. Discrepancy between Isadora Duncan's words: 'The next day we remained in the country, Romeo frequently hushing my cries and drying my tears. I felt as if I were crippled', and those of Simone de Beauvoir in the text.
57. www.gutenberg.org.
58. Stekel, *Frigidity in Woman*. Discrepancy in initials: 'K. L.' in the English translation of Stekel's German text.
59. Ibid. Not in the English translation of Stekel's German text.
60. Colette, *Le blé en herbe. Green Wheat*.
61. Michel de Montaigne, *The Complete Essays of Montaigne*, trans. Donald M. Frame, Stanford University Press, 1965.
62. Juvenal: 'Her secret parts burning are tense with lust,/And, tired by men, but far from sated, she withdrew.'
63. Marie Le Hardouin, *La voile noire*.
64. Jean-Paul Sartre, *L'Etre et le Néant. Being and Nothingness*.
65. Marquis de Sade, *La Philosophie dans le boudoir. Philosophy in the Boudoir*, trans. Joachim Neugroschel, Penguin, 2006.
66. Jean-Paul Sartre, *L'Etre et le Néant. Being and Nothingness*.
67. Colette, *Mes apprentissages. My Apprenticeships & Music-Hall Sidelights*, trans. Helen Beauclerk, Penguin Books, 1967.

Chapter 4 The Lesbian

68. Denis de Rougement, *La part du diable. The Devil's Share*, trans. Haakon Chevalier, Pantheon Books, 1944.
69. Colette, *Aux yeux du souvenir*.
70. Roland Dalbiez, *La méthode psychanalytique et la doctrine freudienne. Psychoanalytical Method and the Doctrine of Freud*.

71. Richard von Krafft-Ebing, *Psychopathia Sexualis*, Rebman, Kessinger Publishing, 1906.

72. Havelock Ellis, *Studies in the Psychology of Sex*, Vol. 2, *Sexual Inversion*, The Minerva Group, Inc., 2001.

73. Colette, *Ces plaisirs. The Pure and the Impure*, trans. Herma Briffault, New York Review of Books, 2001.

74. Discrepancy between Renée Vivien's poem quoted by Beauvoir and Vivien's published version, both translated by Gillian Spraggs.

75. Cited incorrectly by Beauvoir as *Sortilèges*, which is non-existent; poem from translation of *Sillages* (*Sea Wakes*), 1908.

76. Colette, *Les vrilles de la vigne. Tender Shoot*, trans. Antonia White, Farrar, Straus & Giroux, 1975.

77. From *At the Sweet Hour of Hand in Hand*.

78. Discrepancy between Vivien's poem quoted by Beauvoir and Vivien's published version, both translated by Gillian Spraggs; from 'Je t'aime d'être faible' (I love you to be weak), in *At the Sweet Hour of Hand in Hand*.

79. Radclyffe Hall, *The Well of Loneliness*, Wordsworth Editions, 2005.

80. Thyde Monnier, *Moi*.

Vol. II: Part Two
Chapter 5 The Married Woman

1. Emile Zola, *Pot-Bouille*, Everyman/Orion, London, 1999.

2. Bronislaw Malinowski, 'The Bachelors' House', in *The Sexual Life of Savages in North-Western Melanesia*, Liveright, 1929.

3. Colette, *La maison de Claudine. Claudine's House*.

4. Claire Leplae, *Les fiancailles*.

5. Our translation of '*Club des lisières vertes*', source unknown.

6. Stekel, *Frigidity in Woman*.

7. Michel de Montaigne, *The Complete Essays of Montaigne*, trans. Donald M. Frame.

8. G. W. F. Hegel, *Phenomenology of the Spirit*, trans. A. V. Miller, Oxford University Press, 1977.

9. All Montaigne quotes are from *Complete Essays*.

10. Balzac, *Physiologie du mariage. The Physiology of Marriage*.

11. Honoré de Balzac, *Mémoires de jeune Mariés. Letters of Two Brides*, trans. R. S. Scott, Hard Press, 2006.

12. Balzac, *Le lys dans la vallée. The Lily in the Valley*.

13. Søren Kierkegaard, 'Some Reflections on Marriage', in *Stages on Life's Way*.

14. Georges de Porto-Riche, *Amoureuse*, 1891.

15. Colette, *L'ingénue libertine. The Innocent Libertine*, trans. Antonia White, Farrar Straus & Giroux, 1978.

16. *Ce que tout mari doit savoir, Le secret du bonheur conjugal* and *L'amour sans peur.*

17. Colette, *La maison de Claudine. Claudine's House.*

18. Wilhelm Stekel, *Conditions of Nervous Anxiety and Their Treatment*, Liveright Publishing Corporation, 1950.

19. Henri Michaux, 'Nuit de noces'. 'Bridal Night', in 'La nuit remue' – See *Selected Writings*, A New Directions Book, 1968.

20. Pierre Janet, *Les obsessions et la psychasthénie*, 1903.

21. Denis Diderot, *Sur les femmes. On Women*, trans. Francis Birrell, Routledge, 1927.

22. François Mauriac, *Thérèse Desqueyroux*, trans. Raymond MacKenzie, Rowman & Littlefield Publishers Inc., 2005.

23. Colette, *La vagabonde. The Vagabond*, trans. Enid McLeod, Farrar, Straus & Giroux, 1955.

24. *Nature et formes de la jalousie.* Beauvoir's title is mistaken. Lagache's work on jealousy is called *La Jalousie amoureuse (Jealousy in Love).*

25. Marcel Jouhandeau, *Chroniques maritales. Marcel and Elise, The Bold Chronicle of a Strange Marriage*, trans. Martin Turnell, Pantheon Books, 1953.

26. Henry Bordeaux, *La maison.*

27. Rilke to Lou Andreas-Salomé, 8 August 1903.

28. Virginia Woolf, *The Waves*, Hogarth Press, 1931.

29. Gaston Bachelard, *La terre et les rêveries du repos. Earth and Reveries of Repose*, trans. Kenneth Haltman.

30. Virginia Woolf, *To the Lighthouse*, in *The Selected Works of Virginia Woolf*, Wordsworth Editions, 2005.

31. Madeleine Bourdouxhe, *A la recherche de Marie. Marie*, trans. Faith Evans, Bloomsbury, 1997.

32. Bachelard, *La terre et les rêveries du repos. Earth and Reveries of Repose.*

33. In French 'wash boiler', or *lessiveuse*, is feminine, and where English uses the pronoun 'it', French uses *elle*, that is, 'she'. Playing on this ambiguity throughout his text, Ponge gives the wash boiler a feminine identity and presence.

34. Francis Ponge, 'The Wash Boiler' from *Liasse (Sheaf)*; passage translated by Beverley Bie Brahic.

35. Colette, 'La poussière' in *On joue perdant*. 'Dust' in *Playing a Losing Game.*

36. Colette, *Sido.*

37. Jouhandeau, *Chroniques maritales. The Bold Chronicle of a Strange Marriage.*

38. Jacques Chardonne, *L'épithalame.* Epithalamium.

39. Violette Leduc, *L'affamée.*

40. Passage translated by Nina de Voogd Fuller.

41. Bachelard, *La terre et les rêveries de la volonté. Earth and Reveries of Will.*

42. Jules Michelet, *La Montagne. The Mountain*, from *Complete Works*, trans. W. H. Davenport Adams, T. Nelson & Sons, 1872.

43. Dorothy Parker, 'Too Bad!', in *The Portable Dorothy Parker*, Penguin Books, 1944.

44. Friedrich Nietzsche, *The Gay Science*, trans. Walter Kaufmann, Vintage, 1974.

45. *The Diaries of Sophia Tolstoy*, trans. Cathy Porter, Random House, 1985.

46. Ibid. Discrepancy between the French and English translations. In the English text the date is given as April 29.

47. Colette, *La maison de Claudine. Claudine's House.*

48. Marcel Prévost, *Lettres à Françoise mariée.*

49. Janet, *Obsessions.*

50. Edith Wharton, *The Age of Innocence*, Random House, 1999.

51. *Diaries of Sophia Tolstoy*, 19 December 1863.

52. Mauriac, *Thérèse Desqueyroux.*

53. 'Prelude', in *The Short Stories of Katherine Mansfield*, Knopf, 1937.

54. *Diaries of Sophia Tolstoy.* Discrepancy between French and English translations. The date is given as January 17 in the English translation of *The Diaries.*

55. Ibid. In the English translation the date given is September 17.

56. Henrik Ibsen, *A Doll's House*, in *Four Major Plays*, trans. James McFarlane and Jens Arup, Oxford University Press, 1981.

57. Daniel Halévy, *Jules Michelet*, Hachette, 1928 and 1947.

58. Mabel Dodge Luhan, *Lorenzo in Taos*, Knopf, 1932.

59. Jouhandeau, *Nouvelles Chroniques maritales. The Bold Chronicle of a Strange Marriage.*

60. Leo Tolstoy, *War and Peace.*

61. Dorothy Parker, 'Too Bad!'.

62. Jouhandeau, *Nouvelles Chroniques maritales. The Bold Chronicle of a Strange Marriage.*

63. *Diaries of Sophia Tolstoy.* The date is given as November 13 1863 in the English translation.

64. Ibid. The date is given in the English text as October 12 1863.

65. Maurice Halbwachs, *Les causes du suicide. The Causes of Suicide*, trans. Harold Goldblatt, Free Press, 1978.

Chapter 6 The Mother

66. Colette, 'L'enfant', in *Playing a Losing Game*.
67. Helene Deutsch, *The Psychology of Women*.
68. Duchesse d'Abrantès, *Mémoires. Memoirs*, J & J Harper, 1832.
69. Colette, *L'étoile vesper. The Evening Star*, in *Recollections*, trans. David Le Vay, Collier Books, 1973.
70. Cecile Sauvage, *L'âme en bourgeon*.
71. Translated by Beverley Bie Brahic.
72. Isadora Duncan, *My Life*, Liveright Publishing Corporation, 1955.
73. Translated by Beverley Bie Brahic.
74. Colette, *L'étoile vesper. The Evening Star*.
75. *Diaries of Sophia Tolstoy*. Beauvoir attributes this quote to Sophia, but it is in fact Leo's.
76. Jules Renard, *Poil de carotte. Carrot Top*, trans. Ralph Manheim, Farrar, Straus & Giroux, 1975.
77. Simone de Tervagne, *La haine maternelle*.
78. Hervé Bazin, *Vipère au poing. Viper in the Fist*, trans. W. J. Strachan, Prentice Hall, 1951.
79. François Mauriac, *Génétrix. A Kiss for the Leper / Genitrix*, trans. Gerard Hopkins, Eyre & Spottiswoode, 1953.
80. Violette Leduc, *In the Prison of Her Skin*.
81. Stekel, *Conditions of Nervous Anxiety and Their Treatment*.

Chapter 7 Social Life

82. Marie Bashkirtseff, *Ecrits intimes*.
83. *The Diaries of Sophia Tolstoy*.
84. Dorothy Parker, 'The Lovely Leave'. Beauvoir mistakenly calls this short story 'The Lovely Eva'.
85. Virginia Woolf, *Mrs Dalloway*, Penguin Books, 1967.
86. Colette, *Mes apprentissages. My Apprenticeships & Music-Hall Sidelights*.
87. Colette, *Le képi. The Kepi*, trans. Antonia White, Secker & Warburg, 1984.
88. Stekel, *Frigidity in Woman*.
89. Montaigne, *Complete Essays*: 'On Some Verses of Virgil'.
90. Engels, *The Origin of the Family*.
91. Colette, *L'ingenue libertine. The Innocent Libertine*.
92. Janet, *Les obsessions et la psychasthénie*.

93. Joseph Kessel; the real title is *Belle de Jour*.
94. André Malraux, *La condition humaine. Man's Fate*, trans. Haakon M. Chevalier, The Modern Library, 1934.

Chapter 8 Prostitutes and Hetaeras

95. Montaigne, *Complete Essays*.
96. A. Marro, 'The Psychology of Puberty', *British Journal of Psychiatry* (1910).
97. A.J.B. Parent-Duchâtelet, 'De la prostitution dans la ville de Paris' ('Prostitution in the City of Paris'), Brussels: Société Encyclographique des Sciences Médicales, 1838.
98. Dr Léon Bizard, *Souvenirs d'un médecin . . . des prisons de Paris* (*Memoirs of a Doctor of Paris Prisons*), 1925.
99. Dr Louis Faivre, *Les jeunes prostituées vagabondes en prison*, Librairie Le François, 1931. Medical thesis.
100. In the French text of these passages there are grammar and spelling errors that we have not reproduced in English.
101. Pet name for a prostitute's pimp.
102. From internet: bookaddicts.wordpress.com/
103. Ibid.

Chapter 9 From Maturity to Old Age

104. Rom Landau, *Sex, Life and Faith*, Faber & Faber, 1946.

Chapter 10 Woman's Situation and Character

105. Jean-Paul Sartre, 'Les mains sales'. 'Dirty Hands', in *Three Plays*, trans. Lionel Abel, Knopf, 1949.
106. French proverb: 'What woman wants, God wants.'
107. André Gide, *Les journaux d'André Gide. The Journals of André Gide*, trans. Justin O'Brien, Penguin Modern Classics, 1967.
108. Halbwachs, *The Causes of Suicide*.
109. Mauriac, *Thérèse Desqueyroux*.

Vol. II: Part Three
Chapter 11 The Narcissist

1. Dalbiez, *La méthode psychanalytique et la doctrine freudienne. Psycho-analytical Method and the Doctrine of Freud*.
2. Mme de Noailles, *Le livre de ma vie*.
3. Dorothy Parker, 'Too Bad!'
4. Colette Audry, *La poussière*.

5. Balzac, *Le lys dans la vallée. The Lily in the Valley.*
6. 'Ten years' in the English translation of Stekel's *Frigidity in Woman.*
7. Mabel Dodge Luhan, *Lorenzo in Taos*, Simone de Beauvoir's italics.

Chapter 12 The Woman in Love

8. Nietzsche, *Le Gai Savoir. The Gay Science.*
9. Pierre Janet, *Les obsessions et la psychasthénie.*
10. Translated by Beverley Bie Brahic.
11. Colette, *La vagabonde. The Vagabond.*
12. Mary Webb, *The House in Dormer Forest*, Kessinger Publishing, 1945.
13. Isadora Duncan, *My Life.*
14. Comment inserted by Beauvoir and not part of the English translation.
15. Jean-Paul Sartre, *L'etre et le Néant. Being and Nothingness.*
16. Violette Leduc, *Je hais les dormeurs.*
17. Marcel Arland, *Terres étrangères.*
18. Nietzsche, *Le Gai Savoir. The Gay Science.*
19. Fanny Hurst, *Back Street*, Grosset, 1931.
20. Rosamond Lehmann, *Intempéries. The Weather in the Streets*, Virago Press, 1981.
21. The correct title of Lagache's work on jealousy is *La jalousie amoureuse* (*Jealousy in Love*).
22. Dominique Rolin, *Moi qui ne suis qu'amour.*
23. Georges Gusdorf, *La découverte de soi.* Simone de Beauvoir gives the title of his work as *La connaissance de soi.*
24. Nietzsche, *Le Gai Savoir. The Gay Science.*

Chapter 13 The Mystic

25. Gaston Ferdière, *L'erotomanie. Erotomania.*

Vol. II: Part Four
Chapter 14 The Independent Woman

1. *Le numéro 17.*
2. Colette, *Le blé en herbe. Green Wheat.*
3. Clara Malraux, *Portrait de Grisélidis.*
4. André Malraux, *La condition humaine. Man's Fate.*
5. 'Normalians' are students or graduates from the Ecole Normale Supérieure, prestigious school of higher education in France.
6. Colette, *La naissance du jour. Break of Day*, trans. Enid McLeod, Limited Editions Club, 1983.

7. Paulhan, *Les fleurs de Tarbes*.

8. *'Poussières'* in the French: Beauvoir does not specify the author, but this is probably a reference to Rosamond Lehmann's *Dusty Answer*.

9. Margaret Kennedy, *The Constant Nymph*.

10. Stendhal, *Souvenirs d'égotisme. Memoirs of an Egotist*, trans. David Ellis, Horizon Press, 1975.

Conclusion

1. Marcel Jouhandeau, *Chroniques maritales. Marcel and Elise, The Bold Chronicle of a Strange Marriage*.

2. Marx and Engels, *Collected Works*, Vol. VI.

Selected Sources

The works listed below are the published English translations that the translators consulted for Simone de Beauvoir's French quotes, as well as the English-language books and publications themselves, for example, when she paraphrases an author. But the works are also included here as 'selected sources'.

Abrantès, Laure Junot: *Memoires of the Duchess d'Abrantès (Madame Junot)*. J&J Harper 1882.

Aeschylus: *Eumenides*. Translated by Richard Lattimore. University of Chicago Press 1969.

Angela of Foligno: *Complete Works*, Paulist Press 1993.

Bachelard, Gaston: *Earth and Reveries of Repose*. Translated by Kenneth Haltman. Unpublished.

Bachelard, Gaston: *Earth and Reveries of Will*. Translated by Kenneth Haltman. Dallas Institute of Humanities and Culture 2002.

Bálint, Alice: *The Psychoanalysis of the Nursery*. Routledge and Kegan Paul 1953.

Balzac, Honoré de: *Letters of Two Brides*. Translated by R. S. Scott. Hard Press 2006.

Balzac, Honoré de: *The Lily in the Valley*. Translated by Lucienne Hill. Carroll & Graf 1997.

Balzac, Honoré de: *The Physiology of Marriage*. Translated by Sharon Marcus, Johns Hopkins University Press 1997.

Bashkirtseff, Marie: *I Am the Most Interesting Book of All: The Diary of Marie Bashkirtseff*. Translated by Phyllis Howard Kernberger and Katherine Kernberger. Chronicle Books 1997.

Bazin, Hervé: *Viper in the Fist*. Translated by W. J. Strachan. Prentice Hall 1951.

Bloch, Jean-Richard: *A Night in Kurdistan*. Translated by Stephen Haden Guest. Victor Gollancz 1930.

Bourdouxhe, Madeleine: *Marie*. Translated by Faith Evans. Bloomsbury 1997.

Breton, André: *Arcanum 17*. Translated by Zach Rogow. Green Integer 2004.

Breton, André: *Communicating Vessels*. Translated by Mary Ann Caws and Geoffrey Harris. Nebraska University Press 1990.

Breton, André: *Mad Love*. Translated by Mary Ann Caws. Bison Books 1988.

Breton, André: *Nadja*. Translated by Richard Howard. Grove Press 1994.

Breton, André: *Poems of André Breton: A Bilingual Anthology*. Translated by Mary Ann Caws, University of Texas Press 1982.

Colette: *Break of Day*. Translated by Enid McLeod. Limited Editions Club 1983.

Colette: *Claudine at School*. Translated by Antonia White. Farrar, Straus & Giroux 2001.

Colette: *Claudine's House*. Translated by Andrew Brown. Hesperus Press 2006.

Colette: *The Evening Star*, in *Recollections*. Translated by David Le Vay. Bobbs-Merrill 1973.

Colette: *Green Wheat*. Translated by Zach Rogow. Sarabande Books 2004.

Colette: *The Innocent Libertine*. Translated by Antonia White. Farrar, Straus & Giroux 1978.

Colette: *The Kepi*. Translated by Antonia White. Secker and Warburg 1984.

Colette: *My Apprenticeships & Music-Hall Sidelights*. Translated by Helen Beauclerk. Penguin 1967.

Colette: *The Pure and the Impure*. Translated by Herma Briffault. New York Review of Books 2000.

Colette: *Sido*. Translated by Una Vicenzo Troubridge and Enid McLeod. Farrar, Straus & Giroux 2002.

Colette: *The Tender Shoot*. Translated by Antonia White. Farrar Straus & Giroux 1975.

Colette: *The Vagabond*. Translated by Enid McLeod. Farrar, Straus & Giroux 1955.

Dalbiez, Roland: *Psychoanalytical Method and the Doctrine of Freud*. Longmans, Green & Co. 1941.

Deutsch, Helene: *The Psychology of Women*. Bantam Books 1973.

Diderot, Denis: 'On Women in Dialogues'. Translated by Francis Birrell. Routledge 1927.

Duncan, Isadora: *My Life*. Boni & Liveright 1955.

Ellis, Havelock: *Studies in the Psychology of Sex: Sexual Inversion*. The Minerva Group, Inc. 2001.

Engels, Friedrich: *The Origin of the Family, Private Property and the State*. Translated by Alick West and Dona Torr. Marxist-Leninist Library 1942.

Flaubert, Gustave: *Sentimental Education*. Translated by Robert Baldich. Penguin Books 1964.

Freud, Sigmund: *Moses and Monotheism*. Translated by Katherine Jones. Knopf 1939.

Gide, André: *The Coiners*. Translated by Dorothy Bussy. Cassell 1950.

Gide, André: *The Journals of André Gide*. Translated by Justin O'Brien. Penguin Modern Classics 1967.

Halbwachs, Maurice: *The Causes of Suicide*. Translated by Harold Goldblatt. Free Press 1978.

Halévy, Daniel: *Jules Michelet*. Hachette 1928 and 1947.

Hall, Radclyffe: *The Well of Loneliness*. Wordsworth Editions 2005.

Hegel, G. W. F.: *Phenomenology of Spirit*. Translated by A. V. Miller. Oxford University Press 1977.

Hegel, G. W. F.: *The Philosophy of Nature*. Translated by J. N. Findlay and A. V. Miller. Oxford University Press 1979.

Huart, Clément: *Ancient Persia and Iranian Civilization*. Knopf 1927.

Hughes, Richard: *High Wind in Jamaica*. Harper & Brothers 1929.

Hurst, Fanny: *Back Street*. Grosset 1931.

Ibsen, Henrik: *A Doll's House*, in *Eleven Plays of Henrik Ibsen*. Modern Library 1935.

Jouhandeau, Marcel: *Marcel and Elise, The Bold Chronicle of a Strange Marriage*. Translated by Martin Turnell. Pantheon Books 1953.

Jung, Carl: *The Development of Personality*. Translated by R. F. C. Hull. Bollingen Series, Princeton University Press 1970.

Jung, Carl: *Metamorphoses of the Libido and its Symbols*, in *Collected Works of C. G. Jung*. Translated by R. F. C. Hull. Princeton University Press 1967.

Kennedy, Margaret: *The Constant Nymph*. William Heinemann 1924.

Kierkegaard, Søren: *Stages on Life's Way*. Translated by H. V. and E. H. Hong. Princeton University Press 2009.

Krafft-Ebing, Richard von: *Psychopathia Sexualis*. Rebman Kessinger 1906.

Landau, Rom: *Sex, Life and Faith*. Faber and Faber 1946.

Lawrence, D. H.: *Fantasia of the Unconscious*. Dover Publications 2006.

Lawrence, D. H.: *Lady Chatterley's Lover*. Modern Library 2003.

Lawrence, D. H.: *Sons and Lovers*. Modern Library 1999.

Lawrence, D. H.: *The Plumed Serpent*. Vintage 1992.

Lehmann, Rosamond: *Dusty Answer*. Virago Press 2008.

Lehmann, Rosamond: *Invitation to the Waltz*. Virago 2006.

Lehmann, Rosamond: *The Weather in the Streets*. Virago 1981.

Levinas, Emmanuel: *Time and the Other*. Translated by Richard Cohen. Duquesne University Press 1987.

Lévi-Strauss, Claude: *The Elementary Structures of Kinship*. Translated by

James Harle Bell, Rodney Needham and John Richard von Sturmer. Beacon Press 1969.

Luhan, Mabel Dodge: *Lorenzo in Taos*. Knopf 1932.

Malinowski, Bronislaw: 'The Bachelors' House', from *The Sexual Life of Savages in North-Western Melanesia*. Liveright 1929.

Malraux, André: *Man's Fate*. Translated by Haakon M. Chevalier. The Modern Library 1934.

Mansfield, Katherine: 'Prelude', in *The Short Stories of Katherine Mansfield*. Knopf 1937.

Marx, Karl & Friedrich Engels: *Collected Works*, Vol. VI. From Internet site www.marxists.org/archive/marx/works/1844/manuscripts/comm.htm.

Mauriac, François: *A Kiss for the Leper/Genitrix*. Translated by Gerard Hopkins. Eyre and Spottiswoode 1950.

Mauriac, François: *Thérèse Desqueyroux*. Translated by Raymond MacKenzie. Rowman & Littlefield Publishers 2005.

McCullers, Carson: *The Member of the Wedding*. Penguin Classics 1962.

Merleau-Ponty, Maurice: *Phenomenology of Perception*. Translated by Colin Smith. Routledge 2005.

Michaux, Henri: 'Bridal Night', in *Selected Writings*. New Directions 1968.

Michelet, Jules: *The Mountain*. Translated by W. H. Davenport Adams. T. Nelson and Sons 1872.

Mill, John Stuart: 'The Subjection of Women' as reprinted in *Philosophy of Women* edited by Mary Briody Mahowald. Hackett 1994.

Montaigne, Michel de: *The Complete Essays of Montaigne*. Translated by Donald M. Frame. Stanford University Press 1965.

Montherlant, Henry de: *The Bachelors*. Translated by Terence Kilmartin. Greenwood 1977.

Montherlant, Henry de: *The Dream*. Translated by Terence Kilmartin. Macmillan 1963.

Montherlant, Henry de: *The Girls*. Translated by Terence Kilmartin. Harper & Row 1968.

Montherlant, Henry de: *The Master of Santiago*. Translated by Jonathan Griffin. Knopf 1951.

Montherlant, Henry de: *La Petite Infante de Castille*. French & European Publications 1973.

Montherlant, Henry de: *Pity For Women*. Knopf 1937.

Nietzsche, Friedrich: *The Gay Science*. Translated by Walter Kaufmann. Vintage 1974.

Nietzsche, Friedrich: *Thus Spoke Zarathustra*. Translated by R. J. Hollingdale. Penguin Classics 1961.

Parker, Dorothy: 'Too Bad!' and 'The Lovely Leave', in *The Portable Dorothy Parker*. Penguin Books 1944.

Rabelais, François: *The Complete Works*. Translated by Donald M. Frame. University of California Press 1991.

Rimbaud, Arthur: *Illuminations*. Translated by Helen Rootham. New Directions 1943.

Rimbaud, Arthur: *A Season in Hell*. Translated by Delmore Schwartz. New Directions 1939.

Rougement, Denis de: *The Devil's Share*. Translated by Haakon M. Chevalier. Pantheon Books 1944.

Sachs, Maurice: *Witches' Sabbath*. Translated by Richard Howard. Jonathan Cape 1965.

Sade, Marquis de: *Philosophy in the Boudoir*. Translated by Joachim Neugroschel. Penguin Classics 2006.

Sartre, Jean-Paul: *Anti-Semite and Jew*. Translated by George J. Becker. Schocken 1948.

Sartre, Jean-Paul: *Being and Nothingness*. Translated by Hazel Barnes. Citadel Press 2001.

Sartre, Jean-Paul: *Dirty Hands*, in *Three Plays*. Translated by Lionel Abel. Knopf 1949.

Scott, Geoffrey: *The Portrait of Zélide*. Turtle Point Press 1997.

Senghor, Leopald Sédar: *The Collected Poetry*. Translated by Melvin Dixon. University of Virginia Press 1998.

Stekel, Wilhelm: *Conditions of Nervous Anxiety and Their Treatment*. Liveright 1950.

Stekel, Wilhelm: *Frigidity in Woman*. Translated by James S. Van Teslaar. Liveright 1943.

Stendhal: *Memoirs of an Egotist*. Translated by David Ellis. Horizon Press 1975.

Stendhal: *The Red and the Black*. Translated by Roger Gard. Penguin Classics 2002.

Stendhal: *Three Italian Chronicles*. Translated by C. K. Scott-Moncrieff. New Directions 1991.

Tolstoy, Leo: *War and Peace*. Translated by Richard Pevear and Larissa Volokhonsky. Knopf 2008.

Tolstoy, Sophia: *The Diaries of Sophia Tolstoy*. Translated by Cathy Porter. Random House 1985.

Webb, Mary: *The House in Dormer Forest*. Jonathan Cape 1928.

Webb, Mary: *Precious Bane*. E.P. Dutton 1926.

Wharton, Edith: *The Age of Innocence*. Random House 1999.

Woolf, Virginia: *Mrs. Dalloway*. Penguin Books 1967.

Woolf, Virginia: *To the Lighthouse*, in *The Selected Works of Virginia Woolf*. Wordsworth Editions 2005.

Woolf, Virginia: *The Waves*. Hogarth Press 1931.

Zola, Emile: *Nana*. Unpublished translation by Constance Borde and Sheila Malovany-Chevallier.

Zola, Emile: *Pot-Bouille*. Everyman 1999.

Index

THE HISTORY OF VINTAGE

The famous American publisher Alfred A. Knopf (1892–1984) founded Vintage Books in the United States in 1954 as a paperback home for the authors published by his company. Vintage was launched in the United Kingdom in 1990 and works independently from the American imprint although both are part of the international publishing group, Random House.

Vintage in the United Kingdom was initially created to publish paperback editions of books bought by the prestigious literary hardback imprints in the Random House Group such as Jonathan Cape, Chatto & Windus, Hutchinson and later William Heinemann, Secker & Warburg and The Harvill Press. There are many Booker and Nobel Prize-winning authors on the Vintage list and the imprint publishes a huge variety of fiction and non-fiction. Over the years Vintage has expanded and the list now includes great authors of the past – who are published under the Vintage Classics imprint – as well as many of the most influential authors of the present. In 2012 Vintage Children's Classics was launched to include the much-loved authors of our youth.

For a full list of the books Vintage publishes,
please visit our website
www.vintage-books.co.uk

For book details and other information about the classic authors we publish, please visit the Vintage Classics website
www.vintage-classics.info

penguin.co.uk/vintage

The Sonata in the Classic Era

SECHS SONATEN
FÜR ZWO PERSONEN
AUF
EINEM CLAVIER
VON
FRANZ SEYDELMANN,

LEIPZIG,
BEY JOHANN GOTTLOB IMMANUEL BREITKOPF.
1781.